NORAH LOFTS

Norah
Lofts

Jassy

Bless This House

Scent of Cloves

How Far to Bethlehem?

Norah Lofts

Heinemann/Octopus

Jassy first published in 1944
by Michael Joseph Limited
Bless This House first published in 1954
by Michael Joseph Limited
Scent of Cloves first published in 1958
by Hutchinson & Co. (Publishers) Limited
How Far to Bethlehem? first published in 1965
by Hutchinson & Co. (Publishers) Limited

This edition first published jointly
in Great Britain in 1979 by

William Heinemann Limited
15/16 Queen Street
London W1

Martin Secker & Warburg Limited
54 Poland Street
London W1

and

Octopus Books Limited
59 Grosvenor Street
London W1

ISBN 0 905712 33 1

Printed in the United States

Contents

Norah Lofts

Jassy

Norah Lofts

BOOK ONE

GENESIS IN EXILE

'She was a local girl, of rather peculiar parentage. . . .'
So this story is told by BARNEY HATTON, *who lived next door and took an interest in his neighbours.*

I first set eyes on Jassy Woodroffe on the Michaelmas Day before my fourteenth birthday. I was supposed to be working in the garden; but the scene of my labour was well out of sight from the house, so as soon as I heard voices, and hoof-beats and wheels on the road outside, I went to the place where our garden wall had fallen in and watched our new neighbours take possession of the last cottage at the end of the Green.

There was little to hope for of interest or excitement in the arrival of mere cottage people; but I hated gardening and the circumstances that made it necessary for me to do it, so, bored and miserable, I was in a mood to welcome any interruption. I scrambled to the top of the heap of fallen stones, and with the afternoon sun warm on my back, stared across the narrow track which divided the Green from the end of our garden.

The family and their furniture had come in a farm wagon, driven by a surly-looking fellow with a dirty beard. There were three of them, a tall, gaunt, awkward-looking fellow, a woman, brown-faced and very upright, and a little girl whom I took to be about six years old. They climbed out of the wagon, and the surly man got down too, without speaking, and began to throw their furniture out of the vehicle with an air of haste rather than helpfulness. As soon as the wagon was empty he turned it and drove away. It was his manner as much as anything which aroused my interest. His haste and his silence made him seem like a man who was, with the least possible trouble, getting rid of something: I could imagine someone saying to him–take these people as far away as you can and throw them out as soon as possible. And so soon as my imagination set to work on this theme I became interested in the family and watched more closely to discover whether there was anything really peculiar about them.

I noticed several things. First of all I observed that their furniture was very different from that of the usual cottagers. Out there on the Green, huddled together in the rays of the afternoon sun, it looked, as all furniture does out of doors, slightly pathetic. But, piece by piece, it was good. There was a tall clock with a brass face surrounded by a wreath of enamelled flowers; there were several sturdy chairs with red cushions, a dower chest, black with age and curiously carved. There were articles of brass and copper whose high lustre caught the sun's rays; a good deal of china, and far more bedding than there was in any other cottage on the Green. As I took note of this I began to wonder whether these people, like ourselves, had come down in the world. For I was already, for various reasons, acutely aware of social differences, and the sight of this good farmhouse furniture going into a clod cottage reminded me of the incongruity of the tulip-wood escritoire in our own low-beamed parlour.

Thinking in this strain I watched the people who were moving the furniture more closely. I decided that the female was lazy. She went into the house and came out again, never carrying anything of any size, never moving with any decision of purpose. She seemed totally uninterested in what should have been her particular province. The man worked hard, but clumsily, heaving and pushing and pulling like an amiable but not very sensible giant confronted by a task that was only just within his scope. The ruling spirit, the brains of the movement, seemed to me to be the little girl who, alone of the trio, knew what she was about. She issued orders–I was sure they were orders, because some activity always shaped itself upon her words–in a low queer voice of which I could catch the sound but not the sense. Occasionally she would attempt something beyond her strength, and the great man would say, rather helplessly, 'No, no, Jassy, that is too heavy.' Then he would call, 'Sary, Sary,' or the child, articulate for once, would shout 'Mother,' and the woman, moving lithely, but indolent, would emerge from the cottage and lend a dissociated but wiry strength to the business in hand.

I lost sense of time and place in watching them. I began to notice trivial things, the cunning patches in the shirt which the man revealed when he took off his jacket; the fact that his voice, though countrified and unaffected, never uttered a sentence which the Reverend Saunders, my tutor, would have corrected; the difference in the child's manner when she spoke to her mother; and the oddity of the child herself. She was so tiny her head hardly reached the top of the chest of drawers which, with the man's aid, she attempted to shift; yet she behaved like a grown-up person. And she was ugly and beautiful at the same time. Her face, I thought, was queer and hideous. The brow was enormous and emphasized by the way her hair was dragged back and plaited behind. From this great brow her face sloped away to a sharp chin, yet her mouth was so large that it seemed to occupy the whole of the lower part of her face, and although the rest of her skin was the colour of meal, her mouth was so red that even to me, seated upon the broken wall, it shone like a hedge berry. And everything she did was beautiful. When she stood still, regaining her breath after an exertion, when she stooped, or pushed, or braced herself beneath a burden, when she handled anything or hurried from place to place, every movement was perfect. Finally, when every other source of interest was exhausted, I sat just watching her move. I remembered Sharples, Nick Helmar's groom, saying of a colt, 'Bad bone and bad temper, but the movement makes up for all,' and, except for her temper, of which I could judge but little, the verdict applied to this little girl.

Presently the woman came out of the cottage and, without a word to the others, walked away rapidly in the direction of Layer Wood. The child hunched her shoulders and spoke to the man and then went indoors. Very soon a plume of smoke rose from the one chimney of the cottage. The awkward gangling fellow, after a glance at the sky, where the sun was sinking behind those same woods, redoubled his efforts and with graceless haste gathered the rest of his household goods and hurried them under the new roof. In the dimming light I could see the window of the cottage glow golden. At the same moment I was aware that the sun was no longer warm upon me; the sudden chill of an autumn evening had fallen upon the earth. I rose from my seat and went slowly into the house.

It was nearly time for our evening meal. The fire glowed red in the kitchen, and from the brick oven by the side there came a savoury odour. Mingled with it was the acrid, unhappy scent of the smoky fire in the dining-room. Either mother or Meggie, our maid-of-all-work, had been trying to coax the damned thing to blaze.

I took a jug from the row that hung from hooks at the edge of a shelf and was tilting the kettle of boiling water into it when mother, with an apron over her tidy blue dress, hurried into the kitchen.

'Have you seen your father?' she asked.

'No,' I said. 'I haven't been in the yard though. I came straight from the garden.'

'Well, get along and wash then. Everybody's late tonight. I'm not going to wait any longer.' She pushed back her sleeve and jerked a pan from the centre of the fire. Snatching off the lid she prodded the pan's contents with a fork. As she did so I heard the rattle of Dane's hoofs on the cobbles.

'Here he is now,' I said.

'Get along then,' she said impatiently. 'And mind you clean your nails.'

'Clean nails and gardening don't go together,' I said, addressing the words less at mother than at the injustice which demanded that I should work like a farm-hand and yet look like a gentleman.

'What doesn't go has to be driven,' said mother in a more amiable voice. 'Hurry, Barney. This is no time to argue.'

I dashed away up the back stairs, reached my room, washed myself, brushed my hair, and put on a clean neckcloth. When I reached the dining-room the food was already on the table, and my father was standing on the hearth, pretending to warm his back by the smoky fire. Mother was fussing about the table, tweaking a crease out of the cloth and altering the places of the cutlery. Never in a thousand years could Meggie have set a table to her liking.

Father said 'Ha!' as I entered and moved, rubbing his hands, to the head of the table. He lifted the silver dish cover, stared at the small joint thus revealed, and began to carve it. He managed one slice and then, with an air of defeat, looked down the table at mother and said, 'My dear, mumble mumble mumble quite impossible.'

The greater part of father's speech always consisted of quite unintelligible mutterings. I often thought that that this method of talking was the logical outcome of his policy of leaving all exertion to other people. When he spoke, whoever heard him must set to work and guess at his meaning. And that was usually easy enough to do, for he never thought to convey an idea, and his system of mutterings, punctuated here and there by a few loud words, was quite adequate for the business of giving an order or making a complaint. It was not lack of filial respect upon my part to consider him stupid past the ordinary: he was known as the most stupid and most handsome man in the whole county. He was extraordinarily good-looking, with the leanness and the muscular development and the narrow head of a good hound; and since he never bothered about anything or anybody under the sun there was even now, in the forty-ninth year of his age, no line of worry or frustration or ill-humour upon his clear chiselled, high-coloured face, nor was a grey hair visible in the profusion of dark brown curls which clustered about his elegant stupid skull. In looks as well as in behaviour he was like a cunningly-made model of a man, made so that it could acquire certain habits, learn a few phrases, and perform a trick or two. And, like a model man, he would go on and on, unchanging, until at last some cog or bolt within him gave way and failed. Then he would come to a standstill, and it would be very different from the act of dying which overtakes the normal, living human being.

Mother went round to his end of the table and, with her lips pressed together from concentration of effort, severed, efficiently but not skilfully, several slices of the inferior meat. As she laid them upon the plates I stretched out my arm and served the vegetables from her end of the table. She looked at me in a peculiar way she had, possessively grateful, and I wriggled with discomfort in my spirit; because I was not consciously trying to help her, I was not trying to take father's place: I was merely trying to hasten forward the moment when I should be able to start eating.

That half-conspiratorial gratitude of mother's was the final proof–if proof were needed–of her inability to deal with *people*. It was not that she was stupid. In fact, she was an extremely shrewd and intelligent woman. That we had a roof over our heads, a horse to ride, and meat, however tough, upon our table, was entirely due to mother's activities and schemes. She could deal with things well enough; but with people she failed. She never saw that by shouldering all the burdens she left father free to be himself. If, long years ago, she had seated herself on a sofa, and played pretty, and said I want this and I must have that, *things* might not have turned out differently, but *father* would have been changed somehow. This very evening, for instance, if she had remained in her place long enough sheer hunger would have made him hack the tough meat at last. But mother came from a family–the Symmons of Suffolk–who were bustling and ambitious and successful to a man, and I suppose managing and endurance and contrivance were in her blood, just as indolence and carelessness were in father's. So she had failed with him, and she was failing with me, because by her almost cajoling air to me, as though she were asking me to be a prop, to be different from father, to league with her in being bustling and ambitious, she made me obscurely ashamed. And many things that I might have done I did not do out of sheer perversity, because I hated to see myself conforming to the pattern of a son which she had in mind. An adolescent male is a tricky creature, he has many and strange desires, but to be a paragon is seldom amongst them.

We ate almost in silence, as was our custom. But presently, knowing that sooner or later my failure to dig the garden would be revealed and mourned over, I volunteered the information that I had spent the greater part of the afternoon watching the Woodroffes' arrival. We knew the name of the family, because Nick Helmar, to whom the cottage belonged, had mentioned it to father.

'What's the woman like?' asked mother, who was always on the look out for a miracle of cheap efficiency in dairy-work. 'I've been thinking that if I could find a really *good* woman I'd try another couple of cows and let her have a stall in Bywater on market day. Did she look likely, Barney?'

'I don't think so,' I said slowly. 'She looked rather like a gypsy to me.'

'Good gracious! Surely even Nick Helmar wouldn't wish a gypsy on me for a neighbour. What about my chickens? And the drying line at the end?'

'Gypsy,' said father, 'mumble mumble steal from next door. Mumble mumble, risky.'

'Any family?' mother asked. 'A teachable girl would do.'

'Only one, very tiny. She looked about six,' I said. 'But she had the whole business of moving in hand. She and the man–her father I guess–did most of the moving, and she got the fire going. The woman just went off.'

'How peculiar,' said mother.

'Woodroffe's a mumble mumble carpenter. Mumble clever,' said father, with a spark of interest. 'I've got the idea, mumble mumble, old Nick, mumble, great alterations mumble at Mortiboys. Stucco mumble, up-to-date, mumble panelling, new floors, Woodroffe mumble useful. Wouldn't have mumble else. Troublesome fellow, preacher mumble, agitator mumble Nick's sort. Surprised when mumble let him the cottage. Mumble be sorry. Fennel turned him out.'

I tried to fight, as one may try to fight a nightmare, the feeling that had begun to come over me when father mentioned alterations at Mortiboys. Making an effort, I said:

'I thought somehow they'd been turned out by the way the man who drove the wagon behaved.'

Mother–of father I expected nothing–might have asked about the man's behaviour, and then I could have described it and perhaps lost myself in the description and escaped the moments of anguish which were lying in wait for me, just as one may escape a moment of danger or embarrassment. But mother, disappointed of her good woman or teachable girl, had lost interest in the Woodroffes. She rang her hand-bell, gathered the plates, and waited for Meggie to come in with the pudding.

It was a blackberry pie, the last of the season, and I could smell the rich dark fruity scent and see the crisp brown pastry. But I knew that I should be unable to swallow a morsel. I knew how inflexible mother was about table behaviour, and I knew also that if I stayed there and ate nothing she would be suggesting a dose. So I did the one thing left to me. I clapped my hand to my head and said:

'I must go. I've just remembered. I have a task set that will take me four hours, and I haven't looked at it. Tomorrow's Friday.'

Nick Helmar's going to alter Mortiboys now, said the demon in my mind.

'Will ten minutes make such a difference?' mother asked, but she asked it diffidently. The whole business of my schooling was to her mysterious and awesome.

'Indeed it will,' I said.

And *now*, said my demon, Nick Helmar's going to alter Mortiboys.

'Very well,' said mother, giving me a fond, doting glance. 'Meggie shall keep the pie warm and bring you a piece in an hour's time. That will make a little break for you.' And I knew, by the way in which she watched me out of the room, that she was thinking what a boy I was for my lessons, and how probably I should be ambitious and industrious and emulate my uncle, Edgar Symmons, who through sheer ability had worked his way up until he was Dean of Ely. What would she have thought could she have known that as I hastened out of the room I was hating her and loathing father? Father was responsible for the loss of Mortiboys; and mother, though blameless, was capable of hearing of Nick Helmar's sacrilegious plan and of proceeding to cut into a pie as though the news meant nothing.

I reached my room, rucked the mat in front of the keyless door, so that everyone entering would be halted and obliged to give me a moment to recover myself, opened a few books and flung them about, and then went to the window, where, curled on the low wide sill I stared out into the darkness and gave myself to the demon.

Four years ago I had chosen this room for my own because it had the only southward-looking window on the bedroom floor, and on a clear day in winter, when the trees were thin and leafless, it was possible to stare out across the tongue of Layer Wood which licked down into the marshes and see a wavery, ochre-pink line which was the roof of Mortiboys.

I had been born there, under its shelter, so had my father, and his, back and back in an unbroken line, save for one Christopher Hatton, who had been born in Paris during the Commonwealth, since the first Hatton of note, another Barnabas, who, having made a fortune out of leather and twice been Mayor of London, had bought the place in the middle of the sixteenth century when the old monasteries were dissolved.

But Mortiboys was old then, and my interest in it went back beyond the Hattons' possession of it. I even knew and cherished the story of how it was named, away back in the days of Norman William and the Saxons who defied him. The owner of the place at that time, called upon to be William's liege or to surrender the place, 'refused with many oaths,' and when the day of reckoning came, opposed, with his little force of house-carls, the mounted knights. At sunset he was surrounded in the only spot which remained to him–a woodsman's hut in the centre of the woods. There, with the last three of his men dead about him, he set fire to the hut and died within the flames. And the Normans were sufficiently impressed by his performance to name the place Morte de Bois, which name upon the tongues of the common Saxon people was eased down to Mortiboys. Legend had it that his lady, being just with child, visited the new Norman lord on some pretence, and so enthralled him with her sorrow and her beauty that he married her and reared the child as his. If this were a true legend–and there is often a grain of truth in the most far-fetched of them–then that Saxon's blood ran, with innumerable dilutions, in my own veins. For the Norman family stayed at Mortiboys until the sixteenth century. Their history and their property was inextricably linked with the great Benedictine monastery at Bury St Edmunds. When that fell before Henry Tudor's commissioners, Mortiboys came into the market and was bought, as I have said, by Barnabas Hatton the leather merchant. But his son, the one who was responsible for the building of the house, had married the daughter of the original family. And although that other alliance, of the Saxon widow and the Norman lord, may have been merely a romantic story, I often toyed with the idea of its being true. For I could understand, with my blood and my bones and my most inward marrow, the man who refused to relinquish the place and then, beaten, chose to die on the last foot of his own land. I felt that I would have died rather than leave Mortiboys. But alas! I had been carried over the threshold as a mere baby of eighteen months old; for my father, the handsomest and stupidest man in Essex, had parted with Mortiboys, with Layer Wood and the greater part of the village of Minsham All Saints *to settle his gambling debts!*

The Hattons had descended (a word too lightly and often too truly used) from the sensible, substantial burgher who had made a fortune and from his son who had had the shrewd good sense to ally his common blood with the nobility, until they had reached, in my father, a silly, idle, senseless creature who had no thought for anything outside a blind game of chance . . . how would a pack of cards divide, how would a dice fall, which of a number of horses would most rapidly cover a given length of ground, which of two ruffians could hit the other harder. He was, in this respect, just as I was in another, a creature obsessed and without reason. Before he was of age he had run up gambling debts and debts to moneylenders which had well nigh ruined my grandfather. When he was almost thirty years old things had reached the pitch where he must marry an heiress or face ruin. The estate was hopelessly entangled, and the impetus given to agriculture by the French Wars found him too penurious to take advantage of it. So he had married my mother, who, though not his equal by birth, had from Grandfather Symmons, a shrewd man and mean, a pretty little fortune. To marry a Hatton of Mortiboys, even though he were almost ruined and incurably dissolute, had meant achievement to her, and I gathered that she jumped at a proposal from which any girl with money and a better established family would have jibbed. But within ten years or less the Symmons' money had followed the Hattons' into the abyss, and my mother was living a life, identical in its responsibilities and far inferior in its rewards, to that which she would have lived had she married a man of her own class and kind.

For when I was a baby father's affairs reached another crisis, and it was to save himself, literally, from gaol that he sold Mortiboys, house and estate, to his best friend and biggest creditor, Nick Helmar. And it was typical of father's utter lack of feeling that he should then proceed to settle down and make his home where he did, at the Green Farm, Minsham St Mary, which was just within sight, and well within the orbit of the place which he had betrayed and abandoned. Father found the farm very convenient, because he could ride, in just under half an hour, to Mortiboys and there play cards and drink and dine and gossip with Nick Helmar!

In this move, as in everything else, he showed his utter senselessness and lack of perception. And he spoilt life for mother and for me. In another part of the country mother could have begun, without foolery or subterfuge to model the Green Farm on the lines of those which had paid her father so well: and I should never have seen Mortiboys and so conceived an obsession which must last as long as I breathed. At Minsham St Mary mother was like a badly-driven mare, lashed perpetually by penury and cruelly curbed by dignity. For she had friends who remained faithful, women who had known her in the early days of her marriage, and she could not, comfortably, appear before them as a farm-wife. Later on, dignity wore thin and she abandoned pretence, and I believe that the day when Lady Fennel actually found her at work in the dairy was a day of release for her, poor soul. But as I grew older and more conscious of what I had lost, my case grew harder.

I first saw the house on a spring evening when the sky was a sea of colour, green and lilac and primrose, smudged with black clouds. Father, mother and I were driving home from Bywater in the gig, and I remember mother saying, after a glance overhead:

'You'll get a wet coat shooting tomorrow. This sky means rain.'

Father replied with one of his unintelligible murmurs and bore on his rein so that instead of proceeding in a homeward direction we swung left into a narrow lane.

'Where are you going?' mother demanded sharply. 'I'm making no calls at this time of night.'

'Mumble mumble have to,' said father. 'Merely mumble the Lodge for a word mumble Harding. Mumble guns tomorrow.'

The lane ended suddenly in a wide smooth sweep of green turf which was spread like a carpet before a big archway built of narrow pinkish-yellow bricks. On either side of the arch, built of the same material and continuous with it, was a kind of house with little leaded windows and nail-studded doors. Father leaned down and hammered on one of them with the butt of his whip, and a small man with a face of wrinkled leather peered out. Then he emerged and gave father his respectful attention while father mumbled away in an emphatic lordly manner.

While he did so I stared, first at the archway, which intrigued me by its novelty–I had never seen any erection like it before–and then, by leaning forward and making myself lower, at the view framed within the arch. There was a short gravel drive bordered by ornamental shrubs and then the great red bulk of the house, a three-gabled Tudor building with great mullioned windows and a vast shadowy porch. I could, naturally, see little of it, but I loved all I saw. Abler pens than mine have described the sensation of falling in love at first sight; but it is always a person who is reported to have roused the emotion. In my case it was a house; an insensate mass of timber and bricks and mortar, but to me, instantly, the loveliest and most desirable thing on earth. I had no time to sort out my feelings then, I merely stared and stared, so that the swerve of the gig as father turned round on the green sward caught me unprepared and threw me against mother's arm. As I righted myself I said, 'What a beautiful house. Who lives there?'

Father muttered, but in those days, before I had caught the trick of listening to him, nothing he said had much meaning for me. I looked at mother, who said in a queer constrained voice:

'A man called Nick Helmar, a *friend* of your father's.'

'Have you ever been inside it?' I asked, turning back to father and deliberately requesting information of him, for, I think, the first time in my life.

'Certainly I have, mumble mumble, think so indeed.'

'I'd like to go in,' I said.

'Well, it's unlikely that you ever will,' said mother sharply. I was only eight years old then, a timid child, easily snubbed. And I had already discovered that many of my questions which received only mutterings and snappings from my parents could be answered at length, in racy picturesque language, and with great willingness, by Meggie. So I fell silent, and as soon as supper was ended, went to the kitchen and there discovered, luckily or unluckily, a fellow devotee in Meggie.

'You was born there,' said Meggie, applying a live coal to her little black pipe with the tongs. 'And so for that matter was I. Me mother was cook, d'you see, and your grandma was giving a masterous grut dinner party to mark something or other. Wait a bit, I'll remember–yes, 'twas the battle of Queebec. So me mother stayed at her pans till 'twas too late to git home. Me mother had been your grandma's cook till she married Cobb, the keeper, you see, and she allust went up to house when there was a party. But time I was born she din't git home agin, and so I was born at Mortiboys. And it so chanced that Doctor Burrage, he was bid to the dinner and heard about me mother and came out and did her up all nice and tidy. And your grandpa sent her out a bottle of port. She said she never had sich a time with all the nine of us. I was allust her favourite,' said Meggie proudly, 'all on account of that night.'

'Why don't we live there now?' I demanded as soon as I could cut in upon Meggie's flow of reminiscence.

'As to that, you'd better ask your pa,' said Meggie, with unusual caution. 'Or p'raps not, on second thoughts. It's not a matter the poor gentleman might care to tell of.'

'Why not?'

'Because,' said Meggie, studying her pipe with dissatisfaction, 'debts was concerned. Now that's all I know, Master Barney, and you'd do well not to say any more about the matter.'

I sensed a mystery, and for the moment desisted from asking Meggie what exactly a debt might be. But I asked her whether she had ever–apart from her birthday–been in the house, and received in reply an account which lasted until long past my bedtime. Meggie knew Mortiboys from attics to cellars. She had gone to work in it when she was nine years old, and had left only when my parents moved to Green Farm. She knew every draught and uneven board.

'Stands to reason,' she ended, 'only a masterous rich man could live there. Think of the winders alone. Why, in your grandpa's time there was a man and a boy did nothing all day but clean the winders. So many little corners, you see. I daresay it's the same today. And fuel. There's a fireplace there, in what they call the Old Hall, and I tell you, Master Barney, that that do take in a day as much wood as this one do in a week. Right big trees they used to saw into three or four bits and cast on that there fire, and they'd look like little owd logs.'

'What happened then, did we get poor?'

'Now I towd you, Master Barney, that your pa's business ain't for me to talk about. Thass time for your bed, too.'

And to bed I went, with more to think about in the darkness than I had ever had in my life before. My last thought before I fell asleep was about birds. For the last two years I had watched the swallows that nested in spring under the eaves of the farmhouse thatch, and I knew that on both years one, at least, of the birds had been the same. It had a curious white streak on its back. And that bird went away in the autumn to spend the winter in a warmer place, mother had told me; but it knew its old nest when it returned. I was, I decided, like that bird. I had known, as soon as I set eyes on Mortiboys, that it was my home. Sleep, when it came, closed my eyes on the vision of that arch, and the three gables, outlined against the green and lilac sky.

From that day onwards Mortiboys became the main interest in my life. Meggie, relentlessly attacked, gave way and told me all she knew about it, but her information was, naturally, confined in its scope. She could discuss what she remembered and a few trifles which she had heard from her parents; she could tell me, even to the very names, about the men-servants and the maid-servants who had filled the kitchens and attics in her mother's time, and how, gradually, with the fall of father's fortunes, their numbers fell. She even, one evening after a glass of new ale, ventured to give an opinion upon deeper matters.

''Twasn't from your grandpa that your pa got his wild ways with the money. 'Twas from your grandma. A Miss Strawson she was, and her pa, Sir Henry, had gone through three fortunes by the time he was in his middle years. And she was just such another, such a spender as never was. Not enough for her, Mortiboys weren't; no, she must have a house in London, too. If the moon'd been for sale she'd have wanted it, Master Barney, and your grandpa would have got it for her somehow. And how did it end? You can see that for yourself, my dear, here in this poky little place with your mother, bless her! working like a black, though she'd hate me to say it, and only old Meggie, getting masterous stiff in the joints, to do the dirty jobs for you all. So you look out, now, and see that you don't take after your grandpa nor your pa.'

'A fine chance I have of that,' I said bitterly. 'What have I to spend?'

'There's truth in that,' Meggie conceded. 'All the same, I never known you to eat your fat.'

'What's that got to do with it, pray?'

'That show,' said Meggie ponderously, 'a wasteful spirit. Fat is bought with money the same as lean, and will fill your belly as good or better. That is what it do show, and I'm sorry to see it.'

'What I'm sorry about is to think that my grandmother and my father could waste money so that now I mustn't even waste fat.'

'But that's the way it is. What do the good book say? The fathers have eaten sour grapes and the children's teeth is set on edge.'

I pondered that, and for the first time in my life understood metaphorical language. It was like a window opening in a blank wall. I was quite stunned. I said, after a reflective pause:

'It was clever of you, Meggie, to say that. They'–I jerked my head towards the parlour–'may not think you're very bright, but *I* think you're very clever.'

'They're dead right,' Meggie said with a savage note in her voice. 'I ain't bright, don't I shouldn't be here at my time of life. If I'd took advantage like I should I might be cook now, in a grut house, or even housekeeper, maybe. There ain't many that know more about cooking and preserving and bleaching and cleaning than what I do. And here I be, Jack of all work and too old to make a chance. No, I ain't bright.'

I saw that I had hurt her feelings and muttered unhappily.

'No matter,' said Meggie, 'fools and children, they speak the truth. So now I'll say summat to you, Master Barney, as probably only a fool ud say. You forget all about Mortiboys. I noticed you, the whole of this week past, harking on about it. And all you'll do by brooding over it is make yourself miseruble. Looking back never did nobody a haporth of good. You gotta look forrards and mind your book and fit yourself for some sort of job–or if that ain't to your fancy, you must take to the farm and make a living outa that! Do you see?'

I said I did. I knew, even then, that the advice was good. Later on I had a truer estimation of its virtue. But, of course, I minded it not at all. The poison was already in my system, and I did nothing to purge it.

I began to ferret out every fact about Mortiboys. I learned a great deal about its history from a musty volume called *A Survey of Essex*, which told me that the house was built in 1560 upon an older foundation, of which only the Great Hall remained standing. The *Survey* also mentioned, rather lightly, as though the compiler doubted his own story, the legend of how it was named, and how its Norman history was linked to the Saxon. From Nick Helmar's groom, Sharples, whom I encountered upon one of my surreptitious visits to the house, I gained a great deal of information of a very different kind. Sharples was taking a sick horse for a walk in the lane in order to work off the effects of a pill, and he asked me, rudely enough, what I was there for and why I was staring at the house. I told him, for in those days I was frank and outspoken, except with my parents, and Sharples, after inspecting me closely, accepted my explanation and showed himself friendly. He told me about the horse pill, and I asked his advice about Joby, my horse, who had a swollen fetlock, so that I was afoot that day, and had been obliged to walk across the tricky marsh pathway to reach my objective. Sharples seemed to like giving advice, and presently when the sick horse had been walked sufficiently, he took me through the archway and round to the stables with him. My heart beat so hard from excitement that I could hardly breathe, and had to keep dropping behind and opening my mouth to gasp, rather like a landed fish. I was disappointed, and yet somehow relieved, to find that once through the arch we turned aside and did not go near the house. I had a fear that someone might appear and say, 'What boy is this?' and a kind of snobbishness was already at work within me, so that I did not want to make my first appearance in the home of my fathers sponsored by a groom.

Nevertheless I liked Sharples, and he seemed to like me. He said that if I brought the horse along he'd look him over. And I did that, on the very next day, leading Joby over the marshes. So we became friendly, and it was from Sharples that I learned all about the money my father had owed Nick Helmar, and how the estate had changed hands.

'And a bloody bad bargain Master made, too,' said Sharples. 'The house is tumbling down, the grounds are nowt, and every cottage want something done to it. Why he wanted it God only know!'

'I know,' I said softly.

'Why then?'

'Because it's so beautiful.'

'Get away with you. Did you ever see Sir Evelyn Fennel's place–Ockley Manor? Or Baildon Lodge, what Mr Hodge bought for about half what Master give for this?'

'Yes,' I lied stoutly. 'I know them both. They're not a patch on Mortiboys.'

'You're crazy,' said Sharples. We were just outside the archway then, and he moved across to the house part which was his and put his hand to the side of the nail-studded door. He brought it away with a lump of wood, worm-eaten and soft as a rotten cheese, in it.

'Don't do that,' I said in agonized sharpness.

'Rotten!' said Sharples. 'The whole place is like that, too. Here, look through there. See that big window on the left of the porch?' I looked, and saw the great window, with its hundreds of little panes, some of them coloured, jutting out in a square bay. 'When that blow, and God know that can blow bloody hard in these parts, that window flap like a sheet. I seen it. The whole place is rotten.'

'But it's beautiful,' I persisted. 'It's the most beautiful place in the world.'

'Ah, well! You're a Hatton,' said Sharples tolerantly. 'It's like me and my old woman. Plain as a pikestaff, she is. But time I look at her I think about what she was like as a maid, and how she did work on me when I had a mucky poisoned finger and was like to lose my arm. And, I swear I do be blind then to the grey hairs and the wrinkles and the way her teeth do hang like a brukken fence. See?'

This statement afforded me a moment's relief, for it drew my mind away from Mortiboys and rested it upon my fellow men. Life was hard on our country women, most of whom had large families to rear on very little money, and many of whom worked seasonally in the fields as well. A girl who had been quite pretty would look like an old woman who had never been anything but plain by the time she had been married a few years. But, if Sharples was to be believed–and Mrs Sharples was certainly a case to quote from–this was not the tragedy that it might at first seem, if to their husbands they remained beautiful.

I thought of that as I turned away and went down the lane; but when I turned back to have a last look at the gateway and the house, framed within the arch, I forgot everything except Mortiboys again. I had a feeling of exile and destitution; and mingled with it was an ache of longing to be able to go through the arch and walk up to the great porch and to go within, unchallenged, by right that no man could dispute. For the first time I found myself hating my father and my grandmother, who, between them, had robbed me of my birthright. Two extravagant simpletons in succession was too much for any place to bear. If only, if only I had been my father, able to succeed while there was still a fragment to be saved. How careful I would have been, how I would have worked and saved and starved if need be. Why, I would have repaired the place with my own hands, clumsy as they were.

I was eight then, and for the next five years my passion for Mortiboys grew with my limbs. I had, of course, other things to think about and worry over. Mother, much of Meggie's opinion, it seemed, set about training me for a future which would hold little room for idle dreaming. In case I turned out to be a scholar, I must go to the Reverend Saunders and be tutored on three days a week and set tasks to keep me busy for seven; and in case this failed and I must be a farmer, I was always being hustled about the yard and the fields to watch how things were done. And Stoner, the man whom mother employed as foreman, since it was beneath her dignity to deal with the outside work, regarded me as her spy, and hated me and often, with the cruel bucolic humour of his kind, arranged that horrible, ludicrous things should happen to me. Consequently my natural distaste for farm work developed into loathing. And school, for other reasons, was little better. My life within doors, though comfortable enough, was not particularly happy. Mother's designs upon me were very obvious, and made me self-conscious and perverse and conscience-stricken. Father I could hardly look at without being reminded of his folly. And socially, except for father's stubborn contact with Nick Helmar and mother's dwindling circle of faithful sympathetic women–in whom, I often suspected, a kind of gloating sadism was at work–we lived in the awful isolation of the genteel poor, suspended as it were between the comfortable poor who had no appearances to keep up, and the comfortably rich whose place was secure. So I was lonely. And my infatuation, having few counter influences, grew and grew until it was, I suppose, a kind of madness. Like other forms of lunacy, it had tides and moons; sometimes I was just sentimentally sad, sometimes violently resentful. I dreamed great bright dreams about making a fortune in some vague fashion and buying the place back. I had moods of depression when I knew that it was not in me to achieve anything, much less so colossal a thing. And I had moments when, beginning in a word, or a memory, the whole question of Mortiboys and me would swell like a painful abscess and I would go through from the beginning the whole dreary story, and finally cry a little, and then feel better and be able to give my mind to my lessons or to the farm for a while.

One of these moments came upon me when I heard father say, so carelessly, that Nick Helmar was planning to alter Mortiboys, and that was why he had let the man Woodroffe have a cottage. I was just at the point where I was going to shed futile tears over the matter when Meggie brought up my share of the pie. I had snatched up a book as the door jammed against the rucked mat, and I steadied my voice and thanked her. When she had gone, moving very quietly in an effort not to disturb my studies, I looked at the fruit and the pastry and had, I think for the first time in all my mourning for Mortiboys, sensible thought. I thought–well, I can't have Mortiboys, but I can eat this pie. And I did so. Then I worked for a while and went to bed. Before I slept, however, I made an addition to my 'Hate List.' It was headed by father; the second person on it was my grandmother; then came Nick Helmar, who had, after all, wanted Mortiboys, and probably suggested its sale as a method for settling father's debts; and last, much lower, was Sharples, who, although he was friendly to me, said such scathing things about the place. Now I added the man Woodroffe to the list, because he was going to help forward Helmar's scheme for spoiling it. And I thought as I remembered his awkwardness and ugliness, that he would be singularly easy to hate.

But in that I was wrong.

Probably no move in our district, since our own spectacular one from Mortiboys to Green Farm, had given rise to so much gossip as the Woodroffes' move into the cottage on the Green.

At first all the interest centred about Mrs Woodroffe. Every other woman in the village seemed to hate her on sight, and to have more virulent feelings about her as they came to know her better. She was a gypsy slut, a poacher, a maker of spells and, finally, a witch. I believe that their chief grudge against her was her complete immunity from the toils and anxieties which made up their own daily round. On Monday, the traditional wash-day, when every other cottage was a resounding welter of steam and soap-suds and loud complaining voices, when the linen lines ran out their signals for the attack on dirt and thriftlessness, Mrs Woodroffe would leave her cottage and go off on one of her walks. But soon after she was gone the Woodroffe line would blossom out in colour and the small Jassy, probably with a peg or two in her ugly mouth, would step down from the backless chair which she mounted in order to hang out the clothes and resolutely heave the prop into position. A neighbour, prompted by dubious motives, ventured to express sympathy with the poor, overworked little thing.

'I'm eleven,' the mite said fiercely. 'Most people my age are out to work.' It was a shrewd thrust, for the neighbour's own daughter of that age was working in the dairy at Maybrook.

'But what's your mother doing?' the woman persisted.

'Curing a cow at Ockley. Nobody else can do it. And anybody can wash clothes.'

This conversation, as well as all the other gossip, we heard at Green Farm through Meggie, who had cronies amongst the village people. From the same source we learned that Mrs Woodroffe was not a proper gypsy, but a Stannary, a member of a separate tribe stemming from Norfolk. Tom

Woodroffe, said rumour, had found her under a hedge in a storm when he was returning from preaching at Hedstone, had fallen in love with her, married her, and never known a happy moment since. And it was true that she poached; but wise people did not interfere with her. For once, when the Woodroffes lived at Sible Havers, she had been caught by a gentleman and threatened with prosecution. And she had 'whispered' his horses, so that next morning not a single horse would leave its stable until she was sent for and 'unwhispered' them. Romantic as this story sounded, there were uncharitable people in Minsham who did not accept it, but hinted that Sari Woodroffe's immunity, on this occasion, was purchased with quite another coin. Her morals, indeed, were so much suspected that if she were seen, as she was, very occasionally, to be seen, carrying her bucket to the pond which supplied the Green folks with water, those women whose husbands pampered them and usually fetched the water, would turn out themselves, lest, at the common meeting place, some word of civility might pass and lead to other things.

Soon after Christmas, however, the novelty of Sari's doings and appearance waned, and the male Woodroffe became the centre of interest. For early in the New Year he converted Bob Wicks.

Bob Wicks was a rogue and ruffian. His evil temper and his violence were so well known that when he appeared at the little pot-house out on the marshes, known as 'The Evening Star', cautious men would leave the taproom, and that though the customers of 'The Evening Star' consisted for the most part of smugglers and poachers, tough fellows enough. He had twice been in trouble for assaulting women, and there were innumerable other charges laid at his door, but he was still in Minsham and still at liberty, for the simple reason that he was the only smith of any consequence within a radius of six miles. The nearest other one, old Ransome at Ockley, was semi-blind and a victim of 'smith's disease,' that constant tremor of the hands and arms that is the result of the trade. So to sentence Bob Wicks to a spell of gaol would have meant that the Constable–who farmed thirty acres–and the Justices themselves, would have had to go as far afield as Bywater or Baildon to get a shoeing job decently done. Consequently Wicks went on his way unmolested. He lived in a hovel behind the forge, with a thin woebegone wretch who called herself Mrs Wicks, and a swarm of miserable ragged children. He himself was built like a bull, massive and square, and his face was so red that the colour seemed to have seeped into the whites of his eyes, which were netted with red veins. I hated him myself, and had even taken Joby over to Ockley to be shod, but old Ransome was so slow and so shaky, and made such a poor job of it, that I decided against a second visit. Bob Wicks was the subject of one of my father's rare flashes of comprehension. He had met him one evening reeling home, and next day had said, 'Wicks, mum mum, drunk mum lord. Bad colour mum stand it. Do a bad job mum day and mum to jail mum ill-driven nail mum his other mum.'

But that day was still a long way ahead when Wicks rolled home one evening and set about the poor wisp of a woman who called herself his wife. She screamed, just as though she had not been screaming unavailingly for years; and this time she was regarded. For Tom Woodroffe was on his way home from what was called a Revival Meeting at Bywater. He may or may not have known the smith's reputation; having no horse he would not have had occasion to visit the forge, and Wicks was so much a part of Minsham that people no longer mentioned him unless he had just attacked someone or run foul of a keeper. However, warned or not, Tom Woodroffe, hearing the screams and the blows, went straight into the hovel, expostulated with Wicks, and received a blow on the cheek from the buckle-end of the belt which the man was using on the woman. Then he knocked Wicks flat. Such a thing had not happened to the smith since he was big enough to stand up to his father, who had been, by all accounts, just such another. Tom then lifted him on to the wretched affair that served for a bed in that house, and discovering that the Wicks' cupboard was literally bare, went to his own house and returned with everything that was in his own. Judging by what I later knew of the Woodroffe diet, I imagine that this would be only bread and cheese, with perhaps a scrap of fat bacon, but it seemed a feast to the starving family, and for years Mrs Wicks would cry as she mentioned it.

Next day, round about noon, Tom presented himself at the forge. Sharples was there with a couple of carriage horses at the time, so there was a reliable witness. Tom shambled in and said:

'Last night, when you were in drink, I knocked you down because I had no choice. Today, when you're sober, I've come to reason with you.'

Wicks hesitated between desire for instant revenge and the wisdom of not neglecting a job for Nick Helmar.

'You needn't of come,' he said, when he had decided to go on with the matter in hand. 'I'd bin to see you afore, ony I had a job on.'

'I can wait,' said Tom, and seated himself on the bench. Wicks finished the shoeing and then, dropping his hammer, advanced towards Tom, saying: 'And now stand up, you bastard, and I'll reason with you.' He shaped himself for battle. Tom got to his feet and said:

'But you've dropped your hammer.'

'What d'you think. I fight fair.'

'It's as fair to tackle me with a hammer as it is to set about that woman with your belt.'

'That's the truth,' said Sharples, who, like everybody else, detested the blacksmith.

'You keep your bloody mug out of this,' said Wicks, 'and you stop bandying words. I'm waiting.'

'Come on, then,' said Tom, and knocked Wicks flat again.

'There, you see,' he said, as the smith scrambled up bellowing threats and oaths. 'I'm the warning. Go on as you are and you'll see the day when a child can floor you.'

Wicks, mad beyond description, rushed in again, took Tom's fist on the point of his chin, spun round and fell down like an ox in the shambles. Then–gentle as a woman, Sharples said–Tom lifted him and set him on the bench, and wetted his handkerchief and dribbled water on his face.

'Now,' he said as soon as the blacksmith's eyelids twitched, 'be off, my friend. Leave him with me and with God.' So we never knew what shape that queer interview took. Did Tom preach hell fire? Or go on with the physical warning? Or did the fires of Pentecost sit on his tongue? We never knew. But Wicks was never drunk again, and Betty Noakes, of 'The Evening Star,' had to look elsewhere for her ribbons and laces, and Mrs Wicks had no more bruises to show. By the time that Joby needed his next shoes the congested colour was fading a little from the smith's eyeballs.

At first nobody believed in the conversion. That Tom had fought and won, without even taking off his rusty old jacket, had to be believed, for there was Sharples to vouch for it. And as the days passed and the forge children grew fat and Mrs Wicks blossomed, people began to see that some strange and powerful influence was at work. It became a nine days' wonder. But very soon people were asking, 'Why don't he convert his own wife?' And presently I was in a position to give an answer to that question. For to be converted–or corrupted–one must have a soul of some sort. Sari Woodroffe had none. She was exactly like an animal. Evil in her was not a vice, nor was goodness, virtue. Watching her, in the year when I was frequently in the Woodroffe cottage, I learned a good deal about good and evil and the human soul, just as one might learn a good deal about disease by watching a perfectly healthy creature. And I am convinced that Sari Woodroffe was not a woman. She was female, but not a female of our kind. Whenever I saw her I was reminded of the story of the Bywater man who married a mermaid.

After Bob Wicks' conversion I became interested in Tom Woodroffe. Stephen Fennel, who was a fellow pupil of mine, had been sneaking into Baildon to 'The Fox,' which was kept by an old prize-fighter, and had paid a guinea for some lessons. He had passed on to me–since he judged me about his equal in weight and therefore a likely person to practise on–some of the rudiments of the noble art of self-defence. So I was, although I loathed the practice, academically interested in the subject, and I could not understand how Tom had floored Bob Wicks when he was sober. He was so ungainly, such a collection of knobs and bumps and hollow places, he moved so clumsily and seemed so slow and ill-balanced, that it seemed to me as though a mere push could cause him to collapse. So, physically, he interested me, and gradually the interest became deeper. I was going on for fourteen and suffering all the pains of adolescence, amongst which is the quickening of a religious sense. Twice, during the early spring of that year, I listened to Tom Woodroffe preaching, and on each occasion, if willingness to be converted could have brought conversion, about converted I should have been. I longed to share his simple, sincere and lovely faith. But it was quite useless. Whatever response he wakened in me came from my head, not my heart. I remained quite unchanged. But I remained also greatly interested in the man himself, and I was cogitating how best to get to know him, even saving a few odd coins and planning to ask him to make me some small inexpensive thing, when Chance–that capricious, goddess whom my father worshipped so wholeheartedly–threw us together.

Every Monday, Wednesday and Friday I rode over to the Rectory at Minsham All Saints for my lessons with the Reverend Mr Saunders. Mr Saunders was Rector of Minsham St Mary, too, but he lived in All Saints because the house there was better, and nearer the good turnpike road. He was a studious old man, ascetic in his habits, and not very popular in a district where sporting parsons were fashionable. But popularity was the last thing he craved, and I think he would have been perfectly happy to be left alone with his books and his papers and the gentle routine of unavoidable duties. Unfortunately for him, when the two Minshams were enclosed under the Act of 1778, the Squire of St Mary was engaged in a violent feud with the parson who was then the incumbent, and managed, by some trick or sleight of hand, to reduce the tithes on that village to practically nothing. It was the only case I ever heard of where the tithe holder suffered from the enclosures together with the common people. But it had happened, and the Reverend Saunders, succeeding to the livings, paid for his predecessor's quarrel with his lord. Moreover, there were three Misses Saunders, alive and unmarried, and they were all simple in the mind, as though all the brains in the family had been concentrated in the one son. He hated the sight and even the very mention of them, and maintained a separate establishment for them in Water Lane in Bywater, and to meet the cost of it he himself took pupils from amongst what he called the sons of gentry. He detested boys and he loathed teaching, and did his best to avoid resident pupils. But at the time when I suffered under his tuition there were four big boys and one small one lodged in the lofts above the coach-house, and heartily pitied by the rest of us fortunate fellows who could, at the end of each session, ride back to our homes. They repaid our sympathy by envy, and I was most envied of all, for I went to school only three days a week. This was due entirely to our poverty. Mother would have had me there every day if she had had her way, and I did once listen, sweating and apprehensive, while she argued with father that the six guineas tax on the gig every year would purchase me another day a week of education. Fortunately father, though he kept agreeing with her and saying, 'Mum, my dear, mum course. Mum mum yes, yes,' went the next week and took out the gig licence and I was saved. Actually it made little difference whether I went to school three days a week or six, like Stephen Fennel or Lord Latchmore's half-wit, who was being shaped for Eton. The Reverend Saunders never *taught* us anything. He assumed, with little reason in some cases, that we could read English and could stumble through a Latin or Greek sentence. And his method was to select a book for reading, and a primer for working on, roughly within our scope, set us to read it, ask questions on the reading, and whack us soundly for wrong answers. For me the system did very well. I read my English book and, I can say, without boasting, never failed to answer a question; Latin and Greek remained Latin and Greek to me. I recognized a word here and there, but that was all, and I was whacked twice a week as a matter of course. I became hardened to the amount of physical pain which a lazy old man with a cane can inflict upon the saddle-toughened buttocks of a healthy young boy, and since there was no shame, but even a little glory, connected with the beatings, I did not mind them much. Some fellows went through their schooling without ever having been beaten, and they lived in dread of it, exaggerating the pain in their imaginations. Stephen and I, who were whacked so often, were looked upon as little heroes. Stephen was beaten because, being a natural genius at mathematics, a subject upon which the Reverend John never touched at all, he was bored by other lessons and took no pains with them, spending his time in working out curious problems about angles and curves and weights and measures in the margins of his books.

On this particular Monday which sticks in my mind as the day when I first came into contact with Jassy Woodroffe and her father, I had been beaten, as usual, for my failure with my grammar. I had, as usual, eaten my noon meal, one of Meggie's veal pasties, in the company of Stephen Fennel, who had described to me his plan for making a water clock, and given my second pasty and two apples to the little resident boy who complained that he did not have enough to eat, and whose looks bore out the assertion. Then in the afternoon I had answered, without a fault, the questions put to me about the book which I was reading in English. It was a vast tome called *Captain Anderson's Own Account of His Various Voyages*, and when I first set eyes on it I had been thrilled by the promise which the title seemed to hold. But it was the dullest book I had ever read. The good sea-captain had been to many interesting places and seen many extraordinary sights. He seemed to be a brave and resourceful sailor, but he ought not to have attempted to write a book. He never used a short word if he could find a long one, and he never used one word if four could possibly be squeezed in. And in the very middle of a piece of narrative, where the subject was so exciting that even his pomposity could not obscure it, he would digress into a kind of lecture about the wonder of Providence or the mystery of Nature as though he guessed that his pen was running away with him and and was determined to check it. However, I had imagination of a kind and could see, behind the dullness and prosiness, the scenes and the people and the adventures which the captain had attempted to describe, and would probably have said he *had* described. So I could answer and thus escape a beating, whereas Stephen, who was working neck by neck with me, and who had planned a water clock when he should have been afloat in the good ship *Steadfast*, was beaten for the second time that day.

It was March, and Lent had started, so we were let out of school at four o'clock, a relief instituted to enable the Rector to devote more time to the duties which the season was supposed to bring. Stephen and I and two other boys had a brief sharp game of Nobbin behind the coach-house, and I lost a shilling, my only one, destined to last as pocket money for an unspecified length of time. The usual loss for one round was only about fourpence, and I reflected bitterly as I watched Stephen shuffle the cards for a second round, that whereas I had never *won* more than eightpence I had been able to *lose* a shilling. I had to refuse to play again, and since four players were needed the game broke up then, not without acrimony. And then, when we went to the stables for our mounts, I found that Stephen, whose fourteenth birthday had fallen two days before, had a new mare–a sweet, dainty, spirited little thing with a coat which had the colour and gloss of a newly-shed chestnut, and lines which told of blood and breeding. She had been a present from his father, and his mother had given him the silver-mounted saddle and bridle. Even Joby's delighted whinny and nuzzle of welcome could not blind me to the fact that he was only a rough sturdy plug, meant for a farm boy to hack about on.

'Care to try her? You can take her over the fence at the bottom there and I'll meet you on the road,' said Stephen generously.

'No,' I said. 'Thanks. But I'd better be off.'

'It wouldn't stop you. I'll bet a shilling that you'll be waiting on the road by the time I've got there on your horse.'

'I know.' Without offering any explanation I got into my saddle and turned Joby's head towards the gate. 'Good night, Stephen. I'll see you on Wednesday.' Conscious of Stephen's puzzled stare upon my back I jogged out of the gate. I felt miserable and resentful. Poverty, I thought, gripped you everywhere. I was frankly jealous of Stephen, who had likewise lost a shilling and had been able to shuffle the cards with the knowledge that even if the next round cost him as dearly he could pay up like a man; and who had been given such a splendid birthday present. I was fond of Joby, and had been wildly excited when he had been bought for me, but he was just a plug, a boy's mount, a farm boy's mount, and my saddle was shabby, and my stirrups at their longest were now too short. And as far as I could see, I should never be mounted any better.

I gloomed my way out of Minsham All Saints and reached the turnpike. There I hesitated. My mood prompted a visit to Mortiboys, whose rambling red roof showed about a quarter of a mile along the road. But by this time I had gained a certain amount of wisdom and no longer went out of my way to make myself wretched. So I crossed the turnpike and took the road to home.

This road, known as the Upper Road, hugged the edge of the higher land and was long, on account of its windings. The marsh road, called the Lower Road, was shorter, and in dry weather one could ride between Green Farm and Mortiboys in twenty minutes, whereas on the Upper Road the journey stretched out to thirty-five or forty. But in March, unless the winter before had been phenomenally dry, the Lower Road was a sheer lane of mud, covered in parts with water, and nobody chose it unless his errand was urgent. It was much used by smugglers bringing up contraband from Bywater inland. Tonight, riding along the Upper Road in a surly mood which did not welcome the journey's end, I travelled slowly, and the long-drawn-out twilight of the spring evening was beginning when I came in sight of our village green. Just there the road left the higher land and sloped down into Minsham St Mary, and at the head of the slope a man, particularly if he were mounted, had a clear unimpeded view of the village. On this evening, as I looked ahead and saw the Green, dun coloured with the old grass through which the new year's verdure had not yet broken, and the great pond, and the ring of cottages, I heard, made thin by distance, a strange and oddly disturbing sound. It was a weird howling in which ferocity and sadness were oddly mingled. I have heard it since, but on that evening it was new to me, and I was halfway down the slope before I identified it as the mass voice of human beings. By that time, straining my eyes, I could see a knot of people gathered upon the side of the pond which was farthest from the road, and in another second, since distance would not account for their smallness, I could tell that they were children. Some new game, I thought, and wondered why they should, of choice, make so exceedingly dismal a noise about it. It was louder now that I was nearer, and it was remarkably disturbing, like the howling of angry and yet frightened animals.

Now I could recognize, by a few salient blobs of colour on the general drabness of the little crowd, certain individual children. There was the incongruous red patch which Jem Meekings had flaunted all winter on his old buff breeches, Nonny Fayres' grass-green knitted cap, little Fanny Moy's orange scarf, a present at Christmas from my mother, in whose dairy Mrs Moy worked at times. These bright recognizable specks moved as the crowd milled and shifted, but the whole crowd hung together, like a bee-swarm, and it was this fact which, combined with the howling, convinced me that the children were not playing. I checked Joby and rode slowly for a moment or two. I was disinclined to interfere; my position in the village was already an awkward one, and I had no wish to lay myself open to the implied insult of the speechless, sullen stare with which yokels, even young ones, can accuse one of busy-bodying. Moreover, I was in a surly mood myself, and not disposed to be even a putative Galahad. But then I thought of a dog. I could well imagine that howling circle holding in its midst some rail-thin little stray, either paralysed by terror, or futilely ferocious. My imagination kindled easily in those days; and was, at that moment, capable of making me see the dog, its wild glance in search of a protector, the feeble, placating, unavailing wag of its tail. Nevertheless, it was still reluctantly that I looked about and weighed up the position. I was on the road, and the pond, roughly pear-shaped, lay between me and the children. If I rode–and the coward in me knew exactly what advantages belonged to a mounted person–I had to go along the whole of my side of the pond, round the wide part at the end, and so reach them. The narrow, the stem-end of the pear-shape was closed–to a horse, at least–because it joined on to Clem Barber's stackyard, and he had erected a fence to keep his property divided from the Green. But between the rails of this fence and the edge of the water there was a narrow crumbling bank along which an active person, not too heavy, could run. I decided that that was my quickest way. I slipped out of my saddle, said 'Stand' to Joby, hopped over the fence and plunged forward. Once the bank gave under my feet and I fell into the water, splashing even my hat, but I held on to the fence and pulled myself out, angrier than ever and already resolved that I would take a smack at Jem Meekings, a big lout who had annoyed me before. I was within six feet of the edge when the dancing jeering circle broke; little Fanny Moy fell flat on her back, borne down by some pressure from within, and through the gap thus made there dashed a wildly dishevelled crazy figure which I did not instantly recognize as the Woodroffe child. She ran like a hare, and her face, turned my way, was a white muddy mask of horror. The other children who had been facing inwards in a circle, turned about, collided with one another and stumbled over Fanny Moy, who lay where she had fallen and screamed like a pig-killing; but very soon they had sorted themselves and surged forward, a human pack in full cry. There were no words, just primitive sounds of hatred. Every mouth was open, and in every mouth the eye-teeth seemed suddenly longer than usual, fang-like. They were the children of our village; they came to carry away skim milk from the dairy; at Christmas time they sang carols on our porch; after harvest they asked permission to go gleaning in the fields. But tonight they were changed and hideous. All reason had gone out of them; they had swung back across the centuries into the primeval abyss which–according to Captain Anderson–lies behind even the most civilized races. They were so mad that if they had caught their quarry she would have been mauled and trampled before the sanest one amongst them could have realized what was happening.

But I was there. She ran straight at me, so blind with terror that she did not even see me at first. When she did, she thought I was one of the hunters, heading her off, and she screamed like a hare, and like a hare, swerved aside, almost into the arms of Jem Meekings, who was running on one of the horns of the crescent-shaped pack. I caught her by the shoulder, yelling, 'Get along the bank and hold the fence.' She obeyed me, and I backed after her and took up a stand at the edge of the bank, shouting and waving my little riding crop, conscious that it was nothing more than a toy, and longing for a proper horse-whip.

The pack, panting and thudding, checked itself.

'Get outa road, Master Barney,' said Jem Meekings. 'We doon't mean you no harm. Thass she we're arter.'

'Not now,' I said. 'Anybody coming any nearer will feel the weight of my arm.'

'Coo, Master Barney, doon't you go sticking up for the likes of she,' said Essie Beam. 'Rare little drab she be.'

'Put a spell on you like as not,' said a voice from the rear.

'That's witch's stuff in her hands this minnut,' said another.

'Come on now, stand aside, Master Barney. We be ony gorn to duck her, see if she git the davil to howd her up.' That was Jem Meekings, and he took a step forward, and a surge of something I had not felt before, a real lust for violence, rose in me. All right, I thought, and swung my arm. But the silly little crop whistled harmlessly through the air, meeting no resistance. He had thought better of it and stepped back. And the madness was already seeping away from the children. Their mouths were closing, one or two were beginning to stare at their feet and shuffle away to the edge of the crowd. The final, comic note was sounded from the nearest of the cottages. Jem Meekings' mother, a great strapping creature who worked in the fields like a man, from choice, came to the door and called, in a voice that might have been heard in three parishes:

'Jem! Jem! Where's that water? I'll warm your backside for you, my boy!' Jem turned and began to run back to the far end of the pond where the water was deepest and the bank had steps worn in its slope, and the scum and duckweed on the water was pushed away by the regular plunge of the buckets. Other children, reminded of similar duties, or glad of a leader in retreat, followed him. Fanny Moy was already a receding blob and a lessening howl over by the cottages, and in a minute or two Jassy and I were alone.

'You can come back now,' I said, and reached out a hand to help her up the bank. Her thick black hair, usually strained back from her face and tightly plaited behind, had broken loose and streamed about her shoulders. There were several scratches on her face, and the blood was beading along them. Her poor neat clothes were torn and even muddier than mine. Altogether she was a pitiable little object. But she had recovered her self-possession, and although the hand she put in mind was icy cold, it was quite steady. So was her voice as she said, as soon as she stood beside me, 'Indeed, I am most deeply grateful to you.'

'That's all right,' I said awkwardly. 'Now I'll see you home. And we needn't walk, either.' I looked towards the far side of the pond and putting two fingers in my mouth I blew a shrill whistle. Joby was trained to answer it, and I trusted his sense to bring him round the big end of the pond to meet me. But he was thinking of his supper, and chose to imagine that I was whistling him from the farmyard gate. Holding to the road, he set off for home at a rattling pace.

'Stupid clown,' I said angrily. 'He knows better than that. Now we shall have to walk.'

'I'm glad, really,' she said. 'I want to look for my hair-ribbon. I think I know just where it fell.' Her voice was pleasant, low and rather deep for such a small person, and with a smoky quality about it. We began walking. She fumbled about and produced a little handkerchief and began to dab at her scratched face. When most of the blood and mud had been transferred to the handkerchief she tucked it away and shook her hair backwards, raking it with her fingers and smoothing it with the palms of her hands. Her hands were small, with narrow palms and long delicate fingers. They were brown with exposure and rough from hard work, but their shape was delightful, and as I noticed them I realized that I had never noticed hands before. What were mother's like, I wondered.

Perhaps she was conscious of my staring, for she said:

'I must tidy myself before I go in. Father would have such a fright. He shan't even *know* if I can help it. He *abhors* violence.'

'Rumour says differently.'

'Oh, you're thinking of Bob Wicks. That wasn't *father*, that was *God*.' She laughed, and I could see that the scratched side of her face was swelling. It resisted the pressure of her smile and made her look lop-sided and uglier than ever. Yet just at that moment she lifted both her arms and began to plait her hair behind her head, and when the plait was long enough she pulled it forward over one shoulder and worked on, weaving away with her lovely little hands until the plait ended, tapering below her waist. Just as it was finished she said, 'How timely,' and darted to one side, bent and picked up a scrap of yellow ribbon, and having tied it firmly to the end of her hair, tossed the plait back over her shoulder.

'Do I look *fairly* tidy now?'

'Fairly,' I said, 'but I think anybody would guess that you'd been in the wars a bit. Tell me, why did it happen? Why did they chase you?'

She hunched one shoulder and hesitated. 'It's on account of my mother, I think. Well, I know, really. It's been the same wherever we live. And father, too, a little, perhaps. But he doesn't annoy the *ignorant* people so much. He gets wrong with the gentry and parsons. Would you believe that we've lived in six villages in seven years?'

'If you say.'

'We have. Mother likes that, naturally. She's a Stannary. I suppose you know. She shouldn't live in a house at all.' She took out her handkerchief and pressed her check. 'Your mother is very house-proud, isn't she?'

'How do you know?'

'Oh, I've watched. Your drying ground, you know. Your linen makes mine look very mucky. I've tried and tried since I've been here, but mine never looks so good.'

'Well, you're not very big or strong,' I said. 'And actually mother doesn't do the washing in our house. Meggie, our maid, sees to it.'

'Ah, but it's the good mistress who makes a good maid, you know.'

We were near the cottages by this time, and we could see the door of the furthest one open. Against the firelit glow of the interior, Tom Woodroffe's ungainly figure outlined itself. Jassy gave a tiny sigh, half patient, half exasperated.

'He's coming to meet me,' she said. 'Do you think I could *possibly* say that I'd just had a fall? He'll be so upset. And he'll talk about turning the other cheek. It isn't true, you know, I did try that when they first set on me. Mother was nearer the mark. But I can't tell *him* that.'

'What did she say?'

'Oh, once when I was chased at Ockley she said, "Never run. Stand still and draw first blood." And I did get away by knocking over that nasty little Moy girl. But then I ran. So I haven't pleased either of them.'

'It must be rather difficult to please parents with such conflicting ideas,' I said feelingly.

She flashed me a glance eloquent of appreciation and conspiracy, but she said no more, for her father, after searching the Green, had seen us and was loping towards us.

'Jassy,' he said, in an agitated way, 'are you all right?'

'Perfectly,' she said in a funny little prim voice. 'Why?'

'The Moy child ran home a moment since with some horrible tale in which you were concerned.' I heard a little sigh again. 'Jassy, are you hurt?'

'I have a scratch on my face and my dress is torn. Master Hatton here will assure you that otherwise I am. . . . No, father, he must have his due. He did save me. I was in trouble and he did rescue me.'

The big man made a gulping sound, and with his right hand–his left arm was clasping Jassy–reached for mine and gripped it. A torrent of incoherent thanks poured from his lips so that I was embarrassed and began to utter false disclaimers which belied my inmost feelings; for after all I had gone, alone, to the rescue of, as I supposed, a dog; and I had saved her, if from nothing worse than a trampling or a ducking. But my self-conscious murmurings went unheeded. Tom Woodroffe continued to thank me until, with disconcerting suddenness, he broke off, and snatching the little girl up into his arms, said almost tearfully, 'Oh, Jassy, Jassy, why do you provoke them? I've told you before. You're all alone so often. You must be more cautious.'

'But I was,' said the little voice. 'I didn't do anything. I was coming home with a few catkins for grandmother's blue jug. Father, you *know* why it is. How *I* behave doesn't make any difference at all.'

'I must go,' I said, for we were now on the edge of the Green. Tom Woodroffe began to thank me again. I cut him short, saying 'Good night, and walking away. Then, over his shoulder, Jassy called, 'I'm grateful too,' to which I said 'Good night' again and began to run.

When I reached home, in a better mood and very hungry, I found the place in an uproar. Mother had heard Joby and come out to meet me, and found him with an empty saddle. She had immediately concluded that I, who had been riding safely to and from the Rectory for a matter of three years and more, had on this evening met with an accident. When I opened the yard gate Stoner and one of the labourers were just setting out, in thoroughly bad tempers, to inspect the Lower Road with a lantern, and mother was standing over father while he saddled Dane in preparation for a search of the Upper Road. At sight of me mother burst into fresh tears and hysterical expressions of reproach and affection. Father, who probably hadn't yet comprehended the situation, said 'Ha!' and then, looking closely at the girth, 'wants oiling.'

'Leave it now,' said mother sharply, 'and come in.' She put a hand on my shoulder and said, 'Now, where have you been?'

I told her. And I think her marked distaste for the Woodroffes began with that story. Without knowing it she connected the name with her moment of fright. Or perhaps she resented my friendship with a cottager. In any case, my subsequent friendship with Tom and Jassy went forward in the face of a good deal of opposition.

My own reasons for allowing what, after all, was only an incident to lead to a friendship, were so mixed and so numerous that if half of them had not existed the other half would have been motive enough. I was interested in the personality of the man; I still hankered to share the religion which he professed; I had a more mundane fancy to see his workshop and play with his tools; I was curious about Sari Woodroffe; and I had found that Jassy was good company, if only for the reason that her odd manner of speaking and complete self-possession held constant elements of surprise. And I could not forget that she had, quite unwittingly, made me forget myself and my penury and my lost Mortiboys for a full thirty minutes. There was still another reason in which none of the Woodroffes was concerned. In a few weeks I should be fourteen, and I was suffering from the urge to self-assertion which is a common feature of that age; and a routine so dull and circumscribed as mine offered few opportunities for aggressiveness. Nor was mine the kind of mind which could readily invent occasions for mischief. But here was one ready-made. Being friendly with the Woodroffes, in the teeth of opposition, made me feel like a person with taste and choice and a will of his own. The last reason of all, and the least tangible, though perhaps the most powerful of them, was a certain kind of fatalism which had already found an anchorage in my forming mind. I could trace the links of the tenuous chain: I had watched the family's arrival because I was working in the garden and bored; I had been interested in Tom beating Wicks because I had just been introduced to the art of fisticuffs; I had attended two of his meetings because they coincided with the first prickings of my soul; and I had rescued Jassy because I liked dogs. And during the days after that rescue I waited, half credulously, half scornfully, a further sign. For I could not, as things were, begin to haunt the cottage at the Green's end or show any extraordinary interest in the family. So I waited, and ten days after that Monday, sure enough, there was Jassy, looking over the yard gate when I went out to attend to the horses, and she said, trying to keep the excitement out of her voice, and succeeding, though it shone in her eyes:

'Do please come round to our house. Father wants to see you.'

And in the shed at the back of the cottage which Tom had turned into a workshop, untidy and cluttered, he presented me with a little oak desk, admirably and imaginatively made, with more partitions than ordinary, and a little secret compartment, and a lock, and with my initials and the hooded jennet which is the Hatton badge carved into the lid. And from that moment Tom Woodroffe held a place in my heart second only to Mortiboys–and perhaps to mother, who held me to her with peculiar ties of conscience, genuine affection and sheer exasperation.

All told, our friendship was brief enough. He gave me the desk at the end of March, and by the middle of October in the same year he was gone. And I cannot say that he influenced me much. He did not even save me from my infatuation with Mortiboys. Once, during that summer, which was wet and disastrous, I had hopes that he might. For he was, in himself, a completely unworldly person. He showed me how a man who has nothing except skill which he has no time to exploit, a man whose private life is strangely horrible, whose one earthly affection is fraught with fear and anxiety, whose very labour seems abortive, can yet be a happy man, because all his hope and confidence are centred about a supernatural belief. Tom Woodroffe was too busy to earn a living properly; his marriage was worse than a failure, his love for his daughter was a pain, his gratuitous toil on behalf of other men never bore fruit in his time; but he believed and he trusted in God Who had made all things, to Whom all things were plain, and Who would never fail a humble, earnest servant. And he was a happy man. I have never met another.

I had, as I have said, high hopes that I might, by sharing his beliefs, reach the point where to me, as to him, it did not matter where I lived, how I was clad, whether my pockets were full or empty, or whether men esteemed me or not. But destiny, or breeding, were too strong. Tom could not change me.

He taught me things. He had a powerful ally in my imagination, and he made me squeamish about much which other men take for granted. Tailors, for example.

Soon after I had begun to visit the cottage Tom saw, in Bywater, a youth of perhaps fifteen snatch a slice of bread from a child of about four. He spoke to the boy admonishingly, I imagine, and then, noticing that the apparent bully was avidly consuming the bread, was thin and pale, and had a badly bruised face, in a more sympathetic fashion. He learned that the boy was an apprentice at Calthorpe's, the best tailor in the place. He took him into a chop-house and treated him to a bowl of mutton broth and learned, in ten minutes, a great deal about Calthorpe's treatment of the boys who worked for him. Armed with this information–which he implied had been gained by observation and inference–he visited the shop and tried to reason with the tailor, who, perceiving that he was not dealing with even a potential customer, dropped his obsequious manner and roundly told Tom that the treatment meted out to his apprentices was well within the law. There was nothing in their articles to demand that the boys occupied his best bedroom, ate rump steak twice a day, or had leisure to indulge their pranks. He had undertaken to house and feed and teach them, and that he was doing. He defied anyone, even the Sheriff himself, to bring complaints on legal grounds. I can picture the man, so sure of his ground, gloating over the discomfiture of the great awkward ill-dressed busy-body, who merely said:

'Very well, Mr Calthorpe, if you won't listen to the voice of humanity, and the law won't help me, I must try another means.'

Oblivious apparently to the fact that the amelioration of the lot of three tailor's apprentices would put no penny in his pocket, and that obsequious attention to Nick Helmar's wishes would employ him profitably through the coming winter, Tom, with a list of abuses in his hand, set out to visit every gentleman and every farmer who, according to another list supplied by the original protégé, patronized the tailor. Before starting out he worked feverishly in the shed, finishing off commissioned articles, and I know for a fact that he had left with Sari and Jassy every penny he collected on them, trusting himself to the charity of the countryside.

In due course, working on a narrowing circle with our village as its centre, he came, on a June evening, to call upon my father, whose name was on Calthorpe's books, with, at that moment, the sum of fifteen pounds outstanding against it. I was in the parlour at the time when Meggie showed him in, and I noticed the signs of fatigue and hunger on his always cadaverous face. He had caught cold, too, and was almost voiceless, so that conversation between him and my mumbling parent was a test for one's hearing. He offered the paper which bore the evidence against Calthorpe to father, who never read anything if he could help it, and who pushed it away, saying in a puzzled fretful manner, 'Read mum mum must!' Tom read it and it made sorry hearing. Then in his husky shredding voice, he said:

'Now, Mr Hatton, sir, I ask you, can you happily wear a suit of clothes that has been made in such circumstances?'

'Mum never could mum any clothes Calthorpe mum,' said father, still puzzled but emphatic. 'Mum can't *cut* mum. Not that I blame mum apprentices. Mum at all. Mum should mum the scissors. Certainly. Apprentices mum.' Then some idea, misleading, but an idea, dawned in that stupid, handsome head, and he straightened his back and lifted his chin and spoke out quite plainly for a second or two. 'What is all this about? Is

Calthorpe dunning me? Mum mum! You tell him from me, will you, that the things he made me last would disgrace a scarecrow and I don't intend to pay for them. Mum mum! Moreover,' said father thrusting his chin out and looking at Tom with accusatory eyes, 'it's not a bit of use coming here and blaming the apprentices. If they don't work, damme, he should take a stick to them. Mum mum indeed.'

I saw an expression of despair gather in Tom's sunken eyes. He had had, as I heard later, many and various receptions, but never, I am certain, had he been met by such complete lack of comprehension.

'But, sir, you misunderstand me,' he said patiently. 'I'm sorry, perhaps I didn't make my point clear. I came here to tell you how Calthorpe treats these wretched boys, and to ask you, in the name of God and common humanity, not to deal with him again until he acts more fairly to them.'

'Mum,' said father, who, with his head slightly on one side, had really been giving Tom his whole attention. 'I see. Well, all I can say is mum. Never deal with him again. Never. Said so the instant I mum mum that last job. Don't care who knows.'

'But you are withdrawing your custom on account of his bad workmanship, not on account of his treatment of his apprentices.'

'Eh?' Father's face was deepening in colour. The demands made upon his attention were beginning to annoy.

'All this that I read you,' said Tom, thrusting the paper forward again. 'Weren't you disgusted, sir?'

'Utterly disgusted,' said father, and moved to the bell for Meggie to show out this bewildering visitor. He never learned that Meggie, knowing herself indispensable, could ignore bells as easily as insults. I rose from my obscure seat and went over to Tom.

'There you are,' I said. 'That's one more. Now you come along home and get some food inside you and get to bed. I'll walk across with you.'

Tom hesitated, but after another glance at father, bade him a respectful good evening and allowed himself to be drawn outside. As we crossed the little hallway which seemed too brilliantly lighted by the lamp we had brought from Mortiboys, I saw him shake his head, like a big puzzled dog.

'But I wanted your father to put his name to it. Several gentlemen have done that, and four or five even said that they'd write letters independently.'

'I'll write for father,' I said eagerly. 'Our names are the same, and I write a far better hand.'

'Would that be honest?'

'Well, you heard what he said. And that stands for me, too. I'll never patronize Calthorpe, or any other tailor that I know treats boys like that. When you were reading I felt quite sick; and very glad that mother gets old Sam Jolly to make my things, badly as he fits me.'

'Ah, yes,' said Tom with a sigh. 'But later on, when you're a young gentleman of fashion, Barney, my boy, will you bother then?'

'I just said, I'd never wear clothes made in such conditions. If I knew.'

'There's the rub,' he said. He stared straight out into the lovely evening without seeing anything. 'If people *knew*. But they don't, and it's difficult to tell them. I wrote a letter to the *Bywater Gazette* about Calthorpe, but they didn't print it.'

'For a very good reason,' I said. 'They carry his advertisement every week, summer and winter.'

'I hadn't thought of that.'

'And I've just remembered another thing. Don't carry that paper to Jonas Rigger at Marsh Place. He's some kind of relative to Calthorpe, brother-in-law, I believe. I remember his telling Stoner, our foreman in the yard, that he got his breeches made for nothing. He'd set the dogs on you as soon as spit.'

'I had aimed to go there now. But it'd be a waste of labour. So I've finished, save for Mr Helmar, and I can ask him tomorrow when I go along to start work. There're many things I'd sooner do, but I've got to think a bit about the winter's food, I'm afraid. By the look of things, the harvest won't be good this year.'

A sharp pain, as though a hot rod had transfixed me, shot from my skull to my heels, as Tom mentioned going to work at Mortiboys.

'What is going to happen there?' I asked.

'Where? Around here? Scores of people will starve I'm afraid.'

'Oh, no,' I cried impatiently. 'I didn't mean that. What are they going to do at Mortiboys?'

'Pull it down, I should say, from the sound of it. Well, hardly that, but great alterations are planned, I hear. There're going to be a dozen of us at work with a Mr Sedley, a London architect, to tell us what to do. The whole gateway is coming down for one thing. I know that, because before I went off on this job,' he patted the pocket where the papers now rested, 'Mr Helmar asked me my opinion of the wood, and I told him it was rotten as a pear.'

'I don't think I can bear it if that archway comes down.'

'Why, Barney?'

'I can't. And it's all nonsense. It's made of brick, isn't it? What's wood got to do with it? And for you to say that, Tom. I thought you were my friend.'

'Wood has this to do with it,' said Tom, ignoring my outburst. 'Those brick and timber buildings that those old folks put up last as long as the timber and no longer. There're places in that arch, and in the little houses either side, where the beams have gone and the bricks are sagging. 'Tisn't safe any longer.'

'It'd be safe enough for me,' I said violently. 'It's just that Nick Helmar shouldn't live there, with his stinking money and rotten ideas. Mortiboys should belong to somebody that loved it, and would rather cut off his hand than alter one bit of it.'

'I'd go further and say that places like Mortiboys shouldn't have any money spent on them at all–not with wages at seven shillings a week and flour at a shilling a quartern. But that's by the way. Barney,' he put his hand on my shoulder, 'I thought you'd got the better of that weakness. Let Mortiboys go. Haven't we thrashed this out before and agreed that you weren't to ruin your life over a whim?'

'I know,' I said wretchedly. 'I did agree once. But I don't now. Just the mere mention of that gateway going shows me how much I care still. I tell you I'd stop at nothing if only I could have Mortiboys for my own.'

'Barney, you mustn't say such things. Stop at nothing, indeed. Think what that means. Sometimes I fear for you, boy. I had a dread that that place'll twist you and give Satan a hold on your soul.'

'Satan!' I said wildly. 'If Satan would give me Mortiboys–as it is, mark you–he could have my soul and welcome.'

'You're overwrought, Barney, and maybe this isn't the time for me to say much to you, but all the same . . .' and at that moment his voice, which had been growing weaker and hoarser, failed suddenly. He cleared his throat and then looked at me and laughed. 'There,' he said in a whisper, 'God must have known that nothing I could say now would help. I'll get along. And would it be too much to ask you to think over that first talk we had ever about that place?'

My conscience smote me. I had seen how exhausted he was, and I had left my house in order to see him home. And here we were on the darkening Green with me bothering him about my personal problem.

'I'll think of it, Tom. Good night.'

'Good night, boy. God bless you.'

I walked back to our yard gate, and when I had closed it for the night, turned back and rested my arms on the top bar and my chin on my clasped hands. My mind was busy with Mortiboys, seeing the gateway as it now was, the arch of little bricks, the deceptively sturdy timber, the houses with their diamond-paned windows; and then seeing it dismantled, destroyed, gone for ever from the sight of man. I went through the whole story of the Hattons and their home, and although my face was steady and my body motionless, it was as though within me my heart was shedding tears of blood, and through the hollow of my marrowless bones great waves and surges of anger and impotence, of longing and hopelessness, were shaking me to destruction. I could feel my mind reaching out into the empty evening, into the universe, into the past, seeking, demanding strength from something, from somebody, from God, or the Devil, or those Hattons, long dead, who must have loved Mortiboys as I did. I couldn't be left here, one small tortured poor boy hanging on a gate. I must be more, more, more. And suddenly, when the tension had reached an untenable pitch and I was about to burst, something happened. I did, in actual fact, touch something with my mind, and it was like a steady cold hand being laid on my pounding heart. I straightened myself and lifted my face to the sky, where one great star hung unwinking. And I knew that out of the very essence of my soul I had saved Mortiboys. I was as sure that it was going to remain, fundamentally untouched, as I was sure that I was standing by the gate into our farmyard. I began to shake in every limb, even my head wagged, and there was a queer pain, the like of which I had never felt before, in the back of my skull.

I waited until I had some control of myself, and then went into the house, hoping to reach my room without being seen. But mother, who had been trying to get from father an account of the business which had brought Tom Woodroffe into her parlour, was watching for me, and after exclaiming at my pallor–which she attributed to standing in the night air with him–must hear it all again from me.

'It's a wonder he can find time to run around minding other people's business,' she said acidly. 'I thought he was a carpenter.'

'So he is, mum mum,' said father. 'Mm told you when he came mm going to work for Nick mm Mortiboys. Taking down mm dangerous arch I hear.'

Listening to that assertion, which he made as though Mortiboys were not more to him than an Indian wigwam, some of my inflation left me. How could I, just by standing in the dusk and willing something, alter the schemes of a rich, powerful person like Nick Helmar? Reason told me that I was daft. But deep down, below reason and common sense and fear, deeper even than thought or desire, there lay a little grain of certainty. Resting upon it, too exhausted to even think about the matter any more, I took myself to bed.

Six days later the whole countryside was shocked, or excited, or maliciously tickled to hear that Mrs Helmar of Mortiboys had run away with the young architect from London. Apparently he had been her lover for some time, and it was in order to ensure his employment–and easy proximity–that she had worked upon her husband until he gave his consent to the alterations and improvements at the house. Sedley had been staying at Mortiboys for a fortnight, we were told, tapping and measuring and working on his plans; and then Nick Helmar, returning from a ride or a visit, caught the pair in circumstances which could have but one explanation. He had ordered Sedley out of the house, but had not, according to rumour, shown any great animosity to Mrs Helmar, of whom he was dotingly fond. However, when Sedley went she went too. All the workmen were paid off and sent home, three of them, skilled workers in plaster and marble, all the way back to Italy. And the work stopped.

I was stunned by the news, and a little frightened; but I was not surprised. I remembered the cold, unshakable certainty which had laid hold of me on that evening six days before, and I hoped that Mrs Helmar would be happy with her lover, for in losing Mortiboys she had saved it, and in some inexplicable fashion for which mere human language has no terms, I felt that she, and Sedley the architect, and Nick Helmar, the cuckold, had been puppets at the end of a string. A string which I had not pulled, but which I had indicated.

July and August passed, a wet cold summer. The prospects for the corn harvest were the worst for years. And in a two-handed fashion this fact brought Jassy Woodroffe to work in our dairy. Mother, seeing that the harvest would be poor, began to concentrate upon the dairy as a source of profit and was in a mind for more help; Jassy, knowing that bread would be dear, and that Tom would not be engaged in the promised regular work at Mortiboys, was determined to find a situation.

Mother engaged her, largely through my mediation, and dubiously enough. For a few days–until Jassy had caught the knack of the unfamiliar work–my life as well as hers was rendered miserable by constant criticism. But even mother could not long withstand the intelligence, the superhuman energy, the fury of concentration which Jassy could bring to bear upon any task, and within a fortnight mother said, 'She's better than I expected.' That was as far as she would go; but the criticism stopped, though I noticed with amusement that my visits to the dairy were now looked upon with as much disfavour as my visits to the cottage had been.

But there came, in the middle of August, four blazing hot days, memorable because they were the only taste of summer that the year brought us. On one of them–the third–mother went down to Bywater in the gig with father. As soon as they had gone Meggie put on her hat and announced her intention of taking the day off too, and hobbled away to visit her cronies.

At midday I went indoors and, taking a jug, walked into the dairy for some cider at which mother had tried her hand the previous autumn, with indifferent success. But though a sour and windy beverage, it seemed attractive in the unaccustomed heat. In the dairy I found Jassy, bowed over the handle of the churn and crying. She lifted her head as I entered, and I remember being struck by the contrast between her neat, child's figure in the faded lilac print bodice and skirt, her slim brown arms under the rolled-up sleeves, her slender little ankles and feet, and her face. There was a film of sweat on her bulging forehead, her eyes were swollen with tears, her cheeks, usually so pale, were duskily flushed and glazed from crying. Her expression was both miserable and furious.

'Why, Jassy,' I said. 'what's the matter?'

'I don't know. I've done everything I should. And it just won't come.' She began to cry again.

'Wait a minute,' I said. And I filled the jug, drank from it, and turned back to her. 'I'll take a turn, shall I?'

She stood back and I took the handle and turned the churn over. Inside it the cream flopped with a flabby, unhopeful sound.

'It beats me,' I said, 'how you can turn the thing at all. Don't you find it heavy?'

She shook her head. She had almost stopped crying and stood looking at me with an expression which I often caught on her face. It had embarrassed me at first, and I had tried to think myself mistaken. Then, seeing it again, I put it down to the fact that I had gone to help her against the mob of children, and I thought it would wear off in time. But it lasted–a curious mediating look with an element of adoration in it. I had seen it when I said that I would speak to mother about giving her work, and once or twice since then when I had spoken to her about the place. And now here it was again. I turned away from it, uncomfortable, and swung the churn violently. After a few minutes she said, in her primmest voice:

'I'm rested now, thank you. I'll try again. I think you are a little rough with it.'

I relinquished the handle and she began to turn it, smoothly and without obvious exertion, though I could see the sweat start out again on her face. Below her arms and in a pitch between her shoulders, the faded lilac print was damp, darkening with moisture to its original hue. She turned for some minutes, and still the cream flopped, and at last she was drawing her breath in gasps that were quite as noisy and as frequent as the flops.

There was a backless chair under one of the dairy shelves, kept there so that mother could sit sometimes when she was supervising, not working. I dragged it out and told Jassy to sit down while I took another turn. Before I began I took another pull at the cider, and then handed her the jug. 'It's quite awful to taste, but it is cool,' I said.

I turned for ten minutes more and then gave up in disgust.

'Where's old woman Moy?' I demanded. 'Let her do it!'

'She isn't coming today. It's the first time I've been alone with it. I did so want it to turn out well.'

'Go and fetch her.'

'No. I don't want to do that. I won't be beat. Don't you bother though. Leave it with me. I'll do it.'

'I bet you fourpence you won't.'

'I can't bet,' she said primly, 'because I can't afford to lose.'

'I'll bet, all the same. If it comes I'll give you fourpence.'

I sat down on the chair and she took the churn. She swung it steadily, almost persuasively, for another ten minutes. Then she stopped suddenly and all the colour left her face. It was as though she blushed white. Then she said, in rapid succession, three of the worst swear words I had heard, put both hands on the churn and gave it a push that was plainly intended to send the whole thing flying. But the churn merely lurched, ran forward a little, hit the shelf and knocked down one of the wide, shallow pannikins in which the new milk was set for the cream to rise. I got to my feet and stared in helpless horror as the white pool widened about the floor. But even the crash had not sobered Jassy. Beside herself with temper, she jumped with both feet in the milk, snatched up the biggest bit of the broken crock and dashed it to the floor. Then, turning a wild white face to me she said:

'I'm going home now. And you can tell your mother that if she comes there with any idea of beating me I shall kill her!'

'You little devil,' I cried, catching her as she dashed past me to the door. She kicked at my shins, and since that did not release her, dropped her head and bit me on the hand.

'Blast!' I said, and let her go, and stood looking at my bitten hand. The blood was gathering in the two punctures which her eye teeth had made, and I suddenly remembered the glittering fangs of the children who had chased her. And my mind was slipping away to Captain Anderson and his theories about the animal in civilized people, when Jassy, transformed again, seized my hand, kissing it and crying that she was sorry, that she didn't mean it, that she was mad and sorry, sorry, sorry.

'Come and let me bathe it, or you'll fester and die,' she said.

'Shut up,' I said impatiently. 'It's nothing.' I was indeed ashamed that for so small a hurt I had let her go. To restore myself I pointed to the floor and the broken crock and said sternly:

'It's that I'm worrying about. Mother will make you pay for it, you know.'

The spirit of defiance which had been in her a minute since, and the passion of penitence which had succeeded it, gave way to meek sanity. Jassy moved her small hands in a gesture of resignation and said, deeply: 'I know. I'll get another job and some money somehow. How much would it be worth, do you think?'

Immediately I was sorry for her, and thought of the whole pile of similar crocks stored in the cupboard under the back stairs. I fetched one out, and telling Jassy to remove all traces of the other, and the milk, took a pail out to the meadow and milked a cow at the untimely hour of one o'clock in the afternoon.

'You're sure it'll be all right? I wouldn't want you to be blamed,' said Jassy anxiously, as I tipped the new milk into the new bowl.

'It'll be all right,' I promised, and refrained from saying that mother's wrath would hardly visit me in the same fashion as it would have done Jassy. Then I put out my hand to pull the churn into place, and the body of it tilted, and within we heard the unmistakable thump of the butter.

'You did it,' I almost shouted, 'you did it after all.' And being young and easily amused we rocked with laughter at the thought of the butter coming just at the moment when Jassy despaired of it. I took out my fourpenny piece and, when she tried with arguments to refuse it, I put it into her palm and closed her little fingers over it.

Our rather green friendship had ripened rapidly in that hour, and when, with the dairy tidy and the butter awaiting further attention on the cold slab, we went and ate our midday meal together at the kitchen table, we were on better terms than we had ever been before. We talked a great deal and, presently, were telling one another our dearest wishes. Jassy said, with point-blank frankness, that she wanted a farm.

'I might have had one, too,' she said. 'My grandfather and grandmother Woodroffe have a nice little place. But Granny Woodroffe wanted my father to be a scholar and, do you know, she saved her egg and butter money for twelve years so that she could send him to the Grammar School at Bury St Edmunds. And he was so clever and worked so hard that he went from there to Cambridge. That was where he got religion and got into trouble because he wanted to be a preacher, though he wasn't a parson. And that broke Granny's heart. Then he married mother, and his father wouldn't have him home any more. But when Granny died she left him all the things that really belonged to her, the clock and the other things we have in our house. He told me all about Granny and the furniture once, how she loved it and used to polish it. And since then I *have* tried to keep the house nice.' She leaned a meditative face on her hand and added, 'I'm afraid that's as much as I can do towards being *like* her–my granny, I mean.'

'Do you want to be like her?'

'Father would like it. I could hear that in his voice when he told me about her. But then she hadn't a furious temper. Besides, if he thought Granny was the best woman he ever knew it seems odd that he should—' She stopped, looking at me for a moment with clouding eyes, and said, 'But you haven't said your dearest wish yet.'

'Mine is mad and yours is so sensible. You could have yours. You've only to marry a farmer. Mine is impossible.'

'Is it?' If her voice had held more avid curiosity and less sympathy I should have been warned and made up some trivial nonsense. As it was I said, 'I'd like to own Mortiboys.' Her ugly face flashed interest and approval.

'Ah!' she said. 'Back in June, when father worked there for a week, he forgot his dinner one day and I went over with it. I thought that it was pretty. I was sorry about the work stopping, for father's sake, but I was really quite glad to think that they hadn't pulled down that arch and the dear little houses.'

'So was I,' I said heartily. I was pleased, and a little excited, to discover in Jassy a fellow admirer of the gateway, but I was jealous, too. I wanted her to understand that her light and facile admiration of a 'pretty' place was very different from the feelings which I entertained for it. And also, at the back of my mind was a faint, unworthy thought that it was a little presumptuous in her to apply an endearing diminutive to anything connected with Mortiboys. So, beginning with, 'Ah, but you don't understand . . .' I went on to tell her more about my passion, and about Hatton history than I had ever told anyone, even her father. I might even, in my egregious folly, have hinted at how I had saved the gateway from Nick Helmar's vandalism, but before I reached that point Jassy looked up at the clock on the kitchen wall and jumped to her feet.

'I've got that butter to salt and shape,' she said, and went flitting across the kitchen. At the door of the dairy passage she halted and turned back.

'I never thanked you properly.'

'What for?' I asked, still thinking of Mortiboys and forgetting all about the business of the broken pan.

'For saving me again. I am grateful, because I do like working here.'

'Oh, go along!' I said. 'And, Jassy, if you're going to marry a farmer you'll have to learn not to take your spite out on the milk crocks.'

'Yes, I shall indeed,' she said, quite seriously. But as she closed the door she looked round the edge of it, a roguish smile on her ugly little face, 'Still, I brought the butter, didn't I?'

Mother never discovered that the pan was broken, and Jassy was still working in our dairy when the October troubles began.

By October the harvest was in and the price of corn fixed. In October, too, the summer wage rate ended, and the winter one, a shilling or two less on the week, came into force. There was often some slight dispute at this season between the farmers and landowners and the workpeople. Looking back, I think I cannot remember an autumn when there were not complaints and a little mild rioting. Mother, being a payer of wages, took her stand upon two tried arguments: one, that if the men could not support their families on their wages they should have fewer children; two, that if they could not afford to buy the best white bread they should make do with a cheaper kind mixed with rye or barley. Father never argued about the matter at all; he would mumble about the damned Radicals and the country going to the dogs, I, until this autumn, had never given the subject much thought except to agree, blindly, with mother. But this year there was Tom Woodroffe to shatter my complacency. He told me all about the evils of the recent Enclosures; he drove into my unwilling mind many uncomfortable facts about the rise in prices lowering the value of money, so that now, with nine shillings a week a man was worse off than he had been years ago with seven. And he made me miserable without convincing me completely. Because, after all, we were farming and we were not rich, and I did not see how mother could afford to pay higher wages.

'A living wage to labourers would benefit everybody,' said Tom, when I put this point to him. 'If the men in this village, for example, had more money to spend in Bywater, there'd be more trade done in the town, and there'd be an increased demand for your mother's butter and eggs.'

'Then prices would go up and things would be just as they are.'

'Not necessarily,' he said patiently. 'Your farm, and every other farm, could produce as much stuff again without doubling the cost of production. Your place would support twice the number of hens without giving much more work, and to sell forty eggs at twopence would pay better than to sell twenty at threepence. Can you see that? It's the same with everything. These men aren't asking for money to chuck in the pond, they're asking for money to spend. They're customers–or would be. That's what I'm trying to make people see.'

How often I had heard him say those words in the few months I had known him. But that was the last time. The wage dispute in that autumn was Tom Woodroffe's last battlefield.

There had been rumours of rioting in Kent as early as September; but our own district remained quiet for a little while longer. Sir Edward Follesmark, of Sible Havers, who was known as the Mad Squire, had professed himself willing to raise the wages of his own men and to intercede with other employers in the district to do the same. This Sir Edward was the son of the Squire who had cheated the Reverend Saunders' predecessor out of the tithe rights at the time of the Enclosures, and he, like his father, was anticlerical, and, despite his many acres, Radical in his views. He had called a meeting of wage-payers which, since mother could not well appear in public as the owner of Green Farm, father attended. He understood very little of what had happened, but he did come home and mumble that everything was all right. And for once he had the gist of the matter, for from mother's point of view the meeting had been a success: the increased rate was overwhelmingly voted down.

A few days later Nick Helmar at Mortiboys and Jonas Rigger at Marsh End had stacks fired, secretly in the night, as though in warning; and within a week the genuine rioting had begun. Mother, like every other farmer in the neighbourhood, took precautions. Live stock was carefully stalled at night, the shutters of windows were bolted into place, gates were locked and reinforced with faggots and hurdles, and Stoner, his son Phineas, father and I guarded the stackyard in turn. Job Mash and Timothy Rudd, our two labourers, did not come to work during that week, and I wondered to myself in what guise I should next see them. Like everybody else, I had read stories of the French Revolution, and I could not imagine Job and Timothy, so meek and slow, being part of a mob which with threats demanded bread or blood. In that I was right. For when the men visited Green Farm it was in the daylight, mid-afternoon of a golden October day, and they were as orderly and formal as a deputation from Parliament.

Mother, Meggie and I were alone in the house when the men, headed by Tom Woodroffe, stopped at our front gate. Father, in his usual light-hearted way, had accepted an invitation to shoot at Baildon Lodge. Tom came up the short flagged path alone and rang the bell. Mother went to the parlour window and asked in a stony civil fashion what he wanted. I stood at her elbow ready to close the shutter at the first sign of rowdiness. I was–and had been for weeks–in an invidious position. I did not pay wages, neither did I earn any. I was dependent upon mother, and knew that she had struggle enough to make ends meet with wages as they were. But I had also heard Tom's description of the men's case and found it reasonable. So, though I was prepared to defend the farm if it were actually attacked, emotionally I was neutral.

In answer to mother's question Tom flourished a paper and said:

'For myself, madam, nothing. On behalf of everybody here, five minutes of your attention.'

'I am listening,' mother said.

Tom read out, in plain clear phrases, the causes for the present dissatisfaction. He gave, from the paper, exact details of the cost of living and the decreasing value of money. Then, looking straight into mother's face, he launched into an impassioned appeal that the recent decision about wages might be reconsidered.

'We hold the view, ma'am, that Sir Edward's proposal failed to enlist sympathy not on account of ill-will, but of ignorance. We admit that it is difficult for people in a different station of life to rightly estimate the burden which the labouring man has to bear. You, Mrs Hatton, ma'am, and the rest of the landowners are not hit, as we are, by the rising price of food. Therefore, in order that you may not again err through ignorance, I offer you these few facts and ask you to believe, from that evidence and from the solemn word of all those here assembled, that unless wages are increased many of us, with our wives and children, will starve miserably before the winter is out.'

There was a bumbling sound from the knot of men at the gate. A general assenting sound, shot through by a few intelligible words, 'We're starving now'; 'Fix the wages on the price of bread'; 'We must eat to work.'

I looked at the little group and was struck, for the first time, by the miserable appearance they presented. Here and there a young man, as yet unburdened by domestic responsibility, not yet worn down by years of labour, was straight and healthy looking, but they were few. For the rest, although wind and weather had reddened and bronzed their faces, cheeks were hollow, shoulders bowed, knees bent, feet flattened. The common expression was one of anxiety; and after hearing Tom's analysis of their budgets I could understand it. And my sympathy was engaged by their meekness, their remarkable lack of venom. They were only asking, after all, for the right to live. They were not demanding comfort or privilege, but just enough food to enable them to keep up strength sufficient for the day's labour. My vacillating mind sided with them once again. Fidgeting with the shutter I whispered to mother, 'Say that you will reconsider. That will satisfy them and they'll go away.' Mother looked at me dubiously. Then she turned back to the window and said boldly:

'The rise in prices affects other things than food. That must be remembered, Woodroffe.'

Tom inclined his head awkwardly, but with a curiously adequate deference.

'At least you are reasonable, ma'am.' And one of the clear voices in the crowd said, 'You can live without other things. Food must be got.'

And then mother said, and as she said it I was amazed at the cunning of women, and saw why she had so happily seen father ride off leaving her to face whatever might happen that day:

'I have listened, and I have taken in what you have told me. But you must all understand that though I take an interest in this farm, mine is not the final word. However, this I will promise you. What you have said my husband shall hear, and I am certain that if Sir Edward and the other gentlemen and farmers decide to reconsider the matter, he will do likewise. Will that do?'

I realized that I had, for fourteen years, lived with, and for several of them underestimated, a very clever woman indeed. A voice in the crowd certainly said, 'Just words, Mrs Hatton, words,' and another answered it with, 'The master be shooting pheasants. Whass the price o' meat to the likes o' him?' But on the whole the crowd, which had never once been truculent, seemed placated. Tom replaced his battered old hat and the men began to shuffle into a pitiable imitation of marching order, and the visit to Green Farm would have been concluded uneventfully but for Meggie.

The room immediately above the parlour was hers, because it opened upon the back stairs, and she had evidently been listening from her window as Tom Woodroffe read his facts and figures and made his appeal. Now, to mother and me, from just above our heads, came Meggie's rough voice, thickened with tears.

'Wait, wait,' it cried. 'I got suthin for you. I know what thass like to be hungry, and you lot not working this week while you're fighting. I reckon you could do with a square meal. So wait, all on you.' There was a sound of scuffling overhead, and then, down on to our flagged front path and the road beyond the fence fell a shower of coins, vigorously thrown. And mingled with the rattling and little thuds of them came Meggie's hysterical cries. 'Bin saving for my owd age, but that don't matter now. You get your rights and I'll work till I drop. Now you, Job Mash, don't go spending your share on ale; tek your missus and babies suthin home.'

The coins she threw were mostly coppers, and I could imagine Meggie saving penny upon penny and never thinking of changing her hoard into more valuable and easily portable coinage. The shower seemed to last for several minutes. And it transformed a knot of men who had borne themselves with remarkable restraint, even with dignity, into a grotesque, grovelling mob. Tom had seen, with horror, a lout in his teens take bread from a four-year-old. We were witnessess of a more horrible sight, two full-grown men fighting one another for the possession of a penny from a servant maid's poor hoard. And yet Meggie, hysterical as she might be, had been visited by insight beyond the ordinary. These men, seeking their rights in a disciplined and dignified manner, were hungry. They were not working, so they were not earning, and there was not one in a hundred of them who had even enough to keep himself for a week in reserve. They fell upon the money madly, jumping into the ditch to retrieve a rolling coin, pushing and jostling, and looking up to Meggie's window and holding out their hands and caps and shouting, 'To me! Throw to me! Bless you! Bless your kind heart!'

Meggie threw the last coins, cried, really sobbing again, 'Bless you all!' and slammed her window shut. Her loud crying, harsh, as though her physical means for the expression of sorrow was rusty with lack of use–was audible to mother and me in the parlour. Mother had turned white with fury, and her expression boded no good for Meggie. But I could not mind that at the moment, for outside, on our garden fence, awkward Tom Woodroffe was giving another exhibition of incongruous agility. As the brown shower of coppers began to fall I had seen his expression change, become alert, anxious, a little wild. Then he had looked about for some object which he could mount. There was none. Our front garden, with its two flower beds, its flagged path and low box hedges, offered no rostrum. So he went to the fence, tested its strength, and then set first his hands and then his feet on the top rail, which was a mere spline perhaps three-quarters of an inch in thickness. He squatted on it for a second, released his hands and stood up, balanced on that narrow footing. His feet were across it, at right angles, too. He could not stand like a tight-rope walker because the pointed tops of the upright rails broke the surface at intervals of four inches or less. He just stood there, steady as though he were on a rock. And he shouted:

'You've got to give it back, every penny of it. I'm sorry. But you've got to give it all back. Why? I'll tell you why. If you carry so much as a penny you're liable to be charged for demanding money with menaces. That's true. Down at Oslefield in Kent a farmer gave a man eighteenpence in similar circumstances, and the man was charged and convicted. *He was transported for seven years!* If you keep so much as a penny, you are liable to the same punishment. Come on now, into my hat! Into my hat, I say!' He flung his hat to the ground at his feet and stood there, balancing, waiting.

Reluctantly the great bony fists approached the hat, hung over it, opened, and dropped the coveted coin. And as they did so I had a moment's illumination about men and money. Money had enslaved men, and it had established a system of false values. Those men by the gate, every one of them down to the roughest, least likeable specimen of them, were too good to be there grovelling for a charitable copper coin, scooping it up with avidity, and only letting it go–and then reluctantly, wistfully–in the face of a dire threat. And, similarly, there was mother beside me with her whole nature being slowly warped because she had not enough money. One could run one's eyes slowly up the social edifice, rung by rung, and find that lack of money, or the desire for it, was the motive behind almost every action. A few eccentrics, like my father, if indeed there were any others like him, seemed to be indifferent to it; but even he was in a better temper if he had won money at Faro than if he had lost it. And this rule of money was wrong. I had a flashing vision, tenuous, unrecapturable, but real while it lasted, of a world wherein the money value was not supreme. In such a world these men would be reckoned on their merits, good with the plough, careful with animals, clever with tools–yes, even the fact that they were faithful husbands and affectionate fathers would count. In such a world Mortiboys would be mine on account of the love I bore it; whether I could buy it in hard cash would be immaterial–the fact that I would gladly buy it with my blood would be the thing that counted. But I realized, even as the thought came, and went, that to measure what a man is, and what he loves, is impossible; therefore mankind, seeking always the easiest way, had fallen victim to the money value because money is easily reckoned visible, tangible. So there were the men by the gate, threatened with starvation if they did not get an increase of two shillings a week, and there was mother by the parlour window thinking that to give Job and Timothy and young Phineas another two shillings–and Stoner a proportionate rise–would result in her ruin; and that made two shillings, which is a paltry round thing made of adulterated silver and stamped in a special fashion, of more worth than industry and strength, than charity and justice, than human flesh and blood.

Outside on the fence, Tom, balanced in some phenomenal fashion, reached down, retrieved his hat, and held it in one hand while he counted the money. Then, turning his head, he shouted up to Meggie:

'My dear, how much did you have in your stocking?'

'Matter of fower pound ten. I don't want it back,' said Meggie, her voice even more sodden than before.

'Can't you say exactly?'

'Fower pounds ten shillings and ninepence. But you let 'em keep it, Mr Woodroffe, for the sake of the families. I bin hungry when I was a little 'un.'

'That's what we're fighting against,' Tom called back. 'But if we take your money–and it lacks four shillings at the moment–we risk some poor family losing its man and being hungry for seven years. And spies are everywhere.' He swept his gaze round, not excluding either the crowd of his own followers or Meggie herself, or mother and me at the window. Then he brought it to rest upon the men. 'Come on now,' he said, cajoling, 'hand it over. Better a hungry week now than a visit to Botany Bay. There's four shillings missing. *And I think I know where they are.* Now then, shut your eyes every one of you, and those that are able say a prayer for the cause and meantime those with a shilling stuck to their palms, break them loose and chuck them in. Otherwise I give up and you can make your next visit without me.'

I kept my eyes open and I saw the four shillings thrown into the hat. And one of them came from the hand of Kit Barber, Clem's ne'er-do-weel brother, who had no wife and no child and was, at the least, always sure of a meal in Clem's kitchen. He had been keeping the shilling, I was sure, to spend at 'The Evening Star.' And I thought that it was very difficult to make any rules of conduct, or laws, which were to include on a dead level men like him and, say, Bandy Fayres, who, according to Tom, never ate anything but bread and potatoes in order that his wife might have tea and his children bacon and milk.

Tom opened his eyes, dropped easily off the fence on the garden side, counted the money into neat piles, and looked up at Meggie's window again.

'We're just as grateful as if we'd taken it,' he said. 'Put it by again for your old age, and may that be long deferred and easy when it comes. Good day to you.' He flourished his hat and replaced it. Then, scorning the gate, he vaulted the fence, and crying, 'Now for Marsh End, my lads,' took his place at the head of the crowd.

Mother flung back the parlour shutters. 'That man,' she said thoughtfully, 'is the most dangerous of them all, for all he is so civil. He is *enjoying* this!'

I hope she was right. I hope those last days of his were happy. For in less than a fortnight after that visit to us Tom Woodroffe was dead. And he was the only man in our parts–labourer, farmer, landowner or yeoman–to be hurt in any way.

Autumn that year had been as unfriendly as the summer. After a wet September, October opened with a week or ten days of mild blue and golden weather, with mornings and evenings full of pearly mist, and languorous, warm afternoons.

But by the middle of the month the east wind, which is the curse of our weather, was blowing hard from the sea, bringing heavy clouds and fogs that might have suited the end of November. Bywater was reporting unusually high tides up the river, and there was every sign of a long, hard winter ahead.

And still the wage disputes were not settled. Sir Edward's second meeting had, after a more embittered, rancorous course, reached the same conclusion as his first. And then the men were going round again, this time demanding, not a further consideration of their claims, but a point-blank 'Bread or Blood.'

The landowners and the farmers had retaliated by sending for a troop of Yeomanry from Colchester, and three labourers had been arrested and convicted of breaches of the peace. Shortly afterwards all the men in our neighbourhood had returned to work, though they were still out at Summerfield, not far away. After a week it was thought unnecessary to preserve the state of near-siege which had been making life so uncomfortable, and life swung back into its old pattern.

On the last Saturday in October my parents were invited to Ockley Manor to a party given to celebrate the engagement of Mary, Stephen's sister, his elder by some years. Mother was almost tremulously delighted by her invitation, though outwardly she affected to be indifferent. But she said, 'Naturally, Lady Fennel remembered the old days,' in a voice which betrayed to me, at least, that she had not, until the card was safely in her hand, had implicit faith in her ladyship's good memory.

However, the invitation had come, and the rioting had ended, so that the guests felt able to ride and drive abroad after dark, which was lucky, for if Mary Fennel had chosen to get herself engaged a few weeks earlier she would have had very few guests at her celebration. Mother, rigged out very grand, though complaining bitterly about the old-fashioned cut of her gown, had shrouded herself with pelisses and shawls and climbed into the gig beside father, who very handsome and, in some incongruous way, apparently dressed in the latest style, had driven away as though it meant nothing to him that every other married couple would arrive at Ockley in a carriage with a pair of horses and a coachman. I envied him as much as I pitied mother.

So Meggie and I were left alone in the house, and we were spending the evening on the pattern laid down by happy ones in the days long since, when I was not considered to be fit company for my parents in the parlour. We had a great red fire in the kitchen which seemed to be the only apartment at Green Farm with a really serviceable chimney, and we had a prolonged supper which included all our favourite dishes. And now, as the weather grew rougher and I thought with relief that at least mother would be safely at Ockley, and that I had not to watch in the stackyard, Meggie and I settled down to make toffee. The sugar and butter were ready, and there were filberts which it was my job–and how pleasant it had once seemed–to crack and split for the embellishment of the top of the 'stick-jaw'. Meggie (who in deference to my age and the long time which had elapsed since mother had spent an evening from home, had lighted the fire and set my supper in the dining parlour when I came in from an afternoon with Stoner, wet and cold and in a mood for company) was quite pathetically delighted when I said that I would prefer to take supper with her and then sit by the kitchen fire.

'And make toffee, eh? Like old times?' she said, with a wide grin that showed the fewness of her teeth.

But I knew, almost before the evening had begun, that old times are gone for ever and can never be recaptured, and that to attempt to relive even one evening of a childhood which has been, or is rapidly being, outgrown is to invite an experience which brings pain more than pleasure. Now, as Meggie set the pan on the fire and the familiar toffee scent sweetened the warm air, I thought back with wistful nostalgia to the days when Meggie, in a good mood, could make heaven for me; when her tales were the most thrilling in the world, and her rustic jokes the funniest. In all material things this was an evening after the old pattern; but I had grown away from the simple little boy who knew nothing about money, or Mortiboys, or other people's troubles.

Still, for Meggie's sake I must pretend. And to pleasure her further I took off my wet boots and wore a pair of slippers which Meggie herself had given me for my birthday. They were made of felt from an old hat, I believe, and they were fearfully and wonderfully decorated with scrolls and twirls of woolwork and a wobbly B.H. on each toe.

The wind shrieked in the big chimney and we could hear the rain thrown violently against the window behind its cosy red curtain.

'I'm glad that we haven't to watch the stacks tonight, anyway,' I said, dragging my chair nearer to the fire. Then I remembered that I ought not to gloat over that to Meggie. For she was on the side of the men, and they had been defeated.

'I'm glad you're not out this wild night, Master Barney,' Meggie conceded. 'But I'm sore at heart for the poor chaps. Still, we oo'nt talk about them sort of things and spoil our cosy evening.' And this conciliating speech, kindly and well meant as it was, chimed sadly with my recent thoughts about the inevitability of change. Once no question of parochial politics could possibly have come between Meggie and me; now, despite ourselves, we were on the opposite sides of a great gulf. She was on the wage-earning side of it, and I was growing up on the other. That was why we must not mention the matter.

'I think thass beginning to be heavy,' said Meggie, lifting the spoon and letting a golden stream pour back slowly into the pan. 'Oon't be long now.'

Just then the gate of the yard slammed heavily against the wall.

'Damn that gate,' I said crossly. 'I left it on the latch and didn't fasten the chain, so that they could get in easily. But I can't let it bang, it'd be all to pieces in an hour.'

'Don't you go out in them slippers,' said Meggie. I said 'Damn' again and reached for my boots, and had just inserted the toes of one foot when there came a small but urgent tapping on the kitchen door.

'Someone at the door,' I said, and took my toes out again.

Meggie pulled the pan aside and said grumblingly, 'Who on earth can that be at this time of night?'

She rose and moved stiffly to the door. As soon as she had pulled aside the heavy curtain which hung there all the winter, the door opened and Jassy Woodroffe edged her way around it.

'May I come in, Meggie, please? I want to see Master Barney.'

'I'm here, Jassy,' I said. 'What can I do for you?'

She ran across the space between the door and the hearth and flung herself on her knees, clutching at me with wet cold hands. The red shawl over her head and shoulders was dark with rain, and beneath it her thin cotton skirt hung limp and soaked.

'Please, please,' she said, 'take me to Summerfield. If you'll take me to Summerfield on your horse I'll serve you the rest of my days. If only you'll take me to Summerfield there's nothing I won't do for you, for ever and ever.'

'Why, Jassy?' I said rather helplessly. 'Why do you want to go there?'

'I'll tell you as we go. Please. Father's there and he's in danger. Deadly danger. I know. I'll tell you how I know on the way. I've got to get to Summerfield quickly. I did start to run and then I thought of you. You like father, don't you, and you have got a horse. Please, please do come.'

'Where's your mother?' asked Meggie in the hard voice which she reserved for Jassy and other people of whom she disapproved. Speaking to Jassy about Sari, Meggie's voice sounded like a stone hitting a rock.

'She's at Horringer sheep fair. She won't be back till tomorrow. Oh, Barney, please take me! It's a matter of life and death and every minute counts.'

'You're not to go,' said Meggie, as I began to fumble with my boots. 'Do you hear me? Your parents are away and you're under age and I'm in charge here, Master Barney. I'm not gorn to hev you out on such a night, running into danger, gorn God-know-where on behalf of a lot of rag-tag-and-bobtail like this'n!'

'Be quiet, Meggie,' I said. If in my rushed, bewildered mind I had had the slightest doubt of the wisdom of such a journey, this crumb of opposition dispersed it.

'Be quiet I will not,' said Meggie. 'Summerfield is a mighty rough place. Allus hev bin. You ain't gorn to Summerfield, Master Barney, except that be over my dead body.'

'Dead or alive, you can't stop me, Meggie,' I mumbled bending over my boots.

'Oh, thank you, bless you! I'll never forget it,' cried Jassy, with a shudder that made her wooden shoes rattle on the stone floor.

'Shut your noise, you daft little faggot,' Meggie shouted. 'It'd be a fine thing if the last of the Hattons went out and caught his death of cold, or got in with some rough doings all on account of you and your pa. Be off home with you and tend to your own business. Don't come here bleating and disturbing decent folk.'

'Now, Meggie,' I said, standing up and stamping my boots into comfort, 'get me my greatcoat, if you're so mindful of my health. And remember that Tom Woodroffe is on the same side as you are. You ought to be concerned for him, too.'

'I ain't concerned with nowt except keeping you here safe and sound,' said Meggie, not moving. So I reached down my coat myself, and from the peg beside it took the thick old cloak, worn by Meggie and mother impartially when they went out in bad weather to feed the hens. I held it open towards Jassy. 'You'd better have this,' I said. Jassy ran towards me, her big mouth quivering in her white face; Meggie moved towards the door and took up a stand with her back to it. I laid the cloak on Jassy's small wet shoulders over the shawl and we both turned towards the door. Meggie, I thought to myself, would never actually engage in a physical struggle, and if she should I was, I knew, more than a match for her. But as we moved to the door I saw Jassy glance at the clock which wagged a deliberate pendulum against the whitewashed wall. She stopped. I looked at the clock, which showed that in three minutes it would strike eight o'clock.

'I didn't know the time,' she said in a small voice. 'Father had his watch and the grandfather stopped this morning. I didn't know the time. It's too late now, thank you. It's too late!' I had never heard any words spoken so tragically, so doomfully, in all my life.

'How do you know it's too late!' I asked, and my voice was small, too, hushed by my sense of being in the presence of something uncanny.

'I know,' she said. With her eyes fixed on the clock's face she waited. Neither Meggie nor I made a sound or a movement, but the wind threw itself violently against the house and the rain rattled on the window. The clock gave the grating jerk which preceded the chime and then struck solemnly, eight times.

'He's dead now,' said Jassy. 'I heard the church clock chime just as it happened.' She turned her white demented face to me and cried, 'He's dead. They've killed him.' She put both her hands to her head and, with her face hidden, drew two or three long sobbing breaths. The cloak which I had laid on her shoulders fell off and hit the floor with a soft thud. I found myself able to move again and ran forward, taking her by the elbow and leading her to the chair which I had recently occupied. It was like guiding a blind, paralysed person, for she kept her hands pressed to her face, and strong vibrations, part sobs, part shudders, shook her body so that she seemed incapable of movement. When she was in the chair I took off her soaked shawl, poked the fire to greater heat, and muttered stupid, unconvincing words of comfort. She went on shuddering and sobbing.

'Get the cordial,' I said to Meggie. 'You can see that I'm not going out, so don't stand there like a fool.' For Meggie had made no move. I should hardly have believed that she–always so kind to us–could have maintained such detachment in the face of a child's sorrow, however mysterious its cause. She moved to the cupboard, unstoppered the cordial, a powerful restorative made by soaking ripe raspberries in cheap brandy, and poured some of it into a glass.

I took it and leant over Jassy. 'Here, drink this,' I said, 'it'll make you feel better.' But she might have been deaf. She stayed crouched in the chair, with her hands pressed over her face. Sounds like the rending of calico came from her chest, and her shudders rattled the chair, the poker in the fender, and the things on the mantelshelf. I stood helpless, with the glass in my hand, and Meggie, moving to the far side of the hearth, stirred the toffee with that same air of detachment. I felt awkward and silly, and finally vented my feelings by saying, 'Leave the blasted stuff alone!' Meggie looked at me like an unjustly-chidden dog, pulled the toffee pan clear of the fire and sat down in her own chair, vastly injured and offended.

After perhaps ten minutes, incredible stretched minutes which had nothing to do with that wagging pendulum, Jassy drew two great breaths, steadied herself, and dropped her hands in her lap.

'I shall always remember that you were *willing* to come,' she said. She lifted her face to me, and I was irrelevantly aware that she was not ugly any more. That brow was no longer a bulging, disproportionate deformity, it was the seat of calm; and her mouth, resolutely controlled, seemed smaller. But it was her eyes, so blue-grey, so clear, as though washed by her tears–though I had seen none fall–which fixed on mine in a look of indescribable gratitude, made me conscious of beauty. They also made me uncomfortable. I said again, 'Drink this,' and she took the glass, drank its contents as though it had held water, and then turned that clear, adoring gaze on me again.

'Now,' I said in a brisk, sensible voice. 'What is this all about, Jassy? Why should you think that something happened at eight o'clock? Did you have a dream? Or was Tom threatened? Or what?'

'No,' she said, looking down at her hands, which she had clasped again after giving me back the glass. 'I just *knew*. I saw it, you see.'

'Saw it? I don't understand.'

'No. Nobody would, except mother. She can't see herself, but she understands it. And I've never seen anything until this evening.'

'Then you mean that you saw–or imagined–something happening at Summerfield. But, Jassy, that's all rubbish. Come along now. I'll guarantee Tom is home. He was just a little late, and you were worried and got into a state. Let's go. I'll come with you, and if he isn't back we can get the fire and his supper ready.'

'I was doing that,' said Jassy, 'when I saw it. It's no use, Barney. I *know* he's dead. He was killed, just as the clock struck. A man hit him. I saw him do it.'

'But Jassy, you couldn't. You were here at eight o'clock. The only people you saw then were Meggie and me.'

I spoke urgently. I was, in the heart of me, scared. I didn't want to believe that Tom Woodroffe was dead, and I just as passionately did not want to believe that Jassy, at some moment before eight o'clock in the evening, could be in a cottage at Minsham and see what would happen at that hour in Summerfield, a good six miles away. I had had my own experience with supernatural prescience, and, although I did my best to forget it, it had opened a crack in my mind. I knew how certainly and how dangerously that kind of thing could smite at the solid foundations of actuality.

'Yes,' Jassy said, quite calmly, 'I daresay it sounds mad. But it is true, all the same. I was putting wood on the fire. I had everything ready, the table set, and the pot on, and the kettle just about to boil. I didn't know the time. I knew I went from here at five, and I tried not to be ready too early in case the meal spoiled. I had a piece of wood in my hand when I began to see, and I had it in my hand still when I ran out of the house. I was just going to put it on the fire when I couldn't see the fireplace at all. Instead I saw an open space with a sort of broken stone thing in the middle. There were a lot of men, crowding round a man who stood on the stone thing, shouting. I couldn't hear anything, but I knew he was shouting, by his face and the way he moved his hands. And the men were getting very excited. Several of them had torches, and when the man in the middle stopped and wiped his face, they waved the torches and looked as though they were all going to move off somewhere else. But then father jumped on to the stone and held his arms above his head and started to talk. It looked as though he was trying to calm them down. I saw two men drop their torches and stamp on them, and the rest shuffled about as if they couldn't make up their minds. Then some men on horseback came into the space and the crowd broke up and began to run away. And one of the men brought his horse close up behind father and hit him on the head. I saw him fall, and I knew he was dead. I could *feel* that he was. It was awful. Hit from behind, like that. He looked so astonished. And then I heard the clock strike, and as soon as I could *hear* I seemed to come to myself. And I thought that if I could get to Summerfield before eight o'clock I could warn him. So I ran along as far as Clem Barber's, and then I thought that I might not get there in time. So I came to you. And you were coming. You would have saved him if you could. I shall remember that, always.'

'I still think you were dreaming. You were tired and fell asleep over the fire and had a dream. Don't you think that's possible?'

'No. I wish it might be. But I know what dreams are. You wake up and know that you have been dreaming. This was different.'

'Well,' I said weakly, 'if it is true, Jassy, I'm very sorry. Very, very sorry.'

She stood up slowly, but quite steadily, and reached down to take her shawl from the floor. She held it in one hand and rested the other on the back of the chair.

'Thank you,' she said calmly. 'Yes, you liked him. Many people didn't. The rich men hated him because he tried to make them see reason, and the poor men hated him because he tried to make them see sense. And between them he's dead now. That's what you get for being *good*.' The faintest trace of wildness crept into her eyes and her voice. She let go of the chair back. 'For being good,' she repeated. 'You'd better mark that, Barney. Because you could be good too. I can see it in you sometimes. But now you know. Don't let being good make a mess of your life, like he did.' The little wild flash faded and her face went calm again. 'I'll go home now. And thank you once more for being willing to help me. Good night.'

I started forward with a hasty muddled protest against her going back to stay in the cottage alone. I made a whole series of suggestions. But she said quietly, 'I don't mind at all. I'm often alone. Thank you.' She had lifted the curtain and slipped through the doorway before I could speak again.

'Leave her go,' said Meggie. 'She's best by herself.'

'D'you think it's true?' I asked, forgetting my annoyance with Meggie's behaviour in my desire to discuss the thing. 'Or will Tom be home when she gets there?'

'She's right enough,' said Meggie, quite carelessly, drawing the toffee pan towards her. 'I allust knew there was something queer about her. And now me toffee is ruined.'

Next day we heard all the story. In essentials it did not differ from Jassy's. The agitation in Summerfield had outlasted that in other places because, in the early days, a farmer had set his dogs on a peaceable crowd of men who had visited him with their request for a consideration. One dog had bitten a labourer, and he had turned and throttled it. The farmer took action, valuing the cur at thirty shillings, and the bitten man had been sent to gaol. His fellows had regarded this as legal discrimination against them, and been very bitter about it. Tom Woodroffe had gone over to Summerfield because, he said, knowing nothing of the law, the men were likely to land themselves in deeper trouble. On the evening in question the brother of the imprisoned man, a simpleton converted into a firebrand by circumstances, had mounted the ruined Market Cross in the centre of the place and urged the men to burn every stack in the district. Tom Woodroffe was advising caution and milder, legal measures when the mounted Yeomanry charged and dispersed the crowd. And it was Phil Rigger, son of Jonas, and nephew of the tailor Calthorpe, who from personal spite exceeded his duty and struck Tom down.

In our house, and at our table, this event shared attention with the account of Mary Fennel's dinner and ball. And whenever it was discussed I could only think of two things. One was Jassy's voice saying, 'He looked so astonished.' There was something in that plain statement which made Tom's death real to me. And the other was the memory, constantly recurring, of the man himself at work in his shed. I could only remember how, given an order for a plain wooden box, the cheapest of its kind, destined to carry a poor girl's few clothes to her first place of service, he had carefully asked her full name, and when the utilitarian job was completed he had carved, on the lid, her initials and surrounded them with a wreath of daisies, which somehow lifted the dull box into another sphere, making it an individual thing, a thing of beauty. Every time I thought about it I could feel the tears burning in my throat. I reached the state where I could not bear to look at the desk he had given me, and had to put it away, not because it reminded me of him so much as because it made me realize that, to him, a servant girl's wreath of daisies had been as important as my hooded jennet; and in that fact was implicit the whole of the man.

So dead, he might have done for me what living he had not been able to do, wrest my mind out of its material groove and save my soul. But just then, about ten days after the tragedy, Nick Helmar himself stopped at our gate and bellowed an invitation for father to spend the following Thursday with him, and catching sight of me, he added, 'Bring the boy along, too. He'll be company for Dilys, and he can guide you home!' He burst into a gust of laughter in which father joined; for not long before that father, returning home not too sober, had, ignoring Dane's protests, ridden straight into Clip End Bottom and almost drowned himself.

That invitation split our home in two, and half of me was on one side half on the other. Partly I sided–though not for her reasons–with mother, who was determined that I should never come under the influence of Nick

Helmar; and part of me supported father, who held, mumblingly emphatic, that it was time I learned something of polite society. I wanted to visit Mortiboys, yet I dreaded it. And between my own indecision and my parents' arguments, I had little time or interest to spare for other things. So I heard, as it were with the rim of my mind, that Sari Woodroffe was selling everything in the cottage and going back to her own people. Once, it is true, I did have a flash of feeling about that, and saw her, a strange wild creature, trapped by some momentary passion, bearing captivity badly, yet bearing it, and now at last set free. And I did ask what Jassy was going to do. Meggie, who seemed to know everything, said that Jassy had fallen out with her mother over the selling of the furniture and stoutly refused to go with her to the Stannaries. So then I asked mother if she would consider giving Jassy house-room and letting her continue to work in our dairy. And mother said, 'No. She and Meggie don't get on. It wouldn't do to have them under the same roof. If the child likes to live with another family she can go on working here.' That answer set me against mother. It lacked generosity. There was no favour entailed in employing Jassy, who worked so hard and was so clean and clever. And a word from mother would have settled Meggie, I knew. But she was not willing, at heart, to saddle herself with an orphan. I saw that, and so my mind veered away from mother and was less willing to please her by staying at home on the momentous Thursday. So even there Jassy Woodroffe had an influence on my affairs.

And when, very late on the Thursday, father and I came home, he reeling with liquor and I equally drunk from experience, Meggie was waiting up for us. She gabbled, as she helped father out of his boots, of the gossip she had heard during her evening in the village. Amongst the things she mentioned was that the Woodroffes had gone–Sari to Billericay, where a fair was in progress, and Jassy to Baildon. Where? To a job, Meggie reckoned. She added, as an afterthought, that some time during the afternoon Jassy had called to say good-bye to me.

I was touched. But I was exhausted from a day of intense emotion. I had, in one short day, in one timeless, immeasurable day, added to my old love and found a new one. I was dazed, more drunk than father. Jassy, and everything connected with my past life, except my passion for Mortiboys, was very far away, completely unimportant. My ears heard of her going, but my heart was deaf.

BOOK TWO

COMPLAINT FROM LESBIA

'She was a person of some education. . . .'
So this story is told by ELIZABETH TWYSDALE, *who ran, very successfully, A School for Young Ladies.*

Jassy Woodroffe was brought to me by my old maid, Amy Partridge. I was taking my Senior embroidery class, and I remember, in the way one does remember incongruous trifles, that I was showing Hilda Besson how to mitre the corner of the new altar cloth for St Giles', which was our special article of work that term, when the message that Mrs Partridge was waiting to see me was brought in. I fastened the needle and told Hilda that she had better not attempt to go on until I had demonstrated a little more fully. Then I went into the hall, a little impatient at the disturbance, but determined to conceal my feelings, since I owed Amy a good deal. Also it was more than likely that she had brought me a present. Since her marriage and her prosperity she had taken a delight in making me little offerings–a cake made after an old Hampshire receipt; a bottle of wine; a fresh cheese or a jar of honey.

And I was right. For today Amy had brought Jassy Woodroffe.

They stood in the hall where, at that hour, the pale afternoon autumnal sun poured through the two windows and the transom. Amy, who was still in her rather ostentatious mourning, looking bigger and more imposing than ever standing there beside the tiny child who wore a print dress of a very familiar pattern. It had been cut down from one of those which Amy had worn when she was in my service. It had been tucked and seamed until it fitted her perfectly, and it was stiff with starch. And I remember that my first thought was one of wonder as to what Amy was doing with a little girl in tow; and my second was the mental comment, 'What a very neat little girl.' It was, then, the most striking thing about the child, that meticulous neatness. Her hair was pulled back, plaited in a long tail and then turned back on itself and tied with a narrow, stiff little bow. Her white cotton stockings were spotless and taut; her thick new shoes highly polished. She stood neatly, too, with her back very straight and her head held well, and her feet at the right angle. A very neat, pleasing-looking little girl. Probably, I thought, a young relative of Amy's, sent from Hampshire to taste the charity of the aunt who had, by a late and surprising marriage, become the proprietress of the prosperous little 'Red Dragon' inn.

By why bring her here? I thought, as I greeted Amy and began to move across the sunny hall towards my private sitting-room.

'Just a minute, Miss Beth,' Amy said, hesitating before she followed me. 'I want you to take a good look at this young person.'

I did as she requested and surveyed again the small figure, from the top of its smooth black head to the toes of its shiny black shoes.

'That's right,' said Amy, her eyes following mine. 'There, now the lady's seen you, dearie, you just sit there and wait for me.'

The child moved, almost soundlessly despite the thickness of her shoes, and sat on the hall chair, sitting I noticed, as neatly and compactly as she stood, with straight spine, indrawn feet and hands folded in her smooth lap. Amy and I went into the sitting-room and, as soon as I closed the door–while, in fact, I had the knob still in my hand–she turned and said:

'Miss Beth, I've come to ask a favour of you.'

I guessed what it was and was instantly wary. The child was a relative, and Amy, flown with pride and heady with prosperity, had no better sense than to come seeking a place for her in my school for young ladies! How dreadfully awkward. How tactless of Amy. And how on earth, without hurting her feelings and alienating her affection, could I refuse such a request?

'Well, Amy, you've done me many in your time,' I said, with more amiability than I felt, 'so tell me, what can I do for you?'

'I want you to take that little thing,' she said, jerking her head with its feathered hat towards the hall.

'You mean . . . into the school?' I asked cautiously.

'Lor' no, Miss Beth! Would I ask that? I got a bit of sense in my head. In the kitchen, of course.'

I tried to conceal my relief.

'Who is she, Amy? And how old? Has she ever been out before? Tell me about her,' I said, sitting down and thinking how silly I had been to doubt even for a moment Amy's sense of propriety.

'She ain't nothing to me, in a manner of speaking,' said Amy, easing herself in a chair and beginning to take off her tight black gloves. 'And I must say that I don't know much about her. She come to my door late last Thursday night arsting if I could give her a job or tell of one. You get a lot of people arsting that at a public house, you know. I was going to shoo her off quick when something struck me. She look at you very straight you'll notice, and she spoke nice, and though she was dressed very poor she was tidy. So I arst her in and had another look at her. Then she told me her name and about her dad. Woodroffe he was, killed in the stack riots at Summerfield about a fortnight ago. P'raps you remember about it. A decent sort of chap, I heard, though he never come in my place. Not that sort.' There was an odd note in Amy's voice, and I remembered, with amusement, that until Walter Partridge came wooing, Amy had always had a puritanical dislike for what she called strong liquor and everything connected with it. And it was still plain that, though she had, for two years, run the 'Red Dragon' single-handed, and run it very well, she had, in her heart, more respect for those who were not her customers than for those who were.

'And her mother?'

'Not much,' said Amy briefly with her old disapproving look. 'One of them Stannaries, half gypsy like. Run off and left the poor little old thing. Notwithstanding,' she added, with an obvious effort to be fair, 'her, or somebody else, have brought the child up right well.' She proceeded to give me a list of almost incredible length and scope of what the child, tiny and young as she appeared, was able to do.

'How old did you say she was?' I asked, conscious that I had put the question before, but uncertain whether Amy had answered it.

'She's twelve. Maybe you reckon, Miss Beth, that that's a bit young to be so handy, but I tried her out. Why, only yesterday she baked me as good a batch of bread as you'd find in a day's march. You'd find her wonderful useful.'

And it was then, at that moment when some answer was obviously demanded of me, that I first had an inexplicable, but very definite, feeling that I did not want to employ Jassy Woodroffe.

It was completely without reason. Good girls for the kitchen were harder to come by every year. Each generation of working-class youth seemed to be more ignorant, less teachable, harder to deal with than the one preceding it. I could, at almost any moment, find a place for a clean, neat, handy girl. And Amy, who had had full charge of my kitchen until her marriage, knew it. I have no doubt that she brought Jassy Woodroffe to me in exactly the same spirit as she would have brought me one of her little faithful presents. I knew perfectly well that I ought to be–and normally would have been–extreemely grateful to Amy, who still had my good and comfort at heart.

Yet, knowing all this, I found myself, to my own surprise and Amy's manifest impatience, making foolish and inadequate excuses.

'Are you certain, Amy, that you wouldn't like to keep her yourself? You could find her work, and she'd be company for you, too.'

'Ah, that's true. And in a manner of speaking there's nothing I'd like better. But a house like mine, Miss Beth, ain't the place for a decent little girl. That's no good being mealy mouthed about it, you can't run a pub like a school. Betsy Flitch and Lottie Prout they do draw the men, and they're decent girls *in their way*, I see to that. But if she was there she'd be bound to come acrost them, and that wouldn't do her no good. I thought it over and said to myself, "No. The school's the place for her." That's why I brought her. Your girls get a good home and a quiet place, as I know.'

'But it seems to me that her gifts are going to be wasted, Amy. You know what I want young girls for, scrubbing and scouring and to do the grates and shoes. If she can cook . . . and do the rest of the things you say she can, don't you think it's rather a pity that she shouldn't go to, well, some old lady like Miss Dimmock, who can only have one maid. She'd be a godsend there.'

'I wouldn't let her go there,' said Amy stubbornly. 'All alone in that great old house, worked to the bone and near starved.' She tilted her head and looked at me curiously, 'I thought you'd be pleased, Miss Beth. You and me know the new-fashioned girls, and I can tell you this is one of the old sort. Real good. Is it on account of her size you don't like her?'

What could I say? I had a queer feeling that Amy and I were on a very narrow path, and that Amy, on the inside, was resolutely, but gently, urging me off into the gutter. I was surprised and oddly weakened by my own indecision. Why didn't I want the child? I had a notion that there might have been something about her which I had not really noticed, but which had stayed in the back of my mind, influencing it. I had seen a very neat little girl–but did she squint or show some other deformity?

'Ask her to come in, will you?' I said.

Yet, when the child stood there before me I could see nothing. Her face was not pretty, but what could matter less in a maid? She had an extraordinary forehead, far too big for her face, and her mouth was too large. But I had, for eighteen years, been dealing with young females, and I knew as well as anyone living that a girl's looks can alter unbelievably between the ages of eleven and seventeen.

And her manner was impeccable, modest, frank, and, in an unusual way, self-confident. She was, in fact, the very girl I would have picked out of any dozen applicants for work.

But I didn't want her. I grew quite flustered with the confusion in my mind. It was so plain that a refusal to employ the child would puzzle Amy and offend her; and there wasn't even a shadow of a reason for such a refusal. I am not in the habit of giving way to my whims, and it was unthinkable that I should turn to Amy and say, 'Take her away, she gives me a peculiar feeling. I don't think she's lucky.' But, as I realized how unthinkable such a statement was, I knew that that was exactly what something within me wanted to say. I did feel, in that very first afternoon, that Jassy Woodroffe boded me no good. And that in itself was ridiculous. There we were, a twelve-year orphan, seeking menial work, and the middle-aged head mistress of a prosperous school, with that work in her gift. How could she hurt me? Mrs Whiting, Amy's capable, short-tempered successor, would see that she did not even waste my food, or soap or floor polish.

I took another look at the child and decided that my reluctance to take her was probably due to her dress. It had been Amy's, and it reminded me of the days when Amy, growing old in my service, was apt to take advantage of her position, was growing sour and dictatorial. That was it. Nobody would ever realize how much relief I felt when Walter Partridge fell a victim to Amy's almost obliterated charms. And the print dress, fetched out, cut about, sewn and tucked and starched, reminded me of the time when Amy was a resident tyrant, not a visiting friend.

'She don't each much,' said Amy. 'And being so young she wouldn't expect more than her keep and twenty shillings a year, would you, dearie? She could come and drink a cup of tea with me now and then. And it'd be a pleasure to see to her clothes myself.'

What could I say except, 'Very well, Amy'? That my farewells did not show quite the expected glow of gratitude was made clear to me by Amy turning and saying, 'I reckon you'll be glad I brought her along, Miss Beth.'

I remembered the days when Amy's loyalty and labour had saved me from the most degrading results of a penurious marriage, when but for her I should have had to scrub and scour; I remembered those days, too, when the school was starting, wobbly on its legs, and Amy had done the work of four women. I relented and said exactly what was expected of me.

I thanked her, quite fulsomely, for bringing Jassy Woodroffe into my house. And turning back to my Embroidery Class I thought how typical of Amy to begin by saying that she was asking a favour and to end by forcibly extracting thanks.

I went back to my class, and all thought of Jassy Woodroffe passed from my mind. During the next few days I certainly saw her, for although Mrs Whiting was competent and, I think, honest, I am one of those women who believe in keeping an eye on everything. But now that the moment of deciding whether to employ the child or not was over, I had no further interest in her so long as she performed her duties. I should think that it was quite six weeks before I was called upon to give Jassy my full attention again.

It was cold weather and near the end of the term. I was spending the evening in Katharine's room, as I almost invariably did. It was not until long after that it went through my mind that there had been something significant in my regular climbing of the stairs, carrying my work and settling down by Katharine's fire, prepared to stay silent if she was working, or to talk as entertainingly as I could if she were in a mood for conversation. When I did notice the significance I thought bitterly–yes, it is always the dog who is allowed into the parlour, never the master, who for a favour spends an hour in the kennel. But that is neither here nor there. At that time, the December after Jassy's coming, those evenings by Katharine's fire were the happiest part of my day.

Katharine was writing at her desk and I was putting the last finishing touches to the altar cloth. Suddenly Katharine hunched her shoulders and said, 'It's cold, Beth. Put on another log, will you?'

I peered into the queer basket of African native workmanship which Katharine had bought at a missionary bazaar and insisted upon using for her logs, though it was ugly and took up a great deal of room, and saw that it was empty. I rang the bell, rather angrily. Katharine's comfort was my nearest and dearest concern, and I was annoyed to find that on this bitter December evening she had been left without fuel. Suppose, I thought, this had been an evening when I was playing whist at Mrs Dulcimer's, or had visitors of my own: Katharine would merely have looked into the basket, seen it empty and gone back to her writing, too remote or indolent or careless to ring her bell, and she would have caught cold, perhaps even been ill.

A gentle tap interrupted my increasingly furious thoughts, and there was Jassy, saying quietly, 'You rang, ma'am?' to Katharine.

'No,' I said. 'I did. I'm very much annoyed to see that Miss Hamilton's log basket has not been filled this evening.'

'I'm sorry,' the child said, and moved forward with that odd soundless grace which I had noticed before, and lifted the thing by its ugly out-sticking handles, which always reminded me of a yokel's ears.

'Saying you're sorry isn't enough,' I said, and something–heaven knows what–made me add with unusual spitefulness, 'Mrs Partridge spoke so highly of your ability that I can only attribute such a lapse to carelessness. Don't let it occur again.'

The mite changed colour and set the basket down. Something about that sudden pallor and the way the basket went down prepared me for insolence, and something else, in me this time, rose to meet it. I was prepared to make an issue of this moment. Why? But she said, with a gentle politeness behind which some other emotion lurked:

'This room isn't usually my concern, ma'am. Daisy is crying with toothache, so I answered the bell.'

Then I was aware that Katharine had stopped writing and was staring at us.

'Very well, fill the basket,' I said. 'And make haste. The fire is very low.'

She lifted the basket and went away. Katharine, with her pen still in her hand, twisted on her chair and said:

'What girl is that, Beth?'

'One of Amy Partridge's finds,' I told her. Katharine and Amy had never got on well, and so I was impelled to add, 'She is a very good little girl.' But even as I said it I thought, why did she set the basket down in order to answer? There was something subtly truculent about that gesture, as though for two pins she would have refused to fill it at all.

'She came last week one evening,' said Katharine, screwing her short-sighted eyes to look at me. 'I find her extremely fascinating, Beth. Her movements. Have you noticed?'

'Yes. Girls are usually so clumsy. Even our girls–in school I mean.'

'I wonder,' Katharine said, 'would it cause a lot of shifting and bother if I had her instead of Daisy to look after this room?'

'Well,' I said in the voice of slightly facetious indulgence which I often used towards her in order to cover more real emotion, 'I daresay it could be arranged.' And then, as soon as I had said it, I thought sharply–you agreed to that out of habit; it was a stupid thing to do. But why? Why shouldn't Katharine have the best? Why shouldn't she have the quietest, most capable little maid? Why? There was no answer. No answer at all. And within a moment Jassy was back, her slight figure braced against the weight of the heavy basket.

As she set it down I said, 'Thank you.' But Katharine, reaching out with her hand which held the pen, halted the child on her way back to the door.

'In future,' she said, 'you're going to look after me. What's your name?'

'Jassy Woodroffe, ma'am.'

'What? What before Woodroffe?'

'Jassy.'

'Jassy. Is that a name? What does it mean?'

'It is short for Jacinth, ma'am. I was named after a stone that is mentioned in the Bible. In the Book of Revelation.'

'Ah, yes. I remember,' Katharine said. 'A list like a poem. I knew it once. "The first foundation was jasper; the second, sapphire; the third a chalcedony; the fourth an emerald." Lovely names. Well, Jacinth–but I shall call you Jassy like everybody else–good night.'

'Good night, Miss Hamilton. Good night, ma'am.'

She closed the door softly and I began to set the logs endways on the dying fire. The flames leaped upwards. Katharine left her desk and came, rubbing her thin hands together, towards the glow and the warmth.

'You never told me,' she said.

'Told you what, Katharine?'

'About her,' she said, with an inclination of her head towards the door.

'About Jassy Woodroffe?' I asked in genuine astonishment. 'But why should I? I never tell you about the kitchen staff or anything of that kind.'

A curious, dreamy expression dawned upon Katharine's face.

'Kitchen staff, no. God spare me that! But a nymph, Beth. Surely you saw that. Why, even her voice is full of wood smoke. Wood smoke; Woodroffe. Marvellous. And Jacinth to crown all. Hyacinth. No. The extra letter spoils it. Jacinth stone. Her eyes should be blue. Are they?'

'How on earth should I know?' I asked, a trifle impatiently. 'I don't engage girls for their eyes. Or their names.'

'Perhaps you should. Perhaps that is the secret. That one I have now–Daisy Snell. What could one expect of Daisy Snell? I shall expect a good deal of my nymph, Beth.'

'Well,' I said, 'don't go calling her a nymph to her face, Katharine; or asking her if her eyes are blue. You'll spoil her if you do, you know. Girls don't understand that kind of thing. They think you're soft and take advantage.'

'Oh, of course,' Katharine said more briskly, and with a certain air of closing the subject. 'I know that. It was, just for the moment, the combination of those names and that peculiar grace. Don't grudge, Beth. Delight comes rarely.' She leaned forward, rubbed her hands in the flame light, and then went back to her desk. I put in the last stitch and folded my work. Then, leaning back in my chair, I looked across the room to the circle of lamplight in the centre of which Katharine was sitting.

The lamplight was cruel. It showed how the years had hollowed her cheeks and eye-sockets and dimmed the flaming russet of her hair until it looked as though a film of ashes rested on it. A lover–in the ordinary sense of the word–a lover would have been sad at that moment, staring through the lamplight at the wreck of the beauty which had once been hers. But I had never loved Katharine for her beauty; I had been the pretty one, always; and that made what had happened to me the stranger, the less easily explained. I could well imagine how some plain, lumbering woman might fall in love with another who had beauty and liveliness. Why should I . . .? But there was no sense in going over it again. I had, as a rosy, flaxed-haired, spoilt little girl of nine years old, incurred an infatuation for this pale, red-haired half-cousin of mine, who had been sent home from India because the climate was killing her; and I had never shaken myself free of it. To think about it now was foolish. Yet there seemed to me something that demanded thought, and I looked away from Katharine to the fire and tried to remember. Ah, yes. She had said 'You never told me,' when she was speaking about Jassy Woodroffe; rather as though she had expected me to run to her with the news that I had engaged a new kitchen maid. And that set me wondering. Did Katharine feel, perhaps, that she was not consulted enough? But that was nonsense, too. She loathed all practical affairs, and it was my duty, as well as my delight, to shoulder all that side of the business of keeping school. When we first set out in partnership it was agreed that I should attend to all the housekeeping, interview parents, supervise the girls' food and clothing and general well-being; while Katharine taught what and how she pleased, and for the rest remained in her sitting-room, as private and comfortable as a gentleman in his study. That was the arrangement, and I had adhered to it. It had worked perfectly for eighteen years. But tonight she had said, 'You never told me'; and she had leaned out towards that child and said, 'In future you're going to look after me.' She shouldn't have done that. It was for me to say. Suppose I had taken up one of her girls' exercises and marked it?

I pulled myself together, mentally and physically, sat up in my chair and resolutely banished such thoughts. It was near the end of the term and I was needing a holiday. That must be it. It was unlike me to be introspective and resentful of trifles. With Katharine, too!

I don't think that Jassy Woodroffe was mentioned again until the Easter term was within a week of its end. Spring was early that year and the weather was warm. Amy had brought me an armful of daffodils from her garden, and I had put half of them in a glass bowl and had carried them up to Katharine's room when I went on my usual visit. I remember standing by her table, gently moving back into place the heads which had massed together during the journey upstairs. Katharine, as usual, was busy amongst piles of papers, and as I stood back from arranging the flowers, she patted some loose sheets into place and looked up.

'Beth,' she said, 'I want to take Jassy Woodroffe into school after the holiday. As a pupil, you know.'

'What?' I said. I could hardly believe my ears, and my frank incredulity certainly rang in my voice.

'You sound astonished. Is it such a fantastic suggestion?'

'Fantastic?' I said. 'It's unthinkable.'

'Why?' Her tone was mild and questioning; but I had the idea that it was adopted merely in order to mislead me, so that I might voice the obvious objections only to have them disposed of–like setting up skittles for another person to knock over.

'You don't need me to tell you why, Katharine. What would you say if anyone suggested introducing a kitchen maid into school?'

'That would depend upon the girl, surely.'

'Not at all. You couldn't do it with *any* girl. As much for her sake as for anything else. What do you imagine the other girls would say and do about it?'

Katharine shrugged her thin shoulders; the expression of contempt which she often wore when talking of the pupils was strong on her face.

'I am indifferent to what they might say, and I am prepared to deal with anything they might do.'

'Prepared to deal . . .' I repeated. And it flashed through my mind that she must be ill, demented, delirious. Prepared to deal . . . Why, she had never dealt with anything in her life.

'It wouldn't be fair to the child herself, Katharine. She's cleaned their shoes, handed their plates . . .'

'A social injustice that I propose to remedy, Beth. She understands all that. I've explained it. Actually, I think there'll be less difficulty than you imagine. The girls seem to like her very well.'

'How can you know that?'

'I've seen them in conversation with her–laughing, you know the way they go on.'

'You should have told me then. I dislike the girls and the maids being friendly. It always means that they're bringing in indigestible food, or carrying notes, or some such nonsense.'

Katharine gave a loud, fierce sigh. Her thin red eyebrows ran together until they made one line, and she waited–a disconcerting trick she had at times–for an appreciable time before making a fresh start. Until someone of whom you are weakly fond has tried that trick on you you have no idea how discomforting it can be.

'Have you, Beth, any personal opinion upon this subject?'

'Yes,' I said. 'I have. We've always been very particular about the girls we accept. We agreed that Miss Gould made the mistake of taking anyone who could pay the fees, and so her school lost caste. We've built it up again. Why, only last term I refused to take the little Jepson girl, Jepson, the miller, you know.'

'I don't know. I'm sure I never had anything to do with it. Could even a miller's daughter be more stupid than Mamie Pierce? Or more exasperating than Dilys Helmar?' She closed her eyes and put her hand to them, her thumb at the corner of one, her first finger at the corner of the other, in a gesture that conveyed a curious combination of arrogance and weariness.

'I'm sure I don't know what we're talking about,' she said, when she had comforted her eyes for a moment. 'I happen to have discovered that this child has a mind worth educating. I propose to try my hand at it. God knows I spend time and energy on dolts and fools. It'll be a pleasure to teach somebody worth teaching.'

'What do you imagine the parents will say when the girls tell them that one of the kitchen maids is now in the classroom?'

'I've no idea.'

'Well, I have. I can imagine it very well. I shall have nothing but complaints and withdrawals. It's all very well for you, Katharine, to take this high-handed attitude about it. The school is our livelihood, after all; and the parents make the school possible.'

I said that in a reasonable, if argumentative way. I did not intend to provoke her. But she was suddenly furiously angry and, in anger, the living image of the fiery, red-headed old Scotsman who was our mutual relative. 'Send them along to me!' she shouted. 'I'll tell any pie-faced piffling parent that this is my school, and if they don't want their drooling offspring in it they can take 'em away. God knows there're brats enough in the world. We'll get some new ones whose shoes Jassy hasn't cleaned. I could do with a clean sweep.'

'Katharine . . .!' I began.

She put up one hand.

'Beth, please. Any more of this and I shall be angry. I think you might let me have my way for once. Just once.'

'Have your way?' I gasped. 'But, dear, you always have your way. Come, Katharine, you must admit that. Nobody ever crosses you.'

'You do,' she said, still angrily. 'I make a simple, sensible suggestion regarding a matter that is important to me, and you instantly start to make a coil about it, dragging in the possible opinions of a lot of middle-class dunderheads, and talking about some miller I never heard of. It's intolerable.'

I just gaped at her. I had known for almost a lifetime that she had the easily irritated temper of the constitutionally nervous person, but she was usually too indolent to display her anger. And then it occurred to me that she was, over this matter of taking a maid into the school, more actively and nearly concerned than she had been over anything for years. She was, in fact, so set upon it that even my mild reasoning was fiercely resented. And I had, after all, only ventured an opinion for which I was asked; and I was only pursuing a policy which had worked admirably for eighteen years. My feelings were deeply injured.

'I had no intention of crossing you,' I said. 'I should be the last person to deny that you had a right to bring anyone you liked into your school. For it is, we know, your school. I'm only sorry that you should find it necessary, after eighteen years, to remind me of the fact.'

'Now you're angry,' she said, suddenly retreating into her usual helpless, slightly puzzled manner. 'I didn't mean anything by calling it my school. God knows it's the last thing I should ever be possessive about. I only wanted to make it clear that by taking Jassy as a pupil I am within my rights.'

'Very well,' I said, mustering my dignity. 'You'd like me to arrange for her for next term?'

'Please, Beth. But not now, naturally.' For I was going towards the door. I knew that in a few moments I should be in tears, and it annoyed Katharine to see me cry.

'I've remembered something that I must do,' I said.

I went and sat in my own room. The words, 'This is my school,' rang in my ears. Of course it was her school. It had been bought with her money. But it was Katharine herself who had suggested that I should assume the responsibilities and position of Head of it.

'How should I know when somebody needed a pill? Or how many rice puddings to order? Besides, the mothers will like to leave their precious darlings with a nice respectable widow with charming manners.' She had said that herself. And for eighteen years I had worked and planned, cajoled, reproved, interviewed, soothed and supervised all on her behalf. Now, over the question of Jassy Woodroffe, Katharine could flash round and say, 'This is my school.' It was like laying bare a sharp dangerous rock.

I wept with self-pity. And weeping, remembering how Katharine had spoken to me, remembering how my opinion had been swept aside, I began to hate the real culprit, Jassy Woodroffe.

Within the next few days I received evidence that Katharine, so remote and indolent, had been nearer the heart of the school than I, who seldom considered anything else. For two days after that momentous interview Dilys Helmar came, in the hour between lessons' end and supper, and knocked on my door.

I had, during all my years of acting as Head in Katharine's school, sedulously avoided having favourites amongst the girls, and although, being human, I was bound to have preferences, I had always concealed them. But Dilys Helmar was very dear to me. If I could have been given a miraculous power to rearrange my life I should have Katharine for my husband and Dilys for my daughter. It was, I must admit, odd that I should be fond of two such extremely different people–Katharine so clever, bookish and eccentric; Dilys so lovely and silly. But there it was. If a fire had broken out in school I would have saved Katharine first and Dilys second.

Dilys had come to us about a fortnight after her mother had gone off with another man. She was a delicate, sensitive, rather precocious little girl, and the upheaval in her home life had affected her badly. During the last summer holidays she had been ill–and, I think, neglected–and had not been able to return to school until the middle of the term. During that absence I had often thought about her, left to the care of servants, I was sure. I had once seen her father, and he had impressed me most unfavourably. Since her return to school I had kept a very watchful eye on her.

She came, on this evening towards the end of the Easter term, into my sitting-room and stood, rather nervously, just inside the door. I said, 'Come to the fire, my dear, and sit down.' I pointed to a stool. She sat down and I looked at her, half appreciatively, half professionally. Yes, she looked a little less fragile, a little less nervous; and having satisfied myself upon that score, I could take delight in the lovely shape of her face, the golden halo of her hair, the lustrous softness of her great golden-brown eyes. She was the loveliest little girl we had ever had in school.

'Well, Dilys,' I said, 'what have you come to see me about?'

'About Jassy Woodroffe, Mrs Twy-Twysdale, please.'

'Oh, what about her?' I asked, and I thought, so it's starting! The girls had heard the news and talked it over and sent Dilys–as the most important pupil in school, to make a protest. And, I thought angrily, I shan't attempt to deal with it. I shall turn it over to Katharine; she was the one who spoke so boldly about dealing with complaints.

'We d-d-didn't think she'd have any c-c-clothes.'

She opened one of her clenched hands and held out to me a little netted purse, quite heavy by the look of it. 'So p-p-please, we made a little c-c-collection, and will you g-g-get her some?'

'Well,' I said, completely astonished, 'it's very kind of you, Dilys, very kind of all of you. But I think that Miss Hamilton and I will be able to deal with her clothes. We hadn't really thought about them yet. Jassy must be quite a favourite with you for you to have thought about making a collection.'

'Oh, yes. She's very am-m-musing,' said Dilys, with one of her lovely smiles.

I was visited again by that same spitefulness which had made me snap at Jassy herself about the unfilled log basket.

'Isn't it a pity,' I said, 'that you can't master your stammer, Dilys? It doesn't matter much now, but later on, when you are a young lady, it will be a terrible handicap. I thought Miss Ogilvy was going to give you voice exercises.'

The delicate wild-rose colour on her oval cheeks deepened painfully, and I felt a certain remorse at having vented my spite against Jassy, whom I hated, upon this child, of whom I was fond.

'She d-d-does, Mrs Twysdale. I am better, indeed I am. It's only when I'm ex-excited.'

'Am I to understand that you are excited about Jassy's entering school?'

'Yes,' she said, speaking very slowly and carefully. 'It is like a story, isn't it? It hasn't happened before. We thought she would look nice in a red dress.'

She stood up as she spoke and, coming towards me, laid the little purse gently in my hand.

I suddenly thought that I understood. The girls had evidently adopted Jassy Woodroffe just as they might have adopted and pampered a stray kitten. That remark about a red dress was very significant. It reminded me that our girls had most of them outgrown their dolls, and the next objects of that kind of affection–their babies–were still far away in the future; but the instinct to be fond of something small, and to dress it, was active in them because they were female.

'We'll see about the dresses,' I said, 'though I can't promise that I shall use your money. And Dilys, here is something that I want you to remember, and to tell the other girls. Jassy will be happier and derive more benefit from school if you don't spoil her. The kindest thing you can do is to treat her exactly as though she were a new pupil you have never seen before. Do you understand that?'

'Y-yes, Mrs Twysdale. I think so.'

'And now, tell me, have you had any more headache lately?'

A guarded, almost secretive look came over the lovely little face like a shutter.

'I'm better now, thank you,' she said. I saw her eyes look towards the door. A kind of anger seized me–oh, go along then, I thought; go back and talk over Jassy Woodroffe's dresses, and next time your head aches don't expect sympathy from me.

'I'm glad to hear that,' I said. 'Good night, Dilys.'

But when she had gone, with a last smile of remarkable sweetness, I sat for some moments thinking about Jassy Woodroffe. It was an absurd thought, but it seemed to me that, without knowing, and certainly without intending it, that mite of a child had poisoned my relationships with three people. I should always feel some resentment towards Amy, who had forced me into employing her; I should never forget that the nearest thing to a quarrel between Katharine and me had been on her behalf; and now I was annoyed with Dilys.

I remembered my first foolish feeling that Jassy was not lucky to me. Suppose there was something in us more perceptive than our reason; older than thought; more direct than sense? Suppose I had been warned, but, relying upon reason and thought and sense, had disregarded the warning because it came from a quarter which I could not identify? What then?

I put the ridiculous thought from me.

Once, in the school's early days, we had an assistant named Alicia Copping–a youngish, capable, willing woman, but an insufferable colleague because she was such an unmitigated bore. I could never exactly point to the root of her capacity to bore until one day Katharine said, 'That woman is a natural bore; she mentions *everything*.' It was, like most of Katharine's sayings, pungent and shrewd; and after Miss Copping had gone from us we would jokingly refer to Coppingising. I should be guilty of it if I recalled or related every little thing about Jassy Woodroffe during the years she was in school.

But certain things stand out, painful and unforgettable.

She ended my evenings in Katharine's room.

I went up, as usual, one evening after supper, prepared to drink tea, and to talk if Katharine felt like it, or to work quietly if she were reading or writing, and saw, as soon as I opened the door, Jassy Woodroffe seated at the desk. She had some books spread out before her and another in her lap, supporting a sheet of paper upon which she was writing. Her heels were hooked into the rung of the chair, and her face, bent over the paper, was parallel with her lap.

Such a posture, since it must inevitably lead to rounded shoulders, a sagging neckline and a protruding chin, was forbidden in school, and almost automatically I paused by the desk, moved away a book, lifted her paper to the cleared space, and said, 'Never sit like that to write, Jassy. And put your feet on the floor.'

I had spoken quietly, but my voice, or my presence, had shattered something within the room. It was as palpable as though I dropped a glass on a brick floor. The child looked up with a glance so cold and hard that it was almost one of hatred, and Katharine, looking round her chair back and blinking towards me, looked like someone just wakened from sleep. Never in my life had I been so conscious of being an intruder.

'Oh, hullo, Beth,' said Katharine, almost in a whisper. She motioned me towards a chair with a gesture too vague to be called a nod. I sat down, put my feet on a footstool, and took out my work. I had a feeling that I was unwelcome, but I ignored it. I had been spending my evenings here in this room before Jassy Woodroffe was born; I was not going to break a habit on her account.

It irked me even to preserve silence; after all, she had the whole day to study in. However, I worked silently until three quarters of an hour had been measured on the face of Katharine's clock. Then I cleared my throat and said in a deliberate, normal voice:

'Miss Hamilton, there was a matter which I wished to discuss with you.'

Katharine, turning her head and speaking as though to a sleep walker, said softly, 'Jassy. Jassy. I think you'd better leave off now.'

There was a distinct and audible sigh. Then the sound of papers being sorted and books closed and replaced. Then a deep voice said:

'Thank you very much for letting me work here. Good night, Miss Hamilton. Good night, ma'am.'

We bade her good night, I briskly, Katharine with a kind of lingering fondness.

'Well, Beth,' she said, as soon as the door was closed, 'what was this urgent matter?'

'Urgent matter? Oh, nothing. I thought it was time she went away. I hadn't anything of importance to say, but I was tired of sitting mute. What was she doing?'

'Making up for lost time. You see, in some ways she's very backward. I told her she could come here and read a little in the evenings.'

'But that's disturbing you. She could read in the Small Classroom. That's never used in the evenings.'

'It isn't heated either.'

'We could keep the fire in, if this extra study is essential.'

'She doesn't disturb me,' said Katharine, with–or did I imagine it?–the slightest possible emphasis upon the first pronoun. 'I fancy concentration must be contagious. I've worked better myself tonight than for a long time.'

'In fact, I disturbed you both.'

Katharine looked at me with some embarrassment.

'Sewing isn't quite the same thing,' she said evasively. 'I always feel that you would rather talk, Beth. So even when we're quiet I have a kind of–well, almost guilty feeling.'

'You should have told me that before,' I said.

'One gets into habits . . .' It was said in a curiously inconclusive way, but it was more eloquent than most completed sentences. All my skin went hot. Years and years and years I had been going to Katharine's room in the evening, never thinking, but concluding that I was welcome. I had sat for hours resolutely restraining my chatter and she had been conscious of strain all the time.

'I'm sorry, Katharine,' I said. 'I'd no idea. As you say–habit. But that can be altered. What would be your suggestion?'

'Suppose you left the bookworms together until half past nine, and keep tea back till then. Then we could drink it together and have our little talk. Would that suit you?'

'Perfectly. You should have suggested that before, Katharine. Surely you know that I only want to do what suits and pleases you.'

She looked at me curiously. 'Such knowledge often nips suggestions in the bud, Beth.'

So after that I spent most of my evenings alone until half past nine, except on the occasions when I invited Miss Ogilvy or Miss Smithers, whichever was not on duty, to sit with me, or went out to Mrs Dulcimer's. And my life was that much duller and poorer, and my hatred of Jassy Woodroffe mounted steadily.

Still, for a little while, there were the holidays. I had always looked forward to them, for then I had Katharine absolutely to myself. And we could shake off our dignity and our responsibilities and get back, in a way, to those days of childhood in Hampshire when we should have laughed and stared incredulously at the idea of being schoolmarms, carefully calling one another Miss Hamilton and Mrs Twysdale.

We had established a regular routine for holidays. At Christmas we stayed in Baildon, snug by the fire, mildly entertaining the few friends we had made in the town and being entertained by them. At Easter I was usually busy, for we did our spring-cleaning in the holiday, and there were visits from the sweep, and blanket washing, and a thousand things to see to. But often in the afternoon, if the weather were nice, we would hire a carriage from Storey's and take a drive. In the summer we took a real holiday at Brighton, where the family of one of our pupils who had fallen on evil days entertained summer visitors at reasonable rates.

For a year after Jassy's entry as a pupil this pleasant routine was maintained. And I must admit that, in my blindness, I had never even feared that the holidays were threatened. As each one came round Jassy went off to stay with Amy Partridge, and I gave her no thought until school opened again.

But during the Easter holiday of the next year, I came one morning out of the parlour with a pile of curtains and covers which were to be washed in my arms and almost ran into Jassy, who was standing in the hall. I was not even surprised to see her there, imagining that Amy had sent her with a message.

'Good morning, Jassy,' I said. 'What brings you back to school this morning?'

'I want to see Miss Hamilton.'

Oh, do you? I thought.

'About lessons? About books?' I asked.

'In a way, yes.'

'Look,' I said, 'Miss Hamilton works hard during the term, Jassy; she needs a holiday like everybody else. I can't have her bothered. You run along back to Mrs Partridge and give your books a rest. If you've nothing else to do you can lend her a hand about the place.'

She gave me the hard cold stare which I remembered. But she said, quite gently; 'I have been working since six this morning. And I wouldn't bother Miss Hamilton. I've got a book to return and just a question to ask.'

The pile of soft material in my arms was unsteady and annoyed me. So did the sight of Jassy Woodroffe, standing there looking stubborn; looking also almost unnaturally neat and fresh in a pink cotton dress and a wide hat tied with a ribbon. I spoke sharply:

'Leave the book on the chair. I'll take it to her. And you must save your question for next term. I can't have girls running in and out during the holidays.'

'Miss Hamilton told me I could . . .'

'Miss Hamilton is too kind. I won't have her imposed upon. I should have thought that you might have enough perception to realize that you already receive far more than your share of her time and attention. Run along now, there's a good girl.'

She favoured me with another long stare, and incredible as it seemed, I could feel the strength ebbing from my legs; my heart began to pound, and one of the hot flushes which were the curse of my middle age rushed up, suffusing my face, my neck and my ears. We seemed to stand there for a long time, fighting one another with our eyes. Then Jassy turned abruptly, put the book on the chair which I had indicated, and walked away without a word. The door closed gently behind her.

I went to the service door at the back of the stairs and, since my hands were full, thrust it open with my shoulder. I pushed too hard and, as soon as I was on the other side, it swung back sharply and hit me on the elbow. The pile of curtains and covers quivered and fell to the floor.

Crossly, I began to pick them up, and as I did so I thought I heard the front door open again. Kicking my feet free, I shot back into the hall, and was just in time to see a fold of pink dress whip round the bend of the stairs. A glance at the chair told me that the book had gone.

I went and sat down in the comfortless, stripped parlour. I felt weak and furious. The only thing which would have relieved me at that moment would have been to charge up the stairs, take the little hussy by the back of her neck and bundle her out of the house. I was surprised–even a trifle shocked–by the violence of my feelings. But I could not vent them without risking a scene with Katharine, who was obviously so infatuated with the girl that she had given her grounds to believe that she would be welcome at any time. There was the real trouble. Jealousy more than outraged dignity was causing me this pain.

However, within an hour I was rational again. In future, I thought, I should see that the front door was locked and that the servants had orders not to admit Jassy during the holidays. And, I reflected, this morning's visit could not be of long duration, since dinner was ordered for twelve o'clock. Katharine and I were taking a drive that afternoon, and the carriage was to come at one.

It would be the first drive of the holidays, and I wondered whether I could persuade Katharine to go to Colchester. The shops there were far more attractive, and better stocked than those in Baildon, and I enjoyed seeing them, and the bustle and stir of the people, and taking tea in the Blue Parlour Tea Rooms. Katharine preferred to drive the other way, into the–to my mind–gloomy country on the edge of the marshes. And perhaps today, after all, I would defer to her wishes, as a penance for the hard thoughts I had been indulging.

Just before dinner I went upstairs to my bedroom to wash my hands. When I reached the half-landing from which Katharine's sitting-room was reached the door opened, and there was Katharine, with Jassy close behind her. The girl was not in the least discomfited; she met my eyes with a look of supreme serenity.

'I was just coming to look for you, Beth,' said Katharine, not even remembering that we always addressed one another formally before the pupils. 'I thought it would be nice if Jassy stayed to dinner and took the drive with us. . . . My dear, you're quite out of breath. Have you been working too hard, or is it the stairs? Come and sit down a moment.'

For the first time in my life I shrugged away from Katharine's outstretched hand.

'I'm all right,' I said. The harshness of my voice frightened me. 'Perhaps you'd ring the bell and tell Emily about setting another place. I'm just going to wash my hands. Dinner is ready.'

My dressing-table faced the door, and as I entered my room I caught sight of myself. My face was quite white except for two burning red circles high on the cheek-bones; and my eyes were glassy, as though with fever. Small wonder, for I was consumed with a threefold fever of fury and frustration and jealousy. I crossed to the wash-stand, saying over and over again in a whisper, 'I can't bear it, I can't bear it!' My hands were shaking so violently that in pouring water from my ewer I spilt it and soaked the front of my skirt. I dabbed at it frantically, and then, turning from the wash-stand, with my hands still unwashed I began to pace about the room, finding some small comfort in movement. As I walked I framed scathing or pathetic sentences in my mind. I told Katharine exactly what I had done for her in the course of nearly twenty years, how I had served and protected her, pandered to her; how even this morning I had been working hard while she, serene and remote in her room, had been entertaining the girl who had defied me, and had been concocting a plan which was to rob me of the one small pleasure I had counted upon.

I walked round and round, ranting, denouncing and imploring in silence until there came a quiet tap on the door.

'Yes, Emily,' I cried, for since Jassy's promotion there was only one person who tapped like that.

'Miss Hamilton said to tell you, ma'am, that dinner is on the table.'

I opened the door, ready to voice a decision which was only framed as I laid my hand on the knob.

'Emily, will you please tell Miss Hamilton that I can't eat any dinner, nor can I drive this afternoon. My head has begun to ache suddenly. I shall lie down now. I don't want to see anyone.'

'Shall you like a cuppa tea?'

'No, thank you, Emily.'

'Will I draw the curtains?'

'Yes, you might do that.'

Left alone in the dim room I turned the key of the door and flung myself on my bed. I lay for a long time, still talking to Katharine in my mind. Then I fell asleep.

When I woke I felt no better, but my common sense was at work again, and I saw that I should do myself no service by shutting myself away and sulking. I rose, washed, put on my nicest dress, and did my hair carefully. I had been downstairs a few minutes when the carriage arrived and Katharine was back . . . alone.

She inquired sympathetically about my headache and said what a pity it was that I had been unable to take the drive.

'But I ordered it again for tomorrow afternoon at the same time. I hope it's as nice a day. It was lovely today. We turned off the Bywater road and went to look at the house where Dilys Helmar lives. I had no idea it was so near the main road, or so interesting. Jassy knew such a lot about it. Apparently part of it dates back to pre-Norman times. I must look it up in Hopkins' *Survey* and see how much of the entrancing story Jassy entertained me with has a basis in fact. Poor Jassy, I think she rather hoped to see Dilys, but there wasn't a sign of life about the place, and I didn't like to keep the carriage outside too long.'

'Have you invited Jassy for tomorrow?'

'No. When we set her down I hadn't thought of ordering it again. A pity. The air would have done her good. Perhaps I could send round in the morning.'

'No,' I said. 'No, Katharine. Let us go together tomorrow, please. I've had so little of your company lately, you know. And . . . well, in front of a pupil we have to keep up a certain dignity. It spoils that holiday feeling.'

'I'm afraid I forget dignity with Jassy. She's such good company. And full of country lore and sayings. I don't remember when I've enjoyed a drive more. Still, tomorrow shall be your day, Beth, dear. Shall we go to Colchester?'

'Please,' I said. And I thought of the beggar in the Bible who supported life on the crumbs that fell from the rich man's table. Loving can be very ignominious.

Jassy was in and out of the house almost all the holiday, and I made no further effort to circumvent her. But there formed in the depths of my mind a hard little bud of a plan. Remembering the impudence with which she had defied and disobeyed me over the matter of that first visit, I concluded that she could not be so meek and law-abiding as she appeared. That action seemed to have within it the suggestion of practised duplicity. I decided to watch her closely; to keep my eyes and ears open and see if I could not seize upon something which, properly presented, would lessen Katharine's opinion of her, or even lead to her dismissal from school altogether. Meantime I must watch myself as well, taking care to make myself pleasant and indispensable to Katharine and endear myself to her, so that when I finally had a case to present against the intruder it could not be weakened by a charge of jealousy or peevishness.

But some months passed before I had a legitimate cause for complaint. It was a June evening, almost ten o'clock, and the long slow twilight was darkening when Miss Ogilvy, with her hair slightly ruffled and a harassed expression on her face, came into my room. Miss Ogilvy took turns with Miss Smithers, our other assistant, to be on duty in the evening supervising the girls' study and recreation and preserving order.

On this evening she came quickly into my room, stared at me with a boldness very different from her usual meek manner and said:

'Mrs Twysdale, you really will have to do something about that Jassy Woodroffe. I've just spent an hour with Cecily Drew, she's half crazy with hysteria.'

'Sit down, Miss Ogilvy, and compose yourself. What connection is there between Cecily Drew and Jassy Woodroffe?'

'This afternoon, during the walk, Jassy and Dilys Helmar walked at the rear of the seniors, Cecily and Margie Phelps at the head of the juniors, which means, as you know, that Cecily was directly behind Jassy and Dilys. Jassy was telling Dilys about this being St John's Eve . . . and a lot of silly rubbish about old country customs of looking into mirrors at midnight and seeing the man you would marry, and so on. Cecily, of course, overheard all this superstitious nonsense. Whether she was planning, as I believe some of the others are, to get up at midnight and study mirrors and bowls of water, I don't know. But I do know that she went to sleep and dreamed about it and woke screaming, and it's taken me a full hour to quiet her.' Miss Ogilvy drew a hissing, much-needed breath and went straight on before I could speak. 'I've often wanted to speak to you about this matter, Mrs Twysdale, but it seemed none of my business. However, now the time has come and I shall say it. I wonder at your decision to make Jassy Woodroffe a pupil; I disapprove of it, and I say straight out that I think she has a bad influence on the girls. Tonight is only one of a hundred little things.'

I confess that Miss Ogilvy's attack startled me. It was like seeing a soft white rabbit with pink eyes suddenly behaving like a bull dog. Miss Ogilvy, who had been very fair and had drifted almost imperceptibly into white-headedness, was not unlike a rabbit. She had no chin to speak of, her teeth projected, and her pale blue eyes had reddish rims. I had never known her to criticize a rule, or to question an order; she was as unobtrusive, as reliable and as uninteresting as the chair in which she sat. But tonight she bristled with fury, and her manner was the quintessence of accusation.

'One thing at a time, Miss Ogilvy, if you please,' I said, as calmly as I could. 'First of all, this is not the first time that Cecily Drew has waked screaming. She is rather highly strung and has occasional nightmares. I don't think we can accuse Jassy Woodroffe of deliberately frightening her. Can we?'

'No. I didn't make that accusation. My complaint was that the Woodroffe child is conversant with, and talks about, many things which the average girl of thirteen, if she be gently reared, knows nothing about. She is old for her years. Her upbringing is questionable, and if my opinion had been asked, as it never is, I should have had a good deal to say about introducing her into a school for young ladies.'

I said: 'As a matter of fact, Miss Ogilvy, the idea of doing so was—'

'Miss Hamilton's. There's no need to tell me that, Mrs Twysdale. I guessed it all along. And that brings me to another point. I've been here long enough to make several observations, and I must say that it strikes me as singularly unfair that Miss Hamilton is the *only* assistant whose opinion is ever asked, or whose wishes are ever studied. I might tell you that that fact has been responsible for many upsets in the past. The rest of us aren't blind, you know. And I don't mind telling you that when Miss Copping had given in her notice she said to me, "I'm going to teach in a school with only one Head in future." That just shows you. I've borne it because I like you, Mrs Twysdale, and I can see that Miss Hamilton is a very clever woman and I get on quite well with her. But when it comes to bringing up a girl from the kitchen just to please one teacher and to plague the rest, it does seem to be carrying favouritism a little far.'

'Do you mind leaving that matter for a minute, Miss Ogilvy? Oh, yes, I'll explain later. Look, I was just about to take tea. Perhaps you would join me.' I rang my bell and ordered two cups to be placed on the tray, and then returned to Miss Ogilvy.

'Tell me, Miss Ogilvy. You say that Jassy Woodroffe has a bad influence on the girls, that she is a plague to you and Miss Smithers–and the visiting teachers too, I assume–and you say that Cecily Drew's fright is only one of a hundred things you hold against her. Can you, will you, explain as clearly as possible exactly what you mean? It would help me enormously if you could.'

Miss Ogilvy's truculent expression faded and gave way to one of bewilderment.

'It's very difficult to put into words, Mrs Twysdale. It is indeed. Like when you say that she didn't deliberately frighten Cecily. She probably didn't; but she had the *power* to frighten her, and she used it. She just is different, and probably for that reason she has a great attraction for the other girls. Therefore they notice what she says and does. And she is far more mature than they are for her age. So harm is done. For instance, do you remember when there was a lot of bother about the Senior table not eating their soup?'

'Yes, I do. They just refused it, and when I substituted bread and water as a punishment they accepted it with exaggerated delight. I thought it was some kind of fad about soup being fattening, as I believe it is held to be; and since those girls had their figures to consider, I discontinued serving it to that table.'

'It wasn't a fad, Mrs Twysdale. It was because Jassy Woodroffe would not eat soup. And she said, "If you'd seen it made, as I have, you wouldn't eat it either." She hinted that discarded pieces from the plates were always scraped into the stock-pot, and after that none of the seniors would touch soup. She may have been telling the truth . . . she may have been lying. But she spoilt the idea of soup for everyone who listened to her.'

Miss Ogilvy's expression showed very plainly that she had been amongst the listeners. I felt impelled to say, in self defence:

'Every week four pounds of neck of mutton, or four pounds of beef shin, are ordered specially for the stock-pot. I could show you the bills, Miss Ogilvy.'

'They wouldn't prove that Mrs Whiting didn't scrape the plates into what was originally a good mixture.'

'No. I'll look into that, though perhaps it might not be such a *very* disgusting thing to do. It's all boiled again. However, I will give an order.' I drew my writing tablet towards me and made a note. 'Thank you for telling me, Miss Ogilvy. You should have done so sooner. You are so much more in personal touch with the girls. What else have you noticed about the Woodroffe child?'

'Nothing else so concrete, perhaps. In class she is attentive enough; in study hour she is inclined to whisper and make the girls laugh too much. And she tells fantastic stories about her past. One of them concerns herself, how she was going to be drowned by a mob of children and was saved at the last moment by a handsome young man who was the Squire's son. Harmless, perhaps, but palpably untrue, and I am, myself, opposed to encouraging girls to take a silly romantic view of life. You never know. Some of them are senseless enough to deliberately get into a scrape in the belief that a handsome young man will rescue them. There's that . . . and, oh, lots of stupid little things, like pretending to foretell the weather, and cast fortunes for the girls. Nothing bad enough to make a fuss about; but not what I have been accustomed to. And I must say, Mrs Twysdale, I don't like it.'

'No,' I said slowly, 'nor do I.' But even as I spoke I knew that the core of Miss Ogilvy's complaint lay in those words, 'Nothing bad enough to make a fuss about.' There was–and to me this was the only point–nothing which I could carry to Katharine and prove that my foreboding had been justified. And that was what I wanted; that was what I had waited and hoped for. But it had eluded me. Miss Ogilvy had failed to give adequate grounds for her hatred of this child. For hatred, nothing milder, had transformed the white rabbit into a bull dog. And, as in my own case, it was hatred, not of the child's actions, but of her essence. A feeling of helpless frustration swept me. I knew precisely what Miss Ogilvy meant; I wanted to support her; and I thought ironically that had Jassy been a pay-feeing, ordinary pupil I could have banished her at once; I need not even have told Katharine why. As it was, I was powerless.

I looked at Miss Ogilvy, wondering what to say next, and I suppose my helplessness showed on my face. For suddenly, as if all my lost confidence had flowed across the room and entered into her, Miss Ogilvy stood up, looking more erect and purposeful than I had ever seen her.

"This puts you in an unpleasant position, Mrs Twysdale. I can see that. In fact, I feel quite sorry for you; though I could have told you, before the end of my first term, that such a situation was bound to arise one day. Never once, in the twelve years I have been with you, have you crossed Miss Hamilton in any way. And naturally you find it difficult to disregard her wishes in this matter, after giving her her head for so long. But if you like I and Miss Smithers, who feels the same about this matter, will go and have a straight talk with Miss Hamilton. After all, we are in the majority, and though we may not be so clever, or so self-willed, surely we could, backed by you, make some impression. . . .'

She broke off as Emily brought in the tea tray and set it down. The moment while the girl was in the room gave me time to think–not clearly, but hurriedly and frightenedly.

'I don't think that that would have any effect at all, Miss Ogilvy. Until we can produce some more conclusive evidence of the girl's bad influence we could hardly hope to shake Miss Hamilton's infatuated determination to educate her. Moreover, unfortunately, I spoke very frankly when the idea was first proposed; so I'm afraid that complaints as indefinite as yours would merely be attributed to my spiteful influence. Miss Hamilton would think that I had conspired with you and Miss Smithers and then sent you to say what I daren't say myself.'

I was too confused to realize the implication of my words, but I did so as soon as they were spoken. Miss Ogilvy's face enlightened me. She came a step towards me and then said in a curious voice:

'Did you say "daren't," Mrs Twysdale? You must excuse me if I speak frankly. It's a matter that I've given a lot of thought to, and about which I feel very strongly. Earlier this evening I quoted to you Miss Copping's words about this school having two Heads. Now why is it? Why must Miss Hamilton's word be law here? Why does she never take an evening duty; or escort the girls to church; or go with them on their walks; why does she have a sitting-room to herself while the rest of us share? And why, for heaven's sake, daren't you cross her, or even criticize her, about this preposterous notion of bringing a ragamuffin up from the kitchen to upset the whole school?'

It was like the eruption of a volcano, or the bursting of a boil. The words simply bubbled from Miss Ogilvy's meekly-formed mouth, and a blob of froth came with them. She looked mad. And it was suddenly clear to me that beneath her meek, uncritical exterior these questions had been rankling for a long time.

I lost the last inch of my head. Or is it that, faced by any attack, mental or physical, the instinct for self-defence overrides everything else? Either way, I spoke out, senselessly, disastrously. I said, 'I think Miss Ogilvy, I had better be frank with you and give you a truthful answer which will satisfy all your questions. This school belongs to Miss Hamilton. In order to spare herself from the bother of the practical side of it she allowed me to pose as its Head. Actually I have no more *power* in it than you and Miss Smithers. If she wished, she could install any efficient woman in my place. So you see the position. So far as diet and staff and similar matters are concerned, my word is law. But when it comes to dictating to Miss Hamilton about personal affairs, I am as helpless as you are.'

I said all this, looking straight into Miss Ogilvy's face. A series of remarkable changes were taking place there. First she looked like an old cow that had been pole-axed; then confusion and embarrassment replaced the stunned expression; and, finally, she looked at me with nothing less than vindictive loathing. When I had finished she clutched her hands together in front of her hollow waist, stuck out her receding chin, and glared at me.

'I see,' she hissed. 'I see. So that's how you've deceived me for twelve years. I've been saying "Yes, Mrs Twysdale; no, Mrs Twysdale; certainly Mrs Twysdale," and it meant nothing at all. And at the same time I've hardly let a day pass without making some stab or another at Miss Hamilton's privileges. Really, when I think of the times I've said "Some people are lucky!" meaning her to overhear . . . well, really, I wonder she hasn't dismissed me right away! Naturally all these things we've resented so much are her *rights*. She was the one we ought to have respected and considered. It isn't fair. I don't know what to think or do. I can never apologize sufficiently. As for this other matter . . . of course, it's her school. She wants Jassy Woodroffe in it, who am I to question that wish? Really, Mrs Twysdale . . . when I think that in another minute I should have been attacking her on the subject. No, it isn't fair. It isn't fair at all.'

Even in my wretchedness I could derive a sour amusement from the little turncoat's change of attitude. I could see why Katharine had so often said, 'I wonder why Miss Ogilvy stays, she always sounds so discontented.' Poor thing, she had shot her barbs at Katharine and always turned a meek face to me. And now everything she had ever said to Katharine or *at* her must stick like choke-pears in her throat. But under these superficial thoughts the main part of my mind was given over to fury and rancour. For almost twenty years I had been the figurehead of the Baildon Academy; now, with my own hand I had smitten down that imposing figure, revealed it as the myth it was. And who had forced me to do so? Jassy Woodroffe. In this one evening's work was the justification of that sly dread which I had felt when I first set eyes on her. My guardian angel had stood by, warning me, on that day when Amy Partridge brought her, and I had disregarded the warning. My punishment had begun.

I pulled myself together, resolute to save what remained.

'Sit down, Miss Ogilvy, and have a cup of tea. We can both do with one. There are two other things which I ought to make clear to you.' I poured the tea quickly, and after a second's hesitation Miss Ogilvy seated herself again and accepted the cup I offered her. 'Now,' I said, 'I was compelled to speak frankly to you and in a way I don't regret it. And I am willing to overlook a certain insolence in your immediate response to my information. But the first thing you must understand is that this matter is a secret. It was arranged between Miss Hamilton and me at the very beginning; it was for her convenience, and while she accepts me as Head of the school you must be willing to do so too, if you want to stay here. The second thing is this. It would be very unwise of you to make a display of your sudden transference of loyalty. Oh yes, Miss Ogilvy, this interview has been extremely illuminating. I know that after this you are prepared to treat me cavalierly and reserve your yeses and noes and certainlys for Miss Hamilton. She would resent that, not only on her own behalf, I can assure you of that. By all means curb your criticisms in her presence, though that advice is redundant; otherwise, you would show wisdom by going on exactly as before. Have I made that plain? You must remember that Miss Hamilton and I have been friends from childhood. Long years of loyal affection have bound us to one another.'

I spoke confidently. I could see, by the shaking of Miss Ogilvy's hand as she held her cup that my words had found their mark and were having the effect I desired. Now that I had recovered from that momentary madness, brought on by the feeling of extreme helplessness, I was competent to deal with Miss Ogilvy. Katharine might rule me, exploit and defeat me, but that was her privilege, hers because I had given it to her with my love. But I was not having any nonsense from anyone else.

Yet, even as I spoke my brave words about loyalty and affection, even as Miss Ogilvy, in the last stages of confusion, spilt tea into her saucer and turned back into a white rabbit before my eyes, the shadow of Jassy Woodroffe rose before me, monstrous and menacing. A shadow which could threaten and frighten, but which could not be fought, because it was only a shadow.

Next morning at breakfast, which we all took together, I was conscious of Miss Smithers' eye looking at me furtively and with speculation. I knew instantly that Miss Ogilvy had told her something, at least, of the previous evening's interview. But, although I watched for it closely and was prepared to check the first sign, there was no lessening of respect either in her manner or Miss Ogilvy's.

I spent the morning, while I went about my duties, in pursuing the thoughts which had been with me during the hours of a sleepless night. And during the afternoon, acting upon considered judgements, I sent a request that Jassy Woodroffe, instead of going for the usual walk, might come to my room.

I was aware, directly I had sent the message, of a mounting and senseless nervousness. I had to force myself to sit still in my chair, not wander about the room fingering things. My digestion went wrong and my dinner lay like a lump of hot lead in my chest. And all the time I was arguing fiercely with myself. I had had a complaint about the girl and I had sent for her to talk to her, just as I should any girl in the circumstances. Wasn't that right and fair? What more could even the most devoted partisan wish? And yet . . . and yet . . . I wished I had let the matter slide. Some deeper wisdom in me knew that my only hope for success in this affair was to turn a completely blind eye, an utterly deaf ear upon Jassy Woodroffe and wait patiently for the day when she would tire Katharine, or bore her, or, failing that, simply grow up at last and be gone. That way I should survive her, both at the Academy, and in Katharine's esteem. Interference was dangerous. Yet, knowing this, I seemed to be driven to interfere.

Presently there was a gentle tap on my door and my enemy–for that was how I now regarded her–entered. I kept her standing, and I regarded her deliberately for a moment; it was a method of approach which I had often found useful. Even truculent girls will lose confidence if silently regarded. But today, perhaps because I was not completely sure of myself, or because this girl was not like others, it did not work. She did not drop her eyes, but stood still, regarding me; not defiantly, but with a calmness which was even more unnerving.

'I sent for you,' I said at last, 'because I have been receiving complaints about you.'

'Yes?' It was a question, not an acceptance of a statement. That low voice of hers, which Katharine dotingly called full of wood-smoke, was extremely flexible. She could infuse a simple word with a great deal of meaning. That 'Yes?' said, 'Oh, have you indeed? And who has been complaining? And why?'

'Yes, indeed,' I said. 'For instance, what is all this nonsense that you've been spreading about the way soup is prepared? I should hardly have imagined that you would have suffered from undue fastidiousness in that respect.'

'The soup?' she said slowly. 'Oh yes. I never ate mine. Having been in the kitchen I knew that Mrs Whiting will put practically *anything* in the stock-pot. The other girls pestered me to know why I didn't eat it, and finally I told them. I thought it quite likely that they might mind too.'

'Such extreme delicacy . . .' I began angrily, trying at one and the same time to snub the little upstart and to remember whether I had ever seen Mrs Whiting at the stock-pot, and thus confusing myself and leaving the sentence uncompleted.

She interrupted me, answering what I had intended to say, her grey eyes very clear and pale in her biscuit-coloured face.

'I've often lived on very poor food, but I happen to be particular. At home I got it ready myself, and I wouldn't put turnips or carrots in soup without washing them. Nor would I spit in the frying pan to see if the grease was hot enough to fry in. Mrs Whiting does that. I'd rather be hungry than eat her fried stuff.'

My dinner, which had not digested, had included pancakes. My stomach heaved and my mouth stiffened with nausea.

'I didn't know that!' I said sharply.

She said nothing, but 'Well, you know now' shone in her eyes.

I was angry with myself for that cry of disguest and weakness, and mingled with my anger was something else. I realized that this child had, in some curious, inexplicable fashion, the gift of making things bare. She had, on the first day I saw her, clarified the position between Amy and me and made me realize that I didn't really like Amy as much as I thought, as much as I wanted to. And it was through her that Katharine had, in a few words, made our relative positions plain. Now she was exposing horrors which had existed, all unsuspected, in what I had always thought my well-run, speckless kitchen.

I wanted to say, all at once, 'Tell me more. What other filthy tricks have you seen out there?' and 'How dare you mention such things? Even if they were true decent people wouldn't notice them.'

I wished I had left the wretched soup till last, but I knew I had fastened upon it as the most concrete complaint I had to proffer.

'That wasn't all,' I said, knowing that I was going from bathos to bathos. 'Other complaints about you include frightening the young girls with foolish stories and pretending to tell fortunes for the elder ones. I know that your training has been defective, and you are perhaps to be pitied rather than blamed, but surely your own intelligence must have told you that the school is not the place for that kind of superstitious rubbish.'

She appeared to be casting back in her mind.

'I don't think I ever frightened anybody,' she said slowly.

'Cecily Drew was in hysterics last night over some nonsense about St John's Eve.'

'Not from anything *I* said. I don't think I've ever spoken to her at all. Certainly not yesterday.'

'I'm not talking about that,' I said, a little wildly. 'Can't you realize that it's your general attitude that is at fault? You may not have spoken to the child, but you brought within her range of notice a lot of silly chatter which ordinarily would never come near her . . . the sort of thing that only old country cronies talk about. It musn't happen again, do you understand that? If you are going to stay here and justify Miss Hamilton's very high hopes of you, you must try to forget your unfortunate past and settle down to be an ordinary young lady; not try to make yourself noticeable by silly stories and sillier pretensions.'

For the first time during the interview her facial expression changed a little. Her eyes narrowed and her lips moved. It was as though the whole calm surface of her face shifted a little. She said, quite sharply:

'I never *pretended* anything. When there was nothing there I said so.'

'What do you mean? Are you seriously claiming . . .? Why, that is even worse. I cannot have this kind of thing in school.'

'But I haven't *done* anything,' she said on a rising tone. 'Dilys Helmar comes from my part of the country and told the girls about my mother being a Stannary. Then they started crazing me to tell their fortunes. Nine times out of ten there was nothing to tell . . . but now and again . . . there is! When Hilda Besson was sent for because her mother was supposed to be dying I helped her to pack, she was crying so hard she couldn't do it. And while I was kneeling by her valise I *saw* her mother walking with Hilda in a garden, walking very feebly with one arm in Hilda's and a stick in the other hand. And I told her. I only said: "Hilda, they may say she's dying, but I'm certain she'll get better." And she did. When Hilda came back she told the girls about it. That's all.'

I stared at her in horror. But for a moment I could find nothing to say. The confident matter-of-fact way in which she spoke of the incident was as impressive as her actual words were shocking.

'It's all nonsense,' I said. 'You may have had an idea that Mrs Besson would recover–but to claim that you foretold her recovery is rubbish and not far short of blasphemy. Only God can tell what the future holds.' I paused for a second and then said, less violently, 'Well now, I've tried to point out to you just where your behaviour, your general attitude falls short of what we require and expect of our pupils. I hope to have no more complaints about you. You have been singularly favoured in being taken into school at all, you know; you must endeavour to repay the kindness you have received by being worthy of it.'

I usually ended interviews over discipline with some such homily, pointing out any natural advantage a girl might have–intelligence, a good home, kind parents, and so on–as the reason for good resolutions. And almost always the girl left me tearful or apologetic. But Jassy Woodroffe merely looked at me for a moment and then, with a little perfunctory bob, turned towards the door.

Instantly–and I only realized afterwards that it was as soon as her eyes were off me–I was aggressively angry. I thought of all the nice girls, well-born, gently-reared girls, whom I had reproved, and often for no greater crime than undue levity and high spirits, who had gone from that very door with words of apology on their trembling young lips. In justice to them, if not to myself, I could not let her go away like that. I said sharply:

'Jassy Woodroffe! Is that how you turn over a new leaf? Aren't you even going to say that you're sorry?'

She turned back and walked to my table.

'I'm sorry that I annoy you,' she said. 'But I do that just by being here, don't I? You never liked the idea of taking me into the school. Miss Hamilton told me so. I try to annoy you as little as possible and to keep out of your way. But I can't help being myself, and it would be silly to apologize for that.'

It was as though I had been reading, not hearing, the words, and as though 'Miss Hamilton told me so' had been printed in thick black type, a shout on the page. I felt sick. Such disloyalty to me, such proof of intimacy with this creature. I looked at her, loathing her face with its pale tan and its great red mouth and horrible eyes, loathing that ridiculous mode of hairdressing, even the taut, conscious neatness of her body. What could Katharine see in the vulgar little wretch that she should prefer her to me, talk about me to her?

I should have liked to shout, to call her horrible names, to smack her on both cheeks of that insolent calm face.

'I have now lost all interest in you,' I said, mastering my rage and speaking coldly in order to prove to myself that I could control my desire to scream at her. 'I have tried to do my duty by you and to study your welfare. But you are a vulgar, coarse, unresponsive girl upon whom kindness is wasted. In future, whatever you do I shall regard with indifference, knowing that one cannot make a silk purse from a sow's ear.'

For a moment I thought she was going to attack me. Her eyes had a dangerous glitter. Then she swung round towards the door. The edge of my little table caught her thigh, and instead of recoiling, or trying to save it with her hand, she pushed against it, with deliberate violence. It tilted and fell over. My little vase of flowers, my tea-caddy, and the miniature of my mother fell to the ground. Walter and Su-Chong and flower petals mingled upon the carpet.

I knelt down, picking and sorting and mopping and tears fell upon the wreckage. My hands were too shaky to be safe to deal with the miniature's broken glass, and as I stared at them I thought that now was the time to go to Katharine, and then she could see to what a state her protégée had reduced me. I forgot that Katharine hated to see me cry, forgot that displays of emotion disgusted her. I just wanted to run to her and say, 'Look what Jassy Woodroffe has done to me.'

Surely, I thought, making for the door, even Katharine's doting patience with the little wretch would come to an end now. Even she must see that we could no longer harbour a girl who deliberately pushed furniture over.

I was a little mad, I think. I twisted my sodden handkerchief round the finger which had caught on a splinter of glass and ran upstairs, dashing into Katharine's room as though the devil were after me. She said, 'Who's that?' very sharply as I opened the door. But I was inside the room before I realized that she was not alone. I might have known, I thought, halting myself clumsily and feeling that I must scream and scream and scream–for kneeling on the hearth, with her head in Katharine's lap, was Jassy Woodroffe, crying as though her heart had broken. And Katharine, who had always seemed to possess a fastidious abhorrence of physical contact, was passing her hand over the girl's hair.

She looked towards me as I stood by the door and said in a smooth, quiet voice, 'I'll be down in your room in five minutes.'

Perhaps she found even Jassy's tears exasperating, for within five minutes she was in my room, staring at my over-thrown table, which I had purposely forborne to right. But I had, in the five minutes' grace, mopped my face and tried to regain my composure. The sight of Jassy Woodroffe crying had staunched my tears.

Katharine came into the room quite briskly.

'Now,' she said, rather as though she were addressing a refractory class, 'perhaps *you* can tell me what all this is about, Beth. Upon my soul, I'm glad to see you alive and well. From the way Jassy is weeping and wailing I thought she'd committed mayhem at the least.'

'Look at that!' I said pointing to the mess.

'I expected worse,' she said, stooping and setting the table on its legs. 'And your finger? She didn't *bite* you, did she?'

'Would you have minded if she had, Katharine?' I asked bitterly, for her callous levity cut me to the heart.

'Oh yes. I bar biting.' She looked at me, trying, I knew, to coax me into smiling. But this was no smiling matter. So she changed her manner abruptly. 'Beth, dear, don't look so tragic, *please*. I hear from her own lips that she behaved atrociously, and she shall apologize on her knees if you like. But please, please don't make a tragedy of it.'

'I don't have to make it one, it is that already,' I said. 'I little thought that I should live to see myself insulted, all but attacked, by a pupil in this school, and then hear you standing up for her.'

'Oh, but I'm not doing that, Beth. There's been no time, and she wasn't in much of a state for me to give her a proper dressing down. But I shall do so, I assure you. What I want to know is how it all started and what it's all about. She says she lost her temper when you abused her. Why did you abuse her, Beth?'

'I didn't. I tried to reason with her. Last evening Miss Ogilvy came to complain . . .' I began. I was halfway through my account of that visit when Katharine said suddenly:

'Can we have some tea? I know it's early, but I feel like tea. No doubt you do, too.'

I rang the bell and gave the order and went on with my story, halting for a moment when the tea came and then proceeding. When I had finished Katharine set down her cup and said:

'And that's all?'

'Isn't it enough?'

'Enough? Yes.' She walked over to the little elbow chair by the window and sat down. 'Tell me, Beth, suppose it had been Dilys or Mamie or Hilda who had refused the soup and dabbled in fortune telling, as you call it, would you have taken it like this?'

'I would have reproved them, certainly. And they would have accepted the reproof. Not knocked over my table and spilt my little treasures.'

'That's true. But, Beth, we must remember that Jassy isn't quite like them. I've talked to her a good deal, and her early life sounds most peculiar, a radical ranter on one side, a half-gypsy on the other. Then consider her mind, active and receptive, fed until lately upon nothing but the Bible and folklore; and then the kitchen, with nobody but ignorant and superstitious people for company. Don't you think that exonerates her a little? No, no, I'm not making excuses; I'm stating a case.'

'Her case!'

'Well, she's the culprit; she needs counsel for the defence, doesn't she? Or did you provoke her; do you need defending, too?' She looked at me again with a twinkle, inviting me to smile.

'The worst thing about it is that she says you told her that I objected to taking her into school. That seems to me to be a real breath of loyalty, Katharine.'

'Oh, dear! None was intended, I assure you. I merely warned her that you were not predisposed in her favour and that she must behave impeccably. I had an idea that in some matters–table manners, for example–she might offend you. Beth, please, don't make all this of more importance than it is. I like the child, I enjoy teaching her, her company delights me; you find her irritating, rude and distasteful. But then you like Dilys Helmar, who to me is the essence of all that is detestable in the female sex–selfish, deceitful, coy and precocious; but if you told her I didn't like her I shouldn't make a coil about it or bring up the question of loyalty.'

'There's a difference.'

'Where?'

'Dilys doesn't live in my pocket for one thing.'

'If she hadn't a home for the holidays, or a friend in the world except you, you might feel like offering her that amount of hospitality. Anyhow . . . I can assure you that Jassy is truly penitent, and if she apologizes and takes any punishment you care to name, will you forgive her?'

'I don't want to punish her, and I don't want her apologies. I want her to keep out of my way and to refrain from upsetting the school.'

'I'll see to that then,' said Katharine. The lightness had gone from her voice and manner. She sounded tired. I thought, she knows as well as I do that Jassy Woodroffe stands between us like a thick hedge; she seems not to care, but perhaps at heart she does. With Katharine one never knew.

I looked at her; her long thin hands lay along the arms of the little chair; her thin straight shoulders, long thin neck and beautifully moulded head were outlined against the light of the window; her skirt of grey silk shot with purple was spread sedately. I began to weaken with that old lust of the eye which knows no reason. And at the same time my heart was moved, as it always was when I was not angry with her, by her fragility. Age was making me stout and florid–it was dealing with her as it deals with leaves and laces, making her frail and brittle. I thought–she's fifty; with her as with me, life is passing; and her years have been emptier than mine. I remembered that I had had a husband. (And I had chosen him making a disastrous choice, because he was the only man I knew who had something of Katharine's quality, and I was simple enough then to think that a girl must marry someone!) Yes, I had had a husband, and above all I had my love for Katharine herself, which had given much of my dull work some of the charm of a vocation; and I loved the school. Katharine had only had her books. And now the one thing that gave her pleasure was to share those books with Jassy Woodroffe? Couldn't I accept that?

After all, I thought, with my eyes still upon Katharine, the year or two of Jassy's schooling would pass and we should be left together. I must make no wound which would leave a scar to ache in those after days. I must not allow this alien influence to embitter our relationship.

I felt calmer; happier than I had been for months. I regarded Jassy impersonally, as though she were some nasty little pet animal with which Katharine was temporarily infatuated. That reduced her to her proper size.

That made her bearable.

'We'll forget her,' I said, rising to pour fresh hot water into the pot.

'That's noble of you,' said Katharine in a voice of relief. 'But she must apologize for knocking over the table.' She ended the sentence rather vaguely and, looking at her, I could see that her mind had wandered. She was staring at the tea-tray.

'I'm just about to pour you another cup,' I said.

'I think I'll take *her* one,' said Katharine, who had had countless cups carried to her and never, in my memory, carried one to anybody. 'Oh, there isn't a cup. Never mind, the basin will do.'

I set down the pot suddenly. I could no longer hold it. Utter surprise and fury and a kind of hysterical mirth warred in my mind until I wondered if I were going crazy. I had just thought of Jassy as a pet dog . . . and here was Katharine carrying her tea in a basin. All the suppressed emotion of the last hour found vent upon my lips in a crackle of quavering laughter.

'What's the matter?' asked Katharine, filling the basin and lifting it carefully. 'Oh this! I suppose it does look odd. But really she was in a state. This'll pull her round and prepare her for a wigging.'

She smiled and moved towards the door.

After that I ignored Jassy Woodroffe as one may ignore a constant nagging pain, not acute enough to be desperate. There were moments when it called for all my resolution to do so; for in the next holiday, when it was time for our visit to Brighton Katharine decided that she needed sea air and insisted upon her accompanying us. And after that she spent all the holidays with us. She was, I must admit, helpful and unobtrusive, always willing to run an errand for me as well as for Katharine, polite in her manners, pleasant of speech. But she was there, and she was obnoxious to me.

However, time was passing rapidly, as it does pass when one is busy and has reached middle age. And from time to time I saw a gleam of hope. One such came on the day when Jassy changed her mode of hair-dressing. I remember the morning when I saw her first with all her long black plaits coiled and twisted and pinned across the back of her skull. Ah, I thought, you're growing up, my girl, and your days at school are numbered. You'll go away and find new people to charm and subjugate; there'll be a few letters for Katharine, and perhaps another holiday with us, and then it will end. And I shall still be here. Perhaps then Katharine will look round and see where the real friendship lay.

Most of our girls left at the age of sixteen. The majority of them looked to be married within two years, and that was not so long a time to spend in finding a husband and learning to run a house. Now and then a girl with a vain mother who resented having to produce a marriageable daughter, or a girl whose matrimonial chances were outstandingly poor, or a girl whose home life was peculiar, would stay for another year, or even two. Dilys Helmar had stayed and would soon be seventeen. I suppose it had occurred to no one to remove her. But most girls left at the end of the term following their sixteenth birthday. And Jassy's birthday fell in the Christmas term. I felt certain that I could look forward to her removal from my life at Christmas time.

Almost as soon as the term began I began to wonder what arrangements Katharine would make for her protégée's future. A post as governess in a family or as teacher in a school seemed the obvious choice for her. She had quickly made up–with Katharine's help–the arrears in her education, and had developed, as even I was bound to admit, into that rare thing, an intellectual girl with a usefully practical side to her nature. Her needlework was as good as her other lessons, and if I could have brought myself to give it she would often have had a word of praise from me.

But I did not envy the person or persons who would soon be giving her employment, for it seemed to me that she was bound to make trouble wherever she went. She was, in fact, like a highly flavoured dish which one is bound either to dote upon or to loathe. I was sure that wherever she found herself there would be, close at hand, someone who liked, and someone who hated, her. So dissension was inevitable. But I cared nothing for that so long as she was removed from our roof, under which she had done damage enough. I waited eagerly for some word which would show that Katharine was making some plans for that removal.

No such word was spoken, and September ended. The weather broke early, and it was on a night of violent wind and rain that I woke suddenly and lay for a moment thinking that the storm had wakened me. I always slept with a little lamp, dimmed by an opaque shade, burning by my bedside, for a night call to a sick child, though not of frequent occurrence, was not unknown, and it was an advantage not to be obliged to make a light when my hands and eyes were heavy with sleep. Turning my head on my pillow I looked at the table where the lamp burned and where my clock stood, its face so arranged that the light caught it. It was twenty minutes after midnight. A bad time to wake, I thought. Just then I caught the rap of knuckles on the panel of the door, cautious but imperative.

'Hullo,' I called. 'Just a minute.' I dragged on my dressing gown and went, barefooted to the door, which I unlocked and opened. Jassy Woodroffe stood on the mat outside. She held a candle, and by its light I could see that her face was very pale.

'Mrs Twysdale, it's Dilys. Could you come?'

'Certainly,' I said . . . thinking, oh dear, this weather! The winter round of chills and coughs has started already. I turned back to grope for my slippers, asking, 'What is the matter with her?'

'I don't know. She fainted a little while ago and I can't get her round.'

'You shouldn't have tried. You should have come to me at once.' I snatched up the little medicine chest which always stood on my cupboard just inside the door and stepped into the passage.

'How long ago did she faint?'

'About . . . I . . . oh, perhaps a quarter of an hour.'

It flashed through my mind that never in all my experience had I known anyone to faint in bed, save in cases of severe illness, but I said nothing. I thought I would soon see for myself, and lighted by Jassy's candle we passed hurriedly along the corridor towards the stairs which led to the upper dormitories. I was suddenly conscious that Jassy, who usually moved less noisily than other people, was tonight making more noise than I was, and glancing down I saw, below the hem of her dressing gown, the toes of her stout outdoor shoes.

'Why are you not wearing slippers?' I asked.

'I . . . just put on what came handiest.'

'Well, try to walk quietly, we don't want to wake the whole house.'

We reached the stairs, and when I put my hand on the rail I was conscious of dampness, and remember thinking how quickly humidity penetrated–or was the roof leaking again. That was all. The next moment I was inside the square room which Jassy and Dilys shared with Mamie and Celia, since they were now the four eldest girls in the school. Dilys lay perfectly still and deathly white against her pillow; the covers were neat and undisturbed. There was a strong smell of burnt feathers in the room and a mug of water, some of it spilled, stood by the bed. Mamie and Celia on the far side of the room lay apparently fast asleep. It struck me as odd that Jassy's moving about, fetching water and burning feathers, had not disturbed them, but I was, at that moment, too intent upon Dilys to have time for suspicion.

But I did say, as I opened the chest and drew out the bottle of ammoniated salts, 'Where did you get the feathers?'

'From my pillow,' said Jassy.

I raised Dilys' head and held the salts under her nose. She sagged like a half-empty sack and seemed as impervious to ammonia as to burnt feathers. Seeing this I reached into the medicine chest again and brought out the brandy flask.

'Empty almost all that water back into the ewer,' I said to Jassy, pointing to the mug on the floor, 'and then hold it here.'

I poured a little brandy into the teaspoonful of water she had left in the mug and, with my left arm around Dilys so that her head lolled against my shoulder, I held her and pressed the mug to her lips. After a moment which seemed like an age of anxiety she gave a little sputter, and then I could feel a difference in her body, as though the half-empty sack were slowly filling. Presently she opened her eyes and stared at me, quite blankly for a second or so, and then with terror. Trying to loosen herself from the clasp of my arm, she said sharply:

'Jassy! Wh-where are you? Jassy!'

I felt again that deadly stab of jealousy. Always in Dilys' previous little bouts of indisposition she had clung to me, and I had remembered that she was motherless, and because of that, and because of her loveliness and a kind of weakness in her, I had fussed and pampered her more than I should have done another girl. Now, bracing herself away from me, she was calling for Jassy Woodroffe.

Jassy stepped forward into the ring of candlelight and said:

'It's all right, Dilys. I'm here. Everything's quite all right.'

Dilys looked at her blankly. It was as though a shutter had come down over that first expression of terror. For a second I feared she might be going to faint again. Then she looked at me and said, 'Mrs Twysdale . . . I . . . I . . .'

'It's quite all right,' Jassy said again, speaking slowly and distinctly, as though addressing a person slightly deaf or stupid. 'I'm here . . . and so is Mrs Twysdale. I had to fetch her, you know, because you fainted and were such a long time coming round.'

There was a note of apology in her voice. I said calmly: 'Of course you had to fetch me. I only wish you had called me before.'

I was watching Dilys as I spoke, and saw her great eyes slowly filling with tears–not drawn to them by the fumes of the ammonia salts, for her chin and mouth were quivering, though she was obviously fighting for control.

'Do you feel ill?' I asked. 'Have you a pain?'

'N-no, thank you, Mrs Twysdale, I'm quite all right now. Really, I'm qu-quite all right.'

'But you did feel ill, my dear, when you called Jassy. . . . What was wrong?

Try to tell me, Dilys, then I shall know what to do for you. Girls don't faint in their beds for nothing. Is it . . . are you . . . is there any reason why you should feel faint just now?' The question was embarrassing to everybody, but it had to be asked. I saw Dilys' wide eyes, with their dilated pupils, seek Jassy's face, and turning my eyes to follow her glance I *thought*, thought, yet could not be sure, that I caught, as it were, the tail end of a nod. Yet when Dilys said meekly, 'Yes, Mrs Twysdale,' I thought to myself–yes, it was a nod. Jassy was signing to her to be frank and admit it. And I thought–that's one thing to be said for a rougher upbringing, it makes girls less squeamish about the natural functions of their bodies. I was considerably relieved. I turned to the chest again and took out the bottle of essence of ginger, which, mixed with sugar and hot water, I always prescribed for menstrual pains.

'Jassy,' I said, 'you're as familiar with the kitchen as I am, and your legs are younger. Run down and make a stick fire and heat just a cupful of hot water. Let it boil and bring up the kettle and a cup with a spoonful of sugar in it.'

Jassy said, quite brightly and willingly, 'Certainly, Mrs Twsydale,' but Dilys, with her eyes on Jassy again, forming an eloquent appeal which I could not understand, said, 'No, *truly*, Mrs Twysdale, I'm all right now. I don't want anything except to go to sleep. Tr-truly I haven't got a pain at all.'

'Nonsense,' I said. 'A hot drink will soothe you and do you good. Is there another candle, Jassy?'

Jassy tiptoed across to the chest of drawers which stood between the beds where Mamie and Celia were still sleeping the sound sleep of the very young and brought another candlestick. The candle which Jassy had brought down with her, and which had lighted the room all this time, was standing on the similar chest between her bed and Dilys'. Being nearer to it I reached up and held it towards her so that she might light the other from it, and as I did so the snuffer loosed from its peg and rolled to the floor at my feet. While Jassy was shielding the new, frail flame with her hand, I stooped to pick it up. It had rolled past my feet, just under the edge of the bed, and now lay in a pool of water, which I saw, as I stared at it, came from a heap of clothing under the bed.

'What on earth have you here?' I asked, laying hand on the pile. Then I dragged it out–two blue cloaks, heavy and sodden, came out first, then a skirt, almost as wet, and then, piece by piece, every garment which a girl would usually wear.

As I lifted out article after article from its hiding-place I looked at the two girls. Horror, and the peculiar look which comes from guilt discovered, were written on both their faces.

'Take off your dressing gown,' I said to Jassy, when I straightened myself. She did so, and stood revealed, fully dressed; and her skirt was as wet as the one which lay on the floor.

And oh! I thought, if only, if only Dilys weren't concerned in this. And hard on the heels of that first impulsive thought came the knowledge that she was! My pretty, delicate little favourite had been involved in some nefarious adventure with Jassy Woodroffe, against whom my guardian angel had warned me, from whom my every instinct had shrunk.

'Where have you girls been?' I said.

Dilys, with a faint despairing cry, turned and buried her head in her pillow and began to cry. The small, whimpering sound, oddly like that of a trapped animal, held the whole room for a moment. Jassy stood quite silent beside me for a moment. Then she said, in a loud, almost aggressive voice:

'I went out to see my mother, Mrs Twysdale. And Dilys came with me to keep me company coming back.'

I heard–with another ear than those with which ordinary sounds were conveyed to me–three separate sounds. One, a kind of gasp, came from Dilys on the bed, and the other two, not unlike the first and yet quite different, came from the beds on the other side of the room. Dilys' gasp expressed relief, a relaxation of tension; those of Mamie and Celia were more akin to astonishment.

'Your mother?' I cried, wheeling round to face her. 'Where have you been meeting her? And why?'

'She . . .' there was the slightest possible hesitation . . . 'wanted to see me. She wanted to ask me if . . . after all I wouldn't change my mind and go with her. She left me a message to meet her. I didn't know, of course, what she wanted, so I went. But I told Dilys about it, and she said she would come with me because the meeting place mother mentioned is quite a long way away, and Dilys didn't think I should go by myself.'

It was like–oh, it was like hearing that a pet lamb, with a blue ribbon round its neck, had offered to accompany a wolf cub on an errand through the night.

'Is that true?' I cried, putting a hand on Dilys' shoulder and forcing her to face me.

'Y-yes,' said Dilys. 'Yes, that is how it was. Jassy wanted to see her mother and I went with her.'

And still unconvinced, unsatisfied, I swung round to the two beds on the other side of the room.

'Mamie,' I cried, 'Celia! Stop pretending to be asleep. I know you've been awake all along. What do you know of this?'

They tried, pathetically, to give the effect of having just wakened from sleep, with 'What, Mrs Twysdale?' and 'Oh, ma'am!' and yawns and stretching.

'Do you know anything about Dilys and Jassy creeping out after dark and coming back at midnight?' I insisted.

'Oh, no, Mrs Twysdale. I've been asleep. I haven't heard anything,' said Mamie. 'Have you, Celia?'

'Nothing,' said Celia, 'nothing at all. We just came to bed and went to sleep.'

I turned back to Jassy and Dilys.

'Why didn't your mother come here and ask for you?'

'She wouldn't have dared.'

'Where did she leave the message? And who conveyed it to you?'

'She–she asked Mrs Partridge and left the message with her. I'm sorry, Mrs Twysdale, to have caused such a lot of bother. At the time it seemed the best way–the best thing to do. But I see now that I ought to have asked you. But I hoped you didn't . . . I mean I thought perhaps you wouldn't have liked it. I mean to you–well, the Stannary people wouldn't seem respectable.'

'Jassy . . . don't,' Dilys murmured.

'Well, it's true,' said Jassy, giving Dilys a hard, fierce look. 'And truly, Mrs Twysdale, I didn't want Dilys to come. She only did it because she is kind. I'm sorry. But nothing need have come of it, only the wind was so rough and it rained, and Dilys came over faint. So–so I was frightened and called you. I'm sorry.'

'I should hope you are,' I said heatedly. 'Dilys might have died. And after all the pains I've taken to look after her and everything. Why, when I think of what might have happened to her–to you both . . . out in the darkness, so late . . . I tremble to think. Of course, I might have known. I'm not surprised at you, Jassy Woodroffe, breaking rules and . . . and . . . But to take Dilys with you, that is reprehensible indeed. Really, Dilys, I'm surprised at you. You, at any rate, must have known that no young lady goes out unescorted after dark. What came over you?'

'That was why, Mrs Twysdale. That was why. Dilys was so shocked at the thought of my going alone that she offered to come with me. Please don't blame her. It was entirely my fault.'

'So I think. And you'll hear more of this in the morning. For the present, kindly get undressed and into bed. But before you do so, tell me, how did you get out of the house?'

'By the pantry window.'

'But that is barred.'

'One bar is rusted and lifts away. It's been like that for a long time.'

There was a curious, almost accusing note in Jassy's voice, almost as though she were implying that if I had done my duty and looked to the bars of the pantry window all this could not have happened. I experienced the same odd, futile feeling that had come over me months, years before when I tackled her upon the subject of pretending to tell fortunes. Involuntarily I looked towards the bed where the other offender was crouching with the white sheet drawn up to meet her equally white face. In the space of a minute a whole train of thought, at once furious and frightened, sped through my brain. Suppose, I thought, anything should have happened through this night's work, how on earth could I have explained it to Mr Helmar? This was what came of taking half-gypsy kitchen girls into a school and allowing them to associate with and corrupt decent young ladies. Why, Dilys might have died of exhaustion and exposure.

'How could you?' I cried in a high shaking voice. 'Dilys, you should have known better. What's happened to you? How could you suddenly become a party to such slyness, such deceit?'

'It was my fault, Mrs Twysdale.' Jassy spoke from behind me.

'You don't need to tell me that,' I exclaimed, wheeling round. 'I never expected anything else from you. But even *you*, you that are so clever about other things, might have known that this was no fit errand for Dilys. The dark and wild weather and bad company are nothing new to you. Had you gone by yourself I should hardly have complained. But to take Dilys with you. . . .'

'Pl-please, Mrs Twysdale . . . I did want to go. And Jassy must have *carried* me from the end of the road. I can't remember anything after reaching the top of the hill. She was . . . she was thinking about me.'

And something of justice in my mind added that Jassy had fetched me, and so run the risk of discovery.

'I can't talk about it any more,' I said. 'I'm far too upset. But please understand that you are both in disgrace. I'll talk to you again in the morning.'

I took up the candle and, forgetting the medicine chest, came out of the room. At the foot of the stairs I thought that I should not sleep again that night unless I took two of Dr Pillinger's Sedative Tablets. And they were in the chest which I had left upstairs. Turning, I wearily retraced my steps. As I opened the door of the bedroom I heard Jassy Woodroffe's voice, rough, forceful:

'Don't be a fool, Dilys, swallow it for God's sake. It'll make you sleep and forget everything.'

She had emptied my precious brandy into the mug and was thrusting it under the nose of Dilys, who was crying as though all the sorrows of the world were hers.

The last thread of control broke in me. I slapped Jassy with all the force in my body, first on one cheek, then on the other. She reeled under the blows, then, recovering herself, dashed the mug of brandy full in my face.

In the morning, wakening to Emily's knock, I was immediately conscious that this was not merely another day. This was an occasion. I put my hand to my face and then, jumping from bed with an agility which had not been mine for many years, I went to my dressing-table. I looked a fright. My nose was swollen to twice its size, and as black as a boot, and on both my cheeks there was a curved incision where the sharp, chipped edge of the mug had broken the skin. Well, I thought, even Katharine can hardly overlook this. And I went back to bed–pulling my bell on the way–with a very light heart indeed. For not only had I now a cast-iron complaint against Jassy Woodroffe, but I felt that the worst had happened. My instinctive distrust of her, my long years of foreboding, were now ended. And I was relieved to find that my dread and hatred had culminated in nothing more serious than a bruised nose and a cut face. This is the end, I thought. And when Emily answered the bell I told her, placidly, that I had had a slight accident and should take breakfast in my room. When Miss Hamilton had breakfasted–not before, I said–I should be glad if she would put off classes and everything and come to see me.

Emily brought my breakfast and I enjoyed it as, I discovered, I had not enjoyed food for a long time. I was eating my last piece of toast when there was a knock on my door, and, thinking that Katharine had been very quick to obey my summons, I called, 'Come in.' But it was not Katharine; it was Amy Partridge, not in her calling attire, to which I had become accustomed, but in a cotton working dress and an uncompromising mob cap on her head.

'I hear you've had an accident, Miss Beth,' she said.

'Yes . . . but it's very slight, and I feel very well, Amy. Sit down and tell me what brings you here at this hour.'

'I woon't want to worry you if you feel poorly,' said Amy. But she took a chair by the side of the bed and was obviously bursting with news.

'I'm quite well enough to hear anything you have to say.'

'Well, thass like this here,' said Amy, tucking a stray end of hair into her cap and looking at me with the excitement which members of her class invariably betray when conveying bad news. 'Mind you, thass only a suspicion, I had, but I thought I ought to let you know right away.'

'Yes, Amy. What is it?'

'You know, Miss Beth, that I was with you when you started the school and, in a manner of speaking, I look on it as my own. So if I'm mistook you must excuse me. . . .'

'Yes, Amy.'

'Well, I'm of the opinion that one of your young ladies, Miss Beth, is sneaking out of a night to do a bit of courting, if I may put it so frank.'

'Oh!'

'Well may you say "Oh," Miss Beth, and you know I'd be the last to worry you. But there's been a few things going on that I couldn't miss seeing.'

'Just tell me,' I said, thinking–but Amy was supposed to give the message, and even Amy could tell a mother from a lover, and ahah! now Jassy Woodroffe, I have you doubly damned.

'Well,' said Amy again, 'it's like this, Miss Beth. Back in August, in your holiday that was, there was a young officer from Colchester barracks stayed at my place to do a bit of fishing. And while he wuz there Mr Helmar, you know, from Mortiboys on the Bywater road, dropped in for a drink and got talking and found that this young feller wuz a card player as well and arst him out to his place. And the whole of this term that young man hev been coming back, nut on his way to Mortiboys, but sort of hanging about at my place till dark, then going off somewhere and coming back late. Thass happened several times. And he don't go to Mortiboys because he don't take his horse. . . .'

'Well?' I asked.

'Well,' said Amy, rather shamefaced, 'I daresay you know, Miss Beth, what funny ideas you get about people, and I got the notion that this young man had got in with the moonlighters–smugglers, Miss Beth. It seemed sorta mysterious to me that he come so regular and stayed out just so long and then went off so early in the morning. And I didn't want my decent house mixed up in such business. So last night I sent my man, Jess Horrocks, to foller him.'

'Yes,' I said. And although I knew what was coming I had the irrelevant thought that it was not fear of smuggling which had prompted Amy's spying, but sheer plain curiosity. She was always a martyr to it.

'Jess come back and reported to me. He said that our young gentleman only went to the edge of the Grove–you know, Miss Beth, that's the top end of Layer Wood. And he waited there till two young ladies come along, both wearing blue cloaks with hoods. One of them stopped and set on a gate, and the other went into the wood with our young gentleman. By that time the rain wuz coming down cats and dogs, so Jess, lazybones that he is, thought his job wuz done, and come home. But when he said two young ladies in blue cloaks with hoods, I minded to myself that that wuz what your girls wear. So I sent him back with orders to foller the young ladies this time. Which he did. The one that had been in the wood wuz crying by that time and carrying on very hysterical, Jess said. He come back behind them all the way to the corner, where one seemed to take ill. Anyway, the other had to help her along. And then Jess turned back. I give him a rare flea in the ear for nut going to help the young ladies, but he said his orders wuz to foller, not carry them. He's sharp at that kind of back-answer, for all he is so half-witted. Well, so then I thought to myself, Miss Beth, that it looked as though this might be some of your concern. So I come to tell you just what I know myself.'

'I'm very grateful to you, Amy. You have done just what you should. I'll certainly look into the matter. Of course, you must bear in mind that the girls weren't followed to this house. They may have come from somewhere else in this Square.'

'I thought of that afore I come bothering you. And I been going through in my mind. Thass a funny thing, but I don't reckon there's a *young* maid, much less two, at any house round here, excepting Mrs Shuttle's Fanny, and she walk peculiar. Jess'd have noticed that.'

'Or again,' I said, still conscious of the fact that Dilys was involved in this, and that her reputation must be protected, 'it is possible that two of the maids, Emily and Ivy, say, might have borrowed a couple of cloaks to wear in the rain.'

Amy just looked at me. And the look conveyed her opinion that we were playing some kind of game. The next move was hers.

'Ah!' she said, 'that is possible, of course. But I noticed that Jess said "young ladies." He's a roughish fellow and would have used other names, being cross at being sent out in the rain I reckon.'

'Well,' I said, accepting the checkmate, 'that seems to narrow it down. Tell me, Amy, did this man notice any other thing which would help in the matter of identification? I hope you asked him.'

'As a matter of fact I did. But all he could say wuz that one wuz dark and one wuz fair.'

'Oh! And the dark one went into the wood and the fair one sat on the gate.' I had made a false move, led away by my own private assumption. Amy's stare convicted me.

'I never said that, Miss Beth. As a matter of fact, it wuz tother way about. The fair one met the young gentleman and the dark one waited for her. I reckon myself . . .'

I felt a little sick. Dilys, innocent, motherless little thing. . . . And it is really that other one's fault, I thought. Dilys would never have known about the pantry window, or faced the night walk alone.

'Yes, Amy?'

But Amy had become coy. 'I don't like to name no names in a case like this when nobody can be sure, Miss Beth. But I put two and two together and arst myself which of your girls would my young gentleman be likely to know–him having been out at Mortiboys by invitation, like I told you. D'you see?'

'Yes,' I said, slowly dragging out the monosyllable. 'Naturally you would think that. But Miss Helmar happened to be taken ill last evening, and I spent a good deal of time with her myself. It just shows how careful one must be before jumping to conclusions. But, Amy, speaking of Miss Helmar reminds me of your little friend, Jassy. I've been wondering, has anything ever been heard of her mother? You see, very soon she will have finished school, and we shall have to make some arrangements for her. At such a time one naturally wonders about the real parent. . . .' It was a weak excuse enough, but it served to draw from Amy the actual words which would enable me to give Jassy the lie as soon as the subject came up.

Amy's face darkened. Oh, how well I remember that sullen cold look which told of outraged dignity.

'I've never hear anything about her. Nor don't wish to,' said Amy stiffly. 'To tell you the truth, Miss Beth, I've bin disappointed in Jassy. Oh, I know she's a clever girl and all that, and no doubt it was kindness in Miss Hamilton to make such a pet of her. But she spoilt her. I don't care who hear me say so, she spoilt her. She oughter remember–Jassy, I mean–who set her foot on the ladder, so to speak. But she don't. And though that wuz nice of Miss Hamilton to take her away for the summer holidays along with you, the least she could of done wuz come and see me before and after.'

'And didn't she?'

'Not her. I reckon I ain't good enough for a visit these days.'

'I only hope then,' I said, with infinite guile, 'that when . . . when we've finished with her here, she won't try to foist herself on you . . . expect you to do anything more for her.'

'She'd be out of fortune if she did,' said Amy firmly. 'I done with her after them holidays. Besides, for another thing, I don't want any wenches round my place. Men after liquor is bad enough. No, I'd done with her. She wuz a nice little thing in her way, but as I said before, Miss Hamilton spoilt her.'

'I think you're quite right, Amy,' I said. And although there remained a regret in my mind that it should have been Dilys who had kept the rendezvous, my heart sang. When I did what I had planned, what I was still planning to do, there would be no Amy to side with Jassy, to speak up, to frustrate me. In fact, everything was playing into my hand.

'Well,' I said. 'I can't tell you, Amy, how very grateful I am for your loyalty and your shrewdness. You have been a great help, as always. I must begin to look into this matter at once. For one thing, the cloaks–if they were our girls–will still be wet. So I must get up.'

'Emily said your candle blew out in the dark and you run into the edge of the door, Miss Beth. That must of hurt.'

'It did. But it's better now.'

I saw Amy's eye begin to measure how a door could bruise one's nose and cut both cheeks.

'It didn't happen exactly like that, Amy. One day, very soon, I'll tell *you* all about it. But not now. I must get up. So if you will excuse me. . . .'

Amy rose. Then, with the effort of her kind to extract the last, the ultimate word of gratitude, she said:

'I hope you don't think I bin trying to worry you, Miss Beth.'

'On the contrary, you have helped me very much, Amy, and I am more grateful than I can say.'

She was gone at last. And as soon as the door had closed behind her it opened again and there was Katharine, wearing a look of concern.

'My dear, your poor face! However did it happen?' she asked. And then, just in her own way, not waiting for an answer, she went on:

'That Amy! What on earth did she want at this hour? And what a time she stayed! I came up as soon as Emily gave me your message, and I could hear her going on and on. Couldn't she *see* you were feeling poorly?'

'She came on very serious business. And in a way it was connected with my nose.' I leaned back, remembering the line I was to take in this affair, and put on a plaintive, gentle air. 'Katharine, I hate to tell you about it. I'm afraid it's going to hurt you a great deal.'

Katharine sat down on the stool in front of my dressing-table, her back to the mirror and her face to me.

'I suppose it's about Jassy Woodroffe?' she said guardedly.

'Yes. How did you know?'

'By your face, Beth. A special kind of look comes over you when you speak about her. But go on. Don't spare my feelings. I'm all agog to know how she and Amy and your poor face are connected.'

Now, I said to myself, go slowly, keep calm, and let the facts speak for themselves. And very carefully, speaking gently, without passion, I told the whole story, beginning with my midnight alarm call, and going on with Amy's story. But I did not mention the fact that Amy's man, Jess Horrocks, had noticed which of the girls had been keeping the tryst; nor did I, at first, refer to my second visit to the bedroom or Jassy's attack on me.

I watched Katharine's face as I spoke. I was at once pleased and sorry to see that its ivory pallor deepened, and that the lines on it hardened as I came to the crucial point of the story. I was glad that she was taking the thing to heart, and at the same time sorry to give her pain. But I steeled myself and thought, after all, if you will nurture a viper in your bosom it must be plucked out, harshly if necessary, and though the process may be painful, it is salutary.

When I had finished she inclined her head a little and said quietly:

'But your face, Beth. You haven't told me how that happened.'

'I wish I need not. Kathy, dear, I wish I could say that I just had an accident. Look, don't ask me any more about it. It was just an accident.'

'My dear Beth,' she said with a grit of impatience in her voice, 'don't be so transparent! I can guess what happened. At some time or another during the events you have described, Jassy hit you. Isn't that so?' I nodded, conscious of chagrin that the moment of dramatic revelation had been forestalled.

'I thought so,' said Katharine. 'You see I know her–knew her, quite well. She has an ungovernable temper. But I say I *knew* her because what you have just told me reveals a completely new facet to her character. I should have said that she still was a little immature for a love affair, and far too honest for such duplicity.'

'Well, now you know,' I said.

'Yes. Now I know.'

She was wearing a little shawl over her shoulders. It was knitted in dice pattern, in two shades of lilac; and now, taking the corner of it between her fingers, she studied it with a frown of concentration, as though she were trying to sort out the pattern into so many lines of knit and purl. But I knew that her stare was blank, and that her mind was busy. After a moment or so she looked up and said:

'Beth, I think we ought to hear what the girls have to say. Could you bear to have them in here?'

'One at a time, or both together?' I asked, rather to gain time to think about her question than because I wanted an answer to my own.

'Together, I think,' said Katharine. And with that she went over and pulled my bell. Emily appeared so promptly that I guessed she had not been far away, and for the hundredth time I wondered at the rapidity with which, in an establishment like ours, news of anything unusual could spread and set eyes and ears straining for further information.

While we were waiting for the girls to appear Katharine walked to the window and stared out of it without speaking. When they knocked on the door and I called to them to come in, she turned and I saw that in the second between the time when she stared from the window, looking worried and distrait, and the time when she turned to face the room, she had put on dignity as definitely as if it had been a garment. I had often wondered to myself how anyone as vague and careless as Kathy, occupying to all appearances a subordinate, if favoured place, could manage to maintain perfect discipline in her classes. Now I saw that she was capable of putting off vagueness and carelessness and of assuming so stern an air that even I, guiltless and entirely in the right, began to feel uncomfortable, and to examine my case anew, seeking for a weak spot.

Dilys came first, looked wilted and ghastly. Even her lovely halo of golden hair had lost some of its virtue and seemed to cling damply to her scalp. And a sodden cold fear struck me. Suppose, I thought, this turns out to be a question not really concerned with me and Kathy and Jassy, but with Dilys' deflowering and ruin. For just a moment I had a crazy idea that only Dilys mattered, only Dilys was real, and the rest of the coil was mere silly nonsense, woven out of jealousy, my jealousy, and spite. Then I felt again the sharp impact of the mug's rim, and the sting of the brandy in my eyes. I straightened myself and tugged at my pillow, thinking with satisfaction that Jassy's moment had come. She followed Dilys into the room and shut the door softly. She looked just as usual, perfectly neat and composed. I thought–angrily, of course–she is composed, she thinks she will get away with her lie: she doesn't know about Amy's visit. But actually I believe that if she had been going to her hanging she would have looked the same, for she was incapable of feeling anything except anger, and that only under provocation. She had no nerves, no heart.

'Mrs Twysdale is not feeling well, which is hardly to be wondered at,' Katharine began, 'so you will kindly give me your attention. Both of you.' For Dilys, after one shuddering glance at my face, had looked away, then back again, and was staring at me with penitent horror.

'I should be interested to hear exactly what you have to say for yourselves.'

'I–I–please, Miss Hamilton,' Dilys began. But Jassy, with a contemptuous movement of her hand, silenced her, and said in a low firm voice:

'It was entirely my fault, Miss Hamilton. Dilys had very little to do with it. I wanted to meet my mother, who is a very peculiar person, as I have told you, and who arranged to meet me in what you call the Grove. Dilys, being my friend, and afraid of the dark herself, insisted on coming with me. Then it rained and blew a gale, and we had been walking very quickly, and she fainted. When I couldn't bring her round myself I fetched Mrs Twysdale, who did. Mrs Twysdale also discovered our cloaks and the clothes I had taken off Dilys in order to put her to bed properly. And then I explained where I had been. That's all.'

'That is not all,' said Katharine in a voice of ice, 'and you know it. Go on.'

'That is all that concerns Dilys, Miss Hamilton. Mrs Twysdale left us, implying that the whole thing would be thrashed out in the morning. Dilys began to cry and I saw the brandy flask which had been left behind. I poured what was in it–there wasn't much–into the mug and was trying to persuade Dilys to drink it when Mrs Twysdale came back. She slapped me and I lost my temper. And I hit her with the mug.' She swung suddenly towards the bed and addressed me. 'I'm truly sorry about that. But very early in my life I learned to hit back in self-defence if anyone attacked me, and I just didn't think. I know that that is no excuse.'

'I'm glad you realize that.' Katharine's voice changed from dry rebuke to a small, almost an appealing note. 'And that, Jassy, is all you have to say? It was . . . your mother whom you met?'

'Yes, Miss Hamilton. My mother.'

Katharine's big brown eyes, deeply set in their hollow sockets, flashed a look at me. Then she looked back towards Jassy and said:

'Then it is my sorry duty to tell you, Jassy, that you are a liar. Your own mention of the Grove proves that beyond possible doubt. For you were followed last night. Mrs Twysdale and I and two other people know that you went there to meet a man.'

There was a moment of intense silence. It was as though every one of the four of us had been suddenly encased in ice. Then Dilys with a little scream, flung herself towards me, fell on her knees by the side of my bed and, scrabbling at my covers with her outstretched hands, began to cry and speak at the same time, stammering incoherently.

'I-I'll tell you, I'll t-t-tell you everything. It was me. It was all m-m-my f-fault. P-please, Mrs Twysdale, I w-wanted to all along. I'll t-tell you.'

I put out a hand and gripped her shoulder.

'There's no need to do that, Dilys. I know all about it. It's all right, my dear. No one blames you. Just keep quiet and try to compose yourself.'

But Dilys shrugged my hand away, gripped the bed covers and pulled herself to her feet.

'M-Miss Hamilton, please! L-listen. It was me. I was the one who m-met the young man. Jassy just came with me because I was afraid of the dark. Honestly she d-didn't do anything except c-come with me and wait.'

'This is absurd,' Katharine said coldly. 'First Jassy lies to mislead us and protect you both. Then you lie to protect Jassy. Fortunately, we happen to know the truth. You may go, Dilys. Go to your room and stay there until you have regained your self-control. Then go where you like. This no longer concerns you.'

Dilys, on the brink of a fit, began to shriek: 'W-won't you believe me? It's true, I t-tell you. Jassy didn't even speak to the man. It was me. I–oh–I . . .'

'Stop it, Dilys. Do what Miss Hamilton tells you and go to your room.'

But Katharine had already rung the bell, and with that same suspicious promptitude Emily had answered it.

'Miss Helmar is hysterical,' Katharine said. 'Take her to her room, Emily, and stay with her until she is calm.'

'I w-won't go. You m-must listen to me. I've told you. It was m-me. Oh, oh!' Dilys began to shriek and threw herself backwards.

Katharine took her by the back of the neck, as one takes a puppy, and hustled her through the doorway. 'Go along, you silly girl. And stop that noise.'

She kicked the door with her foot and it closed with a clash. Jassy, a little paler than before, but quite calm, stood with her hands clasped in front of her. Katharine paused beside her. Her mouth moved for a second before any words came, then she said, 'You get out, too. Go to my room and wait.'

Katharine watched while the girl obeyed her, and then she flung herself on to the stool of my dressing-table, facing the mirror this time, and put her face in her hands. For a moment I thought that she was going to break down, and I felt a queer, long-drawn-out thrill. I tasted, in anticipation, the joy of taking Katharine in my arms, of comforting her by clasp and touch, of establishing a physical contact which could never afterwards be denied. The state of awed thraldom in which, all unconscious, she had held me these many years, was about to break and to give place to something altogether different, warm and intimate. I was pushing back the covers and pulling down my nightgown, preparing to leap from my bed, when she straightened herself and, staring into the mirror without, I am sure, seeing her own distraught reflection, said flatly:

'Well, I suppose that is the end of that. She has assaulted you and lied to us both. She must go.'

'In any case,' I said gently, 'she would be going at the end of the term. It doesn't make much difference.'

'I was planning to have her stay on–as a teacher, Beth. I hadn't had time to talk to you about it. But that was my hope. Of course, now . . .' She hesitated for a moment, beating her hands together, while I lay back, marvelling at my luck. How nearly I had escaped being saddled with Jassy for ever. Jassy as a member of the staff! Never, never again would I think that I was unlucky.

'Beth. Could there be a grain of truth in what that other child said?' Oh how cruel to be obliged to dash the hope which had sprung into her voice, into her eyes, into the very way she stood.

'I'm afraid not. Amy was very definite. You know what Amy is, curiosity personified. And with one being so dark-haired and the other so fair. Besides . . . Katharine, I don't want to make a coil about this,' I put my hand very gently upon my injured nose, 'but don't you think she struck me because she was so exasperated at being found out?'

'It certainly looks so. Beth, what shall I do?'

'Do? Why, Kathy, you know as well as I do that once girls begin that . . . that kind of thing, there's no holding them. Even if her time here wasn't nearly ended. . . . Surely, Kathy, there is but one thing to do. Send her away as quickly as possible.'

'But where?'

'There's the man,' I said, risking a little callousness in order to remind Katharine of him.

'The pity of it!' Katharine said. But I could see that my last shot had gone home. Yet still she hesitated, standing rather helplessly in the middle of my room.

'Katharine,' I said, 'you don't like the job of sending her off. Let me do it. I'll give her five pounds.'

'Ten,' Katharine said. 'There's some money in the top right-hand drawer of my desk, and the key is in my handkerchief box.' I got out of bed and began to put on my slippers and dressing-gown. 'Beth . . . are we being hasty? She's so young, and so pretty. I dread to think . . .'

'Kathy,' I said, 'look at my face. Can you do that and doubt that she is well able to stand up for herself? Remember the boldness, the barefaced lying.'

'Yes, yes,' Katharine said hastily. 'You are right, Beth. I'm beginning to think that you were right all along. Go and tell her, then, please. I'll go to my class.'

She hurried away, almost as though something were pursuing her. I went over to the dressing-table and began to tidy my hair. The glass reflected the faint, but unmistakable, smile of triumph which curved my lips. It's been a long war, I thought, and I bear the marks of battle. But I have won.

I went downstairs to the half-landing, crossed it and opened Katharine's sitting-room door. Jassy was sitting on the window seat, reading a book. She looked up expectantly, but her expression darkened at the sight of me. She closed the book and stood up.

'Miss Hamilton sent me to tell you what I have no doubt you already know–that it is impossible for us to keep you here any longer. You must pack your things and leave at once.' I went to the door of Katharine's bedroom, opened it, crossed to her handkerchief box, and found the key. Back in the sitting-room I unlocked the top drawer of Katharine's desk and saw, muddled amongst papers and ends of sealing wax and odd lengths of string, a number of gold coins. I picked out five sovereigns, and then hesitated. We were not wealthy; the school was prosperous and we lived comfortably, but there had never been, would never be, much actual cash to spare. Besides, I thought, even to give the little wretch five pounds is a gesture of unthinking generosity. After all, she struck me. And a little cold spring of doubt began to bubble up through my mood of triumph. I should have had nothing but hatred and spite for anyone who had hurt Katharine in any way. Jassy had smashed a mug into my face, and Katharine had said, 'She has a violent temper,' and proposed to give her ten pounds!

Never mind, I thought, once let me get her out of the house and I shall be able to reinstate myself with Katharine. And suddenly, with almost a superstitious impulse, I snatched up a further five coins. I would save that sum somehow by self-denial. I put the money together in a little shining tower and pushed it along the desk.

'You understand,' I said, 'that we are not bound to give you anything, nor to concern ourselves in any way about your future. But we both feel, Miss Hamilton and I, that you are to some extent to be pitied as well as blamed. So we are giving you this so that you may be able to start honestly in the world if you choose to do so. Take care of it. Ten pounds is a large sum of money.'

I gave the pile another little push. But Jassy made no move to take it. She stood quite still, with her hands hanging down, half hidden in the folds of her skirt.

'I don't want it,' she said flatly. 'I don't want anything except ten minutes alone with Miss Hamilton.'

'That's quite impossible,' I said. 'For one thing, Miss Hamilton is far too much distressed to face another scene. For another, she has not the slightest wish to see you again. Surely you must realize that. Take your money and come upstairs and collect your things.'

'I must see Miss Hamilton first.'

I made a final desperate effort to keep my temper.

'For goodness' sake don't make yourself ridiculous,' I said. 'Miss Hamilton has finished with you. Do you imagine that she would even listen to what you have to say? She especially asked me to send you away because she is naturally too disgusted to have anything more to do with you.'

She levelled at me the cold hard stare which I remembered and then, without speaking, sat down again on the window seat, opened her book, and bent her head over it. I had never seen such a gesture of studied insolence in my life. The blood rushed to my head so violently that the throbbing in my nose redoubled itself. And at the same time the little cold spring of fear became a great flood. I could see what would happen if Jassy came face to face with Katharine again–she would tell her the whole story, and Katharine, in a passion of repentance, and relief, would blurt out her offer of a place on the staff, and for me everything would be over. Fear and anger, both dangerous passions, filled me. I took a step forward and cried, 'Shut that book, do you hear me? Shut that book and listen to what I have to say. Unless you go willingly, with what dignity is left to you I shall ring that bell and ask for Jessop to help me, and I shall throw you out and your things after you. I mean that. You've been told to go, and if you refuse I shall have you treated as I would any other intruder.' She did not even look up, and I turned and marched to the bell. I was still, I thought, to all intents and purposes, mistress in this place. I rang bells and they were answered, I gave orders and they were obeyed. Jessop, the sturdy old veteran who minded the garden and kept the pump working and sawed wood and did a bit of painting, would think nothing of carrying Jassy downstairs if necessary. It is not a method I should have chosen, but then the choice was not mine. I took the bell pull in my fingers.

'You'll only make yourself look silly,' said Jassy behind me. 'I shall stay in this room until I am dead, whoever tries to throw me out.' She spoke gently, but with such conviction that I turned my head to look at her, still holding the bell rope in my hand. She had left the window and taken a stand behind Katharine's desk. As I looked at her she laid her hand on the heavy pewter inkpot which stood there. Almost conversationally she said, 'The first person who tries to touch me will get this on the skull.'

I knew that she meant it. I remembered the–the exaltation of fury with which she had dashed the mug in my face; remembered the sting of the brandy in my eyes and nostrils. Oh God, I cried to myself, what did I do on the day when I let this creature in? I glanced at the clock on the mantelpiece and saw that Katharine's class would be over in eighteen minutes' time. A kind of panic seized me; my blood seemed to run backwards and forwards in my veins, quivering with frenzied agitation. But I forced myself to calmness.

'What good will it do you to stay here and see Miss Hamilton again?' I asked reasonably. 'She will only be more annoyed to find that you have disobeyed her last request, which was that you should leave the house as soon as possible. I assure you that nothing you can say to her will make her change her mind.'

'I don't want to make her change her mind. I just want to explain something to her.'

Her hard little face softened suddenly. I saw her lower lip tremble. She bit it fiercely before she added:

'Miss Hamilton has been so–kind to me. I don't want her to think . . . There's something I must tell her before I go.'

Inspiration came to me. I glanced at the clock again and saw that the inexorable hands had measured away another two minutes. Sixteen minutes. Sixteen minutes to get her out of the house. Once she was in the street, I thought, I should be safe. Even if she wrote to Katharine it would mean nothing, for all letters came to me first. Fussed as I was, and short of time, I failed to examine my new idea thoroughly. I said rashly:

'I think I know what you have to say. You want to tell Miss Hamilton that what Dilys said just now was the truth and that you merely accompanied her. Well, I have already told Miss Hamilton that. And as you can see, it has made no difference. No difference at all. Because, you see, it is not just for stealing out at night that you are being sent away. Do you really imagine . . .' I heard my voice go suddenly high and shrill, '. . . do you really imagine that you can behave as you have done, that you can strike me, and then, with a few words about quite another subject, creep back into Miss Hamilton's favour? You overestimate yourself. By breaking rules last night you merely gave Miss Hamilton a valid excuse for ending a business which, begun in charity, has become intolerable to her. She wants to be rid of you and . . .'

I broke off. Jassy had come out from behind the desk.

'I'll go,' she said, quite meekly. 'I only wanted to tell her that, so that she shouldn't think I'd been–well, worse than I had. And she might have helped Dilys, too, perhaps. But if she knows, there's nothing for me to say.'

She moved towards the door. And after another glance at the clock I said, 'I'll send Emily to help you to get your things together.' Emily had often packed for girls who were called home in a hurry, or for sick ones who were fetched by over-anxious parents. She could get Jassy's few things together in ten minutes, and that left three for me to hustle her out of doors. thank God, I thought, Katharine's class this morning was in the large classroom, which was built out at the back of the house.

Jassy opened the door, and as she did so I heard the sound of hasty feet on the stairs and the swish of a silk skirt. Katharine, hatless, looking mad, looking distraught, swung round from the top of the stairs on to the half-landing and collided with Jassy, who was by this time outside the door. They fell together, and then, clutching and clinging, were carried by the impetus of Katharine's haste over the threshold and into the room.

'Oh,' Katharine cried, still holding Jassy by the shoulder and speaking in a voice that hung between sobs and laughter. 'Oh, thank God I got back in time. You're still here.' I saw her arm slip round the girl until, from clutching her shoulder she was holding her in a close embrace. Jassy's face was turned inwards, and over the top of her head Katharine looked at me with furious accusation.

'Why didn't you tell me?' she demanded. 'How could you deceive me so? If I hadn't gone to Amy.... Oh, Jassy, my dear, do please forgive me. How could I ever have thought . . .?'

She put her other arm about Jassy's neck and, bending her head, began to kiss that crown of black plaits. I felt quite sick. This was Katharine, always so cool and dry and distant, Katharine to whom the slightest physical contact had always seemed repellent, Katharine who had never permitted more than the briefest brush of the lips on, say, a birthday morning, or before and after a longish separation. Katharine, positively slobbering over that little bitch. And I knew, although the hated face was hidden, that it was calm and hard and calculating, and that under those plaits the evil brain was busy, scheming how this development might be turned to its own advantage, how Katharine's thraldom might be riveted stronger and closer.

Sick fury drove out my fear. I no longer minded that Katharine knew how I had deceived her, knew to what lengths my hatred had carried me. I said boldly:

'Katharine, I should like to talk to you for a moment. Alone.'

'I have something to say, too.' She loosened her clasp, put a hand under Jassy's chin and tilted her face, looked at her dotingly for an instant, and then kissed her on the forehead.

'Jassy,' she said, speaking normally, as though the girl had just entered the room, 'I want you to do something for me.' She crossed to the desk and took up a sheaf of exercises. 'It's my grammar hour with the Juniors. Take it for me, will you? Here are their papers. They can correct their errors and then . . . well, you'll know what to do next. At the end of the hour come back here.'

'Yes, Miss Hamilton.'

The door closed behind the girl and Katharine turned to me.

'Now,' she said. But I was no longer capable of feeling awe for Katharine. She had shown me her weakness. I made a direct, savage attack.

'Of all the disgusting sights I have ever seen,' I began, 'that was the worst. If anyone had told me that I should live to see *you* slobbering and kissing a schoolgirl I shouldn't have believed them.'

'Nor would I if the same prophet had foretold that you would ever lend yourself to such spiteful duplicity. Amy told you this morning, as plainly as she dared, that Dilys Helmar was to blame. And you were willing to let me send Jassy away for that.'

'It was your own jealousy that made you willing to send her away, Katharine. I see that now. Nothing else she could have done would have made you willing to lose her. I may have kept to myself the name of the girl who went into the wood, but the fact remains that though Jassy Woodroffe only sat over a gate and waited, she is still guilty of breaking a rule and stealing out of the house at night; she is still guilty of attacking me with a mug, and of telling lies. If a man had touched her she was to be sent off with ten pounds; untouched, she is to be reinstated, hugged and kissed. There you have the truth, Katharine, and a revolting truth it is.'

Katharine made an effort, a visible, painful effort to compose herself, to take refuge again in that cool dry shell under which she had hidden from the world. She walked to a chair and sat down in it, saying: 'Sit down, Beth, and try to calm yourself. I want you, if you can, to explain why, knowing that Dilys was the culprit, you withheld that information and allowed me to think Jassy was to blame?'

'I've just told you–not in so many words perhaps–but the real reason is in what I have said. Katharine, you have simply lost your head over this girl. I haven't. So I was capable of seeing that her behaviour, whether she actually went to meet a lover or not, was reprehensible. Dilys Helmar is weak and silly, but alone she would never have gone out in the dark; she wouldn't have known about the loose bar in the pantry window; she would not have been able to think up an adequate excuse. Do you realize, Katharine, that if I hadn't found those wet cloaks Jassy Woodroffe would have fooled me–us–completely, and this clandestine business would still be going on? Then, when she is discovered, she has a lying tale all ready, a tale that takes every advantage of our ignorance of her family. After that, although I may have been hasty when I saw her slopping away my medicinal brandy, she attacked me violently, almost maniacally, and really hurt my face. I had merely slapped hers with my open hand. Can you blame me if, seeing that this multitude of real differences had no effect on your attitude towards her, I took advantage of the one point which I knew would move you. I did it for your sake, Katharine. If you could only be saved through your jealousy, then you must be made jealous.'

Katharine brought her open hand down on the arm of her chair in a slightly theatrical gesture:

'My God,' she said, 'you're the one who should talk about jealousy!'

I realized that she was looking at me with hatred. And I suddenly remembered that the jubilant thought with which I had wakened that morning, the joy and relief with which I had imagined that now, in breaking the skin of my face and bruising my nose, Jassy Woodroffe had fulfilled all my feelings of doom and foreboding about her. What a crass fool I had been. Here before my eyes, now, was the final and unmistakable sign of her work. She had made me make Katharine hate me! The anger and the disgust which had supported me seeped away all at once. Dread and self-pity took their place. My knees felt weak and I was glad to take the chair which I had ignored when Katharine had told me to sit down and be calm. I sat down, but I was not calm. The strain under which I had been living for so long combined with the emotional stress of the last few hours suddenly took a cumulative effect on me. I began to babble. I said things without previously arranging them in my mind, so that when the words were formed and audible on the air I heard them with a shock of surprise and horror. I could neither control what I said, nor stop saying it. It was as though the unconscious control which–even in passion and anger–censors and edits one's speech, had suddenly ceased action. Staring, hypnotized, into Katharine's eyes of hatred, I said:

'Yes, I am jealous too. Just now, when you clasped that little hussy in your arms and kissed her I would have killed you both if hatred would have done it. And why not? I love you, Katharine. I've never loved anyone but you. I loved you the moment I saw you, and I've gone on loving you ever since. And because of that I've worked and slaved for you; how hard you'll never know. My one aim in life has been to protect you, to please you, to make life easy for you. Never once in twenty years have you ordered a meal or mended a stocking. I've behaved to you as though you were my husband, because, in my mind, that was how I regarded you. And what have I had in return? A casual word of thanks now and then when you could look up from a book and remember to speak to me. And I bore it, thinking that you were naturally cold and unresponsive, thinking that you were dry and cool and casual. Then along comes this little nobody, this waif from the gutter, and you give her all the affection that is my due. How could I help being jealous? I, who have waited for a smile from you, gone happily all day on the memory of one kind word–I must stand by and see *her* kissed and cuddled. For twenty years I have served you and loved you, without making a single demand. And now I have to realize that I mean so little that if Jassy Woodroffe breaks my nose and lets a man handle her, she is cast off, but if she breaks my nose and keeps her caresses for you she can remain as your petted favourite. Could anything be more disgusting, more nauseating?'

I broke off, breathless with emotion. While I had been speaking Katharine had drawn herself a little straighter and stiffer in her chair as though she were trying to escape some vile contamination. A spot of dusky colour burned high up on her pale cheeks. But when she spoke her voice was calm and cool.

'God knows of what you are accusing me, Beth. You sound to be beside yourself, but I hope you're capable of believing that I never laid a finger on the girl until ten minutes ago.'

'But you've wanted to,' I cried, out of my own bitter knowledge. 'You've wanted to. Otherwise why did you change your mind so suddenly when you knew that it was Dilys, not she, who went to meet a lover?'

'Isn't that obvious?' she asked with a kind of angry patience. 'If Jassy had developed a taste for illicit adventure that kind of scene would have been repeated again and again. And a fine life you would have led me. Until I saw Amy, what defence had I against you and your talk of bad influences? Later, knowing that Jassy merely went out to accompany that little fool whose fear of the dark is greater than her lechery, I had reason on my side. With Dilys gone I think Jassy will be content to stay in her bed.'

'That means, I take it, that you intend to keep her here?'

After a second's hesitation Katharine said, 'Yes. I mean that.' I began to laugh.

'Katharine Hamilton,' I said, 'I've gone all these years in the belief that you were an intelligent, honest woman. Now I know what you are. Very well then, choose your Jassy, keep her. Get her to run the house for you, and teach classes, and mend your clothes. I've borne all I intend to. I'm going.'

I got up from my chair. Katharine jumped to her feet too, and stood confronting me.

'Don't be a fool, Beth. Where would you go?'

'Anywhere. What I have done here I can do in another place. I won't stay here to be tortured by the sight of that little harpy turning you into . . .'

'Don't let's bandy names,' Katharine said sharply. 'Look here, Beth, God knows if you feel offended with me, you've given me plenty of cause for offence too. Can't we leave it at that? Can't we settle down and make allowances for one another? We're neither of us young, and we're both working on the same job. Couldn't we come to some amicable arrangement?'

It was a placating speech, but I was not deceived. Aha, I thought, the mere threat of being left to yourself brings you to your senses.

I said deliberately, 'I will stay with you, Katharine, on one condition–that Jassy Woodroffe leaves the house today.' I felt that delicious uprush of power which visits those who make conditions. The dusky patches on Katharine's cheeks faded, leaving her face as white as paper. She came close to me, thrusting her face before mine and speaking venomously.

'God knows I've tried to be reasonable and patient, but there is a limit to everything. Go then, if you want to go, and take your filthy mind and its vile insinuations out of my house. You profess to feel disgust with my behaviour; *you* are disgusting with your talk of love and service. I'm not blind, Beth. nor stupid. I knew, before the end of the first term, that it was a mistake for us to set up house together. If you could know the number of times that you've sickened me with your yearning eyes and little furtive touches, with your protection and understanding! And the hours and hours of boredom, either listening to your fatuous chatter or seeing you there, greasy with virtue, bursting with the effort not to talk, with "Katharine musn't be disturbed" written all over you. Years and years! My God, I've paid for having my stockings darned! But I bore it. I would have borne it for ever. Then, when by the merest chance I do at last find a mind that runs along with mine–a cool, eager, companionable mind, capable of staying for five minutes on a mental plane–all you can do, when you've failed to poison my mind against her, is to accuse me of some beastly perverted intercourse which is nothing but the reflection of your own warped mind. Yes, go away. It's the best thing you can do. I'll see that Lawyer Aldritch has some money for you by tomorrow.'

She swung round, turning her back on me, and stood by the desk, purposely moving things about on the top of it. I looked at her, thinking that I should not see her again; that it was all over; that the years and years of service, the love and the consideration were worse than useless; they were ridiculous. And where should I go? What should I do? I, who had set out so blithely this morning to oust Jassy Woodroffe, had myself been ousted.

'Katharine,' I said, 'Katharine!'

She remained silent, ignoring me.

'Please,' I said, 'Katharine, you must listen. I'm sorry . . . I . . .'

'I'm not going to start all over again,' she said in a cold, distant voice. 'You have chosen to go. Please do so.'

'But Katharine . . .'

'I've nothing else to say,' she said. Swinging around again she swept over to the bell and pulled it. Was she proposing to humiliate me finally by ordering my removal? I stumbled towards the door. On the half-landing was Emily, running.

'Oh, ma'am,' she gabbled, 'Miss Ogilvy says to come at once. Miss Helmar is off in a carriage and nobody can stop her.' She broke off to stare at me. 'Oh, ma'am.'

'Tell Miss Hamilton, Emily. I am unwell.'

'That Jassy Woodroffe's gone too, ma'am,' said Emily.

'Miss Hamilton,' I repeated.

With tears running down my face I went on towards my own room.

BOOK THREE

NEUROSIS IN ARCADY

'She was, by all accounts, an admirable housekeeper. . . .'
So this story is told by DILYS HELMAR,
who brought her to Mortiboys.

I was still on my bed, crying about Charles, when Jassy ran in, breathless and looking distracted, and said, 'Dilys, they know all about it. I didn't say a word, but apparently we were followed and watched.'

I sat up on the bed, and the ache in the back of my head, which had been growing in intensity for hours and hours, made me feel sick and dizzy.

'For God's sake, don't faint again!' Jassy said, beginning to fan me with some papers she held in her hand. 'You've got to think up some excuse. Could you say it was your brother whom your father had banished from home or something? You'll have to think of something, Dilys. They're having a fearful row. They'll probably send you home.'

'They won't send me home,' I said. 'I'm going. I shall go crazy if I have much more of this. Twizzy's reproaches would be more than I could bear just now.' I swung my legs off the bed and stood up. The pain in my head made me shut my eyes and groan. 'God!' I said. 'My head.' I thought of my valise, stowed away under my bed, and of stooping to the drawers to lift out my things. 'I can't pack,' I said, speaking to myself. 'I'll have to go just as I am.'

Jassy flung the papers she held on to my bed. 'I'll pack for you,' she said in rather a savage voice. 'I'm supposed to be taking the Junior Grammar class, but it can't make any difference. Old Twizzy is determined to sack me. I can see that.' She stooped and dragged the valise out and then jerked open my bottom drawer. She looked small and forlorn and rather desperate.

'Come home with me,' I said impulsively. Jassy sat back on her heels.

'Do you mean that, Dilys? To Mortiboys?'

'Yes,' I said, 'to Mortiboys! It's the last place on earth anyone in their senses would want to go. But at least we shan't be asked a lot of questions, or be slavered over, there.'

'Wouldn't your father mind?'

'I don't suppose he'll notice.' Jassy looked at me rather puzzled, but she said soberly:

'I'd like to come. For a little while. I've got to go somewhere. You're sure it'll be all right?'

'It'll be awful. But your being there won't make it any worse, if that's what you mean.'

I rested my head against the back of the bed and shut my eyes again. Jassy kept moving about. She was very deft and rapid in all her movements, and almost before the pain ebbed enough to allow me to begin to think again, she said, in a much firmer and more confident voice:

'I've packed. Shall we go before anything else happens?'

'Did you find my purse?'

She handed it to me. I opened it and took out five shillings.

'Give that to Jessop and tell him to run to Storey's and order the carriage to be at the corner in ten minutes.'

Sitting still had eased the pain in my head and I could begin to think. I thought about Charles, about all the hopes I had had, about how I had loved him. I began to cry again, hopelessly. I did not hear Jassy come back into the room, and was unaware of her presence until she put her hand, not very gently, on my shoulder.

'The carriage is ready. We can go,' she said. I turned and clutched her by the arm. 'I'm glad you're coming with me,' I said.

As we rolled along in the carriage I tried to force my grief out of my mind by thinking of other things. I glanced at Jassy, sitting very upright beside me, and realized again how fortunate I had been in having her for a friend. Apart from the way in which she had stood by me in the last few weeks, she was very definitely the only girl of all those I knew and had known whom I could take home to Mortiboys. I should have hated even Margaret Tucker, whose father was a corn-chandler, though a very successful one, to have entered my home in these days. Jassy was different. She came of a poor, humble family, she was not likely to be critical of Mortiboys whatever it was like. She had told me herself that she had lived in one of the cottages on the Green at Minsham St Mary; and I knew that she had worked as a servant in the school kitchen. My home, however strange and disreputable it might appear to anyone else, would not shock her. Moreover, she was not pretty enough to cause any trouble from Old Nick–and that was a matter which must be considered nowadays. For the last three years, ever since the man Sedley had written him that peculiar letter informing him of mother's death, Old Nick had been completely insane. He would go to bed with anything provided it was young and comely. The present unacknowledged mistress of Mortiboys–unless he had made a change since the beginning of term–was a swarthy, sloe-eyed creature called Melia, who had come into the house as parlour-maid. Her sudden promotion had done more than anything since mother's elopement to upset life inside the walls of Mortiboys, for she seemed to be related to almost all the other servants, and during the August holiday, when I had complained that our dinner was uneatable, Agnes the cook, taking advantage of the fact that she was Melia's aunt by marriage, or some such rubbish, had raised a fine scene, and Old Nick had rounded on me with several choice curses.

Remembering this, and other things, I said quietly, so that the driver should not overhear:

'Jassy, I think I ought to warn you that my home is a very peculiar place.'

'Is it? It looks lovely from the outside.'

'When did you see it last?'

'At Easter, three or four years ago. Miss Hamilton brought be for a drive this way.'

'Oh yes, I remember. And the next term, when I gave her a wrong date she said that I ought to have imbibed history with the air I breathed. Little she knew.'

'What was it you wanted to warn me about?' asked Jassy in her matter-of-fact little voice.

'Well, for one thing, it doesn't even look the same outside now. Two years ago the archway blew down in a gale, and at the same time the whole window in the Great Hall blew out, and half the tiles came off the roof. The place looks a ruin now.'

'Why wasn't it mended?'

'That's what I'm trying to tell you. Old Nick–Father, that is–is quite dotty, and one form his madness takes is that he won't have anything mended, not even a window.'

'Why ever not?'

'Well,' I said, 'sometimes I think it's just his perversity. At other times I'm certain that that is his way of taking revenge on the place. It was over the repairs to Mortiboys that Sedley and mother met. I told you about that.'

Jassy nodded. 'That is a romantic revenge, in a way.'

'Romantic! It's horribly uncomfortable.' I leaned my head on my hand, trying to steady it from the intolerable jolting, and added, 'And everything is a mess, and the muddle; the servants are out of hand and father is drunk half the time. So now you know what to expect.'

'Anything will be preferable to school,' Jassy said comfortably.

I did not answer. Holding my head I sat with my eyes closed until the carriage swerved sharply and the increased bumpiness of the road told me that we had left the turnpike and were in the lane. I sat up and tucked my hair under my hat. Within a few minutes we were in front of the ruined archway. Nothing had been done. It lay as it had fallen, the little house where Sharples had lived and the whole arch a mere pile of pinkish bricks with ends of dark broken beams protruding like the limbs of buried people. The other cottage, where one of the keepers lived, was still standing and still inhabited, but the fall of the main arch had torn away the outer wall of one of its bedrooms. The small empty room with its plastered walls and its door and window was somehow more unsightly and pitiable than all the rest of the ruin.

The entry to Mortiboys was blocked by the fallen bricks, but a rough track, skirting the pile of bricks, joined the lane to the drive. Storey, careful for the springs of his carriage, drove in at a funeral pace and pulled up by the porch. Ten minutes ago I should have denied that I could possibly have felt more wretched, but as we alighted my depression increased. The desolation of my ruined home matched so nearly the desolation of my broken heart. The great porch, with its black benches and beams, yawned like the mouth of a monster about to swallow us. Storey put the valises on to a bench, and as soon as he was paid drove away.

I pushed open the heavy door. Inside it was lighter, for on the left of the hall was the great window which matched the one in the Great Hall which the gale had emptied of glass. It was made of hundreds of small leaded panes, set into the stone mullions, and around the edge was a border of coloured panes, some of them bearing coats of arms. Pale, watery shafts of sunlight came in by this window, but they served only to show the untidiness and dustiness of the hall. On the right-hand side the great stone fireplace was piled high with grey wood ash. There was no fire and the ashes had not been taken away for at least a week. Filmy grey flakes of it lay over everything. From a half-open door at the back of the hall came the sound of untuneful singing mingled with the indolent, intermittent sweep of a brush.

I left Jassy standing, looking round with a bird-like look, in the middle of the hall and went over to the doorway. I was glad to see Janey; she was a little slut, but young and as yet unspoiled and quite civil. She scrambled to her feet and looked at me as though I were a ghost. 'Miss Dilys! Whass the matter? Are you took sick?'

'Yes,' I said. 'I'm sick. I want my bed made and a fire lighted. And I've brought home a friend to stay with me. There must be another room got ready for her.'

'I'll tell Melia.'

'Tell Mrs Capps.'

'Mrs Capps ain't here no more, Miss. There's only Melia and Cook and me. And Moult, of course.'

'I see. Where's my father?'

'He's out somewhere. He's bringing three gentlemen home with him for dinner at six o'clock. Thass why I got to straighten this place.'

'Well, leave it now,' I said, trying to fight off the nightmare feeling of being in a strange house amongst aliens. Mrs Capps' going was the last straw. I hadn't liked her, she was a surly, bitter old hag, but she had been a peg–unstable and rotten as everything in Mortiboys–but still a peg which had held the place together a bit. Melia was really in the saddle now.

I went back into the hall. Jassy was standing where I had left her. She looked tiny and chilled. Out of my own desolation of spirit some impulse of hospitality struggled to the surface.

'I'm sorry,' I said. 'It's even worse than I expected. I shouldn't have asked you here. I wouldn't have come myself, but there was nowhere else to go.' I sat down on the nearest chair and began to cry.

'It's all right,' Jassy said, keeping her distance. She was not one of those girls who pat and paw you and exasperate you to further tears as soon as you cry. 'I like it. It's a fine place. You'll feel better when you've had a rest. Couldn't you go to bed for a little while?'

'There's nothing I'd like more. But my bed won't be fit to sleep in, and if Melia has anything to do with it, it never will be.'

'We'll see about that. What's through there?'

'The library. We use it as a parlour.'

'Then there'll be a sofa. Come on, Dilys. You must lie down.'

'But Janey's cleaning there.'

'She can clean it when you've rested. You've some right here, Dilys. It's your home.'

'It isn't. It's father's. And he'll want that room cleaned by six o'clock. He's got company.'

'Good Lord, how long do you think it takes to clean a room? If you'll lie down there for an hour I'll have your own room ready.'

I groaned. I should have stayed at school and faced Twizzy's questions and reproaches. There was no place for me here. And certainly there was no place for Jassy, especially if she thought she was going to organize things and stand up for me. But I couldn't say or do any more. I let her lead me into the parlour and settle me on the sofa with two cushions under my head and a shawl over my feet.

As soon as I lay down the worst pain in my head seemed to be a little blunted, and a not unpleasant wave of exhaustion swept over me. I had spent the night crying and now I was hungry for sleep. But I lay for some minutes in a state of tension, momentarily expecting Melia to come bouncing in to turn me out so that Janey could go on working. At best I expected Janey to enter and go on with her brushing. But everything was still. Presently I fell asleep.

When I woke Jassy was standing by my side, arranging a tray on a table. The sofa had been rolled back a little way from the hearth, where a bright fire was blazing. The room was perfectly clean and tidy.

'What time is it?' I asked, testing my head by lifting it very carefully from the cushion. There was no pain at all.

'Just four. You've had a good sleep. Do you feel better?'

'Immensely better,' I said, sitting up completely. And I did. Sleep is a wonderful thing. Five hours of it had laid a soft kind of buffer between my mind and the raw ache of last night's interview with Charles, the nerve-jangling fuss of our last hours at school, and the desolation of that wretched homecoming. I was still heartbroken, but I was physically sound again. I looked at the tray, which was properly set out, with tea and two piles of sandwiches. Then I looked at Jassy. Her face was shiny, her forehead was marked with a dusty streak, and one loop of the plaits at the back of her head had come unpinned and was hanging loose.

'You've been working like a slavey,' I said remorsefully. And I thought that no one else in the world could have cleaned that awful room so thoroughly without waking a person asleep in it.

'Who is Melia?' asked Jassy, narrowing her eyes at me across the teapot.

'Father's paramour,' I said flatly.

'I might have guessed that, I suppose. She seems to resent my being here.' She paused and thought for a minute. 'Look here, Dilys, this is going to be horribly awkward. I think I'd better go away tomorrow.'

I cried out and stretched my hands towards her in a burst of desolation.

'No, Jassy, please. Don't mind what Melia says, or even father. I'll stand up to him if necessary. But you must stay with me just a little while. Till I've decided what to do, Jassy, please. It won't always be like this, I promise you. They'll leave us alone presently, and we'll go riding to get out of the house. It won't be so bad.'

'Well,' she said, not very willingly, 'I'll stay a little. If you promise to tell me the moment you would like me to go. To tell you the truth, I've had my bellyful of living where I wasn't wanted.'

'I want you,' I said. 'You may be certain of that. Will that do?'

We set about the tea, and as I ate and drank I worked myself into a state of rebellious self-confidence. I would have Jassy. Whatever happened she should stay as long as she liked. Neither father nor Melia was going to separate me from the only friend I had in the world. That wasn't asking much, I thought harshly; there'd never been a servant on my side, father hated the sight of me, Charles had deserted me. There was no other word to describe that cautious, chilly explanation about not being able to marry for years, and the unfairness of tying ourselves down with promises now that the regiment was ordered abroad. Jassy was the one person in the world who cared whether I lived or died, was sick or well, and I would cling to her as long as she would let me. Pull devil, pull baker! I thought.

And at that moment father walked in. He came in as he always did, just as he came from the fields or the woods, without even wiping his boots. He propped his gun in the corner, threw his game bag on the floor, dropped his hat on the first chair, and came striding towards the hearth. I got to my feet and stood still, though the long vibrations of terror and loathing and perverse affection which he roused in me coursed shudderingly along my veins.

'So you're back,' he said. His voice sounded neither pleased nor angry, and not–thank God–the least bit curious.

'Yes,' I said. And wondered how I could ever have been such a fool. That morning, safe in the dormitory, I had thought that I could creep back and lose myself in the careless disorder of Mortiboys. I had forgotten that this moment must come. Better by far have faced old Twizzy. And that is me all over, I thought, running away from one mess into another worse one. And I thought sickly of how I had hoped that when next I faced Old Nick I should have had Charles by my side, a man of my own, saying that he wanted to marry me. Fool, fool, fool!

'Company too,' said father in that same noncommittal voice. 'Wake up, my girl. Or aren't introductions fashionable any more?'

'This is a friend of mine, Jassy Woodroffe. She's going to stay with me,' I added, remembering my recent resolution, and thinking that I might as well strike the first blow.

'Woodroffe. Woodroffe. That sounds familiar,' said Old Nick when, having acknowledged the introduction with a courtliness which he could assume very easily when it pleased him, he sank down on the end of the sofa. 'Ah, I have it. That was the name of the carpenter at Minsham. As damned interfering a Radical fellow as ever walked. Funny to be reminded of him.'

'That was my father,' Jassy said calmly. 'I don't think he would have asked a better epitaph.'

Father turned and looked at Jassy. Very slowly and deliberately he looked her up and down. It was a look which he turned on me sometimes, and I could not stand it. Jassy merely stared back, her face showing nothing but placid interest.

'He was a good carpenter too,' Old Nick said at last. And there was a trace of apology in his voice.

'Yes, he was that too. And many other things that you wouldn't know about. Mr Helmar, would you like a cup of your own tea?'

'I never drink the stuff. You can give me a sandwich.'

Jassy passed the plate and then refilled my cup and her own. Old Nick munched in silence, stretching his legs to the fire and watching the spirals of smoke which rose from his wet boots.

Presently Jassy said, conversationally, 'I expect you wonder why we are here in the middle of term, Mr Helmar?'

'Well, why are you?' he asked in a voice that would have discouraged me and made me stammer.

'Because we're in disgrace.' Lightly, as though she were telling a funny story, she repeated exactly what she had said to Mrs Twysdale on the night before, ending, 'but Mrs Twysdale wouldn't believe that I went to meet my mother, or that Dilys only came to keep me company. And then I lost my temper and hit her in the face with a mug. I think I ought to tell you that because you're sure to have a letter warning you against harbouring such a bad character.'

'Are you a bad character?'

'I must be, to hit Mrs Twysdale with a mug!'

'You're a damned liar, too,' said Old Nick. 'Little girls who hit their teachers with mugs aren't afraid of the dark; and little girls who are afraid of the dark don't hit their teacher with mugs. You can't have it both ways, young woman.'

Jassy burst into one of her rollicking laughs. Nothing that Mrs Twysdale or Miss Ogilvy had ever said could make her restrain that laugh. She threw her head back and opened her mouth and really made a noise.

'That's very clever of you, Mr Helmar,' she said, checking herself. 'But you see, after that Mrs Twysdale did make such a fuss that Dilys said she was coming home. And since I haven't got a home and jobs are hard to get in the middle of term, she asked me here. I hope you don't mind.'

'It makes no difference to me,' father said. Then, as though his attention had been suddenly arrested, he asked:

'Jobs. What sort of a job could you get?'

'I could teach in a school or be a children's governess.'

'How old are you then?'

'Nearly as old as Dilys. I'm sixteen.'

'I shouldn't have thought it. Then it's high time you both left school.' He got up and went to the cupboard and took out a bottle and a glass, poured himself a drink, and drank it at a gulp. Behind his back I signed to Jassy that we would go upstairs. I thought that we would make our escape while he was still in this amiable mood. We stood up. Old Nick, pouring another drink, stopped and looked in our direction. 'You'd better both make yourselves beautiful and come down to dinner.'

'Y . . . yes, father,' I said, completely surprised. I had never before dined with him when he had company.

'Good God, Dilys,' he said, 'I thought they were going to teach you not to stammer.'

'They didn't teach us anything, but we learnt a lot,' said Jassy saucily. She seized my hand and pulled me towards the door.

Old Nick grunted and proceeded to fill his glass.

Going upstairs I thought that Jassy would probably say that he was a nice man. He had, I thought, been extremely amiable to her; and I knew that most girls, if a naturally surly man doesn't, for once, snap their heads off, get inflated ideas. But I was prepared to bear her comments patiently because she had got us out of an awkward hole. She had even prepared him for any letter Mrs Twysdale might write. However, Jassy dropped my hand and, clasping both her own on her waist, turned her eyes upwards and said, 'What an ordeal! I felt as though I were sitting on top of a volcano.'

'You hid that feeling very well. You did marvellously, Jassy. By tomorrow he'll be used to the idea that we're here and probably won't ask another question about it. He happened to be amiable today. He'd probably shot well. And perhaps you wonder why I am so scared of him.'

'Oh no. I'm scared of him too.'

'I have a special reason to be,' I said, opening the door of my own room. 'You see, whenever he gets angry with me he throws mother at me. I happen to be terribly like her to look at. That sets him against me to start with. Oh, Jassy, how nice this looks. I'm sure you did it.'

I looked round my bright cosy room.

'I had to choose a room for myself, since you were asleep,' she said. 'I hope it's all right. Just across there, the one with a sort of Chinese paper.'

'That isn't a *sort* of Chinese paper,' I said. 'It's genuine. It's reputed to have been smuggled out of China in hollow bamboos. I remember mother talking about it. She liked it, too. Mrs Hatton wanted to take it away with her, but it was too fragile to take down.'

'It wouldn't have fitted into Green Farm very well. But I expect Barney would have liked it.'

'Barney Hatton?'

Jassy nodded.

'Do you know him?'

'In a way. He was the boy who saved me from being put in the pond.'

'You didn't mention his name.'

'No. I was trying to make it mysterious and thrilling. But it was Barney.' A gentler look than I should have thought her rather hard little face capable of assuming shone for a second and was gone. 'He was . . .' she said, and then checked herself to say briskly, 'We've got to make ourselves beautiful. For me that will be a long job.'

The problem of clothes took possession of my mind. 'What dress will you wear?'

'My best one. The red.'

'That isn't suitable,' I said. 'Come in and shut the door. I'll find you one. Anything that fitted me two years ago will fit you now. They're all here somewhere.'

I opened my cupboard and delved towards the back of it where the dresses I could no longer wear were hanging. I had plenty of dresses. The one thing Old Nick would give me was money, and during my long, lonely holidays I often spent whole days in Colchester buying clothes. It was about the only pleasure a holiday brought me. Some of the dresses I wore only once or twice, a few not at all, for I had really no use for the pretty, flimsy ones which attracted me most in the shops. They were too fussy for school wear or for dining with Old Nick, who often had not shaved for three days. And never, until this evening, had I been invited to dine with his guests.

'I'm going to be very grand,' I said, with my head in the cupboard, feeling my hands come in contact with a dress of lilac satin edged with frills of white lace, 'so you must, too.' I knew what I was looking for, and eventually drew it out, a little dress of a colour called hyacinth blue, rather plain and made of heavy silk. The corsage, the sleeves, and the hem were finished with rouleaux of the same material. I had taken it to school, intending to wear it at the concert to which we were taken annually. But at the last minute, dressing in the chilly dormitory, my courage had failed me, and I had decided in favour of something less conspicuous. 'It's just your dress, Jassy,' I said, holding it out. 'I've never worn it either.'

She took it by the shoulders and measured it against herself, peering forward to look in my mirror. 'Mercy!' she cried. 'Look at me. Dilys, you might have told me. My hair!' She skipped to the door, halted on the threshold and said, 'I might have said "Thank you" first, mightn't I? Thank you, Dilys,' and vanished.

I dressed slowly, taking care to conceal as far as possible my resemblance to mother. At school I was always being called stupid, and it was also one of father's epithets for me. In many ways I deserved it. My brain was slower than my feelings, and so I often did stupid things. My feelings, for instance, made me rush home to Mortiboys as a retreat, when a little cool thought would have shown me that it was nothing of the kind. That was stupid. So was my habit of stammering when nervous. Also, I found certain things very difficult to learn. Miss Hamilton accused me of not trying, but the mere effort to concentrate, especially on numbers, made my head ache until I was silly. But in other ways I was not so stupid. I could understand people in a fashion. I knew–and I don't think anyone else in school even guessed it–that Mrs Twysdale was crazy about Miss Hamilton in a peculiar fashion, as though she were a man. That was why Mrs Twysdale hated Jassy so much. Jassy knew she was jealous, but she didn't know *how* jealous. And in the same way I was not blind to the grudge father had against me. When I was young, in those far away days when we seemed to be a happy and united family, he had been very fond of me. Now, even if he could forget for a moment that I was mother's daughter, there was my face and my hair to remind him and jog his spite.

So tonight, because I remembered mother, dressed for the evening with a mass of little curls on her forehead, I brushed my hair upwards and backwards, leaving my brow bare; and because she had always been ivory pale I coloured my face very rosy; and because our mouths were identical in shape I reddened mine, sharpening the line of my top lip and thickening the lower.

And as I worked upon this new and undeniably pretty face I thought how odd it was that though all girls wanted to be pretty and envied you if you were, looks were really no use at all. Charles had thought I was pretty, he had said so. But for some reason, although we hadn't quarrelled and I had been as charming to him as I could, crawling out through the pantry window to meet him, letting him know how dear to me he was, he hadn't wanted to marry me. His relief, once he had said that marriage was impossible, was like something visible and noisy. It shrieked at me. Why? What happened to men? What could happen to a man in the short interval of a week, so that at one meeting he said he loved you and kissed you until you were dizzy, and at the next said in a careful, cold way that marriage was impossible and this must be good-bye? It was nothing I had done or said, for we had not met in the interval. It was just a mystery, and the bewilderment it caused me made the grief just that little bit harder to bear.

Sitting there, staring at my reflection and noting how the pinkness of my cheeks made my eyes seem darker and brighter and my hair more yellow, I wished that Charles could see me now. He had only really *seen* me twice, once in the garden here when he had left the card party for a breath of air, and on the day when I went back to school. Our other meetings had been at night, in the dark. If he could see me now, would he kiss me? The thought sent a kind of sick longing through me, through every part of me; even my fingers ached. And at that moment, even as I was thinking of Charles and longing for him, something shifted in my brain and I was suddenly and incongruously reminded of the boy whom Jassy had mentioned some minutes before. Barney Hatton. He was the first boy I ever kissed.

Five, six years ago. The whole of that queer miserable time came back to me, all flavoured with the taste of that autumn day. Old Nick–only I had not then caught from the servants the trick of calling him that–was still in the worst period of his despair over mother. He had not yet sought any consolation from village girls or from the doxy at 'The Evening Star'; he was merely drinking hard and gambling heavily. And he had not yet settled down into his firm dislike for me; there were moments then when he would treat me with maudlin tenderness and then suddenly push me away or shout at me roughly. And I was young. I did not understand. He had told me, quite kindly, that when Mr Hatton came over to play cards next time he would bring his little boy to spend the day and be company for me, and I had expected a child. I had the swing mended and looked out some toys which I had discarded. I was surprised to find that the 'little boy' was a good deal older and a great deal bigger than I was, a serious, quiet boy, whose manner was a curious blend of shyness and aggressiveness. We were very shy of one another at first, and I asked him nervously what he would like to do. He said, 'I came to see the house.' So I showed him over. We went everywhere, even into those parts of it where I had never ventured before, because, for as long as I could remember, I have been afraid to be by myself far from other people's company. All morning we explored the house. Mortiboys was not large compared with some houses, but being old it was full of passages that turned and twisted, full of sudden steps up and down, and of rooms that led out of one another. Barney hardly spoke at all; he walked and stared as though he were sleep walking, and when I tried to talk to him he answered in a cross tone of voice. I imagined that he was disappointed in the house and felt apologetic, wishing that all the improvements that had been planned could have been made before the trouble broke.

But afterwards, when we ate our meal alone together, and then went into the grounds, he altered. He looked at me kindly and with admiration. I was young, but not too young to know that. And once, when he helped me over a wall and held both my hands because I was afraid to jump, he went very red and seemed to be embarrassed for a long while. At seven o'clock Mrs Capps, who was very strict with me, called me to come in and have supper and go to bed. Master Hatton, she said, was to wait in the hall until his father was ready. So I said, 'I have to go now, Barney. Good-bye.' And, going very grown-up suddenly, he took my hand and kissed it. Nobody had ever done that before and I was pleased. I looked down on his head: his hair was bright brown and very well brushed, and his neck was nice, much younger than his face. When he lifted his face I bent forward and kissed him. I never knew why, except that I thought he was nice and his neck was so young. And he kissed me back, very, very softly.

I hoped he would come again. But soon after that Old Nick and Mr Hatton, after years and years of friendship, had a quarrel, and before it was mended I had been sent to school.

Very soon after that Mr Hatton died. I never saw Barney again.

But in one holiday, when I was fourteen, there was a boy in the stable-yard helping Sharples. And he had the same bright brown hair and young-looking neck. And that holiday I pretended that I did not like riding alone and got the boy, Ned–that was his name, I remember–to ride with me. One day, when he was showing me a cut on his hand, I kissed him too. It wasn't the same at all. It was dreadful. For a long time it made me go hot all over to think about it.

After that I didn't kiss anyone again until I kissed Charles. And that was very different.

And yet, as I rose at last and left my dressing-table and my memories, I was thinking of Barney Hatton. Not of Charles. Charles had gone. Presently the seas would divide us, but that would mean nothing. Deeper and colder than the sea itself was the memory of that cold, careful explanation, that shrieking relief when the fatal speech had been spoken. Charles had gone. But Barney Hatton . . . One day, when my heart had stopped aching, when I was myself again, I would think about him.

I went to see how Jassy was getting on with her dressing. The nice blue dress was spread out over her bed, and Jassy, wearing her old red one, was sitting in a chair reading a book. Her black plaits, very neat and shiny, were re-arranged in their elaborate curves and twists. Her face had its familiar privet-flower yellow pallor, and her mouth, untouched, was redder than mine.

'You didn't like it,' I said regretfully, pointing to the dress.

'I loved it, Dilys. I put it on. It was lovely, but I just felt silly in it. I don't know why. I hope you don't mind. I'm just as grateful, but I feel better like this.'

I looked at the red dress. It was worn and too skimpy. Too high in the neck and with meagre sleeves. But then it flashed into my mind that I had only this morning thought it a good thing that Jassy was not pretty. I realized that in offering her an attractive gown I had once again let my feelings run away with my wits. I said, with false heartiness, 'I think you're very wise, Jassy. Red is your colour, blue is not. You look very nice indeed.'

'But the order was to be beautiful,' she said with a funny little grin. 'Well, you are, Dilys. But I expect you know that.'

It was the first time she had ever mentioned my appearance, and I realized that, amongst the gushing of the girls at school, her reticence had been attractive.

'My looks haven't done me much good,' I said bitterly.

'There's plenty of time. They will,' she said. And again I thought of Barney Hatton.

The dinner party was queer and interesting and rather exciting. Father's guests were Sir Edward Follesmark, whom everyone knew as the Mad Squire, because whenever there were rows about labourers' wages, or about men poaching, he sided with the labourers or the poachers; Sir Evelyn Fennel and his son, Stephen.

Sir Evelyn was a thin, sick-looking man with a yellow face and reddish hair receding from his temples. He was a notorious gambler. There was a legend in our part of the country that once, at the end of a mad and reckless game, he had staked his wife, and lost. The story said that Lady Fennel had laughed and insisted upon paying the winner of the game ten thousand pounds, saying that she could not value herself at less. Whether the story were true or not I could not say; it was only servants' gossip by the time I heard it. I did know that she was a rich woman, and not on good terms with Sir Evelyn. Sir Edward, who was a bachelor, was a stout, short, red-faced man with a shock of white hair. He was always untidily dressed and liked to potter about his estate working like a labourer. He was always delighted if a stranger mistook him for one of his own men. But despite his eccentricities he was the most truly nice and gentlemanly person who ever visited Mortiboys. I had known him all my life, and when I was small he used always to have a present for me in one of his bulging pockets. He was immensely rich and extremely charitable, in thought as well as deed. I think he remained on friendly terms with father after he turned queer because he was sorry for him, not because, like Sir Evelyn and, in the past, Mr Hatton, he didn't care with whom, or where, he played so long as he could get a good game.

Stephen Fennel, who was reputed to be very clever, had just completed three years' study at Cambridge University. I had not seen him since he had been brought, a stocky, silent, critical little boy, to the children's parties which mother used to give at Christmas time. He was the youngest member and the only boy in a family of girls, and I remember hearing someone say that he was very much spoiled. But now, meeting him again, I saw no evidence of that. He had improved, I thought. He seemed anxious to make himself pleasant. I should not have recognized in him the little boy who had seemed to regard all games as childish and parties a waste of time. He was not handsome, his face was already tinged with the sallow yellowness of his father's, and his hair, being black, emphasized it.

The arrival of Jassy and myself in the parlour was obviously unexpected. Old Nick had not thought it worth while to mention that his daughter was home and had been invited to dine. Perhaps he had forgotten the matter. He had drunk a good deal in the interval, though he had found time to tidy himself and to put on the best clothes he had. They were getting old-fashioned, for he had bought no new clothes since mother left him. He and Sir Edward looked quaint and old-fashioned beside the Fennels, who were both addicted to dandyism.

Sir Edward greeted me with his old bluff friendliness, and both Stephen and his father, though less familiar, and obviously masking some surprise, contrived to make me feel that I was, after all, in the right place, and young and pretty and welcome. I had been nervous on the stairs coming down, and outside in the hall, as I heard the voices in the parlour, had longed for a mother or for some older women to take charge of the situation. But it was all right. I looked round immediately the first greetings were over, intending to introduce Jassy; but Old Nick, who had done nothing to ease the awkward moment of entry for me, his daughter, had already taken her rather clumsily by the elbow and pushed her before Sir Edward.

'I reckon you remember this young lady's father,' he said offhandedly. 'Woodroffe. Mixed up in that Summerfield business.'

Sir Edward's kind red face went wooden for a moment, whether with his effort to pin down the name in his memory, or with surprise at Old Nick's reference to a long-ago affair, or–as might be excusable–at this introduction to the daughter of a radical carpenter on the hearth of the parlour at Mortiboys, I could not tell. But within a moment his natural benevolent expression was restored, and enhancing it was the most eager and delicate desire to give Jassy assurance and put her at her ease.

'Indeed, I remember your father, my dear. He was a friend of mine; in fact an ally. I'm proud to meet his daughter. Fennel . . .'

Sir Edward's big booming voice interrupted Sir Evelyn in something he was saying to me, and his subsequent introduction of Jassy had just a grain of truculence in it. Again I thought, in a panic, that I had been careless and inconsiderate. I had just asked Jassy to come home with me, partly for her sake, partly for mine. I had not taken into consideration the social question. For one thing, I had not thought for a moment that Jassy and I would see anyone but Old Nick himself; for another, I should never have believed that her name would strike a chord in his memory and thus attach the tag 'carpenter's daughter' to her. But I could see that Sir Evelyn was puzzled.

'Jassy and I were at school together until this morning,' I said hastily, without thinking of the question which such a statement must inevitably raise.

'Until this morning, eh?' said Sir Edward. 'And what . . .' But just then Moult, very stately and on his best behaviour, announced dinner; and it was Stephen, whom I felt capable of fobbing off, who, next to me at table, asked why Jassy and I had come home in the middle of term.

'I'll tell you another time,' I said. 'It isn't entirely my story.'

He smiled, and saying, 'That sounds very romantic and intriguing,' let the matter drop. But throughout the meal he seemed to take pains to talk to me, asking little careful questions which he could be sure I should be able to answer, and telling me about Cambridge, which I had never seen.

As soon as the meal was over the men went back into the library to play cards, and Jassy and I sat in the hall, where the ashes had been rather half-heartedly removed and a new fire lighted. We talked for some time, mainly about school, speculating upon what kind of letter Mrs Twysdale would write to father, and following the evening routine of school with, 'Now they're at supper . . .' and 'Prayers has just started . . .' and 'Now they're off to bed.' It gave us a very emancipated feeling to be sitting there in front of the dying fire when we knew that the 'Lights Out' bell had sounded.

'Miss Hamilton will miss you, Jassy,' I said idly.

'I was going to leave at Christmas in any case. I think she meant to ask me to stay on and teach. But I shouldn't have done that. I have already written to two places about posts.' She gave a little sigh. 'Miss Hamilton had been very good to me. She was a true friend. That's why I would have had to leave.'

'Because of Twizzy?'

'Yes. Miss Hamilton is better with her without me, than she would be without her and with me. And it was going to be one or the other. I saw that a long time ago.' She moved impatiently in her chair. 'Don't think about them, don't talk about them. When I think of her *face!* Honestly, Dilys, I could die of shame.'

'She hit you first.'

'What difference does that make? It was unforgivable of me. Actually I didn't mind. I'd have done it again this morning, or this afternoon. But now, being back here, and hearing Sir Edward speak of my father. He'd have been horrified. Father, I mean.' She tugged a handkerchief out of her sleeve and suddenly, to my horror, began to cry. I had never before seen her shed a tear. To make matters worse I heard the door of the salon open, a sudden sound of voices, quickly hushed by the door's closing again, and then a rather hesitant step. Stephen Fennel was coming across the hall towards us. Jassy brushed her face with the handkerchief and, falling on her knees, began to rake the fire together.

Stephen said, 'I have earned a little respite, I think. May I?' He indicated the vacant place on the settle by my side. He sat down, and Jassy, quite calm now, turned from the fire and, drawing her feet under her, sat on the rug.

'Dilys,' he said, 'I want you to do me a favour. Ask me one day and show me all over the house, will you?'

'A poor favour,' I said lightly. 'But of course. Come when you like.'

'I want to see the Great Hall.'

'But you've seen it. Don't you remember coming to parties? We had them in there.' I nodded my head to the big, heavily-nailed doorway beyond the fireplace. 'It's horrid now. The window blew out, you know, and it hasn't been mended. The birds fly in and out and the rain comes in. There's nothing to see.'

'Nothing save one of the finest hammer roofs in England and, I believe, a genuine twelfth-century minstrels' gallery. I have become interested in such things since the children's parties, Dilys. I'd hoped you had forgotten them. I was a horrid child, interested only in congruent triangles and things of that kind. Cambridge has taught me a great deal.'

'If it's given you a taste for ruins,' I said, 'you can satisfy it easily by coming to see Mortiboys–and Jassy and me!'

'Delightful flowers often blossom amongst ruins,' he said sententiously. And I thought of the stocky, silent little boy who had seemed to be so critical of everything. How queerly people developed as they grew up. What had I been myself in those distant days? So sure of myself; so delighted with my dress; so inflated because it was *my* party. Nothing of that little girl remained–except perhaps the delight in finery. I slid my hand over my satin-shrouded knee. No! That was wrong. People developed, and here and there they were pruned a little by their circumstances, but the core of them altered very little. And as that thought went through my mind, with its offshoots of memories about the conditions that mould one, I heard myself asking, to my own intense surprise:

'Stephen, what happened to Barney Hatton?'

'Ah,' he said, smoothing back one rebellious strand of his black hair. 'Of course, there is a connection between the Hattons and this place. I was at a loss for the moment. He's still at Green Farm, for all I know. Mrs Hatton died last winter. Mother went to the funeral, I remember. But I should think Barney is still there. By all accounts he has sunk every penny he had in the place. He's taking his farming very seriously, I believe.'

'I thought of him,' I said, 'because once, ages ago, I showed him over the house. It wasn't such a ruin then. But he didn't seem to like it much.'

'Barney worshipped Mortiboys,' said Jassy in a hard, fierce little voice.

'Indeed,' Stephen said, dismissing the subject. 'I suppose I must go back now. But Dilys, remember you have promised to show me the house. And I'd like it too, if you–and Miss Woodroffe too, of course, if she's still here–would come over and see us. Mother would like that, I know.'

'We'd like it too,' I said. 'Jassy and I would love to make some visits.'

'I'll send word then making more definite arrangements. I'm delighted that you're home again, Dilys.'

'So am I, for some reasons,' I said.

'Another conquest,' said Jassy, as the door closed behind him. 'What it is to be pretty.'

'Don't talk to me of conquests,' I said bitterly. I glanced at the clock. 'Just this time last night . . .'

'It seems ages ago,' said Jassy, getting up and stretching like a cat. 'Another life in fact.' And although that glance at the clock's face had given me a momentary stab, I could not contradict her. It did seem ages ago.

Mounting the stairs with Jassy I thought that after all feelings were good guides sometimes. I had been right to come home. The day's happenings reared themselves like a barrier between me and last night's heartbreak. Even Stephen–though never, never could he raise in me a tenth of the feeling that Charles had done–but even Stephen, with his obvious admiration and his desire to see me again, contributed to that barrier.

And yet, when Jassy had said good night, and I had hung up my dress and cleaned my face and got into bed, misery, sheer plain misery had me in its grip again. For an hour I sobbed into my pillow, wanting Charles, wanting nothing, nothing but him; living again those happy moments when he had said that he loved me, and that horrible moment when, without actually saying so in words, he had informed me that he didn't. And then, when I had cried myself into an empty hollow shell, a thought struck me. Was my trouble merely that I wanted to be loved? Not that I myself loved too easily or too well? It was feasible. Nobody had loved me yet. Mother hadn't, or she would not have left me behind. Father didn't, or he would have gained some comfort from my presence. Charles hadn't, that was plain. And so, aware of a great lack in my life, I ran round seeking love, like a hungry puppy seeking for food, and, like a puppy, courting rebuffs and disappointments.

Under the impact of this self-revealing thought I sat up straight in bed. Had I ever loved Charles, really? Or had I just been pleased and flattered by his attentions to me? Had he actually been very wise in leaving me as he did? Had he guessed that deep down inside myself I was incapable of loving anyone except Dilys Helmar? Was that true? My head began to ache, as it always did when I tried to understand something that was beyond me. My headaches were queer. I had watched, and even questioned, other people and found that their heads ached in the front. Mine came at the back, beginning with a dull numbness at the back of the skull and growing more violent until I should not have felt worse if someone had struck me repeatedly with a heavy club. But tonight, I did not, as I usually did, relinquish the problem that had started the pain. Sitting up, holding my head in my hands, I went on thinking about love and being in love, about how much of it all was an outgoing towards the other person, and how much a mere adoration of oneself as reflected in the other person's affection. I thought until the pain reached a stupefying pitch. Then I rolled over, covered my cold shoulders and fell asleep. But in the morning I knew that I had had an experience. I was not young any more. I was as old as Eve.

Within a week it felt as though Jassy and I had been at Mortiboys half a lifetime. There was a queer timelessness about the days; I had noticed it before when the holiday had seemed longer than four terms on end. Except when, as on the night of our homecoming, Old Nick had company, no one consulted the clock at all. The master's wishes, within the limits imposed by Melia's whims, ruled the house, and Old Nick's habits were as irregular as his moods. I–and Jassy with me–kept out of his way as much as possible. When we did meet, which was generally at the evening meal, he sometimes ignored us entirely, or, especially if he had been drinking, was surly to me while extending towards Jassy a kind of savage raillery which she bore with astonishing good humour. Sometimes she succeeded in making him laugh. She had, more than anyone I ever knew, the knack of making a simple thing seem funny, or of seeing the ridiculous side of something which other people had always accepted without humour. More than once there had been trouble at school because she made girls giggle over things which had been there for years and never before occasioned a glimmer of mirth. But Jassy's quips and jokes at Mortiboys I could not wholeheartedly enjoy, because there was an element of danger even in father's mirth. Occasionally it seemed to me that he resented the amusement that Jassy afforded; anyway, he would often follow his bark of laughter with some surly, snubbing remark. And I felt happier out of his presence.

Fortunately the weather was good. And Sharples, at my request, produced an aged, steady horse called Major, which he considered a suitable mount for a beginner; so Jassy and I, with a timeless day ahead of us, could roam where we wished.

One mellow October morning we left the stable-yard, skirted the great bulk of the house, wound our way past the wreck of the gateway, and halted. I know now that the same thought was in both our minds. But it was Jassy who said:

'Let's go to Minsham All Saints, Dilys. I'd like to see the place again. And the Lower Road will be all right today.'

The Lower Road, impassable in wet weather, was indescribably lovely that morning. It was sunk between hedges that glowed with the fruit of hawthorn and the wild rose, and frothed with the feathery tangle of wild clematis. Great beeches, burning amber, stood at intervals in the hedges, and the leaves that had already fallen carpeted the ground. Now and then, through a gap in the hedge or a space between the trees, one could see the marshes, very green and flat, patterned by the silver of the creeks that wound through them.

'That's Green Farm,' said Jassy at last, pointing a finger towards a crooked red chimney. 'Barney Hatton's home, you know.'

'I didn't know. I've never seen it,' I said. My voice was cool and ordinary, but a little spurt of excitement rose in my stomach and thrust its way upwards.

The road ended, opening out to a wide green with a pond at its further end and a circle of low cottages on its outskirts.

'That's where I used to live,' said Jassy, pointing to one of the cottages. 'And there's the pond where Barney saved me a ducking. And here's Green Farm.' I followed her pointing finger and saw a low, thatched farmhouse, set slantwise to the Green, with a narrow garden in front and a bigger one dividing it from the cottage which Jassy had indicated. It looked comfortable, but humble. Very humble after Mortiboys; and the Hattons had lived at Mortiboys!

'Shall we,' said Jassy in a small, diffident voice, 'shall we call on Barney? I would like to see him again. He was such a nice boy. I'd like to see what he's grown up like.'

'I don't mind,' I said.

'Oh, not if you don't want to. I'll go by myself if you'd rather.'

'I'll come.'

'This way then,' and she turned Major's head towards the right and just ahead of us, set at an angle, I saw a gateway set between two low buildings of flint.

Jassy slipped out of the saddle–she was already adept at mounting and dismounting–opened the gate, led Major through, and held it open for me. Then she closed it and, with unnecessary precaution, for Major would have stood for a week, slipped his rein forward and twisted it round a post. She did it all as neatly and expertly as she did everything with her hands, and when she lifted them to settle her hat I was surprised to see that they were trembling.

'I wonder if Meggie is still here,' she said. Then she skipped over the cobbles between the yard and the back door of the house and, flexing her little fist, beat on it with, I thought, unnecessary vigour. There was no answer and presently, after making a grimace to me over her shoulder, she hammered on the door again. And within a second the door was flung open and a veritable crone, wrinkled and bent and furious, thrust her head around its edge. Astonishment wiped away the fury for a second and then was replaced by an even more venomous expression.

'Jassy Woodroffe,' exclaimed the crone in the high shrill voice of the very deaf. 'I wondered who it wuz, beating the door fit to bring it down. What brings *you* here?'

'It's Meggie,' said Jassy, and there was a genuine pleasure in her voice. 'And you look just the same.'

'Who did you reckon I'd look like?' I saw her little bright eyes, almost lost in the mass of wrinkles, sweep Jassy from head to foot, taking in every detail of the old green habit of mine which we had spent hours in fitting and altering. 'You've got very fine. Who's that with you?'

'Miss Helmar from Mortiboys?'

'Mortiboys did you say?' Jassy nodded vigorously. The crone bobbed in my direction and I smiled at her. Her expression of bewildered resentment would have made anyone smile.

'We've come to see Barney. Is he at home?' Jassy shouted.

'Master Barney is ploughing the Twelve Acre.'

'Twelve Acre? I know. All right, Meggie, we'll find him.'

She was turning away from the door when the old woman said crossly:

'Hold your hurry. You can go traipsing about in the fields if you've a mind to, but Miss Helmar, do she want Master Barney, should come in and wait, proper fashion.'

I resented this difference on Jassy's behalf and said stiffly, 'Thank you, I'll stay with Jassy.'

'Best both come in then,' she said, and held the door wide while I dismounted and fastened Gyp, who, unlike Major, would not have waited a moment, but have been off round the yard seeking, Satan-fashion, what she might devour.

Meggie led the way through a warm and cosy kitchen which gave the impression of having been lived in always, along a dark passage and into a parlour which felt and smelt like a tomb. Everything in it shone with cleanliness, but the cold air was heavy and undisturbed. No one had sat down in that room for a long time.

The old woman pulled forward a chair and said, 'Please to sit down.' Then she shuffled over to an ornate corner cupboard, painted white with pretty little wreaths of gesso work picked out in natural colours. She took out, with slow deliberation, first a silver tray, which she set on the centre table, then a brown jar with a lid, then two slender fluted wine glasses and a decanter full of some pale yellow wine.

'Thass ony cowslip, but thass my own make, and good though I say it. Help yourself, Miss Helmar, and take a biscuits. Now I'll go and ring the bell and Master Barney'll be here in no time.' Her wrinkled hands, the colour of earth, hovered about the tray for a second, rearranging its contents, then, with a nod, as though the ritual of hospitality had been duly observed, she shuffled away. A moment later the sound of a deep-tongued bell rang through the house.

'Surly old thing,' I said.

'She wasn't surly to *you*,' said Jassy composedly. 'She hates me like poison. She always did. Not that I ever did her any harm. Still, she has a good heart. She once gave away all her savings. And I bet Barney is served better than . . . than most people.'

'Don't spare my feelings,' I said. 'Always complete a sentence, Jassy Woodroffe. Barney is better served than we are at Mortiboys.' It was a goodish imitation of Miss Hamilton's voice.

'Yes, ma'am,' said Jassy meekly. Then in her normal voice: 'But it's true.

I'd like to see Meggie set about those sluts at Mortiboys. Actually she did come from there. So did that and that and those . . .' She pointed to a little escritoire elaborately inlaid and decorated with ormolu, to the side of the carpet, which had been cut to fit the room and bound on the raw edge with braid, and to the long curtains of faded rose-coloured velvet which dwarfed the small window. 'And the whole of her life was cut down and cramped in just the same way.'

'Whose? Meggie's?'

'No. My thoughts were wandering. Mrs Hatton's. And heavens, how she would have resented my knowing that!' She gave one of her funny little sighs and turned abruptly to the table. 'Shall we sample Meggie's brew? This room is like a tomb.'

I heard the neck of the decanter chatter against the edge of the glass. She's nervous, I thought. And my own nerves leapt in response. There was something so formal and deliberate about sitting there in that cold, unwelcoming room, waiting for Barney to come in, interrupted from his work. This meeting, after the lapse of years, should have been casual, almost accidental. We should have looked over the gate and found him there in the yard, and the gulf between our childhoods and the present might have been bridged by the mere act of recognition. This musty room, this almost ceremonial wine, that bell tolling its summons, made the whole thing ponderous and horrible.

Almost without thinking I emptied my glass and set it down, noticing too late the sweet, light, floral quality of the wine.

'Jassy, let's go. Let's say we can't wait. I really *can't* wait. I can't breathe in this room.'

'Sh,' said Jassy. She stood by the table, her glass an inch from her lips, listening. She looked like a deer, disturbed in the depths of a forest. She had always a curious ability to take up graceful, almost embroidered attitudes. That was why so many people thought she was pretty, despite her big mouth and odd-shaped face. 'That *is* Barney.'

I remembered looking towards the door of the parlour and noticing that its white paint had worn thin and dull, and that the white china knob and finger-plates, with their little painted flowers, were cracked and chipped. And I remember hearing a heavy footstep in the long dark passage, hurried and eager at first, then faltering, until at last there was a distinct pause between the final step and the opening of the door.

Out of the blurred whirl of first impressions I gathered that the most striking thing about Barney was his size. He was enormous. His head reached to the door jamb, and his shoulders cleared the posts by an inch on either side, no more. He wore a blue shirt, faded to grey on the shoulders and outsides of the sleeves, a pair of brown breeches, heavy leggings, and thick boots to which, despite recent scraping, the sticky mud of the fields still clung in places. He had shaved that morning, and his hands and forearms had been washed within the last few minutes. They were not perfectly dry; little spirals of steam were still rising from them.

Jassy, though she may have been nervous a moment before, made one of her lightning recoveries. She ran forward like a child, stretching both hands.

'Barney. You remember us, don't you?'

'Of course.' A slow smile lightened the rather harsh lines of his face. He took her hands, and then, dropping them, stretched out his right to me.

'I'm afraid we have disturbed you,' I said. 'Meggie told us you were busy.'

'I'm always busy,' he said, with another smile. His lips were thin and very flexible, curving away from sound white teeth. 'And I seldom have a pleasant disturbance.'

'Is this a pleasant one?' Jassy asked.

'Very pleasant. And very surprising. I often wondered what happened to you, Jassy. When Meggie said you were here I could hardly believe my ears.'

'I've only been in Baildon. Sometimes I thought I'd write to you, but I was afraid you'd have forgotten me. And now I'm staying with Dilys, so we thought we'd come over and see you.'

Barney smiled again, and when his bright blue eyes with their rather bristly thick lashes looked at me, I smiled back. And Jassy smiled. But all our smiles did little to ease the queer tension that held us. Barney looked round uneasily and saw the tray.

'I'm glad Meggie remembered her manners,' he said. 'That's more than can be said for me, I'm afraid.' He took the decanter in his big brown hand and filled the glass which I had emptied so hastily. Jassy, as though she were at home, went to the cupboard and reached down a third glass, and having set it on the tray, lifted the lid from the brown jar.

'Meggie's biscuits were famous,' she said, and peeped inside. Then she leaned lower and sniffed, recoiling with a grimace of disgust.

'What's wrong?' Barney asked.

'Look.' She held the jar under our noses. Inside was merely a great heap of blue and green mould. 'Take a biscuit, Miss Helmar,' Jassy said in Meggie's voice. We all laughed. And after that everything was better. Jassy began to chatter, saying, 'Do you remember . . .?' and 'What happened to this person and that?' I sat quietly. Barney and I had only shared one experience, and whether he remembered it or had forgotten it, it was not for me to remind him. But every now and then his eyes met mine, and each time a kind of warm flood seemed to wash over me, and my whole inside quivered with excitement. I thought with resentment of Stephen Fennel and of how easily we had established a relationship. He had only to invite himself to Mortiboys and ask us to go and see his mother. And Stephen was nothing compared with Barney. It was pleasant, of course, to see Stephen's obvious admiration, and to have him treat me as a grown-up; but in a lifetime he could never raise the excitement in me that one of Barney's blue, rather furtive glances could. And when I did speak, I spoke out of peevishness, sudden and untactful.

'Barney, could you come and see us? Or were you drawn into that silly old quarrel?'

It was easy to see how, in so few years, his forehead had taken on that deep gash between the brows and his cheeks those harsh lines. They were the signs of a settled ill-humour which, banished for a moment by our presence, rushed back in answer to my question.

'If you can call that a silly . . .' he began. Then he stopped and made a visible effort to restrain himself. 'I'm sorry. It probably was a silly quarrel at the beginning–most card-table disputes are silly. But it wasn't silly at the end.'

'I don't know anything about it,' I said.

'Then you'd better know. Perhaps you'll side with your father. I don't know how it started, I wasn't there, and my father was never any good at describing things. But he and your father quarrelled about a game, and as neither of them was strictly sober, abuse flowed pretty freely. Father swore he'd never enter Mortiboys again. That didn't matter. He couldn't afford to play anyway, and nobody minded. Even he seemed not to. But afterwards we knew differently. He began to break up and lose interest in life, as though going to Mortiboys and gambling had been the only thing that had held him together. Within nine months he was dead. I don't blame your father for that, Dilys. Nobody but a fool could do so. They'd quarrelled, and if the affair couldn't be patched over, well, one was as much to blame as the other. But . . .' he leaned forward, resting his weight on his hands, which were gripping his knees, 'that wasn't the end. When he was dying, father, who could never string a couple of sentences together lucidly, suddenly began to talk. For forty-eight hours he talked. You could have called it raving if it hadn't been so sensible. And the burden of it was that he wanted to see Nick Helmar. He delved into the past, tracing the friendship from the beginning, going through and through all the things they'd done together, saying how Nick had been his only friend in the worst of his trouble, and so on, interminably. He even blamed himself for the quarrel, saying that he should have known better than to provoke Nick, who was no longer himself. And then he came back to the old request–that Nick be brought to see him. So I rode over to Mortiboys in the middle of the afternoon and asked your father, Dilys, to ride back with me and make his peace with a dying man. *And he wouldn't come!*'

'He was drunk.' It was half a question, half a statement.

'He wasn't drunk. He wasn't sober, quite. But he understood. I told him that father blamed himself for the quarrel, and he dismissed that as though it meant nothing. And he wouldn't come. When I got back father cried. He cried. And I'd always thought he had no feelings at all.' Barney shifted in the chair, throwing his weight back so the chair creaked. 'Oh,' he said impatient, 'I know it meant nothing. He was living in the past, as the dying often do, and he was thinking, not about a crazy sot of sixty, but of a boy, a young man, who had been his friend. But I had been to Mortiboys, I had pleaded as I'd never pleaded for anything before in my life, and I can't forgive the utter callousness, the ghastly cold-heartedness, that your father showed, Dilys. I'm sorry. But I shall carry that silly old quarrel, as you call it, to my grave. I wouldn't speak to him if we were the last two men left on earth.'

'No,' I said slowly, watching Barney as he stood up with his head almost touching the low sagging beam. 'I don't blame you. I'd feel the same. And I can believe father would behave that way. There's not a scrap of kindness left in him. A crazy sot–you were right.'

'And so you can't come to see us,' said Jassy, breaking the silence with her prim little voice. 'Well, that wouldn't matter if we could come and see you. Would it?'

Barney turned to her. 'Dilys might not want to come. He's her father.'

'Haven't I as good as told you that I feel as you do about it. Only I'm sorry for him sometimes. Because he was different once. It's what happened to him made him as he is. But, of course, Barney, all this wouldn't make any difference to you and me.'

'You and me,' I said, and with the words the most overwhelming excitement came on me. I looked at his thick muscular neck, reddish brown, growing paler nearer the edge of his open collar; raising my eyes, but keeping my lashes lowered, I looked higher, at that thin-lipped mouth, so bitter and yet capable of such a sweet smile. You and me. You and me, Barney Hatton, one day, alone together. I thought of Charles. And the only emotion the thought roused in me was one of increased excitement. I would do better this time. I would get more out of this. I felt faint, and Jassy's voice came from a long way off.

'Does Meggie still go into the village on Thursdays?'

'She hasn't missed yet.'

'Then shall we come on Thursday? And shall we bring some food? I could cook it. It would be fun.'

Why hadn't I the sense and the presence of mind to suggest that? Yet it was better. Secrecy. Let no one know. Give no one cause to guess. Shelter behind Jassy's eager friendship. You and me . . .

'I've plenty of food,' Barney said.

I knew he was looking at me, and I knew in what way.

'Thursday, then,' I said and stood up. 'It's time we went, Jassy.'

'Yes. What time shall we come, Barney?'

'I work till six. Give me half an hour to tidy myself.'

'Slippers?' Jassy asked. Barney laughed.

'How I hated them! Even Meggie's devotion would quail at the idea of making me a pair now.' He looked down at his enormous feet. It was curious to notice how, as soon as he spoke to Jassy, his manner became very easy and friendly. It was as though he still, at the back of his mind, regarded her as a child. I was glad.

He came with us to the yard, untethered both horses and helped me into my saddle. I thought about what his hands would be if they were not respectful. Jassy, agile as ever, scrambled up from the mounting block and, looking round, said:

'You've made great improvements, Barney.' I also looked round and saw that the yard, though nothing more than a farmyard, was far neater and in better repair than the premises at Mortiboys. The walls of all the buildings were pitched to shoulder level and whitewashed above. To the right of the house was a cartshed, and all the wagons and farm carts were drawn up level with their shafts pointing the same way. Beyond was a pigsty, and the pigs were stomach deep in clean straw. I thought of Stephen's remark that Barney was taking his farming seriously. The idea was still a trifle grotesque. But as we rode through the gate which Barney held open, I looked down to say good-bye and he looked up, and it was as though we looked clean into one another's minds. And if he had been a travelling tinker man, and Thursday's rendezvous fixed for some place under a hedge-row, I should have been there.

'We'll take the Upper Road and make the full circle, shall we?' asked Jassy. I nodded and we rode the length of the Green and past the pond without speaking again.

'Well?' Jassy said, as the horses slowed down at the slope which carried the road to higher ground.

'Well?' I said, on exactly the same note.

'He's a *lot* older, isn't he?'

'We all are.'

'That's true,' she said, and gave a little sigh. And for some reason neither of us mentioned Barney again until, on Thursday morning, Jassy said, 'Is your father likely to miss us this evening?'

'I shouldn't think so.'

'Would he mind your going to Green Farm?'

'Probably not, but it would give him an excuse to shout at me.'

'Well, then, if any questions are asked, we'll say that we're going to see an old aunt of mine.' So she had been thinking ahead to this evening as well. But being Jassy, she had been thinking practically.

Barney and I were shy again at first. At least, shyness is not an adequate word for the state of feeling between us. It suggests a youthfulness, a gaucherie which was not actually there. It was rather the kind of deliberate constraint, mingled with nervous tension which can be seen in players before a game begins. And in my case it was combined with a feeling of unreality. Now and then, as he and I moved about the kitchen, obeying the orders of Jassy, who had instituted herself cook, with all a cook's privileges, I would look at the pots and pans, at the food we were preparing, and the great red fire in the stove, and think that this was all rubbish, a pretence that deceived nobody, a deliberate waste of time. And once again I thought that Barney and I should have rediscovered one another accidentally, preferably out of doors, and after one look into one another's eyes we should have held out our arms. There should have been none of this business of visiting and playing at cooking. Above all, there should have been no Jassy. She was so obviously enjoying herself, was so exuberant, so truly in her proper element, that it was difficult to escape her mood. She had a white apron tied round her tiny waist, and her sleeves were rolled above her elbows. Her funny little face sparkled with animation; she darted from table to stove, from stove to pantry; she chatted and laughed, and when she burnt her hand on a hot dish she swore luridly. In a way she was irresistible. Even Barney once or twice would turn, straight from giving me a look that fired my blood, to laugh like a school-boy at some of her nonsense. And once I had the queer idea that if I could, somehow, be suddenly spirited away, all the feeling of conflict in the kitchen would be removed, the laughter would grow heartier, and together they would throw themselves into the cooking and presently would make an exceedingly merry meal. At another moment I was almost horrified to find that I was watching Jassy's performance cynically. She's showing off, I thought, giving an exhibition of what a good cook she can be, what an excellent farmer's wife she would make. And I could see that for Barney to marry her would be the most natural, most appropriate thing in the world. They matched. Barney was a farmer, but he was gently born; he was poor, but he was not likely to be happy with the kind of girl who would want to marry him. And similarly Jassy, who orphaned, homeless, penniless, might consider herself very lucky to marry a farmer, would hardly be content with an illiterate fellow who only shaved once a week. In fact, although they had not been born for one another–for Barney was born at Mortiboys and Jassy, where? under a hedge like as not–they had been made, by their particular circumstances, for one another. But it was on me that Barney was turning that look which I recognized, a look compounded of admiration and hurt and sheer naked longing. And looking at Jassy as she leaned over the stove, I thought, afterwards, my lady, afterwards. I must have him first. For I had not at that time either the desire or the intention of marrying Barney. I had wanted to marry Charles. I had been so young and so silly that I had built, upon a six weeks' acquaintanceship, a whole castle of dreams. But that was different. And I was wiser now. Charles, all unwittingly, had shown me that there was a great deal of excitement–though that is hardly the word–pleasure?–nearer, but not exact–a great deal of something, anyway, to be had on this side of marriage, and to be had without any questions as to whether the other person were eligible or not.

Barney was not eligible, but he was supremely good to look at; with every glance he gave me I could see that he was minded to play my game. We only needed to be alone. You and me. You and me . . .

Jassy turned to the table and snatched a spoon.

'Now there's just the gravy to make and it's done. You two had better set the table.'

'There's a fire in the parlour,' Barney said. He looked at me. 'I tried the dining-room, but the chimney smoked too much.'

'It always did,' said Jassy. She pointed to the dresser. 'I've put everything we need on that tray. Dilys, take the cloth.'

Barney lifted the tray and I, with the cloth in one hand, opened the door into the passage, let him pass, and closed it again. The long passage was dark save for the red glow of fire-light which came from the parlour's open door. My heart began to gallop as I followed Barney towards the light. Neither of us spoke.

Inside the room Barney set down the tray, took a taper and lighted several candles. I spread the cloth, and then, still in silence, we set out the table. When the last spoon was in place, the last imaginary wrinkle smoothed from the cloth, we stopped and looked at one another. That silent meeting of eyes may not have lasted more than a moment, but seemed to stretch itself out until, with a kind of hysteria, I thought that we should stand there staring and dumb for ever. Which of us could move? What was the word which would break that silence? I waited. And when at last I did speak my voice was choked and low and hurried–a sick person's voice.

'Barney, do you remember that day when you came to Mortiboys?'

'I remember it. Very well. So do you.'

'Yes. That's why I'm here.'

'That was a long time ago. We were children.' The harshness of the words showed that he was fighting. He moved his hands, seizing the top of a chair and gripping it so that the tan deserted the skin over his knuckles.

'We were children. Now we're grown up. But I never forgot you,' I said. And driven, partly by impatience, partly by a desire to know whether I could move as well as speak, I took a few steps forward and laid my hand beside his. He took me by the wrist, almost roughly, and said:

'Dilys, do you know what you're doing?'

'I think so,' I said, and looked at him again.

He let go my wrist and, with a little gasp, dragged me into his arms.

When at last we fell away from one another I was so dizzy that I had to clutch at the chair again, and without thinking I put my other hand to my bruised mouth. Barney said savagely:

'Now I suppose you're angry. I don't play at love-making. I'm not a fine gentleman.'

'I'm not . . . not exactly playing either,' I said breathlessly.

'You'd better tidy your hair,' he said. And I remembered how his hand, a moment before, had cupped the back of my head, fingers tangled in the curls, pressing me closer and closer. 'Lovely hair,' he said. 'I've dreamed of it.' And then, with another change of voice, 'Set it right. Jassy will be wondering.'

The rest of the evening is lost in a haze in my memory, as though I had been drunk, or drugged. We were all very hilarious, and I suppose that the meal, cooked by Jassy, was good. But for me there is a gap in the evening between Barney's saying, 'Jassy will be wondering,' and the other moment when, tidying the kitchen, we whispered, while Jassy was in the pantry, that we would meet next evening in Saints' Spinney. And after that there is another gap, which lasted until I was in my room with the door shut. Then I sat down and looked at myself in the glass and thought, well, Dilys Helmar, what have you started now? And sanity seemed to flow back then.

I slept very little, and in the patches of wakefulness, and as soon as I woke in the morning, a part of my mind, the little practical part, was busy with the problem of what to tell Jassy. I found myself, for several reasons, none of them individually conclusive, completely unable to say to her that I was going to meet Barney alone. And this although, in the affair with Charles, which now seemed so stale and was actually so recent, she had been my confidante and accomplice. For one thing, my whole instinct veered towards secrecy; it always had; it was only my fear of the dark and my lack of knowledge of any exit from the school which had driven me to confide in Jassy in the first place. For another thing, I thought that she might feel hurt by Barney's preference. I did not imagine then that she was in love with him; in fact, it was difficult for me to imagine Jassy being in love with anyone, she was so practical, so self-contained and–to my eyes–so immature; but it was plain that she liked him, and that she had regarded that evening at Green Farm as a friendly meeting, a meeting of three friends. It seemed rather hard to banish her suddenly, to say–we're not three, we're two together and you're one, alone. And there were other reasons, silly little ones, like vanity. I knew, for instance, that if I said to her that I was in love with Barney, she would think that my broken heart had healed very quickly, which was true, but not a matter I wanted comment upon, because that would make me feel silly and frivolous. And if, again, something happened and Barney, after six weeks, withdrew and left me, I didn't want Jassy to be thinking that I could never keep a man for long. Oh, there were many reasons why I did not want to take her into my confidence this time. On the other hand, not to do so made the whole thing very awkward and complicated. Ever since we came to Mortiboys we had done everything together. It was difficult to stop doing so suddenly.

In the end, after I had worried the problem until midday, I told her that I was going to visit Stephen and his mother. And even that was a little awkward because, after I had blurted out the words in an ecstasy of relief at having thought of something, I realized that by not taking her with me I might appear to be slighting her. The last thing I wanted to do was to hurt her feelings, and I turned hot and red when, after I had spoken, the full significance of the speech struck me. I cursed my slow brain.

'It'll be extremely dull, and Lady Fennel will ooze sympathy and I'll feel better if I'm by myself,' I said. And then realized that excuses simply underlined things. With that a premonitory dull thud went through the back of my mind and I grew angry. The devil, I thought, why should I explain and excuse? I've got my own affairs to see to. I can't muddle everything on Jassy Woodroffe's account. And of course, like most of my emotional efforts, it was all wasted. Jassy, neither concerned nor hurt nor very much interested, simply said:

'Stephen will come home with you, I suppose.'

I felt a little ashamed and very much relieved. To lend an appearance of truth to my story, I left Mortiboys in the middle of the afternoon, rode in the direction of Ockley, turned off the road, and followed a path back to Saints' Spinney, and then, tethering Gyp out of sight from the road, sat down under the trees and waited until Barney came. It was dusk before he did so, and I was terrified. Unlike most girls who fear burglars, and footpads, and men-under-the-bed, I was never frightened of any human being except my father. But if I were the last person left alive on earth I should be frightened as soon as the sun had gone down. Always with the dusk there came upon me a feeling of being watched and a great dread lest I should hear or see something that should not be heard or seen. Not ghosts exactly. Stories of figures in winding sheets, or with their heads under their arms–and Mortiboys abounded in legends of such–seemed always a little too concrete and ordinary to terrify me. But I was afraid of being alone, far from other people, and I was afraid of the dark. And when Barney came, rather before time than after, he found me standing close to Gyp, almost gibbering with terror. I had moved over to the horse instinctively, and had patted her nose and held my hand on her neck because at least she was alive and warm. Then I had been taken with the fancy that my fear might infect her . . . suppose she suddenly looked at me and said, 'I'm frightened too' . . . that was the kind of thought that came to me in the dark when I was alone. Mad? Perhaps that was it. Perhaps all the time what I was afraid of was being mad. When Barney came I could hardly speak. For a long time I could only cling to him and shiver. And then, all at once, I was myself again, and my frightened clutch merged imperceptibly into a resumption of the passionate embrace which had begun last evening in the parlour of Green Farm.

I was, on that night in Saints' Spinney, young, in years at least; and my experience held only the memory of a child's kiss, a stable-boy's moment of mania and a young soldier's passing fancy; now I am old, I have had three husbands and lovers innumerable. But I knew then, with the flow of my blood and the beat of my pulses, what I know now in the coldness of my mind and the mill of my thought–that only once, only once to anyone does the perfect moment, the ideal physical counterpart come. I say physical deliberately, and far, oh far, from decryingly. All my feelings for Barney were concerned with his physical being, with that bright brown hair, the size and strength of him, the thick neck, the thin mobile lips, the blue eyes, the sound of his voice. I never, at any time, wanted to share his thoughts, or cook his food, or mend his clothes. If he had been ill he would have been immediately repulsive to me, because the very charm of his strength would have been defiled by his weakness. And for the same reason I did not want him to talk to me–except very trivially. I didn't want him to think. I was a stranger to this thoughts. I hated it when he had scruples, when he tried to plan for the future, when, in fact, he tried in any way to alter and shape a thing which, to me, was perfect and whole as it was. I wanted us to go on for ever, or, since that was not possible, for as long as could be managed, two people, with no past, no future, no ties, no background, walking away from the rest of the world, away into the sanctuary of a wood, or an empty room, and there enjoying to the full the sensations that they were capable of rousing in one another.

And for a time I had my way. So short a time really. The leaves were already on the ground in Saints' Spinney the first time we met there, and when it was over the bluebells were only just coming up spikily under the new bright green of the hawthorns. Only so short a time was I able to stay his scruples, hush his talk, and shut the rest of the world away. So short a time; but those few months remain with me, a passionate, not a sentimental memory, a measuring stick against which all other relationships are revealed as poor substitutes. And if, at any moment of my after life, Barney Hatton had suddenly appeared and said, 'Come to Saints' Spinney,' if I could have gone in secrecy without making complications, I would have gone and blessed God for the chance. But nothing is so simple in this world.

The first complication made itself evident on that very evening as soon as I returned to Mortiboys. It was late, for Barney and I had lost all count of time, and I had imagined that Old Nick would be shut in the library and Jassy gone to her bed. But as I entered the hall, before I could see anyone, I heard a gurgle of laughter and Jassy's voice saying, 'Oh, very nimble! Now I owe you five shillings. And I haven't a penny in the world.'

'But debts of honour have to be paid.' That was father's voice, more amiable than it had been for years.

'I know. But you shouldn't have made me bet. All the same, I never thought you'd get my Queen. Hullo, is that Dilys?' I saw her head with its coronet of plaits rear up over the back of the settle. Damnation, I thought. Now something will be said about Ockley and the Fennels. I walked round the end of the settle and saw father sprawled in a low chair close to the hearth. Between his knees and Jassy's was a small table bearing a chessboard and some of the pieces. On the other side of the hearth a similar table was drawn up, and on that stood a tray with a coffee-pot and cups, a decanter of port wine and one glass, and a plate with three biscuits left on it. Something told me that for once father had been imbibing more coffee than port wine. But as soon as I appeared round the end of the settle he reached over and filled the glass.

'Well,' said Jassy, 'did you enjoy yourself?'

'Pretty well,' I said, and made a little face at her, trying to tell her not to pursue the subject.

'We've been playing chess,' she said, instantly responsive. 'It was the only game we *both* knew. But Mr Helmar doesn't like a game that isn't a gamble, so I bet him he'd never take my Queen. He just did. And now I owe him five shillings. Wasn't it rash of me?'

'We'll call it even. You've made the only drinkable cup of coffee I've had for a long time. It's a pity you went to school. You'd have made somebody a good servant,' said Old Nick with one of his unaccountable offensive changes of mood. He stood up, knocking over the chessmen as he did so.

'At that price I'll make you coffee all day long,' Jassy said, without a sign of discomfiture. She stooped and picked up the pieces. And from a stooping position she looked up, smiling, 'Nevertheless, when I'm rich I'll remember that I'm much in your debt, Mr Helmar.' Looking up like that and smiling she was suddenly pretty. The light of candles seemed to catch and emphasize the glossiness of her hair, the long eyelashes. I wondered if Old Nick noticed, and glanced at him. He was turned to leave us, so that his face as he looked at her was sideways. And he was looking at her with a look I didn't like.

'Good night,' he said abruptly, and strode off towards the stairs. The next moment Moult, as though he had been watching and waiting, appeared and bolted the main door, and stood ready to put out the candles.

'Are you ready for bed, Dilys?' Jassy asked in an unusually clear, high voice. 'Or would you like a cup of coffee? I made it, you know. Your father says nobody in this house can make coffee fit to drink. It's still hot.' And she in her turn made a face at me.

'Yes, I would,' I said.

I sat down and Moult vanished.

'Why shouldn't you be considered ever?' Jassy demanded, turning to me, coffee-pot in hand as soon as the door of the kitchen passage had closed. 'If I were you I'd assert myself. Why should you be hurried off to bed just because your father has chosen to retire early? The servants are above themselves.' She handed me a cup of coffee. 'Actually it isn't very hot. But they sickened me. Tonight when I went to make it they all behaved as though I were stealing their birthrights. They need taking in hand.'

'I know,' I said. 'But you see, if I do it there's a row and *I* am blamed. You're different. And Jassy, there's something that I feel I must say in that connection.'

'I'm listening,' she said, dropping down on the hearth and locking her arms about her knees.

I dragged myself out of my dreams of Barney and tried to think of what I ought to say to Jassy. I ought to tell her that Old Nick was not to be trusted; that Melia was only one of a whole series of creatures who had ruled him for a moment; that he had a taste for young things; that the way she talked and looked almost invited his attentions.

And then it occurred to my slowly-moving brain that the best thing of all would be to get rid of her entirely. I did not want to be obliged to make excuses to her every time I went to meet Barney; nor did I want my return to be made in the middle of a domestic scene like tonight's, with Old Nick sober and capable of asking questions.

Also I felt tired. I did not want to concern myself with matters concerning Mortiboys and Old Nick and Jassy and the servants. Nor did I want a lukewarm cup of coffee, however cleverly made.

'It's nothing important,' I said, putting down the cup. 'And I'm tired, Jassy. Tired to death. Let's go to bed, we can talk in the morning.'

She looked at me oddly. 'All right, Dilys, I'll just put these away.' She packed the board and the chessmen, saying, 'They're nice,' once in a low voice as though to herself. Then she said:

'Now, for your soul's sake, ring that bell and when Moult comes tell him that you're going to bed and he may put out the candles.'

And I did as she said, because when she looked at me with those very clear grey eyes of hers I found it easier to comply than to thwart her. It had been the same years before, when she had asked me to lend her my history book.

But when we had said good night and she had gone to her room and the door of mine was closed, I was my own mistress again. And I decided that she must go. She must leave Mortiboys for everybody's sake. Her own, since I did not want her to follow Melia in the list of Old Nick's lights-of-love, and my own, since, with her gone, my affair with Barney would be easier, less supervised. And, curiously enough, for Old Nick's sake as well. Jassy would be less easily shuffled off than Melia and her predecessors. There was something about Jassy Woodroffe which was unfathomable. And suddenly, thinking about her . . . unwillingly, for I had willing thoughts only of Barney at that moment, I was reminded of a curious toy which I had once had years, oh years, ago. It was the shape of a woman in a bell-bottomed skirt, slightly obscene because the skirt belled out so much that the underclothes beneath it were visible. And no matter how hard you tried to stand her on her feet or lay her on her side, she always tipped over and stood on her head. That toy puzzled me for a long time, until somebody explained that there was a ball of lead inside the woman's skull. After that she ceased to fascinate me, and I had forgotten all about her until, lying wakeful, and thinking about Jassy, I was reminded of her. Jassy was like that. She had inside her an overwhelming balance. Only she always stood on her feet. You could do what you liked, you could not upset that inward, hidden balance. And it was half in mischief, half in trepidation, that I thought to myself in the darkness–what will she say, and do, when I tell her tomorrow that she had better leave Mortiboys?

The mischief had gone from the thought in the morning, and only the trepidation and a kind of pity remained. There was a sense of guilt, too. For, but for me, Jassy would have been safe and sound at school, petted by Miss Hamilton, and leisurely pursuing her own little secret schemes for moving on to a post of her own choosing after the Christmas holiday. I decided that I must make her some financial compensation, and was glad that, whatever else I lacked, I had plenty of money.

I chose my moment to speak when we were in the garden, searching amongst the autumnal wreckage for the last late-blooming flowers. The gardens at Mortiboys were in better shape than the house, for Old Nick took no interest in them, and probably never noticed that they were as trim and fertile as in the days before the tragedy. We had found, without much difficulty, a sheaf of blooms and coloured leaves, and having reached the end of a path, where a stone seat was placed near the high red wall in such a position that it caught every ray of sun and was sheltered from all but the west wind, we sat down.

I felt nervous, and I knew that directly I started to speak I should stammer badly. But at the back of my mind was the thought that tomorrow, tomorrow, only a few hours away, I was to meet Barney again; and that it would be impossible to pretend to Jassy that I was going again, so soon, to Ockley. That was my main thought; but attached to it, and in its way quite as potent, was the fear that if, making some excuse, I did get away, Jassy would again be alone with Old Nick, making quips and smiling in that damned innocent way and simply asking for trouble. I was *compelled* to speak. And finally, after a nervous clearing of the throat, I said:

'J-Jassy.'

She looked at me. 'Uhh?' she said, and then looked down again at the sheaf of flowers, pulling the stems into line, taking out a late rose and sniffing it. 'What's worrying you, Dilys?'

'You,' I said. 'I–I–this is a hateful thing to say, Jassy, but h-honestly I think it would be better if you d-didn't stay here.'

She laid the rose she had been sniffing carefully back on top of the sheaf.

'You needn't worry about that,' she said quite calmly. 'I said that you had only to tell me when you wanted me to go. When shall I? Tomorrow?'

I was quite dumb with astonishment. The least I had expected was a demand for some explanation.

'It–it isn't absolutely what *I* want, Jassy. I brought you here, and so far as

I am concerned you could stay for ever. B-but there's father.'

'I see. He's sick of me.'

I wondered, for a reeling moment, whether I might let that stand. It would be an easy way out. But, on the other hand, I was always so unlucky that the deception was bound to be exposed. Father would show surprise at her going or something. So I said:

'No. It's not that. I'm sorry, Jassy, it's my fault. I should have known that this was no place to bring you. What I'm frightened of is that father will find you attractive and make a nuisance of himself. Actually last night . . . I saw signs of it then. I . . . I don't feel comfortable about it.'

She looked at me. Her eyes were quite serious, and as clear as water, but her big mouth was curling at the ends.

'Bless your soul, Dilys? What a one you are to worry about nothing. I can handle him.'

And somehow I was immediately confirmed in my conviction that for her own sake she must go. Old Nick had, for three years, shown a marked preference for kitchen-maids, village girls, all young, comely and lowly bred. And there was, despite her cleverness, something of the kitchen-maid in Jassy. It came out when she said, 'I can handle him.' There was a coarseness about it, and about her voice as she said it. And behind, beyond that, there was a pitiable ignorance which made me feel very old and experienced. I knew how physically inferior a woman was, and I knew how her own senses will war against and weaken her in that preliminary encounter. Jassy was thinking, innocent little thing, that her wits and her nimbleness and her will could save her . . . against Old Nick, wine-flown and amorous!

All thought of my own affair, of Barney and our tryst tomorrow, had left me by this time. I really was, wholeheartedly, anxious to protect Jassy, who seemed so young, so vulnerable in her arrogance.

'You don't understand,' I said. 'You have only seen father on his best behaviour. I've been watching him for years. I really think you'd better go, Jassy. And you must let me give you some money. Because it was my fault you left school and will have two months to wait before the new term . . . and the post you spoke of.'

'Say *lend*,' she said, still in that easy composed way. 'And it needn't be much. Perhaps I could get a place before the end of the term. Then I'd only need my coach fare. Barney would give me a bed and something to eat for a little while, until I was settled.'

'Barney?' I said, astounded. And despite those hours in Saints' Spinney, despite the things we had said, despite the kisses, a feeling of quivering insecurity came over me, shaking every nerve in my body. I had a vision of Jassy flitting about that kitchen, with a crisp white apron emphasizing her neat waist. Everything that I had thought about the suitability of a match between Jassy and Barney rose again and hit me, this time painfully. A kind of inner wisdom began to work in me, too, an instinctive wisdom, and I knew that the more Barney and I assuaged our hunger for one another secretly, severing our ties from the world and ordinary things, the more attractive would be the sight of Jassy, open as the air, commonplace as bread, cooking at his fire, sitting at his table, making her place in his home.

'You couldn't do that, Jassy,' I said. And so rapid had my thoughts been that there seemed to have been no pause at all.

'Why not?'

'It–it wouldn't be seemly. What on earth would people say?'

'Rude things that wouldn't worry me a bit. Besides, don't you think Meggie is sufficient chaperon?'

'No. I'm sure it wouldn't do. It wouldn't do at all.'

Her voice was a little harder when she said, 'I've got to have a bed, haven't I? Barney is the only other person I know in the world. I'm not going back to school, if that's what you're suggesting. Nor to Mrs Partridge. She's Twizzy's friend. So if I leave Mortiboys I shall go to Green Farm. I've no choice.'

I tried to think of something, 'If you had some money, Jassy, you could . . .'

'I'd rather not borrow more than I must. Don't be ridiculous, Dilys. Barney is my friend, and he has a house with seven bedrooms. I could work on the farm for my keep.'

As she claimed Barney's friendship I thought, yes, there is a friendliness between them, and with that my head began to ache. The dull pain hit me with a great thud and my brain went dead. It was the old, familiar feeling of a light having gone out which I knew so well.

'You'd better stay at Mortiboys. But you'll have to be careful, Jassy. Try to keep out of Old Nick's way, especially when I'm not there. And don't be–well, perky with him. I think he likes it.'

For just a second I imagined that her queer little face wore a look of triumph. It was gone instantly, and my head was aching so badly that I could not think about it much. But when she twisted on the seat, so that she was facing me fully, her face was, not kind, she was never that, but smooth with a comfortable matter-of-factness.

'Dily, look. But for you, as you say, I should at least not be in search of a bed. It would suit me very well to stay here until Christmas. Suppose we make a bargain. You go your way and I'll go mine, with no questions and no vicarious responsibility. When you want my company you can ask for it; and if ever I want your protection I'll let you know. We're not children.' She stood up, with the sheaf of flowers in her arms. 'I'll put these in water and then I'm going out on Major, by myself. I've never done that yet.'

She gave me a smile, a perfunctory yet sweet rearranging of her features, nothing more, and moved with her own peculiar grace away along the path to the house. I was amazed at the way in which, without any categorical phrases, she had cut to the very centre of the problem. 'You go your way and I'll go mine.' What did she know? Or guess? And was it by deep craft or by simple sincerity that she had driven me into saying, 'You'd better stay at Mortiboys'? She was, of course, very clever at lessons; yes, and she was very guileful. But so long as her guile was working for me I had not troubled to estimate its depths and possibilities. One thing was certain: I had, by this morning's work, forfeited her friendship. That smile was proof of that. And my dead aching brain managed to remember that Jassy did not forgive easily. Mrs Partridge had fallen from her favour because she had criticized Miss Hamilton. Now I had given offence by an apparent breach of hospitality. Oh, God, what a muddle! And how my head ached and ached!

Then I remembered that significant phrase, 'No questions and no vicarious responsibility.' That meant that tomorrow night, when I went to meet Barney, I need give no explanation. Tomorrow night, Barney. And for the first time in my memory my brain relighted of its own accord. Usually I could only be cured by sleep, or by a merciful interlude of unconsciousness which people wrongly called fainting. But today I was healed by a thought. The pain went. I was mended. I sat for a little while enjoying the sunshine and thinking about Barney. And when at last I went back to the house and saw Jassy, mounted on Major, rounding the far corner of the house, I was able to smile and wave, signifying that our bargain was a good one. She could stay at Mortiboys, and we could each go her own way. And with an uprush of physical well-being I thought, and if Old Nick gets her it won't be my fault. I warned her; God knows anyone so clever ought to be able to look after herself.

I gave myself up, body and mind and soul, to Barney. Each time we parted we fixed a meeting for some time in the immediate future, and the days in between had no taste, no flavour, no sense in them. There was a poet named Marvell whose work we did not study at school, but Miss Hamilton once lent Jassy a book of his poems, and in one of them, which I read, though I don't suppose Miss Hamilton would have believed that I could understand it, was a phrase which I remembered:

But at my back I always hear
Time's wingèd chariot hurrying near.

That exactly described me. I knew that one day, any day, today, even, or tomorrow, something would happen which would drag Barney and me back into the world. Signs and portents were not wanting. The first time we really lay together and I gave up the virginity which I had protected from the stable-boy with my riding-crop, and from Charles with more subtle defences, Barney had been miserable and penitent and talked about marriage. And it was as though an icy hand had been laid on my breast where lately his warm one had wandered. I didn't want to marry Barney and have everyone talking and thinking what a bad match I had made. I didn't want to live at Green Farm and count pennies and learn, through sheer necessity, the business of housekeeping and butter-making and rearing calves and chickens. I wanted just what I had. Barney, and secrecy, a world of my own. So I said that there was no need to talk about that yet; wait until after Christmas.

Christmas leapt at us. There seemed no time at all between my saying 'Wait until after Christmas,' and the season itself. On Boxing Day, Jassy and I were asked to the Fennels', where there was a large, merry party, and Stephen flattered me by singling me out by his attention. We stayed overnight, and on the way home it began to snow. It snowed for three days and four nights; it lay to a depth of five feet in the open, and there were drifts deep enough to engulf a mounted man. We were isolated at Mortiboys, and father, who had planned a shooting party for the third day after Christmas, and who was, besides, unused to being cooped indoors, fell into such a surly temper that it was at the risk of one's life almost that one went near him. He even quarrelled with Melia. And although Jassy and I, crouched over the fire, listened to his bellowing and roaring, and then saw Melia, very red-cheeked and with her head held high, flaunting along the passage, we took little notice. They had had at least three violent rows since we had been home. It did go through my mind that Melia had lasted as long as any of his wenches, and that he was about due for a change, and I said:

'Now, I suppose, Agnes will take umbrage and we'll starve.'

'And deserve to,' Jassy said noncomittally. 'This is where you should step in and take advantage of the rupture and straighten things out in that kitchen.'

'And look a fool when they make it up again. Not me.'

'But you ought to get some practice. When you're married you'll need to be able to control your servants and run a house.'

'Time enough to think about that when it comes. Besides, I shall have a housekeeper. And I'd like to know what has put the idea of my marrying into your head?'

'Lady Fennel herself,' Jassy said, with a peculiar smile. 'Oh, not to me, of course, but I heard her talking to another woman. She seemed most enthusiastic about having you for a daughter-in-law.'

Despite myself I felt warmed and comforted. That short stay at Ockley had reminded me of what I was in danger of forgetting–how pleasant and orderly life can be in a house where people are normal and kind and sane. And I was touched to think that Lady Fennel did not hold it against me that my father was a mad, drunken old reprobate who slept with his maid servants. Oh, if only Stephen had one-tenth of Barney's attractiveness! Oh, if only Barney had been heir to Ockley Manor! I sighed and crouched nearer to the fire, thinking how ill life was arranged.

The third day after Christmas seemed interminable and dull. Yet two momentous things had happened already. For father's quarrel with Melia bore immediate results; and later on, looking back, I realized that Jassy's few careless words about Lady Fennel had fallen into my mind like a pebble falling into a pool, quietly, but starting a ripple which will widen. For on that afternoon I felt for the first time that one day, when I was older and Barney had tired of me, or I of him, it would be nice to marry Stephen. It was as though, running wild in the woods, I had heard, from the open window of a house, a voice calling to me to come in, and tidy myself and behave like other people. I was not ready to do so, yet. But it was pleasant to know that I should be welcome within the circle when I chose to mend my ways.

The meal that evening was, as I had predicted, horrible. Old Nick, who had not been quite sober all day, began to curse as soon as the food was put before him. He cursed Moult and Agnes, the food itself, and then, looking along the table in a manner that reminded me of a bull about to charge, he shouted, 'And you. Both of you. Damned parasites, like all women; sitting about on your backsides all day. One of you could have seen that there was something fit to eat.' Beginning like that he worked himself into a fine fury, ending by telling me that I was just like my mother, without a thought beyond my own silly face, and then rounding on Jassy, who, he said, was a greedy harpy who made no return for her keep. Moult had retired to a little distance from the table, and stood there with an injured expression of self-righteousness on his face. And despite the feeling of sickness which attacked me, as it always did during father's rages, it was with some amusement that I saw the heavy silver dish cover suddenly hurtle through the air and strike Moult plumb in the stomach.

'Don't stand there grinning like an ape, you ——,' father bellowed. 'Clear this muck and bring some bread and cheese. And tell that fat —— in the kitchen that she's sacked. They're all sacked.' He lifted the whole dish, and it was about to follow its cover through the air when Jassy sprang up and snatched it.

'I'll see what can be done with it,' she said, and tripped away.

Father dropped back in his chair, breathing loudly, his face a dusky red. He was never ashamed after one of his fits of temper, for shame after an outburst or a breakdown is only possible when one is conscious of criticism, either from within or without. Father did not care a sweep's curse for anything that Moult of Jassy or I might be thinking, and his faculties for self-criticism had withered long ago.

'Bring me a bottle,' he said to Moult, as he was slinking out in Jassy's wake, and when it was brought he emptied three glasses in rapid succession, and then loosened his neck-cloth.

'When's that little bitch going?' he asked, no more pleasantly, but with a faint rebirth of reasonableness.

'On the t-tenth,' I said, moistening my dry lips. I thought to myself that Jassy had almost too sedulously obeyed my instructions to be careful. Now he had turned against her. He had never before seemed to resent her presence, or shouted at her personally, or called her names. Probably in his dark confused mind he missed the smiles and little good-humoured retorts which Jassy had used towards him before I warned her. Though, of course, with him, you could never tell. He wasn't reasonable; and for women he seemed to have no feelings except lust and loathing, nothing in between, and even those two were very much mixed.

'She's worth a dozen of you any day.'

'Yes,' I said. There was some truth in the remark, and had there been none I should not have dared to contradict him.

'Don't be mealy-mouthed about it. That's your mother all over again. Sweet, sweet and rotten. Yes and no. Mealy-mouthed. Sweet as honey and full of poison. Are you listening?'

I put both hands on the edge of the table and pulled myself out of my chair.

'I–I–must go, father.'

'Sick? You look it. Go on then. Get out.'

I made for the door, tore it open, slammed it behind me and leaned back against it. Once out of that odious presence I felt better. It was only my nerves that loathed him. The day was long since past when anything he said could really hurt me. There had been a time when a scene like this evening's would have made me cry for hours from misery and bewilderment. But now my mind was calloused. I was afraid of him, as one may be afraid of a mad wild animal, but as soon as there was a stout door between us the fear was gone, and so had that feeling of quivering nausea. In fact, standing there with my back pressed to the panels of the door I thought what a fool I was, now I had missed my meal. Why hadn't I had control enough to sit still and let him say what he liked, throw things at me if he had a fancy to, but not let myself be driven from the table?

As I thought this the door that led to the kitchen quarters opened, and there came through it, first, a very savoury and appetizing scent, then Moult, bearing a large tray, piled with dishes, and then Jassy, empty-handed, fastidiously wiping her fingers on her handkerchief.

She looked at me without surprise and asked gaily:

'Stood out?' 'Standing out,' as we called it, was a punishment at school, and the idea that Old Nick had said, 'Stand out for twenty minutes,' was slightly amusing. I smiled as I stood aside to let Moult enter.

'No. I was silly. I began to feel sick and just ran away. I wish now I hadn't. Something smells good. What is it? You haven't had time to cook anything.'

'I didn't need to. Come and look what I've *found*.'

Before I had time to protest that I couldn't go back into Old Nick's company she had taken me by the elbow and whisked me into the room. Moult had set the tray on the side table and was standing, dubious and a little scared, looking at father, who sat where I had left him, staring down at the cloth upon which he was tracing patterns with his fork.

'I'll see to it,' said Jassy, dismissing Moult with a jerk of her head towards the door. Then she laughed and, taking up the largest dish, set it under father's nose and lifted the cover.

'Does that make you feel better, Mr Helmar? It should be good. It's your servants' supper.'

'Good God!' said father, looking into the dish, where, neatly skewered and perfectly roasted, four plump partridges reposed upon a bed of bacon curls and squares of toast. He stared at the dish for a moment, and then, in a voice of ordinary anger, subtly and yet unmistakably different from the kind of perverse animal rage to which we were accustomed, he said, 'This is insufferable. I'll go into that kitchen and I'll . . .' He began to raise himself on the arms of his chair.

'No, no,' Jassy cried. 'Eat it while it's hot. Everything else can wait.'

She darted about, bringing dishes of vegetables, and gravy, serving us all with neat despatch, and at the same time relating, with comic gestures and amusing touches of mimicry, the horror of Moult and Agnes and Melia and Janey at seeing their supper snatched from under their noses. Father, with his fill of wine in him, and his fill of food going down as fast as he could shovel it, changed his mood, forgot his grievance against us and deigned to laugh at last. Finally, when Jassy removed his empty plate, he looked down at the patterns he had been drawing on the cloth and said, 'That reminds me. I have a proposal to make to you, young woman.'

'Are you going to make an honest cook of me at last?' Jassy said, laughing. He stared at her, astonished.

'That's just it,' he said slowly. 'If you'll give up this tomfool job you're going to, and undertake to run this place so that a man may have a modicum of comfort, I'll pay you whatever you ask, and give you a better home than you'd have in any school.'

Jassy set her chin on her hand and looked at him, pursing her mouth. She looked astonishingly like a monkey at that moment.

'That's a nice offer, Mr Helmar. But I'd have to make lots of conditions.'

'Let's hear them.'

'A completely free hand for one thing. And the sack for everybody except Janey. Then, let me see, when I leave, if you send me away that is, I want fifty pounds. You see, I have a job to go to on the tenth. But if you fall out with me it might happen to be mid-term, and I should need money in the interval. Is that fair? And the job I was going to meant my keep and six pounds a term. Is that too much?'

'No. I think I can stand that. Anything else?'

'I can't think of anything at the moment. Yes, I'd want that fifty pounds deposited with a third person. Sir Edward Follesmark would do.'

'You don't trust me?'

'I trust you so far.' She put both her hands in her lap and leaned forward and said what I wouldn't have dared say for a thousand pounds: 'I've got to think of myself, Mr Helmar. At any moment you may find another Melia, and under her influence you might not be fair to me. I'm sorry, I don't want to justify your accusations about being a harpy or a parasite, and if you employ me I shall give you value for your money. But,' and her eyes just flickered in my direction and returned to rest, cool and calm, on his congested face, 'just recently I've been threated with the prospect of having no bed for the night. That's not going to happen again if I can avoid it.'

'And by God you're right!' He looked at her as though he had never seen her before. She smiled at him in a friendly ordinary fashion. It was like seeing a baby being friendly to a great savage dog. 'All right, it's a bargain. And as a token, here's a term's money in advance.'

He threw his great gross body back in the chair and began to fumble in his breeches' pocket. He drew out, not without difficulty, for his pocket was tight against his fat thigh and his hand was podgy, five guinea pieces, two five shillings, two florins and a shilling. He made a pile of them and pushed them across the cloth.

'That wasn't in the bond,' said Jassy, 'but it's very acceptable.' She took up the coins and dropped them into her pocket, all save one five shilling piece. She took that between her finger and thumb and held it over his hand.

'That chess game,' she said, with one of her sweetest smiles. 'Debts of honour must be paid. Please forgive the delay.'

Old Nick opened his hand slowly and took the coin. When it lay in his big red palm he looked at it for several seconds before putting it in his pocket.

'And now,' Jassy said, jumping to her feet. 'I'll go and make some coffee. New brooms, you know.'

Next day the snow thawed and the wind began to blow. On New Year's Day Jassy and I rode into Minsham All Saints to visit a family called Wicks whom Jassy remembered, and which might be expected to provide fresh labour for the Mortiboys kitchen. And when the errand was completed we called at Green Farm, and in the restraining presence of a third person I met Barney again for the first time since before Christmas. There was subtle excitement in meeting a lover so. And Jassy told him all about what she called her new job, giving a vivid and very animated account of the evening when she had stolen the servants' supper.

While she was telling it I sat quite still and quiet, feasting my eyes on Barney and thinking now that the snow had gone we could renew our sweet, stolen meetings. It was like being dropped out of a warm, soft bed into a pool of icy water to hear him saying:

'Look, I don't want to offend either of you, but if it isn't too late for you to take that other job, Jassy, I think you ought to change your mind. I can't help hearing gossip, and if *half* of what I hear is true, the less you have to do with the master of Mortiboys the better. Dilys, do forgive me, but you know as well as I do, that in staying there, in any capacity, Jassy puts herself in–well, a dubious position, to say the least. There's nobody else to say it, so I must.'

He threw a glance of apology at me, and then looked at her with an expression that was oddly protective, almost fraternal.

'I think Jassy knows what she has undertaken. If she doesn't it isn't for lack of warning,' I said. 'And I'm there, remember.'

'But you won't be for long. Darling, I think we might as well tell Jassy.

The first person we've told. Jassy, before you commit yourself to staying at Mortiboys you ought to know that Dilys won't be there much longer. She's going to marry me.'

My first feeling was of furious anger. 'Barney,' I cried, 'I never said–I never. You're—' I was, literally, at a loss for words. And then, as I turned my eyes from side to side, trying to fix upon something which would give me firmness and lucidity, and to frame some kind of sentence of shelter . . . for I felt as though I had been suddenly dragged into the open stark naked, I saw Jassy's face.

I can't describe it, save in a series of negatives. It hadn't turned white; it hadn't altered in any way I could specify; and yet something had happened to it. You can see the same thing if you look at a building, or a scene, in bright sunshine, and then again in, say, the strange light that precedes a thunderstorm. Nothing in the scene or the building has changed . . . and yet no one could deny that there is a difference. It was like that. I knew, with a certainty beyond any shaking, that the news meant something more to her than the mere fact that it conveyed. But that stupendous self-control of hers did not desert her. She rose from the chair and came and kissed me, a mere fleeting brush of her lashes on my cheek.

She said, 'I'm surprised, of course. I didn't know you knew one another well enough. But I hope you'll both be very happy.'

I felt like a fool. But I had recovered enough self-possession to say, with what I hoped was dignity, 'Really, Barney, you shouldn't have said that. Even if we do get married, ever, it won't be for ages.' I turned to Jassy and said, 'For heaven's sake don't tell anyone.'

'You said leave it until after Christmas,' Barney said stubbornly. 'It's that now. And mewed up here for four days I've been thinking. We couldn't go on as we were, Dilys.' He came over and laid his hand on my shoulder. And I knew, in that instant, how closely love and hatred lie together in the human mind. The touch of his hand, after what seemed a long absence, sent the familiar wild thrill through my body; but this time it was mingled and adulterated by the desire to hurt him. But for Jassy's presence I should have slapped him across the face.

I looked round the low, heavily-beamed parlour, where the unsuitable furniture seemed to be ducking to avoid contact with the ceiling; I thought of the kitchen and the farmyard outside. Mrs Hatton, the farmer's wife. Absurd, grotesque!

Jassy rose from her chair and, drawing her gloves through her fingers, said, 'There's a receipt I want from Meggie. I'll just go and ask her for it.'

Still with a hand on my shoulder, Barney stretched his other arm and took her by the elbow as she passed us. 'Jassy, after what I've told you, you will change your mind about staying at Mortiboys, won't you?'

'Why should I?' she said, looking at him with cold, clear eyes. 'I wasn't counting on Dilys' company for long. Only I thought she was going to marry Stephen Fennel, not you. It's nice of you to worry about me, Barney, but it's quite wasted. Mr Helmar and I understand each other.'

She shrugged herself free of his hand and went out of the room.

'There, you see,' I said, 'you've done no good, and you've put us in a completely false position.'

He dropped his hand–and something in my inside dropped with it.

'Why false?' he asked, rather ominously.

'Well,' I said, with the feeling that I was being forced slowly and inexorably towards the edge of a precipice, 'for one thing, I never said I'd marry you. You never even asked me properly. And if you had, and if I'd said I would, I wouldn't want anyone to know for a long time. It makes it all so public. It spoils it so.'

'Look,' he said, and putting a hand behind him he dragged up a chair and sat down so that his knees touched mine; then he took both my hands and held them, palm uppermost, in his, 'I'm sorry if I annoyed you by blurting it out just now. And I'm sorry that you don't think I've asked you properly. I didn't know that you were a stickler for ceremony. But I'm asking you now. Dilys, will you marry me, just as soon as possible? I haven't a great deal to offer you, but I'm doing very well and I can give you a comfortable home. You know I love you; you've given me reason to think that you love me. There's no reason for waiting that I can see. Well, darling . . .?'

I said, 'Barney, why must it be marriage? Why can't we go on as we are? I do love you. This last week when I haven't seen you has seemed endless, I haven't really been alive. But I don't want to be *married.* It'd spoil everything. I can't explain it. I just know it would. It may be very queer of me, but I don't want my love all muddled up with a row with father, and my trying to keep house, and people talking and you seeing me in the morning before I've done my hair.' I was almost crying, Barney said gently:

'You're over-romantic, darling. You can't live your whole life in Saints' Spinney, you know. And you needn't take the whole burden on yourself. I'll see your father, and Meggie will keep house, and if it's any comfort to you I'll promise not to look at you until your hair is done–though I'm sure you look lovely with it tangled. Come on, say you'll marry me, and that's all you need do.'

'I can't,' I said, crying outright now, for my head had started to ache.

He pushed back his chair and stood up. Going to the window he said in a curious low voice, 'Tell me one thing, Dilys. Is the whole idea of marriage distasteful to you, or is it that you don't want to marry me? Is it that you love me, up to a point, but think that I am ineligible as a husband? You must forgive the bluntness of that, but I've wondered often, and it's a thing I must know.'

It was so exact a summing-up of the situation that I had a crazy impulse to cry, yes, that's just it.

It would have been such a relief to say, with utter frankness, yes, that's just it, Barney; I love you, quite madly, and I know I shall never love anyone else in the same way, but I can't face living here and being a farmer's wife.

But suppose I said it, what would be the price of such relief, such frankness? Barney would be, quite rightly, disgusted, and he would refuse, justifiably, ever to have anything to do with me again. There would be no more meetings in Saints' Spinney.

So I said–and I was so conscious of my falseness that my voice seemed to ring like a base coin–'It isn't that, Barney. That's a horrid thing to suspect. It's just that having you, like this, with no one knowing or being angry or making a fuss about it is the nicest thing I've ever known. I don't want to spoil it. It's like having something precious that I don't want people pawing over with their filthy hands. I haven't had much happiness, Barney.'

The last sentence, at least, rang out genuinely, with a break of self-pity in it. He turned to me, instantly responsive, with his 'You poor little thing' expression on his face. But then he checked himself deliberately, and the scowl and the lines in his cheeks were darker and deeper than ever as he demanded:

'Then what did she mean by saying she thought you were going to marry Stephen Fennel?'

I saw danger in that question, and for once I was inspired, not paralysed, by it.

'Jassy has an inflated opinion of my attractiveness–probably because she isn't very pretty herself. If any man pays me the slightest attention, even picks up my handkerchief, she imagines that he is in love with me. And Stephen is very mannered nowadays. He is the same with every woman he meets.'

'There wasn't any reason why she should say it then?'

'No reason at all,' I said, with the confidence of half-truth. 'Honestly, Barney, if Stephen came into this room at this minute and begged me on his bended knees to marry him tomorrow I'd laugh in his face.'

And that was strictly true. The idea of marrying Stephen one day might be couched in my mind, dark, hidden, like a germinating seed, but I was going to have Barney again and again before that day came: Barney in Saints' Spinney, in the heart of the night, in our secret place under the trees; Barney on Thursdays sometimes in that low, dim, over-furnished bedroom just over our heads. Again and again. So that when, replete at last, I married Stephen, or anybody else, I should not expect from him what he had no power to give, that starry delight, that rounded completeness. No one but Barney had that in his gift.

I stood up and went over to him where he still stood, a little dubious, a little reluctant.

'Let's go on as we are for a while, darling. There'll be years and years to think about settling down. This only comes once.'

'Easter, then?' he asked, holding me at arm's length, but with the old look coming back into his face. 'You'll marry me at Easter?'

'Maybe,' I said. 'Only let's not talk about it any more for a long time. You've made my head ache dreadfully. There are so many things worrying me, Barney. Don't you be a worry, too.'

He gave me a slight shake.

'If only you'd stop being such a little ninny and marry me right away, all your worries would be over.' But I said, 'Now, Barney . . .' and the shake ended in a breathless embrace. I gasped, 'Thursday, Barney? Come for me on Thursday.' Too far ahead, too long to wait; but the woods would still be damp from the snow.

'And now I must find Jassy,' I said, pulling myself free.

She was in the kitchen, scribbling away with a frantic squeaking quill on a scrap of packing paper. Meggie, with a more contented expression on her face than I had ever seen there, leaned back in her chair, dictating in a lordly fashion, some highly complicated directions.

'Now just one more, Meggie, if you don't mind. Once–on Good Friday it was, I remember–you made a sharp sauce for the boiled fish. Tell me that one and I won't bother you any more.'

'Well,' said Meggie, 'you take some butter. No, thass no use asking me *how* much. I told you that afore. That depends how many you're making for. Say a bit the size of a wallnut for each pusson. And you melt it and take some best flour and you mix it . . .' The dictation rambled on. IN the middle of it I looked at Barney. He was contemplating Jassy's bent head and scribbling hand with a peculiar expression in which tolerance and kindness and–yes–a kind of admiration were oddly mingled. Suddenly, as though she were conscious of it, she looked up at him, held his eyes for half a second, and then stared down at her paper as though she had seen something distasteful.

'Well, thank you very much, Meggie. I shall be everlastingly in your debt,' she said brightly, jumping up and waving the paper to dry the ink.

'You're kindly welcome,' said Meggie, in a voice quite unlike the one she usually used towards Jassy. 'And anything else you wanta know, you only gotta ask.'

We mounted and rode in silence through the village. The silence was beginning to become oppressive, and I was thinking for a word to break it when Jassy said abruptly:

'When are you being married, Dilys?'

'Not for ages.'

'But it's settled?'

'You heard what Barney said?'

'Yes. I heard.' There was another silence. Then she said, 'I don't suppose I ought to say this, Dilys. But everybody is so eager to give me good advice, I think I'll pass a little on. If I were you I would ask Barney one question before I married him. I'd say, "Are you in love with me or with Mortiboys?" Just that.'

I said, 'Please, Jassy, don't give me anything else to puzzle about. I've got a dreadful headache. Just tell me as plainly as you can, why I should ask that stupid question. What has Mortiboys to do with Barney and me?'

'Isn't it obvious? Mortiboys will be yours one day. And I happen to know that Barney is crazy about the place. I just thought that you ought to make sure. That's all.'

I was furious. The idea that Barney had chosen me because of Mortiboys!

'Barney is in love with me.' I said. 'He knows that I hate Mortiboys, and once I'm married nothing will ever get me back there. If I inherit it, as I suppose I shall, though I've never thought about it, I shall sell it at once. I loathe the place.'

'So long as Barney knows that,' she said.

'He knows,' I said. 'And for all that he's crazy to marry me at Easter.'

'You said ages.'

'Well, Easter is ages, when you're in love.' But some part of me wasn't there, wasn't engaged in taunting Jassy. It was thinking–well, of course, since you don't intend to marry Barney, the question doesn't affect you much, but is there a grain of truth in that notion? Is that why Barney is so set on *marriage*? I knew really, with my blood and my nerves I knew it, that when Barney and I were together the fact that one day Mortiboys would be mine meant nothing. Yet, at the same time, the idea sank deeply into my mind and lay there, side by side with the idea that Lady Fennel would welcome me as her daughter-in-law. Grains of mustard seed both of them compared with my passion for Barney, but both capable of bearing fruit.

'Besides,' I said inconsequently. 'Old Nick might easily marry again.'

'Yes, of course,' said Jassy. She set Major to a sharp canter which put an end to the conversation.

That night I had a nightmare. I had been prone to them as a child, and I think they accounted, in part at least, for my horror of the darkness. They had grown less and less frequent in the last few years, and I had hoped that I had outgrown them. But on this night, having gone to bed with a headache and put my head thankfully on my pillow, and counted, as I always did, the hours until I should see Barney again, I fell asleep and then seemed to wake suddenly when my door opened and let in a sharp cold draught. I was dreaming, of course, but I seemed to sit up in bed, a little frightened, and to look towards the door. A faint grey light filled the room, and by it I could see, near the door which was now shut, though the draught continued, a shapeless figure, rather tall, which was slowly approaching my bed. In a moment, during which terror mounted and I tried to call out but was–as one is in nightmares–voiceless, I could see that my visitor was a woman, muffled in grave-clothes and with a kind of scarf round her head which was nothing but a skull; yet there was a sparkle of jewels from the place where her ears should have been. That was specially horrible. She came close to the bed and said, in a low very mournful voice, 'Mrs Hatton. Mrs Hat-ton.' I knew that she was not naming me Mrs Hatton, but was announcing herself, Barney's mother. The sharp draught came nearer as she moved forward. It came from her in some way. She said: 'I lived here, and I lived there. But you don't love him. You don't love him.' She spoke the last words in a fierce, denunciatory tone and stretched out her fleshless hand very, very slowly. I knew that she was going to touch me, to shake me, as Barney had done that morning. And I knew that if she did touch me I should die. I tried to move away from her, and I tried, tried repeatedly, to scream. And at last I succeeded. Out of the soundless mouthings I heard at last the faint semblance of a word–Jassy. And I kept on screaming and screaming Jassy, Jassy, Jassy, until there was Jassy, solid and real, with a candle in one hand and her other hand on my shoulder, shaking me.

'Oh, thank you,' I gasped. 'I was dreaming. A dreadful, dreadful dream.'

'You were making a dreadful noise,' she said shakily, and I could see the candle spilling grease from the unsteadiness of her hand. 'You frightened me.'

'I'm sorry,' I said. 'I'm really sorry, Jassy. But I couldn't help it. I was having the most *terrible* dream.' I pushed back my bedclothes. 'Get in, Jassy, you're shuddering. Stay the rest of the night with me.'

'No,' she said, rather curtly. 'You're all right now. Look, I'll light your candle. And you know I'm within call.'

'Oh, do stay,' I begged her, humble in my terror lest the dream might come again.

'Give me a blanket then, and I'll sit in a chair.'

'You'd be more comfortable in bed. There's plenty of room.'

Without answering, she pulled one of my blankets free, wrapped herself in it and sat down on my low chair, putting the candle beside her.

'You won't sleep,' I said.

'I shall be all right,' she said impatiently, and blew out the candle.

'Are you angry with me?'

'Angry? No.'

'Then why won't you come in the bed?'

'Because I prefer not to. If you keep on about it I shall go away.'

'I'm sorry,' I said, and was silent for a few minutes until I thought of something.

'Jassy,' I said quietly. 'Did you know Barney's mother?'

'Of course I did.'

'Did she wear ear-rings?'

'What are you talking about?'

'Did she?'

'Yes. Always. I never saw her without them. Even in the dairy. Why do you ask that?'

'She was in my dream.'

'Oh! Begging you to be a good wife to her son?' There was a dreadful gibing bitterness about the question. It made me wonder. Presently, when it was too late to say anything, I realized that I had left the question unanswered.

The weather that year was kind to lovers. January was so mild that when, towards its end, there was a second brief fall of snow, the white patches, as they melted in the shrubberies, merely gave way to other whiteness, stretches of snowdrops, frail and secret under the glossy leaves of the evergreens. Winter and spring meeting and for the moment indistinguishable. After the thaw it was mild again, and very early in February the birds were mating with shrill sweet cries and sustained volleys of song in the first morning light. The evening skies had those colours of apple green and daffodil which hold, as no words can do, the whole essence of the spring.

I shall remember it always. Old, old and hackneyed, that theme of love and springtime, feeling the lover's kiss in the pale sun, seeing the lover's smile in the first green tip of the lilac buds, sharing that full-throated burst of bird song, being near the heart-beats of the urgent earth. Here and now, my love, so little time, more and more.

There was a life, of course, apart from Barney, away from Saints' Spinney. There was Mortiboys, swept and garnished, full of new servants and good fires and succulent food. There was Jassy, very busy in her quiet way, a little withdrawn and preoccupied. There was father, rather like a surly old bull whose stall has been cleaned and hung with posies, full of an almost perverse determination that the 'modicum of comfort' which he had demanded, and obtained, should not fundamentally sweeten his temper. To Jassy–as was only her due, who had made a home, as it were, in a shambles–Old Nick preserved, though at times with an obvious effort, a scrupulous politeness; but to make up for it he attacked me more frequently and more savagely than ever. And then there was Stephen, coming more and more often, driving me (alone now, for Jassy declared that she was too busy for frivolity) over to Ockley on visits which I would gladly have prolonged but for the fact that when I was there I must do without Barney, driving me down to Bywater, into Colchester for a day's shopping, and to Baildon to a concert at the Assembly Rooms. As Stephen grew more attentive I began to dread the moment when he would ask me to marry him. I was certain of its imminence, and often whiled away an idle hour wondering what I should say. And I always ended my meditations with the renewed certainty that I was a fool. Once more I had let my feelings get the better of my sense. There wasn't a girl in four counties who wouldn't have been glad to marry Stephen, who would, in course of time, inherit Ockley, which was beautiful, an estate in superb order, plenty of money, and a title. And yet, whenever I thought about him I ended with a hunger for Barney and a firm determination to play for time. If only they would both be patient all would be well. I knew, I had known from the first, that my passion for Barney was a form of madness from which, one day, I should recover. And how awful it would be if, in my madness, I committed myself irrevocably, and regained my senses only to find that I was Mrs Hatton, chained to Green Farm, finished, done. How madly then, from amongst my chickens and calves and butter-pans, should I envy Stephen's wife. Whereas, given time, and a little luck, I might regain my senses and find myself safe at Ockley, and although I should always be interested in Mrs Barney Hatton of Green Farm, I should not envy her at all, for even her love would be, and I should know it, second-hand. If only both Barney and Stephen would have patience.

Stephen was not particularly menacing. He looked at me with eyes like a spaniel's, and he was as manageable as one. I was, as most girls are at that moment, master of the situation. I could have made him propose at any moment, and I could, with little more difficulty, fend him off for a time. But Barney was different. He had enjoyed a husband's rights–and after that things were never quite the same again. In the ultimate act of love man achieves a moment of mastery which has a lasting effect. He may love the girl as much, he may treat her with careful respect, but a certain awe is gone. He is no longer so easily handled.

About six weeks before Easter–which was late that year–Barney re-opened the subject of our marriage. He did it with crafty kindness, saying that there were some alterations and improvements which must be made at Green Farm, and since the busy season was approaching, they must be begun at once.

'So, darling, though I promised not to mention the matter again until Easter, I'm driven to do so. You must say definitely now. Otherwise you might have to come into the place as it is.'

'I said I'd tell you at Easter,' I parried. 'I might say then that I agreed to marry you, but I might not do it until next year.'

We were sitting at that moment on the trunk of a fallen tree in the very heart of the Spinney, and there were masses of primroses spread out like moonlight under the trees. Barney began to uproot a nearby plant with his toe.

'Dilys,' he said, after a moment or two, withdrawing his foot and twisting round so that he faced me, 'something that I don't like comes over you whenever I mention the future–not just marriage, but anything ahead. You alter, you become a different person. Even your face changes.'

'I know,' I said. And I thought–he is truly in love with me; no one who wasn't would be so observant. And a bit of my mind ran off on down the road to the future, thinking how difficult, in fact impossible, it would be to deceive Barney finally. He would always know, for instance, how much I disliked the farm.

'I am different,' I went on. 'When we're here, ordinarily, I'm happy and free, but as soon as you begin to talk about the future everything is spoiled. I'm unhappy and bothered.'

He said, quite roughly, 'To hell with this whine about everything being spoiled. You say that incessantly. What's spoiled by a decent suggestion of marriage? Surely to God you must see that we can't go on for ever slinking about this wood, or just having the house to ourselves on Thursdays. We're in love, we're both free. Isn't it the natural thing to get married as soon as we can?'

'Perhaps I'm not natural.'

'What do you mean?'

'Well–I doubt whether, if you'd taken up with a nice natural girl, she'd have met you here more than once. I think most natural girls would have been shocked the first time you kissed them, Barney, and that's a fact.'

'God knows that may be true,' he said in rather an astonished voice. 'But Dilys, my love, don't hold that against me. I'd been in love with you since I was fifteen. I was mad for you and–let's be honest about this–you didn't mind *then*. And whatever I've done, however I've behaved, you might remember that before we went from here that night I'd spoken about marriage. Hadn't I? Hadn't I?' he repeated, as I did not answer immediately.

'Yes,' I said. 'And with slight pauses you've kept on about it ever since.'

'Without getting a proper answer,' he said. 'And I'm going to have one tonight, Dilys. I've done playing. Are you going to marry me at Easter or not?'

'No,' I said. 'It's too soon.' There, I thought, that'll teach you not to rush me into decisions.

'You're not in love with me any more.' And that was true. At that moment I hated him, just as I had hated him in the parlour at the farm when he had told Jassy that we were going to be married. And I knew, quite certainly, that if, by any fantastic chance, I did marry him, I should hate him instantly and for always.

'It isn't that, Barney. That's a stupid thing to say. Weren't we just now . . . didn't you *know* then? But whenever I try to explain how I feel about things you get angry and shout. I'm just not ready to be married.'

He waited for a moment and then said, deliberately and offensively:

'You're ripe for it, anyway. God knows what you'd have taken up with if I hadn't been handy. A stable-boy, I should think. You're blushing. I'm right then.' He swallowed so hard that I heard the movement of his throat. 'I've known it all along, really. Ever since that first night. You've been playing for time. You've used me just as fine young gentlemen use dairy maids, to ease your itch until you can find somebody fit to marry. It's a pity I'm not your friend Stephen Fennel, isn't it? By God, Dilys, I've loved you for seven years, and I'm ashamed of myself for doing it. You're nothing but a whore.' And it was all so true. Every word of it was true. Yet I did love him. In a way. Love has so many ways.

'I could make you take that all back and regret having said it, couldn't I?' I asked. 'If I said I'd marry you at Easter you'd be ashamed. But I'm not going to take advantage of you. I'm going home.'

'Very well,' he said. 'And you'll go alone.'

'I mean to,' I said, and glanced round, estimating the quality of the darkness. 'Good-bye, Barney.'

He strode off without replying. And I knew that he was hurt in his most sensitive part, and that it was the same as mine. I could not bear the thought of being a farm-wife; and Barney could not bear the thought that he was socially ineligible. Oh, how clear my damned mind could be at times! But that realization forged another link. For once I was in sympathy with him.

And at the end of a fortnight, five days of which I spent at Ockley in Stephen's constant company, and the whole of which I spent in turning the matter over and over in my mind, I rode over to Green Farm and found Barney working in a field. And I said, 'I'll marry you at Easter.'

I meant it then. If there is, as they tell us, an All-Knowing, All-Seeing God who can assess our motives and weigh our desires, He knows that at that moment I was sincere and genuine. I had had a fortnight without Barney and five days with Stephen, and I was in a position to judge between them. And at the Day of Judgment, if it ever comes, God may remember that morning, as I rode back, leaving Barney dazed and happy in the field. I halted Gyp in the farmyard and looked round and was penitent because I had ever thought deprecatingly of it. I looked at the low house, with the windows so near the eaves; I looked at the pigsty and the cobbles and the pump and accepted them all. They were Barney's background, and they should be mine. If happiness could only come to me through humility I would be humble.

Perhaps that was the last flash of sanity I ever had.

I rode back to Mortiboys. I was determined that I would tell Jassy at once. And I would ask her to be present when I told Old Nick. Then I would write to Stephen and also to Lady Fennel, who had been very, very kind and motherly to me during my stay at Ockley. The worst would be over then.

My head began to ache as I rode home. It began a little differently, not with a sudden thud and onslaught of pain at the back of my neck, but gently, so imperceptibly in fact that I hoped, by riding slowly and breathing deeply of the fresh spring air, to avoid the full force of it. It was still aching, but not badly, when I handed Gyp to Sharples and went into the house, inquiring of Janey Jassy's whereabouts. I found her in a disused bedroom into which, over a period of weeks, she had been gathering all the linen in the house. The great bed, every chair, every chest now bore a neat pile, and there were others on the floor. In the middle of the room stood a chair and a table. Jassy sat on the chair and the table bore a variety of needles and threads, patches already cut, and bolts of tape. She was mending a pillowcase.

I went and sat on the window-seat.

'Jassy,' I said, 'I've just seen Barney and I have promised to marry him at Easter.'

'So you have made up your mind?' she said. 'Am I supposed to be surprised?'

'Well, I am a little myself, to tell you the truth.'

'Why? You're in love with him, aren't you?'

'Yes.'

'And he is with you. So that's all right. As I told you on New Year's Day, I hope you'll be very happy.'

And I thought, it's a funny thing, but I can't talk to you any more. Once I could. Look at the things I told you about Charles. What's happened? We aren't friends any more. Why? And the back of my skull gave a jab as I remembered that the change had come on that very New Year's morning. No, it hadn't, I argued with myself, it was before that; it was on the day when I told Jassy that she should leave Mortiboys. She hadn't *liked* me since then; but she hadn't shown it until after New Year. I remembered that night when I dreamed of Barney's mother. Jassy had hated me then. But I had been so entranced in my own dream that I hadn't noticed. What else had I missed?

'I wanted you to be the first to know. And I wanted to ask you, Jassy, whether you'd be with me when I tell father. You know how he is with me. This will probably give him a great opportunity for shouting at me. I'd like you to be there.'

'I'll break it to him if you like,' she said, but not kindly, scornfully.

I answered the scorn. 'No. Thank you, Jassy, it was a kind offer. But I'll do it myself, if you'll just be there so that he doesn't rage too much.'

'This evening?'

'Please. I think I shall lie down for a little while. My head is nagging but I may stave it off.'

I lay down for over an hour, I sniffed my smelling bottle, I bathed my brow and my neck with vinegar, but my headache grew steadily worse. I got up, intending to write my letter to Stephen, but when I sat down before the paper I couldn't write at all. It was just like being faced with one of Miss Hamilton's tests. Now, as then, I knew what I wanted to write, but there was a great gap between the knowing and the setting down. I gave it up, thinking, as calmly as I could, that there was no hurry, tomorrow would do. I rang the bell and asked for a pot of tea, which, in this new Mortiboys, arrived at once, hot, fragrant. I drank several cups and swallowed two of my headache tablets in which I had once had faith, but which I had begun to doubt. Then I went and walked in the garden. But it grew worse. By the time when I had to face Jassy and Old Nick at the table I was stupid with it. There were spaces when I couldn't hear what they were saying, or see anything except little grey whirling circles.

Then we were in the library, where there were fresh chairs, more comfortable ones, fetched from somewhere, and the covers and the curtains were clean and crisp. I saw Jassy looking at me, and I made an effort and said: 'F-Father, I've got something to tell you. I h-hope you won't be angry. I'm going to marry B-Barney Hatton.'

'Barney Hatton,' father repeated. 'Is that the best you can do?' He didn't sound angry, just nasty. But it was a difficult thing to reply to, and I couldn't think of anything to say. I thought well . . . I've said it, and that's all I need say. I wished I could have gone away then. For it was too good to be believed that Old Nick would content himself with that simple comment. And, indeed, he was already gathering himself for the assault.

'I suppose the day has gone when it was customary for the would-be suitor to ask a father's permission before making a proposal,' he began. It was a mild rumble like that, we are told, which heralds a volcanic eruption. 'Is that so? Am I an old fogey to resent being *told* that my son-in-law is chosen?'

'N-no,' I said doubtfully. 'But I didn't think you'd care who I married so long as you weren't b-bothered.'

'A shrewd conclusion. But isn't it a pity that you selected a lout who hasn't even the manners or the upbringing to know how these matters should be conducted?'

'Barney offered to come and tell–I mean, ask you–but I didn't think that you would want to stand on ceremony.'

'That's a pity. Because there was one thing I should have enjoyed telling that young man.'

'Would you like him to come?'

'God forbid. You may take him a message. It's this . . .' and he bellowed suddenly: 'Tell that little —— that he won't get Mortiboys by marrying you. D'you hear that? I know his breed. That fool of a father of his never shuffled his cards without thinking that he'd got the place in his hand again. I could read it all over his damned silly face. And at the end . . . but we won't go into that. You'll not care to hear what kind of a low cheat your beloved's father turned out to be. But if his whelp thinks that by marrying you he's playing a trump, you may undeceive him. It may change his mind before it's too late, for what use you'd ever be to a farmer would puzzle God to explain. Jassy, get the bottle.'

'I don't want Mortiboys,' I said, 'and I don't think Barney does.' I felt impelled to say something. But as I spoke I recollected that Jassy had also warned me on the same subject, and my voice was not very certain towards the end of the sentence.

'Don't keep saying that you don't think this and you don't think that. We know that you can't think. If you could you wouldn't think about marrying Barney Hatton. Have you ever seen the place where you'll live? Thank you. Well, now, we must all drink to celebrate this momentous occasion.'

He poured out three glasses of wine, slopping it as he always did, and holding his own glass for a moment as though about to propose a toast. But perhaps nothing sufficiently insulting occurred to him; he drank without speaking. Jassy lifted her glass and said, for the third time, 'I hope you'll be very happy, Dilys.'

'Happy!' Old Nick snarled, refilling his glass. I stood up. At the back of my dim aching mind I had a thought about how different this should have been. One's only daughter. . . . But I was used to him. I was not really hurt; in fact, I thought I had escaped lightly. Now I could go to bed, press my head into the pillow, sleep, and wake tomorrow a new woman. Blinded by the grey circles I almost felt my way out of the room. But when I reached the haven of my own bed I hardly slept at all. Even in the darkness, even with my eyes closed, I could see the sickening whirls, and my head thudded until my finger and toes throbbed to the rhythm of the pain.

Next evening I rode to Green Farm again, planning to be there when Barney came in from work. There was no longer any need for secrecy. Need? Had there ever been need? Barney had evidently told Meggie, who was highly delighted, bobbing and smiling, and assuring me that she would serve me till she died, and see that before she did so she had someone else adequately trained. But my head was still aching. I had never known it to ache for two consecutive days before, and I was half mad with sleeplessness as well. Meggie, smiling and bobbing, seemed a long way away, and I had to make an effort to hear her. But waiting in the parlour, by the hastily-lighted fire, I thought that everything would be all right when Barney came. I remembered the time when the mere thought of him had cured my head; now, surely the sight and the touch of him would heal me.

It didn't. Barney, too, seemed a long way away; Barney, too, seemed to be speaking from a great distance. Even when he kissed me, kissed me with a strange new tenderness as well as a renewal of old passion, I remained limp and unresponsive. I was driven to excuse myself, saying that my head ached. Quite soon, attentive and concerned, he rode home with me, and in the lane, near the broken archway, we parted, not with our usual kisses and embraces–last kisses, infinitely prolonged; last embraces, snatched, parted, returning, desperate because so long must elapse before they were renewed–instead of these there were requests upon his side that I should go straight to bed and not worry, that I would leave everything to him; and upon my side a faltering renewal of apology that I had spoilt our evening together. I was crying from exhaustion and pain and disappointment before I could get out of the stable-yard.

That night I slept in short broken snatches. And my head still ached. In the morning I was unrecognizable. My hair, usually yellow and very curly, looked lank and thin, quite straight and almost colourless. My eyes were half-closed and surrounded by brownish shadows, my nose was sharp, and my whole face sunken and doughy. Before I could face anyone I was obliged to curl my hair and paint my face, and then I looked like an old woman masquerading as a girl. And everything I did, even things so familiar as making a toilet and dressing myself, I did slowly, making an effort to remember, pausing, lost for a moment in a daze of pain and stupidity, and then going on again.

Old Nick had gone when I went down to breakfast, but Jassy was still at the table, lingering over a cup of coffee. And presently, when I had looked at her and, with incredible difficulty, thought about what I had seen, I realized that she was not looking herself either. And I thought, perhaps I *am* mad. Perhaps I am imagining things. And yet the limp, straight hair which I had just handled was real enough. I made an enormous effort and said, 'Jassy, you don't look well.' She straightened herself a little and said, in a more friendly and intimate voice than she had used towards me for some time:

'I've just been having one of my funny fits. You remember Hilda Besson and her mother–my seeing her getting well?'

'Yes,' I said, with a faint spurt of interest, for that story had been a nine days' wonder at school.

'Well, it happened again just now. Dilys . . . it was true what he, your father, said the night before last. It sounded an idle, impetuous threat, but Mortiboys will never be yours. I saw it, quite plainly, belonging to somebody else.'

'Who?'

'I can't tell you that . . . it wasn't plain enough. I was just sitting here drinking my coffee and looking at the wall, and I saw other people in it. Owning it. It's difficult to describe, but I am quite sure about it.'

'Well,' I said, and truthfully, 'as I told Old Nick, I don't want it. There's nothing I want less. Though I suppose when I'm married to Barney I should be glad of the money I could sell it for. But I can't even bother to think about that. I've had a headache for three days now, and it's getting worse.'

She looked at me without sympathy and said in a funny, thoughtful way, 'Barney always wanted Mortiboys back, when he was young. He talked about it to me once. I never forgot it.'

'You're hinting again that he's marrying me for the place,' I said with a sudden spurt of anger that sent a sickening thud through my head. 'That's the second time you've said it. I think it's mean and cruel of you. And you're utterly wrong. I saw Barney last night and told him what father had said. It didn't make the slightest difference.'

'Oh, I don't suppose it would. I'm not suggesting that he isn't in love with you, Dilys. A blind baby could see that on that first evening when we had supper there. It's only . . . well, it seems a pity that he shouldn't have *both* his loves.'

It occurred to me again that she was in love with him. And this time I was certain. I ought to have felt sorry for her, but mingled with my headache, and my miserable state of mind, the knowledge served only to make me furiously angry.

'Well, that's one thing you can't arrange,' I said spitefully. 'You seem to be omniscient, but you're not omnipotent. Barney must put up with Green Farm, and me!'

She remained quite unruffled, looking straight at me from under slightly raised eyebrows. After a little silence she asked in an ordinary voice. 'Would you care to come to Colchester with me? You haven't long to shop in.'

What would Mrs Hatton need? Clogs against the farmyard mud? Oh, Barney, weren't we happy in the Spinney? Soon, very soon, there'll be a drift of wild anemones there. Lovely, lovely! But you shouldn't pick the windflowers and take them home and put them in water. They wither. They shrivel and go grey . . . shrivel like a pretty face that has to be painted. Like my face. These wild feelings that you and I have known, Barney, can't be taken indoors and chained to the kitchen table. They shrivel and are gone.

And indeed, *all* feeling had gone from me: the warm, strong ones which had begun during my absence at Ockley, and which had sent me running to Barney in the field; and the small humble feelings with which, only three days ago, I had looked upon Green Farm and accepted it as my future home. I didn't even feel like a girl any more. I was just a vague body attached to a head which ached and ached.

But I still said and did what was expected of me. I went to Colchester and tried, as I followed Jassy from shop to shop, to think about things I needed. The effort to concentrate ended in the drapers' where Jassy was buying curtain material: the counter upon which the stuff was piled suddenly leapt up at me and hit me in the face. When I was conscious again I was in a kind of storeroom at the back of the shop, and my first thought was that now my headache would be better. But it wasn't. And after that I knew that I should have it for ever. Sleep hadn't cured it; Barney's presence hadn't cured it; and now I had been unconscious and still it was there. No feeling for me any more, except pain in the head.

Days began to pass in a mad, whirling muddle. I made no preparations for my marriage; I never even wrote the letter which would tell the Fennels about it. Sometimes I stayed in bed and Jassy, with a kind of angry solicitude, brought or sent me horrible concoctions composed largely of the loathsome red juice of raw beef. One of the new maids she had instituted was a grotesque ugly idiot girl, all but dumb, and it seemed always to be she who presented me with Jassy's doses, except when Jassy came herself.

Sometimes I got up and roamed about the house. Now and then, when the curtain of darkness which seemed to divide me from the world lifted a little, I thought that something was happening between Old Nick and Jassy. She seemed to be using all her wiles on him, and he was responding. It would end as I had told her it would; but I had warned her and could do no more, even if I had wanted to.

Of Old Nick himself I was not frightened any more. I was past feeling fear. Once when he was offensive to me I rounded on him and said everything that I had had in mind, for years, to say. I could hear my own voice, a long way off at the end of a tunnel, saying the most rage-provoking things. Jassy was present, and perhaps for that reason he merely laughed and said, 'You rail like a farm-wife already.' She put her hand on his arm and said:

'Don't mind her. Getting married upsets a girl's nerves.'

'Does it?' he said. 'Does it?'

They looked at one another and laughed a little. It was hateful to see them like that. But I couldn't mind.

Finally, out of despair I dredged up the notion that I might feel better if Barney and I could go once more to the Spinney where we had been so happy. Since I had gone into the field and told Barney I would marry him, we had been meeting openly and behaving with the restraint usual in such cases. But at last I persuaded him to come to the Spinney, instead of taking me over to Green Farm and making me wring out inadequate remarks of admiration for the improvements he was making to the house.

It was a lovely evening, mild and windless. I made my face carefully and curled my hair. I drank a cupful of the red juice and swallowed four of the useless headache tablets. I put on a muslin dress, unseasonable but pretty, and over it a warm pelisse which I could discard in the wood. For hitherto at least I had always been warm enough in Barney's arms.

The oxlips were in bud, in warm corners facing south they were already in flower, shedding a sweet, apricot-scented fragrance on the air. The bluebells, not yet broken, stood up spikily, their buds a darker blue than the flowers would be. Larches were green again and there were spatters of blackthorn, dazzlingly white, in the hedges. It was, indeed, an evening made for lovers.

But one was made and ill and the other bewildered. I thought, I *will* escape. I *will* break through! I will get back to the joy we knew. There must be something left of the feeling that made me ride from Ockley determined to marry Barney; I must find it again.

I tried. Heaven knows I tried. I threw myself into Barney's arms. I kissed him as I had never, even in my most ecstatic moments of rapture, kissed him before. I waked such passion in him . . . but in myself nothing. There was nothing–though we lay in the old place; though Barney was as strong and ardent a lover as the wildest dream could fashion. There was nothing in me except pain and despair.

A thin-sliced moon came up over the pointed tops of the larches and I could smell the oxlips. I lay and thought: it's over, it's over, and it will always be like this. There is nothing for me in the future except this no-feeling and Green Farm. . . .

Barney put his arm under me and drew my head into the hollow of his shoulder. I could feel the wild racing of his heart growing slower and steadier. He said, 'You're tired, my love. I've tired you.' I began to cry softly from disappointment and hopelessness. Years and years, I thought. Even the Spinney had failed me. This was what it was to be dead . . . or very old, so that there was nothing except the brittle dry framework left. And a head that ached and ached.

Barney was puzzled by my crying; puzzled, but gentle and kind. If I had been capable of feeling then I should have been ashamed.

On my way back to Mortiboys I suddenly found myself clenching and unclenching my hands. I tried to stop it, but they moved without any connection with me. I was frightened and thought I would like to ask Jassy about them. Her behaviour to me was curious of late, but she would be kind. And she was sensible and would know if this were madness. But she was nowhere to be seen. When I had looked everywhere I thought of Old Nick's room. I wondered. I went into my own room and lay in the bed, trying to sleep, clenching and unclenching my hands.

Next morning I stayed in bed late, and about mid-morning, while I was slowly and laboriously dressing myself, Janey came up with a message to say that Mr Fennel was waiting below.

I was dressed, but my hair was hanging like string, and my face, freshly washed, was ashen. But I went straight down, thinking that now, since I had never managed to write, I could tell Stephen my news and he would go away and that would be the end of that.

I don't think he recognized me at first, or was so shocked that he could not speak. He just stared as I went towards him, and at any other time I should have been amused at the sight of all his gallantry and mannerisms dropping away and leaving just Stephen, uncertain and unpoised.

I said weakly, 'Hullo, Stephen!' And then he seemed to gulp and swallow in his throat. He said:

'Dilys! What on earth is the matter? What have they been doing to you?'

'No one's done anything to me, Stephen. I'm just not well. My head aches and aches and I can't think. I'm glad to see you though. I've got something to tell you.'

He glared round the hall.

'It's this damned place,' he said blurtingly. 'You shouldn't have come back here. I told mother so, but she . . . Never mind. Look, I brought the carriage. I have to go to Bywater. I hoped you'd drive with me. Do you feel well enough?'

'I can't,' I said. 'It takes me so long. This hair. And my face. I have to make it every day, Stephen. I have no face left.'

He gave me a peculiar look and I thought, ah, here's somebody who isn't used to me. He notices. He knows I'm mad. But Stephen said very gently, as though speaking to a child:

'Is it just your head, Dilys?'

I nodded.

'They've done it between them . . . made you ill, I mean. I'm going to take you out of here. Do you feel well enough to come with me now in the carriage?'

'To Bywater?'

He gave me another peculiar look. Then he nodded.

'Yes. I think I could come to Bywater. The air might do me good, and I want to talk to you, Stephen. Can you wait?'

'Only while you get a hat. Don't bother about your face, or hair.'

'But I look so . . .'

'If you go upstairs you'll be an hour. I want to get out of this place.' He looked round and saw, tossed down on the wide window sill, the hat I had intended to wear the night before. Just as I was leaving I had felt its weight too oppressive and had thrown it off and forgotten it. He picked it up and offered it to me. I put it on my head, knowing but not minding, that it must look absurd and dreadful over those limp strands of hair. As soon as my hands fell to my sides Stephen seized one of them and led me, with restrained haste, out to the waiting carriage. There was a rug lined with glossy dark fur on the seat, and when I was inside he tucked it round me. Then, telling the coachman to drive slowly and avoid bumps in the road, he sat down by my side and folded his arms.

We did not speak until the carriage bounced softly out of the lane and turned on to the high road. I sat thinking that in a moment I would tell Stephen about Barney. But the effort of trying to frame the sentence made me feel so ill that I began to doubt whether I should actually live until Easter. With a kind of amazement I began to consider the possibility that I might be going to die. Except for the amazement I felt nothing, not even self-pity. In fact, I should be better dead than married to Barney in my present state.

At the end of the lane Stephen raised himself, touched the coachman's shoulder and said, 'Home.'

'Not Bywater, sir?'

'Home,' Stephen repeated sharply and sank back.

'I'm taking you to mother,' he said. 'She'll look after you.'

'But, Stephen, I can't stay there. I haven't any clothes.'

'We'll find some.'

'But there's another thing. The thing I wanted to tell you. I've been meaning to write to you for days and days. But I couldn't. Stephen, I've promised to marry Barney at Easter.'

Stephen changed colour a little, but he neither exclaimed nor protested. he twisted in his seat so that he was looking at me, and when he had run his tongue over his lips he asked, in an ordinary, conversational tone:

'Are you in love with him?'

'I have been. Now I don't know.'

'Why did you promise if you weren't sure?' he asked, very reasonably.

'But I *was* sure. That is what makes it so queer and dreadful, Stephen. I was quite sure. It was the only thing to do. The only decent thing, too. I made up my mind when I stayed with you last–you remember? I was thinking about Barney all the time.' Stephen's sallow face seemed to shrink a little, but I went on, not minding. Pity was another thing that I had ceased to feel. 'I went straight back and told Barney I'd marry him–he'd been asking me for a long time. Then, on that same day I began to be ill, and now I don't want to marry him . . . or anybody else. And there's nothing your mother can do for me, Stephen. I think I'm going to die, I might just as well do it without bothering anyone else.'

I could hear my own voice, slow, full of effort, like the voice of someone speaking in a troublesome, unfamiliar language. Then I was aware that Stephen's attention had wandered. He was staring up at the back of the coachman.

'I don't know whether he can hear or not, but it's a risk. Don't say any more for a moment. Crisp,' he said, and then, rising again, tapped the man on the shoulder. 'Crisp, when we reach Green Drive turn in and stop.' There was silence again until, inside the Green Drive, the man halted the carriage and looked back over his shoulder, awaiting his next orders.

Stephen moved over to the seat which backed the box. 'Give me the reins,' he said. 'Thank you. Now walk to the end of the Drive, Crisp, and sit down. I'll wave when I want you.'

The man must have been blind and deaf. Blind to my appearance and deaf to what I had been saying before Stephen checked me, for he went off with a conspiratorial smile, very sly and knowing.

Stephen hooked his arm through the loop of the tight-stretched reins and settled in his seat.

'Now Dilys, tell me all about it.' The one scrap of my mind which, through all my troubles, had remained unimpaired, observed that there was something very comforting, almost feminine about him. We might have been two oldish ladies settling down for a cosy heart-to-heart chat. I suddenly realized that I had not had anyone to talk to since Jassy's withdrawal. It may have been for that reason, or because there was something almost hypnotic about Stephen, but anyway I heard my queer, distant voice telling him everything.

It was, I think, rather more than he bargained for when he said, 'Tell me all about it.' But I didn't care at all. I did not mind if I hurt or shocked him. That remote, detached part of my mind saw, without any emotion, the increasing sallowness of his sallow face, the pained, startled widening of his eye-pupils, the clenched discomfort of his hands. To me they counted as nothing compared to the relief I felt from the mere telling of my story.

When it was finished and I was silent again, he licked his lips and moved them, mouthing some soundless words which might have been epithets of disgust. I did not care.

'Are you . . . do you think you're going to have a baby?'

I had never, never for one moment thought of that.

'I don't know,' I said. I tried to count, but the counting part of my brain, never very active, had been dead for a long time. 'I might be. It's more than likely.'

I looked at him as I spoke. Why not? I did not feel ashamed. I saw a dusky red flash surge up into his sallow face and imagined that he was about to order me out of the carriage.

'You poor little thing,' he said–and I did feel surprised. 'You poor little lost thing!' He seemed to throw himself forward, was jerked back by the loop of the reins over his arms, freed himself impatiently and rather comically, and threw himself forward again so that he was kneeling on the floor of the carriage with his arms round me.

'Darling, you mustn't marry him. You don't love him, you just said as much, and he doesn't love you, or he wouldn't . . . wouldn't have taken advantage of your sweet innocence. You poor darling, with no one to help or advise you! Worried to death, ill with worry, and nobody even noticed. . . .' He ran on, repeating himself in this strain for several minutes. Then he said, more calmly: 'Dilys, I came to Mortiboys this morning to ask you to marry me. I spoke to your father last night when he was at Ockley, but I left it too late and he was drunk, he didn't seem to understand. But I'm asking you now. Will you marry me and let me look after you?'

'You can't want to marry me *now*,' I said.

'Now more than ever. I've loved you ever since that evening when you came home from Baildon–oh, before that really, but I didn't know. I'll be so good to you, darling, and make up for all the misery you've had.'

'But I promised Barney.'

'To hell with him! He ought to be hanged. Taking advantage of you so.'

'I was as much to blame–or more.'

'Don't say that. You don't know what you're talking about. Darling, the innocence of you. . . .'

But it wasn't innocence. Not in Saints' Spinney–that was pure lust; and not now–that was just not caring what I said because it didn't matter.

'And suppose there *is* a baby?'

'No one need know. We'd be married immediately.'

'You're crazy,' I said.

I pushed him away from me a little and looked away down the green ride. My head was throbbing so hard that the trees seemed to be dancing, closing in and then parting again. But I realized suddenly that the quality of the pain had altered a little. It was pain, not paralysis. I could think. And I did think. I weighed, as I had so often done before, Stephen against Barney. But this time it was different. For now I could remember that last night in Saints' Spinney, when I had looked up at the moon and thought–it's over, and it will be like this for years. Barney had never meant more to me than the lust of the flesh, and that had failed. Now there was nothing to set in the scales against Ockley, and money, social security, snobbery. I cared for neither Barney nor Stephen. I was foolishly certain at that moment that even if I lived I should never thrill again to any man's touch. I was not clear enough in my mind to know then what I knew so bitterly later, that the rift in my mind would heal because it had been caused simply by the effort to accept poverty and the farm and social outlawry in order to have Barney's body. How could I guess that when the wound of that decision had healed I should be the old Dilys, burning with the old fire that only Barney could quench, going on and on, all the years of my life, seeking the forfeited pleasure, unsatisfied, for the joy I had lost? No, thinking that all feeling was dead in me, I could not see beyond Ockley.

'Truly, Stephen, I don't know what to say. I'm in such a muddle. All my life has been a muddle.'

'Say that you'll marry me and I'll put it all straight.'

'I wish I could believe it.'

'You must. You shall. I'll show you. May I try?'

I nodded. He raised his face and kissed me. Then he stood up and, in an excited way, waved his handkerchief to Crisp, who came running.

BOOK FOUR

LUNATIC ECLIPSE

'Sometimes, you know, I wonder whether that dumb idiot girl couldn't have told a story. . . .'

So this story is told by BELINDA WICKS, *who was subject to Visitations.*

There is a whole name–it is Belinda Wicks; but when people are kind they say Lindy. When they are not kind they say Latchety or Loony. Not kind are most. Loony is for people who are wrong in the head. I was right in the head once, but when I was little our father came home drunk and threw me off the bed. I fell on my head and there was pain. It was short, but afterwards I was not like the others. I can talk, and I can understand what other people talk, but when I say words they come out thick, like red flannel, or sometimes they don't come at all. So I nod my head, or shake it and make signs.

I am little, too. But I am strong. I can lift things and run very fast. And I can remember a lot. There are the things people say when I am there that they do not think I understand because I cannot talk. But I remember. I can even remember a man called Tom Woodroffe that put the fear of God into our father so he didn't get drunk or knock us down any more. But it was too late for me.

That man Tom Woodroffe gave our father a book. There were pictures in it. There was one picture with an angel in it rolling a great stone away from a hole. The angel was shiny white and there was a ring, like the outside of a plate made of light, on his head. It was lovely.

Then one day there was a wedding, and I went because it was my sister Agnes to be married. And in the church window, high up, there was the same angel. Bigger, but the same. Even the birds' wings of it were the same. I sat very still and looked at it and wondered how it could be there, big, and in the book at home, small, but the same. Then there was a sweet smell, like a rose bush, just near me, and when I looked the angel was there. It said, 'I can be where I like.' I said, 'In two places?' And the words came out right. The people all looked at me and shushed. The angel said, 'Never mind. I will talk to you another time.' I said, 'Where? When? Please tell me.' Then it was gone, and our mum signed to my sister Jill to take me outside. Jill was angry and said I ought not to have come. I said, 'I saw an angel.' The words didn't come so clear as when I talked to it. But she heard and said, 'Aah, you're loopy!'

After that there was the angel many times with me. It could be as big as a house or as small as a daisy. It talked to me and I could talk to it.

There was the time when I could go to work. Our mum got me places. She said I could work very well. And I was cheap. But the people never kept me long. Every time I came home our mum said, 'So you're back again. Oh dear!'

Then one day She came. There was a good shape of her. There was a bad one, too, but it wasn't there then, or very often. She was kind, and when She knew my name, She said it 'Lindy,' like a bird singing in a bush. She said she was looking for some help in the kitchen at the big house, Mortiboys, and our mum said about me being able to work and being cheap. And She said I could go. I was very glad.

The house is big. I lost myself sometimes. There were many servants, and they were just like the others where I had been before. They teased me and called me names. Sometimes when they do that my good shape is there and I run away or hide; but sometimes it is the bad shape, and I stamp and shout at them. One day I was crying and stamping and saying–but it was all wrong and thick–how much I hated them, when She came in and said not to tease me, people should be kind to the afflicted. She smiled at me, too.

That night the angel came, very small, and stood on my bed. It had a long white string, shiny like silver, in its hand, and it tied one end of it round my heart. It said, 'Now I am going to tie the other end round her heart and you will be joined together always.'

I said, 'Will She know?' The angel said, 'No. You are the one to know.' Then it flew away and the string pulled tight. I knew that the other end was fastened. I was happy because we had been tied together, and after that there was always a pull when I was out of her sight. Sometimes it hurt. But when I was with her it was loose and did not hurt. I tried to be near her when I could. Even in the night. If it pulled hard I would get up and creep away through the dark house and sit outside the room with the pretty paper where She was asleep. And in the day I tried to be near her too. Sometimes She saw me and said, 'Lindy, what are you doing there?' and sent me to my work, but kindly, smiling. So I made myself very small and quiet to be near her and She not to know.

There were some others in the house. There was the Master. He was an ugly shape all the time. It was bad temper, and he hated everybody. He was like our father before Tom Woodroffe put the fear of God in him. He was the same colour, and shouted the same way. There was the same smell, too, a bad smell. When I was in the front part of the house because to polish the floor was my work there, I knew when the Master was near because of the smell, and I would go away quickly or hide till he was past. There was a good shape to him too, like there is to everybody, but it couldn't show much. Once I saw it when She was with him.

The other person in the front of the house was Miss Dilys. She was lovely to look at. At first I thought she was a little bit like my angel, but that only the top. Her real shape wasn't settled. She was like the weeds in the pond, wavery and washed about. Once she said that the sight of me made her sick. She was a bad shape then. And sometimes when she talked to Her she was bad too. But not always.

The Master and Miss Dilys and She took their meals in the dining-room, and other times they sat in the hall or in a room called the library. There were screens near the doors to keep out the cold. I used to hide in the screens. It was easy because I am small and can move without making a noise. I was in the screen when Miss Dilys said she was going to marry young Mr Hatton from my village. Miss Dilys was a good shape that night, but the Master was bad, and She was bad too; but whether She was good or bad the string stayed strong and tight. No matter what She did I was tied to her. And that night She cried. I knew because I was outside the room with the pretty paper and I was listening. But She only cried a little. Presently, She started to swear. She used words no lady knows about, only rough men and boys. I shuddered outside the door and knew that the bad shape was inside. Mostly, when people are a bad shape, I want to run and hide, but not with her. I wanted to open the door and go in and touch her and make her better. But I didn't dare.

Then one day a little while after that the Master and She had some talking. I did not understand it, but I can remember some.

He said, 'I'll put it in my will.'

She said: 'A will is too easily altered. It must be as I say. That is my one condition.'

He said, 'It shows a lamentable lack of faith.'

And She said, 'It also shows common sense. I may never be in a position to dictate terms again.' Then he laughed and said She should have been a highwayman.

Not long after that Miss Dilys got ill. When she was ill her shape was very watery and her hair wasn't like my angel's any more. There was a kind of cloud round her. I could see even when she passed me in the passage. It got thicker every day until she was just a dark cloud wandering. Then one day she went away.

There were some days and she came back. There was a man with her. He was not much himself, but when he looked at her he bloomed like a tree. I was polishing the stairs when they came and stood in the hall. I was polishing the stairs for the second time, because She was in the hall putting daffodils and pussy willow in water. I had gathered them early in the morning and put them outside the room with the pretty paper. Very early morning it was, but She wasn't in that room. I knew because when I got there the string was still tight, and when I had put the daffodils down I let it pull me where it wanted to. And it pulled me to Master's room and then loosed a little. I knew She was there. I nearly picked up the flowers and put them outside that door. But he might think they were for him, and perhaps She didn't want anybody to know. So for two reasons I left them where they were. Now She was putting them in water and I was polishing the stairs again just to be near her. When I was near her and could see her doing things I had a smooth feeling, like a cat being stroked. Or cream. Once I ate some cream when nobody was looking, and it was like that, smooth and sweet. But to be near her was better. It was better than anything.

Miss Dilys and the one they called Stephen came in and they did a little talking. Miss Dilys said, 'I haven't come home for good, only for a few things I wanted. Jassy, will you give father a message for me? I've changed my mind. I'm going to marry Stephen after all.'

I was looking. When Miss Dilys said that she went a very wavery shape indeed, bad and good, bad and good, and then bad, bad. The one they called Stephen, just bloomed. He was lovely then, like a bush of flowers, but She went very evil. There was nothing left but her bad shape, temper and swearing. Very frightening. She said:

'You're what?' And Miss Dilys said it again. Then She said:

'You're a heartless little hussy. God knows you weren't worthy to clean his boots, but he loved you. You'll break his heart.' She said other things too, swearing things that only rough men and boys knows.

The young man shouted too, and said he wouldn't have Dilys spoken to like that.

Then She was quiet and said, in a most serious way: 'Dilys, is it because of the money? Don't mind about that. You will have Mortiboys one day, I promise you.'

'But it was you who said . . .'

'I know what I *said*. But I promise you: if you marry Barney you shall have it.'

Miss Dilys began to say, 'It's too late . . .' and the young man was angry, and he was afraid too. Fears smell bad and I knew. He said, 'You talk like a mad woman. Since when has Mortiboys been yours to promise, pray? Dilys, dear, I beg of you, come away, don't listen to her.'

She put her hand on Miss Dilys' arm and held it between the wrist and the elbow, and said, 'But Barney loves you, Dilys. And you promised.'

The young man was very frightened. And because of it he took her by the shoulder and tried to shake her hand off Miss Dilys. There was my sweeping brush there, and when he touched her I took it and ran down the stairs and beat on his head.

'Lindy! Lindy!' She said, and pulled me and shook me.

The young man put his arm round Miss Dilys and took her to the door. 'This place is Bedlam, or worse,' he said. 'Never mind your things. You shall have everything new.'

Miss Dilys said, 'But there is a portrait of my mother, and the pearls she gave me.'

'I will pack everything and send you,' She said in a little tired voice, 'because I see that possessing things is the most important thing in life with you.'

Miss Dilys looked back, 'At least I am going to be *married*,' she said. And there was a sneer.

'Don't start anything else,' the young man Stephen said, and pulled her away through the door. When it was shut She started to laugh. But it turned into crying. She sat on the settle near the hearth and cried. It was hard angry crying as well as sorrowful. The string in me pulled tighter and tighter until at last I was so close to her that I could see every hair on her head. I did not know why she was crying: I had stopped them hurting her. But I was sad too. And I put my hand on her skirt where it lay on the floor. She saw me and looked down. She put her hand on my shoulder and I nearly burst with joy. She said, 'Poor Lindy. I expect you wonder what it is all about. I do myself. Nothing ever goes right for me.'

She didn't say anything about hitting with brushes.

After that there was a time. And She was kind to me. She let me carry the bunch when She picked flowers in the garden, and twice I went to Colchester to carry the things She bought; and we had cakes in a shop. They were pink, and it was like eating roses.

There, and in the garden, it was good; but in the house it was bad. Though She gave me a dress and some shoes and a petticoat that was hers. The hem of it was raggy and She said could I sew, because the hem could be cut off and then it would fit me. I never cut it. I did get some scissors and start, but it was like cutting her, and my toes curled and my hands were cold. So I put it under my pillow and at night I held it. I was afraid that one day She would say, 'Where is the petticoat?' But She never did. It was like hitting the young man on the head, a secret that we never said, even to ourselves.

We were all right in the house, but it was bad with her and the Master. Up to that time he didn't shout at her; but then he started. Behind the screens and in my own hiding places I watched and listened. I heard what they said, but it didn't mean anything. Only that there was temper. And a change. He called her names. He said She was a cold bitch to strip a man and cheat him. She said, 'I do my best. What more can I do?' He said, 'If I had another place to settle on you maybe you would do better, eh?'

Once when he was shouting She said, 'Don't shout at me. I am not one of your doxies.' And he said, 'You're worse than any doxy. I've had better than you for a guinea.'

That time She laughed and said, 'You must balance your good bargains then against your bad one.' And then he hit her. And I forgot that I wasn't to be behind the screen. I ran out and bit his hand. That time She was angry, and said did I ever watch or listen or spy on her again She would send me off. I fell on my knees and beat my head on her shoes and begged her not to say that. After a little She said all right, but if I spied again I must go. Then the Master said, 'She must go now. Do you think I would have her here after this? The mad ——, ——' He said names that were not right. Not true. Bad, bad names he called me. He said to go away at once. I hung on her skirt and cried. And She begged him. She said, 'You shan't ever see her. But please let her stay. She is fond of me, and she works hard and is cheap.'

But I could feel cruelty grow in him, and he said I must go for biting him in the hand. But it was because She wanted to keep me. That was why.

It was the time of falling leaves and rain and wind. The sad time. And when he had said that I should not be there another day, he went out. He did not mind the weather. She came and said that I must stay in my little room until She had thought of a place for me. The little room was all mine, because the others said they would rather sleep three in a bed than share with me.

I sat and listened to the wind. I am sorry for it. It cries and taps on the window and says, 'Let me in, please; please let me in.' Sometimes I open the window and let it in and it runs round the room, quiet and happy to be indoors. That day I let it in because it cried and said, 'How will you feel when you are shut out?' So I let it in, and it put its cold hands on my face.

Then She came, but not till late, nearly dark. I thought She had come to say that She had found a place and I must go. I began to howl like the wind. But She said, 'I want you to help me, Lindy. The Master is taken very ill. I must nurse him. If you do exactly what I tell you you can be a great help to me.'

The doctor was there, and he gave me a bowl with rings marked inside it. I held the bowl when he made a little slit in the Master's arm, and the blood ran out up to the ring in the bowl. The Master's face was the colour of the darkest poppy, and he breathed like bellows. But some of the poppy colour and some of the breathing ran out in the bowl.

Then She said to empty it and have something to eat and come back because I was to sit up with her in the night.

I could not eat, though always I did what She said; but this time not, because the string was so tight I could not swallow, because of them all She had picked me to sit in the night with her and because I was not sent to another place.

There was a happy time. In all my life that was the best time. There was a little room with a door to the Master's room and a door to the passage, and we sat there together by the fire. There was a couch, and in the night one of us lay on it and the other watched to hear and call if he made a noise. There were trays, and I carried them. I went down to eat in the kitchen sometimes and heard the talk. They talked a lot. They were afraid he would die, and what then? They said how he had taken ill and been brought home on a gate. They said how would anybody get better with her and a loony to nurse him?

I listened to it all. But it did not matter. Only there was the time when I thought about his getting better and driving me out. I hoped he would die. The dead ones do not hurt anybody, though some people will not go in the churchyard at night.

The happy time lasted. In the morning I would go down and make tea.

One morning the wind cried and I let it in, and it sat very quiet combing its hair. But when I had made the tea and was going to turn the wind out–because if I left it in there was trouble because it would touch things–it stood up and altered itself and was my angel. I was surprised. The angel kept its hands behind its back for a little time, then it said, 'Look. I am going to tie you together with this now.' And I looked and there was a cord like the other, but not white and shiny. Red it was, like the blood in the bowl. I went back round the table and said, 'But it will hurt more. The white one is sore when I am away from her, and this will be worse because when he is better I must go away.'

The angel said, 'Ah, but if I tie this you will never have to go away. You will be together for always.'

'But it is the colour of blood,' I said.

'That is right. You love her, don't you?'

'Indeed I do. Our mum loved our father, and my sister Jill loved the young chap that was hanged for poaching. But I love her, and that is the best. But I wish there was another colour.'

The angel said, 'This is the colour to tie you for ever.'

So I was glad, and it tied it in a knot round my heart next to the white one, but harder. Then it went away, and soon there was a great pull.

There was talking in the bedroom, and when She came out for the tea She said, 'He is better. He is sensible this morning.' She went to the window and pulled the curtain and looked out. She was not glad. And if he was better he would send me away. Only the angel had said together for always. Perhaps She would come too.

There were some days. He was better quickly and shouting just the same. He would not eat the food for sick people. Or drink tea and milk. He said he was poisoned and flung the food about. He said he was a man, not a baby, to suck slops. He said to bring him a bottle.

But the doctor came and said not much to eat and nothing strong to drink.

The happy times were over. There were bad ones again. She was white and thin. Once in the night when She was alseep She said, 'Oh, Barney, Barney,' and woke up with crying.

There was a day when he could get out of bed and sit in a chair by the fire. She said to me in the little room, 'Soon he will be about again, and I am afraid you must go then, Lindy. But I will find you a kind place and keep an eye on you.'

The bedroom door was shut and I looked at it and made faces. My bad shape was there. And She looked at the door, too, and did not make faces, but there was hate in her eyes. Even our bad shapes were tied together for always like the angel said. I wanted to tell her, but I could not.

That night She said, 'You can go to your bed. Lucky Lindy!' And when I got to my room there was my angel, smaller than a finger, sitting on my pillow and shining like gold. It said, 'Bend down and I'll whisper to you.' I bent down and there was a smell of roses. The angel said, 'She doesn't want him to get better.' I said, 'I know. But what can I do about it?'

The angel said, 'She is very sad.' And then the two cords that were round my heart began to tug and pull. There was great pain, like toothache. There was so much toothache in the pain that I put my finger in the hole where our mum dug my tooth out by the root with her scissors.

I said, 'It is like toothache. But the tooth is gone.'

The little angel danced on the pillow and said, 'Yes, toothache. Think about toothache. You must think about toothache.'

I said, 'Why? The tooth is gone. Our mum rooted it out with the scissors.'

'But before that there was medicine.'

'Yes,' I said. 'There was medicine.'

'Think about that,' said the angel and flew away.

From next door they knocked on the wall and said, 'Shut up, Loony, or we'll come and make you.'

I got into bed. There was a rose smell on my pillow. And there was the toothache pain in my heart. I thought about the medicine like the angel had said.

Next morning when I went up with the tea I thought I had better be sure. I practised on every stair, saying, 'Don't you want him to get better?' And when I got into the little room I said it out, as clear as anybody. She gave me a frightened look and said:

'Who said that?' I tried to say. 'I did. Myself.' But the words came wrong, and I had to point to my chest and nod, and point downstairs and all around, shaking my head to show that nobody but me had said it. She said, 'Don't say it again. Do you hear me?' But She didn't say that it wasn't true. So then I thought about the toothache medicine.

It is good for all pains. It is in a black bottle with a rag round the cork to keep the strength in. It has two smells. The top smell is sweet, like a field of hay just cut. The underneath one is sleepy, like holding a poppy too close to your face. And it has two shapes. One is good and one is bad. When people say, 'Well, it's kill or cure,' they mean the toothache medicine. Two drops will cure you, at least for a time, but a lot of it will kill you. Even when you have only two drops, a drop and a drop on a bit of sheep's wool in your tooth, you must spit all the time. You mustn't swallow your slaver. Because the medicine is poison.

Our mum keeps the bottle in the sag of the beam in the bedroom. There was a time when my tooth was bad first when she would give me a drop and a drop on wool to hold in it and spit hard. But afterwards, when the cure had gone out of it, she took the scissors and rooted the tooth out. There was bad pain and my face was very big on one side. But it got better, and now there was just a hole.

There were two days and the Master was better all the time and shouting, and saying he would not have slops any more, and open the window the room was stuffy, and shut it the draught was blowing his head off. All of those two days I was trying to say that I wanted to go home and see my mum. But the words came wrong and She did not understand. Though She tried.

Then the angel came again and said, 'Say what you want to say to me. Yes, that is right. Now say it again. That is good. Tomorrow you will be able to say it.'

And next day I said, very clear, 'Please may I go home?'

But it was the wrong thing to say. She looked startled and sorry.

'I thought you were happy here, Lindy. What is the matter? Have they been teasing you again?'

I shook my head hard and tried to say what I meant, but it was all thick and flannelly. Then suddenly I saw the little angel, perched on the edge of the mantelpiece and laughing. I said, 'You told me wrong. I should have said I wanted to go home for one hour. One hour, for a visit.'

'That's right,' it said. 'Now you've said it. Good-bye.'

She looked round and then at me. She said, 'You are a funny girl, Lindy. For a moment I thought you were speaking to somebody else. A visit. Yes, of course. You may have a whole day off if you like. You've earned it. I don't know what I should have done without you.'

She put her hand on my shoulder. 'Come along, we'll go and find a little present for you to take home. You'd like to take your mother something, wouldn't you?'

There was happiness in me and thankfulness, and I was proud, too, because of what She had said. She took me to the big pantry and She filled a basket and put a little cloth over it. There was half a game pie with the gravy set in a jelly, and there was a piece of pork and a plum cake.

Then I was outside the door and the cords began to drag at me. I ran very fast. I said, 'Please cords be kind and let me run. I am being as quick as I can go. You need not pull at me. I am going back.' A boy in a farm cart heard me and laughed and jeered. I didn't mind. The hurry pain came in my body too, but it was small beside the cord pain in my heart, and it went away when I stopped and touched my toes.

I went by the Low Road because that is the short way. But it was bad for fast running; the leaves were so thick and the rain made them slippery. When I got home I was breathing like bellows and the sweat was running down my face.

Our mum had a sick look; the old sick look when I came home other times. She said, 'So you're back again. Oh dear, what shall I do with you?'

I shook my head and smiled and pointed back to show that I had just come to visit. Mum understood. So she was glad and gave me a good bun with currants, a Sunday bun. But I could not eat it then. I put it in my pocket. Then I showed her the basket and, while she was opening it and saying nice things, I went into the bedroom and reached up to the sag in the beam. The bottle was there, and there was some medicine in it. I put it in my pocket with the Sunday bun.

Mum wanted me to have pie. There was tea, too. But I could not stop. I took the basket and made mum understand that I was in a hurry and would stop another day. Then I ran back to the big house as hard as I could go.

I went to the little room and listened. She was inside the bedroom with the Master. He was growling at her and saying I shall get up tomorrow, you're in league with that —— fool of a doctor to keep me here under your thumb till I die, but I'll show you. She said not to say such things. The pain got better slowly, now I was near and could hear her talk. Then I went to my own room. I was glad that they would rather sleep three in a bed than share with me. I took out the bottle and smelt it. It was just the same with the sweet smell and the sleepy smell folded over each other.

There was my bun too. I could eat it then.

When I went in the kitchen She was there, making the Master's dinner.

Cook was angry. She didn't like it because She cooked Master's food. But She said that there were always grumbles, and She liked to know whether they were right ones or wrong ones. So She cooked.

When She saw me She was surprised and said, 'I didn't expect you back yet. Did you enjoy yourself?' I nodded. The others scowled because they didn't like her talking to me friendly. Then She said, 'Now you are back I think I shall take a little walk. Mr Helmar may be able to get up tomorrow, and I may not have a chance then.' I helped to carry up the dinner, and I heard her tell him that She was going out for a few minutes. He grumbled, but he didn't stop her. She shut the bedroom door and whispered to me that She would be in the garden. If he rang his bell or called, not to let anybody else get to him, but fetch her at once. I thought that was because She was kind, because he had not been getting better so quickly that day and was in bed again.

I sat very quiet, listening for the bell, or a call, and ready to run, like I can run, very quickly to her. But the door opened behind me and there he was, not red any more, but white and smaller, in his bed gown and a nightcap on his head. He said fearful curses when he saw me, and called me the witch's devil, and said to get out of his sight and out of his house, and never let him see my ugly face again. I started to run, but he called after me to send somebody with a bottle of brandy. 'Can you understand that much? B-r-a-n-d-y. Brandy. Quick. With a bottle inside me I can deal with that she-devil. Brandy, do you understand?'

I nodded and ran down the front stairs to get to her quickly in the garden. But at the bottom of the stairs was my angel. It said, 'This is your chance. Remember the toothache medicine.'

'But I don't know brandy,' I said. 'I hear the words he said so loud and slow, but they are in the dark for me.'

'Any bottle will do,' the angel said.

I knew where they were. It was nearly dark in the dining-room, but I found them. There were many, and alike to me except one not quite full to the neck. I took its cork out and filled it up with the toothache medicine.

I was afraid he would not have it when he saw me with it. I went in, very frightened. He was back in the bed, and he roared at me like Mr Barber's bull. But I held up the bottle and then he was different. It was slyness and as if we were in a secret together.

'Good girl,' he said, very pleased.

There was a jug on the table near the bed, a blue jug with a silver lid on it.

'Empty that muck in the slop jar,' he said, 'and fill it up from the bottle. Can you manage that?'

I nodded and poured away the good barley water She had made him.

'Now take the bottle away. That'll fox my beauty and the fool of a doctor. And mind you, not a word to anyone.' That made me laugh. But he was angry again, and said, 'It's come to a pretty pass that I should lie here dependent on an idiot to get me a drink to keep a little life in me! But I'll show 'em; I'll show 'em yet!'

I thought to take the bottle and hide it in my room because there was a smell of toothache medicine about it. On the back stairs Cook met me. She was angry about the cooking, and because I was the one to sit up in the night. She was always looking to find a fault with me. She looked then and saw the bottle. She said nasty things about that She and I drank the poor Master's wine when he was fobbed off with pap, and them that lived longest would see most.

I put the bottle under my bed with my petticoat that I could not cut. It seemed funny to put his thing and her thing together like that.

There was the night, and I did not sleep much. On my mind there was the toothache medicine working in him, and our mum saying not to swallow what was on the wool, but spit hard and not be poisoned. Nobody knew to tell him except me, and I had done it. There would be good times always now, with us together like the angel promised.

In the morning I made the tea and went to the little room. She was asleep on the couch, very white and tired looking.

When She woke up She said, 'Are you early this morning, Lindy? Or have I overslept? I was disturbed. The Master was sick.'

Sick! Sick! I had not remembered the time when the poaching chap was hanged and our Jill swallowed the medicine, and mum made her sick with the feather in her throat. So much there was to remember, I must forget some. The room in the head will not hold it all. So he was sick, and there would be a new place for me and not good times again.

She put on her robe and went carefully into the bedroom. I waited to hear roaring. But it did not happen. There was a great stillness. There was never such a stillness, not even when the wind has been howling and then I let it in.

She came back into the little room. And then there was a sound. My heart knocked like father's hammer, and so did hers. They knocked together, quick and heavy; together for always like the angel said.

She said, 'Pour me a cup, Lindy, quickly. He is dead. Yesterday he was not so well, and now he is dead.'

He hadn't sucked it all up. There had not been tickling of the throat with a feather. So it was all right.

She said, 'I must let Miss Dilys know, and Doctor Stamper.'

When the tea was drunk She went back in the room and brought out the blue jug with the lid and all the other things he had used and put them on the tray for washing.

On the stairs going down I smelt the jug, and there were the two smells still, sweet like new hay and sleepy like poppies near the face; but there was another smell, too, sharp and strong. That was brandy. But I washed the jug and all the things with the cups.

There was too much talk. With me, when anything is done it is ended. With me it was all over with the washing of the jug. But not with the others.

I didn't hear all the talk that day, because I stayed near her, as near as I could. The cords were very tight that day. But there was bad talk when Miss Dilys came with her husband, the young man that had been like a blossoming tree. She was married now. Mrs Fennel, they called her. And in the kitchen they said to her all about the illness, how nobody went near except us two, and how he said he was poisoned, and how She always cooked because of the complaints. I heard it all afterwards when She was in the front of the house and Mr Fennel–he was very much busying himself all day–said, 'To say the least, you seem to have taken a good deal of authority into your hands, Miss Woodroffe.' He was nasty then.

She said, 'Oh, of course it appears so to you. But there is something that you do not know. I may as well tell you now, since you are bound to know. Your father married me, Dilys.'

Miss Dilys said, 'I don't believe it. When?'

'On the seventeenth of February this year.'

'A week after I . . . just when I was . . . Why on earth should he do that?'

'For the usual reason I imagine.'

Mr Fennel said, 'But why this secrecy?'

'It was Mr Helmar's wish. I think he was ashamed of it. He had had too many women, too easily. But he had lost them easily too, and the idea of marriage was his–though you will hardly believe that.'

'Hardly,' Mr Fennel said. He turned to Miss Dilys and said, 'Dilys, you understand what this means. She's taken Mortiboys from you.'

There was some silence, and a bad cold air in the room.

Then She said, 'We were free people, free to make our own bargain. Marriage was what he wanted, strange as that may sound to you. And I made my own condition, which was that he should make Mortiboys over to me then and there. It was all done in Lawyer Aldritch's office, perfectly legal and above board.'

There was some more silence. Then She said, 'So you see, Mr Fennel, your attack on me is unjustified. Who should tend a sick man but his wife? Who else should assume authority? It was not even as though you and Dilys had been on good terms with him.' She stood up very straight and breathed in, quite loud, through her nose. 'As for this ridiculous kitchen gossip about my having starved him and neglected him, Doctor Stamper will deal wth that when he arrives. Four days ago he congratulated me upon my nursing, and the way I was keeping his eating and drinking under control.'

'You have sent for the doctor?'

'Does that surprise you?' she asked him in a rude voice. Then She came away and left them. I came too. I did not understand much of the talk, though I remembered it all just as they said it. But I did understand that She had been Mrs Helmar for a long time. That was funny. I had seen them both in many shapes, but not love once. Love is easy to see. Mr Fennel had it, especially that first time. It is enough for one to have it out of two. But two without it. That was funny.

Doctor Stamper came. There was some more talk. Everywhere in the house there was talk and guessing and people's bad shapes saying nasty things. And then here was poison. All at once everybody was saying poison, poison, poison. The frightening started in me then, because of the toothache medicine. That was poison.

At first I was frightened that they should say I did the poisoning. Because I did it. And then they would take me away and the promise the angel said would not be true. But afterwards it was worse than that, because they said She did it.

It was Doctor Stamper said it, and Miss Dilys and Mr Fennel, and Cook and the others. It was the talk. It never stopped. Talk and talk. And then there were questions too. The world was full of men with big mouths asking questions.

And in the kitchen they said She would hang, and serve her right. Then I was mad and shouted and beat on my chest and got a bottle and tried to show what I did. Somebody held me still, and in the stillness somebody said, 'She knows something. She helped, that is why she was such a favourite.' There was more talk, with me in it that time.

There is a thing called accomplice. That was my name then. I was accomplice. I did not know what it means but it was good. They put us together.

I did not know whether to be sorry or happy. I was happy to be with her, and for everybody to talk about us as if we were one person; but if it was to be hanging, I was sorry. Because I did it. And hanging is a bad thing. I know because of the young chap that was hanged for poaching. If there was to be hanging it must be me to hang. But I wanted us to be together until it started.

They took us away. They put us together in a little room, small and dark all day, with a smelly bucket in the corner. She was very quiet, not sad. It was harder than sadness. It was like setting a trap for a rabbit and catching a stoat in it; the stoat is not scared like a rabbit, but is angry and still, but the stillness is watchful; it will get away if there is a chance. Like that it was. Except that She was sorry about me. Over and over She said to everybody to let me go. She said She was innocent, and that would be proved; but that against me there was not even a shadow of a case. Nobody took any notice.

I wanted to tell her that it was me to hang. I tried and tried to say about the toothache medicine and the bottle and the poison that I did. But the words were worse than ever. When I tried the words were just red flannel and a thick angry noise. The floor was dirty and I drew on it with my finger, a brandy bottle. I showed how it was not full and then full. I made her look. She said:

'Oh yes Lindy, the cook mentioned seeing you with a bottle. Was it brandy?'

I nodded my head loose.

'But that didn't *kill* him,' She said. 'You mustn't think you killed him. Brandy was bad for him, but it wouldn't be fatal. He was poisoned.'

I nodded again, and beat on my chest and tried to talk.

'But you didn't do it. Poor Lindy, to think that! No. Somebody who hated me did it. Such an obvious way to choose. But who? Who?'

She tried to keep us clean. But it was hard. The room was dirty and the smell of the bucket in the corner was everywhere. It was in the food. But there was a comb and She did our hair every day. One day when She was combing mine it stopped suddenly. I looked and her shape was there but She was gone. She stood still with the comb in her hand and her eyes were dead, staring at the bare wall. I was frightened and was still, too. It lasted a little time. Then She put the comb down and covered her face with her hands, moaning. She said, 'I've never seen a false vision.'

After that there was a difference. It was a rabbit now, not a stoat. The fight was gone out of her. And She was very, very kind to me. Once She said, 'Lindy, you work well and understand simple orders, but I wish I knew how much you understand of all this. If we hang . . .' only in her voice I could hear that the *if* was very small, '. . . I have brought you to it.' She looked at me in the face, very close and serious. 'But you don't understand, poor Lindy, or you'd hate me. As I hate whoever brought me to this.' She jumped up and stamped and swore and said, 'May they rot in hell for ever.' And that was me! I did it. I cried and knelt down and beat my head on her feet. She pulled me up and wiped my face and comforted me.

If only the angel would come and then I could tell her. I could tell her and She could tell everybody. But the angel didn't know about the little smelly room at Colchester. It was still looking for me at Minsham. It was a Minsham angel, in father's book and in the church window, and at Mortiboys. Not here.

There was a big room next, divided into parts like a stable with loose boxes. There were many people in the places. She and I were in one place together. There was one man alone with some hair made out of a horse's tail on his head. There was a bunch of flowers too. And the smell was better than in our room.

Then was the time of the talk and the questions. And the words were hard. I can remember words that I cannot say and words that I cannot understand. But not then. There were too many. People dressed up just to ask questions. And to tell things. Some things were true and some were not true. They said about the quarrels. I had been there when She and the Master quarrelled, but I had not seen the others there. They said they knew though. They said things they had heard her say. How? How could they hear those things? And they said about the food. Over and over they said about her getting the food ready herself. But that was because he had complained so. And poison. They said about when he flung the gruel away and said he was poisoned. But it was the doctor said gruel and not the steak the Master wanted. And they said about me. They said I was a lunatic, but I did everything She said. That was true. But She had never said to me about poisoning him. That was my angel.

There were days in the big room. And always when we were back together She was quiet and low and very kind to me.

Then there was a day when I could smell a rose. I looked at the horsehair man and his flowers, and there was my angel. I shouted loud. I daren't waste a minute saying to the angel why didn't it come sooner. It might go and I not have said what was important. I just shouted very loud:

'I did it. I did it. She didn't . . .' I could have told them all about it, but they shook me and stopped. A man hit me, quite hard, on the head. And She said, 'You mustn't interrupt.' I looked at the angel. It was looking kindly. 'You tell them. You tell them it was me, and how I did it,' I said. But they stopped me again. The angel said, 'Hanging is nasty, but not long,' and then it was gone.

It was worse after that. I had done badly again. They thought I could talk if I wanted to. And they believed I did it; but they said, and it is a hard thing to understand, that I was the hand but She was the mind. They said the word accomplice again.

After all the men talking and the questions there was the time when She talked herself, and it was like a bird singing, but not like a bird in a flowery bush any more. It was like the last twittery songs before the sad cold weather starts. It was as though She knew that saying things wouldn't do good now. All the same She said them; She said all the things that I would have said, and more. And She spoke for me. I thought there was more heart in her when She spoke for me. But it didn't do.

Then there was a solemn time and the man with the horse-tail hair talked. It was plain that he was against us. Part of it was like Parson's talk. But it was for me really, not her. I had done it. When he said 'secret deadly weapon of poison,' it was me he meant. Then I must interrupt. I shouted and waved my arms, and beat on my chest. I did the taking of the bottle out and filling it; I pointed in my mouth to show that if there was hanging it was me to do it. But they didn't mind. They held me and made me be still. They were very angry.

When I was shaken and battered to be quiet there was some great silence. There was some black put on the horse-tail hair and the man said solemn words about hanging.

After that they took us away and put us back in the little room.

So it was hanging. I tried to tell her what the angel said, 'Hanging is nasty, but not long.' That would comfort her. But the words would not come. I cried and tried to show her on my neck–nasty, but not long. But She did not understand. She thought I cried and held my neck because I was frightened of the hanging. She was frightened, too. I could smell the fear on her, but She tried to comfort me.

Next morning–only it wasn't day and night in that dark place–but it was morning because the man threw the food at us; then She did not clean us, or comb our hair. And the food She left. I wondered and tried to ask. Then She showed me her hands. They were dead; the fingers were white like candles and the nails were blue. The white fingers were doubled in over her palms, fixed and dead. So I held the water for her to drink; I would have held the food too, but She turned her mouth away. Afterwards I did our hair and cleaned us.

The man called Lawyer Aldritch came. He was good and sorry, and spoke as though he didn't think we did it. She changed then and was eager again. They had a hard talk. She said, 'You are sure that it will be in order?' He said, 'Yes. As I made clear at the trial, you did not profit by the . . . death of your husband. The property was already yours. If it had been willed to you it would have been different. As it is, it is yours to do what you like with.'

Then She said about leaving it all to young Mr Hatton in our village, and Lawyer Aldritch wrote it down.

'You must sign it,' he said. And She held out her hands to show him. 'But I will sign it,' She said, 'if it is the last thing I do on this earth.' She took the pen in her mouth. Lawyer Aldritch called in two men and they stood, very solemn, while She bent and twisted her head, making marks on the paper. Lawyer Aldritch sweated a lot. The men wrote their names and went away.

There was ink all round her mouth and I wiped it, but not all, there was a mark still.

She said: 'Well, that's done. And I have done what I set out to do, though not this way. However, I have done it.' It sounded so sad, and so ending, like when She said, 'the last thing I do on this earth,' that I began to cry again. She tried to put her arm round me. Then She said, 'Could you, would you write a letter for me?' Lawyer Aldritch said, 'Certainly, I will do anything I can. Will this poor creature disturb you? Shall I have her removed?' But She said, 'No. Lindy never disturbs me.'

He dipped his pen and She said the letter. She said She had left him Mortiboys, and hoped he would enjoy it, because did he remember a hot day when the butter wouldn't come and he said what he wanted in life. She said about the time when he and Miss Dilys were going to be married, and the Master said no Mortiboys for them, so then She thought to get it and give it to them. She said She married him because if Mr Hatton married Miss Dilys it didn't matter what happened to her.

It was a long letter, and sad past crying. Even I stopped crying, and Lawyer Aldritch wiped his face and moved his glasses about. She said Mr

Hatton must please believe that She didn't poison Mr Helmar; what was wrong was to marry him when She only loved Mr Hatton, and had done ever since he saved her from the pond. And She ended not to let the way Mortiboys came to him spoil it, but to enjoy it because if not her whole life had been wasted.

Lawyer Aldritch took his glasses off, and wiped the sweat and round his eyes as well.

She said, 'I hope that is clear. This isn't quite like *writing* a letter, you know.'

Lawyer Aldritch started to say that it was quite clear, but his words came out wrong and broken, too. He said something about heart-breaking.

She went back towards the wall and stood there. She said, 'I hadn't thought of that. I just wanted to make it clear . . . so that he should know *why*. But I don't want to make him miserable.' There was a little time. Then She said, 'I'm sorry, Mr Aldritch, after making you write it, but tear it up for me, will you, please? Yes, that is best; then he'll think I left it to him because I didn't know anybody else.'

Lawyer Aldritch looked at the letter and at her, and he wiped his face some more.

'I don't like the responsibility of doing that . . .' he said.

'No. All right. Lindy, come here and tear this paper, please.'

I was glad to do what she said. I tore it in little bits and they fell on the floor. She said, thank you: and She said it to Mr Aldritch too. He mumbled some words and went away.

Then we were together, like my angel said. She sat on the board that was for sleeping and I sat on the floor with my head against her knees, like a dog. It was quiet. She was quiet, too. It was like the end of something. Presently She said, 'Everything is over now, Lindy, except the hanging. Look at me.' I turned my head. 'I wish I knew how much you understood. We're only dying a little early, Lindy. Can you understand that? Everybody starts to die as soon as they are born. And you were afflicted, and I was always unlucky.'

I tried once more to tell her what my angel said about hanging. But the words would not come and I was afraid to make a noise, trying. Then She said it. The very thing. She said, 'Hanging is a nasty business, Lindy, but it doesn't last long.' I nodded and smiled to show that that was what I wanted to say. 'We must be quiet,' She said, 'and try not to make spectacles of ourselves. Can you understand that? Whatever they do to us, we must be quiet.'

I nodded again, and sat very still to show that I knew about being quiet. She twisted so that one of her arms, with the poor dead hand at the end of it, lay over my shoulder. She said, 'If you can understand anything, Lindy, understand this. I'm sorry from my heart that they dragged you into it. But it wasn't my fault. I'm innocent, too. I tricked him, and I hated him, and I wished him dead. But I didn't do it either.'

It was no good trying to tell her again, or to beat on my chest and disturb her hand. So I sat still. I would be very quiet. I hoped they would do the hanging on me first, so She would see me quiet and be pleased with me.

Bless This House

Norah Lofts

EPISODE ONE
Elizabethan

THE APPRENTICE

We—that is, my Uncle Francis and I—finished the building of Tom Rowhedge's new house at Merravay on the last Saturday in October in the year 1577.

The weather had changed that day and it was bright and clear, with a hint of frost in the air. It was still sunny when, at mid-afternoon, Uncle Frank stepped back to survey the last bit of the work that had fallen to his share, the carving of the great newel-post at the stair-foot. I knew he had finished although I had my back to him and did not look round. I heard him grunt as he straightened himself; heard his foot on the floor as he stepped back; heard the sound of his horny hands rubbing together with satisfaction. Presently he spoke:

'Well, Jonathan boy, thass done. And though I say it, as sound and pretty a job as any I ever see.'

I said 'Umm' behind my teeth. If he wanted praise for his work, I thought, let him look elsewhere. Not that praise would be lacking, for every bit of his skill and craftsmanship had gone into that staircase and it was a job any man might rightly be proud of. He waited for a moment as though expectant of some further response from me, but I went on with my own last job, the fitting of the wide seat into the space under the big window on the far side of the hall. I hoped that he would go away, go home and leave me in peace. My thoughts, though far from pleasant, were preferable to his company.

He moved over to the place where our rush baskets yawned on the floor. I heard the clank of his tools as he laid them away; and then the gurgle of ale as he drank from the wooden bottle.

'Are you dry?'

'No,' I said.

He fumbled about in the bag in which we carried our noon-pieces. There was food in it, for he had eaten lightly at noon, being anxious to get back to his newel-post, and I, not to be outdone, had also gone back to work with my hunger unsatisfied. I now heard the squeak of a knife against the crisp crust of the loaf, and then the moister sound of an onion being sliced.

'Care for a bite, then?'

'No.'

He chumbled his food in his usual noisy way.

'How long do you reckon it'll take you to finish?'

If I said a short time he would wait for me; if I said a long one he would offer to help me.

'I don't know,' I said.

He strolled over towards me, wiping his mouth on the back of his hand.

'You keep on at that rate, boy, and you gotta hour's work. Thass where you're weak yet, Jonathan–reckoning up a job. You want to be able to cast your eye over a job and reckon exactly how long it'll take; otherwise, when a customer say "How much?", you'd be all at sea, like. You'll hev to go a bit more careful when you get this end near the brickwork, don't you'll skin your knuckles. And, you know, I *still* think them pegs is cut a mite short. I quite see there ain't the wear and tear on a window-seat that there is on stairs–still, you want a job to last. Every peg in them stairs'–he turned and looked at his handiwork–'is six inches long. Ah, them stairs'll be there, sound as they are today, when your children's children are old 'uns with children of their own.'

Wonderful! I thought. Tom Rowhedge's children and theirs, and theirs, scampering up and down, all safe and secure because every peg in 'them' stairs is six inches long and driven by an honest man. Oh, for God's sake go away and leave me alone! With my very teeth on edge, I waited for him to say that he'd give me a hand. However, when he spoke he said:

'I'll just go and hev a look at that well-cover; then there's another little job I wanta do. I'll be back time you're finished. Ony go a bit wary, like, when you get to the corner. Once knew a man bark his knuckles on a new wall that hadn't had time to get friendly, and a rare lot of trouble he had. His fingers was stiff to the end of his days.'

'I'm always careful,' I said shortly.

He left me. I heard the big door beyond the screen open and close, sweetly for all it was so newly hung.

Well, God be thanked, I thought, that's over. These last two months when Uncle Francis and I had been working alone in Tom's house had been about as much as I could endure. But it was over; when the last of my too-short, new-fashioned pegs was driven home Tom's house would stand, sound and beautiful, all ready for occupation.

I had only two more to drive when a chance glance through the window showed me Uncle Francis, with a short axe in his hand, striding away across the clear space which was to be the garden, and in which there was already a sundial, like the hub of a wheel, with tiny young box hedges radiating out like spokes, marking off the beds where next year the flowers would bloom. He jumped, nimble as a boy, across the dividing ditch, and set off across the meadow in the direction of Layer Wood. This afternoon the lowering sun shone on the thinned blazing leaves of the beeches, and the contrast between them and the few dark firs that grew amongst them was as startling and lovely as it was in the spring of the year when the firs looked black against the bright translucent young green. Wondering what in the world he was up to now, I drove home my last two pegs and laid my tools away. Then I lifted the ale bottle and shook it. It was empty. Quite reasonably, when I said I wasn't thirsty, Uncle Francis had drained it. I was reminded of one of the hateful old sayings which he quoted at me when I was a child and refused something and then regretted it. 'He who will not when he may, when he would he shall have nothing.' My uncle was never at a loss for a proverb, and he produced every one as though it were mint new.

Setting the empty bottle back in the basket, I remembered another of silly sayings: 'More ways of killing a cat then choking it with butter.' Most applicable in my case, because I had just remembered where I could get myself a drink. At Eastertime, just before the bricklayers, the tilers, the plasterers and ordinary carpenters had finished their work and were about to leave, Tom Rowhedge had paid us a day's visit and had stumped about all over the house, laughing and shouting, wildly excited, extremely pleased with all he saw. He had brought food with him, a whole ham, a great silverside of beef, a barrel of ale, a butt of wine and a little keg of French brandy. There'd been an hilarious feast.

I was sick that day; and although I hoped nobody had noticed me when I crept away, Tom had. Next morning, very early on his way back to Bywater where his ship lay, he had halted his horse by our house and, without dismounting, rapped on the door. I opened it. He looked down at me and said:

'I was sorry you took sick, Jon. You still look a bit green; have a care to yourself. What I came to tell you was–they finished all but the brandy, and that I laid by for you when you feel better. It's in the buttery cupboard and the key's under the beam. I must go. God keep you, Jon. I'll see you at Christmas.'

He rode off into the mist of the August morning, leaving me with this new bit of his kindness lying like lead in my sick belly.

Now I took from my basket the horn cup which Uncle Francis had not troubled to use when he drank and carried it along, through the passage that led to the kitchen quarters, into the buttery, which smelt clean and fresh of new wood and new whitewash. I found the key and opened the cupboard, and there was the little cask. I drew myself a cupful of the brandy and sipped it, somewhat disappointed. I had never tasted brandy before; the duty on it was heavy and put it beyond the means of working men, but I had heard about it and had expected something wonderful. And plainly Tom had thought he was doing me a special favour when he hid it for me. I thought it lacked the flavour of good ale and it hadn't the same mouth-filling quality; one's thirst didn't leap to welcome it and there was something rather choky about it. However, it was something to drink; and as it went down it was warming. I was grateful for that, because I'd been working hard and grown hot, and the buttery, placed on the north side of the house for coolness, struck me with a sudden chill. So I emptied the cup and filled it again. And then, quite suddenly, I understood why people who could afford it would buy brandy whatever the duty on it. I felt warm and light and taken out of myself. I could look back and regard all that had happened to me as though it had happened to another person. Nothing hurt any more. Everything was very clear and bright, but it was like a story, or like–if one could imagine such a thing–a series of vivid pictures in which people moved and talked . . . and I watched, understanding, sympathising, one with the person whose story it was, and yet detached, interested, unhurt.

I suppose it was natural, since I was sitting in Tom Rowhedge's house drinking Tom Rowhedge's brandy, that I should begin by remembering, or my recalling, or my re-seeing, with my first meeting with him. I'd seen him before because we were both at King Edward VI's Grammar School; but he was a lordly great boy of thirteen and I was a lowly worm of eight, so between us there was a great gulf fixed, a gulf wider and deeper and more carefully guarded than any which the adult world knows, a gulf neither of us would have dreamed of crossing even if we had been blood-brothers. The sight of him walking with his father into the little apothecary's shop which my father kept in the Friargate, and which I was 'minding' on this August morning during my first holiday, covered me with the blushing confusion only experienced by schoolboys. It was made all the worse because I had just then a private and particular reason for trying to appear indispensable to my father, but I knew I couldn't serve Mr Rowhedge nimbly and satisfactorily under Tom's eye, so I weakly rang the bell which summonsed Father. He came and quickly served Mr Rowhedge with the horse-pills he wanted.

'Your boy, Martin?' he asked.

'Aye, and a right helpful little fellow,' said Father.

Tom's father eyed me as though I were an animal he thought of purchasing but had doubts about.

'Bit pingling-looking, ain't he? Either you work him too hard, Martin, or else you give him the wrong physic.' It was understandable that old Rowhedge, accustomed to looking at Tom, and perhaps to catching sight of his own reflection in a polished pan, should think that I looked very small and pale, for their faces–very much alike–were broad and red and shining with health.

'He isn't much of an advertisement for my trade, certainly,' said Father in his precise way. 'But apart from his little trouble–and that is mending–he's healthy enough. He seldom ails.' Please God, I begged, don't let the great oaf ask what is my little trouble! 'And he has a head on him,' Father went on fatuously. 'Doing well up at the school, aren't you, Jon boy?' Oh, horror upon horror! In front of a big boy, too.

'Tell you what, Martin,' said Mr Rowhedge. 'It'd do him the world of good to come out to Slipwell till th'end of the holiday. Famous good air out at Slipwell. A chestful of that and a bellyful of good farm food'd make a new boy of him.'

My face felt redder than a poppy. The man meant well, of course, but I resented his remarks about my appearance, and I was embarrassed beyond measure at the suggestion that I should go and stay in Tom Rowhedge's house. Good heavens, he might be obliged to speak to me.

'What d'you say, Jon? Would you like that?' Father was never the man to make up another person's mind for him.

I looked helplessly at Tom; and he was grinning at me.

'You could be my crew,' he said. 'I want somebody small and light.'

That was nothing less than an order. So I nodded, being beyond speech.

'You can ride back ahind of Tom,' said Mr Rowhedge. 'The cob'll never notice your weight!'

The holiday thus carelessly suggested changed, not the course but the flavour of my life. Not because of anything in itself but because it forestalled and prevented me from asking Father to let me leave school. I'd had a half-year at King Edward's School, and that was quite enough for me. I was almost certain that I had only to tell Father what it was really like and he would not wish me to remain. But the holiday had slipped away without ever presenting me with the ideal opportunity for stating my case; Father was very busy. He had his shop and his workroom, he had his hobby, which was helping an eccentric old neighbour to set up and work a little printing press upon which they aimed, one day, to print Greaves' *Herbal*, and he had also to do all that was done on the domestic side. My mother had died when

I was very small, and Father's experience with hired help had been discouraging. So, being anxious to have his whole attention for my horrifying tale, I had avoided all those occasions when it seemed likely that he would say, 'Don't bother me at the moment, Jon, boy', or 'Oh yes. Yes. Yes, I'm listening', when it was obvious that he was doing nothing of the sort. I had concentrated upon helping him so earnestly, so devotedly that he would deem me indispensable. And my reward for that was to be in the shop when the Rowhedges came in, and to be whisked off to Slipwell all in a minute and finally find myself, at the end of the holiday, riding back to school behind Tom. I'd hesitated and I'd lost.

By the time that school closed for Christmas the idea of leaving would have filled me with dismay.

The change was in me, not in the school. The rising bell still clanged at six in the morning; we still washed in cold water, seven or eight to a basin, and woe betide him whose ablutions were scamped; we still hurried down to the great cold classroom and did two hours' work before attaining the dubious comfort of breakfast, a hunk of bread thinly smeared with lardy-fat and a mug of the sourest, flattest liquid ever called ale. No item of the routine varied. After breakfast we were turned into the yard to warm ourselves with rough play, and the bullies were busy, the tricksters played their practical jokes. Then we worked again until midday, each misunderstanding, each mistake, each scrap of detected inattention calling into play the formidable birch which Dr Trudgett always carried under his left arm, whence it could, in the blink of an eye, be transferred to his right hand, which, for all it looked thin and frail, was as strong as a blacksmith's.

When I had planned my school-leaving campaign I had especially meant to emphasise the difference between the Dr Trudgett whom my father knew and liked and the Dr Trudgett whom the classroom knew and feared. Father had for many years had dealings with the schoolmaster, because, when King Edward had established the school on the site of the old Abbey of St Dunstan, the first headmaster had saved from ruin the little herb garden which the monks had tended. In later days this had become a source of steady income to his successors, for most of the herb gardens attached to the monasteries and nunneries had been allowed to perish through lack of care, and in my day apothecaries and physicians from as far away as London sent to Baildon for their supplies. It was through buying herbs from the school garden that Father first got in touch with Dr Trudgett, whom he came to admire very much, saying–and that was high praise–that he was a most enlightened man. And I can believe that standing in the evening light amongst the sweet smelling herbs, discoursing upon this subject and that, Dr Trudgett showed to advantage. Possibly Father showed to advantage too; for when the idea of sending me to school was mooted Dr Trudgett welcomed it, despite my disability, which Father, in his honest way, felt bound to mention.

'I have enough healthy ploughboys,' he said. 'And more than a few good scholars have been subject to just such fits as you describe in your boy.'

He had added that most boys came to school too late, and that in his opinion I should begin at once. And so I went to school after the Christmas in the year when I was eight.

But Father had never seen Dr Trudgett in the classroom. Never heard him say to some pallid, trembling blunderer:

'You cannot reckon seven times eight! That must be mended, sir. Bend over and count aloud.'

Seven times eight is fifty-six, and fifty-six strokes from Dr Trudgett's birch would set the blood running from a boy's breeches.

That was the kind of thing I had intended to tell Father. But I never did. For as soon as I entered upon my second half-year, having in the first mastered the painful rudiments, I found that I had the makings of a scholar. There is no vanity in that statement; it is a quotation from Dr Trudgett's own dictum.

Within a week of our return to school I went to the head of the bench, and I stayed there. Before Michaelmas I moved to the next, where nobody was less than twelve years old. I was fuddled at first, but I was so eager, so desperate to get along with this fascinating business of learning, that I even ventured to hold up my arm and ask for enlightenment when I did not understand. And more than once Dr Trudgett would say, 'That is an intelligent question!' and he would explain, painstakingly.

Within the classroom all began to go well; and outside, too, in the yard, on the holding of forty acres where we worked, for Dr Trudgett's benefit, in the afternoon, and in the big dormitory at night, things were better. I mean for me. And thanks for that were due to Tom Rowhedge. I might now be roaring ahead with the Trivorium–that is, grammar, logic and rhetoric–and rather more than holding my own with the Quadrivium, though my arithmetic was faulty yet, but I was still a small boy, weak-fisted, and a born butt for fools because of my funny fits. But after that holiday, when I had been the meek, easily ordered 'crew' of the boat that Tom had built and loved to sail on the river at Slipwell, he had assumed a kind of responsibility for me. By doing so he showed, not merely physical courage but a boldness of spirit, a disregard for custom and tradition. He was thirteen years old, very big and strong for his age, but he was not yet amongst the biggest of the boys, and he was a lamentably poor scholar. He still had his way to make in his own sphere. Any other big boy would have withdrawn himself and ignored me once we were back at school; but Tom did not. And one day, finding me in trouble, he said, 'Leave him alone or you'll have me to reckon with.' The boys who were bullying me were bigger than Tom and higher up in the school. But they were taken by surprise at his unorthodoxy and remembered his reputation as a fighter. They jeered, of course, to cover their discomfiture, but they drifted off without having accomplished their purpose, which was to see if I could be teased into having a fit. And after that I noticed a great lessening in the torment to which I had been subjected.

I don't think I could have been teased into a fit. Nobody teased me, that I can remember, when I lived at home with Father, and there I had fits pretty frequently. In those days they took me unaware. There would be a kind of crackling sound, like that of a stick fire newly lighted, in my ears and a flash or two of light before my eyes. Then the shutter came down and there was darkness. When I came round I felt a little weak and dizzy, but quite all right, except that once I had almost bitten my tongue through. After that–I suppose I was about six years old then–at the first crackle I used to thrust my thumb into my mouth and wait, looking like a thumb-sucking zany, until the shutter fell. And soon I was wary enough to seek privacy at the first warning sign. At school, of course, that wasn't always possible, and to the louts my fits were a source of amusement. Dr Trudgett, on the other hand, one day when I had one in his presence and came round, dizzy and apologetic, said:

'Don't worry about it, Borage. I've always been inclined to think that the Apostle Paul was similarly afflicted. He speaks often of a bodily weakness, and men have been at a pains to name it, attributing to him everything from lameness to lung sickness. But I think the clue lies in his experience on the road to Damascus. Tell me, do you see a great light?'

'Not a great light, sir. A feeble flash or two.'

'And do you hear voices?'

'No voices, sir. Only a faint crackling.'

'Well, you are young. And you are not an apostle. And you are not a saint. And probably I am talking nonsense. I merely wished to point out to you that your ailment is no reason for shame; nor for idleness. . . .'

I certainly was not idle, though that was small credit to me. I learned as naturally, as eagerly and with as much pleasure as other boys played. When I returned to school after the Christmas when I was ten years old I was placed on the top bench but one, and I vowed to myself that by Easter I would deserve, even though I did not attain, a remove. Tom Rowhedge, who before Christmas had occupied the very seat in which I now sat, did not return to school, having realised his dream of going to sea. His father, with three elder sons to work the farm and share it, was anxious that he should seek a livelihood elsewhere and had sent him to school with the intention of making a merchant of him. But Tom chose for himself, and the old man had promised that when he was as much at home on the sea as he was on land he would buy and fit out a ship for him.

It was February, and I was halfway up the bench and with six weeks still to go before Easter when it happened.

The usher, Master Richards, was taking the evening class when the message came for me to go to Dr Trudgett's room. Boys near me whispered their jibes or their commiserations, according to their nature, and indicated, by dumb show, what I might expect when I got there. But walking along the dim passage, which in the old days had been a cloister, I could not, search my mind as I might, hit upon any fault or any offence serious enough to rate being called out from evening study. Even my arithmetic–always shaky–had seemed correct when I checked my answers with those of a boy who very seldom made a miscalculation. Still, one never knew. . . .

Dr Trudgett was not alone in his grim little room; I was aware of that, though I did not look at the visitor. I took a swift glance at my master's face and saw that something had upset him. He had a pale face as a rule, but anger always painted a thin pink glaze over his cheekbones. It was there now, and I dropped my eyes quickly and stood looking down at my own feet, while my trepidation mounted. However, Dr Trudgett spoke kindly:

'Come in, boy.' He turned on the stranger and said, 'Well, here he is, and you can see for yourself what I said. He's not cut out for manual labour. He has a modicum of brains, though. I had hopes for him.'

'Had', not 'have'; even then I noticed the tense.

I looked up, this time at the other man. He was a big, thick-set fellow, clad in the drab-coloured homespun which workmen wear on Sundays and holidays when they discard their working clothes. His deeply tanned face was heavily furrowed and wore a brooding look; the frown-scars on his brow, the way the thick eyebrows jutted and knotted prepared one for a glance of some ferocity, yet his eyes, surprisingly light and blue, had a mild and kindly look.

'I'm your uncle, Francis Sheply,' he said, 'and I'm afraid I've brung you bad news.'

I had never heard of him in my life; I was unaware that I had any relatives at all.

'Yes,' said Dr Trudgett. 'Perhaps you'd better sit down, Borage.'

More puzzled than ever, I took the chair he indicated and sat down on its edge, glancing from one face to another, waiting for one man or the other to break the bad news, whatever it might be. I hadn't a suspicion, even then.

'Your father is dead,' said my uncle. 'It seems he cut his thumb a while back and never heeded it, but it turned to blood-poisoning and his end come very sudden. He on'y just had time to send for me and bid me care for you. And that, my boy, I'm right ready to do.' He gave me a smile of kind reassurance which lighted his dark face strangely, and then he looked at Dr Trudgett and added firmly, 'According to my lights.'

Dr Trudgett ignored this and came and laid his hand on my shoulder.

'You've sustained a heavy loss, Jonathan. You have my sympathy.' His hand increased its pressure for a second before it withdrew. 'Cry if you want to,' he said. 'There's easement in tears.'

But there were no tears in me just then. I sat there with every feeling in me stunned, save only a half-fearful curiosity. Dr Trudgett moved towards the window embrasure and with a jerk of his head indicated that my uncle should follow him.

'About this other business,' he began in a low voice, 'we must beware of making a hasty decision. And one thing to remember is that the lad is subject to fits. It seems to me that your plan for him would offer certain risks.'

'He'll be under my eye. And he might well take a fit when he was sharpening a quill! There's another thing too. For a boy like that a quiet outdoor life might work a cure. Too much striving indoors and fretting his brain may be the root of the trouble.'

'Nonsense!' ejaculated Dr Trudgett. But it seemed to me that even *he* had realised that Uncle Francis Sheply was not a man to be turned by direct opposition. He said more persuasively:

'Let us defer the matter for a while, say until the end of the half-year. That can do no harm. And if you are thinking of the cost–as I can well understand you may be–think no more of it. Martin Borage chose to pay the fee, but there are provisions in the foundation for poor scholars, and there would be no difficulty, no difficulty at all.'

''Tisn't the cost. The boy is no pauper. Martin Borage had money saved and owned his freehold. There'll be enough to set Jonathan up in business when the time comes.'

This simple–and interesting–statement seemed to set fire to Dr Trudgett's always easily in imflammable temper.

'Then in God's name, man, *why* do you suggest taking him away?'

'Because, on his death-bed, Martin Borage sent for me and I gave him my solemn promise to handle the boy as though he was my own. Martin Borage and me was never friends, but the boy is my sister's child and therefore my flesh and blood, halfway at least. So I give my word, and my boy he is from this day forward. And no boy of mine would spend his young years sitting on a school bench.'

'Why not?'

'Because I don't hold with it.' That was the first time I heard those words fall from my uncle's tongue, and I did not understand their deadly significance. I sat there, apparently disregarded, with my head in my hands, listening avidly; and I knew now roughly what the argument was about. I trusted Dr Trudgett to rout Francis Sheply. I didn't know then that when Francis Sheply said 'I don't hold with it' there was no more to be said.

Dr Trudgett, equally ignorant, said:

'And what, pray, do you mean by *that*? Why do you not hold with schooling?'

'I never said I didn't hold with schooling. I said I didn't hold with a boy of mine heving schooling. There've been schoolmen since the beginning. But 'tis plain to me that things was better–aye, a far sight better–when learning was kept where it belonged, to the great and the godly that was born to it in the station of life to which God had called them.' (The smooth, pat, cultured phrase sounded strange on his rough tongue.) 'To my mind, things hev gone wrong through them that should be butchers and blacksmiths and shepherds getting a little learning and getting blown up with pride and argufying about what they don't wholly understand nor hev proper respect for.'

'I *see*,' said Dr Trudgett dryly. So did I. I knew at that moment what my uncle was; backward-looking, would-be Papist. To him and to his sort Thomas Wolsey was a butcher, Thomas Cromwell a blacksmith. I understood why my uncle and my father had never been friends; I'd heard my father and his crony the printer talk about my uncle's kind; unprogressive, reactionary people whose cardinal belief was: 'As it was in the beginning so it shall be, henceforth and forever more.' Years and years ago there'd been a lot of them; thirty thousand of them in the north of England had actually rebelled against the King. The Old Men and the New Men had come to blows, and the Old Men had been defeated. But in lonely places, in a few stubborn minds, the old fires, carefully hidden, still smouldered.

I waited now for Dr Trudgett, with his shrewd wit and sharp tongue, to put my uncle in his place. He began with one of those calm, oblique statements which so often presaged devastating trouble in the classroom.

'You are indeed a bold man to say that to *me*!'

But before he could proceed my uncle cut in with:

'Aye. And I'm sorry to run down in your hearing the trade you make your bread by. 'Tis as aggravating, I do see, as though somebody should say to me that carpentering and joining was a wicked waste of time. Just the same, feeling and thinking as I do about all this here new learning and the making of bad schoolmen out of what might hev been good workmen, I can on'y do my duty as I see it; and that is to take and make a good craftsman out of Jonathan here, same as I would my own boy.'

Afterwards, thinking it over, as I did endlessly, I wondered whether Dr Trudgett was conscious, as I was, of the blow dealt to his dignity and authority by the opening words of that speech. Without–I am sure–wittingly intending to do so, this rough country carpenter had reduced Dr Trudgett to his own level, a man with a living to earn. He stripped him of his gown, of his birch, and under cover of a half-apology said, 'If everybody thought as I think, you'd starve!' Whether Dr Trudgett saw it as I saw it I never knew. Certainly he did not turn and rend my uncle as I had expected and hoped he would. He said, still in a reasonable voice:

'But he is not your boy; that must be remembered. His father sent him to school, and, so far as we can tell, intended him to remain there. His wishes should be considered. Also, I think, the boy's own. He is very young, but his understanding is beyond his years. This is hardly the time, perhaps . . . the news has been a blow to him. Really, I do feel that this should all be left for the moment. Why must such an important matter be decided this evening?'

'Thass a long walk from Nettleton to Baildon,' said my uncle simply. 'Altogether, time I see Martin Borage decently buried and get meself home again I'll hev lost three days' work. I don't want to hev to come back in the summer and go on argufying about what, to my mind, is plain at this minute. As for the dead man's wishes, 'twasn't you he sent hot-foot for as soon as he knew he was dying; 'twas for me. And though, poor man, he was past saying much, maybe sending for me had meaning. There's many a man,' said Uncle Francis firmly, 'that hev lived in error die knowing the old ways is best; and maybe Martin Borage at the end knew it too. Otherwise, why did he send for me, a day's walk away and no friend of his?'

'He was probably not in his right mind,' said Dr Trudgett sharply.

My uncle swung round; he brought one of his great hands clenched into a fist, down on the end of the table.

'There you are!' he cried. 'Thass the way it go now. Tossing the words hither and thither, spinning a web as sticky as a spider's to catch a man's wits in. He was out of his mind, you say; because when he was dying he saw how he'd been wrong with his pills and his potions and his new learning and his printing and his sending his boy to be stuffed up with pride. With his last breath, with his eyes darkening, a man incline to repentance–else why send for me that was dead set agin all *he* believed in. And so he's out of his mind. That'll do, sir; there's naught more to be said. I see how the wind blow here, and it is as I allust suspected. No fit place for the boy I hev took for my own.' He moved around the table and touched my arm. 'Come along, Jonathan. Thass time we was moving. Go fetch your duds, if you want 'em. You're coming home to bide with me and your aunt, and I promise you it on't be our fault if you ain't happy here.'

I moved my arm away from his hand and stood up.

'I don't want to go with you,' I said. I turned to my master: 'Please, sir, permit me to stay here.'

'With the best will in the world, boy,' said Dr Trudgett. He bit his lip and beat his finger-tips on the table; he seemed to be thinking deeply and rapidly. My uncle drew back a little. One could see how the deep grooves on each side of his mouth had been carved; his smile, no longer kindly, deepened them. 'As an orphan,' said Dr Trudgett quietly, 'Jonathan now falls under the jurisdiction of the justices. It is too late now, but tomorrow morning I will consult Mr Aldridge upon this matter. I am prepared to abide by his decision. And you?'

The sardonic smile on my uncle's face deepened.

'That hare on't run, sir. 'Twas Mr Aldridge himself that Mr Turnbull, the attorney, called in to witness the will he'd drawed up in such a hurry. I can give you the wording. "I appoint the brother of my wife, deceased, Francis Sheply, carpenter, of Nettleton in this county, to act as guardian to my son Jonathan and to hold for him, in trust, for the which he shall answer in the Day of Judgement, such property as I die possessed of, until he shall come of age." Thass plain enough, ain't it? And time the attorney did the writing I said, "Martin, rest easy about the boy; he shall be to me as my own." But, of course, if you doubt my word and hev a fancy to waste your time, and mine, we'll beat it out in front of the justices.'

'I hardly think you would have invented that legal phrasing. Well, in the circumstances . . .' He turned to me. 'I'm sorry Jonathan. You have the makings of a scholar and could have been a credit to the school. It's a very great pity.' He stood for a moment looking directly into my eyes with his boring gaze, and when he spoke again it was in his brisk, bracing schoolroom manner. 'We mustn't waste energy on idle regrets, my boy. You *can* read, you've had a thorough grounding such as few people attain. Any man who can read has a door open in his mind which no-one but himself can close again. Keep yours open. I hope you'll remember something of what you have learned, and I hope, too, that you will so apply yourself to your new trade that your uncle's prejudice against schooling for common people withers away.'

The words were so final, so completely valedictory, that the expostulations and protests forming in my mind died away. There is something frightening in the sight of someone whom one has regarded as omnipotent suddenly yielding to a superior authority.

'I believe you already possess a book of your own. A *printed* book, is it not?'

'Yes, sir. A Gospel of St Matthew.'

Dr Trudgett went over to the cupboard where his own books, a dozen or so of them, lay, and after some deliberation selected a chunky little book, clumsily bound in a linen cover.

'My father gave me this,' said my master. 'He wrote it and made it himself. He was bedridden many years. He devised this plan for making me wish to *read* Latin for pleasure. See . . . each story begins in English, and then, at the turning-point of the tale, goes on in Latin. I hope the day will come, my dear boy, when you will read on and never notice the change of language. And now I see that your uncle is impatient. Go and collect your belongings.'

They were few enough. A change of linen, a spare pair of shoes, my printed Testament, and a sea-shell given me by Tom Rowhedge as a parting present. I owned a knife too, and a foot-rule, and several quills and a dozen coloured marbles; but they were in the classroom, and I did not intend to risk, for their sake, the open question from Master Richards, 'What are you about, Borage?' the whispered questions of the boys. I laid my spare shirt flat on the floor, piled my goods on it and made a bundle. I remembered my cloak and retrieved it from the pegs in the dormitory passage. All the time something in my mind, relentless and sterile as the knock of a passing bell, kept saying, 'This is the end, the end, the end.'

On my way back to the room where my uncle waited I passed a little slit window where one June evening, towards the end of my first half-year, when I was miserably unhappy and fully determined not to come back after the holidays, I had stood and looked out and seen my father, with his big basket on his arm, going across the yard towards the herb garden to collect his supplies. The sight had called to mind happy summer evenings in the past when I had been with him; and I had cried a few hot tears of homesickness and self-pity which I had imagined came from affection. Now I stood by the same window, and suddenly, great boy though I was, I was crying again. And now I was wise enough to realise that I was not weeping for my father, who had always been so kind to me. For that I blamed Francis Sheply. If he had come with his news and gone again without interfering with me . . . then I should have had tears to spare.

If, during my first wretched half-year at King Edward's, Uncle Francis had arrived, and whisked me away, I should probably have settled down in Nettleton and thought myself happy and lucky. My uncle lived very comfortably indeed. The cottage had been built by my grandfather, and stood, with the adjoining workshop, in two acres of ground. We had our own cow, a number of pigs, a good many hens and ducks and geese; the garden produced all, and more, than we needed in the way of fruit and vegetables, and my Aunt Mary devoted her entire life to the management of her household. Except to go to church on Sunday morning, she never set foot outside her own domain. She had no contacts with the outer world; Uncle Francis did what little marketing was needed, and even over so personal a matter as a new pair of shoes she would say. 'When you pass Jim Farrow's next time, my man, bespeak my winter shoes; and tell him to allow for the growth of my bunion.' And presently my uncle or I would fetch home the shoes and she would try them on and say, 'They do very well. Thank you.' She spoke less than any woman I ever knew; in fact she never made an unnecessary remark, and for days on end would only open her mouth to say, 'Supper's ready', or 'Would you like some more?' On the evening, when we arrived at the cottage, tired, cold and hungry, Uncle Francis said to her:

'Martin Borage is dead. This is his boy Jonathan. I brung him home to live with us,' and she looked at me–quite kindly–and said:

'He's welcome. I'll set another place.'

I am not sure that she ever knew my name. She fed me and washed and mended my clothes, looked after me tenderly when I chanced to be sick, addressed me as 'you' and referred to me always as 'the boy'. For all the impact I made on her I might have been a new bit of livestock Uncle Francis had brought home. And at first, so far as I was concerned, she might have been livestock too, an animal, domesticated, superlatively well trained: later on I found myself wondering about her. Had she once been otherwise? Had she come to this cottage a lively, ordinary, pretty young bride? (That she had, once, been very pretty, was obvious even yet.) And had she perhaps had likes and dislikes, a personality of her own; and had she come up against the deadly, overpowering character of my uncle and suffered a defeat and retreated and taken refuge in making herself simply another of his tools? Was her silence, her complete negation, a defence? After I had repeatedly thrown myself against his never-to-be-shaken, never-to-be-ruffled, so reasonable unreasonableness, I did sometimes wonder. I did sometimes consider following her example. Why speak, for instance, when what you said was without effect? Why not give in, become just another useful, inanimate tool?

It seemed plain to me, from the very first, that I should never be a good carpenter, even with the best will in the world. Material, the dead stuff I worked with, was against me. I might cut two pieces of wood, cut them with the greatest care, each, say, four inches long; when I had them nailed together–not when I measured them tentatively, mind–one would be slightly longer than the other, and the protuberant edge could never be neatly sliced off, because it would develop an unsuspected knot, or go splintery. With even so simple a business beyond me, with every tool I handled going blunt or demented or purely vicious, my life was misery; and always there was Uncle Francis looming up, kindly, watchful, determined. 'Now look, boy. You wanta take your hammer'–or 'your saw', or 'your chisel'–'like this and put your hand so . . .', and I used to think furiously, 'It isn't *my* hammer, damn you, it's your damned hammer! Take your damned hammer, damn you, and do your own damned job!' (My repertoire of abuse, even mental abuse, was pretty restricted.)

One day, irritated past caution, I said:

'Now do you see? Can't you realise that never in my life shall I be a good carpenter? I just haven't the aptitude. Please, please, Uncle Francis, let me go back to school and do something I *can* do.'

'Don't talk so silly,' he said placidly. 'Didn't they ever teach you at school–"If at first you don't succeed, try, try, agin"? If not, they oughta. Come on now, you give your mind to it. Thass really the trouble with you, you know. Your heart ain't here, yet. You still would rather be a half-baked clerk going round ready to sell your soul for a bit of scribe-work than a master carpenter like I mean you to be.'

'And what right,' I said hotly, 'have *you* to choose what I should be?'

'Every right. You was left to me to bring up as my own.'

'That was a mistake,' I said, putting into word the certainty which I had fingered over many times. 'My father was frightened. He was dying, suddenly, and he wanted to be sure that I had a home and somebody to look after me. That was all he meant. He wanted *you* to take *his* place, not that *I* should take the place of the son *you* never had! Can't you see that? My father cared about people being able to read and write . . . he'd turn in his grave to know that I was wasting my life here banging silly nails into bits of wood.'

'Now half you a minute.' (That was one of his irritating country expressions, meaning 'Wait half a minute'.) 'You got this all wrong, boy. Look here. As you say, I never had no son of me own, and many a time I hev wondered why God should see fit to hev me childless when I hev a house and a holding and a good honest trade to pass on. And many a time I hev thought of taking a boy to rear and bring up in my craft. But something hev allust bin agin that idea. Then suddenly there is my own sister's boy handed to me. And maybe, as you say, your father was frightened, as well he might be, called to meet his God with all his sins on him; but he was in his right mind; so why, as I said to the man to his face, why didn't he hand you over to your Dr Trudgett or leave you and his bit of money to the justices to take care of? I know why. God guided him. God knew that you and me would fit in like a neat bit of dovetail. I saw that plain. And nobody, least of all you, my boy, can tell me any different.'

Firm conviction is a contagious thing; and so is–well, what can one call it . . . superstition? I know I stood there with my face still hot with fury and felt a cold finger trail down my spine. Stated with such confidence, the idea was just feasible enough to be uncomfortable.

It made *me* so negligible. Here's a boy for Martin Borage to send to school and take pride in. Right about turn! Here, Francis Sheply, is the boy you always wanted, a boy to train to be a carpenter!

But what about me?

Dr Trudgett had often pointed out the distinction between the theories that were, as he termed it, 'susceptible to proof' and those which were not, and later that day it struck me that Uncle Francis's theory about my destiny fell into the former class. So that evening after supper–it was early summer by this time and daylight lingered–I stuffed my bilingual *Tales from Boccaccio* into my jerkin and, with my Testament under my arm, strolled out, saying that I was going to Layer Wood to read. To have taken two books would have aroused suspicion, but the one visible one under my arm merely provoked Uncle Francis's dry comment that at this rate I should soon know it off by heart.

I walked to the wood, found the path and started to run. The path was a short cut from Nettleton to Clevely, and when I emerged from the wood, close to Rawley's Farm, I was near the main road to Baildon. I walked again when I was near enough to Rawley's to be under observation, and then, once on the road, ran again as though the devil were after me. I walked through Minsham, and then ran again, and so continued through the thickening darkness. I was more than halfway to Baildon before I was thoroughly exhausted. Then I lay down in a dry ditch and slept until the light of the new day and the chorus of birdsong which greeted it waked me.

I was in Baildon, washing my hands and face and smoothing my hair over the horse-trough in Friargate, just before nine o'clock, and at the schoolgate as the bell rang for the beginning of the morning class. I couldn't have timed it better. I was in the passage just outside Dr Trudgett's study door when he emerged, settling the birch under his arm, twitching his gown into place, on his way to the classroom.

I said, 'Sir.'

He halted, looked at me for a second without recognition, and then said, 'Ha, Borage! So you've come back, eh?'

'Yes, sir,' I gasped; and then, because I knew he was impatient and time was short, and this no place for beating about the bush and being diffident and deferential, I gabbled on. I told him that I couldn't bear life at Nettleton, couldn't bear being a carpenter; please, I said, please, couldn't I come back; couldn't he, wouldn't he take me in and, if my uncle came in search of me, say that I wasn't there.

'Dear me,' he said, when I had gabbled myself to a standstill. 'In one respect you tell the truth, at least. That your mind is withering. In good truth, that is so. I always thought you were a sensible fellow. And now you invite me, *me*, to conspire with you in the telling of a lie–and, what is worse, a stupid lie! How could I "hide" you, as you so flippantly suggest? To begin with, you would have to re-enter as a poor scholar, and your qualifications for that estate would involve the submittance of your name, your antecedents and circumstances to the justices and the governors. Besides, do you seriously imagine that when your uncle raised the hue-and-cry for you I should perjure myself on your behalf? Really, Borage it is a plan of which any intelligent boy on the bottom form would be ashamed!'

'It was all I could think of,' I mumbled.

'The obvious thing, I suppose. So obvious that your uncle and guardian is probably at the gate this moment? Come in here a moment.' He opened the door of his room. 'Now, tell me truly–is it merely that you dislike the work, the way of life, or is he unkind to you? Are you ill-fed? Ill-treated?'

'Oh no,' I said, rather wildly, because his suggestion that my uncle might already be on my trail threw me into a panic. 'He's kind to me. It's just that I don't like it there. I don't want to be a carpenter. I want to come back to school. I want to go on learning. I'd rather be here and be beaten every day for misconstruing or miscalculations than do woodwork with my *kind* uncle.'

'Few of them,' said Dr Trudgett, jerking his head in the direction of the schoolroom, 'would agree with you.' He brooded for a moment. 'It does all seem a pity, a very great pity indeed. I was grieved at the time, I remember. But your uncle is within his rights, and honestly, Borage, there is nothing *I* can do. In Utopia, I suppose, education will be compulsory and men like your uncle will gnash their teeth in vain . . . but this is not Utopia. How old are you, Borage?'

'Thirteen in November.'

'Eight years to wait. In eight years you will be of age and your own man.' He scowled, trying to remember. 'And your uncle mentioned a little property. Look,' he said, and his expression lightened, 'I do believe that you are one of the rare people who do seek after learning and wish to pursue it. If you can practise your reading and not let your mind rust, it would not be too late in eight years' time. Come back to me then. You'll be twenty-one in November–providing I am still alive we will spend the Christmas holiday together; we'll work fourteen hours a day. And then you shall go to Cambridge. The Master of Peterhouse is an old friend of mine. . . . It shall be managed, Borage. Tell me, can you remember when you were five . . . anything that happened when you were about that age?'

'Why, yes, sir. On the day itself I broke a precious flask in my father's workroom, and I remember him saying that were it not my birthday I should go supperless to bed for meddling.'

'And that seems long ago?'

'No, sir. When I speak of it it seems like yesterday.'

'Well, that was eight years ago. In a similar length of time you will be free to sate your hunger for learning. And now you must go back and do your duty by your uncle, thanking God that he is, as you say, kind. Many are not. Wait . . . I have another thought. Nettleton . . . of course! Simon Dodson is priest of that parish; a very learned man, though his stutter has prevented his gaining preferment. *He* could help you; he has books, ability . . . and, I doubt not, is lonely and fears, as you do, the withering of his mind. Have you not become acquainted? I will write to him on your behalf. Two old King Edward's boys in one small parish, and not friends? Strange!'

'But he is married, sir.'

'And how should that prevent is noticing a good mind dying for lack of sustenance on his doorstep?'

'My uncle strongly disapproves of married priests, sir. On Sundays we go to church and my uncle pays his dues. But only to escape the penalties. Privately he calls Master Dodson "the leader of the Geneva Jig" and outside the church door has no truck with him.'

Dr Trudgett wrinkled his brow.

'The Geneva Jig; what is that?'

'A derisive term, sir, applied, by a Catholic gentleman of Cornwall I believe, to the psalms as arranged for congregational singing.'

'A man of your uncle's mind?'

I nodded.

'I see. So closer contact with Simon Dodson would be an embarrassment to you. What a pity! Yes, yes. Come in,' he cried as a timid knock sounded on the door. And there was a boy, sent by Master Richards, to ask with all respect whether the bell had been rung loud enough. . . .

I knew that to the end of my days I should remember the lonely, deserted feeling which came upon me as I saw Dr Trudgett settle the birch and twitch at his gown as he sent the boy running to say yes, of course he had heard the bell and would be in the classroom in a moment. There was a close organisation, a little society going its way, and he had his place in it . . . and I had once had mine. But no more! I was outside of it; and I was alone. I had the thought that as I felt then the dying might feel. All this activity, all this routine in which I once had a share is going on without me. . . . Horrible.

I stood in the yard for quite a long time. I could hear the murmur of voices, and twice the unmistakable smack of the birch. And I looked ahead at eight long years of Uncle Francis saying 'I don't hold with it', and the subject being closed. I thought, I won't go back. I'll go on and I'll find another school; I'll say my name is Jon Carter or something like that, and that I am an orphan. . . . I'll get in somewhere, somehow.

Of course I was young, immature and romantic.

I was not yet sure that Uncle Francis's theory had been disproved.

Presently I gave myself a shake and remembered that if Uncle Francis really were looking for me this would be one of the places he would search. So I trotted out of the school gate and away down the hill to the market-place, from which roads led off in all directions. I intended to take the one to Colchester, which went on, I know, to London. But by this time I was extremely hungry. The stomach has its habits, and mine was used to being stuffed full of bread and bacon and home-brewed ale at seven o'clock each morning. It was now almost ten. And on the corner of the market-place and the road to Colchester there was a baker's shop. A smell to make the hungry mouth water issued from the new loaves which a pleasant-faced, stout woman was taking from a big basket and laying on to the shelves. I halted, sniffing. I hadn't a penny in my pocket; yet the idea of begging took a bit of getting used to. While I hesitated the woman looked out and saw me.

'What do *you* want?' she asked, her voice far less pleasant than her face would have led one to expect.

I would have said 'Nothing' and moved on, but the thought struck me that I must get used to asking for what I wanted, what I needed, what I must have . . . and I might as well start now.

'I want a penny loaf and I have no penny.'

'Oh!' she said. 'Well, I have a weevilly flour-bin that should be emptied and scoured out against the new lot coming in this morning, if you like to do that for me you can have a loaf . . . when the job's done.'

Such a chance might not occur again between here and Colchester, I thought, so I said I would do the job, and she led me through the shop into the bakehouse, showed me the bin and the bucket and the scrubbing-brush and then stood and watched while I took off my doublet and laid it, with my books, on another bin.

'Have you run away from school?' she asked.

'No.'

'Yet you ain't a Baildon boy; nor you don't look like a beggar,' she mused.

'I'm on my way from one school to another, if you must know,' I said.

'No need to be rude. And do well into the corners,' she said. She went away to the shop; but presently she was back and stood there telling me about the accident which had happened to her husband. 'So I'm single-handed,' she said. 'And before you go you can help me open the yard gate, then it'll be ready for the miller. But you can eat your loaf first.' She inspected the bin and seemed pleased, and when she brought me the loaf she had split it and laid a piece of meat within. I wolfed it quickly and then went to help her with the gate, a tall heavy one which had sunk on its hinges and opened with the utmost difficulty. As I tugged it the last stubborn foot the woman said, 'Well, ain't that timely. Here is miller.' I looked out and saw the wagon; and then the miller–Jacob Woody of Nettleton.

'Well,' he exclaimed, 'I'll go to sea if it ain't Jon Borage. You wicked little varmint. There's your pore uncle standing at the cross-roads asking everybody to cry you. . . .'

I had turned as he spoke and was making for the shop, thinking that I could be through it and away up the Colchester road before he had climbed down from the wagon. But the woman had already slammed the door and was standing guard of it, saying:

'There, I knew it. I had a feeling. . . .'

'By cock,' said the miller, now on his feet in the gateway, 'if you was mine I'd give you a rare walloping. Up all night Francy Sheply was, and half a dozen more with him, reckoning you'd took a fit. Hollering and hunting all through Layer with lanterns they was, and down by the river. And now there he stand, wasting a working day, asking everybody what pass to look out for ye and hev you cried everywhere and pass on the word. I should hope he'll give you a hiding–and there's one on account.' He raised the whip he had in his hand and aimed a blow at me. Without warning the crackling, flashing darkness whirled down on me, and when I came to my senses again I was lying on the wagon floor and the wagon was rumbling into Nettleton. I'd had no time to push my thumb into my mouth and consequently my tongue was so badly bitten that I couldn't speak or eat for several days. When I could speak I said to my uncle, 'I'm sorry you were alarmed about me; but I still don't see that you had the right to have me cried as though I were a stray horse.'

'Oh! Well, I shall hev,' he answered.

At the end of that week he had me up in front of the justices and I was formally apprenticed to him for seven years, with four years of journeyman status to follow. Until I became twenty-three I should be, virtually, his bondsman. Incongruously enough, at the same time he moved his order for flour and meal from Jacob Woody and gave it to the miller at Clevely. Woody, when he brought me home, had said frankly that he had struck me, and Uncle Francis 'didn't hold' with that.

Well, so far as any theory concerning God's intentions and man's destiny was 'susceptible to proof', my uncle's idea that he and I were intended to be dovetailed together seemed to have stood the test. Half-convinced, but even more resentful, I began to settle down.

I was fifteen when I made my next, rather less amateur bid for freedom. By that time I had grown a good deal and my fits came more and more rarely. Uncle Francis was fond of pointing out that he had been right about the health-giving effect of manual work. He delighted also in my increasing handiness and skill, for by this time I had had sense to see that if I must be a carpenter I might as well be a good one; there had been a time when I had done slovenly work deliberately, but that became boring in the end. I might finally have found some pleasure in my work, but for the fact that Tom Rowhedge came home from sea just at the time when my uncle and I were working on a new barn at Slipwell. There again the finger of destiny might be perceptible; for Slipwell was eight or nine miles from Nettleton, and it is unlikely that Tom would ever have known that I was in Nettleton, or, knowing it, have troubled to seek me out.

Tom was now twenty, an enormous, handsome, swaggering fellow, with a darkly tanned face and a huge copper-coloured beard and thick gold rings in his ears. At no time in our lives had the five years' difference in our ages loomed so large. He had done his five years at sea–and from things he occasionally let drop in conversation I gathered that they had been years of great hardship; even Tom, who was tough and plucky, confessed that during the first months he had contemplated running away *from* sea more often than, when at King Edward's, he had dreamed of running away *to* sea. But he had survived and was now to reap his reward; his father was going to fit out a ship of which Tom would be master. Old Rowhedge could afford that–as well as paying other people to build his barns, because he had been made very prosperous through the peculiar thing which was happening at Slipwell. Farther to the north the coast was sinking into the sea, at Dunwich whole streets and great churches were being lost, but at Slipwell the land was rising. There were old men there who could remember their fathers recalling the time when the marshes at Slipwell were useless, wet and reedy and actually under water for eight months of the year. Gradually, over the last hundred or hundred and fifty years, the marshes had risen and were now useful grazing ground for sheep. True, the animals were scrawny, but old Tom Rowhedge was not interested in the amount or the quality of the mutton they produced; he reared them for their wool, and since wool was in great demand just then, he was making a pretty penny.

I can only suppose that Tom, once the excitement of his home-coming had died down, was lonely and found it easier to talk to someone who had *seen* a globe and knew the difference between America and Africa, even if that someone were only a fifteen-year-old carpenter's apprentice, than to his father and brothers and the men in the village, whose idea of a far-distant place was Colchester or Dunwich. Whatever the reason, during the weeks when he was at home he seemed to seek my company, and often while I was working he would lounge about and talk, or even lend a hand to the job I was doing. And in the evenings we often walked together. Towards the end of his stay, softened by his friendliness, I spoke of myself and tried to tell him something of my wretched discontent. Tom, like Dr Trudgett, asked whether my uncle was kind to me.

'Completely, entirely,' I said. 'But you know, Tom, you can murder a fellow by cracking his skull with an axe, and you can also do it by pushing a featherbed over him and holding it down long enough. That's how his *kindness* feels to me. I'd far rather he fetched me a clout occasionally and gave me a shabby breakfast and let me go and read with Master Dodson.'

'Don't wish for clouts or bad food,' said Tom. 'But why shouldn't you read with old Dodson if you want to?'

'Because Uncle Francis doesn't hold with him! I see pretty clearly now what's in his mind. He's rootedly old-fashioned, as bad as a Papist, and he thinks all the new ways are just temporary things. So it's the duty of people who think as he does–and there are more of them than you might think–to rear up a generation of young ones with the same ideas. It'd be such a pity, wouldn't it,' I said sourly, 'if when the old ideas became fashionable again nobody remembered exactly what they were!'

'I can't exactly see the old ideas coming back,' said Tom. 'The new 'uns fit far too easy. Married clerics, for example. Who'd want to go back to the old ways when it meant giving up a nice little bed-partner like Agnes Dodson. She must be at least twenty years younger than he is, wouldn't you think?'

I'd never noticed Mistress Dodson. My interest in women was still so completely childlike that I still reckoned them adorable if they handed out cake when one worked for them, and detestable if, halfway, through a job, they changed their minds and wanted something altered. Also at this moment I was irritated by the switching of the conversation from the general to the particular.

'I don't know how old they are,' I said. 'I only know he has a lot of books, more even than Dr Trudgett; and I'm not allowed to do more than answer him civilly if he greets me. That *does* stick in my craw. Together with a lot of other things.'

'What things?' Tom asked–accepting my change of subject more good-humouredly than I had accepted his.

'Well, this apprenticeship, for instance. Seven years and then four. Positive slavery, and all over the country the system is on its last legs, and he knows it. Only the old-fashioned people bother nowadays; and a good thing too. Don't you think it's iniquitous that until I'm twenty-three I can't get a job, or choose where I live, or get married. . . .'

'And are you anxious to get married?' Tom asked with a smile.

'Don't be silly. It's just a rotten system whereby a person who doesn't want to do a job at all is tied to it in such a way that when he gets out of bondage he's too old to do anything else. That's the old way, the good old way!'

'Aye; I can see. It's hard tack for you. And there ain't much I can do, Jonathan. Now if you had a hankering for the sea . . .'

'But I have,' I said, not with complete truth, for until Tom had returned with his wonderful stories and his fine clothes and gold rings I had never actually envied him his trade; his freedom to choose it–yes, I had envied that.

'Well, then . . . if you really mean that, boy, maybe we could come to some arrangement with your uncle. It costs a bit to break or transfer indentures, I believe. . . .' He scowled. 'But a handy boy like you, trained carpenter and all, and light in the rigging, would be a very useful thing to have. And I'd see you got your sea-legs, Jonathan, a damned sight easier than I did.' His eyes began to sparkle with the old boyish enthusiasm I remembered.

'It needn't cost you anything,' I said proudly. 'My father left me fifty pounds. Uncle Francis has it locked in the chest by his bed; and every month he adds a shilling to it. It's *just* possible that if I offered him that for my freedom . . . Oh, Tom, if only he would!' It seemed, for a moment, almost likely, for Uncle Francis was, within limits, a money-minded man. He would not put money before his principles, and he was not the kind of 'careful man', of whom there were many in our neighbourhood, who would live meagrely in order to save a penny, but he would, and often did, haggle for an hour over the price of a job he was to do, or of material he had to buy, and I never knew anyone get the better of him in a bargain.

That evening I suggested to Uncle Francis that he should cancel my indentures and allow me to go to sea with Tom, and in return take my fifty pounds for his own.

He laughed his rare laugh.

'You really are a silly young fool, Jon,' he said. 'The most I ever heard of paid for indenture-breaking was twenty pounds, and that was a gentleman's son that was apprenticed to the wine trade, and both his father and two brothers older than him died in one week of the winter sickness, so he must buy himself out and go to look after his manor. And here's you, my own flesh and blood, offer me fifty to do a thing I wouldn't do for ten times the money! Where'd you be in a year's time, a silly great gaby like you? Tom Rowhedge can look on the sea as a playground–soon's he's sick or sorry there's a plough waiting for him at Slipwell. You'd be just a half-timed apprentice, no more use than a half-baked loaf. You just oughta go down to Bywater one day and take a look at the old sailormen on the quay there, poor old hulks with one eye, or peg legs, or empty sleeves. They was all going to make their fortunes, once. Now they wish they'd stayed at home and learned a craft. And thass what you're going to do, boy, willy-nilly. And the day you finish, a right craftsman like me, able to hold your own with all comers, with fifty pounds in your hand, and a bit added, you'll thank me from your heart. Then that went so fast, with a three-years apprenticeship–they've cut to that now, God forgive 'em–poor handless critters that couldn't make a kitchen shelf–they'll look up to you and call you master. Aye, you'll bless the memory of your uncle that wouldn't let you runagate, wasting your substance or your time. And thass my last word, Jon,' he said, his face growing sombre again.

So Tom Rowhedge sailed away in quest of fortune and I stayed at home, mastering the carpenter's craft and in my spare time reading my two books, trying to keep open that door in my mind of which Dr Trudgett had spoken, until the rather horrible day came when I realised that I was not *reading* any more; I knew my Gospel and *Tales From Boccaccio* by heart. It was useless to ask Uncle Francis to give me money to buy a new book, he didn't hold with reading. However, I was now well on into my eighteenth year; in fourteen or fifteen months I should be a journeyman, drawing a journeyman's small wage. The first thing I would buy would be a book, I thought.

And then I fell in love.

Her name was Elizabeth–Elizabeth Rawley, and she was the youngest of five pretty girls who owed no part of their charm to their ribbons and laces and such falderals, for their father was an old curmudgeon, noted for his meanness even in our parts, where 'carefulness' was regarded with respectful admiration. He was very unneighbourly too; and as his farm lay on the far side of Layer Wood, on the boundary of Nettleton and Clevely, the Rawley girls were hardly known to us by sight until Old Rawley fell out with the parson at Clevely over a load of hay. After that he elected to attend our church, as he was entitled to do since he had land in both parishes, though the church at Clevely was much nearer his house. We knew about the dispute concerning the hay, because it was the kind of news which Uncle Francis would seize upon and drone on about as another sign of the bad new times; he sided heavily with the parson of Clevely, who, since he was unmarried, was more to his taste than our Master Dodson. So we were not surprised, one Sunday morning, to see Old Rawley walk into church looking like an angry old bear, and followed by his wife and four daughters. The eldest girl had been married a year or so previously, and the grudging, meagre wedding-feast had been a matter of gossip ever since.

It was a lovely warm summer morning, and all but the elderly women were wearing light-coloured gowns or dull ones brightened by a bit of cambric or ribbon. The Rawley girls wore a kind of uniform, untrimmed gowns of grey homespun, and plain straw bonnets. But they were young, and they were pretty, and they were new to us, and that morning there was a good deal of fidgeting and head-turning among the younger men–and some no longer young.

It happened that they were just in front of me, so close that I could smell the lavender in which those ugly dresses had been laid; and presently I noticed that although, from the back, they looked so much alike there were differences in size and shape. And whereas three of the girls had yellow hair, one had black. Little tendrils of it crept out from under the bonnet's edge and lay, soft and curly, like little feathers against the whiteness of her neck. Unfairly, I immediately began to credit her with all the sweet smell of lavender. Then I noticed that she was the smallest and slightest of the four . . . and something began to move in my stomach which was entirely new and rather painful and yet altogether delightful and exciting.

The moment service ended Old Rawley led the way out, and they all followed, looking neither right nor left, but I did catch a glimpse of the dark-haired girl's face, and it was, to my mind, the prettiest of all. The others were pink-cheeked and touched by the sun, but she was pale–pale as the windflowers which shimmered through Layer Wood in the spring.

I ceased to look forward to the moment when I should earn a wage and be able to buy a book. My forward-looking narrowed itself down to a seven-day stretch–the next Sunday morning. The curious feeling in my stomach grew. Presently it no longer depended upon the sight of her; it was all there, all aquiver, when I thought about her.

Then there came a memorable evening when I was taking the short cut through Layer Wood. I was alone, for lately Uncle Francis had trusted me with simple jobs, and this one, the building of settles either side a hearth in a house at Clevely, was well within my scope. I was walking along a ride thickly bordered by blackberry bushes, when, just ahead of me, I saw my little dark-haired girl. She was jumping and snatching at something in the bushes. I quickened my step and saw what had happened. She had hooked down a branch where the berries grew larger and in greater profusion and the spray had sprung back, taking her crooked stick with it. As soon as she saw me she desisted from her effort to recover the stick and, turning to a lower bush, began to pick busily. It was a chance not to be missed. Yet I almost passed by, because at the idea of speaking to her my heart began to thump so heavily that I went dizzy and a kind of blackness came in front of my eyes. I was reminded of my now all-but-outgrown affliction, and thought with terror–suppose I had a fit now! A thought to remember with irony later on. The dizziness did not crackle, however, nor did the darkness flash, and I finally got back enough breath to say chokingly:

'Let me try.'

It was too high even for me; but I had my tools with me, and it was the matter of a moment to walk into the wood, find a crooked hazel, and cut another.

'Oh, thank you,' she said, and smiled, and I saw how sweetly her mouth curved over her small teeth, and how long her eyelashes were. Everything in me moved towards her with pure love.

'Wait a minute,' I said, and taking the stick I had made I hooked down the one she had lost; then there were two sticks, and two people gathering the berries.

We hardly spoke. I asked her name and she told me, Elizabeth; and the word was full of music and wonder, as though that had been the first time it had ever fallen on human ear. I told her that I had seen her in church, and she said yes, she knew. My shyness wore off with a rapidity that astonished even me, and when the basket was full to the brim I was bold enough to ask:

'Will you be blackberrying tomorrow?'

'Oh no. Thanks to your help, I have enough.'

'Let's throw some away.'

She was shocked. 'Oh no. I couldn't do that.'

'Well, what will you be doing tomorrow?'

'Making the jelly, I expect. I have the little jobs while the others help to bring in the corn.'

'And what about the next night?'

'Oh . . . well, if the jelly sets I might carry some to my Aunt Thomasin. I usually do, and then, later on, she gives us some of her quinces.'

I knew where her aunt lived.

'If you could make it about this time on the day after tomorrow, I should be finished work and I could meet you here again. If you like,' I added.

'It isn't what I like. It's Father. He'd be very cross. He'd be cross if he knew I was talking to you now.'

'Why?'

'We're not allowed to talk to people–well . . . men, or boys.'

'Then he shan't know. I'll meet you here, about this time, the day after tomorrow.' Already that moment had a luminous golden haze around it.

'All right,' she said dubiously. 'But if it rained, or if the jelly didn't set or anything . . .'

I carried the basket to the edge of the wood. She was ill at ease again and finally almost snatched it from me.

The next evening but one was quite fine; but though I waited about in the ride until it was pitch dark she didn't come; nor did she any evening for the rest of the week. And when on Sunday all the other people stood about after church, greeting one another, gossiping, exchanging the week's news and making the most of what, for those who lived in outlying places, was the only meeting during the week, Old Rawley walked straight past and away, and though I was so close to Elizabeth that I could have leaned forward and kissed her she never even glanced at me.

The next week–though my work at Clevely was done and it was awkward to manage the time–I spent the evenings in the woodland ride; and the next Sunday was as unrewarding as its predecessor. It was plain to me that some action was needed.

The following week was the Harvest Fair in Baildon. Everybody had a holiday on that day. Even Uncle Francis took the day off; not because he approved of the various devices for parting labouring men from their hard-earned coins but because the fair was one of the 'old customs' and mixed up in the merrymaking there were genuine stalls where goods and stores for the winter could be purchased at less-than-market prices. My father, who had never respected anything merely because it was old, had heartily disapproved of the fair on account of the low prices, which, he held, were uniust to the regular shopkeepers in the town.

However, the fair gave me an idea, because on that Sunday, staring at the little curls on Elizabeth's neck, I thought how easy it would be, if she were almost any other girl, for me to ask her to come with me to the fair. And so my idea fell into my head.

Some kind of sentiment prevented me from parting with the book Dr Trudgett had given me; so I sold my Testament back to the printer who had been my father's friend. He scolded me heartily until I said, 'But it is useless to me now. I know every word in it by heart.'

Then he ruffled the pages and said, 'Is that so, indeed? Tell me then what follows the words, "This fellow doth not cast out devils but by Beelzebub the prince of devils." Go on from there.'

'"And Jesus knew their thoughts and said unto them, Every kingdom that is divided against itself is brought to desolation; and every city or house divided against itself shall not stand. And if Satan cast out Satan . . ."' I went on, glib and flawless, while the printer stared.

'Enough!' he said at last. 'As you say, you need this no more. How come you to have such knowledge of it?'

I told him that it, and one other, had been my sole reading for five years.

'Oh, then,' he said, 'you wish another book . . .' and began to gabble about how much he would allow on the Testament against a new one, what new ones he had, and so on.

I was furious with myself not to have thought of making an exchange before; and I was furious with myself, because even then, even with my plan in mind, I *was* tempted. I wanted another book, I was hungry for one. So I said gruffly what I wanted was money for the Testament–what would he give me?

I went straight to a stall of trinkets and bought a pair of shoe-buckles, very plain, but good of their kind.

Next evening I walked boldly up to Rawley's door. The lower half of it was closed, the upper half open, and when I reached it, angrily and loudly announced by the yard dog, every member of the family seated about the supper table was turned towards the opening. I saw Elizabeth's creamy pallor change to the grey-white of ashes as she recognised me. I hated myself for frightening her and tried to shoot her a reassuring glance.

Old Matt Rawley was in the process of lifting a thick slice of brawn balanced on a thicker piece of bread towards his mouth. He arrested it just long enough to ask:

'Whadda you want?'

I held out my hand, in which lay one of the shoe-buckles, now somewhat battered and scratched and far from new-looking.

'On Sunday morning,' I said quickly, anxious to put Elizabeth out of her torment, 'I picked this up in the aisle just after you'd gone past, and I thought it might belong to one of the young ladies.'

One could imagine the flutter of interest and inquiry that such an announcement, made from some distance, would cause in any other family of five women. Around the Rawley table no one said a word. And only Elizabeth moved. She leaned back in her chair with a gesture of relief.

'Whad is it?' Matt Rawley demanded.

I took that as invitation to enter. I'm in, I thought.

'Shoe-buckle, ain't it?' he said, as I laid the object beside his plate. 'Any of you mawthers hev such a thing?' His fierce little eyes swept round the table, as though daring any daughter of his to admit to the possession of such an ornament. One by one they said, 'No, Father.' Then Mrs Rawley said:

'My Sunday shoes have buckles. May I see? No. Mine are quite different.'

'Oh well,' I said, 'I just wondered. I'll give it to Sexton. Whoever lost it will be asking on Sunday.'

'It was kind of you,' said Mrs Rawley in her quiet little voice. It was from her that the girls had their prettiness and their gentle ways.

'It was a pleasure,' I said. Then I turned about to Matt, who was proceeding with his supper.

'By the way,' I said, 'I suppose you know about your gate at the top there.'

'What about it?'

'It's down, post and all. I wondered. I noticed you'd got stock in the field.'

He shoved the last piece of brawn into his mouth and jumped up. 'You young fool, why the hell di'n't you say so afore. Stand there blithering about a pack o' nonsense time my cows get out. Come on. You can gimme a hand.'

He blundered out into the yard, muttering. 'One of them brutes musta rubbed agin it. 'Twasn't very stiddy certainly, but 'twas all right last time I hitched it.'

And it had been all right–that is, no more tumbledown than anything else on the ramshackle place–when I unhitched it. Now it lay flat, with two broken bars; and the post with its rotted end lay beside it. I'd done a thorough job there if I never did another.

'Thass past mending,' Matt said. 'That musta bin the devil of a shove. I wonder if the brute as did that got out.' He turned and stared towards the cattle, shadowy in the gathering dusk. 'They seem all right. Eight. D'you make eight? Your eyes is younger'n mine.'

I agreed that there were eight. He then began to direct me how to help him prop the gate in such a way that it would form a temporary stop-gap. The broken, sagging thing was difficult to handle, but when I dropped my end and wrecked it still further Matt Rawley's temper gave way.

'You clumsy young b——, you!' he said.

I put up a good show of resentment.

'Can I help it if your gate is so rotten that it falls to pieces in my hand? You should thank me for trying, not call me names. But for my warning you you'd have your cows in the pound by the morning.'

'Thass true. Thass true, too, that but for your "help" I'd hev propped this up. Broke past mending now, it is, thanks to you.'

'It was that before I ever touched it.'

''Twas not. By all rights you oughta make me a new one real cheap.'

'Make you a new one!' I said, and laughed.

'Ah, so you should. Call yourself a carpenter, don't you? And go round breaking folkses' gates!' He was well away now, scenting a shrewd bargain.

'That does sound bad,' I admitted. 'Well, what would you call cheap?'

'You oughta do it for nowt! I find wood and you do the work. You brook it arter all.'

'One bar,' I said.

We argued very happily for ten minutes and finally reached an arrangement satisfactory to us both. I was to make him a new gate in my spare time in return for sixpence and my supper. I pointed out firmly that if I came direct from my ordinary work and worked until darkness fell I should miss my meal at home; and he said:

'Damn it, I'll give you some grub.'

I think that apart from the Bywater merchant who had married Caroline Rawley I was the only person ever to be invited to sit at the Rawley table. Surely a good augury!

I did not hurry over the gate and managed to spend four evenings at the farm, eating four obviously grudged suppers with Elizabeth just across the table. She never spoke and hardly looked at me, but it was joy to see her; and on the third evening, by cutting my finger a little and walking up to the house to ask for a bit of bandage, I did manage to find her in the kitchen alone; and short and furtive as the meeting was, it served my purpose, for we were able to arrange not only our next meeting but a whole series of meetings for the future.

Each Saturday one of the Rawley girls went to Thomasin Griggs's lonely little cottage to clean and cook. The old woman was Matt Rawley's sister and very like him. She was a widow, childless, and possessed considerable property in Baildon. The girls took strict turns because the capricious old creature demanded it, saying that Susan was the best brass-cleaner, Ellen the best washerwoman, Cecily the best cook, and Elizabeth the best company. They themselves adhered as strictly as possible to the rotation because the three-mile walk through Layer Wood and a hard day's work under a carping old woman was anything but a pleasure, especially in winter. Weather was never allowed to interfere with the routine, for Matt Rawley had great hopes of his sister; hopes never justified for when she did die she left all her property to found almshouses in Baildon for 'poor respectable tradespeople'–presumably those who had paid extortionate rents for the little shops which she had owned.

So every fourth Saturday it would be possible for me to meet Elizabeth and walk home with her. And with that, being young and simple and undemanding, we were, for the moment, quite content.

We did, of course, speak about other meetings, less furtive, less far separated; but the very mention put Elizabeth into a panic. She explained to me the origin of her father's order about not speaking to men.

'He's been strict like that ever since Caroline married.'

'But why?' I asked. For everyone agreed that Caroline Rawley had married marvellously well. James Braddock, a well-to-do wool chandler, was surely a good match for a girl from an outlying farm, however pretty she was.

'Well, you see, Father and James Braddock had arranged that Caroline should marry him when she was seventeen, and then when the time came Caroline didn't want to. She had got to know somebody else and wanted to marry him instead. She always was headstrong, and though Father was mad as a hornet she stuck out a long time. He beat her–real hard I mean, not just a clout–she was really black and blue; and then he locked her up, and every day she had just a crust and a mug of water. So, of course, in the end she had to give in. But it took a long time. And then Father said he'd see that none of the rest of us took fancies like that into our heads and we were never to look at or speak to any man. Truly, Jon dear, when you came to the door that time I felt quite *sick*. I was afraid you might say something and he'd know. Father's beatings are nothing to laugh at.'

'I can believe that,' I said. 'All the same, when the time comes I shall marry you, you know. It might be quite easy. When I am twenty-three I shall have a bit of money and a trade to my hand.

'But when you are twenty-three I shall be twenty-two. Father will have promised me before that!' The thought struck me dumb; and she went on calmly, 'Susan is getting married at Christmas; she's very lucky, her man is young and cheerful and nice to look at. Ellen is promised, and she's not much more than a year older than I am, and though her man is old–he's got children older than Ellen–and he's bald and hasn't got many teeth, she will be well off and she will get away. Cecily now will never be married at all.'

'Why not?'

'Well, there are two reasons. Cecily isn't–well, not very pretty. I don't know whether you noticed, but she isn't as pretty as Susan or Ellen. And she is a very good cook. I've never known her spoil a dish; and whatever she makes, even pease porridge somehow tastes better than ours. So Cecily is the one who is to stay at home and look after Father and Mother when they are old.'

'He's got it all arranged, hasn't he?' I said savagely.

'Oh yes. Even the farm. Because we have no brother–and do you know he still throws that at Mother, oh, almost every day–that is why Susan has such a nice man chosen for her. Robin Fulger has only just a little farm, but it's next to ours and the two are going to be put together, and when Father is old Robin will work them both. And when they have a boy he's to be called Rawley!' She made this announcement with a kind of pride and pleasure and plainly shared her father's satisfaction over the arrangement. To me it was just one more instance–a particularly glaring one perhaps–of the dreadful domination of the old over the young.

'What beats me,' I said, 'is how your father sets about his match-making. Nobody ever sees you except at church.'

'There's the stall,' she said, as though that explained everything. Seeing my mystification, she explained that they had a butter stall at Baildon Friday Market. It was there that James Braddock had seen Caroline and the bald, almost toothless man had seen Ellen.

'With Robin Father just went and arranged with *his* father. He'd had his eye on Robin for a long time.'

'Do you go to tend the stall?'

'Not yet. Ellen and Susan so far; but when Susan marries, then I shall go.'

'Well, after Christmas I shall play hookey and come and visit the stall sometimes,' I said. But that was one of what I called my unacceptable remarks. Elizabeth seemed to fear and dread any reference to the future or to any kind of contact other than these Saturday-evening walks through the wood.

'Father is there, and very watchful,' she said.

Susan was married at Christmas, and *she* had a proper wedding because Robin Fulger's mother insisted on it, saying she wasn't going to have her son married like a hedge tinker. After that Elizabeth went to market every Friday, and I had to wait for the third Saturday–Susan's marriage did do that for us–before I could ask my searching questions. Had anyone hung about the stall and then talked to Matt Rawley; had anyone spoken to Elizabeth, stared at her, bought more butter than seemed normal? Every Friday I could imagine the dreadful thing happening.

One spring day I did as I promised and made an excuse to go into Baildon on a Friday. I did the errands that had been entrusted to me and then went and sat in the church porch, which overlooked the market, and watched. It seemed to me that every man in Baildon that day seemed to linger and stare as he passed the stall where the two pretty girls were selling the butter and the eggs and the little cheeses. And I looked ahead, half in panic, half with assurance. In November I should be nineteen and my apprenticeship would be done. If I could get my uncle's consent to my marriage I could present myself to Matt Rawley as a suitor for Elizabeth's hand. I wasn't rich, but I had more than sixty pounds laid by, for Uncle Francis had been meticulous about adding the shilling to the coffer's store, and I had a trade. I wasn't such a hopeless suitor. What I earned during the next four years would pay for Elizabeth's food and she could share my bed. (God, what that thought called up!) And she would be a help to Aunt Mary in the house. On the other hand, if out of timidity or diffidence I waited, some oaf, some lout, some beastly, bald, toothless, rich old man–or, worse, some rich and handsome young one–would step in. And I could not lose Elizabeth now; we'd never done more than kiss one another, or walk handed, but she was part of my very vitals.

The business of speaking to my uncle went badly from the start. The idea agitated me so cruelly that at my first attempt I went down in a fit before I had given him any notion of what I wanted to talk about. It must have been eighteen months at least since I had been so taken, and I was as surprised as he was. He had the sense to push a wad of linen between my teeth, and for that I was grateful. I could at least talk when I came to myself.

I could talk, and I was calm and lucid. I said that I had found the girl I wanted to marry, but that if I waited for four years I was afraid she would be married to someone else, so please would he give me his permission to be married at once. I outlined my plans for the arrangements of bed and board.

'And who is the wench?'

'I'm afraid that there are reasons for not telling you that until I have your consent, sir.'

'Somebody you're ashamed of?'

'Not at all.'

'Is it Bess Whymark of the Evening Star?'

'Good God no! Never mind the name. I'll tell you when you have said yes or not to the question I asked to begin with. Will you give me your permission to get married before I finish my journeyman's time?'

'I will not.'

'Why?'

'I don't hold with married journeymen. For one thing, they don't tend their work properly; and for another, it's awkward. You talk glib about sharing your bed and this house as ain't yours to share. Hev you thought what that mean? Hev you thought about your Aunt Mary, who's been good to you? Hev you thought about the three young 'uns you might breed in four years? How'd they fit in in a quiet house?'

'All right,' I said. 'Then will you give me your permission and pay me a proper wage–you could take it out of the money you hold for me. Clapper Green's cottage is empty. I could hire that and live there. Uncle Francis, it's my very life you hold in your hands; I must get married soon. I can't wait until I'm twenty-three.'

'Hev you gone and got a girl into trouble?'

'No. Of course not. What do you think I am? Look, promise on your honour not to tell. It's Elizabeth Rawley, and you know what her father is.

He'll marry her off to the firstcomer who makes a good bid for her. And that mustn't happen.'

'Now thass what I tell you about changing times,' said my uncle, bringing one hand down on his knee. 'When I was young a man got a roof to his head, a bed of his own, a chair and a table and a few pots and pans, and *then* he looked round for a wench to wed. You young 'uns nowadays got no foresight, you go at things like a bull at a gate. Do you really think Matt Rawley'd let his girl marry a fellow with four years still to do at his craft and not so much as a saucepan to his name? He've done well with his wenches, Matt hev, and the one you're sick for is the pick of the bunch, you young fool. He'll hev an alderman for her, don't I'll go to sea.'

'That's just what I'm afraid of,' I cried. 'If you can see that, you must see why it is essential that I speak for her *now*.'

'Well, lucky I'm here and hev a hold on you. I can at least stop you making that much fool of yourself. See here, Jon boy. The best plums come at the top of the tree, and to get 'em you hev to hev a ladder. The time'll come, maybe–I hope and trust it will–when you'll be a master carpenter with a place and a business and 'prentices of your own . . . that'll be your ladder. *Then* you can look about and pick a wench whose father'll be glad to listen to you and treat you respectful. And that'll be seemly. But to go to Matt Rawley and ask him to give his girl to come and tuck in *here*–thass just asking him to kick your teeth in, and he *would*.'

'I'd risk that. If you would just give me your permission.'

'Well, I ain't give it, and I shan't. I got my pride like other men, and part of it is to see you a right proper craftsman, finished and set up; not to be kicked on to Matt Rawley's dungheap for a silly, handless young fool.'

The mention of *his* pride went to my temper like a flame to faggot; I stormed at him, my voice rising shrill and shaky, using abusive terms I hardly knew I knew. But he was not to be moved, and I realised that the noise I was making was no more than the yelping of a newly tethered puppy, half choked by the chain. And lest, as with a puppy, my rage die down into a whimper of self-pity and my tears come and shame me before my uncle, I was obliged to dash out of the house, leaving him in every way the victor.

In the September preceding my nineteenth birthday Tom Rowhedge came home again. He had been away for more than four years; and if his previous absence had changed him from boy to man, the second one had worked an even greater change. Tom came home a rich man and a hero. He'd sailed from Bywater in the ship which his father had fitted out for him and with very little else, save his wits; he came home with money in his pocket, the title-deeds of Merravay in his hand, and with his fame running before him like a courier. It is true that he had sailed away a whole and handsome man and returned with a patch over an empty eye-socket and an ugly scar seaming one side of his face . . . but most men would have given an eye to have his story.

He had made two or three modestly profitable voyages to Continental ports, carrying cargoes of wool and bringing back wines and silks and spices; and but for his kindness of heart and his easily roused enthusiasm might have continued in that trade, one of a thousand men who followed their bent, made a living and remained unknown. But one day, in a low tavern in Calais, he fell in with an old English sailor who said he was a Devon man, and dying, and who was trying to beg a passage home because he wanted to be buried in Totnes. Hard drinking and the new pox which had raged through the seaports ever since the trade with Africa had been established had made this old man a very repulsive object to look upon; and as Tom Rowhedge confessed to me, though he felt sorry for him he didn't fancy his company 'on my nice clean ship'. However, pity won the day, and Tom made room for the derelict, who, once aboard and sober, seemed to take a new lease of life; even his horrid sores sloughed off. He began to talk. He said he had once been John Hawkins's gunner, and he could give what sounded like a first-hand account of the disaster of San Juan de Ulloa; and he did know about the trade in blackamoors. He knew where they were to be bought, and what one should look for in buying them; he knew where they should be sold, and what prices should be asked. There was, he said, a fortune to be made in the trade, because the settlers on the Spanish Main, having worked and whipped all the Indians to death, were now working and whipping the negroes at such a rate that the demand was enormous, while the supply was small and dwindling, because Spain had forbidden the colonists to buy slaves transported by any but Spanish ships; and what with the searching and the fighting that resulted, none but the hardiest and bravest of the English would engage in the trade.

'Look what happened to Jack Hawkins hisself back in '68. . . .' The old man told his tale again. But he added that there was fortune to be made even yet by those who had the pluck to take the risk. Tom's ambition and enthusiasm took light; the old man, whose name was Jabez Trengrove, decided to postpone his death for a while and make one more effort to acquire that fortune which had lured him to sea so many years before. In return for showing Tom the ropes of the new trade, and acting as gunner if necessary, he was to have a tenth of the profits. So they made all things ready and set off for Africa.

As Tom told me this story–sitting on the lid of the dower chest on which I was carving a bride's initials and the date–I realised that he combined, in an unusual degree, a kind heart and a complete lack of imagination. Brought face to face with any kind of misery, he was moved to immediate pity and to alleviating action; but misery unseen was, for him, non-existent. So he sailed off in the highest spirits in his 'nice clean ship', eager to engage in the dirtiest trade on earth. But when Trengrove had found the river which he remembered and led the way ashore and Tom saw the slave stockades for the first time, 'Then,' he said, 'I began to have my doubts.' Trengrove talked him out of them. He seems to have had a glib tongue. He said that, left to themselves, the blackamoors ate one another, or were eaten, either by their human enemies or by crocodiles and lions: their customs were hideous, their diseases innumerable, and their expectation of life practically negligible. In fact, he said, the best thing that could happen to them was to be shipped to the Indies or the Spanish Main, and nothing but their hopeless ignorance made the slave trade, the stockades, the collars and the bonds necessary. If they had the sense of lice they would swarm aboard and beg to be taken away. Tom let himself be persuaded–the more easily perhaps because he was just falling victim to the fever which attacks every white man on his first visit to these unhealthy places. Trengrove concluded the bargaining, loaded the blacks and brought the ship out to sea. They were south of Cape Verde Islands, where they meant to water, when Tom was well enough to leave his bunk.

'Most of the time I was sick, Jon, I'd either been building that first little boat of mine–you remember?–or back at King Edward's; and wherever my mind was my nose was conscious of a most horrible stink. If I was in my boat I used to think it was the river mud; if I was at school I thought they'd burnt the pease porridge again. But that day I was clear in my mind and knew I was aboard my own ship, and what in hell the stench could be I couldn't think. . . .'

When he knew, when he had tracked the dreadful smell to its source and seen, in the low, stifling hold, meant for the stowing of wool bales and wine barrels, the black men and women lying closer than salt herrings in a keg, on boards thick with the slime of their own excreta; when he learned that on an average five died each day and were tossed overboard with no more ceremony than if they were maggoty apples, his horror and indignation knew no bounds.

'But you must of knowed,' Trengrove said. 'You must allow for half or rather more to die. The Middle Passage sieves them out, see? The good 'uns live and the weak 'uns die, and you know them you sell is good stuff. That allust have been that way, and allust will.'

'Not on *my* ship,' Tom said.

Trengrove's one fear was that Tom would allow the slaves out of the hold. He told a terrifying tale about a slave-ship where the captain had thought that exercise and fresh air might reduce the death-rate. One evening the batch being exercised had turned on the unwary crew and overcome them. They'd spared only the boy who had been in the habit of bringing them water. After that the ship had drifted, since there was no one capable of steering her, and finally they'd set her on fire. The boy, and the black woman whom he had been 'given' as a sign of favour, had been picked up and told the tale. 'You don't want that to happen, do you?' Trengrove asked.

'We'll air them ten at a time, then, and have the space where the ten have been swabbed down.'

'Well, that'll keep us busy till we get to Curama,' Trengrove said, lightly because he was relieved.

'I shan't wait for Curama,' said Tom. 'I shall unload them at the first place I come to.'

'Now, now,' said Trengrove. 'We agreed on Curama. The prices there are the best in the world.'

'B—— the prices!' said Tom.

Notwithstanding the alleviation in their lot, the negroes, homesick and seasick, continued to die. And Tom continued to fret despite Trengrove's repeated assurance that they were making the passage with a phenomenally low death-rate. One morning, when they were still full ten degrees west of Trinidad, Tom sighted a smear on the horizon.

'Land,' he said to Trengrove. 'Know anything about it?'

'An island,' said Trengrove laconically. 'You'll see a lot of them between here and Curama.'

'Spanish island?'

'Could I know? There's scores of 'em in these parts. No bigger'n peppercorns lots of 'em. Chaps that ain't got nothing else to do land on 'em sometimes and stamp about and sort of christen 'em, either with their own name or the name of their favourite saint. I daresay that little dot is to let, in a manner of speaking, and if you were so minded and weren't all sail set for Curama you could land there and call it Rowhedge Island, or St Thomas.

There'd be nothing to show for it, and the next silly b—— that came along'd give it *his* name. See. Islands about here mean nothing till they've been took over and built on. This is the New World, remember.'

'I see,' Tom said; and turning, he called out to the man at the helm to change course and steer for the smudge on the skyline.

'So you want to discover an island, do you?' asked Trengrove, gibing, but good-humoured. 'Well, no doubt it's been discovered before and will be again. Islands are difficult to put a mark on.'

'If this one is suitable for the purpose I'll put my mark on it,' Tom said.

'How?'

'I'm going to chuck the blacks on to it.'

And that, despite Trengrove's frenzied protests, was exactly what he did do. He landed himself first on what he described as a dish-shaped island about as big as Nettleton parish. The little peppercorn of an island bore no sign of very recent human occupation, but men had lived there once. He found some ruined huts smothered with creepers; a spring of water with the rock under its lip worn away where at some time women had rested their vessels. The clear water teamed with fish, and there were tall trees bearing bananas–a fruit which Tom tried to describe to me.

'I landed them there, Jon, boatload by boatload, and at first they were puzzled and fearful, but when they began to understand they were like children let loose in a cherry orchard. It was wonderful. I felt like God! They dashed into the water and splashed about and sang and swam and shouted; they shinned up the trees after the fruit. They gathered flowers and made great wreaths to hang round their necks and my neck. And I stood there and stared at them and realised what they'd cost me! After four years of being my own master, I'd got a ship without a cargo, a crew to pay, a savagely angry partner and not a penny piece in the world.'

'So *then* you decided to turn pirate, Tom?'

'Well, not exactly. What I meant to do was to come back to England and either ask Father for a loan or, if he couldn't manage it, mortgage my ship for three or four voyages. I had to pay the crew, I had to give Trengrove his percentage–he'd have gone stark staring crazy, I reckon, before we got home–he was near to raving then; so when the old *Sancta Theresa* hove in sight it was like an answer to prayer, Jon.'

It was, of course, just Tom's luck that the *Sancta Theresa* was stuffed as full as she could hold without sinking, with silver from the mines at Santiago and with treasures from Cruzco, the Indian capital which the Spaniards had been stripping for nearly twenty years and hadn't yet picked clean. There was more wealth in that one vessel than a hundred small ships like Tom's could have earned by honest trade in a hundred years.

The little *Mermaid* brought the *Sancta Theresa* into port at Plymouth like a small dingy sheepdog bringing a great gilded sheep into the fold, and there were wild rejoicings. By law and tradition the greater part of the immense treasure went into the Queen's coffers, but the share which fell to Tom and Trengrove, whom he insisted upon treating as his partner because he said that but for him he would never done more than ferry across the Channel, was enough to make them moderately rich for the rest of their lives. Nevertheless Tom was astonished and immensely flattered when the Queen sent for him.

I suppose that before he dies Tom will tell the tale of that meeting a thousand times; but I was amongst the first to whom it was told, for Tom rode straight from London to Slipwell afterwards and sought me out on the second day after his arrival in order to give me the present he had bought for me in London. Strange man, he had remembered that on that evening when I poured out my heart of discontent to him I had mentioned my great dearth of books; and riding out of London he had stopped in Cheapside and bought me three! Malory's *Morte d'Arthur,* More's *Utopia* and Tottel's *Miscellany of Poems.* For a moment, with them in my hand, I also felt rich. Perhaps that is why I always think of Tom's interview with the Queen (about which he proceeded to tell me) as taking place in bright sunshine.

'What was she like, Tom?' I asked.

'Not like anything, except, maybe, the figurehead of a ship.'

He said that innocently, almost unintentionally, and then, quite suddenly, saw the value of it. He slapped his hand on his knee.

'But that's it exactly,' he exclaimed, astonished by his own perceptiveness. 'That's what she's like–the figurehead of a ship just newly painted.'

'Is she beautiful?' I had by that time a measure for beauty; I had my tallystick. *My* Elizabeth was beautiful; I was eager to hear how Tom's Elizabeth stood with that measure.

'Oh no,' Tom said. 'Not as a woman; but then how could she be? She is old–over forty, you know. But nobody in his senses would think of that! I mean . . . who asks the age of a figurehead? If it is significant, and freshly coloured . . .'

I could see that he was still a little dazed by the one leap of imagination he had ever known. So I said invitingly:

'But she was significant, then?'

'Oh yes. Not like anybody you ever saw, or thought about. She sat at the end of a big room at Whitehall Palace. That is difficult to describe too. You see, Jon, it's bigger than Nettleton Church, and empty–except for the people, of course. And she sat at the end of it in a chair, with a crowd of people about; all in very bright, rich clothes. Well, then somebody said my name very loud, and the lords and ladies drew back a bit, so there was all that big open space for me to walk over; and I felt, Jon, like we used to feel when old Trudgett used to say, 'Come up here, boy', only worse. The floor seemed to rock, you know. But I got across it and went down on my knee like a fellow outside had told me to . . . and then . . .' He broke off with a laugh in which there was some embarrassment.

'Yes, Tom, then?'

'Well, she patted my head, as though I'd been a good dog that had caught a hare for the pot! And she thanked me and said several pleasant things. Then she said, 'Stand up and let us look at you.' So I stood up, and I felt a thorough fool. And she said something about being handsome and what a pity it was about this. . . .' He laid a finger to the patch and the scar. 'And then she must have made some sign, though I didn't mark it; for all the people skipped away except for the two guards at the door. And then she said:

'"I would knight you, Thomas Rowhedge, if I dared; but I dare not. And lest you think me a coward for saying I dare not, I will tell you why. His Majesty of Spain has a curious habit of misconstruing my actions and chooses to think that I commission my brave men to sack his ships; a thing I have never done, in peace, and never should. It would be so *unnecessary*! You smile. You have, I see, an understanding humour! Then you will understand that to set Sir Thomas Rowhedge on the rolls would–shall we say?–*remind* those who watch that it was Thomas Rowhedge who brought the *Sancta Theresa* to port. And just at this moment that would be unwise." I muttered something about not looking for any reward of that nature, and then she said again, "But you have lost an eye, my good man, and that is a great pity." And she stared at me as though the loss of an eye were a very great matter. I mumbled again, and what I said was perfectly true, Jon–after a bit you *can* see quite well with one eye. And then she asked me where I came from, and I told her Slipwell, where Essex joins Suffolk; and she asked me what my father did, and various other questions which I would have resented from anyone else.

'Suddenly she snapped her fingers. Her hands are longer and thinner and whiter than anyone else's, and she uses them more, Jon. She snapped her fingers and said, "On that border there is a place called Merravay, is there not?" "Yes," I said, "lying between Slipwell and Nettleton. There is a ruined castle there and some acres of good land gone derelict since my Lord of Norfolk went to the Tower. . . ." I chopped off there, it being a sore subject and verging on the political. But she laughed and said, "I see you carry your sea eye ashore with you, Tom Rowhedge! Derelict it is, and that is a pity. Well, since I am reminded of that estate, and since I have it in my gift and can dispose of it without a trumpeting that will sound in the ears of Spain, Merravay is yours!" And even while I was thanking her, you know, it seemed strange that, with all she has to think of and to manage and control, she should remember Merravay.'

'They say she never forgets anything.'

Tom gave his old cheerful chuckle. 'Well, *that*, as old Trudgett used to say, is "susceptible to proof", Jon. Because then she asked me what I should do with Merravay, and I said I should build a house there and get the land under plough again, and make a place to retire to one day. And what do you think she said? "I shall visit you," she said. "Indeed a house in that quarter will be a convenience to me. There is Hengrave, in Suffolk, which is a pleasant place indeed, and Framlingham, which I dislike heartily because of its associations; and Essex is thick with great houses; but, hitherto, on the border accommodation has been meagre. So look for me at Merravay, Tom Rowhedge." That was her last word, Jon. And next day a pale-faced fellow brought along all the papers, sealed and signed.'

'Well,' I said; and 'Well' again. And then I recovered myself a little and said, 'It will have to be a big, grand house, Tom.'

'Not too big.' He had been sitting on his old accustomed seat–the sawhorse in our workshop; now he rose and began to walk about amongst the shavings and sawdust. 'After the open sea, Jon, a man doesn't crave space; he longs for something cosy and close. I'll have a small house, but everything fine in it. After all, I'm the one who has to live in it. Look, this is what I've been thinking . . . tell me what you think of this. . . .' He took a splinter of wood, brushed away the shavings and litter from a space on the floor and began to draw on the bare earth thus exposed. 'Let's say a fair-sized hall–then if she *does* come there'll be room for her, and everything–about what? Fifty feet long by twenty wide; the door coming in here, with a screen, nicely carved to keep the draught out; the stairs going up *here* to the gallery. See? Now on this side a smaller room; twenty by twenty–that's big, isn't it? Big enough for me, anyway; with a huge hearth, and I shall sit at table with my back to it. Then I'll have the kitchens directly to the rear, so that dishes come hot to table; brewhouse, wash-house, storeroom–we needn't bother about them at the moment. Then look. The stairs come up here. Nothing over the hall, I think. People are beginning to floor over the hall nowadays, for economy's sake, but I needn't bother about that. The hall goes to the roof–apart from the gallery, that is. You see, I have to bear in mind that she might come, and then we'd need a gallery for the musicians. Gallery along here, and then sleeping-chambers could lead off. How many would I need, Jon? Eight? Ten?'

'You couldn't get many over the one chamber and the kitchens,' I said. 'Unless you had another floor.'

'Oh, must I? I fancied a small house.'

'Then have another room here,' I said, taking the stick from his hand and adding my contribution. 'See, that would balance better. The big hall across the front, two rooms, each half as large as the hall, behind, and then kitchens behind them. That way, if you didn't want very big sleeping-chambers, you could manage.'

'One must be a fair size. Suppose she stayed the night.'

'One big one, then, running this way, see?' And then I suddenly remembered something which I had heard. 'No, Tom,' I said. 'That won't do at all. This plan is working out square. And I'm told that nowadays all the new houses are being built on an E as a compliment to the Queen. And if there's a likelihood that she will visit and perhaps even spend a night here, and she gave you the land and knows the house is new built . . . by cock, Tom, if ever a house had to be an E it is this house of yours. Now, let me see.' I scrubbed my foot over the lines already drawn and set to work again. I'd never planned a house before, never indeed thought of a house in terms of planning, but it seemed to come easy to me, and in a few minutes I had it drawn out on the floor.

'There you are, Tom,' I said, pleased with myself. 'There's your E. There you have your big hall, with the gallery above, and the kitchens handy behind it. Rooms to the left and right can be many or few, large or small to suit your fancy, so long as you build forward to make the top leg and the bottom, and set the porch in the centre for the third. Turn the face of the house to the south, lad, so your buttery and larder and storerooms stand cool on the north, and at one end of the gallery above make a great bed-chamber with another window to catch the morning sun–a chamber fit for a Queen.'

I stared at the lines scratched in the earth and the sawdust, and out of them I saw a stately house, a beautiful house, rear itself. A poem built, not with words but with timber and glass and stone and brick. . . .

'By cock!' said Tom, clapping me on the back. 'Now I can *see* it. Till now I've been in the dark. I had in mind some snug little place to tuck into when I got too old to go to sea. And when I told the Queen I'd build a house I meant in time to come. But now . . .' His eyes took on a far-away look. 'Ah, Jon, I see it, with every timber seasoned oak, and red bricks for the walls. Come along with me, now, and let's go see where we'll set her. . . .'

So I rode pillion behind him again, as in our boyhood days, taking the track out of the village which could only be used in fair weather and which led on through Slipwell to Bywater.

Away back in the time of the Normans there had been a castle at Merravay, and there was an old story which said that in those days the sea had covered all Slipwell and the man who reared the castle had been warned that one day the sea would come up and engulf it; the name 'Merravay' was supposed to have its origin in that threat. The castle had been ruined and deserted for many generations, and now all that was left was a broken tower, no more than ten feet high. In more recent times, when the land was held by the Duke of Norfolk and tilled on his behalf, labourers had lived in the tower under a roof of reeds laid flat across it. This thatch had rotted and fallen inwards like the crust of an ill-made pie, but inside the thick walls the mark of old, ancient fires could still be traced; and somehow that was pitiful. And the whole place had a sad, desolate air, so that even Tom, little fanciful as he was, turned his back on the ruins and said:

'The stones can maybe be used for barn or byre; for the house I'd lief even the foundations were new.'

We walked forward and came to a dip in the ground where the moat had been. The water had drained away long since and it was now no moister than a ditch, and, like a ditch, was full of ferns and dead meadowsweet. Beyond the ground rose, gently but surely.

I looked about me, seeking the likeliest site. Then I turned and faced the sad ruins again. Between them and the edge of the moat where we stood were two great trees, unlike any I had ever seen before, very sombre with their almost black foliage. I did not know their name then; but later on, while we were building, I heard somebody say that he had been told that they were cedars, probably brought home as saplings by some owner of the castle who had been on Crusade. And it is true that there was a Crusader's tomb in Nettleton Church. That morning, without knowing their value or their history, I could see their virtue in relation to our plans, and I said:

'Tom, if it were my house I'd set her between those trees. 'Twill be years before any tree you plant is grown high enough to give shade in summer or shelter in winter. And if you put the house there you'll have this space for a garden and the dip will make a boundary between garden and field. . . .'

'If she'll lay there, Jon. Let's pace it out and see. . . .'

The space was exactly right, and the ground was level there.

'But they're melancholy things,' said Tom, eyeing the black trees with small favour.

'The whole place has a melancholy air,' I agreed, 'but that is because it has been long deserted. And when your trees have grown these can come down.'

So it was decided. On the way home Tom said he would ride straight on and engage Clem Hubbard, a master mason, to do the building. 'And you and your uncle must care for all the woodwork, Jon.'

'It would please me to have a hand on your house, Tom; but an apprentice can't pledge for his master. You must see *him* about the business.'

Privately I entertained a grave doubt as to whether Uncle Francis would take kindly to the idea of working on a house that was to be built with money stolen from the Spaniards, who were real Papists, on land given to Tom by a Queen in whose authority my uncle barely believed. He might easily not hold with it. I was surprised when, a few days later, he came to me rubbing his hands and saying gleefully that we had work for two years ahead, building Tom Rowhedge's new house at Merravay. Some nasty carping streak in me made me express my surprise in one of my sweet-sour remarks, and he said:

'Bless the boy, what a simpleton it is! Why, even in the good days, when

Queen Mary sat on the throne, the English hated the Spaniards and robbed 'em whenever they could! Why, if I met a Span'ard I'd rob him myself, if for no other reason than because a Span'ard put an end to the owd ways in England.'

'How do you make that out?'

'Plumb easy. 'Twas a Span'ard married Queen Mary and used her so ill that she died broken-hearted. Anybody that was half a man 'ud hev stayed by her and bred a bevy of sons to stand between the throne and the bastard. . . .

Even for Uncle Francis, in the privacy of his home, that was very plain speaking; he knew it and checked himself and looked, for a moment, ill at ease. Encouraged by the sight of his rare discomfiture, I said mercilessly:

'But that is what I meant. If you think *that* of the Queen, you must think also that Merravay was not hers to give, however you skim round the idea of Tom's deserving a reward.'

'Nor I do, in a way,' he said slowly. 'But 'twas wasted as it was, Jon. Been laying waste these many years. Surely 'tis better in Tom's hands.' He recovered from the little setback which his slip of the tongue had occasioned and became his usual, ever-right, moralising self.

'You oughta be owd enough now, boy, not to pick holes in your own blanket. Take a look round you. Whass been ordered this month? A dower chest and a coupla milking-stools! We ain't had a proper big job for months, and with the harvest so bad we ain't likely to get one. We should all go down on our knees and thank God for Tom Rowhedge and the fine big house that'll mean bread for us and a dozen like us for the next coupla years.

As well as being pleased with the prospect of steady work for a long time, my uncle was enjoying a sense of importance; for, as Tom had told the Queen, Merravay lay about midway between Nettleton and Slipwell, and so our carpenter's shop made a convenient headquarters for the conferences which were necessary before the house was begun. Tom's loyalty, or his lack of imagination, had led him to make the thing as purely local as possible. Clem Hubbard, the master builder of Baildon, had said confidently that he could build a palace or a cathedral so long as he had a free hand and a plan to go by. He put his faith, he said, in a good foundation; building, like gardening, was a matter of digging deep enough; given eight feet of sound foundation underground, you couldn't go wrong. He was exactly like my uncle in his devotion to rule-of-thumb sayings and in his faith in his own ability. My uncle, who to my knowledge had never worked on anything bigger or more important than Rowhedge's new barn, and who really specialised in small, meticulously finished work, was equally confident when he talked about king-pins and beams nine inches square. He pinned his faith in sound wood. If you stuck to oak, well seasoned, and used plenty of it, and didn't scamp your pinning, you couldn't go wrong.

There were several such meetings in the warm, apple-scented evenings of that September before Tom went back to his ship. And they were always held in our shop. Sometimes there were as many as ten of us gathered about the bench; for the man who made bricks at Maldon and the man who was supplying the timber and the lead-worker from Bywater who was to cast spout-heads bearing a Tudor rose, the initials TR and the date 1577–these and their sons, or their journeymen, must all have a say. And unless it happened to be Elizabeth's Saturday for visiting her aunt, I was there too.

Midway through the chatter and the amicable argument we would hear the scream of the well-pulley and know that Aunt Mary was hauling the jug of ale from the deeps in which it had been cooling, and presently she would come in, quiet as a ghost, with the ale and mugs and a plate of saffron cakes and a dish of damsons.

At first, in the centre of the bench there lay a piece of paper bearing the plan which I had drawn on the floor; it was always referred to as 'Jon's picture'; presently it was joined by other pictures. Tom said, 'I want the bricks laid herring-bone fashion, Clem', and it had fallen to me to illustrate what he meant. It was the same with the spout-heads. But though they valued the 'pictures' as guides in what was–had they admitted it–pretty uncharted territory, they never allowed me to feel in the least important because I had made them. Nothing *really* mattered save good deep foundation and sound, well-seasoned timber. And as I once said to Tom, 'If in the end you get a house that is anything but a glorified barn, you'll have me to thank!'

So, on the first day of October we stood in the mellow sunshine while Tom took spade in hand and cut the first sod. Then Uncle Francis came forward with a handful of salt and gravely sprinkled it in the sign of the cross over the broken soil, and said, 'Bless the ground on which we build, and the house that we build.' And even those of the company who thought that very old-fashioned said 'Amen'. Uncle Francis, though he was a carpenter, a master man, then took spade in hand and began to dig with the best, saying as he did so, 'Well begun is half done!'

Then the mass of day-labourers whom Clem Hubbard had engaged fell to work and began to dig the foundations along the lines which we had previously pegged out by the plan.

In that same week Tom rode off to Plymouth, where he had left his *Mermaid* for refitting. He was returning to the Continental trade, having had, he said, his bellyful of adventure. He said he intended to crowd in as much trade as he could in the two years while Merravay was building, 'For I doubt, Jon, whether, once the place is finished, I shall ever willingly leave it again.'

I said then the thing that had been on the tip of my tongue many times. 'When you settle down, Tom, you'll have to get married.'

'I know,' he said, and laughed. 'The trouble with me is I like so many wenches so much! I should have been a Turk!'

'And you never saw one you preferred above all?'

'No.'

'You will,' I said.

'I hope so,' he said, quite gravely. 'The house will need a mistress.'

I think it was then that my feeling for Tom suffered damage. It began like the hairline crack in a plaster wall which, left untended, will widen and let in the frost and the rain until it brings the wall down. And once the thing had happened I was surprised that it hadn't happened before; but it is true that, until he spoke of installing a wife at Merravay, I had not envied him. He had, and he was, everything that I had not and was not, and during my first wretched year at Nettleton I had often thought, Lucky Tom to be allowed to choose his own trade–but that was all. Nor had I envied him his luck, his money, his fame, his meeting with the Queen; in fact, because he was my friend, and always so kind to me, I had felt a vicarious pleasure in his success. None of it was an encroachment upon *me*. But now I thought, quite bitterly–Yes; *you've* only to look round and wag your finger and you can marry any girl you fancy, whereas I . . .

However, I saw him off pleasantly and was flattered, because, although my uncle and Clem Hubbard set small store by me, Tom said openly, 'Jon knows what I want the house to be like. We planned it together and he made me see it; so if any question arises he is to decide.' And all through the next year I was tolerably happy. The work was far more interesting and absorbing than any I had ever been engaged on before; working with a number of men was a pleasant change, saving my spirit from the constant rub of my uncle's company; now and then I was able to exercise a certain authority in the making of a decision; and so far there had been no mention of anyone 'speaking' for Elizabeth. She still stood, each Friday, behind the butter stall, as open for offers, had folks but known it, as the dairy stuff she sold; and I still endured agonies for great stretches of time. I would meet her on a Saturday and walk from Thomasin Griggs's cottage to within sight of Rawley's, and my first question was, 'Has anything happened?' So far she had always said, 'Nothing'; and I could then be happy until the next Friday, when she went to the stall again. And that was a childish snatch at consolation, like whistling in the dark, because I knew perfectly well that someone might be making approaches to her father at any moment of those six charmed days, even at the moment when we were walking along the woodland ride telling one another that all might yet come right. Nevertheless I always felt better between the Saturday when I saw her and the following Friday; and then there were fifteen days to wait before I saw her again.

Still, the weeks and the months flew past–all the faster for this constant looking forward, this constant awareness of time–and I was twenty. In three years I should be free. Often we spoke of that. Often Elizabeth said, 'I do want to marry you, Jon. I know I like you better than I shall ever like anyone. But I couldn't stand up to Father. Even Caroline couldn't, and she was very brave.' And I would remember that she had been only a child when Caroline had defied that dreadful man; the beating, the locking-up on bread and water, the final capitulation had all made a deep and lasting impression on her. She couldn't be blamed for that. So I would say, 'But you would let me know. I wouldn't just let you go. I'd do something!' And she would say, 'Of course, Jon. I'd let you know. And now let's talk about something else.'

Generally I then went on to tell her how Merravay was growing.

It grew apace. And it was beautiful. Though I say it, I who made the plan and said where the windows should be set and what patterns should be carved over the hearth at which–on cold nights at sea–Tom dreamed of warming his back, it was a beautiful house. I came to love it. There were times when it seemed more mine than Tom's.

He only saw it twice. He came home in the first February, when the walls were about roof high and the inside no more than a skeleton, and he stamped about a bit and then said to me:

'The old men have done a good job, so far. But it looks raw and kind of lonely. I think I should put the garden in hand.' He looked away towards Layer Wood and grinned a little sheepishly. 'It sounds a bit lordly, Jon, but I happened to fall in with an old man who had a deal to do with the laying out of the garden at Hampton. He's crippled now–in fact he was begging in Plymouth when I found him–but if one took the trouble and had him carried about . . . He still *knows* about gardens,' he ended almost defiantly.

'And what is lordly about that?' I asked.

'He worked for the Queen, and for the King, Jon.'

'And now he begs.'

'Yes. Isn't that sad?'

'He was lucky to fall in with you,' I said.

They brought the old man in easy stages to Nettleton, where Tom arranged him lodgings at the Evening Star. And my uncle made a little wheeled cart, in which for the next few months he sat like a goblin directing the layout of the garden. Nobody liked him much, for though Tom's kindness had brought him up from the gutter he acted in a very disdainful way towards us all, calling us Johnny Go-to-Ploughs, and bumpkins. Also he always held a long staff across his knees and did not hesitate to strike out with it if anyone annoyed him or got in his way. Once he even hit out at Clem Hubbard, who had stepped on a bed of young wallflowers. But he planned a garden such as had never been seen in our parts before, where even quite big houses, such as Mr Turnbull's at Baildon, had gardens which had grown up haphazard and were more for use than ornament.

Unfortunately for me, the more Merravay grew in beauty the more I loved it, and the more I envied Tom. And every time I envied Tom I fell to brooding over what might have been my lot if my uncle had let me buy myself out and go with him to sea when he invited me. *I* might then have had some money and could have been building a house–nothing like so stately as this one, of course, but a pretty little cottage for Elizabeth. Thoughts like that were hard to bear, and on the day when Tom arrived just at Easter, bringing food and wine and brandy and making an impromptu feast, all my stomach seemed to go sour and I was sick, physically sick. (I'd heard Dr Trudgett pour scorn upon the theory of the ascendancy of the various humours in man; but a bilious humour certainly had me that day.)

Soon after Easter the bricklayers were paid off, and then the tilers; the lead-beaters came and fixed the handsome water-spouts and the guttering and lounged about waiting for a wet day to test their work and then went away satisfied. Finally only Uncle Francis and I were left at Merravay, putting the finishing touches.

The previous Saturday had been one of those golden-haloed days which came once in three weeks for me, and the fact that it was a drear, dismal, drizzly day, like so many had been that month, did nothing to lower my spirits. Truth to tell, I rather liked a wet Saturday night, for then I could make Elizabeth walk under my cloak for quite a bit of the road–though we must always make sure that she did not arrive home too dry-looking–and now and again when we came to a particularly splashy place in the path I would lift her over. So light and warm and fluttery she was then, like a bird.

The evening promised well. At six o'clock it was almost dark and rain was falling. I waited at my usual place, as near to the old woman's cottage as I could well be and yet remain out of sight should she look from the tiny window; and when Elizabeth carrying her basket, rounded the corner I opened my cloak and said, 'Come under', and put my arm about her as I had done on a dozen similar evenings. But this evening, instead of coming under and nestling up to me like a bird, she said:

'No, thank you, Jon,' and began to walk briskly along the path.

'What's the matter?' I asked. 'Is anything the matter?'

I thought she shook her head. 'Well, then, why won't you walk under my cloak? You'll be soaked before you get home.'

She walked more quickly until she was almost running. I reached out and took her arm, but my handhold was mostly cloak, and she shook me off quite easily.

'Glory to God,' I said, 'what is wrong with you tonight?'

And then I saw that she was crying. Even that didn't bring me to a sense of disaster, for old Thomasin Griggs took an infernal delight in tormenting her nieces, and it was nothing new for Elizabeth to emerge from that cottage in tears; but ordinarily she would run to me and tell me about it and I would kiss her and talk nonsense until she cheered up again.

'Is it the old she-devil?' I asked, hurrying along, just behind Elizabeth, for the path was so narrow that two people could only walk abreast if both willed it. 'Tell me, honeysweet; it'll be better if you tell me. What did she do to you?' This time I had a firm hold of her arm and pulled her to a standstill, swinging her round so that I could see her face, so small and pale and sweet in her hood, and only just visible, what with the trees' shadow and the early dusk.

'It isn't her,' she said in a voice that was a crying voice but still more or less familiar. Then, in a wild high one that I never heard before, she said, 'It's you and me, and Father . . . and Tom Rowhedge.'

'Tom Rowhedge,' I repeated stupidly. 'What's he . . .?' Then, of course, I knew. Unto everyone that hath shall be given . . . but from him that hath not shall be taken away even that which he hath.

'Darling, try to stop crying,' I said; for now she was sobbing uncontrollably and I couldn't think as clearly as I needed to.

'When did this happen? When he was home at Easter?'

'I suppose so. I don't know. I do remember that week because we had market on Thursday because of it being Good Friday week. And he came and talked to Father, and then he rode beside us as far as Goose Green and Father asked him to supper. And on Easter Sunday he came again. . . .'

'You never told me,' I said harshly. For it was that kind of thing which I had dreaded each time I asked her if anything had happened since I saw her last.

'I didn't know. He never said anything. Nor did Father until the night before last when we heard that Chris Huxstable had died when they cut him for the stone.'

She was still sobbing wildly and twisting my hands in hers, and her last sentence was the kind of *non sequitur* that occurs in delirium. I thought for a moment that she was raving.

'Chris Huxstable? What's he got to do with it?'

'Father said–oh, Jon, this is horrible, but he said it. . . . Chris Huxstable spoke for me as long ago as last Christmas. But he was sick then and didn't want to be married till he was better. If he would have married me out of hand Father said he'd have struck hands on the bargain at once, then I'd be a widow and rich. But Chris said he'd try drinking the Walsingham water, and if that didn't shift his trouble he'd be cut. So you see, Jon, Father couldn't say aye or nay to Tom Rowhedge at Easter because Chris was still at Walsingham then. But the water didn't work and so he was cut and he died, and when Father heard he just said, "Oh. Well, my girl, you'll have

Merravay instead of the tannery; and it smells sweeter." And that, truly, was the first I knew.'

'God!' I said. 'I'm glad of hell! There should be hell for men like your father. He'd have given *you* to Chris Huxstable, who stank of rotting hides and his own corruption till you could smell him a mile off. Darling, Lisbeth darling . . .' I clutched her to me, shuddering, aghast at the thought of what she had escaped. My mind rocked. 'Tom is young and clean,' I said. 'But he shan't have you! And Tom is my friend . . . he wouldn't want to take my sweetheart.' I had a sudden flash of enlightenment. 'Honeysweet, I'll wager anything in the world that Tom spoke for you out of kindness. Tom has the kindest heart in the world,' I said; 'he'd want to save you from Chris Huxstable.' I felt her stiffen under my hands.

'Thank you for that, Jon,' she said, and pulled herself away and began to walk on.

'Oh, what have I said now? Lisbeth, you know I meant no offence; you know, don't you, that I think you so sweet and pretty and altogether desirable that the King–if we had a king–might well seek your favours and count himself lucky if you smiled on him. But what I said about Tom is true . . . he is kind; and I'm quite sure that if I tell him that you are my sweetheart he will withdraw his offer.'

Alas, the farther I plunged the deeper I went in the mire.

'You think it was so lightly made?'

'No, no. But Tom would understand. He has so much, Lisbeth. . . . I have so little . . . nothing but my love. . . .'

All wrong, all wrong!

'If you talk him into withdrawing, then it will be another Chris Huxstable for me,' she said. 'And though I must bear my father's arrangements for me–because he is my father–I cannot see why you and Tom Rowhedge should bandy me about as though I was a marble. . . .' She spoke angrily and began to walk again with short, sharp steps. Some sort of madness flared in me and I said:

'I'm beginning to think you *want* to marry Tom. Is that it? Maybe you think you're like Susan–lucky?'

'When I think of Chris Huxstable I know I am!' She stopped again and wiped the back of her hand and the cuff of her sleeve across her face. 'Don't be angry, Jon. We knew all along that we could never be married, didn't we? These times together . . . they were very sweet I shall always remember them; but they were like something in a song, or a story, not a bit of real life. . . .'

She sounded very old suddenly, old and wise and calm. An appalling sense of loneliness fastened down on me. She had gone over; she was now on the side of the old men who arranged things without taking any count of human feelings.

'If you're so philosophic and resigned all at once,' I said unkindly, 'tell me–why were you crying when I met you?'

My bleeding vanity yearned for one word of comfort to staunch its wound; I wanted her to say that she minded too. She gave me as honest an answer as any man ever had from a woman, I think.

'I was afraid you might be angry with me, Jon. I always cry when I'm frightened.'

'And for *me* you have no feeling at all?'

'Oh, that isn't true. Truly, Jon, ever since the night before last I've been thinking. . . . I know it sounds a strange thing to say . . . but I wished you'd never sought me out and talked to me and walked with me, because then I should be so glad that it was Tom Rowhedge and not Chris Huxstable that I'd be the happiest girl in the world.'

'Oh,' I said. I stood for a moment so coldly furious that I wanted to break her in pieces, and then all at once I saw what those words implied; poor little darling! Pity for her, and self-pity, and fury, and my feeling of being deserted all churned together in my mind, and far off, like distant thunder, I heard that warning crackle.

'Run along,' I said. 'Somebody calling . . . your father! Go! And be happy!'

I did not see her go. I had just time to turn round and thrust my thumb into my mouth when the crackling, flashing dark, saying be happy, be happy, BE HAPPY, closed down on me.

When it cleared the rain had stopped and the moon was high and the mud of the puddle in which I had been lying had soaked to my skin.

Sitting there in the freshly whitewashed buttery of Merravay, I could look back and see all my life up to that point quite clearly, and quite dispassionately. But after that there was a blur. I couldn't eat more than a few mouthfuls without sickening, and I learned that there are many levels to sleep. Ordinarily one dives in and is received in the cradling depths, but it is possible to float just under the surface, to be no longer fully wakeful, to be a prey to dreams, and yet not quite asleep. I did that every night; and every day I went to Merravay and worked, and sometimes my uncle would say things–like he had just said that about my children's children and the stairs at Merravay–which pressed on my hurt.

But the brandy was good. It seemed to take the place of the food which sickened and the sleep which eluded me. For the first time for a week I felt like myself. I set the cup on the shelf and stood up. I thought–Well, this is Merravay, the house which I planned and Tom paid for; the house in which Elizabeth will live. I shall never come here again; so I will look it over now.

This is the hall; twenty feet by twenty as we planned, with the screen to keep out the draught of the door. And, by God, the screen carving is beautiful; solid oak carved to the delicacy of lace; the best job Uncle Francis ever did. And here is the staircase, solid and sound, every peg six inches long, and such a lovely piece of carving on the newel-posts: Moses with his staff turning into a snake. . . . I told Uncle Francis that story; he can't read, he doesn't approve of reading, he really wishes back the time when nobody in a village could read except the priest–and that in Latin; and yet he liked that story, and used it. So here is Moses, looking very much like Mr Nicholas Aldridge, J.P.–just his beard, I swear; and just about the look of surprise that he would wear if his walking-stick turned into a snake. But it's a fine piece of work, and I hope when the Queen comes she will notice it. Elizabeth will have to make a curtsey to the Queen. And the Queen, if she is a woman at all, will envy her complexion and probably ask if she uses rose-water or witch-hazel for it. And Elizabeth will surely give her an honest answer; she's extremely honest, my Elizabeth, Tom's Elizabeth. . . .

Ah well . . . here's the room Tom dreamed of–a fine square room with a good hearth; the board above it nicely carved too, though not so magnificent a work as the Moses. This is Tudor roses–very right and proper, because it was the Tudor Queen who gave Tom Merravay. And who thought of that pretty touch? Jon Borage, bless him! Never at a loss. Tudor roses in this chamber, and in the other, across the hall, there's a sailing ship. And in both rooms there's this big fair window, with a window-seat. In the morning Elizabeth can sit here in the sun; and in the evening she can cross the hall and sit in the other and still have the sun. And be happy! Be happy! BE HAPPY! Better not think about that.

But you want her to be happy, don't you? Of course I do. She never did me any harm. She was my little honeysweet love, my darling, my little bird; but the plums worth gathering grow at the top and you have to have a ladder. You have to have a ladder, and you haven't got a ladder, have you, Jon Borage? You haven't! You have to have a ladder.

Come on, now. You're upstairs. Here is the gallery where the musicians will sit, will sit, will sit and play when the Queen comes. Will anyone notice that it is carved in the lacy pattern and matches the screen by the door? At this end of the gallery is the state bedroom. You'd better face it, you know; they'll surely use it on the wedding-night. What, here? Yes; here. You know, Jon Borage, you are a fool. You could have taken her maidenhead; you know you could. Any night last summer when the hawthorn was in bloom and the cuckoo was calling. What a fool, what a cuckoo you were. There was your chance! She loved you then; she used to cling to you and kiss you and walk under your cloak when it rained. If you'd taken her then . . . and she'd quickened, he'd have been glad–Matt Rawley would have been glad–to have you make an honest woman of her. Oh, but she is honest; she told me why she cried . . . hardly any other woman would have done that. And then when your uncle asked. 'Have you gone and got a girl into trouble?' you could have said 'Yes', and then he would have been all agog for you to marry her. Do you see? But she was like a flower, to be handled gently. Oh, yes, gently; brought to market with the bloom on her–'Fresh violets!' . . . Oh, the fool that you were! Cuckoo! Cuckoo!

Pass we on. Here are six bedchambers, all square and sound. There'll be a little boy one day, and his hair will be copper-coloured and his cheeks will be rosy; and there'll be a little girl with black hair and a skin of cream. And maybe Elizabeth will say, 'He shall be Thomas Jonathan.' Would she dare? Why not? I never did them any harm; I planned this house. He'll say, 'Of course, Jonathan; good old Jonathan . . . why does he never come to see us?' And the little girl will be Elizabeth Thomasin. Why Thomasin, darling? Because and because . . . but that is a secret. Because while that cuckoo called and while that hawthorn bloomed something that might have happened didn't happen . . . because life, like sleep, has different levels, and on one level . . . Yes, darling, on one level you belonged to me.

There'll be guests and there'll be servants.

Let's go down again. What a fine kitchen! You could roast an ox by that hearth; doubtless you will. When the Queen comes. And at this end by the little fire . . . blackberry jelly, my sweet. You'll stand here and seal the jars down with a bit of pig's bladder, and you'll carry them across here into the storeroom. . . . I shall always see your little purple-stained hands dropping the glossy berries into the basket. Will you see mine? Truly, my dear, I hope not; because you always knew that we had no future. You saw what I refused to see. So make your blackberry jelly, make your curtsey, make your little boy and your little girl and be happy! Be happy!

And what of me?

I was back now in the hall, in the place from which I had started, near the window farthest from the stairs. And as clearly as I had seen what life held for Tom and Elizabeth, I saw what was left for me. Nothing. Nothing for my mind, because Uncle Francy didn't hold with book-learning; nothing for my heart, because he didn't hold with apprentices marrying. . . . I looked down a dark, cold, narrow tunnel of years, a slipway to the grave; and despair, the last, the worst enemy of man, came upon me. I saw myself going on and on through all the changing seasons, empty-minded, empty-hearted, with just my hands busy. Stools and cupboards and coffins. Even Merravay, which I had planned with joy, was finished now, and such a job would never come my way again. I was nothing and had nothing to hope for. . . .

And I saw, with piercing clarity, who was to blame. My uncle had taken me, spoiled and deformed me as surely as though he had sawn off my head, cut out my heart and used my dead hands for hammers. If he had done that, in a physical sense, they would have hanged him; as it was, they praised him for his charity to an orphan! The Bible was wiser . . . it bade us not to fear those who killed the body but to fear those who killed the soul. It also said that man could not live by bread alone . . . bread, years and years of earning bread, eating bread, caring, thinking, knowing nothing of anything but one's bread. It wasn't bearable. . . .

I stood there and I died.

He bustled in, carrying in his hand the lopped-off top of a fir tree.

'Had to go a long way in to get a well-shaped one,' he said. His voice rang very loud and clear in my ears, the voice of someone shouting down a well. I saw him clearly too, every line and furrow in his face; and the bits of sawdust on the lock of hair that showed under his white carpenter's hat looked as huge and distinct as cobblestones.

He went over to his tool-basket and took out a length of white ribbon, which he folded and hacked into lengths with his knife.

I sat down on the window-seat and watched him. He propped up the little tree and began to tie the bits of ribbon to its boughs. 'This is for prosperity,' he said, 'and this for health.' He mentioned long life and happiness, fertility and charity. Then he tied the last knot to the topmost bough and said, 'God bless this house.'

And I sat and watched him.

'In the old days, Jon,' he said, straightening himself, 'every house that was reared was blessed. And who can deny it, the houses stood better and the folks were happier. You and me are alone now, boy, and there's none to mock; so, though I know you don't feel about the old things as I do, we'll go now together and put the bless-this-house on Tom Rowhedge's roof.'

The old things. The old way of thinking that a carpenter's boy must stick to his bench; the old way of apprenticing boys so that the master's will was law; the old way of making girls marry the man their father chose; the old superstitions; the idea that an omnipotent, omniscient God would look kindly on a house because of a bit of fir tree and some ribbon knots. Horrible, obscene!

Alive, I might have ventured some futile protest. But I was dead. I rose and followed him out of the house and into the yard at the back. The space was paved with stones, even as eggs, so that on wet days no one would need to don clogs to cross it. My uncle took a ladder and reared it against the back porch.

'Now you on'y hev to stand by,' he said, 'and when I hev it fixed you say

"Bless this house", and Heaven'll be so pleased to see us holding to the old custom the blessings'll come tumbling thick and fast.'

He climbed up the ladder and gained the roof of the porch. After that it was easy for the planes had been so set that a man could gain access to inspect the tiles or clear the snow from the gutter between the gables. I saw his long knobbly legs in their coarse grey hose and the seat of his soiled, baggy breeches disappear. I heard the scratch of his nailed shoes on the tiles. Then there was silence, and after a space his voice.

'God bless this house,' he said earnestly.

The stick-cracking sound began in my ears. And this time the voices about which, long ago, Dr Trudgett had inquired did make themselves heard. First, very faint and faraway, the voice of my father saying things about the chains which superstition clamped upon men; then Uncle Francy's voice saying that he didn't hold with schooling, and did I think Matt Rawley would let his daughter marry a fellow with four years still to do at his craft; and then another voice, soft, persuasive and unrecognised. The voice of hope. . . . Yes, at this moment, when all hope was ended, there was the voice, the indomitable voice, saying to me that Elizabeth and Tom were not married yet; that there was money in the coffer; that death cancelled indentures and the world was wide.

For a moment everything seemed marvellously clear, and I thought what a fool I had been not to think of this sooner. Then the darkness and the confusion which I knew so well began to close in. A darkness shot with sparks and flashes of horrid light. In one flash I saw him coming, carefully, spiderlike, along the ridge of the porch and towards the ladder. I put my left thumb in my mouth, for I knew what the whirling and the darkness and the lights portended; but at the same time I laid my right hand on the ladder. The sound of its fall came sharp and hard through the crackling noises; the sound of his fall was just a soft thud. The voice in my head began to scream as it drew away into the distance.

And then it was quite dark and very quiet.

INTERLUDE

That autumn was long remembered. Seldom, if ever before in the course of their long history, had the parishes of Nettleton, Clevely and Slipwell been shaken by such a series of dramatic happenings.

There was first the tragedy–the almost double tragedy–at Merravay. The ladder had slipped under Francy Sheply's feet and cast him to his death; and the boy Jon, finding him thus, had been taken with a fit of such severity and length that he, too, was taken up for dead. Indeed the hastily summoned helpers who lashed planks into rough stretchers and carried them back to Nettleton were convinced that they carried two corpses.

This story, exciting enough in itself, was lent a peculiar embellishment by the behaviour of Mary Sheply, who claimed to have had a warning. Because she was so silent and unobtrusive a woman people tended to believe without question her story of how, just at sunset on the day of the tragedy, she went to fetch a last pail of water from the well and had 'a feeling' that something untoward had happened. She ignored it for a while; but when supper was ready and darkness complete and neither of her men had returned, she–who never ventured forth alone–walked into the Evening Star, looked round and, not finding what she sought, said:

'Is there a man here who will come with me to Merravay? I have a feeling that something has happened to my husband.'

On the way, accompanied by three or four kind-hearted fellows, she spoke again.

'I should have come at first warning, before it was dark.'

Afterwards they took pains to assure her that even an earlier arrival could have done nothing for Francy. They said, too, how fortunate it was that she had acted in time to save Jon; for that night brought a sharp frost, and lying there, with the life at such low ebb in him, he might have died too. As it was, he was up and about again in time to follow his uncle to the graveyard, where the sad rites were considerably enlivened by his falling into another fit.

The account of these disasters had just reached the most outlying farm and cottage when, from the centre of Nettleton village, a new story began to ripple. The story of Jon Borage's almost inconceivable conduct. After all, said the gossips, he was an orphan, and Francy Sheply had been a father to him–far more dutiful and conscientious than many fathers were in these days. The gossips could name one or two men who had done less for their own children than Francy had done for Jon. And Mary had done her duty by him too. One would have expected that he would now turn about and do his bounden duty, which was obviously to stay in Nettleton and ply the carpenter's trade and keep a roof over Mary's head. But no! A most amazing thing had happened.

Francy Sheply had died on a Saturday and been buried on the following Friday. On that Friday Jon had fallen into a fit and for several days had been carefully and lovingly tended by his aunt. On the following Saturday he had risen from his bed and staggered to the chest where his uncle had kept his savings. The total sum amounted, they said, to just over one hundred pounds sterling. The boy had claimed fifty.

Mary Sheply, suddenly garrulous, had reported the scene.

'Jon said to me, "This was what my father left me. Francis Sheply put it away–I hope before your eyes," and I said, "That is true. I saw him do it." And then he said, "He added a shilling for every week of toil I bore, but that I will not take. That is yours." And I said, "But it is yours by right, boy." But of that he took no notice at all. He took his fifty pounds and said that now he would go to Cambridge. But when he said it he shook and trembled and his face went all awry so that I feared he would be taken with another fit. But he did not. He grew calm and told me the value of the timber and the tools and what I should ask for them; and then he kissed me and thanked me for my care of him. And I said, "Do you go straight to Cambridge?" because it was in my mind to pack him some food in a poke against the journey. And he said he had something to do first. "If this thing had come about two years ago," he said, "I could have gone straight with a free heart, but now it is late." And with that he left me.'

Sympathetic hearers condoled with her, the victim of such monstrous ingratitude. But she said, 'He was always longing to be elsewhere. I knew from the first; but my man was not one to be gainsaid. Now he is gone, and it is better so.'

This story had not reached the outskirts before another was hard on its heels. And the next happening, because it might have fallen upon any one of the villagers, took pride of place. In order to fall from a ladder one must climb one; in order to be deserted by an ingrate nephew one must adopt one; but anybody, anybody walking in the darkness alone, might be set on as Elizabeth Rawley was. And the thought–'That might have been me'–lends a sharp edge to one's appreciation of another's narrow escape.

Elizabeth Rawley had left her Aunt Thomasin's cottage at the usual time. As usual during winter, she carried a small horn lantern as well as her basket. What was unusual–and this gave rise to endless speculation as to whether or not the attacker had had information or motive–was that on this evening the basket, instead of containing some trivial domestic offering, held part of Aunt Thomasin's wedding gift to her niece. Thomasin Griggs was mean and miserly, but Elizabeth was her favourite niece and the cloud of senility was thickening about the old woman's mind. All day, ever since Elizabeth had told her of her betrothal, which she did as soon as she arrived, Aunt Thomasin had been diving into chests and cupboards and bringing out articles–some worthless, some of value–and piling them together, saying, 'All for you, my dear; all for you.' Elizabeth, before she left, had loaded her basket, leaving the rest of the pile to be carried home gradually; and being a shrewd girl, she had selected the most valuable of the goods, since there was considerable likelihood that Aunt Thomasin's mood would change and the articles return to their hiding-places. So she had in the basket a fine copper skillet, a pewter meat dish, two silver spoons, a horn mug bound with silver, and a three-parts-finished patchwork quilt, work upon which had outlasted the old woman's eyesight. Laden with spoil and in high spirits, she had set out for home.

Two hours later, without lantern, without basket, with her clothing torn and muddied and her mouth bruised and swollen, she staggered into the kitchen at Rawley's in a state of hysterical collapse. It was a long time before any coherent statement could be drawn from her. Questions, cosseting, hot milk laced with a spoonful of Matt's precious hoarded brandy having failed, the father's temper gave way and he shouted at her to stop that blether and speak or he'd try what a clout would do. And so presently the story came out. A man, a stranger, had jumped out of the bushes, hit her in the mouth, knocked her down in the mud and run off with her basket.

'And was that all?' Matt demanded.

Elizabeth nodded, putting her hands to her mouth.

'All? And enough, surely,' her mother said.

It was Cecily who said, 'But you're over an hour late, Lisbeth. And this all sounds so quick.'

'I lay dazed; and . . . having lost my lantern in the scuffle, I walked slowly,' Elizabeth said. And having said that quite calmly, she broke down again; so that they saw that further questioning would be useless. Grieved as they were for the loss of the skillet, the dish, spoons, mug and quilt, but thankful that the thief had been content with taking what was replaceable, they got her to bed.

With the first light of morning Matt Rawley walked along the woodland ride intent upon the recovery of the lantern. Elizabeth said that when the man jumped upon her she dropped the lantern and it went out, so there was a chance it had been overlooked; and it was a good lantern, worth fourteen pence.

Such carefulness merits reward. The lantern lay there beside the path, and nearby the stiff bleached grass and some bushes with broken twigs bore out Elizabeth's story of a struggle having taken place. Matt retrieved the lantern, walked on as far as Thomasin Griggs's cottage and told her the tale, briefly, and then returned home. At some point along the path his attention was caught by a gleam of scarlet amongst the dun of the thicket; investigating, he drew out a patchwork quilt. The thief had evidently thought it too bulky, or too recognisable, and thrown it away. Which proved him a fool; for Elizabeth had prudently rolled the two silver spoons and the mug in its heavy folds.

After that Matt walked slowly, keeping, as he said, his eyes skinned, though hardly expecting to find further treasure. He did not leave the path, or search very thoroughly, which was perhaps a pity; for everything which Elizabeth had lost was there within a stone's throw. The quilt, a bulky bundle, had not made quite such an arching flight as the other things, that was all. And on the other side of the path, in the little hazel coppice from which Jon Borage had once cut a crook for Elizabeth's blackberrying, there was something else which would have interested Matt Rawley very much.

But that was to lie hidden, with its hopes and its despairs, its love and hatred, its frailty and its sins, for almost three hundred years.

Through all the dark of that winter women feared to venture out alone and men talked sternly of what measures should be taken to suppress such sturdy beggars and vagabonds as the one whom Elizabeth Rawley had encountered.

At Christmas Tom Rowhedge came home and married Elizabeth Rawley and took up residence in his fine new house; and in the August of the following year Elizabeth, who should have known better than to indulge in such activities when heavily pregnant, slipped from the stool on which she was standing to turn her ripe cheeses on their rack. The fall precipitated the birth, and the child—a boy—was born some six or seven weeks before his time. That, of course, accounted for his frail and delicate appearance.

In June of the next year, 1579, Her Majesty the Queen kept her promise to visit Merravay. Tom Rowhedge, honest man, knowing his limitations, forbore to attempt the masques and plays which other of her hosts–often less well founded than Tom–devised for her entertainment. On the lawn, now grown smooth and green, which stretched between the house and the edge of Layer Wood, he set up a maypole; and there, until sunset, the young people of three parishes performed, under the indulgent royal eye, exactly the same ritual dances–'Gathering Peascods', 'Hayman's Hoff', 'Granny Go Far'–as they ordinarily measured upon the village green. And when the sun was down the rural musicians moved with their fiddles and their horns and their cymbals into the gallery of the great hall and played while a mixed company sat at feast below. Tom made the one courtier speech of his life when he said:

'Your Grace commands even the seasons. Ordinarily such food and such company come together only after harvest; and then we call it a horkey.'

And the Queen said, 'I have never been present at a horkey and this pleases me well.'

And once she looked round and pressed her long thin hands together and said, 'This is the very heart of England. My thanks, Master Rowhedge, for bringing it so close to me.'

In the morning, just before she rode off for Framlingham, she brought up, out of that memory of hers where nothing was ever mislaid or mislabelled, the recollection of her half-intent to knight Tom Rowhedge.

'Now I can do it and the Spanish ambassador will feel no prick. I can knight you, Master Rowhedge, for the best hospitality I have known on this journey.'

That evening young Thomas Rowhedge, with a good dose of poppy-head syrup soothing his stomach, slept peacefully while his father and mother, careful folk, supped in the small west-facing room upon the remains of the feast of yesterday. Tom Rowhedge, worrying the last fragment from a chicken bone, suddenly paused and stared at the fireless hearth above which wreathed the Tudor roses which Francy Sheply had carved.

'Lisbeth,' he said, 'I reckon that now we'll rate a crest; and I know what it shall be. My ship is the mermaid, and my maypole pleased the Queen. We'll have a mermaid with a maypole behind her. If that is to your fancy.'

Elizabeth thought that that would do very well.

And then Tom said:

'You know, all these two days Jon Borage has been in my mind. He it was that planned the house–"fit for the Queen", as he said. I wish he could have been here to see her in it and to see . . .'

He broke off, astonished, because his wife had begun to cry in a wild, distraught fashion.

Quite understandable, of course; so much strain and excitement, for a woman in her condition. . . . she was carrying her second child, the boy Matthew who was, in looks and liveliness, greatly to surpass his brother. Young Thomas, however, remained his mother's favourite, and largely due to her unremitting care, lived to inherit Merravay, to become one of James I's original baronets, to marry late in life and beget one child. Unfortunately a girl.

EPISODE TWO
Mid-Stuart

THE WITCH

Chapter One

Yesterday, when I asked Master Turnbull to add to his kindness by sending me some writing materials, he, thinking that I intended to write letters, warned me to be very careful what I wrote. He is sceptical of the charge they have brought against me and hopes for an acquittal. I am less hopeful, perhaps because I am less certain of my innocence.

Most people accused of witchcraft–and the number so charged has greatly increased in the last few years–violently and vehemently repudiate the accusation, but some, whom I privately suspect of being crazy, admit it and go to their doom muttering curses and incantations and expecting, I fear, some magical intervention at the last moment. Even those who proclaim their innocence seem to know about things which mean nothing to me; they speak of incubi, succubi, familiars, midnight brews, sabbaths and covens; but now and then I have a troubling suspicion that these things are only the rubbish which clutter the edges of that unknown world, and that maybe I missed them and went straight to the heart. Perhaps I am the only person who, asked whether she were a witch or not, could truthfully say, 'I do not know.' I do know that some very strange things have happened to me, or through me.

The first occurred when I was eleven years old. I was then living at Merravay with my father, Sir Thomas Rowhedge, who was almost bedridden, and my grandmother, Dame Elizabeth, who bore me a grudge because being the only child of my father, I had been born a girl. I was very young indeed when a conversation between my father and grandmother sent me stealing into the kitchen to ask old Betty, my friend and comforter, 'What is the difference between a boy and a girl?' Betty said 'They're a different shape, love' and gave me a piece of pork crackling to chew. The untimely gift and the note in her voice convinced me that of the two shapes I was the wrong one.

My grandmother was always busy with the affairs of the estate and the household, and with looking after my father, whom she loved so dearly that she was jealous of the very hound he fondled. He was busy, too, with the books he read and the poems and plays which he wrote; but he was kind, and

I should have spent more time with him had not my grandmother stood between us. As it was, I sought company in the kitchens and yard, and at the time of which I am writing I had found the–to my mind–perfect friend. His name was Robin, and he looked after sheep. His father had been hanged for stealing and his mother had married our shepherd and had three or four children by him; there was little room for Robin in heart or home. Once he was sure that I was friendly and no spy for my grandmother he accepted my company gladly, and we had merry times together. Despite his hard life, he was cheerful and kind; he knew many songs and old stories; he could make wonderful whistles out of an elder twig, and he could sing like a blackbird.

One October day he told me that on the following morning he was to walk over to Ockley to fetch home two dozen sheep which my grandmother had bought from the Fennel flock. I said I would go with him and take a bag-dinner; he was always hungry. I also said I would try to get a horse, then he could ride pillion to Ockley, and coming home we would ride and tie. I was rather proud of my skill as a sheep-drover.

It was a blue-and-gold morning with a singing wind, and I was skipping blithely over the cobbles of the yard on my way to the stables when my grandmother rapped on a window and demanded to know where I was going. She was immensely annoyed. It would look well, would it not, she asked, for me to appear at Ockley as a sheep wench! And what had I in the bag? Betty had seen to it that I had a thoroughly good bag-dinner: two crusty loaves, a cold pheasant, a hard Suffolk cheese, six apples, and some walnuts. 'A little food,' I said. But when I was back in the Ship Chamber and my grandmother took the bag from my hand and swung it so that it caught me a clout on the side of my head it did not seem so little. All day, as I sat by the spinning-wheel to which she condemned me, my head rang and throbbed.

I watched Robin go trudging off alone; I knew he would have nothing in his bag but a slab of cold porridge. And he would think me faithless. He should have come back at five, and I edged my wheel nearer the window so that when he came I might wave and indicate by grimaces what had happened to me; but dusk came and then full dark, and still he had not come. We were at supper when someone ran in from the kitchen to say that Sheep Robin was back and that he had lost four sheep on Strawless Common, where a great dog had run out and scattered the flock. He had searched as long as the light lasted but had only rounded up twenty.

The sheep were some of a breed which my grandmother had coveted for a long time, and the loss sent her into a screaming fury. Carrying with her the chop bone which she had been picking, she hurried into the yard and shouted to Robin that he must go back and search again, and that if he didn't bring back the sheep she would see that he was hanged as his father had been. When she returned to table my father said mildly, 'That was a dire threat; the poor boy may have taken it literally.'

'I meant it so,' she said; and leaned over to hack herself another chop.

I spent most of that night on my knees praying to God to help Robin to find the sheep.

I was early about, and hopeful; but he had not returned, and shortly before noon my grandmother despatched Robin's stepfather and another man to help with the search. They came back at dusk. They had found no trace of the sheep; but they had found Robin, hanging lifeless from the bough of a tree on the edge of the common.

My father was quite peevish and said, 'There, what did I tell you?'

My grandmother said, 'I consider it proof of guilt.'

I could only think that Robin would never sing or whistle or laugh again. And he'd had such a poor life; even his last day had been darkened by disappointment. It was quite unbearable. I imagined him searching and searching, growing desperate, tired to the bone, cold, hungry and frightened. . . .

Once safe in my own room I cried and cried. Then, remembering my prayers of the previous night, I grew savagely angry with God. 'King of kings, whose power no creature is able to resist,' it said; couldn't He have called those sheep back, wherever they were? 'Not a sparrow falls,' it said, but Robin had dangled, lifeless. And who cared? Nobody but me.

And then there came into my mind, neat and complete as though somebody had spoken it in my ear, the remark, 'But you must allow for the Devil!' And then out went my candle.

There was nothing unusual about that; for though we made our own and had great stores of them, my grandmother doled them out meanly, and I was quite used to undressing in the dark; but the failure of my candle drew my attention to the passing of time, for it had been new that night. I hurried into bed, and there I began to think about the Devil.

I am trying now to be entirely honest. I did actually find *comfort* in the thought that the Devil had, on Strawless Common, defeated God. I much preferred that thought to the thought that God hadn't cared, hadn't helped Robin. I thought all the way back to the story of Eden. God, all-loving, all-wise, had surely wanted people to be happy and healthy and good; it was the Devil who spoiled it all . . . and since so many people were miserable and sickly and bad the Devil must indeed be very powerful. The lifeless, voiceless thing, lately a singing boy, which they had cut down and put under a sack in the barn to await an unhallowed cross-road grave seemed to me to prove the power of the Devil.

But I must insist that though, at that moment, I was forced to acknowledge that power, that was all I did. I did not applaud it; I was indeed sorry. I was on God's side. . . .

Having pursued that line of thought to its conclusion, I began to think more practically. I was certain that Robin had neither lost the sheep through carelessness nor connived at their removal from the flock. But I knew how in quiet country districts like ours stories passed down from generation to generation, and I thought that what I wanted now, all I could want for Robin, was that in years to come when men told the story by the fire on winter nights they should add, 'And, after all, those sheep were found.'

Suddenly that became a matter of the utmost urgency. It sounds absurd now . . . but at that time I was only a child. . . . I reached out in the dark and took in my hand the last whistle which Robin had made for me. I said, in my mind, 'Robin, I swear by this whistle that I will . . . I must prove your innocence.' And then it happened. I saw, as clearly as I now see this quill and this paper, a disused claypit, so long abandoned that grass and nettles and willowherb had grown about its slopes; and seven wind-bent young hawthorns leaned over its edge. I thought, Ah! That is the place, and in the morning I shall go there and find those sheep. And I fell asleep as though I had been pole-axed.

At first light I stole out of the house, saddled a horse and was away. There had been a light hoar-frost and all the world was webbed over with a grey-white shining veil.

I rode blindly, making for Strawless Common, which I had never seen, but I knew its direction and I had heard it described, and roads in our part were few. I recognised it when I arrived–a great rough stretch of common land, a space of rabbit-burrowed turf, dotted with gorse bushes, blackberry brambles, heather clumps and stunted hawthorns. At one edge a few clod cottages stood, and the animals belonging to the cottagers–sharp-boned donkeys and cows and goats–lived on the meagre pasture of the sterile land; and beyond these unsatisfactory grazing places the common stretched away to Ockley. I realised that I might search all day, every day for a week without finding what I sought; so I did what I have heard of fog-bound travellers doing. I laid the reins on my horse's neck and said, 'Now go.' He seemed to pick his way as daintily as a dancer, skirting a heather clump, rounding a bush, avoiding a rabbit hole; and all the time I wondered why, free of guidance, he had not turned and made for home. Certainty mounted in me as he moved, and I was not one mite surprised when at last he checked and there was a row of seven wind-bowed hawthorns, with their berries shining darkly red under the frosty cobwebs. I slipped out of the saddle, said 'Stand' and walked forward, passing between the trees.

And there was the pit, full of grass, nettles and willowherb, and at its bottom four woolly carcases, horribly mangled and bloody, and standing guard over them, roused from glutted slumber by my approach, was one of those great fierce herd-hounds which poor men keep . . . and keep hungry to foster their natural fierceness.

I knew with a certainty beyond all doubt that on each woolly bloodied haunch there would be the Fennel mark, the arrow of red ochre cancelled out by a tarry stroke . . . but I meant to see. When I faced my grandmother with the truth there must be no undermining shadow of doubt. I began to let myself down into the pit. The dog resented that. As I slid and shuffled along the slope he raised his hackles and began to circle about his kill, and when a final slither brought me to the comparatively level ground of the pit's bottom he came forward menacingly. And all at once I was furious with him. Granted he was hungry . . . he had killed Robin and was now prepared to defeat me in my determination to clear the dead boy's name. Damn him, I thought. I was armed only with a little switch, which I carried more for show than use, for my horse, well fed and well trained, needed neither stimulus nor correction. As a weapon it was negligible, and evidently the dog thought so, for as I stepped forward he came on, stiff-legged, his eyes shining green, his muzzle wrinkled back to show his long fangs. And something snapped in my head.

'You devil!' I yelled at him. 'I'll kill you. I'll kill you!' I raised the little switch and went forward. I saw the menace in his eyes turn to terror; the wrinkled snarl smoothed out. His tail dropped; he pivoted round on his hind legs and went tearing across the pit's bottom and scrambling up its far side.

I made sure of the marks on the wool and then turned and began to climb back towards the hawthorns. When I was almost at the top the thyme-covered hummock on which my feet were braced gave way and I was left with my hands frenziedly digging into the edge of the pit while my feet sought for hold in the raw clay. And it was then that I called to my horse, as though he were a person. 'Come here,' I said. And he came. 'Nearer, so that

I can take hold of the bridle,' I said. And when I had gripped the rein I said, 'Pull!'

I swear that at that moment there seemed nothing strange or unnatural about it at all. When I mounted and rode back to Merravay to face my grandmother there was nothing in my mind except simple triumph because I had proved Robin's integrity. And later on all the wonder I felt was concerned with the fact that I had had a vision of the place where the sheep lay. That the dog had feared me and the horse obeyed me did not seem strange at all. Yet it is all this talk about animals, horses and dogs which is to be my undoing. . . . And even as I feel bound to protest that no animal has ever been my 'familiar' I know full well that if on any market day I leaned from the little slit of a window which admits light and air to this cell and said to a herd of beasts on their way to the slaughterhouse, 'Turn about and face the blows and go the other way', they would do it. I know they would. They would do it because I *know* they would. But does that make me a witch?

Chapter Two

All through the next year each change of season reminded me of Robin and started the pain anew. I wept for him when the first lambs bleated, when the first hawthorn buds broke white, when the first cuckoo called. Fortunately for me, my father, who was not without guile in his own way, countered my grandmother's complaints about what she called my 'runagate behaviour' by determining to teach me to read and write. The next few years passed rapidly and without incident, at least so far as this confession is concerned.

There came the harvest time when my grandmother said, perhaps truly, that at fourteen I was too big to go and help in the fields; my part in the corn-gathering was henceforth to be confined to the baking of big flat saffron cakes known as 'harvest buns' and the making of the very small small-beer which was provided for the workers at this season. Working with and under the eye of the old woman, whose resentment towards me seemed to increase with the years, was far from pleasant, and I was not wholly sorry, God forgive me, when my father took one of his 'summer colds' and needed all her attention. We were all used to his indispositions and the way my grandmother behaved when he was ill, and this time everything followed the ordinary pattern, even to her taking Dido, his favourite hound, by the scruff of her neck and hauling her out from under the bed and shutting her into a shed in the yard. On the third morning of my father's illness my grandmother, coming into the kitchen, reported that he was much better, and later in the day, cheered by this news and knowing that there were buns and beer in plenty, I took advantage of her preoccupation to wander out into the lovely sunshine, and presently I found myself in the harvest-field. It was at some distance from the house, part of the land known as New Holding because it had been added to the Merravay estate during the previous twenty years. The women, scantily clad and wearing bright sunbonnets, followed, with rakes and pitchforks and bundles of twine, shocking and stooking the corn behind the men who wielded the scythes; they laughed and sang as they worked, and almost before I knew what I was about I was amongst them, as busy and as merry as the best of them. And then, all suddenly, through the happy noise, there came the melancholy howling of the hound. I said, 'My father is dead!' and, dropping the sheaf I held, I burst into tears.

They crowded about me, asking how I knew, and I must have sobbed out something about the dog. There are those who claim now to have seen a great black dog run through the stubble towards me, but that, I am perfectly sure, is nonsense. I am equally sure that those who say that at that moment they all drew away from me in terror are lying; I can clearly remember how they all crowded about me, and how, in a cluster, we moved back to the house, where we learned that what I had said was dismally true.

There followed some weeks of unrelieved misery. Unostentatious as the bond between me and my father had been, it was real enough, and his death was a loss to me in many ways. However, there is no place here for detailed description of my feelings.

Since I was a girl, the title passed, naturally, to my cousin Rawley, who was the son of my grandmother's second child. About this Matthew Rowhedge there was some slight mystery, darkly hinted at by Betty, who could, now and then, say things of startling malignancy about my grandmother. Dame Elizabeth had never been fond of or fair to her second son, though by all accounts he had been a strong, handsome, lusty boy, the sort upon whom any normal woman would have doted; apparently my grandfather had much preferred him to my father, who had been ailing and bookish even as a child. My grandfather had died untimely, gored by a bull, and soon afterwards Matthew had gone to sea and had not been seen at Merravay again. He had died in the Caribbean long ago, leaving a wife and son whom my father had supported for a while.

I think–though I have no proof–that it was a shock to my grandmother to learn that my father had willed Merravay to his nephew, Rawley. The place was not entailed and could have been left to her, or to me, but no doubt my father's sense of seemliness had demanded that the original land should go with the title. The fields and the empty house at New Holding and the recently purchased Slipwell meadows were left to my grandmother for her lifetime, and then to me; and if I married while she was alive she was to provide me with a dowry of five hundred pounds.

I was secretly grieved by the realisation that I should never own Merravay, which had always seemed to me to be the most beautiful house in the world, and I was depressed at the thought of going to live in the New Holding house with my grandmother, who now began to speak openly of the move. Only once did she express any resentment.

'I've slept in that room for fifty years and more, and had a mind to die in it,' she said.

'It is possible that Rawley might let us stay here,' I said hopefully. 'The house is large enough.'

'I should never dream of asking a favour of him,' she retorted; then she added, 'Of course, if he *asked* me to stay that would be another matter.'

Rawley was at that moment on the high seas on his way home from Bermuda. Mr Turnbull, the attorney, who had drawn up Father's will, had sent him news of his inheritance and in the intervening months made some half-hearted attempts–easily frustrated by Dame Elizabeth–to assume some authority at Merravay pending the heir's arrival.

'I am capable of continuing the management and am prepared to give an account of my stewardship,' she said.

What she was not capable of doing–and vast was her annoyance–was to read the letter which, at the end of almost a year eventually arrived from Rawley. Unwillingly she handed it to me. She could do the most complicated reckonings in her head or with the aid of a tally-stick, and she never forgot a fact or a figure, but she had never learned to read.

Now, as I broke the seal, and looked with dismay at the vile, almost illegible script, she leaned on my shoulder, breathing audibly and giving me little nips in her impatience.

'Well,' she snapped, 'in what manner does he write?'

I began to read the letter, slowly, word by word as I deciphered it.

'Never mind that. In what *manner*, fool? Civil or cool, or what?'

'Very civil, I think. . . . Oh yes, indeed. He says it will be a month or more before he has set his own affairs in order. He says he would be vastly obliged if you would "see to and handle and manage all things", as he understands you have done in the past.'

'Is there mention of Master Turnbull?'

'None.'

She straightened herself, and I could feel the certainty of present power and the hope of its continuance flow through her, heartening as wine.

'He sounds like a young man of good judgment. Fetch your tools, girl, and write to him straightway.'

When I came back she was holding the letter in her hand, gravely studying the marks which made no sense for her. Then she looked up at me with an expression which I had never seen turned on me before, appraising, as though I were a colt or a heifer whose value she was assessing.

'It is a pity that you are so plain and like a pikestaff,' she said. 'A young man of good sense might think to marry you and hold the land entire. Here, take it. . . .' She pushed the letter into my hand.

'But ma'am . . .' I began.

'I want no buts from you! Sit down and make ready to write. . . .'

For once I was grateful to her for cutting me short, for my sentence would have ended, 'Rawley is married already.' Then she would have demanded to know how I knew; and for that I had no answer, and her suspicion that I had not read the letter properly would have been the least of the unpleasant results. But I did know! What is more, I knew that Rawley's wife was in some way strange, was small and pale and beautiful, and that there was a fragrance about her, the scent of some flower I had never smelt.

Chapter Three

I had seen and smelt aright. Rawley had married a Spanish girl, the daughter of a man with great estates. It has been a runaway match for Isabella's father had had no intention of allowing his lovely daughter to marry a penniless English sailor.

I was completely enchanted by Isabella from the moment I saw her. I was just at the age when, for all I was so ugly and coltish, I was on the verge of becoming a woman, looking half longingly, half reluctantly into the world of femininity and feminine things in which Isabella moved with such grace and assurance. I had never had a sister or a girl friend; I had no memory of my mother, and my grandmother, though Betty swore that she had once been pretty and charming, had long ago put aside the trappings of sex. So when Isabella allowed me into her room, let me look at and finger her things, let me watch her at her toilet and even brush her long black hair, I was like some earnest young apprentice in the presence of a master craftsman. And she was extravagantly kind to me, partly because she and my grandmother were at loggerheads from the start and took opposite sides in everything. Also, of course, those first months at Merravay were lonely for Isabella. Rawley had much to learn and was out on the land most of the day, spending the evenings with Dame Elizabeth, now his mentor. She had set herself to convince him that she was indispensable, and Rawley, out of his element, easygoing by nature, and, truth to tell, no match for her in wits, seemed content to consult her and lean upon her. There was no more talk of leaving Merravay, and it looked as though the old woman would attain her wish to die in the great room which was always spoken of as the 'Queen's Chamber'.

Rawley and Isabella came to Merravay in the winter, and that year the cold was severe even for our parts. Isabella, huddled in a shawl, went shuddering about as chilled as a butterfly which has outstayed its season. My grandmother, always scant of sympathy and utterly ignorant of warmer climates, attributed Isabella's misery to the fact that she undressed to go to bed and occasionally took a bath. One should, said my grandmother, don a good flannel shift and petticoat at Michaelmas and keep them on, day and night, till Easter; that way one stored up heat.

There came an April morning when the wind veered round and the sun shone. I had been in Isabella's room fitting on a dress which she was making for me. She sewed beautifully and had taken my wardrobe in hand. Her room was in the west 'leg' of the house, and at that hour, at that season, was cold and sunless. When we came out on to the gallery we stood warming ourselves in the sun and chatting. Isabella had been telling me about her distant home, which sounded like a palace to me, and I suppose it was pride and loyalty to Merravay which made me say, 'You've never seen the best bedchamber here, have you? The Queen once slept in it.'

Making sure that my grandmother was downstairs on her rounds of kitchen, dairy and buttery, I opened the door of the room to which I had so often gone in fear and trembling and the certainty of punishment. I intended now to display to Isabella the grandeur and beauty of the apartment with its two great deep-set windows, its noble fireplace, its walls lined with wood so neatly and finely carved they looked as if they were hung with linen, the little dais on which the vast bed stood. Long familiarity had blinded me to the other aspects of the room. My grandmother used it for other purposes than sleeping. There were tally-sticks, samples of wool and seed, specially choice medicines for all ailments, human and animal, great rolls of flannel and print for the servants' annual dole, and, besides, a medley of ill-assorted articles which had been put there to await the moment when my grandmother could give them her leisurely attention. The windows had not, I think, been opened during her occupancy, and the room stank of wool, of horse liniment and sheep-dip, and, perhaps, a little of unfastidious old woman. The fire had been allowed to go out, but the sun shone in strongly and, as well as lighting up the cobwebs on the scarred old tally-sticks and the general disorder, made the room as warm as summer.

'It is the most warm room of the house,' Isabella said.

'And it could be beautiful,' I felt compelled to add.

'The smell is that of the slave cabins,' Isabella said. 'Come away!'

But she had made up her mind, and within a few hours the war of the Queen's Chamber had begun.

There was more in it than two women fighting for the possession of one room. What they were both after was proof of Rawley's allegiance. He loved Isabella quite fanatically; he wanted her to be warm and comfortable; he recognised her right, as mistress of the house, to the best bedchamber; but somewhere along the road Dame Elizabeth had extorted or tricked out of him a promise that so long as she stayed at Merravay and helped him she should remain in that room; and this was the lambing season, when even the toughest, most knowledgeable old shepherd did not mind asking the dame's advice and would say with topsy-turvy pride, 'Ah, her's a masterpiece! That'll live, she say; and live that do, though I give it up for dead!'

While the fight raged there came, as there always does as soon as the poor lambs are dropped, a spell of really bitter weather; and one evening Isabella, shivering by the fire, asked me to run up to her room and bring down her little shoulder cape, which was made of velvet lined with fur and which had a snug, upstanding collar.

The days were beginning to draw out into those long evenings which are so sad in cold weather, and I did not take a candle. I looked into Isabella's clothes closet, sniffing the fragrance, and failed to find the cape on any peg. Then I looked into her chest and was on the point of lighting a candle to aid my search when I thought of the shelf in the closet. I reached up and my fingers touched the fur. Then I realised that something else, something hard, had come down with the cape into my hand. It was a little doll.

My first thought was sentimental and female; Isabella was going to have a baby and had made it a doll already! I knew she wanted a baby more than anything, and I was glad for her. With the cape over my arm and the doll in my hand I went towards the window, beyond which the sunset sky, coldly lilac and green, was beginning to darken. then I wondered why Isabella had made a doll so ugly . . . so exactly like my grandmother.

My grandmother still wore a great wheel ruff in the old style, a ruff which it became more and more difficult to get dressed properly as one after another of the old servants who had learnt the art died off. She also wore the stiff padded panniers which King James I had forbidden to be worn at Court, years ago, because they took up so much room. Old Betty had once told me that the ruff and the panniers were exact copies of those which Queen Elizabeth had worn when she visited Merravay and made my grandfather a knight. Perhaps, I thought, she had also said that to Isabella; and perhaps Isabella, much as she disliked my grandmother, had seen the romance of it and had wished her child's first toy to link with the tradition. And then I thought, How careless! For one of Isabella's best brass-headed pins had been left in the doll, stuck in in such a fashion that the point protruded at the back of the bodice. I pulled it out and would have put it in the little pin-box where it belonged, and then I remembered that by doing so I should betray the fact that I knew Isabella's secret. I was not supposed to have seen the doll at all. So I pushed the pin back, carefully, into the thickness of the panniered skirt where the point was hidden and couldn't scratch anyone as it had so nearly scratched me.

Then I realised that the room seemed suddenly darker and colder and that I had an uncomfortable feeling of being alone, a long way from the warm, inhabited part of the house . . . and yet perhaps not quite alone! I hurried back to Isabella.

Two or three days later when my grandmother was coming downstairs she slipped and broke her thighbone. We carried her to one of the side rooms; and knowing the seriousness of a broken bone at her age, I felt a little sorry that she was, after all, not to die in her own chamber. However, she did not die. The bone knitted, though crookedly, so that she was lame and lopsided from that time on. She could no longer walk upstairs and refused to be carried; so the tally-sticks and all her other treasures were brought downstairs. On level ground she could move, slowly and awkwardly, but indefatigably, and Jack Lantern made her a little cart, like a chair set on wheels, in which she could be pushed about out of doors.

After a week's scrubbing and polishing and airing the Queen's Chamber was ready for Isabella.

Chapter Four

Time passed. The confidence which I awaited from Isabella never came, and beneath all the increasingly gay social life which was beginning to enliven Merravay–for Rawley was convivial and popular–there was just a trace of discontent and anxiety; there was, each month, a day or two when Isabella was gloomy and downcast, and I would think, Poor Isabella, disappointed again!

So we came to my birthday, which was in June, and we must have a party with the Fennels, the Blackwoods and the Headways to eat supper with us and afterwards play hide-and-seek and other merry games in the garden in the warm dusk and afterwards dance in the hall. Lady Fennel, who had a loud, hearty voice, asked me how old I was; and when I said, 'Sixteen', she said, 'How time passes! Think, by Yule I shall be a grandmother!'

Mrs Headway said, 'Mary has lost no time! Why, she was married only at Candlemas.'

'Ah well,' said Lady Fennel, 'I always say a good tinder strikes first time and a damp one never will!' They laughed. I happened to look at Isabella and saw her white-rose pallor take on a tallowy hue, and the bones showed in her nose.

Two nights later there was a full moon; I had no curtains to my window, and the light, falling full on my bed, woke me. After a while I got up and went towards the screen which in winter stood between me and the window to exclude the draught, and which in summer leaned, folded, by the wall. It would now serve to shade me from this extraordinarily vivid and strangely melancholy light. Hanging over the screen at that moment was the exquisitely made petticoat which Isabella had made and given me for my birthday. I had not laid it away in my press because I was waiting for some rose-leaves which I was drying to be ready enough to sprinkle in its folds. It was so lovely, with its delicate stitching and fine embroidery, that I meant to lay it up with care to await some really special occasion. As I lifted it from the screen I thought about that special occasion . . . for most girls of my age that would mean my wedding-day; but I had little hope that anyone would fall in love with me. I was so tall, so thin; and in me the Rowhedge red hair, instead of being dark chestnut, was a pale, very unbecoming tawny, and it was short, very curly and springy, so that even my grandmother had never succeeded in making a parting in it; it grew like a lamb's pelt. Also I had pale-green eyes, and in summer hundreds of freckles.

I was thinking these purely personal thoughts as I took the petticoat in hand, and then everything rushed out of my mind except terror. Not for myself; for Isabella. I knew in that special way of knowing that she was in danger, horrible danger. How, lying there in her own bedroom with Rawley by her side, she could in in danger of any kind I could not think; but I knew she was. Then I thought that she might be ill. My first impulse was to go running along the gallery; but even under the impact of terror some sense remained with me, and I thought that if this were all nonsense and they were asleep they would hardly thank me for going to their room. But if she had been taken ill Rawley would have made a light. I ran to my window, from which theirs was visible. I looked out. I don't think I even saw their window, for my eye was caught by something which moved, accompanied by a sharp black shadow, across the smooth turf of the lawn. It had almost reached the point where a deep decline separated the garden from the field. There, in old times, when the castle of Merravay was in being, the moat had lain.

The moving figure–and I was almost certain that it was Isabella–disappeared into the dip and then emerged again in the cornfield and began to move towards Layer Wood. It was Isabella, and my first thought was that she was walking in her sleep, for never consciously would *she* leave her warm bed and go wandering in the night. I had been led to believe that nothing untoward ever happened to sleep-walkers; so I wondered again why I should have the certainty that she was in peril. Then I remembered.

Years and years earlier, when I was very young, I had been a frequent visitor to Layer Wood, going there in search of wild flowers and the very small, very sweet wild strawberries which grew there in profusion; until one day I pushed my way through a little hazel thicket and had been so frightened, of nothing, seized with such sheer reasonless animal terror that I had dropped my basket and run home like a rabbit. Ever since I had avoided that spot, and called it, in my own mind, the Bad Place. Now Isabella was walking straight towards it.

I pushed my bare feet into my shoes and, hitching up my nightshift, ran out into the moonlight. I could, at need, run like a stag, and if I had stopped to put on my stockings and fasten my shoes I might have saved time. As it was, my feet, slippery with the cold sweat of fear, came out of my shoes at each step, until finally I discarded the shoes altogether and ran barefoot over the sharp tufts left from the hay-scything in the field.

Isabella was in the wood when I reached her; and she was wide awake.

I gasped out, 'What are you doing?'

She said shortly, 'A thing of importance. You must help or go away.

Better, I think, you should go.'

'I can't leave you here, alone. This is a bad place. . . .'

'A right place. Now lend me your hands and stay silent or go. And never speak, never, of what you see.'

I stayed; I helped. Does that make me a witch? Does a kitchen slut handing a dish, passing a spoon thereby become a cook?

I hated it all; I hated it so much that by the time the thing was done I was well on the way to hating Isabella herself. When it was over she sat down exhausted on a fallen tree trunk, and it was I who stamped out the fire and buried the poor drained body of the little white cock who would never greet the sun again. Then I picked up the doubly sullied bowl.

'That must be broken,' she said. I hesitated, for it was one of new set and pretty, yellow with a brown rim. She took it from me and smashed it against the tree trunk. It fell into four almost even pieces. She counted them and then fitted the pieces together, as though to make certain that none was missing.

'Is a pity. It will be a girl. But that is the beginning only. I shall call her by your name.'

'Do you really believe . . .?'

'Oh yes. It is a thing very old, brought by the slave people from Africa, but very sure. And all that was left to do, Alice. Marrying Rawley, who is heretic, has made me incommunicate; not even the little saints would ask for me. But by next year this time I shall have baby. Let us go home now.'

In April of the following year the baby was born; and it was a girl. But it was not named for me; for Isabella died within half an hour of its birth, and it was left to my grandmother, the only person unaffected by the tragedy, to choose the name. She chose Thomasina.

Chapter Five

Rawley took refuge in drunkenness.

My grandmother bore with him patiently at first, but as the sum of months mounted she took on a censorious tone. One day she told him that *she* had always found hard work the best cure for heartbreak.

'How could you know? You never loved anything but a tally-stick!' he said bitterly.

Another day she suggested–I think with good intent–that he should leave Merravay and return to the sea for a while. She said she would look after his affairs for him.

'I'm damned sure of that!' Rawley said nastily.

Things worsened between them as he grew more and more sottish, and one evening as he slumped over the supper table she snapped out:

'If you are so uxorious that being widowed makes a sot of you, the best thing you can do is to marry again.'

Rawley cried out like an animal, a wordless sound of pain; then he picked up his heavy silver tankard and flung it at her. She put up her hand and by the luckiest chance caught the tankard by the handle. Setting it with exaggerated care on the table, she said coldly:

'That is exactly the action of a spoilt child whose toy has been taken away.' Then with dignity, despite her limp, she walked away and Rawley lowered his head until it rested on the table.

'She shouldn't say such things to you,' I said. Filled with pity, I went near and laid my arm across his shoulders. I meant to comfort him as one comforts a child, and like a child he turned to me, making a little muffled sound, half groan, half sob, as he thrust his head against me. I stroked his head and said, 'Poor Rawley!'

Then all at once it was 'Poor Alice!' I began to tremble, sharp pain transfixed me, I was dizzy, I was gasping for breath.

Rawley moved, freeing himself.

'Dear little Alice,' he mumbled. 'Kind. Mustn't upset yourself. Be all right.' He patted me as though I were a dog and went lurching away, not to the Queen's Chamber but to a small bare room which actually *smelt* of his misery.

And that is how I fell in love with Rawley.

The pain continued in me and grew worse, and added to it was a terrible shyness. I was so afraid that he might guess what I felt about him that I dared not look him in the face; I could hardly speak to him and avoided his company.

The slow months passed and there came the time when rumours about Rawley and Phyllis Whymark, the girl from the Evening Star, began to creep about. Strange as it may sound, I could see exactly what it was that Rawley sought and found in her; I liked her too. There had been a time when she used to drive geese up to the London market, and she would come to Merravay some days before the setting-out day to dip the feet of the geese in tar, which hardened and protected them from the wear and tear of the long journey. I used to steal out to watch this process, to enjoy her easy, wryly humorous conversation and to gaze with admiration upon a girl, not much my senior, who could undertake that long, hazardous journey alone. Her mother was a woman of notorious bad character; but though I wouldn't have staked a pin on Phyllis being a virgin, she wasn't a whore either–the respect with which men spoke of and to her proved *that.* With her nimble wit, earthy philosophy and salty humour she was just the company for Rawley at that moment, and she would never in any way remind him of Isabella. But for the fact that I was myself in love with him I should have regarded the affair as a blessing.

Not so my grandmother; she was scornful and furious, and in her fury precipitated the very situation she dreaded, for one day she faced Rawley with the rumour and he whipped round and said that if the idea of his having Phyl Whymark as his mistress was so shocking and repulsive the only way of mending the matter that he could think of would be that he should marry her! And despite the aching of my heart, I could not deny that he could have done worse; there was something vital and vigorous about that young woman; if Rawley married her he would never miss his grandmother, for Phyl was capable of running Merravay or anything else. The very way she walked showed that.

Probably the old woman recognised her match; for as soon as she had convinced herself that Rawley meant what he said she began again to make preparations for leaving Merravay and going to New Holding. She took a high-handed attitude towards the affair, an attitude which I could but admire.

'Don't for one moment imagine,' she said, 'that I shall stay here working myself into my grave to keep that base-born slut in comfort! I leave you to go to ruin at your own gait.'

She began to gather her gear together, and at last there came the–to me–dreadful day when she told Jack Lantern to take out all the sacred tally-sticks and burn them. I knew then that there was no hope.

Later that day she told me to make ready anything I wished to take with me to New Holding; the servants would convey the baggage next day, make fires in the house and arrange it, and we should follow on the day after.

I went up to my room feeling that life was over. I must turn my back on the man I loved, the house I loved and go forward through the joyless days in bleak and bitter company.

Since my grandmother had decided to leave Rawley to his fate she had been less strict about candles, and I went to my room with two long, new ones.

I had few possessions, and I was too wretched to care much what I took or what I left; but at the very bottom of my chest I came upon two things which I had hidden there because the very sight of them gave me pain. One was the petticoat which Isabella had given me on my birthday, the other was the last little whistle that Robin had ever made. I couldn't leave them behind, nor could I take them with me. I thought of the Dame's tally-sticks and decided that her action was seemly. I carried them over to my hearth, and, taking my candle, tilted the stick so that the flame licked at the fine linen; but before it was smouldering the candle fell out of the stick, rolled away and went out.

In the dark once more I felt my way to the my chest, took up my brush and began to brush my hair; thinking as I did so about the whistle and the clay-pit; about the petticoat and that night of full moon.

This is what confuses me. I performed no ritual; I said nothing; but I *thought*, and as I thought I became aware of a kind of power, something welling up in me, so that instead of thinking to myself, I wish Rawley would marry me instead of Phyllis Whymark, I was thinking, breathing, willing, *being* to myself, He shan't marry Phyllis Whymark, he must marry me! I will it; it shall happen.

Chapter Six

The next day passed without event, save that my grandmother suddenly remembered a couple of silver spoons and a mug.

'They were of small value measured by all that has come into this house since,' she said, 'but they are mine and must go with me.' That sounded reasonable enough. But when the things were found she said, 'They are dear to me though I had overlooked them. They were with me in the mud that night. Then I flung them into the bushes and my father found them. A very stern man was my father; he was to blame for everything.'

The idea of her ever throwing anything of value into a bush was somewhat startling, but I was too miserable to give it much heed.

Rawley did not come near us that day. Darkness fell, and my grandmother and I sat down to our last supper at Merravay. I thought she looked pale and a little tired, which was not to be wondered at. We ate, with small appetite, in silence until she said abruptly:

'Chris Huxstable is dead, you know. He was cut for the stone and died. So now you'll have Merravay, my girl, and that will smell sweeter than the tannery!'

'I beg pardon, ma'am; I don't understand.'

'No–well, you're young. But I give you warning. You never *have* anything. Whether it's a stinking tannery or a beautiful estate, you don't have it: it has you; and when it has sucked your very marrow they'll cast you on the dungheap. That happened to me, clever as I was. But they didn't have it all their own way, you know. There was a time when I had nothing; and the few things I had I must throw away to make it look like a robbery. And it was so muddy too! But I was so happy. So happy. I've never been happy since.'

I was alarmed and shocked to see that tears were running down her face. I had never seen her cry before; even when my father died she had shed her tears behind a closed door.

'I think you are feeling unwell, ma'am,' I said, rising from the table and going to where she sat. 'Come, let me help you to your room.'

She took my wrist in her thin hard old hand, and I could feel the unnatural heat of it.

'You must decide,' she said. 'And now; there is no time to waste. Will you come or won't you? Fifty gold pieces will last a long time, and I'm not without skill. You'll never lack.' Her voice changed, losing its urgency, its curious echo of youth. 'That is what he said, you know. And then it was so muddy and I wondered how I could explain. But I did. I fooled them all.'

'Of course,' I said soothingly. 'Come and lie down now.'

In the kitchen, whither I went to fetch a hot brick, for the old woman's feet were as cold as her hands were hot, I found Jack Lantern trying to persuade the cook to put two hedgehogs in the oven for him. He had found them on his way back from taking our baggage to New Holding. The cook refused to have anything to do with such uncanny creatures, and he went off disgruntledly muttering that he would cook them himself.

Apparently he did so, over a fire made of Dame Elizabeth's tally-sticks. Later on he swore that the fire was out before he left it and went to sleep off his orgy, and that may well have been true. A spark may have flown up and started a quiet slow smouldering in the thatch of the stable while he was enjoying his strange repast. It was hours later, hard on midnight, when the glare and crackle of the fire and the screams of the frightened horses trapped in the stable roused the house.

When I reached the yard the roof of the stable was all ablaze, but all the horses save three at the far end, beyond an eight-foot-high partition, had been got out. Just over the partition a portion of the flaming roof had fallen inwards, setting fire to the partition itself. Jack Lantern had actually made one dash past the flames and attempted to drive the three horses out, but they had refused to face the blazing barrier and were now rearing and screaming against the farther wall. I could see instantly that though the partition was aflame there was still a passage between its end and the wall.

The opening in normal times was wide enough to admit a man with a forkful of hay, and I knew that I could save the horses if they would just do what I told them. Darting and shrugging away from those who would have restrained me, I ran in through the opening that was arched and bordered with flame and seized the first horse by the mane. My hands were as steady as they ever were at table, my voice as calm as though I were exchanging the time of day with a passer-by. 'Steady, now,' I said, 'trust me; there is room. Steady . . . you're safe with me.' Three times I did it, and as I followed the last horse past the flames and into safety the whole roof, with a snarling roar, caved in. Smoke and flames and bits of blazing debris seemed to reach towards me. I lurched forward and fell into Rawley's arms.

They are saying now, of course, that I went to and fro through the flames exulting and unhurt. That is hardly true. I suffered no serious damage, but my hair and eyebrows, like the manes and tails of the horses, were singed and the skin of my face and arms was scorched so that it peeled off like corn husks and left me painfully raw. They lie who say that, tempered by the fires of hell, I emerged from a burning stable unscathed. . . .

But . . . but ought I to deny the power of the Power which had come to my aid so timely? In twenty-four hours I should have been at New Holding and Merravay might have burned to the ground without my knowing. I had willed that something should happen to take Rawley from Phyl Whymark and give him to me . . . and what I willed had come to pass.

This is no love-story, and these things are too intimate to set down here. It suffices to say that while they were larding my raw flesh with goosegrease and then powdering over the grease with flour so that I was grotesquely masked, and my close pelt of hair, crisped and blackened, was flaking about like ash, Rawley came and knelt by my bed and told me how he had felt when he saw that burning stable and heard that I was within. And I shall always cherish the knowledge that he was coming to me through the flames.

Chapter Seven

And after that for almost twenty years nothing strange took place. Life proceeded in normal, placid fashion. We were very happy.

I was one of Lady Fennel's 'good tinder' kind. Within a year I had borne a child, a boy, whom we called Charles. He was a happy, healthy, handsome little boy, and with him and Thomasina, who now seemed like my own, I was well content.

My grandmother lived only a short while after the night of the fire and was never again wholly sound of mind. At the end I had her carried up into the Queen's Chamber, so that she might die there as she had wished; but it was a wasted gesture, for she seemed to imagine that she was lying in Layer Wood and complained bitterly about the mud.

Tucked away between the woods, the river and the sea, we at Merravay led, I can now see, a life that was isolated, self-contained and perhaps unduly complacent. It was life after the antique fashion, in which a hailstorm that flattened a wheatfield or a bad batch of butter seemed of more dire importance than the disputes of bishops or the conferences of kings.

We were warned, of course. As early as the December of 1637, Sir Walter Fennel, sitting at our table, full of our food and wine, suddenly leaned forward and asked Rawley:

'Have you paid your ship-money yet?'

'Some time since. Why?'

'Pity,' said Sir Walter, cracking a walnut between his fingers. 'I was one who didn't. And now I see that this Buckinghamshire fellow, Hampden, is refusing to pay and letting his case come into court. And not a penny will they get from me until I see which way the cat jumps.'

'I can tell you that now,' said Rawley cheerfully. 'They'll make him pay–and next year put up his dues!'

'That remains to be seen,' said Sir Walter. 'After all, Hampden rests his case upon an indisputable fact–that ship-money is illegal.'

The old sailor in Rawley knew a brief resurrection.

'God above us! We've got to have ships, haven't we? And how can we have ships without money?'

'Taxes should be levied by Parliament,' said Sir Walter, something stubborn and pontifical creeping into his voice.

'But we haven't had a Parliament for eight years! And when you wail about ship-money you should remember, Walter, what a mass of taxes the Parliament men would have levied if they'd sat there all that time with nothing else to do.'

That seemed to me a sound argument; and since Rawley was holding his own so well, I forbore to say anything.

'Well . . . of course, if that is the attitude you take . . .' There was something a little ominous about Sir Walter's unfinished sentence; and although for a long time after that conversation our families continued to meet and maintain friendly relationships, something sour remained and would reveal itself from time to time in remarks such as, 'You're a King's man, aren't you, Rawley?' or 'Don't say such things in Rowhedge's house–he's Royalist, remember!'

One day Rawley said to me, 'I'd give a shilling to know where Fennel gets his information. To my certain knowledge he's not been in London these last three years, yet everything that's said and done there is known at Ockley within a week–if we can believe him.'

Next time I saw Lady Fennel I asked her the question, and she was pleased to tell me about the weekly newsletter to which Sir Walter, the Headways and Blackwoods subscribed and which they shared. An enterprising fellow called Shuttle had started the scheme to supply news to country places, and the service was now so swift that a newsletter sent from London on Wednesday morning reached Ockley on Saturday afternoon. I promptly ordered a copy for us, and then, when I found it to be violently anti-Royalist, I also subscribed to another, which was equally biased on the other side; but though we read–or rather I read while Rawley listened, yawning–and talked about what we read, the whole business seemed remote, unimportant. So unconcerned were we that when, in 1640, the King did call a Parliament which promptly declared ship-money to be illegal, the first thing Rawley said was, 'Now Walter will be happy! Let's ask him to supper and see his shining face!' I also remember, quite clearly, that we were at Ockley when the news came that the Queen had left England and gone to Holland.

'That means war and nothing less,' said Sir Walter. 'She's off to beg, borrow or steal money; and with the powder and shot and the foreign mercenaries thus provided, the King'll shed out English blood!'

'But the Queen has gone to convey the Princess to her husband, which is reasonable enough,' Rawley protested.

'The Princess is a child of ten!' Sir Walter snorted. 'It's time you faced facts, Rowhedge; or do you mean to sit on the fence till you're pushed off?'

I suppose that was our intention, if we could have been said to have any at all; but in the end we were forced into taking sides. By our own son.

Charles, then aged seventeen, was at Cambridge; and one day in June we received a letter from him. Instead of the usual rather rambling amusing discourse to which we were accustomed, this letter contained some terse instructions.

'Please send, as quickly as possible, my mare and a sound packhorse, my warm cloak, my silver cup and ten pounds. Let young Lantern, or Bill Woods–or, better still, both if you can spare them–come to ride with me. I am for Oxford.'

'Oxford,' said Rawley. 'What in the Devil's name does he want with Oxford? Didn't we thrash out the question and settle on Cambridge for his learnings?'

'He is going to the King,' I said.

'That is nonsense! Now that I will not allow,' Rawley spluttered. 'This is a grown men's quarrel, whipped up by old fools. If it comes to blows, let the old men give and receive them. Sit you down, Alice, and write to him bluntly and say I bid him stay where he is. Or, better still, come home. Aye, that is it. If this matter of learning is so light that it can be abandoned to go gallivanting off to Oxford, then the boy might just as well . . .'

I never heard the end of that sentence. I stood there with Charles's letter in my hand, and the thing which had not happened for so many years happened again. I saw my son, grown older and thinner and brown of skin, standing in a strange place. He stood between sky and sea, both blue with an intensity of blue that our skies, our seas never knew. There was fierce, vivid sunlight, and queer trees with feathery foliage which shook out a warm spicy odour. He looked well and prosperous and assured, and something remained of his old boyish merriment, tinged now with bitterness. . . .

'Here,' Rawley said, slipping his arm about me, 'bear up, Alice; don't take it so hard. He hasn't gone yet, and by God he shall not go! I'll ride myself to Cambridge and knock sense into his head if needs be.'

'He'll go if he has set his mind to it,' I said; 'and if he goes he must go well equipped.'

'He won't go,' said Rawley stubbornly. 'He won't want to go when I've had my say.'

'I will come with you,' I said, 'to take leave of him, in case . . . And we will take what he asks for, in case . . . But of course I hope that you may persuade him.'

I knew then that it was a vain hope, and when we reached Cambridge I was more than ever certain. The whole place was in an uproar. The town and the surrounding countryside was strongly Parliamentarian but the colleges were for the King. Behind the closed gates the young men were making ready, melting down their silverware, gathering their gear, looking to their weapons. They were all in wild, hilarious high spirits, like children about to go on some long-promised treat, and of course poor Rawley's arguments and persuasions were no more than leaves in a wind. In fact there was one moment when it seemed as though the contagious enthusiasm might make a convert of him.

Despite my inner certainty that Charles was not going to his death, that he would live to be at least thirty, I parted with him in agony, for I did not believe that I should ever see him in the flesh again. I was also miserable for Rawley's sake and wished that I could have told him what I *knew*. But that was impossible. For one thing he would have thought me mad; for another, there was some deep instinct which informed me that these were not things to speak of.

All I could do, as the battles of Edgehill and Newbury and Chalgrove Field followed one another, was to say, 'I feel in my bones that the boy has taken no harm. I should have known, Rawley. I am his mother.'

Chapter Eight

At Merravay, through all these troublous times, life went on much as usual. Except for the Hattons at Mortiboys, all our neighbours were inclined to the Puritan cause, but there was no fighting in our district. Known to veer the other way and with a son rising rapidly in the Royalist ranks, the worst that befell us was that we were regarded a little askance and avoided, rather as though we had a case of plague in our house. Sir Walter Fennel, most Puritan of our neighbours, forswore our company, but he still sent his mares to our Barbary stallion. With the Blackwoods we remained on cordial terms, because two years before war broke out Thomasina had married young Robert Blackwood. When her firstborn was christened Robert Rawley we were asked to the ceremony; and the Royalist cause being in the ascendant, we were not unwelcome to the other guests. But as time went on matters became more difficult.

For one thing, a Huntingdon squire named Oliver Cromwell came back, after the first Battle of Newbury, to raise new forces in East Anglia. He had said, of the Parliamentarian forces, 'Do you think that the spirits of such base fellows will ever be able to encounter gentlemen that have honour and courage and resolution in them?' and he had vowed to raise an army of his own from men of honour and courage and resolution. In due time there came to us at Merravay a manifesto, a demand for men and money.

The moment I had it in my hand I saw–just as I had seen the clay-pit, and Rawley's wife, and Charles aged thirty in a far place–a really horrid sight, a mass of mouldering bones, hanging in chains above the heads of a great crowd of people, all jeering and pointing, rejoicing in the grisly sight.

'From whose hand?' I asked. 'Who wrote this?'

'The General's own,' they told me. I drew Rawley aside and said, 'Though it would be expedient now to trim our sails a trifle, have nothing to do with this man. I have a feeling that he will come to a bad end.'

Rawley stared at me, astonished. 'What could I have to do with him, Alice, even if he were headed for the throne itself? With Charles on the other side!'

(This incident seems strange to remember now, when Cromwell rides so high and I lie so low. But that 'eye in my hand' never saw wrong, and the end is not yet!)

One day soon after that Rawley was in Baildon, in the yard of a hostelry called the Hawk in Hand, where he stabled his horse, and one of the hostlers came up and said, rather furtively, 'The young master is with the King, ain't he, Sir Rawley?' We had never made a secret of that, so Rawley said, 'Yes.'

'Well, if ever you want to send him owt, bring it here. We've got ways of managing.' And shortly after that we began to receive cryptic little messages from Charles, demanding money. We sent it, cautiously and suspiciously at first, but it always reached its destination, and was always acknowledged in terms which made sense to me but would have meant nothing to anyone who had intercepted the letter. One little note, for instance, read: 'Who used to be a notorious gambler? Wouldn't he put up a stake?' And that sent Rawley riding to Kit Hatton, who would have bet on which way the wind would blow tomorrow, and Kit raised two hundred pounds, which went down the 'Tunnel', as we called this line of communication.

Then came the second Battle of Newbury, and next time Rawley visited Baildon he found the Hawk in Hand closed down. For many weeks during that long cold winter we had no news of Charles at all, and what other news we received was all discouraging.

One evening Rawley and I were sitting in the Ship Chamber when I heard a stealthy tapping at the window. I thought it might be a gull. In bad weather they came up the river and grew bold, tame as barnyard fowls, and I often put scraps on the sill for them. I looked and saw something–too large to be a gull–move behind the pane.

'Rawley . . . there is someone by the window.'

For the last week or so Rawley had been convinced that he was being watched wherever he went. He rose now in anger and said, 'Spying on us at our fireside now, are they?' He went and unlatched the casement and flung it open and then stepped back with a cry. Charles put a leg over the sill.

'Dear hearts,' he said, 'I hope I did not alarm you.' He pulled off the woollen cap he wore and came to kiss me. All his lovely glossy curls had been shorn, and as soon as I had recovered myself I said, 'Oh, Charles, you look like a Roundhead.'

'That was my intention. I've got so far on my looks, but I dared not trust them where I was known. That is why I came to the window. Mother, can I have something to eat, at once. I've a great deal to say, and I must be on my way in an hour.'

I began to bestir myself. I ran to the kitchen and brought food and the ingredients for mulled wine, for the boy was soaked to the skin. Then I went to his room and picked out the plainest and shabbiest of the clothes he had left behind at the beginning of that Cambridge term, which now seemed like a lifetime ago. Old as they were, they were too fine to fit the role he had chosen, so while he sat by the fire eating with the voracity of a wolf, talking all the while, and Rawley mulled the wine, I busied myself by cutting off the bits of fur and velvet and the fancy buttons as I listened to his talk.

The King, he said, had men in plenty, for the reverse at Newbury had brought forward many formerly lukewarm; but he was tragically short of arms. However, arrangements had been made; the King of France had no wish to see his brother-king defeated and was sending weapons of war.

'To get them in . . . that is the trouble. The Cropheads hold all the ports, and places like Plymouth and Poole where we hold the land inward are too well watched and guarded. So we thought of the east, where they hold both port and land and so feel secure and are less careful. And we hope to land arms at Hull, and Yarmouth . . . and Bywater!' He broke off and eyed us over the bread and bacon which he was stuffing into his mouth.

'A bold scheme,' said Rawley thoughtfully. 'Under their very bows as it were.'

'I'm glad you're in favour of it,' Charles said quickly, 'because this is what you must do . . .'

It all sounded wildly fantastic, as unreal and unlikely as the games children play or the dramas that unfold themselves on a stage; and when Charles finally stood up, looked up at the hat from which I had removed band and buckle, and said, 'Still far too jaunty,' and pulled on the sodden woollen cap again, I stared at him, feeling that it was all–his visit, his talk, his disguise–part of a dream from which I must surely soon wake.

'There,' he said. 'Now don't I look like Jeremiah-O-Lord-Arise-Scatter-Thy-Enemies Jones? And now can you get me a horse? You'll find the one I came on in the Low Meadow. It's foundered, but it was a good horse and could be again.'

A few minutes later, out in the windy dark, he kissed us and mounted. We said, 'Be careful of yourself' and 'God keep you'.

'And you. And speed you in all you do.' Then, raising the old cap, he cried, 'God save the King!' softly but as though it were a battle-cry. He touched the horse with his heel, and in a second the double dark of the night and the avenue's shade had engulfed him.

We never saw him again, but I know he is alive, somewhere.

He left us wholly committed to the King's cause.

Chapter Nine

It would be tedious to describe in detail the campaign of subterfuges, shifts and lies upon which we then embarked. What we had to do sounded simple enough. We had only to provide transport for the arms between Bywater and Merravay and warn the innkeeper of the Red Lion at Colchester, who would then make the next link in the chain. (Almost without exception the innkeepers were Royalist, because they feared that the Puritans, once in power, would close their houses.) Had Rawley and I been a simple farmer and his wife, used to driving our own teams, it would have been easy enough; as it was, it demanded great cunning. We had decided not to involve any of our servants–not so much because we did not trust them as to avoid the slightest risk of an indiscreet word, an ill-timed significant glance. Consequently we were obliged to behave as though these old faithful friends were all enemies. To me fell the task of carrying the warning to the men at the Red Lion, and many were the devices to which I was driven to shake off, even for a few minutes, the servant who had for years attended me whenever I rode so far. Twice, I remember, I went to the length of having a tooth drawn by a man who had lately set up as a tooth-dragger in a room behind the inn. Sometimes, too, I chose to ride the Barbary and saw to it that the servant was mounted on a slow-moving horse and pretended that it was past my power to hold the great black horse to the pace of the plodder.

We tried never to repeat a story or to play the same game twice; and as the weeks mounted into months we had the satisfaction of knowing that the arms had at least reached Colchester safely and been sped on their way. Now and then when the King scored one of his spectacular–but, alas, indecisive–little victories we could look at one another and think that perhaps, with our scheming, hard riding and sacrifice of sleep, we had contributed a trifle towards it.

One day in May we were notified in the usual manner that a load waited at Bywater. This time we were providing the team and wagon in the least troublesome though most expensive way. Rawley was going to Bywater, where he meant to buy the best that the market offered. After nightfall he would drive it to the place where the Colchester men with their vehicle always waited–a lonely place where a tongue of Layer Wood ran down to meet the road to Bywater. There he would stay with it until later next day and then drive it home. Such a procedure would be easily explained in view of the approaching haysel and harvest.

I had decided to use the tooth-dragging again as my excuse for a visit to Colchester, though this time I had decided that I would not carry the pretence quite so far. Rawley and I rode out together as far as the cross-roads, and there, in the sunshine under trees where crinkled young leaves were unfolding, we said goodbye to one another.

Colchester, which was a completely Puritan town, was very dull that day and full of soldiers. As soon as my errand was done I started for home, not even bothering to look into the shops, which, if they had anything gay and pretty–which I doubt–kept it well hidden. I decided to ride round and visit Thomasina, who was expecting another child at the time. Truth to tell, I always found the day before one of these night ventures intolerably long and trying; I was not cut out for a life of risk and excitement; I could too easily imagine the number of things which might go wrong. I should find Thomasina's company soothing and diverting.

She was, as always, delighted to see me, but I thought that the behaviour of the other members of the family was strikingly cool and formal. The King's cause was no longer flourishing as it had been at the time of the christening of Robert Rawley Blackwood, and Thomasina's mother-in-law, with whom I never had been much of a favourite because long ago she had hoped to marry one of her many daughters to Rawley, said with a dark look that if things went on as they were doing the war would soon be over and there were those who would be sorry for the attitude they had taken. The Blackwoods had recently had soldiers billeted on them, and spoke highly of their behaviour. These soldiers of the New Model Army were models indeed; they neither drank nor swore; they did not steal; they left the maids alone. And think of it! When some went to billet on the Hattons at Mortiboys and Mrs Hatton said, quite untruthfully, that she thought they should move on, as they had a case of suspected plague in the house, the sergeant in charge had said, 'God will take care of His own!' and moved in, uncaring.

Still, even the barbed chatter served its purpose in keeping my mind off the journey which Rawley must soon make with the wagon so heavily loaded that even the best team he might buy could only move slowly through the night. So I stayed on until the shadows were long across the lawn in which Mr Blackwood took such pride, and it was dusk when I reached Merravay.

The day had been very warm and my sticky clothes were turning chill on me, so I went to my room to wash and change. I was taking my time over it, thinking that in a few minutes Rawley would be setting out; then I could linger over supper, walk in the garden for a while . . . anything rather than go to bed and lie there thinking about that slow progress through the dark. There was no doubt about it–Rawley was dearer to me than any cause, even though, through Charles, I owed it my allegiance.

I was putting on my dress when a servant came to tell me that some soldiers had arrived, seeking accommodation for their horses and themselves. That had happened before–not often, because Merravay lay far back from the road, but often enough for us to be used to it and for me to know that all that Mrs Blackwood had said about Puritan soldiers was quite true. In fact, as I ran down, hastily fastening my dress, I thought it was a pity that soldiers of the New Model Army were so very abstemious. Otherwise I would have opened a cask of good brown ale and made sure that when they lay down they slept soundly. Although the place of rendezvous which we had chosen for our transactions with the Colchester men was at a safe distance from the house, its very existence made me nervous and vulnerable to thoughts of danger.

It was only a small contingent–a captain, a sergeant, and eight troopers; they asked civilly for what they might have demanded or taken without a word. They looked tired, so did their horses, but when I suggested that the animals should be turned loose in the pasture the captain thanked me and said he would make his own arrangements. As I turned away, leaving him to do so, Sir Walter Fennel rode into the yard.

It was months since I had seen him face to face, for since the decline in the social relationship between our families the strictly 'farmyard' business which he had had to do with Rawley had been conducted out of doors. He greeted me with surprising cordiality, and then, looking towards the open cartshed where the soldiers were installing themselves, he said:

'Ah, I see you have company. Is Rawley home yet?'

'No. I do not expect him until tomorrow morning.'

'But he has only . . . I called this morning and your servants said that he had gone to Bywater. I hoped he'd be back.'

I was heartily glad that *this* time there had been no secrecy, no subterfuge, no juggling with means of transport or even with time.

'He could have been, of course. But Rawley is an old sailor, remember, and once he gets to Bywater, where there are ships to look at and sailors to talk to, he likes to take his time.' I smiled. 'In the meantime, is there anything I could do? I know a little about most things.'

'Thank you, Alice; no, there is nothing. . . . Unless you cared to invite me to supper. I have been in the saddle all day and it would be late before I reached home.'

I managed, with difficulty, to conceal my enormous surprise.

'It would be a pleasure,' I said. 'It is a long time since you honoured our table.'

Fear, or fear's beginning, began to move, cold and slippery, in my stomach. Across the yard the soldiers were watering their horses . . . but they had not unsaddled!

'Since you will stay I think I will invite the captain to join us,' I said. I would have him under my eye.

Sir Walter strolled across with me, and I thought–I could not be sure, for I distrusted my knowledge-engendered suspicion–that a significant glance, a look of recognition and confirmation, passed between the two men.

The captain accepted my invitation, and I led the way into the Ship Chamber, where I excused myself, saying that I must go to the kitchen to speak about extra places at table. I did not close the door; and having gone, with a tapping of heels and a rustle of silk, across the hall towards the kitchen quarters, I stole back along the wall.

'. . . a bigger force,' I heard Sir Walter say.

'Others are posted and patrolling. No loophole this time,' said the soldier.

Before I had reached the kitchen I had known–and thrust aside–the impulse to do the obvious and dangerous thing. My first thought had been to run straight out, leap on the black horse and make a dash for Bywater. But the soldiers were in the yard and before I could get the horse out of the stable they would have ringed me round. Besides, such an act would be a confession of complicity. Then I thought of making an excuse to ride out openly–to say, for instance, that I was anxious about Thomasina Blackwood and must go to see how she was faring. But that, even if they accepted it, would accord ill with my having invited them to supper, and most certainly Sir Walter would have insisted on accompanying me. No, I must think of something more crafty.

Chapter Ten

The meal lasted a thousand years. I sat there, noting the thickening darkness outside the windows. In May the nights are short, and Rawley, if he had not already set out, would be about to do so. Slowly, creakingly he was moving towards the trap.

I was very gay. I gave, I think, a good impersonation of a woman with nothing on her mind save the entertainment of her guests; and that fitted in well with what I had to do.

When the meal was over I rose and moved to a side-table, where a silver dish held the last wizened apples of the autumn's crop.

'Now,' I said, 'I must ask you to excuse me for a few moments. Every night, without fail, I give my black horse his apples, and he is more of a stickler for ritual than Archbishop Laud ever was!'

Laughter greeted that sally; but in the glass above the sidetable I saw them look at one another and make ready to move. Forestalling them, I said:

'You, Sir Walter, know my Barbary and his antics, but perhaps the captain might be entertained to see his performance.'

They followed me out. In the yard the creak of leather and rattle of chains informed me that the troopers' horses were still ready.

'We should be fair,' I said. 'I expect your horses like apples too.'

'They're not accustomed to pampering, ma'am.'

'Just this once,' I said. I held apples to the questing velvet muzzles; I spoke into the long, twitching ears. Then I opened the door of Barbary's loose-box, called to him, and he came. He danced as I told him, rearing and pivoting on his back legs; he held up one hoof, then another; he whinnied to order. I handed the dish to Sir Walter at last and said:

'His best trick, for some reason, he will only do when I am on his back. Captain Allbright . . . please.'

He helped me to mount.

'Kneel!' I said to the great black horse; and he buckled his knees and lowered himself. 'Give him his reward,' I cried, and as Sir Walter held out the apple I leaned over, saying 'Good boy, *good* boy!' Then I spoke into his ear. And at once he was up, a great mad thunderbolt of power, striking out back and front, gathering himself for the great leaping bounds which carried him out of the yard–not towards Bywater but in the other direction. I clung to his mane and screamed for help.

We thundered out of the yard and were halfway up the avenue before I spoke to him again and steered him across the fields into the marshes–safe now, thank God, for the spring had been early and dry. Headed for Bywater by the shortest way, I got myself astride him and, lying low on his neck, said, 'Run now; run as you never ran.'

I reckoned that Rawley would still be on that part of the road where it ran alongside the river. It would be the action of a moment to back the team, unhitch and let the incriminating load roll of its own momentum into the water. Rawley could go back to his bed at The Ship, and the horse and I would finally come to a standstill somewhere quite incredibly far from Bywater. I might even stage a minor accident. . . .

Nobody, I thought, could blame me for over-estimating my control over a horse which most people already regarded as a dangerous demon, and certainly no one would believe that the refusal of the troop horses to budge an inch could be in any way due to me! Later I learned that they did stand fast, even when prodded with pikes; and I learned, too, that nobody had any difficult in believing that I had bewitched them.

I founded the wagon just where I had reckoned. It was blazing fiercely, and of the four or five dead men around it one was Rawley.

So now I do not care what they say about me, or what happens to me; my spirit is already dead in me. My flesh shrinks from the thought of death by burning. Yes, that appals me, and I can only hope that what Thomasina said on her visit to me is true–that the smoke chokes the victim before the flesh chars and the boiling blood bursts the veins.

There, I have set it all down, honestly. And what does it all amount to? Five times in my lifetime–is it five? There was Robin's whistle, Rawley's letter, the petticoat, Charles's letter and Cromwell's manifesto–yes, five times something which I have held in my hand has communicated something to my mind. Twice–once over the matter of Robin's innocence and once in the matter of Rawley's affection–I have imposed my will on my circumstances. And always I have been able to make animals obey me implicitly. Does this amount to witchcraft? Am I damned, not only in this life but in the life to come? I cannot remember ever wishing or working ill to anyone. I cannot, even now, wish positive ill even to those who tell those twisted, lying stories about the transparent black dog in the harvest field.

No, if I could wish anything it would be that I might die, quickly, easily, before the faggots are lighted.

INTERLUDE

Lady Alice Rowhedge was found guilty of witchcraft and condemned to be burned. In the brief interval between the delivery and carrying out of her sentence she was taken back to the cell in the old Bridewell in Friargate at Baildon. She must have gone and stood by the narrow windows, unglazed and rendered still more narrow by a rusty iron bar. What happened happened so swiftly that people going home from the trial and arguing about her guilt, or her innocence, actually saw *and stepped aside to avoid a small black dog which was proceeding along Friargate in peculiar circular fashion, seeming to wish to bite its own tail and crying as it went.*

Alice Rowhedge–with what was almost her last breath–said that she saw the dog and imagined that it had a thorn in its flank. She called it and it came, and she put out her arm, not without difficulty. The dog bit her, sinking its teeth into her hand, not once but many times, for on account of the narrowness of the window and the angle at which her arm was held she could not easily withdraw it. The dog ran on as far as the corner, where a blacksmith, recognising the nature of its ailment, clubbed it to death with his hammer.

Inside the cell Lady Alice told the gaoler what she had done and what had happened, and added, in what he called a wondering voice, 'No dog ever bit me before!' Then, in almost no time at all, she fell into frenzy, and from frenzy to coma, and died.

Only the most stubbornly rational people–and they were rare at the time–reminded themselves and their hearers that the dog was real enough to have been killed by a blow from the blacksmith's hammer, and that its wretched little carcass had laid on his dunghill for days, plain for all to see. the vast majority believed that a dog of quite another kind, the dog of the harvest field, had come to save the witch from her just deserts.

An abbreviated version of the story which she had written while she was awaiting trial was printed under the title of A Witch's Confession, *and a copy of it found its way into every household where one literate person lived; and even the least superstitious people were forced to admit that she* had, *after all, died before the faggots were piled. Her story, with many variations, many embellishments, was told by the winter fires and under the summer trees–told so often that it became part of the folklore of the region.*

After the King had been executed–another thing to argue about, for even in Suffolk, where most men had been against him, there were those who thought that such an extreme action boded no good–Merravay was taken in hand by the Commissioners and divided into three portions. The two that consisted of land only found a ready market, but the third, consisting of the house and gardens and about thirty acres of land, was hard to dispose of. Merravay itself had become a place to avoid, for dark and sinister stories were creeping around. And the house, staring there blank-eyed across the fields, deep in its grounds where the nettles and brambles encroached upon the pinks and lilies and roses of Lady Alice's garden, grew daily more like a place where ghosts would walk than a place where people should live. Only little boys, inspired by greed and bold in company, would venture there on sunny afternoons to snatch nuts from the shrubbery and pears from the sheltered walls; then, retreating with their loot, they would tell tales of strange things seen and heard and resolutely braved.

One such party, early in a new season of nuts and pears, did receive a genuine fright; for Phyl Whymark, the woman from the tavern, suddenly appeared from the house and ordered them to be off and not come back. Merravay was her property, she said.

From a safe distance the boys mocked her–mocked her claim to ownership. But it was valid enough. And the older people, with longer memories, said, 'Ah, so she got it, after all!'

EPISODE THREE
Restoration

THE MATRIARCH

Chapter One

There's no doubt about it, I ain't as spry as I was!

It's as much as I can do to stagger out here into the sun and drop down in this chair like a sack of meal.

But then I reckon I must be close on ninety. Nobody can know for sure; they kept no count of birthdays when I was young. I got meself born, and I've kept meself alive, and when I come to take stock I can't help thinking that I ain't done so badly. A mite of luck, but in the main hard work and mother-wit hev got me where I am today.

And where am I today? I'm sitting in the garden at Merravay, and I can look to right and left and straight ahead; and for all I'm so long-sighted, as far as I can see belongs to me–my own, my very own.

Maybe I was meant to hev it; for there was a time, long ago, though to me that fare like yesterday, when Sir Rawley Rowhedge was minded to marry me. He would hev done, too, but for the spells put on him by that whey-faced cousin of his–her that would hev burned for witchcraft if the Devil hadn't snatched her away. Nowadays folks make mock of witches and such like–more fools they! I could tell 'em something; but I don't. What happened betwixt Rawley and me was our business then, and I've kept the secret all my life.

Till I took up with Rawley I'd kept meself to meself, and that weren't so easy. For one thing, my mother was a byword for loose-living; for another, I went up to London every year, driving geese. We lived rough, sleeping in stacks and ditches along the road, and I was reckoned to be pretty.

When Rawley took up with me and spoke serious about marriage I reckoned that was the reward of virtue–the virtue I'd often fought tooth and nail for; and when he fell under the spell and jilted me and give me fifty pounds I reckoned that was the wages of sin. Between the two there was a bit of my life I never cared to think on. He was a right proper man, Rawley was, and I could never bear him much grudge; it wasn't his fault.

I was heart-sick, but people like me don't brood over their feelings–leastways not their softish ones–and I pucked meself up and reckoned meself lucky to hev the money. And nobody was scornful to me. People reckoned he'd just hung about our place time he was drinking to drown his sorrow, and the one he was thought to hev jilted was Miss Blackwood.

I looked round for a way to put the money to good use. I did think about heving a pastry-cook's shop, for I was a fair hand at cooking; but there'd be no customers much in a village, and I hated all towns. Moreover, by this time my mother was dead and there was only one of my brothers–if you can call 'em that–living at home, and the way he was going on he didn't look like making owd bones. So I thought I'd wait a bit; and if he drunk hisself to death in good time, I'd spend my money making the tavern a better sort of place, the sort travellers would pull in at.

I found out a lawyer man that everybody spoke well of and went and arst him about putting money somewhere safe where it could breed a bit. I laugh to myself even now when I think about that first little business betwixt Mr Turnbull and me and where it all led to in the end.

I'd no sooner laid the money away safe than I found I was in the family way. Christ in glory! I was so savage I could hev kilt myself. I'd allust set myself to be a cut above my mother, who'd had a bastard most years, and here I was, going the same road.

There was a chap or two would hev married me if I'd played my cards right, but I was still sore for Rawley and couldn't fancy any of 'em. So I told myself I'd get out of this fix as I'd got into it, secretwise.

First of all I tried every old-wives' cure I ever had heard of, mainly through hearing my mother say she wouldn't touch 'em. I jumped off ladders and heaved the heaviest things I could find, and one night went and stood in cold water up to my neck. But my John was a sight stubborner then than he ever was in later days. In the end I knew I'd either got to stand and brazen it out or get away. I towd my brother I was off to London to try to pick up a little money and threatened him well what I'd do if he burnt the place down or anything else silly time I was away, and off I went.

I knew where to make for–the Poultry Market, where hundreds of geese waddled in and were killed and dressed every day, and where anybody that could see and had two hands could hev a job.

I wasn't exactly a stranger, and my home was nothing to be homesick for, but, God, I was miserable that time. I hated London, and the Poultry was a stinking place even for London, and the people I worked and lived with were low, scum of the earth. Still, it was a good place to hide in.

I worked hard and laid by a shilling or two, and when my time came near I bargained with the woman at the house where I'd been sleeping to let me hev a room to myself for a bit. She towd me about a place started up by some kind ladies, a laying-in place for poor women, but I didn't want nothing like that. Nor I didn't want her messing about. I towd her so. The night I went back feeling a bit queer I give her two shillings.

'Thass rent till I get about again,' I said. 'And you keep outa my way.'

She laughed. 'You don't know whass coming,' she said. 'You may be hollering for me afore you've done.'

'I may holler, but you keep out. I paid for his room, and if you bust in I'll claw you,' I said.

I shoved a brukken chair under the knob of the door and settled to wait. I'd helped my mother more times than I could remember; I knew just what to do . . . and what not to do.

Next day, or the one after, I meant to go out of that room with my waist in the right place and nothing to show that any man'd made free with me.

I was my mother's second or third, and by the time I was of an age to help her she'd hev a baby as easy as she would wring out a cloth, so I'd no idea what heving a first baby meant. By noon next day, when the baby was born, I was that wore out with the pain and the struggle that what I had planned should happen damn nearly did happen, willy-nilly. But I roused myself enough just to take a look at the thing that had caused me such a lot of trouble . . . and with that one look I was undone. John and me hev been through a lot of things together, but I never loved him more than I did at that minute.

Chapter Two

I could hev stayed in London, where one bastard more or less didn't matter, but I wanted my child to grow up in a healthier place; so, regardless of shame and gibing, back to Nettleton I went as soon as I could face the trudge. And once there I cast round in my mind for some way of making a little money at the same time as I tended the baby and looked after what trade there was at the tavern.

I hit on pork pies.

I've worked hard all my days, but never harder than in the next few years. I reared, killed and cleaned my own pigs, sold the choicest joints and made the rest–down to the shreds of meat that I could scrape from the toes and the jaws–into pies. There was the tavern too; and a baby that I tried to bring up clean and healthy, and my brother well-nigh as helpless and a sight more nuisance. But I managed.

All this time the witch, Alice Rowhedge, was living smooth and soft up at Merravay. She'd had a baby too, a boy, a fine handsome little chap, but not a patch on mine, or so I thought. Hers was more like Rawley, with the same copper-coloured hair; my John took after me, and that was lucky. I could see Rawley in him, though.

I had kind of cherished the notion of getting him a bit of schooling and give him a push up in the world that way; but he never took kindly to learning. Any other sort of work he was a wonder at, very willing and very strong.

The years went by, my brother died, John grew, the war broke out and the tavern trade dwindled, but the pie business flourished, and John and me had laid penny to penny till we'd got another fifty pounds to set aside with that that Rawley had given me; and we was looking about for a bit of land to rear more pigs and geese on, when Captain Samuel Fletcher came into our lives.

Him and half a dozen troopers arrived one afternoon and billeted theirselves on us. The men went into the bar-room what was hardly ever used for its proper purpose, for what with the rules and the scowlings, you could hardly sell a drink them days. Captain Fletcher follered me into the kitchen and after beating about the bush for a bit arst me if I could let him hev a sup of something. I was wary and said no at first, but then I see he wasn't trying to trap me, he was a proper drinker and he wanted something badly. So I went down the cellar and brung up some good owd October ale and a little brandy that I'd been howding on to. He was as happy as a yard dog let off the chain for a bit.

He got to telling me what he suffered in Colchester, where the taverns were shut down, and I towd him how I was planning to get out of the trade and get some land, and he said, 'Ma'am, take my advice and wait. There'll be land going begging when this is over.'

'How so?' I asked.

'Once Cromwell is safe in the saddle,' he said, 'he'll take the land off all them that fought for the King. And once they get to breaking up the big estates, mark my words, land'll be mighty cheap.'

'Not about these parts. Them with land about here are all for Parliament.'

'I know one who isn't,' he said, making a knowing sort of face. I arst who, but he was a man who could keep his own counsel even in his cups, which is a thing I respect.

Then he suggested that he should give me a regular order for pork pies.

'Delivered to me, at Colchester barracks. And to my mind, ma'am, all a good pork pie needs is a drop of something to wash it down.'

'And to *my* mind,' I said, 'there's nothing easier to carry in and out than a nice bit of washing. You send me your dirty linen. . . . For send bare pies amongst a lot of soldiers,' I said, 'I just dare not.'

We understood each other.

Thass funny to think that about this same time the witch up at Merravay was setting about her bit of smuggling.

I've never been much of a thinking woman, I been too busy; but now and then thoughts'll go through your head time your hands are busy, and one thing I thought once is this. Loving a person and hating one are alike in this–you take note of what they do, where they go and what happen to them. I *hated* Alice Rowhedge so much that if somebody'd stood at the cross-roads and said her name in a whisper I'd hev heard it.

Well, things went wrong with her and she was carted off to gaol. At first we thought it was for helping to get arms to the King, and there, of course, there was nothing I could say; but when it come to witchcraft that was different. I knew she'd put a spell on Rawley; men don't suddenly, overnight, fall in love with their ugly cousins that hev been living under the same roof with them for years. Alice Rowhedge was there when Rawley's wife died, but he hadn't turned to her then, he'd turned to me. So, though I wasn't going to say aught about the one spell I *knew* she'd worked, I could and did say about the time when I was stooking at Merravay. . . .

Chapter Three

After a bit the thing what Captain Fletcher said would happen did happen. They put Merravay up for sale; but I could hev cried with vexation because of the way they did it. No separate fields and pastures the same as I'd been counting on. Three big lots they cut it into; the New Holding land and the Merravay land next to it was one–and Sir Walter Fennel bought it; the Slipwell land and the other part of Merravay on that side was another–bought by Mr Blackwood of Muchanger; and the house and two fields and meadows made the third. It was as plain as the nose on your face that Sir Walter and Mr Blackwood had had a say in the dividing–not that I minded their getting what they wanted; what raised my gall was the thought of the two fields and meadows near the house, any one of which would have suited my purpose, all going back to wild while the house went to rack and ruin. Nobody wanted that lot, for people who looked to live in a great house wanted more land, and people who wanted a little land didn't want a great house. So there it stood, shorn of its acres, useless as a ship gone aground.

I was still smarting when, one day, Captain Fletcher came grinning into my place, and I rounded on him pretty sharp.

'That was rotten bad advice you give me,' I said. 'But for you and your land going begging I'd hev bought Croop's meadow time that was for sale. I went and let that go; and now I shan't never get the bit of land I hanker after.'

He grinned, and I went on: 'And I should like to clout the head of the fool who divided it.'

'Clout away,' he said, and stuck his close-cropped skull towards me.

'You!'

'The same, ma'am. I'm one of the commissioners. The army is in command now. Bless you, I thought I'd done you a good return for favours received. I knew that neither of the bespoke customers needed a house . . . so I tucked away a nice little thirty acre bit *under* the house, so to speak . . . and then you go for me like a vixen!'

'If you did that you're more of a fool than I thought you! Thirty acres and a mansion–what use is that to a poor woman like me? All I've managed to scratch together in twenty years' hard grind is a hundred and fifteen pounds.'

'Well, offer me that!'

'For Merravay and thirty acres. Man, you're mad.'

'Maybe. Go on, make a firm offer and it's yours. Not today; not tomorrow . . . but before the year's out. "In default of better offer", see? We must do things orderly.'

'But suppose you have a better offer,' I said, very dry in the mouth.

'Well,' he said, dragging out the word. 'I'm only one of four, and there're strict eyes everywhere; but there are ways and means. For one thing, it's a very bad-reputed house. They say the witch walks there. Of course . . . that wouldn't bother a sensible woman like you; but, being an honest man, I should be bound to warn any prospective buyer. Shouldn't I?'

'You ain't mocking me?'

'I'm dealing with you, ma'am, as you dealt with me, fair and square and underhand. And now, have you anything to wet the bargain?'

I never said nothing to nobody, not even my John, in case things should go wrong. The best part of a year went by, and sometimes the impatience in me was like a pain; another season wasted and me getting older and the land going back to wild. They say in our parts 'Fallow hath no fellow', but they only mean for a year.

However, the day came when Captain Fletcher visited me again, this time with another man, and all very strict and stiff. They had come to tell me, they said, that since no better offer had been made for Merravay they would take mine, ridiculous as it was.

'I don't know about ridiculous,' I said. 'There ain't so many people want a house where queer things arc to be seen and heard, nor land so weeded over that you can't tell ploughland from pasture. I made my offer afore the weeds had got such a howd!' That changed his tune for him!

Chapter Four

Knowing what I knew about Alice Rowhedge's power, and hearing all the stories that were springing up and spreading about the house, it is a wonder that I didn't feel a bit funny going to live there, especially as I'd been one to speak against her; but, to tell the truth, I never give the haunting a thought. I went up alone to look at the place for the first time as soon as I'd handed over my money and got the keys. There'd been a red climbing rose over the porch and part of it had come loose and grown right over the door, so I had to fight my way in, scratching myself something cruel. I'd expected it to be musty and dampish and darkish inside, but it wasn't; it was warm and dry and sweet-smelling, and there was nothing but the silence to show that nobody'd been there for a long time. I walked all through, thinking about the uses I could put some of the rooms to, and if I thought of anybody it was Rawley–which room had he slept in, where had he taken his food? And what would it have felt like, I wondered, to hev come in, married to him, with the place all furnished? I'd hev been shy and awkward, and scared of the old grandmother; now I was bold and certain of myself, and knew I'd got the best bargain in the world. Maybe that suited me better, after all.

I was in the kitchen then, looking round and planning how John and me'd live there, how he'd come in when the day's work was done, and how I'd be getting the meal ready time he washed. It'd suit us fine, I thought. And then I heard the laughing. High and shrill and merry, as though somebody'd heard my thoughts and laughed with a–Ah, so you may think! Alice Rowhedge had always been a one for laughing when she was little, given half a chance. For just a minute I went cold, and caught my breath. . . . Then I realised the the laughing came from the garden, and out I went and found six or seven little urchins getting pears off the trees by the wall. I towd them to be off and not come back, and they ran a little way and then stood and mocked me, 'Owd Phyl Whymark, 'tain't your place.'

'Oh yes it is!' I said. And that was the first time I said it. And somehow after that it seemed true. And–So much for ghosts! I said to myself. Let that be a lesson to you.

I'd been to Mr Turnbull, of course, to get back my money and the interest it had gathered, and I'd asked him, this time, to lend me fifty pounds to buy stock with. He said something about security.

'You write yourself a paper,' I said, 'to say that do I die or come to ruin you're to hev fifty pound worth of stock.'

'But if you were ruined, Mistress Whymark, there might be no stock.'

'Well, the house and land can't get away. Write it so.'

He coughed and fidgeted about with the things on his table, then he said:

'I think it would be bad to burden a property with a mortgage so soon. Tell me–you hold your tavern freehold, do you not?'

'I did; but I just fixed to swop it with Matt Bowyer for his owd mare and wagon.'

'Has that transaction taken place?'

'We talked about it last night. . . .'

'The licence to brew and sell ale is in order, I take it?'

'Oh yes; but that ain't worth much these days.'

'Slightly more than a mare and wagon, I think. I believe I could get you fifty pounds.'

He did, and six months later they made a loop of good hard road that just reached the old tavern, and the coaches came. But I didn't grudge it; I'd been prepared to take an owd horse and wagon for the place, so I hadn't been wronged; and the new road made it easier for me to get my stuff to London. I began on that right away, heving no truck with the little towns what could get more stuff than they needed. My time in the Poultry Market had taught me what a hungry place London was. Whereas geese might open at two shilling apiece in Baildon or Colchester and drop to eightpence when folks'd sell at a loss rather than trail 'em home again, in London there was always a hundred daft people rushing about to find a goose after nightfall, even on Christmas Eve itself.

At first, heving set everybody plenty of work to do, I'd go up with John to show him where to go and how to do his deals, but he took to that the same as he always took to anything real and in the way of work; so then I could stay at home. I had broody hens sitting and fatting hens penned all over the ground floor of the house. I had geese in the orchard and sheep under the trees in the avenue, pigs in the yard and calves in the meadows. Sometimes it fared to me that I was feeding half London, I poured food out at such a rate; cheese and butter, bacon, meat and table fowls, eggs and cream. I used to work till I was past speech, well-nigh deaf and blind. I never did stop except to throw a bit of food into meself and John when he was home; and at night I used to drop on to my bed in my clothes as though I'd been stunned. And I know that old Noah packing his Ark never got so many living creatures into a square yard as I did at Merravay. Every penny I made I put straight back into the place, and in ten years I never bought myself nothing but footwear and a herring now and then. I couldn't grow herrings and I was inordinate fond of them.

Chapter Five

One morning–a lovely June morning it was–I noticed my hands while I was milking; and they was the hands of an owd woman, all gnarled and twisted like tree roots. And I did a bit of reckoning and knew I must be fifty, maybe a bit more. Getting along; soon be going downhill. . . .

That day I said to John, sudden like:

'Did you ever think about getting married?'

He gaped at me. 'I been thinking,' I said. 'I'm getting on. I should like to see my own grandchildren.'

'You ain't sick, are you?'

'You know I'm never sick–ain't got time. But I reckon that if you're going to marry you should do it soon. You're thirty.'

He didn't say anything, or seem to think any more about it, and I reckoned that that'd be another thing for me to handle. So I looked around for a good strong girl, a farmer's daughter, likely to be a good help to us, but at the same time bright and lively. And I picked just the one, a girl named Hester Fulger that made beautiful lace in her spare time. I thought I'd ask her to dinner one Sunday, for though I'd never had no advantages I knew how things should be done. Any girl bidden to Sunday dinner to a house where there was an unmarried man knew which way the wind was blowing. But afore I got so far with my plans John went off to London on his next trip, was away two days more than I'd counted on, and got back just as the late summer dusk was coming down, bringing a girl with him. He walked into the kitchen howding her by the hand, and before I could speak for the surprise at seeing her he said, 'Mother, this is Alison, my wife.'

I never see, in all my days, a poorer, more dwindling, more scared-looking creature. She was clean and had a sort of prettiness, with her great tangle of curls and huge eyes, but she was about the size of a twelve-year child that has never had a square meal in all its life and expected everybody to give it a clout.

'Married?' I said; and the word went on ringing through the kitchen.

'Two days ago,' said John.

'I'm afraid this has given you a shock,' said the girl. Her voice surprised me; it was sweet and clear and very sure.

'I am a bit took aback,' I admitted. 'Hev you and my boy been long acquaint?'

'Two years,' she said. I wanted to ask where he had found her. I tried to take comfort in the fact that she was too shabby to be a street whore. I turned back to the stove to hide my mortification.

John said, 'Whass for supper?'

'A bit of gammon and peas.'

'That'll do. Only Alison can't eat fat, so give her my lean and me her fat, will you.'

It was only a little thing, but I do believe it was the first time in all his thirty-odd years that he'd handed me an order. While I dished up he took her cotton bonnet and hung it on the peg over his working clothes and set her in a chair by the table, as if she was the Queen, and she turned her great eyes about, taking it all in, missing nowt and saying nowt. I took my place, feeling ill at ease, but trying not to let the upset put me off my food, trying to think of the next job waiting for me. It was no good–there across the table she set, my daughter-in-law . . . where I'd meant to make a bid for Hester Fulger. Oh, it was hard!

She ate very dainty, taking her time, and now and agin wiping her lips on a bit of handkerchief. And for all her eyes looked so scared, she wasn't as nervous as I was; for though I couldn't find a word to say and could only look at her and then away agin, quick, she looked me full in the face as if she was taking my measure, and once she smiled, a right sweet friendly smile, but not as if she was asking me to like her, more as though *she* was minded to like me. In one of my sharp glances I noticed her hands; thin and small they were, like a little bird's claws, but red and rough with hard work. Taking them into account and the smallness and the frightened look, I guessed that John had picked her up out of pity, same as he might a stray kitten. There was a very gentle streak in my boy. Nice for her, but what about me, counting on a good strong girl to take on when I got older; and what about the healthy great boys I'd pictured in my mind's eye?

Next morning when John took his place aside me at the early milking I said to him sharp and sudden:

'What come over you, boy? And where did you find such a dolly?'

At the Shepherd and Dog, just behind the Poultry where he lodged in London, he said. He'd had his eye on her for a long time, feeling sorry for her, doing menial, ill-suited work. 'She looked like a flower on a muckheap,' he said.

I nearly said that we hadn't much use for flowers at Merravay; but I held my tongue. He was my boy; we'd stuck together through thick and thin; and if he wasn't as bright and sharp as I could hev wished at times, maybe he wasn't to blame for that. I wasn't going to quarrel with him on account of that little bit of thread!

Then presently we went in to our breakfast, and there she was, with it all ready and neatly set out. She'd found, somehow, the one tablecloth I owned, the one I'd washed and got ready against the day I arst Hester Fulger to Sunday dinner! And she'd put a few rosebuds in a mug in the middle of the table and got water hot so as we could wash our hands. Something new had come to Merravay . . . and I suppose you couldn't say that it wasn't wanted.

So in time we shook down together; though there were odd minutes when I was minded of the Bywater man what caught a mermaid in his net and brung her home and married her, minutes when I would think–What a tool for a busy woman to hev to put up with! She couldn't push, she couldn't pull, she couldn't lift. She wasn't unwilling, she just hadn't no strength. She'd wash–she was a great one to wash–but by the time she'd got the things soaked they was too heavy for her to lift and wring out; and though she took to the dairy work very kindly, when she churned I had to heave the cream in and then listen till she called, so I could tip the butter out, do she'd turn the churn over trying. There was things she could do that I couldn't–read and write and reckon in her head–and she sewed beautifully; she mended us up very tidy. I never was much good with a needle, and I never had time.

She quickened sooner than I'd thought for, but she carried the baby so ill that I often wondered whether it'd come to anything. I used to look at her and think of myself in like case and think maybe, in a rough and ready way, the burden is fashioned to the back. What she'd hev done, wringing geese's necks and taking their insides out up to the very day, God alone knows. Then her time came and for a bit we reckoned we'd lose her, and it was then that I knew I had a fondness for her. My best Dutch cow calved the very same day . . . but I stayed by Alison, though John had fetched the doctor and I wasn't needed all that much.

The baby wasn't the poor pingling little thing I'd expected, and in a way braced myself to take and add to my load. A great lumping girl it was, and Alison said it must be named Phyllis for me.

Less than a year later Alison was in the family way again, and this time we all had hopes of a boy. Young Phyllis was doing well; the place was prospering. Things looked fair and pleasant for us, and then the blow fell. And what a blow it was!

Chapter Six

Along came Mr Turnbull one afternoon when I was just laying the oak logs to my smoke-oven to cure a couple of pigs and say he's sorry to bring me such tidings, but the fact is that Merravay, and all the land to it, do now by rights belong back to Sir Charles Rowhedge what fought for his lawful King.

We'd known, of course, that the King was back in London; good for trade that was, too. We knew owd Oliver–the tavern shutter–had been dug up and hung in chains . . . just like the witch in her writings said she had seen him. (A rare stir in Nettleton that caused.) But apart from the men what had signed the order for the owd King's killing they said nobody was to be punished . . . but I could see in the blink of an eye that Mr Turnbull, what had been a good business friend to me, thought it right and fair that I should be cast out of Merravay . . . and if that wasn't punishing!

'But I paid for the place. All legal and above board.'

'Ma'am,' he said, 'you made a token payment to them as had no right to sell. Count yourself fortunate,' he said, 'that so small a sum was involved. There are those in England today, thousands of them, especially in the West Country, who are going to lose property for which they paid the full market price.'

'Lose it? You mean just go away and leave it . . . have nothing.'

'Not perhaps so precipitately as that. Sir Charles, who has been engaged in the nutmeg trade in the Dutch East Indies, has arrived in Amsterdam, from whence he has written to me. I have written to inform him of the–er–position, and he will probably come to see about things for himself. But I thought it only fair to warn you that Merravay is no longer yours. . . .'

I set the logs right and closed the door of the fireplace, opened the oven and saw the smoke flowing smoothly through. I took up one half-carcass and hung it carefully on the hooks. Two pigs . . . four sides of bacon . . . mustn't waste or fumble . . . they at least were *mine*. But I felt sick.

'You have done well out of your venture, taking it all in all,' said Mr Turnbull, as though he was chiding a child for sulking when a treat was over.

It was true, I'd made profits; but they was all out there, walking about, eating their heads off, past profits carefully bred back to make future ones . . . it'd have been better if I'd bought meself diamond rings, or stuffed money into a mattress. Cut the ground from under me, and my stock was nothing but a liability–or so much dead meat!

I shut the door of the smoke-oven very carefully so as not to check the flow.

'I sincerely hope,' said Mr Turnbull, 'that you will be successful in finding alternative accommodation. You are lucky in having had a little warning . . . I have heard of others less fortunate.'

But what comfort was that to me?

There followed another bit of my life that I don't ever want to think about.

One thing that made me mad was that when those who'd sided with the King had held on and been fined and sold some land to pay the fines the people who bought that land weren't to be turned out. Not far from us the Hattons had been fined and sold a bit of the Mortiboys estate, and the man who bought that was reckoned legal owner still. I'd bought Merravay at bargain price, that I'd never deny . . . but it was the best price Fletcher and his friend could get. I'd bought it, bought it . . . worked and slaved over it, put my money back into it, and I had less rights than a squatter. It didn't seem fair. They talk about angels in disguise; Captain Fletcher was the Devil got up to look like an angel, so far as I was concerned.

Still . . . I plucked meself together again; it was no use setting down and crying. I took a sharp look at my stock, and I knew there was two things I must, at all costs, save out of the wreck–my brood mares and my Dutches. The mares had a story of their own. Lady Alice Rowhedge had done her riding on a famous black stallion; and after she was tried there was talk about killing him, but Mrs Blackwood, who was Rawley's daughter by his first wife, took the animal away to Muchanger. There she was the only one with a good word for him; he behaved like the Devil, savaging stable-boys and always trying to break out and get back to Merravay. Maybe he started the stories of Lady Alice riding that bit of road.

When I first went to Merravay I bought, cheap as I could, a work mare that was owd, had had a hard life and was past all foolery, you'd have said. My John, who was good to dumb beasts, fed her up and fussed her and she got right frisky, and one fine morning we found her and the witch's stallion in the meadow together. In due time she dropped a foal, a mare, that was a rare freak, because put to a work horse she'd give you one twice her own size, heavy and solid out of the ordinary, and put to a riding horse she'd drop something lighter and swifter and more shapely than was ever seen in our parts. Whatever went into her came out *more*; if you'd put her to a jack ass she'd have handed you something with ears a yard long. I'd reared two of her foals, one heavy and one light, and they'd dropped some extraordinary young 'uns, the heavies heavier and the light 'uns lighter than any ever known. I meant to howd on to them two mares come what might.

Then there was my Dutches. They had a story too. While old Oliver was still fighting the Dutch one of their ships was brought into Bywater. The captain had had his wife and child on board, and he'd got a cow and her calf too. They was for sale–by orders of the Mayor of Bywater–one day when I happened to be there; and lots of folks had gathered round the pen to see them, they being curiously marked, pied, black and white. I noticed that when the calf–a heifer–had suckled its fill the cow's bag wasn't half empty, and I thought–Thass a good yielder. I made up my mind that if the bidding wasn't too sharp I'd try for the pair myself. And though folks had come to stare few made bids for animals they didn't reckon to be a canny colour, so I got them cheap; and then, keeping a sharp look-out, I heard of a man called Stebbing, in the Yarmouth trade, that had brought a cow and a bull of the same kind back from one of his voyages; and I swopped the bull's service for my heifer calf, and for a year or two we went hither and thither till I had a herd. He never got one because most of his animals died, eating yew.

Dutches give more milk, and more cream to it than any kind known, and I could ask almost any price I fancied for a heifer calf.

So the first, the least thing I must do, knowing I was to be chucked out of Merravay, was to find pasture and shelter for my Dutches. And till I began to try that I never knew how much people was against me. No! No! No! Nobody'd rent me house room.

In the end I was so desperate that I thought of Strawless Common. So I went out there and tried; but there wasn't a cottage to let and the grazing rights went with the cottages, and the rough lot that lived there said if I put my beasts on it they'd stone 'em.

It was coming home from Strawless that I heard the witch laughing.

I ain't a fanciful woman, as I'd proved; but I hadn't ate for days, nor slept for many nights, and I was ill with worry. For many a long year I hadn't given the witch a thought, except that now and again, with my broody hens setting in her big hall and my motherless calves sucking gruel in her withdrawing room, I'd thought–Ha! And it's me and my boy and my creatures that hev Merravay now!

And now she was laughing at me. Her boy was coming to drive me out and I couldn't find a corner for my mares and my Dutches. Them that laugh last, laugh loudest . . . and she was laughing last. And I heard her, just like she used to laugh when she was little and could get away from her Granny and come out where I was getting the geese ready.

Hearing the laugh, it struck me I was going crazy, and small wonder. Alison I couldn't bring myself to tell, her being in the state she was; John was gone to London, all ignorant of what was toward; there wasn't anybody that I could talk to.

I got back to Merravay, and there was Phyllis tied into a chair, and Alison, wearing a pretty apron, with a meal that I had no taste for, waiting. And she said, 'There's a letter for you, Mother Whymark,' and she took it from behind the salt jar on the dresser.

I took it and turned it about in my hands. I knew Mr Turnbull's seal. I laid it on the table and made a show of eating, feeling sick and sicker. . . . I knew what was in it . . . the date by which we must be gone.

Alison lugged Phyllis off to bed, and as soon as I was alone I broke the seal and looked at my letter. A date, I reckoned, might be set down in figures. But it was just a mass of words. I set there staring. Alison came back and began to gather the crocks.

'Leave them,' I said. 'Look, you'd best come and read this to me. But I don't want you to fret. I've known about this'–I tapped the letter–'for a week or so now, and I ain't yet worrited my way out. But I shall, my dear, don't you fret. Just read out what it say and let's know the worst.'

So she read it out. It was all a mass of long, learned words, but the gist of it was plain enough. Sir Charles Rowhedge had decided that he never wanted to see Merravay again, since he had heard from Mr Turnbull the details about his father's and mother's deaths. So he'd given the lawyer the office to sell the estate, either in whole or in parts. For the house and thirty acres now in my 'temporary possession' Mr Turnbull thought a thousand pounds a fair price and was giving me the benefit of the first refusal.

'There you are, my girl,' I said, when she'd done. 'That's what I've been living with these last weeks. We're homeless. And whass worse, I can't find a place for my Dutches!' Then I remembered the state she was in and that we was hoping for a lusty boy, so I pulled up short and patted her shoulder and told her again not to worry. I'd think of something. I'd manage.

And as I said that I heard the witch laugh again; and suddenly something went snap in my head. I knew I was walking up and down, up and down the length of the kitchen, beating my hands together and talking, talking, telling her everything that I had tried, the rebuffs I'd met with, the hatred I'd uncovered. I knew I was doing wrong, for Alison started to cry, and I turned on her and said, 'Cry. Go on. Be glad you *can* cry! I wish to God I could.'

Then she was taking me by the arm and pushing me into a chair. 'You must be calm, Mother Whymark,' she said. 'You'll wake the baby and drive yourself to distraction. We'll think of something. We're not ruined yet . . . Look, I'll get you something to drink. Something to put heart into you . . .' She walked towards the dresser and I thought she was going to get a mug and fill it with milk, and I said, 'It's kind of you, Alison, but milk wouldn't settle in me now. I feel right sick. But I'm all right. I'll steady meself.'

She stood by the dresser and laid her hand on the side of it and looked at me very odd.

'I couldn't help finding out,' she said. 'There was such a mass of cobwebs behind it that one day I got a man from the yard to shift it for me. You needn't have bothered to hide it from me. Working in an inn set me rather against it. . . .'

I didn't understand; and when I see her, what never could heave anything, take and try to shove the great dresser aside I was afraid she'd took leave of her wits.

'What are you doing?' I asked, sharp like, 'and what are you talking about? You come and set and calm yourself.'

She gave the thing another piteous little push and said half-crying, 'I can't budge it. You ought to have had more foresight and kept at least a little brandy where one could get at it.'

'What brandy?' I got up and went over to her quickly, calm and sensible again now that she'd gone distraught.

'The brandy that's in the cellar.'

'What cellar?'

'Down behind here. . . .'

'I never knew,' I said. I took and give the dresser a mighty heave, and there, sure enough, was a door, matted with cobwebs again. 'Christ in glory!' I said.

'I thought you'd put it there on purpose. I'm sorry . . . I've wronged you in my mind.'

'This dresser'–I gave it another bit of a shove–'was here when I come; I thought it was a fixture. Mrs Blackwood took the movable stuff. You say you been down there, Alison?'

'I peeped. I wanted to know what you were hiding from me.'

'Git a candle,' I said. I pushed the door and it give way; it wasn't locked though there was a great keyhole. A short flight of steps, made of red brick like the house, led down into the dark. Alison come along with the candle, and bidding her be careful I led the way down.

It was a great cellar, and as far as the light of the candle reached we could see the casks a-laying on the brick stillions and the bottles on the racks. I was dumbstruck. But I could see what had happened. Rawley had been fond of his liquor and had some connection with ships and foreign parts; when the war started he'd laid in stuff to last him a lifetime; and when the end come, somebody, some faithful servant, maybe, failing to lay hand on the key, had done the next best thing and shoved the great dresser in front of the door. And but for Alison's craze to root out spiders nobody'd ever hev known what was hid. So here it all was, French brandy enough to float a ship in a manner of speaking, and other things as well; wines from France and Spain and Madiery, and the clear fiery stuff that the Dutch drink. It was like some poor toper's dream. In one little bin there was even a lot of home-made stuff, cherry and damson and sloe brandy in pretty little flasks sealed with pig's gut; they gleamed red and purple like jewels in the candlelight as I hauled them out.

Rawley's gift to me, made all unbeknowst. That was the thought that went through my head. And there was a picture too; Rawley laying dead in his blood, the witch gone on her last wild gallop, the soldiers prowling through the house, and some foresighted creature shoving that dresser in front of the door!

And then it come to me what all this stuff was worth. With the King back and everybody wishful to make merry there was a great dearth of real good liquor in the land. Put with the mite I'd saved, what I could raise selling off stock, the price I could get for this wondrous store might just save us. And with that thought I come over all weak and wobbly.

'Ally, we're saved,' I said, and I leaned myself up against a cask and began to cry like a baby.

Alison turned and scuttled up the stairs, leaving me in the dark. And I thought of the witch laughing at me, just a minute since, and Rawley saving me. I'd allust known it wasn't just a lustful passing fancy he'd had for me . . . he'd meant me to be mistress of Merravay, and spite of all, spite of the spells and everything, it had come about.

Alison come back with a couple of mugs. She took up a bottle at random and very nimble knocked of its neck against the wall. She splashed some of the liquor into the mugs. It was Dutch snaps, and snap it did. It fair took my head off. 'Oh, Ally,' I said, when I got my breath back, 'if you hadn't been such a spider chaser!' And I started to laugh.

Chapter Seven

So the time come when we began to see the fruits of our labours. London kept growing and prices went up, and we was all ready to make the best of 'em. I was still working from dawn till dark–and beyond, but in such good heart that the work came easy. In the year 1670–the year when Alison bore her son at last (her second child had been a girl, called for *her* mother, Maud)–I had enough money and enough pluck to buy back the New Holding land from the Fennels. They'd put a lot of money into some wild-cat scheme for starting a company to trade against the big East India Company, and they'd come to grief and had to sell acres to get clear. And after that nothing went wrong for us; we was proper farmers at last, not just dealers and hucksters.

There was one more baby, another girl, named Agnes, who turned out just like me to look at but feather-brained. The owdest, young Phyllis, hadn't my looks, but she was most like me inside. A right dangerous little girl when she was young, for you had but to say, 'No, my dear, you can't manage that yet!' and next thing you knew she'd managed it, and stood there looking at you, a bit sneering. Long before she could reach the table she'd stand on a stool and make bread, grunting and clenching her little teeth and kneading away at the dough as if it was her enemy. Maud, the next one, I hadn't much use for, a whining child and jealous of Phyllis, who was two years older in age and twenty in all that mattered. The boy, called John like his father, came just right–when things was going well; he hadn't Phyllis's fighting spirit; very easygoing he was, happy and idle. Just the stuff to make a gentleman of.

Alison often said I spoiled John, and maybe I did. *My* John took and died the year after Agnes was born. He wasn't much over forty and there should hev been long years ahead of him; he'd never ailed to my knowledge, and the day he died he ate his dinner as usual. It got dusk and then dark, and in the end I went to call him to supper and there he was, dead on the stable floor with a bucket of water overset beside him. That was a sore blow to me; and it changed something inside me. All the scraping and striving didn't seem much good when folks take off and die young like that. He'd never had much out of life except hard work and hope for the future, and just as the good times was coming . . . So maybe I did pander to the boy, giving him what I'd hev liked to give his father.

And the money kept pouring into Merravay. There'd been two laws passed that did me a power of good. One kept out the cheap foreign corn, and the other kept out the cheap Irish cattle. In Ireland, I was towd, there's rain every day and the grass is knee high; the Irish put a bull and some cows in a field and they lay down on their beds and wait till 'tis time to drive the young down to the cattle-boats. Costing nowt to rear, they sold very cheap and was a thorn in the flesh to such as us. Owd Oliver was allust fighting the Irish, but he never had the sense to deal 'em a blow that way. King Charles did, and I blessed him for it.

I was able to lay money by now, as well as set the house to rights and send Johnny to a right good school that Alison knew about.

Alison came into her own at that time. Never in all my days had I touched a curtain, nor trod on carpet, nor seen any eating tools except a knife, a two-pronged metal fork and a horn spoon; I was more ignorant even than girls what had gone into service. But Alison knew all about such things.

I liked everything she bought, it was all good solid, handsome stuff, and I paid for it gladly. Johnny had to hev a proper home to come back to and not be ashamed; but feel at home in the rooms that Alison furnished I just could *not*. I felt I must walk on tiptoe and speak in a whisper. All them lovely shining things was mine, but they didn't know that, and there was no way of letting 'em know. They just shone at me, scornful.

And then there was clothes. All my days I'd worn a short skirt, well clear of the mud and dust, and a bodice with sleeves that'd roll up out of the way; on my legs I had knitted hose, and on my feet what was called in our parts 'high-lows'–higher than shoes to keep out the mud, and lower than boots to be easy to get in and out of. A good pair, well nailed, would last ten or twelve year and they shape to your feet; they get wet and fold in the right place, and though they seem as hard as wood they're a lot more comfortable than any soft shoe. But of course in my rig I looked what I was, an owd work woman.

That didn't suit Alison; so she bought a roll of plum-coloured silk and she made a dress. Lovely she made it, with lace ruffles and everything . . . Lord, if I could hev had that when I was a wench! But I was too owd. the waist of it nipped me so I had to breathe careful, and the skirt was so long and full that I tripped over it and nigh fell flat on my face.

The girls laughed and Alison got cross with 'em, fearing I'd mind. I just said, 'Unhook me, then I can laugh too.' For there is something good and comical in sparrers got up in pheasants' feathers. But I said, 'I'll wear it Ally; I promise you. 'Tis a beautiful gown and I thank you for sewing it. I'll lay it by and keep for the weddings.'

And then Ally said, in a bitter sort of voice that she didn't often use, 'Weddings! Where're they going to find husbands, I'd like to know?'

That was what we call a 'lickser', meaning anything–a question, or a job, or a situation–that hev you licked. There was Phyllis, on the plain side, mighty proud and masterful, handy and smart, she'd hev made any man a good wife. But what man? The poor was scared of us, the better sort scorned us. There we was, so far as marrying was concerned, neither flesh, fowl nor good red herring. No decent sort of farming man would hang round a plain girl, however good, for fear of being thought after her money. And I doubt whether Phyllis would hev taken a poor chap.

And there was Maud, a bit better-looking, but a misery and given to good works. Cracked on the parson, she was . . . but he was married well and truly, with six little 'uns.

And there was that good-looking scatterbrain Agnes without a thought in her head except horses–but it was early days to worry about *her*.

But the days mounted up; same as the pence that turned into pounds. And it come to the time when Johnny was finished at Cambridge and was coming home for good. Alison said, 'I just hope that he'll take an interest in the land and the stock. That is his only hope. . . .' She'd been ailing for a bit, so I was gentle with her and just said:

'Hope of what?'

'A happy full life,' she said. 'He'll have no friends here, will he? Nobody to talk to . . . associate with. And I'm so afraid that he'll turn to London, where any young man with money to spend is welcome and fussed over. . . . It's such a pity . . . because, given half a chance, he could fit in here so well.'

And I groaned to myself. I could send Johnny away and buy him an education and give him everything that was needed to make a gentleman of him. But there was no denying that once back at Merravay he'd be just the grandson of owd Phyl Whymark, who'd come from the tavern with her bastard, got Merravay for a song and made a fortune.

I said, a bit harshly, 'Ally, when I was his age I was hard put to it to keep myself and my child with food to eat. And I still reckon that two meals a day and roof overhead is the main thing to strive for. The rest is just trimmings! Either they come of their own accord or they ain't worth worrying about.'

But for all that, I was as glad as anybody when it turned out that Johnny wouldn't lack company for a while, at least; for when he come home that summer he brought his own with him. And what company too! Young Lord Thrapston, no less, that was son to the Marquess of Whardale–lucky for him to be born in the purple. for he was a nitwit if ever I see one. So far as I know he never did but one sensible thing in his life, and that was taking up with our Agnes.

Just at this minute he was in trouble; he'd got into debt and gone gambling, and his father, a very furious owd man by all accounts, had said he'd have his hide when next he set eyes on him, so he dussn't go home and had to go what he called 'to ground' till such time as his aunt, as was away drinking some special waters at a place called Bath, could get up to Leicestershire and talk the owd man round. So, without a roof to his head or a penny in his pocket, he was glad to accept Johnny's invitation to ride home with him and stay with us for a bit.

He wasn't like anybody we'd ever seen before. Since he'd gone to school and all that Johnny had allust seemed sort of frisky and nonsensical to me; but set aside his friend Toby, Johnny looked as sober and solemn as a Baptist minister. Still, daft as Toby was, allust larking about and laughing, he had a way with him, though not much to look at, too much nose and not enough chin; and I reckon that Johnny had warned him to look out for *me*, for he did seem to go out of his way to be civil.

He'd been with us three weeks when he had a letter from his aunt that set him whooping and halloing as though he'd started a fox. She'd talked his father round, as he had said she would, and he was free to go home; and I was looking forward to the day when he did, for Alison would keep me rigged out in the silk gown, and in place of my comfortable high-lows a pair of thin shoes, no more than slippers, in which my feet seemed to hit the ground cruel at every step. But he didn't shift and he didn't shift, and there was Agnes looking as mischievous as a monkey . . . and next thing I knew they was talking about being in love and going to get married.

Oh-ho, I said to myself, so the wind is blowing from that quarter again, is it? Well, it ain't going to blow Agnes what it blowed me! Maybe there's a body in Leicestershire clever with spells too! Though that weren't really what I feared–more the father and the argumentating, and maybe Auntie shedding a tear or two. So I took Agnes by the scruff of her neck and shut her in her bedroom, and I took his lordship and I talked to him like he'd never been talked to before. But he held he was serious- he'd never seen a girl like Agnes, he said, nor ever would again, and he was ready to marry her tomorrow.

'Then you'd best go down and fix things with parson,' I said, 'for next time you see Agnes will be at the altar at church!'

He said so long as I was willing for him to see her there that was all he arst, and he grinned at me cheeky and went and got on his horse and rode off hell for leather.

But he didn't come back and he didn't come back. And Alison cried and scolded me as if I was a babe, using all the long words she knew. She said that but for my interference all *might* have come right; I'd scared him off and ruined Agnes's chances. Johnny remembered hearing of somebody up in Norfolk that had a hunter to sell and took hisself off to get free of the unpleasantness. Phyllis and Maud went about looking smug and self-righteous.

After a bit I let Agnes out, and she was no mite concerned.

'He'll come back,' she said. 'And if he don't there's other fish in the sea!'

But he didn't come back, and I was priding myself that at least, thanks to me, there was no harm done and trying to make Alison see a bit of sense and make the other girls keep a civil tongue in their heads to Agnes for the whole of that week and the best part of the next.

And then he did come, bringing the aunt he set such store by with him. She was a widow, a Lady Pernherrick, very rich, and as odd as they're made. The main thing, out of the confusion she chucked us all into, that I remember is her looking Agnes over as if she was a horse she half meant to buy and saying:

'Hmmm, not bad; not bad at all. Time we had some new blood in our family. Getting very parrot-jawed.'

Agnes bore the scrutiny just right, looking neither shy nor saucy, nor put about; she'd been in the dairy when the owd dame arrived and was wearing her print dress open at the neck and rolled at the sleeves, and she did look pretty as a picture. Alison behaved very comely too, though fussed inside, I know. She got busy with refreshments, and Agnes said:

'Now, if you'll excuse me, I'll go back to my butter; it was on the turn.'

And his young lordship looked at me and said, 'With your permission, Granny Whymark, I'll go with her.'

Chapter Eight

After that, little by little, I began to loosen my grip on the family, though I kept howd of Merravay. It was partly the company that made me fall into the background. There was no lack of company once the news of the wedding got noised abroad. I fitted Agnes in the proper manner and I gave her six hundred pounds for a dowry; and you could see people think, as if their heads was glass, that what was good enough for the Whardale family might just about do for *them*. If it'd happened sooner I reckon Phyllis and Maud would hev got husbands too, but they was a mite owd and not much for looks, and there was allust a shortage of young men in our parts–among the gentry, I mean; and of course after Agnes's catch the others wouldn't look at nothing less. So the comings and goings and the match-makings all fixed upon Johnny. I'd hev been the last to grudge him company, but 'twas no use pretending that I took to the Fennels and the Headways and the Blackwoods, neighbours though they were and try as they did to suck up to me late in life and say I was a 'character'. When I was trying to hire a bit of land for my mares and my Dutches, and willing to pay whatever might be asked, they'd had no doings with me. So I never mixed with 'em, and kept myself to myself when there was parties.

There was a time when it looked as though Johnny might marry Miss Caroline Blackwood, and that give me a bit of worry. For they were cousins of a sort. Mrs Thomasina Blackwood was Rawley's daughter by his foreign wife; she'd had a lot of children, and Miss Caroline was the last of 'em. With animals I'd bred cousin to cousin, and closer relations too, many a time; but now and again I'd wake in the night and picture to myself Johnny marrying Miss Blackwood and bringing forth something not quite as it should be, a kind of punishment for me keeping my secret all these years. But there was nowt I could do except hope for the best, and things worked out all right. Johnny went off merry-making with Agnes and Toby and came back engaged to marry a young cousin of theirs. Poor as a church mouse she was, for her father'd been one of the King's men that had stayed and been fined heavy and sold land that had to stay sold; but she was a lady in her own right, which was one in the eye for the neighbours. I was mighty well pleased.

And, oddly enough, it was over Johnny's getting engaged that me and Phyllis had the nighest thing to a set-to that we ever had.

'I suppose you're *pleased* about this,' she said in a tight, sour voice.

'I ain't sorry,' I said. 'Somebody young and well-bred is what I allust hoped for for Johnny.'

'For Johnny!' she said in a wild way. 'For Johnny! That's all you ever think of, you and Mother. Maud and me could work like black slaves and feed in the kitchen like labourers, but the house must be set out for Johnny! Maud and me could work without wages and be grateful for a new pair of shoes so the money can pile up to make our brother a gentleman and he can marry a lady who'll despise us and treat us like dirt!'

'Howd on, now,' I said. 'I look to live long enough to learn her her place if she come treating anybody like dirt. While there's breath in my body I'm mistress here, and master, too, and don't you forget it!'

'But even you can't live for ever. What's going to happen then? Johnny'll have Merravay, of course; he's the boy, he's the heir! No matter that he can't tell a bull from a bullock and is wasteful and careless and brainless. Oh, I can see him, with his lady wife to help him, going through what we've sweated to store up like a knife through butter. . . .'

'Do we start measuring sweat, Phyl, I reckon I'm still a bit ahead of you. Naturally property go to the man that carry on the name and family–so it allust was, so it allust will be. Granted you've worked, good and hard, and been careful and managing and saving, and I been pleased to see you so. But 'twould be no manner of use you having the place, for you're another that can't live for ever, and you're a bare branch. . . .'

With that she bruk out crying, a thing she hadn't done since she was a toddler, and then only with rage. Cried and carried on, saying how unfair everything was, and that she'd give her whole life to Merravay and now was to be chucked out, and how I was taunting her with not being married. Finally I spoke to her right sharp.

'Here, that'll do, my girl!' I said. 'D'you take me for a fool? Thass right bad luck to talk of death and willing, but I'll tell you this for your comfort. Nobody but yourself'll ever chuck you outa Merravay. D'you think I'm one to forget how when you was a little mawther you'd help me with anything you could set hand to? You should know me better. Moreover, I ain't blind to what Johnny is; but he is as I made him, as I planned he should be. So I've made my will, all right and proper, and there 'tis set down by Mr Turnbull that you and Maud are to hev a home here at Merravay and one-quarter of the profits between you–and thass fair, for Johnny will hev a wife to keep and a family to rear, God willing.'

I'd made that will after a lot of thought and turmoil. And Phyllis's share had been part justice and part craft. I knew my Johnny and I knew my Phyllis too. She'd see her share didn't dwindle, and looking after part she'd be bound to look after the whole.

But was she grateful?

'I'd rather you left me something of my own, Gran. A bit I could make something of. Leave me New Holding; the house is half down, but it'd do and it's good land. . . .'

'But I've been scraping and striving all my life, Phyl, to get the land *together*; I can't go mincing it up. The more acres together the cheaper to work and the bigger profits. Why, girl dear, I mean to buy back the Slipwell land if ever 'tis for sale; I might live to see that day.'

'Buy back!' she spat at me. 'As though it had once been yours! Land and money, land and money, that's all you ever think of. I'm trying to talk to you about *my life*. If Merravay had been mine I'd have given my life to it; but it isn't and never can be! And I'm not a brick of the wall or an acre of land that you should treat me as part of it. All right, get your land, keep it together. And in the end you'll lay under it! Under six foot of graveyard clay, like the rest of us.'

The funny thing was I'd allust thought Phyllis was fond of me.

'Aye, so I shall. And I shall lay quiet and with nothing on my conscience about the way I've treated you, you young hussy!' I said.

But I wasn't really angry with her. She got her temper from me, and her land hunger. She was the most like me of the lot. But that was all the more reason for chaining her down.

However, as it happened, two things got together to make me think things over. One was that I couldn't take, try as I would, to Johnny's wife. She was pretty, with eyes the colour of bluebells and hair the colour of primroses, and she was small and sweet-mannered, but I distrusted her from the start. I could do with some gentry–Lady Pernherrick I'd truly liked and one or two more that came to the wedding. It was the woman in Lady Rosemary roused my gall; I'd have felt the same about her whoever she was, wherever she'd come from. Sly, a worker-round, and spiteful.

The other thing was that when Caroline Blackwood married somebody in the West Country her owd father and mother decided to sell Muchanger and go and live near her. An owd admiral wanted Muchanger but not all the land, so I seized my chance to buy Slipwell; and that brought me close to Mr Turnbull again, and one day I opened my heart to him.

'You know how I've left the main part of my property,' I said. 'But I don't feel right easy in my mind about Phyllis. I want her to stay here as long as is possible, but I can see trouble that might brew. If it so happened that her temper was too much tried . . . I'd like her to hev something to fall back on. But it mustn't be open . . . do she wouldn't try at all. And I want her to try.'

So he set his wits to work, and in the end I altered my will entirely. She was to stay at Merravay and hev her share as arranged so long as she wished. But if she married–I put that in for cover–or at any time decided to leave Merravay and break with Johnny she was to consult Mr Turnbull. And I left the New Holding land, not to Johnny, but to a trust until otherwise claimed, Johnny to pay a peppercorn rent which was to provide a harvest horkey for the workmen. It was all wrapped up in whereases and aforesaids and renewable tenures and conditional something elses, but he'd got it clear. If ever Phyllis and Johnny parted company New Holding would be hers. But she wouldn't know that till the break was made. So she'd stand still till the end and howd her own . . . I hoped for all their sakes.

With that done there wasn't much for me to bother about. So now I take things easy. When the sun shine I creep along to a sunny place between the porch and the jut of the house and just sit there. The garden hev come on wonderful; the stone pot things that once made handy feeding troughs for my beasts are set back on the wall and they're full of flowers, stiff tall things called tulips that come from Holland, like my Dutches. And over the wall there's a field of corn, doing well; thick and green with hardly a weed in it. And beyond that and to both sides 'tis all mine, gathered together with hard work and a bit of luck.

But I ain't as spry as I was . . . and often, time I've got meself out here and looked round and done a bit of thinking, I'm right glad to shut my eyes and hev a bit of a doze. . . .

INTERLUDE

The death of old Mistress Whymark–as she had come to be called in her later years–caused hardly a ripple. She was immensely old and had been, for some time past, feeble of body and inclined to wander in her mind. Her last will and testament gave pretty proof of her senility.

She was not forgotten. Her achievement took its place in the folklore of the neighbourhood and was often mentioned as an example of what sheer hard work and tenacity of purpose could do. Her name was generally mentioned with respect; money was money, after all; and in that period of wild and often fatal investments, when so many fortunes vanished overnight, the possession of solid money and untrammelled acres attained an enhanced importance.

The old woman's shrewdness and driving energy appeared to be passed in greatest measure to her eldest grand-daughter. Mr John Whymark was careless, good-natured, open-handed and convivial, and much–particularly in the early days of the marriage–under the thumb of his pretty wife. Miss Phyllis Whymark adopted an attitude of opposition which in time became almost involuntary.

In any dispute about management and husbandry she had one strong ally, her dead grandmother; and she could always say:

'But I can't allow that. That would jeopardise Maud's share and mine. I must guard our interests.' Also it became increasingly plain that when Phyl's judgement was respected things prospered; when she was crossed they tended to go wrong.

Accepting her authority in most things, Mr Whymark, nagged by his wife, sometimes defied her over matters of personal expenditure. 'God knows what you do with your money, Phyl, surely I can do what I like with my own!' The most contrary thing he did was to plant an avenue of lime trees and turn two good fields into parkland. Miss Whymark, having invoked Granny's name in vain, with a monotonous mention of turning in graves, actually wept over the waste of good ploughland. She avoided the avenue, and on the rare occasions when she went to the village she would plod on foot across the fields and emerge near a miserable little holding called Church Farm, from whose few acres a man named Fulger wrested a poor living for himself and his family.

There she would sometimes see a thin lanky boy and a thin small girl immensely busy at tasks only just within their capacity to tackle. The sight gave her peculiar pleasure. So young, so hard-working, they would get on in the only way which Miss Whymark valued–Granny's way.

Then one day, on skirting the yard of the smallholding, she heard sounds of merriment. The ertswhile admirable Fulger children appeared to have acquired a very beautiful little pony with a fine saddle and harness.

More spoiling, thought Miss Whymark, quite sadly; and she walked on, wondering, as she so often did these days, what the world was coming to.

EPISODE FOUR
Early Georgian

THE GOVERNESS

Chapter One

The first actual money that Luke and I ever earned was sixpence a week for enjoying ourselves, and that was in May of the year 1720. Luke was twelve then and I was ten, and we'd both been hard at work for as long as we could remember, but we'd had no wages–nor looked for any, until the day when Father came home and said:

'Old Mrs Maybrook called me across the road today as I came home from the smithy. That child is to have a pony and it is to be stabled here, there being no room for it at their place. She'll pay two shilling a week for its feed and grooming and you two'll tend it. You'll have sixpence a week–to save.'

'How'll she buy a pony? Through the parlour window?' Mother asked.

Years and years of being married to Father hadn't quite got Mother out of the way of making little jokes. I could see the point of that one, and if Father hadn't been there I should have laughed and Mother and I would have gone on wringing the last bit of fun out of it. The point was that in the whole three years that the Maybrooks had lived in Nettleton nobody had ever seen Mrs Maybrook out of doors. She'd moved into Ivy Cottage, a very gloomy little house near the church, and there she lived with a surly old maidservant and a little girl–about my age–who was reckoned to be her grand-daughter. Anything to be done out of doors the servant did, but now and again when she was ill Mrs Maybrook would rap on the parlour window and attract somebody's attention, then stand back in the shadow and give her orders and presently put the money on the window-sill. The old man who sometimes did a day's work in their little back garden said she acted the same way when she gave him his directions; he said it was because she was so pocked she didn't look human.

Everybody was sorry for the child. Even Luke and I, who worked hard and were often scolded and punished, wouldn't have changed with her, cooped up in that dull house with two old women. It was nice to think she was to have a pony.

I don't know how Mrs Maybrook managed it, but it came within a week, and it was as pretty and dainty as a lady. Luke and I fell in love with it at first sight and gave its toilet far more attention that we gave our own, which was apt to be scanty, especially on cold mornings. We harnessed it up and tried it; we'd never ridden a proper saddled pony before. It was just my size, but Luke, who was very big for his age, looked like a duck's egg in an ordinary egg-cup. I told him so and we both laughed, and Father put his head out of the barn and said, 'Stop that foolery.' He always feared that if you were laughing you were wasting time.

'And,' I said softly, when Father had taken his head into the barn again, 'you look a bit like Jesus on the ass's foal on Palm Sunday.'

Luke said 'Shush', very shocked. But it was true. In those days he had a sweet, patient, long-suffering kind of look, and that, with his clear grey eyes and mass of light brown curly hair, gave him a saintly air, as if he didn't quite belong to this world. He was a proper Fulger; Father must have been very handsome before hard work and bad temper scored the lines on his face. I took after Mother, small and brown-coloured, and lively and merry–when we were let to be.

The afternoon came when the old maid from Ivy Cottage hobbled along to our place, holding Luella by the hand. I'd seen her before, of course, but never close to, and never dressed up as she was that day. She had proper riding clothes, made to her measure–dark-green velvet they were–and a little hat with a feather. In her hand she carried a small crop with an ivory handle.

Luke and I always kept the pony fit to go into a parlour, and in a moment we had it saddled and let it out, very proud.

'There you are, love. There's your pony,' said the maid.

Luella did not move forward; she stood there looking timid and reluctant.

The old woman turned to us and said, 'Now don't you let her fall off, or the creature run away. And bring her back at four, up to the house. I can't come out again.'

Luke looked at me; so, though I was a girl and the younger, I had to speak up.

'We were told to look after the pony. We can't take her out on it. We both have jobs to do.'

'Your father about?'

'He's ploughing. If you want to ask him you must go to him and don't speak till he turns at the furrow's end.'

'You're sharp!' she said, with disfavour. 'Mind you don't cut yourself!'

She stumped off and I looked at Luella.

'Most likely he'll say no, so you'd better let us help you on now.' She looked at me and at the pony and at Luke, and then back at me again; then she said:

'To tell you the truth, I'm rather scared of it. This wasn't my idea at all.'

That was the first time I had heard her speak, and for a moment I could only stand and go on hearing her voice after it was silent; she spoke so clearly, with such sweetness, the words coming out so gently and yet so firmly. I could hardly bear to use my own voice after that. I said, as coaxingly as I could, but sounding gruff and rough all the same:

'There's nothing to be scared of. It's easy! Look, shall I show you?'

I scrambled on to the pony and rode round the yard.

'He's as gentle as a lamb,' I said.

I brought him to a standstill near her and hopped off.

'Now you try.'

Luke spoke for the first time.

'I'll set you up,' he said, and came forward.

I held the pony's head and Luke went to lift Luella. Immediately the pony pivoted sharply, so that Luella almost fell with Luke atop of her.

'Now, no fooling about. That ain't what you're paid for!' said the old servant, hobbling back. 'Yes, thass all right; your dad was sensible. So just be careful. There's no need for her to be venturesome; she ain't going to be a jockey.'

With that she departed. Later on, when I knew the Maybrook household better, I realised that this incident was very typical. There was the care and the carelessness side by side; the pretty pony, the elegant clothes, the escort to our yard; but whether the pony were gentle or vicious, Luke and I fitted or unfitted for responsibility, nobody bothered to ask.

Chapter Two

That was the beginning of happy times for us. Over the plough handle Father had bargained, sixpence an hour for our time. ('I never reckoned Father rated us that high, boy,' I said to Luke. 'Just think what we earn in a week!')

It was a mercy we weren't paid for results, for Luella never did master the riding; to the end it took both our efforts to get her on and less than nothing to topple her off. And the pony was no help. He was an angel with Luke and me, and a devil with her. But once she got over her first fright of him she didn't mind; she'd laugh and say 'You ride him' to whichever one of us was due for a turn, and then, with the other, she'd play 'Tag' or 'Granny Grumble', or just saunter along and pick flowers. She'd never had any young company before and seemed to cling to us; when we parted she'd watch us out of sight and keep waving and calling.

Towards the end of September that year there came a day which we, being hardy, called 'fresh', but Luella soon had a blue-white face and chattering teeth; so we took her off the pony and all had a good game of 'Tag' to warm her up: however, she caught cold and didn't come out for several days. Then one day the old maid came stumping along to ask if I could go and keep her company. Highly elated, I put on my Sunday gown and shoes and went to Ivy Cottage and spent the afternoon in a paradise of dolls and draughts and dominoes and musical-boxes. That day I didn't see Mrs Maybrook; the servant brought tea and cakes to the room we played in, and we drank the tea from the dolls' cups and cut the cakes into tiny pieces to fit the little plates. I'd never spent such an afternoon in all my days and went home dazzled.

Soon after that there was another message from Ivy Cottage. I saw the servant arrive and leave, looking utterly disgusted; and waited, with my heart in my mouth, to know what she had come for. Nothing was said that day, but when Luke and I were in bed I could hear Father and Mother threshing something out in the kitchen below, Mother's voice quick and eager, Father's slow and grumbling.

In the morning Father said to me, 'Tuesdays and Thursdays you get up early and do all your jobs and then go along to Ivy Cottage; and mind how you behave.'

It was not to play, this time; it was to have lessons with Luella's governess, Miss Pelham. They thought Luella would learn better if she had company.

Luke, seeing me off, said, 'Dog's nails! I wish I could come too!' (In the old days people used to say 'God's nails' when they wished to be emphatic and 'Damnation' when they were annoyed; now, because of chapel and the text 'Swear not at all', they said 'Dog's nails' and 'Tarnation' instead.)

Although Luella had chattered freely while we were out together she'd never said anything about her home, and we'd never asked any questions; and it was quite a surprise to me to discover that Mrs Maybrook was not her granny but her mother. Mrs Maybrook was very little older than my mother; it was the scarred face and widowed way she dressed that made her seem so elderly. But the mystery remained, even when one was close to, almost part of the family. It took me a long time to gather, bit by bit, that Luella's father and brother–a good deal older than she–had both died of the smallpox which had ruined Mrs Maybrook's looks; and that Luella had only escaped because she was put out to nurse. I knew enough about things then, even, to know that only rich, fashionable people put their children out in that way, and the idea didn't go alongside the dull little house, the one servant, and Mrs Maybrook's clothes, and other evidences of very modest means. At the same time, everything in the house was on the rich side, velvet curtains and silver things and such; and once, when Luella and I were playing 'dressing up' and she was a princess, Mrs Maybrook let us have things out of her jewel-box. I can believe now that they were neither so many nor so wonderful as they seemed to me at the time, but it did seem strange to me that she should have rings and brooches that she never wore, and only one cross old servant and a man odd times for the garden.

She had a voice exactly like Luella's, but with sad notes in it; she was a sad creature. There were times, though, when she was different. Now and then, on those winter afternoons when Miss Pelham was ready to go and catch the coach back to Baildon–it touched Nettleton on Tuesdays and Thursdays; that is why the lessons were on those days–Mrs Maybrook would drift in, carrying a square bottle with a gold pattern on its sides and two little glasses that matched.

'You must have something to keep out the cold, Miss Pelham,' she would say. Miss Pelham would say, 'That is very kind of you', and take her glass and sip daintily. Then she would go . . . and times, if the road was slippery or there was anything to carry, she would take me with her, which Luella and I hated . . . other times I could stay for a little while; and then Mrs Maybrook would fill her glass again, and again, and grow merry, telling us funny stories and making jokes and imitating everybody, even Miss Pelham; not unkindly, but in the funniest way. Then her voice lost its dreary sound and was like music. She could say my name, 'Deborah', so that it didn't sound plain at all. I used to sit there, listening to her and thinking what a shame it was about her face, and how she was paying me to play and to learn, which I'd always wanted to do. (Father had asked a shilling an afternoon for me, though I still did my work at home!) And for Christmas that year she gave me a red woolsey dress.

Then the spring came and the outings started again. I was glad for Luke's sake, because, although I always told him every single thing that had been done or said at Ivy Cottage, he had felt cut off.

One morning, late in April and lovely weather, Luella said, as we heaved her on to the pony:

'Let's go to Merravay.'

That suited me, because Merravay lay near to the woods, which, I'd heard tell from children with more time for idling, was a famous place for flowers. I ran to get a basket, and when I came back I found that Luke had turned the pony's head towards the fields.

'It'll still be a bit miry at Vinefields Bottom, Luke,' I said. 'Wouldn't it be best to go through the village and up at the front.'

'You couldn't get near. They've built a great wall round and put a gate with lodges. And two fields gone to waste planted with trees. Didn't you know?'

'Oh, I want to go *near*. I want to see the house,' Luella said.

'Why?' I asked.

'Oh . . . I've just heard a lot about it.'

'So have we–and nothing in its favour, eh, Luke?'

We had heard enough about Merravay. Within the living memory of people like our old Great-aunt Hester, who lived with us, the Whymarks had made a fortune at Merravay, all out of sheer hard work; and the old woman who had done most of the work had lived to be ninety, so in holding her up as an example to the young the old people could very truthfully say, 'Hard work never killed anybody!' Sometimes when Aunt Hester droned on about it I used to think to myself–Maybe not, but hearing about it is killing me! Of course I daren't say it, and of course nobody ever did die of boredom or Great-aunt Hester would have been knee deep in corpses.

From our little field the ground sloped down to the swampy bit where the king-cups grew, and then up and up. We reached the top of the rise and were at the edge of a field of young corn. On its farther side was Layer Wood, and to our left, slightly downhill, stood the house. Luella turned the pony and sat there, staring while Luke and I took a good look at the place about which we had heard so much.

It was a big house, with many windows and clumps of chimneys; the bricks of the walls and the tiles of the roof were a pretty colour, an orangy pink, like hawthorn berries when they first start to ripen. The colour showed up pleasantly against the dark green-black of two huge trees and the shining green of the lawns. But . . . it was just a big house.

'Oh,' said Luella on an outgoing breath. 'Oh. Yes, it is beautiful. Better even than I expected.'

She seemed quite overcome. So I looked again. The field at whose edge we stood was divided from the garden by a deep ditch that was like a long narrow horse-pond drained dry in a drought. On the house side the dip was topped by a low wall the same colour as the house, and along its edge there were some things like fir cones made of grey stone, and between each pair of cones there was a big grey vase full of yellow flowers–daffodils maybe. Back of the wall there were yew trees, like those in the churchyard but cut into shapes. All very pretty, neat, well cared for, but it didn't rouse in me the kind of excitement that came on me when our lilac tree bloomed, or when I thought of that distant wood full of primroses.

'Isn't it beautiful? Luke . . .' Luella turned to him.

'Lookit the stacks!' he said, craning his head. 'Eight, ten, and I can only see a corner of the stackyard. Dog's nails! And lookit the far side, out towards Slipwell. Beasts without number!'

'All got together with the sweat of the brow, lad,' I said, imitating as best I could Aunt Hester's voice. 'Do you work as hard you may do as well. Hard work never killed anybody.'

But the joke fell flat. They just went on staring. So I looked towards Layer Wood. Except for a few hawthorn trees that were freckled with green and some firs which stood here and there along the edge, the whole wood seemed to swim in a purple-pink haze as the swollen buds shone in the sunlight. I could just imagine how the pale tide of primroses shimmered under the trees.

'Oh come on!' I said. 'You've seen the house. Let's go to Layer.'

Luella ignored me, but Luke shook himself free of his trance and said, 'Aye, come on. Our time'll be up!'

'You go,' said Luella. 'I'll stay here.'

'And the pony'll run away with you as soon as we've gone,' I said petulantly.

'Oh, take the pony!' She dismounted in a way which, but for her smallness and lightness, would have been comically clumsy.

With me on the pony and Luke loping alongside we soon reached the wood; and it was just as flowery as I had heard it was. The primroses were huge, the biggest I had ever seen, and the most fragrant. Every stem was four inches long, and I made up my mind to borrow one of Mother's precious glasses, so that the pink tips would show, blushing and beaded in the water. In those days flowers meant a great deal to me, and while I gathered the primroses greedily I saw with delight that the bluebells and foxgloves and windflowers were coming on. It was like Heaven, only there the flowers, they said, never died; so how, if the primroses lasted the year round, the later ones would find room was a mystery. But I remembered that once, when I had voiced a similar perplexity about something I had heard in Chapel, Father had sternly bid me to bear in mind that with God all things were possible.

As we went back–Luke riding this time–we could see Luella standing just where we had left her.

'Can *you* see anything to stare at like that about the house?' I asked.

'Only the stacks. Thass a rare pity, Deb, that we ain't got more cornland. Still, I reckon I'll make my fortune out of beasts!'

As we pelted down towards Luella we called, but she only waved a hand and went on staring.

'She's daft,' I said.

'Daft as a hen with its head off,' Luke agreed; but his tone was tolerant rather than critical.

It took all our persuasions and finally mention of the scoldings and beatings that awaited us if we outstayed our time to get her to move, and when she did she looked back and said:

'I wish I lived there.'

'Why? It's so lonely,' I said, 'I'd rather live in *any* house in Nettleton. What d'you say, Luke?'

'Not *any* house, Deb,' he said cautiously. 'Say Squirrels, or Curlew, or Monks.' He named the three best farms in the parish.

'But that is a beautiful *house*,' Luella said dreamily. 'I shall come here again.'

'So shall I,' I said, thinking of the bluebells and foxgloves.

Yet, for one reason or another, we never did, though all through that spring and summer we had many pleasant outings; mainly without Luke, who, to his disgust, was kept at home to do 'real' work, though, so far as I know, Mrs Maybrook still paid for his time. Not that it mattered, except to Luke, for I was quite capable of managing the pony.

Chapter Three

Then came the winter day when both Luke and I fell victims of the sweating sickness which carried off more than a few that year.

Mother, who had great skill with herbs and simples, set about brewing one of her noxious remedies. It was market day and Father went off to Baildon, promising to bring back a lemon if he could find one not too dear. And then through my whirling throbbing head shot the remembrance that this was the day when I should go to Ivy Cottage for my lesson.

'You must let them know,' I moaned.

Mother said that with all this illness about they would guess, but my muddled mind had fixed on that, and I kept on till at last she said:

'Well, I daresay Aunt Hester could make her way there at a pinch. It's a straight road and everybody's gone to market now.'

Aunt Hester took kindly to the idea.

'Aye, I'll go. And I shall take some of my lace to show the lady.'

I was vaguely against that for no reason I could exactly name, but I was too grateful that she should go at all to say anything. In her youth she'd been a great maker of lace. I always thought that was what ruined her eyesight. She'd made so much that she still had furlongs of it laid away in well-chalked linen to keep it from turning yellow. It was sixty pounds, saved from years of lace-making and lent to my father, that ensured her a home with us. Even after her eyesight failed she had gone on peddling lace until some knave in Baildon paid her with a bad shilling. Now and again one of her regular old customers would come and buy a length out of the chest, and that was always a great day, but such days came seldom.

Mother said, 'Yes, do', and went on pounding away at the rosemary and nettle leaves with the rolling-pin.

Aunt Hester was so long on her errand that we had drunk the brew and were so muddled in our heads that I was never quite certain whether this happened or whether I dreamed it. . . .

It seemed to me that she came back, blundering as usual over the threshold and clinking some money in her hand and saying that Mrs Maybrook had bought a dozen yards of her best three point, and adding:

'I know something.'

'Say it then, say it. Can't you hear my calves blaring?'

'I know who old Mrs Maybrook is.'

'Well, we all know that!'

'Ah, but thass just what you don't know! She's Miss Blackwood, my Miss

Caroline that used to live at Muchanger.'

It seemed to me that Mother began to pay attention.

'How d'you know? Did she make herself known to you?'

'No, but I heard her voice. And I've told you a dozen times that the strength of my eyes have gone elsewhere, nobody hear like I do, and I'd know her voice anywhere.'

'You hear well, I will say. But if 'twas so surely we'd know. The gentry, the Fennels and the Headways, would all be around her for the sake of old times.'

'Ah, but they don't know. 'Tis only my ears know. She's come down in the world and lost her looks, but she crept home at the end, same as I should have done if I'd moved with the family that time. She never wanted to go, Miss Caroline didn't. . . .'

'Well,' said Mother, 'well, fancy . . . oh, them calves! All right, all right, I'm coming.'

It seemed to me that after she had gone Aunt Hester pottered about, muttering to herself about somebody who'd been treated badly, played fast and loose with, been homesick for years and now come home to die. And it seemed to me that presently she turned to me and said that this was a secret, not to be mentioned.

I may have dreamed it all, for presently I was riding wildly on a seesaw, putting a wreath of buttercups round our sow's neck, quarrelling with Luke about who should lick the honey-spoon, and a thousand other things which I can't remember at all.

Then I was clearly myself again, and Luke and I both had quinsies in our throats. And one day when Luke could speak he asked who was looking after the pony.

'The pony's gone,' Mother said.

'Gone where?'

'How should I know, child? A man came and took it away. Now you know as much as I do, so don't ask any more questions.'

It wasn't until we were almost well again that we learned that both Mrs Maybrook and the old servant had caught the sickness and–as Mother said, not having anybody to make them a good brew–had died.

'Then who sent for the pony?'

'The man mentioned Mr Turnbull. But it was your father he talked to, not me.'

'And what happened to Luella?'

'Mr Turnbull is looking after her.'

So that was the end of being paid to be idle and to have lessons. And most likely we'd never see Luella again. What a hateful world we had struggled back to.

One day I said to Aunt Hester, 'You were right about her coming back to die.'

'Who?'

'Mrs Maybrook.' But she pretended not to know what I meant; and then I could not be sure what I had remembered and what I had dreamed.

Chapter Four

Father worked harder than anyone I ever knew and had the worst luck. Nothing he ever did turned out right. When I was nearly thirteen we were so poor that it was decided to put me to service, a fate which, being the only girl in the family and always with a job in my hand, I had hoped to escape. I'd heard some horrid tales about the way servants were treated, and Aunt Hester's admonitions to me–and she should know, she had been in service all her life till her eyes failed–did nothing to reassure me. They were so much concerned with humility, and, truth to tell, I was at that time rather a proud little girl. I'd always been quick and handy and good at contriving, and sometimes even Father, who was quicker with blame than praise, would say, 'Let Deb try', when there was anything particularly tricky to do. Also I'd done very well with the lessons at Ivy Cottage; Miss Pelham knew who paid her, of course, and so refrained from comparisons, but Mrs Maybrook herself said my writing put Luella's to shame. I could sew neatly too, and I had once cherished hopes of being apprenticed to the dressmaker in Baildon; but for that one had to pay a premium and then earn nothing for four years at least. So it was service for me; and because Lady Rosemary Whymark happened to come–on Lady Fennel's recommendation–to buy some of Aunt Hester's lace for edging handkerchiefs and Aunt Hester happened to mention that I was in need of a place, it was to Merravay that I went as a kind of maid-of-all-work when I was just one month short of thirteen years old.

I'd been there six years and worked my way up to be Miss Sophie's personal maid, and even to do most of her ladyship's sewing, when I heard that the three young Whymarks were to have a new governess and that her name was Maybrook. I began at once to think about Luella.

In all that time we'd had but one bit of news of her. One day Luke had done a thing quite unlike himself, he'd gone to Mr Turnbull's office and asked about her. Mr Turnbull, Luke said, was very civil and kind and told him that she was at school in Epping, quite well and happy, and that he saw her regularly and would, on his next visit, say that someone who remembered her had inquired after her. 'But for all that he never asked my name,' Luke said. Sometimes, before I left home, he and I would occasionally say, 'Do you remember?' and Luella would come to mind. But for six years I had only seen Luke on my free day, the last Saturday of each month except December, and he was always busy and growing up so swiftly that our childhood, our shared memories, had fallen into limbo.

Now, hearing the name Maybrook, I could only hope that Luella hadn't been reduced by circumstances to become a governess . . . or that if she had she was not the one doomed to come to Merravay. I'd lost count of the governesses who had been there in my time, but I could say for certain that they had all been miserable. It was, without any obvious reason, a most unhappy household, full of undercurrents, changing allegiances, conflicting loyalties.

At first sight, and afterwards, down on my knees scrubbing and polishing, I thought Merravay a large house, but the whole of Suffolk would hardly have been wide enough to contain its inmates peaceably.

The master, Mr Whymark, was a very easy-going, good-natured man for nine-tenths of the time. He would shut his eyes and ears to the perpetual squabbles about him and often let them develop when a word from him could have quelled them. Then he would suddenly lose his temper with everybody, just and unjust alike, and stamp and shout and either fling out of the house or shut himself in his library and get drunk. Every time he did that the disputants would drop the original quarrel and begin blaming one another for upsetting poor John.

Lady Rosemary was that sad thing–a pretty woman who was growing old and resenting it. She still had eyes like frozen forget-me-nots and a great sheaf of honey-coloured hair in which the white ones hardly showed at all, but the skin round her eyes and under her chin was crinkled like young beech leaves, and she was too stout. Provided that she believed that you were devoted to her personally she was pleasant to work for, though tyrannical in her demands. She seldom lost her temper and could say the most waspish things in a cool, controlled voice. Once, they said, she had been extremely poor, but an uncle who had gone to Virginia at the end of the war had left her a good deal of money and a tobacco plantation, so she could afford to indulge her whims. Yet most of the rows in the house were concerned, directly or indirectly, with money. For living at Merravay were two Miss Whymarks, and the elder was parsimonious past all belief. Even my poor mother, who never had a penny to spare, was not so mean, so watchful, so worried over candles, logs, wasted crusts. Most people think of ruin as something which might, if they are not careful, come upon them some day; Miss Whymark faced ruin, and spoke about it, every day of her life. She also made constant reference to her Granny–the old tavern-keeper who had bought Merravay in Cromwell's time and whom Aunt Hester so much admired; Miss Whymark evidently admired her too and kept her memory green by acid remarks about 'the old days' and 'Granny's time', and the probability of Granny turning in her grave. For some reason which I never understood, Miss Whymark wielded enormous power, both within doors and without, and everybody went in dread of her. But there was this to be said in her favour: she was the same every day, and if you worked yourself silly, never answered back, never wasted a grain of salt or a half-inch of candle, you did at least know where you were with her.

With Miss Maud it was entirely different. She was just as queer–not with meanness, for she could be extravagantly generous, but with imagining that she was being slighted and insulted. Even over food. Whatever was carved she would cast sharp little glances at all the portions, and unless hers was ostentatiously the best she'd push it away, burst into tears and run off to her own room, where she kept great stores of sweets and cakes and a little outfit for making drinking chocolate. She was as susceptible to gross flattery as she was to imaginary insult and was forever taking sides, having favourites, carrying tales. Nothing was real to her, and for that reason she was very dangerous. Still, she did a lot for the Church and for the poor, of whom there were plenty, especially after Strawless Common was enclosed and the cottagers were turned off.

Of the eight children born to Lady Rosemary five had survived; the deaths had occurred to the middle ones of the family, so now two were fully grown and three still in the schoolroom.

Mr Roger was old enough to be soldiering abroad when I first went to Merravay. He came home during my third year there, invalided out of the army, looking very sickly and much older than his twenty-seven years. After staying at home for eight or nine months he went off to Virginia to see to some business in connection with the tobacco plantation, and he had stayed away. I had seen little of him; he was very quiet, though restless in the house, and well liked by those who came into contact with him.

Miss Sophie had grown to young-womanhood during my time; she was two years older than I. When she was older and more settled she would probably be considered handsome, for she had inherited her father's brilliant colouring and height, but she was too thin and awkward to be a pretty girl. She was clever in a way which was no help to a young lady of her kind; she read everything she could lay hands on and could talk about what she had read. Lady Rosemary checked and chided and snubbed her at every turn, and did her best to prevent her from reading; consequently Miss Whymark encouraged her and frequently snatched up the London papers as soon as they arrived and carried them off to her room, where Miss Sophie could read them undisturbed. This action was purely perverse upon Miss Whymark's part, for the whole world might have sunk under the sea or gone up in flames without rousing in her one flicker of interest provided Merravay remained untouched.

The three young children, Miss Julie, Miss Arabella and Master Billy, were, despite their material comforts, more pitiable than enviable, for around their innocent heads unpredictable disputes of ancient origins were likely to break out at any moment. They were pampered, scolded, admonished and cosseted by the four adult women according to mood or arbitrary situation. So they were growing up secretive and defensive, prepared to regard all grown-ups as potential enemies. Very often in the lapses between governesses it fell to my lot to take them for walks, while Miss Sophie took charge of their lessons, which she did very happily and efficiently. She had offered to take on the work permanently, but her ladyship scoffed at the notion. 'You don't need anything else to round your shoulders and screw up your eyes, dear,' she said. When they were without a governess they took their midday meal with the family, and the sessions at table were very trying.

One of them might leave a little scrap of fat on the side of the plate.

'We were told to eat what we were given,' Miss Whymark would say. 'If we had wasted good food things would be very different here at this moment.'

'Poor Julia is like me; I never could eat fat. Leave it, darling.' The indulgence in her ladyship's voice could not disguise its challenging quality.

'Well, let us hope these good times will continue, so that we can afford such fastidiousness. We should be ill prepared for a setback now, what with the waste of good food within and the waste of good land without.'

The grass had grown smooth over the fields that had been turned into parkland, and the young trees were branchy, but no resignation had grown over Miss Whymark's resentment at the loss of the arable land.

'Surely, Phyllis, the reason why most gentlemen's residences stand in parks and not in fields is to show that they can afford to spare a little ground.

And for the same reason there is no need for the children to lick their plates as though they were starving dogs.'

At this point the master would get up and go. Then Miss Maud, if she were at odds with Lady Rosemary, would make her contribution: 'Every time I go into the village I see *many* poor little children who would be only too glad to eat that meat. Julia dear, clear your plate in gratitude to God, who has provided so well for you.' But if she had fallen out with her sister Miss Maud would take a different tone: 'Really, Phyl, what a fuss to make about a little bit of fat! All the scraps go into the swill-pail!'

Her ladyship was then quite likely to say, with marked ingratitude, that the swill-pail was not a subject to mention at table.

With slight variations of subject and side-talking, this kind of scene would be repeated more frequently than anyone could believe possible.

The new governess–Luella or another Miss Maybrook–had the house by the ears some days before she arrived.

On a late January morning I was seated by the big window in Lady Rosemary's room, the one known as the Queen's Chamber. Her ladyship had attended a ball at Baildon on the previous night, risen late and was sitting by the fire, drinking her morning chocolate. I was mending a lace flounce which had been trodden on and torn. At the moment Lady Rosemary and Miss Whymark were allied against Miss Maud, who was vehemently supporting the rector over the tithes; and as a sign of the brief, uneasy allegiance Miss Whymark came into her sister-in-law's room and accepted a cup of chocolate.

'Johnny has a new bee in his bonnet now,' said her ladyship conversationally. 'He thinks that governesses don't stay because we are so unpleasant to them. He read me a lecture on kindness to poor creatures. For what it is worth I pass it on. . . .'

'If you have Miss Runackles in mind, Rose, I can only say that to me waste is waste, and the hussy who wastes in this house gets short shrift whether she is governess or scullery slut.'

'Johnny also thinks,' the cool voice went on, 'that the room we give the governess is dreary.'

'Perhaps he would like her to have my room,' said Miss Whymark very tartly.

'Well . . . of course he is very muddle-minded,' said her ladyship, not denying or confirming the possibility of such an audacious suggestion. 'But naturally I should never entertain such an idea. No, actually I intend to give Miss Maybrook Sophie's room.'

'But Sophie won't like that!' said Miss Whymark.

'No. But the move might serve to draw her attention to the fact that at Ockley there are eighteen bedrooms of which she could take her choice. I haven't told you about last evening! I was so infuriated. There we stood, having just arrived, and Sir Frederick came across to us, making it quite plain that he had been waiting for her. She said, 'Oh!' And what do you think Johnny did? Whisked her off into the dance, under the poor boy's nose. A father dancing the first dance with his daughter. There I stood, not knowing where to look or what to say. I was never more mortified!'

'Johnny isn't in favour of forced marriages,' said Miss Whymark in a voice that indicated that she, too, thought them obnoxious.

'What a strange term! *Forced!* It just happens that that poor infatuated boy sees something in Sophie that eludes everyone else. That he is the most eligible young man within fifty miles has hardly any bearing on the matter; he is the *only* man not entirely senile who ever looks at her. But I could see how dashed he was. A few more incidents like that and she won't have a partner at all.'

'She's still very young.'

'She's twenty-one. That may seem young to you, Phyl. To me it seems dangerously old. I've seen too many girls go right through the wood picking and choosing and come out with a crooked stick at last–or no stick at all.'

That was a direct challenge to Miss Whymark, for there was a legend in the house that both the old ladies had been very choosy in their youth.

'Well,' said Miss Whymark, very slowly and clearly, 'I should be sorry if you hoped, by putting Sophie in a poky room, to influence her attitude. For *I* have seen what happens when people marry for the sake of a comfortable home.'

That was a frank production of the well-gnawed bone. To my astonishment her ladyship ignored it.

'The one good thing about this idea of pampering governesses,' she said in a ruminative voice, 'is that it made Johnny see sense about the alterations. A house where the simple business of allotting everyone a habitable room causes such a commotion is obviously too small or badly planned. And when you think that one day Roger will bring a wife home, and that there are still two girls in the schoolroom . . . well, something must be done. Anyway, Johnny at last sees the necessity, and I am going to write to that man Kent this very day, before he has time to change his mind again.'

That put spark to tinder and started a row of quite extraordinary violence. The idea of altering Merravay came into direct conflict not only with Miss Whymark's parsimony but with her sentiment as well. Merravay had been good enough for Granny; it should be good enough for anybody.

They wrangled, entirely forgetful of my presence, for several minutes.

'For two pins I'd persuade Johnny to build an entirely new house, fit for civilised people to live in, and leave this Merravay barn to you.'

'Nothing would please me more,' said Miss Whymark, stamping off to take counsel with Miss Maud.

I had finished my work, but was wise enough to stay with my head bent and my hands apparently busy for a moment. Suddenly her ladyship became aware of me.

'Deborah,' she said, 'I am planning some changes. Daisy can do what is needed for Miss Sophie, and I want you to take charge of the schoolroom. I seem to remember Miss Runackles complaining that the food there was always cold and the fire unsatisfactory. We want Miss Maybrook to be comfortable, so that will be your main duty in future. Of course you will still have time to do things for me. Yes, that is a very neat piece of work, hardly detectable. Hang it away carefully.'

Her ladyship was going to keep her bargain; the new governess was to be comfortable. And poor Miss Sophie was going to lose her bedroom and her maid . . . Daisy was a heavy-fisted, hard-breathing halfwit.

The quarrel about altering the house went on, making itself felt in many strange ways. With Miss Whymark more violently economical than ever; with Miss Maud rushing out of the drawing-room one evening in tears, wailing, 'Little did I think when I used to get up in the dark on winter mornings that I should live to see . . .'

And finally with Mr Whymark standing in the hall and shouting at the top of his voice:

'For God's sake, Phyl, stop dragging Granny in. Bless her heart, *she* spent money on Merravay as soon as she could afford it. Why shouldn't I? And let me tell you that if she is turning in her grave it's because you're trying to make her out as damned mean as you are. She wasn't, by God, she was a riotous old girl! Though why the hell she fixed up such a punishment for me I shall never know. . . .'

Chapter Five

The day of Miss Maybrook's arrival came; it was a day when the coach did not run into Nettleton, so it was arranged that the cart from Merravay should go and fetch her from Baildon. But it turned out a pouring wet day, and at mid-morning Lady Rosemary decided to send the carriage instead. She had forgotten that this was one of the days when Miss Maud, carrying her own little locked tea-caddy, was to go and favour the rector's wife with her company, her criticism and advice, all washed down with the best Suchong.

At two o'clock, from the window of her room where she was changing her dress, Miss Maud saw Jack Lantern putting the horses to the carriage and screamed down that he was early, the fire wouldn't be lighted in the rectory parlour. Lantern shouted back that he was off to Baildon and would drop her on the way.

'That will not do,' said Miss Maud, and still wearing her shabby dress, with her hair in disarray and the tea-caddy clutched to her breast, she scampered downstairs, muttering that fifty years ago, when she had sat up all night dressing fowls for market, she'd imagined that she was laying up comfort for her old age. Was some chit of a governess to be considered before her now?

Her ladyship, appealed to by the coachman, said laconically that if she had said once she had said a hundred times that a place like Merravay should have three carriages, and it was entirely Miss Whymark's fault that there was but one.

Miss Whymark said of course the two errands could be combined; Miss Maud got into the carriage and said she should scream if it moved an inch before three o'clock. In the end it was decided to send the slow cart to Baildon after all, and the governess was expected to arrive, no doubt soaked to the skin, some time between six and seven o'clock. So soon after five I made a handsome fire in the schoolroom and the children settled down by it to roast chestnuts, gloomily speculating upon the nature and appearance of their new governess.

I was drawing the curtains when I heard my name called and ran down. Her ladyship was standing in the doorway of the drawing-room, with Miss Whymark close beside her. Halfway across the hall Miss Maud, just back from the rectory, was rubbing a few rainspots from the tea-caddy. Briggs, the footman, was just behind the screen, slowly closing the door and lingering to see and hear as much as possible. And just inside the screen stood Miss Maybrook–Luella, explaining, in the voice that took me straight back to childhood, that, having decided that she was not to be met, she had hired a post-chaise!

I have seen a flock of sheep with young lambs, all at variance with one another, turn, as one animal, to face a strange dog, drawing together, heads outward, presenting a united, defiant front. It was just like that. A governess . . . hiring a post-chaise . . . seven shillings . . . what was the world coming to?

Having told me to take Miss Maybrook to her room and then show her the way to the schoolroom, her ladyship backed into the drawing-room, followed by the Miss Whymarks. Briggs stuck his nose in the air and stalked into the kitchen to make his report. Luella and I stood face to face.

She was much altered. But for the voice–and of course the name–I doubt if I should have recognised her. I had always thought of her as a pretty little girl. Even making allowances for the effect that her clothes and her cleanliness, her smooth hair and skin had had upon me, I still think that as a child she was pretty. But all the prettiness had vanished. She looked at least thirty years old, pale and thin, hollow-cheeked and sharp-nosed. Her eyes were enormous, slightly prominent in their hollows, with thin, veined lids edged with long lashes and set under thin dark brows which ran from a little frown mark over the nose upwards and outwards to her hair. Her mouth was enormous too, deeply curved, with the lower lip turned out in a wistful, discontented, yet very sweet way. I stood and stared at her, thinking that if I had met her in a street and she had asked the way I should have told her, unknowing, and then gone on, wondering why I was suddenly thinking of Mrs Maybrook and Ivy Cottage.

'But you're Deb . . . Deborah Fulger, surely. Do you remember me . . . Luella Maybrook?'

'Of course,' I said.

'How lovely,' she said, and stretched out the hand she had ungloved. I had taken care of my hands, making excuses to myself about the impossibility of doing fine needlework with rough fingers, but as I put mine out to meet Luella's it looked and felt, for all my care with the goose-grease and witch hazel, as big and coarse as a ploughboy's. Hers was nothing at all. There was just nothing of her except those great eyes, that mouth and the voice.

'Oh, I am glad to see you again,' she said as I lifted the shabby little valise. 'I've thought of you and Luke so often. Those happy days we had. And then I didn't even say goodbye to you; you were so ill. I always meant to write to you; but I was so miserable, whenever I started to think about those days I just cried, so the letter never got written.'

'Luke once asked Mr Turnbull for news of you. He said you were well and happy.'

'He may have thought so. He wanted to, I expect. Men can believe anything they want to. Well and happy . . .' she said with surpassing bitterness. 'Still, I survived. And here I am. I owe that to Mr Turnbull at least. Deborah, what are they like? The children?' By that time we had reached the bedroom door, and I said, apologetically, 'I meant to light the fire, but I didn't think you could be here for at least an hour.'

She told me about the taking of the post-chaise.

'They all seemed *shocked.* Are they poor, Deb?'

'Heavens, no! The old one who stood in the doorway is fanatically *mean.*' I set the valise on a chair and went across to open the door of the clothes closet, which in this panelled room wasn't easy to see, and as I did so I told her a few things about the characters of Merravay's inmates and what to be careful of . . . 'that is, if you *want* to stay here,' I ended.

'But I do. Of course I do. It did seem the greatest good fortune . . . when I heard from Mr Turnbull I could hardly believe . . . I always so wanted to live here.' She made a funny wry face. 'In my innocent childish dreams, Deb, I used to plan that someone left me a fortune and I bought it; or I married a very rich man who bought it for me. I never saw myself coming here as a governess. . . . Still, here I am, and I must make the best of it. But that's enough about me. Tell me about you. Have you been here long, and are you happy?'

'Six years; and I'm *settled.*'

'And Luke?'

'He has the farm now. He's doing quite well. My father died very suddenly two years ago.' For some strange reason I heard myself saying aloud something that had been in my mind ever since Father died–something I never had said, or dreamed of saying, to anyone. 'We all thought he was vilely bad-tempered, but the truth was that he'd been ill for a long time and nobody knew.'

Luella had been bent over the valise. She straightened and turned to me.

'Poor Deb. Does that worry you? You mustn't let it. How could you know? Perhaps he was proud of not complaining. And, anyway, as far as I can remember, he *was* a cross man, well or ill. I used to shake in my shoes if he looked at me. And think how he used to shout at Luke, who was always trying so hard.'

That speech soothed a sore place in my mind. Father had grown more and more cantankerous and had made Mother and Luke most miserable. He'd sent me to service and took my wages every quarter without saying so much as thank you. When Aunt Hester died and left her sixty-pounds share in the farm equally between Luke and me he never even told us, and there were times when I felt I positively hated him. Then one morning he'd walked into the kitchen and said 'I feel queer' and fell on the floor. Mother could see that he was past her help, so she sent Luke full pelt for the doctor. Father was dead when he arrived; but he was young and curious, and there had been two cases in our neighbourhood where women were suspected of poisoning their husbands, so he stripped the body. He found a lump the size of a bladder of lard in Father's groin and said it was a wonder he'd kept on his feet, leave alone done so much work, because he must have suffered agonies.

After that I had felt very badly about the way I had felt towards him. I'd wake sometimes in the night and think of him, mad with pain and taking it out on Luke and Mother; and working on and then dying, like a sick horse. And I'd think how he'd never known any success, and never had a drink or any fun, not even a really good meal. It seemed pitiable and heartbreaking.

'I know just how you feel,' said Luella. 'One of my pupils died suddenly after being peevish all day and I'd chided him. Oh dear . . . I think of it still sometimes; though Heaven knows I paid for that! My next place was quite unbearable. So bad that I left without giving notice or waiting for my wages. *That* is why I wrote to Mr Turnbull; I knew he still had a little money left over, and I just asked him to send me some. When he sent it he said he'd heard about this job.'

We had not closed the door behind us, and now, far off along the gallery, I could hear Miss Whymark's stumping tread.

'I mustn't stand here talking,' I said, 'I'll show you the schoolroom. Then I'll light this fire and afterwards you can unpack in comfort.' As I spoke I thought how delightful it was to have someone to talk to at last; and how very remarkable it was that Luella should be prepared to take up our friendship where it left off, not a bit conscious, apparently, of the difference in our positions.

We met Miss Whymark just where a lamp hung on the wall, and as she was carrying a candle, and I was too, we could see one another clearly. I stepped back, and she stood and regarded Luella with cold curiosity. I felt that she had come up to see what prodigal act this extravagant taker-of-post-chaises had committed within ten minutes of her arrival.

'You look very young for a responsible post,' said Miss Whymark–surprising me. 'How old are you?'

'Twenty, ma'am; and I have had three years' experience.'

'You look delicate too.'

'Apart from a cold, I have ailed nothing since leaving school, where I had all the childish complaints–an advantage to a governess.'

'That is a highly unsuitable dress you are wearing.'

I had been a little surprised when Luella took off her shabby hooded cloak and revealed the dress. It was sombre in colour, a deep lavender-grey banded with purple velvet; it was not over-extravagant in style, but it looked costly.

'I'm sorry you should think that, ma'am,' said Luella in a voice which held interest, a trace of surprise, but no embarrassment. 'Lady Hereford gave me this gown, since I had no mourning of my own.'

'Mourning?'

'For little Lord Henry, who had been my pupil, poor child.'

Oh dear, I thought, this is a bad beginning; two titles mentioned so soon, and Miss Whymark had scant respect for the aristocracy. I waited for some scathing words. But when she spoke, after another long assessing look, Miss Whymark said civilly:

'Well, I have no doubt you are hungry after your journey. Schoolroom supper could be early this once. Deborah will see to it. Good evening.'

Unperturbed by the encounter and quite unconscious of her luck, Luella followed me to the schoolroom, where the children, counting upon a later arrival, were in the middle of their chestnut-roasting. They looked up guiltily.

'Hullo,' said Luella. 'You do look cosy. And what a lovely smell. Oh, chestnuts! Now how could you guess that I should be hungry?'

She knelt down on the hearth, holding her hands to the fire and turning her gaze almost gravely from one flushed young face to another. Some kind of trust was established immediately, for before I had finished drawing the curtains and making the table clear for the untimely meal they were peeling nuts for her and saying: 'Have this, it's bigger.' 'No, this, it's cooked all through.' 'No, this once, Miss Maybrook; I did it specially for you.'

Downstairs in the kitchen I found that Briggs had reported that the new governess looked harmless enough.

Chapter Six

Her ladyship had lost no time in sending for Mr Kent, and before my February Saturday was due (a day to which I looked forward most eagerly, because I could tell Mother and Luke about Luella) he arrived to look over Merravay and work out the best way to make it larger and more up to date. Such improvements had been in her ladyship's mind ever since she and Mr Whymark had visited the house in Leicestershire where the Miss Whymark who had made the fashionable marriage lived. Moreover, at Muchanger, a nearby house, a beam that was said to have smouldered for six months–which might be true, for it was solid oak and measured two and a half feet each way–burst into flame in the middle of a windy night and half the house was burned down. Muchanger had been rebuilt in the new style, and after that her ladyship had nagged and cajoled and finally bargained to get Merravay altered.

I saw Mr Kent arrive on a mild blue-and-white February morning. He was shabby, he looked awkward and surly, and he rode on what was plainly a hired hack. But I was interested in him, because, secretly practising my reading at every opportunity, I had saved old papers from the lighting of fires, and seen in one a brief account of a quarrel he had had with someone who employed him. And I thought him lucky to have been chosen by Lady Rosemary to work on Merravay, because she was a lady who was very much copied, and if he pleased her it was more than likely that he would be altering houses in Suffolk for years.

He alighted and then walked all round the house, staring, before he rang the bell. Then he went in and was closeted with her ladyship and plied with refreshments for almost an hour. The master, like Pilate washing his hands, had left the house early and gone to shoot at Mortiboys.

Presently her ladyship, with a lacy scarf over her head, went out with the architect, and they paced up and down for a while and then crossed the dip and stood in the field. Mr Kent waved his arms about and looked like a scarecrow in a high wind. And then he was back in the yard, wrenching the hired horse from the first good meal it had had in its whole life, poor thing, by the look of it, and off he rode, with his head sunk between his shoulders, and a dour, defeated look on his face. I guessed that he had failed to satisfy her ladyship, and I felt sorry for him.

But it wasn't that at all. From the conversation which Briggs overheard that night at table the truth drifted down to us. Mr Kent had refused to touch Merravay. He said that he had never before seen a house, particularly an old house, which his fingers hadn't itched to improve; but Merravay as it stood was perfect. He wouldn't touch it himself, and he hoped God would strike dead anyone who attempted it.

Here Briggs had the exact words to report. Her ladyship had said:

'So I said to him, "Mr Kent, houses are made to be lived in, not looked at!" and he said, "Aye, and paper is made for wrapping things; and there are shops in London now where they'll slap a pennorth of brawn in paper for you. But if some lout went to wrap my pennorth in a page of Shakespeare's sonnets I'd cry shame on him . . . as I do on you." Then he asked me who designed this house and said whoever did it was an artist. And then he went off.'

That was the first–I might say the only–time that I ever heard of a man sacrificing a chance of winning bread and butter, not to mention fame and fortune, for the sake of an idea. I still could not see exactly what was so special about Merravay, though I went to the top of the field and looked again, hard, earnestly. Nevertheless I could never think of Mr Kent, obviously poor and in need of a job, riding away from a promising, sizeable one because he didn't wish to spoil something he thought beautiful, without respect and a kind of awe.

Soon after that came the last Saturday in February, and, according to my habit, I left the house just before the midday meal. Since Father's death I had gone home more gladly, for Mother's merry spirit, never entirely subdued, had bobbed up again; and Luke regarded me as a shareholder in the farm. Mother thought, or pretended to think, that part of Father's trouble had been due to bad feeding, so nowadays she kept a good table; and, curiously enough, the extra outlay was not noticed, for in the very things where Father had failed, try as he might, Luke was succeeding.

I was hurrying home, thinking of the welcome and the toothsome dishes that awaited me, and of all the things I had to relate, when I met Luella and the children coming in from their morning walk. She asked me where I was going and said she would like to come with me.

'I'd like it too . . . but . . .'

'Oh, they have plenty to do,' said Luella. And they all three began saying what they should do–work on a sampler, mount and label a collection of winter berries, read. No other governess had succeeded in teaching Billy to read, but Luella had made him a book of his own, called 'William Whymark's Book'. It has pictures of familiar objects, with short sentences printed under them. The first picture was a little boy, lopsided of face; under it it said, 'My name is William Whymark. I am a nice little boy, and I will learn to read.'

'Run along, then. Don't make a noise, and have lots to show me when I come back,' said Luella. Falling into step beside me, she said, 'After all, teaching them to be self-reliant is part of the job.'

'You're very clever with them,' I said. 'Their other governesses seemed to hate the sight of them and yet were afraid to take their eyes off them. And always complaining. Not entirely without cause. They once put a frog in Miss Runackles' bed!'

'How detestable. I should retaliate with three hedgehogs if I could find them!' She linked her arm in mine. 'Will your mother mind my suddenly appearing like this? Oh, I do so want to see her, and Luke, and the place again. I always longed to be asked into your house. Oh, what a long time ago it all seems.'

We walked along briskly, talking of this and that. She said what a good thing it was that Merravay wasn't to be altered.

'It would just have been too ironic if they'd started to tear it down the moment I came back.'

'I confess,' I said, 'that I don't understand it all. What is it that attracts you so much?'

'Why do *you* love flowers so much?'

'I've never asked myself. I just love them. They're beautiful and . . .' I groped for a word which would express the inexpressible, handicapped by the fact that I was never called upon to converse about ideas. 'Well, silly as it sounds, they seem to *promise* me something. Don't ask what, Luella; I couldn't tell you to save my life . . . but it is true, just one flower can seem to promise something that hasn't to do with hard work, meals, making ends meet, being down to earth. . . .'

'That is it, exactly. All things that are just beautiful carry that promise . . . in different languages to different people. . . .'

'Promise of what?' I asked, half fearful.

'I should think . . . Heaven. Tell me quickly, Deb–when you think of Heaven what is it?'

'Layer Wood in every season at once,' I said without hesitation.

'Yes. And I think, "In my Father's house are many mansions" . . . all like Merravay. And the idea of many mansions in a *house* has precisely the same magic . . . other-worldly . . . preposterous touch as your every season at once. D'you see?'

We went on, walking and talking so fast that we made ourselves breathless. . . . Presently Luella said:

'Do you still read a lot?'

Despite my effort at control, the red colour flared into my face. My reading at Merravay was a guilty secret. I felt that the purloined key of the bookcase and the most lately 'borrowed' book, both safe under my bolster, must be imaged in my eyes, I saw them so clearly as I asked, uneasily:

'What makes you ask that?'

'The words you use, the way you put them together . . . that's all.' She was sharing my embarrassment. I realised that during this walk, with its delightful resumption of good-fellowship, I had forgotten to keep my usual check on my tongue. Guilt and secretiveness had now such a hold on me that I was careful never to use, in ordinary circumstances, any word that Daisy might not.

'Well . . .' I said, decided to tell a half-truth, 'yes, I do. After you went away I was at home for a year and I didn't see a written word of any kind. When I went to Merravay I was surprised to find that I *could* still read. So for practice I read the papers when they are weeks old and used for lighting the fires. And I write too. I copy pieces out of the paper sometimes, and I write what the weather is like and what flowers are blooming. But nobody up there knows, Luella, and I don't want them to.'

'Why ever not?'

'I might find myself in the schoolroom!' It was a stupid reason, but all I could think of at the moment. Fortunately at that moment we reached our yard gate and she had no chance to ask why I feared that fate.

Mother and Luke were astonished to the point of incredulity to see Luella, but delighted, too; and when the exclamations ended we settled down to what, I think, must have been the merriest meal ever to be eaten in that house. Since Father's death Mother had resumed her making of home-made wines–elderberry, cowslip, and blackberry–and now, with many apologies for their lack of maturity, she produced samples of all kinds and we grew very lively. Luella seemed to slip into place with unbelievable ease–even the silk dress did not strike an incongruous note. Only her voice, her clear laugh, did that.

We lingered over the meal, and then Mother and I went into the backhouse to do the dishes. Luella offered to help, but Mother would not allow that, and we left her with Luke by the fire. After a few minutes Luke put his head and one arm around the door and picked up the wooden pattens which Mother used for walking in the yard.

'I'm going to rack up now,' he said, 'and Miss Maybrook wants to come with me. I'll take these.'

From the unglazed hole in the wall that served our backhouse for a window I watched them crossing the yard, Luella walking clumsily in the pattens and laughing at her clumsiness. At the miry part by the pigs' pen she stumbled and Luke took her elbow to steady her. Luke was laughing too, and I realised suddenly that I had never seen him really merry before. In Father's time he had been suppressed and subdued, and then, at a stride, he had passed to responsibility and the deadly seriousness that goes with ambition. But he was laughing now.

'She've turned out a lot better than I should've expected,' said Mother, dropping a pinch of wood ash on a greasy plate and scrubbing vigorously. 'To tell the truth, I allust thought she was a mite dim-witted.'

'Ah, that was because she couldn't manage the pony,' I said, thinking that even then she had managed *us* and we had managed the pony for her. I looked back over the month she had been at Merravay–a whole month, and nobody, not even Miss Whymark, had yet found a word to say against her....

That evening Luke drove us back to Merravay in the cart. He and I were the best of friends. At Father's death he had told me that a third of the farm was mine, but I had always gone back on foot, feeling very cherished and privileged if he strolled with me, in winter, until the lights of the house were visible across the fields. It had never occurred to him to drive me, and in justice to him I must say that the idea of being driven had never occurred to me, either.

Chapter Seven

Quite early in March another architect, of whom her ladyship had heard a good report, came to make a visit of inspection. He was young and good-looking, well dressed and full of confidence. He measured and tapped, walked about the house and stared at it from various angles, and then retreated to the library to draw some preliminary sketches. When they were complete Miss Sophie borrowed them and brought them to the schoolroom to show Luella. I was there, and she invited me to see them too. She was well disposed to me just then because, though it was no longer part of my duty, I helped her with her hair and her clothes. I had, one evening, almost been caught doing her hair when her ladyship came in, suddenly, to tell her daughter which dress to wear; luckily I heard her voice and hopped into the clothes closet and hid myself. Afterwards we laughed almost hysterically together and some sort of barrier fell and never went up again. Luella also helped with the constant titivation of the wardrobe–even her ladyship would ask her advice; for with Lady Hereford Luella had lived in London and had opportunities to see the ladies of fashion.

So now we all three bent over the sketches as though they were dress patterns. I could see at a glance that Mr Armitage's alterations were to be fundamental; the house's new face was to be flat, with many windows set in rows, and instead of the deep old porch the new door was to have a pillared portico.

'I tried not to like it,' Miss Sophie said. 'Poor Aunt Phyl is so upset because what she calls "Granny's Garden" will now be built upon; and the window tax will be calamitous. But now I have *seen* it . . . Don't you think it is impressive–and so well designed?'

'It would be fine on any other house,' said Luella. 'I shall go on hoping to the very last minute that something occurs to balk these plans.'

'Well, nothing will,' said Miss Sophie in a pleased way. 'Mama is delighted with them, and with Mr Armitage. . . .'

Two evenings later, after the architect had ridden away, Mr Whymark came to a belated realisation of the extent of the alterations planned, and once again there was no need for us to wait for Briggs or Parker to bring news from the front of the house to us in the kitchen. The master, really angry and a little flown with wine, could make himself heard at Slipwell.

Where, he demanded to be told, was it proposed that they should live while the whole of the front of the house was pulled down? Yes, he knew he had promised, though how the devil he'd been such a fool he didn't know; but he'd only meant a couple of extra bedrooms and new doors and windows if she set such store by them. Live in a house with no front he would not!

There was then a babble of female voices, the words indistinguishable, and then the master's voice again.

'You keep out of this, Phyl,' he roared. 'All right, you agree with me. I don't want your blasted agreement. It's this everlasting pull devil, pull baker that's been the ruin of this house. Am I never to have any peace? It's a bit late in the day to point this out to you all, but this is *my* house, and you'd do well to remember it. All of you. Parker! Bring a fresh bottle to the library!'

And it was then, according to Parker, that the door opened and Mr Roger walked in, saying:

'This sounds just like home!'

He had always looked old for his years, and he had aged considerably in the two and a half years he had been away. A wig was now more to him than a sign of rank or mark of fashion, it was a necessity. The yellow-sallowness of his skin had darkened and his face had fallen into grooves and lines–all melancholy; he looked rather like a hound. But he had a smile of singular sweetness; it was not merely a stretching of the lips and a brightening of the eyes, it was a lighting up, a rearrangement of his whole face. My work, of course, did not bring me near him, and Merravay, despite her ladyship's complaints, was big enough to allow two people under its roof to meet by accident very rarely, but on the few occasions when I did see him I found myself waiting for that smile, the sudden flash of sunshine in a sombre sky; it reminded me irresistibly of Mother's wryly merry looks behind Father's back in the old days.

Mr Roger's arrival did a good deal to console her ladyship for the blow dealt her over the alterations. For four or five days everything was pleasant and lively and excited; parties to celebrate Mr Roger's safe return, and reciprocal parties in other houses. And then everything changed.

For all this part of the story I had to rely upon what Luella, coming home with me in March and April, could report.

Mr Roger had gone to Virginia, it seemed, because the overseer of the plantation–sometimes called the agent too–had died and it was necessary to appoint another person, completely trustworthy and knowledgeable. That was soon done, but by the time it was arranged Mr Roger had become deeply involved in the business of slaves and slavery. When he had learned all there was to learn about the slaves on the plantation, which would, one day, be his own, he had set out and visited dozens of others–places where rice was grown, and cane-sugar and cotton.

What he had seen and heard appalled him. He had all the facts set down in a number of little black notebooks; the numbers of slaves on various plantations, how many died, were bought, sold, born each year; their weights, their rations, hours of work, diseases and punishments. He had come back to England with all this carefully gathered and meticulously recorded information, and with the staggering but firm intention of trying to have the whole system abolished. He began by offering her ladyship a paper upon which she had only to write her signature and the two hundred slaves on her Virginian property would be free. That must be the first step, he said, because it would be a hopeless handicap to his campaign if people could turn round and say that his mother was a slave-owner.

Legally–as Luella pointed out to me–her ladyship, being a married woman, owned nothing; but in point of fact Mr Whymark had always refused to have anything to do with the American property. I imagine that he resented it because it had made his wife independent, able to follow her whims. He now pursued his established course. To Mr Roger, when appealed to, he said. 'It is for your mother to decide', and to his wife, 'You must do as you think best. In your place I'd sign.'

Two days later he said he didn't intend to have his life made miserable by the discussion of the woes of a lot of black fellows he'd never set eyes on, and forbade the mention of the subject in his presence.

The sense of conflict made itself felt throughout the house. We all, willy-nilly, began to take sides. I had no particular love for her ladyship; she had treated me fairly, but had never done anything to endear herself to me, and I knew very well that if, one evening, lacing her into her gown, I had dropped dead she would have minded the resultant confusion and loss of time far more than my demise; but I could see her predicament. Mr Roger was her eldest son, her best beloved child; he had been absent for overlong and she was delighted to see him home; she was mildly shocked by a few carefully selected incidents which he related to her and she wished to please him. But he admitted that by freeing her slaves she would, temporarily at least, reduce her income; and since she was now going pig-headedly towards a modified alteration of Merravay she needed the money because it bolstered her authority.

Miss Whymark, because anything likely to reduce her ladyship's power seemed most desirable, was for doing away with slavery. Miss Maud said that if the slaves could be sure of enough fat pork and meal to keep life in their bodies they were better off than many poor people in Nettleton. Miss Sophie, anxious to do anything, short of marrying Sir Frederick, to please her mother, said, not without truth, that a careful investigation of the ordinary farm labourer's conditions of life and labour would expose some shocking facts. Luella, partly because she was very tender-hearted, and also–I think–because loss of money would restrain her ladyship's rebuilding, was firmly on Mr Roger's side; and when she found that he needed several copies of his charts and facts and abstracts written out she offered her services.

I was, I think I can say with truth, an entirely disinterested abolitionist. And it was not Mr Roger who had converted me. It was somebody called Thomas Rowhedge who had been dead for almost a hundred years.

Soon after I first went to Merravay a brick in the breast of the chimney in the Ship Chamber became porous and a great dark patch came through the plaster. During the process of taking out the faulty brick it was discovered that the panelling on one side of the chimney was not solid; it was the front of a cupboard, and the cupboard was full of ancient books. When they had been cleaned and their leather bindings polished they were housed in a special glass-fronted bookcase in the library, and during my time as maid-of-all-work it was one of my tasks to dust them occasionally. It was then that I discovered, to my delight, that I had remembered how to read. For a week or two I contented myself by peeping into the books and reading a page at random while I was supposed to be dusting, and then one day I came across a thick, leather-bound book, written by hand, and noticed the name 'Alice' recurring. A Lady Alice Rowhedge who had lived at Merravay many years before, and who had been–they said–a witch, had become a part and parcel of the folklore of our district, and many a winter night I had sat by the fire at home and listened to Aunt Hester's tales about her. A dark, shuddering curiosity seized me as I handled this book, and presently, when I left the library, it was hidden under my apron. Five minutes later it was under my pillow. I was fortunate in having been put to sleep in a little room directly under the rafters, reached by an almost perpendicular ladder which even Miss Whymark in her visits of inspection never climbed, cruelly cold in winter and roastingly hot in summer–a lonely, unenviable eyrie of which I remained in undisputed possession.

That book was, from my point of view, disappointing, but it had given me a taste for reading in bed, and for several weeks after that I 'borrowed' books from that case. Then her ladyship caught Miss Sophie reading something which she said was most unsuitable and she locked the case and carried off the keys. The case left open contained books of surpassing dullness: most of them were ones which Mr Whymark had had when he was a young man at Cambridge College; some of them weren't even in English. By that time the reading habit was strong in me, and when I had been reduced to carrying *A Mirror for Magistrates* to bed with me I realised that I had only to ask her ladyship for the key under pretence that the locked books needed dusting. I never gave it back to her.

Amongst the books with which I was thus guiltily free to indulge was a slim, handwritten one containing a play called *The Middle Passage*. Under the title Sir Thomas Rowhedge had written:

> 'This Drama is rooted in a True Story, told me many years since by my Father who was himself the Sea Captain.'

It was all about slaves and the things they endured on their journey from Africa to America. It made terrible reading, but there was poetry in it too.

In the end the captain, to the detriment of his pocket and the extreme fury of his partner, turned them all loose on a desert island, saying:

> *'It may be that you die here. Even so,*
> *Die as free men whose hands, too late unbound,*
> *Have failed to wring a sustenance from this soil;*
> *That shall be my blame too, an added guilt*
> *To that I bear already. But from hence*
> *It shall not be my profit. Not for me*
> *The Judas coin with blood upon its rim.'*

I didn't believe, of course, that a rough sea-captain would talk that way to black men, or that they would understand him if he did; but it was good to read, and it set me against the slave trade and everything connected with it. So when Luella offered to make the copies for Mr Roger I volunteered to help her. We used to work in the schoolroom at night, after Miss Whymark had made her last round and the house was quiet. Despite the fact that Luella had had years of schooling and much more practice, I still wrote the better hand; but if Mr Roger ever noticed the difference he never said anything. He himself sat in the library all through the lovely month of April, sorting the papers and scribbling away like a clerk. With every passing day her ladyship regarded him with more disfavour, and when he began sending letters to Sir George Fenstanton, who was our Member of Parliament, and trying to enlist his interest in the business she went about with a tragic face, burst into angry tears frequently and said, not caring who overheard her, that to have thankless, unloving children was the hardest fate a woman could have; she said that Mr Roger was trying deliberately to ruin her, to take the roof from over her head, the bread from her mouth.

During this same month of April a rumour began to creep about the kitchen that Sir Frederick Fennel had proposed to Miss Sophie and been refused. This remained rumour until, during the Easter week when the balls began again after the Lenten lapse, I received first-hand proof of it.

Her ladyship's own maid, Kate, Luella and I were helping to dress her and do her hair, and I was watching for an opportunity to slip away and see what sort of mess Daisy had made of Miss Sophie's hair, when the young lady herself, wearing a wrapper, came in.

'Mama, do you wish me to wear the yellow or the blue?'

Without turning her head, upon which Luella was erecting one of the new high fashionable coiffures, her ladyship said, quite sweetly:

'Neither, my dear. I do not intend that you should accompany us this evening. Since you have decided to emulate your aunts you may as well stay at home with them. Miss Maybrook! That last pin pierced my scalp!'

Not altogether by accident, I thought, catching sight of Luella's face. Even the fanatically devoted Kate looked troubled. The cold venom, the unkind timing of the announcement had not been pleasant to see.

'As you wish, Mama,' said Miss Sophie.

'She'll learn,' said her ladyship, pleasantly. 'I can see that I have been over-indulgent with my children, and the result is a headstrong wilfulness. Still . . . it may not be too late to rectify matters. . . .'

Rectifying the results of almost thirty years of what she called indulgence towards Mr Roger took the form, a few days later, of refusing to entertain Sir George Fenstanton and the Bishop of Bywater. He asked her at table, in

Briggs's presence, so we all knew exactly what had been said.

'If those two, lately at daggers drawn, propose to visit you together, Roger, we know why! All right, Johnny, I am not mentioning the subject! I may not be clever, but I have sense enough to see that when a politician and a churchman get together some third person is about to be robbed. I do not intend to receive them under the roof that they and you are trying to rip from over my head.'

'Don't talk such nonsense, Rose,' said Miss Whymark. 'This house stood here years before any of those black men were born and will stand long after they're all set free or dead. I do resent the way you talk as though Merravay depended upon a few poor slaves.'

'Did I or did I not say that I wouldn't have this thing discussed in my presence?' Mr Whymark shouted.

'Roger brought it up. That's all he thinks about,' put in Miss Maud. 'I tried to make him interested in the poor Thackers, turned out in the road with eight children; but no, they ain't black enough to . . .'

Then, Briggs said, they all began to talk together. Mr Roger accused his mother of trying to build a fine new house out of dead negroes' bones; Miss Whymark accused Miss Maud of spoiling the Thackers, who should shift for themselves. 'It was a regular bear-garden,' said Briggs.

That evening Luella said that we must work extra hard over the copies; she had seen Mr Roger some time during the day and he had told her he was off to London in the morning and wanted the papers to take with him.

We worked late thinking the house asleep, and when Mr Roger came in I was caught unawares. There was no time for me to lay down my quill and pretend to be busy with some much-belated domestic task as I usually held myself ready to do.

He had been working too; there was ink on his fingers and a blob of it on the end of his nose. He had discarded his wig, and the few remaining strands of rust-coloured hair were all on end. His neckcloth was loosened and he looked more like an overdriven scrivener than the heir to a fine estate.

He took in the situation at a glance.

'Ah! So that's how it's done. I often wondered. Bless you, child. I thank you from my heart. As for you'–he turned to Luella, who was ruling a line to frame a column–'but for your help I should have been another month. I truly cannot express my gratitude . . .'

She laid down the ruler, stood up and stretched and yawned, as gracefully and unselfconsciously as a cat. He stood smiling, the lines in his face softened out and changed as a dark furrowed field changes under the touch of the sunshine. And then as he looked at Luella the smile died out, and for a moment,–or less, for a mere second–before his face resumed its everyday expression, there was something else. . . .

'You know I take this as a symbol . . . that two young people should sit up o' nights, spoiling their pretty eyes to help the cause. It proves to me that once the facts are known all right-minded people . . .'

He broke off at a sound beyond the door.

'Miss Whymark . . .' said Luella in a horrified voice.

'It's all right . . . she's with us . . . I'll explain.'

The door opened after a knob-fumbling pause and there was Mr Whymark.

'Thought I heard voices,' he said in the staccato voice which came upon him when he was drunk. He stared at us all. 'Wanted to see you before you go. Off tomorrow? That right? Wanted to say . . . all a great pity, very great pity. Mustn't mind your mother, y'know . . . very excitable. Always was, always will be. 'Nother thing, too, wanted to say. Ah, yes. Mustn't get carried away. Take little chaps that climb chimneys. Know what? They all die before they're twelve. On paper, my boy, on paper. 'S'fact. Read about it t'other day. Die before they're twelve. But you go 'long Goose Lane, old Sweeper Armstrong, claims to be ninety, put's son to the trade, Young Sweeper, as old as I am, lot healthier; regiment of youngsters, all climbing chimneys and lively's crickets. See what I mean? Mustn't get carried away; make crass fool of y'self.'

'I see exactly,' said Mr Roger. 'I won't do that. Everything I say is soundly based on fact.'

'So you reckon to set Thames on fire with all that paper, eh?'

'I hope to convince somebody who can. Sooner or later.'

'Well,' said Mr Whymark, staring round aimlessly for a moment. 'Well, wish you luck, m'boy. Ha . . . 'nother thing. Money. Can't do without it, y'know. More pull in a good dinner and a bottle of the right stuff 'nin all the talk in the world. And even if you do turn the black chaps loose don't mean we shall go on the parish. Plenty money here, trust old Phyl for that.'

'I have all I need at the moment, sir,' Mr Roger said, the smile lighting his face again. 'But I thank you for the thought; and even more for your good wishes.'

''Snothing,' said the master, waving his hand in the air. 'Just heard voices and came along, say a friendly word. G'night.'

He wheeled round with a lurch and then, arrested by something, turned again and peered at Luella.

'You . . .' He drew back, shaking his head. 'Just f'r a moment, mistook you. Very peculiar thing. . . .' Muttering, he took himself off.

'If they were *his* he'd free them tomorrow,' said Mr Roger, gathering his papers together.

'Because it would–for him–be the easiest thing,' said Luella.

Mr Roger looked up sharply. 'All too true! Do you see through everybody as clearly as that, Miss Maybrook? Let's hope not, eh–er–Deborah? Still, that sort mustn't be discounted, you know; they have the will to good; in mass they form a power called public opinion. Well, thank you again, both of you, more than I can say. Good night.'

'Well, that's over and done with, thank God,' said Luella, yawning again as she dropped the lid on the ink-bottle. 'And tomorrow is your free day, Deb. Your mother did say . . . but would it be more change for you to go alone?'

'Of course not. And I'm sure they'd both be horribly horribly disappointed,' I said.

Chapter Eight

She came home with me in April, and we gathered primroses together again; and in May when the cowslips were in flower and the lilacs shyly showing their colour. My days at home had always been very cheerful since Father–poor man–had died, but Luella's coming contributed something else, something special. Both then, and later, I gave hours of thought to the problem of Luella–and not without cause. I never put my finger exactly on what it was she did to people and for people, but I think I was near it when I concluded that she was a little like a flattering looking-glass. She was always herself and allowed you to be yourself, but in her presence, under her response to you, you were a little more how you would like to be. That, and her boundless capacity to enjoy herself . . . and, of course, the other thing which still eludes me, the thing there is no word for. It wasn't that I was charmed with her and therefore imagined her to be charming; there was the way in which the children had taken to her, the fact that in strife-ridden Merravay she had no enemy.

On our April day she asked again to be allowed to help with the dishes, and my mother laughed and said, 'All right, then, love, come along', and taking one of her own print aprons she wrapped Luella in it, greatly amused because it was so much too wide. 'The backhouse is a hovel,' said Mother, 'my bowl is cracked and the dishcloth is the tail of one of Luke's owd shirts, but you'll hev to excuse all that,' and plainly she knew that Luella would, otherwise she would never have let her cross the threshold of the scullery.

In May that year the weather turned gloriously warm, and on my free Saturday I decided to wear my summer 'tidy' gown, but it had rotted while it was laid away and split when I put it on. So I donned one of my clean working prints and rather morosely set out, side by side with Luella, who was wearing a sprigged muslin, light and airy and very pretty. I grumbled a bit and she said:

'Ask Luke to buy some stuff for you next market day, and I'll make you a dress just like this. You need six yards, and three yards of ribbon. You should have a cherry colour. We could sew in the evenings and have it ready for the next outing.'

'We shouldn't be able to collect the stuff till then,' I said, still depressed over the split dress.

'Don't be so silly. Luke could bring it up, couldn't he? Or you could walk down to fetch it. It's light till nine.'

The gulf between us, so often firmly bridged by her friendliness, by the memory of old days, by the hospitality of my home, suddenly yawned. Miss Whymark–I think because she was afraid that servants would *feed* their visitors–had made a rule forbidding relatives and friends to call upon them except in cases of emergency, in which she must first receive the caller and hear the business. As for running home to fetch a parcel . . .

Embarrassed, and more cross than ever, I explained this.

'She really is . . .' said Luella, as always instantly understanding. 'Well, all right. I'll fetch it for you. After all, in my last post I had a free day each week. . . .'

Luke, of course, willingly accepted the errand; but when we explained about Luella coming to fetch it, alone, on the evening of market day, I saw something happen to his face. And I thought to myself–yes . . . like everybody else he had fallen in love with her, or maybe he has been all along. It was natural, perhaps inevitable. But I was filled with foreboding.

That deepened when, about ten days later, as we were putting the final stitches to the new dress in the last light of a lovely, lingering summer evening, Luella said:

'There, Deb, it's lovely, and you'll look lovely in it. And I promised Luke that you'd ask for permission and we'd go to the fair with him.'

'The Midsummer Fair!' I said, aghast. If there was one person in our district more averse, more opposed to the two fairs that took place, one at midsummer and one at the end of harvest, than Miss Whymark herself was, it was my brother Luke.

'Yes, the Midsummer Fair,' said Luella, biting off her cotton.

'But Luke . . .' I began and stopped. No point in letting her know how completely off his head she had driven him. It must be that; nothing else would explain this sudden change of front. 'Luke doesn't realise,' I said. 'Miss Whymark never allows anyone to go to the fairs.'

'But I promised. I never have seen a real old country fair. But I've heard about them. Deborah, they still have *mummers*, simple little plays done in mime, just like the medieval days . . . now, in the eighteenth century! Did you know *that*? And climbing greasy poles to win a pig, and prizes for making the ugliest face through a horse-collar . . . All the old things that have amused people for hundreds of years; and all dying out except in remote places like this. Deborah, I would love to see it.'

'Well, *you* can. I can't. That is one of Miss Whymark's rules. No fair-going. You see, there is another side to it. People go wild and get drunk and shamelessly rowdy. They reckon that two-thirds of the bastards in the villages around . . .'

'Deborah, there are people who go blind because they read too much, people who die of overeating and overdrinking. The world is full of fools. . . .'

'I am just trying to explain how Miss Whymark sees it.'

'And I am trying to explain how *I* see it. Look, I'll ask her for us both. I did promise Luke.'

'But it isn't a thing that decent people . . . Oh, Luella, how can I explain? It's all so outdated. Poor, rough people stick to the old things, they don't know any better . . . but the others move on. . . .' Was Luke, my dear brother, so serious, so ambitious, really one of the 'poor rough people', or had Luella's desire to see the mummers persuaded him?

Suddenly it came to me that I was worrying myself unduly. Six years under Miss Whymark's inflexible rule now enabled me to say, quite light-heartedly:

'This isn't for us to decide, Luella. You ask Miss Whymark.' Stupid old woman, she betrayed me! She couldn't, she said, permit me to go because that would create a precedent of which the other servants would take advantage. But she was sympathetic . . . mark that . . . sympathetic with

Luella's desire to see the mummers, and if she was *sure* of a reliable escort . . .

'I wouldn't have credited it,' I said, when Luella told me.

'She even asked me, since I *was* going, to take note of the prices of cheesecloth and knitting needles. She wrote the Baildon prices down, and if the fair ones . . . Deb, what is the matter? Why are you looking at me like that?'

'I've just thought of something else, Luella. You see . . .'

The thing I had to say seemed to choke me.

'Well?'

'You see . . . when a girl goes, by herself, to this particular fair with a man it's supposed to be a sign . . .'

I still couldn't say it. Luke, so simple, unable to read or write, dear to me–oh, very dear to me, a good man, but for all that, with his muddy boots, sweaty shirt, hard hands, not to be thought of. . . . A cat may *look* at a king, but . . .

'A sign of what?' asked Luella crisply.

'Special favour,' I gulped out. 'You see . . . lots of country men are shy, they can't say things. So to make it easy for them there are these old customs. And the Midsummer Fair . . . it's easier for them to say "Come to the fair" than "Will you marry me?" But it means the same.'

'Deborah, really. I never heard anything so entirely old-fashioned! It's just a spectacle, something to look at. And Luke didn't ask me alone . . . we were both supposed to go. Practically his last words to me when we parted were joking ones about minding to have this dress ready for you. And it is; and you shall go. I shall ask her ladyship . . .'

'Luella, please! If you did that Miss Whymark would make my life a misery for months. She'd take it as a direct insult and never rest till she'd . . . why, she might even give me the sack. Even if you did ask and got permission I simply dare not go.'

'This really is a very difficult household,' said Luella. 'I had set my heart on going, and I promised Luke.'

'I'm not preventing you. I'm just pointing out what it means.'

'Luke has more sense. Still . . .' She broke off and brooded for a moment, winding a strand of hair about her finger. 'You may be right. But there's so little time now. If we could catch Lantern we could send Luke a note.'

'Luella, you know he can't read!'

'Well, he said he would wait for us at the end of the avenue at ten o'clock. One of us must run down and explain. I don't trust Lantern to deliver a verbal message.'

'There again,' I said, 'I can't go galloping off at ten. . . .'

'Very well, then, I will.'

She set off next morning just before ten, wearing her working dress and no hat. I lingered over my work in the schoolroom, wishful to hear how Luke had taken the disappointment. She didn't come back. Presently the children had finished the tasks she had set them, and I took them out for a long walk, starting off along the avenue. There was no sign of her. It was a perfect fair-day, warm and sunny, with a little brushing breeze.

She came back at dusk. Her peculiarly white skin was powdered with freckles across the nose and brow, her hair was a tangled froth of curls, and out of their hollows, deepened and darkened by fatigue, her green eyes shone like water. She was laden with fairings: a pair of fine white stockings for me to wear with my new dress, wooden dolls with painted faces for Miss

Julia and Miss Arabella, a monkey on a stick for Master Billy. She had even remembered Miss Whymark's needles and a great roll of cheesecloth. And she had had a wonderful time–a perfect day, she called it.

I had saved some oatcake and a glass of milk from the schoolroom supper, and she settled down to it, talking all the time. 'I really shouldn't need any food at all. Luke and I have been eating and drinking most of the day. But I am hungry. Oh, I must tell you about the plays. Deborah, you would have enjoyed them; they were enchanting. . . .' She rattled on while I lighted the candles. Then, as she tilted her head back to drink her milk, the heavy tangled hair swung backwards and I saw something glitter in her ears.

'Did you get a fairing too?' I asked.

'Oh yes, these. . . .' She loosened the ear-bobs and laid them in my hand; little daisies with petals made of silver and a scrap of yellow stone for centres. 'Aren't they *pretty*? The prettiest on the booth. Luke gave me them. And I gave him a wonderful pocket-knife. . . .'

So now, by all the traditions of our countryside, the wordless proposal had been made, and accepted, and Luke had every right to regard her as his pledged sweetheart.

But that was too absurd even for me to say aloud.

Chapter Nine

Nevertheless, on our June free day, which came round soon after, I could detect a subtle change both in Mother and Luke. That was not really so surprising. To people of leisure and education it might seem strange to build any permanent plans upon the foundation of four or five visits and an outing; but for working folk that was the way. With free time so scanty and distances–on foot–so great, the business of courtship must be reduced to the minimum and rely largely on symbols. I'd known many girls get married on the strength of an invitation to Sunday dinner and two or three subsequent walks.

It was not that Luke made any open display of feeling–he was not the kind to do that–but his eye dwelt upon Luella with a possessiveness that was new; and when, in the evening, I remembered that it was time to call for the new shoes which Farrow, the cobbler was making for me he was not slow to say, 'Then if you start out a bit afore us, and Luella and me walk the field way and take it easy, you'll just about get there together.'

'We'll wait for you, Deb,' said Luella. 'At Vinefields Bottom. You know, where the pony once threw me off into the mud.'

Such references to our childhood days were often on her tongue, and hearing this one I wondered whether she realised that those days had gone, that we were not children any more, that walking with a young man through the fields on a June evening might have some significance. I pondered the matter all the way to Goose Lane. I told myself reasonably that there would be nothing so startlingly strange, so fundamentally incongruous in her falling in love with Luke. He was very handsome then; the long-suffering, saintly look had disappeared, his face had hardened and now wore an expression of resolute intent which, if it were balked, as Father's had been, might deteriorate into the same surliness. He was ambitious, too, and seemed, so far, to be lucky in all his dealings. He would make a good husband . . . for some girl. . . . But, perhaps because I had so chancily attained the state myself, and had been so hard put to it to maintain my hold, I did set a disproportionate value on being able to put thoughts into words. I knew that for myself I could never contemplate marriage with an ignorant man, and therefore it was highly unlikely that I should ever find a husband, and I knew that compared with Luella I was ignorant indeed.

But then I had never been in love. Was Luella?

July and August passed all too quickly, as they always did, as May and June had done. Soon winter, with the mud and the biting wind and early dark, would be upon us again.

In July Mr Roger came home, for the Parliament gentlemen had all gone to their country homes to overlook their harvests. He told Luella, who told me, that he had gained a hearing from one or two influential people and 'planted a seed here and there'. Her ladyship seemed pleased to see him again, and had evidently decided to treat his activities as a form of unimportant sickness from which he was almost recovered and which need not be mentioned any more.

The corn ripened and harvest began, and soon everyone was thinking about the horkey, the highlight of the Merravay year.

As was their custom, her ladyship and Mr Whymark went to stay with his sister, Lady Whardale, in Leicestershire, leaving home a week or ten days before the feast. They had made a point of being absent at this season ever since the two fields were turned into parkland, for at the horkey Miss Whymark always made a speech at the table, and that year she had been tactlessly blunt in her remarks about how Grandmother Whymark would have felt about the innovation. Her ladyship, younger then, and more impetuous, had jumped up and protested and there had been a scene.

The horkey, ancient custom as it was in fact, at Merravay was entirely a Whymark festival–Miss Whymark's festival. Some money had been left by the old lady, and just for once in the year Miss Whymark spent lavishly; she had even been known to contribute a little of her own money in a year when prices were high. In fact any careful observer–as I, in my necessarily limited way, was–might mark a change come over Miss Whymark the moment that the master and mistress drove away. During the fortnight of her undisputed reign she was less carping, more genial; partly it was excitement over the feast, and partly, I think, a kind of endeavour to cast the blame for the unpleasant atmosphere usual in the house upon the absent Lady Rosemary. And relief may have had something to do with it too.

Two days before the event, when we were already beginning to bake and boil and clear the centre of the great barn where the long table was set out, Mr Armitage arrived.

Her ladyship had written to him earlier in the year, cancelling the ambitious plans for the new front in a mood of angry despair. Later her spirit revived and suggestions for the extra rooms and some modification of the frontage had been made, and she had written again, asking the architect to pay another visit. Perhaps he was annoyed, or wished to assert his independence, for since then nothing more had been said or done. Now here he was and her ladyship was in Leicestershire.

Miss Whymark was not so busy with her plans as to forget that she was opposed to any alterations to the house. But she did not make the obvious move of sending away the young man who had come to make plans for its alteration. On the contrary, she set herself to woo him. She insisted that he stay, she lodged him well and fed him better, and several times during the next day or two dragged herself away from her delightful preparations to walk about and talk to him. Once when I went to find her and ask something I heard her telling him what Mr Kent had said about the house. There was no doubt that she was a wily and forceful old woman . . . probably not above a little bribery; it was quite possible that her ladyship might return to find that Mr Armitage had deserted the cause.

There came the day when the last load of corn, decorated with ribbons and boughs and flowers and topped by 'The Maiden', was dragged into the stackyard; and another year's harvest was safely in. The first cask of ale was broached and then the labourers went to their homes, whence they would return, washed and reclad, accompanied by their womenfolk, to sit down at six o'clock to partake of the hospitality of a woman long dead.

The meal lasted for a long time, for these were guests who did not, every day, eat their fill, and Miss Whymark had provided nobly, with succulent cold roast sirloin, hams, pork pies and pasties, pickles and sauces, tarts and jellies, cakes, biscuits and sweetmeats, all washed down with ale in plenty and tea, and home-made lemonade. This year, as usual, she made her little speech, glorifying her grandmother's memory. She could say 'Those of you who are old enough to remember with me . . .' in a very moving way which set the older people nodding their heads and thinking sentimentally of days which seemed golden in retrospect, not because of old Mistress Whymark's goodness and kindness but because they themselves were young then, and more vigorous, more hopeful. This year Miss Whymark struck what was, for those of us who understood the situation, a very topical note.

'We meet here, every year, to remember, to look back. It is a custom, an *old* custom, and none the worse for that. There are those in this world'–she looked directly at Mr Armitage–'who do not fully realise the value of the old, the tried, the proved. There are those who cannot see that there are some things so old that they are nearly holy. . . .' She went on at some length, and a great gloom descended upon the company, who, hearing the trend of the speech and missing, perforce, its point, began to wonder what it boded. Later on I heard speculations voiced . . . Was this the last horkey? Was everybody over fifty going to be sacked? Was Miss Whymark going to retire?

When she ended her speech and the applause had died down, Mr Armitage, quite uninvited, rose to his feet.

'Madam,' he said, 'you have entertained me royally, and your speech has given me a great deal to think about. May I, in return, attempt to entertain you? I cannot, alas, sing for my supper like the boy in the nursery rhyme, but I can . . . Ah, I'll start with Master William Whymark. He looks a nice little boy, doesn't he–I believe his book says that he is a nice little boy. I am astonished to find him so greedy! What can he be doing with this and this and this?'

Quick as light, from Master Billy's ear, from the back of his collar, from his curly topknot of hair, he produced an orange, a mince-pie and four sugar plums.

Before the laughter had died down, and while the children still stared, wide-eyed, he turned to Miss Whymark.

'I'm practically a stranger here, but I have seen, in a short time, that yours is a hard task, Madam,' he said dolefully. 'You have all these rapacious, wasteful creatures to look after. Let me see if I can help you a little. Is that of use?' He took a candle out of her cap, another from her fichu, an egg from her elbow, two sausages from between her shoulder-blades. The slight edge on his words delighted the company, everyone of whom had, at some time, suffered under Miss Whymark's parsimony. She was flustered and astonished, but true to her character; as he juggled with the egg she called out, 'Be careful; be careful.' And then the mirth was unrestrained.

Through it he said to Parker, 'We know you are careful of the silver, but must you carry it on your person?' From Parker's pocket he drew four silver spoons.

When he had finished he sat down, not in his old place but next to Luella; near enough for me to hear him say:

'That went well, didn't it? Was I word perfect?'

'You were wonderful,' she said; 'you remembered every tiny thing. And how you could and do the juggling as well . . .' So she had pointed out the idiosyncrasies upon whose frank but not unkindly mention so much of the success had depended. Mr Armitage looked at her approvingly and settled down with a smoothed, pleased look; he evidently liked being told that he was wonderful. Luella had done it again.

Then there was the dancing, with old Mortlock and Young Lantern playing their fiddles and Miss Whymark stepping stiffly out, first with Parker and then with the bailiff and two or three more, in strict order of seniority. A few old people stood or sat aside, remembering, with discomfort, the implied threat of possible changes to come and picking their teeth. The young ones romped through the ancient dances, and the presence of Mr Roger, Mr Armitage and Luella added to the extra-merry mood which the juggling display had ushered in.

Luella romped like a child, completely unselfconscious, utterly given over to the process of enjoying herself. Once, and not so long ago, I should have done the same; now I derived more pleasure from watching. And amongst the things I saw that evening and marked and remembered, was the expression on Miss Sophie's face as Luella, one arm linked in Mr Armitage's, the other in the clean-smocked shepherd's, rollicked through the movements of 'Three Meet'. Envy, admiration, wistfulness, wonderment –they were all there.

A fortnight later, when Mr Armitage had gone his way and the master and mistress were home again and the chestnuts–always the first to hope or despair–were showing some lemon-yellow leaves, everyone was surprised that Miss Sophie, returning from one of her solitary rides, announced that she was going to marry Sir Frederick Fennel 'very soon'. I was not surprised. I knew the exact moment when she had made that decision. For I also, in moments when my lack of certain things has been borne in upon me, have thought–Ah, but this and *this* I have and may be sure of!

The engagement–Miss Sophie's grasping at the one thing she could be sure of–pleased everyone; and several people, recovering from their surprise, claimed credit for bringing it about. Her ladyship held that it was her stern treatment which had resulted in the change of mind–the thought of another dull home-keeping winter had brought the silly child to her senses. Mr Whymark said that he had always been of the opinion that so long as the girl wasn't pressed or bullied nature would take its course. Miss Maud said, frankly:

Well, I gave her some advice, based on my own experience. I said, "Roger will bring a wife home one of these days and you'll find that living in your brother's house isn't all honey, however kind *he* may be!" That made her think!'

The wedding had been arranged for the second week in October. How many people, I wondered, saw the significance of that? Miss Sophie's birthday fell in the following week; she would be twenty-two. She would be married before she was twenty-two. In her present mood that mattered.

It mattered to me too; for I lost my September Saturday, because there was so much to do, cleaning the house and making ready for the Whardales, who must, of course, come to the wedding and must stay at Merravay. And if I had ever yearned and longed to go home for any reason but sheer homesickness, it was just then.

For when I went home, with Luella, on the August Saturday, Mother had said, 'You girls must fend for yourselves today. Mr Loveridge, across at Squirrels, stuck a fork through his foot day afore yesterday and I'm seeing to the brews and plasters.'

She was very busy and important, and sure of her skill in cures; she said he would mend.

But in little more than a week Jack Lantern, who brought us the village news, told us that Mr Loveridge was dead. I felt, on the verge of my mind, sorry for his wife, a town-bred woman and helpless, and his six-year-old son; but they would be all right, in a way, for Squirrels was their freehold and a good farm. It would sell easily. Another week passed, and Jack Lantern, not without a trace of awe in his voice, said to me one morning, 'So that brother of yours has took over Squirrels! Well, to be sure, some people get on in this world!

My curiosity swelled like a boil, and one day when Luella told me that she was going into Baildon with Miss Sophie to buy materials and engage the services of the best local sempstress to help with the dresses, I said, 'Luella, please make some excuse and stop at the farm and ask what this is all about.'

She came home with quite a story. Mrs Loveridge hadn't had complete faith in Mother's remedies and had called in the doctor, who had made mock, in a pleasant way, of the plaster of dock-leaves and iris roots which she had applied, taken it off and put on his own. According to Mother, Mr Loveridge's foot had started to rot from that moment and he died. The widow immediately veered round and was full of remorse and kept saying that if only she had trusted Mother . . . Then Luke had looked after the business of getting her harvest in, as he would have done, as a matter of course, for any neighbour in similar plight, and so she felt kindly towards him. And she didn't want to stay in the farm herself; nor did she want to sell it, because there had been Loveridges at Squirrels since the beginning of time. And the upshot of it all was that she had agreed to let the farm to Luke on a ten-year lease, on condition that when her boy was fourteen Luke would take and teach him to run it, and that he would not cut down the rose that sprawled over the housefront, or the lilacs which Mr Loveridge had planted to screen the privy.

Squirrels had always been well handled and the land was in good heart; such a farm was very rarely for hire, and in getting a lease on it Luke had had a piece of luck that fell to no more than one in a thousand.

Luella had had no time to gather details, and I did not know then that Mrs Loveridge, despite her distress and her sentiment, had fixed a rent which, if Luke worked twenty-four hours a day, kept his health and met with nothing but good fortune, might still leave him a small margin of profit.

During the next week–the one before the wedding–I heard from Jack Lantern that Luke had already found a tenant for our old house, but was going to keep the land. The tenant was a cousin of Farrow, the bootmaker, a kersey weaver whose lungs had weakened; he wanted the house, the orchard and a shed or two where he could keep a goat and a few chickens to eke out what he could earn by field labour in good weather when he felt able.

To hear all this in bits and pieces was very irksome, and as soon as the wedding was over and the house guests gone I asked Miss Whymark if I might run home for an hour one evening.

Luke was out and Mother was alone in the middle of packing and sorting, muddled, distracted but happier than I'd ever seen her in my life. Despite the fact that the light was failing and I had but a short time to stay, she loaded me with bundles and baskets and hurried me off, across our orchard, through a gap in the hedge and over the meadow that divided the two houses. A well-defined track showed me how often she had come and gone that way during the last few weeks. She talked incessantly, breathlessly, as we scampered along.

Squirrels was a good big solid old house, with one or two panelled rooms and a multitude of cupboards.

'Now this is what I call a farmhouse!' said Mother, with deep satisfaction. 'It's like the one I was born in. Ah, I give up a bit when I married your poor father! But then I thought and hoped he'd get on; and why he never did is a mystery–he worked hard enough. Still. . . . And to think that I can get out my bits of brass and copper that my granny give me that've been in a box under my bed all these years and never had room to set out. Oh, I'll hev a nice kitchen again! Now come and see what'll be the parlour . . .'

We stood in the thickening twilight in the big square room. It had two windows, and red roses, which must not be cut, grew all about them, with a belated bud or two close to the panes.

'You know, Deb,' said Mother, in a less excited voice, 'I never said a word, but I hev worrited myself of late. I could remember how *I* felt once the first glow had wore off and there I was, with that place in the passage where you knock your head twenty times a day, and nothing but pegs on the doors for your clothes. Well, that just show, no sense in worrying. Things kind of work round, if you wait. And Luella'll hardly know she ain't at Merravay, once this is set out. . . .'

The chilly little wind of the autumn night moved in the rosebush and set the buds tapping against the window.

'You seem . . .' I began, and stopped. 'Isn't it a bit soon to take for granted that Luella . . . Or do you know something I don't?'

'Well, bless my soul! Naught's been *said*, at least to me; but surely we all know. Why, she went with him to the Midsummer and everything. And look how they carry on, laughing and skylarking about. What could be plainer? And him talking about buying a *carpet*!'

What could be plainer?

The wind was in the big chimney now, making a plaintive sound; and the buds, the last, too-late buds, tapped at the glass, as though asking for shelter.

'I don't know,' I said. 'Sometimes . . .' But what could I say?

Mother suddenly laughed with just a hint of mischief.

'I know what ails you, my girl. You're just a thought jealous. You marnt be that, now. Your turn'll come. . . .'

I was spared having to answer that because she suddenly clapped her hand to her mouth.

'Dog's nails! I left a beef pudding in the copper. It'll hev boiled dry, and that boy ain't had a proper meal since the day afore yesterday. We must get back. You can see the bedrooms another time.'

Luke was swilling himself under the pump when we trotted into the yard. He seemed surprised to see me.

'I been wanting to hev a word with you, Deb.'

'I mustn't stop now. I'll see you on my day,' I said.

'No, I'll come a step with you.'

'But you're hungry and the pudding's spoiling.'

'That can wait.' He picked up his jacket and shrugged himself into it and then called to Mother that he'd be back in ten minutes.

I was terrified that he was going to talk about Luella; but he began with a half-shamefaced apology.

'I ought to hev talked it over with you, Deb; but time was short, and I knew I'd never get a chance like that again. Now I've got to spend what is yours by rights, as well as my own, stocking the new place; and if you should want to get married I couldn't give you your portion straight out like I allust meant to, see? But you'll be better off in the end. In two or three years' time, if my beasts go ahead like they are doing now, and corn keeps its price, we'll be well-to-do, Deb. Only just now we must sow before we reap, see?'

'That's all right, Luke. I'm not thinking of getting married. You're welcome to use my share for as long as you like. I'm glad you've had the chance. I hope everything goes well with you.'

And now don't say anything else. Let me go back with my doubts; let me not have to say anything about what is too formless, too uncertain to be put into words.

I mentioned the meal waiting.

'Just a minute,' he said. 'That ain't all. I been wanting to talk to you about . . . Luella and me.'

Exactly what I had dreaded.

'You see, like I said just now, putting money in afore we can take it out I'm going to be short of *spending* money. It was in my mind to ask her at Christmas. Back in the old place I could've spared a guinea or two to hev things nice. Now that look to me as though we've got the parlour and nothing to put in it. But I don't want her to think I'm shilly-shallying. What d'you think I oughta do, eh, Deb?'

Despite his quietness, he was usually so sure of himself, his plans, his rightness, that this clumsy, hesitating bid for help and direction struck me as horribly pitiful.

'You should talk to her,' I said at last.

'Well, I hev tried. But, you know, I ain't handy with words, and she sort of head me off and go rattling on about something else. She 'on't be serious. . . .'

Deadly serious himself, of course, he was attracted by her apparent lack of seriousness–just as, no doubt, long ago, that dour man, our father, had been attracted by Mother's lightness of heart. Strange how things fell into pattern.

But I knew that Luella could be serious enough when she chose to, and my foreboding deepened with the thought that when she headed him off she did it deliberately.

'I ain't asking she should scrub floors and feed calves. Time we're married I mean to hev hired labour; and if I can't, damn-all-to-Hell, I'll sit up a nights and do things with these hands. You tell her that, Deb, and tell her thass up to her to say whether we do it at Christmas or wait a bit.'

'Damn-all-to-Hell, Luke, d'you know what you're asking? I can't go telling her things like that before we even know whether she wants to marry you or not. Have you even made it plain to her that *you* want to marry her?'

'I been more or less courting her since the first day she come back, ain't I. You never see me so much as look at any other female, did you? I took her to the fair . . .'

'That's just it,' I said angrily. 'All these silly old customs. A man has a tongue in his head, hasn't he, and could ask a plain question without making such a morris dance.'

'Well, a word in season wouldn't cost you nothing, Deb; and it'd clear the way for me a bit,' he said, unruffled by my sharpness. 'Thass all right for folks that are handy with words–I ain't. I start and get all tied up, and then off she go on another tack and I'm lost. You just edge a word in for me, some time when you're having a chat. Eh, Deb?'

'I'll see. I think the best thing for you to do is to show her the house and everything next time we come, and then ask her. Then you'll know where you are. And, Luke . . .'

'Yes, Deb.'

'You mustn't . . . I mean, don't count too much, or be too much disappointed. You see . . . nowadays, everybody doesn't attach such importance to things like going to a fair.'

He laid a heavy hand on my shoulder.

'Hev you got any reason to say that? Any reason to think . . .'

'No. Truthfully, Luke, none at all.'

No reason for anything I said, or thought; no reason for feeling cold and empty and sad and sorry for everybody. . . .

Let him ask her and have done; the thing had been on my mind, a vague disquietude, ever since the February evening when he had driven us home.

Chapter Ten

That last Saturday of October was one of those rare lovely autumn days; it began with a mist like a bloom on a grape and opened out to a noon of marigold-yellow and closed with an evening of hyacinth-blue, full of the scent of apples and burning leaves. Luke wasn't home when we arrived; he had gone to one of the farm sales, of which there were always plenty at that time of year. Mother, Luella and I spent the afternoon moving the last few things across from our little old house into the new one. I was glad to be so busy, for I was as nervous as though I were the one who was to make the proposal, or to receive it. For one thing, I was terrified lest Mother should say something tactless and premature to Luella; but I wronged her there. Luella, of course, threw herself into the moving, the rearranging, the admiration of the rooms, with exactly the enthusiasm which she would have shown over a doll's house which two children had just acquired.

At dusk Luke came home, pleased with his purchases. He was wearing his market clothes, buff breeches and a bright blue coat with brass buttons. He looked extremely handsome, solid, reliable and genial.

We sat down and ate the first meal that Mother had cooked in that kitchen. When it was over I saw Luke look at me and tighten his mouth.

'I reckon you've seen the house, Luella. I want you to see the barn. Mrs Loveridge said 'twas a thousand years owd and used to be the main house. 'Sbig as a church.' He lighted two lanterns and led Luella away.

Mother and I washed the dishes. Then we polished and set out the cherished pieces of brass and copper ware.

'And there's another thing,' said Mother suddenly. 'There's room for *me* here. I allust wondered whether the time'd come when Luella might feel about me the way I did about your Great-aunt Hester. Not that I *grutched* her house room, poor soul, but she did fare to be allust underfoot. That 'on't be so here. So long as I'm useful I can busy myself, and when I'm useless there's a room for me to be out of sight and out of mind.'

'I hope that time is a long way ahead,' I said. I wondered what was happening in the barn.

After what seemed a long time they came in. My first thought was that Luke had balked his fence, for he did not look like a man whose suit had been accepted, or rejected; and Luella, very white and small-faced, looked even less like a girl who had been proposed to. For one demented moment I thought that she had expected Luke to speak and been disappointed when he didn't.

They admired our handiwork; we all ate plum cake and drank a glass of elderberry wine. Then Luella said:

'It's a nice night, Luke, and the horse has been out today, so we'll walk home.'

'Right you are,' he said. 'I'll walk with you to the avenue at least.'

'But you're tired too.'

'A bit of walk 'on't hurt me,' he said. Voice, manner, everything, just as usual. Just as usual his leave-taking, with his mention of seeing us next month 'or maybe afore'.

We began to walk through the deeper darkness of the avenue, through the light, brittle fallen leaves which gave off a dry autumnal scent. Luella walked in silence, and I was just about to say some trivial thing when she said:

'Luke just asked me to marry him.'

'I'm not exactly surprised,' I said; though I *was* surprised to know that he had done it after all. 'Well?'

'I don't know what to say.' Her voice sounded far away, lost. 'It's very difficult, Deborah. Marriage is such a *final* thing. . . .'

'That, I should imagine, is what people in love like about it.'

'In love . . . when you're all dazed and dazzled, when you're not yourself at all. In that state you have to make a decision that affects your whole life, everything you do, and have, and are, from that moment on. It's a frightening thought, Deb.'

'Yes; I suppose it must be.' But what did you say to him? Tell me, without my having to ask.

'You look round,' she went on in that remote voice, 'and what do you see? Most people would say they married for love . . . and they end up like the Whymarks. I'm inclined to think that the more you follow your heart the worse you feel when you wake up one morning and find that it misled you.'

'I think you're unduly cynical, Luella. Is that bound to happen?'

'I think that love–not the kind part, the friendliness and the working together; they last–but this thinking that the sun rises and sets with the one person, and the . . . the physical part, that *is* bound to wear off. Time alone would . . .'

'What did you say to Luke?'

'Almost exactly what any well-reared young woman is told to say in the circumstances.' She gave a sudden laugh, harsh, almost hysterical. 'That I wasn't sure–and that, God knows, is true–that I must have time to think. Straight out of the book, Deb, word for word.'

Well, that suited Luke exactly; no wonder he'd looked so calm. My spirits rose a little. This seemed an apt moment to say my few words. And since he had come into the open himself it would do no harm to mention my certainty that he would make her a good husband and was utterly devoted to her.

'I know. I know. Anyway, if I do marry him I shouldn't mind the work. I should delight in it. And I could help in other ways–read the papers for him, and do accounts, for he'll end with a bigger business than he can keep in his head, smart as he is in his quiet way. . . .'

'Luella, you *are* in love with him!'

'Yes. Oh yes, I am. At least I have this . . . Oh, Deb, you'd never understand. In some ways you're still such a child; you have never . . . I mean all your ideas are out of a story book. Fall in love and live happily ever after. Dear Deb, I hope *you* will. You might. You *are* single-minded!'

'You're not.' It was half question, half statement. 'Luke is,' I added, as she did not answer.

'I know. And they're the ones who get their way in the end.'

'In this case, I truly hope so.'

'Thank you, Deb. That was a pretty speech!' She laughed in the old light-hearted fashion, thrust her arm through mine, and, saying that it was turning cold, hurried me towards the house at such a pace that further speech was impossible.

I felt quite gay too. I believed that she was being a little coy and shy and girlish.

Early in November somebody got up and made a speech in Parliament about the slave trade and its iniquities; and then the papers took up the subject and printed some articles and dozens of letters. Mr Roger's name was mentioned several times. But the time was not ripe yet. My turn to study the papers would not arrive for two or three weeks, but I heard all about it from Luella. Her ladyship, faced with the fact that what she had determined to regard as a foible, a bit of child's play, was being seriously discussed in London, reverted to her earlier attitude, and tears and angry recriminations became an everyday occurrence. At the end of the week Mr Roger went to stay at Ockley with Miss Sophie, who, as soon as the wedding-ring was on her finger, had proceeded to take a subtle revenge on her mother. It was a simple one too; it consisted of charming, affectionate behaviour to everyone else and cold, flat, formal behaviour to her ladyship. A typical example was one morning when she arrived, carrying an enormous bunch of lilies, the like of which I–nor indeed many people in England–had never seen before. They were shaped like the white ones which fill cottage gardens in June, but they were pale pink in colour and splashed with purple at the heart. And this was November. At Ockley they had hot-houses.

'Sophie, how beautiful!' said her ladyship.

'They are pretty,' said Lady Fennel coolly. 'They're for Aunt Maud, for the church.'

'I'm afraid the cold will kill then,' said her ladyship after just a second's recoil.

'If they can survive here . . .' Lady Fennel shivered inside her furs. 'This room is like an ice-house. How poor Deborah can sew at all! No wonder she has chilblains. Have they started this year yet, Deborah?'

'Ockley is too warm,' said her ladyship. 'And that is why, in my opinion, Freddie takes cold so easily. Such a pity! I always think a man with a heavy cold . . .' She made a grimace of disgust.

With things on such a footing between them it was natural enough that Lady Fennel should now take sympathetic interest in her brother's cause.

On the last Saturday of November I had to go home alone. Luella and the children had gone to Ockley for four days. The rector at Ockley was a very old man and fond of old customs; he had revived a winter merry-making known as a church-ale, a thing which, like the horkey and the Midsummer Fair, few villages had had since Cromwell's time. There were mummers there too. If her ladyship resented the fact that now every member of the family except herself had been invited to Ockley for some special occasion she gave no sign, merely saying that it was instructive for the children to see things which would be done away with by the time they grew up.

From that visit Luella returned in rather low spirits, which I attributed to the cold which she had caught. Ockley was splendid, she said, and Lady Fennel had been more than kind, and the church-ale had been most entertaining. But all this I gathered by questioning; the usual rippling enthusiasm was absent.

I passed on to her the invitation which Mother had sent, for her to go home for Christmas, any day, all days when she was free. I, of course, did not go home at all in December.

'I don't like to go to your home to be merry, Deb, while you have to stay and work,' she said. 'Anyway, I can't begin to think about Christmas yet. This cold and everything. . . .'

'Poor Luella,' I said. 'I believe you should be in bed. You look feverish.' I put out my hand to touch her forehead and see. She shrugged away from me.

'*You* shouldn't hang about me. You'll catch it. I'm all right. I'm better. It's just . . .'

The days moved on and it was the seventeenth of December. The day of the Christmas Market, when they judged the fat bullocks and gave the prizes. After the judging the beast was sold, with butchers competing heartily for it; then it was paraded round the town with the crier going ahead, ringing his bell, calling out the weight of the bullock, the name of the man who had reared it and of the butcher who had bought it. Everybody then ran hot foot to the butcher's to bespeak a joint of that beef for Christmas, and it was a standing joke that whatever the bullock weighed alive it weighed two tons dead, since no one was ever disappointed of his order. Joke or no joke, it was a fact that the winner of the first prize put ten pounds into his pocket, sold his animal in a competitive market and gained himself a reputation as a breeder.

It was one of those days with a hard dry wind when fires burn fiercely, consuming solid logs as though they were paper. Midway through the morning I carried a fresh basket of logs to the schoolroom, and just as I reached the door it opened and Mr Roger, whom I thought to be at Ockley, stepped out.

'Ha . . .' he said, in a manner quite unlike his own. 'I hoped I'd see you–er–Deborah. Wanted to wish you a happy Christmas and . . .' He pressed a guinea into my hand and laughed. 'To buy a new pen with, bless you!' He patted me on the shoulder and went running downstairs.

The children were not in the schoolroom; Luella was alone, looking so small-faced, so pale and shaken that I dropped the log basket and ran to her, asking:

'What's the matter? What happened?'

'Nothing. Nothing, Deb.' She linked those little white bird's-claw hands and moved them up and down in a distracted gesture. 'I must get the children in. He told them to run away for a minute and they did, without their coats, in this wind. They'll catch their . . .'

She moved towards the door. I reached out and grabbed a handful of her skirt. I heard my voice, thin and strangling, say:

'What did he want? What did he say to you?'

'Deb . . . I can't. I've hardly . . . later on . . . Deb, please.'

She put out one hand and pushed mine away with it, then lifted it to her cheek, driving her knuckles against the flesh. Then she was suddenly calm. There was a rustle of silk, a waft of perfume from behind me.

'So you came too,' Luella said. I turned.

'I thought it best. Nobody knows better than I how nasty Mama can be,' said Lady Fennel. 'Good morning, Deborah.'

It was both greeting and dismissal, delivered in the way that gentry are born with. But I didn't move.

'Look, Lu, I think this may be very unpleasant. You'd better come back with me, now.'

'I must get the children in.'

'Deborah can do that. You come and get some things together. I know, my dear, I saw every sign of storm. Let Roger face it. . . . There, what did I tell you?'

From downstairs there came a wailing scream, and then the sound of commotion; voices, doors slamming.

'I've had enough scenes to last me the rest of my life,' said Lady Fennel, coldly. 'I'm having no part in this one. I came to spare you. Come along.' She took Luella quite roughly by the elbow and began to hustle her out of the schoolroom. I caught her by the other arm.

'He asked you . . . and you . . .?' I knew, of course, but I wanted her to tell me. To my surprise, she gripped my hand and used it to steady herself against the impetus of Lady Fennel's pull.

'Wait a moment, Sophie. I can't just run away like this. I haven't committed a crime! Yes, Deb. Mr Roger Whymark has asked me to marry him, and I have said I will do so.'

'That is all I wanted to know,' I said. 'I hope you'll be as happy as you deserve.'

'And Mama,' said Lady Fennel, 'is going to call you ugly names and derive great pleasure in ordering you from the house. You're a fool, Lu.'

'I know.'

'And you're shaking with fright. Mama will come screaming at you, and you'll fall in a fit, that's what you'll do.'

'I am not frightened. Why should I be? I am worried about those children. If you, Deborah, would be so good as to go and look for them I could stay here in case her ladyship should wish to speak to me; otherwise I must go myself.'

'I'll go,' I said, and went to push past them as they stood in the doorway.

'I still think . . .' Lady Fennel began.

The children, when I found them, were wearing their coats and hoods; and because I wanted a little time to think, and thought that they would be as well out of the house for a while, I took them for a long walk along the edge of Layer Wood, where we were sheltered from the wind. So I missed what was, by all accounts, the most spectacular and noisy scene ever to take place in Merravay.

When we got back the house had the air of having been battered into silence. Her ladyship had taken to her bed; Miss Whymark had taken refuge in her accounts; Miss Maud had gone to the rectory with her story; and since Luella was nowhere about and her brush and comb and a few other things were gone from her room, I gathered that she had, after all, gone to Ockley. Mr Roger was still in the house, waiting for Mr Whymark's return from the fat-stock judging. And of course rumour and counter-rumour had the house by the ears. They even said that her ladyship, at one point, had thrown a vase at Miss Whymark, who was taking Luella's part.

I should have found it all very interesting and very amusing–if it hadn't been for Luke.

I should have thought it very right and proper, highly suitable–if it hadn't been for Luke.

I should have regarded it as highly romantic, especially as Luella had such strong feelings about Merravay–if it hadn't been for Luke.

But there it was. My dear, serious-minded, single-minded Luke had been jilted–there was no other word for it–and I honestly felt worse than if I had been jilted myself.

At intervals through the day I had thought about how he would take the news, and every time I felt as though someone had kicked me in the stomach.

And there was Jack Lantern, about to go home carrying the news; and Miss Maud, even now, telling the story at the rectory. I couldn't leave Luke to hear from the lips of a casual gossip.

At seven o'clock I put the puzzled children to bed and I did what I had never done before, walked away on a working day without asking leave. Whom could I ask, anyway–go to Mr Roger, reading in the library, and say, 'I must go and tell my brother that you're going to marry the woman who for the last seven weeks has been making up her mind to marry him'? Look him in the eye and say, 'You be careful! She's in love with Luke Fulger; she's marrying you for another reason. She doesn't believe in love because it wears out'? All so true, so reasonable . . . and too fantastic to consider for more than a moment.

I battled against the wind all the way home; and there was Mother alone.

'Luke meant to go to Baildon, but he heard of a sale–a man died over at Minsham and he thought he might pick up a few things cheap. And what brought you, my dear?'

As she asked the question she opened the door of the oven and took out a loaf of currant bread whose readiness for withdrawal from the oven she tested by turning it over and rapping its bottom with her knuckles and then holding it to her ear to listen to its response.

'Ah, they're done,' she said, and busied herself. The scent of hot bread was for once not appetising to me.

Presently we heard the creak and rumble of wheels.

'Ah, so he got a wagon. He took just the horse, in case.'

He'd got the wagon. He was pleased. He came in. He ate great helpings of the mutton-and-apple pie–ordinarily almost my favourite dish. Tonight I couldn't look at it, though I had had nothing to eat since breakfast. I felt like a hangman watching a condemned man take his last meal. And then I felt I was exaggerating; and I wished I'd been in love myself and had some other standard than books to judge by; and I wished that Mr Roger had died in Virginia, or on the high seas; and I wished that Luella had never come back. And I wished, almost most of all, that it hadn't fallen to me to break this piece of news.

Most of the time we were talking about Christmas, and finally, when he had eaten his fill, Luke got to his feet, took a candle in hand and said to me:

'You come here a minnit, Deb.'

He led the way into the cold, almost unfurnished parlour. On the old table that used to be Aunt Hester's there were two parcels.

'Thass for you, with my best wishes,' he said, pointing to one of them. It was a cloak, grey and smooth and fine; a lovely cloak, lined with red. Choking sick, I thanked him and did what he was obviously yearning for me to do–looked at the other, smaller parcel. A little fur tippet. Small, but so smooth and light and silky that I could see that it was the best of its kind . . . even her ladyship, though she had bigger and more, had no better.

He took it up in his great brown work-scarred hands.

'She'll like that. I did what you said, Deb, and asked her straight out, like, and she ain't in no hurry; so seeing's I got time to get carpets and such-like I reckoned I could get her a pretty present. . . . And that is pretty, ain't it?'

And if I cry now . . . just cry and run away without saying a word as I long to do . . . he'll be like Mother and think I'm jealous! Oh God, what did I ever do that you should bring me to such a pass?

'It's lovely, Luke. Lovely. Fit for a queen. You have the best of taste. But my cloak is even better. It'll last me a lifetime. Oh, Luke . . .' I leaned against him. 'I am grateful . . . and I do love you. . . .'

'Why, Deb,' he said, 'there ain't no need to carry on that way about a little owd Christmas present. Tell you what, you put it on now. I'd'a kept the horse hitched if I'd known you was here. S'nasty owd night.'

'The wind was against me coming. It'll blow me home. I will wear the cloak, Luke, and I'll be proof against anything. Will you come a step or two with me?'

We stepped out into the tearing wind, turned the corner of the house into a sudden calm and stopped to gather our breath. And then, like a surgeon who must inflict agony and can best show mercy by being swift, I laid hold of his arm and said:

'Luke, I came to tell you. Luella is going to marry Mr Roger.'

He said nothing. His arm went stiff under my hand and I heard the breath go out of him. Presently I heard my own desperate voice explaining, consoling; and then we were at our yard gate, across the road in the teeth of the wind again, under the lighted window of the Evening Star, in by the way that the coach passengers used, into a warm, blazingly bright room; still with my hand stiff on his stiff arm; and still he said no word.

In the bright room, loud with voices, confusingly full of men, I turned and looked at Luke. The wind-whipped red was still in his cheeks, but all round his mouth and the root of his nose there was a white shadow as though a chalky finger had brushed them. And his eyes were blank, stunned.

A man–landlord?–wearing an apron, bald, holding a ladle, came bustling about.

'Well, if it isn't Mr Fulger himself. Just talking about you. Congratulations, I'm sure. Mr Everton, sir. . . .'

Another man, red-faced, beefy, thumping Luke's wooden shoulder, shaking his wooden hand. Congratulations indeed. Thirty years in the cattle trade, never seen, never hoped to see, a better beast than the one which had just won Luke the fat stock Christmas prize.

'And what shall it be, sir? On the house, I insist. This is a great day for Nettleton. We're pleased and proud indeed.'

Ha, I thought . . . Luke is an up-and-coming man who has just taken over a big farm and never set foot in this place before. But it was possible that they were pleased.

'Brandy,' Luke said, breaking the silence at last.

'And the young lady. Will she partake on this great occasion?'

'Brandy,' Luke said again.

I put on a false, gay, rallying voice. 'Luke, you forget. The news must have stunned you. I will take a small glass of Madeira, if you please.'

I might have been thrust into a place where no lady should be, but I would show them I knew what a lady might drink. And though to mention being stunned by news was so cruel that I flinched as I said it, it was sensible too. It offered some excuse for the way he was behaving.

'But you must have known there wasn't a beast to touch it,' said Mr Everton. 'Why, alongside yours the rest all looked like Pharaoh's lean kine . . .' Somebody asked facetiously what breed that was; somebody else said well, be fair, the second-prize winner had beef on him too; somebody took Luke's glass away and gave another, full. When he had drunk that he drew a long deep breath.

'I clean forgot the bullock, Deb. Little owd Weaver took it in for me and I got thinking about the sale; then my supper, and then . . . Clean forgot.'

'You've got that sort of a mind, Luke. And if you'll think steady about the next thing and never look back you'll be all right.'

Then they were surging about him again, asking him questions, refilling his glass. Every minute took us one pace away from the dreadful thing; so I waited, patiently, though I would not let anyone fill my glass again.

The wag-on-the-wall clock over the fire jerked along to nine.

'I must go,' I said. 'I shall be locked out.'

'It isn't every day you have a thing like this to celebrate,' said the landlord.

'She's right, though. Must be getting along.'

'We'll hope to see you again, Mr Fulger.'

'Aye, and afore long,' Luke said.

The moon had risen and rose high, with wind-driven clouds scudding across her face, so that moments of pitch darkness were followed by moments of brilliant, unreal light. Once the lights of the Evening Star were behind us we might have been in the middle of the desert; it was not a night to tempt anyone abroad, and in winter the village people went to bed early to save fuel.

Luke and I walked in silence; that and the rushing wind, the fact that the one glass of wine in my empty stomach had seemed to affect my weight, and the confusing alternations of light and dark made everything seem unreal and dreamlike. Wake up and think–What a hateful dream! Thank God it isn't true!

Then all at once I heard the sound of horse's hoofbeats. We were on the stretch of road which led only to Merravay and then on to the Lower Road, which nobody used in winter because of the mud.

The wind made it difficult to be sure of direction, and for a moment I thought the sound came from behind us–that would be Mr Whymark coming home, very late, from the Fat-stock Show. But next time I caught the sound I was sure that it came from the road ahead of us, and it was coming towards us, fast.

And suddenly I thought of Lady Alice. It was on just such nights as this that she was said to ride abroad. Ordinarily I regarded the legend with some scepticism, but tonight I was in a state to believe everything. I grabbed Luke's arm and said:

'Can you hear a horse?'

He listened. 'No.'

That increased my cold panic; for it confirmed the stories of how two people could be walking, arm-linked, through the night and one would see and hear the phantom while the other declared that nothing but the wind went by.

'I can. And it's coming from Merravay and the Lower Road. *Her* ride. Oh, Luke. It's Lady Alice!'

'Don't be so sawney,' he said, and listened again. 'I hear it now. 'Tain't galloping.'

I, too, heard the pace slow down; but then, sometimes, passing people, she did slow down and lean from the saddle the better to cast the evil eye on them. Every story I had ever heard came back into my mind. I cast about for somewhere to hide, but the hawthorn hedges on either side of the road were as high and solid as walls.

'At least stand back,' I whispered; and I pulled him close to the hedge.

The horse, moving at a steady trit-trot, was close to us when the cloud moved and the whole road sprang into light. Luke and I, in the shadow of the high hedge, were partly hidden. I cringed and closed my eyes. But at the last moment some strange compulsion came upon me. I *had* to look. And there was Mr Roger on his brown horse with the white blaze.

Fright had driven every bit of sense out of me. With relief as sharp as pain, I said, 'It's Mr Roger.'

In the next half-second I was alone under the hedge. Tattered by the wind there was borne back to me the sound of hooves, of pounding feet, of Luke's voice calling.

The moon went in again. In the sudden blinding darkness I dragged myself from the hedge in which I had been half embedded and set out towards them on legs that seemed to be made of flannel. Two dozen yards of road stretched on and on, an endless journey.

Then it was light again and I had reached them. The horse stood broadside on and Luke and Mr Roger were grappling together. Urgent in my mind was the thought of Mr Roger so light and thin and brittle-seeming, Luke so heavy, thick-muscled and strong–two such ill-matched men mustn't fight. I shouted to them through a mouth stuffed with chaff and put out my flannel hands and seized Luke by the coat tails. Something, elbow or fist, came up and hit me under the chin, sparks of light burst out from the top of my head. My teeth had gone into my tongue and my mouth was filled with blood. I tried to scream again, but nothing came but a blubbing sound. I spat and just managed to call Luke's name.

Another cloud moved. There was a thump, a grunt, and the slither of feet in the mud. Then quietness. The next burst of light showed Luke on his feet, Mr Roger spreadeagled on the ground. His wig and hat, still wedged together, lay between him and horse.

I wavered forward and knelt down and set my hands on him. I'd handled enough dead fowls and rabbits in my time to know the 'dead' feel. It wasn't there. Immediately my mind began to work again, smoothly and sensibly.

'He's only stunned,' I said. 'Take his hat . . . ditch that side . . . get some water.'

Running home as I had done, I had gone in my apron. I took it off and used it to dribble the cold water over his face. Then I remembered that most gentlemen carried flasks when they rode abroad. Luke found it and handed it to me, but Mr Roger's flask had not been unstoppered lately; I had to hand it to Luke to unscrew. There was no more than a teaspoonful of brandy in it, and careful as I was it seemed to run from his mouth uselessly.

'I never meant to kill him,' Luke said. I went on dripping the cold water.

'Perhaps . . . the doctor . . .' I said at last, thinking sickly of all the miles between us and Baildon.

Luke turned towards the horse. Stopped and stripped off his coat and the knitted fisherman's jersey which Mother had knitted.

'Keep him warm,' he said, handing the garments to me. As I was wrapping them I saw Mr Roger's face begin to twitch. His eyelids flickered, opened, closed again.

'It's all right . . . he's come round,' I said.

His eyes opened again, looked at me, recognised me.

'Deb,' he said, in a puzzled way.

'Yes. It's all right. We'll look after you.'

'Shouldn't speak with your mouth full,' he said in an inconsequent way, giving me that singularly sweet smile. After a moment he said, 'I'm all right. Was I thrown? Belle'd never . . .' He began to struggle up. Luke leaned down and lifted him as though he'd been a child who had tumbled.

'Fulger,' said Mr Roger. 'No coat. Cold night too.'

'We're quite near the Lodge, sir,' I said. 'Could you sit on the horse if Luke lifted you? Or shall he carry you?'

'I can walk. I haven't broken anything. My wig . . . where is it? Feel the cold, you know.' I set his wig, muddy as it was, on his head.

'All this is very odd,' he said in the same bewildered way.

'I hit you,' Luke said in a humble, broken voice. 'I'm main sorry now. I was out of my . . .'

'Don't bother him now,' I said. 'Let's get to the Lodge.'

'Ockley,' said Mr Roger clearly. As he said it he sagged, bowed forward, with a stream of blood and vomit gushing from his mouth. And once more my hands knew; live weight and dead weight are not mere butcher's terms.

It was Luke who broke the immeasurable silence.

'I'll carry him to the Lodge. You get back to Mother and warn Tad Thatcher on the way.'

Tad was constable that year.

'I can't do that. They'll hang you.' My bitten tongue had swollen, every word cost me agony, but I must talk now if I never did again.

'I kilt him.'

'You did not. You hit him. It was an accident. You had cause; and drink in you too. But they wouldn't . . . No, Luke, if I can manage . . . this must be between us two for ever.'

'A man should take his punishment.'

'You'll be punished . . . your conscience . . . all your life,' I said cruelly. 'But there's Mother . . . worked so hard, helped you–d'you want her to end in the poorhouse and me be branded murderer's sister all my days? Don't ruin us all for one unlucky blow. Let me look at you!'

I inspected his face.

'He hit me more about the body like,' he said simply, and I found that heart-breaking–summing up as it did in so few words the dead man's lack of viciousness even when attacked.

'Hands,' I said sternly. One knuckle was barked a bit.

'Suck it.' I ran my eye over his clothes. If he'd gone to the Fat-stock Show he would have worn his best and the mud on his breeches knees where he had knelt would have shown. On his stained workaday ones it was unnoticeable.

'Put on your other things. Now listen. You must do exactly what I say. Back to the Evening Star. You set me on my way . . . went back to celebrate. Buy drinks for everybody. Go home. Don't say a word . . . ever. Do that and I can save you.'

'But, Deb . . . I'd as lief hang as live now. . . .'

'So you think now. You wouldn't when you found yourself in the lock-up. For Mother's sake, Luke. Hurry. Be too late soon.' Oh, if I could only get him moving. What could I say?

'Most likely they'd hang me too, Luke, for helping you. I can't hide my mouth.'

That did it.

'But what'll you do, Deb? Alone here with *that*. Murder can't be hid.'

'Never you mind . . . less you know . . . better. For God's sake, move!'

The moment he turned and began to walk woodenly away I set the horse's head towards Merravay and dealt it a blow which set it galloping off. With any luck it might go rushing past its own gate, and even if it failed to do so the people in the Lodge would have heard galloping and be unlikely to be able to say positively whether they had heard one horse or two.

Then I waited for a little while. I was not frightened. I stood there in the dark, alone with a man just murdered, and worked everything out as though

I were doing a sum. Afterwards, as long as I lived, I was to go through the whole thing in my dreams, starkly terrified, and wake screaming; but then, when it mattered, I was calm.

I ran to the Lodge and shouted and threw things at the window until Bert Baxter put his head out. Presently I was mumbling out my story–so exact in many details; how I had just left Luke and turning the bend in the road had seen Mr Roger struggling with a man. How I had been hit myself. The man–a stranger–I said had thrown himself on his horse and galloped away. The Baxters had heard a horse. . . .

At some point of my story somebody whipped round and asked what I was doing out that night, and even for that I had an answer. I had so wanted to know whether Luke had won the fat-stock prize.

INTERLUDE

Deborah Fulger's story was accepted without question. People found it easy to believe that the assailant was some highwayman lying in wait for some market-merry farmer jogging home from the Fat-stock Show. Only a stranger to the district would have gone into ambush on a road that in winter led nowhere except to Merravay.

Sir George Fenstanton, who had been extremely fond of Roger Whymark as well as interested in his schemes, had another theory. He believed that Roger Whymark's premature and abortive anti-slavery campaign had alarmed someone with vested interests, someone powerful and unscrupulous enough to hire an assassin. Occasionally, in his cups, he was heard to say that he could make a shrewd guess, and that if only he had a shadow of proof . . . but that was never forthcoming.

In the early days of his grief Sir George swore that he would continue Roger's work; but he was not the stuff of which reformers are made, and in the end his contribution to the cause was accidental and posthumous.

During his lifetime he had gathered together and had printed and bound in fine morocco leather every word which Roger Whymark had ever written on the subject of slavery. Decades after his death a friend of his grandson's, a man named Clarkson, rode over from Bury St Edmund's and was shown into the library to wait because Sir Philip was down at the stables overlooking the dosing of a favourite hunter. The monograph lay, as it had lain for years, on the writing-table, side by side with a silver inkstand, arid as the Sahara–Sir Philip was no scholar. Mr Clarkson, a hopeless print addict, picked it up and began to read and never noticed that the ten minutes he had been asked to wait had stretched to fifty. When his friend, soiled, sweating and apologetic, did arrive he raised a face upon which horror and excitement conflicted.

'This,' he said, holding out the monograph, 'is the best prepared and correlated mass of evidence on any subject that I have ever seen. Years old, of course, but nothing's ever been done. Conditions are worse now, if anything. Would you mind if I borrowed it? I'd like Wilberforce to see it.'

Sir Philip, who could read if he had to, just as he could bear toothache, said that Clarky could have the whole damn library for all he cared.

'Who exactly was this Roger Whymark?'

Sir Philip knew all about that. He described the tragedy and went on to say how after it the family had split up; they'd built a fine new house at New Holding and only an old aunt and the family governess had gone on living at Merravay. They'd sealed themselves in by planting a shrubbery across the top of the avenue.

'Like in the story Sleeping Beauty. *Only they weren't. At least, I never saw the old aunt; the other I did, once. Enough to frighten the French. She's dead now, and she left the house back to the Whymarks. I hear old Bill's trying to sell it.'*

Sir Philip naturally knew about the Whymarks, whose eccentricities and bargains and quarrels had been the subject of dinner-table chat. He was not familiar with the story of Luke Fulger, who at the opposite end of the social scale had become a legendary figure. Humble people still spoke of him as proof of what could happen when a man let success go to his head. Sober, hard-working sensible chap that he seemed, he'd won the fat-stock prize and that had ruined him, for he went on drinking to his victory till the day he died. There never was, there never would be again, such a drunkard as Luke Fulger was. From the night of the Fat-stock Show onwards nobody ever saw him sober.

And when he died his sister Deborah, the best sister ever man had–she'd stuck to him through thick and thin and even found him a wife, hoping to reform him–had put a stone over the grave. A plain stone, with just his name, the dates of his birth and death and the words, 'He will be long remembered'. And those words were truer than most such cut in stone over graves; for people were still saying, as naturally as they said 'Hard as iron', 'Drunk as Luke Fulger'. Not that anybody ever was, of course.

EPISODE FIVE
Late Georgian

THE NABOB

Chapter One

This evening, entering the house, I had, for the first time, a sense of ownership; that inner confidence of possession which says, 'Mine! My house! My hearth!' Why that feeling should strike with such poignancy at this late hour I cannot imagine. It has always been fairly plain that I had only to outlive Father to inherit Merravay; and he has been dead for almost a month. Moreover, for six years, ever since his stroke, I have been master here; but it wasn't until today when I made my will, naming as my heir a young man for whom I care very little, that I felt the place to be really mine.

In the room which I invariably use when alone, a comparatively small and cosy apartment with a little ship forever sailing across the chimney-breast, all the papers relative to Merravay were still lying about. I say 'papers', though this is so old a house that some of the deeds are written upon leathery parchment in script that is, to me, almost illegible. A name, a date here and there, stands out.

Unlike Ockley, where the Fennels have lived, father and son, for three hundred years, or Mortiboys, which the Hattons claim to have been in the family from Saxon times to within living memory, when Chris Hatton staked it on a gambling game, Merravay has changed hands several times–good business for the lawyers. Even when, as happened in 1729, it passed from Whymark to Whymark, it was the subject of formal and complicated transfer. One Whymark received it in exchange for some land at New Holding, where their present family house stands. Earlier, in the middle of the previous century, a Phyllis Whymark appears to have bought it twice! She could not sign her name; instead there is, in each case, a large, firmly inscribed cross, and written below it, 'Phyllis Whymark, her mark'.

I sat for an hour looking through the deeds and thinking. In these dry and dusty documents with their formal phrases one aspect of Merravay's history is told. What of the human stories behind? For wherever living people meet there is a story. I, for instance, have inherited Merravay in the most normal way; I take my place in the company of its owners as 'George Frederick, my beloved son'. Neat, dull, ordinary. But behind that there is a story too. The story of what I paid for my heritage. But the paying has been so protracted and so subtle that I am at a loss to say exactly what I gave. The self-dramatising devil that lurks in us all prompts me to say, 'My soul'; but that would surely be an exaggeration. A scrap of integrity here, a bit of self-esteem there, a little cowardice, a little cynicism, a larger amount of what sometimes seems to be a ridiculous obsession.

It began in the November following my sixteenth birthday when Father came home from India, unexpected, unannounced, and took me away from my school at Withernsea. I had spent ten years all but a term there and been dully miserable all the time. There are, I believe, worse schools; places where boys are starved, savagely beaten, and taught nothing. Ecclestone House was not like that. Mr Ogilvy loved to teach and was, on the whole, sparing with punishment, though he could lay on at times; and nobody *starved*, though a constant diet of bread, potatoes and porridge induced in us a perpetual, nagging residue of hunger for something else, so that we nibbled hips and haws out of the hedges, chewed leaves of wild mint and avidly devoured apples no larger than marbles. Our way of life, our surroundings, were of unrelieved dreariness, all cold and grey and dull. Most of the boys had begun life, as I had, in warm, sunny places overseas, pampered, perhaps spoiled, by native servants; Ecclestone House specialised in caring for boys whose parents were abroad. Only a few of us could look forward to a holiday or to a visit from a relative. In ten years I had only left Withernsea once. Time, thus unbroken by things to look forward to or back upon, stretched endlessly. As a forcing place for scholars Ecclestone House was unsurpassed. With every other outlet for interest closed, all but the most congenitally stupid boys sought what relief mental effort could offer, and Mr Ogilvy could point proudly to many old boys who had done very well in after life.

I was just a dull, average kind of boy, without, I think, much imagination; and to this day I believe that if Father had removed me one year earlier we should have got on well together. That I should have been happier, I know for certain.

But during my last year a new parson came to Withernsea, and very soon evinced interest in the school. Ecclestone House being run on what was known as 'sound Church of England principles', the clergyman was naturally *persona grata* within its walls. He liked boys, he saw that our lives were dreary and pitied us; he also, I suspect, saw us as potential raw recruits to the cause he served. He used to ask us, two or three at a time, to his house, where, having regaled us with strong sweet tea, inch-thick slices of sparsely buttered toast and very solid seed cake–all of which, unluxurious as it was, seemed to us like heavenly manna–he drummed into us, bluntly and openly, the principles of his Methodist-flavoured faith. His religion had little to do with dogma or ritual; it was not highly coloured and perhaps not very spiritual; it was vigorous, earthly and militant; and it boiled down, really, to the simple order, 'Put yourself in his place.' He told us that it was good for us to be cold and hungry, because when we got out into the world we could then sympathise, in the real sense of the word, with those countless people who were doomed *always* to be cold and hungry. By example as well as precept he bore home to us that 'Put yourself in his place' did not mean just another man's place; it applied equally to women, and to animals. Christ's words, 'These are my little ones', he said, meant every living thing on earth except one's self.

To this day I can never think of the Reverend James Carter without thinking of the parable of the Sower and the Seed. So much that he said must have fallen on the stony ground, or in the weed-choked places; but there may be many men in the world who stop for a moment, now and again, and think, and measure, as I have done, their conduct against the standard that he set. And I hope that to bolder, more positive characters than mine he has been an inspiration. To me he has been little more than a hair shirt, worn secretly.

The first person to whom I began applying the principle of justice to all was Mrs Ogilvy. In school she was known as the 'Old Hag' and was credited with every meanness, every furtive shift known to woman. Our parents–those who were abroad–were charged five pounds a year for our clothing; yet everybody knew that only when a boy was about to leave, or go home for the holidays, was he given a new garment. Mended, patched, let out, taken in, clothes were passed from boy to boy in endless line. We held that against her; as we held the dull food, the thin blankets. It was easy to think of her as a harpy, battening upon our privations. Then one day I looked at her and saw her with Mr Carter's eyes, and I saw her as a fellow victim–either of Mr Ogilvy's greed and mismanagement, or of a system which compelled them both to make the lowest possible charges in a competitive market. Anyway, I saw Mrs Ogilvy as a woman, past her first youth, continually harassed, running Ecclestone House with such poor help as could be obtained, since nobody with any choice would work there. She always wore a kind of linen cap in the house and her face sagged heavily, like a hound's, but one day a strand of hair broke loose and fell along her cheek, and mingled with the grey of it there was a glint of yellow, and I found myself thinking that once upon a time she had been young and her face hadn't sagged and her hair must have been pretty. And perhaps Mr Ogilvy–young then, too, though that was unimaginable, even to me–had loved her and told her how pretty she was!

And, oh dear, I thought to myself, how sad everything seems when you start putting yourself into another person's place; and now I can't bring myself to say that my Sunday jacket is inches too small.

So I was wearing it, and the breeches that must be hitched dangerously low if they were to meet my hose, and the shoes with the patches-upon-patches, on the day when Father arrived and Mrs Ogilvy came and told me to make myself tidy and go to the parlour because my father had come.

The man in the parlour, standing by the too-recently lighted fire and sipping, with an air of distaste, a glass of that Marsala known to the school as 'parent-juice', was a stranger to me despite the fact that I had prided myself on my exceptional memory. They say that white children who start their lives in tropical countries mature early; that may be true. Or it might be that for ten years I had been in the same dull place, with very little to overlay the vivid memories of childhood. I believed that I remembered my father, my mother, my ayah. I am certain that I remembered my ayah's ear-rings; three strands of copper wire threaded through a blue bead, and the left-hand bead chipped in two places. But the man in the parlour bore no resemblance to the parent I had remembered, who was red-faced, fleshy, blue-eyed and cheerful-looking. This man was tall, stooping, and very yellow; even the whites of his eyes were yellow. His face was heavily lined and his mouth was a thin, greyish-purple gash. Nothing familiar and nothing pleasant.

I recovered myself quickly, bringing Mr Carter's principle into play, and I thought–Well, he saw me last, a fat, curly-headed six-year-old, all in white, fresh from the ayah's hands, and what does he find! A lanky scarecrow, overdue for the barber, with legs and arms sticking out in all directions. I mustered a sheepish grin. Father came over to meet me, set his hands on my shoulders and kissed me.

'I'd have known you anywhere,' he said. 'The hair alone! Not to mention the nose. . . .' He stood back, looking at me with, for a moment, undisguised satisfaction. Mr Ogilvy, not much interested, for he had grown used to men coming from the ends of the earth to claim boys they had not seen since infancy, muttered something about there being a remarkable resemblance, and went on to say that I had been a good, untroublesome pupil. As he spoke Father's look of satisfaction changed to one of deep disgust.

'They aren't your best clothes, are they?' he snapped.

With a nervous side-sliding glance at Mr Ogilvy, I nodded.

Father said, 'Well, I'm damned. . . .'

He swung round and began to rate Mr Ogilvy, who said:

'I'm afraid that is not my business, Mr Sandell. All that I call the domestic side. . . .' At that moment Mrs Ogilvy, who had hastily changed her gown and put on a clean cap, came sidling in. 'Ah, my dear, how timely,' Mr Ogilvy said. 'Sandell's father was asking about his clothes. They do look a trifle small. Perhaps you should explain that Sandell has grown rather phenomenally in the last week or two.'

There followed a thoroughly nasty little scene. Mrs Ogilvy said–which was not true–that the tailor was making me some clothes. Father pointed to a mend, a patch, a place where the jacket I was wearing had been let out and expressed his doubt that this had been made for me, and fitted me, so lately as last year. He did not lose his temper, he did not raise his voice; coldly, relentlessly he stated his grievance. Mr Ogilvy glared at his wife, and her face, after going dark red with angry confusion, began to quiver. Seeing that, I said, 'It is, Father, entirely my fault. Two Sundays ago, when I put on these clothes, I realised that I had grown out of them. But I knew Mrs Ogilvy was planning for the tailor to come . . . and I didn't expect to grow quite so much in just a fortnight. . . .'

'Quiet a minute, my boy. Let me speak,' said Father. And speak he did, to such point and purpose that Mrs Ogilvy began to cry and Mr Ogilvy offered, with injured dignity, to return Father five pounds if he wasn't satisfied.

'Never mind that, now,' Father said, a little mollified by the offer none the less. 'The boy is alive and looks well, that's all I care about. D'you own a top-coat, George? Get it, then, and we'll go.'

'You mean now? Am I leaving today?'

He nodded, and I went bounding away, so full of joyful excitement that I thought I might burst.

At Hull, where we stayed for a few nights in an inn which seemed unbelievably luxurious to me, though Father had many faults to find with it, I was fitted out with clothes and had my hair dressed; then we drove, by post-chaise, to Peterborough, where my sister Olivia was at school. I asked Father whether he intended to remove her as precipitately as he had done me, and he replied that he wasn't sure; a great deal depended upon Olivia and upon the school. Olivia was almost two years older than I, but we had come to England together in charge of a woman friend of my mother's who was bringing her own children home. Once during our ten years of exile that same woman, kind soul that she was, had invited us both to spend Christmas with her family. I had not seen Olivia since then, though we wrote to each other two or three times a year. I tried to tell Father what she was like, but apart from the fact that she was amiable and pretty I could find little to say. I could inform him that she liked her school, for during that brief holiday I had listened with astonishment, incredulity and envy to her account of it. And when we arrived the home-like, easy-going atmosphere of the place made itself felt in a moment.

Olivia was quite grown up, though she was not now as tall as I; she was dressed in a way becoming to a young lady and bore far more resemblance to the mother I just remembered than to the sister I had seen five years before. She was very pretty, with a face like a kitten's and extremely black hair which grew off her forehead in a point.

She came into the room where we were waiting, a little shy, but demure and with a smile ready. I though that Father would be delighted with her. But his manner was strange, stiff and quite unaffectionate. I put that down to shyness, and to her looking so like Mother, which probably waked sad memories in him. Having shaken her by the hand and asked her abruptly how she did, he stood back and stared while Olivia turned to me and put her arms about my neck and kissed me and rubbed her cheek against mine and said how lovely it was to see me. Then she said:

'And dear Papa! After all these years. Oh, isn't it exciting? Oh, I could cry for joy!' And she did begin to cry.

'Now, now, there's no need to be silly,' Father said.

At that moment one of the Miss Rossiters, followed by a maid with a tea-tray , came bustling in. She was a very animated and garrulous old lady and passed over the awkward moment by asking Father a series of questions that needed no answers. Then she said, 'Come now, Olivia dear, dry those happy tears and pour tea. Exhibit to your papa those pretty manners which we have tried to inculcate.'

Olivia's dimples peeped, her cheeks went pinker as she sat down behind the tray. She asked in the prettiest possible manner:

'How do you like your tea, Papa. With cream? Sugar?'

'I never drink it,' he said.

'Well,' said Miss Rossiter, gaily, 'we know what to say in that case, don't we, Olivia?'

Olivia was obviously disconcerted, but she said:

'I say, "Perhaps you prefer sherry or Madeira. Many gentlemen do."'

'But not to *me*, dear. To your guest.'

More confused than ever, Olivia repeated her words to Father.

'That is right, child,' said Miss Rossiter. 'And *then* you ring the bell.'

Father said later that it was at that moment that he decided to remove Olivia from school. 'Damn play-acting. Time she learned sense!'

Chapter Two

We spent the next few weeks moving about looking at properties that were for sale in the east of England, the part which Father preferred because it was driest; and so, in early February, we came to Merravay.

A handsome old man mounted on a large grey horse met us at the lodge gates.

'The house is rather difficult of access, I fear,' he said when we had greeted him. 'So I came to show the way.' He led us along an avenue of limes to a point where the trees went on but the road was blocked by a mass of shrubs, dark laurels and lilacs just pricked with green buds. On our left several trees of the avenue had been removed to make a gap, and beyond this another avenue of younger trees led away and ended in a great white-pillared house in the Palladian style.

'Of all the stupid things they ever did,' said the old gentleman in a confidential, conversational voice, 'blocking this avenue was the silliest. That is my house.' He pointed to the big white one. 'Merravay lies there.' We could see, at the end of the closed avenue, a cluster of tall, rose-coloured chimneys. 'And now we must take the cart-track,' he said, and led the way between two trees on the right-hand side, to a beaten path only just wide enough to allow passage for the carriage. It ran skirting the closed avenue for a while and then curved to end in the stableyard at the back of the house.

It struck me that Father was well disposed towards Merravay from the first. In other places which we had inspected his first words had usually been of a critical nature. Here, as soon as he alighted, he stared round and said, 'I like that. I've seen several places where what they called the Home Farm was a mile or more away. Difficult to keep an eye on.'

'We could go in at the back. I found both keys,' said Mr Whymark with almost childish pride. 'But I think you should see the front first.' He opened, with some little difficulty, an elegantly patterned gate of wrought iron, set in a length of red wall, and ushered us into a moderately well-kept garden. But he sighed as he looked round.

'Dear me! What an air of neglect. I send over fairly regularly and have it tidied, but it's painfully obvious that nobody has *loved* it lately. Do you like gardening, Miss Sandell?'

'I've never tried. I think I should,' said Olivia.

'Now we'll take this little path and come out at the end of the garden. Of course the best view is from the top of the field. Still, this gives some idea. . . .'

We emerged by a low red wall, set with grey urns filled with daffodil spears, and there we turned to face the house. I thought it very beautiful; and evidently Mr Whymark had some feeling for it too. He looked at it for a long moment and then gave another gentle sigh.

'Isn't it *grim*?' Olivia whispered to me, catching my arm as we followed

Father and Mr Whymark up to the house.

'I rather like it,' I said. And a moment later, when the great door was opened and we stepped into the hall, I suffered that emotion which, in other circumstances, is known as love at first sight.

I was so fascinated by the place, so anxious to look in every nook and cranny, literally feasting my eyes, that I could not wait for Father and Mr Whymark to make their more systematic and leisurely progress. Dragging Olivia by the hand, I went from room to room, upstairs and downstairs, delighting in all I saw. The two men were still upstairs when Olivia and I came back into the great hall, and there I knew the full measure of my enchantment when Olivia said:

'Oh, I do hope and trust Father doesn't buy *this* house! It's *much* the worst we've seen.'

In the past weeks Father had so often checked and snubbed and chided her and told her not to be silly that she had developed a meek, almost mute manner in his company, and when she was alone with me indulged in a compensating exuberance. So I ignored a good deal of the emphasis in her words.

'Why don't you like it? I think it's beautiful!' I looked round as I spoke. The hall was as long and wide and high as a small church. Just inside the door was a fixed oaken screen, most delicately and exquisitely carved. At the farther end a magnificent staircase led up to an open gallery. At the foot of the stairs the banister rails ended in a great solid post carved into the figure of a man, so lifelike that one could see the ripples in the hair of his head and beard. He leaned on a staff, and the set of his shoulder, the bracing of his hands on the staff, gave one the impression that he was holding up the staircase.

'Look at *him*!' cried Olivia, following the direction of my stare. 'Imagine taking a candle and going up to bed past him! Oh, I should be terrified. Dear George, George darling, I do beseech you, try to persuade Father not to live here.'

'But he's a benevolent old fellow,' I said, going nearer the figure. 'He'd wish you pleasant dreams as you passed.' But that wasn't true! There was a sternness about the carved face.

'Oh, but look,' I said, 'it's Moses, with his stick turning into a snake. Why, Olivia, if this were in a church or anywhere except a private house people would go to see it. It's a wonderful piece of carving–it's a work of art!'

I put my hand over the knotted, gnarled wooden ones that clenched the stick, and felt what I can only call a satisfaction. At the same time, through the great window, I saw a view of the garden: the green of the grass, the warm rose of the wall, the dark field, the wood beyond.

'And what a view!' I said.

'What of? A ploughed field and a wet wood. Oh, George, no! Truly it frightens me; there's something terribly unfriendly about it. Hateful.'

'Now that is silly,' I said. 'Considering that it is empty, and has been for five years, I believe, it seems to me extremely welcoming. Think of that one we saw at Kelvedon. This doesn't seem like an empty house at all.'

'No, it doesn't. It's haunted, George, that's what it is. And the ghosts hate us for disturbing them.'

I knew enough by this time to realise that her opinion would not influence Father in the slightest; I had no fear of that. What I minded was that she should say such things about the house I liked so much. So I said peevishly:

'Oh, for Heaven's sake, Olivia. Don't talk such absolute nonsense.'

She saw that I had lost patience and began in her pathetic eager-to-please, frivolous little way to try to make me laugh.

'It was nonsense. I was joking. But, George dear, can't you just imagine . . .' and she started to rattle off an account of just what ghosts Merravay might harbour, headless ladies and men dragging chains.

Charm, particularly charm of speech, is difficult to define and impossible to describe. Odd little turns of phrase, the timing, the glance that accompanies the words, all mean so much. But whatever it is, Olivia had it in full measure, and soon I was laughing and protesting that now she was frightening me.

In the midst of this a sound on the stairs made me look up, and there was Father, followed by Mr Whymark, coming down. Father was looking at Olivia with such cold distaste that the laughter died on my lips. It was a look of physical revulsion, such as a man might turn upon a dish which had once badly disagreed with him.

Mr Whymark said genially:

'I can't tell you how it delights me to hear young voices in Merravay again. I spent my early childhood here, you know. I had two sisters, not much older, and after Miss Maybrook became our governess we had very merry times. She was so kind to us . . . and so gay. Poor girl.' And again there came that gentle little sigh.

Father said briskly that he had still to see the buildings and wanted to get back to Baildon before dark.

On the way home he said that if the question of access could be settled to his satisfaction, which meant that Mr Whymark knocked the cost of making a new avenue off the purchase price, he was prepared to buy Merravay.

'Did he happen to tell you why the old one was blocked?' I asked. I was in that state of mind towards the place which, when turned towards persons, leads one to ask where they were born, what games they played as children, what is their favourite book.

'Oh, some long-winded story about a row between his mamma and an aunt. So far as I could make out, the aunt liked the house and his mamma loathed it–his elder brother came to a tragic end, or something. The aunt owned the land where the New House stands, so they swopped. And they couldn't share the avenue–which, by the way, I don't wish to do either–so she had it blocked. And then some jumble about the aunt leaving it to–why, yes, that governess he mentioned, who lived there all alone apparently, like a hermit, until five years ago, when she died and left it to him. He's been trying to sell it ever since. I should say he's hard pressed for money. Small wonder! He told me he'd been married three times and had eleven children in all. Talkative old fool; but if we mean to settle here it'll pay us to humour him . . . up to a point.'

I was so delighted that Father liked Merravay that I could overlook his attitude towards a charming old gentleman.

Chapter Three

One of the things I had said to Olivia in an endeavour to cheer her, once we knew that Merravay was to be our home, was that no house should be judged in its empty state. Imagine, I said, the difference which carpets and curtains and pictures and furniture would make. That remark was both prescient and an understatement. I had no idea then of what Father intended to do. Lodged in a warehouse at Hull he had five or six enormous crates containing things he had brought from India. Their freightage must have cost a fortune, for each of them displaced its own bulk in tea, or pepper, or cloves, or nutmegs–all very valuable commodities. Father had brought rugs and carpets so silkily smooth, so brightly coloured that it seemed wrong to lay them on the floor and walk over them; he had brought yards and yards of the thin embroidered silk which at that time, I learned, was being hung upon walls in rich houses and imitated in paper for the decoration of homes less wealthy; he had brought cabinets and chests in red or black lacquer heavily gilded; and there were dozens of ornaments too, some beautiful, some grotesque, made of ivory and ebony, of silver and mother-of-pearl, or jade and soapstone.

Even the ordinary household furniture which we bought during visits to London–visits which included my introduction to theatres and tea-gardens and coffee-houses–was all beautiful and all costly: elegant ribband-back chairs, sideboards and tables and chests of drawers in satin-smooth walnut wood.

Father paid me the intoxicating compliment of inviting my opinion about everything he bought. My taste, like any other hobbledehoy's, was unformed and dubious, but I knew what was elegant and pleasing even then. Sometimes the expense worried me, especially as Father often grumbled about it and tried to haggle with the shopkeepers. Once I mentioned the matter and he laughed.

'Bless you, boy, I could buy the shop and the man who owns it and never notice. But it doesn't do to let them know, they'd fleece you.'

Sometimes, when the burden of choice between two things weighed heavily on me, I would say, 'But which do *you* prefer, sir? After all, you have to live with it.'

'You have which you like. It'll all be yours one day.'

Perhaps I dwell unduly on those days, when everything seemed wonderful and exciting, rich, pleasant, colourful and comfortable. But even then . . . there were moments. One I particularly remember. On a miry day, on a bit of bad road, going uphill, the horse in our hired carriage, a poor thin old beast, made heavy going. I said I would get out and walk to the top.

'Damn silly idea! Get yourself muddy,' said Father. He leaned out and called to the driver.

'Get along! Use your whip, man! What's a whip for?'

Settling back, he went on to talk, pleasantly, on the subject which I had interrupted.

I should, of course, have known then.

We moved into Merravay about midsummer, and with the sunshine without and the splendour within there was little to remind us of the day of our first visit. The drawing-room walls had been hung with the silk, a deep maize yellow embroidered with flowery boughs and bright birds. In other rooms where the surface of the panelling did not lend itself to hanging the oak had been painted, white and gold, or pale bluish-green. The great open hearths in most of the rooms had been enclosed with slabs and pillars of marble and provided with basket grates, graceful as Grecian urns. But the hall–the place which at that time I liked best–was almost untouched. Father had decided that the stair-posts and the fine screen would be ruined by being painted, so he had left them and the walls in their natural state, and he had retained the open hearth there too. But to compensate for the lack of colour he had gathered against the dark background all the brightest of his Eastern treasures; the most glowing rugs, the red lacquered cabinet and chest, great bowls and vases of painted porcelain. Just to look at the colour, so lavishly spread, was to know a lifting of the spirit.

It may be because I had left a place of bright sun and gaudy colours and lived so long in grey Withernsea, where the schoolroom floor, the sea outside, the sky above were all the same dull neutral hue, that I was, and shall always be, susceptible to brightness, even to the extent of loving a dirty gypsy woman because of her scarlet neck-cloth, even to the extent of liking to see poppies in a cornfield, indicative of bad husbandry as they be.

I know that when I entered Merravay for the first time after everything was in place I thought–I shall feel pleasure every time I come in here, no matter what happens. I should, in fact, have been perfectly happy during our first months at Merravay if only Father would have been nicer to Olivia.

Nothing she did, nothing she said could please him, that was the truth of it. I'd been long enough with him now to realise that he didn't care for women at all, he always spoke contemptuously of them; but he could be, and often was, perfectly civil when face to face with a woman of his own class. To Olivia he seemed unable to be civil; and at the same time he seemed unable to let her alone and allow her to avoid him, as she tried to do. Like a man with a sore thumb, he must keep picking.

'Where's your sister? What's she up to?' he would say. He would enter the house, 'Olivia! Olivia! Oh, there you are . . .' and launch into some complaint; nothing too trivial, nothing too absurd. He had a curious theory that women must be kept busy, otherwise they got into mischief, grew fanciful, took to tea-drinking and gossip. In this belief he assiduously invented little jobs for Olivia. His linen was badly laundered–Olivia must do it; yet, to judge from the resultant, never-failing complaints, she was worse than any laundress could be and keep a job. The maid who cleaned the silver dropped and dented one of the branching candelabra–Olivia must polish it in future; and it is a fact that from the moment she took on the task he never touched or saw a piece of silver without giving it the closest scrutiny, and nine times out of ten he would find something to rebuke. It was like a sickness. He had bought, in London, one of the new pianos, and Olivia, who had learned to play a little and had a good ear and clever fingers, liked to play. The music she made was always wrong–too loud, not loud enough, miserable belly-aching stuff, a silly tinkle. But when, in despair, she ceased to play except when he was out of the house that wasn't right either. Why had he given all that money for a silly toy if it were never to be used?

It all sounds petty and trivial, almost laughable, and sometimes indeed Olivia and I did laugh together–a little hysterically–about it, but it was hateful to watch, a continual jarring of the nerves. In the beginning I had occasionally put in a politely worded, mildly reasonable protest. 'That's hardly Olivia's fault, sir,' I would say. He would retort, 'It's none of your concern, my boy!' or 'I know what I'm about, George', and I soon learned that by speaking I did more harm than good, for always later on he would be more actively disagreeable to her. I should, of course, have hated it had he taken a similar attitude to me, but at the same time I did not enjoy the pointed contrast. Sometimes Olivia would say, half laughing and half crying, 'Oh, you're all right; you're "*George, my dear boy*", the fortunate fellow who can do no wrong!' And to that I could only reply, 'I believe he's a woman-hater!'

'Then why did he ever bring me here? He could have left me at Peterborough. I was much happier there, George, truly. If this goes on I shall write to Miss Rossiter and ask if I can go back and teach the small girls. I shouldn't want any wages.'

'You'd do better to stay here and get married,' I said.

And indeed as time went on the idea of Olivia's finding a husband and having a home of her own became to me as delectable an idea as ever it could have appeared to a girl herself or to the most scheming match-making mamma. I grew more and more inclined to shuffle off a feeling of guilt and responsibility where she was concerned by thinking that this state of affairs couldn't last for ever; Olivia would soon find a husband and be out of Father's clutches.

Nor was it by any means a far-fetched idea; for one of the fears which Olivia had voiced, the fear that life would be very lonely at Merravay, proved to be entirely unfounded. We had no sooner settled than Mr Whymark invited us all to dinner 'to meet a few neighbours'; and soon we were entertaining and being entertained at least once a week, and sometimes more often. Perhaps it is the ever-present danger of life becoming dull in the country which makes country people really cultivate and bother about their social activities; I know that all around us were people who seemed to enjoy the company of their fellows and to be extremely tolerant of one another's little peculiarities, and to be willing, though with a certain understandable caution, to welcome newcomers into their circle. Very soon Father gave a special Indian dinner, with curries and strong pickles and fruits and sweetmeats and Candy, our negro servant, in his finest clothes moving around like a shadow; and that was a great success. It was plain that the new state of Merravay's interior impressed everyone very much. And Father, without making any particular effort to be agreeable or ingratiating, seemed to strike just the right note, particularly when he confessed that he knew absolutely nothing about English agriculture and expected that for a year or two he would lose money. At that the English countryman's desire to be helpful with dictatorial-flavoured advice came uppermost. Almost every man at the table immediately offered to ride over and just cast an eye on this and that. Then Sir Evelyn Fennel, who lived at Ockley Manor and was related to the Whymarks in some degree, said:

'You'd do better, Sandell, to get a good steward. Otherwise you'll have civil war. Great-uncle William here, on my left, will tell you to plant seeds in the dark of the moon, he is so old-fashioned; while Hodge here, on my right, is so much day-after-tomorrow that he's taken to marling his land.' Everyone laughed.

Father said, 'As a matter of fact I have engaged a foreman who seems to know his job; a fellow called Tom Fulger.'

There was a tiny silence.

'He's knowledgeable enough,' said Mr Hodge at last, a little grudgingly. 'Worked one time for Coke at Holkham. Yes . . . he knows his job.'

'Well, what don't you like about him?' asked Father, going in his direct way to the heart of the matter.

'Damned revolutionary,' said Sir Evelyn. 'You keep your eye on him. He had the nerve to say–and in a public place–that any labourer that was worth his salt was worth ten shillings a week! That's where the rot starts. *They* don't want it; they haven't got the wit enough to think up such nonsense; but you get one or two big-mouthed malcontents like Tom Fulger rip-ranting about and then there's trouble.'

I came to know Tom Fulger very well during the next year or so. During the September after our move to Merravay I had my seventeenth birthday, and shortly afterwards Father asked me in a kindly casual way whether I had any ideas about my future. I had none; I was enjoying my present way of life and asked nothing but that it could continue. I hesitated to confess this lack of ambition and enterprise to a man who so often spoke about 'making opportunities' and 'taking time by the forelock' and so on; therefore I said:

'I haven't given the matter much thought, sir. Have you anything particular in mind?'

'I'm asking you.'

'Well . . .' I said.

'Surely to God, boy you know what you *want*; or what you *don't* want. The world's open to you. Would you like to go to the university, travel a bit . . . ?'

'If it were merely a question of what I should *like*, I should say that I should like to go on living as I am at the moment but to have more to do with the land, the farming side. That does interest me; and if I learned about it properly, one day I could run it for you.'

'Nothing would please me more. But why be so timid about it? It's the thing I should have suggested myself, but I wanted you to choose.'

'Well, I thought perhaps you might think it was . . . unenterprising. That perhaps you thought I ought to go out and tackle the world, like you did, Father.'

'I had to, my boy; if I hadn't it'd have damned soon tackled me. But you're different; you can have what you want, do what you like. And you don't have to thank me,' he said with a note in his voice that I had never heard before. 'You're part of the prize I wrung out of the struggle. When I was your age I was sweating over ledgers in an airless hole in a dirty stinking little place called Kumalore; and God help me if I made a blot. Yes, sir–no, sir–let me kiss your arse, sir–to clods and clowns that hadn't half my brains or my breeding, if it comes to that. And when I see you at the same age, George . . . I'd see you off on the Grand Tour, or to Cambridge, or if you wanted to go and make a young ass of yourself in London it'd all be one to me, because it would be like having it myself.'

I heard those words then and I felt warmly, gratefully towards him for saying them, for lifting the burden of gratitude from my heart, for making so free with all that he had. But later on I saw what lay behind them. I was nothing really, just a peg upon which he could hang another self. That was why I could have a fine new saddle-horse in the same week as he had grudgingly handed Olivia the price of the cheapest possible muslin dress, told her to buy the stuff and sew it herself. But that, as I say, came later. At the moment I was delighted because he was pleased with my choice of occupation, and delighted that I was to stay at Merravay, to know it better, to serve it.

Chapter Four

In that way I became, to an extent, Tom Fulger's pupil. He was a tall lean fellow with a face like a saint in a stained-glass window and a remarkable repertoire of swear-words. His family had lived in Nettleton since the beginning of time and his grandfather had been, by all accounts, a substantial farmer. One day when we were driving into Baildon market he pointed out to me the house in which his grandfather had lived and where his own father had been born. It looked a big, solid, prosperous place.

'That's why I never touch a —— drop of the —— stuff, not even home-brewed,' Tom said, leaving me to guess the connection. 'I had an old great-aunt, my granfer's sister–wonderful old woman too, she was, and kept things together longer than they'd have held otherwise–and I've heard her say that he was all right, doing wonderful well, taking prizes with his beasts and God knows what, and then one day something upset the old sod and he went and downed a glass of —— brandy. And never stopped. Drunk hisself out of Squirrels, drunk hisself out of Church Farm, drunk hisself out of two or three jobs old Deborah got him. They still say around these parts "Drunk as Luke Fulger". And all on account of once being upset in his belly, or maybe it was toothache. Soaking old sod, I hate even to think about him!'

I thought, but I did not say, that probably it was a Fulger trait never to do anything by halves. Tom was the most thorough man I ever knew. And just a little demented. He thought every man, irrespective of whether he owned property or not, should have a vote; he thought every labourer should have ten shillings a week; he thought every child should go to school; he thought all foxes should be shot, all race-horses put to work and only big, healthy bulls allowed to run with the cows. There was hardly a thing which had come under his notice about which he had not had some thought, and most generally his thought was in direct opposition to everyone else's. He afforded me a great deal of entertainment, and presently, when I had come to realise how sound and right all his ideas about agriculture were, I sometimes asked myself whether a man could be so sensible in one direction and wrong in all others. And that, of course, was a dangerous line of thought.

When I look back on that year and the next one I feel like a very old man. I suppose that if one is ever to have boundless enthusiasm and endless energy one has them at seventeen, eighteen. And perhaps the change of diet had an effect on me. I could rise at first light and be out with Tom, who had no nonsensical ideas about 'gentleman farmers' or 'lily-white hands'. Later in the day I could shoot or hunt or ride with Father, spend another couple of hours with Tom, and play cards or dance all evening. I've ridden home from a ball at the Baildon Assembly Rooms, changed my clothes and spent the rest of the night in the lambing-pen and not felt a penny the worse.

Olivia and I had no lack of friends of our own age. Of Mr Whymark's third family two girls and one boy were still under twenty, a gay, high-spirited trio; the girls particularly were allowed more freedom, both of speech and movement, than was common. It was young Phyllis Whymark's hoydenish ways which precipitated a scene in our family.

Father, although thinking little of Mr Whymark's capacity for business, was well aware of his social value and did nothing to discourage friendship between the two houses. Olivia was always at liberty to accept the frequent invitations to the New House, to ride, to picnic, to go shopping with Phyllis, who had developed for her one of those doting friendships in which girls delight. One bright April morning Phyllis came galloping over to know whether Olivia would ride to Ockley with her. Olivia came out to find me in the yard. 'Do you think I might go? Father isn't here, so I can't ask *him*.'

I said that naturally she could go. I had not noticed that before each previous outing she had had to seek permission.

'Oh yes,' she said, when I commented on this. 'Always. Cap in hand, "Please, Papa, may I go?" Just like school. Well, have I your permission, then, George?'

'Oh, don't be silly,' I said, a little embarrassed; and then, to cover the brusqueness, added, 'Enjoy yourself.'

She came in just before dinner. I had spent the day on the farm and come in and cleaned myself early; Father, who had been to Muchanger, was still upstairs, changing. Finding me alone, Olivia lingered for a moment, abandoning the quiet, repressed manner which she now, as a matter of habit, assumed upon entering the house. There was a new baby at Ockley and Phyllis was to be its godmother; there were hot-houses at Ockley and in them strawberries were already almost ripe. The simple, innocent excitements of the day were held out for my sharing.

'Well, miss, and where have you been all day?' asked Father from midway down the stairs. He looked quite savage.

'At Ockley with Phyllis, Papa,' said Olivia, instantly deflated. She moved to the stairs and stood aside to let him pass her, and then began, quickly, to mount them. Father walked to the centre of the hall, and said, 'Come here!' He raved at her for several minutes, going on after he had reduced her to tears.

Once I said, 'Look here, sir, she did consult me, and I . . .'

'Keep out of this, George,' he said, and raved on. Olivia, crying, said, 'But you weren't at home, Papa, so I asked George . . .'

'Will you leave George out of this?' he said furiously, and raved on. Finally he dismissed her to her room, saying that he did not wish to see her at dinner.

I made a cub's move.

'If Olivia has no dinner I don't want any either,' I said.

'Now for God's sake don't you start!' he said, and taking me by the arm he hustled me without ado into the dining-room just as Candy padded in with the soup tureen.

I sat down at my place, realising that I had put myself into a ridiculous position. Whatever I did now, whether I ate or refused to eat, I should look silly. And at the same time–so lacking in dignity is crude nature–I realised that I was extremely hungry. The plate of soup which Candy placed before me both looked and smelt painfully appetising. But I did not take up my spoon. I folded my arms and sat there, feeling a fool and looking like one.

After a moment Father cocked an eyebrow at me and said:

'George, you look exactly like a dog "on trust"! Eat your dinner, boy, and don't be so ridiculous.'

'I know it's ridiculous,' I said, 'because it makes no difference to the situation whether I eat or not! All the same, I think you were very unjust and unkind to Olivia just now, and it isn't the first time, either.'

'Well, suppose we discuss that afterwards. Argument at table leads to indigestion. Richard Whymark was at Muchanger today and gave me a message for you. The pups are ready to leave their mother, and he'd like you to have first choice. Young Stephen Fennel is going over there on Thursday, so if you want the really first choice you'd better try to get there tomorrow.'

'Thank you for telling me,' I said in a voice I tried to make cold.

He was too wily to repeat the friendly overture. The rest of the mealtime passed in silence, giving me ample opportunity to think, 'I am right. I am right,' and then to wonder whether the need to think so repeatedly wasn't in itself a sign of weakness.

We went back to the hall, where a fire was burning. Father took his usual chair and stretched his thin yellow hands to the blaze; then, rubbing them together, he leaned back and said in a conversational tone:

'So you think I'm unjust and unkind, eh?'

'To Olivia, sir; not to me. And that makes it rather hard for me to say . . .'

'Go on. State your case.'

'Well, just before dinner, for instance. You shouted at her that you would not have her careering about the countryside, her whereabouts unknown, her company unapproved and her behaviour uncontrolled. But if you had been here and asked for your permission you would have given it, I think. Well, then, I fail to see how an exchange of words between you could make all that difference to her whereabouts or her company, or her behaviour.'

'Very lucid, George. Very true too. Up to a point. The point being that in leaving the house without my permission she was flagrantly disobedient. It was no crime to go with Phyllis Whymark to Ockley to see a new baby, I agree with you there. But the trouble with females is that given an inch they immediately take a mile; and if on this occasion she escaped without reprimand, next week she would be off without leave on some less innocent errand.'

I almost said, 'That is silly!' but checked the words just in time.

'Well, are you satisfied?'

'I don't want to offend you,' I said, 'but it isn't just today's occurrence. You are, to my mind, very hard on Olivia always. She does her best to please you, but you never are pleased. She's young and inexperienced in housekeeping, but in that matter you behave to her as though she were forty and judge her harshly; and then in other matters you treat her as though she were a child–so she is never right. And it makes me unhappy to watch.'

Remembered, that speech sounds mild and reasonable; but then it seemed bold and challenging, and I waited, with lively apprehension, for the wrath that must surely follow. But Father said nothing. He got up and went to the red lacquer cabinet and took out the brandy. He poured some into a glass and drank it in a manner contrary to his fairly abstemious habit. He was–at least by Suffolk standards, which were all I knew–fairly abstemious and would sit for a whole evening with a similar measure of liquor, sipping and toying with his glass.

Filling the glass again, he closed the cabinet and returned his chair.

'It's a pretty good rule, you know, George, not to bother about what can't be helped.'

It was difficult to find an answer to such a pontifical statement, so I sat still and waited.

'And if a–well,'–he looked up and smiled–'let's say a yellow dog with floppy ears bites you, it's understandable that in future you don't care for yellow dogs with very floppy ears. You agree?'

Father's speech, though often pungent and succinct, seldom tended towards the metaphorical. That it did so now showed, like that gulping of brandy, that this was a critical moment.

'Well, sir . . . that would rather depend. Quite a different yellow dog . . .'

'Bitch, bred of the bitch that bit you?' he asked, raising his heavy eyebrows. 'Have I said enough, George?'

I could have left it there, I suppose. But I said:

'Either too much or too little. You seem to be implying . . .'

'Telling you, my boy, telling. I can't like her, George. That's something you'll have to accept if you and I are to remain on friendly terms. Every single thing about her; her size and shape and colouring, the sound of her voice, the very way her hair grows . . . and that laugh! You may not believe it, but I have *tried*? And it's useless. Simply by existing she sets my teeth on edge.'

'Because she is so like Mother?'

'That stumps you. Well, there you are, you forced it on me, George. You started it. So you'd better know. Your mother isn't dead. So far as I know she's still living in a dirty little bungalow at Kumalpore with a down-at-heel scrivener with the lung rot. And, by God, I hope she's hungry!'

I'd remembered her, pretty, kind and gay; and dead, preserved from change and age, static, enshrined.

'I was busy,' Father said in a flat, harsh voice–'busy trying to make money. I'd always given her everything I could; I wanted to give her everything that there *was*. But women are like that, George. You might as well know it now. Offer them a daisy and they want the moon; climb the sky and drag down the moon by sheer force and nothing will please but the daisy. While I was sweating my guts out *he* was playing his damned little tinkles; putting Hindu songs into English and setting them to music. Hindu love-songs . . . out of a country where women are less valued than cows. My God! The top of my skull still lifts when I think of it.'

I said the only thing I could think of. 'I'm terribly sorry.'

'Why should you be? Sorry for yourself, perhaps. I offered . . . when you and Olivia came home . . . I could have afforded it then–I offered that she should come with you. But the rot had set in; she couldn't leave then. So tuck this away in your mind, George; never let a woman get the upper hand of you;

they're all as false as hell. And now let's forget it. We've survived, and that is the main thing. Have some brandy . . . you look a bit white about the gills. Mustn't take it to heart, you know.'

It was only later on that I realised that my protest, the revelation it had provoked, and the understanding of Father's attitude which the facts had engendered in me, had done nothing to help Olivia or to soften her lot.

And whenever I think of Olivia I think of Candy too, because all my memories and all my remorses are inextricably tangled.

Candy was an African negro whom Father had bought in Zanzibar; he was often referred to as 'my man, Candy'. He had been bought for money, he received no wages. Father regarded him, and he regarded himself, as a chattel.

Coming through the Bay on the voyage home Candy had met with an accident and had broken a leg, so Father had left him in Hull in a hospital for the sick poor, and I only learned of his existence after Father had decided to buy Merravay and was, one evening, discussing the staff we should need in the house.

'A cook and three maids will be plenty,' he said. 'Your sister will make herself useful, and my man, Candy, will be both footman and butler.'

'Who is Candy?' I asked. Father explained, and I, with some muddled recollection of Mr Ogilvy's dissertations about socmen and serfs, said, 'But I thought one couldn't have slaves or be a slave in England.'

'That's as may be,' said Father. 'When you go to London you'll see every other fashionable lady attended by a little black boy. They buy them young, give them plenty of gin and make them sleep in cupboards to keep 'em small. They put collars on 'em, like dogs. I once saw one with a collar studded with garnets and turquoises; very pretty.' He smiled. 'I shan't put a collar on Candy. He's an ugly old devil, but you'll like him; I never saw his equal for getting a shine on boots. You look incredulous, George! See here.' He reached for the paper, turned it about and held it to me, pointing to a column. And there, sure enough, were several advertisements for black boys, wanted, for sale, or lost. The lost ones, I noticed, were all pockmarked and bowlegged; the ones for sale all handsome and very accomplished.

'Well,' I said, 'I never knew that!'

'If you will forgive my mentioning it, George, there were one or two things omitted from Mr Ogilvy's curriculum!' He smiled as he said it, and I smiled back.

'Can he speak–and understand–English?' I asked.

'Well enough. His last master was Portuguese, but I've had him nearly two years. I'd made up my mind to retire and that was my last visit to Zanzibar, and I'd heard such accounts of English servants from people fresh out from home I thought I must make sure of one good servant. And Africans are much stronger than Indians. . . .'

Candy came down from Hull in the wagon with the crates of furnishings, and my first thought about him was that he was very ill-clad for the English climate. It was a day of bitter March wind and he was wearing a pair of thin cotton trousers and a short jacket of the same stuff. His huge feet were thrust, hoseless, into a pair of shabby shoes. He was a good deal older than I had expected him to be, his close-curled black hair looked as though it had been lightly powdered, and he was less black than I had imagined, for at that moment he was the curious pinky-grey colour which negroes go when they are ill, or cold, or frightened.

'Poor thing,' I said, 'he's frozen. He must have some warmer clothes.'

'He's all right; he'll warm up when he starts moving about. What he certainly is is damned filthy.' Father turned to Candy and said, as one says to a child, 'Dirty! Dirty.' Candy's eyes rolled like loose marbles in their sockets.

'Four days, no water, no wash. All ize, ize, No water.'

'Plenty of water here,' Father said. 'Help with this stuff and then wash.'

That was a day when we were only at Merravay in order to see the furniture safely in, and just before dusk we drove back to Baildon to the inn where we were staying. When we went towards the carriage and Candy climbed up beside the driver I was horrified to see that he had taken literally Father's orders to wash. His coat and trousers were now clean, but quite wet and already plastered to him by the wind.

'He's wet, the fool,' I said. 'He'll catch his death. Shall I give him my coat?'

'George, please,' said Father, putting one hand on my arm and pulling me into place beside him, while with the other hand he drew up the rug. 'He's all right. He'll take no more harm than a dog would. You must get that into your head. You might just as well go and give your coat to one of the horses.'

If Candy had sneezed or snuffled next day I could have said, 'There, I told you!' but he did not. He took no apparent harm at all.

The next time–or at least the next time I remember–that I spoke up on Candy's behalf was, oddly enough, the time when I thought he would be too hot. It was when we finally moved into Merravay, and I discovered that Candy was to sleep in the chimney room, which was just a space partitioned off around the main chimneystack of the house. The whole of one side of it was made of the red-brick chimney; there was floor space about six feet long and four wide, and it had no window. Three little round holes bored in the top of the door which divided it from the passage admitted the only air.

'He'll stifle,' I said.

'You'll see,' said Father.

But just as Candy had not frozen, so he did not stifle. I used to remind myself of that, trying to believe that negroes were different, less sensitive. I had to take comfort in that thought if I could, for Father was hard on Candy; just as he was hard on dogs and horses, hard on Olivia, hard on everybody except me. I really must have been the world's worst simpleton, always to think myself exempt; never to guess that he knew all about the hair shirt Mr Carter had slipped over my head; never to guess that I was as much his slave as Candy.

I didn't. I went on my gay, happy way, thinking how lovely everything was and how much I should enjoy myself if only . . . if only . . . if only . . . thinking that Olivia would one day marry and get away . . . thinking that Candy, after all, must be made differently . . . thinking all the coward's thoughts.

Chapter Five

Time slipped away. I found myself devoting more and more attention to the farm. Father took singularly little interest in it, though he would walk around the yard every now and then and make a great fuss if a bucket or a wisp of hay were out of place; he liked it all spick and span and he liked to show visitors round. But the ordinary routine bored him, and I came, almost unconsciously, to look upon my work as a refuge.

Olivia had her twenty-first birthday. Father gave her a pear-shaped ruby on a gold chain and then cut into her timid expressions of gratitude and pleasure with the remark that she was now an established old maid. Some time ago, towards the end of our first year at Merravay, Olivia had put into action her threat of writing to Miss Rossiter to ask if she could go back to Peterborough as an unsalaried teacher. Miss Rossiter had written her a long letter, rich, I suppose, in sorry wisdom. Any girl, she said, who had a home and a father who was willing and able to provide for her should thank God every morning and evening for such blessed security in a world where so many unfortunate females had none. Dozens of women–some as young as fifteen, some as old as fifty–had applied for the last post they had advertised, and almost all had said that they were willing to work for no salary; some had even offered small sums of money as well as their services in return for bed and board. So would dear Olivia–the letter ended–please cultivate a meek and cheerful spirit even when things were a little difficult, and remember always to count her blessings. . . .

When I read the letter I said:

'Well, I never did think it a very good idea. You stay here and get married.'

And steadily, over the next two years, whenever I thought of Olivia I assured myself that she would get married; she was so pretty. But though at parties and picnics men paid her plenty of attention and she never lacked partners at the balls we attended, somehow no young man, to my knowledge, ever sought for Father's permission to marry her; and all too soon she was twenty-one, and Father, when at a loss for other taunt or gibe, could always remark that she was becoming an old maid.

Just before my birthday, my nineteenth, Father surprised me by announcing that he had invited an old acquaintance, a Mr Douglas Booth, to come and stay. My surprise arose from the fact that Father seemed to have severed all connection with his past; and although he spoke freely and authoritatively about India and Indian affairs–then much to the fore on account of the trial of Warren Hastings–I do not remember ever hearing him mention any one of his former associates by name. I evinced some interest in Mr Booth, but Father had nothing much to say about him, save that he had known him years ago but had not seen him since his return to

England. I was left to judge for myself that he was a man for whom Father had some regard. It was arranged that he should occupy the master bedroom, the one which local legend, confirmed by Mr Whymark, said had once been slept in by Queen Elizabeth. And Olivia, whose wardrobe was, for a girl in her position, very modest, was given permission to buy two new dresses.

Mr Booth arrived on the afternoon before my birthday. He was considerably Father's senior, small, very dried and brittle-looking. To begin with, he seemed painfully nervous and shy, but later on his manner showed traces of aggressiveness and self-importance. His carriage, his horse-flesh, his clothes and appurtenances were evidence of his wealth, and he irritated me on the first day because when he was looking over Merravay he followed each favourable comment by another which showed that, compared with his own place in Berkshire, Merravay was very small beer indeed. I remarked upon this to Father, who said:

'Well, I believe Gore Park is quite a palatial. He inherited it from his grandfather, who made a great fortune before the public conscience became quite so tender about such things.'

'Oh,' I said. 'I thought he'd been in India with you.'

'So he was. He held an official post. But he's regarded as the only man who ever went to India and came away with nothing but his pay in his pocket. A phoenix!'

'Is he married?'

'Not that I know of,' Father said carelessly.

That evening Mr Booth regained the ground he had lost in my opinion over Merravay by being very pleasant in a nervous, unobtrusive way to Olivia. He asked her if she played the piano, and she said she did but had not practised lately.

'If it wouldn't trouble you, I wish you would play a little for me. I am exceptionally fond of music and used to play myself . . . before . . . well, my handicap . . . you know.' We had all noticed that the first and second fingers of his right hand were missing; he referred to the loss as though it were something to be ashamed of.

Olivia glanced at Father, who nodded. She went to the piano and played, with nervous clumsiness at first and then with more assurance. Mr Booth named several of his favourite tunes, some of which she knew and some she had never heard of, and he listened with unassumed interest and pleasure. When she had finished he thanked her and said she had a very pleasing touch. Father stayed silent; Olivia blushed.

Next morning, learning that it was my birthday, Mr Booth apologised, too effusively, for not having known and come provided. He insisted that I should accept a very fine seal from his own fob. In the evening, when several neighbours came in to dine, and to dance later on in the hall, he apologised again for his inability to dance–perfectly understandable on account of his age–and instead of retiring to play cards with the other old gentlemen he hovered about, looking like a little grasshopper, on the verge of the gay crowd. I thought him pathetic and once stayed out from the dance to talk to him; but he said he was enjoying himself, the music gave him pleasure and he liked to see people making merry. At Gore Park, he added, there was an enormous ballroom with mirrored walls. 'But seldom used; all too seldom used.'

Next day we went to Ockley to shoot partridges, returning for late supper in the evening. The principal dish was a large game pie, which Mr Booth praised quite fulsomely.

'Yes,' said Father, 'Olivia has turned out to be quite a skilful little housekeeper.'

Even then no breath of suspicion stirred in my mind. I was simply glad that someone for whom Father seemed to have regard should say the things which I often wished to say about Olivia but knew would be ineffectual coming from me. Old, ugly, fidgety and annoying as he was, I felt my heart warming to Mr Booth for pointing Father the way to a better appreciation of Olivia.

A very pleasant week followed. Mr Booth had arranged to leave on market day, so, knowing that I should be up early and breakfast alone, I said goodbye to him overnight. When I shook, with an inward shudder, his cold, scaly, mutilated hand, and uttered the conventional hope that we should soon meet again, he said, shyly:

'Indeed I hope so. I hope to see you all at Gore Park. I particularly want to show you my Home Farm. And the whole estate, of course; eighteen thousand acres in all.'

'I shall look forward to that, sir,' I said, and took my leave.

Next day, coming back from market and about to enter the house from the rear, I heard a little tapping sound from over my head, looked up and saw Olivia signing to me from her window. As soon as I had divested myself of my boots I went along to her room. Pressed against the glass, her face had looked very white and distorted; but that, I told myself, might have been a trick of the light.

She must have been crying for hours, her eyes and her nose were puffed out of shape, and at sight of me she began to cry again so violently that it was some time before I could understand the reason for her distress. Then it came out.

'Oh, George. Father says I am to marry Mr Booth!'

I said–I shall always remember the words–'I wouldn't let you.'

At that she flung herself into my arms. 'I thought you'd be on my side.'

'Of course I am. I never heard anything so ridiculous. Why, he's older than Father! Father must be stark staring mad.'

'With rage, he is. I said I'd rather die.'

I could understand that. This bit of news had scraped from my mind all pretence that I liked the man because he had been pleasant to Olivia and civil to me. I knew all along I had seized on the small bearable things about him because I hated the sight of him and felt guilty for taking such a dislike to any human creature. Now I could admit to myself that I loathed him, everything about him; the dark, reptilian leathery skin, the pale, bright, reptilian eyes, the scanty, scurfy hair and the bad teeth. And that sly, creepy manner. And his age! How could he dare to think of marrying any pretty fresh young girl, leave alone my sister?

'I'll go and talk to Father now,' I said.

Father was dressed for the evening; Candy, on his knees, was easing on the light, buckled shoes.

'Ah, George, I was coming along to talk to you while you changed. I've something to tell you. You're late, aren't you? Run along, I'll be with you in a minute.' Candy rose and went to the chest, sprinkled a fine linen handkerchief with lavender essence and presented it humbly to Father, who accepted it without a glance and tucked it into his cuff. 'Come along,' he said, 'I'm damned hungry. But you must change; you smell, George. What is it–pigs or yokels?'

'I'd better say what I have to say now.'

'Oh. I see. Five minutes, Candy. Well, George, I take it you've been treated to a display of hysteria. I was coming to warn you. I expect Olivia cried on your shoulder and said that she would rather die, eh? Women use these expressions so lightly, you know; many would rather die–by their own evidence–than pass a spider in the open road. you mustn't take that to heart, George.'

He said all this in a light, flippant way which was somehow more deadly than anger would have been.

'I'm not going to stand by and see Olivia married to that little toad,' I said hotly. 'He's old enough to be her father and as ugly as sin. The whole idea is so revolting I wonder you entertained it long enough to tell her about it.'

'Well, I agree that it is rather a striking example of Beauty and the Beast, so far as appearances go; but it's the right way about, you know. Now if you contemplated marrying an ugly old woman, George, I should take a very different view. As it is, I am delighted.'

I could see that. My fury mounted.

'Yes; but then you've never had any natural feeling for Olivia, have you? I happen to be very fond of her, and I won't stand by . . .'

'Don't repeat yourself, George. Time's short. As for that accusation . . . if I were as doting a father as old Whymark I could hardly hope to arrange a better match for my daughter. Mr Booth admires her very much; he is in a position to give her every comfort. I'm sure he'll be kind to her, and once she has forgotten about the handsome young man that every girl expects to find round the next corner she'll be very h . . .'

At that moment the great gold-and-silver inlaid, pearl-and-coral encrusted elephant bell, which Father had brought from India and which served as a gong, rang out.

'I shall begin,' said Father, moving away from me.

I tried to hold on to my bold, angry mood while I hastily washed and threw off my market-day clothes; but when I rushed down again to the dining-room, ready to take up the cudgels again, Father, with a sidelong glance at Candy, began at once to talk upon some trivial subject. He put himself out to be pleasant, and since I knew that to anger him would be of no help I contrived to be pleasant too. Imperceptibly the atmosphere warmed.

Candy put the port wine, the fruit dishes and a bowl of walnuts, the first of the year, on the table and withdrew.

'Now,' said Father, 'we can continue. Bawling her head off and talking about dying, she upset you, I know. She was just being girlish; they always behave that way when they're first proposed to.'

'Olivia was genuinely distressed. And so should I be. God! In her place I should be thoroughly sick at the thought.'

'That is one of the troubles with you, you know. I've often noticed it. You will always go putting yourself into somebody else's shoes–Candy's, Olivia's, even a horse's. That is such a waste. You can't understand how they feel, you only judge by how *you* would feel in their place. Naturally the idea of yourself in bed with old Douglas hugging and kissing you makes *you* feel sick. If it didn't there'd be something seriously wrong with you! Where it's a matter between man and woman it's entirely different. Damn it,

George, have you never seen a fine lady give a hearty kiss to a filthy sweep who had crossed her path and brought her, she thought, luck? Make a little allowance for sex, boy. And for God's sake don't go and encourage her whimsies. It is a pity she got her word in first.'

'That makes no difference. Even if she wanted to marry him, Father, I should hate the idea. He's too old; and ugly; and creepy. I want Olivia to marry somebody nice; somebody she *could* be fond of.'

His thick eyebrows arched quizzically.

'Have you a candidate in mind, George? Take your time,' he said, as I hesitated. 'All these avid suitors take some counting, don't they?'

'Well,' I said, 'I know that just at the moment . . .'

'Come, come,' he said with testy good humour, 'face facts, George. She's twenty-one and there's a dearth of young men. Of old Whymark's eleven, only three were boys, and it's the same wherever you look. Also, much as this will shock your tender susceptibilities, there's this to remember. Love fizzles out and the lucky people are those who have something left when the kissing is done. Can't you see that she's damned lucky to get such an offer? And believe me, once the first coyness wears off she'll realise it. Poor old Douglas, he was too shy to speak; he asked me to prepare the way and then he'd write her a nice little letter. By the time that arrives she'll have come round and be as pleased as a dog with two tails. You'll see. So don't you worry, George; and don't encourage her to keep up this play-acting. And now, since we're alone for once, how about a game of chess?'

In the next few days he ignored the subject.

Olivia and I talked of the matter when we were alone, and she certainly didn't seem to be affecting the deep revulsion she professed; and whenever I was with her I shared her feeling and repeated that of course the idea was absurd, untenable, that of course I was on her side and would support her in her refusal.

Then one afternoon two letters arrived–one for Father, which I didn't see, and one for Olivia. It was a stilted, pompous little letter and it said that the proposal it conveyed was made with Father's full knowledge and approval.

'You see, they settled it between them,' said Olivia.

Father was out that evening. Next morning, having been out for a couple of hours, I came in to breakfast to find him literally forcing Olivia into a seat at the table.

'You will sit there and eat your breakfast properly. Pretty, eh? You look like an old woman who's lived through a famine! You'll eat your breakfast and then you'll write that letter.'

Olivia dared not refuse the food he kept thrusting at her, but she cried all the time; and there is something about a person who is eating and weeping that is–well, unendearing, to say the least of it. I was shocked to find that my pity was giving way to irritation, as pity so often does in the end. After the nasty meal was over Father tried to force her into the library to write but she refused and he started to shake her, and I said, 'Stop that', in a high, shrill voice quite unlike mine.

'Yes. That was a mistake,' said Father as Olivia wriggled out of his hands and ran, loudly crying, upstairs. For the first time since the affair had been mooted he seemed to lose a little of his composure.

'Look here, George. That letter must be answered. More hangs on this than you know. She's carrying coy reluctance just a little too far. Go and see if you can talk sense into her.'

I went up. Olivia turned and said, 'Oh, poor dear George, I've made you fall out with Father.'

I remembered all the things he had said about women being different, and being coy and being hysterical and being silly about spiders and kissing sweeps.

'Now, for God's sake, Olivia dear,' I said, 'be quite honest with me. Is it just . . . ?' She looked at me, and I was ashamed. But, as though she had sensed my Father-instilled doubt, she jumped from the bed upon which she had flung herself and went to her dressing-table.

'He thinks I'm pretty, does he?' she said. She took up the scissors and with three sharp snaps of their blades cut off all the little curls which clustered about her forehead. Then she dragged the points of the scissors down her face from just below the eye to the jaw. The parallel furrows leaped up, beaded with little drops of blood.

'All right,' I said, answering something that hadn't been put into words. 'I'll tell him. Don't you worry any more.'

Father was waiting.

'It's useless,' I said. 'She just can't do it; and I don't want her to.'

'Let's go for a ride,' he said.

It was one of those mellow autumn mornings when the thin mist shreds away and the sky is harebell blue, and everything wears a gentle, wistful look. Father led the way along the narrow headland that divided the front field from Layer Wood, which was blazing with copper and gold and sharp yellow. Single damp bright leaves fell slowly down, spinning.

Speech was impossible while we rode one behind the other; but at the top of the field Father halted and I drew up beside him. From this point one had the best view of Merravay, for the field ran down towards it and the trees rose behind it so that it seemed to be cupped in the loving hand of the earth. This morning the worn old walls, the slightly uneven roof were drinking in the sunshine and giving it back again in a glow of apricot and rose and tawny. A thin column of smoke from one of the chimneys went spiralling up, blue against blue. In the garden the flower-beds were fragile patchwork against the solidity of the lawns, the carved yews.

I had meant to speak as soon as we halted, but having looked at Merravay I was compelled to sit and stare for a moment, thinking that I had never seen it look so lovely.

It was Father who spoke first, breaking the silence by saying, in a rapid, staccato, strangely distinct voice, as though addressing someone slightly deaf or stupid:

'Look here, George; this has gone far enough. I gave you several perfectly good reasons for my approval of this match; there is another which I wasn't particularly anxious to talk about. But since you are so stubborn and will insist on encouraging her I must tell you. You've read all this ridiculous nonsense about Hastings, I suppose. All right! Now when they drop the net for big fish they take small ones too. An inquiry of that nature turns up a lot of things one believed to be done with and forgotten. And I've realised in the last month or so that at one point I am vulnerable. It would be very useful for me to have Douglas Booth on my side.'

'You mean that you did something . . . and now he's blackmailing you?'

Father laughed.

'Really, George, you do so tend to melodrama. If there is blackmail in it, the boot surely is on the other leg. I'm the blackmailer. I've got what poor old Douglas wants; and whether he would ever be called upon to repay me is very much a matter of chance. I just want to make sure that in the event he would stand by me. You're not the only one who likes Merravay, you know. I'm fond of the place too.'

'What has Merravay to do with it?'

'I should not, if it came to the point, sit there waiting for Messrs Fox and Burke to slap *me*, George. My gains, ill-gotten as they may seem to such sentimentalists, cost me dear, and I shall hang on to them. At the first breath of trouble, unless I can be sure of Douglas, I shall sell out and go abroad again.'

He paused to let that sink in.

'And I still think,' he continued, 'that Olivia would be better off in her own home, with a rich and doting husband and a pack of children–she's the sort who would breed once a year–than she will be as governess or companion to a lady! For I tell you frankly, George, and you can tell her, that if she doesn't go to Gore Park she doesn't stay at Merravay. As it is, the effort to be fair and just to her is just a little too much for me, and after *this* . . . if she defeats my neat little scheme for self-preservation by sheer pigheadedness . . . I doubt if I could keep my hands off her. You saw what happened this morning. If she won't go my way, she must go her own, and discover just how much fairness and justice there is in this world.'

I said the only thing possible for me.

'The day Olivia goes out to earn her living, sir, I shall go with her.'

What effect I expected the speech to produce I find it difficult to say. I knew, or thought I knew, that his affection for me, though rooted in his self-love, was firm and strong. But he was evidently one of the 'if thine eye offend thee, pluck it out' manner of men. He turned and gave me a long assessing look and then said in a reasonable way, far more chilling than any sneer:

'Well, if that is the way you feel, George, there's no more to be said. You're a nice-looking boy, you write a clear hand and have pleasing manners when you choose. You'd be worth every penny of eight shillings a week as a clerk; I started with less. In that case Mr Booth can hang himself for all I care. I always had a nagging desire to be a country gentleman, and I thought you liked Merravay. I was prepared to settle and found a family. But without you it would be pointless to stay. So if you've had your fill of it we'll say goodbye to Merravay as soon as possible.'

With that he swung his horse round, set it to the low fence between field and meadow and went galloping off, leaving me with his last words ringing in my ears.

I often wondered whether he used the phrase 'Goodbye to Merravay' deliberately or not.

The next four or five days were as wretched as any I remember. Olivia kept to her room. Father and I met at table after the first evening, when I absented myself and he sent Candy to fetch me. 'I see no reason why we should avoid one another, George,' he said. 'You're young and romantic, I'm old and practical, and we take different views, as men are entitled to do; but let us behave in a civilised fashion.'

My interviews with Olivia were just as trying in another way; she cried and cried and kept begging me to make it up with Father. I had told her, so far, only that Father had threatened to turn her out and I had said that I should go too; I hadn't mentioned Merravay. She had written another letter to Miss Rossiter, explaining that now she was about to be homeless, and begging her to employ her or find her employment of any kind.

'She'll help me now that my circumstances have changed, George, I am positive of that; and truly I should be happy, glad, pleased to go from here if only you hadn't said that you'd come too. It's so much worse for a man to be poor. Nobody expects a woman to have anything, anyway. And I shall have a place to go. It was a kind, noble gesture, George dear, and I do appreciate it, but you're making everything so much more difficult for me.'

Constant crying and misery had marred what looks the scissors had left; and looking at the bristly hair and deeply scratched face I kept thinking–Yes, that was a gesture too; and whom did it hurt?

'Do please say that you'll stay with Father.'

My jangled nerves gave way.

'God damn it all, Olivia, why should I? He's kind enough to me, but the way he treats Tom Fulger and Candy and you sets my teeth on edge. There are times when I hate him, and I don't intend to go trailing about the face of the earth in his company just for the sake of his filthy money!'

'What do you mean by trailing about, George?' she asked, suddenly quiet and intent.

'Well,' I said, confused, 'nothing really. But there is some sort of threat; he may have to leave Merravay. It's some sort of inquiry or something which Mr Booth could ward off if he was so minded. that's one reason why Father is so . . . Oh, for God's sake, Olivia, don't *cry*! I didn't mean to tell you that. I was just trying to show you that I might as well go with you, of my own free will, as wait and be chucked out.'

'And now I've lost Merravay for you,' she cried, and threw herself face downwards on her bed.

'Well, if you can't discuss the thing reasonably . . .' I said, and went away.

On the fourth or fifth morning, at breakfast, Father said to me, 'Has Olivia written at all?'

'Not to my knowledge.'

'Well, tell her to do it today. A civil, decent proposal demands some answer, and there's no point in being more offensive than necessary. Tell her, too, that she'd better start looking about for a post. *I* meant what I said, George.'

The slightest possible emphasis on the first pronoun fired my temper.

'So did I,' I said.

'Then you had both better start looking!'

He ate some food rather more quickly than usual; then, emptying his mouth, said:

'This is all your doing. If you hadn't backed her up she'd have given in within twenty-four hours and written Dear-Mr-Booth-you-do-me-too-much-honour-and-what-kind-of-a-ring-can-I-have? As it is, she thinks you'll bring me round. If George is for me, who can be against me? They're all as crafty as foxes, and she thinks she's on a safe bet because I'm fond of you. I *am* fond of you, when you're amenable, but I'm damned if I'll be blackmailed, even by you. You're turned against me, and I'm one of those who do not love their enemies.'

'A few days ago,' I retorted, 'we were civilised people taking a different view–or so you said. Now you call me your enemy.'

'A few days ago I was counting on your fondness–not for me, for Merravay, George. So we're all wrong. And why God Almighty ever took into His head to make women I shall never understand. Surely His infinite wisdom could have devised some less troublesome way of propagating the human race. Everything ruined by one cock-snitched little bitch's whim . . . encouraged by *you*. You'll remember that to your sorrow!'

He was going to spend the day at Muchanger, and shortly after breakfast he rode off.

I had arranged to work with Tom that day, but suddenly I had no heart for it. My future at Merravay, learning about and then managing the land, the crops and the flocks, was like a path, seeming to lead on and then stopping suddenly. I had no future here.

I wandered idly into the garden. There was a slight autumnal chill in the air that morning, but the sun was shining on the dew that lay like silver on the lawns and sparkled on the thousands of cobwebs which stretched from leaf to leaf. A brilliant cock pheasant rose from a bed of marigolds and flew to the red wall, where he rested for a moment between two of the grey urns and then flew on to the field. The furrows lay striped in dark chocolate and faint purple. The wood blazed with a last desperate fire.

'I saw Father leave,' said Olivia, coming up softly behind me.

'Yes, he's gone to Muchanger.'

'Did he say anything?'

'Yes, he said you must write to Mr Booth today. And he said we must both begin to look about for jobs. And he said everything was my fault.' I tried to speak lightly but failed to keep the inward dreariness from sounding in my voice.

Olivia plucked a marigold and stood staring at it as though counting its petals.

'George, dear, do please give in. I'll tell you something . . . I didn't think either of you would hold out so long.'

I laughed. 'That's exactly what Father said. We must be a very stubborn family.'

'I'm being stubborn for my own benefit, George. You're doing no good at all. I do with my whole heart beg you to make it up with Father.'

'I tell you I don't care about Father.'

'But you do about this place.'

'I shall survive.'

She turned and stared at the house.

'Isn't it strange,' she said, musingly. 'I hated it from the first; you loved it. It was inimicable to me from the beginning. Like a person. Quite apart from any other reason, I shall be glad to leave the house. If it belonged to me absolutely I shouldn't want it.'

'Look, Olivia, we're wasting time again. We must make plans, think what we're going to do.'

'I think I should write that letter first.'

In less time than I expected she came to the door, the letter folded and sealed in her hand. 'I've done it,' she called brightly.

We walked towards one another, and when we met she held out the letter, address uppermost, very clearly written.

'Doesn't that do Miss Rossiter credit?' she asked.

Something cold and gall-bitter rose from the pit of my stomach to choke my throat. Oh yes, I thought, you may well be gay, now. You're leaving a critical parent and a home you hate . . . anything to you will seem an improvement.

Just at that moment Phyllis Whymark arrived; she wanted Olivia to go with her to Baildon to match some ribbon.

'Of course,' said Olivia. 'I was going to take this to post, anyway.'

'What on earth have you been doing to yourself?' Phyllis asked.

'A series of accidents. I burned my hair with the curling iron and scratched my face on a rose bush.'

'I've been in the wars too. Look, young Billy hit me in the mouth with a ball; took one tooth out, clean as a whistle. I shall never get married now!'

'Married!' said Olivia. They went off laughing.

A day at Muchanger seemed to have restored Father's good humour too. Olivia had not returned when we sat down to dinner; but since she was no longer expected at table her absence was not remarked upon, and he seemed to go out of his way to be entertaining, giving me a lively account of his day's doings. It was impossible to avoid the thought that with Olivia out of sight and mind, with Olivia away, we two got along pretty well. A self-pitying consciousness that I had made a fool of myself to no purpose came inevitably upon that thought's heels.

We were halfway through the meal when the door slammed, and before I could do more than hope that Father would not connect the sound with Olivia she had reached the dining-room door and stood there, looking pretty and in some way different. Her riding clothes were worn and shabby, but they had been made for her and fitted better than some of the clothes she had made for herself, and the little cocked hat hid her spoiled hair; the flush of a day in the open did something to conceal the marks on her cheek. But the difference lay deeper than mere appearance. She moved and looked like a free woman at last; as though the shy, demure schoolgirl had spent three happy, successful years somewhere and now looked in to visit us.

Father looked at her, his ordinary expression of cold distaste shot through with positive venom. For the first time in these years she met his look without flinching and stared back, her eyes as hard as his own. My heart began to beat with a nervous flutter.

'This is an unexpected honour,' said Father with heavy irony. 'But I trust that you do not expect to dine here. You are both late and unwelcome.'

'I dined at the New House,' said Olivia. I caught her glance and signed to her to go away, but she stood her ground and it occurred to me that she might be a little flown with wine. The females at New House were very free in such matters and often stayed at the table with the menfolk, sharing the port wine.

'It's all right, George,' she said, answering my sign. 'I have something to say to Father.'

'Nothing that you have to say would interest me, now, miss. Get out!'

'All the same, you should know,' said Olivia hardily. 'I wrote to Mr Booth this morning and accepted his proposal.'

Astonishment held us both speechless for a moment. Then Father said, 'Well, I'm damned!' and began to laugh.

I said, 'Olivia, you didn't!'

'I hope that pleases you both,' she said, and her glance flicked, like the very tip of a whiplash, from Father's face to mine; then she turned and walked, very straight-backed, to the door.

'There you are. What did I tell you? That's women for you, George. Unpredictable as the wind! All that fuss, and she meant to have him from the start.'

'She did not! She changed her mind this morning. And I know when . . . and why . . .' I was almost crying, so sharp and terrible was my remorse, my knowledge of my secret disloyalty, my recognition of a flashing relief.

'You must have been remarkably eloquent, George,' said Father.

'It's nothing to laugh at,' I said savagely, jumping up from my chair. 'And she shan't do it. I shan't let her. I'd sooner see the place burned . . .'

I went blundering towards the door, but Father, from his end of the table, was quicker, and stood there with his back against it.

'Don't be in such a hurry,' he said quietly. 'Such militant chivalry will keep for a minute. Sit down and hear what I have to say.'

'You won't talk me round,' I said. But I let him push me back into my chair.

At that moment Candy returned, and I realised that all this shattering little incident had happened in the time it took to change plates between courses.

'Oh, take it away, and yourself with it,' snapped Father, motioning the dish away. 'Put the decanter on the table and get out.'

As soon as we were alone again he poured wine for us both, and then, for just a second, sat silent, twirling the stem of his glass between his fingers.

'It would be most unkind of you, George, to withdraw, now, whatever it was that you said or did this morning! I mean that. You see, you'd be taking away her excuse for doing what she wants to do, what she has wanted all along to do.'

'I don't believe that.'

'You can test the truth of it presently; but I won't have you, for the second time, go blundering in blindfold. On that first evening, if I'd caught you before she did, I could have explained, warned you, and none of this fantastic muddle would ever have arisen. You see, George, he is ugly and he is rich–a most damning combination where women are concerned. A woman could marry an ugly poor man and still feel noble, or a rich handsome one and feel romantic. D'you follow? What Olivia was waiting for was some reason that would be acceptable to that vanity which women carry about with them like a set of scales–and you gave it to her. Her warped female sense of values would seize with delight on the notion that she was saving you from exiling yourself. I'll bet that she was writing that letter before whatever it was you so fortunately said was out of your mouth.'

To myself I admitted the truth of that–the apparent truth; but his whole premise I could not accept.

'I will take back what I said if she will take back what she wrote.' I tried to remember exactly what I had said–so little, so vague; it must have been my manner rather than my words which had provoked that impulse of self-sacrifice.

'Well, you can try,' said Father, calmly. 'It would, as I say, be unkind; and I think it would be useless too. She knows that such offers don't come every day. Also, if she hasn't whispered it was the most deadly secret to Miss Whymark, who by this time has told everyone within reach, I'm a Dutchman.' He paused while I thought about that.

'I'd rather have her silly, then, than sell herself in a loveless marriage to that little toad on my account.'

'You know, George, you are most devastatingly like a woman in some ways–the way you talk. Sell herself! Loveless marriage! Old maid's twaddling stock phrases! And the way you shift ground. This morning, apparently, you conveyed in some way your wish for the match to take place; the moment it's settled you're all against it. It's time you grew up, you know. Men know what they want and take it by hook or by crook, if they can, and are glad. If you feel impelled to pity *some*body,' he said, a malicious grin beginning to spread over his face, 'pity poor old Douglas. He'll have to line up with me now; and then start at his inflexible age to accommodate himself to Olivia's whims and fancies.'

'Not if I can prevent it,' I said.

'Run along and try,' said Father, settling back and lifting his glass.

Olivia listened politely to all I had to say, but she would not budge an inch. At one point, made cruel by exasperation, I cried:

'I believe Father is right, I believe you want to marry the man after all. And you're the girl who would rather die!'

'I'm not,' said Olivia, giving me a strange look. 'That girl did die, writing the letter. I'm a different girl, George.'

'Oh, don't talk rot,' I said, and my voice sounded like Father's.

'It's true. I am different. Why, I actually heard myself boasting to Phyllis about the glories of Gore Park!'

I gaped at her. So Father had been right about the whispered confidences. Probably right about the secret wish to marry. . . . Despite that creeping doubt, however, I continued to argue and plead until at last Olivia said, 'Really, George, I did think that now I should be left in peace.'

Chapter Six

I suppose that the final, the fatal defeats never come to a man from the outside; they are inflicted from within. And I suppose that those inner defeats are never the result of one great battle–ground is lost inch by inch. What Father stood for as opposed to what I tried to stand for was not triumphant until I began to suspect that he was right; but the struggle had begun long ago. Perhaps as long ago as the day when we met in the Ogilvys' parlour. I could look back and think, if I hadn't been so easily silenced when I tried to speak up for Mrs Ogilvy . . . if I had got out on that hill and walked in the mud, if I had stood up more resolutely for Candy . . . I should have altered, not Father's nature or behaviour, but my own; I should be a stronger character. It was the dreadful weakness of my own character that distressed me most when I thought about Olivia; the weak hysterical support, the weak self-pitying withdrawal of it, the weak tardy effort to replace it.

Outwardly all went very well. The wedding, by Olivia's express wish, took place before Christmas. Father, pleased with her at last, did everything in fine style and gave her a generous marriage settlement. Two of his casual prophecies were fulfilled: she bore her first son within a year and within six years had five, all healthy and surprisingly handsome. And given her inch she took her mile; Mr Booth certainly had to accommodate himself to her whims and fancies. It would be difficult to find a more masterful and exacting wife, a milder, more tolerant husband. Sometimes it is easy for me to believe that Olivia Sandell did die that sunny autumn morning, and went–a wistful little crop-haired ghost–to join the ones she always said haunted Merravay.

I live on, most enviable young man; but something in me had been damaged. For one thing, I could never marry, never again feel at ease with any woman; Father's cynicisms and Olivia's transformation combined to put that out of the question. And with men I became conscious of a feeling of inadequacy. I could still work and do business with them, but I could not share their pleasures. With the passage of time I became misanthropic as well as misogamist, quite against my will.

I never opposed or openly criticised Father again. The impulse would arise, sometimes, especially when, during the trouble time six years ago, wages became a matter of hot dispute, but as soon as I had convinced myself that he was wrong I would remember the number of times when he had been proved right. I never even argued with him again. And he seemed to lose interest in me. Our relationship settled down to a placid coolness to which his illness and long immobility hardly made any difference at all. Six years ago Tom Fulger, long since gone from Merravay, which I was, by then, capable of running on my own, came, as the representative of the farm labourers, to see Father about raising the winter rate of wages to match the rising price of food. Father, who had never liked Tom, lost his temper and had a stroke. A few days later, without telling him about it, I raised all the wages. After six years, during which I visited his room every morning and evening and saw to it that everything was done to alleviate his suffering, he died. And after the funeral I moved into the great bedroom, where I had always wanted to sleep.

Romantic defeated, impulsive warm heart turned cold, unfriended–for that raising of the wages turned every neighbour against me–a self-hater, a weak, poor-spirited fellow, I sit here tonight and know that I am happier and more fortunate, in the final issue, than anyone else I know. For I love, with an unchanging love, something that cannot change. And today, with the willing of Merravay to Olivia's third and favourite son, I have shaken off an old nagging sense of indebtedness. If I liked the boy better my sense of repayment would be that much less complete; willing it to him, as Olivia asked me to do, hurt so much that now I feel I owe her nothing. Tonight Merravay really belongs to me.

INTERLUDE

George Frederick Sandell, Esq., of Merravay, died as he had lived, an eccentric.

Even before his father died he had gained himself a reputation for sloppy sentimentality, and during his term of office as a justice of the peace he caused scandals and made many bad neighbours by his lenient sentences to poachers. In the end sentiment killed the miserable, puling fellow.

A hot-headed agitator called Tom Fulger, who had once been manager at Merravay, sided with the labourers during the riots and stack-burnings which broke out during the demand for higher wages or cheaper food which followed the end of the Bonaparte wars. In Suffolk the Yeomanry was called out one November and Fulger was shot through the head.

What must Mr Sandell do but order a stone to be put over his grave?

Several people thought that the Rector of Nettleton failed in his duty in allowing the erection of the stone at all. The rector, however, perceived a golden opportunity. Mr Sandell was far less regular at church than a gentleman in his position–for the sake of setting a good example–should be. The rector said that when the stone was set up there must be a proper dedication service. He planned to speak very frankly at that ceremony.

Mr Sandell protested that there was no need for a commotion; he only wanted Tom's grave marked so that in years to come, when the workers had got a fair bargain, there'd be something to show whom they had to thank for it.

The day of the dedication dawned clear and bright, a typically English April day. The rector, warned by his wife, who was weatherwise, put on his hunting boots and wore a number of warm garments under his cassock. When the driving sleet came down he stood his ground without marked discomfort. Most of those who had come to watch and listen had understood from the rector's opening sentences that the rector's views were as sound as their own; they retreated to the shelter of the church. Mr Sandell, bare-headed, stood as though in a dream staring at the ornate stone, over which the sleet was sliding, blurring the words:

To the Memory of

THOMAS FULGER

Who in his Devoted Endeavour
to Attain
Better Conditions

for

His Fellow Men

Laid Down His Life

Even when the rector's sonorous phrases had come to an end Mr Sandell stood there. He was seen to shiver as he at last walked to his carriage; and ten days later he was dead of inflammation of the lungs.

His heir was a nephew, who upon taking up his heritage added the name of Sandell to his own of Booth, and was, largely on that account, regarded with considerable suspicion for a time. But he, thank God, had no nonsense about him; he took after his grandfather, the old nabob. He was entirely sound over matters like poachers, wages and trespassers.

He became extremely popular. He married one of the Fennels of Ockley and slipped into place in the county like a hand into a glove. Once again the great hall at Merravay became the scene of gay gatherings. All was well.

EPISODE SIX
Victorian

THE POACHER

Chapter One

In October in the year 1848, when I was seventeen, I was sent to Merravay in disgrace. I had committed the heinous crime of falling in love with the wrong young man; then, forbidden to see or speak to him ever again, I had proceeded to fall–in conventional fashion–into a decline.

My papa, who was very angry with me, approved of Merravay as a place of exile because it was a hundred and fifty miles away from Archie; my mamma, in whom rage had given way to exasperated concern for my health, thought that the good country air and a change of scene would be beneficial. So a letter, explaining the circumstances, was sent to Uncle Alan, and back came an invitation rendered lukewarm by the accompanying apologies. He was afraid, he said, that I would be lonely in this womanless household; and he was afraid that I should find life at Merravay dull in this season; and he was afraid that if they were hoping for some young man in Suffolk to prove a counter-attraction they would be disappointed, there was a great dearth of young men.

The fact that winter was approaching was one reason for Mamma's desire to get me away, for in the garrison town where my papa was stationed at the time the winter was the gay, social season; and since I could not be left at home without arousing comment, or be taken out without the risk of seeing Archie, it would have been a very awkward situation indeed. And nobody cared, I least of all, how dull life at Merravay would be. I felt that every place where Archie was not was hateful; and besides, was I not going to die very soon?

Of course I can look back on it now and laugh, and feel a little sorry for my parents, and put all the blame on *The Posy,* that apparently innocuous little magazine. Until I was fourteen and my mamma, for reasons of economy, dismissed my governess I had nothing but contempt for *The Posy*, for at that time I was interested in everything under the sun except clothes and love stories; but once Miss Tibbenham had gone I seemed to be stranded in a mental desert, and *The Posy*, which my mamma took regularly because it had fashion pages, was the only oasis in that desert. It seemed harmless enough and was highly thought of by all parents. Its fashion pages told us what was being worn just then, and how to reconstruct an old garment to look like new; it had a page of Household Management, mainly hints on how to be mean with food and strict with servants; it had a 'Pretty' page telling us how to deal with freckles and such things; and it had a serial which invariably lasted just six months. Twice a year for three years we were regaled by a new version of the same story; there was always a girl, crossed in love, who fell into a decline and died. Pale, 'beautiful in death', with her long hair streaming, she lay covered with roses in each one of the six stories.

So, of course, when I was seventeen I fell in love, was crossed, and fell into a decline. I had mistimed things somewhat, for unless I lasted out until the summer, which seemed unlikely, there would be no roses for me.

However, I went to Merravay, as to death, and made no protest.

It was a place often mentioned in family circles, generally with an accompanying comment about Uncle Alan's luck and my grandmamma's unashamed favouritism towards him. My grandmamma, whom I could just remember as a strict, intimidating old lady, had spent her girlhood at Merravay. Her brother, who never married, had made Uncle Alan, her third son, his heir, and everyone believed that Grandmamma had ordered him to do so. They said also that my oldest uncle, who inherited Gore Park, had greatly hoped that when Alan went to Merravay Grandmamma would go to end her days there; but she did not. She stayed at Gore Park and retained her martinet sway until the end. A young male cousin of mine had once stayed with Uncle Alan and reported that the shooting in East Anglia was superb but that Merravay itself was a dull hole, and an elderly female cousin, who had for a short time kept house for Uncle Alan after the death of his wife, many years ago, still spoke of Merravay as the most beautiful place in the world; but she was given to easy enthusiasms, as spinsters so often are.

Chapter Two

Complicated arrangements for my safe escort across country were made, and I arrived safely one fine September afternoon and went straight to bed. Self-inflicted as my woes were–or as, looking back, I see them to be–they were real enough then, and I was genuinely ill. Alan's first comment, when he met me at the coach-stop, was that I looked more ill than he expected, and that he hadn't realised that I was 'a doctor's case'.

He was a tall, stout, handsome, self-indulgent and, up to a point, genial man; his wife, of whom he was reputed to have been very fond, and his six-year-old daughter had both died during an outbreak of cholera which had swept through the country like a plague. His son was, according to family parlance, 'damn odd'; he was scholarly and spent most of his time abroad, brooding over the ruins of old cities, Jericho, Babylon, Thebes. My papa and my two uncles whose inheritance had been small professed to pity Uncle Alan for having so odd a son, just as they professed to pity Uncle Frederick, who had inherited Gore Park, for his gout. It consoled them for their envy.

Uncle Alan was obviously ill at ease with a strange young female and an ailing one at that; but he had made meticulous arrangements for my comfort. I was installed in a vast, beautifully furnished bedroom and given a maid, Susan, to attend me. One of the symptoms of decline, as laid down by the stories in *The Posy*, is that the subject should eat nothing, or almost nothing; and I hadn't been in Merravay for twenty-four hours before I realised that Uncle Alan's food was far more difficult to resist than Mamma's 'invalid diet' had been. Mamma's idea had been to offer gruel, steamed fish and blancmange; Uncle Alan appeared to think that if one couldn't eat a roast partridge one might be tempted by oysters, a smoky hot puffy omelette, breast of chicken in cream sauce, or peaches in brandy.

But it was not, I must contend, the food which brought me round. I was still miserable enough to be resistant to that. It was Uncle Alan's embarrassed, clumsy, almost boyish concern which brought me downstairs on the evening of my third day in his house. And after that I had something new to think about.

I went down, making what I thought of then as a valiant effort, thinking that if I were going to die I might as well die on my feet. We dined together and afterwards sat in the drawing-room, an immense apartment, beautifully furnished. He asked me if I played chess–I didn't–or the piano, which I did a little. I played for quite a long time, sometimes with tears in my eyes, because music is of all things the most conducive to emotion. At nine o'clock Clayton, the man-servant, brought in the tea-tray, ordered specially for me, and when the tea was drunk Uncle Alan said, 'Maybe you should get back to bed now.'

I rose obediently and bade him good night and he uttered some of his awkward, kindly intentioned words, so that I almost cried again. Then I walked to the door, opened it, closed it behind me and was immediately seized by what was perhaps the first genuine emotion I had known since Miss Tibbenham had read me some of Macaulay's poems.

It was a highly unpleasant emotion too. Sheer stark terror, and utterly reasonless.

The hall at Merravay is very large; not like the hall of a house at all, more like a church or a barn. But everything that could be done to soften its austere appearance had been done. The stone floor was almost completely hidden by lovely rugs; the furniture was beautiful. On a bed of ash in the huge hearth three enormous logs were blazing, lending their light to supplement that of the two lamps and many candles. There was no reason at all why I should be frightened, should stand there by the closed door of the drawing-room paralysed by terror, with cold sweat breaking out all over me. Nothing to see, save the big, gracious apartment; nothing to hear.

To be frightened was an entirely new experience for me; I was far from being a nervous creature. My sheltered life had prevented me from ever being very greatly tested, but the common everyday accidents of life had never found me wanting. An unruly hired horse had run away with me and finally thrown me, but I rode again next day; and once when Miss Tibbenham and I had been left alone, with only a daily woman, she had gone out to the chemist's one evening, slipped on an icy path, broken her ankle and been taken in by some kind people nearby. I'd slept alone in the house for ten days then–which every girl of twelve wouldn't do! The daily woman had made quite a fuss about it, making me go round and lock every door and shutter the windows before she left at dusk, and predicting the most shocking possibilities.

Now here I was, utterly unable to cross a room because I was frightened. Of nothing!

I stood there shivering and sweating and waiting for whatever it was to pass over. But it didn't. The terrible fear–fear of nothing–mounted and mounted.I wanted to scream, but though I opened my mouth and tried to no sound emerged. How long I stood there I don't know; or how long I should have stood there. I knew that Uncle Alan was in the drawing-room, I had only to take a step backward and turn the handle and I should be with him. I longed to take that step, but I couldn't move.

It was he who moved. He was a pipe-smoker; but he was too polite–just then–to smoke a pipe in his own drawing-room in the presence of a female. After I had gone–and how avidly he must have been waiting for that moment–he came to fetch his pipe from the library, where, I discovered, he usually sat when alone. He opened the drawing-room door and walked straight into me.

The terror, whatever it was, receded at once with the opening of the door, with his first step into the hall.

'Good God!' he said, as his stout warm body hit my cold shaking one. 'I thought you'd gone to bed.'

My first impulse was to gasp out that I had been frightened. But something that was half common sense and half good manners rose up in me and took charge. Poor Uncle Alan, a sick girl thrust on him was surely bad enough; spare him the mad fancies.

I said in what struck my own ears as an amazingly ordinary voice:

'I just wanted your arm . . . on the stairs.'

'Poor girl, poor girl,' he said. 'I didn't think of it. Very remiss of me. Well, here we go. Lean on me.'

He scooped me across the hall and up the stairs and into the warm lighted room, where Susan was busy with the bed-warmer and the hot milk of the bedtime ritual.

I was too near the edge of sleep to come back and start worrying when I realised that from the moment when I had said good night to Uncle Alan I hadn't thought about Archie at all. For the first time in months I slept without crying myself to sleep.

Chapter Three

I have heard old ladies say tartly that a sharp smack of the face is the best remedy for hysterics; it may be that a sharp shock of fear is the best remedy for decline. Certainly I woke next morning with something other than my love-sickness on my mind.

The memory of the terror was still vivid, and as soon as I was fully awake I began to dread a similar experience. Unless I stayed in my room–a thing I felt less inclined to do now than at any time since my arrival–sooner or later I should be obliged to face that walk across the hall alone.

Yet, now that I was capable of thinking about it, and of taking courage in the bright morning sunshine, the place drew me. I felt I must look at it, investigate, search for some explanation. I was up and dressed by eleven o'clock.

The hall faced south and had two enormous windows through which the sun spilled slantingly; on the bed of grey ash two logs burned; the place felt warm and looked gay. I stood at the bottom of the stairs and stared for a long time; nothing sinister met my eyes. With a feeling of daring mingled with scepticism, rather like that with which children play 'Old Man', I went and stood by the drawing-room door, exactly where I had stood last evening. Then I walked slowly round, looking at everything and touching some things and finding nothing frightening at all. I didn't know what I was looking for, but if I had come upon a suit of old armour, or a skull made into an inkstand, or a hideous foreign idol such as I had seen at Gore Park and other places, I should have regarded that as the focus of evil, probably made up some story about it, attributed my susceptibility to my low state of health and been, if not comforted, satisfied. But there was nothing; and finally, having walked all round the hall, I sat down on the window-seat farthest from the stairs, full in the sunshine.

I was on my feet again in a minute. Absurd and ridiculous and impossible as it seems, even to me who was on the search for the absurd, the ridiculous, the impossible, to sit down there in the full sunshine was like lowering oneself into a well of icy water. It wasn't just the deathly cold; it was the awful feeling of misery and despair.

I had bounded away from the window-seat and now stood two feet away from it in a place where the sun lay on the floor. Warm sun.

After a while I walked to the other window, touched the smooth, age-polished wood of the seat there; it was almost hot. I went back timidly, but with dogged curiosity, and felt about the other window. There was no detectable draught, but there was the chill–a chill which not only affected one's flesh but seemed to pierce one's very soul, so that the light went out of the day and there was nothing but utter desolation.

I was familiar, of course, as who is not, with a ghost story or two–the flying skull at Francoy Abbots, Maria Marten, the nun at Borley; but in all of them something was seen, or heard. No story that I knew had ever mentioned cold as a sign of haunting; yet as I stood there I was perfectly certain, as–with very little else to go upon–I am sure to this day, that the far window-seat in the hall at Merravay was a haunted place.

Chapter Four

Apart from exercising craft and guile to ascertain that I never had to cross the hall alone after dark, there was nothing that I could do. I daren't mention the subject to anyone; I daren't ask a question. Now that I had been jerked back into life, and found myself capable of taking an interest –however morbid–in something outside my own affairs I realised how idiotic my recent behaviour had been. Doubtless to other people it had seemed so all along, and if I now started to talk about a haunted window-seat they would be justified in thinking me quite demented. And I must admit that now and again the thought that I might be going out of my mind did occur to me! Obviously I was not a very steady-minded girl. I could now exist for increasingly long periods without thinking of Archie at all, and when I did think it was with hardly a pang–and last week I was prepared to die for love of him. Had I merely fallen into a fresh state of delusion; changed an imaginary grief for an imaginary terror?

All this went on below the surface. Poor Uncle Alan was delighted in the change in me, and attributed it to the air and the food. He began to take trouble over my social life. He had several friendly neighbours; the Fennels, to whom he was related by marriage, were within easy visiting distance, and the Whymarks, though their house was hidden by the trees, were practically next door.

I particularly remember a visit which Uncle Alan and I made to the Whymarks late in October. For one thing, it was the first time that I had been on horseback since early summer when the storm broke over me and Archie. For another, there was at New Holding a very old lady, Miss Phyllis Whymark, who said that she remembered my grandmother and that I was very like her to look at. That pleased me, because my grandmother had been accounted very handsome in her day. Miss Whymark opened her mouth and pointed to a gap in a set of otherwise remarkably sound if yellowed teeth.

'I do so well remember,' she croaked, 'the day after I lost this tooth I went over to Merravay and there was your grandmother, my dear, in worse case. She'd burnt her hair off curling it and torn her face on a bush. We laughed and said that now we'd never get married. And believe it or not, as soon as we were alone she told me that she was going to be married before Christmas. I was so jealous I could have clawed her eyes out! Ah, but that's a long time ago.'

We had lunch at New Holding, and after the meal some of the young ones led me off to see their puppies. As a consequence my boots were caked with mud, and being town-bred and used to my mamma's house-proud ways I didn't enter Merravay on my return. I went to the back door, sent Susan up to fetch my house-shoes and called to a boy in the yard to come and pull off my boots as I leaned against the wall.

The main back door at Merravay had a porch, one side of which, at that hour of the afternoon, caught the westering sun. I moved into the sunny place, braced my back against the wall and lifted my foot and stood there trapped within another circle of the same icy cold, the same deadly misery as lay about that window-seat. It struck with a same impact as a pailful of cold water, strongly thrown. I gasped and gave a violent shudder. The girl Susan, standing by with my shoes in her hand, said:

'You didn't ought to stand there, miss. Thass the one sunny place in the yard and thass allust cold.'

I put my hand on the red, warm-looking wall.

'Yes,' I said carefully. 'It looks warm but it strikes cold.'

The boy tested it and said shyly:

'That fare warm to me like, miss.'

'You got so much muck on your hands, Sam, you couldn't feel nothing,' said the girl sharply. 'You didn't ought to handle miss's boots even with them hands.'

He went very red about the ears, and as soon as he had dragged off the second boot he went hastily away. Susan was still stooped over my shoe, and I said, in as casual a way as I could manage:

'There's the same cold current of air or whatever it is in another place, I've noticed. I wonder if you have ever . . .'

'Ah,' she said, with a wealth of meaning in her voice. 'That winder in the great hall.'

I could have kissed her.

'Set to clean it, I was, soon arter I come here, miss. Never again. No, not if I was sacked for refusing.'

'Because of the cold?' I asked lightly.

'No, miss. Because of the badness. It's there too,' she said, looking towards the side of the porch which we had instinctively left as soon as my shoe was on. 'Thass all very well for folks to mock, but this was the witch's house, when all is said and done.'

'What witch?'

'Oh, thass a long way back, miss; hundreds of years ago. But there's them that hev seen her tearing past like the wind on a great black horse; honest, steady folks, miss.' Susan's face had gone very white and stiff-looking. I shivered, this time from a cold that came within me. I told myself that this was all nonsense, ignorant country superstition. But, after all, I had used the word 'haunted' in my thoughts about the cold place in the hall; and if one were credulous enough to think of a window-seat as being haunted, why boggle at talk of witches? And why also, with a most practical view of the nonsensical, proceed to point out to oneself that the ghost of the witch, riding a ghostly horse, would surely confine its activities to the out-of-doors? I had no sooner thought of that than Susan said:

'I allust reckon, myself, miss, that Lady Alice used to sit by that winder and make her spells and such; and there by the porch I reckon she used to keep her nasty beasts.'

Thinking it over, I came to the conclusion that Susan's explanation was as likely a one as any I should ever think of. And though it left me far from satisfied, it was the only one that I seemed likely to get. I had to adjust myself to it, though; for, perhaps because I had never taken witches very seriously, the atmosphere which lay about that window-seat had seemed to me much more dreadful than any one would have expected to be left there by a maker of spells.

Lady Alice Rowhedge, I discovered, however, had left a mark on more than the atmosphere of her old home. I never mentioned her–both from caution and delicacy–to my uncle; but a chance word, intentionally dropped here and there, brought me a good deal of information. In the country memories are long, and so are lives. One day, over at New Holding, I dragged the conversation round to the subject, and I learned to my astonishment that there before my eyes was someone who had known someone who had known someone who had known someone who had actually seen the witch. Such an almost incredible thing was made possible, I suppose, by the fact that the Whymarks were, as a family, long-lived. There sat this old Miss Phyllis Whymark whose father in his boyhood, had had an old Aunt Phyllis–a very eccentric old woman–whose grandmother, also named Phyllis Whymark, had been present at the trial when Lady Alice Rowhedge was found guilty of witchcraft and condemned to be burned. It had happened in the days of the Civil War . . . but suddenly it seemed as near as yesterday as I sat and listened to the ancient croaking voice telling the tale. I was, naturally, extremely interested, but at the end of her story I was aware of the same lack of satisfaction as I had felt when Susan had first mentioned the witch. Absurd as it seemed–and was not the whole thing absurd?–the 'bad feeling', as Susan called it, which emanated from that window-seat had in it too much of despair, of impotence, of being thrust down into a cold darkness for me to accept it as the result of Lady Alice's activities. And I wasn't satisfied about the porch, either. Why should she, with all the barns and byres at Merravay, have kept her 'nasty beasts' there?

The old lady ended her story with the ritual words, 'All nonsense, of course!' And popped a strong peppermint into her mouth, whereupon I said, with a creditable pretence at casualness:

'That is very interesting. Thank you for telling me. Are there any other phantoms at Merravay?'

She laughed and choked on the peppermint. 'You're just like your grandmother, my dear! Ah, she was a one for ghosts! She once told me something she daren't tell even to her brother that she was so fond of. She once *saw* something.'

'What? Where?'

'A boy, just about to be taken with a fit. In the hall! She said he looked so real that she went to help him and found that he wasn't there at all. Very upset she was at the time, I recall, and I had difficulty in persuading her that it was all imagination.'

'Do you believe that?'

'Dear child, what else could it be? Bodies are shovelled into the ground and spirits go off to God or Satan, according to their deserts.'

'I wonder,' I said. 'I wonder whether a very strong feeling mightn't leave a mark, stay there and go on and on . . . still being felt . . . like weather. I mean if you woke up just after a thunderstorm you'd have the feeling of it, just as you'd know if you woke up on the evening of a lovely warm day. You'd know by the atmosphere . . .'

'Heaven save us,' said the old lady. 'If people's feelings lasted like that the world would be so full of them we should all go about with no room for our own. Isn't that so?'

And that so exactly, though unwittingly, described what had happened to me in the hall at Merravay that I could only say:

'Yes, of course, that is quite true.'

Chapter Five

Well, now I come to the really incredible part of this story.

My Uncle Alan's bugbear was poachers. Quite a large portion of the Merravay estate was taken up by a wood, called Layer Wood. Up to the time when he inherited the property there had been what was called a 'right of way' through it; it was the shortest path between the villages of Nettleton and Clevely. Little girls went there for flowers, little boys for nuts, and all too often, according to my uncle, men went there and 'knocked off one for the pot'. For poor people the times I look back upon were hungry times.

Uncle Alan, who set great store by his pheasants, closed the path at both ends and put up notices. Then he engaged a number of keepers. And finally he set man-traps. By his account–and I must confess that I never heard the other side–he was within his rights; but he met with a good deal of opposition, especially over the closing of the path, which was a right of way by ancient custom which even the rector recognised and supported. However, Uncle Alan had won in the end; Layer Wood was 'preserved' and anyone who trespassed there risked falling into a man-trap, while anyone who poached risked the utmost rigour of the law.

Midway through November, on a very foggy evening, Uncle Alan and I were playing chess, the rudiments of which he had managed to teach me, when there came a noise and a stamping and the sound of men's voices approaching the front of the house from the garden.

Uncle Alan cocked his head and said, 'That's Palmer, by God!' and jumped up and was across the hall and had the front door open before I could catch the table and steady the chessmen which his precipitate departure had disturbed. He had left the door open and I could look through it, across the hall, and see, as though in a theatre, the scene that was taking place there. Palmer, my uncle's head keeper, whom I knew by sight, and one of his underlings, held between them a wretched-looking boy of about my own age.I couldn't see much of his face, for he sagged between the two men, but his very black shaggy hair and something about him made me think of gypsies. Presently, after a good deal of talking in the thick, slurred Suffolk voice which, at that distance, I could not understand, Palmer pushed the boy forward. Then I was almost certain that he was a gypsy. He had one of those big-nosed, high-cheekboned faces which at the best of times have a hungry, haggard look, and for the boy this was not one of the best of times.

It may be weak in me, but I never like to see dogs with their ribs showing, or horses with thin drooping necks, or people who look miserable. This, I know, is no virtue in me; I just hate the feeling of discomfort that they rouse in me. Once when I was quite small I was so affected by the blue fingers of a flower-girl that I wanted to give her my little muff. Mamma explained that she didn't mind cold hands, she was used to them, and would instantly have sold the muff and bought gin with the money, and that I must try not to be a silly little girl. I was no longer little and had–I thought –become rather less silly lately, but my heart went out to the boy who looked so cold and hungry and thin and captured. The other three looked very well pleased with themselves, and presently Uncle Alan rang the bell and Clayton came, and went, and returned with two big mugs on a tray. I thought–Oh dear, nothing for *him*; and he looks as though he could do with it.

Then they all four went out by the door that led to the kitchen quarters, and for a few minutes I had something else to think about. The door between the drawing-room and the hall was open and I was alone: was that the same as being alone in the hall? Would the terror come stalking in? The obvious thing to do was to get up and shut the door; but that I could not do. I could only sit there and wait.

I was pathetically pleased to see Uncle Alan when he came back, and he was pleased to have someone to whom to tell his tale. At last the expense of the man-traps had been justified. In the fog last night that little devil of a poacher would have got away if he hadn't stepped on one of them and been nipped by the ankle.

'*Last* night?'

'So Bowyer says. Anyway, he was there at six this morning, but Bowyer knew he was snug enough; and Palmer was having his day off so he left him there till they made their night's rounds.'

'In a trap. Is he much hurt?'

'Of course not. Just nipped.'

'He must have been very cold . . . and hungry.'

My nice kind uncle, who had pressed all those tasty dishes on me and taken such pleasure in my better appetite, laughed jovially and said:

'He'll be hungrier by the time he gets to Baildon Gaol!'

'Is he on his way there now?'

'Dear child! In this fog? It's worse than last night's. He's in the old buttery. When I first became a J.P. they would insist on hauling offenders up here at unearthly hours–so much nearer, in many cases, than the lock-up in Nettleton–I just had to find somewhere to put them. Now let me see . . . My dear, I'm quite sure you've been cheating. Never in a thousand years would I allow my Queen to be . . .'

'You got up so hurriedly that you knocked the table. I just gathered them up anyhow.'

'Then there's no point in going on, is there? And I apologise, my dear, for the suggestion that you cheated. Your Aunt Mary . . .' He broke off, horrified. I realised that never before had he mentioned his dead wife by name. In a flatter voice, but with obvious, calm resolution he continued, 'She would cheat me, but so prettily. Draw my attention to something, you know. And then move a piece. And I never let her know I knew!'

That was somehow so pathetic, so revealing that the distaste I had been feeling for him because he had laughed about the poacher being hungry melted away, or was overlaid. As soon as I had dismantled the board and was ready he lent me, as was his habit now, his arm to the top of the stairs.

In my room Susan was busy with the warming-pan; the hot milk, which I was supposed to drink last thing at night, stood in the hearth, and a plate of cheese-cakes, a comestible which I had once been edged into admitting to liking, stood on my bed-table.

Conversation, as Susan helped me to undress, turned, inevitably, upon the poacher. Susan, from whom, because she had been sensitive to the cold spots, I hoped for something else, was full of glee because he had been caught. She was Nettleton born and bred and all against gypsies.

'Thass been them all along, miss. Mr George was real soft about them, I've heard my father say again and again. Said they was colourful! But for them and their thieving ways honest folks could still go there for primroses. They come, they take what they fancy, and off they go, leaving us to bear the blame. Now they've got one. And I'm glad!'

She said much the same thing in several different ways; then she said good night and left me.

For what I did next I take no credit for kindness, but for boldness . . . yes. It was not kind of me to wish to feed the boy; it was simple self-defence. I couldn't lay my head on the pillow and sleep knowing that he was hungry; the jug of milk, the dish of cheese-cakes kept yelping at me reproachfully. But it was–considering my circumstances–very brave of me to step outside my bedroom door. Brave because from the first night of the terror my own room had possessed a compensating quality of sanctuary. All terrors bring their own cures. If you are frightened of the dark the first dawn glimmer can scatter them; if you fear spiders the mere removal of one can bring peace . . . and from that, so small a thing, up and up to the very fear of death with its mitigation of the hope of life everlasting, every dread is balanced in the human mind by the compensating factor of dread-removed. To me, once night had fallen there was the terror in the hall . . . and, had I ever been called upon to face it, the similar terror of the back porch. I could take temporary refuge in the drawing-room, the dining-room or the library; my bedroom was absolute sanctuary. To leave it, once I had gained it, called for an effort more violent and more sustained than any I had ever made. To any rational person my dilemma must seem incomprehensible; but to me it was real and painful–either I must get into my bed and lie all night worrying about the hungry young poacher in the old buttery, or I must open the door and go down–not through the hall, for I could take the backstairs, but through the open dark where the terror, though apparently confined to one place, might possibly be at large.

Oddly enough, what the poacher might do to me never once entered my mind.

I had a little blue-silk bag with a pattern worked on it in beads. I set the jug of milk in the centre of it and wedged the cheese-cakes all round. I could hang that on my arm, carry a candle in the same hand and still have one free for opening doors.

The first one I opened timidly. I was out on the gallery which ran along above the hall, which was the haunted place; and before I took a step out I waited. If I felt the cold . . . if I sensed the terror, back I meant to bolt like a rabbit. But there was nothing. I took the few necessary steps along the gallery and then turned sharply to the right, into the passage that led to the top of the backstairs. Halfway along it was the room which one of the Whymarks who knew Merravay well had said was the schoolroom when their family lived there; and at its far end was a ladder which led to the space under the rafters. Compared with the front part of the house this was all ugly and grim and outwardly far more frightening. . . . But it was all right, there was no terror. It's all *right*, I thought to myself. Truly if, just in the passage, I had been joined by two or three friendly and quite unfrightened people I could not have felt more reassured. The knowledge that the terror was limited, that so long as I did not go to meet it in the hall it could not come to me, did a great deal to restore me to my natural confidence.

Except for the setting in of a great iron stove at one of its open hearths, the kitchen at Merravay has been unaltered for generations; and behind it the sculleries, larders, and game-stores made a warren. I found what they called the old buttery by sheer accident, recognising its new purpose from the heavy padlock on the door and the opening in its upper panel. The aperture was no bigger than an ordinary book and divided into halves by an iron bar. Having found what I had set out to find, I hesitated. The boy might be sleeping the sleep of exhaustion, and if so it would be small kindness to wake him back to his woes. I stood and listened, and I heard the straw rustle as he moved. Stepping up to the door, I held my candle high so that he could see me, though I could not see him, and I said:

'It's all right. I've brought you something to eat.'

For a moment there was no answer; then the straw rustled more noisily and there was a dragging, shuffling sound, and into the faint radiance of the candlelight, just behind the bar, his face emerged. A hoarse choking voice said:

'S'that true? You ain't making game of me?'

'Oh no.' I set the candle down and began to fumble in my little bag. I handed him a cheese-cake. I expected him to snatch it and start eating, but he held it in his hand, looking at it as though he doubted whether it were really food. Then he said:

'God bless yer! But if yer could . . . miss, I'm perishing for a drink of water. . . .'

'I have some milk. . . .' But the milk was in the jug and the aperture was too small to allow of its passing. The boy had his face close to the bar now, and I could see the avidity in his eyes, the cracked dryness of his mouth. 'Just a minute,' I said, 'I'll have to get a little mug.' I hurried back to the kitchen and snatched a pewter pipkin from a hook. I filled it and passed it in, carefully. The boy drank, passed it back to me to be refilled and emptied it again. And again, until the last drop had gone.

'God bless yer,' he said again, more clearly. 'You saved me life, I reckon.' He ate a cheese-cake then, cramming it into his mouth so fiercely that the good crisp pastry broke and he lost some crumbs.

'Take your time,' I said. 'There are three more.' I handed them to him one by one. He licked the last crumb from the palm of his hand and asked:

'What made yer do it?'

'I thought you looked hungry.'

'For a minnit I thought you wus a angel.' I saw his face change. Its open pathos gave way to craftiness.

'Miss, lemme out,' he said, and as he spoke he put his face to the opening and stared at me with such urgency, such pleading, and such wiliness that I stepped back a pace.

'I couldn't. Even if I wanted to. You're padlocked in.'

'I know that. But this here winder is on'y boarded over. I on'y want a bit of a tool. Knife'd do. They took me knife. Hand us in a knife, miss.'

I just stood and stared at him, and encouraged by my silence he began to talk so quickly and so brokenly that I only caught a phrase here and there. He spoke about being transported for seven years at least, being loaded with irons, starved and beaten; he said he hadn't touched a pheasant, that there was enough gypsy in him to prevent his having a fair trial.

One had, of course, heard stories about convict ships and settlements which, even if exaggerated . . . And he was young, and so thin.

Also, just at that moment I was feeling a strong dislike for my kind uncle by whose orders a boy who had lain for a night and a day in a trap had been locked up without being given so much as a cup of cold water. And not being country-bred I was insufficiently convinced of the sacredness of pheasants.

At that moment my candle flickered, and looking at it I realised that very shortly I should be in the dark. The effort to think clearly and quickly, the excitement of making a sudden and unconventional decision, fluttered my heart and dried my throat. I turned without speaking and hurried to the kitchen, where I first found a new candle and then looked round for a tool. I looked with a certain wistfulness at a heavy, sharp-edged wedge rather like a big chisel which was used for jointing carcasses; but I was cautious. If the boy failed to get out . . . So I chose an anonymous-looking knife with a short stout blade.

When I got back to the door the boy had retreated to his straw and was crying in harsh gasping sobs which stopped when he saw the light. He came to the opening with tears making little runnels of cleanliness on his dirty face.

'If you don't succeed in getting out you must account for the knife,' I said, and handed it in. He put his mouth to my fingers and slobbered at them like an affectionate dog. 'I hope you do get out and then keep out of trouble,' I said. I was backing away while he blessed and thanked me, and then he said, with another abrupt change of manner, 'Wait, Lady. Look, I got sumpin for yer.' He fumbled about in his clothes. 'They dint find this when they went over me. Got it in me mouth, see! Howd yer hand, miss. I mean it. Buy yerself sumpin pretty. Thass all right, I never stole it. I come by it honest, give yer me word.'

His thin dirty hand had come up to the lower edge of the opening, and between its fingers and thumb was what looked like a golden guinea.

I gasped. Not with the surprise which the boy evidently expected, for he said shyly, 'There now! Go on, take it. 'Sreal!' but with some other feeling for which I have no name. To say that I knew makes at once too great and too small a claim, but there is no other word. I *knew*, instantly and surely, that the gold coin between the gypsy's finger and thumb was connected, in some way, with the hatred and misery and despair which lay over the cold spot in Merravay hall and by the back porch.

'Where . . . did . . . you . . . get . . . that?' I asked.

'Up in the wood,' he said, without a second's hesitation. 'Time I was in the trap, scratching about. Under a lotta leaves that was.'

'*Is* it a guinea?'

'Course it is. Here, see for yerself.' He stretched his hand past the bar. 'I ain't never handled one afore, but I know a guinea when I see one. Take it. It's yours.'

'I don't want it . . . I mean . . . thank you very much for wanting to give it to me. I couldn't take it. I would just like to know . . .'

'Look at it; see for yourself. All right then, hold the candle and I'll tell you. This side there's an old woman on a stool, and some words writ. This side there's a flower, rose outa the hedge. That got the right edge, too, ridgy. Thass a guinea all right. And I come by it honest, like I told yer. And I'd like you to have it . . . Whass the matter? D'you hear sumpin?'

The more he thrust the coin towards me the worse I felt, for the little shining coin seemed to hold the very essence of whatever it was that affected me with such terror. I knew, just as people know the first onset of a familiar pain, that unless I went quickly I should be too frightened to move.

'Goodbye,' I gasped out. 'Good luck.'

'Just a minnit, lady,' he said. 'I wanta get on, but I gotta say this first. I ain't 'Gyptian proper, I don't know the words, but I give yer the blessing. May yer marry a rich man that'll be good to yer and have plenty of strong healthy children and live to be old with yer own teeth, and when yer . . .' But I had started to walk away, to scuttle like a scared rabbit making for its burrow.

In the morning, when it was found that the boy had gone, there was a considerable fuss, which would doubtless have lasted longer and caused me more secret embarrassment had not my cousin Rupert arrived home suddenly. At first I was a little frightened of him; he had an odd, abrupt manner and a way of saying things which would suddenly make you see them in a new way. He had no trace of Uncle Alan's geniality of manner, but now and then, when they argued about things like wages, corn laws and pheasant-preserves, he would say, in his offhand, dry way, a word or two which led me to think he might be, at heart, the kinder person of the two. We didn't get to know one another very well until he had been home for about a fortnight. Then there came an evening when Uncle was out and we were alone together. It drew on for bedtime and I began making my wretched little plans. When my uncle was at home the matter of going upstairs presented no problem. Once he had got the idea of helping me upstairs at night it had become a habit with him; and though I was now quite able-bodied he helped me, and would have gone on doing so, I suspect, if I had lived with him for twenty years.

Suddenly Rupert looked up from his book and said:

'What is it that you're so scared of?'

Questions rapped out like that often receive a truthful answer, and this one did.

'There's something in the hall that I don't *like* by day and just can't face at night.'

'Show me,' he said, and stood up and reached out his hand to me.

'But it's nothing you can see,' I said, feeling thoroughly foolish. 'It's just a–a feeling.'

'Of what?'

'It's two things. *I* feel terrified because of what is there . . . because I don't like such things and don't understand. But the feeling that is there isn't terror, that is the queer part. It's a feeling of utter, complete despair and helplessness, as though–well, as though someone were drowning in the dark. It's something very awful, Rupert . . . I'm not, ordinarily, a coward.'

'Of course you're not. Come and show me where.'

Hand in hand, like lovers, we crossed the hall.

'Do you feel it now?' he asked.

'No. I never do except when I am alone. Then it is so strong that I can't take a step or utter a sound. And it isn't my fancy, truly. One of the maids . . .'

He looked at me sharply and asked in that curt way of his:

'Now who started this, you or the maid? I've noticed often how mere space frightens maids because they're used to huddling together in their little hovels.'

'Oh, I felt it before I ever spoke to her about it, though apparently she had felt it before I came here. And there's exactly the same feeling on one side of the back porch.'

'All very interesting,' he said musingly and–I was glad to see–quite seriously. 'It's strange how eclectic these things are. I only once knew a case where everyone within range was affected. I was myself. We were digging just south of of El Khasan and a workman turned up a bit of a bowl. He went to pick it up but didn't; instead he turned and ran, and so did we all, fifteen grown men, including a stout old German professor who hadn't run for thirty years. Come back to the fire and tell me more about this.'

I told him what little there was to tell. Then I said:

'Oh, and there was the coin . . .'

'What coin?'

'I can't tell about that. It is a secret.'

'You can describe the coin, surely.'

I did so.

'It sounds Elizabethan . . . about the same period as the house, you know. Why can't you tell me? I'm very discreet.'

'You see, I don't quite know how you feel about pheasants . . .'

'I dote on them roasted,' he said, and smiled at me, suddenly young and friendly. 'I'll tell *you* a secret. Time and again I come back to Merravay when my appetite gets the upper hand! I sit down one day to a makeshift meal wherever I am and think–They're roasting pheasants at Merravay! And home I come. Now your secret could hardly be more self-revealing and shameful than *that*! Tell me.'

I felt that I could tell him anything.

'Promise not to tell Uncle Alan,' I said. 'He's been so very kind to me, and he'd be very angry and upset.'

'So would he be if you told him that I came home for the sake of the food! But I promise.'

When I had told him he said, 'In my opinion you were right . . . Well, I'll ask Palmer where that trap lay and I'll go and pry about. Like to come with me?'

'I did find out the place. I could show you. Yes, I think with you I would dare.'

The trap was still in position, and Rupert, after a glance at it, said, 'Most likely he was reaching this way, to haul himself up by these hazel twigs, poor little devil; and the path bank slopes so that a coin may have rolled. I'll try that side first.'

The trap had been set so that anyone who persisted in using the path would fall into it. On the inner side of the path was a little clump of hazels standing in the piled-up drift of the leaves of many autumns.

As soon as I arrived at this spot I began to wish that I had not come. It was a crisp, bright morning, and I had company, but I felt uneasy, depressed in my spirits and afflicted with a curious physical feeling, as though my clothes or my skin did not fit. I looked at the trap and thought of the boy lying there all night and all day, and that was a bad thought too; but below and beyond that there was more. At the same time my morbid curiosity was lively; I knew that we were on the right track. This place, the back porch and the hall at Merravay had some dark connection.

Rupert pushed in amongst the hazels. I started to follow and then drew back.

'I think I shall stay here,' I said.

'Wise,' he said. 'These leaves are soaking wet.'

I looked up and down the path. It had been closed for only a few years and was still used by the keepers, but it was rapidly being grown over; the blackberry brambles particularly had thrust out aggressively so that in places they almost met. I thought again what a pity it was about the pheasants. This must have been a very pretty pleasant path between two villages. I pictured people on it, very trite pictures; little girls in spring gathering primroses, little boys in autumn gathering nuts, and in the long warm summer evenings young lovers wandering with their arms about one another.

Presently I heard Rupert say, 'Ah.'

'Have you found something?'

'I think so. Oh yes!'

'To do with it?'

'I should say so. Stay where you are . . .'

'What is it?' I called, sharply because now I was all curiosity.

'I'm coming,' he called back, and in a moment he pushed through the bushes. He looked a little queer, half excited and half concerned. He had pushed back his sleeves, and his hands to the wrists were covered with soil and bits of crushed wet leaf. Holding the left one out stiffly so that he did not touch me with it, he laid his right arm over and round my shoulders, while the other hand held out for my inspection what looked like a little heap of dirt with several gold coins bedded in it.

'They look like . . .' I pried one loose and rubbed it on my handkerchief. 'It is the very same!' I said. What the gypsy boy had called an old woman on a stool was a queen on a throne, and his hedge rose was the Tudor emblem, exactly like the ones that were the motif of so much of the carving at Merravay.

'You were right. Elizabethan, Rupert; it says so . . .' So far curiosity and what one might call the heat of the chase had sustained me, but now I knew that I felt towards this coin as I had done towards the one in the gypsy boy's hand. 'It feels the same too,' I said, and dropped it back into Rupert's palm. 'Oh, was that all you found? Nothing to tell us any more, nothing to explain? That place in the hall, and by the porch, and now here . . . all connected. And all awful.' The arm about my shoulders tightened.

'Darling,' said Rupert, 'to find so much in so short a time proves my extraordinary prospecting ability, don't you think?'

'I know. Of course. But we're no farther. I wanted something that would explain, that I could settle down with and know that it made me feel this way because of . . . You know, I went all round Merravay for days, looking for a nasty idol, or one of those horrible inkstands made out of a skull . . .'

Rupert gave me an odd swift look, and I thought–Yes, now you'll think I'm morbid and hysterical.

'We'll come back when it isn't so damned wet in there. And with a spade. I'm not used to doing my own digging, you know.'

'Of course not,' I said penitently. I stood looking at the clump of hazels which held–I felt–the clue to the mystery.

'Let's go back,' said Rupert, dropping his arm and offering me the crook of it. 'I do want to wash!'

On the way back I thrust away all thought of what he had not found and we talked animatedly about what he had. He said that the coins must have belonged to a rich person or to a very miserly one who saved small amounts and then converted them into a few pieces, for coins of such value were rare in Elizabeth's day, being worth thirty shillings apiece then, which was five or six pounds by our reckoning. He said, too, that he believed the little lump of stuff in which the coins were embedded was the rotted and altered remains of a leather bag, and that the one piece of gold which the gypsy had found had probably been pushed out by the growth of a root or picked up and dropped by a magpie. And that was all very interesting to me; I liked to hear Rupert talk.

Chapter Six

We did not make our second visit to Layer Wood; the weather turned cold, with a bitter wind from the east and sharp sleet storms. My papa, who within his sphere was a man of influence, succeeded in getting Archie posted to the West Indies; my mamma suffered a recurrence of migraine. So they decided that I had imposed upon Uncle Alan's hospitality for long enough and wrote to suggest that I should go home for Christmas. This suggestion raised very mixed feelings in me. Apart from the terror, I'd been happier at Merravay than in any place where I had ever been, especially since Rupert's return; the prospect of going back to take my place as a dutiful daughter in the strictly regulated treadmill of social life in a garrison town had very little appeal for me. I told myself, pretty sternly, that I had fallen victim to the comfort, the indulgences that I had received at Merravay. And every evening, when either Uncle Alan or Rupert walked with me across the hall and up the stairs, I told myself, with another kind of sternness, that it would be pleasant to return to a place where I *could* go upstairs alone.

I was running all these thoughts through my mind one evening, three days before I was due to go home. Rupert and I were alone in the library, one on either side of the hearth, both deeply engrossed–or so it seemed–in reading.

Because of my imminent departure the last week had been a round of gaiety, and it was very pleasant, I thought, to be alone together again. And I wished that he would put aside his book and look up and talk to me on this–this which might well be the last time we ever . . . Something swelled in my throat at the thought and tears came pushing up under my lids. I stared at my book until I had controlled myself, and then I looked up and thought how strange it was. There we sat, exactly as though we were a couple who had been married for years and had reached the haven of companionship. And oh, I thought, if only it were true! I realised that always, for the rest of my life, wherever I went, whatever happened to me I should be, in some measure, an exile. Perfect happiness, for me, would be to stay here, in Merravay, with Rupert. However, since that was not to be, I must, I thought, take hold of this one particular moment and wrap it up and lay it away in my mind, something precious, something to remember and cherish for ever.

And I was doing that; taking note not only of his face and form but of everything, even the shadow of him which the light from the reading lamp cast on the wall and the sharp earthy scent of the chrysanthemums blending with the faint smokiness of the log fire. This is the moment . . .

Just then Rupert looked up and closed his book with a little snapping sound.

'Charlotte,' he said, 'I want to ask you something and I don't want to be clumsy. You see, from something Father said I gathered that . . .' He halted, choosing his words, and I said boldly:

'Oh, that is all ended. It wasn't *real.* It sounds a strange thing to say, but that . . . whatever it is out there'–I nodded towards the great hall–'put it out of my head completely!'

'How?'

I heard myself saying, in carefully chosen, scrupulously measured words, exactly how I had known that my love-sickness was a matter of imagination. I ended with the words:

'I'm probably giving you the impression that I am utterly shallow-minded, but that I can't help. Honesty compels me to admit that your Merravay ghost, whatever it is, drove Archie clean out of my mind.'

'And the poacher, the gypsy boy–his plight drove the ghost out?'

'Well, no. It was all right . . . I mean I was *just* safe until the moment when he handed me the coin. Then it was terrible!'

'I've been wondering,' Rupert said, 'whether it would make any difference if that end of the hall were walled off. You see, Charlotte, I love you . . .' His face, his shadow, the lamp, the flowers began to whirl round before my eyes in a crazy fashion; his voice, saying things about being diffident in case I was still in love with Archie, about being willing to live elsewhere if I found Merravay too frightening, seemed to come from a long way off. The voice, the words sounded as cool and reasonable and dispassionate as I knew Rupert to be, at heart; but somehow there we were, midway between the two chairs, locked in embrace which wasn't cool or dispassionate at all.

'I've been in love with you, Rupert, ever since the evening when I knew I could tell you *anything*!' I said. Then I thought about the haunted place and how it had shown me the truth about myself and Archie. Even at this moment, when my cup of happiness was full to overbrimming, that mattered somehow. I dragged myself out of Rupert's arms.

'Wait here,' I said.

I went out of the library. I closed the door behind me. The hall was lighted by a single lamp; the 'bad place', the far window-seat, lay in the gloom. I walked towards it. There was the terror; there was the despair; there was the deathly cold. I walked into it and I knew the day must come when Rupert and I must die, and that before that we should grow old and impotent. I stood there, knowing for one concentrated moment all the despair which poor human mortality brought face to face with eternity can know . . . but I wasn't frightened. I thought–That is how it is, how it has always been and always will be. All we can do is to snatch at this moment, the time which is ours, and make the best of it.

I went back to Rupert and said:

'It is all right. Whatever was there is gone. I'm not frightened any more.'

Then he told me that on the morning when he found the coins he had also found a skeleton. He, of course, was used to ancient burial-places and old bones and was not much shaken, but he had feared the effect of his find on me and hurried me away from the place. But his work had led him to an understanding of the importance of burial rites, and therefore he had arranged that these bones should be given Christian burial. Dear Rupert, he believes that that may have brought rest to the uneasy spirit.

He says that the bones lay in peaceful, sleeping fashion, with one hand under the skull and the other laid upon something which, though rotted past recognition, might have been a book; and I know that he believes that someone, when this house was young, used to sit in that window-seat and read and one day went into Layer Wood to read, fell asleep and never woke. That somebody set great store by Christian burial and could not rest without it.

I think otherwise. It wasn't a bookworm, it wasn't a witch who made that emotional mark on Merravay. It was a lover. . . . I know, because my false love couldn't face whatever there was there; my true love could. And those coins were somehow deeply concerned. But it is all a mystery which I accept, just as I accept the fact that I have never lost a tooth and have been blessed with six handsome healthy children, all boys. . . .

INTERLUDE

Strangers to Nettleton still stop to stare at and remark upon a number of cottages which, though too old and individual to be council houses, bear evidence of having been planned and built with more taste and care than is common, and of having been erected, all twenty-four of them, at the same time.

Though their style is ornate and old-fashioned they are pretty enough and they have worn well. They stand, two by two, each with its strip of garden in front, a larger patch to the rear; each with its own wash-house, shed and outdoor convenience, and with two wells to serve the two dozen.

In the centre of each frontage is a lozenge-shaped piece of stone bearing the letters RBS and the date 1875. That was the year when the railway went through to Bywater and Mr Rupert Booth-Sandell sold some land profitably.

In the same year he invested money in the Great Eastern Railway Company, and that was a profitable investment. In 1880 he built what is known as the Institute–used as a village hall to this day. During the following the Tudor almshouses at Baildon, reared and endowed by the terms of the will of one Thomasin Grigg, widow, were found to be finally past repair. Mr Booth-Sandell built new ones, single-storied versions of his Nettleton cottages, because he felt that old people should be spared the effort of climbing stairs. The lozenge on the almshouses displays the initials of Mrs Booth-Sandell.

Those were the settled spacious days and Rupert and Charlotte Booth-Sandell were typical of their class and generation. Until quite recently it was possible to find old men and women who would speak nostalgically of the 'old master and mistress'; of their generosity, their dignity, their family of lively handsome boys, the glory of Merravay during their régime, the way the carriage lights shone on the trees of the avenue when the Booth-Sandells gave a dinner-party, the ox-roasting to which the whole village was invited when Mr Booth, the heir, came of age. Ah, they were the days, and gone for ever.

And if the wages of the farm-labourers were never more than twelve shillings a week, and sometimes as little as ten, nobody was ever stood off in the winter; and the moment there was trouble in the house there was the old mistress on the doorstep ready with an offer of help. And food was cheap, and the new houses, let for one and sixpence a week, had enough garden to grow vegetables for any family, however large.

In 1890 in the glowing mellow sunset of the century, Mr Booth Booth-Sandell, succeeded his father. Gradually the twilight descended.

Things were never again the same at Merravay. For one thing, Mr Booth, for all he was so handsome, never married. Too gay and frisky in his young days, and later on too crusty. But although he was never the man his father was, and of course, seeing how much his father had spent on good works, not nearly so rich, he was popular enough with the village people, for he could be unthinkingly generous, and he was always one for a joke.

EPISODE SEVEN
Pre-1914 War

THE HEIRESS

Of all the self-imposed burdens under which mankind struggles, family loyalty is, I think, one of the heaviest. I notice that modern people tend to be very casual about their obligations in this respect, but those of us who are now called, somewhat scornfully, the Victorians, were so schooled to a sense of duty towards those of our own blood that we must either perform it or suffer pangs of conscience. So I must sit down and pen the invitation which, if it is accepted, will spoil what remains of my life. I have no choice.

The exasperating part of it all is that I never liked Merravay; I never liked my Uncle Booth; I never liked my cousin Maude.

Maude and I and another cousin, a boy who died in his early teens, were the only children in our generation; of my grandmother's six sons one, the eldest, my Uncle Booth, remained unmarried and two others were childless. Maude and I were almost of an age; she was about six months older than I and, in those far-away days visits were often arranged and long journeys undertaken because our parents thought it would be nice for us to meet. I remember her as a thin, leggy child with a mane of very curly pale auburn hair and the freckled skin which often goes with it. She had a high-bridged arrogant nose and curiously narrow, very bright blue eyes. Her parents, who adored her, had spoiled her shamelessly and she had no fear of anything or anybody. I was rather a timid child myself and most of our meetings seemed to end in some kind of trouble which she instigated, mocked me into, and then sailed out of, unrebuked, while I was taken aside and punished. I thought this decidedly unfair; my parents seemed to think that they were omniscient, surely they should have seen how things were, I used to think.

One of the places where we used to meet was the family house in Suffolk, then the property of my Uncle Booth. It lay in a very remote place, amongst fields and woods, but it could hardly be called inaccessible, for the railway ran to within two miles of it. The shooting there was reckoned to be above average, and every year my father and Maude's and my other uncles endeavoured to get to Merravay at some time during the autumn and to arrange their visits to overlap as far as possible. So far as one could judge, this desire to get together at least once a year was not due to any deep-rooted affection; they quarrelled, they criticised one another, they took sides, but they all seemed to enjoy the reunion, and when increasing age, infirmity, and finally death broke up the family circle it was easy to look back and be rather sentimental about it all.

Merravay was a Tudor house and considered very beautiful; remarkable, they said, for having stood for three hundred years without being added to or altered. Of that fact the kitchen quarters bore witness. Uncle Booth had made one innovation; he had installed a bath. Apart from that the house remained, even to the rugs on the floor, exactly as Uncle Booth's great-great grandfather had had it when he came from India and settled down at Merravay. The garden was delightful, but I always thought that the place as a whole was gloomy, and when–as time went on–it became my duty to make occasional visits there alone, doing my duty to Uncle Booth, I always went reluctantly and left with joy.

I was never at ease, for one thing, with my uncle. He was odd and arbitrary, and even in his more genial moments inclined to poke fun at one, to make outrageous statements and watch for one's reaction. His father, my grandfather, was still remembered in the neighbourhood as a liberal-minded, open-handed man. Cottages which in their day were models, almshouses and public buildings all bear his stamp, RBS, and the date. There are boys now at Baildon School and at the universities profiting from the scholarships he founded. Uncle Booth had been known to say that his father had been extravagant in *his* way and thus curtailed extravagance in his heir.

My father died suddenly, and at a comparatively early age, when I was sixteen. We were left badly off, and I think Mother would gladly have gone to live at Merravay; but she was not asked to do so, and if she made any overtures they were disregarded. She was very anxious, however, that I should ingratiate myself with Uncle Booth. The death of my boy cousin had removed the obvious heir. Mother always knew when Maude had been to Merravay and would tell me, rather reproachfully; and I would say, 'But Maude *likes* Merravay.' Maude had told me so herself, times without number. She always said it was the most beautiful house in the world. I think she was sincere too. Often when we'd stayed there together I'd seen her, before breakfast, go running to the end of the garden, scramble up on to the wall between the urns and sit there swinging her long thin legs and just staring, and staring, as though she were in a trance. It would be no hardship for her to spend part of her holidays there; for though she got on with Uncle Booth little better than I did, she wasn't afraid of or embarrassed by him and always had an answer.

Her parents were wealthier than mine and more worldly. At sixteen she was sent to a Paris finishing school, and a year and a half later she was presented and launched upon a London season. Everybody said that she was a raving beauty. Certainly she had got rid of her freckles and gained control of her limbs, and with that blaze of hair and those blue-ice eyes she could not help but be noticeable; but I personally thought that she was still too thin, and too tall, and too high-nosed to be beautiful.

'She'll make a wonderful match, I expect,' said my mother with a little sigh.

Actually I was married first; and if getting a man as near perfection as a human being can be counted for anything, mine was a wonderful match, though it cost my poor mother many a sigh–not small ones, either. I married the local doctor. That was considered little short of disgraceful, especially as he had no private money, no connections, and was only a junior partner. But I knew what I wanted, and for once I was determined to have my way. Uncle Booth could not come to the wedding–he had just suffered his first slight stroke. He sent me a cheque for twenty pounds and a grumbling letter because I had not taken Ian to be looked over.

'I'm afraid you've done for yourself there,' said my mother.

She said it again when, almost a year later, Maude was married, and from Merravay! She said she had always hoped to be married from that house. And of course the enormous hall which takes up such a disproportionate part of the ground floor lent itself for such an occasion. I did not go to the wedding, it was only a few weeks before I had my baby; but I heard vivid accounts of how wonderful Maude looked coming down the great staircase in her wedding-dress and veil. Uncle Booth's present to her was an enormous ruby on a thin gold chain to wear as a pendant; and we were told that some old lady, a remote relative, one of the Gore Park Booths who was at the wedding, said that it was an heirloom which should never have been in our part of the family at all.

My son, my dear Angus, was born while Maude was on her honeymoon in Venice. I was perfectly content. I was very busy, too busy to bother much about anything outside my own household. In the next five years I went to Merravay only once, just for a day to take to Uncle Booth a few things of my father's which my mother, on her death-bed, said she wished him to have. Poor mother, she was hopeful to the last and tried to make me promise to take Angus too; but I travelled third class and it was hot weather. I left Angus at home in his cool clean nursery. The stroke had affected Uncle Booth's speech and made him even more difficult to talk to; otherwise he was unchanged. So was Merravay.

When Angus was five and we were in process of changing his nurse for a governess something happened to me. To my mind. For one thing, I realised that though Maude had now been married four years she had had no child; and I also realised that Ian would never make money. He was too kind, and too careless. I wanted nothing for myself . . . but for Angus, I suddenly knew, I wanted everything. We could, we would, afford a governess . . . but away ahead in the years I could see many other needful, desirable or merely pleasant things which would be, unless circumstances changed, unattainable. And there was Uncle Booth, a man of property; and here was Angus, as handsome, well-set-up, delightful a little boy as there was on the face of the earth. All suddenly I realised how *my* mother had felt about Merravay and why she had cried when she compared the twenty-pound cheque with the great ruby.

I wrote to Uncle Booth suggesting that Angus, whom he had not yet seen, and I should spend a few days at Merravay. The letter which came back was kindly enough, and when we arrived our welcome left nothing to be desired. It was obvious that Uncle Booth had taken pains to ensure our comfort –even to the extent of having two steps made so that Angus could get into the high bath. But almost immediately he started making the gibing remarks which I always resented, even when they were aimed at me alone.

Angus had the grave, speculative stare which all children of that age adopt towards strangers. Uncle Booth stared back at him and then said 'Boo!' so sharply that the child jumped and backed away. I had told him how *he* was to behave, and he was trying to obey orders; he wasn't prepared for foolery on the part of a poor sick old man. To me Uncle Booth said, 'Take him away, Catherine. He's a nice little boy, I'm sure, but he's got such a bedside manner I expect him, every minute, to ask have the bowels worked today.'

I thought that was unforgivable; a back-handed slap at Ian, an insult to Angus. And it was rude to mention bowels, thus gratuitously, to me!

That was not a successful visit. On the last day of it Uncle Booth received a letter from Maude. He laughed over it.

'What a gel that is! Listen to this. "Edward is going to divorce me. May the black sheep come and graze at Merravay before being sheared in public?" Joking about it. That damn fool of a husband of hers doesn't know what he's losing. There aren't many with Maude's spirit. Now you can make yourself handy, Catherine. You can write for me.' He sat down and dictated the letter straight away. A hateful letter. I know it began:

> My dear Maude,
>
> I was shocked and horrified by your news. So far as I know, we have never had a divorce in the family. God knows what things are coming to when a decently bred, decently reared young woman like you can be accused, openly, of adultery . . .

It went on like that, bitter, vituperative. And it ended by saying, 'Of course you may come and hide your head at Merravay–blood is thicker than water, they say; besides, the thing might as well end where it began. So come and wear your penitent's sackcloth where you wore your bridal satin.'

Was it all meant as a joke? He'd told me, often enough, that I had no sense of humour. I could understand and laugh at Ian's jokes; that was one bond between us, we laughed at the same things. For the life of me I couldn't see anything funny in this. In Maude's place I wouldn't have accepted such an invitation even if refusing it had meant that I had to go into cheap lodgings in London.

I went home next day. Maude went to Merravay and stayed there for several months. It was a particularly nasty divorce. Her husband was as vindictive as he had been doting, and a young, titled girl who had had what was called an understanding with the co-respondent committed suicide in a fit of disgust, so there was a great deal of publicity. Everybody expected that in the end Maude's fellow sinner would feel compelled to marry her. Whether he ever offered to or not, the family system of communication –what Ian always called 'the jungle drums'–never informed me; they did tell me that Maude said the young man was a handsome ass and that his asininity was responsible for the whole catastrophe and she did not intend to marry a fool.

She had no need to. She married Sir Theodore Audley; thus gaining, at one stroke, another rich, doting husband, a title, a great Palladian mansion in Wiltshire, an imposing house in St James's Square and a shooting lodge in Scotland. She also gained, and filled as though born to it, a place in that half-raffish, half-royal circle which was such a feature of Edwardian society. She remained childless.

Early in the summer of 1912 the jungle drums informed me that Uncle Booth considered himself neglected by me and mine, and that he was in failing health. In mid-July I received a letter, a formal invitation for a month. One sentence in it roused my resentment. 'Bring your husband,' it said. 'I have reached the state where a private physician seems to be called for.' That didn't seem to me to be the right way to ask a busy man to give up his holiday.

'He's old and crotchety. Take no notice,' Ian said. 'You and Angus go for a month. I'll come down with you and stay a week, and then again for a week at the end.'

'You probably won't,' I said. 'He'll insult you funnily or be funny insultingly and you'll leave and never come back. I wouldn't go near him again if I didn't feel it my duty to Angus.'

'You visit your Uncle Warren . . .' Ian said.

'Because I'm sorry for him. His son died and then his wife, and he's poor . . .'

'And dipsomaniac and dirty! Dear Cathy; at the bottom of your heart, you know, you're afraid that you might seem to be a fortune-hunter. So you feel *bound* to take offence at Uncle Booth.'

'Is it that? Do *you* want me to be nicer to him, about him?' I asked, a little bewildered.

'Makes no difference to me,' Ian said. 'I can give Angus every advantage I ever had, and more. But it does seem to me that you're a bit mixed about your Uncle Booth. He *can't* be worse than Warren.'

'All right. I'll try again. We'll all go and be nice to this poor old rich uncle of mine . . .'

Whether age and illness had improved Uncle Booth's manners or whether Ian and Angus being there made things easier I cannot say. I only know that was the best visit I ever had at Merravay. For one thing, the weather was lovely. It is a little strange how those two or three summers immediately preceding the fatal summer of 1914 seem to glow with more than sunlight. Even Merravay seemed to lose its gloom.

Ian and Angus established surprisingly friendly relationships with Uncle Booth, and Angus was praised for the way he took to riding; he had never had much chance to acquire horsemanship, but he proved to be fearless and to have what they call 'good hands'. 'As good as Maude at the same age,' said Uncle Booth. We understood that praise could go no further.

During the last week Uncle Booth's lawyer came and was closeted with him for the best part of a morning; and after that I did permit myself a hope or two on Angus's account. There was no doubt that Maude would inherit Merravay–Uncle Booth had several times mentioned her devotion to it, as a place: 'She doesn't come to see me, you know. She comes to count those house-leeks on the roof!' But Angus, I thought, had made his mark and would be remembered.

We had been home three days when I heard that Uncle Booth had had another stroke, likely to prove fatal. I went back at once, but he was dead when I got there. Maude had arrived a few hours earlier but had had, she said, no speech with him.

We were alone together there for that evening. Now and then it struck me as rather sad that we should both be so calm. Maude's manner was brittle, but no more so when she said, 'I shall miss him; he was always *there*', than when she said, 'This soup is almost stone cold.' I hadn't seen her since her second marriage, and to me she looked surprisingly young and almost intimidatingly sophisticated. I was almost sure that there was rouge on her cheeks and lips; she wore diamonds in her ears and on her fingers; and she smoked–absolutely naturally and with no air of bravado–cigarette after cigarette, using a long holder that looked to me as though it were made of jade.

I noticed at once that out of the confusion which inevitably follows a death had emerged the idea of Maude being the centre and head of the house. That was hardly to be wondered at. Despite her busy social life and her travels, she had spent much more time at Merravay–though I had stayed there more recently. She was older than I; she was–if Uncle Booth could be credited with such a conventional preference–his favourite niece; and all the servants, being snobs to the bone, enjoyed saying 'Her ladyship this' and 'Her ladyship that'.

It was a lovely late summer evening, and after dinner Maude and I, by common impulse, escaped from the hushed house and went into the garden. Dusk was creeping in from the fields and the wood. Merravay had always struck me as being an unnaturally quiet place, even when allowance was made for its remoteness. Tonight the quiet seemed almost unearthly, although when one listened one could hear the soft mourning of doves, the twitter of smaller birds settling for the night, the clatter of the last train running through to Bywater.

In the rose garden the second-crop roses, which had been buds when I left three days before, were full out, wide-hearted after the day's warmth; and from the herbaceous border waves of heavier perfume from lilies, late stocks and tobacco flowers came to meet us as we strolled. At the very end of the garden, where the urn-topped wall divided it from the field, we stopped and turned, leaning back against the still-warm bricks.

'It is,' Maude said, looking to left and right and then straight ahead to the house, 'the most beautiful, perfect place in the world.'

Ordinarily she had a crisp, light way of speaking, just flicking her words and dropping the emphasis in unexpected places. Ordinarily she would have said, 'The *most* beautiful place . . .' But tonight her voice was deep, caressing, and she gave 'beautiful' its full, brooding value.

Ordinarily I should have questioned her verdict; it was solid, spacious, and had certain historically interesting features, but it was too grim and gloomy to be beautiful in my eyes–very much as Maude was too angular and high-nosed; but the thought of Uncle Booth lying there in his vast high-windowed bedroom, dead and really unmourned, depressed me so that I didn't feel like arguing. I felt empty and forlorn; I longed for my husband, my child, my own neat snug house and garden. All the sadness about this place, the age-old, ingrained gloom which I had always felt, seemed to rise like a tide and engulf me. On a sudden impulse I moved nearer to Maude and took her arm. Inside the billowing chiffon sleeve her arm felt hot, almost feverishly hot, and surprisingly frail.

'It's sad,' I said, without choosing my words, 'to die and have nobody to mourn you.'

Maude jerked her arm away. 'We can't all be founders of families,' she said. 'Who'd you expect to cry over a selfish old bachelor? And he's oblivious to whether we cry or gloat.'

That struck me as exactly the thing which Uncle Booth would have said in the same circumstances.

'You and he were very much alike, in some ways,' I said.

'That's why we got on so badly. We saw through one another. He knew why I came here; he knew what this place means to me.'

That was true. I'd heard him say so.

'That mystifies me, Maude. You have three–is it three?–houses. You see and stay in all kinds of magnificent places. What is it about this place? To me it seems a gloomy old barn, it does really . . . but Ian,–my husband, you know–seemed terribly taken with it too.'

Maude stared straight ahead towards the house, which loomed, dark and menacing, against the fading green of the evening sky.

'I don't know,' she said at last. 'It's just something. . . . The first time I came here I wanted to stay; I asked my father to buy it. I've always come back, and when I'm away I dream of it. It's my place. It is *so* beautiful. It's one of those things which nobody can explain. . . .' She fitted a cigarette into the holder, struck a match and narrowed her eyes against the flame. 'Talking of crying,' she said abruptly, 'I did cry, for pure happiness then, the night Uncle Booth promised to leave it to me. So if I cried now it would be hypocrisy.'

So he had promised Merravay to her. That was no surprise to me; it had been understood more or less all along. Just a thousand pounds for Angus, I thought; just enough to see him comfortably through school and started in life. And there was this to be said for Merravay going to Maude; if Uncle Booth had left it to either of his brothers, Ernest or Warren, the only two left, he would have felt bound to leave money for its upkeep. With Maude that would never arise. So perhaps–with luck–just a thousand pounds for Angus.

Uncle Ernest arrived early next morning. He had spent most of his life in the colonial service and had retired with a knighthood and a pension. He lived in a not-very-luxurious club in London and seemed glad to get to the flesh-pots of Merravay. But he grumbled, almost automatically, at everything. A damp patch and a crack on his bedroom ceiling caused him great concern.

'Well,' he said, looking from Maude to me, 'whichever one of you gets *this* handsome property gets a white elephant, let me tell you. Roof's in shocking condition. Ceiling over my bed! Sword of Damocles nothing to it. Have you seen it?'

'I've seen the one in my own,' said Maude. 'But I've been up in the roof. There's no worm or dry-rot. The tiles just need relaying and replacing in parts.'

'That'll cost a pretty penny.'

'Five or six hundred pounds,' said Maude, as though it were nothing.

'Not that *we* need worry, yet,' Uncle Ernest proceeded. 'Tricky chap, Booth; always was. Probably left the place to Dr Barnardo's Homes. Short of his leaving me my father's gold hunter, which I always coveted, nothing would surprise me!'

'Well, Uncle Ernest had his surprise. Uncle Booth had bequeathed him not only the coveted watch but all his personal belongings, studs, cuff-links, cigar cases, guns, everything in his cellar and the sum of a thousand pounds.

That was one of the first of what seemed an interminable list of bequests. One would have thought that this was the will of an unusually sentimental man who was either fantastically generous or prodigally rich. Dozens of servants, past and present, people for whom Uncle Booth had never had a good word to say, all remembered; the Almshouse Trust at which he had jeered; the Scholarship Fund which he had pretended to deplore. A veritable shower of gold fell upon all; and still there was no mention of

Angus. How rich had he been. What would be left?

At last Mr Turnbull paused, cleared his throat slightly, and read out the final phrases. All the contents of the house were left to Maude; Merravay and the garden to me.

I swallowed something sour and choking that came up from the pit of my stomach into my throat. I felt Merravay, with its medieval kitchens and sagging roof, fall like a dead weight on my shoulders. I knew a moment of bitter disappointment. Then I braced myself. All right–I thought–you wanted to surprise everybody, but I am not surprised; I always thought you were a horrid old man, and now I know it. I could see that the will had been the last of his verbal quips. What perverse pleasure he must have derived in sitting down on that fine August morning and planning a surprise for everybody. Surprise a kitchen slut with a legacy of fifty pounds; surprise Angus, the obvious heir to everything, by not even mentioning him; surprise Maude, who had three houses full of furniture; surprise Catherine, who didn't care for Merravay. I am not surprised, Uncle Booth; but Maude . . . oh dear. For the first time in my life I could think, 'Poor Maude.'

I took a careful glance at her; she was sitting as though someone had taken a sharp sword and run her through. There was now no doubt about whether she rouged her face; the harsh colour stood out like clown's paint, her nose looked like a bleached bone. As I watched she stood up, straightened herself, and without a word to anyone stalked out of the room.

I thought to myself that I would be ashamed to make such an exhibition of feeling. After all, I was equally, or more, cruelly disappointed, mocked. I was a woman who had to look pretty sharply to the butcher's bill, who had to live in a town two hundred miles away, who had a child to provide for. And all that I'd got was a liability. She could have Merravay; I'd sell it to her. Thank God there was one person on earth mad enough to want it and rich enough to indulge the whim.

I muttered a word of excuse and ran after Maude. She was in her room, hurriedly throwing her clothes and toilet articles into a dressing-case. I was breathless from my run up the stairs and along the gallery, but I managed to gasp out:

'Maude, you can have it. I don't want it. I never did. And I couldn't afford . . .'

'Get out of my sight,' said Maude. She cast at me one look in which all the hatred and accusation in the world seemed concentrated; a mad look.

'Don't take it so hard,' I gasped. 'I'm terribly disappointed too. But we can come to some arrangement. . . .'

'I'm not going to *buy* what is mine by right. I never want to see the place again!' She snapped the dressing-case and went to the bell, jerking the pull crazily.

'I'll give it to you. . . .' She gave me another mad look. 'Maude, you must see that it isn't any use to me. I couldn't live in it; I couldn't have the roof mended.'

'Insure it and burn it down,' Maude said. 'Oh, Beales . . . I'm leaving immediately.'

Even the rule about behaving oneself before servants was no rule to her. I said 'Goodbye, Maude', in as normal a voice as I could manage. She swept past me without a word.

Then began the terrible time during which, were I a fanciful woman, I would say that I was justified in all my feelings about Merravay, back and back to my earliest recollection when I was frightened of the place. It had seemed to threaten me, and Heaven knew it now carried out its threat in terms of near ruin. We couldn't leave it empty and uncared for and allow obvious decay to add itself to the hidden flaws; we had to find wages for a caretaker and a gardener. Upon our limited means the great house fastened like a bloodsucker.

I wrote three letters to Maude, each more beseeching than the last; she answered none. A formal letter from a firm of furniture removers, asking for access to the house for four days, informed me that she meant to remove the furniture. I shut myself in my room then and cried a little in secret. There were things of great value at Merravay; if only Uncle Booth had . . . I know the Bible explicitly states that to him who hath shall be given and from him who hath not shall be taken away even that which he hath . . . but I had never expected to be obliged to interpret that so literally.

Once I knew that Maude was adamant I did everything possible to sell the place. Advertisements which stressed its historic value, the scenery, the shooting, photographs over which even Ian would brood and say, 'It really *is* beautiful', appeared in all the papers. Numbers of house agents had it 'on their books'. But the stark fact, which I had recognised before Mr Turnbull had finished speaking, just would not be gainsaid. Nobody wanted a great crumbling house in the depths of the country but with nothing but a kitchen garden attached to it.

One day, when I was obliged to go there, I tried to cheer myself up by playing a game. I arrived at Nettleton Station and drove to Merravay in a ramshackle cab, pretending that I had never seen the place before, had been attracted by the advertisement and had come to inspect it.

It was an experience to frighten the hardiest. Stripped of the furniture, the house was simply not habitable even in imagination. I stood in the drawing-room and looked at the walls, realising for the first time that the silk which covered them had once been deep yellow. Wherever a picture had hung or a piece of furniture stood against the wall, it was bright yellow still, with birds and sprays of flowers embroidered on it in delightful colours; elsewhere everything had faded to a dim greyish buff, marked with brown stains where the damp had crept in. In places it was frayed, in others torn. Imagine any woman standing there and thinking–My drawing-room. That alone . . . and then there were the kitchens, grim vaults.

No, it was hopeless. I realised it then. What should I do? What could I do? I thought of Maude's remark–another one of those that old Booth himself might have made–about insuring it and burning it. Really, if I could have hoped to do so without exposure I should have been tempted. And certainly if I could have wished the place out of existence it would have vanished there and then. But it stood there fundamentally solid enough. The roof might leak, but the timber was sound. I looked at what seemed like acres of flooring, smooth and shining, honey-coloured; at what seemed like miles of panelling, much of it beautifully carved; at the staircase, as good as the day it was completed; at the roses and ships and other things which decorated the chimney-breasts. Had they no value?

Then I went out into the kitchen garden. It was a wildly prolific place; Uncle Booth had employed two men and a boy and the garden produce at Merravay had always been one of the joys of a visit. I had kept on one man, the eldest of the three, paying him a small wage and allowing him to make it up by selling what he could. I had also arranged to have boxes of stuff sent to me by rail, but that was highly unsatisfactory. Now, carefully tended, basking in the sun, the wealth of it–great plump shining strawberries, thick, tender asparagus, early peas–tended to exasperate me almost past bearing.

On my way home in the train I made up my mind. Next day I wrote a letter to the Baildon agent, who, being at hand, could better deal with it. I asked him to try to find a buyer for the kitchen garden, and to sell the house, if he could, to a 'house breaker'. Ian was very much distressed. I said, 'What else can I do? Almost two years, and it's costing us money all the time. If I can get just a thousand pounds . . .'

'For almost the first time in my life,' he said, 'I wish I'd devoted a little more attention to money.'

But it worked out in the end. A builder named Hoggett offered a thousand pounds for Merravay as it stood. The agent, a shrewd and energetic fellow, took him over and persuaded him, on the strength of the staircase alone, to raise his offer to fifteen hundred pounds.

On the last Saturday of July 1914 I received a cheque for the whole, minus the agent's fees, and when I subtracted the sums I had paid out in wages and the cost of my journeys to and fro, and the other expenses, I reckoned that I had almost exactly the thousand pounds for which I had hoped. I'd finished with Merravay.

Nine days later war was declared. Ian joined the Army Medical Corps, and after that I had something else to worry about. I don't think I gave Merravay another thought until the other day when I heard that Maude was hard up and homeless. All her husband's houses passed to a nephew when he died, and Maude had squandered the money he left her, and her own, in unwise speculations and endless house-movings. They say that between 1919 and 1938 she moved house, buying and selling and losing money on every deal, no fewer than fifteen times. That must be an exaggeration.

What could I do but write and invite her to share my tiny flat even though I am told that she once described it as 'one cell in an eggbox'? I suppose the whole thing would strike Uncle Booth as a most delectable joke.

INTERLUDE

When Joe Hoggett wrote the cheque for fifteen hundred pounds and so became owner of Merravay he was putting his name to nothing so mundane as a money order. He was signing a declaration of faith.

Several times during the past weeks he had said, 'Don't you believe it. There ain't gorn to be no war. Stands to reason. . . .'

He knew all the reasons and could reel them off, pat.

On the last Sunday of July he drove out from his neat villa, Jesmondene, on the outskirts of Baildon, to inspect again, this time with a possessive eye, his latest purchase. He took with him his wife and his daughter-in-law, who were always pleased to have an outing on a fine Sunday afternoon, and were today excited by the prospect of seeing Merravay, of which they had heard a great deal. It irked Joe that his son, Joe Willie, was unable to accompany them; his absence quite spoilt the day.

Joe Willie did not share his father's confidence in Germany's awe of the British Navy, in the Kaiser's blood relationship to the British royal family or any of the other things which Joe thought of when he said, 'Stands to reason. . . .'

Joe Willie had been, for the last two years, a member of the Suffolk Yeomanry, the Loyal Suffolk Hussars. Old Joe had nothing against that; he was proud that Joe Willie, son of a working builder, should take his place amongst the sons of farmers and gentry–and be the best mounted of the lot. Joe had taken that showy, spirited black horse as part payment of a bad debt when the Whymarks 'went up the spout', as he termed it. Joe Willie, looking very smart and handsome, had gone off to what he called 'exercises' on this fine Sunday.

Mrs Hoggett and Rosie, after a glance at the outside of the house and a more prolonged stare at the hall, both of which Mrs Hoggett pronounced 'gloomy' and Rosie 'romantic', went off, womanlike, to the kitchen quarters, leaving Mr Hoggett to take–a little shamefacedly, for it was Sunday, after all–a folding rule from his pocket and just run it over, just to make sure, just to confirm. . . . He knew *that he had made a good bargain, really; but his original offer had been for a thousand . . . and though he knew and was sure, he just wanted to* make *sure.*

Once, running rule and eye over the panelling, the thought struck him, cold, stomach-shaking–Do that come to a war and Joe Willie go, it'll be like this a long time, me alone. . . . But then, thass daft. There ain't gorn to be a war. Stand to reason. . . .

In the kitchen and pantries and store-rooms the two women were having a wonderful time. Mrs Hoggett's father had been a butcher and had enjoyed Mr Booth-Sandell's esteemed custom; she had always regarded the family with genuine awe. Seeing the kitchen in which that meat had been prepared for table was a shock to her.

'Well, if I wasn't seeing it with my own eyes I never *would have believed it. Swanking about like that, ever so lordly, and living so shabby. Look at that old sink. All hollowed out with wear. You couldn't clean it, not if you wanted to ever so. Well, I never did.'*

'I don't suppose the old man ever saw his sink,' said Rosie. It was a reasonable statement, but there was just that something in her voice which made Mrs Hoggett suspect that once again she and Rosie weren't seeing quite eye to eye. That often happened; though they were the best of friends, really. Still, it was with a certain asperity in her voice that she said, in the bathroom:

'He did see the bath, I s'pose!' They stared at the mahogany surrounded sarcophagus that stood high and lonely in the centre of a moderately large room.

Rosie agreed, for a moment, that the new bathroom at Jesmondene was preferable to this; then she looked out of the window and wasn't so sure.

Again Mrs Hoggett sensed the lack of response. Rosie wasn't quite the homey, companionable daughter-in-law she'd hoped for, but she suited Joe Willie; and though she seldom said the absolutely right, cosy thing, she never said the downright wrong one.

The three met in the hall. Joe Hoggett was jubilant. He'd been right as usual. The staircase and the fireplaces alone were worth the money; then there was the panelling and the flooring, all solid oak as good as new and better; and the tiles–it was curious how, these days, lots of people building a new house didn't want it to look *new, liked the old tiles.*

'Well, my dears,' he said, closing and locking the great door, 'Joe Hoggett weren't far off the mark there. Thass a bargain all right!'

'When I think,' said Mrs Hoggett, 'how in the old days he'd come to the shop and sit there in his gig and give the window a clip with his whip to draw attention, ever so lordly, and all the time . . . Well, if I hadn't seen with my own eyes . . .!'

Joe Hoggett helped the women into the high dog-cart, gathered the reins, clicked his tongue to the horse and then turned to take one last look at the house which he meant to carve up as a butcher carves up a carcass. The doomed and threatened house stared back at him. . . .

'I call it a shame to pull it down,' said Rosie in a strained, desperate voice. 'It's such a beautiful house.'

'Thass better; thass a beautiful bargain,' said Joe easily. 'You wait till Joe Willie sees what his old dad've pulled off this time!'

But Joe Willie never saw the wonderful bargain; he rode away on his handsome horse, came home for one leave that was reckoned in hours and went to meet death in the Dardanelles. Joe Hoggett's zest for money-making was quenched; there was no point in it now, for Joe Willie had left no child. There was some slight satisfaction in lending Merravay to be used as a military hospital where men less desperately wounded than Joe Willie might be mended, and when, its purpose served, the place came back into his hands he was spiritlessly relieved to sell it to the first bidder.

During the next thirty years the house changed hands seven times. A new law protecting ancient and historic buildings prevented anyone doing with it what Joe Hoggett had planned to do; a brief period in the ownership of a capricious millionaire saved it from falling into complete decay. In 1940, for a fortnight, it sheltered a number of evacuees who would have stayed longer if there had been a cinema and a fried-fish shop within easy reach. Later in the war contingents of soldiers stayed long enough to write rude words on the plaster and carve their initials on the panelling.

Peace came; the old house stood and awaited the next turn of fortune. One thing only seemed certain–the time had come when Merravay must work for its keep.

EPISODE EIGHT
Post-1939 War

THE BREADWINNER

Chapter One

In 1946, when David was what they called 'rehabilitated', we set out to look for a little place in the country where we could cultivate a market garden and bring up a family. We had about three thousand pounds between us; and when we had discovered that people were asking five or six thousand for two acres of chicken-sickened ground and an asbestos-board bungalow so small that David's claustrophobia became rampant at the sight, the miracle happened and we found Merravay.

It was an old Tudor house in Suffolk; quite genuine, spacious and beautiful. It had been modernised after a fashion some years before; it had a banqueting hall and a musicians' gallery and–what mattered more to us–a big kitchen garden and some substantial outbuildings. During the war it had suffered; as David said, looking round, 'The legions have camped here', and perhaps that was one reason why it was for sale so cheaply. They were asking three thousand pounds for it. When I brooded over the possible folly of buying an historic mansion to house two adults and one child I could find three points in favour of the project; first was that even on our first visit of inspection David had stayed indoors for a full hour without making one of his pitiable little excuses to go outside; secondly I could see that–should the market-garden idea fail–there was room here for me to take paying guests; and thirdly I was a fool. 'Knaves and fools all pay in the end, but the fools pay first!' I was fool enough to fall for the charm of the house. Its air of having seen such better days, of falling into decay so graciously, of wanting to be loved and used gently again . . . oh, I don't know! I was just a fool!

We put down our ready money, and I sold the best of the things my grandmother had left me and we bought fifty handsome Rhode Island pullets scheduled to begin to lay in November when eggs, scarce and dear, command good prices. That sounded promising, and we were also encouraged by the fact that the old man who had had charge of the garden (on a 'sharecropper' basis) while the house was empty decided to stay and work for us. He was the recipient of a pension of some kind which made it inadvisable for him to *earn* more than thirty shillings a week. His method of recompensing himself more adequately had worked well in the past, and probably he saw no reason to alter it. But it broke down in September when

I went into a fruit shop at Baildon to try to sell some green figs and was informed that they always bought figs from Merravay which were better than mine. That was indisputable! The wretched old man had risen earlier and picked more discriminately. Attempts–almost pathetically well-meaning on our part, at least–to reach some less cut-throat arrangement met with marked non-collaboration from him, and finally, with the remark that he was used to working for gentlefolk, he left us.

However, that was just at the beginning of the long spell of severe weather for which the winter of 1946-7 is memorable, and as there was nothing to do except feed the hens and wait–and pray–for eggs and look for the places where snow had penetrated the roof, we bore up bravely, saying that there was no better place to be housebound. The hall made an excellent playground for a young child and the fireplaces took kindly to a diet of wood cut from the overgrown shrubbery.

In the spring of that year I made my first tentative suggestion about taking in guests. David wriggled away from it. He didn't actually *say* that an Englishman's home was his castle or that it was a man's duty to provide for his family . . . that was all implied.

And there were, of course, several stones unturned, many avenues unexplored . . . To hell with clichés! We tried goats and bees and mushrooms, we tried dog-breeding; we grew pyrethrum, and scabious and lavender and potted plants. We tried everything!

And then, one day, driving in from Baildon, David overtook Ginger Whymark, whose car had broken down. Once upon a time the Whymarks had been the big noise in these parts; they'd owned Merravay and sold it and built a great new white house nearby and lately sold that to be an agricultural college and moved into their own lodge cottage–a bit added to. The old man had managed to retain the shooting rights and every autumn he had a big party; very favoured old friends screwed themselves into the limited accommodation at the Lodge, the others went to the Evening Star in Nettleton, and soon after David had become–and I had forced myself to be–friends with Ginger Whymark the woman at the Evening Star fell ill on the very eve of one of the old man's parties and Ginger came across to ask a favour . . . would I, could I, put up four decent old chaps? Just bed and breakfast; she could manage everything else.

I'll be honest. I didn't much care for Miss Whymark with her marmalade-coloured hair and her hearty voice and her abounding energy. They said she did all the housework at the Lodge single-handed, bred her dachshunds and looked after an old aunt across the way as well and still had time to hunt or go beagling when chance offered–a reputation which made me respect and admire and . . . is there a word for it? Resent doesn't quite do, nor does fear. . . . Anyway, that doesn't matter. What does is that I seized on her suggestion and took in the old men, who were perfect pets; and when David saw that the sun did not fall out of the sky at the sight of Captain and Mrs Stamford taking base coinage in return for hospitality the way was opened for me to do what I had been longing to do for months–start Merravay as a guest-house. I sold a few of my remaining treasures, a Bow clock, some bits of Chelsea china and a lidded wassail bowl–the only complete one, I believe, outside a museum, in all England–and with the proceeds I bought the necessary furniture and paid for the necessary advertisement and before long my guesthouse was on its feet and staggering along.

Chapter Two

It would be ridiculous to pretend that the guesthouse made much profit; what it did do was to work in very well with David's various activities. Vegetables and fruit, eggs, rabbits and fowls I could have at cost price, and since I could now order with comparative lavishness at the Baildon shops their owners were more inclined to buy what we had to sell. By May of 1950, when the lilacs and mock-orange in the overgrown shrubberies at Merravay were scenting the air for miles around and every day ended in a kind of cuckoo-haunted dream, I could look round, not with complacency but with some satisfaction. We were solvent; people who had stayed once had come again and recommended us to their friends, and Ginger Whymark had heard of someone who had two old horses in need of a good home and we had offered to take them–'meat for manners'–so now we could offer riding as one of the amenities at Merravay. My main worry was that David was overworking. Since the guesthouse had got going he had suffered a decline of spirits, had more than once said something about being a failure and having made a mistake in coming to Merravay. This I attributed to the fact that he was working too hard as well as resenting the establishment of the guesthouse.

The overwork, at least, was remedied. Early one morning, driving back from Baildon, he saw a man sitting by the roadside endeavouring to hammer back–with a stone–the loose sole of his shoe. David's all-embracing sympathy came uppermost; he stopped the car, spoke to the man, brought him to Merravay, gave him a meal and a rather better pair of shoes. The man was a Pole; whence he came, whither he was bound we never knew. When he had eaten and was re-shod he looked at the garden and said, 'I dig. I am not beggar man.' And he dug until the next mealtime; after which apparently his pride demanded that he should dig again. At nightfall he slept in the loft and was then so deeply in debt that he must dig all next day.

He looked harmless enough–a thin, clean-looking little man with closely cropped hair and very bright blue eyes–but, as I said to David, he might be a thief, a murderer, for all we knew.

'Damned good worker, though,' said David. 'We could use him.'

At the next feeding time David asked, casually:

'Know anything about horses?'

Something happened to his tight, bony little face.

'Me. To know about horses.' He dived into an inner pocket and brought out a wallet, grey-edged from wear, held together by a rubber band. He selected and held out to us a photograph of himself in the high boots and trim uniform of the Polish cavalry, seated upon a much too-tall, lively-looking horse. I could think of no comment which would not–by implication at least–be hurtful, but David said, in just the right tone:

'Ha. Cavalry! Yes, I'd say you knew about horses.'

'Against tanks they were no good,' said the little man, replacing the photograph and busying himself with the rubber band. 'Much later I have Spitfire. Was good.'

'The operative words there are "much later",' said David with one of his brief, sudden accesses of bitterness.

'Please,' he said, not understanding. But after that he was, all at once, one of us and we were privileged to call him by his name, which was Stanislav.

Largely thanks to his efforts Merravay was looking its best when Miss Julia Sherwood came to stay with us for a fortnight of recuperation after an operation. Somebody had recommended her; and she looked so frail, so faintly distraught that at sight of her some little-mother-of-all-the-world instinct rose up in me. I plied her with Bovril, Ovaltine, eggs beaten in milk–and in return she ruined me.

She arrived on a Saturday, and on the following Thursday went to town to keep a pressing engagement, she said. David drove her to the station to catch the one good 'up' train and arranged to meet the good 'down' one in the evening. She wasn't on it, and in the morning I had a letter thanking me for my care of her and saying that urgent business had compelled her to remain in London; would I send on her belongings. She enclosed a cheque for the full fortnight.

Nobody in Nettleton was sufficiently hard up or enterprising to deliver Sunday papers, but they were obtainable at the station between the hours of twelve and one, and on the Sunday after Miss Spenwood's departure one of the people staying in the house who was fond of riding rode in to fetch them. I was busy getting the lunch, but I did notice that all my guests had congregated in a little bunch about the papers as though something interesting was afoot. Some particularly gory murder, I thought, knowing the Sunday papers. But while I was clearing the tables the old dear who had fetched the papers lingered, hovered, hesitated and then handed me one paper folded small and said, 'I think, Mrs Stamford, you should see this.' He hurried away, and I looked at the headline, which asked, in bold thick print, 'Another Haunted House Near Borley?' Underneath was a small but beautifully clear photograph of Merravay. Below that was a spiel about poor Julia Spenwood, the fashion editor of the paper, who had been ill and gone to Merravay for her convalescence, and who, after four days, had been forced to flee the place because it was so dreadfully haunted. There was no mention of what she saw, felt or heard, apart from a 'feeling' on the stairs, a 'cold place' in the big hall, but it was a clever piece of sensational journalism. I could see exactly what it meant. It was Miss Spenwood's 'comeback'. Poor old dog Tray, sick and blunt of tooth, had nearly been shut out, but he'd managed by chance to grab a hare and had carried it home and was now reinstated in the very middle of the hearthrug.

A cry of 'Fire' could hardly have emptied the house more quickly. By Monday midday everybody–with some fatuous excuse or another–had departed. The week's post brought me several cancellations, a letter from a medium who wished to hold a seance in our haunted house, a letter from a woman whose own house had been dreadfully haunted and successfully exorcised, and an anonymous communication furiously denouncing me for trying such a cheap advertising stunt. In the next fortnight I received no requests for accommodation, and the only people who came to the house were a few sensation-seekers, hoping, in a half-frightened way, to find another Borley. It seemed to me that I had been ruined by an irresponsible journalist and should have some redress; so one day I put the article and the letters of cancellation into my bag and drove into Baildon to consult young Mr Turnbull, the solicitor who had dealt with the transfer of Merravay.

At home, to David, I had always managed somehow to make light of the disaster, but as soon as I began to describe it to someone who would not be inwardly *hurt* by the implication that I needed to make a living out of paying guests my control wavered. My voice and my hands shook, my head jerked, my eyes filled with tears.

Mr Turnbull listened gravely and–I thought–sympathetically; then he studied the newspaper cutting and the letters.

'Most unfortunate, and, I realise, infuriating for you. But in law, I'm afraid, you have no redress. You see, it would be difficult to prove conclusively that Merravay is not haunted, and even more difficult to prove that Miss . . . er . . . Spenwood was not genuinely of the opinion that it was. And she could certainly produce–not evidence of haunting, but evidence that she was not alone in her opinion.'

'You mean that other people have said so?.

He nodded. 'As a matter of fact my attention was drawn to the subject some years ago–before the war. There was some trouble about lease-breaking. The house was rented at the time. The tenant tried to plead that it was haunted as an excuse . . . that didn't work, of course. But I looked up the story. Very interesting!'

'Tell me.'

'Well, I shouldn't wish . . . though there's nothing actually frightening. . . .'

'That kind of thing never frightens me,' I said. I could have added that I had enough real terrors to contend with, getting into debt, finding a new and really serious leak in the roof. . . .

So he told me the story of Lady Alice Rowhedge, the Witch of Merravay, whom some remote ancestor of his had attempted, unsuccessfully, to protect when she was tried for witchcraft in the middle of the seventeenth century. She was supposed to ride a great black horse, on windy nights at certain seasons, along a certain stretch of road; at other times she walked about in the house, brewing potions, making spells. 'Three hundred years is a long time, Mrs Stamford, but the story seems to crop up fairly consistently. Miss Spenwood wasn't being very original.' He smiled and went on, 'This story, you know, will either die down and all will be as before, or else you may find that your ghost is established and becomes an attraction. Then you could charge half a crown for admittance and sell wildly expensive cups of tea.'

'To a lot of stupid neurotics!'

'Oh, don't be harsh on us! I visited Borley several times; and the fact that the ghost story interested me took me to Merravay in the first place, and as a result, when somebody wanted to demolish it I put a stop to that scheme. You owe your ghost a little, Mrs Stamford.'

'Maybe,' I said, getting to my feet, 'it would have been better for me if it had been pulled down . . .'

His manner grew more serious.

'The guesthouse really mattered?'

'Why else should I bother?'

'Well . . . of course it's not for me to make suggestions. But if you find that people like to visit, but are averse to sleeping in, the house, you could try making it into a club. A relative of mine did that with her white elephant of a house and says it pays and she hasn't to make beds, a job she happens to abhor.'

'That would mean getting a club licence.'

'Which wouldn't be difficult. I could do that for you.'

I thanked him for his kindness. Halfway home I stopped the car and, bowed over the wheel, gave way, for the first and last time, to a bout of lachrymose self-pity. Everything we had tried so far had come to no good and had cost money; even the bee-keeping scheme! And I had just invested in a store of sheets and towels. Now I must go marketing for glasses, liquors and a club licence. It seemed a little too much! But by the time that I had repaired my face, stiffened my courage and got ready a cheerful, optimistic mood in which to meet David my mind was made up. I'd try another thing; Merravay should become a club.

The way one thing links up with and leads to another is very strange. Worry and rancour had taken me to Chris Turnbull, and much resulted from that visit. Not only did he get me the licence, he made the club.

There is another strange thing–the way wars work out for different people.

My war had been dull; and because I was bored by it I had taken a course in cookery, found an unsuspected talent and gone on and on.

David's had been disastrous. He'd just reached captain's rank when he was taken prisoner and pushed into a camp, where he was senior officer. In those days, before it was proved that the Japanese intended to disregard all conventions, David, who knew the rules, often ventured upon his pitiful, futile protests. One of these concerned overcrowding and lack of exercise, and he used the unfortunate expression 'boxed up'. The Japanese to whom he made his complaint said, 'Bad exaggerations. I will show you boxed up. I will demonstrate to you categorically boxed up.' David being six feet tall, the box they made for him was exactly five feet six inches each way, and he spent nearly two years in it. He emerged wildly claustrophobic.

Chris Turnbull's war, beginning with a wound at Dunkirk, had put him into a hospital bed next door to Jimmy Rorke, the film actor, and there had started one of those apparently incongruous friendships which astonish everyone except the participants.

So now Chris could say to me, 'It is nice to have somewhere to bring Jimmy and Mavis when they come for week-ends!' And local people could say, 'Let's run out and have a meal at Merravay. We might see Jimmy Rorke and Mavis Mallinson!'

And I could cook, especially the kind of exotic meal for which people are willing to pay a disproportionately high price. I still think that I could have made a great success of Merravay as a club and dining place had nature seen fit to endow me with cast-iron feet, a solid timber backbone and a dozen hands. As it was, I had to have help; and to need help in England nowadays is to rank with the piteous drug addict, who must pay blackmailing price or perish.

Of course I could always advertise 'bus passes gate'. It did just that, at forty miles an hour, twice a day, making for Nettleton post office, where it stopped. But 'help' didn't like that; and after some harassed and distracted months, some comic, heart-breaking experiences I settled down to run the place with the assistance of one good steady daily woman and a fugitive succession of girls who thought they'd rather like to do a little waitressing–and, of course, the invaluable Stanislav, who took on, voluntarily, the work of a barman. Each afternoon he would stop work, take a bath, put what looked like Durofix on his hair, and, with an expression which would have become his sainted namesake–dogged resignation–get behind the bar and proceed to act with his usual dexterity and care for our interests. Out of the tips that came his way he hoarded enough to buy what I hope is the noisiest motor-cycle ever made; and often, when we had made everything tidy for the night and I had tottered to bed to lie beside David, who had been asleep for hours, I would hear that motor-cycle go roaring away, lonely and raucous, through the dark. Stanislav seemed to need so little sleep, lucky man. My own need was chronic and accumulative. I could have lain down at any moment and slept for a week, a month, a year, for ever. Shopping, catering, cooking, making out the menus, totting up the bills, being pleasant to people; being a wife to David; being a mother to young John, who was now, thanks to the Club, a weekly boarder at a decent little school and whose week-ends must somehow be made to seem happy normal interludes . . . it all took toll, and sometimes I would catch a horrifying glimpse of myself in a glass: light-brown hair dusted with silver; face thin and lined, rouged and powdered too hastily into a caricature of itself; eyes too wary, too watchful. But one day, I told myself, after each such glimpse, things would alter; I'd have time . . . one day I'd go to the hairdresser's; take forty-eight hours off and sleep . . . one day something would happen.

And one day something did. I went to answer the telephone's shrill summons, and instead of the table reservation I expected it was a personal call from London for Mr David Stamford. A friend of his, one Eddie Blenco, much blessed by me because he had once sent me a hundredweight of sugar–he had a plantation in Jamaica–was in London and wanted David to go up to see him. I remember saying, 'You go. The trip will do you good. Stanislav and I can manage.' Somebody, somewhere, filed that remark away!

David went and came back to tell me that Eddie Blenco had had to have an operation which might alleviate, but could not cure, his complaint. He knew that his active days were over and he needed somebody entirely trustworthy to go and manage his plantation.

'But you don't know anything about sugar-cane,' I said tactlessly and saw David's face darken.

'I am prepared to learn. Besides, the place is crawling with people who know everything. What Eddie wants is somebody he can trust to go and look after *them*. And look, Jill!'

He whisked out and showed me a photograph of a long white single-storied house with a deep veranda. In the foreground was a garden, neat but luxuriant, and behind it a mass of palms.

'Ours,' said David in a voice of intense gloating. 'No rent, free service . . . and a thousand a year!'

It was his great moment! Man the provider had gone out and brought home the carcass, and I spoiled it all. I said:

'But what about Merravay?'

He looked at me and said, 'I never gave it a single thought. It was a gaff.

Just a place to get away from.'

That reminded me of the old David; of the dashing headlong way in which we had got married, decided to have a child, bought Merravay. And though I was glad to see this resurrection of the spirit, I felt compelled to say:

'But we gave three thousand for it.' And then the devil made me add, 'I'm not budging from here till I see that money again.'

Chapter Three

Just before he left–which was three months and about thirty disappointments later–David said, 'You must be the most pigheaded woman God ever made. So we paid three thousand for the damned place! Can't you see that we've lived here, three of us, for five years. It owes us nothing! For the last time, will you shut the door on it and come with me?'

'I daren't,' I said. I thought of the chance of his not liking the job, not being able to stand the climate, of the plantation failing, of his falling out with Eddie. Three thousand pounds was three thousand pounds; a nest-egg, education for John, food, a roof, a bridge to the next venture.

'All right,' David said. 'I shall go. I won't smoke or drink; I'll live on sugar-cane; I'll take odd jobs and cheat and swindle everybody and *I'll* give you three thousand for the bloody house. Nobody else will. . . .'

'For the house perhaps not; but for the club as a going concern somebody might. And I just feel I must stay here until somebody does. . . .'

Stanislav promised to stay and look after everything. David promised to find him a place on the plantation. Chris Turnbull promised to keep an eye on us. I promised to take the first reasonable offer for Merravay. Even young John promised to be a good boy.

So David left, and I was appalled by the sense of loss which his going inflicted. Of late we had spent little time together, rising up half asleep, utterly uncommunicative, to go about our separate chores, to meet over hasty meals and eventually to go, at differing hours, back to our work-induced slumber, side by side. There were days when we had hardly exchanged a dozen words; but he was *there.* I could save up things to tell him when the opportunity occurred, could amuse myself by collecting, polishing up, making more amusing or significant the trivial things that happened in the course of the day's work. Now I missed him terribly; far more than I had during the war, for then our brief times together had not led me to rely upon his mere physical presence. I decided that in the past I had never been sufficiently sympathetic towards widows, especially those who had enjoyed a longish married life. . . .

The year crept up to its summer peak and then began to go down the slope which, beginning gently with August and September, would lead precipitously to the winter depths when it would be dark in the morning when I rose–and there would be no-one to speak to–and dark again in the afternoon long before the most avid-for-drink member came into the bar. David wrote regularly; and every letter mentioned the warmth, the sunshine, the beauty of the country, the plenitude of things like domestic labour. Every letter said, 'Put on your hat and come!' And each time the temptation to do so became a little more insidious, to be balanced by the determination not to do so becoming a little more stubborn.

On the last Saturday in August my dear daily woman, Mrs Baxter, told me that she was leaving; she was going to marry the village constable, who lived next door to her. I was not surprised; she was so pink and placid and comfortable that she was sure to marry again. I would have married her myself had I been qualified to do so! But the news dismayed me.

'I'd have done it over Bank Holiday,' she said, 'but I wasn't sure of Annie Coote till this last week.'

'A bridesmaid?' I asked, forcing myself to take interest.

'Bless you, bridesmaids! And Ager my third! No, Annie's for you. She's niece to my first and a rare good worker. And she'll live in. She'll wait too; trained she is. You'll be set up with Annie!'

Touched by this solicitude for my well-being, I gave Mrs Baxter the only thing I owned which had ever evoked her admiration–Granny's bow-fronted china cabinet, which still emptily mourned the treasures I had been obliged to sell. One of her husbands had been a champion winner of fair-ground ornaments and the cabinet would show off the prizes 'a treat'.

And for some time after Annie's installation I would have given her aunt-by-marriage the same thing daily, I was so grateful. Annie was about thirty-six, past the silly age, tireless, willing, quiet. A real treasure until she fell out with Stanislav.

In the beginning she seemed to like him, did little things for his comfort, spoke him very fair, and to say that he rebuffed her would be untrue; he met her overtures with the same monosyllabic courtesy which he used towards me and the club members. Annie, not understanding, felt herself snubbed and rebounded into frank hostility. I noticed the rasping little speeches which he seemed to ignore, but it was difficult for me to interfere until one morning when, carrying in some pot plants, he dropped some soil and fetched a brush and dustpan and swept it up.

'While you're about it you might as well make a job of it,' said Annie. She pointed to some cigarette ash.

'When madam wish me to sweep she tell me and then I sweep,' said Stanislav. His voice and the glance he shot at me were both imbued with challenge. I said–truly–that he had enough to do without sweeping. Annie, with a mutter about dirty foreigners and cheeky Poles, turned away. Best to ignore it all, I thought; but later in the day when Stanislav and I were checking supplies behind the bar he suddenly said:

'To be called dirty by that peasant! Pole I am and proud to be. Yes, despite all, proud! And never will I carry that cow on my motor-bicycle. There is trouble! She wait every time and wish I should carry her. Should I take her on my motor-bicycle and rape her in ditches she like me well. Otherwise I am dirty Pole. I do not forgive her. Never!'

'Well,' I said, 'I'm not suggesting that you should take her as passenger or anything like that, but I wish you'd forgive her and bear with her. She helps me so much. And it's for such a short time. Things are going so well. We've made twenty new members. Very soon I shall sell the club and you and I will be on our way to the Captain.' (Having learned David's rank, Stanislav always used it punctiliously.)

'It is in my mind,' he said, 'that raping in ditches is not such thing as should be said to ladies. Please forgive me, madam. I was too angry!'

I forgave him. I realised that what he said was true enough.

Our waitress at that time was a rather pretty, cheerful, bumbling little girl named Nancy Peake. I'd never been able to teach her much, but she'd taken a liking for Annie and begun to model herself on her, and very often Annie spent the afternoon in the Peake house. One morning–it was late in October but more like November weather, a day of dark drizzle–I was coming back from shopping and overtook, halfway up the avenue, a little thread of a woman who was stumping along through the wet leaves. I stopped and said, 'Are you going up to the house?'

'I am,' she said.

'Get in, then. I'll run you up.'

'But I'm Mrs Peake. And you're Mrs Stamford. I know you, though you don't know me. And I've something to say that 'on't be to your liking, so you don't want to go giving me no lifts! You go along. I'll be there presently.'

I grinned. Unsuspecting, simple fool that I was, I grinned and said, 'Now what could you have to say, Mrs Peake, that would make me unwilling to give you a lift? What is it? Does Nancy want to leave?'

'She don't want to, but she's gorn to. Ah, that she is! We're poor, but we've allust been respectable, Mrs Stamford. Nancy ain't staying in a place where there's carrying on! Oh no! There's right and wrong, and how you and your husband, poor man, fix things between you is your affair and I ain't interfering; but where my Nancy is concerned, thass different. We're poor, but we've allust been respectable; and respectable we stay. Thass all. Thass what I come to say; and I said it, to your face!'

She whisked around and stamped off in the direction of the village. I sat for a moment, feeling stunned and a little sick, and then I realised that it was Saturday; that every table was booked. Without Nancy I should be in a muddle. I turned the car and drove back to Nettleton, hoping that Mrs Baxter . . . Mrs Ager, might be free to 'oblige', as she had occasionally done at a pinch.

Mrs Baxter was pleased to see me, but it was clear that Mrs Ager was faintly alarmed and no little embarrassed. She asked me into the parlour, where the cabinet was now a cage for a menagerie of pottery animals of unlikely proportions, and avoided my eyes as she said that Ager didn't really like her to take odd jobs. 'You see, with Ager there's this, ma'am. He really do hev his position to think of; and to tell you the truth, he ain't quite so easy handled as my others, so you see . . .! I'm sorry. And I wouldn't like you to think that I paid any attention to that Annie and her wicked tongue. Told her straight I did, only last week, that the worst thing up at Merravay was her evil mind. But thass the Cootes all over; speak evil of somebody they must, and now they're done with me they start on you! And I'm right sorry I ever recommended her to you!' Then suddenly her wavering gaze came to rest on my face; her blue eyes were troubled, oddly innocent, and yet corrupt with wisdom. 'You know how it is, ma'am. For one that'll give you the benefit of the doubt there's ten that 'on't.'

It was too late to retire into dignity and pretend that I didn't know what she was talking about; besides, it would have been utterly untrue. I knew. I simply said that I was sorry that she couldn't come and help out that evening and retreated.

Chapter Four

I suppose that anyone with a grain of sense would have gone back, sacked Annie and closed the club, admitting defeat. But at the mere thought of so doing something–mainly panic, I suppose–rose in me and made it absolutely imperative to stay in Merravay until I sold it or died. So I said nothing; I worked side by side with my enemy, and I held out until the first week of December.

There had been a long spell of fog; the worst weather for me, for it made catering almost maddeningly difficult. At six o'clock I'd look out into a white blanket and resign myself to an unprofitable evening; at eight o'clock a dozen hungry people would arrive, clamouring for food. Either the fog had cleared for a bit or else some bold spirit had suggested risking it. Or again there would come an evening when the fog seemed to have lifted, and I'd cook; and nobody came, and Annie, Stanislav and I would eat, all next day, lavishly, heartbreakingly, things like Wienerschnitzel, warmed up. And David's last letter had said, 'Do give it best, darling! If only you would we could still be together for Christmas.' And I thought–If only I could! And I saw three thousand pounds, made visible in the shape of very black pound signs, leggitty little beasts, tearing away from me, never to be recaptured!

However, that morning, the first Saturday in December, dawned bright and clear and the weather forecast said that the fog had finally lifted. The telephone rang and rang; by eleven o'clock every table was booked. My spirits rose as I set about making the pastry.

It was Stanislav's day for having his fortnightly hair-cut; so, with the cart piled high with greenstuff and some pot-plants, he had gone into Baildon early. John was paying his weekly visit of devotion to Ginger Whymark's latest litter of dachshund puppies–a fact for which I was later to be supremely grateful.

For suddenly the kitchen door burst open, and there was Stanislav, one half of his head ruthlessly clippered, the other still bristling with its fortnight's growth; his face was blue-white, his ears blazing red. Without a word he walked over to where Annie sat, cleaning silver, and smacked her face, twice–his palm hit her right cheek, his back-hand her left with a sound like a pistol shot.

Before he could hit her again I had him by the elbow, clutching with both hands and throwing all my weight against him. Annie saw her chance, got up, overturning her chair, and made for the door, screaming like a banshee. Stanislav jerked himself free and would have followed, but I was between him and the door and just managed to rush across, slam it and set my back to it.

'Have you gone mad?' I gasped at him. For a moment he glared at me so savagely that I expected him to charge the door and fling me aside. In that moment I could hear Annie's screams, evenly spaced, diminishing in volume as she fled down the avenue. And I saw the madness–not the fury–go out of Stanislav's eyes.

'She is vile, wicked woman! Such things she is saying of me. I wish very much to kill her!'

'I could see that.'

'If you should know what she is saying . . .'

'But I do. I've known ever since Nancy left. But she was *help*! Now look what you've done, you silly hot-head!'

'This English phlegm! This nation of shopkeeper! Never shall I understand. She is help, and so to be free to be saying untrue vile things so that barber men are winking and making filthy jokes to me. Two times he makes the joke. The first time I am not believing the ears; then I understand. I do not think he makes any further joke today!'

Apprehension seized me.

'Oh, what did you do? You didn't . . .?'

His teeth shone briefly, wolfish.

'I am meaning to knock his teeth down the throat. But they are false teeth he is having and fall on the floor instead. Is funny!'

He gave a short sharp bark of laughter in which I had a hysterical impulse to join. 'Is funny' indeed. . . .

'Now we shall have real trouble . . . police. . . .'

I could see the headline in the paper, 'Pole Strikes Barber'; I could imagine the exposure of motive, all the hints and rumours which I had tried to ignore, creeping to the surface like worms after a rain.

'Can be fined,' said Stanislav. 'Can be in prison. Better than sit in barber chair and hear'–his hot little blue eyes glanced away from me–'dirty jokes about me and that filthy bitch!'

The lie–and all that it implied–touched me. Suddenly something absolutely female and atavistic stirred in me. Angry, bristling, ridiculous little man, he had struck blows and would doubtless perjure himself in defence of my 'honour'. The clash of pennant-fluttering lance on blazoned shield, the 'pistols for two' in the dawn had narrowed down to 'Pole Strikes Barber; Fined Thirty Shillings', but it was chivalrous still.

'Well,' I said weakly, 'all that must wait. The first thing is for you to find another barber and have your hair finished. You can't go about looking like that!'

'Will finish him presently, myself, with horse clippers. Meanwhile . . .' He snatched up the rag which Annie had dropped, plunged it into the plate-polish and began to work on the silver with all the vigour of unexpended rage.

I stood for a moment looking at all those forks and spoons which must be set out in order, collected and washed. I looked at my unfinished pastry, at the slate upon which I had written the names of those members who had booked tables; I thought of the gallons of soup, of the mounds of vegetables. Weakness washed over me like a wave. I had tried, I had done my best, and I was beaten; why not admit it? I couldn't cook for and wait upon thirty people single-handed; nobody could. Moreover, by this time the rumour of Stanislav's assault upon the barber would be all over Baildon, lending point and substance to the scandal. Could I face the furtive, curious eyes?

I had only to lift the telephone, cable first to David, and then make a series of calls saying that, having no help, I was obliged to close the club. Let people think what they liked–they'd think the worst, anyway. And I wanted–oh, how badly–to share with David the exquisite humour of 'but they are false teeth he is having'. After all, I thought, there are other values in the world besides material ones; why ruin your happiness trying to salvage three thousand pounds?

To this day I don't know why I didn't lift that telephone. . . .

But I didn't. And by six o'clock the tables were set and the fires made up; Stanislav with his skull shaven was behind the bar and I was in the kitchen. John, I might add, was in the heaven of heavens because Ginger had given him one of the puppies; its nose was a fraction of an inch too short, or its tail a fraction of an inch too long, so in this world of curious values it wasn't marketable. He'd taken it to bed with him and retired early, and willingly, because he thought it might be tired. They were asleep, curled up together, when I looked in before going down to make my last stand.

Good evening! Good evening! Yes, isn't it lovely to have it clear again. Oh yes, of course you can have dinner. So difficult to make arrangements beforehand in this weather. David? Oh, he's very well, thank you. I heard from him this week. Plenty of sun there! Oh, hullo . . . if only I'd known you were coming I'd have made you one of your special dishes. An omelette will do? Of course. Cheese or mushroom? (Nothing to me, dearie. Dash it off in no time.) David? Oh, very well, thank you. Yes, I hear every week; sometimes twice. A drink? That's kind and I could do with it, but I just must get back to the kitchen. Single-handed tonight. Yes, isn't it awful? Stan's hair? He does look a bit odd, doesn't he? Rather *too* short; maybe somebody 'got in his hair', as they say. (Oh yes, I'm a wit, I am!)

I was back in the kitchen, having 'shown' myself and faced them, or at least those who had come early, when the telephone rang. It was Chris Turnbull.

'Jill! Look, I know it's a bit late, but I've had a young American wished on me. Nice. Mad on old houses . . . so I thought . . . But if it's awkward we'd eat at the Evening Star and then, if we survive, come on later.'

'If you really had my good at heart, Chris, you'd drive out here full speed and take on the bar for an hour while Stan helps me to dish up. I'm entirely on my own tonight. If you would . . . and then eat later, I'd do you proud. . .

After that, what with the steam, the heat, the haste, everything melted into a kind of nightmare. I drowned in a sea of soup, potted shrimps, smoked salmon; I fought my way through a jungle of roast pheasant, filet steaks–with or without garlic, dear member? I climbed great mountains–potatoes, peas, braised celery and what-sweet-would-you-like? I ran marathons–cheese, black or white coffee and can-I-have-my-bill-please? There was Stanislav, useful as another pair of hands to me, never hesitating, never needing direction, never forgetful; breasting the wave, thrusting through the jungle, climbing the steps, running the race by my side. And we did it. At about ten o'clock somebody looked out and said, 'Fog coming up again'; and fifty thousand people said at once, 'But the forecast said . . . my bill, please . . . swallow that down and let's get going . . . good night.'

After that there was a great quiet.

There is something about complete exhaustion which is akin to one stage of drunkenness; time seems to skid about. I heard the last car start. I was conscious of nothing but a grinding agony in the small of my back and a peculiar feeling of being hobbled. I looked down and thought–Good heavens! Elephantiasis! Huge bags of jelly were bulging and shaking where my ankles should have been. Another day like this and I'd have to have one of–no, two of those little carts they tie on to fat-tailed sheep.

Then, without the slightest idea of how I came to be there, I was sitting by the fire in the hall. A cup of coffee and a brandy glass stood on the table beside me. Stanislav was clearing the last things from the deserted tables and Chris Turnbull and a craggy-faced young man with dark-red hair were helping him.

I called to Chris–and, just as in drunkenness, my voice came out peculiarly high-pitched and clear.

'Leave it, Chris; leave everything. There'll be plenty of time to clear up in. I can't go on like this. I'll just have to shut down and go to David.'

'I think that would be wise,' Chris said.

There, I've said it, I thought; that makes it real.

Then I lost another moment, during which somebody must have brought a stool and propped my feet on it. The place was tidy and Stanislav had gone. Chris was sitting opposite me and his friend stood by the foot of the stairs, running his hand caressingly over the almost life-size figure of Moses which stood there. The sight called to my mind the number of things about Merravay which were unique and lovely. Now that I had, by a single decision, severed my connection with the house I afforded a moment of admiration for its beauty and regret at its fate. I looked ahead and saw it deserted again, given over to the bats, the owls, the ghosts.

'It isn't my fault,' I said aloud. 'I've done my best. I could truly say that everything we ever tried here was doomed from the start. Chris, I believe you were right about Alice Rowhedge. She didn't want us here, so she puts spells on us. Well, now she can have it, all to herself.'

'Now isn't that curious,' said the young American, who had been crossing the hall as I spoke. 'Alice Rowhedge, did you say? That was my mother's maiden name!'

FINALE

Between a young Cavalier named Charles Rowhedge who disappeared into the East Indies in 1662 and a Thomas Rowhedge first heard of as one of the few survivors of an ill-fated party making the overland route to California in 1841 there was a gap which nothing but imagination could ever bridge satisfactorily.

In course of time Mr Christopher Turnbull, eager as ever for any activity more to his romantic taste than the routine duties of a country solicitor, managed to unearth the fact that a Thomas Rowhedge, in the island of Banda, in the year 1749, had added his shaky signature to a protest sent by the nutmeg growers there to the Dutch East India Company's Office in Amsterdam. That was the end of the trail in the East.

In the West the name Thomas Rowhedge occurred in a list of five people, all that remained of a party of twenty-three who had been snowbound on Trucksee Lake for five months during the winter of 1840-1. Their trials and escape had been lent some notoriety by the suspicion–and rather more than that, since one man, almost demented by his experience, confessed to it–of cannibalism. Another survivor, in his deposition, was recorded to have said, 'I went by Tom Rowhedge and he never, so I never.' There were a few other small indications that this Thomas Rowhedge had been a person of influence and integrity, and the family which he had founded in the sunny valley of the Sacramento had always cherished his memory.

It would have been nice to think . . . but there was the gap.

There were clues. The tendency to choose Thomas and Alice as names for first-born sons and daughters; the fact that, although the first Californian Rowhedge married a woman with some Indian blood, many Rowhedges were red-haired; and there was a mention of the Rowhedge red hair somewhere in the original Alice Rowhedge's confession. Very little to go on, as Thomas Rowhedge Anderton was the first to admit. And even within his own mind he regarded his feelings with a degree of cautious scepticism. He knew that he had always been extremely, almost excessively Anglophile; he had come to England early in the war as a member of the Eagle Squadron and he had never felt wholly at home anywhere else since then. And he had fallen in love with Merravay at first sight. Long before Mrs Stamford had let fall the name which started his imagination leaping he'd thought that of all the houses he had seen that was the one he liked best, would most like to own.

Properly approached, Chris Turnbull had said casually, Mrs Stamford would take five thousand for it, he thought. Her husband was in Jamaica and she was very anxious to join him there.

That certainly was cheap for a house with a room still called the Queen's Chamber where the first Elizabeth had slept; for a house with a rose garden that had been laid out by a convicted witch . . . and cedars said to be brought from Lebanon seven hundred years ago.

And Amanda, so homesick, so terribly out of place in America, would surely love it.

Also, he wanted it himself. And his experience in wanting things was extraordinarily scanty. His mother, once widowed and twice divorced, the resultant circle of suitors, stepfathers, relatives, friends had seen to it that his wishes were not only met but often forestalled. By the terms of his father's will he had attained an independent income when he was eighteen, and at twenty-one he had inherited the bulk of his Grandfather Rowhedge's solid if unspectacular fortune. He was a very enviable young man, and one who might have been sadly spoilt. But his tastes had remained curiously simple. He had once quite shocked a young newspaperwoman, who was gathering material for a restaurant-sponsored column of nonsense about what and where people liked to eat, by saying that his favourite food was radishes and bread and butter. The young woman, privately thinking this a facetious snub, saved her face by giving the dish the name by which she had recognised–but not deigned to order it–during her one holiday in France, 'radis au beurre'. But it was an honest answer, and revealing. Revealing, too, was his certainty that Amanda, when she heard that he had bought, on the impulse of a moment, an old historic house in England, would be, not merely approving, but transported with delight. For he and Amanda saw eye to eye in everything.

Amanda was half-English by birth and entirely English by education–that was what had attracted him to her in the first place. Her mother, after years of unhappy marriage to a Wiltshire landowner who liked to go to sleep in a chair after dinner and finally allowed himself to be divorced so that he could do so in peace, had gone back to America and her family. She had taken Amanda, aged seventeen and just released from school. Amanda was coltish and shy, years younger, by every sophisticated standard, than her cousins and their contemporaries. Even when she had been coiffured and dressed and equipped to pattern she had failed, dismally, to fit in, and the chance introduction to Tom Anderton came as a godsend, just in time to save her from developing an inferiority complex.

Soon after her eighteenth birthday they became engaged; gratitude on her part, Anglophilism on his, taking the place of love. Their mothers opened the debate as to whether an Easter wedding, with lilies, or a June one, with roses, would be preferable. The debate continued.

One of Amanda's American uncles, who suffered from asthma, always wintered in Florida, and being fond of youthful company, and rich enough to command it, always set out with an attendant bevy of nephews and nieces. This year Amanda was invited; and since Tom had pledged himself, long ago, to act as best man to a friend who was about to marry in London, it all fitted in well.

Just before he left America Tom looked in at a party, where he talked for a while with a quietly-spoken, shy-seeming Englishman who turned out to be Jimmy Rorke. In the course of the conversation Rorke said that he thought the really loveliest part of England was a bit one never heard about–not the famous Constable country; just north of it, over the border, South Suffolk. Tom confessed that that was a part which he had never heard of.

'I go there pretty often. I have a friend there, Chris Turnbull; he's a solicitor in a place called Baildon.' He went on to say that Chris was brilliant, could have done anything, but had chosen to bury his talents, in a way, because there had been Turnbulls practising law in that town for four hundred years and he hadn't the heart to break the line. If Tom should happen to go that way and cared to look Chris up and say . . .

'Maybe I will,' Tom said.

And there had come a time when the wedding was over, and he was feeling lonely and yet unwilling to go home. . . .

That was how it had happened.

With one thing and another he was only just back in time to keep Christmas with his mother, and immediately after he set out for Florida to see Amanda. He took with him two dozen photographs of the house. The ones of the interior, taken in powerful artificial light, were clear and dramatic; the outdoor ones, for which the photographer had been obliged to depend upon the vagrant, pale sunshine of a winter's day, were less successful and suggested a sombreness, a look of brooding age, that was only just short of sinister. But Amanda would understand; when he said that the house was built of old brick Amanda could imagine . . .

She had no need to.

'It's the spitting image of Daddy's house. I knew it! The moment I read your letter I thought–Heavens! It sounds just like Hadwyke! Darling, what can have come over you?'

'But it's beautiful! Here, just look at this. That shows the screen in the hall. Silvery grey and so finely carved. And then this room where Queen Elizabeth . . .'

'Darling, it's always her, or Anne Boleyn! I can't believe they spent their time rushing about sleeping in different places just to give people something to talk about later on. Can you?'

Outside a voice called urgently, 'Mandy! Mandy!'

'Well, we don't have to live in it, do we?' said Amanda, shuffling the photographs into a heap and standing up. 'Get your bathing things, darling. The others are waiting.'

He knew he hadn't even reached first base. She wasn't in the right mood. Now he came to think about it, she hadn't been in the right mood ever since his arrival. There'd been a slight undercurrent . . . as though he'd offended her in some way and she was bearing a grudge. It couldn't be because he'd bought the place without asking her . . . or could it?

He probed the point at the first opportunity, which was not very soon. For something had happened to Amanda during his absence. She seemed to have become very popular. She'd always been rather out of things; now she was the centre . . . it was 'Mandy' here and 'Mandy' there all the time, and she appeared to like it. But at last he did get her to himself and he asked his question.

'Well, since you ask,' she said, 'yes, I do think it was a pretty high-handed thing to do.'

'But, honey, there wasn't much time. This Mrs Stamford wanted to make the sale right away, and I knew that you wanted to get back there and it was the loveliest old place we'd be likely . . .'

'I can't think what made you imagine that I wanted to go back. I don't, Tom. And if I did it'd be Mother and Hadwyke all over again. It was the house that finally got her down, you know. Besides . . . I like it here. And you should have consulted me.'

Fortunately the full irony of the situation escaped him. Being engaged to him had given Amanda just the confidence that she needed to make the grade in her new circumstances. Having made it, she need no more be bothered with this dull young man. And he had liked her because she was English and homesick and different.

If he had come straight home without visiting Jimmy Rorke's friend they would probably have had the June wedding with the smother of roses upon which her mother had set her heart, and a little later on some other catalystic circumstance would have revealed, more disturbingly, how little in love they were. As it was, the broken engagement hardly mattered at all. An old house, thousands of miles away, staunchly facing the blizzard-laden east wind of its four hundred and seventy-fifth winter, had merely forestalled one more divorce.

By the third week in January Tom was back in Nettleton, with the full approval of his mother, who was absolutely certain that Merravay was the Rowhedge ancestral home and that the blood of baronets ran in her veins. When the weather was warmer and he had the place comfortable she was coming, with a number of her cronies, to use the house as a headquarters for her Coronation visit.

He was camping in one room while workmen swarmed through the house, installing bathrooms and central heating. A plump, cheerful woman whom some people called Mrs Coote, others Mrs Baxter, others, again, Mrs Ager, and who didn't seem absolutely sure herself, came up each morning and made his breakfast and tidied his bed. He was completely happy, though at times he would have liked someone with whom he could have shared his happiness and his enthusiasms. And even that he found. . . .

One morning he went into Baildon and was driving back when he overtook a tall girl who was plunging along through the rain. She was ill-clad for such a day. A scruffed old leather jacket shed the water from her shoulders, but below it her tweed skirt hung soggily and a pair of thin, high-heeled shoes sucked at the mud; her head was bare and her bright yellow hair, misted with raindrops, shone like a halo. She carried a parcel which looked heavy and from which the soaked newspaper in which it was wrapped was peeling away.

Tom passed, slowed down, stopped. Despite the unsuitable shoes and the parcel, she was loping along at a good pace and soon drew level.

'Could I give you a lift?' he asked.

'That depends where you're going,' she said, crisply. 'If it's only into the village it's hardly worth while mucking up your beautiful car. Thanks, all the same.'

'I'm going through, to Merravay.'

Grey-green eyes, narrowed against the rain, widened and regarded him with frank interest for a moment.

'Oh . . .' she said; and the single word implied that she had heard a good deal about him. 'Well, in that case I should take it kindly.' Before Tom could reach out and open the door she had done it for herself, had heaved the parcel into the rear seat and lowered herself into place beside him. She brought with her a faint feminine scent of cosmetics mingled with that of wet leather, wet hair and something else dangerously near to being downright nasty.

'This is the second time this week I've broken down, and this time they don't hold out much hope. I shall have to get a bicycle . . .' She pushed the thought aside. 'So you're Mr Anderton. I'm Ginger Whymark–we're the nearest thing to a neighbour you have; we live in the lodge at the end of the other avenue. Tell me . . . is it true that your folks only bought Merravay in order to rip out the stairs and fireplaces and take them off to the States?'

'Why, no! My folks, as you call them, haven't had anything to do with it. My father's been dead nearly twenty years and my mother's quite crazy about the place, so far. She's coming over in May–if I can get it clear by then. I don't

expect she'll want to say long. But I'm staying.'

'It's you then, you own it?'

'That's right. I own it.'

'It was just that you look a bit young to go owning houses,' she said. 'Nowadays, around here, anyway, you have to save hard till you're forty in order to buy a caravan. Still, I'm glad, by God, that that *tale isn't true. I've a very soft spot for that house. I was so* relieved *when the Stamfords took it, but anybody could see with half an eye that they'd never hold out. They were the nicest people, but like children, always trying out something new and never giving anything time to get going. I did try to point that out. It was just the same with my dachshunds. I mean, if at the end of the first year I'd decided–as well I might–that they weren't a paying proposition and gone rushing off into Great Danes or Pekes or something that way the Stamfords would–well, I shouldn't be where I am today!'*

'And where is that!' he asked, matching her frankness.

'I'm recognised as one of the best breeders of dachshunds in England. Not wishing to boast–but Monarch of Merravay simply swept the board . . . Oh!' She put a long, thin, hard-worked-looking hand to her mouth and shot him a glance. 'The place was empty then, when I started, and didn't look like ever being occupied again, and Merravay went so well with Maid, Matriarch, Monarch, Mischief and Midget. Lodge wouldn't go with anything except Lousy!' She laughed, with just that touch of wryness which David Stamford had found so engaging, especially when he was having a bad day. 'And,' she said, meditatively, 'it was meant to be a bit of homoeopathic magic, like African witch-doctors pouring a libation to bring down the rain.'

'Now there, I'm afraid, I don't quite follow.'

'Of course not. Well . . . there was a time when I did just hope that the Stamfords would just hold on until my great-aunt . . .' She laughed again. 'Damn it, she is ninety-four! It had gone through my mind in demented moments that if the dogs did well and she really left me what she says she will because I mend her fuses and chase the burglars from under the bed, and bully her butcher, I just might have . . . But of course that was a pipe-dream. And I couldn't have left my parents. And I couldn't have kept the place up. I should just have moved from room to room, one jump ahead of the rain; and in the end the roof would have caved in on me. But how could man die better? Oh, blast! I was afraid of that!'

Heaving and shrugging, she freed herself of the windjammer and, rearing on one knee, leaned over to wrap the parcel. As she did so the unpleasant odour of which Tom had become increasingly conscious, and which had somewhat inhibited his full response to her chatter, became more noticeable. Was there, he wondered, proper bathing accommodation at the lodge?

'Gah!' said Miss Whymark. 'It's high this week! That is the one thing I don't like about my job. Even when it's fresh I have an absolute horror of horse-meat.'

'I once heard a professor say that all true Anglo-Saxons have,' said Tom. 'He said it was on account of the horse once being a sacred animal and subject to a tabu.'

'That's interesting; feasible too, I should say. Look, I wonder would you mind dropping me here. I've just remembered I must go along Goose Lane and pick up my heavy shoes. Old Farrow promised them for this morning.'

'Down here?'

'Yes. But don't come. It's a vile bit of road and you couldn't turn. . . .'

'I could back, I guess.'

It was all too apparent that Miss Whymark was not accustomed to much consideration.

She re-entered the car, carrying, unwrapped, exactly the pair of shoes one would have expected her to be wearing on such a morning. She inspected the clumping new soles with considerable satisfaction.

'Nice neat job,' she said. 'How he does it I can't imagine; he's as blind as a bat!'

Was it possible that the poor girl had but the one pair of heavy shoes?

'Oh!' said Miss Whymark as they passed the mouth of the chestnut avenue which Nabob Sandell had planted. 'I meant to get out here. Now you'll have to turn in our *avenue and the College traffic has churned it into a bog–tractors, you know.' The avenue of limes–the cause, once, of so much dissension–came into view. 'When my family lived at Merravay this was the avenue up to it. There's quite a fascinating story about the family quarrel which resulted in the shrubbery being planted across its upper end.'*

'I didn't know you ever lived at Merravay.'

'Not me; the Whymarks. Oh yes, we lived there, years before New Holding was built. Now, keep well over to this side . . . ah! Just missed it! That's grand.' Once more she forestalled his effort at courtesy and was out of the car in the rain and the mud, whipping out the parcel before he had pulled on the handbrake. 'Now come in and have a drink. Father has two or three friends staying; they should be shooting, but it's too wet. I bet they've been drinking for hours!'

On the inward side of the little lodge cottage a considerable extension had been made in modern style. Tom could see a wide bay window with a bank of exotic hot-house flowers just behind it; and behind the flowers, drawn by curiosity to the window, were a number of elderly male faces, all of them, Tom thought, bearing a marked resemblance to the late Sir Aubrey Smith. The owner of one face came nearer the window, beamed at Miss Whymark and pointed to the flowers with a gesture of exaggerated complacency and triumph.

'Lovely! Lovely!' she shouted. 'That is Sir Stephen Fennel,' she said, turning to Tom. 'He's brought Mother some flowers. Poor old dear, it was touch and go this year, but he managed to keep his hot-house going by not having a fire himself. He sits at night with his feet in a muff. . . .'

A curious, inexplicable shyness descended upon Tom.

'I mustn't come in now, thanks just the same,' he said. 'I've got some stuff aboard that the men are waiting for.'

'Some other time, then. Any time,' Miss Whymark said, equably. 'And I've no doubt that when Mother hears you are really going to live *at Merravay she'll rout out a hat and pay you a formal call. That is,' she added gloomily, 'if they ever get the car going again. She can't walk far these days.'*

'Well, I'd be glad . . .' he began; but probably that wasn't quite the thing to say. 'I would like very much to show you what is being done up at the house.'

'And I'm all agog to see.' She pondered. 'I tell you what I could do. I walk the dogs most evenings. I could walk that way. I often did when the Stamfords were there. Then seeing it empty again and the rumour of the staircase being ripped out depressed me so much, lately I've avoided it.'

'This evening?'

'There again, it depends. If Sir Stephen stays on, I might. *If not, they'll need me to make a fourth–bridge, you know.'*

'You might even give me a word or two of advice about furnishings. I took over a few things from the Stamfords; but for the rest–well, it's all new to me.'

'My experience of furnishing has been confined to fitting nine-footer sideboards into rooms twelve feet square and *leaving room for the door to open. But, of course, if you really . . .'*

'I do,' Tom started to assure her; then he realised that she was standing, without hat, without jacket, in the rain. And he thought–I'm as bad as the rest, using her rough.

'Come up as soon as you can. I'll be looking for you,' he said quickly, and drove away, followed by her voice thanking him heartily for the lift.

It was raining more heavily now, a silver-bead curtain suspended from a slate-grey sky. The men who should have been crawling about the roof had taken shelter in the kitchen and were busy with yet another brew of tea. One of them, a Nettleton man, was holding the floor.

'Mind you, I wunt want a word of this to git to his *ears. Let him spend every duzzy dollar he got afore he wake up to the fact this ain't a house to be* lived *in! 'Tis well known, in these parts, to be haunted. Ah, I see you grinning into yer mug, young Saunders! That don't alter fax. Why, only year or two back there was a whole crowd of right smart people staying here and they all upped and went, saying they couldn't sleep for the moaning and groaning. Bit in the paper about it, there was. Then you go back to afore the war. Lady Clumberly come down once, just the once and never no more. Work stopped and up for sale again. 'Twill be the same agin now, you'll see!' He drank deeply, and looked with pleasure on his audience.*

'I can remember further back than that even. A sensible owd working chap called Joe Hoggett bought it. He come up here one Sunday arternoon and never set foot in the place no more; and if you so much as mentioned it to him he'd blench and look at yer as if you were talking about Owd Nick. And now I bin in it I know why. You couldn't call me chicken-hearted,' he said modestly (he had gone, very reluctantly, to the 'old' war, and at Vimy Ridge, chiefly because no other course had seemed open to him, had held a machine-gun post single-handed and had been awarded a Military Medal), 'but you wouldn't catch me spending a night here; no, not if you was to offer me a thousand quid.'

'Little Mrs Stamford slepp here all by herself,' somebody contributed.

'Ah. So they say!'

'What about that there Pole?'

The conversation showed signs of drifting.

'But what is it all about! What does the haunting?' asked an electrician from Colchester.

He genuinely wanted to know, but to conceal his serious purpose he winked right and left as he spoke, pretending to be leading on this credulous Nettleton fellow.

'Ah, wink away,' said the Nettleton man, who was sharper than he looked. 'There's them that hev laughed for years about the walls of Jericho tumbling down when Joshua's trumpets blew, and now they've dug the place up and found that they did fall down. Thass the same with this. There's the story they tell in the village; and if that ain't good enough for you, go and look in Baildon museum and see the thing writ out. There was a Lady Alice Rowhedge, hundreds of years ago, and she was a witch and she made spells and bargained with the Devil to get this house for her own. And the Devil did her! So now she can't rest nor cease from tormenting till the Rowhedges hev it again.'

'Reglar Boris Karloff you are!' somebody said. 'Make my flesh creep. Still, so long as I'm out afore dark.'

'And not a word, mind. Don't forget the dollar gap!'

'Time he've finished here the balance'll be on the other side, I should reckon!'

Tom entered, as he always did, for the sake of the joy the first sight of the hall invariably gave him, by the big front door. The lacy screen, the massive, mounting staircase, the figure of the old man leaning on the staff, the eighteen-inch wide, honey-buff planks of the floor, the long taut stretch of the gallery, the Tudor roses over the cavernous hearth–he looked at them, one after another, and knew that his pleasure in them, sharp as it had always been, was today increased. A little dragging sense of loneliness vanished. It would be ridiculous and naïve to bank too much on the strength of a single meeting . . . but he had been definitely attracted to her, even when he was wondering about that odd smell. And of course the set-up . . . shooting-parties and patched-up shoes, hot-house flowers and foot-muffs, formal calls if a broken-down car could grind out two more miles . . . that all savoured of the Deep South. But anything less like a southern belle . . .

Obviously she had the heck of a life, a very bad deal; but it hadn't got her down.

She'd wanted Merravay herself, but she didn't grudge his possession of it. She was glad. She didn't like to see it empty. When she came . . .

Yes, he'd have a fire in the big hearth of the hall–he hadn't tried that yet. He'd put his two chairs and the rug close to the fire. Drinks? He had plenty, and it might be that after the walk she'd be ready to eat too.

And she'd come along, glad to see the lights in the windows, and he'd open the door and say, 'Welcome to my home!' No, that sounded a bit pompous. He'd say, 'Hi there. Come in.'

But the fact remained that after the way Amanda had behaved about it, and the way that his mother had snatched at the whole thing–not because it was what it was, but because of what she chose to make of it–the idea of the arrival of someone who felt–and with more reason–about Merravay as he felt was extremely exciting and satisfactory. Probably, when she'd rested and had something to eat and drink, they'd go over the place together. She could tell him details of that family quarrel which had resulted in the closed avenue; and he could ask her–because it was quite clear that one could ask her anything–what was behind this hint of haunting. Gosh, there were so many things. . . .

Making his preparations, mental and material, for his first visitor, Tom felt that he had come home.

Scent of Cloves

Norah Lofts

PART ONE

Ireland 1649–1657

Chapter One

When the dream reached its horrifying climax she began to scream, and woke herself and lay for a moment with the sound of her own voice and the screaming which had shrilled through the dream mingling in her ears. Then she was fully conscious, in her own bed and the night all quiet about her. Just another dreadful dream.

She hoped she had not awakened the child in the next room, or poor old Maire, already so frightened, and Edward, who usually woke at her first whimper. She moved her hand in search of the comforting solidity of his body and found his place beside her empty and cold. For a moment fear clamped down again; dead, dead, everybody dead. No, only a dream; nothing has happened *yet*.

And there was the difference between this waking and all the other times when she had come out of dreams of terror to find herself safe and unthreatened. This time it was not enough to be awake, for the dream had merely been the extension, seemingly logical and inevitable, of the situation which had overtaken them all. By this time tomorrow the dream might very well be accomplished fact.

Only an archway, hung with a curtain, separated the two rooms and now from the inner one came the sound of a voice, tremulous with terror.

'Lady, what is it? Have they come?'

One must not show fear before servants.

'No. I was dreaming, Maire. Go back to sleep.'

A mumbling grunt answered her, and then there came the sound of steel scratching flint, a faint glow of light that outlined the curtain and that presently pushed aside to show the old woman, fully dressed as she had lain down, her headcloth all awry and the newly lit candle wobbling in her unsteady hand.

'Lady. Indeed and you sounded as if the Devil had hold of you. Or Cromwell's own self.'

As the light wavered nearer Lucy Ashley wiped her sweating face with her sleeve, a quick, furtive movement.

'I told you to go back to sleep, Maire.' The evil flavour of the dream still lingered; she longed to be comforted, not to be obliged to pretend to be calm in order to comfort an hysterical old woman whom it had been difficult to persuade to go to bed at all.

'The sleep has gone from me,' Maire said. She shuffled forward shielding the candle with one brown, wrinkled hand, reached the bed-table by Lucy's side and carefully transferred the flame to the other candle there, saying, as she always did:

'God be thanked, we have light. Lady, lying there, wakeful in the dark, a thought has come to me. A good thought. I remembered my young years when I was a girl, gathering cockles on Cloonmagh beach, and my hair to my waist. And I thought of the caves at Cloonmagh.' She set her candle beside the other and dropped on her knees by the bed, clutching the clothes with her hands.

'Lady, I could lead you and the little one to the caves at Cloonmagh and we should be safe there till the trouble is past.'

'We are safe here,' Lucy said steadily. 'Where could we be safer than in a castle, with strong walls, and a moat, held by the best soldier in Ireland and provisioned for twelve months?'

(All that was true, yet it was taken, jeered the memory of the dream.)

'They took Drogheda,' Maire said.

Lucy had said the same to Edward, and he had laughed, not with forced false laughter but with genuine amusement. 'And who held Drogheda? A mob of Irish, without loyalty or conviction, and a few politicians whose tongues were sharper than their swords. An old woman with a donkey stick could have taken Drogheda. Master Cromwell will find Arghama a very different proposition. I can hold Arghama for a year and he hasn't that much time to spend battering my walls. By that time England will have turned against him, the Scots will be in arms and even his own army will be giving trouble.'

'Drogheda was different,' Lucy now said. 'Here we are all of one mind, and under one command. Sir Edward will never let Cromwell take Arghama.'

'Sir Edward is a bold gentleman, a bold, pretty gentleman, so he is indeed . . . but Lady dear, in the night I was thinking. This Cromwell is going from Drogheda to Wexford, they say; he's not likely to leave this strong castle and a bold gentleman in it, standing behind his back. And him with a great army. Lady, in times of trouble it's safer to be in a secret place. And I'm thinking of the caves at Cloonmagh.' The light from the candles had gathered strength and shone on her face, deepening every wrinkle and showing the urgent fear in her eyes. 'God be good to you, Lady, as you have been to me, but I'm Irish; I have no part in this quarrel. Your King that they chopped the head off, poor man, God rest his soul, was never King of mine. Into Arghama I came six years ago to earn my bread, Bridget in the kitchen and Patrick with the horses, the same way. It is a hard thing if we must die in the English quarrel.'

The bitter words opened a gulf. It was hard to believe that Maire, always so devoted, so humble, so grateful for kindness, could have spoken them.

'Cromwell,' Lucy said, 'looks on everyone inside the English Pale as his enemy. Irish or English, he takes no count of that; the English Pale is Royalist, and loyal, and that is enough for him. The Puritan soldiers are killing Irish peasants everywhere.'

'So they are, God help us. But not in Cloonmagh! In the ancient times when the Horned Men came in the long ships and burned and robbed and killed, the people in Cloonmagh took to the caves and were safe. And in the days of the pirates, too. They say, "Safe as the caves at Cloonmagh." Sir Edward did me a wrong, taking up the bridge so sudden. . . . Lady dear,' her hands scrabbled for Lucy's through the bed-clothes, 'do you suppose, if you begged him, he'd let it down for just so long as I could run across. I'd be blessing you and praying for you all the rest of my days. . . . Though you'd do well to come with me, you and Little Miss.'

'I don't think anything would persuade Sir Edward to lower the bridge again,' Lucy said. 'And you wouldn't be safe outside, Maire. You might meet the soldiers.'

'Not the way I would take. I know a safe, secret way. Lady dear, for the love of God will you *ask* him?'

'I could ask,' Lucy said, unwillingly. 'But I know I should waste my breath.' She could imagine Edward saying, if she has a mind to commit suicide let her jump in the moat, the silly old crone!

'Most times the master is anxious to pleasure you,' Maire said, 'and rightly too, for a sweeter lady never lived. . . .' Suddenly, disconcertingly, she burst into tears, letting loose the pent-up fears and conflictions of feeling of the last forty-eight hours. Through the sobs and snuffles and the harsh intakes of breath a word or two here and there emerged, every one of them dovetailing into Lucy's dream. The gist of it all was the asseveration of what all the Irish, and quite a few English believed–that Cromwell had made a bargain with Satan! Cromwell was to desecrate all sacred things, smash down the images of the saints, destroy every cross and relic, defile altars, stable his horses in churches . . . and in return the devil promised him complete and unchallenged power. Who, no matter how brave, well-prepared and determined, could stand against that?

'. . . in blood and flames,' sobbed Maire, 'this place will go down, the way of the others. . . . The Lord's anointed–and he was that, King of England if not of Ireland–could not stand before him, how then can we?'

Following so hard upon the dream, this was unbearable, and presently Lucy said: 'Maire, be quiet. I will ask about the bridge in the morning if you will be quiet now. Be quiet and go away.'

The relationship between them, upset by circumstances, fell back into balance.

'Would you be wanting anything before I go to my bed?' Maire asked.

'No. Just go and lie down and try to sleep,' Lucy said.

She lay awake after Maire had gone, thinking of many things, but chiefly of her own fears, her shameful lack of courage. She thought of all the stories she had heard lately of women who, in the civil war just brought to its sorry conclusion in England, had acquitted themselves with astounding valour and competence, holding castles and manor houses for weeks on end during the absence of their husbands. No such demand had been made upon her. Edward was down there, in the courtyard or the guard-room, or on the walls, all she had to do was to trust him and maintain a calm demeanour. And she was so cowardly that she woke, screaming from a dream, and thus precipitated a scene with old Maire and gave a promise the keeping of which in anticipation alone filled her with dread.

Over and over again, before the first light of the summer morning turned the narrow window grey, she imagined herself going to Edward and saying: 'I promised Maire. . . .' She doubted if she could do it. I haven't even courage enough for that, she thought dismally. She realized that courage could not be suddenly acquired; you were born with it, or perhaps you attained it by constant practice. She had always been afraid of everything, of the dark, of a bad dream, of making someone angry, of being laughed at, of being afraid. . . .

The window lightened at last, and down in the courtyard the first cock cried. She rose gladly, and moving quietly about the room, dressed and did her hair carefully. No sound came from the inner room and when she was ready she pulled the curtain aside and went in. Maire was sound asleep and the baby was sleeping, too, snug in the heavy oak cradle which had already rocked four generations of Ashleys. Lucy stood looking down on her daughter with love, with the inevitable, fleeting regret for another child who had died, and with a fresh upspringing of fear. She remembered the dream, the child's body, limp and bloody on the end of a pike. Almost she turned then to Maire, to shake her awake and say–If I can persuade Sir Edward to let you go, promise to take the child and keep her safe. . . . But that was foolish, superstitious and disloyal. She turned abruptly, crossed her own room and began to descend the spiral staircase whose steps were worn hollow and the curves of its walls smooth and shiny from the passage of all those who had gone up and down it throughout the years.

She was forming and re-forming the request she must make as she entered the courtyard, where the castle's state of preparation for a siege was evident. Cattle were closely penned along one side, and piles of fodder for them were stacked nearby. Arghama would have fresh meat as long as the fodder lasted then the remaining animals would be slaughtered and their flesh salted down. In a separate pen a newly calved cow was blaring her misery at separation from her calf, and another, due to calve later in the year, stood placidly by. Edward had thought of everything.

The soldiers who had stood guard during the night had begun their breakfast. Edward was not with them and before she could ask his whereabouts she saw him coming briskly down the ramp which led to the outer wall.

He kissed her heartily, and said: 'A quiet night and a bright morning. I hope you slept well. Broken your fast yet? Let's go in then. I'm hungry.'

It was never expedient to make a request of a hungry man. She fell into step beside him. As they passed the soldiers one of the men had just fitted a piece of cold fat bacon on to a slice of bread and was about to lift it to his mouth.

'Spare a crust for a starving man, your honour,' said Edward, in tolerable imitation of a beggar's whine, and took the piece from the soldier's hand. They all laughed. He walked on, cramming the food into his mouth.

'It'll be today,' he said cheerfully. 'There's smoke to the north of us. I'd send out a scout for news, but if I lower the bridge now there'll be trouble.'

'Oh,' she said. 'Why?'

'There's a crowd of country-folk there, begging admission. They've been arriving all through the night, babies and old grannies, and donkeys and all. I could use the men too. . . .'

She could imagine how safe the castle looked to those who were locked out of it.

'It seems hard, doesn't it,' she said falteringly. 'They aren't on either side, and yet. . . .'

'War always hurts somebody,' he said curtly. 'Don't look at me like that Lucy. I'm not to blame. And I can't take in a lot of hungry mouths. I've been up there, shouting to them to turn about and go inland. Cromwell's going straight through to Wexford–his men may fan out a bit in search of food, but they won't go far. The fools out there'd be safe enough if they got well out of his road. But they won't listen. The donkeys have more sense.'

He had begun to eat, quickly but without haste and giving the food his full attention; a hungry man whose next meal might not be quite on time.

'Maire says she knows a safe place not far from here, some caves, at Cloonmagh.'

'Cloonmagh. That'd be no help to them. You can only get there by boat, I believe.' He laid down his knife for a moment and put his hand over hers. 'Sweetheart, don't look so miserable. There's nothing you can do for them now. I'll go up and shout at them again: threaten to shoot if they don't move away. Squatting there like that they're as good as dead already.' He put the last bit of food into his mouth, took a long draught of ale and stood up.

'I'll come with you,' she said.

'You'll only begin to cry and say "poor things" and beg me to have them in. And I tell you frankly, Lucy, I shan't, because I can't. If the twelve Apostles stood there asking to come in I'd be bound to say no.'

Something in his voice hinted to her that he was distressed by the plight of the refugees.

'I won't cry,' she said, and after that, saying and doing nothing to call attention to herself, she followed him out, across the courtyard, up the ramp and on to the wall. The ramp ended in a kind of shelf, wide enough for two men to pass one another with ease, and above the shelf the wall was head high, except for the places where it dropped to waist height. At each of these places cannon were in position, heaps of balls ready and men standing by.

Edward went to the cannon station nearest the drawbridge, and she went and stood beside him. It was a perfect September morning, the sky the colour of a harebell and cloudless. The moat at the foot of the wall lay smooth and glassy, mirroring the sky's blue. Across it four swans moved with stately grace.

'Yes,' Edward said. 'It's smoke right enough. That'll be Shallyran. We're next.' He looked down at the huddle of people on the other side of the moat, pressed together at the spot where the drawbridge, if lowered would touch.

'You must get away,' he shouted. 'Shallyran's burning. They'll be here within the hour. Go inland and keep off the roads.'

They turned their helpless-looking faces upwards and some held out hands, but they made no move to go away.

'Do you think they can hear you? Do they understand?'

'Listen,' he said.

It came up with dreadful clarity. 'Let us in. Sir, sir, in the name of God, let us in. . . .' An old woman went down on her knees and held up prayerful hands; a younger one showed her baby, just about Julia's size. Helpless, stupid as sheep, and as pathetic.

'Tell them about the caves.'

'There are caves at Cloonmagh,' Edward shouted. 'Go there. You can't stay here. You'll all be killed. I can't take you in. Go to the caves.'

A man came forward, tugging at the head of his donkey.

'There's no getting to Cloonmagh without a boat, sir. Take us in. You can't leave us here to perish.'

She saw the sweat break out on Edward's forehead; a drop gathered and rolled down his cheek and fell, with a little plopping sound on to his breast plate. She knew what he was going to say and she knew what it was costing him.

'I won't have you stay here to be slaughtered,' he bellowed. 'If you don't scatter I shall fire on you.'

They moaned and pressed closer together.

'Edward, Maire said she knew a way through the woods to Cloonmagh.' He looked at her for a second, his lips pressed together; then he looked to the north where the smoke was now a grey column, distinct against the sky, and then down at the huddle of people with their bundles and their babies and their cooking pots, their deadly, hopeless obstinacy.

'Fetch her,' he said.

As she lifted her skirts and ran down the ramp she heard him shout that he was sending somebody to guide them all to safety.

Maire was like all the rest of them, like peasants the world over; she owned very little but that little was precious and must go where she went, even in the face of inconvenience and danger. She began, with hardly a word, to gather her poor possessions.

'And Lady, I'll need food too. If I go in the kitchen they'll not believe. . . .'

'I'll fetch you food,' Lucy said, her voice gritty with impatience. 'I'll take it straight to the bridge. Maire, you must hurry. Men who should be busy at other things are waiting on you.'

Maire had hurried; by the time that Lucy reached the inner end of the drawbridge, carrying some hastily gathered food tied up in a cloth, the old woman was there, clutching a great bundle under the shadow of her shawl.

Above their heads, out of sight, Edward was shouting again.

'All you down there,' pick up your gear and walk back twenty paces. Now stay there. Anybody who moves a step when the bridge comes down will be shot. Shot dead, d'you understand. Follow the one who comes out and she'll lead you to safety. All right! Lower awaaay!'

Gently, with the muted screech of well-oiled wheels and chains, the great bridge came down and spanned the water.

'Run, Maire. And God go with you,' Lucy said.

'And have you in His keeping, and all you love,' said Maire. Looking very small, looking like an ant carrying away its egg to safety she scuffled across. She landed on the farther side and cried, 'After me, all of you!' and without waiting to see whether they followed or not, set off, skirting the moat and then making for the woods.

'Bring her up!' Edward shouted. The chains wound in, link after link, and the bridge rose, slanted across the water, was upright. . . . Edward turned and began to descend the ramp. As he did so there was a sharp crack, louder and more reverberating than a musket shot. It was followed by the rippling rattle of an out-running chain. The bridge remained poised for an instant and then fell with a crash which had a desperately final sound.

Despite all their agonized effort to raise it, to hack it through, to blow it up, enough remained to afford a passage across the moat for the Puritan soldiers an hour later.

In one respect reality differed from the dream; Lucy was spared the sight of Julia at the end of a pike, for Maire's confidence in the caves of Cloonmagh as a hiding place had given her courage enough to carry Little Miss away with her.

Chapter Two

Johannes Belderdik, owner and master of the *Sea Maid*, had, in the years before Cromwell's Navigation Act, made regular voyages between Amsterdam and the Irish ports and knew the west coast well. He had never called at Cloonmagh, which was not a port, just a tiny fishing village, set close under the cliffs and remarkable only for its church. The tiny, ancient grey stone building was surmounted by a cross, disproportionately tall, and gilded. It constituted a landmark, and Captain Belderdik was on the look-out for it on this bleak February morning in the year 1657. On this voyage he would put in at Cloonmagh, because that was what he had been hired to do.

A mystery, which he was content to allow to remain so, surrounded his errand. A gentleman, giving the name of Mr Bull, and telling some specious story about wishing to inspect an Irish horse for another gentleman, had approached Johannes and asked whether he would take the risk of carrying him to a small place on the Irish coast, land him, wait for an hour and bring him back again. Mr Bull said that he realized that it would be an expensive trip, since no incidental trading could be involved; but that did not matter; he was willing and able to pay the price demanded.

That in itself deepened the mystery. Holland was full of fine English gentlemen who had followed their young king into exile, and hardly any of them had any money at all; even their card debts had to be settled by IOUs drawn against property now in Puritan hands and only to be recovered when the Restoration came. That Mr Bull had money enough to hire a whole ship and its crew in order to make a visit lasting one hour indicated that something very secret and important must be brewing. But that was no affair of Johannes's. He had only to find Cloonmagh.

It was more difficult than he had anticipated. The weather was bad, visibility frequently obscured by squalls of sleet, and careful study, through his glass, of one little huddle of houses after another, failed to find for him the unmistakable landmark of the tall gilded cross. Finally he knew that he had overshot his mark and must turn back.

'It may well be that the cross has been removed.' Mr Bull said. 'Cromwell passed this way, and we know his attitude towards the holy emblem–the same as the Devil's to holy water, and for the same reason! If all else fails we must put in at one place after another.'

So they turned about and at the next village, of which Johannes said dubiously, 'It could be Cloonmagh–if it had the Cross,' made a careful approach and, when the sounding revealed that the ship could go no nearer, lowered a boat.

'Sir,' Johannes asked, as his passenger prepared to embark, 'do you speak Gaelic? Then you will have difficulty in ascertaining whether this is Cloonmagh or not. I will come with you.'

They landed, in the middle of another squall, on the desolate beach and walked over the wet sand towards the cluster of poor clod hovels. The place gave no sign of human occupation; there was no sound, and not a threat of smoke rising from any roof. But as the sleet-storm cleared they could see, beyond the hovels, set a little higher and slightly apart, the squat stone church, and protruding from its roof, a broken stump, gilded.

'This is Cloonmagh,' Johannes said. 'And it's a dead village.'

'It suits me well,' said Mr Bull forgetting caution for a moment. 'If this is Cloonmagh I have only to follow my directions. I shall be back in an hour.' It was a speech of dismissal. He began to walk, at a spanking pace, towards the church, was lost to sight for some moments and then appeared again scrambling up the cliff and finally vanished behind a screen of gorze bushes and wind-twisted fir trees.

It was not a pleasant day, or a pleasant place for a walk, but after the confinement of ship-board it was good to stretch one's legs. Mr Bull had skirted the houses and made straight for the church, and in order to avoid the slightest appearance of following and spying, Johannes turned in the other direction and walked between the houses. They were a sorry sight, their mossy roofs falling in, the wet walls sagging, gently sinking back into the earth from whose sods they had been built. What had once been little gardens were now a green tangle of winter-defying weeds.

He walked until he had reached the church, stood for a moment regarding the white mass of bird droppings in its little porch, looked up at the stump of the Cross and remembered how often, sailing down to Wexford, he had seen it gleaming in the morning sun or shine wetly through the rain; and then, depressed by the brooding desolation of the place, he turned back. Facing the houses again, he heard, and then saw, something which indicated that the place was not so entirely deserted as it seemed. He heard the food-demanding squeal and grunt of a pig, and saw emerge from behind one little house and go to stand by the doorway of another a great gaunt sow, heavily in pig. In prompt answer to the demand the low door opened and a very old woman crept out, dragging a wooden bucket. She pushed and heaved it a little way from the door, the pig rushed to it, and she crept back into her house.

Then something happened which brought Johannes to a standstill. Out from some hiding place, crouching low and moving with animal stealth and swiftness, came another figure, a bit of fluttering rag, a tousled mass of hair, arms and legs as thin and angular as twigs. An animated scarecrow. It darted to the other side of the bucket, crouched down, thrust its arms in beside the sow's guzzling snout and brought up handfuls of food and shovelled them into its mouth. The sow moved, pivotting round, swinging its bulk, trying to shoulder the intruder away; the child simply moved around and went on feeding. The sow stopped eating just long enough to let out a cry, disconcertingly human, a complaint, a call for aid. A human child eating like a pig, a pig crying out like a child, Johannes thought.

The door opened again, and out crept the old woman, this time carrying a stout stick. For all her seeming frailty the blow she struck would have hurt had it fallen where the old woman intended, but the child was too quick. It was upright and on its feet and running when the stick thudded down on the edge of the bucket and the sow squealed again, this time in angry reproach. Running, the child betrayed its sex–it was a girl. She had filled her hands with the dripping, revolting-looking pieces and as she ran she carried them, one after the other, to her mouth, and was so intent upon running and eating at the same time that she was close enough to Johannes for him to smell her before she noticed him. When she did she stopped short, dropping her hands and staring at him with enormous eyes set in a filthy, blue-white face.

He said quickly: 'Don't be frightened. I shan't hurt you!' but he spoke, without thought, in his own tongue. He repeated the assurance in halting, painstaking Gaelic, unpractised these many years; but even before the words were out he realized that there was no need to tell her not to be frightened of him. She looked over her shoulder at the old woman, now hobbling towards them using the stick as a prop, then she looked at him with an expression of confidence as well as appeal and moved to his side, slightly behind him, sheltering.

'Help me,' she said.

The old woman, now close to them, seemed to sense his partisanship; in a spate of Gaelic, too swift for his understanding, she made a speech of self-justification and complaint. The gist of it–so far as he could make out–was that the girl always robbed the pig and the pig must eat or die.

'The child also,' he said.

The old woman shrugged, a gesture of helpless indifference. She spoke again. The girl had nothing to do with her. Maire had brought her and now Maire was dead; everybody was dead.

The child beside him said: 'Yes. Maire is dead and I am hungry.'

'Have you food in the house?' he asked the old woman. 'I could pay,' he added. An intent, greedy gleam in her eyes raised hope for a moment, but it vanished and a dull indifference took its place again.

Of what use was money, she asked, when there was nothing to buy. What food she had would hardly last for herself until her son came back; everybody was dead, and she would have been dead too except that she had a son who worked at Shallyran.

Rummaging in his mind for the Gaelic words, halting, improvising, he asked her if anyone else lived in the village.

No; they were all dead or gone away.

'And the child has no parents?'

No; she never had any; Maire had brought her; Maire was dead, and soon the child would die too, only by robbing the pig had she kept alive so long.

He looked at the girl. He thought of the good food at that moment being prepared in the ship's galley and made an instant decision, with no more thought, at that moment, of its results than a man would have when he put down a saucer of milk for a starving cat.

'You come with me,' he said. 'I'll find you something to eat.'

Her dirty little face took on a look of pure bliss. Then it was grave again and assumed a 'remembering' look. To his enormous surprise, she stepped in front of him and made him an elegant, competent curtsey and said: 'Sir, I should be very grateful.'

'Come on then,' he said, smiling.

'God be thanked now,' said the old woman, 'the pig can eat in peace.'

The sailor who had been left with the boat was walking briskly up and down, stamping his feet and beating his arms across his chest. He stared to see his captain appear accompanied by a filthy scarecrow child. Johannes lifted her into the boat, thinking how piteously small and light she was.

'Put your back into it, Daan,' he said, 'this child is starving.' Of Julia he asked: 'How long have you lived like this?'

'Since Maire died.'

'How long ago?'

'It was Christmas. . . .' Tears filled her eyes and slowly spilled over, making tracks down her dirty face.

'All right,' he said hastily, 'we won't talk about that. You're all right now. I'll look after you.' He took off his jacket and covered her rags. Washed and fed and properly dressed, he thought, she would be a very pretty little girl. And Geertruida would love her–surely. Geertruida's childlessness had been a great grief to her in the early days of their marriage. . . .

'What is your name?' he asked.

'Julia. Maire said remember always. . . . Shall I say it?'

'Yes,' he said, intent and curious, 'tell me what Maire said you were to remember.'

It surprised him again. He had once heard a grey parrot with a bright pink tail recite in a prim Amsterdam parlour some of the choicest obscenities of the forecastle, and in exactly that same accurate, uncomprehending way his waif now said, in English:

'My name is Julia Ashley. I am English. Cromwell killed my father and my mother and Maire saved me.' She breathed hard with the effort and went on. 'My mother was a good lady and my father was a brave man. I must be good and brave.'

He must now summon up his smattering of English, the legacy of visits to London and Hull and Grimsby in the old days when the two Protestant seafaring nations had been good friends.

'Say . . . that . . . again,' he told her, in English.

She looked at him blankly. Apparently the little recitation was all the English she knew. Asked in Gaelic to repeat it she did so instantly.

'Do you know how old you are?'

She looked down at her fingers, moving them against one another, and finally held up her hands, both thumbs tucked down.

'Eight. You are eight years old?'

'In summer. Maire told me.'

They had reached the *Sea Maid*.

'Well, here we are. We'll soon have some good hot food inside you,' he said.

Eight, he thought, was a good age, young enough to have something left of entrancing childishness, old enough not to be too heavy a responsibility. Geertruida would love her. . . .

PART TWO
Holland 1657–1664

Chapter One

For the third evening in succession, Geertruida Belderdik, having made sure that everything was in readiness for Johannes's return, sat down to await his arrival. She took up her knitting–a pair of long warm stockings for Johannes–but her fingers were clumsy with excitement and impatience and after she had dropped several stitches and missed a line of the pattern she abandoned the attempt, rose to her feet and began to move about the room.

Twenty-two years of marriage to a seafaring man had not trained her to accept with calm the inevitable rhythm of such a life. Still, when he went away she felt the wrench of bereavement; then, when all her tears were shed there was the waiting time, during which she could hardly be said to live at all. The lonely empty days dragged themselves over her, she did nothing, saw nobody, seldom left the house. Finally there was the re-birth, with its own pain, a time when she must count the days, the hours, the very minutes, with so much to be done making ready her feverish welcome, and the exact time was never certain, she must bear the impotent dependence upon wind and weather, she must listen, day and night for the sound of his coming.

Tonight the weather was as bad as it could be. The wind came screaming down from the frozen North and flung handfuls of rattling sleet on the closely curtained windows. Moving about the cosy room she could see, with her inward eye, the *Sea Maid* so small upon the waste of waters, and her very heart shuddered.

She went to the table, where, on a white cloth, glossy with abundance, were set out. Cold ham, smoked sausage, spiced beef, pickled red cabbage, honey, her home-made cherry, her apricot jam, a rich plum cake. In the kitchen various hot dishes were being slowly brought to perfection or kept warm. It had been the same yesterday, and the day before; it would be the same tomorrow, and every day, until he came.

She thought–as she touched everything on the table, moving one thing and then the other, until it was all rearranged–that this was exactly how she had *not* intended to live her life. She had planned that as soon as they were married, he should give up the sea.

There was plenty of money: her father was an East India merchant, not one of the princely ones, but wealthy enough, and she was his only child. Johannes was, at the time of their marriage, one of his hired captains, and in marrying him she had mated below her station. Secretly she had felt confident that that would help her to have her way with him. Secretly she had relied upon her father's wealth to make up for what she thought she lacked in looks and charm.

Towards the money Johannes's attitude had been disappointing, arbitrary not to say cursed and awkward from the very first. Geertruida was not alone in being conscious of the difference in their stations and Johannes was–also secretly–so suspicious that people might think that he had married for money that he had refused to have anything to do with it at all. It took some persuasion on her part to make him consent to live in the big Hoogstraat house. He had his eye on a small place near the water front, he had some pieces of furniture made, and left to him, by his grandfather. Humble hired captain he might be, but he was in a position to provide a home for his wife, and he rather wanted everyone to know it.

Over the house he capitulated; Geertruida pleaded that it would be cruel to leave her ageing father there alone; it was her home, and she loved it; there was ample room there for his cherished furniture; the little house he had in mind could only be a temporary home anyway, there was no room there for children. All sound sensible arguments, such as would appeal to a sensible man.

Over the money he was adamant.

'It's your father's now; and when he dies it will be yours, Geertruida. I want nothing to do with it. I shan't always be sailing other men's ships. When my father dies I shall have my share of the farm, and I shall buy a ship of my own.'

It was then that she had said that she had hoped he would leave the sea. She had been angry, hysterical, tearful, all without effect. Johannes Belderdik married intended to continue–with only the slightest modifications–the life which he had led as a bachelor. He pointed out that he loved the sea, had left his father's farm in Zeeland and served a long hard apprenticeship on account of that love. He demanded to be told what in the world, would he, a healthy seafaring man, find to do with himself ashore. Her father, she said, would find him some kind of a job.

'I have a job, Geertruida,' he said, gravely, 'and I intend to continue in it until I'm beached by old age.'

Beaten down at last, humble as a dog, she had said: 'At least buy a ship now. Let me do that for you.' She imagined that when he was his own master he could at least order his comings and goings, or allow her to do so. In the end the *Sea Maid* had been bought with her money, but when, in the following year his father died, he had paid her back, and she had taken the money, resentful and respectful at the same time.

She had tried, in the early days, to do what many captains' wives did–go with him on his voyages; but she proved to be a hopelessly bad sailor, constantly, irremedially sea-sick, not just for a day or two but all the time. She was sensible enough to realize that a sea-sick woman, in the close confines of a ship, was not an attractive companion. In the end she had stayed at home and begun the pattern of parting and waiting and reunion that simply led to another parting. And never once did she suspect that the irksome pattern contributed to keeping their love alive and fresh. She had never, in fact, brought herself to believe that Johannes loved her at all.

She considered herself very ugly. She had decided that in early childhood, noticing the differences between herself and all the other little girls she knew. She had always been small and thin: her skin was dark, her eyes very black and her hair–also black–quite straight and far too heavy and stubborn to be affected by curling-irons or rags, however tightly wound. All the other little girls were plump and fair-skinned and had light-coloured eyes and hair that was either curly or capable of being made to seem so. To be so different, to be, at the age of twelve, out-topped by blonde beauties of nine–that was bad enough, but when she was fifteen something worse happened. Her father, who doted on her, brought home from his warehouse a length of superb silk, the colour of flame with stripes of a darker shade, almost tawny. It would, he told her, make her a fine new dress.

She had unrolled the shining length of it and draped it over her shoulders and gone to look in the glass. It changed her; against the strong vivid colour her skin looked creamy, her hair and eyes blacker than ever, her mouth a dusky red. She studied her reflection, first with surprise and then with growing displeasure. Then, throwing the silk to the floor she cried:

'I can't wear it. It makes me look like an Indian.'

Perhaps she had expected contradiction; when he said nothing she looked at him with growing consternation and suspicion. She seized his arm and shook it, demanding in a loud voice:

'Is that it? Am I an Indian? Am I? Am I?'

He said slowly. 'Your grandmother was Javanese–a princess. And your mother was the most beautiful woman I ever saw.'

'A beautiful *black* woman!' she screamed in derision.

'She was not black,' he said, speaking with a sternness he used seldom. 'She was beautiful, I tell you.' He paused as though searching for words which would convey that remembered loveliness and found them, fatally. 'Just for a minute,' he said, 'with that silk about you, you looked just like her.'

She gave him a look of pure hatred, spurned the silk with her foot and rushed out of the room.

By the time she was eighteen–and fell in love with handsome, young Johannes Belderdik–the consciousness of being ugly, different, somehow inferior, had imposed upon a nature fundamentally passionate and arrogant, a deceptive meekness and an apparent desire to please. That, and her smallness and the piquancy of her tiny features and unusual colouring made a strong appeal to Johannes. With some diffidence–because of the difference between their stations–he began to pay her attentions which, to his surprise were well received, not only by Geertruida but by her father, who had been troubled by her surly withdrawal from social contacts, her moods of bitter misery and attitude of self-denigration. Johannes had been, and remained, astounded by his luck; his faithfulness to her had been effortless, he knew he had the sweetest, prettiest wife in the world.

Tonight, when she had fidgeted with everything on the table, she moved restlessly about the room, went to the window and pulled back the curtain and saw the sleet sliding over the glass. Not to be borne, this endless dread and uncertainty. No man who loved a woman would subject her to such torment unless he had to. . . .

As she let the curtain fall and turned back to the room with the intention of snuffing a guttering candle she heard . . . and it was more a matter of heart than of ear . . . the sound of a footstep in the street. In a moment she was out of the room, across the hall and opening the heavy front door. The wind helped her, pressing the door inwards and flinging the sleet against her.

The Hoogstraat was inhabited by good citizens and well lighted in compliance with the rule, a lantern at every door, but the sleet was so thick that each lantern was just a yellow blur and for a moment she could see nothing. But she could hear. It was Johannes's step, though slower, less springy than usual. He'd had a trying voyage, she thought. Leaving the door open she ran back to the head of the kitchen stairs and shouted.

'The master is back, Anna.' Then, just as she was, she went into the street. The half-melted sleet between the cobbles soaked her frail indoor shoes, the wind buffeted her and tore at her carefully arranged hair, but what did she care?

She flung herself at him, saying his name over and over. Ordinarily at such a moment he took her in his arms, and because she was so tiny, swung her off her feet and held her high. Tonight, under his heavy, sodden cloak his arms were occupied, clutching something immensely bulky. He never came home without bringing her a present, and as she put her arms about him as far as they would go, she had time to think . . . a roll of the woollen cloth the Irish made . . . a wolfskin. . . .

'Dear Truida! Dear Truida!' he said, as her lips travelled over his wet face. 'Run in! You shouldn't be out in this.'

'You run too,' she said, and felt under the cloak to take his hand. He quickened his pace a little, thrusting her along with the pressure of his body, but he did not free a hand to take hers. At their own door she ran up the steps ahead of him, let him enter, and then, with a great effort closed the door against the wind. And that was always the loveliest moment of all, the moment when he was safely back and the door shut on the weather and all the outer world.

'Safe home once more!' she said, in a voice tremulous with joy. She loosened the clasp of his cloak and gave it a little tug so that it fell with a sodden thump on to the spotless floor.

'What have you . . .' then she saw. The child's head stuck out from the muffling folds, a pale sleeping profile, a tangle of bright hair, tucked between his upper arm and his breast.

She was to think, a thousand times, a thousand thousand times afterwards that that moment was symbolic of it all–herself running to meet him and throw herself into his arms, and his arms not free to take her any more.

'It's a little girl,' he said.

'So I see. Who is she? Why have you . . . brought her here?' She heard the sharpness of her voice.

'I'll tell you all about it,' he said, and looked about for some place to lay his burden, selected a settle on the far side of the hall and gently laid the child down.

Then, too late by an unreckonable age, he took Geertruida in his arms.

When he set her down they both turned to the settle.

'I found her, starving in a deserted Irish village. . . .' He had started his story when Anna, carrying a covered dish, came into the hall. She made a stiff bob and said, in a voice of genuine pleasure, 'Welcome home, Master.'

'Hullo, Anna. Something smells very good. . . .' By that time Anna's gaze, following Geertruida's had lighted upon the child. She gave an exclamation of surprise and the lid of the dish rattled.

Geertruida, who often eased her suppressed irritation with Johannes by snapping at the servants, swung round and said:

'Be careful, Anna. And take that stupid look off your face. It's only a child. By the way you're gaping one would think it was a monkey.'

'You might have thought so if you'd seen her as I did. I have cleaned her up a bit, and she's put on. . . .'

'Dearest,' Geertruida said, 'the food will get cold. You haven't even taken your hat off. And your feet must be. . . . Anna, fetch the master's slippers. Johannes, come to the fire.'

He removed and flung down his hat and then went to the settle. 'We'd better take her in. She might wake up and wonder where she was. Not that she's timid, she's as friendly as a pup. And if there's food about. . . .' He laughed. 'You never saw such an appetite!' He lifted the child and shook her gently. 'I wanted to keep her awake, so that you could see her with her eyes open. She has beautiful eyes.' As he spoke Julia's eyes opened and he spoke to her gently in some foreign tongue.

'Can't she walk?' Geertruida asked in that same sharp way.

'Of course she can. And run. But she hasn't any shoes, you see. We rigged her up as well as we could but the shoes beat us.'

He carried Julia into the parlour and Geertruida drew up a third chair. Johannes set the child down and pulled away the coat in which she was muffled. Geertruida saw that she was wearing Johannes's best shirt, with the sleeves rolled up and a pair of drawers securely tied about her small waist with a length of tarry string. She was now wide awake, looking from one to the other and then about the room. Johannes smiled at her and spoke in that same strange tongue and after a moment she slipped from her chair and curtseyed to Geertruida.

'You see, somebody has taught her manners. I don't think she'd run wild long,' Johannes said in a silly doting voice, as though he had been responsible for training the brat.

Geertruida served the food. The table had been set for two, and she deliberately refrained from ringing the bell and asking Anna to set another place. She sat with her hands clenched together in her lap, ostentatiously not sharing the meal. Johannes did not notice. He ate heartily himself, praised the food and kept pressing the child to eat. Once he drew Geertruida's attention to her pretty manners. Then he began naming the things on the table, the food in the dishes, making her say the names after him. She joined in the game eagerly, laughing at her failure to imitate him perfectly. Her laugh was delightful, gay and musical. And her eyes, as Johannes had said, were beautiful, the soft dark, almost purple-grey of a thunder cloud and set between long lashes that were dark at the roots and just brushed with gold at the tips.

The meal lasted a long time. When it was done Johannes eased his chair back and said, as he always did: 'That was good! God, I am glad to be home.'

And he had not noticed that she had not shared this, their re-union supper. Tears of self-pity dripped–not down her cheeks where they would have done no harm–inwardly, corrosively on to her heart.

The child ate, lingeringly, gloatingly, slice after slice of bread and honey while Johannes told how and where he had found her, speaking of the pig, the old woman, the desolation of Cloonmagh.

Then Geertruida said: 'And what are you going to do with her now?'

For the first time he wondered whether he had taken too much for granted.

'Well,' he said, 'I thought you'd like to keep her, Truida. She's a very nice little girl. I thought, when I'm away, she'd be good company for you. A bit of life about the house. But of course,' he looked her straight in the face and spoke with honest directness, 'if you don't take to the idea you're under no obligation. I could make some other arrangement for her.'

'What? The Klopstock Home?'

'Good God, no! That'd be the very last place. No, I'd find somebody who did want a nice little girl. Or failing that keep her aboard. She was no trouble and the men all loved her.'

'She'd be better here. Would you like her to stay?'

'Of course I should. That's why I brought her home.'

Julia had been following this conversation, turning her eyes from one to another as though she sensed that the talk concerned her. Johannes now spoke to her in the strange tongue, and she smiled and nodded and then broke into that ripple of laughter.

'I told her she was to stay here and be our little girl,' he explained. 'And I told her that she must be quick and learn Dutch because I find the Gaelic very difficult.'

'I'll have a bed made up,' Geertruida said. But she did not ring the bell to summon Anna or Wilhelmina. She went out of the room and stood for some moments in the cold hall, doing battle with herself.

It was true that in time past she had regretted her childlessness but the children for whom she hungered had been great sturdy boys exactly like Johannes, each one a link in the chain binding him to her more closely.

This strange girl-child, appearing out of nowhere would never be a link; she was a wedge. Already she had come between them, spoiled this happy evening.

In the end the long years of hiding her true feelings, hiding even her real nature, came to her aid. Once again it was a matter of pretend, submit. Opposition at this stage would be unwise; give way but be watchful and when the slightest excuse offers itself, edge her out.

She was able to give her orders about the preparation of a room for Julia in a manner which gave no indication that the child's arrival was other than a pleasure to her.

Chapter Two

The thought came to her in the night. Johannes was already asleep and she was lying, drowsy and sated with love-making, under the weight of his arm, just slipping into sleep, when the obscene thought came into her mind as though an enemy had spoken it in a loud clear voice.

She tried, on this first occasion, to refute it, but feebly and with little conviction. It followed so naturally on her secret fears that within a few minutes she had accepted it as truth and told herself that she had always known it to be true. Always, wherever he was bound, even Alexandria or Tripoli, she had visualized the place full of tall, full-bosomed hussies with pink-and-white skins, light eyes and fair hair. That had been part of her misery, that she, who could never bear to have about the house a servant-girl who was not old or positively ill-favoured, must bear the dread that at each landfall Johannes betrayed her.

Every time he came back she questioned him closely. 'Tell me what you did, where you went, whom you saw. I want to share it all with you.' His answers, apparently frank and certainly meticulously detailed could, all too easily, have been lies. People could hide anything from one another: she knew that, for she had hidden from him her conviction that he had married her without loving her. She had never, in all the years, had the slightest confirmation of her suspicions; he was a loving, even uxorious husband, tender, indulgent, passionate, but her wounded self-esteem had been past healing long before she met him, and it had gone on festering despite the balm of a seemingly happy marriage.

And now she knew.

That was a bad night. And from that night on always she woke. Always suddenly, as though someone had roused her, and always just before the clock struck two from the church tower. And always she thought, flinching–I'm not going through all that again! And except that every day added to the weight of evidence, the night's ordeal was always the same.

Always the same. . . .

The child's hair, now that it is properly washed, is just the colour his was as I first remember him, a colour hard to describe, unusual because it is made up of so many; brown, a brown made up of copper, and dead beech leaves and honey, always changing. And her eyes are beautiful; he mentioned her eyes almost before he was inside the house, beautiful, because they remind him of other eyes, set in a pink and white face.

She's eight years old. Nine years ago he went twice to Ireland. I remember every voyage he has made in twenty-two years; the log of the *Sea Maid* is not more accurate than my memory. And this year, with every port closed to the Dutch, at the risk of his life he must go to Ireland again on an errand I always suspected. There was no horse. I asked what colour and did it travel well and he said that there was no horse.

And what a careful plan to fool me! She has not, he said, run wild long; see what pretty manners she has! She had not run wild at all. A week of fasting would strip the flesh from the bones of a child that size. . . .

Who was she? God damn her, damn her, damn her wherever she is; may she rot in Hell forever and ever. . . . May he. . . . Oh, no. I love him; he is mine; he belongs to me. Not true. If he loved me, if he belonged to me he would have given up the sea. . . .

He did not give up the sea because this woman, this child's mother lived on the other side of it.

Presently the clock would strike three.

Sometimes there were fresh things to consider. There was the day when Johannes had told Julia to say her piece for Aunt Geertruida. She had said it and Johannes had translated it into Dutch and added: 'Isn't it exactly like Mevrouw Beet's parrot?' Of course it was exactly like the parrot–it had been learned parrot-wise. It meant nothing–at least it meant a great deal. 'I am English . . .' that was just meant to hide that she was Irish. All part of the plot.

And look how he loves her. 'Where's my girl?' before he has the door open. 'How's my girl?' 'That's my girl.' I was his girl once. Oh, God! Those happy days when I was happy and didn't know it. But she is, very truth, his girl. No man could dote so on another man's child.

Turn over, gently so as not to disturb him; weep, but softly, so that he does not hear. Think of something else, because this one thought, going round and round, will wear your wits away.

Once or twice he woke and found her crying. Why, Truida? Why, my dearest? She had her reason ready. Time was running short, soon he would

be gone again; she would be alone and he in danger from the sea.
The *Sea Maid* was a good ship, he said, and even if he said it himself, he was a good sailor. Nothing to fret about.
'And this time, when I go, you will not be lonely. You'll have Julia.'
Yes, indeed; she would have Julia!

Chapter Three

Outwardly life in the Hoogstraat house went on in orderly serenity, and whenever, in later life, Julia looked back upon this time, she saw it golden with sunshine. Even in winter, when the canals froze and she went skating with a crowd of little boys and girls, the sky seemed to be blue and the snow, when it fell, fell through sunshine.
Her memories of Maire and of the dreadful time after Maire's death, dimmed every day, despite Aunt Geertruida's efforts to revive them with questions.
Aunt Geertruida spared no pains to teach her to speak Dutch, and since, as soon as Uncle Johannes had gone back to sea, nobody about her spoke a word of any other tongue, she acquired it quickly and easily. Then the probing began.
'With whom did you live before Uncle Johannes brought you here?'
'With Maire, but she died?'
'What was Maire like?' That was a question hard to answer; she had never noticed Maire much, she had been accepted, missed and mourned but not observed in a way that furnished a description.
'She was kind.'
'Was she young or old?'
'Oh, very old.' But what did that mean? To a child of eight any person full adult would seem old.
'As old as I am?'
Julia would ponder this, bring her delicate, clearly marked brows together in a frown of puzzled concentration.
'I don't know, Aunt Geertruida, I don't know how old you are.'
'Did she look old? Was her hair grey?'
'Yes. Maire was old. Her hair didn't show. She had a shawl.' Julia brought that proof of memory forward with an air of triumph.
Then possibly Maire was not the mother; the grandmother; bastards often ended up in the grandmother's care.
'Was Maire married?'
'I don't know.'
'Who else lived in the house?'
'Only Maire and me.'
'And Maire taught you manners?'
'Yes. Because she said one day they would come back and she must say that I knew my manners.'
'Who would come back? Julia, try to remember.'
'I don't know, Aunt Geertruida.' She knew that this answer, so often the only possible one, was unwelcome. She tried hard to remember, to catch at

the fleeting memories of those days and have something more to offer. 'There was a place. Maire went there to wash, but they were different people. Not the ones who would come back to see if I knew my manners. Maire cried.'

'Why? What about?'

'She said–"Now they will never know how hard I tried." And she said I must remember.'

'What?'

'What Maire told me. I do remember that, Aunt Geertruida. Shall I say it for you?'

'No, thank you. I know that part.'

Conscious of another failure to please, Julia would sigh. She had known, almost from the first day, that it was necessary to please Aunt Geertruida who did not feel towards her as Uncle Johannes, or even as Anna and Wilhelmina did. Aunt Geertruida never looked at her as though the sight gave her pleasure, and this, Julia, thought was because Aunt Geertruida did not like her hair. She often mentioned how untidy it was. Nothing, no amount of combing and brushing could bring Julia's hair to the state of perfection of Aunt Geertruida's, which looked as though it had been painted on her head, but finally Anna and Wilhelmina between them devised a coiffure which resulted in a cessation of complaint, though it evoked no spoken approval. They brushed it flat with a wet brush, plaited the ends back hard and turned the plait back on itself and tied it with a narrow ribbon.

It was the first thing Uncle Johannes noticed when next he came home. 'What have you done to your hair, my pretty? You look like a skinned rabbit.'

That day Aunt Geertruida took Julia's side; she knew she had done her best. She said:

'That is the only way to keep such a mop of hair tidy.'

'Well, I don't like it. It makes me think of orphans.'

'I *am* an orphan,' said Julia brightly, 'and I'm very lucky not to be in the Klopstock Home.'

Uncle Johannes looked displeased. He untied the ribbon and loosened the plait, ruffling her hair with his hand.

'You're not that sort of orphan,' he said. 'You'll never be an orphan as long as I'm alive.'

'I know,' she said happily.

She knew about the orphans. They lived in a big house on the Heerengracht and when they went for a walk they went two by two and never spoke above a whisper. They had very dull grey clothes that looked scratchy, and their hair was dragged back and their faces were sad. They never joined the other children at the skating; Anna had explained that kind gentlemen gave them food and clothes but couldn't afford to provide them with skates. It was however, not Anna, but Aunt Geertruida who had pointed out that Julia was lucky not be in the Klopstock Home, and Julia, in hearty agreement with the remark, had sensed no unkindness in it.

She never thought Aunt Geertruida unkind. Strict, certainly, and rather sad and gloomy, especially when Uncle Johannes was at sea. Everything cheered up when he was at home and as the seasons wheeled round Julia came to share, though naturally with less violence, Geertruida's pattern of life, the sad parting, the long waiting, and the glad re-union.

Time passed quickly because there was so much to learn; needlework and knitting and embroidery, spinning and bleaching and laundry work; how to cook and how to clean house.

Very soon, it seemed, they were celebrating Julia's twelfth birthday.

Johannes had decided that Midsummer Day should be her birthday. She had said that it was in summer and, 'Nothing,' he said, 'could be more summery than Midsummer Day. Also,' he added teasingly, 'it will help us to remember.'

He was home for that birthday, and gave her a string of coral. Aunt Geertruida had made her a blue dress which laced down the front with a coral-coloured ribbon. Anna had contributed a handkerchief edged with lace she had pegged herself, and Wilhelmina had given her a tame greenfinch in a cage. It was a wonderfully happy day–until supper time.

The parlour faced north and for just a few evenings in the height of summer was granted a brief share of the setting sun's light, not quite direct, but diffused and other-worldly. On this evening, as they sat down to the special birthday supper, the light came in and cast its enchantment upon Julia. It touched the edges of her brown hair so that her head had a nimbus of gold, it shone on the youthful moistness of eyelid and lip, it transformed the unfinished prettiness of her face into something of momentary, dazzling beauty.

Geertruida saw it as she handed the girl her plate and sat for a moment staring as though she had never seen her before. Then her gaze went to Johannes, and she saw that he was staring too, doting, entranced.

All at once she knew that she could bear it no longer. She let the serving spoon drop into the dish with a clatter, put her hands to her face and burst into a fury of weeping.

They jumped up and went, one on either side, to pat and clasp her, to ask, over and over again, what was the matter. The real reason could never be told. Presently she gasped out that she did not feel well, had not felt well all day.

Johannes held one of her hands in his, and laid his other on her forehead. 'You have a fever,' he said. 'Come, up to bed with you. Julia, run and tell Anna to make some hot lemon tea.' He lifted Geertruida and carried her upstairs.

His concern and the concentrated attention soothed her. She drank the lemon, said that she felt better, lay for a while feeling rather ashamed of her outburst, and presently fell asleep.

At some hour in the short darkness of the midsummer night she woke, and now she felt genuinely ill; very ill indeed. All her limbs ached, her head was spinning, her ears buzzed and she felt extremely sick. Soon, miserable and apologetic as in her sea-going days, she was sick and, as in those days, Johannes tended her with matter-of-fact kindness. During the rest of the night the fever mounted steadily and in the morning Johannes sent for Doctor Beets.

The doctor, as soon as he saw her, said he knew what it was; it was the summer fever which had been raging through the poorer part of the town for three weeks or more; now it was appearing in the better class districts. It was nothing to worry about, he said; even without medical attention most people recovered in a few days. He bled the patient, prescribed a nauseous draught, and advised that she should drink as little as possible, despite her ranging thirst.

'It is the fever which demands water,' he explained gravely. 'Deny it and it will depart the sooner.' He then departed himself, having added unassuaged thirst to the misery Geertruida was already bearing.

It was the season for voyages to the Baltic ports and Johannes was due to sail for Riga in three days' time. The *Sea Maid* was re-fitting, and taking on cargo and there was a good deal that demanded his attention but Geertruida clung to him and he stayed at home all day, until, at about six o'clock, the medicine seemed to take effect. She stopped asking for water and complaining of pain, and became drowsy.

He left Julia sitting by the bedside, said he would not be long and hurried away to the docks. Julia was very pleased to take his place, for a long time now one of her private dreams had been concerned with *doing* something for Aunt Geertruida which would convert tolerance into positive affection; this seemed to be her chance.

Johannes returned in the last, long-lingering twilight. As he hurried along he hoped that Anna or Wilhelmina would have had the sense to relieve Julia of her watch–for he had been delayed far longer than he had expected, but as he passed the kitchen window on his way into the house he saw two white caps just visible behind the potted geraniums which he had brought back two years ago, from the Cape and which Geertruida had relegated to the kitchen because she did not like their colour.

He entered the house and ran upstairs two at a time. Before he reached the landing he could hear Geertruida's voice, louder than usual, hoarse and scolding.

She lay high in bed, her face dark and dusky against the white pillows, and she seemed not to notice his entry. She did not cease talking. Julia had left the chair and was standing against the wall, as far from the bed as possible; she turned as he entered but did not move.

'Oh,' she said, 'I am glad you've come. . . .'

'. . . away, right away,' Geertruida said. 'This is my house. You have no right here, it was a plot. . . .'

He stood, poised for a moment between the raving woman and the frightened girl.

'Run along, Julia. Go and get your supper.'

He went to the bed and tried to take one of Geertruida's wildly flailing hands. She tore it away with a loud cry.

'Don't touch me! I've had enough of this pretence. I know how you've plotted and lied and. . . .'

'Julia,' he said, 'I told you to go. Send Wilhelmina to fetch Doctor Beets.'

That set her in motion–and once she had gone, with her frightened white face, he felt that he did not mind what Geertruida said. It was only the fever talking.

Only the fever talking. . . . He tried to remember that as it all came pouring out, unstanchable, sometimes incoherent, sometimes obscure; leaping from complaints about looking like an Indian to complaints about there never having been a horse at all. Only the fever talking . . . but it was Geertruida, telling the truth at last; the truth as she saw it.

By the time Doctor Beets arrived with a soothing opium draught, Johannes knew what had lain concealed behind the façade of his marriage. It was as though, undressing one night for bed, he had discovered his clean flesh rotted with leprosy.

Chapter Four

As soon as Geertruida was quietened he left Anna by the bed and went in search of Julia.

He found her sitting by the untouched supper table in the parlour, she had lighted the candles and drawn the curtains and she looked calm, which was a relief to him. He was also calm, outwardly, but there was a tremor in his stomach, and before he sat down to the table he took a bottle of schnapps from the cupboard.

'You shouldn't have waited for me, my dear,' he said.

'Oh, I wanted to. Shall I cut the bread?'

While she did so he took a drink and felt the spirit run, warm and steadying through his stomach. His mood lightened. He told himself that what Geertruida had said to him hardly mattered, so long as what she had said to Julia had been harmless or not understood. That he must discover, so that if damage was done he could mend it.

'Your Aunt,' he began, setting down his glass and taking up his knife, 'is out of her mind with fever. You do understand, that, don't you?'

'Did she say terrible things to you, too?'

'Terrible!' He pretended, not to amusement exactly, but to something akin, something which would invite confidences without seeming to do so. 'I never guessed there were so many things to be accused of. And that just shows you what fever will do–because in her right mind your aunt doesn't think I have a fault at all.'

'She called me a bastard. Once I heard a boy say to another, "You bastard"–he was angry so I knew it wasn't a nice word. She said it over and over.'

'What happened, exactly. Tell me from the beginning.'

'She woke up and asked me to lift her in the bed. Then she asked me for water and I told her what you told me–about Doctor Beets. And then she was angry. It was all muddled, but it was about you and me and Maire and not wanting me here and my being a bastard. She said I was *your* bastard. I stayed up, not for my supper, I'm not very hungry tonight, but to ask you what it meant. And Uncle Johannes, you can tell me the truth because even if it's not a nice thing to *be*, if it makes me belong to you it would please me very much.'

He said: 'Nothing could make you belong to me more than you do. We belong to one another for the best reasons, because I'm fond of you and you're fond of me.' It occurred to him that, up to a very short time ago, that was the kind of belonging which had been between him and Geertruida. He poured and hastily swallowed some more schnapps.

'I'm not your father,' he said. 'I only wish I was. But your father, I reckon, ranked high. Do you recollect that piece you were taught to say? I do. Your mother was a lady and your father was a brave man. You must hold on to that. And being brave . . .' he hesitated, knowing exactly what he wanted to say but finding the words elusive . . . 'being brave isn't only about not minding being hurt or in danger–all that sort of thing. There's another way of being brave. For instance, now. Just forgetting all those things that were said, and not meant; not minding a bit about what is said: Do you see what I mean?'

'I do if you mean not *crying* about it. But you must *mind* what people say, mustn't you? Aunt Geertruida is ill. But it did sound as though she didn't like me and never wanted me to live here. It is her house, isn't it?'

'Yes. And we live here because she wouldn't move. It was her father's house and when he died I wanted . . .'

I'm as bad as she is, he thought with a sense of shock; have I been brooding over *that* all these years and now go bursting out with it, without even the excuse of fever?

'Nothing she said this evening meant anything,' he said firmly. 'The only thing, the only kind thing to do is for us to forget it all. And it's time you went to bed.'

When she had gone he emptied the bottle and finally fell asleep where he sat.

Chapter Five

In the morning Geertruida, though weakened and still slightly drugged, was herself again. She had missed a day and seemed to think that this was the day after the birthday.

'I must get well quickly,' she said. 'You have only three more days. Oh dear, this was such a short time and I spoiled it, being ill. I spoiled the birthday, too. Really I didn't feel well all day yesterday but I kept about not to spoil the day.'

'Yesterday,' he told her, 'was not the birthday. That was the day before. Yesterday you . . . you slept most of the time. Doctor Beets gave you some medicine and you. . . .'

'Then you leave the day after tomorrow. Oh, Johannes! Oh, why couldn't I sleep and lose a whole day when you're away and time seems so long? I've wasted two precious days then. I must get up at once.'

In the end he promised her that if she would stay in bed and not fret he would defer his sailing for two days. She was delighted.

'Johannes, that is the first time, the very first time you've ever done that for me. I am honoured. Thank you, my dearest. I shall be quite well tomorrow.'

'I hope so,' he said. He knew what she was thinking and felt sick. At the moment he felt that he could never, never as long as he lived, share her bed again. 'It isn't just to humour you, Truida. Things are all behindhand with the ship. I shall have to sleep aboard tonight–probably every night until we *do* sail.'

Twice before he sailed he made indirect reference to what Geertruida had said in delirium.

'Julia is twelve now. It's time we began to think about her future.'

Geertruida, touchingly convalescent, had insisted on going on with her knitting and was counting stitches.

'Twenty-five,' she said. 'What do you mean, dearest, by her future? She'll be married one day.'

'Not before she's seventeen if I have any say. That leaves five years. I've been thinking she should go to school.'

'To school? Girls don't go to school.' Geertruida's voice was calm, but she had taken her finger off that twenty-fifth stitch and was looking at him intently.

'Call it what you like. Mevrouw den Hage has four girls of her own and accommodates five or six others and hires a teacher for them. What's that but a school?'

'A private arrangement to spare Mevrouw's purse, I should say. Do you think she would take Julia?'

'I could ask. Den Hage does business with me. Would you like me to find out?'

Sudden, almost unbelievable happiness welled in her heart.

'It would be a very pleasant and advantageous arrangement for Julia, I have taught her what I know, but that is little and she does sometimes mention a desire to learn to read. Also, now that she is twelve I don't like her to walk in the streets alone. I prefer to stay at home and a servant can't always be spared. . . .'

'You don't think that you would miss her company?'

'I should miss her, certainly, but we must consider her first.'

Then it was true, she had resented the child's presence. And if that was true, so might the rest be; that she believed he had been consistently unfaithful to her.

'I'll go and ask about it now,' he said, and fled from the stifling room.

The other reference concerned the house. Geertruida said something about his retirement from the sea and he said:

'When I do, I shall build a house, somewhere on the other side of the Zee, looking south over the water.'

'You mean leave this house?' she asked incredulously.

'Yes. I never liked it, you know. It gets no sun.'

'You've never said so before.'

'While I'm at sea it doesn't matter. You chose to live in it and you do. But when I retire I shall have a house of my own–that's every man's right; and I shall have an apple orchard and keep bees. Still, that's far ahead. There's ten years' sail in me yet.'

'I hope you will change your mind about that, Johannes. I should like us to have some life together before we are too old.'

And suddenly the idea of retirement was more than ever detestable to him, and he wondered whether, poor woman, she had been right in doubting that he loved her.

In this unaccustomed uncertainty of mind and mood he made his final arrangements, said farewells and gladly made his escape.

Chapter Six

They expected him back on the last day of September, and on the twenty-sixth day of that month preparations for his welcome were already in full swing.

Geertruida, wearing a huge mob-cap to protect her hair, was washing the inside of the window in a back bedroom which Johannes had never entered and probably never would; and under her stern eye Anna and Wilhelmina were beating all the rugs in the garden. The servant at the next door house was standing on a stool gathering pears from an espaliered tree and every now and then she would rear up her head and say something to the Belderdik servants who would stop their thumping to reply. Then Geertruida would rap on the window. So much noise was being made that the door bell rang twice before Geertruida heard it and sent Anna in to answer.

After a few minutes she lumbered into the room.

'It's a Captain Wilhemsteen, of the *Dolphin*, Mevrouw. He asks to speak with you.'

'Did he say. . . . It isn't bad news is it.'

'He didn't say. Just asked for you,' Anna said. But after Geertruida had pushed past her and gone down the stairs, Anna stood, clasping her hands to her stomach. She said afterwards that her inside knew before anyone in the house did.

And it had known rightly. Captain Johannes Belderdik would not be coming home from this voyage. He was dead and already buried in far-away Riga. And he'd been the victim, not of the storm Geertruida had always dreaded but of a simple accident, a silly little accident.

Captain Wilhelmsteen had seen it happen; his ship and the *Sea Maid* lay side by side, *Dolphin* already laden and waiting for the tide, *Sea Maid* taking on casks of tar and turpentine. A hoisting rope, insecurely lashed, had slipped and a cask had fallen, and rolled overboard, carrying a seaman with it. It smashed his leg, too. Johannes, who was watching the loading, dived over to his aid, and the frantic man had grabbed him by the head as he came out of the dive. They'd both gone down to death together.

'It should never have happened,' said Captain Wilhelmsteen. 'That sort of accident doesn't happen once in a hundred years. But happen it did, and to one of the best men that ever sailed. That's all I can say, Mevrouw, except that we gave him a proper funeral and Dick Marsman is bringing *Sea Maid* home.'

Geertruida said nothing. Her sallow face had turned waxy yellow and that was, for a moment, the only sign that she had heard and understood. She remained sitting stiffly upright in her chair and then, quite slowly, she heeled over and lay on the floor, looking so curiously unsubstantial and crumpled that Captain Wilhemsteen thought the news had killed her. He'd told her clumsily and too suddenly. But how could you break such news?

However much you beat about, it had to be said in the end.

As he blundered out to call the servant, he thought of his own wife and the possibility of someone coming to deal her such a blow; and he was ashamed to find himself thinking about that at such a moment.

Geertruida lay for several days in a darkened room, refusing all food and comfort. In the past she had–she believed–often faced the prospect of Johannes's death and had always found a dismal consolation in the thought that she would die too. Now she lay and longed and prayed for death, but did not die. And though death would be the end of her misery she lacked the physical courage needed for self-destruction; lacked, in the final issue, the obstinacy to carry her fast to its logical end. Anna tipped the scales, in the early, death-inviting hours of the morning of the fifth day, by spooning a little brandy into her mistress's flaccid mouth. The spirit, rapidly permeating her depleted body, had a curious effect. It made her very angry with Johannes.

If he'd done what I asked him to, she thought, this would never have happened and I would be spared this misery. He never did love me or he'd have wanted to stay at home with me. The sea and his other women, that was all he ever cared about. He dared to bring his bastard home and expect me to take care of her. Even that I did. Why should I grieve for the death of a man who used me so badly?

Oh! the relief of that anger! The joy of not grieving.

Anna came along with her routine, hitherto fruitless persuasions–a little milk, Mevrouw, a sup of broth, just to please *me*, Mevrouw. This time she was successful, and presently, nourished and slightly tipsy, Geertruida slept.

She woke, of course, to misery again; to gazing down the long grey avenue of the future, cold, helpless. He'll never, never, never come home again. How can I bear it?

Only with the help of brandy could it be borne.

She swung now between moods of sober anguish and drunken anger. In neither mood could she bear the thought or sight of Julia. When she was sad and mourning for Johannes, Julia was the creature who had filched away some of his love and much of his attention, the creature who had spoiled their last days together. When she was angry and reviling Johannes, Julia was the living proof of his heartless infidelity.

There was the real Julia, swollen-faced, red-eyed with weeping, trying to share the grief.

'Poor Aunt Truida. . . .'

'That was his name for me.'

'I know, that was why I used it. . . .'

'Leave me alone. Go to the kitchen.'

'You'd think now of all times she'd like the child's company,' said Wilhelmina.

'Sorrow takes people in queer ways,' said Anna, who had noticed the brandy drinking.

Misery and anger agreed on one thing? Julia must be got rid of.

'The Klopstock Home? Good God, no, that'd be the last place. You're not that sort of orphan. You'll never be an orphan while I'm alive.'

Klopstock Home. Orphanage. Refuge for bastards and unwanted brats. The proper place! And Geertruida knew Mynheer Kinker, one of the

Governors, slightly. One day, in her widow's clothes, well-fortified with brandy, Geertruida was going to walk out and call on Mynheer Kinker. She knew exactly what to say.

Chapter Seven

Mynheer Kinker was sympathetic, but a little puzzled. In June, when Johannes was ashore, he had met him with Julia and had thought what a pretty, pleasant-mannered little girl she was. Mynheer Kinker was very partial to pretty, pleasant-mannered little girls, he'd had two of his own, now grown up and married, alas, and he hoped to live to see his grand-daughters. In the meantime he devoted a few minutes here and there–and a whole hour each January when the accounts came in–in helping to run the Christian Benevolent Orphanage for Girls, more familiarly known as the Klopstock Home. He fully believed it to be a well-run and kindly place but. . . .

He said now: 'Could it be Mevrouw, that this disobedience and naughtiness of which you speak are the result of her grief? I can well remember when Elsa–my eldest, you know–lost a puppy to which she was devoted. She uprooted and stamped upon all my best tulips!' And could naughtiness go farther? his voice and expression demanded.

'It's not that. Not that at all,' said Geertruida. 'Julia was becoming unmanageable long before my poor. . . . One of the last things he did in June was to try to make arrangements to get her out of the house. He asked Mevrouw den Hage to have her but. . . .' She left it there without saying that Mevrouw den Hage had said she would try to make room for Julia at Christmas. Let him find a reason for himself. 'It is a great worry to me, Mynheer. You see I feel so responsible, and if I can't control her I can't be responsible, can I? At the Orphanage the girls always look so very well controlled.'

'I sometimes think,' said Mynheer, pulling at his lower lip, 'that they are a little too well-behaved. But of course when one is dealing with large numbers one must have more discipline than would be desirable in a private home.' He was quoting, word for word the retort which the Superintendent of the Orphanage had made to one of his mild remarks about the orphan's unnatural orderliness.

'Control is just what she needs. I do realize she will be an expense to you. I would gladly make a donation of, shall we say a thousand gilders? Would that cover her keep and everything for four years?'

'Good gracious! That would be enough to . . .' He was about to say–keep *four* of them for four years, but thought better of it and ended, 'send her to Mevrouw den Hage's.'

'Exactly,' said Geertruida. 'If Mevrouw den Hage would have taken her I should have paid, so it makes no difference.'

His mind's eye presented him with two little pictures, one of Julia so happy with Johannes on that summer day, the other of the orphans quietly and listlessly taking their daily walk, with a big, surly-looking girl at one end of the line and the Superintendent's assistant, a sour-visaged woman, at the other. It seemed a pity, but if Mevrouw Belderdik couldn't manage–and really, poor thing, she did look frail and helpless; and she certainly wasn't trying to evade her financial responsibilities.

'Well,' he said. 'In such a case, of course. . . . Let me take the particulars. Now, her name?'

'Julia.' He wrote that and held his pen poised. *Not* Belderdik, Geertruida thought fiercely. There'd been some other name tacked on to Julia in that parrot recital, but she couldn't think of it. 'Maire' she could remember. And it was near enough. Bastards took their mother's name.

'Maire,' she said, and spelled it. 'It's an Irish name I suppose. I explained that my husband brought her. . . .'

'And she is–how old?'

'Twelve last Midsummer's Day.' The effects of the brandy which she had gulped down before leaving the house had been gradually wearing off for some time now, the mood of anger was dying, leaving her vulnerable to the memories of that day. My last happy day, she thought. Then I was ill, and somehow . . . he never slept with me again. And now he's dead. I can't bear it, I can't bear it.

'Mynheer Kinker,' she said, as the quill ceased squeaking, 'all this . . . so upsetting . . . I feel a little faint. Do you think . . . a little brandy, *please*.'

Chapter Eight

For Juffrouw Klopstock, Superintendent of the Orphanage, and for Juffrouw Hoorne, her assistant, each day ended with a pleasant little ceremony–chocolate drinking. In winter they drank it by the fire in Juffrouw Klopstock's sitting-room, in summer on the balcony overlooking the garden. Their position entitled them to certain privileges, more numerous of course in Juffrouw Klopstock's case, but perhaps of them all the chocolate drinking was the most cherished. Chocolate, imported via Spain from the new lands in the west, was a very great luxury indeed; even the very wealthiest people did not drink it regularly. The Juffrouws managed to do so because Juffrouw Klopstock, under her plump pink lethargy, concealed a genius for financial shift and contrivance. For her the chocolate drinking was a symbol of triumph over adverse circumstance; for Juffrouw it stood for social achievement.

All day, every day, Juffrouw Hoorne did Juffrouw Klopstock's bidding, shouldered the whole burden of the Orphanage routine, accepted meekly the orders, the complaints, the reprimands. All day long she went about in a state of smouldering revolt, carrying on a silent, angry monologue— There she goes again, lazy cow, lazy pig! Complaining, complaining, harrying me to death, making me do all the work and taking all the credit. Just because she was born a Klopstock and this was her aunt's house! I won't stay. I won't be treated like this. I'm nothing but a slave.

Then it would be nine o'clock; even the small amount of noise made by the orphans would be hushed and Juffrouw Klopstock's musical voice would call 'Klara! Come along!' And that was the signal for the luxurious moment, the cosy little chat, the easing of weary feet, the salving of the bruised self-esteem. By bedtime the furrows were smoothed from Juffrouw Hoorne's brow, the harrow marks from her soul, and she would retire asking herself where in the world could she find another job where her only work was to see that work was done by other hands, where else could she be sure of a fire in her bedroom in cold weather, drink chocolate each evening and be admitted to the company of a lady like Juffrouw Klopstock?

On the evening when Julia was admitted to the Home the October gales had set in. Outside the leaves were being whirled from the alder trees and dashed on to the ruffled waters of the canal. Juffrouw Klopstock's sitting-room seemed more than ordinarily cosy as the two ladies settled down by the fire, the silver chocolate pot and two delicate china cups on the table between them.

Earlier in the evening the Superintendent had received Geertruida and Julia. Idle as she was, she never missed that kind of contact with the outer world. Juffrouw Hoorne, in her rebellious moments, always thought of this as 'keeping me in the background', and 'making a show of herself'.

'I thought,' said Juffrouw Klopstock, lifting the silver pot, 'that she seemed a very quiet little girl, not at all what Mynheer Kinker had led me to expect.'

'She cried when Louisa gave her her clothes,' said Juffrouw Hoorne.

'Quite understandable. Her own dress was very pretty.'

'I don't like new girls of that age. They don't settle. And if they're rough their language is shocking and their manners appalling, and the few from decent homes, pine.'

'Twelve is rather old,' Juffrouw Klopstock admitted. 'But I couldn't go against Mynheer Kinker.' She answered, as she always did, the complaint which her assistant had not quite dared to voice. 'However, I don't think Julia will give you any trouble. Her origin is very obscure–even Mevrouw Belderdik seemed to know nothing of it–but I'll wager that she is well-bred. She has the *look*. Did you notice her hands?'

If there was one word which Juffrouw Hoorne really hated it was 'well-bred'. Juffrouw Klopstock used it very often, sometimes innocently, sometimes with malicious intent. This evening it was an impersonal observation and had no connexion with Juffrouw Hoorne's lowly birth, nor with her large, red, coarse-skinned hands which had been irretrievably ruined, before she was sixteen, by scalding hot water, icy cold water, sour cheese-whey and salt. Anybody set to work in a dairy at the age of ten would have hands like that, irrespective of breeding, she told herself, as she tucked them under the shawl she had donned before making her rounds of the draughty dormitories.

'I didn't look at her hands. I go by faces, their expressions. I thought she looked surly and too much head-in-air. I should say she'd been spoilt to the point of becoming unmanageable, and then pushed off on us.'

'Well, I know of no one better qualified to manage the unmanageable than you, my dear Klara,' said Juffrouw Klopstock, perhaps a trifle too sweetly.

Juffrouw Hoorne considered the remark. Something, somewhere had gone slightly wrong this evening. Ordinarily, whatever the day had brought, the chocolate-drinking hour found them in full–if precarious accord; tonight, in the space of three minutes, Juffrouw Klopstock had been–she thought deliberately–twice offensive. Well, if that was the way she felt. . . .

'If you mean that as a criticism,' she said, 'I would like to point out that I am responsible for keeping forty noisy girls of all ages so quiet and unobtrusive that you can pretend that they aren't in the house at all.'

That was the first time, in almost nine years, that she had allowed a piece of her private monologue to slip out. She was astonished to hear herself saying such a thing; but, she thought stubbornly, it is the truth.

It was.

The big grand house on the Heerengracht had been built by Juffrouw Klopstock's grandfather, who had made a fortune in the slave-trade, a fact of which he was so little ashamed that when the house was built he had two full-sized negroes, carved in wood, to flank the wide doorway. Juffrouw Klopstock, the orphaned daughter of the old man's younger son, had been brought up there by her aunt and uncle. There had been some thought of marrying their only son, a delicate boy two years her junior, but he had died of the lung rot in his teens. The uncle had died soon after and the two women had lived on alone, the older dwelling in the past, the younger in the glorious future, for the aunt was always saying, 'You'll be well provided for, Ellen.' The years crawled by. When the aunt died she left the big house and the bulk of her fortune to the Christian Benevolent Refuge for Orphans. She expressed a wish that her niece should be appointed as Superintendent.

It had been a calamitous blow, but after a period of bitter rage at the injustice, of furious soul-searching as to *what* she could have said or done to deserve such treatment, Juffrouw Klopstock had settled down to make the best of things. It was still possible to be *comfortable*, and when she had completed a number of what she called, 'arrangements', she was pleased to realize that her position had, after all, improved. She now had authority; she had Juffrouw Hoorne and anything from thirty to forty down-trodden little girls to wait upon her and do her slightest bidding, and the Governors gave her no trouble at all. By adopting a high-handed manner towards them from the first she had bamboozled them into regarding her as patron, not as employee. The place became known as the Klopstock Home and quite a number of people believed that Juffrouw Klopstock's charity was largely responsible for its maintenance.

Oh, yes, what Klara, bristling like a hedgehog, had jerked out, was quite true.

'My dear Klara,' Juffrouw Klopstock said, 'why in the world should I criticize your methods when they are so effective and fit so well with my design. You might as well criticize some of *my* financial arrangements– which benefit us both. Let me refill your cup.'

The smooth devil! thought Juffrouw Hoorne with a mingling of hatred and reluctant admiration; she has an answer for everything.

But this evening the chocolate-drinking had not had its usually emollient effect and for that the new girl, Julia Maire, was to blame. That idea took its place in Klara Hoorne's hard, narrow mind and nothing could ever dislodge it.

Chapter Nine

Julia woke to the clanging of the rising bell. She had cried herself to sleep and her eyes were gummy, her head thick-feeling and heavy. There were five other girls in the small room and as they rose, yawning and stretching, she was conscious of their eyes on her. Their stares were almost impersonal, their curiosity dull–as though they were crows in a field and I was another, just let in through the gate, she thought.

For quite a while nobody spoke to her. Indeed there was very little talking at all, and what there was, was whispered. They dressed quickly and Julia, following their example, began to put on the ugly clothes, the sight of which had, on the previous evening, broken down her fortitude. But it was not, as Juffrouw Klopstock had suggested, the contrast between her own dress and *this* which had made her cry. It was the memory of the time when, from the security of Uncle Johannes's home, she had pitied the orphans in their sad garb. Now she was one of them!

There was an iron tripod in the corner of the room. It held a brown basin, and below, where the legs crossed, a little wooden dish with a piece of rough soap in it. On one side of the tripod stood a jug, and on the other a wooden bucket. Two girls took their turns at washing, and then Julia went forward.

'You're last,' a girl said.

She said, 'I'm sorry,' and waited her turn. When it came there was not a drop of water in the jug. Holding it in her hand she turned with the intention of asking where she could fill it. They stood in a group, watchful, inimical; a ripple of smothered laughter, derisive rather than amused, ran amongst them. Occasions for amusement were rare in the Klopstock Home. . . .

Hateful, she thought, setting the jug down. This is a hateful place and you'd think it was bad enough to be in it, without playing tricks like that and making it worse! She looked at the towel, thin and grey and sopping wet. She couldn't bring herself to put it to her face, but she wiped her hands on it.

The door opened; the giggling stopped. The girl called Louisa who had handed out the clothes last evening, was standing in the doorway, running a calculating glance over everything and everybody.

Last night her flat face with its reddened snub nose and thick eyebrows drawn together in a perpetual frown had been just one more disquieting, disheartening thing. This morning because she had quelled the giggling by merely looking in, she had the face of a friend.

'Please,' Julia said, 'could *you* tell me. . . .'

'You mustn't speak to me till I speak to you. I'm the chief orderly.'

All five faces took on exaggerated expressions of shocked disapproval.

'Good morning,' said Louisa, formally.

'Good morning, Louisa,' said five sycophantic voices in unison.

'You may go down.' She passed on, and Julia, lining up behind the others, could hear, from the next room, her formal greeting and the chanted response.

They moved, in line, with exaggerated care not to make a noise, along the passage and down some stairs, turned a corner, descended some more stairs and came at last to a door which led out into a yard. There, behind a trellis, netted with the bare stems and withered leaves of some creeping plant, six doorless privies stood in a row. They were occupied; they were vacated; occupied again under the eyes of those waiting. Horrible, horrible.

After that, still in line, they went into a large, half-underground room in which there were three tables, two long ones running lengthways and between them, at one end, a square one. One place at the square table was served by a red cushioned chair, like a throne; everywhere else were narrow backless benches. Girls were moving, quietly and busily, between the tables, and the kitchen next door. They set wooden bowls on the tables, took their own places behind the benches and waited. Juffrouw Hoorne entered, walked through the hush to the red chair, and said, 'Good morning, girls.' Everybody said, 'Good morning, Juffrouw.' Juffrouw said:

'God bless this food and make us thankful. Amen.'

There was porridge in the bowls, well-made, pleasantly salted and hot. To eat with it, or afterwards, according to your taste (and that was, Julia discovered, about the only thing which was left to your choice), there were thick slices of bread, one for each girl. To drink there was milk, not the fresh creamy liquid which the Governors visualized when they read 'Milk' on the accounts, but a pale, bluish fluid, twice skimmed, supplied by a cheese-maker with whom Juffrouw Klopstock had made one of her 'arrangements'.

The day was to come when Julia was to eat all her portion and long for more, but on this first morning she was too wretched to be hungry. She sat staring round, loathing all she saw.

At the small square table Juffrouw Hoorne was carving a large joint of pink and white salt pork, and the bread at that table was cut, not in hunks but in slices so that the meat could be laid on it and eaten so. Nobody else in the room had meat; and perhaps, Julia thought to herself, the extra food was provided at that table to make up to the girls there for their afflictions. They were all disfigured in some way; one had an ugly birthmark, one a hare-lip, one a squint. There was a girl with one hunched shoulder, and two scarred by scrofula and two wore expressions of mild idiocy. And there was Louisa, whose fearful scowl was in itself a disfigurement. Julia wondered how it was possible for Juffrouw Hoorne to sit at that table and eat as heartily as she was doing.

Julia was looking, although she did not know it, at one of the outward manifestations of Juffrouw Klopstock's genius. As soon as breakfast was over all these afflicted girls would go off to the saltings, to split and clean fish, and throw it into the barrels.

When Juffrouw Klopstock took over the Superintendency of the Home, girls had stayed there until they were thirteen or fourteen according to their size, and had then been placed out in domestic service; their ties with the Orphanage were severed and whoever, thereafter, profited by their labours it was not Juffrouw Klopstock.

The two simple-minded creatures had helped her to remedy this state of affairs. When they reached an age to go out into the world Juffrouw Klopstock told the Governors that she was gravely worried about them;

they were not capable of holding their own in a workday world and they would be certain to come to grief. Suppose she tried–with permission, of course–a little idea of her own. The poor girls could be found some easy mechanical work, well within their capacity, and they could remain in her care. Their wages would cover the cost of their keep.

The idea was original and that year the Governors took the trouble to look at the girls who were, all too obviously, exactly as the Superintendent had described them. So they went to work in the fish saltings, and from time to time they had been joined there by other girls whom Juffrouw Klopstock deemed unfit to face the world. Their earnings were the matter for some very complicated 'arrangements'. In her accounts, which she kept meticulously in a legible hand, for she had had the advantage of sharing her boy cousins' lessons, Juffrouw Klopstock always proved that this variation of the Home's original purpose was self-supporting, in fact a trifle more than that, but the real profit of the enterprise did not appear in the accounts or anywhere else, it was concerned with the supply of fish, both fresh and salted, to the Home, at a cut rate price. The orphans were appreciated at the saltings, never absent, never late, never seeking other employment.

Nobody lingered over breakfast; Juffrouw Hoorne rose and said Grace again and the labour force marched out, each girl taking with her a packet of food to eat at mid-day, something which would compare very favourably with any other meal carried to the saltings, all evidence that Juffrouw Klopstock did not stint on food.

The other girls remained standing, and somebody whispered. Louisa spoke quietly to Juffrouw Hoorne who nodded and said:

'I understand that you did not wash this morning, Julia Maire.'

Blushing hotly, Julia said, 'I couldn't, because. . . .'

'I did not ask you a question. One rule of the house which you must learn is that girls speak when addressed or when given permission to speak, not otherwise. Another is to be clean, in your person, in your clothing and in your work.' There, at any other time, Juffrouw Hoorne would have left it, but she remembered last evening. She looked at the new girl with disfavour. Julia's neck was very long and slim, and this morning, between the collarless neck of the uniform dress and the scraped-up hair, it looked longer than ever and gave her, despite the burning humiliation in her face, a proud look, easily confused with defiance to a spiteful eye.

'Whatever you may have been accustomed to in the past,' said Juffrouw Hoorne, '*here* you will be clean.'

'There wasn't any water. . . .'

'Be silent!'

'. . . and I didn't know where . . .' said Julia, now as angry as the Juffrouw.

'You will have no supper this evening.'

'. . . to get any.'

'Louisa, show Julia where to find water, and see that she washes, thoroughly. Has any other rule been broken?' Had there been, nobody would have been so extravagant as to report it *now*. This was excitement enough for one morning. What an exciting morning, indeed.

'Very well, you may disperse,' said Juffrouw Hoorne.'

'You'll soon be in trouble if you go on like that,' said Louisa happily.

'But it was *true*. The other girls had used all the water and when I asked you, you said. . . .'

'That you shouldn't speak without you were spoken to first. I'm saying it now. It's the rule.'

'Then it's a very unfair rule.'

'Now you're finding fault with the rules. Your very first day too!'

'But it is unfair,' Julia said stubbornly. 'If you've done something you couldn't help and then mustn't even explain.'

'You keep on,' said Louisa, 'and you won't get supper tomorrow either.'

Provoked past caution, Julia used a word she had heard Uncle Johannes use, but which she would never have let him hear her say.

'Damn the supper! And you, too!'

There had not been such a day in the Klopstock Home for a long time. What the new girl had said to Louisa was whispered round and round. The memory of the morning's scene was still bright; and then in the evening when the coarse salt fish–the orphan's favourite food–was served and Juffrouw Hoorne said:

'Julie Maire, stand out,' and pointed to the place by the wall where she was to stand, near enough to see and smell what the others were eating, that was interesting, too. The new girl stood by the wall and although she didn't say anything–and even she wouldn't dare to–she stuck her nose in the air and had a look on her face which said very plainly that she didn't in the least mind having no supper, and what a very nasty supper it was.

'Well,' said Juffrouw Hoorne, quite happily, 'I've had trouble with the new girl already.' She ran off the list of offences; failure to wash (so much for your breeding!), insolence, criticism of the rules, swearing at Louisa. 'And then, when I stood her out at supper, she stood there looking down her nose as if she despised the good food–and us for eating it.'

'Dear me,' said Juffrouw Klopstock, 'we can't have *that*, can we?'

The words had the wrong sound; not sufficiently shocked, almost . . . almost amused. Once more for some strange reason Juffrouw Hoorne found her inward monologue going on, here, in this hitherto sacrosanct room. That's right, she thought angrily, find something funny in a girl answering me back and making trouble; I don't have enough trouble, I suppose, running this place single-handed.

Aloud she said firmly, 'I don't *intend* to have it. She'll have to learn to knuckle under, like the rest.' The two red spots of colour which might have been painted on her high cheekbones, so even and symmetrical they were, suddenly melted and ran outwards, until her nose and forehead were red, too.

Juffrouw Klopstock looked at her with mild surprise and said, with a genuine intent to soothe:

'She's new, and I expect she has been spoiled. But she looked intelligent. She'll soon settle down.'

Chapter Ten

The settling down was very hard. There was nothing, so far as Julia could see, to mitigate the bleak dreariness of the place. The one seemingly obvious advantage, plenty of company, proved to be illusive; you were lonelier here than you would be in the middle of a desert. In the Klopstock Home everybody was the enemy of everybody else. For this Juffrouw Hoorne's system was partly to blame. It was her task in life to keep the girls busy, quiet and unobstrusive. She was aided by Juffrouw Klopstock's housekeeping, an almost entirely farinaceous diet not being conducive to uproarious high spirits; but even underfed and lethargic girls were capable of chattering in the passages and on the stairs and of scamping their assigned tasks, and she could not be everywhere at once. So everybody was a spy, a willing spy, since it is a rule of human nature that some of your own misery can be lightened by seeing somebody else in worse case. Julia quickly learned that every word she spoke was reported and that every gesture of friendship was regarded with distrust as being likely to lead to some incautious word which she, in turn, would eagerly betray.

You didn't have a friend; you didn't have a moment's privacy; you had very little leisure. Juffrouw Klopstock, in addition to her arrangement with the fish, salter, ran several subsidiary employment schemes with private households. The Home took in washing and plain sewing and embroidery; it was common enough for a lady in Juffrouw Klopstock's social circle–which was wide and growing–to say that she had a superfluity of pickling cabbage, or plums or apples or lavender or fat pork, and that if all those willing little hands at the Orphanage would do the pickling or the preserving, the making into bags or the drying down, and let her have back just what she needed, the rest could go into the store-room at the Home. Charity was a virtue, after all.

It was by way of one of these arrangements that Julia made her bid for escape.

A lady of Juffrouw Klopstock's acquaintance, come down in the world and able to retain only one, rather elderly maid, had in her garden in the summer after Julia's admittance to the Home a heavy crop of blackcurrants, a troublesome fruit, tiresome to pick, tedious to free from the stalks, in fact precisely the job for the Klopstock girls. Ten of them, under Louisa's stern eye, did the picking and struggled home with the heavy baskets of fruit, and practically everyone, during the next few days, had a hand in the preparation, the boiling, the straining, the bottling and the tying down of the preserved fruit with tightly stretched pig-bladder. About two-thirds of the finished produce was to go back to the old lady, and one afternoon two orphans set off, pushing the little low wooden cart often used for such errands.

Juffrouw Hoorne saw them off, and turning back into the house remembered that a piece of plain sewing, just completed, could be delivered along their route. It was ready to hand and she took it up, thrust it at the first orphan to come in sight–who happened to be Julia–and told her to run after the pair with the cart and give it to them to leave on their way.

Julia ran out of the house and then stopped. The two orphans pushing the cart with their behinds stuck out ungracefully, were now at a little distance along the path which edged the canal. She began to follow them, her feet going slowly, her thoughts very fast.

The idea of running away was not a new one- she had entertained it from the very first day and had been watchful for a chance; there had been none, there might never be another. She was now alone, and out in the street, but there were the clothes, instantly recognizable by anybody. Then she realized that she held, folded in her arms, somebody's winter cloak, prudently sent, in high summer, to be relined by the orphans.

The cart-pushers were now much farther away. With her heart beating so violently that it seemed it might shake her to pieces, she turned down the next side street, shook out the cloak and put it on. Then, still walking, quickly now, she pulled at her hair, and shook it loose. The long, heavy cloak was eccentric wear for a hot summer's day, but at least it covered her completely.

Now, where to go? What to do? She realized that she had never carried her plans for escape thus far in her mind. Getting away had always been the problem.

Life in the Klopstock Home had taught her one thing–there was plenty of work in the world; four of the girls with whom she had shared a room had gone into service at the New Year and she had watched them go with great envy. The thing to do, she told herself firmly, was to find a house which looked as though servants were employed there, go to the door and ask if they wanted one.

She was now in a poor street of small, shabby houses and unprosperous-looking shops–the sort of street which Anna, in the old happy days, would avoid, or walk quickly along, talking of 'catching something'. Some children, ragged and dirty–but happy and lively-looking compared with the orphans–were playing marbles in the gutter. As she drew level with them, one of them looked up, pulled a rude face and said jeeringly:

'Got her mother's cloak on!'

She tried to take no notice. With sad lack of originality the others took up the chant and the words:

'Got her mother's cloak on,' followed her to the end of the little street.

The thought–do I look so funny? undermined her small self-confidence.

The shabby street led into another of much the same kind, but that, at its farther end, opened out into a square of good, solid-looking houses, nine of them.

Now she must do it; and the jolt and beat of her heart told her how much she dreaded the ordeal. No good lingering. She walked straight to the first house along one side and knocked on the door.

It was opened by a pleasant-looking, middle-aged woman in a voluminous apron.

'Good afternoon,' Julia said. Her voice sounded strange, very high and shaky.

'Good afternoon,' the woman said, pleasantly.

'I wondered if you wanted a servant.'

'What did you say?' It was not meant deterrently, it was a request to repeat something not quite clearly heard. Julia said it again.

'Why, no. We don't. And if we did we know where to go. I've a niece of my own waiting for a place.'

'I see,' Julia said.

The woman's attitude changed; she laid her hand on the door, which had been wide open, and pulled it half closed. Suspicion wiped the pleasantness from her face.

'Are you a gipsy?'

'Oh, no. No.'

'Or in with thieves or anything.' Her eyes sought the square, all quiet in the sunshine. 'I know that old trick, sending somebody to look for a job and spying about. We've got a savage dog in this house, let me tell you.'

She slammed the door.

'Well, that was horrid, but it was only one house. There were eight more, here in this very square.

'No, we do not. We have more than we need at this moment, idle rogues that they are.'

'No thank you. And we never take chance comers.'

'No. Our mistress always has girls from the country.'

'No.'

'No. The family is away. I'm the caretaker.'

'No.'

'No. We always get our new girls from Klopstock Home.'

And all the time the curious, speculative, assessing eyes, noticing the too-long cloak. Better get away from here, quickly.

Down another street, across a canal–not so nice as the Heerengracht, dirtier, with a dead thing floating.

Now another pleasant street. Try again.

The strange thing was that as her need and urgency increased, her opening sentence, no matter how much she tried to word it differently, sounded more and more false and like something a gipsy or a thief would say. In the end she sounded like, she almost *was*, somebody trying to get in, to spy, to betray.

Twice more she heard reference to the Klopstock Home.

The sun began to sink, gilding the trees.

Presently she was convinced that it was not, after all, possible to get a servant's place in that way. But there were other things. Saltings. The one which employed the orphans couldn't be the only one in Amsterdam . . . but that one must be, at all costs, avoided. The thing to do was to get down near the harbour, find a place to sleep and tomorrow morning keep a sharp lookout, see into which shed the orphans marched to work and pick the one farthest away.

Now the streets became familiar, full of sad memories. Here, and here and here, she had walked, swinging on Uncle Johannes's hand, coming down with him to visit *Sea Maid.* Right here on this corner was the place, half tavern, half eating house, where only last June, on the day before her birthday, returning from the docks, he had said: 'Are you thirsty, sweetheart. I am.' And they'd gone in and sat in a kind of box place, with high sides and a table all scored with names and initials and dates, and he had drunk schnapps from a small glass and water from a big one and she had had a long cool drink that tasted of lemons.

The window was lighted, and except that now it was evening instead of mid-morning, and a whole year and a month had passed, it looked exactly the same; there was the ham on the dish, the pies and the pastries, the little three-cornered cakes.

I'll have no supper tonight, she thought; but without much feeling. In the Klopstock Home she had often been punished, sometimes with reason, more often without, by forfeiting supper. It was Juffrouw Hoorne's favourite punishment. She kept canes of varying thicknesses in her room, and sometimes used them, but she believed that having no supper for a week was more effective. The cane's impact was a thing of the moment, the other meant seven separate reminders that rules were not to be broken. Having no supper was a thing Julia had trained herself to bear, and although a voice in her mind added–and no breakfast tomorrow, it was not hunger which made her stare into the little window. She was looking at the enclosure, made by two facing settles, where she and Johannes had sat, and taken their drinks and laughed . . . he had teased her by pretending that he had forgotten about her birthday tomorrow. . . .

The voice said: 'Feeling peckish, eh?'

She turned; it was a sailor . . . the same clothes, the same face almost as she remembered, the general sort of sailory look, calling to mind Daan and Pieter and all the others who had made such a fuss of her every time she visited *Sea Maid*.

'No. I wasn't looking at the cakes. I was just looking in.'

You couldn't share memories with sailors, nice as they were.

'Well, come in then, and take a good look. I'm going in myself. Home from home I call this place. Come in and keep me company, eh?'

'I haven't got any money. You'd have to pay for me.'

'What'd you want with money? Pretty little girl like you. Come right in and ask for what you want.'

He was the first really kind person she had met for a long time. But then sailors were kind.

'That *is* kind,' she said.

'Come right in,' he said again, and flung open the door.

Only one of the little boxes was unnoccupied, the one immediately on the left of the door.

'Sit you down,' he said, giving her a little push. 'Now, what d'you fancy, eh?'

'A meat pie,' she said eagerly.

'And what'll you drink?'

'Last time I was here I had a nice lemon drink.'

He said something that she didn't understand at all. Something foreign perhaps. He left her sitting there and went to the counter and a fat man in an apron put four meat pies on a pewter plate and then gave the sailor two mugs which he carried carefully to the little table and set down. He then seated himself beside her, and she smelt the old, familiar smell of tar and salt water, and sweat.

'There you are,' he said, 'lay to!'

Now that the food was before her and she was heartened by his kindness, she was hungry. The pies were delicious, the best food she had tasted for a year. She ate three of the four; the sailor ate one, rising now and again to have his mug re-filled. She found the drink he had brought her less agreeable; it didn't taste of anything much, just vaguely musty, and every time she sipped it she choked. He drank it as though it were water.

'You like it, don't you?' she said, and smiled at him.

'Why not?' he said, genially, 'it's the best schnapps.'

'Oh, is that what it is. My . . . somebody I once knew used to drink it sometimes. I'll try again.' She sipped and coughed.

'I think it's for men,' she said; and smiled again.

He asked her her name, and she told him 'Julia' with which he seemed content.

'And what's yours?'

'Hans.'

'I shall remember that,' she said.

'Maybe you will,' he said in a rather peculiar way. 'You live around here?'

'Well . . .' she hesitated. 'Not exactly. Just now I don't live anywhere. I'm looking for work.'

'You've found it,' he said; and as he spoke something happened to his leathery, sunburnt face. It smiled, but in a way that made her feel uncomfortable. And what did he mean?

'Get that down of you,' he said, jerking his head at her mug. 'Perk you up a bit. What'd you like now? One of them cakes?'

'Yes, I would, please. That is . . . if you think you can afford it.'

He laughed, and the sound shared the something that had been in the smile.

'I got money and I don't mind what I spend. That's a sailor's life that is–hard tack and maggotty meat and water that foul you have to hold your nose to drink it, and then good schnapps, and your belly full and a right pretty girl.'

He lumbered away and came back with a re-filled mug and one of the little cakes held between his finger and thumb.

'Get *that* down,' he said, 'time I drink this. Then we'll go.'

'Where.'

'I know a place,' he said, exactly as he had said that he had money.

'You mean you know a place for me? A place where I can work?'

He had to take the mug away from his mouth in order to laugh.

'Now then,' he said, quite good-naturedly, 'don't give me too much of the bloody innocence. Little of that goes a long way. Work, eh?' He laughed and again said something which had no meaning.

She was now liking him less; and she knew why. He was getting drunk. That was the prime failing of all sailor men–except of course, Uncle Johannes; they were the nicest, kindest people in the world, but they did get drunk.

The cake lost its flavour suddenly.

He emptied his mug again and sat for a moment looking at her.

'You don't want *that*,' he said suddenly. 'What you want. . . .' He put his arm, hard and heavy, around her shoulders, pulled her round and kissed her full on the mouth. It was very unpleasant; his lips were wet and his breath smelt of schnapps and something else even more horrid; and that wasn't the way people should kiss other people–more like trying to eat them. She pushed him away with all her might and would have got to her feet but that his arm pinned her down. But she wasn't angry with him, just confused and rather sorry, because he had been nice to begin with, and now was drunk.

Still pushing at him she said: 'You mustn't do that. I think you're a little drunk.'

And he wasn't angry either.

'Drunk am I? Maybe I am but I ain't so drunk . . .' and once again he said something she didn't understand. He lurched to his feet, still holding her, and said: 'Come on, let's go.'

She said: 'But you are drunk and I don't think anybody'd give me a job if you went like that to ask for me. Thank you all the same; I don't think it'd be any good.'

Then all at once he *was* angry; and that was the thing she had been afraid of ever since she suspected that he was getting drunk. Drunk men did get angry all over nothing at all. Once she'd been with Uncle Johannes and they'd seen Daan and Pieter, the best of friends aboard *Sea Maid*, fighting on the quay, trying to kill one another. Uncle Johannes had separated them and knocked them both flat.

It was the same with this sailor; he'd invited her to go in and eat with him; he'd said he didn't mind what he spent, and now he was angry about it, and grudging, shouting about how much he had bought her, and saying many other things which, although she did not understand them, were certainly unfriendly and rude.

He was trying to force her round the end of the settle and towards the nearby door, but she had her hands clenched on the settle's side and her body partly braced against it. They contested silently–except for his accusations and curses–for several minutes, and she looked around the room, searching for one friendly face.

There were none. Four sailors at one table stopped the game they were playing and stared with delighted interest, beginning to laugh and call jeeringly. They were probably drunk, too. A man sitting alone at a table looked up and then down again, indifferent, disgusted. Two gaily dressed women, sitting with another sailor at a farther table, were watching her with exactly the same expression as her room mates had worn when she lifted the empty jug.

Even the fat man behind the counter, though he was watching, had a dull look, as though he had seen similar scenes too often to be much interested.

Suddenly the man abandoned the attempt to push her away from the settle. He lifted his hand and dealt her a stinging blow on the side of the face. It jarred her to her heels, so that her hands dropped from the settle and she staggered.

The sailors let out some hilarious cries.

Now, in no time at all, he would have her through the door; he was reaching for her again. He clutched a handful of the cloak; she twisted out of it, leaving it in his hand, and darted across the room, ducked under the counter flap and came up beside the fat man.

'Help me, please,' she gasped. 'He's drunk!'

The sailor came, lurching and cursing, up to the counter, and the fat man proved to be more of a champion than she had dared to hope. Leaning forward he said:

'Leave her be, Jack. She's nothing but a kid! You go get yourself. . . .'

The sailor broke in, violently. Of all he said Julia only understood, 'You mind your own bloody business, Fatty,' 'cheating little bitch' and 'wreck the place'.

The last words were taken up by the four sailors at the table. The fat man looked frightened.

It was one of the hard-eyed women who saved the situation. She got up and walked down the room, swinging her hips and holding her head high. She slipped her hand under the sailor's arm and said:

'You can do better'n *that*, Jack. What good's a green girl to you? You come along with me.'

Astoundingly he stopped cursing, blinked and grinned and let himself be led away.

'Now you . . .' said the fat man, with a look of annoyance, and then with a disbelieving stare. 'For Christ's sake,' he said, 'it's a Klopstock girl!'

Chapter Eleven

She stayed in the Klopstock Home for almost two years more but she never lived down the escapade. Juffrouw Hoorne, who had always disliked her, had been made to look silly and careless. As long as Juffrouw Hoorne remembered, Julia would have good cause to remember also–and regret.

After that all the most repulsive tasks, the heaviest punishment were hers. She spent a good deal of time locked in the cellar–popularly supposed to be haunted by the ghost of a girl, who, it was whispered, had been locked in there and forgotten until she starved to death. She was almost invariably prevented, on some excuse or another, from going on the daily walk, which was the one break in the long day's monotony, and the days on which she went supperless to bed far outnumbered the others.

It was a life which must either harden or break any nature and something in Julia refused to be broken. In the cellar it was cold and damp and dark, but if there was a ghost Julia never saw it, and it was peaceful there. And who wanted to go on those stupid, deadly dull walks? Not she! The loss of supper, by this time, did matter rather more, but you could pretend that it didn't. And when Juffrouw Hoorne, in desperation, took to caning you could always remember that blow from the drunken sailor's fist and take this pain–less because it had no emotional accompaniment–with an unflinching grimness which, quite plainly, made the Juffrouw more angry than ever.

She remembered how the sailor had hit her, how the fat man had half-heartedly befriended and then betrayed her, and how she had been turned away from all those doors, how the very children had jeered, and her cynicism reached out and embraced all the outer world. The process had begun when Geertruida had ignored her pleadings not to be sent here; it had been delayed by her certainty that if only she could get out of this hateful place things would be better; it had been completed by that brief excursion into the world.

Everybody, everywhere, was an enemy. You walked warily, outwitted the enemy when you could and when you could not bore the penalties as though they meant nothing. You hoped for nothing and cared for nobody.

It took a little girl named Katje to change all that.

Katje was brought in by a kind-hearted old market woman who had seen her begging amongst the stalls by day and sleeping in an upturned barrel at night.

Katje knew her name and that she had once had shoes which some other children had taken away–and that was about all. Juffrouw Hoorne, experienced in such matters, said that she thought she was about five years old and had been homeless for a long time.

She was as pretty as a doll, with a china-white face and black eyes and a mop of black curls which could not be dragged back into the regulation hair-dress because they were so short.

She was not, however, at all pretty when she came in, she was caked with filth and smelt so horrible that the task of cleaning her was naturally one for Julia Maire.

By the time she had cleaned her, Julia, without knowing it, had fallen in love with Katje who had, most marvellously, fallen in love with the Klopstock Home.

'Got shoes again!' she said, with wondering delight, as Julia helped her into a pair of tiny shoes, clumped and reclumped on the soles, patched and repatched on the uppers. (Shoes were a problem. Juffrouw Klopstock realized that clogs cost less and wore better, but they made such a noise!)

For the first time Julia saw the purpose of the Orphanage and realized that although to her it had always been a hateful place, to such as Katje it was indeed what its proper name implied, a refuge. How horrible the poor little thing's life must have been.

She was on her knees, helping on the shoes, and she looked up, her eyes level with the child's.

'You must be very *good*,' she said seriously. 'If you're very good and do just what you're told, you'll be all right here.'

Katje was, for several days, not merely all right but blissfully happy. Three times a day she encountered, with positive enjoyment, food which, whatever its deficiencies by ordinary standards, was wonderful when compared with what could be begged or picked up in the market after the stalls had been cleared away. She rapidly put on flesh, as many poor children did immediately after admission. It was a fact noted and reported upon by Juffrouw Klopstock every year.

For a week, at the risk of breaking rules and incurring wrath, Julia watched over Katje, told her what to do and what not to do, forestalled the tricks always played on any newcomer, and eased her into the life of the place. On the morning when boredom overtook Katje, Julia was in the laundry where she spent most of her time, and her protegée was in the kitchen.

Juffrouw Hoorne had found a simple little job for Katje. She had to grate some salt from a block and then pound it until it was fine enough for use.

There were several other girls there, working away in the near-Trappist silence that the rules demanded. Katje, bored with her job, tried to talk, and was hushed, frowned upon, ignored; later on she would be reported as well, but that she did not know. She was determined to make the others notice her, so she proceeded to show off the simple tricks which had often gained her an apple, a cake or even a small coin in the market place. She turned some expert somersaults, walked on her hands, clapping her feet, and with her hands round her ankles and her head tucked between her knees rolled over and over like a ball. The other girls gave way to temptation and watched, and Katje worked harder. Juffrouw Hoorne, entering the kitchen, found the pudding saucepan boiled dry, and the bread which had been set to rise on the hearth brimming, forgotten, over the edge of the wooden trough. The girls were watching wide-eyed, while Katje stood on one leg, the other stuck out at right angles, arms at full length and shoulder level, as she spun round on one toe. The mortar in which she should have been pounding salt was balanced on her head.

Juffrouw Hoorne cried 'Stop' in a terrible voice, and Katje did stop, so suddenly that the mortar lost balance and fell, and smashed a dish full of sliced apples for Juffrouw Klopstock's pie. The apples were smothered with salt.

'You naughty, naughty, *naughty* little girl,' said Juffrouw Hoorne, seizing Katje by the arm and administering, with each 'naughty' a sound smack on the ear. Katje had often suffered similar attacks during her short life and she defended herself as she had learned to do. She ducked her head and set her sharp little teeth into Juffrouw Hoorne's thumb–that loosened the clasp, and kicked her in the shins–that delayed pursuit, and then she ran behind the table and stood poised to dodge when pursued.

'It was just like dealing with a wild animal,' said Juffrouw Hoorne to Juffrouw Klopstock over the chocolate cups that evening. She wore a conspicuous bandage on the injured thumb and would have been prepared to show, at the slightest hint of sympathy, the bruise on her shin.

'How unpleasant. Where is she now?'

'In the cellar. And not quelled yet, she screamed and banged on the door for hours. A most truculent girl!'

A slight look of uneasiness crossed the Superintendent's placid pink face.

'Neighbours,' she reminded Juffrouw Hoorne, 'always expect places like this to have a torture chamber. If they hear screaming. . . . We don't want any scandal, do we, Klara?'

No sympathy, no support. Criticism, direct or implied, all the time.

'I shouldn't think even old Kinker would expect me to be bitten and the little ferret to go unpunished. I said she should stay there until tomorrow evening, but of course if you'd prefer to deal with her yourself. . . .'

'Good gracious. I shouldn't have the faintest idea what to do. Anyway, she's quiet now, isn't she?'

No sound reached the cosy room, but in the passage at the other end of the house as she went to her bed Juffrouw Hoorne could hear noise coming from the cellar. It was muted by distance, and indistinct but she knew that in the street it would be more audible. Despite her bold, scornful words about Mynheer Kinker, she did not want a neighbour or passer-by running to him and saying that shocking things must go on in the Klopstock Home, for she knew who would be left to bear the blame. She went to her room, selected her stoutest cane, and carrying it, the cellar key and a candlestick, descended the stairs again.

The cellar door lay at the far end of the laundry passage. The yelling and the banging, which had grown louder as she approached, had died down before she reached the passage; when she turned into it she could hear another voice, speaking in a firm, soothing tone.

'. . . I can't. I haven't the key. But I'll stay and keep you company. I'm here, right outside the door, as close as I can get.'

It was being locked in that Katje minded; company and being talked to did little to lessen the wild panic that possessed her. She began again to scream: 'Let me out, let me out,' and beat on the door.

'Katje! you *mustn't* make that noise. You'll be punished more. Katje, please. . . . Oh.'

Julie had seen the light, and behind it Juffrouw Hoorne. She was startled, but almost immediately calm again. She had broken Heaven knew how many rules, and she would be punished, but none of that mattered now. She broke another rule by addressing Juffrouw Hoorne without permission.

'Oh, please, Juffrouw, let her out. She can't bear it. She's going mad.'

'Be silent,' said Juffrouw Hoorne. She set the candlestick on a stone slab near the door and beat on the door with the cane.

'Be quiet, in there!' she shouted. 'If you keep making that noise you will *never* come out! You'll stay there until you are quiet. Do you hear me?'

Katje gave several staccato screams and then fell to whimpering.

'When you have been quiet for a whole day I shall let you out. If you make a sound, I shan't.'

The whimpering, now and again rising to a hysterical scream, went on.

'I can still hear you!' said Juffrouw Hoorne.

'She can't help it,' Julia said. 'She'll go mad. Please, please, Juffrouw, punish her some other way.'

Juffrouw Hoorne had come down with the half-intention of letting Katje out, caning her thoroughly, and sending her to bed; now a fatal obstinacy rose and over-mastered her. That Julia Maire, of all people should be telling her what to do!

'You'd do better to begin thinking about your own punishment!' she said, with venomous relish.

'I don't mind what you do to me, Juffrouw, if you'll just let Katje out. She can't bear to be locked up. She'll go mad.'

'She will stay there until she is quiet. I've said so and I mean it.'

'Then I shall fetch Juffrouw Klopstock.'

In the whole history of the Klopstock Home no one had ever dreamed of approaching the Superintendent except by order or invitation at any time; and it was now ten o'clock at night. The foundations of Juffrouw Hoorne's solid little world rocked, quite literally; for half a second everything went black and moved sharply sideways. She thought again about the possibility of a stroke.

She opened her mouth to say: You wouldn't dare! But Julia had already turned and was walking away along the passage, a ridiculous, yet purposeful figure in her too-short, skimpy night-gown and bare feet. Juffrouw Hoorne took two swift steps and caught hold of the looped-up plait which offered itself as a convenient handle at the back of her head. She jerked at it savagely, turning Julia about and at the same time giving her two cuts with the cane. Pulling at the soft, firmly braided hair gave her a feeling of mastery, a vicious pleasure.

'You insolent little bastard,' she said between her teeth.

Julia bent and bucked and writhed, trying to free her head. Juffrouw Hoorne held on and raised the cane again. The key of the cellar door jerked from her hand and fell with a clatter to the stone floor.

Then Julia went mad; she wrestled with the Juffrouw, she pushed her; she hit her with clenched fists. She stepped by accident on the key, and kept her bare foot on it. Then she gave Juffrouw Hoorne one last mighty shove which carried her some distance along the passage, and stooping, picked up the key.

'Give me that! Give me that key!'

'I'm going to let Katje out and take her straight to Juffrouw Klopstock,' Julia gasped.

Juffrouw Hoorne made as though she would come to grips again, and then thought better of it. The girl was mad, dangerous; nothing but madness could have given that frail-looking body such strength.

'Very well,' she said. 'I shouldn't like to be you, in the morning. That's all.'

Julia put the key in the door and turned it. The door opened outwards, and was heavy. The strength which had enabled her to grapple with Juffrouw Hoorne had gone; she had to exert all that was left to open the door at all.

Katje lay crouched on the top step, silent now, and as the door opened she sprang towards it, almost unbalancing Julia. At the same moment Juffrouw Hoorne pushed the door from the outside. It's swing caught both Julia and Katje, thrust them inwards and downwards. They rolled to the bottom of the cellar stairs together, and above them the key turned again.

Chapter Twelve

'. . . so there they are, both locked in the cellar. And what I want to know now is what we are going to do with them.'

It was the first time that 'we' had been used in such a context and Juffrouw Klopstock lost no time in countering the suggestion it conveyed.

'I should suggest that you give the small one a thorough whipping and find some humiliating punishment for the other.'

'Do you realize that she was coming to disturb you. Past ten o'clock at night.'

'I should have tried to settle things without–I–trust–indulging in a bout of fisticuffs.'

The red colour ran over Juffrouw Hoorne's face. Really, it was maddening; the effort to keep her temper in the face of such provocation made her quite dizzy.

'What I want to know is–how am I going to get them *out* of the cellar. Both those girls attacked me yesterday. I'm not going alone to release them and I can't take another girl to witness what may well be a scene.'

'No,' said Juffrouw Klopstock, sensibly. 'I see that. I will come with you myself, as soon as I am dressed. Dear me, how very tiresome! And I always thought your discipline was so good!'

The release was an anti-climax; they emerged meekly enough. Katje, who had spent the night curled up against Julia and who was fully dressed, had suffered little damage except that she had beaten her hands raw by hammering on the door. Julia, thrust into the cellar in her night-gown, was in a palsied rigor from cold and quite speechless from the chattering of her teeth. One of the blows from the cane had broken skin just above her eyebrow.

'You take the little one, Klara. I'll deal with this,' said Juffrouw Klopstock, and moving more quickly than she had done for many a year, she took Julia to the laundry and made her get into one of the tubs of warm water and kept her there, with a girl bringing fresh hot water to add to the bath, until the rigor was less violent. She then told her to go and get into bed, and a few minutes afterwards came to the bedroom herself, followed by an orphan carrying a bowl of steaming hot porridge.

'Don't imagine,' she said coldly, 'that I'm overlooking your behaviour.

You acted like a wild savage and I am completely disgusted with you. You haven't heard the last of this, by far.'

It was a pity that Juffrouw Hoorne was not present when that speech was made; she was, actually, enjoying the sight of two big girls forcing Katje's raw hands into a bowl of hot salt water. She did not know what Juffrouw Klopstock had said, only what she had done–which was to treat Julia as though she were sick. She brooded over that for the rest of the morning and all through the mid-day meal, and immediately afterwards climbed the stairs and for the second time that day intruded upon the Superintendent's privacy.

Juffrouw Klopstock sat in a cushioned chair with her small neat feet on a stool; she was stitching at the embroidery which occupied so many of her idle hours.

'Well, Klara,' she said and raised her eyebrows.

'About Julia Maire. . . .'

A glimmer of concern showed in Juffrouw Klopstock's pink face.

'Is sh. . . .'

'Oh, she'll be all right. She's very well. Bathed and put to bed and coddled! What I want to know. . . .'

'You saw the state she was in. I only took sensible precautions. We didn't want her ill, did we?'

'I don't want her, well or ill. That's what I've come about. She's fourteen. Two years ago she was unmanageable, but I have tried. I've tried very hard. You don't know what trouble I've had. But I don't intend to have any more. She struck me. . . . Now there she lies, lolling in bed, and when the others go to bed, *think* what a tale she'll have to tell! Before we know where we are every girl in the place will be hitting me to get a plate of porridge!'

Juffrouw Klopstock saw the funny side of that, and laughed.

Something, stretched tighter and tighter inside Juffrouw Hoorne, tighter every day over all these years, snapped.

'That's right. Laugh. All these years I've played your silly game so you could pretend to be a lady. I've done all the work and taken all the blame while you had the money and the praise. I'm sick of it, you hear me, sick to my bones. Every way I turn you get the better of me. Because that little bitch hit me, you take her side. Let me tell you this–unless she's out of this house this very day, I shall be. And then you'll know!'

Yes, she would. Juffrouw Klopstock, successfully deceiving so many people, seldom deceived herself. She knew Klara's value exactly. She used her hard, goaded her . . . but that meant nothing. It was like whipping a donkey: that didn't mean that the donkey had no value.

And out of the whole tirade she picked the single item about which something could be done.

'She shall go this very day,' she said firmly, 'My dear Klara, if I had known you felt so strongly . . . that she'd given you such trouble, I'd have got rid of her long ago.'

Juffrouw Hoorne was conscious of an odd feeling of deflation.

'What will you do with her?'

'That I don't know . . . yet. But I shall think of something.'

'Get up,' Juffrouw Klopstock said, quite pleasantly. 'Dress as far as your petticoat and then come to my room. And be quick.'

The short November day was dying. A sad grey light lay in the bedroom, and in the passages; but Juffrouw Klopstock's room was warm and light.

'Now, let me look at you. That cut on your face . . . something will have to be done about *that*. Loosen your hair.'

When she turned back to Julia she held a pair of scissors in her hand.

'Stand still,' she said, and snipped, pulling the clipped ends forward. 'That hides it well. Now, let us see.' She turned to two dresses which hung over a chair. One was blue sprigged with little flowers; the other was grey with bands of purple. Juffrouw Klopstock held them up, measuring them against Julia.

'Fortunately you're tall. How old are you, I forget.'

'Fourteen last Midsummer Day.'

'You forget, too. It was fifteen. The blue suits you better but the other makes you look ol . . . your age. Put it on. Now, listen carefully to what I have to say. . . .'

'You've been a very wicked, ungrateful girl. You know that, don't you? And you deserve to be punished, severely. But in this world people don't always get what they deserve. If you are careful, and clever . . . we may arrange something for you which will be much better than you deserve. When you're spoken to, speak up. And smile. Try to look as lively and attractive as possible. We're going out and I wish to be *proud* of you.'

She stepped back and regarded Julia critically. She looks very delicate, she thought with some dissatisfaction, far too slender–but girls often are at that age, you can't grow both ways, and she *is* tall. And she's graceful, too, and hasn't, thank God, that cowed look. I may manage it.

'You're really very pretty,' she said, bracingly. 'You may look at yourself in my glass if you like. Now, smile–you see what an improvement that is.'

'Juffrouw, may I speak?'

'Of course. Oh, forget that ridiculous rule. I want you to be *natural*.'

'Where am I going?'

'Out. I am making a great effort to arrange something for you. For your future. You realize, I suppose, that you can't remain here after last night's . . . performance.'

'Oh,' Julia said, and her pallor warmed a little. 'Juffrouw, is it a job?'

'You could call it that. But you must have some training first and you must seem suitable for it. Here is a cloak. When we arrive, push back the hood, but keep that short curl well forward–if that mark is seen you'll be asked how you came by it and that would be quite fatal.'

Juffrouw Klopstock put on her own cloak, a fine one lined and edged with fur.

Along the Heerengracht the lanterns by the doorways were being lighted and a thin rime of frost glittered on the roadway and on the leafless trees. Juffrouw Klopstock set a brisk pace. They took the turning down which Julia had stolen on that ill-fated afternoon, and avoiding the street, where the children had jeered, emerged, from a different side, into the square where she had tried in vain to find work. After that their road was different, though in the same general direction, but they stopped short of the harbour and finally turned into a well-lighted street of tall houses, of which every ground floor was occupied by an office. Through many lighted windows Julia could see the long desks and high stools occupied by frantically scribbling clerks.

They turned in at a doorway. Twelve heads were raised, twelve pairs of eyes stared. The clerk on the nearest stool slid to the ground and came foward and said:

'Yes, Mevrouw?'

'I'm Juffrouw Klopstock, of the Klopstock Home. I should like to speak to Mynheer Dekker.' Her manner, here in this strange place, was as easy and authorative as in the Orphanage; Julia noticed that with admiration, for she was herself embarrassed by all the staring eyes.

The clerk hurried away and came back.

'You wait here, Julia. Possibly someone could find you a seat.'

The clerk offered his own stool, and Julia, blushing, sat down on it, folding her hands in her lap while Juffrouw Klopstock followed up the long room and through a door.

She was gone a long time; then at last the door opened again and there she was in the doorway, smiling and beckoning.

They all looked again as Julia walked the length of the room, so she arrived in Mynheer Dekker's presence pink-cheeked and with that air of shyness which, on a young girl, is like the bloom on a grape. 'Ah, yes,' said Mynheer, 'I see what you mean.'

'Julia, this is Mynheer Dekker.'

She made him the curtsey which Maire had taught her so long ago, and remembering Juffrouw Klopstock's admonition, smiled at him.

'Good afternoon, my dear,' he said, smiling at her. 'I trust you are well. Do you enjoy good health?'

'Oh, yes, Mynheer. I'm never ill.'

'Splendid. And you are fifteen years of age?'

'Yes, Mynheer.'

He studied her attentively. He had small, very bright brown eyes in a clean-shaven, rather yellowish face. He looked kind and she thought that she would like to work for him. So she smiled again with innocent seductiveness.

He made a little noise of assent, 'Um-m-m.'

'It seemed to me such a pity, such a waste,' said Juffrouw Klopstock.

'I must say she does you a great credit. And so does your concern. I hope she realizes. . . .'

'Oh, I told her nothing. It would have been unkind to risk the disappointment.'

'We can consider the matter settled,' he said.

'You have done me a great favour, Mynheer.'

'No, no. On the contrary, Juffrouw. There are plenty of girls, but so few suitable. Things have changed very much lately; the demand has increased and the type of demand has changed too.'

'That is largely due to you, Mynheer,' said Juffrouw Klopstock sweetly.

Mynheer pooh-poohed that but he was obvioulsy pleased.

'And I may leave her now? There would be so much envy. . . .'

'I'll take her round to Mevrouw Helmers myself.'

Juffrouw Klopstock rose.

'Julia,' she said, taking one of the girl's hands, 'you are a very very lucky girl. You are going to be a Company's Daughter–the most fortunate thing that could happen to a girl in your position. I hope you'll be very happy, and very good,' she gave the hand a little conspiratorial squeeze as she spoke the last word.

Julia was confused, she knew nothing about the Company's Daughters or the nature of the good fortune which had overtaken her; but that, for the moment hardly mattered at all. She was out of the Klopstock Home; and it was the Juffrouw's doing. She raised the hand which held hers and kissed it and said:

'Oh, thank you, Juffrouw. Thank you.' And Juffrouw Klopstock took her into an embrace which was surprisingly soft and warm, and said with an emotion that seemed entirely sincere:

'Good-bye, my dear. I know you'll be happy. Bless you!'

Their parting made quite an impression upon Mynheer Dekker, who, like most people had heard several contradictory stories about Juffrouw Klopstock's management.

That evening Juffrouw Klopstock was very pleased with herself and with the day's arrangements. Julia had done her great credit and for a long time the faintest hint of criticism could be met with the incontrovertible remark that it wasn't everybody who could turn a Klopstock orphan into a fit candidate for the Company's Daughters' Home.

She also looked forward to telling Juffrouw Hoorne the news. She had not forgotten the extremely rude and rebellious things Klara had said. She had ignored them at the time, but she remembered. Now Klara would be annoyed to hear that Julia, her enemy, was so well placed, and Juffrouw Klopstock would be able to say in a soft, innocent voice: 'But you told me she must go— What else could I do with her?' That would teach Klara to issue ultimatums.

The soft, innocent remark was never to be made.

Juffrouw Klopstock said, as she poured the chocolate, that she had got rid of Julia Maire, and Juffrouw Hoorne asked where she had gone and Juffrouw Klopstock told her.

'Y . . .' said Juffrouw Hoorne, and her mouth seemed to slip sideways. 'Y . . . y . . . y . . .' she said. Her head shook; the chocolate cup danced in its saucer and then fell to the floor. 'Y . . . y . . .y,' she cried accusingly as the red mist closed down.

The stroke she had so often expected smote her to the floor.

Juffrouw Klopstock had given her donkey one whack too many.

Chapter Thirteen

Her time in the Home for Company's Daughters was very brief, only a year and a few days long, and, in the sense that it was extremely happy, with every day's passing a thing of regret, it seemed very short; in the sense of experience and education, it seemed very long.

There was a great deal to learn.

'You *must* learn to read and write and reckon,' Mevrouw Helmers would say. 'A wife who can do so is a help to her husband, and improves her own status. Look around and ask yourselves what women count for most in this world–the wives of small shopkeepers who understand and help with their husband's businesses. They are indispensable and the men know it. I want *you* to be indispensable to your husbands!'

'You *must* learn about illnesses and how to deal with accidents. Where you are going there won't be a doctor on the nearest corner and a midwife in the next street. And if your husband is a nutmeg planter you may find yourself responsible for slaves as well as for your family.'

'You *must* learn deportment. Girls of very good family go out to the Islands now and when you are married you must be prepared to meet them on their own ground. We can't have your husbands making unfavourable comparisons.'

'You *must* learn to occupy your free time. Life in the Islands can be idle for white women, and it can be lonely. Your husbands will have their work and their interests.

She never for a moment allowed the girls to lose sight of their destiny. They were Company's Daughters, being trained to make good, acceptable wives for the Dutchmen who lived in the Molucca Islands and grew nutmegs and cloves for the Company's trade.

The system was an old one. It had begun in the days when few girls would voluntarily face the long sea-voyage–seven months of it, at least–and spend the rest of their lives in exile; the white men then had been glad of wives of any kind. Then there had been a middle period, when the nutmeg growers had made great fortunes and–as Mevrouw Helmers said–quite important families had been willing to spare a daughter to be the wife of a nutmeg 'prince'. Then there was a slight social slur in being a Company's Daughter, or the husband of one. But the private arrangements, generally made by ships' captains acting as go-betweens between distant husbands and greedy families in Holland, had not always worked out well; several plain girls, disagreeable girls, sickly girls had been shipped out. Mynheer Dekker, who in his young days had spent many years in the Islands, had known several small tragedies, and when he came home and was elected to the management of the Company's Home he had put into practice a scheme of his own. The Daughters were now all picked girls, and properly trained; and they were not sent out, as in the earlier days, just anyhow and to anybody. Negotiations must be conducted, credentials produced, and in most cases the formal marriage by proxy–known as a Glove Marriage–was performed with as much ceremony for an orphan girl as for one of good family.

Mynheer Dekker fully deserved the little compliment Juffrouw Klopstock had paid him.

He had chosen well in making Mevrouw Helmers head of the establishment; she had also lived in the Islands where her husband had been a low-grade clerk. That she had then been, and still was, Mynheer Dekker's mistress, though it had affected his choice to some degree did not make it less a wise one. She was shrewd and practical, knowledgeable and kind.

In all ways, except one–and that vital–she did prepare the girls for their futures; she spoke of 'your husband' in a sensible and realistic fashion; but she shared the prevailing view that 'innocence' in a bride was no drawback. She had been a very innocent bride herself, believing that babies were got by kissing. Learning otherwise had done her no harm at all; in fact the lesson had pleased her so much that in the end she had practised it 'out of school' as it were. She believed that it was a lesson which nobody but a husband *could* teach a girl. It wasn't a thing that could be talked about, there were no words, except rude ones.

The girls, of course, were not innocent at all and the words in which enlightenment was spread would have shocked Mevrouw Helmers very much indeed, as much almost as the discovery that her relationship with Mynheer Dekker was common, though secret, knowledge.

A very pretty, jolly, friendly girl named Frieda was Julia's mentor in this matter, and a promising friendship died untimely. From the evening when Frieda 'told' until she sailed in January for the Moluccas, Julia had to avoid her because she couldn't bear to look at, or touch her.

She thought it was all intensely horrible. As Frieda ripped away the veil she saw again the face of the sailor who had pretended to be kind, the face of the woman who had led him away. 'So that was it!' she thought with sick disgust. *Now*, because Frieda's pretty lips were shaping to them, she understood some of the words he had used when he had abused her.

So that was it. Jolly Mevrouw Helmers and kind Meynheer Dekker, too. Aunt Geertruida and Uncle Johannes. *Quite* unbelievable; and horrible, horrible!

Curiously enough, side by side with this deep revulsion against the physical side of the man-and-woman business, she developed an interest in, a yearning for, something called 'love'.

Mevrouw Helmers thought girls should be able to read, should take delight in reading, and she read to them, and gave them to read, the kind of story most likely to provoke avid perusal. In these pairs of lovers, figured prominently: two French ones, oh, and a very sad story. Héloïse and Abelard; two Italians, and what a tragedy, Romeo and Juliet; two English, long ago but still achingly sad, Tristram and Iseult.

Julia saw them, clean, brightly yet delicately coloured, made of china, moving stiffly against a background of trees and flowers; the young men carried papers upon which they had written poems, the young women walked along with fawns pushing their noses into their hands. They spoke, they said, 'I love you. I love you', but their words had nothing to do with *that*! Sometimes they touched hands. In such an interchange, Julia would gladly have taken part, with a young man, tall and slim, with yellow hair and blue eyes, a younger Uncle Johannes.

That was 'love'. but Mevrouw Helmers never spoke of that. She said, 'your husband', and every time she said it–once Frieda had explained things–Julia saw the drunken sailor, felt his slushy kiss and the weight of his arm.

Being a Company's Daughter was pleasant indeed, but it was a short-lived business, a mere prelude to something else–and very often, when she looked into the future Julia wished that Juffrouw Klopstock had sent her to the fish saltings.

Mevrouw Helmers had a very clear-cut idea of what the prospective brides should know about their duties, but in many other matters concerning the Moluccas and the life there, she was curiously vague. Listening to her might make one believe that the Islands, except for the nutmegs and the slaves–and, of course, the husbands–were not so much unlike the Dutch countryside. Her brisk, practical nature was not one equipped to absorb atmosphere and then, years later, to convey it by spoken words.

The girls currently under the Home's tuition had therefore a choice of two pictures when it came to throwing their thoughts forward to their future home. There was Mevrouw's rather ordinary and unexciting a Dutch landscape with nutmeg trees, some dark-skinned slaves and 'your husband' superimposed upon it; and there was the one composed of rumour, truthful reports, products of over-strained imaginations, of old sailors' tales, ancient letters, things overheard–and that was a picture of a nightmare paradise. This was the one which the girls held up to one another, with shudders, with delight, with yearning, with dread foreboding. They whispered of slave revolts, of nutmeg planters and their families wiped out in one night of fire and rapine and slaughter; they told of a mountain which spouted fire and sent streams of red hot molten metal pouring through groves and houses; there were bats as large as rats which drank your blood as you slept; there were frogs in your shoes and snakes in your bed, sharks in the sea and crocodiles in the rivers. Even cannibalism was not overlooked. But there were also the flowers–twelve inches across, some of them, and of such fragrance that if you smelled them too close you swooned; there were fruits of a flavour unimaginable; there was unending leisure, if you had a baby you did not even have to carry it in your arms, a brown slave did that; there were parties every evening, picnics every day; just to be white in the Islands conferred such status that the humblest Dutch woman lived like, and was treated like, a queen.

Against this colourful and contradictory background were set the individual stories of things that had happened to other Daughters of the Company. There was the girl who sailed in a ship that was attacked by the Moorish pirates and who was sent as a present to the Grand Turk, in whose harem she ended her days; the girl who went to Java and whose husband hated her on sight, made her get into some kind of bath which dyed her brown, and sent her out to work amongst his slaves; the girl who was married to a clerk in the Company's office, but was so beautiful that a rich planter persuaded the clerk to exchange her for the best planation in Macassar.

Nothing too unlikely; nothing too fantastic. Yet some healthy scepticism, some optimistic selection must have been at work, even as, with an accompaniment of shudders and little screams, the tales went round; for most of the girls looked forward with impatience to the time when they should embark into the unknown. The horror stories had the thrill, the fascination of stories of ghosts or bloody murder, but you could never seriously imagine that you, yourself, would play a part in such a drama. Other people saw ghosts, other people were murdered; not you. Stories of the delights of the Islands had, on the whole, a rather more personal application; most of the girls did look forward to a life of leisure, of wealth, of happy marriage and motherhood. Shivering on a cold winter's day they would speak of the delights of living in a perpetual summer; doing the household tasks that they shared they would say how wonderful never to wash a dish, scrub a floor, scour a saucepan again. Brown hands to labour for them was a certainty. So, also, were new dresses; the least self-assured girl was positive that, given a husband, she could find ways of making him give her pretty clothes.

Julia never really saw either picture of the Islands; was never much affected by the threats or the promises of the future; when she looked forward she saw one thing only–'your husband'.

And so the weeks sped on; and the months; inescapable, relentless as death, the future advanced.

One day in November, a mild, mist-moisted day, she and a girl named Marie with whom she had made a pleasant but carefully-not-intimate friendship were in the garden, cutting the very last roses of an unusually protracted season.

'And I hope,' said Marie, snipping the last bud, 'that next time I gather roses it will be in my own garden.'

'Do roses grow there–in the Islands?'

'Yes, all the year round,' said Marie happily. 'Think of it, no winter. . . .'

Mevrouw Helmers opened a window and called them. They went in, their hands full of the damp flowers, drops of moisture clinging to their hair and their eyelashes. They made a pretty pair, Marie all ebony and ivory and rose, Julia leaf-brown and cream and grey. Mynheer Dekker who was in the room with Mevrouw Helmers looked at them with a kind of wistful lechery. He put out one of his brown-speckled hands and touched both their heads, remarking upon the dampness of their hair, to cover the gesture. Then he remarked upon the flowers.

'And you look just as sweet and fresh,' he said.

Mevrouw Helmers watched, without jealousy. They came and went, an endless line of them, pretty young things with all their troubles still to come. Hers–and she had known trouble–were over, she rested easily in a relationship which was as worn and easy as an old shoe.

On the table stood a package which had been opened and then just folded together again, and a bottle of Rhenish wine and four glasses.

'Well, shall I tell them or will you?' asked Mevrouw Helmers.

'I can guess!' Marie cried, clutching the roses to her breast. '*It's our turn!*'

'They just live for the day,' said Mevrouw Helmers. 'Yes, it's your turn, Marie, and yours, Julia. And I may as well say at once that you are both very lucky girls.'

'Both Glove Marriages,' said Mynheer Dekker, with an air of personal achievement.

'When?' demanded Marie.

'At the end of this month.'

'There you are, Julia. I said I hoped the next rose I cut would be from my own garden. And it will! Oh, Mevrouw, who is he?'

'I must be off,' said Mynheer Dekker. 'I'll just drink to your happiness and then you can know all the details.'

Mevrouw Helmers began to pour out the wine. Marie turned to Mynheer Dekker and said, prettily:

'Mynheer, will *you* be our proxy?'

'I shall give myself that melancholy pleasure,' he said, and he took the proffered glass and swung his beaming smile around. The dark girl, bless her, was all right, flushed and sparkling, her ordinary youthful prettiness transformed into beauty by the glow of excitement . . . but the other looked as though she had received a mortal blow. And, of course, it *was* a step in the dark, disguise it how you would. He caught Mevrouw Helmer's eyes, flicked a significant glance at Julia and was reassured by a nod. All that sort of thing could be left in her capable hands. He raised his glass:

'To your future, my dears, may it be happy and prosperous!'

They drank and he left, and before he was well out of the room Marie said:

'May we look?'

'Certainly not. How would you know which was which? Since you are so impatient I'll deal with you first. Here you are . . .' she handed Marie a buff-coloured glove, made for the left hand, its cuff embroidered with scarlet silk.

'You are to marry Hendrik Oltman, who is twenty-six years of age, and a clerk in the Agent's office in Banda Neira. He has good prospects and his disposition is said to be amiable. I congratulate you.' She added quickly: 'Oh, now! You mustn't try it on, that brings bad luck; glove on, wedding off, did you never hear that?'

'I think it will fit me,' said Marie, measuring the glove against her hand. 'And smell it! Doesn't it smell lovely? Hendrik Oltman. I like that name. Marie Oltman. . . .'

'I'm glad that you are pleased. And now for Julia.'

It was a glove of yellow silk with pearls sewn in a pattern on its gauntlet. 'Isn't that pretty? Well, take it, dear. It's for you. Your husband is named Pieter Vosmar and he is twenty-two. His father has a nutmeg plantation on a little island called Rua. You are to be congratulated, too.'

'Isn't it wonderful?' said Marie, and Mevrouw sensibly allowed her to speak for them both.

'Run along,' she said, 'show off your gloves, and make the others envious. This is your day; theirs will come.'

Julia carried her glove straight to her bedroom and there, with a shudder of distaste, pushed her hand into it, grimacing at her own credulity as she did so. Once, she supposed, somebody had tried on her glove and then not been married after all; that was how such superstitions began. Nevertheless she was missing no chance!

The next few days were very trying. Everything centred upon the wedding, everybody shared in the preparations. You were never allowed for one moment to forget that you were a bride-to-be. If it were forgotten for a moment Marie would say or do something to bring it back into focus and somebody was sure to add: 'And Julia, too!' Behind Marie's gaiety her own glumness passed, she thought, unnoticed, but Mevrouw Helmers had seen it and was not surprised–or worried–when, one evening, a mere five days before the wedding, Julia came to her room and asked if she might speak with her.

The thing she had come to say, and which seemed so easy, and sensible, and simple, when she tried it over in her mind, wasn't easy at all. Mevrouw was sewing–on the wedding clothes–and she looked up with a bright kind smile which seemed the very epitome of the general mood, a mood in which she alone could not share.

'Mevrouw, I don't want to be married.'

Mevrouw Helmers hesitated, while she decided between several possible replies and then laughed.

'Oh,' she said, 'the *times* I've heard that, here in this very room!'

It was clever. It removed Julia's sense of being different, of being unsuited for marriage.

'Oh. I didn't know anybody else ever felt that way.'

'Bless you child; everybody's felt the way we do about everything. The world is pretty old, you know. I've prepared dozens of girls for marriage and they took it in one of two ways; either, like Marie, they couldn't wait for the day, or they insisted that they'd rather be dead. And do you know, so far as I can make out, they were as happy, or happier than the others. Sit down, Julia, and tell me what's in your mind. You'd rather be dead, is that it?'

'I wondered whether Betta couldn't go instead of me. She's longing to be married.'

'Now that, at least, is an original idea. Nobody ever suggested that before.

Betta cannot, she must wait her turn. She's only fifteen.'

'So am I.'

A single question and answer elucidated that little mystery. Mevrouw Helmers thought that Juffrouw Klopstock had done rather well.

'It's too late to do anything about that now,' she said. She put out her hand and tapped Julia's knee. 'You forget all about that year, Julia, save it up until you're thirty-nine. Every woman hates her fortieth birthday and on the eve of yours you can give yourself a whole year for a present.'

It was all so cosy, so feminine, so almost irresistible.

'I wish I were forty now. Then I'd be too old to go. Mevrouw, please, couldn't I stay here. I'd do a servant's work. Or go out and get a job.' It was an echo of her pleadings with Aunt Geertruida.

'Now Julia, don't be tiresome,' said Mevrouw Helmers, using the term which, in this easy-going little world, was extremely derogatory. 'The arrangements have all been made. Even if I wanted to I couldn't send Betta in your place, she wouldn't be at all suitable. The Vosmar family is old and important, you don't realize how very fortunate you are. There are girls with good homes who would change places with you, gladly. *Naturally* you have doubts and fears. I've always found that a very good cure is to take the thing that is worrying you and look it straight in the face, and if possible talk it over with somebody of greater experience. Come along now, tell me exactly what is the trouble?'

The very thought of putting it into words made her face burn.

Mevrouw Helmers took up her sewing and made several stitches. Without looking up she said: 'It's the . . . physical aspect, isn't it?' She took silence for assent. 'I do *wish* you girls wouldn't pry and chatter, the blind leading the blind! When it comes you'll find it as natural as eating. That is true, Julia. After all men and women were made and put together in this world by the good God, and He never makes a mistake. Even this reluctance of yours isn't going to be wasted–you'll be all the more delighted when you find how wrong you were.'

She spoke with sincerity and conviction, and Julia recognized the good sense of what she said. But. . . .

'As for staying here and remaining unmarried,' Mevrouw Helmers went on, 'that's a fate I wouldn't wish on anybody. An unmarried woman, whoever she is, becomes in time a pitiable object. And you're so pretty; that young man will *adore* you. Look, you sew on this, it's for Marie, and I'll sew on yours. I want you both to look beautiful.' She planted some sewing in Julia's lap and went on. 'I know Mynheer Dekker isn't a very exciting proxy–I expect you girls think he's old and too fat; but he is so kind and so interested in you all, and so proud when it's a Glove Marriage, so I do want you both to look pretty . . . and happy. Try to look happy, to be happy, Julia. The years go by so quickly. . . .'

In her voice, there was something of the wistfulness which had been in the old man's eyes when he looked at the girls with the flowers in their arms.

They sewed for the rest of the evening and Mevrouw Helmers chatted on, making it all sound safe and ordinary and quite, quite inevitable. As they put away their work she said: 'Are you sleeping well? I thought not. Go and warm a cup of milk and bring it back here.' When Julia returned Mevrouw had a little box in her hand; she opened it and took out a pinch of grey powder which, placed in the milk, instantly dissolved.

That night she slept heavily, and all the next day moved in a placid daze;

nothing, not even her own hands and feet seemed quite real. Mevrouw Helmers repeated the dose each evening until the wedding, and on that day not even Mynheer Dekker, very sprucely dressed and gallant in manner, helping them on with the gloves, kissing them and calling them by their new names, seemed quite real. But she was now Julia Vosmar, properly married, in the sight of God and man, to Pieter Vosmar whom she had never seen.

PART THREE
The Moluccas 1664

Chapter One

They had seen the island of Banda and its little satellite islands come up out of the water, blue blurs which took on, as they watched, the shape and substance of reality. The smaller islands were out of sight now; the ship lay in Banda harbour with the town of Banda Neira, Marie's future home, directly ahead of them. There was the circle of houses and warehouses along the water front, white and cream and yellow, and blue and pink and ochre-coloured, and behind it the massed roofs of many houses, and behind them a climbing sweep of green, rising up to a sharp conical peak, which, the captain had told them, was the Fire Mountain.

He had stood with them by the rail, pointing out things of interest. Then the *Trade's Advance* had stopped moving, coming to rest like a tired swan upon the clear, hyacinth blue water. And the boats had come shooting out from the shore, and he had gone away to meet the men who must see that there was no case of plague aboard, the men who had come for the mail, the Company's agent, Mynheer Aaden.

The two girls stood alone together, and Marie, who had looked forward so joyously and confidently to this moment, suddenly turned pale.

'I do hope he will like me . . . that I shall like him. I hadn't realized. . . . You did, didn't you?' she asked, almost accusingly. 'All along you knew how dreadful it would be.'

'We shall soon know the worst,' Julia said.

The agent came aboard. He had brought two assistants with him, the good penman to make the cargo lists and the strong fellow to take charge of various boxes addressed to the agent's wife.

To the latter he said: 'Yes, I know you've got a wife aboard, and sorry you'll be, my boy. Don't let that take your mind off your duties; I've got a wife at home and she's waiting for what the Captain has brought–or God help him!'

'May I just take a moment to look at her, Mynheer?'

'You may,' said the agent, 'but only a minute. You've got the rest of your life to look at her, God help *you*.'

The girls saw him coming, shouldering his way along with unmistakable intensity of purpose.

'We should have worn our gloves,' Marie said.

He saw them. One small and plump and dark; the other taller and fairer. His heart rose. He didn't give a damn which was which; he'd be happy with either, happy with both, given the chance.

Marie looked at him and hoped; Julia looked at him and feared. His thigh muscles bulged against the thin material of his tan-coloured breeches, black hair fuzzed at the opening of his shirt and along his bare forearms; beads of sweat stood on his broad sunburnt face. He was rather horribly like 'your husband'.

Just short of them he stopped and made a bow, clumsy to begin with and ruined by someone behind him brushing against his hindquarters. To keep his balance he had to take two steps forward, but as he straightened he smiled and said good-naturedly and somehow endearingly: 'That *would* happen to me! May I bid you both welcome to Banda and ask which is Mevrouw Oltman?'

Marie said: 'I am,' and then he knew that she was the one he had favoured all along. He threw his great arms round her and hugged her. 'Oh, I'm lucky,' he said. 'You're so pretty. I never thought you'd be so pretty.'

'And you're handsome,' Marie said.

Julia had taken a step away and stood looking at them. It was just right; exactly what Marie had expected and exactly what Mevrouw Helmers had foretold. The good God had made men and women and put them together. He'd made Marie and Hendrik and had–with a little help from the East India Company–brought them together and for them all was well. But for me . . . the man isn't born to whom I could take so instant a fancy . . . and somewhere here, somewhere very near now, a man is coming who will . . .

She felt sick and turned away and looked over the rail.

Coming in towards the ship's side, very noticeable amongst the other boats was one painted white with a yellow canopy. It was rowed by two brown men who wore short drawers of the same yellow and had metal collars around their necks. They brought the boat alongside, and one took hold of the ship's ladder. As he steadied the boat by his hold on the ladder and the other rower steadied it with his oar, a small man, dressed entirely in pale grey, came out from under the awning and began to climb.

'That must be somebody very important. What a fine boat!'

Julia was surprised to find Marie beside her.

'Hendrik has some work to do, so I have to wait. Julia, don't you think he's *nice*? I do hope yours is too.'

The small man in grey had gained the deck, looked sharply this way and that and now came towards them, and whereas Hendrik had had to push his way through, everybody stepped back to allow this man free passage. A few people greeted him, and he nodded or lifted a negligent hand in recognition.

'It must be the Governor himself,' said Marie, 'and he's . . . yes, he is . . . coming to welcome us.'

And it seemed so. He came straight towards them. He was, despite his short stature, an impressive figure, very upright and taut. His hair, worn long and elaborately curled, was as near as could be to the colour of his clothes; fine lace frothed whitely at his wrist and breast. He halted, looked at them both in a way only just saved from insolence and by its seriousness, and then asked:

'Mevrouw Vosmar?'

'I am, Mynheer.'

As she made her curtsey Julia heard him say: 'Ah.' just an outletting of the breath, but it held relief, as though he had said: 'Thank God.'

He bowed.

'I am Simon Vosmar. My son was unable to meet you himself. I trust you had a pleasant voyage. And now, if you are ready. . . .'

He turned, pivoting like a dancing master and offered her his arm.

Julia said: 'Please, Mynheer . . .' and turned to Marie who was still staring, wide-eyed. They embraced, with a warmth hitherto unknown in their relationship. Mynheer Vosmar watched them with impatient tolerance and, as they exchanged some muddled promises about meeting soon, he said:

'Doubtless you will–unless this young lady is proceeding to Java.'

They both spoke together–I am–she is–Banda Neira.

'Then you will certainly meet–often,' he said, but there was in his manner a contemptuous dismissal of Marie which Julia resented.

'And there is my baggage, Mynheer,' she said. He dismissed that even more contemptuously.

'That will be seen to.'

The bone of his arm under her hand was sharp and frail, but his hand, as he helped her on to the ladder, had an astonishing strength and steadiness.

They took their places, side by side on yellow silk cushions under the yellow awning; the boat's head swung round and they shot away over the silken water, leaving the curve of the harbour upon their right.

'Well,' said Mynheer Vosmar, and the single word had a note of accomplishment, of finality. Something else was over and done with. After a moment's pause he began afresh.

'I'm very glad to see you. I hope you'll be happy in Rua. My son–as I told you–was unable to meet you.'

'I hope he is not ill.' How perfunctorily polite it sounded.

'Thank you, no. His health is uniformly excellent. He had an accident–a long time ago, and he is recovering, but slowly. He is . . . disabled. That is Rua,' he said, pointing to what, at this distance, was no more than a flat dish, filled with feathery green.

As though the mere sight of his home filled him with impatience to be there, he picked up the silver-knobbed cane which lay at his side and rattled it against the boat, exactly as Julia had seen carters rattle their sticks against the front of their wagons. Just like horses the boatmen increased their efforts for a moment or two and then fell back to the more comfortable pace.

'Rua,' said Mynheer Vosmar, 'is a small *island*, but a large plantation; and it is one of the oldest. My grandfather was producing nutmegs there when Banda was still in a state of chaos. And several times, when catastrophes of various kinds have befallen the Banda groves, they have been replenished by young stock from Rua. My grandfather had his own ships; but now that the Company is so . . . so active, I have given up the ships. Otherwise we remain a self-contained community. We even have *cows* in Rua.'

'Is that very unusual?'

'Most. In fact it is singular. Cows need pasture, you see. On Banda, Lonthoir and Api even gardens are rare and regarded as an extravagance. Why grow a rose where one could grow a nutmeg? My gardens are very beautiful. . . .'

He chatted on and seemed content with her brief responses. As he talked she had an opportunity to study his face and attempt to guess from it something of his nature. It was not a genial face; his pale lips were thin and closely folded, his nose delicate, sharply hooked, an arrogant nose; but it was his eyes which drew and held her attention. They were very large and set far forward between fleshy lids; the prominent eyeballs were yellowish and veined with red, the irises a light, glassy grey. She thought suddenly that with his thin legs, his spare figure and huge eyes he was like an insect.

Perhaps she regarded him a trifle too openly, a second too long, for presently he broke off his talk and shifted a little in his seat and looked at her, so searchingly that she found it difficult to maintain composure.

'You *look* to be a sensible girl,' he said at last. 'I must confess that just now I had a moment. . . . The girl who was with you, to whom is she married?'

'Hendrik Oltman.'

'Oh, yes. A stupid young man, breaking his back with a view to being an Agent one day. He never will!' In three words he banished the young man to perpetual obscurity. 'Look, you can see the house now.'

She had seen a white building, enormously long, single-storied, some moments before he drew her attention to it, and thought that it was a row of sheds or warehouses; it was like no house that she had ever seen before.

'That also is singular,' said Mynheer with great complacency. 'It was my grandfather's most original idea. You will find, when you visit in Banda, that the stupid stubborn Dutchmen build, in this climate, houses exactly like the ones they lived in–or admired from a distance–in Holland. They have bedrooms just under the roof, where it is hottest, and then complain that they cannot sleep! My grandfather had travelled a great deal and when he built, combined most sensibly the principles of a native hut and a Spanish-Moorish house. Above us, between roof and ceiling we have ten feet of cool space, and nowhere is the house more than one room deep, so what air there is can blow through. Actually we suffer less from the heat in Rua than they do in Banda. I think you will soon become accustomed to the climate. This is the hottest season. Soon we shall have the rains.' He lifted his cane again and rattled it threateningly.

The island seemed to rush forward, and soon she could see the house in detail. It was thatched and the thatch jutted out far beyond the walls and was supported by pillars covered with creeping, flowering plants. Urns, set between the pillars, brimmed with flowers.

'It's very beautiful,' Julia said.

He gave her a glance of approval. 'I'm glad you think so. I do,' he said.

The boat ran in alongside a little stone jetty. And now, in just a minute. . . .

'Welcome to Rua,' said Mynheer as he helped her from the boat. 'You are shivering, I do assure you, you have no cause for nervousness. None at all.'

He took her elbow in his firm grasp and led her along the stone path, flanked with smooth green sward, and up the steps of the veranda.

'It faces west,' he said, 'and it is very pleasant to sit here and watch the sun set over the water.'

The entrance to the house was through an archway, and there was no door in the ordinary sense; two gates of fine wrought-iron work which, when closed, would fill the archway were flung back against the walls. Within was a large, stone-paved hall, unfurnished save for a few silky rugs, some statues on pedestals and several small flowering trees growing in huge pots of gaily painted pottery. Later on she was to appreciate the beauty of it all, but at the moment apprehension filled her.

Mynheer Vosmar guided her across the hall and out into a kind of stone cloister overlooking a garden brilliant with colour. They turned right and passed at least a dozen doors before he halted and opened one.

'These,' he said, 'will be your own apartments and of course they must be furnished to your taste. I have merely provided what I thought you would need, and a few things that I hoped would please you. But you must ask for anything you want, anything you fancy. . . .'

She looked, without seeing anything, about the two rooms. Mynheer Vosmar said, peevishly: 'Where is that. . . . Oh, *there* you are. This is Juno whose sole duty will be to look after you.' A handsome woman with a skin like brown silk, had entered silently. She carried a tray in her hands. Mynheer Vosmar inspected it critically and nodded.

'At mid-day we eat very sparingly and take our main meal in the cool of the day. You will find it advisable to rest afterwards–I invariably do myself. I will see you again at four o'clock.' He turned away, swung round again with his dancing-master grace. 'Juno understands Dutch,' he said, 'and she knows her duties, but she is incorrigibly idle. You must keep her up to the mark.' He went away.

'Is hot now, Mevrouw, please,' Juno said in a soft, sibilant voice, indicating a tea-pot that stood on the tray. 'Why I am not here . . . see you come, go make tea hot.'

'I should like some tea.' She went towards the table and Juno pulled a chair a little way out, and pushed it a little way in, took up the pot and poured the tea. The tray was laden; there was meat, sliced very thin, a green salad, some strange but delicious looking fruit, tiny bread rolls, fresh butter. But she could eat nothing; even the tea, delicious and fragrant, went down with difficulty. Twice she had braced herself; once on the ship, and once when entering the house, and each time the ordeal had been postponed. Except for the single remark about his being disabled, Pieter, her husband, had not been mentioned; in his talk Mynheer had never said 'we' in a way which implied 'my son and I'; even when he spoke of preparing these rooms for her he had said 'I provided'. He had also said, 'your own apartments'.

It was impossible to sit still. She put down the cup and stood up.

'You do not like?' Juno asked humbly. 'Other things. Much other. I fetch?'

'Oh, no, thank you. It's all very nice. I'm not hungry now.'

'Mevrouw wish to sleep?'

'I couldn't.' Even the sense of being watched irked her and she walked restlessly from the sitting-room to the bedroom beyond. The rooms communicated by an arch hung with silk curtains, yellow, with white dragons. Each room looked out upon one side to the veranda, upon the other to the cloister and the garden beyond; the windows had no glass, only screens of that same fine iron-work. Even at this, the hottest part of the day in the hottest part of the year, the air flow and the white walls, the pale silver-grey of all the woodwork contributed to an impression of coolness.

Suddenly she noticed, standing alone and looking oddly out of place in the luxurious bedroom, her own small trunk.

There was a job for Juno. She called her.

'You could unpack for me, and spread out my other dress to get rid of the creases.'

'Mevrouw has many dresses.'

'This and one other.' And the other was her wedding dress. . . .

'Many. Please, many dresses.' Juno opened a door and showed a cupboard which might have held a rainbow, five or six dresses in different shades of colour, all delicate, hung there.

'Not finished,' Juno explained. 'I make fit. Wear today.'

Just for a moment her mood lightened. The provision of the dresses showed a kindly forethought–and her welcome, though strange, had been kindly, too. The ordeal was still ahead of her, but what better support could any woman have in any ordeal than a brand new dress? She hadn't had a new dress since her twelfth birthday, except for the wedding dress, and that was now seven months old.

'Which one shall I try first?'

Juno put out a diffident finger and just touched a yellow dress.

'Is Vosmar colour. Mynheer has fondness that colour.'

It was a chance to slip in a question.

'And the young Mynheer, Mynheer Pieter. What colour does he like?'

'Mynheer Pieter ver sick.'

'I know. How sick?'

Juno rolled her fine black eyes, moved her brown hands, alongside but not touching her own head, down, down.

'Sick, all sick,' she said.

'But he might like one colour more than another.'

Juno found the perfect answer and offered it with relief.

'Mynheer Pieter like what Mynheer like.'

'Then I'll try that one,' Julia said.

She always remembered that instance of her father-in-law's passion for detail. He had prepared a wardrobe for an unknown woman; how tall, how plump or slender she was and what her colouring would be, he could not know; so there they were, in many colourings, with the lace ruffles stitched in, the eyelet holes worked for the lacings, the embroidery bright on the skirts, but the hems were not turned up and the side seams not stitched. An hour's work would have made any one of those dresses fit any one of the Company's Daughters.

When the dress was fitted, Juno said:

'Mevrouw sleep now?' But it would be impossible to lie down and be still, and think, and wonder, and surmise.

'Mevrouw like bath?' Answering the questioning look Juno laid the dress aside and opened another door. It opened on to a small square room lined entirely with marble, with an oblong bath sunk into its floor. Some tall white jars with double handles, stood on its edge.

'Mevrouw go there. I fetch water and pour,' Juno explained.

'When the dress is ready,' Julia said. 'Now I'm going in the garden.'

'Much hot. In shade please, Mevrouw.'

Mynheer's pride in his garden was justified; it had been carefully planned so as to seem larger than it was; bright, tough-foliaged native flowers, whose names Julia did not know, grew in open beds that looked like strips of embroidery; roses and lilies were cunningly placed so that they were tree-shaded at noon. In one corner a little artificial mound had been made; on its summit was a seat, shaded by a tree whose branches had been trained over it; and when you sat there and looked straight ahead you saw nothing but a mass of shrubs with dark, shiny spear-shaped leaves and great clusters of blossoms in many shades of pink and purple and beyond them the sea, intensely blue.

Julia sat on the seat and looked at the vista, and the sense that she had come to a very pleasant place and that once the worst was over she might be happy there grew. She pondered the 'disabled' of Mynheer, the 'very sick' of Juno, and began to visualize a gentle invalid, confined to a chair, a man who might, perhaps, make no demands upon his wife except that she be a companion to him. She thought of Mevrouw Helmer's insistence that every girl who had the slightest capacity for it should learn to play chess and backgammon, and she thought how strange it would be if, after all her fears, she should find that there was nothing to fear at all. She knew, from the intimate talks which the long weeks aboard ship had forced upon them, that Marie, indeed perhaps most girls, would little relish the idea of an invalid husband. But it would just suit me, she thought.

The faint hope re-awakened her apprehension and she could no longer sit still. She walked to the bounds of the garden on that side. At one point it ended in a wall, which curved round and made a kind of enclosure against the side of the house. Flowering trees lifted their heads above the wall so there was evidently another garden within, but it was not to be reached from without. She turned back, anxious about time, and went into the house.

At four o'clock she was ready, bathed and dressed, her hair smoothly curled by Juno's expert hands. She looked, she knew, her very best; and Mynheer Vosmar, coming for her punctually at the hour, surveyed her with grave approval.

'I am glad you chose that dress,' he said. 'It is my favourite colour. It is supposed to symbolize *Hope*. Did you know that?'

With a faint smile she shook her head.

'Well it is. And hope is something we must cling to. Now, if you are ready. . . .' He offered her his arm again.

For the last time she braced herself. In a few minutes now she would meet the man with whom her life would be linked until death severed the bond; she would know the worst–or the best, of all she had feared, and hoped for so many months.

But, once again, the critical moment was to be deferred. Instead of taking her directly to her husband, Mynheer Vosmar embarked upon a leisurely tour of the house, explaining its peculiarities and virtues as they moved from room to room, and every now and then lingering, gloatingly, before some special treasure. It was difficult at first to give him her attention, apprehensive as she felt about the coming ordeal, and impatient, now that it was so near, to get it over and done with; but gradually Mynheer's calm, yet insistent claim for her attention succeeded, and her interest woke.

The house covered a good deal of ground, being, as he had said only one room thick anywhere; every room looked out on to the veranda at the front and on to the cloister-like passage at the rear. Most of them could be entered only by doors from the cloister, but some were connected, like her own sitting-room and bedroom, by open archways. Coolness and airiness had been the aim; all the walls were white, the floors of stone, or tiles or polished wood.

'The folly of some settlers is quite unbelievable,' Mynheer said. 'You'll see houses made stifling with rugs and curtains and glass windows. And young women still arrive with feather beds and pillows as part of their dower. The resultant heat rash they blame upon the climate, poor fools!' He paused by a cushioned chair and thumped it. 'Stuffed with raw cotton,' he said, complacently.

He threw open another door and said: 'This is the salon. A beautiful room, I think. Too little used, of late; but now that we have a lady in the house again, things will be different.'

Julia stared around, momentarily forgetful of everything save what she saw. The salon was beautiful–and it was magnificent, too. The walls and the high arched ceiling were white, the floor black and highly polished and everything in the room was black and scarlet and gold. Facing one another from opposite sides were two identical pieces of furniture, the like of which she had never seen before, huge scarlet cupboards standing upon golden pillars, and topped by golden domes, and decorated, all over, with entrancing pictures in black and gold, pictures of birds and butterflies and flowers and twisted trees.

'You are admiring the cabinets,' Mynheer Vosmar said in a satisfied voice. 'They came from China. China is supposed to be the closed land, they boast that nothing goes in and nothing comes out–but my father obtained these, many years ago. He furnished the room around them, so to speak.' He opened one of the doors and showed the arrangement of little drawers, all painted, and the arched recesses. 'Do you play chess?' he asked, with seeming irrelevance.

'A little. Mevrouw Helmers taught us . . . just the rudiments. 'I'm not very good at it.'

'You and I must play,' he said. 'I'm not very good either. I've had no one with whom to play . . . for many years.'

Her latest mental image of Pieter quivered and vanished.

They came at last to a door at the end of the cloister. Ahead of them, just beyond the door, a wall ran out at right angles, ten or twelve feet high and thickly covered by masses of climbing flowers, pink and purple, rose-coloured and white.

'Joshua's Trumpet,' said Mynheer, seeing her admiring stare. 'Well named, left to run riot it could have brought down the walls of Jericho.' He opened the door. 'This is my library,' he said. One side of it was lined with shelves, filled with books. She had never imagined that there were so many books in the world, leave alone in one man's possession. Under the window at the veranda end was a big desk, and a chair. There were other chairs, more comfortable and several low tables upon one of which was a tray bearing a bottle and two tall fluted glasses.

Mynheer Vosmar pulled forward a chair.

'At this time of the day I find a glass of wine agreeable,' he said. 'Well-cooled that is. I hope you like wine.'

It was associated with Mynheer Dekker's announcement, and the gloves, and a feeling of nausea.

'I don't think I do, Mynheer.'

'Then you must learn to,' he said, but quite pleasantly. 'I should hardly imagine that your experience of *good* wine is wide enough to justify an opinion. I chose this for you and had it hung down the well, to cool, before I came to meet you.'

All at once the thought struck her that he was deliberately postponing the moment when she should meet Pieter; the lengthy tour around the house, and now this. . . . Was he nervous too? Was the truth something that even he hesitated to reveal? Without knowing it she linked her fingers and kneaded them.

'You are nervous,' he said. 'I assure you, you have no need to be. Nothing is demanded of you except that you should be happy!' He handed her one of the glasses, and raising his own said: 'To your happiness in Rua.' He took a little formal sip. She said: 'Thank you, Mynheer.'

'One thing will be lacking,' he said. 'How much, or how little that will matter to you I do not know.' His bulging, glassy grey eyes looked over her speculatively, and to cover her embarrassment she lifted her glass. The wine was light and cool and fragrant, almost flowery.

'I told you,' he said, 'that my son had an accident. It happened eighteen years ago, when he was four years old. He had a careless nurse, and she left him alone. He fell.' A change took place in his face as he spoke; his eyes bulged even more and reddened, and she was suddenly conscious of his teeth behind his thin lips. 'He bruised his brain, and it has never healed. You must understand that anything resembling normal married life is quite out of the question.' He looked at her with a faintly challenging air and waited for her to speak. For a moment she could not do so; she was so much relieved, and at the same time obscurely ashamed of her relief. Finally she said in a stiff, prim little voice:

'You have my sympathy, Mynheer. And he . . . I am sorry for him, too.'

He looked at her sharply, and with some surprise.

'You may well, in course of time, become sorry for yourself. You may think that I have brought you here under false pretences. In that case, of course, you have no redress. But if you choose to be helpful and amenable you will find me–not ungrateful. I shall, in any case, do my utmost to enable you to lead a full, and interesting, and I trust happy life. That being understood we may as well go in.'

He rose and to Julia's astonishment, took a bunch of keys from his pocket, and choosing the one he wanted, went across to the door which stood in the centre of the book-lined wall. Opening it he gestured her to pass ahead of him into the room beyond.

Chapter Two

It was a large, well-lighted, sparsely-furnished room; and at a long solid table in the centre two men were sitting, one with his back to the door, the other in profile. The one who had his back to her, and who did not turn round, was, she judged, young, he had light-brown, very dry-looking hair, and wore a bright blue jacket; the other man, who rose as they entered, was older, heavily built, and wore dark clothes with plain white linen bands at his throat. His face was pallid, much lined, and jowly.

Mynheer Vosmar, having closed the door, stepped forward and took Julia by the elbow. He then said, 'Pieter' in a voice of peculiar clarity, as though addressing someone slightly deaf who, at the same time must not be shouted at. Very slowly and clumsily, moving his whole body in order to turn his head, Pieter Vosmar looked round.

She had seen that face, or rather that kind of face before. Once on a little girl who lived in the Hoogstraat, a beautifully dressed little girl who never played with other children and never went out alone. ('Fourteen years old, the poor creature and her mind like a baby's,' Anna had said.) Once on a poor boy who roamed the streets with a little cart, sweeping up horse dung and selling it to people for their gardens. He was known as 'Mucky Karl' and some children regarded him with a half-pleasurable dread, and would call him by that ugly name until he was angry and shambled after them, brandishing his broom. ('He shouldn't be loose; he'll do somebody an injury one of these days,' said Anna.)

She remembered this as she looked at the red, puffy face, with its blunt nose and small red-rimmed eyes and loose damp mouth. She tried not to show, in her face, anything of what she felt.

'Stand up,' Mynheer Vosmar said: 'I've brought someone to see you.'

Clumsily, laboriously Pieter rose, turned himself about and with the air of one who makes a tremendous effort, held out his hand.

'Good morning,' he said. He spoke indistinctly, in a thick, flannelly voice. But his face creased into the caricature of a smile, and taking his hand Julia felt her first revulsion melt into pity. She said:

'Good morning, Pieter. My name is Julia.'

'Julie,' he said; and again, trying it over, 'Julie.'

His hand seemed to have no bones, it lay in hers like a stuffed glove; yet it clung, and there was power in it. He pulled her to the table and pointed to a curious tangle of cane and dried grass with which he had been engaged when interrupted.

'Nice,' he said, 'nice basket.'

'A very nice basket,' she said. 'Very nice indeed.' A piteous expression of pleasure dawned on his face. He pulled at her hand again.

'He won't hurt you,' Mynheer Vosmar said.

'Oh, no, I know that,' she said, and allowed herself to be led across the room to where a clavichord stood open on a smaller table under a window.

'Music,' Pieter said.

'I'm sorry. I can't play.'

'Perhaps some day you can learn a simple tune,' said Mynheer. 'He is very fond of music.'

'I'll try,' she promised. She looked out of the window and noticed that it opened neither on to the veranda, nor the cloister, but directly into a small walled garden, a patch of trampled looking grass, surrounded by flowering bushes. She had just time to see that before Pieter tugged her away again; this time towards an archway opposite the door by which they had entered.

Again Mynheer, watchful, reassuring, said: 'It's all right. I think he wants to show you his garden.'

'It's all right. I'm not afraid of him,' she said.

Beyond the archway was a bedroom of monastic austerity; from it an open doorway led into the little garden. Once there Pieter dropped her hand, and moving very purposefully, went to a bush which bore large clusters of pink flowers.

'Pretty,' he said.

She said: 'Very pretty.' And her throat ached with sadness because he, so grotesque and ugly, yet recognized beauty when he saw it.

He began to tear at the bush, grunting, and breathing hard as he bent and broke the tough, leathery stems from which the pink flower sprang. She was aware that Mynheer Vosmar and the man–keeper, tutor, what did he call himself?–had followed and were standing in the doorway, watching and now and again exchanging a few words.

At last Pieter succeeded in ripping away a bunch of the flowers and turning, held it out to her.

'Pretty,' he said. 'Pretty for . . .' he breathed hard, 'Julie.'

'Thank you, Pieter. Thank you very much.'

It was the first time in all her life that anyone had given her a flower, but instinctively she first held it away and looked at it admiringly, then sniffed at it, and then tucked it into the lacing of her bodice. Pieter gave a kind of caper and then lumbered over to the bush again and tore off another cluster.

Again she accepted it, saying 'Thank you,' but holding it in her hand.

'Pretty,' he insisted, 'pretty for Julie,' and looked at her anxiously. She realized that he wanted her to wear this offering, too. She tried to push the second cluster into place beside the first, and Pieter gave his dreadful, pathetic smile and capered and lurched off again towards the flowering bush. . . . How many more?

Mynheer came to the rescue.

'I think that will do for today,' he said. 'Daan, if you were to play that would distract him and we could slip away.'

The man disappeared and within a few seconds the music rang out, masterfully and beautifully played. Pieter ceased his mangling of the bush, turned, and without a glance at his father or his wife, blundered towards the clavichord.

'Come,' said Mynheer.

As soon as they were back in the library Mynheer turned from her and walked to the window. She saw him put his hand over his mouth and grip his lower jaw. He was fighting for self-control and all at once the pity which, half an hour earlier had been merely a matter of words, sprang up in her, real, vital, over-ruling all the other mingled emotions of the moment. She said nothing, but walking over to the book shelves, studied the seried titles attentively.

After a moment he said, in a far more warm and friendly tone than any he had so far used:

'You will excuse me, my dear. God knows I have had time to accustom myself. It was the occasion which made it seem less than usually tolerable. My only son . . . meeting his wife . . . for the first time. It should have been very different.'

She did not know, at that moment, the reach and vastness of his pride in his family, in his name, which was the motive power of his life; the dynastic aspect of the tragedy was hidden from her. She saw a rather frail-looking, elderly man grieving over his son's affliction.

'I'm very sorry,' she said, 'more for you than for Pieter. He seems quite happy.'

Mynheer said, a trifle harshly: 'He has no reason to be otherwise. You did very well. It must have been a considerable shock for you. I thought it wise to hide nothing from you. But you need never again enter that room, unless you wish. He is not, I realize, a pleasant sight.'

'Sad, but not unpleasant,' she said, with a degree of firmness. 'Unless my presence upsets him in any way I should like to help to amuse him. He is gentle, and means well. I found him rather–touching.'

Mynheer looked at her with an expression which she did not recognize as distaste. This product of an Amsterdam orphanage, this virtually nameless nobody had looked upon the heir to Rua and found him 'touching'. Now, surely, he had drained the last dreg of his degradation.

He said: 'I'm sure that if you care to devote a little time to the poor boy Doctor Hootman will be very grateful. But that must be as you wish. Don't look upon it as a duty. You were not brought here for Doctor Hootman's benefit.'

That enabled her to ask the question which, from the moment when Pieter turned his head, had been nagging at her.

'Why was I brought here? I mean, Mynheer, you must have known . . . all along . . . that Pieter did not need a wife.'

He did not immediately answer. He turned from the window, and she from the book shelves, and now they were facing one another across the room.

'That is one thing that you must understand,' he said. 'I have managed to conceal from the world, even from other branches of my own family, the extent and the nature of the damage sustained by Pieter when he had his accident. It has not always been easy. I have let it be known that he is disabled and disfigured and has become of his own choice, a recluse. I believe that rumour–always so kind–has it that he is so grossly ugly that he cannot bear to be looked upon. That I do not mind. My business has been to hide the fact that he is mentally infirm. Obviously, my only son, whatever his appearance, would be expected to marry, one day. You are a pretty girl, and, which matters more, a presentable one. I shall be very proud to say: "This is my daughter-in-law." That will confound the gossiping fools. And if you prop up my story and play your part well, you will find me very grateful.'

'I understand, Mynheer.' She was on the point of adding that she already had cause to be grateful to him. The dark threatening figure of 'your husband' had been laid low, never to rise again; she was grateful for that. But something checked her tongue. Partly it was the selfish caution inculcated by the years in the Klopstock Home. Let him feel himself indebted, let him *be* grateful. Partly it was a flash of unselfish insight. After all, it was only by the merest accident of chance that she, who did not wish to be married at all, had come here to be part of a marriage that was no marriage. Suppose it had been Marie, or any one of any other dozen girls who really wanted a husband and a normal married life. . . . Mynheer had, quite obviously, given no thought to how the girl would feel. Let him be grateful!

She said: 'I shall always do my best to try to please you.'

'Yes. I think you will. I think we shall get on very well together. The situation is unusual, I admit, but I hope you will find that it is not without compensations.'

She remembered suddenly, and with great clarity, her interview with Mevrouw Helmers, and the kind easy voice saying that God never made mistakes. Could it be, dare one for a moment believe it to be, true?

Chapter Three

Doctor Hootman dined with Julia and Mynheer, and by the end of the meal she had formed the opinion that he was a sulky and unfriendly person. Mynheer sat at the head of the table in a high-backed chair which did not match the others; Julia sat on his right hand, Doctor Hootman on his left, so they were face to face across the table. Inevitably, now and again she would look up and meet his eyes–dull brown eyes, heavily pouched, and always he looked away hastily. He did not speak a word to her, nor did he once smile, and when addressed by Mynheer, answered in a brusque way which dismissed her first impression, which was that he was in great awe of his employer.

Mynheer seemed unaware of any discordant note. He talked easily and well, and encouraged her to talk, and tried, repeatedly, to draw Doctor Hootman into the conversation. He was–she was to learn–always at his best at table; for him meals had a certain ceremonial value, and even when he was suffering some emotional stress, he would set it aside and preside at his table with a detached and punctilious courtesy.

He told her the name of the main dish–rysttafel.

'We have it very often, but it has so many variations that I never tire of it. If, after a time, you do, my dear, you must say so.'

She thought she would never tire of it; not only was it delicious, it was so nice to look at. It was served in a great number of very delicate china bowls of varying sizes, all beautifully painted, both inside and out, with flowers and reeds and blossoming twigs. The largest bowl was full of rice, the smaller ones held eggs, meat, fish, vegetables and spicy preserves in a bewildering number, prepared in unusual ways. You helped yourself, Mynheer explained, to a mound of rice and then added whatever you fancied.

'Some of the side dishes will taste strange to you, but you will become accustomed to them in time. At least I hope so. I deplore the attitude of some in the islands who insist upon oversmoked ham and salted herrings. Their leathery Dutch cheese I must forgive–they have no choice.'

He gave one of his complacent glances at the side table, where on a silver dish, in a nest of crisp green leaves, a large freshly made cream cheese lay.

They were waited upon by a brown man, who looked, to Julia's unaccustomed eye, exactly like Juno, but male. His name was Pluto.

'My grandfather,' Mynheer explained, 'instituted the custom of naming all his house-slaves after characters in mythology, and I adhered to it.'

'With some strange results,' said Doctor Hootman, 'Cupid for example.'

Mynheer gave him a sharp look, but said, agreeably:

'That is so; but they are named as babies and who can tell what their looks will be later on. As with dogs; an aunt of mine named a puppy 'Tiny' and it was the size of a donkey when full grown.'

Pluto removed the last plates and then the glistening white table cloth, not folding it carefully for use again, but gathering it into a bundle. Mevrouw Helmers, discoursing upon behaviour, had spoken of gentlemen sitting over their wine, and of ladies retiring with promptitude. But Mynheer was speaking as the cloth was withdrawn, and he went on, composedly. And then Pluto set the table again, with plates of the same flowered pattern, and with huge bowls, piled with fruit, and with small bowls with water in them. Flower-petals floated on the water.

Mynheer finished speaking, and Julia, following Mevrouw Helmer's instructions said: 'Mynheer, I will leave you.'

'Oh no,' he said. 'No formality when we are alone. I want to introduce you to some of our Rua fruits.' He leaned forward and studied the bowls. 'Pears, of course, you know. These are not good. They are Chinese stock but even so the climate is too moist for them; edible and that is all one can say. These are mangoes–I think myself the most delicious of all fruit, the peach, the nectarine and the apricot, all in one, with something in addition. And these, in Malabar, are called *pala*, but the African name is banana–they, I contend are an acquired taste, I have never, myself, acquired it. This curious looking thing is a pineapple–aptly named, don't you think? May I prepare you a piece, at least an inch of its outside must be cut away. . . .'

She tried everything, and everything was delicious. Copying Mynheer she dipped her fingers now and then into the flower-strewn water which was delicately scented. Her sense of having come to a beautiful, comfortable, wonderful place grew, and grew. She thought of her own room, the wide, silk-covered bed where she would sleep, alone, untroubled–for the first time in many months–by the thought of another bed, to be shared by 'your husband'. Oh, how soundly she would sleep tonight! Suddenly and, she felt, with an appalling lack of manners, she yawned.

'How inconsiderate I am,' Mynheer said instantly. 'You must be very tired after such a day. Allow me to take you to your room.'

'I can find it myself, Mynheer.'

'Very well. Juno will be there. Good night–Julia.'

'Good night, Mynheer.' She hesitated, looking towards Doctor Hootman, but he was rather ostentatiously giving his attention to the peeling on his fourth banana. And Mynheer was waiting, holding the door for her. As she passed him she smiled and he said, almost fondly, 'Good night, my dear. Sleep well.'

He closed the door, and turning back into the room, looked at Doctor Hootman's back with a scowl. It was gone however by the time he had reached his own place at the table, and his tone was genial as he refilled his glass and said:

'You are in a peculiar mood this evening, Daan. What's the matter?'

Doctor Hootman raised his heavy eyes, and speaking deliberately said: 'In the comparatively humble station in which I was reared it was thought desirable that a man should be introduced to a woman before he engaged her in conversation.'

'Good God!' Mynheer said. 'Did I omit to do that? I apologize. I must confess I was very much pre-occupied. I fully expected a scene, you know.'

'All the same, I think that the owner of the menagerie, bringing a visitor into the cage, would have said: "This is Doctor Hootman, who has charge of the wild beast".'

'I find that a very offensive comparison.'

'I found your behaviour this afternoon very offensive.'

'Daan, don't be silly. It was remiss of me, I admit; but think of the situation. I should never have thought you were so touchy.'

Doctor Hootman hunched a heavy shoulder.

'No, dealing as you do, exclusively with slaves and sycophants you are bound to become insensitive to other people's feelings. I am not your slave, or your sycophant; merely a hireling. Hired to attend, control and as far as possible, train your idiot son.'

Mynheer Vosmar was not an impulsive man given to words or gestures, but now he brought his hand down on the table with a smack which slopped the wine from the glasses and made several pieces of fruit hop from their dish and go rolling about the table.

'I will not have him called that! Idiots are born, not made. Pieter was like anybody else until that pig of a woman let him fall.'

Doctor Hootman swallowed the last piece of banana, dipped his fingers and wiped them.

'It pleases you to think so. But it isn't true. He was a born idiot; but since, in the first few years of a child's life no great demand is made upon the intelligence, that fact escaped your notice. When you could no longer ignore it you seized upon the nearest excuse–a timely, trivial bump on the head. But that isn't true and nothing you can say or do can make it so.'

It was one of those speeches, stating a truth too impalatable to be accepted, which, aimed at a wider target, have often taken the speaker a long step towards martyrdom. Had Mynheer Vosmar, been at that moment, a mob, with many mouths, every one of them would have been open, yelling, 'To the Stake': 'To the Gallows': 'To the Cross'. His eyes did bulge and redden, but although he was angry, his anger was not pure; it had an alloy of curiosity.

'What makes you say this now? Is it just a retaliation for my lapse of manners this afternoon, or something more?'

Before answering Doctor Hootman lifted his glass and with finicky care wiped first the foot of it, and then the place where the wine had slopped over when Mynheer had hit the table. He sipped, swallowed, and sipped again.

'I was,' he said, 'annoyed this afternoon. Taken for granted, treated like a piece of furniture. Still . . .' he shrugged again, 'let that go. I had another reason for frank speaking. I agree with you that providing Pieter with a wife was a very pleasing little touch to the façade. And you were fortunate . . . she seems sensible. But it is my duty, at this point to warn you.'

'To warn me?' Mynheer said. 'What do you mean?'

'Shove them into bed together,' Doctor Hootman said brutally, 'and you'll have an idiot grandchild on your hands.

Mynheer lifted his glass and with a fastidiousness matching his companion's, wiped it, and the wet ring from the table top.

'You've been with me for eight years,' he said solemnly, 'it doesn't seem possible that you can so entirely misjudge and misunderstand me. I never dreamed. . . . I should no more think of shoving them into bed together as you term it, than I should think of . . . of . . . well, taking Juno into my own bed. I don't believe, and you will never make me believe, that Pieter was a born idiot, but he is an idiot now. The very idea is obscene. And the result might very well be as you say, another idiot. No, what I have in mind is something quite different. Shall I tell you?'

Doctor Hootman's expression, which had relaxed into relief, tightened again, became wary. As though he knew this, he looked down at his plate, and then up again, with a carefully blank face which matched his careless. 'If you like.'

'You've been in my confidence from the first,' Mynheer said, 'and you've done marvels for Pieter. Perhaps you should know what I propose: it may make you feel a little less like a piece of furniture.' His eyes twinkled. 'Listen,' he said.

Chapter Four

Around her, day by day, the new life fell into pattern. It was a life of unimaginable ease and luxury, and of leisure which, as Mevrouw Helmers had warned, might become tedious to anyone incapable of finding occupation for herself.

The day began early. At dawn the great brass tong-tong in the compound sounded the call to begin work. Mynheer always rose then and went to the plantation. Julia, who often slipped out of bed and looked out of the window to enjoy the sight of the dew-drenched garden, striped with sunshine and long shadows, would see the spare, trim figure, stepping daintily across the lawn towards a pergola, thickly hung with roses, which marked the boundary of the garden upon that side.

Almost immediatley Juno would come, with a beaker of cool sweet fruit juice and a pot of the peculiarly fragrant tea. In her soft velvet voice she would wish Julia good morning and inquire if she had slept well, and what she would like for breakfast. Then she would vanish again, to return with an armful of freshly laundered linen, a smoothly ironed dress, clean shoes.

On most mornings, by the time she was dressed and had had breakfast, Mynheer was back, and had had his. During her first week on Rua he devoted what remained of the cool morning hours to showing her over the island.

The nutmeg trees, evergreen, feathery and sweet-scented grew in orderly groves all over the island, and paths ran this way and that through the green gloom.

'It's hardly likely that you would ever lose yourself,' said Mynheer. 'But if you should, don't keep taking side turnings; keep straight on. Eventually all the main paths run out at the shore.'

He enjoyed showing her things and explaining how the 'nuts' were gathered, and dried in racks over slow fires, turned at regular intervals until the outer shells could be broken and stripped away; how every nutmeg must be plunged into a lime bath to be made sterile: the whole wealth and importance of the islands depended upon the monopoly, so no fertile nut must ever be shipped out. Julia watched and listened and tried to remember, hoping in time to know enough to be an acceptable companion to him.

Everywhere they went the slaves were working and there was never any flurry when Mynheer appeared. Rua was a well-run plantation, with just a hint of running by clockwork, she thought. The slaves all looked well-fed and were far better clothed than many she was to see later in the streets of Banda; Mynheer's passion for uniformity extended to his slaves' wearing apparel; even the lowest grade, those who gathered the nuts, even the children, wore neat, taut loin-cloths of the Vosmar yellow, in a coarse cotton material. Overseers wore drawers, like the boatmen.

The slaves were of all colours, from dark blackish brown, to pale coffee colour. There were, Mynheer explained, no Bandanese amongst them. The natives of this island group, having put up a fierce and bloody resistance to the white men had then taken flight; what remained of them now lived on two small islands, 'very fine people, the aristocrats of the islands,' said Mynheer, 'they would not have made good slaves.'

In one of the drying sheds Julia was surprised to see a white man wearing the overseers' yellow drawers and armed with the overseers' cane. He was out of earshot, so she mentioned him, and her surprise to Mynheer.

'If you were nearer to him you would see that he is not quite white, my dear. Very nearly, yes. His mother, I should say, had some white blood, and his father, I know, was a Dutchman. These things happen, you know.' He gave her a little sideways glance. 'Most regrettable, I agree. Such a thing has never happened in Rua.'

'Why is he a slave? If his father was Dutch?'

'The child of a slave is a slave, my dear, whatever his colour. This one, his name is Mercury, was one of a batch I bought some years ago. I tried him as a house slave–that is why he has a house-slave's name, but it didn't do at all. His manners were bad, and he . . . well, he was above himself. He actually used to try on my clothes. I caught him at it, preening in front of my looking-glass.'

'What did you do?'

'Burnt the clothes of course, and degraded him to plantation work. It was kinder really. When he'd learned his lesson I made him overseer, and he is excellent. He hates everybody–which is a splendid thing for one in his position.'

Despite the heat in the drying shed she was conscious of a little chill. In a few words, neither callous nor sentimental, Mynheer had told a tragic story. She cast another discreet glance at the subject of it; he had turned and was now in profile to her. He had a fine profile, with a nose as arrogant as Mynheer's.

'What a sad story,' she said.

'Yes. The least his father could have done–in my opinion–was to free him and have him taught a trade. But he shuffled off his responsibility and we can't alter that, can we? Come along, it is very warm here.'

On another morning Mynheer said: 'Now I will show you the compound. That is one place which I should wish you to avoid. Oh, not that there's any danger; they're all tame enough, but they are primitive and one has to allow them a certain freedom there. You might see some unedifying sights. . . .'

The compound lay, as nearly as she could judge, in the very centre of the island. It consisted of a circle of small, low huts ringing a space of bare stamped earth in the middle of which was a well. A few immensely old, or extremely pregnant women were cooking on little fires outside the doors of the huts, a number of children, too small yet for work, were playing, rather listlessly in the dust. Here, unlike other places which they had visited, their arrival did cause some disturbance. The women left their fires and stood up; the children ceased playing and huddled together.

'I don't often come here,' Mynheer explained. 'Three generations of us, at the very least, to my certain knowledge have tried to enforce some rules of cleanliness. Fifteen years ago I had every hut burnt, the whole compound dug over, tons of sand from the beach spread, two feet thick and stamped down, and these huts erected. But look at it now. Smell it!'

It reeked of too many people, too closely pressed together; woodsmoke, the stink of the pan of rice that had boiled dry, the fat that had flamed, the dough that had gone sour, the meat that had scorched, the sick baby, the burnt rag . . . it was all there, intermingled with the overwhelming, main odour of human excreta. It was the smell of defeat, too.

She looked at the children. All but one of them looked healthy enough and some were quite beautiful. The one was a little boy, three, four years old, with sore eyes.

She said to Mynheer, who, having said 'smell it!' was looking this way and that with evident disgust.

'Mynheer, that little boy. . . . Mevrouw Helmers at the Company Daughters' Home, told us how to make an ointment which she said would cure all sores. I have the recipe for it written in my book. May I try it on him?'

'Just a minute, my dear,' he said. 'Now that I am here, I must look in on Toeg. He was once one of my boatmen, and when we capsized in a sudden storm, he saved my life. If he knew that I had been in the compound and not visited him I think his heart would break.' He moved purposefully towards a hut, almost immediatley opposite the well, and she went with him. 'I think perhaps you had better stay outside,' he said. 'I don't know how far you are capable. . . . Toeg suffers you see, from a very rare, and–if you are capable of detachment–a very interesting disease; but it isn't pretty.'

They had reached the door of the hut, which, even from the outside, looked better kept than the others.

'What is the disease?'

'Nobody knows. It is called, for obvious reasons, elephantiasis. Of course, if you could face it, a visit from you would be. . . . I can hardly explain what it would mean to Toeg.'

'Then I can face it,' she said.

Ducking his head at the low doorway Mynheer entered the hut and she followed him. Inside the hut, seated on a solid wooden bench was a tiny, shrivelled brown man with a monkey's face and grey speckled hair. Laid out on a kind of low table in front of him was a leg, one enormous leg, larger, thicker, bigger round than the whole of his body.

As though from a great way off she heard Mynheer say:

'Toeg, I've brought the young Mevrouw. Mynheer Pieter's Mevrouw, to see you.'

A voice, so small, so throaty as to be almost inaudible, said: 'Greetings, Mevrouw. God is kind to let me see this day.'

A small brown monkey's hand came out, and she put her own to it–just touching her finger tips Toeg lifted it to his brow.

'They're looking after you properly?' Mynheer asked.

'In every way, Mynheer, your orders are obeyed.

'You get your meat?'

'Three times in every week.'

'Splendid,' said Mynheer, briskly, sweeping a critical glance about the hut, and seeming satisfied with what he saw. 'Keep that daughter-in-law of yours up to the mark, Toeg; and if you want anything, let me know.' He smiled at the old man affectionately and they took their leave.

Outside Mynheer said: 'Now what were you saying? Oh, I remember. Sore eyes and ointment. The suggestion does you credit, my dear, but I'm afraid there's nothing you can do, in that way. That the boy? Ah, yes, I see what you mean; nasty sight. But your ointment would do more harm than good.'

'Mevrouw Helmers had great faith in it . . .' she said.

'Mevrouw Helmers probably knew more about ointment than about slaves. All these people are very mixed, races, religions, nonsensical observances,' his voice hardened and his glassy eyes reddened. 'I'll give you an example–that child may be Hindu, we have a few here; you put something greasy on his eyes; fat from a cow, sacred animal; his eyes may get better, they probably would, but his grandmother would fall and break both legs; his mother would miscarry and his father go blind; and who would be to blame? You and your ointment. Or he may be a Moslem; then your ointment would be suspected of being made from lard, untouchable pig. Again, his eyes might get better, but he would be unclean for the rest of his life, his aunts would all go crazy and his children be born dumb!' He paused. 'You think I exaggerate? I do not, I assure you. The amount of superstition in this one compound is unbelievable. Within my lifetime a Hindu family here, in this place, were all hell-bent to shove a widow into the fire where her husband's body was burning. I had to go down and rescue her myself, nobody else could stop them. They're best left entirely alone.'

'With their sore eyes?'

'Now you're not to fret about that,' he said in a kinder voice, 'when the moon is right and all the other auguries auspicious, they'll daub on some cure of their own–some holy man's spit and cow dung, or something like that. And it'll work; they'll have faith in it, which they wouldn't in your ointment you see. And faith will move mountains.'

'Even superstitious faith?'

'Any sort of faith. Even–no, not even, most of all faith in oneself.'

After the morning walks, and again after her rest in the afternoon she would go along to Pieter's room and help to amuse him. He always greeted her with every sign of affection and pleasure, smiling his wide, pitiable smile, and rubbing his head against her. Very soon she was hardly aware of his appearance, conscious only of his gentleness, his pathetic anxiety to please and his fondness for her. She had known so little affection, since Johannes's death, that even that of an idiot boy was not to be despised. She developed a corresponding fondness for him, as for an ugly but good-natured dog.

Now, as he completed each piece of fumbled handiwork he would present it to her. 'Pretty for Julie.' He knitted her a scarf of bright purple wool, wide at one end, narrow at the other and full of holes where he had dropped stitches, and little as a scarf was needed in Rua, at that season, she wore it often when she visited him, remembering the hours of frowning, hard-breathing labour that had gone to its making.

Sometimes they went into his little garden, and there she would play ball with him. His movements were too clumsy and unpredictable to allow him to catch a thrown ball, but he loved to retrieve it when it was thrown and bring it back to her to throw again. When she tired he would scrawl on the ground with a stick, or gather flowers–'Pretty for Julie', until her lap was full.

These visits brought her into frequent contact with Doctor Hootman. His original surly manner, which she now attributed to shyness, had changed into one of formal civility, and there it rested. He seemed neither to encourage nor to resent her visits. As soon as she arrived he would turn away and busy himself, tidying cupboards and drawers, preparing something for Pieter's next employment, or simply reading his book. Sometimes he would say: 'Don't let him tire you. Mevrouw'; and occasionally, 'I think that will do; it does him no good to get excited.' His manner towards his charge was unvarying, kindly, authoritative, oddly impersonal. He had two words of rebuke, 'dirty' and 'naughty'; he used them sparingly, but when he did Pieter would hang his head and seem to wilt, to grow smaller, like a scolded dog.

The late afternoons usually found her with Mynheer on the veranda to watch the swift, dramatic going down of the sun over the sea; and often, while the sky flowered and faded, and the earth poured out its many-flavoured scents, and the sea whispered on the beach and slapped against the little jetty, from the compound there would come the sound of music, played on the gamelins, strange, monotonous, rather mournful, muted by distance and sweet, it would come to them and weave a kind of spell, so that to speak, or move, demanded a definite effort. Sometimes Mynheer would touch her hand, or her shoulder:

'It's pleasant here, is it not? I hope you are happy?'

'Very happy, Mynheer.'

'Not lonely? Not bored? Not sorry you came?'

She could truthfully say no to such questions.

'All the same,' he would say, 'I must not be selfish. We must entertain; go visiting; you must make a call on your little friend.'

She grew fond of him, too; there was nothing intimidating about him when you came to know him; the formal stateliness of his manner made his occasional unbending the more to be valued; he was an easy, undemanding companion, and if, now and then his conversation had a cynical flavour she reminded herself that he was old, ripe in experience, and that she was young.

And so the golden, sun-drenched, scented days went by.

The weather grew warmer, or, if not warmer, more oppresssive. The days were not invariably fine; it rained–she thought–quite often, sudden showers falling from what was virtually a clear sky, sometimes even through the sunshine. The rain would cease as abruptly as it had begun, and all the wet leaves would steam. But Mynheer and Doctor Hootman and Juno were all beginning to talk of the rainy season which was coming. The real rain, upon which the crop and everything else depended; the rain which would soak in and cool the earth. They held it out to her–the newcomer–as a kind of promise: 'Soon the rain will come.' 'It will be cool.' Mynheer produced, from some hidden treasure chest, a shawl of fine lace, silky, not quite white, white which had lost its purity from being laid away, for a long time, in darkness.

'When the rains come, my dear, you may be glad of this in the evenings. Tell Juno to hang it out in the sun.'

There came an afternoon when, rising from her rest, she was aware of a change, something missing. The light had altered. It was just as hot–even hotter–but there was no sunshine, and the slight movement of the air, too slight to be called a breeze, which, in Rua, had tempered the heat hitherto and made it tolerable, had ceased to flow between the veranda and the cloister. Pushing her damp hair from her forehead she went to the window and looked out at the garden. Every leaf, every flower, even the hardy cannas, the native orchids, looked limp, their vitality drained away. Something threatened and they cowered under the threat.

Inside the room it was gloomy and stifling. It would be better, she thought, out of doors. She went, moving listlessly to her favourite place in the garden, the seat on the little mound by the bank of flowers–azaleas, as she now knew. The mention of impending rain suggested clouds, but there were none, just a sullen, dark purple-grey pall drawn over the sun and the blueness; under it the sea lay flat, leaden coloured, and the pink and rose-colour and scarlet of the bank of flowers had not so much faded as been drowned in the general gloom.

It was very depressing and after a few minutes during which her spirits sank lower and lower and she began, for the first time, to feel homesick and lonely, she jumped up and decided to go for a walk. In the groves, between the tall trees, it was always shady, and there, she imagined, the change in the light would be less noticeable. She would not, she decided, go far, in case the rain began.

The main path, the one Mynheer took each morning on his way through the compound, began at the edge of the garden, behind a pergola of carefully trained roses. It ran straight, but branching off from it were many paths, well used by the slaves who gathered the nutmegs. Julia knew them all by this time, and knew that by taking any left-hand turn she came through the groves and out at the shore. Ordinarily, in order to take as long a walk as possible she pursued the main path until she was almost at the forbidden compound and then turned off. Today, on account of the threatening rain she took the first turning.

She had been wrong, she realized, to imagine that in the groves the change in the weather would be less noticeable; the purplish gloom, with the strange sense of foreboding which it conveyed, was thick in the narrow path, and the heat was stifling. It was stupid to have come for a walk, the house would have been much cooler. She came to a standstill and stood hesitant; would it be quicker to walk on, reach the place where the path came out on the shore, or turn back and retrace her steps? The gloom seemed to deepen as she stood there. And then she heard the sound, a low, miserable moaning, the sound of someone in pain. She listened, trying to determine from what direction the sound came, never an easy thing to do, and less easy here amongst these closely growing trees. Listening, she realized that she could no longer hear the doves. She imagined that the sound came from ahead of her along the path, but not directly, slightly to the left, she thought. She moved forward, and the noise seemed to come more clearly, but she could see nothing that would account for it. Then she saw, on her left, the opening of a path much more narrow than any of the others which intersected the groves. They were all wide enough to allow the passage of two men with a load of nutmegs slung between them, this was a mere track and not, by the look of it, much used.

In the purple, ominous gloom it had an uninviting, almost a sinister look and she hesitated before entering it. But she was certain now that the moaning came from somewhere along it. A few steps brought her to a length of fencing, made of roughly hewn tree trunks placed close together. The fence ran parallel with the path, was about ten feet high, and had no opening; but it was a mere façade, one had only to step into the grove to get behind it. The agonized sound came from its other side, and now, mingling with it she could hear a clink, a rattle, as though someone were shaking a chain.

Again she stood hesitant. She had a very clear feeling that behind the fence might be something that she would not wish to see, perhaps should not see; much the easiest thing would be to turn and hurry away. But someone, or something–for the moaning noise sounded sometimes human and sometimes not–was behind that fence and in trouble. Also she herself was curious. She stepped into the grove and rounded the fence.

At the back of it some trees had been hacked down and in the space stood a square cage. The bars were five or six inches apart, and behind them she could see something which moved and moaned and rattled a chain. Unwillingly, touched already by dread, she went near and put her face to the opening between two of the wooden bars. A stout post stood in the centre of the cage and attached to it by a length of chain linked about its waist was . . . what? For a moment Julia thought it was some kind of monkey; it was bent over, very brown, shrivelled, and had its back to her as it strained against the chain and towards the bars on the farther side of the cage. And all the time it moaned and whimpered.

As she watched it turned, ran back and then lunged forward again, rattling the chain. With a slow, draining sense of horror Julia realized that it was a woman, skeleton thin and stark naked.

Moving almost unwillingly she went around the cage to the side where the woman was scrabbling at the bars. Then she understood. Just outside, just out of reach, stood a bucket with some water in it and two little wooden bowls, one empty and one containing a handful of rice. She looked from them to the face of the woman behind the bars and was so shocked that she turned dizzy and found herself suddenly addressing God–Don't let me faint, keep me up so I can do something.

She kept up, and she did something. She took the empty bowl, dipped it in the bucket and pushed it between the bars. The woman seized it, drained it, thrust it out again. There was just enough water in the bucket to fill the little bowl three times; the last time Julia set the bowl down and tipped the bucket to pour out the very last drop. When the bowl was returned she said:

'I'm sorry, there isn't any more,' and her voice sounded as though she had been crying for a long time.

She handed in the rice bowl. She noticed the rice as she did so; it had been cooked some time before and in the day's heat had begun to dry and curl again. Even if the three little doles of water had quenched the woman's thirst for the moment such arid fare would quicken it again.

The woman took the bowl and held it under her chin with one hand while with the other she scooped and shovelled the rice into her mouth. She did not chew, she swallowed, just as a dog, watched by another, would swallow food. Four dips, four gulps and the bowl was empty. She handed it back and retreated towards the post in the centre of the cage, squatted down on the heap of filth which lay there, put her elbows on her knees and her head between her hands and from under the curtain of matted black hair regarded Julia with a dull, incurious, animal stare.

People did go mad, of course; there were people so mad they tore off their clothes; so mad that for their own safety and the safety of others they had to be very strictly confined. It was possible that this was a mad woman, and that today whoever had the duty of looking after her had forgotten. One mustn't go jumping to hasty conclusions, imagining the worst. There might be some explanation.

She gathered her skirt, a handful on each side, and began to run, but running meant drawing quick breaths and today there seemed to be nothing to breathe. No air, and though it was still half an hour before sunset, no light; the heavy purple pall pressed down, closer and closer, stifling, blinding. It was like the end of the world. It was like one of those dreams when you run and run, from some undefined but dreadful thing, and run and run, and make no progress.

Breathless and quite distraught, she came to the rose pergola; that, too, was changed, no longer a pleasant, shaded place through which to walk idly, a dark tunnel now, littered with shrivelled petals, going brown at the edges.

It was with the utmost relief that she saw, coming towards her, wiping his neck with his handkerchief, Mynheer. He moved with his ordinary, nimble, dancing master's grace.

'My dear Julia,' he said, as soon as he was within speaking distance: 'I have been worried about you. I should have warned you not to go far today. The rains are about to begin.' A low, long drawn-out rumble of thunder shook the dark pall that hid the sky. 'You might have been caught and drenched,' he said. 'Or frightened by the early darkness. Take my arm, you're out of breath.'

She could not speak. She took his arm gratefully and he hurried her across the lawn towards the house. Another clap of thunder shook the very air and a few, very large, very deliberate-seeming drops of water showered down.

'I should have prepared you. I do blame myself,' Mynheer said, as they reached the steps of the cloister. 'It came very suddenly. My dear, it is only thunder, there is no reason to be alarmed. You are trembling. Come and sit down.' He led her to the salon and up to one of the red and gold covered chairs. She sat down, mastered her breath, and said:

'It isn't the thunder. I've just seen something *horrible*.'

'In the compound?' he asked sharply.

'No. In a cage. A woman . . . on a chain . . . in a cage . . . starving.'

'Oh.' The single word rang out as it might have done had she hit him in the face. 'She isn't starving. She is keeping Ramadan–a Moslem fast.'

Horror receded. If the torment was self-inflicted, part of some strange creed . . . then it was different. Sick pity gave way to a puzzled, unwilling admiration. She steadied herself, brushed back her damp hair and wiped her hands on her handkerchief.

'She looked so awful. I thought she might be mad.'

'She may be, now. She was sane enough once,' said Mynheer, and his voice was cold, cruel. Julia, looking at him, startled, curious, saw the exact expression which had been on his face when, on her first day, he had mentioned Pieter's fall.

'Is she ? Oh, no!' she said, putting her hand to her mouth.

'She is Psyche. She was Pieter's nurse. She was a Moslem so she must keep the Fast of Ramadan; that means that for a full lunar month nothing, no food or water, may pass the lips between the moment in the morning when a white thread can be distinguished from a black one and the same moment in the evening. One evening, at the end of a parching day, she left him, to fetch herself a cup of water, and he fell. So, since Ramadan meant so much to her, more than her duty or my child's well-being, I decreed that she should keep it for the rest of her life.' The disturbance in his face had not invaded his voice, he spoke calmly and with great simplicity.

'How cruel!' she said.

'That I can hardly deny. What I can deny is that her suffering has matched mine, or could, if she stayed there for a thousand years.'

There was something frightening about his absolute calm, his imperviousness. It denied the friendly, almost fond relationship which had built up from day to day between them; her opinion, anything she might say, meant nothing to him. Knowing this, sensing the futility, even the unwisdom of saying anything more, she yet felt compelled to attack.

'You can't even be sure that she *was* to blame. I knew two people who looked exactly like Pieter, in Amsterdam. They hadn't both had falls!'

How can you be sure of that? In any case this is quite irrelevant. Pieter fell and is as he is, and Psyche is where she is. 'And think,' his voice lightened, became sardonic, 'of the merit she is acquiring. In the next life she will doubtless be Mahomet's plumpest houri–or better still, his favourite camel.'

She thought of the cage, the woman squatting on the heaped filth . . . of the cold-hearted spite which could take so protracted a vengeance for a moment's carelessness . . . and her soul sickened.

'You see, you must be careful never to provoke me,' Mynheer said. 'I had no idea that you would penetrate so far, or I should have warned you. I'm warning you now. Don't walk that way again. You have no need to go in search of objects of pity, you know. Pity yourself. A married woman without a husband, and with no hope of children.'

The silence that followed his words was broken by the sudden roar and hiss of the rain.

Chapter Five

The finding of Psyche had ruined Julia's sense of being perfectly happy in a perfectly beautiful place. She was like a person who, having bitten into an apple, lowers it and sees the fat maggots crawling; the impulse is to spit out the bitten piece and throw the apple away. But life, circumstances, relationships with other people are not to be so lightly abandoned.

The emotional disturbance, coinciding as it did with the season of heavy, almost persistent rain, when exercise out of doors was impossible, resulted in wakeful nights, haunted by the thought of the woman in the cage, and also by worrying thoughts about herself and Mynheer. He had dismissed the matter entirely, and although for some days her manner to him had been stilted and unfriendly, his to her remained exactly the same, indulgent, paternal.

Lying awake, listening to the drip and patter of the rain, she tried to think, coolly, reasonably, and finally came to the conclusion that merely feeling sickened, sorry, disgusted was not enough. She must *do* something. She decided that as soon as the rain stopped she would visit the cage every day and take some food and some water. She could do it in the afternoon when Mynheer invariably slept.

Once that was decided she felt better about Psyche, less haunted; it wasn't, she realized much to do, but it involved disobeying Mynheer, risking discovery and his wrath and was thus shifted out of the class of easy charity.

That decided she turned her thoughts to Mynheer. She had always hitherto identified herself with Psyche, put herself in the woman's place; now she tried to think of the whole affair from his point of view. He believed–she thought sincerely–that the woman had ruined the whole life of his son and heir; he was angry, and he was, in Rua, completely powerful. In his place mightn't she, mightn't anyone act with similar ferocity. She remembered how willingly she would have killed Juffrouw Hoorne that night in the Klopstock Home. . . .

So, carefully, deliberately, as one might mend a precious, broken piece of china, she endeavoured to repair her mental image of Mynheer. The mended thing served, seemed much the same, would last, maybe for years;

but it had lost something. The fondness that she had begun to feel for him, roughly plucked up that afternoon, never rooted again.

He attributed her mood to the season; spoke often of the delightful weather which would follow the rain, and of the entertaining and outings that he planned. Several times he mentioned Marie, and Julia, while looking forward to that visit, at the same time shrank from it. In the circumstances some comparison of their experiences seemed inevitable, and what could she say?

There came a day when the rain fell less heavily and less persistently and another when the fair periods outnumbered the showers; and then it was sunny again, the world washed clean and everything springing into lush new life.

'Now,' said Mynheer, 'we must see about some entertaining. We've led a quiet life far too long. Not, I must in all fairness, warn you, that the company will be very lively. The men have one subject of conversation–the nutmeg; and the women discourse, I think exclusively, upon the peccadillos of their house slaves, sometimes so gruesomely that one has a slight hesitation in accepting their invitations! It takes a certain insensitiveness, you know, to do, as one lady did to me, first to relate how she caught her cook straining jelly through one of her husband's dirty stockings, and in the same breath ask me to dinner! However, it will divert you to see the dresses and coiffures, and the gentlemen will pay you compliments. And as you listen to the stories you may reflect–as I do–how much better we do in Rua.'

Their first guests were to be the Governor, his wife and a visiting niece, and Captain Kraemer who was in command of the soldiers at the Fort.

'That,' said Mynheer, 'will make six, with us, which I think the perfect number for dinner. It will also come to the notice of the Agent, and he will feel rebuffed. Nowadays, the commercial element has become so over-rated that many people rank the Agent with the Governor. I do not.'

He asked her which dress she proposed to wear, and when she said she had not yet decided, he asked:

'Is there not one, a rather dull, slaty blue?'

'Yes. I've never yet worn it. I thought it the least attractive of them all.'

'I consider it suitable for this occasion. Will you allow me to be judge, or do you resent my interference?'

'I'll wear it,' she said.

That evening, when the dress was on, and fastened, she regretted having been so weak-willed; the dress, of beautiful, heavy silk, was so plain as to be unbecoming. Unlike the others it had no decoration at all; no lace, no frills, no embroidered posies. It made her look old, and staring at her reflection she wondered whether that might be the reason why Mynheer had suggested it; she could think of no other.

'I don't like it,' she said, turning her head to Juno. 'Do you think we could pin in a lace collar or–or something to brighten it up a little.'

'Is dress for old woman,' Juno said unhelpfully. 'Much other dress, pretty dress, Mevrouw.'

As she spoke a gentle tapping sounded on the sitting-room door–the entry from the cloister. Juno padded away and in a second or two Julia heard Mynheer's voice inquiring whether Mevrouw was dressed. She rose, and with a rustling of silk skirts, she went into the sitting-room.

Mynheer had not chosen himself a dull and unbecoming outfit; of a paler grey than usual, his jacket and breeches had the smoothness and gloss of polished silver and the lace at his breast and wrists was particularly fine. He carried a flat, square box, covered in leather.

He looked her over with critical attention.

'It is ugly, isn't it?' she asked. 'Shall I change?'

'Not immediately. Try this first. . . .' He opened the box and held it out towards her. Lying on a bed of faded blue velvet was a necklace, diamonds and sapphires set in very pale gold. The chain was formed by the stones, set alternately, every one as large as a pea, and hanging from it were seven pendants each made of one large sapphire surrounded by a ring of diamonds. As she stared at it, he tilted the box slightly so that the light of a nearby candle shone in the perfect, unfathomable blue and struck sparks of scarlet, green, purple and yellow from the whiteness.

'It's pretty, isn't it?' She knew that his choice of the slight, the faintly derogatory word was deliberate.

'It's beautiful.'

He put the box on the table and lifted the necklace from it, shimmering and glittering.

'Permit me,' he said, and laid it around her neck and fastened it under her hair. The stones fell into place, icily, against her skin.

Stepping back he regarded her gravely.

'Yes,' he said. 'Yes–but see what you think, my dear.'

She ran to the glass. The dress, she herself, utterly transformed; the blue and sparkle seemed to have invaded her eyes.

'I am sometimes right,' said Mynheer modestly. 'When I ordered that dress I bore in mind that my daughter-in-law might be someone whom I could bear to see wearing that necklace. It suits you very well. I hope you will wear it on many pleasant occasions.'

'I don't know what to say, Mynheer.'

'There is no need to say anything. What there is need of . . .' he lowered his voice a little. 'Julia, this evening I'm afraid you must be prepared for a mild form of inquisition. The ladies will hardly miss such an opportunity of satisfying their curiosity. They will ask you all the questions that the people of Banda have been asking themselves for so long–and never quite dared ask *me*. So imagine that Mevrouw Van de Lijn has you in a corner and asks you about Pieter's disfigurement. What will you say?'

She thought for a moment, and then looking straight at him said:

'Mynheer, I shall tell her that Pieter's disfigurement is grossly exaggerated by everybody, including himself.'

Behind the bulging, clear glassy grey eyes something popped up and looked out for a moment, something surprised, uneasy, vaguely respectful. It gave her the look which an expert might give a novice who had proved astonishingly adept at some game. It was not altogether pleased.

Then he smiled. 'A beautifully ambiguous answer, my dear; and nobody else will be conscious of its ambiguity. I couldn't have thought of a better myself. Stick to that and you will do well.'

She experienced, that evening, something she had never known before–a feeling of pride, pride in the place which she now called home, pride in the family of which she was now a member. It was so plain that these people–the most important members of Banda's society, regarded Mynheer with a respect that was little short of awe; even the Governor deferred to him, saying, 'With your long experience . . .', saying 'Now on this I should value your opinion. . . .' And Mynheer, presiding with geniality, with easy dignity at his own table was at his very best. It was impossible not to admire him, difficult not to like him. Here at this table, bright with flowers and the best service of silver-gilt, watching the skill with which he directed the conversation, everyone included, everyone provoked to animation, feeling about her throat the cold clasp of the necklace, being praised, displayed, smiled upon, was it narrow-minded, she wondered, to withhold something, to resist the appeal of his personality, to remember Psyche in her prison?

Half-way through the meal something happened for which Julia was not prepared.

Every evening, just before the candles were lighted, screens of the finest gauze, stretched tight over wooden battens were placed inside the iron grill-work of the windows to keep out the night-flying things which might be attracted by the light. The veranda outside was ordinarily left in darkness, but this evening–she had imagined for the convenience of the guests arriving and departing–lanterns had been placed at intervals between the flower-brimming urns; the windows were pale golden transparencies, traced with black, curving patterns.

Suddenly Mynheer broke off in mid-sentence and looked fixedly at one window, thus drawing everyone's attention to it. Blocked darkly against the lantern light, filling the window, was the whole of one human figure and half another, a jutting hat brim, one shoulder. The one seen fully Julia recognized as Doctor Hootman; the other? Pieter? Even she could not be *quite* certain. Doctor Hootman turned his head and seemed to address his companion, and lifted his hand and laid it on the other's shoulder, and they moved away in such a direction that the man who was half-glimped was never fully seen.

'Pieter and his friend have resumed their walks now that the rain is ended. That is something to be thankful for,' said Mynheer.

There was a moment of slightly embarrassed silence; then the Governor said:

'Such a pity–to take it so hard.' He turned to Julia and said: 'I suppose Mevrouw you hardly notice anything amiss, now. I am sure, that given the same opportunity, we should all become equally accustomed.'

'Only today . . .' she said, and tried out the neat little speech.

Captain Kraemer, with the best intentions, broke in with an account of a fellow officer, a handsome man, who had been shot through the jaw. 'Never could close his mouth properly afterwards, poor fellow. But we soon got used to the sight of his teeth.'

'Ah, but he was of reasonable age,' said Mynheer. 'One cannot reason with a child. Before we realized what was happening Pieter's habit of seclusion was fixed and nothing will alter it now. Still,' his voice brightened, 'he is very fortunate. He had his Doctor Hootman, and he now has Julia, who shares all his pursuits, except music.' He smiled at her, indulgently, mock-reprovingly. Captain Kraemer, who was musical, tactfully took that as a cue and the conversation drifted away from Pieter.

Even the inquisition for which Mynheer had prepared Julia, did not take place. Mevrouw Van de Lijn was engrossed with anxiety about her own child, a daughter, married and living in Holland, and due about now, as nearly as the mother could reckon, to have a baby.

'And whether things go well with her or not, whether I have a grandson or a grand-daughter, I can't possibly know for another seven months. That is what I find so hard. I don't mind the climate, I'm not afraid of a slave revolt, or of the Fire Mountain erupting, or of finding a snake in my bed, but I do mind, I mind very much, these separations and the feeling of being at the world's end, so entirely cut off.'

Using slightly different words she said the same thing several times.

The niece, a plump, pretty but very dull girl, had no thought to spare for Pieter Vosmar either, being intent upon Captain Kraemer whom she hoped to marry.

At the evening's end, however, attention, was drawn to Pieter again. As the guests were leaving, about to make their way from the house to the little jetty where the Governor's prahau with a lighted lantern at its prow bobbed and looked like a dancing firefly, the sound of the clavichord, played in a masterly manner, came from the end of the house where Pieter's apartments lay. It was far from being the pleasant, tinkling tune produced by the average performer. In the wild, stormy music there seemed to sound the cry of a soul unsatisfied, lonely and searching, racked by a measureless yearning. Exactly so might the legendary Pieter have played.

'Ah,' said Captain Kraemer, in a voice of awed appreciation.

'Poor boy! So gifted too,' said the Governor.

His wife gave a little shiver. The music spoke to her of the miles of tossing, perpetually discontented sea which lay between her and Holland where her heart was this night.

Turning back into the house Mynheer laid his hand on Julia's arm.

'My dear, you did splendidly. I was very proud of you. Your manner to that tiresome old mother-hen could not have been bettered. People really *should* learn to leave their private concerns at home.'

It was an unsympathetic speech, and that part of her mind which was now alert for such things duly took note of it. The other part remarked that he, of all men, was justified in making it.

After that there were other dinner parties, and several times Mynheer and Julia went to dine in one or another of the big houses in Banda. There was never time on these occasions to visit Marie, he said, and Julia was glad, she had no wish to appear before Marie finely gowned and be-jewelled.

One day Mynheer returned from a visit to Banda and said that he had made an appointment there for the morning, two days ahead; his business would take about two hours and he thought it would be a convenient time for Julia to make her visit.

'I took the liberty of sending word so that she may expect you. You must take her some flowers, they have no garden I believe.'

Marie lived in a narrow house squeezed between two taller, larger buildings. It was faded pink in colour, and except that it had shutters might have been any house in any humble street in Holland.

She opened the door herself, and Julia had difficulty in suppressing an exclamation of surprise. Marie had greatly changed, grown so fat that she almost filled the doorway; lost all her trimness, all her good looks. Behind her, in the narrow passage stood another woman with two children peering from behind her skirts.

The population of Banda Neira had grown rapidly and since the town could not spread outwards without filching land from the precious nutmeg groves there was a shortage of houses and the Oltman ménage was typical of many. Marie and Hendrik shared a house with his brother, his wife and two children, and an unmarried clerk from the Agent's office.

'. . . and now he wants to get married, too,' said Marie, explaining the situation, 'and we haven't the heart to say he can't, so where we shall be then, I don't know.'

She had lost none of her cheerfulness, of her vivacity, Julia was glad to find. Chattering gaily she led the way into a hot, cluttered sitting-room, called her sister-in-law and introduced her and asked her to put the flowers in water, and shooed away the children.

'Now,' she said, 'let me look at you! And tell me quickly, while we're alone, which we shan't be for long, are you all right Julia?' She asked the question with a peculiar urgency.

'I'm very well. Are you?' But surely it was wrong to have grown so very stout, so pale and puffy of face in so short . . . how long? Good heavens, six whole months.

'I'm as you see,' said Marie, looking down at her bulging figure with some pride. She giggled. 'Almost at *once*. Hendrik is so pleased. He wants a girl to look like me; and I want a boy to look like him. And it *could* be twins, couldn't it, the size I am.'

So that was it!

'I'm so glad for you.'

'I'm glad, too. Mind, I shall be more glad when it, or they, have arrived. I look so awful. It's no use being polite and trying to contradict me. I look as ugly as sin. And the odd thing is, Hendrik doesn't think so. He says honestly that I'm prettier now than ever. Do you think something comes over men who are going to be fathers, a sort of blindness?'

Deep in Julia's mind something stirred. Men and women were made and put together by the good God . . . no mistake . . . even such a veiling of a man's sight. That, she thought, must be real love. . . .

'I wanted to come and see you,' Marie ran on. 'But the Vosmars are so rich and important, and we aren't yet–though Hendrik is so clever and hard-working, he's bound to get on–it didn't seem quite right for me to come to you first. And then this happened. And you didn't come and didn't come. I have been a bit worried about you.'

'Why?'

Marie looked away and a little, unbecoming colour crept into her pasty cheeks.

'Well . . . such tales go round,' she said. 'Don't mind me asking. Is it true that your husband had a terrible accident and is dreadful to look at?'

Once again the neat little sentence served.

'And then there's that frightening old man. Oh, when I saw you go off with him Julia. . . . I did pity you.'

'But he's very kind–to me. I'm not frightened of him.' But that is a lie, every afternoon when I steal out of the house to visit Psyche I can hardly breathe for fear.

'If he's kind, his looks belie him. But I'm glad he is. And what about your husband, apart from his looks? Did you get a nice one? Oh, I like Hendrik so much, I couldn't help wondering about you.'

'Pieter and I get on very well. He's fond of me. He'd do anything he could to please me.' That least was true.

'Well, that just shows. They say he's surly, never sees anybody, never speaks. They even say he's a bit . . .' she tapped her head with her finger and laughed, then, leaning forward took Julia by the hand. 'I suppose you'll think I am crack-brained, too, but truly, when somebody told me that, I was upset. All I could think of was Mucky Karl . . . being married to him! Ughhh!' She gave an exaggerated shudder and was about to laugh again. 'What's the matter? You have turned white,' she said.

Julia made the effort.

'The thought of being married to Mucky Karl is enough to turn anyone white, isn't it?'And he isn't like Mucky Karl; he's very clean (Because he is so well-looked after, Doctor Hootman . . .) Not dangerous either. (Because he is sheltered, not sent out in the street to be jeered at. . . .)

'It turned me more than white,' Marie was saying, 'it made me really sick; but of course that might have been. . . .' She looked down at herself again; then at Julia and said brightly:

'You'll have to have a baby, won't you. A boy for you. Look what he'll inherit!'

Another effort. 'Give me time! Slow starters often go farthest.'

But Marie had succeeded in diverting her own attention.

'They're vastly rich, aren't they?' She looked at the simple dress Julia had chosen to wear for this visit. She didn't quite dare to ask the question directly, so she said: 'I expected you to walk in all silks and satins and covered with diamonds.'

'But I had to come in a prahau. I have a silk dress. . . .'

She could see that Marie was so happy, so contented with her lot that she was safe from envy, so she described one or two of her dresses.

'Have you one of those native things? You know, a sarong and little jacket? Oh, well, Hendrik and I were asked to the Agent's once–I don't like *her*, nose-in-the-air, but that's by the way–and she was wearing one, pink and purple, very thin stuff the jacket, it looked so cool and pretty. I meant to make myself one–you only have to do straight hemming on the sarong, easy–but then this happened, and it didn't seem worth it for a while. But I shall after, if I ever get back to my right size that is. It seems unlikely doesn't it?'

In such girlish chatter the time passed swiftly. The sister-in-law came in, carrying Mynheer's offering of lilies and roses and orchids which she had crammed into an ugly brass bowl; she went out again and returned bringing strong black coffee and some rather stale little cakes. The children stole into the room, soon forgot their shyness and began squabbling and had to be sent out; the lack of garden was deplored. Soon it was time to go.

At the moment of parting, Marie had a resurgence of anxiety.

'You really are all right, Julia? Happy?'

'Of course. You must come and see for yourself.'

'I can't take a boat trip just now. I will afterwards–if you invite me.'

'I am inviting you,' Julia said. How would Mynheer take that?

The prahau swung out of the harbour and headed for Rua.

'Well, and how did you enjoy your visit?' Mynheer asked.

'Very much, thank you. We had such a lot to talk about.'

'Your little friend is enjoying her new life?'

'Oh, very much.'

'Not feeling the heat too greatly?' Such interest in Marie was rather surprising; it struck, for some reason, a slightly false note.

'She didn't complain. Of course in that small house it is hot; and they have no garden. She was delighted with the flowers and sent you messages of gratitude.' That was not true. Marie had handed the flowers to Rita and hardly looked at them when they were brought in. Save for a flash or two in Julia's direction Marie's eyes were turned inward, self-absorbed.

'I expect she told you all the gossip of the town.'

'No. I don't think we gossiped at all.' Or was Marie's mention of the Agent's wife being nose-in-the-air gossip? 'We talked mainly about ourselves, I'm afraid.'

She could feel, without turning her head, that he was looking at her closely. He was wanting, waiting for her to tell him something more. What? Oh, of course. . . .

'She did ask me a few questions about Pieter, which was only natural. My answers satisfied her, and I think, would have satisfied you.'

'I'm sure of that. I rely upon your discretion absolutely.'

He seemed to wait again. Then he said:

'Well, perhaps it is true–as some ladies aver–that men are the real gossips. It seems that my business talk has provided me with a tit-bit that you missed. Unless you saw fit not to mention it to me.'

'You mean about Marie . . . that she is going to have a baby?'

'Yes. Is it true? Then was it modesty that kept you silent on the subject. Or envy?'

She had a sudden, strange, utterly unwarranted suspicion that he had known all along; that he had deliberately postponed taking her to visit Marie until he had, somehow, on his previous trip, heard that she was pregnant. But that was stupid, why should he? And why this sudden probing?

'Neither. I just felt that, in the circumstances, it was a matter better not mentioned between us. That was all.'

'Now why?' he asked. 'Between us there should be complete understanding. We two are alone as few people are; if we cannot confide in one another in whom can we confide? My dear you do, despite the poor little house, the lack of prospects and everything, envy her, do you not?'

What did he want her to say?

'I suppose every woman, if she could, would like to have a child of her own, but. . . .'

'Exactly,' he broke in with something less than his usual courtesy. 'And every woman *should*. It is her *right*!'

In the circumstances, an astonishing, a challenging thing to say. But I can't she thought, go into it with him, now; once I might have. But I must answer. . . . She said: 'Many women remain unmarried, Mynheer. What about them?'

'This is an imperfect world, my dear. The rules are made, hit or miss; often by knaves to exploit fools, or by fools to control knaves. I never pay heed to the rules. I never have. I still say that any woman, married or single, should have a child if she wanted one.'

It all seemed to be leading somewhere, but where?

'That is a very original idea,' she said.

He laughed. 'I'm sure somebody said just those words to the man who first thought of harnessing a horse, or setting the wind to work a mill or sail a ship. Today's innovation is tomorrow's commonplace. Where would the world be if no one had ever had an original idea? I feel very strongly. . . .'

She waited, feeling that the next words would reveal his purpose; make everything plain.

'I talk too much,' he said. 'And for that you are partly to blame. You're very easy to talk to, very sympathetic in the real sense of the word. I often forget that you are so young, and a female. Never mind. One day. . . .'

He left that sentence unfinished, too, and reached out and patted her hand. Then he took up his cane and rapped it threateningly.

Chapter Six

One day during the next week Mynheer made another visit to Banda Neira, this time alone.

'I will not ask you to come with me today, my dear, because my business will take longer. Also I may bring two guests back for dinner and I want you, if you will be so kind, to do a job for me.' He took out his keys and removed one from the chain and handed it to her. 'That is the key of the plate cupboard. Pluto knows what to get out, but I would like you to be there. He will overload a tray and then things fall and are dented. Make him bring out one piece at a time.' He smiled at her as she stood with the key in her hand. 'It is very pleasant for me to have someone to whom I can entrust these little domestic details,' he said genially. 'And of course you must begin to take charge. One day you will rule this house; rule all Rua in fact.'

She said, with sincerity: 'I hope that day will be long in coming, Mynheer.'

'Thank you, my dear. But it will come. That is a fact to be faced. However, I have made every possible provision. . . .'

The vision of the future, thus conjured up, cast a slight gloom over the bright morning. Day to day living in Rua was–apart from the ever-nagging memory of the woman in the cage–very pleasant and carefree, but to look ahead was to see a time and a situation curiously shapeless, empty of the landmarks which ordinary people saw along the years.

She tried to throw off her bewildering and foreboding thoughts by being busy, but Pluto suggested, in the most humble fawning manner, that the removal of the silver should take place in the afternoon. Speaking so servilely, not even looking sulky, he managed to convey to her that her supervision was hurtful to his feelings, so she agreed to the postponement without demur or question. When afternoon came he was so exaggeratedly careful in the handling of the many pieces of the silver-gilt dinner service which was to be used that evening that the afternoon was well advanced before Julia could re-lock the cupboard and go away.

On any ordinary afternoon this would have worried her, but today, with Mynheer safe in Banda, it did not matter. She went calmly to her room, picked up a rather large bag of pale pink brocade with a piece of embroidery sticking out of it, and set off to pay her daily visit to Psyche. Concealed under the embroidery was some food saved from her own mid-day meal and an old wine bottle full of water.

Ordinarily she made this furtive little journey during the hottest hour of the day, when she could be almost certain that Mynheer was asleep. *Almost*, never *quite* certain, and it was always with a feeling of trepidation, an increase of the heartbeat that she went into the garden, sat on a seat and stitched for a few minutes, and then with a purposeless, wandering air, strolled into the nutmeg grove and broke into a brisk walk.

Psyche now knew her, and watched for her coming; every afternoon she was at the bars of the cage on the side from which Julia appeared. Apart from this recognition of identity and purpose their relationship had remained static and Julia was not even sure whether the woman was fully sane or not. On the first few occasions when she had brought the extra food and water, she had been appalled by the way in which she, herself a woman, fully dressed and at liberty, had handed food and water through bars, to another woman, naked and caged as though she were an animal and to mitigate the situation she had tried to talk to her, calling her by name. There was no response; eighteen years of slow torture and solitary confinement had reduced Psyche to something less than human, and eventually Julia could see that this was merciful. It would be unkind, wrong, to make any attempt to recall the mind, the soul, the personality, whatever it was which did distinguish people from animals. Julia contented herself with handing in what she had brought and hurrying away. Sometimes, on her way back she cried a little; and sometimes she felt a renewed upsurge of dislike for Mynheer.

This afternoon Psyche was waiting as usual at the corner nearest the point where Julia entered the little clearing. An extra meal every day for some weeks had done nothing to change her dreadful appearance; under the filthy scaly skin every bone, every ligament showed plainly. Her eyes, under the shadow of the mat of hair, flickered with recognition and avidity, and Julia was glad to think that today there was meat in the bag. She could remember, from her own hungry days in the Klopstock Home, how meat-hungry one could become, even when otherwise sufficiently fed, and how wonderful the sailor's meat pies had tasted.

Ordinarily, as soon as Julia arrived, Psyche, after that single, human-seeming glance, would run, with a clanking of the chain, to the other side of the cage where the water and rice were displayed in their Tantalus inaccessibility. Today, however, she stayed where she was, pushing her claw-like hands through the bars and whimpering. She was more thirsty than usual, Julia thought, because of the delay.

'I'm sorry I'm late,' she said, forgetting her resolve not to attempt any communication, 'come along.' She walked around to the side where the bowls and the bucket stood. Psyche, legs bowed, shoulders bent, ran across with a clanking of the chain. Julia put the bag on the ground by the bars, removed the piece of embroidery and the packet of food and revealed the bottle, standing upright with the pink folds of the brocade bag collapsed around its base. She reached out for the bowl into which she always poured the water. As she did so Psyche's hand shot through the bars and snatched at the bottle, drawing it into the cage. Poor thing, she is thirsty, Julia thought; and, despite all evidence to the contrary, she can still reason. It is quicker to drink from the bottle than to have a bowl filled, handed, in, handed out and refilled. No animal could have worked that out. Yet, Psyche, bottle in hand, was retreating towards the centre of the cage with exactly the look of a cat that has made off with a piece of fish.

'It's all right,' Julia said. 'Drink out of the bottle if you like. But you must give it back to me. I must have it back, Psyche. I must have it back.' She heard a certain shrillness in her voice, and thought, I mustn't frighten her. I must keep calm.

'Drink it and give me back the bottle, for tomorrow.'

Psyche made no attempt to take out the cork. Perhaps she had forgotten. . . . She wasn't even handling the bottle as though she intended to drink out of it. She held it by its neck.

She is mad, after all, Julia thought.

Holding the bottle by the neck and swinging it as though it were a club, Psyche hit it against the post. It broke, the water splashed out and pieces of glass fell down on to the heap of filth. The neck of the bottle, with the cork still in it, remained in her hand until she dropped it amongst the other fragments. Then she bent down, looked at the pieces of glass and quite deliberately chose one. With it in her hand she stood up, and then, with that same deliberation, drew the edge of it across her stringy throat.

It made, to begin with, a cut, like a little mouth with red lips; then, in a flash, the wound, Psyche's hand, the piece of glass which it held were all lost in a gush of blood. Nobody could have believed that that dried-out, emaciated body could have contained the fountain of blood which shot out until it reached the bars of the cage, hit them with such force that it ricocheted and spattered Julia and her dress and the brocade bag.

It all happened so suddenly that there wasn't time even to close one's eyes, or look away.

Psyche did not fall down immediately; the arching fountain of blood had slackened before she fell to her knees and then forward from the waist until her face touched the ground. In this prayerful attitude her body gave one or two convulsive twitches which jerked it slightly sideways; then it was still.

It had all happened so suddenly, and been so unexpected, that it was difficult to believe that it had happened at all. But it had happened. There lay Psyche, dead, with the bits of broken glass around her, and there was Julia, sick and dizzy, clinging to the bars of the cage for support. Despite the heaving of her stomach and the unsteadiness of the ground under her feet and of everything around her, she could think, quite clearly.

Psyche was dead; she was glad of that; her troubles were over. Mynheer would come, at feeding time, see the corpse and the bits of glass. He would instantly suspect Julia, because she had once shown interest in the dead woman. He would be furiously angry. Baulked of the rest of his vengeance what would his vengeance be? There was only one answer to that. He would put her in the cage. She would spend the rest of her life there, naked, chained to a post by a heap of filth. There was no escape. She was on an island, she couldn't get away, there was nowhere to hide: except for Marie, inaccessible in Banda, she hadn't a friend in the world.

She began to tremble, so violently that her hands could no longer clasp the bars, so violently that her head jerked and shook like that of an old person with palsy. I must get away, she thought, away from this place of horror. The idea of drowning herself slipped into her mind. Yes, death in the cool, crystal-clear blue water would be better than facing Mynheer in his rage. He had warned her, said she must be careful not to provoke him.

She staggered out of the clearing and on to the path, turning away from the house and towards the shore. She had taken only a few jerky, shuffling steps when she stopped to listen thinking that she heard other steps coming towards her around the curve of the path. It was so. Mynheer, back from Banda rather earlier than he had expected and coming from that direction towards the cage.

She would have turned and run the other way, or darted off and hidden in the nutmeg grove, but she now could not move at all except to shudder and tremble. She could only stand in the middle of the narrow path and wait.

It was not Mynheer. It was nobody she had ever seen before. A man, giving at that slight distance, an impression of youth unconfirmed, she was to learn, by a closer view. The same clarity of mind which had enabled her to realize at once what she had done, what the result might be, and the hopelessness of her situation, came into play again now as she stood paralysed and palsied and watched him approach. She even noticed that he looked surprised, a little startled at the sight of her, and that as he drew nearer his expression changed to astonishment, and concern.

He came close enough to touch her, looking at the path behind her and into the grove on either side.

'Have you had a fright? What's the matter?' he asked.

She tried to speak, but she had no more control of her jaw and tongue than of her legs, her teeth chattered and that was the only sound.

'I didn't frighten you, did I? I'm harmless.'

He saw the splashes of fresh blood on the front of her dress, the state of her hands where she had clutched the blood-splashed bars. He tried again.

'Have you had an accident?'

Almost unwillingly then he touched her, put his hand under her arm and turned her slightly.

'Sit down,' he said, and helped her down and propped her back against the trunk of a tree. Her head was still jerking so uncontrollably that her hair rubbed against and was caught in the rough bark.

The man carried a brown jacket over his left arm. He now turned it about, searched for and found the pocket and brought out a small, dented silver flask. He removed its top and bending down held it towards her.

'Take a sip of that. It'll pull you together.'

She tried to lift a shaking hand, then tried to shake her jerking head to indicate inability.

'Poor girl,' he said, 'You are in a state.' He threw down the jacket, knelt beside her, put an arm around her shoulders and with his other hand held the flask to her lips, exactly as though she were a baby. Even with his firm hand on the flask it was difficult for her to hold its top between her chattering teeth and some of the liquid jerked out, ran over her chin and on to her dress.

'You got some,' he said. 'Try again.' He tightened his clasp on her shoulders, steadying her, and that time she did better. 'Once more: that's right.' He set the flask down, reached for his jacket and put it between her and the tree as he withdrew his arm. 'Just sit back and wait for a bit,' he said. He capped the flask and put it this time into the pocket of his worn, faded blue breeches. And again he looked this way, that way along the path, and into the trees on both sides.

Whatever it was he had given her ran warmly down from her throat to the pit of her stomach and after a minute or two from there it began to spread out. Every rigor that shook her was now a little weaker than the one before. Presently she tried to move her hand again, and this time it came up at her bidding, she took her lower jaw between her finger and thumb, held it for a few seconds and then managed to say:

'Thank you.'

'Now,' he said, with an air of getting down to business. 'Are you hurt?' She shook her head. 'Then where does all this blood come from?'

'Psyche . . . she killed herself.' The radiating warmth which had run about, loosening the grip of the shaking paralysis, had now reached the very core of her mind; she burst into tears. 'It was awful,' she gulped out between her sobs. 'I was glad for her, but it was . . . an awful way to die.' She drew two, harsh, snuffling breaths, felt in her sleeve, found her handkerchief and used it, and gasped out. 'Unless I drown myself I think he'll put me in the cage instead. Oh, I know it all sounds crazy, but this is a crazy place. You don't know!'

Now the extreme, painful clarity of mind which had enabled her to observe everything so minutely–even to the fact that his shirt had once been fine, and that now its frill was in tatters–had given way to emotional confusion. She hardly noticed that he had slipped his arm around her again and was holding her close to his shoulder and urging her to have her cry out because then she would be able to tell him what was the matter and he would see if there was anything he could do.

With her mind she was hardly aware of all this; but her body remembered that in just this way Uncle Johannes had held her and comforted her when something had gone wrong with her childish world. Since his death her life had been singularly devoid of physical contacts; the drunken sailor had kissed her, she had hugged Katje in the cellar, amongst the Company's Daughers light fleeting kisses had been current, and Mynheer sometimes touched her arm or patted her hand, but nobody, for years, had held her with intent to comfort or sustain. Despite everything, she was comforted.

At last, in the encroaching calm, she was able to say:

'Are you a friend of Mynheer Vosmar's?'

'Let's say an acquaintance. I'll tell you this. If it's trouble between you and him, I'm on your side.'

'Why?' she asked, lifting her head from his shoulder and mopping her eyes.

'Because I'm always on the side of ladies in distress. No, seriously, you're safe with me. What *is* the matter?'

While she had been crying he had been trying to decide her status. She was white, and the soiled dress was pretty and expensive; but amongst the wealthy planters white concubines were not unknown. An agency in Java specialized in the supply of girls for the purpose, mainly Greek or Georgian. . . .

'If there's anything I can do to help, tell me,' he said. 'I haven't much time.'

'I don't see that anyone could help me. Mynheer kept a poor woman in a cage and slowly starved her–kept her short of water, too, so every day I took her some and just now she snatched the bottle and cut her throat. He'll know it was me. She's been there for eighteen years and nobody else ever bothered. He'll put me in the cage instead–unless I drown myself.'

'Or I said I gave her the bottle. . . .'

She moved her head a little so that she could look into his face, and instantly he slackened his clasp on her and shifted his position so that they were no longer in contact.

'Could you do that? Would you?' she asked in an awed voice.

'I don't see why not. He can't do anything to me.'

His eyes she noticed, with some part of her mind, which had disengaged itself from the main problem, were blue; not the soft periwinkle blue of her dream porcelain-figure lover, a brighter, harder blue, and they were narrow, wrinkled at the outer corners as though he were always screwing them against the glare of the sun.

'I don't know,' she said doubtfully. 'He'll be *very* angry, and he's a ruthless man.'

'The most ruthless man I know, and I have known a few. But his anger wouldn't hurt *me*. Don't you fret about that. Let's work it out; I'm coming along this path, carrying a bottle of wine, nothing extraordinary about that. What draws my attention? I've walked this path before and never noticed anything . . . where is this cage? How did you find it?'

'Behind that fence,' she said, looking in that direction and then quickly away again. 'I heard her moaning.'

'All right. *I* heard her moaning. I gave her the bottle of wine. That is, I might say, and will seem so to Mynheer, quite out of keeping with my character, but then the circumstances are somewhat unusual. Will that do?'

She said slowly, 'I don't know what to say. I should be so deeply, so everlastingly gr . . .' She began to cry again.

'Ah, don't!' he said. 'It's over now. You'll just puff up your face and that will look suspicious. And we haven't much time. He'll soon be back. You've got a lot of cleaning up to do. So that shall be our story, eh?'

'If you're *sure* you don't mind the risk.'

'All I risk is that he should burst with fury, and I don't think he will. Tell me,' he said in a different voice, 'what hold has he on you that you should be frightened of him?'

'He's my father-in-law.'

'Your *what*?'

'My father-in-law.'

'Great God in Heaven. You don't tell me you're married to that idiot boy!'

For the first time she felt something shameful about her situation. Hitherto it had been unusual, false, bewildering, but nothing more, in no way a reflection upon herself. Her face grew hot and she looked down as she said:

'I didn't know: it was a Glove Marriage. And of course it is in name only.'

He said nothing for a moment.

'Are they kind to you?'

'Oh, yes, very kind. Today, of course was different. I did disobey him. . . .' That was a reminder. 'Mynheer, if you do take the blame for what I did, when can you tell him? I think he comes to feed . . . her, at sunset every day. If he came before he heard your story he would think of me and if he spoke of it, or questioned or accused me I'm afraid I should give myself away.'

'He shall know that I am waiting to see him, on most urgent business the moment he sets foot on the jetty. Make your mind easy. All you have to do is to clean up; and forget all about it. Especially forget that you ever saw me.'

'Oh, I couldn't do that. I shall remember you and what you've done for me every day of my life.'

'No, just forget it.' His voice changed again. 'Do you see much of Daan Hootman?'

'Every day, several times.'

'He's a good chap. If ever you need a friend he'd stand by.'

'I'll remember that. But I shall be all right. I've learned my lesson. I shall never interfere with anything again.'

'That's right,' he said. He rose lightly to his feet and reached down a hand to help her to hers. 'How do you feel?'

'A little shaky, but all right, thank you.'

'I'll walk a little way with you. Then I'll look behind that fence, so that my story hangs together.'

'It's a dreadful sight,' she said with a shudder.

'Don't think about it. It's over. She's in Heaven, Paradise, whatever you call it, the place where everything is made up to us.'

'You believe that?'

'Sometimes. Anyway, you think that, and remember you helped her on her way. I think you've been extremely brave.'

'I'm not. I'm a coward to my bones. Every time I've come I've been so frightened that I felt sick.'

'But that is the very essence of bravery. Well, I mustn't come any farther; I have an appointment. Just forget all about it and be careful in future. I hope everything will work out all right for you.'

He had stopped in the path and she realized that now she must go one way and he another; that she would never see him again, and must even try to forget that she had ever seen him.

'I haven't thanked you properly . . . but then I never could. And now we have to say good-bye. . . .' Tears rushed to her eyes again. She held out her hand and he took it. Then, suddenly, acting on impulse he gave it a little pull, drawing her nearer, and bending his head, kissed her on the forehead, just where the brown hair grew in a little peak on her forehead.

'That's for luck,' he said lightly. 'You're the sweetest thing I've seen for many a long day.'

She threw her arms round his neck and kissed him on the mouth, for luck, for gratitude, for good-bye, with a kind of innocent passion. He stood rigid and unresponsive for a second; then, under hers, his lips moved, once. Instantly he reached up his hands and caught hers.

'You really must go, it's getting late,' he said stiffly.

She knew that if she tried to speak again she would cry, her throat ached and her eyes were swimming. She began to walk quickly away; but at the path's end she turned and looked back. He was standing where she had left him, his shabby old jacket slung over his arm. He raised a hand and she waved back, taking a last look at him with her heart in her eyes.

As she hurried along the rose pergola she saw Doctor Hootman on the other side of the garden, but he entered the grove from that side by a less frequented path, and she was able to reach the house unobserved.

Chapter Seven

Beneath his stolid appearance, phlegmatic and slow-moving calm, Doctor Hootman concealed a lively and sensitive perception and an imagination more than averagely facile. The instant the man he had come to meet was within sight, before a word or glance had been exchanged, he sensed that something had happened, and that this meeting was in some way different from their former ones. Circumstances being what they were anything different held the threat of disaster and within his big slack body his spirit braced itself for the reception of bad news.

Philosophically he reminded himself that those who play with fire must expect sooner or later to burn their fingers: he congratulated himself that his connexion with the dangerous element had been more or less a vicarious one.

They met, shook hands; and in the doing of it Doctor Hootman asked:

'What's the matter, Charles? You look perturbed.'

'Do I?' Charles rubbed his hand over his face as though to right his expression. 'And well I may,' he said, a faint grin coming and going and leaving his look unchanged.

'Is something wrong?'

'Oh, with the job? No. All safe in Madagascar by now, or should be, and the money lodged. I wasn't thinking about that. It's what has been happening *here*, that's what I want to know, my boy.'

'Here? Everything here is as usual.'

'You're an old oyster. You've got an addition to the family, I understand.'

'Oh, that,' said Doctor Hootman with an air of relief, dismissing Julia as of no importance. 'The jungle drums don't miss much, do they? Yes, in addition to all the other trappings of normality, Pieter has now been provided with a wife.'

'I've just seen her.'

'Good God! Did she see you?'

'We had a long conversation.'

'Most unwise. Suppose she mentions you.'

'She won't. She can keep a secret.' Charles flung himself down on the crisp, aromatic leaves that had drifted beside the path. 'She's had one of her own which I bet even *you* never ferreted out.'

Lowering himself more awkwardly Doctor Hootman also sat down.

'I must confess it had never occurred to me to look into her activities.'

'Well, listen to this.' Doctor Hootman did listen, intently, while Charles told him, briefly, the story of Julia's visits to Psyche and how the last one had ended.

'Next thing I know I shall have a case of apoplexy on my hands,' Doctor Hootman said, speaking as though he relished the prospect. 'He'll be so mad with anger, and the conflict between his fury and the paternal attitude he must preserve will be enough to make him burst a blood vessel.' He hugged his knees and looked pleased.

'He wont' be angry with *her*. Me. I'm the scapegoat. We worked it all out. I was walking along, found the poor wretch and gave her the bottle of wine which I was bringing up as a present for himself. That'll burst all his blood vessels, eh?'

Charles laughed outright, and Doctor Hootman's pleased look warmed for a moment into a smile. They were men of entirely dissimilar character, breeding and experience, with nothing in common except the furtive bit of business they carried on behind Mynheer's back, but that was in itself a strong link. They were a little like two schoolboys in league against a master.

Doctor Hootman's smile soon vanished.

'I don't call that a good move at all. You're not supposed to be here today.'

'I've got a story to explain that, too. Don't you worry.'

'I have reason. It looks to me as though you threw away all caution at the sight of a pretty face. If she were in the condition you describe you could have turned off into the trees and kept out of sight.'

'She was in the condition I described and nobody with a drop of human blood in his veins could have left her in it; or failed to help her, if he could.'

'I don't think he'll believe you.'

'What else can he believe? I've even checked on the bottle. Lovely bottle of Rhenish it was!' His face hardened. 'I shan't give him time for doubt, Daan. I shan't walk in and say, "So sorry, Mynheer, I had the slight misfortune to finish off your victim." I shall tell him straight out that he's a damned filthy swine and that I don't think I can do business with him any more.'

'Yes,' said Doctor Hootman thoughtfully and with approval, 'that does lend a ring of conviction. And it will set him thinking. That's the line to take.'

'It's not a line. It's how I feel. I shall have a hard job to keep my hands off him.'

Doctor Hootman looked with mild interest at the harsh-lined face, now scoured with angry disgust.

'I shouldn't have thought that Psyche's plight . . .' he began.

'Damn it all, I'm not thinking of Psyche–though that was bad enough. It's the girl. Of all the vile things to do, to fetch out that poor innocent child and marry her off to . . . I'm tough bellied, but when she said "daughter-in-law" I did feel bloody sick.'

One of Doctor Hootman's eyebrows moved a little.

'You needn't concern yourself about *that*, Charles. They live quite separately. And theirs is really rather a touching relationship. She plays with him as though he were about four years old and just a little backward, or as though he were a dog.'

As he spoke, something deeply buried, most intricately coiled at the very roots of his mind, moved, cold and sluggish, a snake stirred from its winter sleep.

'She seems to have made quite an impression on you, Charles. Was she equally taken with you?'

'She probably wouldn't recognize me again if she saw me. Poor girl, she was half out of her mind with distress and terror. She'd got an idea that he might put *her* in his cage. She said she thought of that every time she went–but she'd gone, just the same. That's pluck, if you like. Every day, in cold blood, not the way we work. And getting nothing out of it either.' Some memory moved; the planes of his face shifted, the look of troubled disgust gave way to a half-rueful smile.

'She was grateful,' he said. 'What's her name?'

'Julia.'

'Julia,' he tried it over; he liked it; it suited her. He caught Doctor Hootman's eye, and broke into a self-derisive laugh.

'We can't all be like you, you old eunuch! It's a hell of a long time since I *saw* a white woman, much less talked to one.'

'The brown ones are well spoken of.'

'They're all right; but they do so stink of that nutmeg cheese.' He turned his attention to more immediate matters.

'Get hold of Mynheer, Daan, as soon as he lands, and tell him a man–you can say a rough looking character if you like–came to see him and you shut him in the library. Then, from your lair you can listen to the explosion.'

'I'd like to know what excuse you'll give for being here today–unbidden by him.'

'Stern business–and it happens to be true. London seems to have tapped another source and the price dropped by two shillings a pound.' So he probably will burst, and I'll have killed the goose that laid the golden egg. For once I don't care. There's always the nutmeg. Your gleanings are in the same place, I take it. Good. I think this time we really must make an effort to get some to America. It's amazing, isn't it, how they don't grow. You and I alone have shipped out enough to start a forest, and we're not the only ones. And the demand goes on.'

'We should be grateful for that. Now, as regards the patrols.'

'I'd clean forgotten.'

'You are not yourself this afternoon. The seventeenth; the twenty-third; the first of next month. But the Lonthoir run, on the fifteenth is full moon. So have a care then.'

'Thank you, Daan,' Charles said warmly. 'It's due to you we've eluded them so long I do verily believe. He's a mean swine about that, too. He has all the information, and every one of his own little jobs is pin-pointed, timed to a second, but never another word or hint that a poor struggling chap could take advantage of. I'd be interested to know who supplies his information.'

'I don't think anybody does,' said Doctor Hootman, rising and brushing, with scrupulous care, every bit of clinging leaf from his dark clothes. 'A patrol officer, in his cups, one evening dropped a hint about general principles of routine, varied by tide and the moon; and after that, clever fellow, he could work it out for himself. On the first of the lunar month, as regularly as it comes round, he sits down and makes his little chart; at which I look next time I pass. Well, I'll go ahead; wait ten minutes and then follow. I'll be on the look-out. I hope your luck holds.'

'Thanks. And Daan. . . .'

'Yes?'

'Keep an eye on . . . Julia.'

'I can promise to do that. I also admire courage. I have my human side, you know.'

He walked, unhurried and ponderous, through the grove where the twilight was thickening and all the island scents were intensified, as though the earth had let out a deep breath of relief as the sun went down. As he walked he snapped his fingers coaxingly at the snake which had just moved in his mind. Come out little snake, let me inspect you and see whether you are what I wish, what I hope you might be. Are you just a harmless little grass snake, or a deadly viper?

He could remember every word, every inflexion of voice used on the evening of Julia's arrival when Mynheer had said: 'Listen . . .' and then unfolded his audacious, incredible scheme. Every word had been a blow to his own plans and hopes. But now, after what had happened this afternoon, it was just possible, just barely possible that Julia might be a weapon snatched from Mynheer's hand and fitted to his own.

Doctor Hootman was neither religiously nor mystically inclined. Ignoring Providence and Destiny he was therefore forced to bend a superstitious knee in the worship of another controller of human lives, the great goddess Coincidence. Coincidence was responsible for the fact that the ship on which he had sailed as doctor-surgeon and spy for the owners, should sink in the Banda straits and that he should be without a job, awaiting a passage at the very moment when Mynheer Vosmar was searching for new medical attention for Pieter. Again it was Coincidence which had ordained his meeting with Charles Youngman; they had, literally walked into one another in the dark, got to talking, chanced to make one another laugh, and so founded a partnership which had been very profitable. So far, so good. Had Coincidence now stretched out her long arm and simply by throwing a man and a girl together offered him the ghost of a chance of defeating Mynheer's scheme and prospering his own?

Pondering these things, not with optimism but with a calm determination to make the most of every opportunity, Doctor Hootman plodded back to his place of imprisonment, while Charles lay in the dusk on the scented leaves and thought of Julia and how she had kissed him.

He kept coming back to that. His mind was like a dog tied to a stake with a good length of rope. It ran this way and that. He thought of Daan's unlimited nutmegs and of all the people who were anxious to buy one, just one that was fertile, that might grow into a tree which would make a crack in the solid stone front of the Dutch monopoly. He thought of the patrol boats making their futile, regular prowls on the look-out for smugglers. He thought of his fellow outlaws, the disillusioned, dispossessed, risking their lives for ten guilders, living in squalor and daily danger, but gallantly and cheerfully. He thought of Mynheer, and how, presently his eyes would redden and bulge and how the froth would gather at the corners of his mouth. He thought of Psyche, once a woman, now dead, like a dog, on the dunghill. And he thought of a long avenue of elms, noisy with rooks, that led to what had been a gracious house, tawny-pink in the English sunshine, now a heap of blackened rubble.

But always his thoughts came back to Julia, to the memory of that sweetly innocent and yet passionate kiss and the way it had stirred him.

Ten minutes. So many of his jobs called for perfect timing that he could gauge a given period to a few seconds without the aid of a timepiece. He rose, brushed himself down.

He might never see her again. There was no room in his life for sentiment. He told himself that he was overdue for a whiff of nutmeg-cheese.

Chapter Eight

When Mynheer returned, with his guests, from Banda, she was bathed and reclad, and the dress she had been wearing that afternoon, had been washed and hung at the back of the closet. Outwardly she looked calm enough, but the marrow of her bones still thrummed with a hidden vibration; and she decided to stay in her room until Pluto rang the miniature silver tong-tong as a sign that dinner was on the table. However, after a few minutes Mynheer himself came and tapped on her door.

'My dear, could you come and entertain my guests for a short time? Daan has just informed me that I am wanted. I know what it is–a business that won't take more than five minutes, but it seems rude to leave these gentlemen alone.'

She went with him to the veranda where the two gentlemen sat in the cane chairs with drinks before them. Mynheer made the introductions and slipped away.

Now was the moment for applying one of Mevrouw Helmers's little rules of behaviour. 'Always remember that gentlemen like to talk about themselves and their business. Open with a question or a remark which invites them to do so, and then sit and listen, pretending to understand, but now and again asking a question, so that they can explain to you. They like explaining, too.'

It was a sound rule. The gentlemen talked, the sun went down in all its blossoming glory; the gentlemen refilled their glasses, and talked again. Mynheer's five minutes stretched out to thirty, and Julia, with her guilty knowledge of what was being said, and experienced, somewhere else in the house, grew so uneasy that it was difficult for her to stay still.

At last, however, Mynheer stepped on to the veranda, and from within the house came the sound of the tong-tong. He apologized for the delay.

'Really, a most trivial bit of business that anyone could have dealt with,' he said. 'One day I shall get an agent. . . .'

She could see that, during his absence, he had been intensely, violently angry. His always prominent eyes were bulged out and the whites of them very red, and the hand which he laid on her arm as he made his apology had the same tremor as was shuddering through her own bones. His manner towards her, however, was unchanged and her heart went out in gratitude to the man who had rescued her.

The meal was lengthy, the conversation, however, often brought back to general topics, constantly drifting away again towards business. She wanted to escape and knew that, in their hearts, the men would be glad when she went. The shadows of Doctor Hootman and Pieter passed across the screen, and were duly commented upon and she was thinking that now, in a moment she might rise and go, when the man beside her, abandoning a spirited attack upon some new rule of the Company, turned to her and said: 'I expect like most ladies, you spend a good deal of time making pretty things with your needle, Mevrouw.'

Needle! Embroidery! My bag!

Caught off her guard her hand went to her mouth; she could feel her face change.

'Mynheer . . . that has reminded me of a promise I made and failed to keep.' She turned to the head of the table. 'I promised Marie that I would begin, at once, to make her something. . . .' The vagueness and the confusion would be attributed to the something being connected with a baby, unborn and therefore unmentionable; when she had gone Mynheer would tell the others and they would laugh!

'You haven't lost much time, my dear,' said Mynheer indulgently.

My bag! she thought. Now I must go . . . in the dark . . . to that dreadful, dreadful place, alone. Or, worse still, perhaps Mynheer has been already–that would account for the delay. Perhaps his smooth manner was assumed because there were guests. . . .

The trembling within–though when she looked down at her hands they *looked* steady–had now reached the paralytic stage, and though she wanted to jump up and rush out in search of the bag she felt unable to move.

Pluto, moving soundless as a shadow, paused by his master's chair, spoke in a low voice. Mynheer nodded.

'My dear, Pieter would like to see you for a moment.'

A new, and rather telling touch to the masquerade, she thought.

'I'll go at once,' she said, and willed her legs to support her as far as the door. Mynheer smiled at her with approval. He couldn't know; nobody could be so consummate an actor.

In the cloister she stood still for a moment, leaning her hot face against one of the cool stone pillars, steadying herself against its solidity. She was glad that this latest ruse gave her a chance of speaking alone to Doctor Hootman; he would know whether Mynheer had rushed straight to the scene of tragedy; he might even know whether he had believed the invented story or not. And he could, certainly, tell her something about the man who had helped her.

'Ah, Mevrouw,' said Doctor Hootman, opening the door of Pieter's room. 'I trust that this little proof of a happy connubial relationship was well received.'

It seemed to her that there was a marked, though subtle, change in his manner towards her; the words, with their hint of derision, seemed to place her on Doctor Hootman's side of some invisible boundary line. She wondered whether she dared ask him to go out and retrieve her bag. It was, she knew, a good deal to ask. Before she could find the courage, or the words to make the request he had turned from her and gone to one of the cupboards in which Pieter's clay and beads and paints were all tidily arrayed. When he turned back he had the brocade bag in his hands.

She said, 'Oh,' in a fading voice and groped her way to a chair, tears of sheer relief filling her eyes and rushing saltily into the back of her throat.

'I did consider putting it on your favourite seat in the garden,' Doctor Hootman said. 'Then I thought you might remember it and be worried.'

She swallowed painfully.

'I did remember it, just now, at the table. I nearly died. . . .'

'That must have been a bad moment,' said Doctor Hootman sympathetically. 'All is well now.'

He sat down on a chair on the other side of the table and looked at her. There was something new in his regard; it was–she searched for a word–it was speculative.

'You're a brave woman,' he said. It was a statement made without intent to praise, without admiration, without surprise. It was like his expression, speculative.

'Oh no. All along I've been terrified.'

'Indeed? I wondered whether you realized what a risk you were taking; whether perhaps Mynheer's paternal, indulgent manner had led you to think that you could do what you liked.'

'Far from it,' she said, with a little shudder. 'This afternoon I was half out of my wits. So much so that I didn't even ask the name of the man who helped me.'

'I gathered that you were somewhat distressed.'

He did not volunteer the name.

'Was Mynheer very angry?'

'He was so angry,' said Doctor Hootman with ghoulish relish, 'that he almost fell into a fit. By your charitable–and if I may say so, somewhat sentimental–action, Mevrouw, you have compelled two very stubborn men to break two of their own most inflexible rules. The man who helped you by taking the blame for Psyche's mishap has what we might call a business connexion with Mynheer; he never comes without an appointment, and on those occasions he is invisible to me. You understand. He and I, on less frequent occasions, meet, less formally perhaps, and then he is invisible to Mynheer. Today, in order to tell his tale he did an unprecedented thing, presented himself without an appointment. And when he had told his tale Mynheer, in his turn, did an unprecedented thing. He sent for me. So there we were, all three together,' he nodded towards the library and something that was not quite a smile lightened his heavy face. 'Very funny, really. It took all my skill and resource to have Mynheer ready to meet his guests in time. I don't suppose he has been so enraged since the day of Pieter's accident.'

'You knew about Psyche?'

'I know a number of things. I have learned not to interfere.'

'So have I.'

'I wonder,' he said. 'In this case, I must admit your temerity astonished me–if you knew what you risked. But then, I know very little about women. They look frail, but I suppose they can be resolute where their sentiments are concerned.'

He made the statement, but it had a questioning sound.

'I don't think it was sentiment. It was a kind of self-defence. I used to wake in the night and think about her. It made me so miserable, I had to do *something*. I know it wasn't much, but it probably comforted me more than it did her.'

Doctor Hootman's expression changed, took on something of astonishment, something of–yes–respect!

After a moment he said: 'Mevrouw, that does as much credit to your head as to your heart. Many people are kind, as you say, from self-defence, but those who realize their motive are very few, and those who would admit it still fewer. Yes now and again justice is done. You deserved your miracle this afternoon.'

'It was a miracle–that he happened to be there and was willing to take the blame. Doctor Hootman, what is his name?'

'To me he is known as Charles. Whether that is his name or not I don't know.'

'I was so confused and upset . . . but afterwards, thinking about it . . . his voice . . . he isn't Dutch, is he?'

'Oh no. He is English. The situation is very complicated and very changeable. Some years ago the English Royalists were welcome in the islands, you know. Cromwell was the enemy of the Dutch, therefore his enemies were regarded as friends. Then, when Cromwell gained the upper hand he demanded a few small islands as compensation for the so-called massacre of Amboyna, and naturally all the settlers there were not Royalists, and not welcome neighbours. There is a tendency, now, to lump them all together and to dislike them all. So each time Charles sets foot in Rua he takes a risk. When he comes to see me he takes another, a risk within a risk. I trust you to remember that, Mevrouw. I hold the secret of the truth about Psyche's death and you hold the secret of Charles's connexion with me.'

'I shouldn't dream of mentioning him to anyone,' she said warmly. 'After the way he helped me! I'd sooner die.'

A girlish extravagance of phrase? Possibly. Doctor Hootman's hand went to his chin, finger and thumb moved in a rhythmical stroking.

'His behaviour this afternoon was quite out of character, I must say.'

'In what way, Doctor Hootman?'

'I should have thought him capable of passing by on the other side, or, if expedient, stepping *over* any number of weeping women in the pursuit of his unlawful occasions. The life he and his little group lead is not conducive to impulsive acts of chivalry.'

He said the words with deliberate provocation.

'I thought you were supposed to be his friend. He spoke well of *you*!'

'I intended no criticism, Mevrouw. I was merely commenting upon the surprising contradictions of which man is capable.'

'I don't think that even there you are right. When something happens, and people have to act quickly, without time to think, then they show their true characters. I thought about that when I was trying not to be frightened about going to that place. You can't become brave all in a moment; and you can't become kind all in a moment either. I think Charles helped me this afternoon because he is kind, and brave.'

'You may be right, Mevrouw.'

He wondered whether to leave it there. But an opportunity of this kind might never come again.

'All the same,' he went on, 'you mustn't underestimate the force of emotion. You, for example, say that you were frightened, yet you acted with courage because something in Psyche's plight appealed to you. I think much the same thing could be said about Charles's behaviour. Something about you must have made a strong appeal to him. He asked me your name, and was very anxious to know whether Mynheer treated you kindly–a subject upon which I was able to reassure him.'

She said nothing to that, but the expression on her face told him that the words had not been wasted. After a moment he asked, in the voice which suited the change of subject.

'Well, the whole affair ended fortunately. In future Mevrouw, you should be careful about allowing your will to come into conflict with Mynheer's.'

'It never will again,' she said, with some firmness.

'Can one be sure?' One of his eyebrows lifted.

'Reasonably sure. It's unlikely that I should find another Psyche, and short of that . . . Even then I think I might think twice about it.'

'I suggest that you leave now, Mevrouw. The two fat fellows believe you to be with Pieter, but Mynheer knows otherwise and he might wonder what you and I have so suddenly discovered to talk about.' He rose as he spoke, lifted the embroidery bag and handed it to her.

The blood had spattered it too, and the brownish-black spots stood out starkly against the pale pink shining stuff. She took it gingerly, with a resurge of horror and disgust. She would throw it away at once. Then she remembered that he had handled it, had contrived to return it to her. Immediately it became the most precious of all her possessions. She would clean it as well as she could, and if–as she feared was the case with her dress–some stains remained, stubborn and immovable, she would regard them as reminders, not of the evil thing, but of the kindness and comfort with which they were equally associated. They would be her link with the man she might never see again.

'It may never happen,' said Doctor Hootman, moving towards the door, 'but if it ever should . . . If Mynheer were away for instance, or some other circumstance made it quite safe to do so, I would try to arrange that Charles could see for himself that you were well and happy. That is if that should be agreeable to you.'

'Oh yes, indeed it would. Thank you. Doctor Hootman. Thank you, too, very much for all you have done today.'

'It was a pleasure, Mevrouw. Good night.'

He fastened the door and went back to his chair; he did not take up his book. Busily and intently he wove and twisted and knotted the filaments of his thoughts, a gigantic spider, spinning a gigantic web.

Julia went to bed but it was a long time before she slept. Whether she lay with eyes open or closed, there passed before them, in a series of little pictures, all the events of the day. They came and went, their choice beyond her control. It was useless to turn shuddering from the memory of Psyche, drenched in her blood, and to think–I'll remember Charles instead. Then no picture came; just a few disconnected fragments which added up to nothing, had no life or meaning. An old shirt with a torn frill: a pair of very blue eyes, the white lines running out against the darkly tanned skin: brow and cheeks scoured by harsh living: a mouth firm against her own. But just before she fell asleep every other memory of the day receded and she saw him whole and clear, just as he had stood at the opening of the path and waved his hand. Once again her heart, her whole being moved out towards him.

Somewhere in the very heart of the night, she began to dream. She was in the cage, chained and naked, just as Psyche had been. She knew why she was there, she had offended Mynheer and that was her punishment. She was not, however, unduly distressed because Doctor Hootman had promised to help her and she had only to wait for his coming. Then he came, but not alone. Mynheer and Pieter were with him. Mynheer carried his silver-knobbed cane and Pieter had a piece of knitting which was ravelling out as he walked. They came and stood by the bars and looked at her, and then they began to laugh. They all laughed in the same way, mockingly. She realized that she had been fooled. She had no friend. She would stay here, shamed and tortured until she died.

She woke, moaning and shuddering, with the sweat of cold terror crawling over her skin. Even when she was fully awake and sensible the evil aura of the dream remained, as a foul taste will linger in the mouth.

But it was only a dream. It was the natural, and inevitable result of the day's excitement. She was in no danger. Charles had seen to that. She thought of him, at first with gratitude, and then, all at once with longing. Now the things of which Frieda had whispered, things which so long had lain indigestible, a source of discomfort, became assimilated, became part of her being. *Now* she understood. With just the one, the chosen person, that would be possible . . . wonderful . . . right.

She lay quite still, stunned by the revelation, and her girlhood slipped away. She could think now with a rueful, tolerant amusement of her immature idea of love, two porcelain figures against a background of flowers! What nonsense.

Her thoughts shifted. She recalled, with a new, bitter understanding, some of the pitying things Mynheer had said to her about herself. 'A married woman without a husband, with no hope of children.' She recalled also Charles's words, 'married to that idiot boy.'

She realized for the first time, the full extent to which she had been defrauded.

Chapter Nine

Suddenly all Mynheer's talk concerned a young kinsman of his, Nicolas Vanderplasse, who was coming to spend three months at Rua.

'A long-standing, vague arrangement,' he said, 'which couldn't have fallen out more happily. If he'd come last year he would have found Rua intolerably dull, and I should have found the effort to entertain him quite exhausting.' Nothing betrayed the fact that he was giving Fate credit for a timeliness which was of his own contriving.

He went on to explain that amongst planters of standing in the islands, there was a system of exchange not unlike that which had existed in mediaeval times when a boy would go and learn his knightly duties in another man's hall.

'Whether the young scamps really learn more than they would at home is debatable, but it does them good to get away; some of these planters are born and die in the same spot without moving more than twenty miles either way. The custom does contribute in some small measure to the dissemination of new ideas, and of course in some cases it helps to mitigate the danger of inbreeding. With Nicolas the wife-hunting does not apply, he has been betrothed from childhood to the daughter of a man who was Governor of Amboyna, a suitable match in many ways but in one regrettable; all the women of that family are plain and dull, a horrible combination. I am sure he will envy Pieter very much.'

'Does he know about Pieter?'

'He knows what I have chosen the world should know. You, my dear, and Doctor Hootman are the only ones I have ever taken into my confidence. Of course, on so prolonged a visit, and with a kinsman, things will be a little difficult, but we must do our best. It can't be helped. You, I am sure, will support me to the best of your ability.'

'Of course. You see, Mynheer, the truth makes me look very silly.'

He pondered that for a moment, sucking in his cheeks so that his eyes seemed more than every disproportionately large. Then he said, and the simple words went to the heart of the matter with a frightening shrewdness:

'But the truth is known only to us three. Does Doctor Hootman's awareness of the situation embarrass you?'

She knew that it did not; it never had done. Even Marie's reference to Mucky Karl had been, only an awkward blow to be parried. It was Charles, saying, 'You don't mean to tell me that you're married to that idiot boy?' which had shown her the truth; and Mynheer's words came perilously near to asking, 'Who else knows?'

She braced herself, looked him in the eye and said:

'I sometimes think about the servants.'

'The slaves. My poor child. I never realized. I should have explained. Pieter has his own staff; a Hindu widow who counts herself fortunate to be alive at all; she does the menial work, and an Ethiopian whom I went to some pains–and was lucky–to acquire; he takes charge during the hours when Daan is free. He is, in point of fact, dumb. The Ethiopians have an amiable custom of making the punishment fit the crime, the hand which steals is cut off, and so forth. Echo, as I named him when he came into my employ, when he could speak told a lie, apparently. My dear, don't look at me like that, it was not my doing. I merely report a fact. So you see, you need have no thoughts about the slaves' thoughts! As for the outer world, they gossip and they speculate, but so long as we work together they can *know* nothing, and in the end we shall utterly confound them!'

It was not the first time that he had made such a reference to the future, and whenever he did so she had imagined that he was stubbornly clinging to the hope of some improvement in Pieter's condition; that had always seemed pitiable and now, in the light of what Charles had called Pieter, 'idiot boy', it seemed doubly so. Her feeling must have shown in her face, for he said:

'I know now that he will never recover. I hoped. I told myself that the brain was delicate, out of reach of balm and plaster, that it must heal of its own accord, take its own time. I expected a change when he was twenty-one. There was no change; I have now resigned myself to the likelihood that there never will be. But . . . life must go on. And I am fortunate,' his voice brightened, 'in having such staunch support in Doctor Hootman. Sometimes, before he came, the burden did seem unbearable. And now I have *you*.'

Thinking that he was counting her as an ally in the task of concealment, the pretence that Pieter was merely disfigured and misanthropic, she said:

'I shall do what I can to help.'

'I believe that.' He came towards her and put his hands on her shoulders. She could feel the dry heat of them through the stuff of her dress. His manner changed, so did his expression.

'I think God sent you. I did Him a small wrong, and in return He thrust me into torment that makes Hell look like a summer garden. He took all I had; a cruel usury. Night after night I've wrestled with Him like Jacob of old, demanding not mercy, but justice. And now for the first time, I see a little hope, a gleam of promise.' He seemed to be overcome with emotion, strangled by it, his eyes popped and his whole face quivered. Dropping his hands, he turned and went quickly away.

Mynheer had last seen Nicolas when he was fourteen, six years ago, but he could have picked him out from a score of young men of the same age, identically clothed; he was so very much a Vosmar, with such a close resemblance to himself as a young man; even his eyes, grey and set well-forward now, would be protruberant in years to come. He had the kind of good looks that come of youth, of perfect health and cheerfulness, and at the moment of meeting everything about him was touched by a not unpleasing shyness.

As Mynheer greeted his young kinsman, his heart contracted with a sickening spasm of pain. Just so should Pieter have been. Oh, what pride, what measureless pride would he have taken in a son like this.

The greeting he extended was cheerful, however, and as soon as they were seated in the prahau, he began to talk about the Pieter who did not exist; partly because he derived an obscure comfort from describing the mythical figure. It afforded him the same relief as a cover drawn over a dead face; the truth lay there, but it no longer stared up stark and bare.

'I think,' Mynheer began, 'that I must prepare you as regards Pieter. I suppose you've heard something from your parents.'

Nicolas, who had heard a good deal of speculation and comment, said tactfully:

'We all knew that he had had an accident and that it had made him very . . . shy.'

'Shy is an understatement. His passion for retirement has reached the point of mania now. I know he is greatly to be pitied, but he makes things very difficult. He has his own apartments, from which he never emerges, except sometimes for an evening walk. Even his meals he insists upon taking alone. Well, not entirely alone; he has a great friend, a Doctor Hootman. They are inseparable companions.'

Nicholas mumbled that it was all a great pity.

'A great pity. And I, a few months back, made a most regrettable mistake. I encouraged, I *urged* him to get married.'

'Oh.' Nicolas's voice held surprise. None of the stories current in the Java branch of the family, stories fabricated from guesswork and embroidered with suspicion, had ever hinted of 'poor Cousin Pieter' being a suitable subject for matrimony.

'You never told us,' he said.

'No, I meant to write, but to tell you the truth, I was so disappointed by the way things turned out that I lacked the heart to spread the news. She's such a sweet girl, pretty, charming, willing to overlook . . . a really dear girl. And I had such high hopes. I really thought she would cure him; I thought that for her sake he would exert himself, face things. I thought the mere fact that a sweet pretty girl didn't shrink from him would give him confidence. She never did; from the first moment her manner has been perfect. I can't speak too highly of her. It may seem a strange thing for a father to say, but by his treatment of her Pieter has somewhat alienated my sympathy. That is Rua, over there.'

The boy stared ahead eagerly.

'I've heard so much about it, from Mother. She used to spend a good deal of time here as a child, didn't she?'

'Yes, she and my father were cousins–he was much older, of course. There was a great affection between them. I've heard him say how sorry he was that she married in Java. Let me see now, you are betrothed, are you not?'

'I'm to be married almost as soon as I get back.'

'Indeed. How time flies. And it's one of the Hoogenbeet girls, isn't it. Greta or Christine?'

'Fancy your remembering their names.'

'My memory is pretty good. I never knew the girls, they were very small when their father retired; but I knew Mevrouw Hoogenbeet! That probably accounts for my remembering; one didn't forget anything Mevrouw Hoogenbeet told one! My word, no. She was a most terrifying woman.' He laughed irreverently, almost boyishly. 'Dear me, yes, it was once my misfortune to be in Amboyna when the Governor gave a ball, and there being nobody of much importance handy, I had to lead out Mevrouw. I know I'm no giant, but honestly, she seemed to me to be about seven feet tall.'

Nicholas's shyness dropped away. The Java family held Uncle Simon in grudging respect; he was very, very rich; he was very, very proud; he was more than a little eccentric; he was hard to please; critical, arrogant, a very difficult character indeed. Nicolas, weighed down with orders to be on his best behaviour, had embarked with some trepidation. And now, suddenly he found himself telling Uncle Simon of a secret fear that he had never mentioned to his favourite brother.

'Everything I hear about Mevrouw Hoogenbeet fills me with alarm,' he said. 'I'm terrified that Greta will be like her.'

'She can't be as tall; rest assured of *that*.'

'How can you know?'

'Because Mynheer Hoogenbeet was much shorter than his wife, and my observation tells me that girls are almost always shorter than their fathers, just as boys are almost always taller than their mothers.'

'Is that so?' asked Nicolas, much interested.

'It seems to me a natural law, to keep the human race from breeding giants and dwarfs. Most men marry women slightly less tall than themselves–they lack Mynheer Hoogenbeet's courage, you see! Then the boys over-top their mother, the girls stop short of their father and a rough kind of average is kept.'

'Well, thank you, Uncle Simon. That's the first word of hope or comfort anybody has ever offered me. All I've heard was about Mevrouw Hoogenbeet's size and strong-mindedness and economical housekeeping!'

'She was virtuous, too!' said Mynheer drily. 'You know, I often think these early betrothals, glove marriages and marriages by proxy are a regrettable necessity. Take my poor Julia who surely deserves, if ever a girl did, to be happily married. It may be quite revolutionary of me, but I am inclined to think that there should be some element of choice in a matter which after all, is going to be an important factor in two people's lives. I don't say the whole decision should rest with the young–if you'll pardon my saying so, few of them have sufficient judgement, or experience to make such a momentous decision; but they should be allowed to meet first, to talk together, find out if they are agreeable to one another.'

'That's exactly what I think,' said Nicolas eagerly. 'You not only thought so, you acted on what you thought and believed, didn't you, Uncle Simon?'

It was a mistake.

Mynheer's face went stiff and cold.

'You know my story? Yes, I acted. But of course that kind of . . . Never mind. I can tell you this, though. Nicholas. I've no doubt that when your female relatives discuss my affairs they say: "Serve him right!" But if I had the choice to make again I would act exactly as I did then, even if I knew what would result. Two years is a short time. A week is even shorter. But a week with a woman you really love is worth a lifetime of the other thing. That's not something I should say to you, perhaps. Look you can see the house now, the long low white building.'

Again Nicolas stared out, but the conversation was, for him, too intimately interesting to be lightly abandoned. It was the first time in his life that he had taken part in that kind of talk; in his home accepted customs were not criticized and, despite his twenty years and imminent marriage, he was treated like a child.

'The thing is,' he said tentatively, 'that the system seems to work. I mean, for most people. Most marriages seem fairly happy, don't they?' It was a thought from which he had derived a little comfort when he visualized himself as a married man.

'That,' said Mynheer, 'is the most damning indictment. Fairly happy. Who wants to be fairly happy? Scale the peaks of ecstasy, yes! Even if, afterwards you're thrown down, like Lucifer. Taste the golden apple once, even if it turns to wormwood in your mouth. How much better than the dull jog-trot of "fairly happy".'

This was heady talk.

'Oh, I do agree. But some of us are doomed to jog-trot. Take me, for example. To tell you the truth I'm *not* looking forward to my marriage. But there it is, all arranged. And I have never seen any woman for whom it would be worth while to defy the rules and upset my father and . . . and everything. Perhaps that kind of, well, romance only happens to a few people.'

'Perhaps. I think it also offers itself to many others who refuse it out of cowardice or a silly regard for what you call "the rules". I'm inclined to look behind the rules and ask myself who made them, and why. "Thou shalt not covet they neighbour's wife", for example. Why, in God's name, if she's covetable? That one, I'm sure was slipped in by some very unattractive fellow who had a *supremely* covetable wife.'

The son of a very strict, reformed Dutch family experienced a slight sense of shock which made him jerk out:

'But Uncle Simon, that was one of the Commandments that God gave to Moses.'

'Was it?' Mynheer's voice was elaborately casual. 'I rather suspect that many of those edicts suffered some change during the process of being carved in stone. A lengthy business, you know. I for one, would hesitate to order my life on what may have been a slip of the chisel.'

After a second's blinking astonishment Nicolas threw back his head and laughed. Something innate, inherent in his Vosmar blood, long subjected to the Vanderplasse stream, leaped up to embrace its own.

'Uncle Simon,' he said, 'you're not a bit what I expected. Oh, I think I'm going to enjoy my stay in Rua. Mother often said it was like nowhere else on earth.'

'I don't know about that. I do most sincerely hope that you will be happy. I shall do my best to make you so. I hope you'll be company for Julia and that you will, as far as possible, ignore Pieter; that, believe me is the kindest thing you can do. And now, here we are. Welcome to Rua.'

Chapter Ten

Nicolas Vanderplasse was twenty years old, a perfectly normal, healthy young man who had been rather strictly brought up, and who had his full share of the sensuality which is so often found in sons of puritannical fathers. He had made his first visit to a brothel when he was seventeen, staggered by his own daring, knowing it to be sordid and mercenary, and overcome by a paralyzing sense of guilt. Nevertheless, he had returned. At the same time, as though to restore the balance, he had developed, and for rather more than two years maintained, a slavish, mooningly-romantic relationship with a married woman who, at the age of twenty-five was as much his senior as she was junior to her fifty-year-old husband. It had been an affair of soft glances, sweet speeches, a snatched kiss here and a handclasp there, of dreams without any hope of fulfilment. It had died a natural and quite painless death with the beginning of her first pregnancy.

Like most other young men of his age and in his situation, he would then have begun to look forward to marriage as an answer to the demands of both sides of his nature, and to dream of the wife about whom he could feel both romantic and passionate, but here was a handicap, peculiar to him. The ghost of Mevrouw Hoogenbeet still stalked the islands. Fifteen years had passed since Mynheer Hoogenbeet's retirement from the governorship of Amboyna, but the memories and stories of her size, her parsimony, her tirades and her bullying persisted. Was it possible that Greta, daughter of such a woman, could be lovable? Nicolas doubted it and had begun to look upon his marriage as a life sentence.

However, he had still some months of freedom and he intended to make the most of them. Setting out for his visit to Rua he had made up his mind to sample–along with anything else that offered–the pleasures of the compound, the 'Brown Satin' as men called it. This was a thing which decent men, men of sensibility, avoided on their own plantations, or even on those in their vicinity, since it was not altogether agreeable to see recognizable family features emerging from some small brown face.

He had forgotten this intention, and almost everything else within a week, having fallen in love for the first time. Here was the very girl of whom–but for the shadow of Mevrouw Hoogenbeet–he would have been dreaming; lovely to look at, with grace and charm, delightful to talk to, a girl to adore, and one who could, at the same time, by a glance or the brush of her sleeve wake unimaginable hungers.

The setting too, might have been specially designed to be the background of a love affair. Nicolas had been born and bred in the islands; the colours and the scents were not new to him as they were to Julia. But now all the world was made new. The wealth of flowers, loading the air with fragrance, the brooding green of the trees, the sunsets, the water creaming on the pale beach, the silver and ebony of the moonlit night all offered themselves to eyes hitherto blind. The very doves, mourning in the nutmeg trees, ceased to be greedy marauders, the planters' enemies, and became the disembodied voice of enchantment.

And there was in Rua also, unconsciously yet immediately assimilated, a sense of moral freedom, almost of laxity. Here nobody watched, nobody criticized. 'You two young people must amuse one another.' Uncle Simon had said as soon as he had introduced them, and after that he seemed to show no more interest or curiosity in their comings and goings than he did in the flight of the birds. His only concern was that they should be happy. At home industry was, in its own right, a virtue, so great a virtue in fact that even the appearance of it was sought after, those who were not actually busy affecting to be so. Uncle Simon's attitude was the reverse.

'I go out when the tong-tong rings, and I see everything started. If you care to come with me that is as good a time as any to see how things work. After that, on a properly organized plantation, the business should proceed smoothly. I look in here and there at various times of course, where and when I'm least expected; and I invariably check on the stores myself. But you don't have to turn out every morning, Nicolas. Young people can sleep on, and they should. They should also be grateful that they can. I wake at dawn now, wherever I am, and once awake I must be stirring.'

Most mornings Nicolas managed to wake and accompany his uncle on the rounds; and during those hours together the insidious process of undermining the home standards would go on. Uncle Simon laughed at things which would deeply have shocked Nicolas's father, and mocked at things regarded with reverence at home; and although Nicolas would often be disconcerted by the levity and the mockery, almost always, immediately afterwards he would think, 'But he's right', or 'I often felt that way myself'.

One of the most startling, and pleasing of Uncle Simon's attitudes was that which he adopted towards youth. At home youth was something slightly deplorable. 'You'll know better when you're older'; 'You're too young to understand'; 'You're just a silly boy'; 'Remember you are addressing your elders.' In Rua youth was given its due. 'It's the best time, my boy, make no mistake about that. Whatever the years bring they take away the capacity for enjoyment.' 'It's one of life's ironies that by the time a man can afford the best wine he has lost his palate'; 'Half the rules are made by old men to prevent young ones doing things that they themselves can no longer do.'

Once he spoke, in terms of age, about Julia who had just left them in order to make her morning visit to Pieter.

'I hate myself sometimes,' Uncle Simon said. 'I should have persuaded him to marry an older woman. Thirty would have been the perfect age. How can a girl like that care what an interesting book he is reading? That is his main topic, you know; books! Life at one remove. She's at an age when life should be *lived*, not read about, talked about. Pieter, poor boy, never had any youth, he has to accept a substitute, but she . . . It's like seeing a bud flung out on the dust heap with a bunch of dead flowers.'

None of these speeches was momentous in itself, but each made its small contribution; and when the time for plain speaking came the atmosphere had been established.

It began with a morning walk. Julia had by this time become aware of Nicholas's infatuation and was trying to acquire the art of avoiding sentimental scenes without injuring his feelings. She had learned that it was advisable to have a definite destination when they took a walk, and, if possible, some impersonal topic for conversation.

'This morning I'm going to show you some trees which even your uncle doesn't know the names of, and see if you can tell me,' she said.

'I doubt if I can. They must be rare if he couldn't name them. What are they like?'

'Red.'

'There are dozens of red trees. And of course there are different names in different places for the same tree. At home we had a tree, with a red trumpet-shaped flower, which we, and everybody else around us called Cardinal's Hat, but my Macassar cousins, when they came to stay, called it Bee Bloom. We had one of those is-isn't-is-isn't arguments about it and I got a walloping for not being polite to guests.'

'These are quite a walk away, we mustn't dawdle.'

'I never knew anyone who liked to walk so fast as you do, Julia. And you've been here such a short time, you should feel the heat. But I can't imagine you getting hot and red in the face. Your face always looks as though it were made of ivory or alabaster or something like that.'

They came at last to where the trees stood, all in a group together. Their tops were thickly massed with flowers of a deep, rich red colour which made a pleasant contrast with the feathery evergreen of the nutmegs and of the lofty Canariums which over-topped and shaded the groves.

'There, aren't they pretty? Why, Nicolas, what is the matter?'

He was staring at the trees with an expression of astonishment and profound dismay.

'They're . . . they're *cloves*!' he said in a voice of disbelief.

'Well, is that so astonishing?'

'Julia dear! There isn't supposed to be a clove tree in all the islands, except in Amboyna. My God, if the Company knew! Uncle Simon must be *crazy*!'

'He doesn't know what they are. I asked him when I first saw them and he said: "Oh, just a native tree".'

'That's quite impossible. He's lived here all his life and they used to be quite common. Then the Company decided to concentrate the clove-growing in Amboyna and every tree elsewhere had to be cut down. My father had to get rid of his, I've heard him speak of it. You can't go against the Company these days, you know.' He looked at the pretty, sweet-scented trees and shook his head in a puzzled way. 'Where does he sell them?' He answered his own question. 'He *can't* sell them. So why on earth does he take such a risk? And waste the space. It beats me.'

'I think it's quite likely that they've always stood there, and he thought they were pretty, so he kept them.'

'Ye–es; with him that is just possible. Rua is his kingdom, isn't it? My mother always says he acts as though he were Royalty. Which makes it all the harder for him–Pieter, I mean.'

'In what way?' asked Julia carefully.

'Staying at home, not showing off, not cutting a dash as the heir apparent. Uncle Simon cut no end of a dash when he was young, or so I've heard, and no doubt he'd have liked his son to be the same.'

'I think it more likely that he thinks his heir is his heir and therefore permitted to behave just as he chooses.'

'That's a shrewd remark. That's one thing I do like about you, Julia. Most girls as pretty as you–not that there are many–never say anything worth listening to.'

'Will you mention the clove trees?'

'You bet I shall. I shall warn him, too. Rua may be a kingdom, but the Company rules an Empire, and even Uncle Simon is only one of its satraps.'

'It's *what*?'

'It comes out of the Bible. Somebody, probably Nebuchadnezzar, had princes and satraps. I was brought up on the Bible. Weren't you?'

'Not really . . . which is rather strange, though I never, I must admit, thought about it until now. I spent quite a long time in what was called, officially, "The Christian and Benevolent Refuge for Orphans," otherwise the Klopstock Home. It wasn't very Christian, or very benevolent, but it was completely Klopstock. To be quite honest we didn't all have cloaks, but for the daily walk that didn't matter because some of us always had to stay in to finish work, or for a punishment or something. But for Sunday church if we had all gone there weren't enough. I think that must have been the reason . . . we never did go.'

'You don't realize how lucky you were. At home the sermons last two hours. I can remember several that lasted even longer.'

The innocuous, unprovocative comparison of their upbringing and experiences lasted all the way back to the house.

Doctor Hootman always left the table promptly after dinner and Julia soon followed him, leaving the gentlemen to their wine. On this evening, as soon as they were alone, Nicolas said:

'Uncle Simon, you *do* know a clove tree when you see one?'

'I should hope so. I'm not blind or in my dotage.'

'Then you know you have quite a number here, in Rua?'

'Of course. I know every tree on Rua. Why?'

'Why? Because if the Company ever found out they'd . . . they'd. . . .'

'Fine me. A sum of money, large by their standards, negligible by mine, which I should not pay without protest, my boy.'

Nicolas's eyes widened and bulged in a way which foreshadowed how like his kinsman he would be in later years.

'*Not* without protest,' he repeated. 'To whom could you make a protest in a case like this?'

Mynheer did not answer immediately; he offered the wine and then refilled his own glass.

'The Company,' he said mildly, 'is very large, and like most over-grown things is not constitutionally very sound. Also, like all large things it offers a wide target of vulnerability. In Holland there are many–in very high places–who view with grave concern this insistence upon monopolies and the over-riding of civil rights. Only the other evening the Governor of Banda, here at this table, said that it was only when he dined out that he took precedence of the Company's Agent: he described himself as a mere figurehead, rapidly becoming a figure of fun. By what right does the Company–that conclave of merchants and stockholders–dictate to me what I should grow on my own ground? Those clove trees have always grown there, and as far as is humanly possible I have preserved this estate as I received it . . . as I hope to pass it on. Is that a crime? They could never prove that I had sold a clove. No man can do the patently impossible. I should have quite a case, Nicolas, which properly handled might easily do the Company more damage than they could do me. And I would see that it was properly handled.'

Nicolas looked at Mynheer with admiration; he had heard, for as long as he could remember, complaints about the Company's growing autocratism, but he had never before heard words of open defiance. He was, however, except where women were concerned, of a realistic turn of mind.

'That's all very well,' he said. 'Meantime they could refuse to ship your nutmegs, and then where would you be?'

'Here, I trust. And losing no sleep, I assure you. I grow nutmegs because nutmegs have always been grown on Rua; but I do not, thank God, depend upon the nutmegs for my daily bread, or other small comforts.'

Nicolas had always know that the Rua branch of the family was far wealthier than his own, but to talk of being independent of nutmegs hinted at riches of a fabulous kind; in the islands everybody, everything depended upon that small, brown, shrivelled object. But not, apparently, Uncle Simon. . . .

He said in that special voice which people reserve for talk of money in large quantities.

'It must be nice to be so rich.'

'It is nice to be independent–and in these days that demands money.It was not always so; the first Vosmar to own Rua had no money at all, he was independent by virtue of his strong body and indomitable mind. But those days are over.' He paused, as though paying past history the tribute of a moment's silence. Then he said: 'Yes, I am rich. I inherited a fortune, and by careful manipulation I have made another. Far more money than poor Pieter, with his simple tastes, will ever know how to spend.' He sighed, and with an air of abandoning the subject, lifted his wine glass and sipped at it, daintily.

'You're the eldest of, which is it, I always forget, four, aren't you, Nicolas?'

'Out of date, Uncle Simon. There's baby Benjamin.'

'Of course. That's three boys. And two girls to be provided with dowries. You won't–to begin with, anyway, have too much to do with, will you?'

'I should think not.'

'Well,' Mynheer said, 'I've taken a liking to you; you are my kin, and as I said just now I have more than Pieter would know what to do with. Mark you, everything I inherited goes to him, it couldn't be otherwise. But of the money I made myself I propose to leave you a share, or give it to you in my lifetime if you prefer; I think one needs money more in youth than in age. This isn't a sudden decision, my boy. Long before you came I had meditated it, and decided that if you turned out to be a real Vosmar, as you promised to as a boy, and if I took a fancy to you, I'd do something substantial for you. And I will.'

This was the realization of a family hope which had peeped slyly out from behind the arrangement of the long visit. For some time references to Rua had abounded with little unfinished sentences concerning the one, rather unsatisfactory son, probably in delicate health, certainly taking no part in running the estate, and the chance which awaited Nicolas if he ingratiated himself with his relative. Now here it was. And all he could find to say was:

'It's wonderfully good of you, Uncle Simon. I don't know how to thank you.'

'Then don't. I don't want thanks. It will please me to think that you can enjoy some slight independence. Will you take brandy?'

'No, thank you,' said Nicolas, with a slight self-righteousness.

'Do. To keep me company. I have something else to discuss with you. To my mind a much more serious matter.'

'Oh. What is it?'

Mynheer knew the value of silence. Without speaking he poured brandy into two glasses, pushed his chair back from the table, crossed his legs and carefully removed a tiny thread which clung to the knee of his pale grey breeches.

'It concerns Julia . . .' he said, and noted, with satisfaction a slight deepening of colour in the smooth pink and white boyish face. 'You're in love with her, aren't you?'

Put like that it sounded like an accusation; and coming so soon after the talk about money hinted at a bargain, an attempt to buy him off. Aware of this, yet unwilling to deny the first genuine love of his life, Nicolas played for time.

'What makes you say that?'

'If there is one thing that annoys me,' said Mynheer testily, 'it is to have a question answered by another. I asked you, are you in love with Julia?'

Julia was Pieter's wife and Uncle Simon was Pieter's father; and however lightly and irreverently he might speak about one's neighbour's covetable wife, it would be a very different thing when it concerned the family. And a love affair with Julia however delightful, could only last for three months. The money would last forever.

'I find her extremely attractive,' he said, 'but I do assure you, I've never touched her or said a word that couldn't have been overheard.'

'That still doesn't answer my question.'

'Very well, then, I am,' said Nicolas sulkily. 'How could I not be? I know she's Pieter's wife, but that is difficult to bear in mind, the way things are! But I swear. . . .'

'Never mind that. For the rest, you have said it exactly. It is difficult to bear in mind that she is Pieter's wife. I'm not in his confidence, or in hers to that extent, but I'll tell you this. I'd wager my last guilder the girl's a virgin still. And I tell you this, also, and I say it as sincerely as I ever said anything in my life. If Julia could have one romantic, successful love affair, nobody would be more delighted than I!'

Now thoroughly taken aback and scarlet to the edge of his hair, Nicolas could only gulp out:

'Why?'

'I have many reasons. First of all, I'm sorry for the girl. Think of her position; married to a man who, just because his face isn't acceptable, won't offer what is. My second reason is more selfish. I don't know how well you understand women, I flatter myself that I do. All women need an emotional anchor. If you consider that a moment you'll perceive its truth. Some women live on mere memories, some take to religion, some lavish their affections on pet monkeys or dogs. They have to have something; and what they don't get in one place they look for in another. Unless my poor Julia is given, very soon, some emotional and imaginative ballast I shall have trouble. She'll take a lover and there'll be scandal to deal with. One really satisfactory love affair would give her something to remember, dwell on, be sentimental about for the rest of her life. I know that is true, Nicolas. I remember three old Vosmar aunts–the Macassar side, before your time; all unmarried, two miserable, sour, spiteful, horrible old women, the third quite content and happy; the man she was betrothed to had been drowned at sea, but she had her memories. I think of her very often. I would like Julia to have a memory, at least.'

It sounded very sad and romantic, and very far away from the brisk, cool-hearted, hard-headed household in which he had been reared.

'I'm very fond of Julia. I'm sorry for her. But I doubt . . . I mean, there are her feelings to be considered, too.'

'By your own account you have never tested them,' Mynheer reminded him. 'It would hardly be maidenly for her to show her feelings, would it? She's very young, quite untouched . . .' He contrived somehow to give the last word an unmistakable lasciviousness. Spurred by it Nicolas dared to say:

'And suppose we did . . . and suppose she had a baby.'

'I hadn't thought of that. My thoughts always ended with Julia. Well, do you know, I think that would be even better than an empty memory. A child can entirely fill a woman's life. And she'll never get one out of Pieter at this rate. I don't think that that would be a tragedy at all. But that *is* carrying speculation rather far, don't you think.' He smiled and then said in a voice which struck exactly the right, seemingly irresponsible note: 'Dear me, I'm afraid this has become a most unorthodox conversation. Quite reprehensible. How shocked and alarmed your dear parents would be! And really I only want everybody to be *happy*. Youth passes, and life passes and I've learned that it is what one misses that one regrets.'

Chapter Eleven

Until Nicolas allowed his feelings for her to become obvious Julia had enjoyed his company very much. She was a little shy with him at first, for he was something entirely new, the first young man with whom she had been brought into contact; but as soon as he found his Uncle Simon so very different from the formidable person of family legend, his own diffidence disappeared and his naturally good spirits rose, so that it was impossible to be shy with him for long.

In the beginning the only jarring note in their gay companionship was his deep and persistent curiosity concerning his cousin Pieter. He had hardly believed what he had been told on arrival–that it was unlikely that he would see his relative; but as the days went on and Pieter remained invisible he became understandably inquisitive. It was not a subject to discuss with Uncle Simon, so he turned to Julia.

'Exactly in what way is he disfigured, Julia?'

Once again she gave the ready-made reply about the disfigurement being exaggerated.

'How much exaggerated? Is he awful to look at?'

'Not in the least.' She could say that with truth now; she had become so accustomed to Pieter's appearance that she could hardly remember the shock it had been when he first turned his head.

'You can bear to look at him?'

'Of course. Don't I visit him every day?'

'Now you know, that is an odd thing to say. *Visit*. Wives don't visit their husbands.'

She coloured with self-annoyance.

'We spend some time together. Is that better? He has pursuits that I can't share and he has Doctor Hootman for company.'

'There's a curious character if you like!'

'In what way?' She turned to a discussion of Doctor Hootman with relief.

'Secretive,' Nicolas said, after a little pause during which he sought for the right word. 'As though, behind that dull, solid look all kinds of things were going on. I've often glanced at him suddenly and seen him staring at me, measuring me up. Then he'll look quickly away.'

'I think he's shy, too. He used to look at me like that when I first came. He's quite nice, really!'

'But what a way to live! Pieter presumably has a reason for his behaviour; but you'd think anybody else would go crazy. I should.'

'Doctor Hootman probably enjoys a quiet life.'

She was astonished to find how easily evasive and deceptive sentences would slip out. She would come from Pieter's room and find Nicolas waiting for her.

'And how is Pieter this morning?'

'Very well, thank you.'

'What's he doing?'

He was painting when I left him. A grain of truth there. Pieter enjoyed applying blobs and strokes of colour to his queer-shaped bits of pottery. And it was almost true to say, when she had left him busy stringing his beads, 'he was doing some sort of sums.' He was adding one to one. And if he were cutting up paper with his blunt nosed scissors it could be called 'paper-work'. Nicolas was given to believe that Pieter, though a recluse, led a full and busy life.

But things changed. Nicolas began looking at her differently, long-resting, yearning looks. He began saying things which she found embarrassing, made attempts to take her hand. And his attitude towards Pieter changed, too, became derogatory and spiteful.

One day, when she had parried a question, he looked at her closely and said:

'Poor Julia; you can't really bear to talk about him, can you?'

'I am talking about him now; or so I imagined,' she said a trifle sharply.

'Without telling me anything.'

'There is nothing to tell. And if you were Pieter, would you wish your wife to discuss you with someone else?'

'If I were Pieter,' said Nicolas, ceasing to walk and speaking with a dreamy intensity, 'if I were Pieter I shouldn't care what I looked like. If I were ugly enough to frighten the English, if my head grew out of the middle of my chest—' (that was, actually, how he visualized his cousin, a hunchback) 'I shouldn't act like that. If I were lucky enough to be married to you, Julia, I should go round saying, "Don't look at *me*, look at my beautiful wife? Look what I've *got*!".'

In the cool, prim voice which she used more and more often nowadays, she said:

'It's impossible to say how you would feel, or act, in another person's place.'

'I know one thing. I'd give my right arm to change places with him.'

She thought of the marred red face, the ape-like stance, the heavy-hanging hands; of the whole, empty, futile life. She spoke vehemently.

'Nicolas, don't say that. You don't know what you're saying!'

'Why shouldn't I say it? I would change places, not just with him, with the humblest, poorest little clerk, if I could be married to you.'

He spoke sincerely, and was looking at her with admiring, passionate, almost worshipping eyes; and except for embarrassment she had no feeling at all. He was young and handsome, very likeable, and falling in love with her, and it meant nothing.

'Pieter had no right to get married at all,' Nicolas went on. 'He hasn't the slightest idea how to treat a wife.'

'I don't know why you should say that. He's very fond of me. And very kind to me.'

'Kind!' He repudiated the word with scorn. 'Decent men are fond of their dogs and kind to their slaves. He doesn't love you.'

'How do you know?'

'If he did he wouldn't let you be here, with me, now. He'd be as jealous of me as I am of him.'

'He doesn't know the kind of thing you're beginning to say to me, Nicolas. And I wish you wouldn't. It just makes me uncomfortable and doesn't do any good. I am married, and very soon you will be yourself.'

'Must you remind me of that?' he asked roughly. 'When I was riding my hobby-horse and Greta was in her cradle our parents put their heads together and struck a bargain. Was that anything to do with me? Did anybody give one thought to *my* feelings? And the same with you. Somebody shoved a glove on your hand and somebody else said a few words. And they dare to call that a marriage! Then we see somebody else and we know, in our hearts . . . in our very bones. . . .'

All unwittingly he was describing what had happened to her; that unlooked for, uninvited recognition of the one, the only possible person. On that day, when Charles had kissed her and she had thrown her arms around him and kissed him, if he had said, 'Come with me', she knew she would have gone, anywhere, to the world's end and never even remembered that she was married.

Was it possible that Nicolas felt like that about her?

'It's like everything else,' she said, 'there has to be some sort of order, some sort of rule. Otherwise it would all be such a muddle. If you tried to go by *feelings*. . . . You see, they so seldom fit. Everybody seems to be in love with somebody who isn't in love with them.'

He supposed this to be her way of intimating that she was not in love with him. But what did she know about it? He remembered the way in which Uncle Simon had said 'untouched'. By comparison he felt infinitely experienced.

'Oh, no,' he said. 'Sometimes two people are in love with one another. And then everything is wonderful.'

She looked at him, and for a moment tried to imagine Charles standing there in his place, saying such things to her, gazing at her in that way. It was to imagine the impossible. Not Charles's style at all, some instinctive knowledge informed her. But this was no time to think of that. Once again she must deal with this situation without hurting Nicolas's feelings.

'I've never known a case like that,' she said, with an assumed lightness. 'Those I've read about always came to a bad end.' As soon as the words were spoken they had a ring of doom. 'Suppose,' she said, 'just *suppose* that I fell in love with you; think how miserable we should be when the time came to part.'

'But we should have had something, Julia. We'd have known what happiness was. We'd have something to remember.'

Ah, but *I* have that, already; a very small, shadowy thing, but I have it and nothing else must be allowed to cut across, to come between me and what I remember.

It occurred to her suddenly that what she had said a little earlier might be entirely true–everybody was in love with somebody who wasn't in love with them. That might be why Charles had so firmly loosened her clutching hands. . . . Well, all the more honour to him. She must profit by that example.

'I don't love you, Nicolas. I like you very much, but that is all.'

He was sufficiently infatuated to tell himself that he liked her all the better because she was not 'easy'; because she was, he thought, loyal to Pieter and her disastrous marriage. He was too young to hear in the words 'I like you' the fatal denial of all hope. In fact, with no great difficulty, he was able to read into them a properly maidenly, entrancingly shy promise of a warmer emotion.

So the languorous spice-scented days went on, and passed through the fields of the sunset into warm spice-scented nights full of stars. And presently Nicolas's stay in Rua had reached the half-way mark.

Chapter Twelve

There came a day when Mynheer announced that he would be absent for a night.

'I'm going to the Governor's very dull, gentlemen-only dinner party,' he said. 'And as I have some business to do in Banda tomorrow morning, I shall stay there and return about mid-day. I daresay you two will make shift to entertain yourselves. Oh, and Nicolas, I've opened a bottle of what, if it lives up to the shipper's promise, should be a rather special wine. Try it at dinner, will you, and give me your opinion.'

In the later afternoon, dressed in his best and followed by a slave bearing a large bouquet of Rua flowers for Mevrouw Van de Lijn, whose efforts to make a garden within the walls of the Fort had proved unavailing, Mynheer stepped into his prahau and was rowed swiftly away.

Julia spent the afternoon with Pieter. Ever since she had allowed her tongue to slip and say 'visit', she had prolonged the time she spent with him, and occasionally had refused to keep Nicolas company on the pretence that she had promised to do something with Pieter. Part of this pretence was a keeping faith with Mynheer, part of it was habit, and part was the result of the feeling of shame which she had felt when Charles had remarked upon her marriage; she was now anxious to hide the truth for her own sake.

This afternoon Pieter was busily and happily and messily making clay pots. They were all lop-sided and flawed, but she admired them profusely and when she left he presented her with the largest of them.

The candles were lighted, and she had changed her dress and Juno was putting the last touches to her hair when there was a knock on the door between her sitting-room and the cloister. Juno put down the brush and went to the door, and Julia heard, with surprise, Doctor Hootman's voice. 'Tell Mevrouw that Mynheer Pieter wants her for a few minutes.' She called:

'I heard. I'll come at once.'

Most likely, she thought, he wanted to give her another pot. Amenable, and easily handled as he generally was, he had cantankerous moods now and then. At such times, unless given way to he would scream with rage and throw himself to the floor. Doctor Hootman would hasten to give way. 'Indulging his whims, however fantastic, does him less harm than throwing himself about like that,' he had once said. So if Pieter had forgotten that he had just presented her with a pot and was determined to give her another, Doctor Hootman would protest up to a point and then, with a shrug, say: 'Very well,' and send for her.

She crossed the library and tapped upon the door of Pieter's room. Doctor Hootman opened it and said:

'Come in, Mevrouw.'

Charles stood by the table.

She said: 'Oh!' in the awed, rapt voice of someone confronted by a heavenly vision. And then she just stood and stared, and Charles stared back at her.

She had never, really, expected to see him again. The memory of him had been something laid away, sealed over, having no connexion with ordinary every-day living. Now there he stood, living, breathing, real, just by the table where, a little while ago, she had been helping Pieter with his pots. There were no words. She could only look and look. . . .

Charles was dumb, too. Unlike her he had not cherished his memories: whenever they hovered he had beaten them off. He'd met, by accident, a girl whose looks and personality and situation combined to make an appeal to him, but he was a realist and he had faced his feelings realistically. There was no room in his life for love of any kind, certainly not for a mooning, hopeless love such as this might be if he let himself go. Nobody but a crass fool would give a second thought to a girl met once, a girl who was married. In common with others of his background and generation he was familiar with the song contained in Ford's *Music of Sundry Kinds*.

> 'There is a Lady, sweet and kind,
> Was never face so pleased my mind;
> I did but see her passing by,
> And yet I love her till I die.'

That sort of thing belonged to the poets; if it had ever been part of ordinary life it had been part of a life which had begun to die when the King raised his standard at Nottingham and had breathed its last at the Battle of Naseby. Aged sixteen, his father's sword heavy in his hand, a borrowed horse between his knees, he had been present by the death-bed. The old golden age was gone and gone forever, with its love, and its Ladies, its songs, romance and chivalry. Elmhurst was a fire-blackened ruin, and he was an exile, lucky to have got away alive. There is a Lady–think that, think of those eyes and the way her hair grows in a little point on her forehead, and of that sweet curve of the lip, and think of the sheer pluck–and *then* where are you? There are deprivations and yearnings enough, without contriving more for yourself. Fool! A pretty little Dutch girl, with a kind heart. You did your best for her. Forget it. Here a job, there a job, everywhere a pretty little guilder; an unlimed nutmeg, an unsupervised clove, a close brush with the patrol boat, one more brick towards re-building Elmhurst and to hell with everything else!

Daan had said: 'Come up to the house, Charles. Mynheer is away for the night. We'll make free with his brandy.'

And then he had said: 'I promised Mevrouw that if ever it could be managed I would arrange that you met. She feels that she never thanked you properly.'

'I don't want her thanks.'

But he did want to see her. Just to prove . . . what? That she was merely a pretty little Dutch girl; not the dream-provocative memory-troubling Lady who had passed by and waked a love that would never sleep again.

So Daan had sent for her. And here she was.

Into the silence, so loud with unspoken things, Doctor Hootman said: 'I must begin getting my charge to bed.' He went into the bedroom, closing the door gently behind him.

'I thought, since I was here, I'd like to see how you were,' Charles said awkwardly. 'You're thinner than I remembered.'

So he had remembered.

'You look just the same.' Just the same, even to the torn frill of the shirt that had once been fine.

'You haven't been getting into any more trouble?'

'Oh no. And thank you for bringing back my bag. I was in such a state. I didn't think of it. And I didn't even ask your name.'

'You know it now?'

'Oh yes. Charles.' There was something special about it, and about using it to him, for the first time.

'And you're Julia. I asked. So every now and then I can say to myself, I hope everything is going right with Julia, or, I wonder what Julia is doing this fine morning.'

What an utterly asinine thing to say! Sounds as though . . .

'I've thought of you, too. Every single day. And I never even hoped I'd see you again. I don't even know where you live.'

'I live on a little island called Ay. There are about a dozen of us. In a hut. We live like pigs.'

'Which way does it lie, your island?'

He took a mental bearing and jerkd his head.

'Oh. One of my windows looks that way. I shall be able to look out . . . and think. . . .'

'Of me, in my hut? If it's in the morning you can think of me lighting the fire. I most imprudently let it be known that I have a talent for lighting fires, and so I was saddled with that job.

'I often had it, in the Klopstock Home; it was one of the unpopular ones.'

None of these words meant anything at all. it was their eyes that were doing the real talking.

'Doctor Hootman told me that you are English,' she began afresh.

'That's right; but I've lived in the islands for a long time now.'

'I think I'm English, too.' To establish a bond even so impersonal as a shared nationality was delightful and exciting.

'What do you mean, *think*? Don't you know?'

'Not for certain. It was in Ireland that I was found, but I could say a piece in English. Uncle Johannes told me what it meant in Dutch; and it said I was English. He believed I was.'

'Who was Uncle Johannes?'

'The man who found me. He was a sea captain. He knew a little of several languages.'

'Say me your English piece.'

'In English? I don't know whether I remember it. It's so long ago. And even then he said I said it like a parrot. But I'll try.'

Slowly, dredging up each word from the depths of her memory she repeated the simple identification which Maire had taken such pains to teach her.

'Ashley,' he repeated as she came to the end. 'That's English enough. In Ireland you say. When?'

'I was eight then–when Uncle Johannes found me. And I shall be seventeen in June.'

'How long were you with Maire?'

'Oh, all my life I should think. I can't remember anything before. She said she taught me to walk and to talk.'

'You were a baby then in '49. Cromwell in Drogheda. That'd be about right. I think you could claim to be English. We're a long way from home, Julia.'

'Perhaps that is why . . .'

'Why what?'

She floundered a little. 'Well, that day . . . I was all confused, half out of my mind, but later on, when I thought about it, it was just as though we weren't really strangers. As though I had recognized you.'

And it had been so with him. Miscall, deny it how you would, you recognized the Lady who just passed by . . . that was why the one glance was enough.

'So the Dutchman brought you out of Ireland. What then?'

'He was drowned. His wife didn't like me, so she sent me to an orphanage and I ended up in the Company's Daughters' Home. And then I came here.'

He said abruptly: 'They don't often live to be old.' The jerk of his head showed where his thoughts had jumped; and as though it had been a signal, there came from behind the closed door a low grumbling sound, like distant thunder, Pieter's indistinct flannelly voice raised in complaining protest. 'Things might work out right for you, yet. I'd like to think so.' He brushed his hand across his face with a gesture of helpless confusion oddly at variance with his general demeanour. 'I've worried about you, a bit; though God knows I've worries enough of my own and I can't do anything for you.'

'I'm all right,' she said quickly. 'You mustn't worry about me.' But it was sweet to think that he had. 'What worries have you?'

He laughed. 'All concerned with mental arithmetic and similar sordid things. I'm all right, too. You and I have survived the break-up of a civilization, Julia. We should reckon ourselves lucky to be alive.'

The noise in Pieter's room was now loud and continuous. The words, 'Julie. Want Julie,' emerged quite clearly, and were followed by a bellowing roar, a purely animal sound of rage and distress. There were several heavy but soft-sounding thuds, one of which made the door shudder. They could hear Doctor Hootman's voice, firm and soothing, too low pitched to be distinguishable above the noise.

'He knows I'm here,' Julia said.

As she spoke the door opened a few inches, was sharply slammed. The bellowing cries rose to a crescendo, and then the door opened fully and Doctor Hootman and Pieter, locked in a Laocoon embrace, came hurtling into the room.

Though physically over-borne Doctor Hootman was still in charge of the situation, and still calm.

'Take him, Mevrouw; distract his attention,' he said, and released his hold on Pieter who plunged straight at her, quiet now except for gulping sobs of rage. He burrowed his head into her shoulder and clutched at her, saying; 'Julie, Julie,' over and over again between the sobs.

Doctor Hootman placed himself squarely in front of Charles.

'You must go. One word would be enough! I couldn't let the noise continue. We have a guest in the house.' The calm of his voice was just touched with anguish as he spoke the last words.

Julia hugged Pieter to her, keeping his face hidden in her shoulder. Charles, hustled by Doctor Hootman, went to the door, and there turned. Over the large, nuzzling head thatched with the dry-looking hair, she smiled, and because they must not speak she put into the smile all the unspoken things. That was what Charles carried away with him, the memory of Julia, sweet and lovely and brave, smiling at him as she soothed the poor boy.

Just before the door closed he raised his hand: and it was not in salute to a pretty little Dutch girl. . . .

Doctor Hootman turned back into the room and said with genuine regret: 'Mevrouw, I am *sorry*! I simply dared not risk the disturbance.' Pursing his lips he looked at Pieter who had stopped crying and was stroking Julia's sleeve. 'I've never known him so violent; or else I'm out of condition. Come along now, Pieter. You've seen Julie and Julie has seen you being very naughty. Very naughty indeed!'

'Naughty,' Pieter admonished himself heartily. 'Naughty indeed!' But he did not assume the scolded-dog aspect ordinarily educed by the use of the word. On the contrary he seemed pleased with himself.

'Seen Julie,' he added.

Doctor Hootman's heavy eyebrows knotted in a little frown.

'Some sort of animal instinct at work there.'

He might have been speaking to himself, and Julia almost allowed herself to assume that he was, for to speak it was necessary to drag her mind away from its dream.

'What do you mean?'

Doctor Hootman looked at her, hesitated, and said:

'That he knew you were here. We shall have to be a little more firm, I think. Come along, Pieter. Time for bed.'

'Time for bed, Good morning Julie,' said Pieter, and allowed himself to be led away. At the bedroom door Doctor Hootman turned.

'I think, if you will excuse me, Mevrouw I shall dine here. With Pieter of course.' He added the last words with the now familiar, derisive grimace with which he always marked any additional act of subterfuge.

She wanted to be alone to re-live, to remember, but she could hardly leave Nicolas to dine alone. She must wait. Tonight though, his yearning looks and sentimental words were more than usually irksome. They encroached; they also, in her present mood, provoked a tiresome form of pity. She could believe now that Charles was not without feeling for her and to come direct from the meeting which had inculcated that belief and be beset by Nicolas's pleading glances made her feel like somebody newly rich, his wealth not even yet counted, immediately accosted by a beggar.

'This is an occasion,' he said, as they sat down to the table. 'We've never dined alone together before; we never may again. Oh, Julia! When I think of Pieter who could have that pleasure every night of his life. . . .'

Pluto's entry gave her an excuse to frown so that that sentence died on the air.

Nicolas tried again, and again, until her short, and finally impatient replies gave him the key to her mood. He realized that he was becoming slavish and he had heard, or read somewhere that with women slavish tactics were seldom successful. He must be gay and charming.

The wine helped. After two glasses of it his spirits and his colour rose, his wits and his eyes brightened.

'Uncle Simon was dead right about this wine, Julia. It is special. Let me . . .' he leaned forward and filled her glass. 'I suspect that my father – himself a schnapps drinker–warned Uncle Simon that I was a wine-bibber as well as an idle scamp. So in his presence I always feel self-conscious if I have a second glass. Though I don't think he'd mind. It's odd, don't you think, how some parents seem to enjoy decrying their children–you'd think they'd be ashamed. I must say that–quite apart from other reasons–I'm not looking forward to my return to the family roof. For one thing my father will expect me to have acquired, in three months, all the secrets of Uncle Simon's success in business. And not one have I ferreted out. Careless, unobservant rapscallion that I am.'

Encourage him to continue with this easy kind of chatter.

'Tell me about Java, and your home and everything,' she said. He filled his glass again and with willingness launched into a description of his home and family. He could, when he wished, talk very entertainingly, and he did so now, with just enough exaggeration to be amusing.

'My mother,' he said, 'is one of those women who can see danger in *everything*, and can prove her case with a hair-raising tale. She must have known, intimately, the victims of more fatalities than anyone else in the world. For instance, if she saw you, sipping that wine, sitting on that solid chair she would certainly say: 'My dear, do be careful; I once knew a woman who choked to death, drinking a glass of wine. And my sister's second cousin by marriage once sat in a chair, just as you are doing, and it broke under her. The fall injured her so that she never walked again. So do be careful." She honestly would.'

Of his father, he said, with a slight decline of amiability.

'He was named Jacob, which was fortunate because it gave him the notion that he is one of the Bible patriarchs. I very narrowly escaped being called Reuben. My mother had to beg, on her knees, for Nicolas. She saw danger in Reuben as the name for her first-born, you see.'

'What danger?'

'Dear me, you are ignorant, Julia. Reuben was the eldest of twelve!'

'I see,' she said, laughing.

'Benjamin she did accept, with good cheer, when my youngest brother was born.'

He chatted in this fashion, re-filling and emptying his glass. Then he said:

'Now I feel like making some music. I can play, too. But only when I'm happy. Let's go and brave Pieter in his den and ask if I may play his clavichord.'

'Oh no!' she said. She heard the real horror in her voice and knew it to be disproportionate to the occasion.

'He always retires early. If we disturbed him he would never forgive us.'

'That's just it. He should *be* disturbed,' said Nicolas, with the intransigence of the near-intoxicated. 'I'd ask nicely. I'd say: "Cousin Pieter,

I haven't come to stare at your scars or lick your sores. I just want to play your clavichord." Who knows, it might be the turning point in his whole life; the opening wedge, as it were.'

'He'd be very upset, and very angry. He'd blame me. Please Nicolas, don't even think of it.'

'The idea is abandoned. Nobody could resist you when you speak so earnestly and look so seductive.'

'If you really want to play, there is a clavichord in my sitting-room.'

'You never play.'

'I can't. But your uncle, when he furnished the room provided everything that any kind of woman could possibly require. Therefore I have a clavichord.'

'I've never seen your room. Come along, I will make you such sweet music as will melt even your stony heart.'

'You won't, you know,' she kept her voice light and casual. 'If you have that in mind, Nicolas, I warn you, you'll be wasting your time.'

Too late she realized that it had been stupid to invite him to her room. Done without thinking, to divert his attention from Pieter, it might easily be misunderstood.

He stumbled a little as they went along the cloister and the memory of the drunken sailor revived in her mind. She would have been wiser to let him go blundering along to Pieter's apartments; Doctor Hootman could have dealt with him.

At the door of her room she wondered whether to say: Now, if you come in, you must promise to behave. But that had a kind of implication, of coyness which might precipitate the very thing she wished to avoid. A brisk matter-of-factness was probably the best defence.

She opened the clavichord and placed the candles near it, reserving one for herself on the far side of the room.

'There you are,' she said to Nicolas, who was idly wandering about the room, looking at the furnishings. 'I shall sit here and go on with my work while you play.'

He surprised her by playing, even in this slightly tipsy state, remarkably well. The music he made was nothing like Doctor Hootman's wild sombre cry of discontent; he played light, graceful little tunes. They were all love songs and after a few minutes he hit on the idea of turning and announcing each title in a half-teasing way, laughing at her over his shoulder.

'Now this one is called "You are my Chosen". Oh, how I wish I could sing. I'll teach you the words, Julia then you can sing them. "You are my chosen, the one that I love" . . . that's the first line. Say it after me.'

'I can't sing at all.'

'Have you no talent – apart from the talent for making people love you?'

'You're hear to play my clavichord, not to catechize me!'

She went on stitching and he turned back to the instrument.

Presently he said: 'I play well, don't I. Better than Pieter, don't you think?'

'Differently.'

'How very miserly! Julia, sometimes I think you must be in love with him, and he so surly he won't even speak to his own cousin. What is it? Pity? Would you be kinder to me if I wore my scars on my face instead of on my heart?'

It was asked flirtatiously rather than seriously and she replied in the same manner.

'No. I couldn't be kinder to you. I'm already so kind that I find it a strain.'

He began to play again, passed from one tune to another and reached, at last, one different from the rest. No longer light and gay. A sweet, haunting melancholy tune that seemed to hold all the sadness of good-byes spoken forever.

It had its effect on Julia who ceased stitching and folded her hands on the embroidery bag with its eloquent stains. *His* hands had touched it, and in holding it, she made some kind of contact. Her mind, her heart went winging out, over the sea to Ay.

The music, and the wine he had drunk, took effect on Nicolas. Slavish adoration, pretty speeches, yearning looks brought no return. A man should be masterful, ruthless, possessive. Youth went over and life passed by, and a man on his way to a life sentence was justified in snatching at a flower to take with him–even if it grew in another man's garden.

With his fingers still drawing sorrowful sweetness from the keys, he turned his head, and saw upon Julia's face a look which he had never seen before, unguarded, dreaming, desirous.

He left the clavichord and crossed the room in a single swooping motion, gathered her into his arms, and saying, 'You do love me, you do, you do,' set his mouth to hers.

The fact that he was kissing her in the way that she would have liked to kiss Charles, in the way she longed to be kissed by him, added to her sense of outrage.

She turned her head, and freed her mouth, and put both hands against him, thrusting him away.

'I don't! You forget yourself. Leave go of me!'

He was beyond control now. The touch of flesh on flesh, even the way she struggled, fired him; and the weeks of meek adoration had to be paid for as well as the threatening years of a loveless marriage. He put his hand to the back of her head and forced her face round; he fumbled at the lace of her breast.

Drunken sailor, drunken Nicolas. All one.

With a wrench that seemed to break her neck she got her mouth free again and screamed. Useless. She knew that even as the single shrill sound rang out. Doctor Hootman was at the other end of the house; the slaves even farther away and heedful only of the bells.

Yet immediately somebody tapped on the door, not loudly, but with insistence. Nicolas heard it, too, and his clutch loosened. She gave another push and he stood up. She ran her hands over her hair, drew in a breath and managed to call, 'Come in.'

The door opened, rather slowly, as though stiff on its hinges and there was Doctor Hootman, looking mild and vague, blinking like an owl against the light.

'I had to come,' he said, with a note of apology in his voice. 'I heard music. . . . Music from a hand far more skilled than mine . . . or Pieter's. Yours, Mynheer?'

'I was playing.' He sounded sulky and curt.

'Most beautifully,' said Doctor Hootman. He lifted his big, heavily-haired hands and rubbed his eyes.

'Coming in from the dark, so many candles all together, quite blinding,' he said.

He might pretend not to see anything, but the sound of the scream still hung on the air.

'I spoilt it,' Julia said in a voice so high-pitched and unsteady that it, as well as the scream, needed explanations. 'I put my hand into my bag and a needle ran into my finger. Just for a second I thought a snake had crept in.'

'That could very easily happen, Mevrouw. I've seen your bag lying in the garden.' He turned to Nicolas who had recovered some show of composure. 'Mynheer Vanderplasse, I had no idea that you were such a musician. Would you mind if I stayed and listened for a while, if Mevrouw would give me permission, of course. One becomes, as you will understand weary of the same old tunes. All yours were fresh to me.'

'Do stay. Sit down, Doctor Hootman.'

Nicolas said: 'I only know a few tunes. I've played them all and to repeat them would bore me.'

Doctor Hootman, who had almost taken a chair, stood, uncertain, hesitant.

'Perhaps you would like to try *my* clavichord,' Julia said. 'Your old tunes might sound differently.'

'Mevrouw, to do that would be to invite the inevitable, and I am sure, invidious comparison.'

There was a moment's bristling silence. Then Nicolas said, rudely:

'Not from me. I'm going to bed. Good night, Julia.'

The door slammed behind him and before the sound of it had died away Doctor Hootman was at the clavichord.

'I must play, Mevrouw,' he said. 'To a young man as angry as that one another comparison might suggest itself, old and ugly as I am. However, flown with wine as he is, he will soon sleep.'

He played on for about five minutes, then ended a tune abruptly and stood up.

Julia said at once: 'Doctor Hootman, thank you! How did you happen to be near enough?'

'I often take a little stroll after dark.' He sat down on a chair near the table where the candle stood.

'I'll assume that my intervention was welcome,' he said. 'So we need not talk about that. Mevrouw, not long ago you told me that you would never again allow your will to come into conflict with Mynheer's.'

Why should he say that, *now*?

'Yes, I did. And I meant it. Doctor Hootman, are you implying that what you interrupted. . . .? I assure you that that was entirely against my will. You must know that. You heard me call out.'

'Mevrouw, please! Of course I understand that. Otherwise should I have dreamed of interfering?' He paused, looked at her gravely, then looked down and pulled at the fingers of his left hand with the thumb and first finger of his right so that his knuckles cracked. 'I think the time has come,' he said at last, looking up again. 'Mevrouw, you must forgive me if I speak plainly. I'm no good at trimming things up, and I don't think it is a subject which can be broached delicately. I can only tell you the facts. What almost happened here this evening, and would have done, but for me, may have been against your will, but would have been in direct accordance with Mynheer's.'

'What?' It occurred to her that Doctor Hootman had also–in Mynheer's absence–made free with the bottle. 'Do you *know* what you are saying?'

'I am telling you that if you are truly compliant with Mynheer's will you will take that pretty nincompoop as a lover and pray that next year there will be a fine new branch on the Vosmar family tree.'

She stared at him as though he had struck her in the face or used some word of extreme obscenity. Then commonsense pushed its way through stunned incredulity and recognized the truth. It was true; everything, from Mynheer's talk on the way home after her visit to Marie to his absence this evening, all fitted in.

'I told you it was plain speaking,' Doctor Hootman said. The blood had rushed into her face and he courteously refrained from looking at her for a moment.

'He spoke to you of this?' she asked in a low, shamed voice.

'On the night of your arrival. Mevrouw, you must not mind my knowing; rather be glad.' His voice changed and took on an easier, more conversational tone. 'I had, of course, quite understood the purpose of his elaborate deception, family pride was at the back of that; a wife seemed to me to be an unnecessary complication and risk. I said something to that effect and then he told me the plan he had been cherishing all those years. When that young man was a mere child this visit was proposed and Pieter's marriage was timed to dovetail in with it–a few months to spare so that his wife might have time to become fretful and discontented and begin to ask what life held for her. Have you never noticed how often Mynheer has said things calculated to make you sorry for yourself?'

She nodded:

'You see? Nothing overlooked, nothing left to chance. It is the careful work of many years which you have in your power to crown with success or doom to failure. The young man's mother was a Vosmar. I have no doubt that Mynheer includes in his plan a prolonged tour of the islands, proudly and assiduously pointing out that the Vosmar family features have been reproduced once again.'

'Don't,' she said. 'You make it all sound so horrible–just like animals.'

'It is. That is what we are, not being Vosmars. Another Holy Family, and you know where that has ended?'

She nodded again.

'Not a pleasant plan, but in its way masterly.'

'Is it? It seems to depend so much on chance. Nicolas might have hated the sight of me.'

'Every man has his price, Mevrouw; and Mynheer is very rich. Not, I hasten to add, that that has been necessary in this case but it was an eventuality for which Mynheer was well-prepared.'

There was a silence. Then she said:

'I don't think I could do it. It goes against something . . .' she pressed her clasped hands to her breast. 'It's so sickeningly cold-blooded. No, I couldn't.'

Doctor Hootman seemed to settle more firmly and comfortably into his chair; he crossed one leg over the other and linked his hands around his knee.

'Then Mevrouw we must consider. I think that we should first look at the gravity of the situation. An heir Mynheer must have, and he will go to any lengths to get what he needs. He never fully believed that Pieter's accident was responsible, so he dared not marry again. Imagine having to conceal the existence of two idiots, invent a secret life for them both–that would have taxed even Mynheer's ingenuity. So you see what a normal child means to him, not an heir only, but a perfect vindication of all these years of make-believe. Opposition isn't going to be easy, or safe.'

The fright showed in her eyes.

'It's always best to face a thing squarely. It is hardly likely that Mynheer, having come so far, will let one girl stand in his way. The world is full of girls.'

'He'd kill me.'

'Not with my consent. I am,' he raised and shrugged one heavy shoulder deprecatingly, 'of no particular importance, but–I play my part. The fact that Pieter has outlived so many of his kind is my doing, and at least half the façade Mynheer has raised in my work. I should use my influence to see that you got away with your life.'

It seemed an outlandish promise to be made, here in this quiet, luxurious room.

'Before we go into that, look a little more closely into Mynheer's proposal. It is not without attractions, you know. You could be mother to the heir of All the Vosmars, a Queen Mother, in fact; pampered, revered. Mynheer would not be niggardly in his manifestations of gratitude. Many women would not, in the circumstances, mind acting as brood mare.'

'That's what I said,' she exclaimed sharply. 'Like animals. Horrible!'

'Well, you may change your mind. If you stick to that, you will be dispensed with, and replaced. Poor Pieter Vosmar, in addition to his other afflictions will suffer sudden bereavement, but, being the resilient character that he is, he will soon find another wife.'

Even at that moment something in his tone jarred.

'Don't,' she said, 'none of this is his fault!' But this was not time to think about Pieter. 'Where should *I* be–if not dead?'

'That is where I should come in. I am in Mynheer's confidence; and I should be watchful. Up to this point he has been content to let things develop naturally. On his return he will begin to exert pressure. The day will soon come when he will say, will you or won't you? If you persist in your refusal he will begin to plan your removal, but I shall forestall him. My plan is already made.'

'Already. What is it?'

'Remember Mevrouw this which is new to you has been known to me for several months. I have had time to think. When danger threatens–and make no mistake about it, it will be deadly danger–I shall get you away, safely. It will appear as though, too hard pushed, you drowned yourself.'

No dream had ever seemed more fantastic.

'Where should I go?'

He looked her full in the face and said:

'To Ay.'

Yes, she knew; he could see that. He went on smoothly:

'I have friends there into whose keeping I could safely commend you.'

'Charles lives in Ay.'

'That is so. He told you? He seems to have become very communicative all of a sudden. Well, don't you think that you would be safe there? In Ay, with Charles?'

She almost laughed. The impulse to laughter was there but she was afraid that if she yielded to it she would cry as well and pretending to be drowned, and then popping up safe and sound in the one spot in the world where she longed to be pushed fantasy past the place where it could be taken seriously.

'Really, Doctor Hootman, that sounds so much like the ending of a fairy tale that it makes me wonder whether any of the rest of it is true.'

There came across his face that same look as when she had explained her reason for taking food to Psyche.

'Look,' he said, leaning slighty forward. 'Isn't all the evidence in favour of Mynheer's plan being cold fact? Think carefully. What would have happened tonight had I not been ready, waiting?'

'Yes,' she said, 'that could be true.'

'Isn't it also a fact that being a man accustomed to his own way he will be dangerous if thwarted?'

'Yes.'

'I can't actually *prove* that I would not like to see you murdered; but can you take that for granted?'

'Yes. Yes, of course.'

'Very well, then; that brings us to the point. What could I do except get you out of Rua? And where else could I send you? What is so fantastic, so much like a fairy-tale about that?'

'It would be such a happy ending,' she said, simply. The hot colour rushed into her face again.

'Mevrouw, after all our trials, don't you think we deserve a happy ending?'

Something peculiar happened to her mind; she could only see herself saying: 'Let me do that', and lighting the fire for Charles. 'Let me do that', and lighting the fire. 'Let me do that', and lighting the fire. Over and over again, like a clock which had stuck and went on striking the same hour.

Doctor Hootman uncrossed his legs and shifted in his chair.

'You'll have a day or two to think it over, I expect. Your best plan, for the moment, is to appear to encourage the young man when you are in company and discourage him when you are alone. You have your full share of feminine guile and inventiveness, I think.' He looked at the work-bag. 'Remember that you can count on my support if it is needed; but don't, too hastily, decide to oppose Mynheer. Life in Ay would not be luxurious. There is a good deal to be said for being a brood mare. I wish you good night, Mevrouw.'

The cloister lay sharply black and white in the moonlight. As he walked its length, moving from light to shadow, Doctor Hootman linked his hands and lifted and lowered them in a gesture very much like that of a man giving himself a congratulatory hand-shake.

Julia had known nights of uneasy, broken sleep, of sudden jolting wakenings and bad dreams before, but that night, for the first time in her life she did not sleep at all.

Chapter Thirteen

'You look unlike yourself, my dear,' said Mynheer. 'Is anything the matter?'

He watched for the betraying blush, the evasive glance, and was disappointed.

'I have a headache. I was lying down when you called me,' Julia said.

It was mid-day when he returned and he had come straight into the house calling her name. The thought of facing him sickened her, but she must do so sooner or later, so she had come out of her room and found him in the hall, with a large parcel, wrapped in white linen, lying at his feet.

'I'm very sorry,' he said, in his kindest voice. 'How long have you had it?' It wasn't credible that after all his careful staging a headache should have intervened. . . .

'It came on in the night.'

'Well, I've brought you a present which I hope will cheer you, even if it won't cure a headache. Look.'

He whisked away the linen and revealed some folded softness, a shimmer of blue and silver which lifted and shaken out by his nimble hands revealed itself as a sarong of silk and a little jacket of gauzy stuff.

'It'll be cool to wear, and I'm sure you'll find it very becoming.'

He expected, and awaited, some exclamations of admiration and of gratitude. She forced herself to say:

'Thank you, Mynheer. It is very pretty,' but the words came out listlessly.

Tainted, sinister, like every bit of kindness he had ever shown her. Decking out the brood mare!

'Your head *is* bothering you, poor girl. I'm sorry I disturbed you. Go and lie down again and tell Juno to rub your head for you. They have great cunning in their fingers and can often shift a pain.'

As she turned to walk slowly away, he asked:

'Where is Nicolas?'

'I couldn't say, Mynheer. I have not seen him this morning.'

'Never mind. I shall find him. I expect he is seeing to things for me. I hope your headache will soon vanish.'

He went off briskly towards the plantation. When she reached her own doorway, instead of entering the room she turned, and leaning her arms on the cloister wall, put her aching head in her hands, and stared out into the garden. Mynheer was just about to enter the rose pergola.

From that distance he looked very small; and perhaps for that reason she made another effort to think well of him. There was something admirable in the way he had faced, what must, to a man of his disposition, have been an intolerable situation.

If I'd been different, she thought, his scheme, fantastic as it is, might have succeeded. Many women would not have found the bargain unduly one-sided. She thought of the hard-eyed woman in the tavern, who, for some trivial sum, was eager to sell herself to a drunken sailor. The rewards here were very large, and Nicolas was young, attractive. Many women . . . but then I'm not any other woman, I'm myself. I am as I am, I can only be myself, be guided by what I feel and know what is right for *me*.

Mynheer met Nicolas on the path and greeting him observed that he also looked unlike himself. His eyes were bloodshot, the colour less smoothly spread in his young face and his eyes *were* evasive.

They exchanged a few remarks about the morning's work.

'You seem to have taken my place most satisfactorily,' Mynheer said. 'No need for me to go any farther. It's getting hot, too. Let us go and sit on the veranda and drink some well-cooled wine.'

'Not for me, thank you,' said Nicolas with a grimace. 'I drank too much last night.'

'Indeed? For you I prescribe lime-juice, then. Does *your* head ache? Julia's does. What did you get up to last evening? a Bacchanalian orgy, eh?'

'I drank too much and I. . . . Uncle Simon, I think I'd better go home. If you don't mind, I'd like to go to Banda today, and wait there for a ship. After what happened last night I don't think I can face Julia again.'

'Good gracious me!' said Mynheer, putting his hand on Nicolas's shoulder. 'Was it so bad? What happened? Or is it too dreadful to tell?'

'I got drunk. Not very drunk . . . in fact I didn't think . . . but that was a very subtle wine, or something. Anyhow, I lost my head and threw myself on Julia and . . . well, you can guess what happened.'

The patchy pink in his face was engulfed in hot scarlet.

'That's just what I can't do. Nor can I see, in anything you have told me so far, why you should see it necessary to leave Rua. Did she . . . rebuff you?'

'Rebuff! She acted as though I were trying to rape her.'

'Which was, of course, far from your intention?'

Nicolas shot his favourite relative a look of utter loathing, and said nothing.

'So she rebuffed you. Well, she wouldn't be a woman if she didn't do that at least three times! Surely you realize that.'

'Once is enough for me. Thank you!' said Nicolas between his teeth.

'Dear me. You are in a bad way. You're beginning to make me suspect that your feelings are seriously involved–to be taking the thing so much to heart. But I should be sorry if you cut short your visit–for my own sake, and for other reasons. Your father would look for some explanation.'

'I could tell him the truth,' said Nicolas, who was in a self-destructive mood.

'He'd be delighted to hear *that*,' said Mynheer drily. And the boy's sense of reality held up to him the vision of his father's face, the thin humourless lips, the hard, strict stare. No; if he went home he would have to give an invented, an acceptable reason.

'I wouldn't do that,' said Mynheer, giving the shoulder under his hand an affectionate little squeeze. 'No harm has been done, you must make allowance for maidenly modesty and coquettishness, clumsily displayed. Poor Julia; I'll warrant that at this very minute she is trying some new dress or some new way of doing her hair in order to charm you.'

'Or Pieter,' Nicolas said.

Mynheer's hand fell away. 'Did you say Pieter?' he had asked before the long-established censor within had had time to say–Careful, now careful!

'I think you've been wrong about them all along,' said Nicolas, with some slight satisfaction at being thus able to shift a little of the blame. 'I've been thinking things over this morning and I've come to the conclusion that she's in love with Pieter–which makes my behaviour the more beastly. . . . And ridiculous,' he added.

'Well, of course,' said Mynheer, now completely on his guard again, 'that would be most desirable. I should have said that no woman who wasn't blind deaf and equipped with the hide of a rhinoceros could possibly love anybody who had treated her as Pieter had treated Julia. But of course there are women who like to be ill-used.' His voice was thoughtful. After a pause he said: 'Perhaps I've been a little blind myself. I've seen no sign. What makes you think so?'

'Nothing that I could put into words, really. Partly the cheerful way she goes off to spend time with him; and she won't talk about him. I admit I was . . . I mean I *am* . . . curious about him. You never. . . .' He broke off and began again. 'To you, I suppose it all seems ordinary, you're used to it. But imagine if you went to stay in Java, or Macassar and there was a member of the family whom you never saw, wouldn't *you* be curious?'

'I most certainly should,' Mynheer agreed. 'So Julia won't talk about him. That could be evidence on the other side.'

'No. What she does say is all in his favour–I realize that now. The fact is, what with one thing and another, I've made a complete fool of myself.'

'And I concerned myself unduly, or prematurely, about her happiness. I wonder. I don't usually make mistakes of that sort–and I see them together, you know.'

'I saw her face last night. I was playing for her . . . it was her look as much as anything that was my undoing. She's in love with somebody, and it certainly isn't me.'

Mynheer thrust his hand under Nicolas's arm.

'I'm to blame then, I misled you.'

'I should have lost my heart–without any help from you, Uncle Simon,' the boy said, in an easier way; merely talking about it eased some of the sting. 'But had I known, I'd have kept better rein on myself. As it is you do see why I can't stay here.'

'I don't see that at all; but if you feel like that I have an alternative suggestion. I was in conversation with an acquaintance of mine, Gerard Barnevelt of Lonthoir, at dinner yesterday. I spoke of you and he extended an invitation for you to visit him. I think that would be a valuable experience, now that you are in this vicinity. I flatter myself that I run Rua with moderate efficiency, but my methods are my own; there are others, and perhaps you should see something of them.'

'I should like to do so,' said Nicolas. 'When could I go?'

'Not today, I'm afraid. It could probably be arranged for the day after tomorrow, if I sent a message at once.'

'That leaves me where I was as regards Julia.'

'Do you carry a seal, Nicolas?'

'Yes . . . why?'

'Valuable?'

'It's silver.'

Mynheer dived into his pocket and brought out his chain of keys from which his own seal swung. It was made of gold, inset with a large emerald upon which a bold V had been deeply cut.

'I'll wager this, against yours,' he said, 'that her manner, when you meet, will be charming. You see, I'm still not convinced. However, we shall see. . . .'

Under the soothing stroking, the gently prodding movements of Juno's firm fingers the headache eased, and finally she slept, waking when the swift twilight had invaded the room and it was almost dinner time. Instantly the memory of the information that Doctor Hootman had given her, and of the pattern of behaviour he had told her to follow, settled like a heavy yoke upon her spirit.

Pale cheeks could be tinted, but even when that was done there was something wrong about her looks. Mynheer's eyes were sharp; and Nicolas's she dreaded to meet. She thought that perhaps if she wore the native dress it would divert attention from her face and account for her different look.

It was a wise choice, for the awkward moment of meeting was all taken up by exclamations of admiration, skilfully guided by Mynheer into a discourse about native weaving; how was it possible that human eyes, human fingers, could have worked so successfully, on material so fine as the gauze of the little jacket; the threads were finer than the finest hair; and wasn't it remarkable that primitive people, completely untutored, should have such perfect sense of design? The native Bandanese ironwork, for example, was said to be extraordinary.

'Of course it may be that the word primitive is here misleading. The arts of the so-called primitive people, in this part of the world at least, may be *remembered* things, the last echo of a vanished civilization. They say that all these islands are, or rather were, the tips of mountain ranges of some submerged continent. Lost Atlantis, perhaps; who knows? Arts would survive a cataclysm of that kind because they depend upon the individual who could hand on what he knew to some likely youngster . . . just as, in a shipwreck, one might save a pair of shoes while a whole valuable cargo went to the bottom.'

With this kind of conversation, impersonal, speculative, yet well within his listeners' range, he enlivened the meal; and Julia, catching Nicolas's sheepish, immediately eager smile, smiled back. All seemed as before.

Presently Mynheer, leaping chamois-wise from one subject to another, mentioned Nicolas's imminent visit to Lonthoir.

'And how we shall miss you, my boy,' he said.

'When do you leave?' Julia asked Nicolas. He glanced at Mynheer, and he answered for him.

'I have despatched the message. I suggested the day after tomorrow, unless that is particularly inconvenient for Mevrouw Barnevelt.'

Across the table Julia's eyes met Doctor Hootman's. They were inscrutable and almost immediately he looked down at the food piled on his plate.

It occurred to her that all he had said to her on the previous evening might have been the product of his imagination. It was a strange life that he led; hours and hours on end, locked away there with nothing but an idiot for company, emerging for an hour at dinner time and then going back to his books. It was possible that he invented things to amuse himself and had reached the point where he no longer could distinguish the real from the fancied. And no wonder when, in Rua, the two were so intricately entangled. Mynheer was now saying, for instance:

'Daan–if Pieter hasn't retired when you go back, ask him to wait up, will you? A proposition was put to me this morning upon which I should like his opinion.'

'I'll go now, and see if I can catch him,' said Doctor Hootman, and rose and hurried away.

A few minutes later Mynheer rose.

'This business with Pieter won't take more than fifteen minutes,' he said. 'If you two like to go into the salon and set up two chess boards, I'll take you on both at the same time. You'll find a second set in one of the cabinets, Julia.'

Walking along the cloister Nicolas said: 'Julia, I want to apologise for my behaviour last evening. To say that I was not sober, I know is no excuse, but I hope you'll take it into account.'

'Let's not speak about it, or think about it any more,' she said.

'Will you forgive me?'

'I have.'

They entered the salon and she went to the cabinet where the chessmen she and Mynheer used as a rule were kept.

'Set these up,' she said. 'I'll find the others.'

He stood there, holding the lacquered box in his hands.

'I wasn't just being drunk and . . . lascivious, you know,' he said in a rather miserable voice. 'I do love you, Julia.'

There was something touching about him this evening, in this shamed and subdued mood, and with the first brightness of his good looks blurred he looked younger instead of older, as he should have done. She looked at him without speaking for a moment.

'I'm sorry, Nicolas. I wish I loved you. I really do. But I don't. And there's nothing I can do about it.'

For the first time he seemed to accept this.

'I wish to God I'd never come to Rua,' he said. 'Never set eyes on you.'

There was hope for him then, if he felt like that, she thought, turning away to search the cabinet for the second set of chessmen. I've only seen Charles twice; I may never see him again; I have nothing to hope for; but I wouldn't *not* have known him for anything in the world.

But perhaps there lay one of the differences between women and men.

She found what she was looking for, and crossed to one of the tables and began to set out the game. Nicolas still stood holding the box she had handed him and stared at her gloomily.

'Uncle Simon's story was the only bit of family lore I ever found in the least interesting,' he said at last. 'Little did I think that mine was going to be the same–only more hopeless.'

'What was his story?' Julia asked, hoping to divert him.

'He fell in love with a nun.'

'With a nun?'

'On his way to Holland for his wedding with a girl to whom he had been betrothed for years.' A tinge of that pleasure which comes from having a dramatic story to tell crept into his voice.

'What happened?' Julia asked.

Nicolas moved then, sat down by the other table, and began, slowly, to set out the pieces between sentences.

'They wanted him to be married in Holland; his father, and grandfather, had been travellers in their day and his father thought he should see something of the world. The woman was on the same ship; she was Portuguese, going back to Lisbon from Goa. Older than he was; and she'd been a nun for years; and was so well-connected that she was practically royal. But this is where the case was different,' there was accusation now in his voice: 'she did love him.'

In his youth, before his eyes bulged and his colour faded and his flesh shrivelled, Mynheer must have been good-looking, very much like Nicolas, and there would be that charm of manner, the glib tongue, the flashing intelligence. Yes, easy to imagine.

'What happened?' she asked again.

'She got off the ship at Lisbon; he went on to Holland and talked himself out of his betrothal. That was more serious then even than it would be nowadays. They made a great fuss and demanded compensation for all the chances the girl had missed through being promised to him. Then he came home and tackled his family.'

What, he wondered, was Uncle Simon's father like? Stern and strict, like his own? Tolerant, understanding, unconventional, like Uncle Simon? Still, it must have been a scene. Imagine any young man, expected home with his wife, walking in and saying: 'I didn't get married. I've fallen in love with a nun.'

'So he set to work,' he went on. 'It took him five years. Letters to everybody concerned, the various families, and the Head of the Order, and to the Pope himself–and all of them taking seven months each way. And more compensation to be paid. But he got his way in the end.'

'You mean he married her?'

'Yes. She was Pieter's mother. And within two years she was dead. My mother always says that that, and Pieter's accident, came as a judgement.'

Mynheer believed that, too? She remembered what he had said about having a feud with God; and about God being just, after all, and sending her to Rua. Suddenly that linked with what Doctor Hootman had said last night. Her momentary doubt of his sanity vanished.

Her hands went limp, fell on to the board, knocking over several pieces. Against what had she pitted herself, what defied, what foiled?

'It's quite a story, isn't it? And Uncle Simon told me himself that it was all well worth it. Two years with the woman of your choice, he said, was worth a lifetime of the other thing.'

His manner changed suddenly; he stiffened in his chair gripping its arms with white-knuckled hands.

'And that's made up my mind for *me*,' he said in a harsh voice with something of hysteria in it. 'I shall not marry Greta Hoogenbeet. Nothing, nobody can make me. She can marry my brother and I shan't marry at all. It's too much to ask that when you're in love with one person you should be forced to go through the actions with somebody else!'

Just the way I feel, she thought, but I should protest, dissuade him, he'll ruin his life. It's no good his trying to copy Mynheer, he isn't made the same way, made of the same stuff. . . .

Before she could speak Mynheer himself came into the room, saying cheerily:

'Well now, are you both ready? Ladies first, so I'll start with you, Julia. My *dear*! How many times have I told you? What can you be thinking of?'

Chapter Fourteen

Two days later Nicolas departed for Lonthoir, and dinner that evening was a quiet meal. Mynheer spoke little and was distrait of manner. When Doctor Hootman, with his usual perfunctory, 'If you will excuse me . . .' began to push back his chair, he said, brusquely:

'Sit down, Daan. I have something to discuss with you, and we might as well do it over a glass of brandy. I'll join you later my dear.'

Julia left, and Mynheer sat silent, his elbow on the table, his clenched fist pushed against his cheek, silent for so long that even Doctor Hootman's equanimity cracked a little.

'Help yourself,' Mynheer said at last, indicating the brandy. 'You'll probably need support when you hear what I have to say.'

He'd heard–one of them had spoken about the interference that evening. Doctor Hootman braced himself.

'Well,' Mynheer said heavily. 'I have to confess myself defeated. It–just–wouldn't–work. After all those years of scheming and waiting and planning. A crushing blow, Daan. A mortal blow to hope.'

'They always seemed to get on very well together.'

'Dogs play prettily–when the bitch is not on heat!' said Mynheer coarsely. 'And in this case that was the trouble. He was head over ears, poor boy. . . .' He brooded for a moment, then said, in a brisker tone. 'Well, that's over and done with, and there's the future to be faced. How old are you, Daan?'

'Forty this year,' his voice betrayed surprise.

'I wish you were younger. Still, you'll outlive me. I'm fifty-five and the years are beginning to tell. As you know . . . I'm not the man I was.'

'If you could take things more calmly,' said Doctor Hootman in a smooth, false voice.

'I might as well tell you to take things less calmly. We take things as we must. However, that's by the way. I've made new arrangements; they involve a radical change in your position, Daan; one that I think, I hope, will be welcome.'

'What change?'

'When I die, I shall leave all I have to Pieter who cannot even write his name, who cannot, must not, be seen by anyone from outside. Did you ever ask yourself what would happen if my plans came to nothing?'

'I never carried my speculations so far. Keeping Pieter amused and occupied, lending colour to the story . . . that has sufficed to exercise my wits.'

'It all works in. You are recognized as his friend, his resident doctor, the one man whose company he tolerates, but it would hardly do, after my death, for you *suddenly* to emerge as his man of affairs. That rôle you must begin to fill *now*. I propose, from this evening, to stage a very gradual retirement. Then, when the change comes it will seem no change at all; people will be accustomed to doing business with you. I shall begin taking you about with me, introducing you and getting you familiar with the routine of running the plantation.'

The bulging glassy eyes looked–and looked in vain–for sign of emotion on the heavy-jowled face.

'Well,' cried Mynheer at last, in a more sprightly voice than he had yet used this evening; 'talk of taking things calmly! I tell you that in everything except name you are to be my heir and you sit there as though I had offered you a cup of tea!'

'I'm stunned,' said Doctor Hootman. It was largely true. He was astonished beyond measure, not only by Mynheer's latest plan, but by the way he had taken the failure of his former one. At this very table, on the evening of Julia's arrival Mynheer had confessed how long that plan had been in his mind, how deeply, how entirely he counted upon its success. Now, with hardly a whimper, he had abandoned it and was off on another tack. Why? The world–as he himself had said to Julia–was full of girls. Was Mynheer breaking up? Not very old yet; but his life had been full of hidden stresses; did he feel, as some men did, the beginning of failure within him? Did that reconcile him the more easily to failure without? Or was there, somewhere, carefully concealed, a trap in this new arrangement? Mynheer had a devious mind.

But I think I am a match for him, thought Doctor Hootman.

'Stunned,' he repeated.

'Well, you've always had my confidence, and stood by me; and I shall feel that Rua–and my poor boy–are in safe hands. I shall begin to initiate you into the business tomorrow and then in ten days' time I think I shall ask you to undertake a journey for me–to Macassar.'

Instantly it was all plain. Ha! said Doctor Hootman to Doctor Hootman as the light broke. *He wants me out of the way!* He does know of my intervention the other evening; probably he knows more; the girl may have betrayed something. I probably made a false step in speaking so freely to her, but it was necessary. Now, with me on my way to Macassar and Nicolas back from Lonthoir, anything may happen.

'Macassar,' he said thoughtfully. 'That's a long way. I don't think. . . . It's Pieter I'm considering now. How will he manage?'

'Pieter must be weaned as it were. You can't perform the duties of nurse *and* agent, Daan, that is evident. Echo can look after him.'

'Echo is useless,' said Doctor Hootman, quite angrily. 'He was dying of apathy, in Echo's charge, when I first came here.'

'There's the girl now, don't forget. She is, I think, genuinely devoted. She'll keep him amused.'

'Yes, there is that.' Doctor Hootman's voice was doubtful. His mind raced forward, weighing, assessing. 'Pieter is, so to speak, my life work . . . it isn't so easy just to hand over.' He took a gulp of his brandy. 'I can spare time to learn the business, I should indeed like to do that. I waste a good deal of my evenings, just reading. I could go to Banda with you, or for you if you wished. But to be away so long, the first time I leave him . . . that does need thinking over.'

Now, if the voyage to Macassar is just a ruse to get me away, he'll insist, Doctor Hootman thought; and if his suggestion is sincere he will compromise.

'Yes,' Mynheer agreed. 'Anyhow, one of us must go. The *Queen of the East* sails from Banda to Java in about ten days' time, and she will call at Macassar. I bespoke a passage on her this morning before leaving Banda. Whichever one of us sails in her will be sure of congenial company–Nicolas will also be aboard.'

'Nicolas! ! !' The single word, uttered in complete amazement seemed to ring out and vibrate in the silence. 'But his time isn't up.'

No. But he's of no use to me now. I don't want him back here, making sheep's eyes and sighing. Also, between you and me the young ass began talking of breaking off his betrothal. The sooner he's back under his father's thumb the better. I shall arrange that whichever one of us sails for Macassar can take along what gear he left.'

'I see,' said Doctor Hootman.

There was no trick then; no double dealing. It was an honest, straightforward arrangement. Nicolas aboard the *Queen of the East* and no other Vosmar nearer than Macassar. Safe. Better than safe. Promoted, elevated . . . everything handed to him on a platter. Was it possible? Could he believe?

'Of course,' Mynheer went on, 'if your devotion to duty–and I'd be the last to deny that it is admirable and does you great credit–is going to confine you here, this new scheme of mine can't work. If, in the future you are going to act for Pieter, you must begin to act for me, now; and not boggle about a journey that will involve a few weeks' absence. Anyway, think it over, Daan. If you decide not to go, I shall; and if I go to Macassar, I shall go on, to Java.'

'To Java. Why?'

'Because if you don't go to Macassar I shall understand that you can't leave Pieter and therefore can't become what I want you to become. I shall consequently be compelled to make a different arrangement. I shall bring back a Vanderplasse boy. I'd prefer to have Nicolas, but he is the heir, they'd hardly spare him, and there is this complication of his lost heart to consider. There is, however, a brother, barely a year younger. I admit that the idea has certain attractions. Have done with all this pretence; tell the truth and adopt the boy legally. That might be best.'

Doctor Hootman took a gulp of brandy, and then, under cover of the table, wiped his sweating palms.

'I didn't say I *couldn't* go; I was just wondering how. If Nicolas isn't coming back here it alters the situation. Alters it considerably. I thought that he was, and I could imagine Pieter in a screaming tantrum, me not here to control him, Nicolas in the house, all ears. After eight years, you know, one thinks of these things, almost without thinking. Without a guest in the house–which also means that Mevrouw would be free to give a little more time to Pieter–yes, I think I might go.' Then, like a gambler risking all his winnings on one final throw, he added: 'Of course, to adopt a young Vanderplasse would be a solution, and as you say, easier; but I do beg you, before you do *that*, give me time to get well away; I may be thick-hided, but I don't think I could face the talk and the scandal that would result from the divulging of the truth.'

Mynheer did not wince; he had faced that thought himself.

'That is the drawback,' he agreed. 'Then I take it that what I propose is agreeable to you? I add that I think you have earned everything you'll get, Daan.' He lifted his glass and said: 'I drink to your happy future.'

Mynheer came tripping into the salon and took his place at the chess table.

'I'm sorry to have kept you waiting so long. I've been persuading Doctor Hootman to take a little holiday, and an uphill task I found it. He is so conscientious.'

Her whole inside seemed to fall away. It was true then. And somehow he knew that Doctor Hootman had promised to help her, so he was sending him away.

'Don't look so concerned, my dear. Is it that the thought of assuming more responsibility for Pieter distresses you? It really need not. Echo is perfectly competent. And Dann does *need* a holiday. He should have gone as soon as the rains stopped–but then Nicolas's visit was imminent. I confess that when we have a guest Daan *is* as indispensable as he likes to imagine himself at all times.'

He had looked down at the chessmen, moving, with pernickety little nudges, one or two which were not in the exact centre of their square. Unobserved she could moisten lips gone suddenly dry.

'What about . . . when Nicolas . . . comes back?' she asked.

'He isn't coming back. He's decided to curtail his visit and join the *Queen of the East* at Lonthoir. I thought you knew. So it looks as though you and I, my dear, will have to entertain one another. Now . . . my turn to be white, I think!'

So it was all over. That was, if it had ever existed. Her mind and spirit, having performed so many mental and emotional somersaults, relaxed and gave way to exhaustion. The will-of-the-wisp delight which had danced at the final point of Doctor Hootman's scheme–that in the last event he would find some way of sending her to Charles for protection–flickered away into darkness. And even that, at this moment, seemed not to matter much. She had never really believed it, anyway.

Now the future stretched ahead, serene, if dull. Making pots with Pieter; playing chess with Mynheer. She remembered the moment when she had felt that to be oneself was to fulfil one's destiny. My destiny–stop with Pieter; chess with Mynheer.

He beat her with more than his usual ease, and leaning back said: 'Don't be discouraged; remember I was playing this game before you were born.'

'I don't concentrate hard enough.'

'No. And concentration is the secret. That and a certain flexibility. . . .'

He looked at the board as he spoke but it was not of a mere chess game that he was thinking.

Chapter Fifteen

There followed some peaceful, ordinary days, during which, except at the dinner-table, she saw little of either Mynheer or Doctor Hootman. The latter's holiday was, Julia was given to understand, to combine a business errand, and in preparation for this the two men spent many hours in the library with books and papers spread before them.

They also went to the plantation together in the mornings and late afternoons, and the change in Doctor Hootman's way of life had a rapidly visible effect on his appearance and demeanour. He looked healthier and his manner was cheerful, almost buoyant.

Echo and Julia took over the duties which Doctor Hootman had relinquished. It was the first time that Julia had been in close contact with the huge, dumb Ethiopian, and her original feeling of pity for him gradually gave way to one of exasperation. He knew the value of his disability and traded on it. He performed, with clockwork regularity and precision all his actual duties, but he took no interest and never pretended to. It was a machine attending a machine.

With Doctor Hootman in charge Julia had never entered the room and found Pieter idle, but now, very often, though the materials with which he busied himself were laid out on the table, she would find him sitting empty-handed, with Echo on the other side of the table, his arms folded, his eyes fixed on the wall, his thoughts who could tell where?

Doctor Hootman was to leave on a Thursday, in the morning. The *Queen of the East* sailed from Banda in the afternoon. The library that morning was deserted, the books and papers put away. In Pieter's room Echo sat with arms folded as usual, but Pieter was busily and happily employed applying some ready mixed red paint in blobs and strokes on the sides of his collection of clay pots. Julia noticed that he, like the so-called primitive people, had a definite sense of design although his fingers were so clumsy that the pattern was laid on irregularly. Still it was there.

He rose, overturning the paint pot, and seized her hand.

'Julie. Good morning. Look. Pretty.'

'Very pretty.'

Doctor Hootman came to the door that led into Pieter's bedroom; he carried a shirt in his hand.

'Good morning, Mevrouw,' he said affably. 'I wanted to see you. I'm packing. Would you mind coming into Pieter's bedroom?'

He saw the spilt paint and strode to the table.

'Clear that up!' he said furiously. 'Don't just *sit* and stare, you black fool.'

'I'll come and paint with you in a moment,' Julia said to Pieter. 'Do one for me now. A pot for Julie. A pretty one.'

'Pretty for Julie,' he said, plunging the brush into what paint remained.

Doctor Hootman's room lay beyond Pieter's and through the open doorway she could see his bed, with a little open valise on it, and some clothes thrown about. Doctor Hootman stood by the door that led into the enclosed garden.

'Mevrouw, I have a favour to ask of you. You and you alone can enable me to go away with any peace of mind.'

'I'd do anything to contribute to that, Doctor Hootman. What do you want me to do?'

'Look after Pieter,' he said, with a peculiar urgency. 'Echo is useless, worse than useless; he has a most undermining effect. It's visible already. Pieter holds out something and says "Look" and he won't even move his eyes; and to anyone like Pieter that is discouraging. It's as though he hit him.'

'Oh, I will. I meant to anyway. I shall spend almost all my time with him.'

'Thank you,' he said, with some feeling. 'It matters to me. Very much.' His gaze slid away to the garden. 'There was something else I wanted to say to you. It makes me feel rather foolish. About the other evening. . . . The way things have turned out, I expect you think I was exaggerating, or inventing?'

She hesitated for a moment, and then said: 'Well, I did wonder.'

'It was true enough, so far as it went. But I misjudged Mynheer.' He stared into the garden. 'Yes . . . an error of judgement. Anyway, you have nothing to worry about now, I think. And–perhaps this sounds a little like exacting usury–you will remember that when you looked like being in an awkward situation, I did promise my support, for what it was worth. So, if you find *him* a strain, as I know you must, well, bear it for my sake, will you, please?'

'Of course. I don't think you need worry. Echo can do all the dull jobs and I promise I'll keep him amused.'

'You think I am over-anxious. Perhaps I am. But you see, I've devoted myself, for eight long years to keeping a spark of something. . . .'

He broke off as Pieter came blundering into the bedroom, carrying a pot to which the paint had been so hastily and liberally applied that it was running off again and dropping like gouts of blood to the floor.

'Pretty. For Julie,' he said, holding it out.

'You see? No control. No interest. Pieter, dirty! Dirty! Let it dry. It must dry. Dirty Julie's dress. Dirty Julie's hands. Back on the table. On the table. To dry.'

Slowly Pieter turned and ambled away.

'That is another thing, Mevrouw. He will obey if you say a thing firmly enough and often enough. It's like a weak sagging bell pull, the first jerk won't ring, but if you keep on, and hard enough, you get some response. Oh, and *another* thing. . . . I don't think this will happen, I hope not anyway, but if he should on any account fall into a tantrum, don't let him throw himself about, and don't let Echo handle him roughly. Send for Mynheer.' He brushed his hand over his forehead. 'Really,' he said, 'I don't think I should have agreed to this. I should have refused.'

'I think all this anxiety is really a sign that you need a holiday.'

'I need a holiday. But there are many things I need more. I hope you can manage.'

'I'm sure I can,' she said.

That evening she and Mynheer dined alone for the first time. He remarked upon it, saying flatteringly that he preferred her company to all others, and having said that proceeded to talk as entertainingly as he had ever done at any party. Listening to him, fascinated, and now and again provoked to laughter, she took another step towards adulthood in the realization that it was possible to derive pleasure from the company of someone of whom one disapproved. And from that she passed to the admission that it was impossible not to admire his tough resilient spirit. If indeed he had planned as Doctor Hootman had said, the outcome must have been a shattering, a crushing disappointment; but of that there was no sign. There he sat, neat, sprightly, composed, gaily juggling with words as light and iridescent as bubbles.

He ended a story concerning a native Bandanese, named Shal Ahmi who had successfully fooled everyone in the islands a few years earlier and succeeded in organizing the only really successful slave revolt that had ever taken place; and then said:

'Now tell me what you have been doing all day.'

She had devoted her time to Pieter and somehow he, to whom hours and minutes were all one, timepieces without meaning, days and months nameless, had sensed–she thought–that he had been the centre of extra attention. When she had left him he had clung to her and had lifted her hand and kissed it again and again, wet, slobbering kisses like a dog's, just saved from being distasteful by virtue of the otherwise inexpressible feeling which lay behind them.

'I do see,' she said, when she had given a brief account of their activities that day, 'that for purposes of concealment, Echo is perfect: but I don't suppose Pieter can understand that he *can't* talk to him, and Echo doesn't try, by look or gesture, to make up for his dumbness. There's something flat and dead in the room when they're together. You can feel it when you go in and it settles down again behind you as you leave.'

'Yes, it is a pity. But anyone who can talk to Pieter, could talk about him. Menials, I mean. And he must have an attendant.'

After a moment's silence, he went on:

'You have become genuinely fond of my poor boy, have you not?'

'Oh yes. He has some endearing ways, like a child, or a. . . .'

'Or what?'

Her face reddened. 'I was about to say a dog. But not in any derogatory sense. I'm very fond of dogs. I always wanted one.'

'My *dear* Julia! How many times have I told you to ask for anything, anything at all that you wanted? Then you sit there calmly and tell me that you have always wanted a dog. Why did you never ask?'

'I don't know. Well, for one thing I didn't know whether people did have dogs in the islands.'

'Of course they do. And even if they did not, in Rua we have what we want. What kind of dog would you like?'

'One of those small, long-eared spaniels,' she said promptly. 'Mevrouw Helmers, at the Home, had one, so tiny she could carry it in her sleeve. They were very fashionable because King Charles kept them when he lived at Breda; people called them King Charles's spaniels. Mevrouw Helmers's, though it was so small, was as brave as a lion. Once a drunken tinker came and was abusive because we had no work for him; Mevrouw Helmers said: "See him off, Spider", and that little dog did. I did admire it.'

'You shall have one, as soon as possible. I don't know whether I can find one in Banda, but I will try. What a pity you didn't mention it sooner. Daan could have added it to his list of commissions. What shall you call it?'

'Charles.'

'Oh. Yes, yes, of course. You know, Julia, your choice is very revealing.'

Did he mean her choice of dog, or her choice of name? What did he know? How did he know?

Colouring again and avoiding his eyes, she asked:

'In what way, Mynheer?'

'Women,' said Mynheer in his smooth, controversial way, 'can be divided into many different categories, plain or pretty; witty or dull; but the deepest division is between the maternal and the courtesan types; and what they *like* is the surest sign. The maternal type likes things small, the courtesan type has a preference for large things. You, my dear Julia, are an outstanding example of the maternal type. The afflicted boy, the little dog, they make an appeal to you.' He smiled at her, then looked away. Twirling his glass slowly between his fingers he added in a most casual manner: 'But to poor

Nicolas, handsome, healthy and head over ears in love with you, you could be, and were, quite cruel.'

Her heart which had begun to leap and thud when she had wondered if the word 'Charles' had betrayed her, and then steadied down, began to flutter again. So it wasn't over. It had, at least, to be talked about.

'I tried not to be, Mynheer. I didn't want him to fall in love with me. When he said he had, I discouraged him as gently as possible.'

'Why?'

'Because, although I liked him, I didn't love him. And I bore in mind that I am married.'

'Yes,' said Mynheer, his voice grown heavy. 'You are married. And your husband, as a token of his esteem and affection, can give you a lop-sided clay pot. Is that enough?'

'It . . . has to be, Mynheer.'

'From Pieter, yes. I will say this, Julia, sincerely and from my heart, your acceptance of an intolerable situation has, from the beginning filled me with admiration. I told you once that you would find me not ungrateful. Were you blind to what I offered you?'

It was one of those dangerous questions to which either yes or no was an answer which gave recognition to what lay behind the question. She parried it feebly.

'I don't think I understand you. Everything you have given me I have accepted, gratefully.'

'I didn't say given: I said offered. I'm not heartless, Julia. I was obliged to find Pieter a wife. All these years I have presented a picture of him to the world, disfigured, misanthropic, but *normal*; and normal men, especially when they are heirs to great estates, have wives. I deliberately chose a Company's Daughter because I felt that a girl who had known some privation in her youth would more easily find some compensation in the comforts and small luxuries which I could offer, but I *knew* very well, that in the end they would be inadequate. Man does not live by bread alone. I brought Nicolas here deliberately, knowing that he would fall in love with you, as any young man would. I hoped that you would fall in love with him and accept, from him, all that Pieter could not give you–the pleasure of love, the joy of motherhood. Don't be embarrassed by this plain speaking; I am old enough in years to be your father, in experience, infinitely older. I am being frank with you, be as frank with me. Dear Julia, why did you refuse?'

'Mynheer, one cannot be in love to order.'

He made a little gesture of dismissal with his hand.

'Tell me this then. On the day when you arrived in Banda, if Nicolas had met you, if he had been your husband–what then?'

'I often thought of that. In that case he would have been my husband. It would have been my duty to love him, or to behave as though I did.'

He gave her a long, hard look.

'So you did at least consider it?'

'Yes. Nicolas was always very charming to me. He said he loved me. I thought about it. Any woman would have done.'

Mynheer put out one of his slender, well-kept hands and laid it over hers.

'My dear,' he said earnestly, 'think again. You have behaved impeccably, your loyalty and restraint have been beyond all praise; but facts must be faced. In Pieter you have no husband; from him you will have no child. You are young now; you do not realize the measure of your loss, but it *is* a loss, and in the years to come, when it may be too late, your awareness of it will grow, every day. This situation which I freely admit is of my making cannot be altered, but it can be mitigated. This would not be just an ordinary, sordid little adultery–if that is a suitable word to use–not just a passing love affair. Nicolas is deeply, genuinely in love with you. He has given proof of that; he has dared to write to his father saying that he will not honour his betrothal. That surprises you?'

'No. He spoke of it and I tried to dissuade him. I was appalled by the thought of his angering his family and spoiling his whole future on account of a passing fancy.'

'It is not,' said Mynheer, 'a passing fancy. I can assure you of that. And Nicolas's future can be safely left to me. His father has other sons. . . . Nicolas could remain here. In everything but name you could be husband and wife. Of what account, Julia, is a bit of ceremony, when set beside a real, overwhelming passion?'

None, she thought; knowing that if things had worked out as Doctor Hootman had foretold, she would have gone to Charles without hesitation, abandoning her marriage as lightly as she would have discarded a torn handkerchief. But this was different.

She could see Mynheer waiting for an answer. She said slowly:

'Mynheer, I hope that what you call an overwhelming passion will prove to be mere boyish infatuation. But in any case, the sincerity of Nicolas's feelings does not affect mine.'

He withdrew his hand. Now he is angry, she thought, and braced herself.

'Well,' he said, folding his hands together, 'you're honest and sincere. That gives us something to go on. Will you, just for a moment, look at it from another point of view. Mine.' She saw him change colour, his yellow-grey complexion turned greyer and all the lines in his face seemed to deepen and darken. When he spoke it was with difficulty, in strong contrast to his usual glib facility with words.

'This family,' he said, 'is old, honourable. We've been here a long time, but that is no more than a moment in our history. In the Netherlands, under the Spanish Inquisition, a Simon Vosmar died for his faith . . . at the stake, with the agony pear in his mouth. His son, Pieter, escaped with his life and nothing else. With his two bare hands he set to work to restore the family. He laid the foundation of all that you see here. He named his son Simon, and *he* named his Pieter. A long, unbroken line. Today you have been painting pots with Pieter Vosmar, the last of that line. I am to blame. I invited the curse and it fell. Doctor Hootman wonders, you may have wondered yourself, why I never married again. Anyone stricken as I have been does not invite a second blow.' He unfolded his hands and took hold of the edge of the table, leaning forward. 'Julia, you are my only hope; you alone can redeem us.' He paused and swallowed twice, painfully, audibly. 'Give me another Simon Vosmar, give me a bud to graft on to this barren stock. Let me once hold your child in my arms and cry Nunc. . . .'

He broke off; a frightening change took place in his face. The bulging glassy eyes swivelled upwards, exposing the red-streaked whites; little blobs of foam formed at the corner of his mouth. Apparently conscious of them, he snatched up his table napkin and pressed it to his lips, saying through the muffle of the linen: 'Nothing . . . trifling indisposition . . . leave me . . . go!'

She had jumped up and stood indecisive. She could remember Mevrouw

Helmers saying in her bright airy way; 'And then you *may* have fits to deal with. The symptoms are. . . .'

The symptoms she had listed so blithely bore a horrid similarity to what was happening to Mynheer. His whole body arched and strained as though it were in the grip of two maniac hands twisting against one another. His teeth clamped down in a rigor which held the table napkin firm after his hands had fallen away to clench on empty air.

And then, just as suddenly as it had set in, it was over. His eyes rolled back into position, his teeth loosened and the table napkin fell to his knees. He gave a great sigh, his whole body relaxed, and the perspiration broke out over his face and head so profusely that as she watched his curled silver hair went lank and the colour of lead.

But he was indomitable. With a shaking hand he lifted the napkin and mopped at his face and neck.

'This is nothing. Don't be frightened.' He breathed as though he had been running, and the sweat continued to pour off him.

'Can I do . . . or get you anything?'

'Glass of water, please.'

She poured it and would have held it for him, but he insisted upon taking the glass himself. When he had drained it he said, more steadily:

'I'm sorry, Julia. It happens if I let my . . . emotions get the upper hand. Nothing to worry about.' He managed a ghastly smile. 'You see how much it means to me. Think about it. Think about it.'

Terrified of provoking a further attack she said:

'Yes, I will. I'll think about it.'

Chapter Sixteen

They did not meet again until dinner time of the next evening. Mynheer appeared to be fully recovered and was in a genial mood. Julia, after another night spent in agonized indecision, had the worst headache of her life, so violent that she was incapable of thought and sometimes barely conscious. Amusing Pieter during the afternoon had taxed her fortitude to its limit and she longed to creep away to her room and lie down in the dark; but to do so would look like evasion and merely postpone the evil moment.

Mynheer, and the table between them, and the room around them kept being blurred out, as though whorls of fog were being blown about. Just as on the previous evening he chatted, courteously, entertainingly; sometimes she did not hear what he said, when she did, she made some kind of answer. The sight and smell of the food sickened her and the two or three mouthfuls she forced herself to take were as tasteless as straw.

Mynheer was oblivious, or affected to be oblivious to her state; and at last Pluto, moving noiselessly as a shadow, placed the fruit bowls and the decanters on the table and withdrew. This the moment, she thought. It was like being on the gallows, with the noose round her neck and the cart under her feet about to pull away. But there was still time . . . she could say yes. . . . All night and all day the arguments had gone on, chasing one another round inside of her dizzy skull and here she was, still uncertain. . . .

'You slept badly?' Mynheer's voice was kind and solicitous.

'I didn't sleep at all.'

'Poor Julia. Try a little brandy.'

'It would make me so . . . ill.'

'It wouldn't you know. Believe me, it is the best restorative. Try just a sip, to please me.'

He poured some into a glass and handed it to her. She lifted it. The scent of it had started its evocative business before the liquid tilted to her lips. She set the glass down. She was not conscious that it was brandy which Charles had given her that day on the path, or that it was brandy, poured by Mynheer, which had, by its mere scent, called him so vividly to mind. She only knew that now, all at once, she was certain.

'I have thought,' she said, so firmly that she was surprised by the sound of her voice. 'I tried to look at it from your point of view, Mynheer. But I know that even if I said I would, in the end I shouldn't, so it's best to say so.'

There was a long silence. The grey whorls of fog blurred everything. Out of the fog, from a great distance away, Mynheer said, kindly, sincerely:

'Don't distress yourself, Julia. I'm very much disappointed. But the decision was yours to make, after all. It's the end of my hopes, but not the end of the world.'

Such calm acceptance, the last thing she had expected, broke down all her defences. She put her head in her hands and began to cry. Mynheer rose and came round the table, put an arm around her shoulders and with his other hand stroked her hair.

'I've been inconsiderate,' he said. 'I asked too much of you. Poor Julia, poor little girl.'

His kindness filled her with a sense of guilt.

'I would have done it, if I could. I tried,' she gulped out.

'I know. I know. Now don't think any more about it. Come along to bed and have Juno rub your head until you fall asleep. Please, Julia, the thought that I have upset you so much distresses me more than I can say.'

He helped her to the door of her room, snapped out an order to Juno, bade her good night and went away.

She lay in the bed, soothed by the movements of Juno's firm brown hands, feeling as though she were recovering from a long and serious illness. The whole episode was closed now. She had made the right decision and Mynheer was not even angry. Her peaceful thoughts merged into sleep.

She began to dream again. This time it was a happy dream. It was a bright beautiful morning, with a little breeze blowing from the glittering sea. She was wearing a new dress, white sprigged with green, and she was playing with Pieter, not in his private garden but near the rose pergola at the back of the house. Doctor Hootman came walking under the clusters of flowers and said, 'Pieter, fetch Julia one of your pots.' Immediately, with that disregard for time and place which is the prerogative of dreams, they were all standing in Pieter's room and Pieter was holding out towards her the same pot, dripping with red paint which he had attempted to give her on Thursday morning. She saw that it was not red paint at all, but blood.

'It's blood! I can't take it,' she said.

'Of course it's blood. What did I tell you?' said Doctor Hootman.

She woke, with his words ringing in her ears.

It was dark in the room. Juno had put out the candles and stolen away. A feeling of cold, sharp terror laid hold of her, so that her flesh pimpled and her hair crawled on her scalp. Fool that she'd been, to be so easily deceived, to think for one moment that Mynheer would accept, in a few weak words, the defeat of a plan so vital. Paralysed with fear she lay and remembered everything that Doctor Hootman had said–that Mynheer would not let one girl stand in his way, with the world full of girls. Dispensed with, and replaced.

Somehow, in some uncanny way, Mynheer had known that Doctor Hootman was her friend, so he had been sent away. She was alone here, and helpless. His very restraint this evening now had a sinister implication; he was no more *angry* than one is with a pen which will not write–throw it down, choose another.

Cold sweat crawled over her. Even at this moment Mynheer might be coming near, intent upon smothering her as she slept.

But, unrecognized, unacknowledged, there ran in her veins the blood of the man, who, with his drawbridge jammed and his enemy approaching, had said: 'We'll not be taken like rats in a trap. We'll do some damage before we die,' and had ridden out, with a half a dozen mounted men behind him in one last desperate charge.

I can't, she thought, just lie here, waiting. She forced her clammy quivering fingers to make a light, and then, carrying the candle, went into the sitting-room whose door led to the cloister. It was closed, as usual, but not locked, though there was a key. She turned it, and then, after several minutes' struggle, dragged up a small heavy chest. As she tugged at it she thought: And I won't be poisoned either; I shall eat and drink only in the evening, at the table where he is, and only of what he is sharing.

Almost at once, with this resolution made and the chest looking oddly out of place by the door, she had another change of feeling. All this is mad, she thought. Between Mynheer and Doctor Hootman I've been driven out of my mind.

The night's thoughts and actions seemed crazier than ever in the morning, with the sun spilling great golden patches on the floor and Juno bringing in the silver tray with the clouded beaker of cold fruit juice, the pretty painted tea-pot, the flowered cup. Nevertheless, she made an excuse to send the woman away, and when she had gone, emptied the beaker and most of the tea down the sluice which took the water when she bathed. She did it with regret and some sour amusement. It seemed a silly waste, but. . . .

When she was dressed she went along to Pieter's room where Echo was keeping watch but doing nothing more.

'What would you like to do this morning, Pieter?'

'Beads,' he said positively. He had a large number of them, big solid beads of many colours, bored with holes large enough to be threaded, without a needle, on lengths of lightly waxed string. He knew the names of the colours and showed a certain artistry in the combinations he chose. He never strung them haphazardly, but with great care, naming each colour as he threaded the bead. 'White one . . . now red . . . green one.'

As usual, all he made was for her. 'Pretty for Julie.' When he thought a string was long enough she snipped the thread, tied the ends together, and slipped the necklace over her head. When, towards the middle of the morning, Mynheer came in, she was wearing a necklace of red-white-and-green, one of red and green, and one of red and white. Pieter was breathing hard over a fourth, a green and white one.

Looking at Mynheer cautiously she saw that he did not look well; his face was grey; and he, ordinarily so light and nimble in his movements, this morning walked slowly, leaning on his silver-knobbed cane. But he spoke with cheerful kindness.

'Good morning, my dear. I trust you slept well. Hullo, Pieter; you're busy.'

'Pretty for Julie,' said Pieter, breathing hard.

'Very pretty.' Mynheer turned to Echo. 'You can go and get your dinner while I'm here. I'll send for you when I want you.'

He came near the table and just touched Julia's beads with the tip of his finger.

'He does choose colours well,' he said. 'There's *something* there, isn't there? And he *is* affectionate. Dog-like, as you said, my dear.'

There was something rather pitiable in the way in which Mynheer was trying to find something in Pieter's favour. The phrase, 'resigned at last' came into Julia's mind. And her heart smote her because of her night thoughts.

Mynheer sat down, and after watching Pieter's fumbling yet persistent efforts for a moment, said: 'Oh, Julia, do something for me, will you? On the top shelf in the library there are some black books, numbered. I want number three. The steps are in position, you won't have to search. I don't feel like climbing this morning.'

'You don't look very well,' she said, rising.

'Oh, I'm all *right*. Growing a little old, I suppose.'

'White one . . . now green,' said Pieter.

She went into the library and climbed the steps. The books were there, to her, even at the top of the steps, only just within reach. She found number three, and was balancing with it, swaying a little under its weight, and prepared to descend when she heard Pieter scream. The noise was nothing like that which he had made on the evening of Charles's visit, nothing like any sound she had ever heard him make; it was a shrill cry of animal pain and terror. It came again, and again, and then, in the same piercing voice he called 'Julie! Julie!'

She threw down the book, scrambled from the steps and ran across the library, hearing as she did so another sound, the thwack, thwack of somebody beating a carpet. She pushed the heavy inner door and stood on its threshold for a second, immobilized by horror and disbelief.

Pieter cowered in his chair, trying to protect his head with his hands, from one of which still dangled the string of green and white beads. Mynheer stood over him, raining down blows with the cane, seeming to aim at his son's head but not heeding where the cane fell.

She was across the floor, and had Mynheer's arm in both her hands, bearing down on it with all her force and weight, in the time it took her to think that he had gone mad. Nothing else could account for the insensate fury of the unprovoked attack, nor for the superhuman strength in that seemingly frail and brittle arm. It was as strong as steel, and when it lowered she knew that it did so in answer to Mynheer's will, not to her frantic efforts. Still, it did lower.

Pieter, who had screamed each time the cane struck him, broke ito a dismal whimper.

'That's just a start,' said Mynheer a trifle breathlessly. 'If I must, I'll beat him to death. Stand over there and watch.'

'Mynheer,' she said, as steadily as she could force herself to speak, 'you're not well. You don't know what you're doing.'

'Don't talk to me as though I were an idiot, too! I know what I'm doing. You don't like to see your dog hurt, do you? Stand back there then, before I hit him again.'

She took a pace backward. As she did so, Pieter, still holding his hands over his head, crouched low, scuttled across to her and pushed his face into her skirt. Red weals were coming up where the cane had hit him, and one of his ears was bleeding.

She put both hands on his shoulders and said: 'It's all right, Pieter.'

'Now you can listen to me,' said Mynheer. 'So far I've given him a flick or two with this light cane, but as God is in Heaven, I swear I'll beat him until he is dead unless you give me your word to do what I want you to. Without you he's of no use to me, the slobbering idiot. I've only kept him alive all these years because to have a grandson a man must have a son. I hate him. I always have.I've never looked at his ugly face without wanting to smash it in, beat it to pulp. And now I will–and you will watch if I have to tie you in a chair!'

Against her knees Pieter burrowed, whimpering. She looked down at him, and then into Mynheer's bulging eyes.

'You know I'd bear you twenty grandchildren rather than see Pieter hurt,' she said.

But Pieter had been hurt; and she had been tricked. Anger as well as acknowledgement of defeat moved in her; and a desire to hurt him.

'I only hope,' she said clearly, 'that the Vosmar madness won't come out in Nicolas's child.'

'You dare say that to me!' said Mynheer. He stepped forward, raised his hand and slapped her face, twice, on one cheek with the palm, on the other with the back of his hand. He had to reach over Pieter to do it, but the blows were heavy enough to jar her whole body and sharp enough to bring the stinging tears to her eyes.

Moving back he said: 'I have you now. What I've suffered from your airs and graces, you little bitch from the gutter!'

He glared at her with pure hatred, and she glared back at him through the water standing in her eyes. The marks of his fingers stood out, bright scarlet on her ashy face.

Between them Pieter lumbered to his feet, lowering his arm and loosening his fingers so that the string of beads fell rattling to the floor. He turned himself about.

'Bad!' he said. 'Bad. Hit Julie.'

He began to shamble forward, his head lowered, his heavy head swinging.

'Keep away from me,' cried Mynheer, stepping back and raising his cane. But Pieter kept on.

Just too late Julia called: 'Pieter. No!' Mynheer had lashed out, hitting Pieter across the face, and Pieter gave a great bellow of rage which drowned her voice. Bellowing he put his hands around Mynheer's throat and began to shake him. Mynheer's dainty little feet chattered on the floor and then slipped. His fall brought Pieter down, too, but the puffy, limp-looking hands did not loose their hold.

Julia ran forward and took Pieter by the collar, crying:

'Pieter. No. No. Pieter, stop.'

It was trying to restrain, trying to talk to a gorilla.

'Bad! Bad! Hurt Julie! Bad! Bad! Bad!' said Pieter, at each word lifting Mynheer a little way from the floor and then smashing him down again.

She let go the collar, ran to the bell and tore at it, and then ran shouting to the door. Tearing it open, she found herself face to face with Doctor Hootman. Except that he wore a hat, had a two-day growth of beard on his chin and carried his little valise he might just have been returning from one of his casual strolls.

'They're killing each other,' she screamed at him and jumped aside so that he could rush past her. He did rush, and by the time she had turned herself and followed him back into the room he had his arms hooked into Pieter's elbows and had dragged him clear. He said, and the mildness of his voice, the word he chose, brought a sob-giggle of hysteria to Julia's throat.

'Naughty Pieter. Naughty! Naughty!'

Pieter gave himself meekly into the hands of accustomed authority.

'Bad. Hurt Julie,' he said once more. And then, with bright recognition. 'Good morning, Doctor Daan.' He put his hand to his bleeding ear, looked at his fingers and said in a tone of rebuke: 'Dirty. Dirty.'

Doctor Hootman was on his knees by the broken thing that lay on the floor. He opened Mynheer's frilled shirt, laid a delicately explorative hand on his breast, held it there for a minute and withdrew it.

'Nothing can be done about *that*,' he said, getting to his feet, 'except be thankful that it didn't go the other way about. . . . Mevrouw, sit down,' he caught her as she swayed, 'put your head on your knees.' She felt his hand on the nape of her neck bearing down. She heard him say, 'Pieter, go in the garden. Garden. Get some flowers. Go and get some flowers for Julie.'

Over her bowed head their voices went on.

'Bad,' Pieter said again and again. 'Hurt Julie.'

'Julia will be all right. Not hurt. All right. Go and get her some flowers.'

'Dirty! Dirty!'

'I'll clean you. Soon. Flowers first, Pieter.'

'Pretty for Julie.'

'Yes, pretty for Julie.' Doctor Hootman's voice never lost its patient insistence, but she heard him give a sigh of relief as Pieter went lunging away.

'Mevrouw, are you feeling better? Stay as you are. I think I have some brandy here.' He removed his hand from her neck. She heard him moving about. Then he said:

'Here, drink this.'

She lifted her head and said helplessly: 'I can't,' and began to cry.

'That's right. Have a good cry. You'll feel better afterwards.'

He set the brandy within reach of her and went over to what lay on the floor. He stooped, and took from Mynheer's pocket the chain of keys; held them cupped in his hand for a moment, and then took out his own, a mere two or three held together by a thin leather strap, worn and greasy from much handling.

Mopping at her streaming eyes and still sobbing Julia watched him weighing the two lots of keys against one another; his face wore a look of immense gratification. With a sudden movement he opened one of the drawers in the table, the drawer in which he kept a few of his personal belongings, and tossed the leather-held keys into it. The others he slipped into his pocket. Then he came over to her and asked kindly:

'Better now?'

She nodded. As soon as she thought her voice was to be trusted she said:

'I thought you had gone to Macassar.' The words were followed by a great sob.

'So did I,' said Doctor Hootman drily. 'So did he! But Nicolas was supposed to board the ship at Lonthoir. When there was no sign of him I disembarked. I realized that I . . . that we had been outwitted. Well, he'll never trick anyone again.'

'Oh, don't!'

'It must have been very distressing for you. Try not to take it to heart. It is much the best thing that could happen. Oh, dear! How quick it can be about some things,' he said, as Pieter, clutching a few crushed flowers, came blundering in. He laid them in Julia's lap, and when she did not instantly acknowledge them said on a questioning note:

'Thank you?'

'Thank you very much indeed, Pieter.'

'I must bestir myself,' Doctor Hootman said. 'There's a great deal to do. Do you feel able to get to your room, Mevrouw? Then go and lie down. There's nothing to worry about now. Nothing at all. Just leave everything to me.'

She stood up. Her legs felt too long and very hollow. Like someone very old, or very sick, she handed herself across the room, from the table to a chair, and to another chair, to the edge of the open door. She had to pass the place where the dead man lay and though she meant not to look that way some kind of fascination made her, at the last moment, turn her head.

Doctor Hootman was spreading his handkerchief over the dead face.

Chapter Seventeen

At the head of the table Mynheer's chair was empty.

Otherwise everything was as usual. There was no sign of the confusion and break with habit associated with the sudden death of the master of the house. The silver tong-tong had announced the meal punctually, and Pluto, with his expressionless trained-house-slave face, brought in the dishes. It was difficult to realize that Mynheer was not merely dining in Banda.

There was, however, one slight difference. Tonight Julia wore the dress in which she had arrived; the plain, dull, serviceable garment with which every Company's Daughter was supplied, and which, with the gayer wedding dress, comprised all the wardrobe considered necessary. And tonight she wore no jewels.

'Good evening, Mevrouw,' said Doctor Hootman, taking his accustomed place to the left of the vacant chair. 'I trust that you feel rested and restored.'

'Yes, I do, thank you,' she said. He had been, she thought, wonderfully considerate. She had gone to her room and had sat there, sick and shivering, for half an hour, cold despite the mid-day heat, unable to do anything except go over, and over again, the terrible events of the morning. Then Doctor Hootman had come along, with a glass in his hand, saying that he imagined she would welcome a sedative. She had taken it and slept all through the afternoon. When she woke everything that had happened in the morning seemed to have run backward in time; she could remember every shocking detail, but the sharpest edge of emotion was dulled. That, and the apparent ordinariness of everything, gave her a feeling of complete unreality.

'If you are agreeable,' said Doctor Hootman, 'we will wait upon ourselves. There are several things to be settled and not much time. Very well, Pluto, you may go.' As the door closed he said: 'It is remarkable, though not, perhaps, surprising that the tragedy has been accepted with such calm. Rua has always run as though by machinery, and like a machine it goes on.'

She remembered; but with that same sense of it being long ago, and drained of horror, Mynheer's attack upon Pieter.

'It would be hypocrisy for me to pretend to any grief,' she said.

'Exactly. No doubt everybody feels the same–to some degree. Of course, if Pieter were capable of occupying that chair, some show of mourning would be expedient. For myself, I feel that the man was a fiend and that the world is well rid of him.'

'How *is* Pieter? I should have gone along to see him, but I slept so long. I had only just time to dress.'

'He is somewhat shaken. Not by the thought of what he did–he seems to have forgotten that. But he cried when I dressed the wound on his ear and showed signs of very considerable disturbance. Of course, nobody has ever struck him before in his life. I have once or twice been obliged to use force to control him, but I have never hit him, even with my hand. I am astonished that his father should have done so. What happened, Mevrouw? Can you bear to tell me?'

She told him, and even in the telling it was a tale of long ago. Doctor Hootman listened attentively, but without ceasing to ply his knife and fork; he nodded now and again and once or twice looked at her sharply.

At the end she said: 'I don't know why, but it all seems to have happened much longer ago than this morning.'

'You have slept. And your mind is putting up its own defence. All in all, you have had a very trying time. If I could I would spare you all exertion now and say leave everything to me. In a sense, certainly, you can leave everything to me, but there are things which I am forced to discuss with you, because I need your help. With the funeral.'

'You know best about such things.'

'Ah, but this is no ordinary funeral!' He looked from his now empty plate to her untouched one. 'Mevrouw, you have eaten nothing!'

'I'm not hungry. I don't think I shall ever be hungry again.'

'Try, at least,' he said. 'Try some fruit. Drink some wine. I know you have suffered a severe shock, but you need your strength now. One more effort and you need never make another as long as you live. That one effort must be made, or we are both undone.'

'In what way, Doctor Hootman?'

Before answering he rose and carried his plate to the side table, then removed hers and set a clean plate and two bowls of fruit before her.

'We face,' he said, coming back to his place with a fresh plateful, 'a problem quite unique, or so I should imagine. You are aware, Mevrouw, of the picture of Pieter which Mynheer always presented to the world. We can't, at this point, expose its falsity. That would be fatal.'

'I used to wonder,' she said, 'what would happen when Mynheer died, but today I haven't even thought about it. I haven't had time.'

'I have,' said Doctor Hootman drily. 'I've had eight endless years. Mevrouw, try at least to drink a little wine while I acquaint you with the results of my long thinking. . . . We must, at all costs, conceal the fact that Pieter is not, in the legal sense, competent. If we do not I can foresee danger from two quarters. First, the family. Both branches, in Java and Macassar, are well-to-do, but Mynheer was, by an incalculable margin, richer. Once let the secret of Pieter's condition leak out and down they will swoop, like vultures. You realize what that would mean?'

'They would want Rua,' she suggested.

'They would take Rua. Before we knew where we were, another pop-eyed Vosmar would have the plantation, and his wife would rule the house. You, Mevrouw, would be reduced to the status of unpaid companion. It isn't only at formal dinner-parties, you know, that wives take precedence by their husband's rank. The family would always speak of "poor Pieter" and you would be poor Pieter's wife. We now the Vosmar attitude towards the defenceless.'

He filled his mouth, chewed vigorously and swallowed, washing the mouthful down with a great gulp of wine. His lips left a greasy mark on the glass, and, with a little inward shudder she looked away.

'So much for the family,' he said. 'The other threat comes from the Company. Land tenure in the islands is largely dependent upon the Company's goodwill. Rua is undeniably Vosmar property, but how long would they allow it to remain in the possession of an idiot? The Company, remember, is all-powerful, far above mere law. And there is a land famine. I am positive that on the slightest excuse, or no excuse at all, someone would whisper "maladministration". You and Pieter–strictly for your own good, of course–would then become wards of the Company. I trust I am making myself clear, Mevrouw.'

'Very clear, Doctor Hootman.'

'Good. So here we are, back at the problem of the funeral. Mynheer was a prominent man; many people will come to see him laid with his fathers in the family burial place. The Governor and the Company's Agent will be among them.'

He shovelled more food into his mouth, chewed, drank, swallowed and hastened on.

'I cannot help but feel that any man, however sensitive as to his appearance, however retiring, would feel it incumbent upon him to attend the funeral of his own father. After all, we have proved–God knows with what effort–that he can stand up and walk.' He shot a glance at the screened window. 'Is it feasible that he should absent himself from the graveside? All our efforts have not prevented suspicions of a mental rather than a physical affliction getting about and unless Pieter Vosmar puts in an appearance at eleven o'clock on Monday morning, those suspicions are going to be confirmed–with the results that I have indicated. You see our quandary?'

'Yes,' she said. But it was his quandary; she could understand but not share it.

'Well; does any solution occur to you?'

With idle unconcern she fingered the idea of making some disguise for Pieter. A hat pulled low, a collar turned up. Useless! The way he stood, the way he walked betrayed his state as clearly as his face did. And people would approach him, making the proffering of condolence and excuse to satisfy their long-standing curiosity.

'I can see no way out of it,' she said.

Doctor Hootman spooned up the last mouthful, pushed his chair from the table and leaned back.

'Fortunately for us both, I can. We must provide a substitute. Someone who knows what Pieter is and whom we can trust. Now. . . . Does the name occur to you?'

'Not. . . . You don't mean Charles?'

'I do indeed! Who else?'

This was the end of being remote from it all; now she was entirely involved.

'He wouldn't do it,' she said.

'Show him a guilder and he would do anything,' said Doctor Hootman incautiously. He realized immediately that he had struck a wrong note and hastened to cover it. 'He has every reason to be mercenary. He lost everything in the Civil War, and though the actual land has been restored, the house is a ruin. His mother and brother live like peasants; the brother actually works in the fields. Charles, like those with him, lives in daily danger for the sake of money, and in the hope of one day returning home. For *him*, at least, that day is much nearer than he dreams–if *we* play our cards with skill and care . . . and courage.'

Now, she knew, she must think for herself.

'Tell me exactly what you propose to do?'

'Well, first, as regards the funeral. I suggest that when the mourners have assembled, you and Charles come, at the last moment and stand inside the burial ground, near enough to be associated with the ceremony, but far enough away to avoid close inspection. That would be in keeping with what is known of Pieter's character. No one there will be familiar with Charles, or with Pieter; why should they suspect anything? I can disfigure him, probably with a scar, convincing enough at a distance. And, of course, it is a funeral; a handkerchief held to the face would be allowable.'

The last words enabled her to recognize the nature of her objection. It all sounded sly and shady, out of keeping with everything that she remembered, or had imagined about the man she loved. A false scar, a false face of grief. . . . Not Charles! Yet, after all, she had only seen him twice; Doctor Hootman, presumably, knew him much more intimately, and believed he would do anything for a guilder.

I *don't* believe it, she thought stubbornly.

'All other considerations apart,' said Doctor Hootman, 'I am sure that Charles, no more than I, would wish to see you at the mercy of the family or of the Company. Once the funeral is safely over it is all smooth sailing. We shall have estabished that apart from his aversion to contact with people, a harmless eccentricity, there is nothing wrong with him. From the privacy of his room he will conduct his business, through *me*. I have amused myself by perfecting a style of handwriting and a signature–most impressive–quite unlike my own. And, by a supreme irony, Mynheer, before sending me out on a goose chase, carried his attempt to deceive me to the point of initiating me into such of his affairs as had hitherto been kept from me. I assure you I can run Rua, even to the Company's satisfaction.'

Smooth, feasible, cunning. Why object? Somebody must run Rua; Pieter could not, so why shouldn't Doctor Hootman? All she minded, at this moment, was the thought of that macabre bit of masquerade by the graveside when respect, and that kind of love which without respect must die, perhaps would die.

'I'm sure you could,' she said. 'But it does mean keeping up all that burden of pretence. Mynheer's family pride was involved; we haven't that excuse. Do you think that perhaps we over-rate the threat from the family and the Company? I am Pieter's legal wife and I am in my right mind. You understand the business. Couldn't we come into the open, admit what Pieter is and act for him?'

Doctor Hootman did not answer immediatley. His hand went to his chin. His jowls had darkened.

'The drawback to that, Mevrouw, is that it leaves us just where we are. You the wife of an idiot, and me the hired man. Frankly I visualized a rather more attractive future for us both.'

'Whether we pretend or not that is what we are; I'm Pieter's wife, you're his agent.'

'Ah . . . but let us look a little farther into the future. I will now allow myself the use of a sentimental expression. Poor Pieter. Poor Pieter's kind seldom live long; it is rare, I believe, for one such to come of age. Eight years ago, when I took charge of him, he was moribund, dying, very slowly and easily of apathy and boredom. He sat in a chair, Mevrouw, with his hands on his knees, staring at the wall; Echo sat opposite, staring at nothing. Twice a day they walked, for fifteen minutes, round and round the little garden. Pieter was dying and Mynheer dared not call in Doctor van Nagel who lived in Banda Neira and who might talk. I happened to be handy. I saw at once that the situation had possibilities, vague, I admit, but my own circumstances, at that time were such that even the frailest hope was something to be exploited. *I set myself to keep him alive.* And I succeeded. Every one of those trivial little activities has been a peg, holding Pieter Vosmar and life together. Oh, I know,' his voice took on, suddenly, the complete sincerity of irritability, 'it's nothing to boast of; in itself nothing to show for eight years' work, but he is *alive* . He has lived to finish his basket, to make a clay pot, to thread another bead, to hear me play the clavichord. You understand me? *Deprived of his activities he will die within three months.*'

Her mouth had gone dry; it was difficult to speak with the necessary casualness.

'And you will so deprive him?'

'Immediately after the funeral.'

Once, long ago, she had told Mynheer that she thought he was cruel; she was wiser now.

'And then what happens?'

'Then, Mevrouw, we come into our own. That sane, non-existent Pieter Vosmar will have made his will–as any childless man would upon coming into his inheritance. To you he will have left the bulk of his fortune; to me, his close, indeed his only friend, he will have left his estate, Rua.'

'I see,' she said.

There was so much to see. Not only the future. The past was all at once brilliantly illuminated. Now she saw why Doctor Hootman had been on guard that evening, why he had, with a promise of support and help to escape, encouraged her not to fall in with Mynheer's plan. An heir to Rua had no place in his schemes. And his schemes were as far-fetched, and as cold-blooded as Mynheer's.

Once more, just when she had thought that the worst was over, she found herself facing something worse still.

Doctor Hootman seemed to mistake the reason for her long silence. He said, defensively, almost placatingly:

'You must not grudge me my share, Mevrouw. Remember what my life has been these eight years. Every day, all day, shut away with an idiot for company; using words of one syllable and using them over and over again before they roused a glimmer of understanding. It has often seemed to me to be a miracle that I retained my own sanity. My God! When I look back . . . the drudgery, the uncertainty, the sheer humiliation. If ever a man earned anything, I have earned Rua.'

She said hastily: 'Oh, I agree. I don't grudge it. I don't want it myself, is that what you were thinking? After all that has happened here, I should like to go away and never see the place again.'

'And that is exactly what you can do, Mevrouw. Very soon. You will be rich and free, and still young. I have imagined, in my sentimental way, that there is a mutual attraction between you and Charles. If that develops you can go back to England with him and use some of your wealth to rebuild his house. If it does not–well, you are a very attractive woman, and you will be rich; you will also enjoy what you have earned. I use that word advisedly; you also have had your trials.'

The one essential was that he should continue to believe her to be co-operative.

'Oh, we've earned it,' she said with a pretended heartiness. 'But . . .' she hesitated and managed a rueful smile. 'You'll think this very sentimental of me, I'm afraid. Without knowing what he did this morning, Pieter saved me from a dreadful situation, and that makes me feel that I don't want anything that depends on his being dead. There must be some other way.'

Quite amiably Doctor Hootman said: 'I am open to suggestion, Mevrouw. Bear in mind, though, that while you appear to be willing to forego your reward, I am not.'

'Suppose,' she began, tentatively, 'that I took him away. You could just as easily pretend that a sane Pieter Vosmar existed without the real one locked in that room, couldn't you?'

'Rather more easily; but I think you under-estimate the difficulty of the removal. It involves–to say the least–a passage on a ship. Remember, dark stories, which have shown a strong tendency to survive despite lack of substantiation, are already rife in Banda, hinting that Pieter Vosmar is not quite as he should be. If one day Mevrouw Vosmar boards a ship, dragging behind her thirteen stones of plain idiocy, wouldn't that give rise to comment? Inquiry?'

'I suppose it would. I'm not a very good planner, am I? Then couldn't we just wait?' Without being aware of it she lifted her head and spoke in a firmer manner. 'I can't just stand by and watch him made miserable and hurried out of life.'

'I've done my waiting. Eight years of it. At any moment during that time Pieter might have died. Where should I have been then? Another three months of waiting for the end will be all that I can bear!' His voice changed, became soothing. 'He won't suffer, you know; he'll just die, gently and gradually, as very old people do. For his kind he *is* old. And you need not stand by and watch, Mevrouw. You need never see him again. Nor need you feel any sense of guilt. You have made your protest and your earnest but quite futile effort to suggest an alternative plan. You may comfort yourself with the thought that neither you nor anyone else can stop me now.'

Any further hint of opposition, or even of half-hearted agreement would now be fatal. Once again she was in conflict with a ruthless and determined man, with nothing but her wits for weapon.

'If you can assure me that he won't suffer . . .'

'I can do that. He won't even know what he lacks. All these years he has been kept alive by what you might call artificial means. I have supplied the stimulus, now I shall remove it. That is all.'

Like saying that a person kept alive by breathing; put a pillow over his face, remove the stimulus and that is all.

'When do you expect Charles?' she asked.

'Tomorrow. I sent him the usual signal and he should come at the usual time. He will be expecting to see Mynheer on business. I think he will be pleasantly surprised.'

'I've so often wondered about that business.'

'There's no harm in your knowing,' Doctor Hootman said pleasantly. 'In defiance of all rules Mynheer continued to grow cloves, and of course the ordinary channels of disposal were closed to him. Charles was his outlet. Dear me, that reminds me! Those trees must come down. Tomorrow. They're at some distance from the burial ground and well out of sight, but somebody might go wandering, somebody with really keen, experienced scent might even smell them. I am deeply obliged to you, Mevrouw, for bringing them to my mind. How easily one overlooks even vital things.' He brought his glance to bear on her with an intensity that seemed to have actual physical weight and said, more slowly: 'Amazing as it may sound I had forgotten the cloves. I thought that Charles would act for me on Monday partly from desire for money, partly for your sake, partly even to oblige me: I had overlooked, until this moment, the most powerful motive of all, the need to save his own skin. On Monday morning Rua wouldn't be a very healthy spot for an English clove-smuggler unless he *was* in disguise, would it?' The facial change which was not quite a smile became visible again.

So that was it. And she did not for a moment believe that the thought had just occurred to him. He'd withheld it, produced it at the last minute, a fine, flourishing, clinching move. She wondered if her face had changed, if the leap of her heart into her throat had been seen and noted.

'I've thought of another thing, too,' she said. 'Wouldn't it look better, more natural, more in order, if Nicolas were at the funeral?'

'Admirable! Actually I had thought of that. I sent for him this morning. He should be back by tomorrow evening. His presence is necessary; it will, as you say, make everything seem in order. I regret it, though. I think his morbid curiosity concerning Pieter constitutes our one real danger. A faked scar across the width of the burial ground is one thing, face to face quite another. Pieter will just have to refuse to see him, promise to do so and then postpone the meeting, write him a letter, send him a message, anything. We must deal with that as it comes. After all, Mevrouw, neither you nor I are novices in the art of deception. We shall manage.'

'Of course,' she said. She knew now what she must manage. Tomorrow she must meet Charles as soon as he set foot on Rua, warn him and send him straight away again. Then she must see Nicolas and tell him everything; that would save Pieter.

Now at last she lifted her glass and said:
'Success to the plan, Doctor Hootman.'
'Success to our plan, Mevrouw.'
Was he deceived? Did he believe them to be one and the same? How could she tell?

Another bad night; and this time, in the heart of it something new; this time side by side with the old confusion and fear and feeling of weakness and despair there came a real and very urgent temptation. Why not give in? The situation had changed. To have given in to Mynheer would have meant going against her own feelings and against her deepest instincts; to give in to Doctor Hootman would be in exact accordance with them. Why not do what she wanted? Why should she bother whether a hopeless idiot lived another year or so of useless life? Who had ever bothered about her? She remembered Aunt Geertruida's treachery; the miserable years in the Klopstock Home; the superficially kindly but fundamentally ruthless system which had shipped her out to Banda. Exploited, she thought, exploited all the way along.

She reverted to the ethic of the Klopstock Home, to the person she had been there before Katje came. The world was a hard, heartless place, and only the hard and the heartless could hope to survive in it.

Then the other arguments began. She hadn't survived in Cloonmagh by virtue of hardihood or heartlessness, but because of kindness and pity. Johannes had saved her from starvation; Charles had saved her from Mynheer's wrath; Pieter pitiably acquiescent when he was attacked, had risen up in her defence. . . .

Tomorrow, somehow, she must out-wit Doctor Hootman.

Chapter Eighteen

Fifty years later, when she was an old woman, one of the trees in the long avenue from which Elmhurst took its name was found to be unsafe and had to be taken down. On that clear cold day in the English winter she walked, leaning on the arm of one of her grandsons, to see the end of the venerable tree. The sound of the axes striking home took her straight back, across half a century, across half a world, to that Sunday in Rua.

'It might have been yesterday,' she said suddenly.

'What might?'

'The day when your grandfather asked me to marry him,' she said. And the boy who had never been farther afield than Canterbury, saw in his mind's eye a piece of English lawn, shaded–since this was in foreign parts–by palm trees, and in the shade a pair of china figures, all pink and white and blue and bearing no resemblance to his grandparents, placidly plighting their troth and sealing it with a chaste kiss.

That Sunday in Rua had not been like that at all.

In the morning she had gone to see Pieter. His face and neck were marked with long narrow blue-black bruises and his ear was swollen to twice its normal size. He was pleased to see her, took her hand and rubbed his head against her shoulder, but something had gone out of him.

'I'm so glad you felt able to come,' said Doctor Hootman briskly. 'I have so much to do and I didn't want to leave him with Echo. He's not himself today, not himself at all.' He gave Pieter a glance of worried exasperation. 'Off his food; most unusual. Try to amuse him, Mevrouw.'

'Of course,' she said.

'I've decided that when those trees are down, the flowers and the foliage must be buried, not burned. The scent would probably hang about till tomorrow; so I must get trenches dug. But I'll relieve you as soon as I can.' He hurried away.

She asked the routine question: 'Well, Pieter, what shall we do today?' and for the first time he was unresponsive.

'Cut some paper for me,' she suggested. That was a favourite occupation, but this morning, though she rustled the paper invitingly and placed the scissors in his hand he showed no interest. At last, with a small inward shudder she suggested threading beads.

'No! No!' He spoke loudly and vehemently.

It was wrong to say that he had no memory, no feelings. Deep inside he was probably just like everybody else; the real Pieter was locked away inside this defective mind and clumsy body as a man might be clamped into a suit of armour.

'No,' she agreed. 'No beads today. We'll go in the garden. Garden. Ball. Shall we play ball?'

He rose and took her hand, but instead of tugging her towards the door, he went towards the clavichord.

'But I can't . . .' Then she thought, oh, what does it matter? I can make some sort of sound.

She sat down and Pieter crouched beside her on the floor, resting his head against her thigh. She touched the notes gently, experimentally, making no attempt to link one with the other.

'Yes,' he said in a satisfied voice and sighed with content.

From far off she could hear the regular, rhythmical blows of the axes on the clove trees and soon she found herself striking the notes to the same rhythm. Presently Pieter put up his hand and took her wrist and lifted her arm and draped it about his neck as though it were a scarf. With her left hand she continued to touch the keys until, looking down at him she saw that he had fallen asleep. On his poor face the innocent, defenceless look, shared by all sleepers, even the most guileful, even by Doctor Hootman, was very marked and instinctively she tensed the arm which lay about his thick red neck. So far as was in her power, she would protect him.

Charles must be warned, Nicolas must be taken into confidence. Her heart began to race and shudder as she thought about time, and opportunity, and risk. . . .

To escape from the house in the afternoon had been relatively easy when one was eluding Mynheer whose habits were regular; Doctor Hootman must be watched. He returned to the house at mid-day, but the axes worked on through the heat. She dared not go out until he had gone again; he might wish to see her; he might even be watching her movements. The latter possibility became almost a certainty as the afternoon wore on. She had taken a chair into the now-shaded cloister from which she had a clear view of the path he would take on his way back to the plantation. The warm air was heavy with the scent of crushed cloves which were being thrown into shallow trenches, covered with soil and stamped down. The lovely, forbidden trees were, by a few hours, preceding their owner to the grave.

At last she saw what she had been waiting for, the heavy sombre figure making its way across the garden and through the rose pergola where every rose lay flat and open-hearted in the heat. She forced herself to wait a little and then set off in a state of nervousness which made her expect to find Doctor Hootman lurking around every corner, in every shadow.

This afternoon she must take the path which ran past Psyche's cage. It was the way Charles had come on that fateful afternoon and she hoped to meet him there again today.

There was still something sinister about the path; even now the doves seemed to avoid it. The axes had ceased to sound as Julia crossed the garden and now the afternoon had an ominous silence. She hurried past the cage, not looking that way, and was then on the spot where she had stood, sick and shaking and heard the footsteps. If only she could hear them now!

Once around the curve she was on new ground. The path narrowed and began to slope upwards; when at last she came to the edge of the grove and could see the sea, it lay between twenty and thirty feet below, at the foot of a sheer cliff thickly clothed with ferns, with pink azaleas and the far-flung, twining wreaths of the island honeysuckle, brilliant yellow and scarlet, and so heavily scented that here the crushed clove odour was no longer detectable.

At this point the sea had taken a bite out of the island, making a little cove, a perfect place for surreptitious landing; shielded on either side from observation.

All this Julia noticed, but she failed to see or, seeing, failed to realize as significant, that today the little cove was awash with the incoming tide. The narrow strip of beach at the cliff's foot was already under water; presently the sea would reach the level where the lowest ferns grew. It would be hours before any boat could beach there.

Ignorant of this she went to the cliff's edge and stared out into the shimmering blue distance. She willed Charles to come, and to come quickly, with an urgency which left her as exhausted as a fierce physical effort would have done. Nothing stirred on the silken skin of the sea.

The watched pot, she thought, reverting to Anna's idiom, never boils. Look away, walk this way, that way along the cliff top, counting the steps. Stare down at the flowers and count five hundred, a thousand, two thousand, three, and then look up and see the dark speck on the blue. . . .

Always the sea was empty. In the west, on the other side of the island the sun began its rapid slide down the sky. The slanting light turned to liquid gold on the face of the water and for a few minutes it was impossible to stare at it, even with squinted eyes. Now, now, while she was blinded, he would come. Turn away, look into the thickening green gloom of the nutmeg grove and then look back and see . . .

But when she faced the sea again the only change was that the brazen-gold had softened and was streaked with rose, with amethyst, with daffodil, colours which, even as she watched, began to blur and merge into grey.

Soon it would be dark. Before dark she must be back in the house. Up to the moment when she told Nicolas everything she must retain Doctor Hootman's confidence, otherwise he would find some way to keep them apart. Though she had failed to meet and warn Charles, she might, even yet, save Pieter. And to do that she must get back to the house.

She had run a long way before the comforting thought struck her that perhaps Charles did not intend to come to Rua. Perhaps Doctor Hootman's message had miscarried. Perhaps he had some other business on hand. Perhaps in some secret, underground way, he had heard of Mynheer's death and so seen, in the 'usual' signal, warning of danger. In that case everything would be simple and easy; just take Nicolas along to Pieter's room and it would be done.

When she reached the pergola she adopted the sauntering gait of one who had, in the lessening heat, merely taken a stroll, and it was as well that she did so, for Doctor Hootman was standing on the steps that led up to the cloister and he was scanning the garden even as he placed a hand on the arm of Nicolas who had evidently just arrived. Two of the house slaves were carrying his little travelling trunk towards the door of his room. Both men saw her and came towards her, but Nicolas by breaking into a run, reached her first and put his arm around her in a brotherly, comforting gesture. He began to say 'Poor Julia, it must have been awful for you . . .' and by interrupting him she had just time to say:

'I must see you alone. There's so much to tell,' before Doctor Hootman joined them.

'Mevrouw,' he said, 'I have looked for you everywhere. Pieter is being most difficult about tomorrow. You must talk to him.'

His voice was heavy with hidden meaning and she understood that Charles had come.

Nicolas, taking the words at their face value said, tightening his arm:

'You can leave that to me, Julia. Ever since I heard the awful news I've been thinking about Pieter. He'll have to drop all his nonsense now, and I think I should be the one to tell him so.'

'It may come to that,' said Doctor Hootman, 'but I feel that Mevrouw should try her persuasions first. I left him thinking things over.' That sentence, too, was dark with implication. 'Perhaps it would be as well to leave him for a little while and refresh ourselves. Mevrouw has eaten nothing all day, you, Mynheer have been travelling, and even I . . .' He spread his hands.

'You must have been very busy,' Nicolas said.

They went into the room with the Chinese cabinets; the room where Julia had played chess with Mynheer and been told that concentration was the secret. If only she could concentrate now! The news that Charles had come, after all, and was here in the house, altered things; and something in Doctor Hootman's manner of conveying that news had warned her that he did not wholly trust her.

A cloth had been spread on one of the tables and set out upon it were the dishes always served in the islands on casual occasions, small cakes, fruit, fresh and preserved, highly spiced and pickled vegetables and pieces of meat and fish capable of being picked up in the fingers and popped into the mouth. There was also a bottle of wine, which Doctor Hootman, with a nice show of courtesy, left for Nicolas to handle, while he set about the food.

There began, and lasted for about ten minutes, what, in retrospect, Julia thought was perhaps the most fantastic little scene of all. Nicolas was young enough to find any death disconcerting and sudden death particularly so. He had been genuinely fond of his Uncle Simon and for the whole of his stay in Rua he had been a witness to a most affectionate relationship between him and Julia, a kindly one between him and Doctor Hootman. He took it for granted that they shared his grief over the death, his dismay at its suddenness and everything he said had the effect of making Mynheer seem an ordinary man, to be, like other men, sincerely mourned.

'It was so appallingly sudden,' he said. 'He was in good health when I left.'

'Not quite so good as it seemed, Mynheer. He was very sensitive on the subject, but he had had one one or two minor attacks in the last few months. He was aware of his state; that was one reason why he was beginning to delegate more and more responsibility to me. I was about to travel to Macassar on business for him, was I not, Mevrouw?'

'Yes. Oh yes,' Julia said.

'Was it a stroke?' Nicolas asked.

'Of a kind. A seizure. There's this to be thankful for, he didn't suffer at all.'

'I still can't believe that I shall never see him again. He was quite unlike anybody else, wasn't he? So amusing, and understanding, and kind.'

As he said these words he looked at Julia as though asking her to agree and confirm. He had not shaved that day and the faint golden downiness on cheek and chin made him look very young. She forced herself to say:

'Yes, he could be very kind.'

Their eyes met, and in his she saw, behind the distress something else move, sharp and active. He was remembering her words upon meeting.

'You do look poorly, Julia,' he said. 'Let me take you to your room.'

'Mevrouw *must* see Pieter first,' said Doctor Hootman.

'Why can't I do that for her?'

'For the simple reason that being confronted by a stranger–which is, with all respect, what you are to him–would merely upset and anger him and leave him less open to reason. Mevrouw has far more chance of success. In fact if Mevrouw cannot persuade him to make an appearance tomorrow I don't know who can!'

'Now I'll tell you something,' said Nicolas more brightly. 'The Barnevelts with whom I have been staying asked me a lot of questions about Pieter. They could hardly believe that I had stayed here for weeks and never set eyes on him. When they realized that I wasn't lying and knew no more than they did they told me some of the stories that are going round about him. They weren't pleasant, I assure you. And if Pieter shirks his own father's funeral . . . well!'

'I know, I know,' said Doctor Hootman, worriedly. 'He must be persuaded.'

'That kind of rumour does no good–with the Company I mean,' said Nicolas. 'In Java we had a neighbour who had so many bouts of fever that his memory was affected. They kicked him out, tactfully, of course. They said there was a danger that he might ship out unlimed nuts or something.'

'Had he no wife?' asked Doctor Hootman without looking at Julia.

'Oh yes, and a son, but only a child. They couldn't run a plantation.'

'You see, Mevrouw, it is essential that these ridiculous rumours are quenched tomorrow.'

'I still think I should talk to him,' Nicolas said. 'I'd contrive to act in such a way as to convince him that he hasn't all that much wrong with him.'

'That,' said Doctor Hootman, 'would be extremely easy. When you see him, you'll be surprised to find how little is wrong with him. Don't you agree, Mevrouw?'

'I always said so,' she said dully.

Suddenly she could bear it no longer. 'Let's go and get it over with.' She stood up.

'I shall take a little walk,' Nicolas said. I'm still cramped from the boat. Then I'll come back here and hear how you succeeded. And if he's still stubborn I shall have a good straight talk with him.' The ghost of the old spite was in his voice. 'I think you all pay too much attention to his fancies and foibles.'

'Perhaps,' Doctor Hootman said easily. 'But you see . . . to those who *know* him. Pieter is very lovable.'

And that, also, was for her ear alone.

'When did Charles arrive?' she asked, as they went along the cloister.

'A few minutes before you came back from your walk. Had you been in the house you would have had the opportunity for a little private talk.'

Was that said ironically? Did he know why she was not in the house? A swift glance at his face gave her no clue.

'Is Charles against the plan?'

'As I said, Mevrouw, I left him thinking it over. His immediate response was unco-operative. But I admit I had done no more than outline the situation when that boy arrived.'

They halted by the library door and Doctor Hootman took out Mynheer's bunch of keys.

'Now I have to lock *this* door,' he said, with an almost humorous look. 'It becomes more and more like Bluebeard's castle.'

The door opened and Charles, who had been lolling in a chair, jumped up. For the third time they stood face to face.

He held out his hand and she put hers in it; he put his other over hers so that her cold, unsteady hand was sandwiched between his two firm, warm ones. They looked at one another without speaking for a moment. He looked unconcerned, at ease, quite oblivious to the fact that he was in any danger. She tried, through her dumb hand, her dumb eyes, to convey some hint of the real situation, but he did not understand. He increased the pressure of his hands and said, in a voice warm with sympathy:

'Poor little girl, you have been through it. But it's all over now. Come and sit down.'

'Yes,' said Doctor Hootman, turning from his relocking of the door. 'Sit down, Mevrouw, and let us get this thing settled; there will be time for everything else afterwards. All the time in the world. Well, Charles; have you thought it over?'

'I have,' Charles said. He sat down in a chair beside her and linking his hands, dangled them between his knees.

'I'm sorry to be disobliging, Daan. There isn't much I wouldn't do for a guilder, but I must draw the line at hiring out as a mummer.'

'Now look here . . .' Doctor Hootman said, his jowls beginning to darken. Charles cut in:

'What's more, you should thank God that this wasn't something you could rush into on your own. The old chap's death gave you a jolt, Daan, and you've gone a bit off course.'

'Morally, you mean?' asked Doctor Hootman with a look of the blankest astonishment.

'Morals be damned!–I ask your pardon, Julia. Practically, man, practically. You've thought up a scheme that nobody with a grain of sense left in his head would entertain for a moment.'

'I refute that,' said Doctor Hootman, who had recovered his composure. 'My plan is, above all, eminently practical.'

'How much do you know about this?' Charles asked, turning to Julia.

'A good deal more than you do, my friend,' Doctor Hootman answered for her. 'We were interrupted, you know.'

'Then you can see that it's crazy, can't you?'

She weighed her words with every hint of warning that an innocent-seeming speech could carry.

'Doctor Hootman has thought about this plan for years, Charles. He thinks it's feasible, and he's very . . . very set on it.'

'A slight understatement, but good enough. And you call it crazy. Why?'

'It's crazy because you couldn't carry it through. You've lived here, Daan, how long? Eight years. And you watched old Simon fool everybody; so you think you could do it too. You might–only don't count on me, but you could find another dummy–just muddle through the funeral. Afterwards you'd come a cropper. Say what you like about Simon Vosmar, he had a sort of power. People were scared of him. They didn't press his guard too close, even with questions. You ask yourself, how many men could have carried off such a thing for so long? Also, remember he *owned* the place. Nobody came here except by direct invitation. You wouldn't have that authority. Before you knew where you were somebody would up and say: "Who the devil is this Doctor Hootman to stand between me and the man I want to do business with?" Or, "I'm going to see Pieter Vosmar; if he doesn't want to see me he can order me off himself." Can't you see that?'

She remembered suddenly a bull-baiting which she had seen, for five horrified minutes, in Amsterdam; lured there, all unknowing by her young skater friends. Here was the dog, tail awag, eyes shining, begging the bull not to make a mistake!

'The thing wouldn't hold together for three months,' Charles said.

'It has no need to. Three months is all I need. And low as you rate me, compared with Mynheer, I *think* I could make shift to hold the busybodies at bay for so long. Of course, my dear Charles, our conversation was cut short. We never looked beyond the funeral, did we? Grief, the press of business inseparable from sudden demise would surely protect Pieter Vosmar from intrusion for three months. And after that there would be nothing to hide.'

'He'd still be here, plain idiot.'

Perhaps when he knew what Doctor Hootman planned for Pieter he would realize what kind of man he was and be on guard. That thought made her say, quickly:

'But Pieter wouldn't be here, Charles. Doctor Hootman thinks that if Pieter is deprived of all his little occupations and interests he won't live very long.'

The silence seemed to stretch itself out to give everyone in the room a chance to contemplate the future in terms of Pieter dead. Doctor Hootman spoke first.

'Here chivalry compels me to point out, Charles, that over this detail

Mevrouw did register a protest. But I managed to convince her that his–I assure you, painless–death would benefit us both. You see, the mythical, sane Pieter Vosmar is going to make his will. Mevrouw will get his money and I shall have Rua.'

This time the silence was longer. She forgot even Charles's danger as she waited. This was the touchstone. What you were mattered, in the last extreme, more than what happened to you.

Charles got up, very slowly and deliberately, and took a position, just in front of, and facing her, with his back to Doctor Hootman.

'Julia,' he said, 'this isn't the time or the place to say such things'–and he did look as much embarrassed as a man forced to take a bath in public might do. 'I do love you, very dearly. Ever since that first day I've thought of you day and night, but I wouldn't have said so except that I don't want you to think . . . God knows I wish you were free; but not this way! It'd make it all so easy, but every time I looked at you, I'd see myself blubbing into a handkerchief by the grave of a man I disliked, or that poor fool pining for his toys. It'd ruin everything. If I say no to this, Julia, don't go thinking . . .'

His voice trailed away because, screened for a moment from Doctor Hootman's view, she was screwing her face into grimaces of warning and conspiracy.

'It is so many years since I saw a play,' said Doctor Hootman, 'that if time permitted I should enjoy this touching scene. As it is . . . Charles, will you oblige me by leaving the irrelevancies and saying whether or not you are prepared to help me tomorrow?'

With one last, puzzled look at Julia, Charles turned about, and threw himself into his chair.

'With the mummery, no. I thought I had made that clear. I'd be the last to deny, Daan, that you've earned whatever you can walk away with; you've probably earned Rua, but you can't walk away with that, so pick something easier, and I'll help you. Collar the cash box or a sackful of silver plate, or a whole load of unlimed nuts.'

'That's the English all over,' said Doctor Hootman. 'Noble sentiments, dignified behaviour and mercenary motives. You're looking ahead to the time when Mevrouw may inherit everything.'

Offensive as the speech was Julia welcomed it; surely *now* Charles would see that Doctor Hootman was not his friend and would realize the truth of the situation.

He said, quite unruffled: 'You're wrong there, and I can prove it. Call the nephew or whatever he is, in, and hand over to him and Julia can come away with me tonight, just as she is.' He swung round to Julia and said: 'I'm taking a lot for granted, but I'd look after you. Married or not makes no difference, I'm yours for life.'

'For God's sake,' said Doctor Hootman, 'will you stop talking sentimental rubbish! I've told you what I propose to do. I need Mevrouw. Will you get into your thick English skull that nobody, nothing is going to turn me from my purpose. Now, for the last time, are you going to help me?'

'No. Get that into your thick Dutch skull.' He said it without rancour.

'Then I must think of an alternative,' said Doctor Hootman, quite calmly.

'This time think of something that won't take you straight to a rope's end at Banda Fort.'

Yes, it was possible to love a man and yet think him a fool. She longed to say–It's you who'll end in Banda Fort if you don't agree.

Doctor Hootman's hand had gone to his chin.

'Work this into your meditations, Daan: murder is murder whatever the means. If you want to be rid of the poor fool, I'll take him, too. You can play your game of invisible man whether you've got a lunatic locked up there or not, can't you?'

'And I should feel secure, shouldn't I, with the heir and his wife roaming about in Ay! Let's have no more inane suggestions. I am in process of realizing how immensely stupid I have been.' He dropped his hand and leaned forward as though they were two children to whom he–an adult–was telling a fairy story which had just reached the exciting climax.

'I have, I think, the perfect solution. I've known all along that it would be a little difficult to convert your rugged good looks into something that would account for Pieter Vosmar's behaviour. I could have done it, but it would not have been easy. This is. Pieter Vosmar shunned the sight of men because, poor fellow, he had coloured blood. It *will* crop up you know, even in the third generation; most people accept it. But a Vosmar wouldn't. It won't be beneath Mercury's dignity to stand by the grave tomorrow; and the beauty of it is that the closer he is inspected the more obvious will be his reason for hiding. Charles I owe you a deep debt of gratitude.'

'You've lost all touch with reality, shut away with an idiot and your own thoughts for company. You can dream of these schemes; you can't carry them out. Who's this Mercury?'

'A slave. Quite three-quarter white.'

'And you seriously consider a scheme that depends on him? Wake up, Daan! What about the other slaves?'

'No other slave will be at the graveside. Mynheer would as soon have had his cows at his funeral.'

'All right. Think for a moment of how you're putting yourself into this Mercury's hands.'

Oh, stop it! Stop arguing with him. Stop treating him like a dear old friend slightly demented. Think about yourself.

She dared not speak. It was just possible that having found a satisfactory substitute Doctor Hootman would let Charles go; and once he was gone, provided she had not committed herself she might get a chance to talk to Nicolas.

'I put myself in nobody's hands,' said Doctor Hootman. 'Not in yours which, like Pilate, you have so carefully washed; nor in Mevrouw's, so dainty and gentle. I know her; she'd ruin everything for the sake of an idiot who can't tell Sunday from Monday!' There was venom in his voice. 'Luckily she is also sentimental about *you*. So tomorrow she will lean, very lovingly and convincingly on Mercury's arm; because you, my English, clove-smuggling friend, will be here; pledge of her good behaviour! Even the tide served me, you see. If you had landed in the usual place she'd have met you with words of warning on her lips.'

So now it was all out.

'That is quite true,' she said quickly. 'I am against your plan–because of Pieter. But I promise, I give you my word, if you let Charles go I'll do anything you tell me to; tomorrow and afterwards.'

Charles reached out and took her hand.

'Thank you,' he said. 'But you can't bargain with a crazy man. All right Daan, what now?'

Doctor Hootman stood up, took the keys from his right hand pocket and transferred them with a tantalizing little toss into his left hand. His right hand he put into his pocket again, and kept it there.

'What now? Why, now you can continue your love scene while I find Mercury and get him dressed and ready to meet his kinsman.' Still facing them he edged sideways and backwards towards the door.

There was now in the room, in the whole situation, an air of unreality and of falsity which had not been there before, even when they had been talking at cross purposes. She, at least, knew where it originated–in Charles's behaviour. Why didn't he *do* something? Just to sit there, without even a protest, holding her hand and looking at it as if it were the most wonderful thing in the world . . . all wrong, somehow.

She decided to try something on her own. More than once during the last few minutes she had been aware of a sound of movement in Pieter's room. If she mentioned it now, and Doctor Hootman went to investigate, as he most surely would, he would cross the room; Charles could shoot out his legs and trip him, make a grab for the keys, do something. She twisted her hand and dug her nails into Charles's palm, hintfully, and said:

'Doctor Hootman, I can hear Pieter moving about.'

He laughed outright, a hearty, delighted laugh.

'Dear Mevrouw! Who once found a snake in a work bag? No wonder you love her, Charles! She's wonderful. I could almost love her myself.'

'But it is true. I can hear him.'

'His movements have ceased to concern me,' said Doctor Hootman. He gave his attention to putting the key into the door with his left hand and without turning.

Then Charles jumped.

It was like the leap of a panther, swift and sudden and silent. One second he was lolling, holding her hand and the next he had Doctor Hootman by the linen throat-band and was grappling for the keys. The older man was so much taken by surprise–Julia thought–that he did not even remove his right hand from his pocket. All he did was to put the keys behind him, a curiously childish, futile gesture. When Charles reached for them and began to twist his wrist, maintaining at the same time his grip on the neck-band, Doctor Hootman said in a choking voice: 'You're throttling me. All right, have them!' And he flung the keys to the floor. It was all over in half a minute, an oddly spiritless and unvicious little struggle.

Without letting go of the linen, Charles half stooped and reached for the keys. Then Doctor Hootman's right hand came out of the pocket, its fingers clenched round the barrel of a short pistol. As Julia screamed he brought it down, with deliberately measured force, on the back of Charles's skull, just behind the ear. Charles's body gave a convulsive jerk and went limp. As his hands loosened and his arm lowered, Doctor Hootman caught it, breaking his fall and letting him down, quite gently to the floor.

She ran forward crying: 'You've killed him.'

'Nonsense,' said Doctor Hootman cheerfully. 'One does not kill a hostage. A mere rabbit punch which will keep him quiet for half an hour. I've hit many men like that before sawing off a limb. A ship's doctor must be his own surgeon, you know. You'll find brandy in that cupboard, but don't give it to him while he is unconscious; many people have been choked that way.'

He unlocked the door and as she knelt by Charles she heard the key turn on the other side and the sound of his footsteps going along the cloister.

Despite the re-assuring words and the logic behind them 'she was frightened when she looked at Charles's face. His eyelids were only three-parts closed and looked stiff and wooden. All the bones in his skull seemed to have become prominent, pressing in white patches against the sun-tanned skin on brow and nose and cheek. But he was breathing, shallowly and a little noisily, and his heart was beating.

The wound was nothing; a thin sluggish trickle of blood ran from it and beaded slowly at the edge of his hair, and even that stopped as, under her eyes, the swelling began. The bump grew visibly and with incredible rapidity. She took comfort, remembering Mevrouw Helmer's theory that the more an accident or illness manifested itself the less dangerous it was. From that her mind moved on to the methods of restoring people to consciousness. Hartshorn was best, but she had none. Burnt feathers were good, but the cushions at Rua were stuffed with raw cotton. Quills? Yes, on the desk, a jar of swan feathers, dyed yellow to suit Mynheer's whim.

Patiently she held them, one by one, to the candle flame and passed the resulting stinking, black, blistering mass to and fro under the white-boned nose. Nothing happened. Doctor Hootman knew his business. Presently she gave up and sitting down on the floor took Charles's head in her lap. Conscious or unconscious she thought drearily, made no difference. They were trapped now. Doctor Hootman might make crazy schemes but he was sane enough to know that they both knew too much. How it would all end she couldn't even guess, but it would be badly; like all the lovers in the stories.

Except for the sound of Charles's breathing the room was very quiet. Now and again a night bird cried raucously in the groves. Now and again an insect would throw itself against the window screen; otherwise it was so quiet that she could hear the sea slapping gently at the jetty and whispering on the beach.

And then she could hear something else; Pieter was still moving about. Ordinarily he slept heavily from his early bedtime until dawn; but he had been unlike himself all day; he had slept during the morning . . .

She had seen Doctor Hootman toss his own keys into the table drawer.

Pieter knew one object from another; if he wanted his scissors it was useless to offer him his knitting.

Pieter was obedient and anxious to please.

It was so frail a chance that she was almost reluctant to recognize it; but it was a chance. She laid Charles's head on the floor, rose to her feet and went to the door of Pieter's room tapped on it lightly and called his name.

Absolute silence answered her. She had expected him to come blundering to the door and then, perhaps, to become enraged at not being able to reach her. But he had a kind of rudimentary conscience he was probably standing stock-still, stricken with guilt.

She tried again. 'Pieter, it's Julie.'

No sound. Was it her imagination which attributed a strained, listening quality to the silence? Or had the sound of movement itself been imagined?

'Pieter, I want to come in. Want to see Pieter. The door is locked.'

No reply. No movement. Only that feeling that she was not speaking to emptiness; the feeling of someone there, listening, almost holding his breath.

'Doctor Daan's drawer, Pieter. The key. Look for the key in Doctor

Daan's drawer. Get the key, Pieter. Let Julie in.'

It was like trying to thread a fine needle with coarse thread while wearing three pairs of gloves on your hands. The effort to impose her will, to make him understand and act, was so great that she seemed to be in the dark, all the light of her consciousness poured out, streaming away towards him. Sweat broke out on her forehead and under her eyes and rolled down her face like tears. His mind was so limited, a key might be outside his range of recognition; the key might not even be there; Pieter himself might not be there. Oh, God! Our only chance . . . this door once open and I could run through, into Pieter's little garden and over the wall, I could find Nicolas. . . .

Doctor Hootman's drawer always screeched a little when it was opened and that sound now, harsh in the silence, turned her faint. Her hands tingled and pricked as though touched by nettles. He *was* there. He did understand.

She knew that to her racking impatience every second seemed like an hour and she restrained herself from asking–Have you found it? A question would only distract and confuse him.

'It's a long key, Pieter. Long key.'

All was quiet again. She could imagine him standing there, perhaps even with the keys in his hand, blankly wondering what next to do.

It was almost impossible to speak calmly.

'The long key, Pieter. In this door. Push it in.'

He could thread a bead on a string, he could unlock a door. But he had to be told things over an over. She went on telling him, agonized because she could not hear him come towards the door. The sound of the key, pushed, with the minimum of fumbling, into the lock sent the tingling prickle all over her. She thought; of course he came quietly, he is barefoot.

She tried to speak encouragingly to him, but she lacked the breath. She could only implore him, turn it, Pieter, turn it, wordlessly, with the very pounding of her blood.

The lock clicked. She put her hand on the latch and for half a second it resisted her, as though he were trying it from the other side. Then it moved and the door opened.

But it wasn't Pieter who stood there with bits of leaf and twig in his hair, his face and shirt-front smeared with green from the mossy boughs.

It was Nicolas.

Chapter Nineteen

Now she knew full, perfect happiness. People said that the times when you were happy went by unrecognized, that only afterwards, when you looked back, when the joy had gone over, you said nostalgically–I was happy then. That wasn't true; she was happy, and she knew she was happy and revelled in it.

One shining happy day slid into another, there were no nights. There were no anxieties, no responsibilities. Even the effort to speak was not demanded of her.

It was a blue and white April day on Cloonmagh; the clouds raced across the sky and their shadows raced over the shining sands. All the air was full of the fresh clean scent of the sea, softened and sweetened by the fragrance of some unseen gilly-flowers. She ran on the beach and the sand squeezed between her bare toes. Maire was there, not the sad, emaciated Maire of the later days, but the earlier, just-remembered Maire, full of hope and strange old tales. Maire spoke of another bright shining day in the future, when the proper people would be back in Armagha and they would go there together and Maire would say: 'You see she knows her manners.' They were lucky and gathered a good basketful of cockles and took them home and cooked them and ate them with crusty, fresh-baked bread. Delicious. She ate greedily and Maire rebuked her: 'Eat dainty, darling, as a lady should.'

Then it was summer. She wore a pretty cool dress and her loosened hair brushed against her neck. She walked along the sun-filled streets with Uncle Johannes, on the way to the docks to visit the *Sea Maid*. He was talking about his next voyage which was to be to Africa, and he promised that if, before he sailed, he could get Aunt Geertruida to give consent, he would bring her back a little monkey for a pet. They paused by a tavern on the corner and he said: 'Are you thirsty, sweetheart? I am.' Inside it was cool and smelt pleasantly musty. She drank something deliciously flavoured with lemons.

It was no season, one of the warmth-laden, spice-filled island days. She sat on her favourite seat, overlooking the bank of flowers, all pink and purple against the sapphire sea. Charles sat on the ground beside her, his face peaceful. He lifted her arm and put it around his neck. He said: 'I love you very dearly.' There was still no need for her to speak. She tightened her arm around his neck and bent down and laid her face against his hair. They understood everything.

She was in her own room, playing the clavichord better than she had ever heard anyone play. Wonderful music. Because of it she did not hear the door open, and Psyche and Katje were there beside her before she was aware of them. But she was not startled; they looked so well, and so happy. She held out her hands to them and Katje said: 'We came to tell you that we're in the place where everything is being made up to us.' She wanted to say: So am I; isn't it wonderful? But there was no need. They knew.

Even her beloved little green bird was there in its cage. It stood on the window-sill of her bedroom between two pots of scarlet geraniums. Pieter came and looked at it and said: 'Pretty. Pretty for Julie.' His coming struck the first jarring note. Unlike the others he did not look well, or happy. And he was idle. There were all his things laid out on the table behind him and he was doing nothing. She knew that she must make an effort to rouse him. To him she must speak. It was more of an effort than anything she had ever done, worse than lifting the heaviest wash-tub in the Klopstock Home.

'Pieter, cut some paper. Cut some paper for Julie.' She held out the blunt-nosed scissors, snapping their blades invitingly.

From somewhere immeasurably far away someone said:

'Pieter is quite all right. There's no need to worry about him.'

And she knew that that was true. Nicolas would look after everything.

She was free to go back to the happy places, the loved happy people.

The wind began to rise in Cloonmagh. It came from the east, a leaping shouting wind. It whipped the sea in the little bay so that the grey-green, smooth, curved-marble waves were edged with lace and mountain high. One, higher than the rest reared up, held itself suspended, translucent. It would drown her. She must run, run, run! Too late. She was caught, lifted, tossed about, limp and light as a strand of seaweed. Drowning; drowned. No, washed up and left by the receding wave, in her own bed.

It was evening and the candles were lighted. Two faces were looking down at her. One was a woman's, pale and fat and plain between the edge of a little linen cap and the collar of a print dress. I don't know you! The other was a man's, thin, sharp-featured, with a bright, birdlike eye. I don't know you either.

The man said: 'There. I told you there was no reason for alarm. Merely a matter of time and good nursing.'

That's because I opened my eyes. What a mistake! But I shan't speak. If I don't speak I can go back, and back, and back. I shan't speak. I shall close my eyes, give myself to the wave's sweep and swing and be carried far away.

The voices pursued her for a little while; one said something about a natural, healing sleep and being much better tomorrow; the other, female, rather lugubrious said something about a daughter. A sleep, a daughter . . . but they are not my people, this is not my place, I shall go away again.

The happiness however was not to be recaptured.

She heard Nicolas's voice and the woman's. Now she must wake properly; she must speak to Nicolas. There was so much she didn't know, and must know.

She opened her eyes; there was Nicolas, looking anxious, and the woman. She was familiar after all; Mevrouw Van de Lijn, the Governor's wife would look like that, with her face bare of paint and powder, and out of her party dress. What was she doing here?

Nicolas was now on his knees by the bed. 'Julia, Do you know me?' He spoke as though a sound might break something.

'Nicolas. . . .' There he had stood, in the doorway, and she had known that he had climbed the wall of the little private garden and must have come through Pieter's room, and knew everything. That was where reality had broken off; she had thought–He knows, it will be all right now, and then she had gone down into the dark.

'Everything's all right, Julia,' he said, in that same muted, careful voice.

'Charles?'

'Perfectly well and all right. I promise you. Nothing in all the world to worry about. You just lie still and get better.'

'Pieter?'

'He's all right. I'm taking care of him. I'm taking care of everything.'

'You know about it all?'

'Everything.'

Mevrouw Van de Lijn came to the other side of the bed, lifted her a little and held a glass to her lips. Milk, creamy and very cold. Lovely.

She wanted to know more about Charles; but her mind was active now; mustn't talk about Charles in front of the Governor's wife.

'Everything is all right? Everybody safe?'

'Safe as houses. You go back to sleep again, Julia.'

She heard Mevrouw's voice. 'I wonder who Charles is?'

'A cousin she was fond of, back in Amsterdam,' said Nicolas. Good Nicolas, taking care of everything: knowing just what to say.

Next time she woke everything was quite different. It was morning, she knew by the way the sun came in from the window on the cloister side. She was alone in the room and as soon as she woke misery assailed her like a savage animal that had lain in ambush for a long time awaiting this moment. Her mind was perfectly clear, she remembered everything; she remembered Nicolas saying that everything was all right–but how could she believe that? All the dread possibilities of the situation she had abandoned when she fell down by the door, now came thronging back; how could Nicolas have dealt with everything, with two senseless people flat on the floor and Doctor Hootman coming back, pistol in hand. How could she have allowed herself to be so easily lulled by a few soothing words?

In addition to everything else there was something badly wrong with her head. It felt cold, and when she turned it on the pillow it felt light and strange. Hesitantly she raised her hand and touched her head. She had no hair, no hair at all. The whole of her head was covered with sharp bristles. No man ever had hair so short. Who on earth had cut her hair, and why? Did they cut mad women's hair, or criminals'? Had she been mad? Did they think she was somehow incriminated with Doctor Hootman's wicked plan? Was it perhaps one of the duties of a Governor's wife to act as guard to the mad, or the wicked? And what had really happened to Charles? What were they hiding?

She began to cry and instantly the door of her bathroom opened and out rushed Mevrouw Van de Lijn, clad in her petticoat, her face and arms beaded with drops of water and a towel in her hand.

'My dear, my dear,' she cried, hurrying to the bed. 'What is the matter? You mustn't upset yourself–the very worst thing. You're better, everything is all right. It's over now, all over. There, there, just be calm.'

'I don't *know* anything. I don't even know what day it is. I don't know what happened. Why are you here? And my hair. Who cut my hair?'

'I did. You have been ill you know. The doctor advised it.'

'Doctor Hootman?'

'Oh no, no. Doctor Van Nagel, from Banda. You see we had to put wet cloths on your head to cool your brain, and the hair was in the way. You mustn't fret about that. It'll grow again. I can say that for certain. My own little girl had to have hers cut, and do you know, it grew again in the loveliest curls you ever saw, though it had been straight as a poker.'

'Why are you here, Mevrouw?'

'I've been looking after you, my dear. I came for the funeral and I heard you were ill, so I stayed and took care of you.'

That was very kind. But is it true?

'Oh, I was glad to do it. I welcome anything that takes my mind off my worries and helps to pass the time till I hear. My daughter–I don't expect you remember. . . .'

'I do. Yes, indeed. She was to have a baby and you must wait seven months.'

'You *are* better. Fancy you remembering that.' Mevrouw began to dry herself vigorously.

'You came for the funeral, Mevrouw. Was it yesterday?'

'No, my dear. On Monday. Today is Friday. You have been ill, you know. Four whole days. We were very worried; but Doctor Van Nagel assured us there was no need. He said you must have living under a great strain ever since you came to Banda, and that this was Nature's way of giving you a rest. You do feel better?'

'I feel quite well. Mevrouw, what happened at the funeral?'

Mevrouw Van de Lijn had turned to the chair where her print dress, freshly laundered and smooth from the iron, lay. She began to put it on, and spoke in a rather absent-minded way.

'What happened, dear? Well, Mynheer Vosmar was buried, and then young Mynheer Vanderplasse brought my husband and the Agent into the house and disclosed to them what Mynheer Vosmar had hidden all those years. It was a great shock to everybody, of course, a great shock.'

Nothing about an Englishman, a clove-smuggler, being brought to justice.

Mevrouw, busy with the buttons of her bodice, turned around.

'Some people are inclined to be critical of Mynheer Vosmar's behaviour, but do you know, I understand. If such a thing had happened to my little girl I might have acted in the same way, if I had been able to.' She looked at Julia and it was evident that her maternal feelings suffered some cleavage, mother hen against mother hen. 'All the same, it was very wrong and heartless of him to bring you here and involve you. You must have had a horrible time. Thank God, I *know* the man my daughter married. If I didn't I should have gone mad by now, to think that such things were possible.'

'I want to see Nicolas,' Julia said.

'He always looks in at about this time, when he comes back from the plantation for breakfast. How fortunate it was that he was here, all ready to take charge of everything. I wonder if poor Mynheer Vosmar knew that his days were numbered and took that precaution.' She had finished her dressing, and came to the bed; expertly she lifted Julia and pulled the pillows around to support her. 'I'm a handy nurse,' she said. 'I've had lots of practice. My daughter was never very robust; that is one reason why I am so concerned about her at this time.' Punching the last pillow into position she said: 'I think I hear Mynheer Vanderplasse now.'

She rustled away. Julia heard from the sitting-room a few sibilant words, much better, almost herself, talk too much, nothing to upset. What did that mean?

Nicolas came tiptoeing into the room.

In some way for which there was no accounting in physical terms he had aged. The thick shining fair hair, the fresh complexion, the clear, slightly prominent grey eyes were all just as they had been; but the stamp of authority and responsibility–yes, and of a calf-love outgrown, were on him now, ageing him by ten years. One day, and not so far ahead, he would be the very image of Mynheer.

He said: 'Hullo, Julia. You really are feeling better? I'm so glad. You look almost like yourself.'

'I look hideous,' she said, 'but never mind that. I have so many things to ask you.' She dropped her voice. 'Is Mevrouw Van de Lijn out there?'

'No, she tactfully decided to drink her tea on the veranda.'

'Nicolas what happened? First of all, what happened to Charles?'

'He went back to Ay. I had to hustle him off. I couldn't keep him here, with half Banda coming to the funeral, could I? But he was fit to go and I know got back safely.'

'How do you know that?'

'We arranged a signal. I realized that that would be the first thing you would ask. And he, naturally, wanted to know about you. So we arranged to use the old signals, but with different meanings. There's a tall tree on Ay and another on the tip of Rua; through glasses they're visible, and with flags of different colours–that's how it's done.'

'And he got back safely, and nobody knows about him?'

'That is so.'

She rested back more easily against the pillows.

'Now tell me all the rest. How did it happen? Where is Doctor Hootman?'

'You don't need to worry about him, Julia.'

'I'm not worrying. I just want to know. There's a great gap in my mind. I must fill it in. That door opened and there you stood, and I saw you and I thought, he knows, now I can give up! That's the last thing I can remember. Now, Nicolas, please, go on from there.'

The look, half smile, half grimace with which people acknowledge a comic element in a situation not fundamentally amusing, came into Nicolas's face.

'Well, there I was, with the two of you flat on the floor. I knew nothing–and I'd just seen Pieter, I wasn't feeling too steady myself. You remember, the moment we met, you said you had something to tell me, and I gathered, from the way you stopped talking that you didn't want Hootman to hear. Then you went off and I got to thinking . . . all that mystery you know, and things the Barnevelts had said. I thought I'd see for myself. So I climbed the wall. . . . Julia, I am profoundly sorry for the way I used to talk to you about Pieter. It must have added to what you had to bear. And I'm sorry for the rest of my behaviour, too. Of course, as soon as I understood . . .'

'Go on, finish the story.'

'I stood there, not knowing why you had been locked in, or who the man was, or anything. I knew where Uncle Simon kept his brandy, so I got it, and went from one to the other of you in a dotty sort of way, like a hen with two chicks, a hen with its head off at that. It made no difference to you, but it brought him round. He's . . . he's a good fellow, Julia. He got himself up and pulled himself together and said to me: "You're the cousin or something, aren't you?" and in no time at all he'd explained everything, what Hootman was up to, and why, and why you were scared, everything.' He broke off and looked at the pale, sunken face on the pillow, with its violet-lidded eyes and the naked look the lack of hair gave it. 'Mevrouw Van de Lijn said I shouldn't talk too much, Julia. Everything is all right, be sure of that. I'll tell you all the rest another time.'

'Go on, go on,' Julia said. 'I want to hear it all now. It's like starting a story and having the book snatched away. I can bear it. If you don't want to upset me you'll tell me everything, just as it happened.'

'Charles said that Hootman was slightly crazy and had a pistol and would be dangerous. So we made a plan to disarm him. When we heard him coming, Charles, whom he expected to see, sat in a chair and held his head and I got behind the door. He came in, very cock-a-hoop, and said that Mercury was delighted to oblige and was having the time of his life going through Uncle Simon's wardrobe. As he turned to lock the door I pounced out and took his pistol away. And that was the end of that.'

'But not the end of the story. Go on.'

Nicolas's lips curled with distaste.

'He went to pieces. He dropped into a chair, put his head in his hands and he . . . cried. Being so big, that somehow made it worse; he went to jelly. I tried to be sorry for him, but I couldn't. Charles was. I will say for the

English they do love their enemies once they're disarmed! He got him some brandy and said: "Bear up man. It's the end of that little gallop but it couldn't have lasted anyway." I tried to be generous, too, and said he could stay on and look after Pieter; whereupon he cried the harder.'

Little boys in the streets of Amsterdam had a game which they played whenever they could cajole a butcher to give them a pig's bladder. They blew it up and kicked it about until the toe-iron on somebody's clog, worn thin and sharp, pierced it. Then the air would seep out with a long-drawn hiss and that was the end of the game. She could visualize Doctor Hootman, similarly punctured, similarly collapsed.

'So then?'

'Then Charles lost his patience and got up and gave him a shake, and said: "You're a doctor, do something for her!" Her being you. He said you'd come round in time. So Charles and I carried you here and Juno put you to bed. Then we had a sound good supper; we talked about the signals and he went off.'

'Do you know a signal asking him to come here?'

'Of course. I'll run it up whenever you like, Julia.'

'That's very kind.'

'Just,' he corrected her. 'I remember that it would have been much to his advantage to play Hootman's game. And to yours.'

She raised herself a little higher on the pillows.

'Now tell me about Pieter.'

'There's nothing to tell. He's there. That's all.'

'Is he *doing* anything?'

'What is there for the poor thing to do?'

'Who is with him?'

'That great dumb negro.'

'Where is Doctor Hootman?'

'You don't have to worry about him, Julia.'

'Is he dead?'

'Yes.'

'Did he kill himself? I can see by your face. That doesn't upset me. He's better dead. He'd lived all those years on hope. When that was gone, what had he to live for?'

'I offered to keep him on here,' Nicolas said, not understanding. 'And Charles offered to take him to Ay. He said they were all rogues and vagabonds there, and that a doctor would be very welcome. Hootman said he'd do that, and went to get his things. He had a pair to the pistol we'd taken from him, and he shot himself. There, now you know everything.'

And it had done her no harm; she looked better, restored and lively.

'Thank you very much, Nicolas. Now you go and have your breakfast. I want mine. Could you come back in about an hour?'

'Of course. As soon as you feel well enough we must have a serious talk. But for the present I just want you to understand Julia, that although I'm looking after things for you, I don't wish in any way, to usurp your authority.' His voice had taken on a faintly pompous tone.

She said: 'I'm very grateful to you for looking after things.' And now it seemed quite safe and quite ordinary to say, 'Dear Nicolas.'

When he returned she was in the sitting-room, wearing a wrap and propped up in one of the long chairs with a leg rest brought in from the veranda. On one side of her stood the clavichord, open, and on the other a solid table, cleared of all its small ornaments. The rugs had been rolled up and everything fragile put away. It reminded him of a room prepared for the spring-cleaning upon which his mother, a good housewife, insisted even in this land where no spring came.

Julia cut short his protests at finding her out of bed; his questions about the altered room.

'I want you to fetch Pieter here to me. I'm too wobbly to walk, and I don't much fancy that room any more, but he can come here and I can amuse him. The change of scene in itself will do him good and there's no reason now to keep him locked away. Bring all his stuff, Echo knows where to find everything.'

'Honestly, Julia, I think you're making an unnecessary exertion. He doesn't know one room from another. And if he had stuff to do why doesn't he do it. I've never seen him do anything except sit.'

'That's just it. Unless he's roused he'll sit there till he dies. His toys are his link with life–but there has to be somebody taking an interest. I understand all about it. Doctor Hootman has kept him alive for eight years.'

'And now you're going to keep him alive?'

'To the last moment. Charles said it. When we come together we don't want to be haunted by thoughts of Pieter.'

After what seemed a long time she heard their footsteps, Pieter's clumsy and shuffling, Nicolas's sharp and precise. Then they were in the doorway, Nicolas holding Pieter by the arm.

Nicolas, who had not known him until this week, probably thought he had always looked like this, but Julia was appalled by the change in him. He looked twenty years older, there were even some white hairs amongst the dull dusty brown ones; he had shrunk, and all his clothes were too big for him. Like a parasitic plant which has no roots of its own, severed from its host, he had begun to dwindle and droop and die.

His dull, uncomprehending, earthen stare wandered about the strange room. Nicolas's face took on a what-did-I-tell-you? it-is-hopeless look, and he withdrew his arm, glad to be free of the contact. Behind them Echo loomed up in his Ethiopian darkness, his arms piled with the bead boxes, the clay, the cane, the string.

Julie said: 'Pieter. Good morning Pieter. Come to Julie.'

His dull stare swung round, focussed and brightened.

'Julie,' he cried, 'Julie!' It was the voice of the lost one who has been found.

He lumbered over towards her and then, just short of her outstretched hand stopped short, lowering his head and looking at her suspiciously out of the corner of his eyes. Something wrong. Something different. On top of all the things that had been wrong and different lately.

'It's Julie,' she said, in a steady, re-assuring voice.

'Julie! Yes, Yes! Julie.'

He gave his pathetic, wide-open smile and came forward. When he was near enough he lifted one of his limp red hands, slowly, awkwardly as though it weighed very heavy. Tentatively, experimentally, he laid it on her head. Then he said, with delight:

'Pretty! Pretty for Julie!'

How Far to Bethlehem?

Norah Lofts

This book is dedicated with
admiration and gratitude to
EDWARD WAGENKNECHT
who suggested the theme

PART ONE

NAZARETH

90 miles

At some time, too long ago for even the oldest people to remember, the well in the village had failed. The heaviest rains in winter could not replenish it, so it was abandoned, and for at least three generations water had been fetched from a spring which broke out from the rocks on the other side of the hill. This meant that the water-carriers, always women and children, must walk for half a mile, uphill, then down, with empty jars, and half a mile, uphill and down, with full ones.

Women, practical and short of time, had soon found a way to shorten and to ease that journey. Avoiding the road and the hill they cut through the fields that girdled the base of the rising ground, and over the years had trodden a path which halved the length of the journey and was all on the level. In the rainy season the path was muddy and the daily procession of feet churned the mud until it was as sticky as porridge; and for that, too, the women had found a remedy. Certain days in Spring and again in Autumn were marked as stone-carrying days when everyone using the path in either direction brought a stone, dropped it and trod it in. This custom was older than any memory, but it was still faithfully observed, with the result that between his humble village and its water supply ran a path as hard and firm and flat as the new roads that the Romans were beginning to lay to link city with city.

The solidity of the path had served the women in another way–and not so long ago. Former owners of the land had respected the path as an established right-of-way, one of those ancient things protected by tradition. Seven or eight years ago the field had changed hands and the new owner had questioned the right of people to use part of his land as a public footpath. He intended, he said, to plough up the path and sow corn right up to the base of the hill. The stones, layer upon layer of them, dropped by hands long dead, had defied the ploughshare and the straining oxen. He had then, in a fury, declared that he would fence the path off at both ends. But before he had time to do so his wife had been brought to bed with a child, and several of the village women, pitying her because she was a stranger–and married to such a churl!–had shown her small kindnesses. And apparently even a churl could feel gratitude for nothing more was said about closing the path; indeed the right-of-way was tacitly acknowledged by the placing of large boulders, smeared with ochre, at intervals between the path and the arable land.

Nowadays not only women used the path; horsemen and the drivers of pack animals were glad to take the short cut and avoid the sharp incline; but they could only use it in winter when the field was bare. The packs were often wider than the path and would have brushed against the standing corn, bruising and breaking it; also the animals would snatch a mouthful in passing. So every Spring, early or late according to the clemency or otherwise of the season, on a day decided by the Rabbi and village elders, posts were planted at each end of the path and bits of red rag tied to them. And there they remained, gradually losing colour in the fierce summer sun until the harvest was in and the field gleaned.

The daily journey for water though time-consuming, and on days when one did not feel vigorous, tiring, had its happy aspect. It was a social occasion, a daily, communal outing. Women mustered all along the village street in little groups, greeting one another, calling exhortations to haste, sorting out their children, sending those who were old enough to do so running ahead so that their behaviour could be overlooked and their ears out of hearing of the gossip. There was little chance that any woman could be sick or in trouble of any kind and stay alone and neglected. If she didn't come out, either to join the group to which she belonged or to give some excuse for not doing so, something was wrong and must be investigated. On the path and at the spring every bit of gossip was exchanged and repeated; there was a good deal of laughter over homely, very parochial little jokes, and a good deal of tongue clucking, some outbursts of sympathetic indignation, sly eloquent glances, some nudging of elbows. Every one of them at some time or another had grumbled, to herself, at least, about the daily trudge and wished that she had a well in her own yard, or access to this mysterious piped water that was said to be available in cities like Sepphoris; but there was not one who would willingly have foregone, even in the worst of weather, this daily women's hour.

There was no acknowledged rule about it, but on the whole women walked in groups according to age and status, it being unseemly for unmarried girls to listen to talk about marital or obstetrical problems, and boring for settled married women to be obliged to listen to the chatter of the young and frivolous.

On this particular March morning everyone was unusually gay because, at last, after a lingering winter, Spring had come. Overnight the wind had died down, the clouds had vanished and the sun was shining in a sky the colour of hyacinths. Soon, of course, they would all be tired of the sun, would shrink from it and the all-pervading dust, would hide from it in their little thick-walled, mud-roofed, vine-shaded houses and long for clouds and cool breezes: but nobody thought of that on this morning. Spring had come and everybody welcomed it. Especially the young.

Four young women walked together; two and two because the path was narrow. They did not quite conform to pattern because one of them was married, the mother of one child and pregnant again. Rachel walked with her friends for several reasons. One was practical. They could be trusted to carry Joshua, turn and turn about. He was a fat, handsome, lazy little boy, nineteen months old, and he could walk but preferred to be carried. Married women had no patience with her; they said she spoiled him: they said, set him down and walk away, he'll follow quick enough: they issued really horrid warnings about what would happen to the unborn child if she insisted upon lifting and carrying that great lump of idleness. Not one of them seemed to realise that if she spoiled Joshua it was because he was the only joy her marriage had brought her. There was her other reason for wishing to walk with the girls. She'd had no wish to be married; she disliked the man her parents had chosen for her. Despite Joshua and the bulge below her girdle, she still felt unmarried, wished that she were, sometimes dreamed that she was, and on the daily exodus to the spring liked to pretend that she was.

On this morning they were talking–as girls tend to do in Spring–about clothes. Not new ones, new clothes were rare in their lives, but about the light-weight summer clothes now to be brought out and refurbished; turned perhaps, or dyed, embellished by a few stitches of simple embroidery.

Susannah, shifting Joshua from one hip to the other–really the naughty little boy grew heavier from one day to the next–said:

'You, at least, are sure of a new dress, Mary. What will you choose?'

In Rachel's mind the word 'sackcloth' formed itself; but she did not say it, because the others might see, behind the jest, something of her own private little hell. Nor would it be apt. Mary's parents, unlike her own, had allowed her to have some say in the matter, and the man she should marry in two months' time was good and steady and looked kind. Ephraim, probably sensing Rachel's aversion to him, had not been kind. . . .

Then Rachel and Susannah and Leah became aware that Mary had made no answer to this, surely most important and easily answered question. They looked at her and Susannah said, 'She's off again!'

They had grown up together and the three others knew that Mary had these curious lapses; times when she seemed not to hear or see or be with them in any but the physical sense. They'd learned from experience to leave her alone; for five minutes or so she'd behave like a sleep-walker, and then blink and smile and take up the chatter where it had broken off. But before they had learned this, when they were still very young, they'd tried to rouse her.

Once, abruptly, she'd been very sick; and once she had cried, so long and so violently that they had been frightened. Mary's mother, Anne, was well known for her sharp tongue and hard hand, and although she herself was never overtly indulgent to her daughter, anybody who made Mary cry was in for trouble.

So they'd learned. Amongst themselves they'd talked about it naturally, and reached their own childish conclusion. Mary's grandmother had been a woman of the desert who had fallen sick and been left for dead by her tribe. Mary's grandfather, a merchant in a small way, had been coming home with his two camels, had found the woman, brought her to his home and in due time married her. Desert people were known to be different; when they were thirsty or hungry or exhausted or tired they could absent themselves from their suffering bodies and so survive, in some mysterious fashion, where other people would have died. There was something about the desert, the three little village girls had agreed, prophets and holy men often came out of the desert. And as they grew older, they noticed small differences in their well-loved friend, a peculiarly free-striding manner of walking, a way of holding the head, an outspokenness which was startling in one so modest, and these lapses.

Rachel, looking at Mary and seeing her state, wished with all her heart that she could similarly absent herself from the connubial bed. Leah said:

'Look the red rags are out. Spring has come!'

'No more donkeys,' Susannah said, shifting Joshua again. 'What a blessing. I hate walking through dung!'

'We're lucky,' Leah said. 'We have wood. There are places where women have to gather it and use it for fuel. Imagine having to wait till a donkey passed before you could cook your dinner.'

'I don't believe it,' Rachel said, and an argument began.

The girl named Mary had sighted the red rags and felt the now familiar feeling of sadness and foreboding and desolation. Spring had come; and with the short smooth path closed to them, the donkeys, with their heavy loads, must face the hill. Uphill they slowed down a little, downhill they stumbled, and their riders or their drivers were always too ready to prod or strike. For her the bad season had begun.

She did not hear the question about her wedding dress. She was thinking, with something very near resentment, *why me*? Nobody else cared. A donkey was a donkey, a thing, a beast of burden, provided by God to help men with the business of transporting himself or his goods from place to place. If its pace slowed and a shout proved insufficient incentive to greater effort, a stick or a goad must be used. That was how all reasonable people looked at it; and to think differently was to invite scorn, wonder, amusement. Once, at the sight of a piece of quite gratuitous brutality, she had spoken out, and some of those who heard had laughed, some had been embarrassed for her; the man she had rebuked had been abusive, and, worst of all, had hit the poor donkey even harder.

And perhaps ordinary people were sensible; it seemed a pity, almost wrong to allow the sight of a red rag and all that it implied to mar such a lovely morning of sunshine and birdsong. Being miserable about donkeys did them *no* service. So stop it; think about something else. Think about Spring.

It had always been her favourite season, not merely on account of its beauty but for its promise. Every year, for as long as she could remember, she had felt that before the first flowers faded and the young leaves darkened, something wonderful would happen to her. Many times she had stood by a hawthorn tree, the green and the white just breaking and been certain that some quite unique experience was about to be hers. The silken petals of the first anemones could affect her in the same way–as though they held some secret which if she stayed quite still, and waited, would be revealed to her. Nothing had ever happened, nothing had been revealed. On one Spring day, wishing to know whether this feeling were peculiar to herself or part of ordinary human experience, she had so far overcome her natural reserve as to speak of it to Susannah, the most wholly sympathetic of her friends. Susannah said:

'Yes, of course, I feel it too. Everybody does; even birds. It simply means that you're looking forward to getting married.'

Mary had almost accepted that. Susannah was a sensible girl, and thoughtful, too, and the explanation was almost feasible, but not quite; the expected thing was less ordinary, less capable of being put into words. In fact it had been silly to try to talk about it at all, because there were no words.

And now it was Spring again, and she was not only looking forward to being married, she was properly betrothed; she was in love with Joseph and recognised her good fortune in that respect, was grateful to her parents for allowing her to exercise some choice; she was looking forward, with eager anticipation, to her wedding day, to having a husband and a house of her own, and presently, by God's favour, a child. She pictured him, a sturdy little boy, rather like Rachel's Joshua. Yet for all this, the feeling of immanence, of waiting for something wonderful, was with her still, and honesty compelled her to admit that it had nothing to do with Joseph, her feeling for him, or the little house adjoining the workshop.

At this point she returned to herself and her companions and reaching out her arms took Joshua from Susannah, saying:

'My turn now.' She settled him on her hip. 'By Abraham's beard,' she said, 'you're heavier today than you were yesterday. If this goes on we shall have to hire you a litter!'

The girls exchanged satisfied glances; that was the way, leave her alone; she always came back, as sweet and good-natured as ever. Susannah repeated her question about the wedding dress.

'It's blue,' she said. 'And I didn't choose it. It was my mother's. Mother could never wear it, it is too long for her and to cut it would have been a shame: it is such beautiful stuff. My grandfather bought it in Damascus.'

'Just blue?' Leah said. 'Isn't that Mary all over? I never knew a girl who cared less about clothes. Her wedding dress; and it's blue, and beautiful stuff! What kind of blue and what kind of stuff?'

'It's about the colour of . . . of flax flowers, and I think it is silk.'

There were sounds of appreciation, not unmixed with envy. Leah said sardonically, 'She *thinks* it is silk!' She and Susannah then began to speculate as to when it would be their turn, and to describe the dresses in which they would like to be married. Rachel, looking back sourly to her own wedding, thought how much more suitable a mourning robe would have been than all the family finery in which she had been decked; and, unwilling to talk about marriage, fell into conversation with Mary about Joshua.

So, chirping like birds they came to the place just where the field path and the highroad were divided by the out-thrust buttress of bare reddish rock from which the water sprang. A very ordinary Spring morning in the twenty-fourth year of the reign of Augustus Caesar.

Chapter Two

Years and years of wear from the pressure of the mouths of water-jars held against the rock to catch the spouting water had altered the formation of the spring which now gushed into a circle of eroded stone which looked as though it had been placed there for the convenience of the women. Each woman rested her jar against the rim, tilted it slightly and waited until it was full. Newcomers to Nazareth, or women who had had occasion to visit other villages, said that this was a quick and easier way of getting water than hauling a bucket up from a well by a rope.

Few people were in a hurry, most of them indeed were willing to prolong the business, nevertheless there was some rough order of precedence. Married women first, according to age; then girls. And every morning, as the women, like figures on a frieze, moved, stooped, waited, straightened themselves and set their jars on their head, half-way through the married women's line somebody was certain to say, 'Michal's turn.' And there would be laughter.

Mary, part of the frieze, standing aside with the other girls would wait for the poor joke and wonder that now, after two years, it should still have the power to amuse. Sometimes she felt impatient with them; at other times she would think–It is the measure of the fundamental dullness of their lives. She would wonder, too if twenty years hence her life would have narrowed down to a point where she must relish an ancient jest and one that had never, at first coining, been very good.

There'd been a time when Michal, a pretty, lively young woman, had taken her rightful place at the spring; then her husband had died, leaving her in a pitiful plight, no relatives at all, nobody to be responsible for her or to fend for her. She'd been reduced to doing the most menial jobs about the village in return for a meal or a bit of cast-off clothing. Then suddenly she had ceased to solicit jobs or charity, had appeared in a brand-new dress one day, the next with scented oil on her hair, soon with bangles on her wrists. There were whispers and raised eyebrows and hard looks and suspicion, soon confirmed. Her tumbledown little house stood on the outskirts of the village, almost next door to the inn on the road to Sepphoris, and men had been seen going in, and coming out.

She must have been very stupid, Mary thought, or very brave, for morning after morning she had joined the exodus to the spring, amazed at first and then tearful to find herself treated as though she were invisible, until she came too near; then she'd be pushed past or jostled. She seemed to think that if she persisted the morning would dawn when she would find herself forgiven and accepted again. She'd had three new water-jars broken and two dresses soaked before she realised that the women had outlawed her–for ever.

After the last 'accident' Mary, then very young, and strictly brought up to respect her elders, had spoken out in a way that Rachel and Susannah and Leah knew.

'It's a shame!' she said, as Michal, finally admitting defeat, fled back along the path, with no water and her pretty dress spoiled. 'She did *try*, until she was nothing but skin and bone. We should be sorry for her!'

They'd rounded on her with an astounding ferocity.

'Shame is it? I agree, so it is to hear a girl so young speak in such a way.'

'I'm glad your mother didn't hear that,' said the woman who intended to inform Mary's mother at the first possible moment.

'I *was* sorry for her. Many's the job I found for her, things I could well have done myself. And when we killed a sheep I remembered her.'

'And bread she never lacked; my husband saw to that,' said the wife of Hilliel, the Rabbi who was also the baker.

Susannah attempted to take Mary's jar.

'I'll fill it for you. You run home,' she whispered.

'I'm going to fill my own jar. I haven't done anything. I only said I thought it was a shame. And I still do!'

They were all going to say the same things again, but more vehemently, when an old woman moved and stood near the girls and said to Mary:

'You're young, dearie, and very innocent. You'll learn later that a woman like that is a threat to every married woman. Men are frail creatures. Let it go, now, let it go.'

That morning the chatter on the return journey was loud and vociferous. Imagine Anne's daughter, *Anne's daughter*, saying a thing like that! And what was the world coming to when any girl so young should not only rebuke her elders but, when in turn rebuked, be defiant? Did you see how her eyes flashed? If my daughter ever dares . . .

Mary knew by the expression on Anne's face that she had been informed. What she did not know and never would was that the informant had obtained little satisfaction from the interview.

'Maybe she spoke out of turn,' Anne said, 'and she'll hear about that from me. But as for sticking up for a harlot, worse nonsense than that I never heard, even from you, Rebecca! Why, the girl's so innocent she wouldn't know what Michal's doing nowadays. That wouldn't occur to you, would it? She thought it was a shame to treat her so because she wouldn't understand *why*. My daughter's been properly brought up, let me tell you.'

To Mary she said stern things about respect to elders and being careful about one's reputation. Michal she did not mention either by name or reputation, still being careful of her child's innocence. But of course the girls knew all about it and often discussed it; they thought it was a terrible way to earn a living.

Nowadays Michal drew her water very early in the morning or in the afternoon; and every day, when the procession reached a certain point, the joke about her turn was made, and the women laughed and Mary thought of their dull lives, and of her own, so like theirs, except, of course, for what went on in her head.

On this morning the four girls were last at the spring and then delayed a little because it was Leah's turn to carry Joshua and he had decided not to be carried by her; Rachel must carry him. They argued about this, saying, 'You shouldn't; he's too heavy,' and each in turn inviting him, cajoling.

'Joshua, you ride on me; I'll be your horse,' Mary said. But Joshua had his mind made up and knew already that one male mind made up is a match for any number of women.

'I'll take your jar then,' Mary said. To carry two jars, one on your hip, one on your head was easy enough, but it took a second or two to lift and arrange both without spilling a drop, and the others had rounded the rocky point and were on the path by the time that she was ready to follow them. She had her back to the highway when she heard the hurried, stumbling hoofs, the laboured breathing of the burdened, the cheerfully callous exhortations of the driver.

Don't look! she told herself. There's really nothing you can do about it, and what you see will haunt you all day and even more at night when you lie down and shut your eyes. Hurry round the rocks without looking, get on to the path, join the others, think of something silly to say.

But you always looked; you were compelled to, if only in the hope that it might not be quite so bad as you feared.

She looked. It was very bad. An aged, decrepit donkey. Three bales, one on either side; a third poised across them. The driver was just a boy, not ill-looking; in his weather-darkened face his eyes were bright and his teeth very white as he gave a rueful grin.

'The short way's closed, I see. That would happen today of all days. Now we've got to get up this hill.'

'Oh, please,' she said, 'don't prod him. He's very old and very small for such a load.'

'Just what I said. My very words, this morning. I wanted the black one, half his age and twice his size. With a wreck like this how can I make the journey in one day? I mean to, though!'

He gave evidence of his intention and Mary made a sound of distress.

'You don't want to fret about donkeys–pretty girl like you.' His voice was friendly; his glance ran over her with approval, a near-flirtatiousness. Something in her shrank from the glance, but if he considered her pretty, could she use his admiration to help the donkey?

She said, 'I *do* fret about them. It may be silly but to see one hurt hurts me. Look, if you'll let him take his time up this hill and not prod him, I'll walk with you, and when we come to my home I'll give you a honey cake and a cup of wine.'

'You're a funny one,' the boy said. 'Where do you live?'

'Just over the hill; in Nazareth.'

One part of her mind broke off to consider what her mother would make of this offer of hospitality to a chance-met donkey-boy.

'I've got to make a stop there,' the boy said; 'and any other time I'd be only too pleased to eat and drink as well. It just happens that today I'm in a hurry. My brother's wife has a child–a boy, and tonight he's giving a feast. It would be just my luck to get a long journey, a half-dead donkey *and* an extra load, and the short cut closed.'

The boy was wasting no time; as he talked he kept moving and Mary followed him. They were now climbing uphill.

'If you really mind about donkeys,' the boy said, giving evidence that he did not, 'you could save us a few steps by telling us where the carpenter lives. That bag,' he prodded the uppermost one, 'is for him, iron stuff, nails and door hinges and handles. And they're heavy. These,' he prodded the side bales, 'don't weigh much really, dyed cotton stuff. Then along comes my master and says–You'll be going through Nazareth, drop this on the way. Just my luck.'

She said, 'I know where the carpenter lives. I am betrothed to him.'

'He's a fortunate fellow,' the boy said, concealing under gallantry a certain feeling of surprise. She had an elegance, not of clothing or of manner, or speech, nevertheless an elegance and a delicacy that made it hard to picture her as the wife of a village carpenter. But his interest in her was peripheral. If he hoped to be at the feast tonight he must keep moving. The donkey struggled and made little sobbing sounds. In its browny-grey coat the places where the goad went home ran red.

Suddenly she said, 'I can't bear it, I can't bear it. Please, please, let me carry the heavy bag.'

He was so astounded that he ceased prodding the donkey.

'Don't be silly. Break your back, that would.'

'No,' she said, 'I'm strong. I'm really very strong. I can carry that bag and you won't even have to turn into the village street. You can go straight along and save time.'

The boy realised the truth then. He'd fallen in with a mad woman. Pretty, young, properly dressed, she'd been alone at the watering place; without asking his name she had invited him to eat honey cake and drink wine in her house; she minded about donkeys and said she was betrothed to the village carpenter. Madness was the one and only explanation.

And mad people must be respected; they were possessed by devils. And they were strong. In his own village there was a madman who could straighten a horseshoe between his hands.

He saw himself, at the feast this evening, making a bid for attention–What do you think happened to me this morning, just outside Nazareth? I fell in with a mad woman. And they'd all think of somebody old, with staring eyes and wild grey hair.

He said, 'If you want to carry it, lady, you may. But it is heavy. And nails make an uneasy load.'

She had already set down the two water-jars she carried in the shade of a bush at the edge of the road.

'I can carry it,' she said. The donkey, unprodded, had slowed, come to a standstill, and stood, drawing breath.

Hardly believing what he was doing and yet thinking what a story this would make, the boy unhitched the bag of iron stuff and laid it upon Mary's back. She put her hands over her shoulders and took the sack by its ears. The donkey, relieved of its heaviest bale, gave itself a little shake.

'Here we go then,' the boy cried. 'Oy! Oy!'

They moved, considering the incline of the road, at a spanking pace. Mary walked beside the donkey; she could see its eyes, so gentle, so entirely hopeless. The knowledge that she had eased this load, this one journey, braced and encouraged her. And then, suddenly it seemed, the donkey had tripped ahead and she was alongside the boy.

He tried to think of something that could be said to a mad woman.

He said, 'You all right?'

'Quite all right, thank you.'

'In some places,' he said, 'where women carry heavy loads, they wear head-bands. They help, they take some of the weight. But after a time they leave marks, like pack galls.'

She seemed to be making rather heavy work of it and an obscure feeling of guilt afflicted him. She asked to do it, he reminded himself. He'd told her it was heavier than it looked.

'I told you it was heavy, didn't I? Had enough? Let me shove it back on him.'

'I'm managing,' she said, trying not to sound breathless.

She was amazed at the heaviness of the comparatively small sack. Like every other woman of her kind she was accustomed to carrying things, bundles of washing, of firewood, of gleaned corn, baskets of winnowed corn for grinding, baskets of vegetables, water-jars, Joshua; but none of them had ever seemed a quarter the weight of this. The position perhaps; she wasn't used to carrying things on her back; and the boy hadn't exaggerated when he said that it was an uneasy load; points of some of the nails came through the sack and dug into her.

Think about something else. That was a trick she'd learned early when set to do tedious jobs like grinding corn or shelling beans. So she thought about the fine new house which Joseph was helping to build just outside Cana. The nails would be intended for decoration of the outer doors, nail-studded doors were evidence of wealth in a country where iron was scarce and expensive. With rows of nails and iron hinges and handles it would be a very imposing door indeed. The thought crossed her mind that Joseph would not be pleased if he knew that she had carried this load uphill! He was a very kind and considerate man–it was that which had first attracted her to him.

Then, quite unbidden, another thought slipped into her mind. A hideous thought. There was another use for nails; the Romans used them for that slow, terrible punishment known as crucifixion. The Jews stoned their malefactors, and a man could be knocked senseless in three minutes, and dead in five. On the crosses men hung and suffered for as much as three days. Oh, why must she think of that now? Wasn't this load enough, pressing down, hindering the breath, making every step a painful labour?

The boy could hear her breathing now–worse than the old donkey at his worst.

'Give over now,' he said, almost pleadingly. 'It was a daft idea. You'll do yourself a damage.'

She lifted her head and saw that they were almost at the top of the hill which was marked by a group of trees, old gnarled hawthorn bent by years of prevailing westerly winds. And she saw the little donkey, plodding on with his lightened load. She shook her head at the boy and the drops of sweat flew off and spattered the dust. She drew in a breath that hurt her chest like a knife-thrust and said:

'I-shall-get-to-the-top.'

The maddest, most stubborn woman he'd ever encountered; but the guilty feeling moved in him again. He lifted his donkey goad, intending to dig it into the sack and so lighten it for her. But the stick slipped, or the sack swayed and the point struck her in the side. A little blood from the goad, and some from the wound, crept out and stained her grey gown.

The boy was almost crying. 'I didn't mean to do that! It was an accident, an accident!' he cried. 'I was trying to help you! Give up, now do! I should never have let you try it.'

She seemed not to hear, or not to understand. And he knew that at the feast tonight he would not entertain anyone with his encounter with the mad woman from Nazareth; it wasn't amusing any more. It would be quite a time before he even wanted to think about it.

Mary plodded on, ten steps, counting now; change to seven, seven was a special, mystic number; seven and another seven; must be almost at the top now. And then, swift as flame leaping through dry sticks, pain ran through her, possessing, engulfing; a pain such as she had never known before; a pain that made every other pain a mere discomfort. She cried out in a voice that was to ring through the donkey-boy's dreams for years; the sack fell with a rattling thump and she stood swaying, her hands pressed to her body, and then gently collapsed.

The boy stood and swore in three languages. What now? Sling her across the damned donkey and take her into the village. That'd mean carrying the sack himself, and a waste of time finding out where she lived. That wouldn't do. He took her by the shoulders and pulled her to the side of the road, under the shade of the new-leafed trees. She seemed very light and soft between his hands; and she was pretty. It was a shame that a girl like that should be so crazy. He had half a mind to get his water-bottle and wet her sleeve and dabble it across her face, try to bring her round; but that meant a further waste of time. And he was a little frightened. After all he had struck her and she was mad; she might come round in quite another frame of mind and accuse him of attacking her. So with another half-guilty, half-apologetic look at the pretty pale unconscious face, he left her; took up the bag and refastened it to the back of the donkey which had snatched this unusual opportunity to take a mouthful of grass. He'd better deliver the bag and get on his way as soon as possible. She'd come round, and she wasn't far from home; or somebody would come along with more time and a less-loaded beast. She'd be all right. But he wished it hadn't happened.

'Oy! Oy!' he cried, and was ready with his goad; but the old donkey had got its second wind and the road was downhill now, there was hardly any need to prod.

Chapter Three

It was all exactly right, that was the beauty of it; the thing that she had, through so many Springs, expected. Colours sang, music was sweetly scented, scent took on lovely shapes; there was snow, made of white roses, and the stars fell like rain, the moon tasted of honey and all the beanflowers were butterflies, and the hawthorn, from which she had always expected a revelation, was an awning, green and white against blue, over this wonderful place where beauty was one and indivisible. This was heaven and to see an angel did not astonish her at all. . . .

Chapter Four

Rachel said, 'Where have you *been*? We dawdled and waited; and Leah ran back to the spring, but you weren't there. Are you all right? Have you had a fall?'

She could truthfully say, 'Yes, I had a fall.' Some explanation, however makeshift and temporary, was needed. 'After you'd gone, somebody came along, taking the hill road, so I took it too, and I fell. But I've brought you your water.'

'I was waiting for it,' Rachel said. If she'd had more time, if she hadn't been so scared that Ephraim might come in and scold because his dinner was belated, if Joshua hadn't been pulling at her skirt, Rachel would have questioned her friend more closely. But she could guess. Mary had had another of those spells when her mind was elsewhere, not seen some unevenness in the road, and stumbled; she'd spilled the water and had to go back for more. Following this line of thought she said:

'How lucky the jars weren't broken.' And that sounded heartless, so she added quickly, 'and that you didn't hurt yourself. But you have been crying.'

Suppose she said–Yes, from wonder and joy, and went on to explain; suppose she were Rachel, standing in the low doorway and Rachel were herself, telling such a marvellous tale. Would I, in her place, believe it? Will *anyone* believe me?

She held out her hands, grazed and dirtied.

Rachel said, with solemnity, 'Mary, when you're married you won't cry over a grazed hand. Thank you for bringing the water, I must make Ephraim's dinner now.'

Moving on towards her own home she thought–Whom can I tell, with the slightest hope of being believed?

One's mother seemed the obvious person, until one was face-to-face again with that practical, bustling woman, waiting, at the moment, for fresh water and slightly irritated.

'What a time you've been! Every day it seems to take longer and longer. In my day we went straight there and back, with a good clout if we lingered. And what have you done to your hands?'

'I fell.'

'Carrying the great boy of Rachel's!' Anne said. 'So that's the end of that. You can just say that I forbid you to do it again. God gave children legs to walk with. Your dress is filthy too, dust and grass stains.' The blood she did not notice for Mary was careful to keep her arm close to her side. At the first opportunity she slipped away and changed her dress.

The day wore on; such a day as no woman had ever lived through. The sun and the warmth had induced a house-cleaning fever in Anne; every mat, every blanket must be taken out into the yard and beaten, every candlestick cleaned, the big chest rubbed with beeswax. And Mary was much less helpful than usual. In the end Anne said, half serious and half sarcastic:

'You didn't by any chance hit your *head* when you fell, did you? You're acting as though you were half-witted. What ails you?'

Turn to her and tell her the plain truth and what would happen? She'd drop dead. She was pious in her way, and like all pious Jews knew the prophecies about the Messiah and his virgin birth; but she would never be able to believe that her own daughter, whom she was scolding for letting the beans boil dry, was that chosen one. So belief and disbelief would work in her as new wine often worked in old, hardened casks; they split; and Anne's limited, orderly mind, asked to accept and contain this marvel, would split and she'd drop dead.

She realised, as this momentous day drew to its close, that the only person she could tell was Joseph. He must, in any case, be told because he was so nearly concerned. Would he believe her? She cherished one hope here; since he was so nearly concerned, since so much depended upon him, God would surely have prepared him already. God was omniscient, He would know that without Joseph's help and support . . . Don't think of that! God was just; Joseph, too, on the long walk back from the house outside Cana, or in his workshop, would have been visited and enlightened.

To be with someone who knew, who understood and believed, was such a wonderful prospect that she could hardly wait for the moment when, supper over, she could slip away and find him.

Chapter Five

She knew, before a word was spoken, that that hope had been groundless.

He was in his workshop, making the most of the last of the daylight, setting his tools in order and brushing some shavings from the bench to the floor. When her shadow darkened the doorway he looked up, recognising her with an expression of pleasure, and then, seeing that she was alone, with surprise.

He lived by himself and properly brought-up girls like Mary, with mothers like Anne, did not come visiting, almost at dusk, men who lived alone, even if they were officially betrothed. Once or twice a week Anne, who believed that men left to themselves ate nothing but bread and cheese, would invite him to supper, and sometimes, afterwards, Joachim, Mary's father, would go to make his hens secure from the foxes and Anne would absent herself for a little while, and they'd be left alone; but she'd never come to his house unaccompanied and his first thought was that something must be wrong. Carpenters were often called upon when accidents happened for people believed–not without some reason–that a man who could dovetail two pieces of wood together so smoothly that they seemed to have grown that way, could replace a sprained joint or set a broken bone.

If God had informed him, she thought, he would have come to welcome her, reached out his hands to hers and begun to speak of the wonder. As it was he said:

'Mary! Is anything wrong?'

'No,' she said. 'Nothing wrong.' Disappointment made her voice sound small and woeful. And it was impossible to avoid the thought that had she come to report some physical disaster–the roof of the house fallen in, Anne's ankle sprained, Joachim's leg broken–she could have counted upon him absolutely. Sympathetic, kind and sensible, in any ordinary situation he could be relied upon to do the right thing and do it well. But in this situation . . .

The very sound of her voice dismayed her. She had come to share with him the most marvellous news that anyone, ever, anywhere, had had to impart. It should have been announced with joy and pride and the singing of trumpets.

She said, a trifle more firmly, 'I came to see you, Joseph, because I have something to tell you, something for you alone.'

His heart gave a great downwards thud. He aligned the handle of a chisel and the handle of a saw with meticulous exactitude. He knew what she had come to say. She didn't, after all, wish to marry him. All along he'd found it difficult to believe in his luck. She was so young, and so pretty, so well-brought-up. He'd been immensely, and pleasantly, surprised when her parents had seemed to encourage him; and when, after quite a time of trying to pluck up courage, he had made his formal request to Joachim and he had said, 'You'd suit me; but we must find out how Mary feels,' he had suspected that Joachim was making an excuse, not liking to say 'No' outright.

The trouble was that he was too old for her; age mattered in a society where widows had a very poor time. Any careful father was bound to look ahead and choose for his daughter a man who wasn't likely to die before he had reared a son capable of supporting his mother. Of course, with a rich man it was different; he could provide for a wife. Unless they died early, in childbed, women tended to outlive men and that fact must be taken into consideration when arranging marriages.

However, Mary, so pretty and graceful and gentle, Mary, who could have married anybody, had agreed to marry him, a carpenter in his late thirties, not a native of Nazareth, a man who had plied his trade in many far places–he'd even been in Egypt–before settling down. An enormous gratitude had blended with his love for her. Amazement too. And if she had come here this evening to say that she had changed her mind, thought better of it, he would not be truly surprised. Sad, disillusioned, but not surprised. He'd bear the blow as a man should, not whimpering; and for her wedding to some younger, luckier fellow, he'd make her a chest, carved all over with lilies, her favourite flowers.

Having, by the arrangement of the tools, gained time to brace himself, he looked up.

He said, 'You're shivering. Come into the house and I'll rouse the fire.'

She preferred the workshop. The little house that adjoined it, in which once or twice she had, with her father and mother, on formal visits eaten little sweet cakes from Hilliel's shop and drunk wine, had the inexplicable pathos of a place where a man lived alone. It had always been, on those occasions, clean and tidy, but the scent of over-cooked food had hung about. And once–whenever she recalled that visit, her heart moved and melted–Joseph had procured from somewhere a bunch of the white, sweetly scented lilies that she loved; and he'd shoved them into a jar of indescribable ugliness, so narrow-necked that the lilies were pressed together, stiffly crowded, and coloured ochre, orange, red and a peculiarly sharp yellow.

She said, 'I'm not cold, and it is lighter here.' That was true, the workshop faced west and the last, level rays of the sun–the sun which had risen this morning on a seemingly ordinary day, and was now about to set at the end of a day that had seen the miracle, the germinal birth of a whole new world–shone in at the wide door.

'Sit then, please,' Joseph said, and he brought forward the plain stool on which, sometimes when he was tired, he sat at the workbench. As he carried it he brushed his hard work-hardened hand across it to remove any dust or sawdust.

'Now,' he said, and, moving backwards, perched himself at the end of the workbench which was already in shadow. 'Tell me. You look troubled.' She would be troubled, if she had come to tell him what he suspected, for she had the tenderest heart in the world.

She said, falteringly, 'It's a very hard thing to say. So hard to put into words. . . .'

She looked so pale, he thought. Despite the errand he attributed to her in his mind his heart moved towards her; he wanted to make things easier for her.

'If it's anything to do with *me*,' he said, stoutly, 'out with it. I've taken a few knocks in my time. One more won't floor me.'

She said, 'Joseph, today I saw an angel . . .'

It was still light enough, even where he sat, for her to see his face, shocked, then incredulous and presently frankly appalled. She told him everything, as though by adding detail to detail she could overcome his disbelief. When she mentioned the sack she had carried he turned his head, she looked in the same direction and saw the bag standing there, in the corner. But that proved nothing. She had no proof. She had a fantastic story which must either be taken on trust or rejected, and even as she talked, even as she described the angel, she could see Joseph rejecting it. She could also, in her mind's eye, see herself facing the women at the watering place.

She ended, 'I'm not lying, Joseph, I am not mad and I was not dreaming. It happened, everything, just as I have told you. And it *was* prophesied that a virgin should bear a child who would be our Messiah. I don't know why I should have been chosen–I'm as confounded as you are; but the angel said I had been; he called me blessed amongst women.'

She stopped speaking and in the dim, sweet-scented workshop there was silence which stretched on and on until at last Joseph said, as though someone had him by the throat, choking him:

'It is written that the Messiah should be of the house of David. I can trace my lineage back to Solomon. But if you are, as you say, already with child, I am not its father and my lineage has nothing to do with it.'

She said, 'He will need an earthly father, too.'

No truer word was ever spoken, Joseph thought; and wondered that she could speak with such gentle detachment. What about her need for a husband? Why wasn't she weeping and tearing her hair?

He could not rid his mind of the memory of the donkey-boy, young, handsome, an obvious young rogue. Horrible, almost impossible to think of, but this was an evening of impossibilities. Suppose that on this Spring morning . . . But then, how could she know, so soon, that she was pregnant? A moon must run its course before any woman could be certain.

But maybe she didn't know that. Maybe she didn't know anything of such matters. Her life had been very sheltered. He had heard of girls so innocent that they thought babies were begotten by kisses. Such girls were rare, but they did exist, and Anne's daughter might well be one of them.

Remembering the boy's shining eyes and white teeth, he thought, magnanimously, that he could forgive a kiss or two. Yet how out of character that seemed! And so did the concoction of such an elaborate and impious story.

'Did he touch you?' he asked abruptly.

'No. He stood under the awning and spoke to me. He said his name was Gabriel.' Her voice took on an awed, remembering tone. 'He was almost too beautiful to look at, and he had a lily in his hand. He told me another thing too. He said that my cousin Elisabeth had been pregnant for six months and she is well over child-bearing age.'

This piece of evidence, susceptible to proof, carried less weight with Joseph than it might have done, since he had never seen Elisabeth. He said:

'I mean the donkey-boy.'

'Yes. He hit me. By accident he said, and I believed him. But not on the head, if that is what you are thinking. Here under my arm.' Then the full implication of the question struck her and she lifted her head a little and spoke in a different voice. 'The boy,' she said, 'was a young lout, ill-treating his donkey. But if I had so far lost all respect for myself and my family and *you*, Joseph, do you really think that I am wicked enough to tell a story involving holy things? Or stupid enough to tell a story so difficult to believe? Think how much easier it would have been to have torn my clothes and run screaming that I had been assaulted. Then I should have been sure of sympathy, and everybody would have believed me. I don't think you do.' She looked at his face, wrenched with indecision and misery, and felt sorry for him. 'I cannot blame you,' she said, more gently. 'You saw no angel. And I, who did, still find it difficult to believe. I know that the coming of the Messiah has been foretold, hoped for, prayed for–and never more than now; but all day I have asked myself–Why *me*? Yet, when you come to think of it, God has made strange choices before. Jacob and David, quite ordinary until they were chosen. Now I am chosen. I vow to you, Joseph that everything happened exactly as I have told you.'

She longed for him to say, 'I believe you.' She waited. And because he loved her he wanted to say the comforting words for which he knew she was waiting; but the whole matter was too great, too solemn to be thus easily accepted. He couldn't say that he did not believe, he wouldn't say that he disbelieved; so he sat dumb, looking puzzled and wretched.

She thought–I have failed. And with that thought another came. Isaiah, in his prophecy of the Messiah, had used the words, 'He is despised and rejected of men.' The rejection had begun here, tonight, in this wood-scented workshop. The first to reject him was the man who might have been a father to him. She unclenched her hands and folded her arms across her body, protectively. Not rejected by me, she thought. It is hard to believe but I know it is true, and if I must I will manage alone, and still think myself blessed, despite all the ridicule and the scorn and the pointing fingers.

Again Joseph wondered that she should be so calm. If what she said about her condition was true–however it had come about–unless he stood by her she was in a sorry plight indeed. Anne and Joachim loved her, but their very love would be the measure of their shock and horror. In them, as in him, doubt would war with faith, credulity with incredulity. . . .

He said, pitifully, 'I don't know what to think. I need a little time to think things over.'

She stood up then, and her veil slipped back from her hair, which, freed of the confinement, loosened itself and caught the last rays of the sun and made a halo about her pale, calm face.

She said, 'I came, hoping that God, having chosen me, would have given you a sign, or that you would have faith enough to believe without a sign. I was mistaken. But there is no need to fret or be unhappy. If it is God's will that this child should have an earthly father, one will be found. It may be that he needs none. *My* father is another who can trace his lineage from David! Good night, Joseph.'

Outside, with the sun suddenly sunk behind the hill's shoulder and the dusk thickening, the night wind chilly after the warm day, she was afraid. Alone, and cold, and afraid. No longer the blessed, the chosen, but an unmarried girl with a child in her womb, and upon her tongue a story that nobody could believe.

She could see now why the angel had said, 'Fear not'. There was so much to fear. Her parting words to Joseph had been bold, almost defiant, but now thinking of her parents, her friends and her neighbours, she quailed.

For the first time she saw the width of the gulf that divided what people professed to believe from what they were actually capable of believing. At this very moment if someone went to her home and asked her parents–Do you believe that Messiah will come? They would say–Yes, yes, indeed. Put the same question to Hilliel the Rabbi and he would answer–Indisputably, it is so written. As late as this morning Joseph, confronted by the question, would have professed his belief. Yet tonight he had been incredulous, despite all her efforts to state her case in a manner likely to lead to belief. She had forced herself to speak calmly, not to weep, or gesticulate or plead. She had known, instinctively, that had she cried and made an appeal to his pity Joseph would have weakened and accepted the situation without accepting the truth. That would have been very wrong. So quietly, rationally, she had offered him the facts, and he had not believed her!

The night grew darker, the wind colder; the feeling of loneliness grew. As she neared her home she knew that she must enter and present her usual untroubled countenance; she could face no more this day. So she leaned for a moment against the thorn fence which her father had planted to keep out the foxes. She felt the prick of the long sharp thorns and thought of the donkey goad. Chosen of God, and then abandoned. She sent a wordless cry, winging through the night–My God, my God, why have you forsaken me?

Chapter Six

Joseph, left alone, first thought–I should have walked home with her. But she'd gone so suddenly, and there'd been so much to think about.

He got up from the bench, moving slowly and heavily, like an old man and went into his living-room. He'd spent this day at home, so he'd eaten at midday; bread and cheese would serve for his belated supper. He set them on the table, brought a knife, sat down and felt sick. Up to that point his mind had been engaged in listening to the story, trying to assess its truth and finding possible alternatives. When he had once glanced at the future it had been on Mary's behalf.

What of his own?

His own future, as well as that of Mary and that of an unborn child, lay in his hands; he must make a decision and at the moment he felt incapable of doing so.

His last task before taking on the job at the new house near Cana had been to make a new gateway and a length of fencing for a man who owned a small vineyard, and as part payment he had accepted a large jar of wine which he had set down in the coolest corner of the workshop, intending to save it and contribute it to the wedding feast. He was, by habit, an abstemious man.

Now he rose, took a jug, went to the jar and broke the stamped clay seal, poured a jugful of the wine and hurried back into the house. In the workshop the stool on which Mary had sat was still in position, and something of her presence seemed to linger there, too. He thought uncomfortably that if, at the end of his thinking, he decided that he didn't believe her and did not intend to marry her, he would never enjoy working in that place again. In fact he doubted whether he could go on living in Nazareth, where, even if he could avoid seeing her, he would hear about her.

Get away, he thought. And the question Where? was easily answered. He could go into the hills and join the guerrillas, the nameless ones, the night-walkers.

He thought about them as he sipped his wine and felt it warm and sustaining after the shock.

It was almost sixty years since the Roman, Pompey, had intervened in the Jews' disastrous civil war, had taken Jerusalem and made Palestine a province of the Empire; the great majority of the Jews had settled down, if somewhat warily and uneasily, under Roman rule. But there were others who refused to accept the fact that the war had ended; there were men who remembered their families massacred, either by the Romans themselves or by their tool, Herod, whom they had made King of Judea. There were ardent patriots, religious fanatics, men with grievances, and they had taken to the hills and seized every opportunity to make a nuisance of themselves. They killed sentries, destroyed stores, stole horses, sabotaged the new road and water works, occasionally even ventured an ambush by daylight. At infrequent intervals individuals or small groups were captured and executed. In official quarters there was a tendency to underestimate their numbers and to decry their activities; there were even Jews who deplored their existence, maintaining that they consisted mainly of lawless men, fugitives from justice; but most people admired their courage and their cunning, and the stories of their reckless, spectacular exploits helped to keep alive the spirit of even the tamest town-dwellers, backing up the conviction that in the end nobody but Jehovah and his appointed servants could govern the Jews.

Into the ranks of the nameless ones Joseph could disappear tomorrow and be lost. And if what Mary said about her state was true, nobody could blame him; or, if they did, he'd never know.

He drank again and was seized by self-pity. Wasn't it hard, he thought, that at his age, having led a wandering life in youth, and now prepared to settle down, he should have to uproot himself again. He liked his little house; until this evening he had liked his workshop; he liked Nazareth and his neighbours and his customers. Never before had he felt himself to be part of a community; seldom before had he stayed in any place long enough to reap where he had sown in the sense of establishing a reputation for good sound work. Here he was known, Joseph the carpenter, respected and trusted. Must he abandon it all?

The alternative was to stay and face a very distasteful situation. An espousal was a serious thing; to cancel it was almost like breaking a marriage. But even if a couple had been married for twenty years and hadn't co-habited for a time, due to separation or ritual abstinence and the woman had said she was pregnant because an angel had spoken to her, the man would be fully justified in putting her away. Wouldn't he? *Wouldn't he?*

He'd have to give his reason, of course. And he could just see Anne's face, wrenched by shock and horror, Joachim's distorted by anger; and Mary's, full of sorrow and reproach. His fundamentally kind nature shrank from that prospect.

There was another alternative; he could accept her story. He drank again, and then, scowling, went through the whole account again.

He was now down to rock-bottom, weighing and measuring exactly the faith in which he had been born and reared and to which he had paid allegiance, always.

He believed in God; the one and only God who in six days had made the heaven and the earth and all that were therein; the God of Abraham, Isaac and Jacob, who had enabled Daniel to face a den of hungry lions and Shadrach, Meshach and Abednego to walk unscathed through a fiery furnace, seven times as hot as an ordinary one. These, and a hundred other miraculous stories, he had listened to a dozen times and never doubted; they were now as much a part of him as the callouses on his hands. But they were all long ago, part of the fabulous past, part of 'once upon a time'. Then, take the prophecies; did he believe them? Naturally; every pious Jew did.

Messiah would come, in great power and glory, to deliver His people. But that was all in the future. That was to be one day. . . .

There, you have it, he said to himself, lifting the jug again. Belief in the past things and in the future things is easy; but here and now, that's different. Do I believe that Mary, the woman to whom I am espoused, this morning was visited by an angel who told her that she was to bear the Messiah, and that upon that word she became pregnant?

And the answer to that was a downright 'No'.

There it was, and there was no help for it. No use blaming oneself for one's disbelief, belief was there or it was not there; it could not be commanded. He wished with all his heart that it could be. Because he loved her; he wished he could have given her the answer she wanted. He loved her so much that he wished she had come to tell him that she preferred another man. That, he felt, he could have borne. What he resented–he was facing facts now–was the fact that she had tried to deceive him.

She wasn't stupid; that was one of the things that had attracted him to her. Other women went to the Synagogue and, if they were young, clattered their bracelets and looked covertly at young men from the edges of their veils and thought their young, silly thoughts; if they were older they were glad of a chance to be at peace and rest for a moment, or watched how their children behaved. *She* had listened and remembered; and today had tried to use what she had learned.

And yet, and yet, trying to dismiss her as a light, deceptive creature, he could not forget her calm, the dignity and assurance of her last words.

Suddenly he thought–Poor girl, how she will suffer!

The thought of it, and the wine he had drunk, made him break out into a sweat. If he repudiated her, what would they do, Anne and Joachim, so respectable, so orthodox? Hide her away, say she was ill, smuggle the baby away the moment it was born and put it out to nurse somewhere far away? Anne was sharp-tongued, Joachim, if displeased–Joseph had once or twice seen him so–sullen and surly. What a terrible life the poor girl would have.

And as he thought of that the last alternative presented itself, and even as he entertained it he knew that it was something that only a pot-valient fellow would consider.

Why not marry her?

He loved her and she needed him. Why make all this coil about what you believed and what you didn't believe, and God and the prophets? If she had been frail, all the more reason why he should be strong. And he wouldn't, by any means, be the first man to rear another man's child and grow to be fond of it.

She was very sweet and very innocent; somebody had taken advantage of that sweetness and innocence; and she, in turn, had tried to take advantage of him. But that was because he was her only hope. She had agreed to marry him, and he owed her something for that. And he realised that he was, compared to her, old, and a very unromantic kind of fellow. He looked back on his own youth, remembering its fancies and its passions, its moments of ecstasy; it would ill become him to sit in judgement. . . .

Yes, he thought; he'd marry her, because he loved her, because he was sorry for her and because it was the easiest way out for all. And if by some fantastic chance her story should be true, and nine months from now she bore a baby with . . . Exactly *how* would the Messiah be born? With wings? With a crown on his head, a sword in his hand? With a countenance of such shining glory that no man could look on it?

How very peculiar that none of the prophets had given the slightest information about that. Dream-ridden, impractical men, they'd spoken of a conception without sin, and of a virgin birth. It had been left to a carpenter in Nazareth, an ordinarily sober fellow who had missed his supper and drunk more in an hour than he ordinarily did in half a year, to ask–How?

He said to himself, Man, you're tipsy! Get to your bed.

But, tipsy or sober, credulous or incredulous, he had decided to marry her; and for that he was always to be thankful. In his ordinary, human, unenlightened state he had, from love and pity, made his decision.

He lay down, and fell asleep. And presently the low dark room was filled with a golden light, and there was the sound of music, and the sweet scent of flowers. There too, exactly as Mary had described, was the angel, a dazzle of whiteness and beauty with great wings, and a lily in his hand. Gabriel!

He would have risen, would have fallen to his knees, but he was paralysed.

'Joseph, thou son of David,' Gabriel said, 'fear not to take unto thee Mary, thy wife; for that which is conceived in her is of the Holy Ghost.' If he could have spoken then Joseph would have said that he had already decided; but awe held him speechless. 'She shall bring forth a son, and thou shalt call his name Jesus; for he shall save his people from their sins.'

Then it was dark again, and silent. The night wore away and in the dawn Joseph woke.

Very often, he knew, dreams were conjured up out of what had happened during one's waking hours; twisted, sometimes almost unrecognisable, but you could, if you gave your mind to it, find the link. It did not seem to him unduly marvellous that he should have seen, in a dream, an angel exactly as Mary had described him, even to the lily. But there was one thing about this dream that could not have been the product of anything he had been told or imagined. That final phrase–'from their sins'. That was, and the sensible, practical carpenter recognised the fact, something new, something he could never have imagined or dreamed. Messiah, when he came, was, by common belief, to save his people from the conquerors; he was to re-establish the throne of David, justify and reinstate a proud people. But Gabriel had said 'for he shall save his people from their sins', and that was such an original, revolutionary idea that it could only have come direct from God.

And although the idea that God, the one and only God, had through a dream communicated directly with him, the village carpenter, just as He had communicated with specially chosen people in the past, in the once-upon-a-time, Joseph felt curiously calm. He now understood Mary's attitude on the previous evening. 'Rest in the Lord and wait patiently for Him.' 'The Lord is my shepherd, I shall not want.' The certainty was like a rock. Yet, as over even the most solid rock, a climbing plant may throw its comparatively unimportant growth, over the certainty there were the purely human considerations; he must get to Mary and assure her; he must make arrangements for hastening on the wedding.

The village was hardly stirring when he walked to her house. The door was still closed and he knocked on it. Mary opened it and her face, already pale, whitened when she saw him. He took a step backward and signed to her to follow him.

'Have you told them?' he asked in a low voice.

She shook her head. She had come home, feeling forsaken of God, and thinking that she must tell them, the sooner the better, and found them both busy, preparing the eggs that her father would, in the morning, take into the market at Sepphoris. Anne, with a damp cloth, was wiping each egg clean from the clawmarks, the dung, the bits of nesting chaff, and Joachim, taking them one by one, was holding each egg against the candlelight. To sell an egg with an embryo chick in it, or with a blood spot or a meat spot, would be to lose custom. In Sepphoris ordinary housewives, or the slaves who bought for bigger households, must always be able to say, 'The eggs we buy from Joachim are always fresh.'

She'd stood there for a moment, visualising what would happen if she suddenly gave them the news. She'd tried Joseph the one to whom, mentally and emotionally, she was closest and he had not believed her. So from her parents she had turned away and gone to bed.

'I'm glad of that,' Joseph said, in answer to her shaking of the head. 'I've come to ask you a great favour.' He was aware that in the shadowy room behind the open door somebody was moving, listening, alert. He raised his voice a little. 'I know weddings and the preparations for them mean a great deal to brides and their mothers. But Cana is seven miles away, I have to leave early and I get back late. I'm tired of coming home to a dead hearth, tired of making my own breakfast. . . .' Whoever moved in the shadow had come nearer, was listening intently. 'The day after tomorrow,' he said, 'is the day for weddings. I've come to ask you, Mary, to marry me then, instead of two months hence.'

Even had he not had his dream her face would have been sufficient justification. Joy, gratitude, wonder, completely transfigured it. He had thought it over, he believed it.

She said, 'Oh, Joseph!' and looked on him with love.

'What is this? What is this?' demanded Anne, able no longer to remain a silent listener and coming to the door.

'I want to put the wedding forward,' Joseph said.

'I heard you. There's selfishness for you! Marry the day after tomorrow–with the guests bidden for eight weeks ahead. So you're tired of fending for yourself and to spare yourself just that short time more you'd do Mary out of her wedding day. In the whole of my life I never heard anything so preposterous!'

As in the early days, faced by Mary's mother he felt all hands and feet and angular elbows. He said, as awkwardly as though his request had been made from purely selfish motives:

'I thought if Mary didn't mind . . .'

Mary said, 'I don't, I'd be glad.'

'You be quiet,' Anne said. 'You're so soft, you'd stand by the door and give away your nose for a whistle if anybody asked you!' The tone in which she said that was almost rough, yet she was expressing, for the first time, fully and freely, her inmost opinion of her own daughter. She was so tender-hearted, so easily troubled, so altogether, in Anne's opinion, unfitted for the hard battle that was ordinary life, that somebody must stand up for her, protect her, save her from herself as it were. And Anne had hoped that Joseph would be that somebody. That had been her only reason for showing him any favour; he was getting on in years, he wasn't and never would be rich; but she had thought him kind and reliable. Now he was the very one to come along with this most selfish suggestion.

'We,' Anne said, giving the contemptible fellow a fierce look, 'have relatives, on both sides of the family, scattered all over Galilee and Judah. I have a brother in Capernaum and another in Bethsaida; Joachim has two sisters in Sechem. And there's Zacharias,' she said, naming, with some pride, the husband of Mary's cousin who was a priest in the Temple. 'How do you think they're going to feel when they hear she's been married without their presence? It's all very well for you to come strolling along and suggest getting married the day after tomorrow, just because you've spoiled your breakfast. Things aren't done like that in decent families.'

Mary said, 'At least my dress is ready.'

'So it may be. But nothing else is.'

Joseph felt rather than saw that Mary was looking at him with appeal. What could he say?

Speaking almost as the words came into his mind he said:

'What I said to Mary wasn't the whole of it. When we set the day I didn't know this job was coming up, did I? Now I can see I'm going to be so busy that it'd be very inconvenient to take three days off then. This week I could do it.' From first to last a properly celebrated wedding in humble families went on for three days, with richer people it could extend to six.

'Too busy to attend your own wedding!' Anne exclaimed. 'That's the first time I ever heard that.'

From behind her Joachim said, as he fastened his girdle:

'What is going on here?'

Anne turned and in the short sharp words informed him. Joachim looked at Joseph, who appeared to be embarrassed and awkward, at Mary, who seemed to be on the brink of tears, and at his own belligerent wife. And he thought–Why of course, they're in love and it's Spring, poor fellow he doesn't want to wait any longer. On top of this understanding thought he felt the instinctive impulse to side with one of his own sex.

'Well,' he said, when Anne had finished, 'I can't see so much amiss with that. Unless Mary minds. It's her wedding; it's for her to say.'

'I'd like to be married the day after tomorrow,' Mary said.

'That's settled then,' Joachim said before Anne could speak. 'Now perhaps one of you would come in and give me my breakfast.'

Speechless, Anne flounced into the house.

Mary said, 'Oh, thank you, Joseph! I can never thank you enough. You do believe me?'

'I believe you,' he said.

Her joy at being believed was so transcendent that he decided not to mention the dream yet. He'd save that for an unjoyful day. Looking ahead he could see plenty of that sort to come.

PART TWO

PYANGYONG

6,000 miles

At the foot of the stone stairs that led up to his tower, Melchior turned and looked at old Senya; she'd never been, in his opinion, particularly bright, and now, with age, her wits, as well as her hearing and eyesight, were failing. He had to say things over and over again, and even then could never be sure that she had heard and understood. Her own few remarks she repeated so often that had he taken any notice of what she said, he would have found the reiteration quite tiresome.

Wrapped up against the cold, muffled and shrouded in the remnants of several garments, once of varying colour but now from age and dirt a uniform dun, she crouched by the pitiable fire.

'Senya,' he said. She was his slave, but as always he addressed her with gentle courtesy. 'Senya, you did understand me?' Her head, like a tortoise's, emerged from the carapace of wrappings and turned towards him. 'I am going up now and I shall not be down until tomorrow morning. Don't call me and don't cook any supper for me.'

He had told her that twice before and she had merely nodded and grunted. This time she said:

'Master, there is nothing to cook. Nothing. Nothing at all. When what we have is eaten we shall starve.'

'I'll think about that tomorrow.'

She had been muttering about the nearness of starvation for quite a long time now, sometimes he took no notice, when he did he always soothed her by saying he would think about it presently.

'The pig is hungry, too,' she said in her flat old voice. He was the cleverest man in Korea, maybe the cleverest man in all the world, but in many ways he could act like an idiot, and he was acting that way about the pig. It was good housekeeping to have a pig in a pen to eat the household scraps and a panful of meal now and again, and this year, as in former years, she had bought a little pig, the runt of a litter; very cheap it had been because the man who had sold it thought it would be dead before she got it home. What she had been trying, without success, to make Melchior see for the last fortnight, was that when there was so little for people to eat there were no scraps for pigs, and when there was no money there could be no meal. The pig was losing flesh; and its hungry squealing, shrill enough to pierce the constant buzzing in her ears, made Senya perpetually aware of its plight. However, Melchior was her master, the pig was his, bought with his money–she looked at the little jar which stood in a niche in the wall, an empty jar now–and she would never dream of doing anything about the pig until Melchior told her to.

'I'll think about the pig, too; but presently.'

In the bitter depths of her heart she said to herself–Always presently, always tomorrow, shuffling things off; so he has brought ruin to himself and hunger to us both.

But when he had disappeared around the first turn of the spiral staircase and was reasonably certain not to turn back and tell her again what she had fully understood in the first place, she roused herself, took a knife and, with a savage, a self-mutilating cut, halved the bit of stale bread, the bit of hard cheese that lay on the bench. Then, opening the door, she stole out into the bitter wind and went to where at the base of the tower there was a basket, attached to a long rope. She slipped her offering into it, covered it again and went back to the fire.

Only a few minutes earlier, showing him the poor portions of bread and cheese, she had said, 'Master, this is all we have!' And he had for a moment brought his mind back from the wide fields of the sky where it ranged, and he had looked closely at the food.

'Enough for today,' he had said, quite contentedly. 'Halve it between us.' It had never occurred to him to say–Halve it fairly because for years it had been understood that whatever there was was to be thus divided. And under his eye, attentive for once, she had made a fair division. Now she had given him half her portion; because he was her master, and because she had loved him slavishly for more than fifty years. He wouldn't notice; he never noticed anything; at least not anything on that level; that was why they were in this sad state.

The pig, having seen Senya come out and go in again without throwing him so much as an outside cabbage leaf, squealed angrily. Senya, going into another of the little rooms at the base of the tower to smooth Melchior's sleeping mat and his blanket, thought–He did say tomorrow! and thought how good a bit of roast pork would taste.

Melchior, climbing steadily, indeed briskly, the spiralling stairway that clung to the tower's inner wall, deliberately put the old woman's words out of his mind. Poor, poor, yes, he knew they were poor; but one good thing about eating scantily was that you stayed spry and lively. How many men of his age, seventy-five, could go up and down these stairs as he did, he asked himself. Very few. Leading the life he did–he had not set foot outside the tower since he'd sold his last bit of land, and that must be at least five years ago–if he had eaten full, he would be heavy and scant of breath, an occupant of a carrying chair. As it was, only lately had he rigged the rope and the basket as a means of getting things to the top; previously he had carried them.

Undoubtedly the worst thing about being poor was the cold. It was Spring now, the snows had melted, the frost-hardened earth was softening, but this process added a dampness to the chill of the wind which blew from far inland where it was much colder than in sea-girt Korea. He could see the damp on the stone wall, feel it in his bones. Years ago, when the tower was newly built, there had been braziers here and there on the stairs, and no fewer than three in the room at the top. When he'd moved here he had brought three slaves, Senya and two young males who had scampered up and down the stairs carrying food and water and fuel for the braziers. In those days he'd had a bed in the room at the top, and a big bell in an aperture; he had only to ring it. . . . He did not grieve over the vanished service, the lost comforts, but he did feel the cold. He was glad to wrap rags like bandages over his cloth shoes and well up his legs. And all through the winter he wore his one wadded robe, a good garment in its day, now stained and faded. But Spring was on its way; the winter solstice was three months past. In a rush the warm weather would come, and he could wear his other, unwadded robe, and Senya, as in other years, would take this one and wash it, beat the lumped wadding into fluff; and the sun, shining into the room at the top of the tower, would cherish and revive him.

Poverty, self-imposed, was tolerable. He had, he knew, only himself to blame for his state. He'd been a most fortunate young man. His grandfather had come out of China in the train of that great, that almost legendary warrior, Wiman, and in the carve-up of the conquered territory he had received enormous tracts of land which had passed eventually, undiminished, to Melchior. If, when he had come into his heritage, the tower had been built, he could have stood at the top of it and looked in every direction and known that all he could see he owned.

His father he could not remember; both his parents had died young and he had been reared by his grandfather, who, because he was a Chinese and had no learning, had a great respect for it. One day the boy Melchior had made some remark or observation–he could not remember the exact circumstance–and his grandfather had said, 'I think you may be a clever boy. You shall go to the university in Pyangyong.' Pyangyong at that time prided itself upon being one of the most cultured cities in the world. Korea had, long ago, been colonised by Chinese who had brought their own culture, their own learning with them. General Wiman's invasion had been a re-conquest, almost an invasion of barbarians; and there had been times, when in the muted, learned atmosphere of Pyangyong's schools Melchior, because of his ancestry, had been made to feel that he was almost a barbarian. That had made him pursue his studies more diligently. He'd learned eagerly, everything, even some rudimentary Greek. Less than a hundred and fifty years before the great Wiman conquered Korea, a Greek named Alexander had marched into Asia, intending to conquer India. He'd failed–Melchior now knew exactly why–but his tongue had spread along the routes, had established itself in many places, become a means by which men of widely diverse cultures could communicate. In Pyangyong, where no born Greek had ever been, a place that no Greek had ever heard of, the young Melchior had learned Greek of a peculiar kind, together with history, mathematics and astronomy.

Astronomy had been from the moment he was introduced to it, emotionally his darling and financially his downfall. The moment he had come into his inheritance he had built this tower, at vast expense. Glass; that was the trouble. He must have glass, and only one country in the world knew the secret of its making. Egypt, a place immeasurably far away. But intrepid traders, voracious traders had held open the tenuous lines between East and West. Ask in Pyangyong–as Melchior had asked–for glass, and it was like dropping stone into a pond; the ripples spread. Months, even years, later, you had glass, fragile stuff, carefully packed, gently handled, carried on the backs of camels, donkeys, horses and mules and men, moved by stages, paid for by stages, but arriving at last and costly beyond all reckoning. He'd grudged nothing; he had planned a great tower with a glass dome, and he was not surprised or dismayed by the fact that when at last it stood on the hill-top, just as he had visualised it, nine-tenths of his heritage was expended.

And in a way he had been right not to care; he had what he wanted; and he had a tenth of his patrimony left, and that would have sufficed to keep any ordinary careful man for as long as he lived. He simply hadn't been careful. Could he be expected to come down, in the middle of some calculation, or the careful drawing of a chart, to deal with a dishonest steward, a defaulting tenant? The idea was absurd. He'd said–I'm busy. He'd said–I'll deal with that tomorrow. Now and then, faced with the problem in some way that forbade escape or deferment, he'd said, 'I'll sell something.'

With what remained of his estate he could not be bothered. Nor could he be bothered with friendships or any social contacts that made demands upon his time. When the tower was new there were men who had known his grandfather, men who had studied with him in Pyangyong, men with marriageable daughters. All splendid people he was sure, but to him as troublesome as flies in summer. Hundreds of times he had said, 'Yes, thank you, I will come,' in answer to their invitations. Then he had forgotten all about them.

So his fortune had wasted away and his life had narrowed. Now on this very cold morning, with Spring imminent, he owned his tower, a small vegetable garden in which, presently, Senya would plant vegetables, Senya herself and a hungry pig. Nothing else in the world.

And there was not a happier man in the world. . . .

Downstairs, Senya, having straightened Melchior's sleeping apartment, moved back to the fire and looked at it with a gloomy eye. It was almost dead and she must go out in search of fuel. She looked at the miserable scrap of bread and cheese that remained and realised that she must do something about food, too.

In the past she had been in the habit of going down into the valley and hiring herself for some hours during the busy season, doing field work for which casual labour was welcome. Bent double, she'd planted rice in wet paddy fields, and then cut and carried it. She'd planted vegetables too, and gathered them. She'd picked and packed fruit. She'd cleared fields of stones and with the same stones built fences. She'd spent hours and hours in the stinking place where hides were scraped and the hair, mixed with glue, was beaten into felt from which hats and shoes were made.

Of these activities Melchior knew nothing. She'd timed her goings out and her returns very carefully. She never left the tower until he was safely at the top, and she was always back by sunset which was the usual time for the evening meal. He had not, of course, noticed her small but invaluable contributions to the household expenses. It must be at least five years since Melchior had sold that last strip of land and had come in, trusting her absolutely, and put the money in the jar that stood in the niche. Even his bemused mind must have recognised something of the situation, for he had said, 'That's the last, Senya. Make it go as far as you can.'

Having said that and set the jar back in its niche he had gone straight up the stairs to what he called his work and she, in her mind, called his toys. And she had gone across to the jar and counted the coins. How wicked, she thought, the way good men are cheated; had that field been mine I should have haggled and sold it for at least twice as much as this. And then she had realised, for the first time, fully, that Melchior not only trusted her–she had known that–but that he was depending upon her.

So, shameful as it was for a slave born in the family house and reared therein, to do such a thing, she had gone and sought casual labour. Always far down in the valley where she was not known. And always, if questioned, she had said that she came from Pyangyong. Sometimes she had added the information that she was a widow.

It had worked until last year. Then something had gone wrong inside her head; far worse than the buzzing in her ears. When she stooped–and all field work involved stooping–she'd turned dizzy. Naturally she had ignored this, just as she had ignored her aching back, her stiff knees and elbows. But, working on through the dizziness, she had fallen and lain unconscious. She always came round, as good as new, and no harm done; but she'd had such spells so often, in so many different fields and orchards, that now no one would employ her. There was a superstitious belief that to have a worker die, at work, brought bad luck.

There were still things she could have done, inside houses; she could have cooked, preserved fish and meat, mended, done anything that did not entail much stooping; but the trouble was that in the valley there were only rich families who had slaves and servants of their own to do such work, or poor ones who would never hire domestic labour. The same problem had bedevilled her one or two begging expeditions; the poor had nothing to spare and in the big houses the servants had chased her off, calling her a dirty old woman.

Today the situation was desperate, she must go out to find fuel, and, if it were humanly possible, something to eat tomorrow.

When she opened the door the pig squealed in anguished anticipation; she gave it a calculating look as she passed. Nothing but skin and bone now, and it would be worse tomorrow. Tomorrow she must, by some means, gain Melchior's attention and make him understand about the pig. It seemed strange that such a clever man should be so stupid about simple things.

Still, she was his slave and she must do her best for him. In addition, she loved him very much. She had lost her heart to him more than half a century ago, when she was fifteen and he a handsome young man of twenty. Oh, how handsome he had been, tall and slim and elegant, with such bright eyes and glossy black hair, and such beautiful manners. The old master had been alive then, the tower did not exist and they were all living in the magnificent house that stood half-way down the slope, overlooking the valley. She was the youngest of the female slaves, and the prettiest, and it was quite usual for masters, young or old, to take a comely slave girl to bed. She remembered the dusks of summers long ago, when the young master was home from his studies, and the night wind blew softly and she'd haunted the courtyard outside his bedroom and yearned for him. She'd done her best to attract his notice, putting oil on her hair and scent on the palms of her hands. If someone then, with the gift for seeing, had told her–You'll live alone with him for thirty years, sharing a fire and a dish, how wrongly she would have interpreted it, how overcome with joy she would have been.

Bodies grew old, she thought, shuffling down the hill; handsome young men turned into thin, frail ones–but she still thought Melchior good-looking, for his age; and in comely girls the sap dried up, till they were like old twisted trees and nobody would believe that once they had worn flowers behind their ears and been desirable, and almost died of their own desiring.

In the end even desire failed.

But duty remained; and a kind of fondness, and that was why she was out here in the biting wind with the mud seeping through the rags that wrapped her feet instead of remaining indoors and thinking that it was a master's duty to provide his slave with at least one meal a day.

After a time she drew level with the big house under whose warm-coloured, curving tiled roof both she and Melchior had been born. She had never visited it to ask for employment or charity; it was too near the tower; she might be recognised and so bring shame upon Melchior; and Melchior, looking out from his tower, might even have seen her. Also she had felt a curious reluctance to go back there where life had run so comfortably in the old days.

This morning she thought about the past. The old master had possessed a sternness unknown to his grandson, but he had been just, and there had never been a mistress to make things hard. The old mistress had died in childbed, and Melchior's mother had died, with his father, in the time of the great sickness, two years before Senya herself was born. In the comfortable house life had been pleasant; plenty of fuel, plenty of food, plenty of tea. Of all the things she had lacked in recent years Senya missed tea most. It came from China and was very expensive, so it had been one of the first things to be cut out. Melchior seemed not to notice; he drank hot water without comment or complaint, but Senya still yearned to see the green leaves uncurling and yielding their flavour and fragrance, and the water changing colour. Between a bowl of hot water and a bowl of tea there was all the difference in the world.

She came back to the present. Either the wind was stronger than usual or meagre feeding was telling at last in increased feebleness; she was making very slow progress. Ordinarily she would have been in the valley by this time and here she was, still skirting the wall that surrounded the big house. It offered some shelter from the wind and she paused to gather strength. Through an archway she could see into the main courtyard. It wore its winter look. The big tubs of lilies had been taken indoors and every rose tree had been loosened from its stake, bent over and swathed in sacking. Very soon now it would look very different. Spring, when it came, came at a bound. She remembered now, for several years, she had watched the rose trees being unshrouded and straightened, and the lily tubs brought out, with excited anticipation. Maybe on some warm, scented evening *this* year Melchior would notice her and she would be able to give her maidenhead where she had already given her heart. That was all she asked.

It had never happened; and all that wasted hope and emotion might have been a sadness and a hurt to remember, but for one thing. If she had failed to make her humble way into his bed, so had women not so humble. Many men, with silk-clad, tiny-footed, jewel-shining daughters, had desired that rich, handsome young man as a son-in-law, and Senya had watched fearfully, feeling that she could hardly bear it if he took a wife without first taking her, yet knowing that she must bear it and give no sign for fear of ridicule. That misery, at least, she had escaped. Melchior had taken the sky as his bride, and such a rival any woman could accept, not gladly, but with fortitude.

She stood in the shelter of the wall and realised with dismay that this morning, even if she forced herself on, down into the valley, she would never climb back again. Old, yes, she was old, her ears buzzed as though bees were swarming there, and when she stooped she grew dizzy; but she'd never felt feeble before. Now she did, her legs trembled under her and she felt dizzy without stooping. It occurred to her–and it was a shocking thought–that if she was to have anything to offer her master when tomorrow morning he came down from the tower, she must ask for, and obtain it from *this* house.

She turned and looked back at the tower, a long grey finger pointing to the sky with a glass dome at its tip. It seemed far from where she stood, skulking in the shelter of the wall, to where her master was, high in the glass dome. But he had that wonderful glass, the thing he claimed to have invented.

Some years ago, but she could remember the day with clarity because it was the one and only time that he had ever shared his real life with her, he had come down with a tube, like a section of bamboo in his hand and he had said, 'Look through that, Senya, and tell me what you see. No, put it to one eye and close the other, now what do you see?' It had been summer-time and the door in the base of the tower had been open and he had handed her the thing with its end pointing outwards. So she had obediently closed one eye and applied the other to the end of the tube and seen nothing, a blue, and she'd been confused, torn between her wish to please him, since the toy was evidently of importance to him, and her inability to guess even what it was that she was expected to see. And then, suddenly, she had seen. A tethered goat, eating grass.

She'd said, 'I can see a goat.'

And that had been exactly the answer he wanted. He said:

'Now, take the glass away and look in the same direction, Senya. Can you now see the goat?'

She could not.

'Try the glass again.'

She did so, and there was the goat, so close that she felt that by reaching out her hand she could have touched it.

'I see it now,' she said.

Then he'd snatched the thing from her and said, 'It brings distant things close, doesn't it? It will be of inestimable value to me in my work.'

After that she had felt less happy about her own work, fearing that even when she was far away in the valley he might turn the glass in that direction and see her as plainly as she had seen the goat and the grass. But in time she had realised that he only turned the glass upon the stars or the moon, and the fear had left her. This morning however, because she was about to do something that outraged her own standards, her fear of being observed sprang up again, lively enough to make her turn and look before rounding the corner of the wall and making, in a furtive way, for the entrance to the kitchen courtyard.

Although she had never yet been back to what in her mind she always called *the* house, she knew who lived there. A big fat man who had made a fortune from running houses of prostitution in Pyangyong. A very disreputable way of making money, as the man had realised. So, with one child born and another about to be, he had sold his houses, moved into the country and bought Melchior's family house and several little farms. He was said to be an oppressive, unmerciful landlord. It was also said that his temper had been embittered by the fact that people in other big houses would not befriend him, called him Bawd-master and did not seek to ally their families to his by marriage. All this Senya had heard from the tongues of gossips. She had heard it said, also, that her master was at fault for so demeaning himself as to sell the house of his fathers to such a man.

And now, after all these years, she was about to demean her master even further, and demean herself too, by begging at the kitchen door.

It was terrible, and she knew it; and it was all her master's fault; he'd wasted his substance, just as he was at this very moment wasting the pig which, killed a week ago, would have provided several succulent joints, and killed tomorrow would hardly have enough fat in it for basting.

The kitchen door was firmly closed against the cold; but even her buzz-ridden old ears could hear the sound of voices, of laughter. When she knocked there was a momentary silence, then a voice said, 'See who that is.'

Another voice said, 'Ordering me about! Go yourself, lazy-bones.'

The first voice said, 'Lazy-bones, am I?' And there was the sound of a scuffle and more, louder, laughter.

Senya knew, intuitively that there was no master, no mistress, within this house. She remembered hearing somewhere that the Bawd-master, old now and his bones creaking, often took himself and his family south to winter in a less rigorous climate.

Slaves left in charge, she thought, growing arrogant and fat in idleness, the worst possible people to beg from. This opinion–based on experience–was confirmed when the door was opened by a young woman who said, after one glance:

'Whatever you're selling, we don't want any.'

With the suddenness of a lightning flash from a summer sky, the idea came to Senya. She said in a wheedling, cajoling voice, not her own:

'You'll want what I have to sell, dearie. So will those within. I can read fortunes. True ones. By the lines in your palm, or by the tea-leaves in a bowl, I can tell what Fate has in store for you.'

And wasn't it marvellous! She could have said, I'm starving, my belly is empty, my legs shake and my head spins from hunger, and they'd have turned her away. A few words of rubbish and there was the girl at the door all attention, and a voice from within saying, 'A fortune-teller, is it?' And in less than a minute she was inside the warm, the food-scented, the oh-so-familiar kitchen.

Melchior climbed the stairs and reached the one at the top, much wider than the rest, with, straight ahead of it a solid door, and to the right an aperture with a slatted shutter. This he opened and hauled up the basket, which, as was his custom, he had packed himself. For some reason quite outside his comprehension old Senya appeared to resent this sensible labour-saving device; she had offered to toil up the stairs with whatever was needed, and when he had pointed out to her that they were both now too old for such needless exertions, she'd turned sulky. Whenever she packed the basket something went wrong with the contraption because she seemed unable to understand the necessity for packing the basket in a balanced way. So now he did it himself. He knew–or thought he knew–exactly what was in the basket today. At the bottom a few handfuls of charcoal for his brazier; the last of the supply; a full jar of water, and as a counter-balance on the other side a larger wine-jar containing a very small amount of rice wine, also the last of the supply. Between the two his half of the bread and cheese. Ample for all his needs for the next twenty-four hours. He carried the basket into the glass-roofed, circular room and set it on the floor. Then he looked about him with that sense of satisfaction, of home-coming, which the room never failed to evoke.

All around the room, broken only by the entrance door and another leading to a little side chamber, ran a wide flat bench, set at just the right height for a man standing or sitting on a high stool to work at. On this bench, this morning, several charts, drawn on paper or parchment, and smaller pages covered with closely written figures or words, lay exposed. Others, neatly rolled, lay on shelves beneath the bench. In the centre of an empty space stood a box without a lid; in it lay his tools, his astrolabe, his compasses, his lodestone, and the glass which Senya remembered. There were pens, too, and sticks of coloured chalk, ground to a fine point; there was a knife and an ink-jar.

The centre of the room was clear except for the three-legged brazier and a tall ladder with a stout strut at the back of it and at its top a platform upon which a man could sit or lie. The whole place was noticeably neat, even clean. Dust was never allowed to gather upon the oldest, the least used chart or map.

It was noticeably cold, too, perched on the hill-top, and above bench level all of glass: he looked wistfully at the brazier, already laid with a few dry twigs and lumps of charcoal. But he must not be extravagant. Soon, when the sun reached its midday height, the tower would become warm; then when it went down and night fell it would be colder than it was now; he must reserve his fire for the night. So he tucked his hands into his sleeves and went and stood by one of the charts, studying it.

He wondered if there were, somewhere in the wide, outer world, anyone who, looking at this chart, would understand it. There were astronomers in Pyangyong–it was there that he had gained a rudimentary knowledge of the subject, but, and this thought roused no pride in him, they were not of his calibre. How could they be? He had given his whole life to the study; they were men of divided interests; they gave lectures, reared families, took regular meals and spent a great deal of time in useless talk.

There were astronomers in the West, too; he even knew the names of two cities famous for their experts, Babylon and Alexandria. But, a thin smile moved his lips as he thought, they hadn't done very well by Alexander. If he had been on that great General's staff he could have warned him that his attempt to conquer India was doomed to failure, a waste of time and money. Mars in decline, Saturn in the ascendant. Hopeless! He could have foretold, too, the break-up of the Empire Alexander did succeed in establishing; in the third house there was every augury of disintegration and division.

To be honest, though, there had in the last month or two been moments when he would have been glad to talk to a really skilled, truly learned fellow scholar; not in order to indulge in the futile, wrangling arguments such as he had witnessed and sometimes taken part in during his student days. He would have liked to hold out this chart and say, 'What do you make of it?' Not because he was unsure of himself; a pregnant sky was as unmistakable as a pregnant woman; some new thing was augured; probably a comet; he would have welcomed another opinion about that.

He was now well away, and no longer aware of the cold; and Senya need not have feared his observation. If by any chance he had looked out and downhill and seen her about to enter his old home he would merely have thought that she had shuffled out to have a gossip with some of her own kind. There had been a time when she would go out with some regularity and stay away for hours; women had an infinite capacity for gossip.

When Melchior had decided that he could no longer afford the house and the tower, and had also argued that to live on the spot would be more convenient, he had taken Senya, the two young male slaves, and enough furniture and gear for their needs. The rooms at the base of the tower were small, however, and much had been left behind and sold with the house. So the kitchen looked very much as it had done when Senya left it. The great chopping block still stood in one corner; several enormous cooking pots hung on the wall, and on a shelf were the blue and white, lidded jars, left behind with some regret. Not that she'd have had any use for them lately, being unable to afford the spices and exotic herbs they were designed to hold. Onions and salt had been the only flavourings she had used for years, and the onions had been home-grown.

There were three people in the kitchen. The young woman who had let her in, an older woman with a full-fleshed face and hard-looking eyes, and a boy on the verge of manhood. Their easy, holiday-making air confirmed her guess that they had been left in charge of the house; she knew the situation; little to do, nobody to oversee them. Here they were, at midday, drinking tea and eating, what were they eating? She used her nose as well as her eyes. Delicious! Small savoury dumplings, packed with chopped pork and herbs. She'd made many in her time. And if her master would agree to the killing of the pig before it starved to death, she would again–if by some means she got some flour, some herbs.

The woman said, in a rousing, challenging way:

'Well, what about these fortunes?'

Senya, disturbed from her meditations, started and blinked. What fortunes? Then she remembered, and said:

'Oh yes, the fortunes. By palm or by tea-leaves? And I have to be paid, you know.'

'We could have guessed that! In cash or in kind?'

On any previous day, asked that question, she would have said, 'Cash.' She was a shrewd, shrill bargainer and down in the village invariably managed to get more than her money's worth. But now–she thought swiftly–she simply didn't feel able to walk the rest of the downhill way, face the bustle and shoving in the market, haggle, and then, carrying bundles, climb all the way back. And she thought of the store-room that adjoined the kitchen; in the old master's day it had been a treasure house of good things. Hams and strings of sausages and bunches of salt fish had hung from hooks, there'd been barrels and sacks of flour and honey, soya meal, dried peas and beans, rice, jars of oil and vinegar and wine. She turned dizzy again at the thought of the abundance. And doubtless it was the same now. The Bawd-master had a bad reputation as a landlord but nobody had ever suggested that he was a stinting, niggardly master. So she said:

'Pay me in food.' And as she said the words she could see herself carrying away food for two, perhaps even three, days. And she could see Melchior, tomorrow, coming down from the tower top and being so surprised and pleased to find that she, whom he had left with a bit of bread and cheese, had somehow, miraculously produced a real, belly-filling meal. He wouldn't ask how; he'd just enjoy it and say, as always, 'Thank you, Senya, a very good meal.'

'Food it shall be, then,' the woman said. She was plainly the one in command, probably the cook. 'I'll have mine in the tea-leaves.'

The girl said, 'Me too.'

The boy said, 'I think I'll have mine by hand.'

Senya watched, enviously, mouth-wateringly as the two women drained their tea-bowls. And then she did her very best. She knew absolutely nothing about telling fortunes, but she did know what everybody wished to hear–impossibly favourable things. She was handicapped by her lack of knowledge about this household; in kitchens you found born slaves, like herself, bonded people, who must serve a certain term, and free people working for hire. And since status governed the future with an iron hand, a would-be fortune-teller must needs by very careful. She was careful; and she managed to offend every one of them. Staring into the meaningless pattern made by the tea-leaves and thinking of what she would have wished to hear when she was this woman's age she told the cook that she would have children, beautiful children, and the cook, now the secret mistress of the old Bawd-master, chanced to desire nothing less. She told the young woman what surely any girl would wish to hear; many lovers, she said; and the young woman, who had one lover to whom she was utterly devoted, heard in that her doom. For the boy, regarding the delicate, uninformative palm that he offered, she foretold a future that was possible to any young man, slave, bonded or free; because of all things the army was the most powerful; masters of every kind were always being asked to contribute to the army–that was a polite way of putting it. So she told him that he would be a soldier and a very successful one. The boy, a homosexual, who was waiting for one of his master's friends, a rich man of the same mind, to buy him and dress him in silk, was not pleased by this prospect.

It struck Senya, as the boy withdrew his hand, and she abandoned the trance-like attitude that all the fortune-tellers she had ever encountered had adopted, that they were an ungrateful lot. What had they expected? How had she failed?

The cook said, 'Well, that is that. Now we will pay you.' She poured hot water into a cup and sprinkled tea-leaves on it; she took a long-handled spoon and caught one of the savoury dumplings, and put it into another bowl.

'There you are,' she said coldly. 'Eat and drink.' The three of them withdrew a little, whispering amongst themselves, saying each one speaking from his own inner dissatisfaction, that this was no true teller of fortunes, just a dirty old woman who shrank from downright begging. Take no notice, they said.

To Senya the bowl of tea was very welcome. In good conscience she could drink it and enjoy it; but the lovely little dumpling presented a problem. If only she could get it home, unbroken, what a meal it would make for her master when he came down from his tower tomorrow morning. Five minutes in a pan of boiling salt water and it would be as though it had been freshly made. Draining her bowl of tea, looking at the dumpling and repressing a fierce desire to eat, to taste it, she said:

'I would like, if you please, to take it home with me, to eat just before I sleep. One sleeps ill on an empty belly.'

She could see, by their faces, that they were now hostile. And the hostility took the form of opposition, even to that simple request.

The cook, thinking what pregnancy would mean to her, said:

'Eat it. You asked for food, and that is food. Eat it!'

'I can't,' Senya said, thinking how awful, how unthinkable, it would be for her to eat a delicious savoury dumpling while her master ate stale bread and sour cheese.

They whispered together. The cook said:

'Eat it. You shall have something to take home with you.'

'Eat it,' the girl urged, wondering how long it would be before the one, the chosen, deserted her and she must console herself with the many.

'Eat it,' the boy said, contrasting what she had foretold with what he had hoped for.

So she ate it and it was so delicious that she abandoned the restrained manner of eating which she had adopted when, years ago, Melchior had said–Come, sit and eat, Senya, while the dish is hot. She allowed her teeth to clash, her lips to slap audibly, and somehow that added to her enjoyment of the dumpling.

Then, all suddenly, the boy said:

'I've seen you before. It's bothered me, all the time. You serve that crazy old man who lives in the tower.'

Shame and disgrace; Melchior's slave, going about trying to tell fortunes, begging for food.

She said, 'What tower? What crazy man? I come from Pyangyong.'

'Then you must,' he said, 'be sister to the old woman who awaits upon the madman in the tower at the top of the hill.'

She could not disgrace her master, so she denied him.

'I may have a sister of whom I know nothing. And I know nothing of madmen in towers. I am from Pyangyong. A poor widow.'

The cook said, 'And you want something to eat this evening. I will fetch it.'

Well, that was what she had come out for; something for her master to eat tomorrow; and she had achieved it. Scooping up the last bit of dumpling, Senya said, 'Thank you. Thank you kindly.'

The cook came back and handed to Senya one of those woven reed baskets in which fish and fruit were often carried. Such baskets were made by blind children in Pyangyong; some charitable ladies saw to it that there was always a supply of reeds, and they bullied shopkeepers into buying the baskets. A large household could collect four or five in a single day, and it was regarded as an unworthy act ever to hand back the baskets; if you had a use for them, well and good, if not they should be burned or dug into the garden to rot and enrich the soil; only thus could the orphans continue to eat, the ladies to be charitable. The basket she now had in her hand was closed by a sharp wooden skewer which pinned its edges together. And it weighed beautifully heavy. She was so glad that she had chosen to be paid in food, for no sum she would have dared to ask could have bought so much solid heavy provender.

She pushed her hands into her ragged multiplicity of sleeves and bowed, expressing her gratitude again and again. The hostility she thought she had sensed had vanished by this time, and they all smiled at her. The boy said, 'Enjoy your supper!'

'Oh, I shall. I shall indeed. There is enough here for many meals. On the morrow's morrow I shall still be blessing you.'

They smiled.

After the warmth of the kitchen the outer air struck even colder than before; and because she had lied she was compelled to walk away, downhill, as though making for the valley and the city beyond it. That was not all wasted effort, though, for she found, half buried in the thawing mud, a sizeable log, and later, when she had turned and was climbing back by a path which did not lead past the big house, she found several small bushes which the winter had killed; she grubbed them up, roots and all. She was fully loaded as she made her way up the steep incline below the tower, breathless and rather dizzy, but too happy to mind. Food and fuel for two days.

The pig squealed when it saw her and then again, even more loudly, when she passed it by without a glance.

She re-lighted the fire first, feeding the feeble flame twig by twig and then putting one of the roots in place. The log was damp, and she laid it in the hearth where it could dry out a little. Then, as excited as a pampered wife who on New Year's Day had received a prettily wrapped parcel the contents of which she could not guess, she opened the basket and gave a yelp of dismay. There was nothing edible in it at all.

What had weighed so heavy were some shards, the broken remains of a heavy jar, and a piece of dried plaster from a crumbling wall, and a great bone, bare and bleached.

She remembered the way the three had whispered together–planning this; the way the inexplicable hostility had given way to smiles; the latent cruelty in the way they had forced her to eat what she had wished to bring away. Who could have believed that there were people in the world so lacking in all feeling, so downright wicked as to have played this heartless trick on her? I did them no harm, she thought. And all at once she was crying.

Her life, pleasant compared with that of most slaves, and quiet, had for years been a hard one; she had suffered her share of aches and pains, but she came of a hardy stock, possessed of an animal-like patience and fortitude and she hadn't wept since she was a girl, taking the wilted flower from behind her ear, smelling the wasted scent on her palms, knowing that it was all useless. She had wept then, slow sensual tears. Now she wept tears of rage and disappointment, and guilt because she had eaten the dumpling, because she had let herself be deceived. Oh, how she longed to punish them all; not realising that she had done so; that the cook would lie down tonight counting days on her fingers, and the young girl wonder how she could bear many lovers when she loved but one, and the boy dream of the harsh fabrics, the discomforts, the rigours and dangers that made up a soldier's life.

She cried for some minutes, with harsh, angry-sounding snorts. Then she realised that the light was changing. Soon it would be dark.

The day was ending. What a wasted day. The night would come, and the morning; her master would come down from his tower and she would have nothing to offer him except the half-portion of a half-portion of bread and cheese–and they both seemed to have grown smaller while she was away. The thought brought her back to her ordinary dumb, doggedly enduring self. She mopped her eyes and blew her nose on one of her sleeves and asked herself–What can I do?

Outside, the pig also saw daylight declining and cried aloud his hunger and despair.

I shall kill the pig, Senya said to herself.

Never before, in all her years of servitude, had she acted in defiance of an order, even an unspoken one. Every time that she had mentioned the pig, during these hungry days, she had been inviting Melchior's order. It had not been given. That might be simply his usual dilatoriness about everyday things, or it might imply that for some obscure reason of his own he did not wish the pig to be slaughtered. But she intended to kill it. For many reasons.

One she recognised; plain sense; an unfed pig lost flesh.

Another she recognised; there was nothing else to eat; and it took some time to dress a pig carcass and make it fit for food.

Another she recognised; she now had fuel.

One reason, good and valid, she never even thought of. The feeling of fury, the desire for vengeance, had been building up in her ever since she opened that basket. Rage must be vented on something or somebody. The pig was the only available victim.

Savagely she sharpened the knife on the hearthstone.

A pig-killing is never a pleasant process; and when the butcher is an old woman, enfeebled by long malnutrition and already exhausted by effort and emotion, and the pig is young and lively and madly hungry, several macabre touches are added to what is at best a bloody business. But her mind was set, and she had him cornered at last and she cut his throat, slash, slash, slash, one for each of the people who had made a fool of her that day. Once it was done she was calm. Outside, in the pen where the pig had spent his short, hungry little life, she disembowelled him, carefully saving such of the offal as was edible. Then, as dusk fell, she dragged the body indoors and with one last expenditure of energy, managed to get it suspended from a hook. She added another root to the fire and set a pan of water to boil. Soon, slowly, because she was tired, but doggedly, she began to dress the carcass.

For Melchior, high in his tower, the time had passed unmarked. The sunset, pink and purple, golden and a clear cold green, spreading all over the sky to the west, brought him to his senses. This day was almost spent. And inside the tower the cold had clamped down again. The sky was still clear however.

He lit his brazier, not without difficulty. In his vague way, on the outer rim of his mind he had never ceased to wonder at the fact that Senya, in many ways so witless, could set flint to tinder and in almost no time have a fire going. Whereas he, who could, had he been asked, have explained exactly why flint struck on iron made a spark which lit the tinder, must strike twenty times. But in the end he had his fire, the twigs caught and he blew upon them, gently, and presently the charcoal caught and began to glow and give off a faint warmth.

He then took the water-jar from the basket, and opened the door to the little side chamber which was a stool room, with a chute which ran all the way down the side of the tower into a cess-pit at the bottom. He made use of it; then he poured water into a bowl which stood on a tripod, a bowl which even then would have commanded a good price and which presently was to be priceless, to him just a pretty, useful bowl, and carefully washed his hands. The used water he poured down the chute. Amongst all the other things which he must deal with tomorrow was the bringing up of at least two full jars of water so that the chute might be thoroughly flushed. Senya's awkwardness about the rope had somewhat defeated him there. Clever as she was at making fires and in other ways, she had never quite managed the business of sending up that extra jar of water that was needed. But no matter. If he had been right in his calculations, tomorrow he would be a free man, able to give his mind to things like flushing the chute and providing food for himself, Senya and the pig. He was not so stupid as not to have realised that Senya thought him foolish over the pig. He knew, very well, that a young pig must be fed, must be fattened all through the months until autumn when it would be fit to kill. But until this moment he had forseen a situation in which he might need another sheet of paper, and the pig was his one saleable asset. So he had been able to ignore Senya's hints, and the pig's squeals; for work came first, and he was prepared to say, 'Take the pig and sell it and bring me back a piece of paper or parchment whichever is handiest.'

He went back into the tower room and sat down by the brazier. He reached for the basket and found the bread and the cheese. More than he had expected to find. Enough for twenty-four hours, he had told himself, and here was enough for two days. The old woman's whining voice, talking about imminent starvation, came back into his mind. Women *worried* so, he thought. Food and fuel, the contents of the cooking pot–that was about as far as their minds could reach, poor creatures! And he felt a little guilty pang; he might have seemed oblivious to the plight in which he and Senya and the poor little pig were involved; but actually he was not. He'd seen this crisis coming quite a long time ago, and he knew how he must deal with it. Tomorrow or the next day he must go down to Pyangyong and offer to teach. To a man of his kind, after so many years of quiet, dedicated, study, of separation from the world, the idea was appalling, but he had faced it, and faced it now, without flinching.

He'd been, he realised, careless and remiss, especially lately, but he'd been absorbed. Tonight–unless his reckonings were very much amiss, and after a day's final, critical scrutiny he couldn't see how they could be–a comet would start on its elliptic course. Melchior's Comet. He had foretold it, on his charts; he had marked its probable course. And having seen it, having proved his worth as an astronomer, he would go down and hire himself out for regular salary; and old Senya could have her tea, her honey and flour and soya meal and everything else which he knew she had missed and craved.

Eating his meagre meal, slowly, fastidiously, he refused to think of himself, back in his old age in the crowded corridors, the packed halls of the university, facing all those lumpish young men, sent–as he himself had been sent–to get a smattering of learning. There might be one, just one, similar to himself, just one who cared for learning for its own sake, not as a means by which to gain respect from the vulgar, or to obtain a job. That one might be worth teaching.

Mumbling the stale bread, the hard cheese, he thought of that potential one and refused to think of the hundreds who had no wish to learn.

Then he took one mouthful, no more, of the rice wine, to clear the crumbs from his mouth. And he was ready. The sunset had died into a faint yellow line between the earth and the sky. Now, now, he thought, I am about to know whether I was right or wrong. He took his glass from the box and carefully climbed the steps of the ladder. For some reason always on the ladder, never on the stairs, he remembered that old men were prone to fall and their bones were brittle. One day he was going to think about this oddity, it had something to do with the solidity of what you climbed upon; on the stairs you didn't see how far away the earth was; climbing the ladder you were conscious of the floor. Also, of course, he must carry the precious glass as though it were his child, his son, his first-born. He mounted carefully, full of expectation.

When he descended he came down the ladder like a cat dislodged from a wall. It was black night except for the stars and a small pink glow from the brazier. He found a stump of candle, made a light, pulled his stool up to the bench, reached for the chart and his tools and set to work. He breathed in quick, shallow gasps and his heart thudded so heavily that the vibration shook his hands. He had been right; the sky had been pregnant, and it had brought forth, not the comet that he had expected, nor an ordinary star to add to the existing myriads. He had half foreseen, and then witnessed the birth of the star of stars. Now he must make certain adjustments to his chart and work out the full meaning of what even his cautious mind recognised as a phenomenon.

When he had finished, in the bitter cold hour before dawn, he said to himself–Greater than Alexander! And he thought–It may be that I am the only man alive who knows this, and if that is so . . . He straightened his bowed shoulders to take the weight of the enormous responsibility. The expression of awe upon his face gave way to one of determination.

He reached for a map and spread it. It was unsatisfactory; all maps were; too many blank spaces. It was curious that men had never yet succeeded in making maps of the solid earth–which could be walked upon and surveyed–anything like as complete and accurate as the charts which he and others had made of the unreachable sky. But no matter. There would be other maps, in other places. The one he held had been made on the assumption that Pyangyong was the centre of the world; map-makers in places blank on this map would have worked on some similar assumption; he would have to find his way as he moved.

Now he must think practically. Amusement brushed the surface of his mind as he remembered that on this day, just dawning, he had intended to be practical; had meant to go into Pyangyong and stick his head into the scholastic yoke and work for his keep, like an ox. There was a joke, one which it was unlikely that he would ever be able to share with anyone. For a moment the completeness of his loneliness appalled him. And so did his penury. He had no money, no friend from whom he could borrow.

But he had one asset, his tower. And for that there was only one potential buyer–the University of Pyangyong. He felt a momentary regret that he had not bothered to keep on good terms with the governing body of the University; he had refused, or neglected invitations to lecture to the students or to dine with the faculty. Still, what he was offering to sell was unique, they must realise that. If they failed to, if they hesitated or haggled he must sell it to a speculator, not for what it was, the best observatory in the world, but as a collection of stone from which many houses could be built, and a collection of glass, enough to glaze many window openings . . . but he hoped that it would not come to that.

Pushing away the distasteful thought he busied himself; he took his chart and the map, rolled them tightly and slipped them into a hollow bamboo case. He pushed those of his tools that he thought he might need into the loose front of his robe. Then, holding the tiny wafer of candle in his hand, he looked about the room in which he had spent his life, his youth, his energy. He never expected to see it again. He was, after all, seventy-five years old and he was setting out on a journey such as few men had ever faced. Destination unknown. There would be deserts and mountains and rivers; there might be wild animals, robbers, places where war was being waged. He thought of all the hazards and did not quail. Only one thing mattered, and that was that he should get there in time and tell what he knew, what the stars had told him.

From habit he closed the door carefully behind him and then hurried down the stairs.

The room at the bottom smelt of smouldering wood, and of an old woman who had not washed or changed her clothes since last summer, and of something else which he could not identify. Senya lay asleep by a fire; in better days, with fuel more plentiful, she had often scorched her outer clothing, but there was little danger of that now. Against the wall there was something pale, something that had not been there in the morning. He raised the dying candle and peered. Ah, the pig! Killed and dressed.

Even in his haste and excitement he had time to think how strange it was that she had known! When people lived in close company, as he and Senya had for so many years, it seemed that they developed a link–Greek expressed it best, telepathy. He had sometimes thought that this was a subject worth investigating. Once, up in the tower, he had been stricken with such pain in his back that he had only just managed to crawl downstairs, and when he reached the kitchen Senya had been brewing the stinking liniment that he needed. And another time, in Pyangyong, buying paper and ink he had suddenly thought–Salt! and had bought a block and carried it home and Senya had said, 'I needed salt, master.'

Now she had known, by that same peculiar means, that he was about to make a journey and would need food to take with him.

He roused her gently. Credulous people believed in dichotomy, soul and body; they believed that when a person slept the soul left the body and that if the body were too abruptly wakened the soul might not find its way back. Melchior held no beliefs of that kind, but he was not a man to scorn the beliefs of others, so he called her name, softly, then more loudly and only when she stirred and groaned did he put his hand on her shoulder and give her a little shake. She opened her eyes and said, in alarm:

'It is morning?'

'Very early morning. I see you have killed the pig.'

She gave him the lie which had come to her overnight, comforting, sleep-inducing.

'Master, the pig died. The pig died of hunger.'

'You had the good sense to dress it at once. It will be edible,' he said. And she saw that he was pleased that the pig was dead and ready to eat; she wished she had not lied about the manner of its death.

'I scalded and scraped it, master,' she said with eager servility. 'If you wish you can have liver for breakfast.'

He said, 'I have no time for breakfast. I must go into Pyangyong. But I should be very glad if you could cook some of the meat, cook it well, with salt, so that it keeps. I could take some on my journey.'

'Your journey? Master, what journey? To me you said nothing of a journey.'

'I knew nothing, until a little time ago. I must go now. I must be in Pyangyong early; to sell this tower and buy a camel.'

'A camel?' She had an irritating habit of picking a word from what he had said and repeating it. 'Master, where would you be going on a camel?'

'That I do not know. To the south-west. I shall learn as I go. Senya, I shall need my hat.'

It was so long since he had been out of doors and needed his hat that for a moment she stood, perplexed, saying the word 'hat' over and over. Then she remembered that she had put it carefully away, and went and fetched it, and offered it, respectfully. He set it on his head and it was incongruous wear with his soiled, faded robe, for it was a hat of quality, made of good felt, black, and lacquered all over to make it rainproof. She wished she had had more warning; he could have stayed in bed one day and she could have washed his robe.

'Now,' he said. 'I don't know how long this business will take. I shall be back as soon as possible. Meanwhile, cook some of the meat, cook it hard, with plenty of salt, so that it travels well.'

He stepped into the morning air, which though cold seemed a trifle less so than yesterday's.

'And if you need fuel,' he said, astounding her, 'there is a fence around the pig-pen, and as there is now no pig, it may be burned.'

She realised that she herself would have gone past the pen a hundred times and never thought of that.

Then, picking over all that he had said in so short a time, she recalled that he had said he intended to sell the tower. *And what is to happen to me?* I'm old and feeble, nobody would give a handful of meal for me. I'm old, I'm useless, my ears buzz and if I stoop I fall down; I am of less worth than a worn-out donkey. The tower is my home. When it is sold I shall be homeless, after all these years. The thought was all the more shocking because she had never, in all her life, given her personal future so much as a glance; well-born families such as Melchior's never discarded their slaves, however old and tiresome they might become; broken in body and sometimes of mind the old creatures squatted about, certain of their rice bowl and a spare-rib to gnaw on.

I shall starve to death, out in the open, like a dog with no owner, she thought; and again she wept.

Weeping she tugged up the stakes of the fence and made the best fire the little kitchen had seen for years; weeping she hacked away at the pig's carcass, choosing all the best pieces for him to take with him. The salt of her tears fell into the brine as she cooked. Yet she cooked carefully. He might be planning to abandon her, but he was her master still, and her beloved. He'd ignored what she had offered, so shyly, so passionately, all those years ago; he'd ignored her warnings; though courteous always he had ignored her warnings; and now he was about to ignore her plight; but that made no difference.

It was after midday when he came back, riding on a camel. Not a good one. A single glance from her smoke-reddened, tear-blurred eyes told her that. It was an old camel, with a hard life behind it. He would have done better to let her do the buying; but then how could she? Yesterday she had been unable to even reach the village, she could not today have walked to Pyangyong.

He was pleased with his camel, and with all his other arrangements. And he had not forgotten her.

'I realised,' he said gravely, 'that this had been your home for many years, Senya; so I included you in the contract. You are to be the caretaker.

Students will come and go, because this is now the chief observatory in Pyangyong, and so long as you feel able to stay here and keep the place tidy, you are the caretaker. But you are also a free woman; and when you no longer wish to work you will receive a pension–enough to live upon. You do understand me, Senya?'

She began to weep again and to thank him; but he cut her short.

'Is the meat ready?'

'It is cooked, but still hot. Master, you are not leaving *now*! The light is fading; soon it will be night.'

'I intend,' he said, 'to travel much by night. And I must leave at once.'

'But why? Why is there such haste?'

'Because of what I know. I fear that only I know this thing. There is a warning to be given. And not a moment to waste.'

She packed as much of the still-warm, greasy meat as she could cram into two of the reed baskets, and then went out and helped Melchior to attach them and the bamboo chart case to the camel. Then she stood back.

Now all was done; the last service rendered. The heart which she had thought broken on summer evenings long ago, broke anew.

Something of her dumb misery made itself known to Melchior.

He said, 'You have served me so well, Senya, that I never missed the others. I think I shall call this camel by your name.'

The misery was not eased; he tried again.

'You will be safe and comfortable. I put it all in writing. You are a free woman and will be paid for what you do here; and when you can no longer do it, you will still be paid. You understand?'

She took his hand and bowed over it.

'May all the gods and the spirits of your ancestors and of mine, have you in safe-keeping, wherever you go, my master.'

He looked at her, seeing her properly for the first time now that he was unlikely ever to see her again. Poor old woman; poor faithful old woman, grown grey and bent in his service. He stooped and for a second laid his cheek against hers. A gesture of love.

At last! she thought, and felt repaid for everything.

PART THREE

BETHPHAGE

15 furlongs

The relatives to whom Anne had referred with pride, Mary's cousin Elisabeth and her husband, a temple priest, lived in a hill village within walking distance of Jerusalem; and there Elisabeth had made a garden which was justly famous. Elisabeth herself, by nature a woman somewhat silent and reserved, warmed when speaking of her flowers and herbs, her fruit and vegetables. She would say that the garden was her own creation; and that was true. Just over forty years earlier, when she had come, a bride of seventeen, to this house the ground around it had been an unsightly waste, its thin soil trodden hard over the stones that lay near the surface, and nothing grew except a few tough weeds. Former occupants of the house had used the space as a drying ground for linen and a place to throw rubbish.

She had begun to work on the garden immediately after her arrival, for then she found time heavy on her hands. She had been the eldest daughter of a large family, always busy. Now, with Zacharias so often absent on his temple duties, she was much alone with little to do. She was not the kind of woman to make friends quickly.

Zacharias in his spare time had helped to clear away the rubbish and to remove the largest of the stones and to dig a little. He was a leisurely mover and teased her about the haste with which she worked herself. Gardens, he said, weren't made in a year. She was too reserved and shy to tell him that she wanted all the heavy work done in a month or two because she hoped soon to be in a condition which would render digging and stone-hauling unwise. As she worked she often thought to herself–Next year! She saw a plump healthy baby lying on a mat in the shade, then taking a few tottering steps.

But at the year's end she was still able to work; to gather basketfuls of stones and take them out and throw them amongst others on the hillside and then refill the baskets with the fine silty soil which the rain washed down from the hills. She had planted trees, a fig tree near the house door, almond, apricot and plum and apple trees along her boundary; young trees that would grow as the child grew. For she was certain of a child next year.

So year had succeeded year and hope had died a long-drawn-out death. By this time she knew her neighbours and had more than once heard women with several children mourn a new pregnancy. 'Another mouth to feed,' they said. Once, when her herb garden was well established and known, a woman had come to her and after some half-sentences and evasions had voiced an inquiry and a request. 'There are seven already and my man is poor; how shall we manage?' Elisabeth, explaining with some embarrassment, that she had nothing of that kind in her garden, had thought how inexplicable, how seemingly unjust God was. An eighth child to a woman already over-burdened, and her own arms still empty.

The woman had found what she sought and almost died of the bitter brew and that child was never born.

Nobody, not even Zacharias, had ever heard Elisabeth repine. Only her garden knew how often, coming back from the well or from the market, she would walk with rapid, agitated steps and wring her hands and cry, 'God, my God, why? What have I done? What has he, your servant, done that we should be cursed?' The flowers had held their innocent faces towards her, offered their perfume for comfort. Very slowly, grudgingly she had abandoned hope, and, without realising it, had allowed the garden to fill the empty place in her life. In some ways it was like a child; it needed constant attention; it progressed in little steps; it was something that she had made. In hot dry summers she would go twice, three times to the well; on the much-travelled road into Jerusalem she would gather dung. The garden flourished and was beautiful; even the fence that divided it from the road was a thing of beauty, thickly covered with morning glories, so gloriously blue, and thicket roses, coloured like a summer sunset. And all within the fence, the flower-beds, the herb patches, the vegetable strips were neat and tended and precise, the living embroidery which she had worked upon the stony hillside.

And it had been, appropriately, in the garden that the miracle had happened. It had been an autumn evening, mild and mellow, and she had been gathering fallen leaves and heaping them in a corner where through the winter they would rot into the cool, dark substance which in the early summer of next year, spread around the roots of trees and flowers, would help to prevent the soil from drying out.

Zacharias had come to her there, looking, as he always did after his spells of duty in the Temple, pale and tired. She had risen, rubbing her hands together and said:

'Supper is ready.'

And he'd mouthed at her, his lips moving but making no sound. He used his hands, touching his lips, beckoning her into the house.

She thought–He's had a seizure! And a great weight of guilt fell upon her. She hadn't valued Zacharias as he should have been valued. She'd thought always about the child, and then she had transferred her attention to the garden, not realising that despite all she had been singularly blessed, having a good husband.

'You're sick,' she said. But he shook his head and would not take the arm she offered to help him into the house. And she, watching him, saw that he walked as usual, if anything more vigorously.

'What is it?' she asked, and he shook his head and smiled.

Inside the house he had gone straight to his own special table, taken up a waxed tablet and his stylus and written something and held it out to her. She could read a little. Early in their marriage, sensing her unspoken discontent, he had taught her to read, even to write a few words. But her heart had never been with her studies, and his vague hope of turning her into another Anne, a woman he knew, childless, a widow, but happy because she was studious, had been defeated. Still, Elisabeth could read, and having read what he had written, and re-read it, in case she had made a mistake, she had looked at him and said:

'Can you hear? Nod, if you can.'

He had nodded.

She said. 'It is impossible. I am too old.'

He snatched back the tablet and wrote, 'Remember Sarah.'

She said, 'Yes, I remember Sarah, but that was all long ago, in the days of the Patriarchs. Nothing like that could happen *now*.'

She was expressing the feeling of many Jews of her time; the age of miracles was past.

Zacharias wrote again. 'Great things impend. This child will be the forerunner.'

She read the words and looked at him a little fearfully. Except for her barrenness they had been a happy couple, but there were great tracts of his mind, even of his life which she could never hope to understand. He was a priest; he was allowed by right to enter the inner court of the Temple where no lay person could go; he was deeply religious, almost a mystic.

She asked, 'How do you know?'

Bit by bit, writing brief, succinct sentences, he told her how, in the middle of his duties at the altar, he had seen an angel, Gabriel, who had said that their prayers were to be answered and that she would bear a son, to be called John; a very special child who was to prepare the way for the Messiah.

'And I was struck dumb,' the last sentence read.

Her fear and her uneasiness grew. One did not contradict one's husband; one did not argue with a priest of God. But she was unable to rid herself of the thought that he had been taken ill–visions often accompanied illnesses.

'Otherwise are you well?' she asked.

He nodded and wrote, 'I am happy. You?'

'Yes,' she said, untruthfully, 'I am happy.' In truth she was puzzled, incredulous, miserable about her incredulity and worried about him. All that evening she fussed over him, treating him as she would treat a man who had had some severe physical shock. When, just before bedtime, she presented him with a steaming bowl of her famous herb brew which her neighbours had come to regard as a panacea for anything short of a broken limb he had broken into silent laughter, and reaching for his writing tablet, wrote:

'I am not sick. I am to be dumb until the child is born. Punishment for disbelief. Be warned!'

It was the first time in over forty years of married life that he had ever shown any sign of levity, and that, somehow, increased her uneasiness.

Long after he was asleep she lay by his side and thought it all over and asked herself–How shall I know? In her child-bearing days a woman's life was ruled by the moon. A disturbance, an interruption could be noticed, interpreted with joy or with dismay. She knew; there was no woman in the world, she thought, who had more closely checked her reckonings. A day's delay and she had hoped . . . But it was a full ten years since the moon's courses and hers had ceased to be connected. Ten years ago since she had, at last, abandoned all hope. And Zacharias' admonition to remember Sarah had a peculiar sting. For quite a few months she *had* remembered Sarah with whom it had ceased to be after the manner of women, and she envied that long dead woman very greatly. But ten years . . .

Zacharias remained dumb and Elisabeth remained dubious. But changes came, things the most realistic and incredulous of women could hardly overlook. Her skin regained its lost bloom, her hair its lustre; the early-morning nausea made itself felt. And her body, like a ripening fruit, began to swell.

One day she could say to Zacharias, without any reserve at all, 'It is true!'

And on his tablet he wrote, 'I told you!'

She was unthinkably happy, but embarrassed, too–and there again, ashamed of her embarrassment as she had been of her disbelief. Women always pretended that they could not reckon, but they were sharp enough where another woman's age was concerned. There wasn't a woman at the well or in the market who wouldn't know that Elisabeth, the wife of Zacharias, was fifty-seven years old, and even if she could bring herself to tell them the truth, was there one who would believe it? Not one. They'd look on her as a poor self-deluded creature, afflicted with one of those slowly killing growths in the womb, pretending to believe that she was with child. The herbs she grew and the draughts she made from them had brought her into contact with many people, sick of mind or body and she knew about the fantasies such people wove. She hated the thought of such a fantasy being attributed to her.

So she had refused to leave her house. Zacharias had written his protests and she had said, 'When the child is born, I will go out with it in my arms, or ask them in to see.'

Everyone in the village knew that Zacharias had lost his power of speech and imagined that this fact had so upset Elisabeth that she was unable to go to the well or to market. A girl, extravagantly rewarded for such service, delivered water daily and Zacharias bought everything that was needed in the markets of Jerusalem. That Elisabeth's distaste for going out and exposing her state was no mere whim had been proved to him by her attitude to her cousin Mary's wedding. It was due to take place when Elisabeth was in her eighth month; a good time, really, all the early inconveniences and dangers over and done with, and a pregnant woman, moving slowly, commanding deference, could take, amongst friends and relatives, her rightful, proud place.

But Elisabeth had said, 'I cannot go. I love my cousin Mary, and if I could see her alone I would gladly go. But there's Anne–imagine how she would look at me; and there'll be women of my age trying to arrange marriages for their grand-daughters. Zacharias, I could not face it. Please, write and say that your duties at the Temple will prevent us from attending.'

He had intended to write, but he had never been obliged to do so, for in Elisabeth's sixth month, Mary's wedding date still two months away, they had had word that Mary was already married. Rabbi had communicated with Rabbi, link by link, a chain that reached over the eighty intervening miles, and Zacharias and Elisabeth were in due time informed that to suit Joseph's convenience, the marriage had been put forward by two months. It had therefore been a small wedding, and had lasted only one day.

Elisabeth was relieved, and yet concerned. It sounded as though Mary, that sweet, gentle creature, might have chosen a selfish man. After all, a girl's wedding day was her one great day; and she shouldn't be cheated of it to suit the bridegroom's convenience. If a man had never given the woman he chose any consideration and meant never to give her any, he usually allowed her that one great day, thinking nothing of his own convenience.

'I hope she will be happy,' Elisabeth said, looking back over her own marriage which, apart from that one lack, had been so very happy. 'We must send her our gift.'

They'd spent time and thought on it; nothing of wood, Mary was marrying, they knew, a carpenter, so she would be well supplied with anything in that line; and Elisabeth, though she had not seen her Aunt Anne for some years, knew that anything practical, linen, blankets, bowls, could be counted upon to come from her.

'She's very fond of lilies,' Elisabeth said. 'And I will send her a dozen good bulbs; but from us there should be something more.'

She knew that with Zacharias in regular employment and–as in Nazareth they would still think–childless, something generous would be expected of them. And one day, without warning, Zacharias, setting down the stores he had carried, and smiling, showed her the exact thing. It was a coin, known as a rose jekkal, the rarest and most valuable coin in the world. Not only for its worth, for its beauty. On one side, not imprinted but embossed, there was a full-blown rose, exact, even to a thorn; on the other there were symbols, words perhaps, in a language nobody could read. For the rose jekkals came from far, far away and if four of them reached Jerusalem in a single year, that was the most. They were eagerly sought after and the woman who could hang a rose jekkal amongst the coins of her head-dress was a proud woman indeed.

Zacharias held the lovely coin on his palm and invited her approval; dumbly, like a trained hound.

Elisabeth said, 'For Mary?' and he nodded.

She said, 'It is beautiful; and, with the lily bulbs, a fine gift. How clever of you. Where did you find it?'

He wrote on the tablet which he now always carried.

'At the money-changer's stall.'

It was just right; a thing of beauty, a thing of value, a suitable accompaniment to the lily bulbs. And yet, Elisabeth thought, turning to the hearth, not right, in some mysterious way. Mary, as she remembered her, had such a lovely brow, so calm and smooth, with the hair growing back from it in such a pretty way. For some reason it was difficult to imagine Mary, the young Mary, with the usual coin collection dangling between the curve of her eyebrows and the curve of her hair. It would seem a deformity.

Nonsense, nonsense, Elisabeth told herself. Mary, like every other married woman, would now begin to make the collection of coins for the head-dress which constituted in fact, every respectable family's nest-egg. And Mary, who loved even the wild cornflower, would love the rose.

Lifting the pot from the hearth, she said, 'We must find a trustworthy messenger to carry it.' And she said again that it had been clever of him to obtain it. She said, 'If I thought I could get in and out of Nazareth without seeing Anne, who, though she is my aunt, is younger than I, I would take it myself. I think that Mary is the one woman in the world whom I could tell, and be at ease with.'

Zacharias wrote on his tablet, 'Go.' He was sure that she had only to cross the threshold and she would be released. It was said–though he'd never tested the theory, that one could confine a hen by drawing a chalk circle; and there were times when Elisabeth, in her present state, seemed to him to be similarly confined by a barrier of which only she was aware.

While the subject was still under discussion they received a letter, written in a large, squarish hand and in the black graphite with which carpenters marked measurements on rough boards. The journey had smudged it but it was legible. It said, simply, 'My name is Joseph, Mary my wife, who is your cousin, would like to visit you. Friends leave for Jerusalem on the twelfth day of the month and she could come with them.' The bearer of the letter, a pedlar, in Jerusalem to stock up with what he called 'pretty things' said that he was intending to return to Galilee and would carry their reply. Zacharias wrote that Mary would be most welcome.

Elisabeth, though delighted at the prospect of seeing Mary and having her under her roof, was perturbed again. In the first months of one's marriage, if it were a happy one, one did not give much thought to cousins, or propose an eighty-mile journey in order to visit them. She remembered how, last time they met, at the wedding of another cousin, her Uncle Joachim had said that when Mary was old enough to marry he hoped it would be to someone she *liked*. Elisabeth, a conventional woman, could see an element of danger there; girls so often liked men for all the wrong reasons. How, at the age of sixteen or seventeen, if properly reared, could they know anything about men, know what to look for and what to avoid? Such things were better left to parents who had some standard judgement, some experience, and cool heads. Mary might have made a mistake, been misled by good looks or a persuasive tongue.

And yet the letter had something frank and straightforward about it; and would a selfish man–and such the wedding arrangements had indicated Joseph to be–have written at all, been willing so soon to spare his bride from his bed and his hearth?

She turned the letter about as though it might have some hidden information to offer; and in a way it had, for it was written upon the back of a draft obviously from the skilled hand of an architect; the plan of a large house, almost a mansion, and in the lower left-hand corner were the words–'House of Nathaniel in Cana'. A possible explanation occurred to her; Cana was seven miles from Nazareth, and if Joseph were working under pressure he would not get home until well after dark, on some nights perhaps not at all. He might have qualms about leaving Mary alone. Mary might not wish to be left alone. Against the explanation must be set the fact that Mary's parents were in the village. . . .

Well, she must wait; when Mary came she would tell her everything, no doubt, for despite the disparity in their ages on the few occasions when they had met they had always been congenial.

The family with whom Mary was travelling as far as Jerusalem was on its way to attend a Bar-mitzvah of a young relative there, and they were very merry. The weather was fine and warm, not yet the blistering heat of high summer; in the fields the crops were ripening, poppies and cornflowers abounded, vetches and honeysuckles threw their tendrils over every fence and post. The father of the family had made this journey several times before and knew many short-cuts, through fields and by-ways, and Mary was always glad to leave the highroad where sights, distressing to her, were to be seen.

After Gibeon, however, they kept to the road and joined up with other foot-travellers, for the hills were full of robbers, apt to attack any small party.

There was so much chatter and laughter that there was little chance to think much. A mile short of the city their ways parted. The head of the family issued a hearty invitation to her to enter the city with them and partake of the hospitality in this relative's house–everybody was welcome on such occasions; and it was a shame–he said–to be so near and miss a chance of seeing Jerusalem. But she was anxious to see Elisabeth, and anxious to be alone. So, thanking him, she said that she could see the city under Zacharias' guidance almost any day. And when they had made certain that she had only a short distance to go, and that over a safe road, they left her.

It was now seven weeks since the angel had visited her and they had been seven weeks of unreality and confusion. The wedding, so hastily arranged, yet, in Anne's capable hands, so correct; a girl's great day; to her part of a waking dream. Clad in her grandmother's beautiful gown, receiving compliments and good wishes and gifts, she had felt utterly detached from it all. She thought of women she knew–some of them women to whom marriage had brought little happiness–who cherished some trinket or piece of clothing, whose worn faces would brighten, whose harsh voices would soften as they said, 'I wrote it at my wedding.' Yet here she was, with as much reason to be glad and grateful that she was being married as any woman ever had, looking at the smiling, friendly faces and thinking–If only you knew!

She'd looked at Joseph, too–the one person who did know–and saw with consternation how he had changed in a handful of hours. He'd always worn his years lightly, taking few things seriously except his work, and her; he'd always worn a cheerful, care-free look, in accord with his roving, foot-free life; it had been so easy to visualise him shouldering his tools and going off to see what the next place had to offer. That was all gone now; and his new air of responsibility which would have been right and only slightly touching in a young man just embarking upon the serious step of marriage, in him was very touching, giving him an elderly, almost a troubled look. She made up her mind to be the best possible wife, always cheerful, patient and kind; she would love him forever and try to make up . . . Her thought jolted to a standstill. Make up for what? Being chosen by God?

And so it had gone on.

Rachel, with the lazy Joshua astride her hip, had offered her a present, a handsome oil-jar. 'I'll hope you'll be very happy, Mary,' she said, and all her willing could not prevent her voice from revealing her doubt that any woman could be really happy in marriage. Then, in a different tone, she had added, 'And I hope you'll have a boy, like this, but less lazy.'

And Mary had thought, dizzily–Suppose I said that I knew I should have a son, and that he will be the Messiah. Rachel would recoil, and probably be so shocked she'd drop Joshua.

The grooms lifted and carried her to her new home; and she thought–You little know whom you are carrying beside me! And there the ritual vase, the symbol of virginity, was broken, and the feast began. Joseph had cleared the workshop for the purpose, and Anne, loudly complaining that she had had time to do nothing, had done marvels. There was wine which Joachim had been saving for the wedding, and Joseph also had a jar; he gave it a peculiar look as he produced it, saying that it was not quite full . . . as though that mattered!

The feast had been very merry; most of the guests lived lives on or only just above subsistence level and were as much exhilarated by the food as by the wine, though there was plenty of that, the company being so much smaller than it would have been if held on the appointed day. (Years later, she was to remember this, to think–There was plenty of wine at my wedding, and out of kindly pity for the embarrassment of a family less well-provided, make a suggestion that was to result in what was to be known as the first miracle.)

Then it was dusk; there were children to put to bed, animals to feed, hens to shut up against the prowling foxes. The company began to disperse. Anne threw her arms about her daughter in one last, protective gesture; from this hour on the kindness and the chiding and the sheltering care must come from another, from this fellow who, in Anne's view, suddenly seemed quite incapable of taking her place as Mary's guardian. She said, 'My dear, I wish you every joy,' and then, hearing and despising the tremor in her voice, said sturdily and rather crossly, 'It has been a pleasant day. But there should have been three!'

The age-old feud between the loving mother and the husband had claimed another victim.

Joachim, very slightly inebriated–and why not? It was, after all, his daughter's wedding–sobered up suddenly and took Joseph by the shoulder and said in a voice not completely void of menace:

'Use her gently. You understand me?'

'I do indeed,' Joseph said. And he thought–That is the final irony; if only he knew!

Quiet had fallen upon the little house, and on the workshop, littered with the remains of the wedding feast.

Watching her own hands as though they were those of another woman, Mary had lighted, in her own house, her own lamp.

Joseph said, 'What a day this must have been for you!'

'And for you,' she said.

And he had thought, God is not blind. Far better me than some untried, amorous boy.

He said, 'I shall sleep in the shop. I've slept in many worse places. You take the bed and I hope you sleep well.'

She'd reached out and taken one of his big work-hardened hands in hers.

'Joseph, this was not of my choice. It happened. It happened to us both.'

'Yes,' he said. 'It happened.' Something almost like resentment tinged his voice as he thought of what the present moment might have been, but for what had happened. Hard on them both.

'It happened,' he repeated, 'and we have to take it as it is. You don't look to me as though you've slept much these last two nights. Try to sleep now. This is God's doing and we must leave the outcome in His hands.'

She said impulsively, 'I know why you were chosen, Joseph! You're the best man in the world.'

He said, 'No. I reckon I just happened to be handy.' He shouldn't have said that, he knew as soon as he had said it, and made a clumsy attempt at a joke. 'Praising myself! It's the best thing you can say of a carpenter–he's a handy man.'

In the morning the struggle between the real and the unreal tilted a little. She was in her own house, using her own bowls and knife and spoons, taking bread from her own crock and making Joseph his piece to take with him to eat at midday. He went off to work and presently Rachel called for her to go to the spring. She was grateful to Rachel for having broken through the rule about married women walking with married women; she dreaded their eyes, their sly questions. They knew, or pretended to know, many signs which told whether a marriage had been successfully consummated or not. Rachel said, 'Are you happy?' and she said, wholeheartedly:

'Very happy. I have a good man.' And there was that thought again–If only you knew how good.

Leah and Susannah joined them and chatted girlishly about the wedding; and suddenly, there with her friends, on the familiar path she was overwhelmed by loneliness. She thought with longing of Elisabeth and wished with all her heart that she lived nearer.

Towards evening, making a meal with which to greet Joseph on his return, things seemed ordinary again and continued so until, in the middle of eating, Joseph said:

'Mary, I've been thinking, on and off all day. What are we going to tell people? And when?'

'I don't know? I wanted you to believe me, and you did. Beyond that I haven't thought. But I suppose we must . . .' She shrank from the thought of the disbelief, the jeers, even from the commotion that would be aroused by those who did believe. Almost sternly she said, 'It is the truth. And it is something that concerns every Jew.'

'Every Jew,' Joseph agreed quickly, '*and a lot of others as well.*'

'What others?'

'Herod for one.' As he spoke the name of the King, far away in Jerusalem, she realised how narrow her own imaginative view had been; limited to Nazareth, to–to be honest–the women by the spring.

'I thought of him on my way to work this morning. He's got less right to the throne he sits on than I have; and he knows that. I can't imagine he'd dance for joy to hear that the promised heir to David's throne will be born in nine months' time.'

'That is true–but I should never have thought of it.'

You could see why a child–even such a child as this–needed a father and a mother; this was the kind of thing that men thought of, and women did not.

'There's another thing, too, the Romans. I know our beliefs mean nothing to them, but they'd see danger. The Jews aren't all that settled yet. Start a story of Messiah about to be born and the national feeling would stir. The Romans know that, and they'd stop at nothing to forestall it. This is something we should take into account, Mary. They, or Herod, might easily do you an injury. Herod is a master-hand at arranging accidents for people he wants out of the way. And there is yet another thing. . . .' There was the faint hesitation, the near-embarrassment with which she was to become so familiar. 'Nothing you were told sounded as though we were to go shouting from the house-tops.'

'No,' she said slowly, thinking back. 'That is true.'

'Then why not wait,' he said, rather as though they had been arguing. 'Once he's born he'll be the Son of God. How he'll be born or what we should expect is a mystery to me, but once he's born, God will take care of him, or perhaps he'll be born able to take care of himself. It's you I'm concerned with now, and I can see danger for you. Silence may be part of the plan. After all, you didn't go running to tell your mother, did you? You came to me. And now I have this feeling . . .'

She said, 'I should be glad to tell nobody. It's such a very difficult thing to put into words.'

He nodded. 'I know. With most situations there's some guide, other people have been the same way and left their tracks. We're in a situation nobody has ever been in before. We have no guide. I think it would be wise to say nothing until we have some sign.'

'Unless,' she said, 'I should see Elisabeth. I might not even have to tell her; she might know. Gabriel told me about her, he may have told her about me.'

He was amazed, as he was to be again and again by the simple, matter-of-fact way in which she spoke of the archangel–as though he were a neighbour, not the awesome, shining presence from the thought of which his own mind shied away.

He said, 'Yes, it is a pity she doesn't live nearer.' And there the conversation ended for the moment. Into his mind, though, had flashed the thought of how lonely she must be with a secret of such magnitude that he had urged her not to share with anyone. It was different for him. He had his work, his work-mates. Now that the anxiety that had been with him all day was allayed he knew that there would be hours on end when he would not give the matter a thought.

But the thought of her loneliness, brief though it was, had dropped a seed which rooted and grew, and one day–again as he ate his supper, he said:

'How would you like to go and visit Elisabeth?'

She said, 'I would like it very much. But how can I? Who would look after you?'

'That same stout fellow who's looked after me since I was so high,' he said, measuring a height from the floor. 'Joseph, the carpenter.'

She laughed. 'You couldn't be in better hands. But think of my mother; all her plans for the wedding spoiled because you didn't like coming home to a dead hearth; and then, in a few weeks I go gadding off to make a visit.'

'My fault,' he said. 'I underestimated–a thing that has brought many good carpenters to ruin. You could tell your mother, and anyone else who was interested, that we're now working such long hours that it would be better for me to sleep on the site. The masons have reared a good lodge and they'd admit me, I'm a craftsman. I've only made that trudge in order that you shouldn't be in the house alone. . . .'

'Is that true?'

'In part; for your mother, wholly.'

'Then she'll suggest that I go back home.'

'Not if I have made other arrangements. And I have. I've been keeping my ears open. Joel and all his family are off to Jerusalem very soon. You could travel with them. Suppose I wrote to–what is his name?'

'Zacharias.'

'To Zacharias, and made all the arrangements? Then you could go to your mother and say Joseph has done this and that and she will not question it. Would you like that?'

'More than anything in the world. . . .' And then she realised. What a cruel, what a dreadful thing to have said. There were forms of brutality that had nothing to do with sticks or goads.

'I didn't mean that the way it sounded,' she said. 'I love you, as no woman has ever loved a man before–not having the reason for love that I have. But as we are . . . and if you are sure that in the masons' lodge you will eat well . . .'

'Masons,' he said, 'eat like kings, every day. So much building is going forward that when they contract they can stipulate two meat meals every day. Shall I write the letter?'

'If you would. If you are sure. . . . You see, you know, you believe, and you understand; but there are times when a woman needs another woman; and Elisabeth is the only one, the only one to whom I could talk.'

'I'll write it now,' he said.

So now, here she was, within sight of Elisabeth's garden which she had never seen, but recognised from descriptions given by various members of the family and, more modestly, by Elisabeth on the rare occasions when they had met and sat and talked together, quietly in the midst of hubbub. That a miracle should have happened to Elisabeth was not in the least surprising to Mary; Elisabeth was a rare person; she had borne that curse of a Jewish woman, childlessness, with great gallantry, without a complaint, without jealousy of luckier women. She'd endured loneliness–his Temple duties often kept Zacharias away from home for two or three days together; and out of her frustration and solitude she had made beauty on a bare hillside.

As Mary walked, swiftly now, eager for their meeting, towards the place of colour and perfume that was Elisabeth's garden, she saw her cousin emerge from the house door, empty a bowl at the foot of a tree and then stoop and straighten up with a bunch of yellow flowers, marigolds, in her hand. And it was true, Elisabeth, in the fifty-seventh year of her age, was heavily pregnant.

She had never doubted it; Gabriel had told her and she had believed, just as she had believed what he had said about her own state; but there was a difference, a very great difference, between believing in your mind and seeing with your eyes.

She hurried forward, calling her cousin by name and Elisabeth, on her way back into the house, halted and turned and came to open the gate in the flowery fence.

'Mary!' she said; and Mary said:

'Oh, how I have longed to see you!'

They were about to embrace and then Elisabeth took a step backwards and turned pale and sweat sprang out, like beads on her brow and upper lip.

'*You!*' she said. 'You, Mary! *You* are to be the mother of the Lord to whom my son is to be the forerunner. You, blessed above all women.'

Mary said, 'You did not know?'

'Until this moment, no. But the child did. It leapt as I spoke your name. So late and never a movement, I was worried. But he leapt, recognising you and the child you are to bear.'

'Gabriel did not tell you?'

'I never saw him. He appeared to Zacharias, in the Temple. He was dumb-struck, and dumb he has been ever since. Did you . . . did you see him, Mary?'

'Yes. He told me about you.'

'The chosen, the blessed one,' Elisabeth said. And because ordinary words were too ordinary, too worn to be used at this moment, there in the flowery garden they broke into one of those antiphonal chants of the kind which from time immemorial their race had used as a vehicle for praising God. Chanting and extempore song-making came easily to Jews in emotional moments. Deborah, in song, had celebrated the defeat of Sisera; David, in song, had lamented the death of Jonathan.

'Blessed is she that believed,' chanted Elisabeth; and Mary sang: 'My soul doth magnify the Lord . . .'

The meeting set the tone for the whole visit. For two happy months Mary lived in an atmosphere of understanding and acceptance so complete that on one occasion she brought herself to mention to Zacharias some of those prophecies that caused her such foreboding.

Zacharias reached for his tablet and wrote, 'He shall see of the travail of his soul and be satisfied, it is written. You too.'

Elisabeth read the words aloud, and added, 'John may have a hard life, also. The path of the forerunner is never easy.'

They agreed that all that they could do was to ensure the children a happy childhood, to rear them to be strong. They were oddly in accord in never doubting that to begin with, at least, these would be ordinary human babies. Without realising it they were thus rejecting the pagan ideas that had come to Israel with the Seleucid invaders, stories of gods and goddesses born in some supernatural way, springing to birth full-grown, armed, with winged feet and similar fantasies.

In Mary's company Elisabeth's reserve and fear of ridicule or pity disappeared completely; she moved about the village again and allowed Zacharias to write letters announcing her news. Two female relatives offered to come and tend her in childbed.

'They are experienced; and it would be more seemly,' she said to Mary, almost apologetically, for it meant that Mary's room would be needed.

'I must go home,' Mary said. 'Joseph will need me. The house at Cana should be near completion, now.'

Zacharias, inquiring round through another priest, found a group of pilgrims to Jerusalem, about to return to Galilee; and with them Mary walked home, knowing that the first thing she must do would be to tell her mother that she would have a child in mid-winter.

Anne's feelings–greatly to her own surprise–were divided. She was delighted with the news, delighted at the prospect of becoming a grandmother; to her delight she gave loud and repeated expression; but she also thought–Poor Mary, so soon! She'll hardly be accustomed to being a wife before she'll be a mother, hardly be used to managing a house before being called upon to manage a child as well. And all the natural fears that women have when told such news by their daughters rushed uppermost, exaggerated in her case by her protectiveness towards this child of hers who was so unlike her; not very robust, too sensitive. These feelings took expression in a great outpouring of advice, some sensible, some sheer superstition. She also said, again and again, how fortunate it was that they lived so close to one another; 'I'll look after you,' she said.

The visit to Elisabeth had bridged for Mary the gulf between the real and what seemed unreal. She knew now; and to her mother and her friends she no longer felt the impulse to say–If only you knew! She could think of the day when they *would* know; when what had been revealed to her would be revealed to them. And she turned upon them the smile that was to embrace the world.

CHAPTER FOUR

JEXAL

700 miles

Every time that Gaspar rode into his city with its towers and its arches and its tinkling fountains something happened between his shoulder-blades, a prickling uneasiness, as though he were a dog whose hackles were rising. Always, somewhere between the Gate of the Rose and the Fountain of the Maidens, he would turn to Kalim, or whoever rode on his right, and make some remark. 'Jexal looks well today,' or 'How it stinks, this place,' or 'Still standing, I see.' Such words would bring him reassurance; it *was* his city, the heart-beat centre of the region he had won by his sword.

He never thought of it as his home; if he lived here and ruled for sixty years, and went out and came in again every day of those sixty years, it would never be, he knew, with any sense of home-coming. In the desert three black huts, a few hobbled camels, a dung fire smoking into the evening air never failed to move him with the sense that he was rejoining his own; to a lesser degree he could feel it in the grasslands, where a huddle of clay huts stood by a patch of bean and rye, and there was the smell of sheep and dog barking. In the city he would always be a stranger. Its people had accepted him with despicable alacrity, had settled down, were smiling and placating; the city itself stayed inimical.

On this morning, at the usual place, he turned to Kalim and said, 'Our city has put out the banners!' It was true; in the ten days of their absence the place had burst into bloom; trusses of flowers, pink and purple, blue and white and yellow, hung over every balcony, sprawled over every wall. In the open spaces around the fountains the trees had shaken out their green.

He had heard people say that it was the most beautiful city in the world. It was immensely old, and for the last thousand years had been very rich. The soft-living, careless people had planted trees and flowers, had reared beautiful buildings, made fountains, when, in Gaspar's opinion, they would have been better employed in looking to their defences and bringing up their boys to be hardy and brave. He'd watched the city for a long while before he finally moved against it; more than once he had entered it on foot and mingled with its people in the streets and markets. They were arrogant in their assurance; buying and selling, eating and drinking and making merry was all that mattered to them.

When, at dawn on a summer morning, now almost four years ago, he and his Five Hundred had swept in, the city had been taken as easily as a peach from a tree.

Kalim, in answer to his remark, smiled, showing his splendid teeth, and said:

'Very gay banners.'

Gaspar returned the smile with a ferocious scowl.

'You're riding behind me again! How many times must I tell you that I want none of that nonsense?'

Any hint of the formality that hedged kings about roused the same uneasiness in him that the city inspired. He was the leader of the Five Hundred; that he could accept, it was a right he had won, being able to out-ride, out-fight, out-wit and, if necessary, out-fast them all. He expected loyalty and demanded obedience, but lately they had tried to give him more. There'd even been a suggestion that he should wear the crown and call himself King–and that suggestion had not come from the city people, but from the members of the Five Hundred. The idea filled him with horror which was almost superstitious. The city rot setting in, he thought.

To Kalim he now said:

'Nine times out of ten the man who rides second is plotting against the one ahead!'

'That I should live to hear you say that to me!' Kalim exclaimed. Then he mastered his rage and said, 'I'll tell you something, Gaspar: you're becoming a fearful man.' It was, and he knew it, about as insulting a thing as one member of the Five Hundred could say to another. He hastened to explain. 'Fearful not of hurt or of death, but like a child in the dark, fearful of what is not there!'

'What I fear is there, Kalim; I know its face, I know its name. Anything, anything that could tend to make us like them!'

He jerked his thumb towards a group of Jexalians, out for the first time in their summer clothes, standing idly admiring the prismatic colours made by the sunshine in the spray of the fountain.

'You're still upset about Lakma,' Kalim said shrewdly.

Gaspar turned in his saddle and looked towards the last riders in the group.

'Upset? Not any longer. I've settled him. I hope,' he gave a rueful grin, 'that I've settled that for good and all. I have only ten fingers; Lakma broke one for me.'

'You broke his head,' Kalim said dryly.

Gaspar allowed himself a more wholehearted grin as he remembered how, three months earlier, Lakma, one of the Five Hundred and a man of mature age, not a silly boy to be easily persuaded, easily forgiven, had wanted to marry, to take as his legal wife, a girl of the city, a daughter of the defeated ruling family, a princess. 'You want to *marry* such rubbish!' Gaspar had said, in horrified astonishment. 'Take her, use her, such women were made for use; but to stand up in the sun's eye and mingle your blood with her dregs! Man, have you thought? If you do that, and she bears a boy, he will be entitled to your place in the Five Hundred, to your horse and your sword. A half-breed, with soft straight legs and black eyes!' Nothing more scornful could be said of any man's potential offspring; the race of which the Five Hundred was at once the remnant and the flower had eyes as blue as a summer sky, and believed that boy babies were born with bowed legs, ready shaped to a horse's barrel.

'That I will not take, even from you,' Lakma said.

'It is a truth that I will not withdraw.'

'Then we fight,' Lakma said, leaning upon his immemorial rights.

'The weapons to be of your choosing,' Gaspar agreed.

They could fight it out on horseback, using staves or swords, or on foot, barehanded. Lakma had chosen a mounted contest with staves, and he approached the conflict with a divided mind. If he won he must be prepared to accept the duties and responsibilities of leadership, a daunting thought; on the other hand the girl, very young, very appealing in her dark, exotic way, had fired his blood. As soon as the fight had begun he had no time for thought at all, for Gaspar had fought like a madman; his place as leader was at stake, and so was something, to him equally important–the absolute necessity of preserving, pure and untainted, the blood of his people.

In the end Lakma had taken the crack on the head which had dismounted him, and it was some days before he was in a fit state to speak the ritual words, 'You are right. I apologise.' Gaspar had relented then, and the errand from which they were now returning had been taken for Lakma's benefit. A small party of them, led by Gaspar, who always took advantage of any excuse to get out of Jexal, had ridden into the desert and hunted until they found four black tents by a spring of water that sprang from an outcrop of rock and then ran away and was lost; and in the tents there were three females, not yet mated. 'Take your pick,' Gaspar had said, Lakma had chosen the youngest, the most comely, and together they had stood in the Sun's eye at midday, he had slashed his wrist, the girl's father had slashed hers, their blood had been mingled and the marriage was made. A sheep had been killed and roasted, and at the feast Lakma had professed himself well pleased with his bride. They were bringing her back now and within a year, with any luck, she'd bear him a son, with blue eyes and red hair, and before he could walk he would be riding on a sheep's back, getting ready to be a horseman, in time to be one of the Five Hundred.

Now they were clattering across the bridge, so rightly called the Golden Bridge, for, though nobody thought of it nowadays, it was to this bridge across the tumbling river that the city owed its origin and prosperity. The bridge made possible the continuation of the trade route towards the East, to the fabled lands of India and Cathay. Once a simple, serviceable structure of stone it had been many times enlarged and beautified. This morning the water swollen by the melting of the snow in the mountains was emerald green, marbled with white foam.

'Lakma,' Kalim said with a pretence of resuming a conversation, 'left marriage too late. Whims multiply with the years.'

Gaspar's scowl returned. He knew what *that* meant. And in his heart he admitted the rightness of it; it was ridiculous that he should go about arranging marriages for other men and remaining celibate himself. But marriage demanded intimacy, and he had never attained that, even with his men, even with his grandfather who had reared him. For as long as he could remember he had been self-contained, self-possessed. The idea of going, unclothed, unarmed and submitting himself, even for the briefest space, to the embrace of another human being was repulsive to him. Yet, paradoxically, he regretted not having a son. If now he ever saw a woman whom he *could* marry–and he simply could not imagine what kind of creature she would be–and she bore him a son, the boy would be handicapped by his youth in comparison with the sons of other members of the Five Hundred; be he never so hardy and bold and worthy of leadership, it would take him years to attain it.

He said, 'Kalim, when you find me entertaining a whim, tell me; in blunt terms. Then *you* can break my finger and I'll break your head, if I can.'

Kalim gave a little snort of laughter. *That* was what gave Gaspar such an ascendancy, not only over the bodies of the Five Hundred but over their minds as well. He always saw through what was said to what was meant; he always went straight to the point and he never lacked an answer. Even when he was old and feeble–and let that day be long deferred–he would be a man to be reckoned with.

They were now approaching the Palace, an ornate building to which successive kings of Jexal had made additions and alterations. Three hundred years earlier, Alexander had marched through Jexal on his way to India and the Jexalians, following their established policy, had welcomed him. The then reigning king had arranged for one of his sons to go to Greece, 'to learn the ways of the West', and that young man, when he returned had set his mark on the Palace, and to less degree on the city.

Gaspar hated the Palace more than he hated the city; it provoked in him, in exaggerated form, the same uneasiness. For more than a year after his conquest he had slept in one of his people's felt huts, reared in the Palace gardens, and he would have been sleeping there still but for a rumour that had reached him. The people of Jexal were saying that he dared not sleep in the Palace because he was afraid of the spirits of the old kings. On the night of the day when that rumour reached him he had moved into the Palace and slept in the vast bed, all golden posts and silken hangings, in which the last king of Jexal had slept on the night that had ended with a bloody dawn. He'd slept there alone, lying down as he always did in his tent, wearing his leather breeches and with his sword to hand. With the doors wide open and the window unshuttered it had not been too unbearable, had not inflicted too great an outrage upon his distaste for houses, his dread of being shut in.

In former days one wing of the Palace had housed Palace officials; there were hardly any left now and the apartments were occupied by members of the Five Hundred who were unmarried, or whose wives were amenable to communal life. Some women had preferred houses of their own and they had had wide choice of the splendid establishments formerly occupied by Jexalian grandees.

Another wing had been given over to administrative offices. Gaspar had reduced officials to the minimum, he had seen no reason why a man who checked the market dues shouldn't pour himself a glass of wine when he wanted one, or why customs officers needed uniformed public servants to help them on with their shoes. The administrative service was now much depleted and about three times as efficient as it had been.

One official Gaspar had retained. He had been known as the Grand Vizier, and he was still the Vizier, but no longer Grand. He was fat and flabby, as all officials–indeed most Jexalians past first youth–tended to be, but he had his wits about him. He'd been cunning enough to hide himself well away when the city was sacked, and sensible enough to appear before Gaspar wearing a plain brown woollen robe, and lucky enough to speak the tongue of the ordinary people who had dealings with the country dwellers. True he spoke it with a lisping refinement, but it was understandable; and what he said made sense. He had said, 'Lord, you have taken this city. Fifty miles down the river stand the ruins of a city similarly taken when my grandfather's grandfather was a young man. Trade died there and the people perished or fled. A few goats now graze there amongst the fallen stones.'

'I know it. I have camped there.'

'A city lives by its trade,' the Vizier said. 'And trade needs men who can read and write and keep accounts and make visitors feel welcome and safe. Fighting men are not shaped for such work.'

That was true, Gaspar reflected. And although he hated the city and all its ways, he had taken it, he knew, because he wanted it. As it was, rich and prosperous. Who wanted to be master of a mass of deserted ruins? What he wanted, he realised, was an ideal city, rich and prosperous, lively and flourishing, but not soft and decadent. So there and then he and the Vizier had made their bargain, and it had worked out very well; the Vizier had traded in his former grandeur and its accompanying insecurity for a less obvious but far more real power and Gaspar had, here and there, abrogated part of his authority, saying, 'Maybe you know best about that.' Jexal had continued to flourish.

In former days whenever the King of Jexal had moved in or out of the Palace there had been a great commotion; trumpeters had blown upon their silver trumpets, attendants had stood, evenly matched on each side of the twelve shallow steps. Gaspar had done away with all that. The small cavalcade clattered into the space between the fountains and the serried cypresses flanking the Palace steps and Gaspar swung himself from the saddle and left his horse to the boy who had come running. The others, reining in, prepared to disperse. Gaspar waited until Lakma, with the girl uncomfortably perched on the saddle before him, drew level, and then put his hand on the man's knee. 'I wish you joy,' he said, and turned, and began to mount the Palace steps which were so shallow that any active man must take them three at a time.

His Vizier was waiting for him, ready to report upon what had happened in the departments for which he was responsible during the last ten days. None of it was important. He had never been able to rid his manner of servility, but at least he had learned to stand upright and speak like a man, and not to keep saying 'Lord'. He ended his account by saying:

'Benjamin, the carpet merchant arrived yesterday. Is it your wish to ask him to supper?'

Gaspar brightened. He liked the old Jew who visited Jexal every second year with a long train of handsome mules and went away laden with the choicest products of Jexal's looms. On Benjamin's former visit he had been scornful of the Vizier's suggestion that he should receive the old man. 'A carpet pedlar!' he had exclaimed.

'He buys our best,' the Vizier had explained. 'He is a man of substance, noted for his honesty. He is also a speaker of tongues and a great carrier of news. As you say, a carpet pedlar, but an aristocrat of pedlars.'

'That would be something to see!' Gaspar had said. 'Ask him to supper.' They'd had much interesting conversation then, and he now looked forward to another. But two years! How fast time flew in a place where it was reckoned; in the desert, with little to mark one day from another, it had moved slowly.

'And, Lord, there is one other thing,' the Vizier said.

'Yes?' He spoke sharply, knowing that nowadays the Vizier only used the honorific term when broaching matters of importance–in his own eyes at least.

'The boy, Malchus, very humbly asks if you could spare him a moment of your precious time.'

'Malchus?' For a second Gaspar was at a loss; then he remembered. The old king had had several wives and the youngest of them, when the city was raided, had hidden herself and her two children; they had remained in hiding for a week, and when they were discovered the blood-lust had been appeased. The girl, Ilya, had been twelve or thirteen then, the boy some two years younger, and Gaspar had said, more in contempt than charity, 'I don't make war on children!' And *that*, he now reflected sourly, had cost him the use of a finger, for it was the girl, Ilya, whom that fool Lakma had wanted to marry.

'What does he want with me? If my memory serves I told his mother to apprentice him to a useful trade.'

'She did so,' the Vizier said in a voice carefully void of all expression. He could remember the two beautiful, pampered children, their old father's darlings, petted by competitive courtiers and officials, Prince Malchus and Princess Ilya. . . . Four years ago, and in another world. 'He works as a smith. He chose that, being fond of horses.'

'Very sensible. And what does he want from me? Permission to set up his own business?'

How he bristles, the Vizier thought, at any mention or reminder of the old days in Jexal.

'He did not state his business. Today is the spring Festival of the Horse, and although it is no longer a public holiday–by your command–the smithies are idle. So he came and I allowed him to wait and said that I would tell you he was here.'

'I'll see him,' Gaspar said. 'In the Balcony Room.'

It was the only place in the whole huge Palace in which he felt moderately at ease, and that was because, strictly speaking it was not a room at all; it was a bulge in the corridor which led to the private royal apartments. Once, more than five hundred years earlier, a Queen of Jexal had paused there, looked through the lacy marble of the wall and seen beyond the cypresses and the flowers of the garden and the green river tumbling down. It was, she had declared, the best view obtainable from the whole Palace. Her doting husband had had the wall removed, the floor extended, so that she might the better enjoy her view. The doted-upon Queen and the King who had doted upon her were long since dead and forgotten; for many of their successors the balcony had been only a draughty place, to be hurried through, between the public audience chambers and the private rooms; but Gaspar had seized upon it as a place where he could feel moderately at ease and not suffer the shut in, stifled feeling that the rest of the Palace inflicted.

The boy, Malchus, came in and Gaspar looked at him with interest and curiosity and distaste and grudging admiration, all mixed. Fourteen? Fifteen at most, but with none of the awkwardness of the boy-meets-man stage. He was roughly, even poorly clad in a tunic of undyed homespun, now a trifle tight; his shoes were such as only the poorest wore in Jexal, that prosperous city, wooden slabs shaped to the foot and held in place by a thong which passed the great toe and its neighbour and tied about the ankle. And at the end of his thin boy's arms his hands hung, disproportionately large, coarse, scarred, ingrained with black that no amount of washing would remove. Yet he seemed quite at ease . . . at home. At home! Gaspar thrust that thought away, but with a commentary; he always felt at home in a felt tent, he'd been born in one; this boy had been born here, so naturally . . .

'Well,' he asked harshly, 'what do you want with me?'

Malchus said, 'I was advised not to say "Lord" to you or to use any other term of respect. So please do not attribute the omission to incivility.'

'What do you want?'

'I wish to call your attention to the plight of my sister Ilya.'

'I know all about her. She's given me quite a lot of trouble. Lakma, one of my men, wanted to marry her. I made him think better of it.'

'Yes,' the boy said. 'That is why I am here. Ilya is now almost seventeen years old; she is very beautiful. It is time she was married.'

'Marry her off, then.'

'That is easily *said*. My ambitions for her are, I assure you, moderate. Our nobles fell in the battle. Lesser men, but rich enough to keep her in comfort, many look upon her lustfully, but they avoid us, partly through fear of how you might regard their linking themselves to the royal house. I had one hope, which your man Lakma seemed about to fulfil.'

'And I prevented him.'

'You did. Could you tell me why?'

'I don't hold with mixed marriages.'

'Have you ever thought about them, coolly, without prejudice?' the boy asked. 'Believe me, I have not come here to anger you. You rule, we obey; but this is one city, it cannot for ever be occupied by two peoples. Marriages would weld them into one.' Then, while Gaspar was thinking of some retort that would suitably express his anger at this audacity, Malchus said quickly, 'Not that I ever thought Lakma a fit match for my sister. It would be much more suitable if you yourself married her. As Queen my sister would command the loyalty of all our people.'

Gaspar glared at him. The audacious young cub! He wanted to stamp, to shout, to laugh and jeer; but there was something about the boy's manner, so matter-of-fact, so fundamentally dignified, that he checked himself, gripping his hands, hurting the stiff, ill-set finger.

'The loyalty of your people?' he said sneeringly. 'And what's that worth? Didn't I win it between dawn and midday?'

'The loyalty of fear,' Malchus said. 'There is another. The loyalty of the heart.'

'And *that* made a brave show, didn't it–when we rode in?'

'More than three thousand died.'

'So they did. Like sheep, running this way and that.'

'Taken unawares,' the boy said hardily. 'For a thousand years my people had been here, living in peace in this valley, cultivating the arts and the skills that can only flourish in peace. That is true, you know. *Your* women can do no more than to tread wool into felt; they never have time enough, or peace enough, to set up a loom.'

That was truth and Gaspar faced it with distaste; but, skirting round the situation in his mind as once he had skirted around Jexal on his horse, he hit upon the boy's vulnerable spot.

'We're barbarians,' he admitted. 'And now I'll ask you something. Where's this loyalty of the heart you talk about? You would wish to marry your sister, first to Lakma, then to me. By the sun, if I had a sister I'd slit her throat sooner than see her give a cup of water to those who had killed one of her kin!'

'That,' Malchus said, 'I do not doubt; but then–Lord, you said it yourself. You are a barbarian.'

'And I rule here,' Gaspar said. 'Do you realise that for that saucy remark I could have your head?'

'My head,' the boy said, 'you are welcome to. For a long time it has been nothing but a nuisance to me! If you want to see me quake, threaten my hands!' He held them out as he spoke, unsightly with their callouses, a half-healed blister, but steady. Gaspar had a fleeting doubt whether he, unarmed and helpless in the presence of an all-powerful enemy, would have been so steady. To make up for that doubt he spoke with increased gruffness.

'I want neither your head, your hands, nor your sister, boy.'

'Have you ever seen her?' Malchus asked. Before Gaspar could snap out his answer, no and he had no wish to do so, the boy turned, gracefully, without haste and called, 'Ilya.' Evidently a prearranged signal, for immediately from between the pillars that separated the balcony room from the inner corridor the girl came forward.

Gaspar's idea about what made a woman desirable were based upon strictly practical considerations. A marriageable girl should be young, upright and strong, equally ready for child-birth or hard work; she should bear the signs of health on her skin and hair, she must be one of his own race. That her demeanour should be modest and her attitude meek was taken for granted; all decent parents saw to that.

In no way did this girl, born a Princess, conform to these standards. She was pale, with the pallor of an indoor life, of careful protection from wind and weather; this, and her huge, artificially darkened eyes, gave her a look of ill-health; she was very slim, almost frail, with delicate wrists and ankles, narrow hands and feet. Her black hair, exactly like her brother's, clung in little lustrous curls to her head. Gaspar's sharp eye noticed even that her ears had been pierced for the wearing of ornaments, but she wore none; and her dress, something the colour of the water of the river just below the balcony, though of silk, was worn, in places mended. A fine wife she'd make, he thought contemptuously, visualising her carrying and hauling, drawing water, collecting dung for the fire, grinding corn and cooking, all without interrupting the process of breeding and bearing. What in the world had got into Lakma? he wondered. Then the girl looked him straight in the eyes and he wondered no more. . . .

His first reaction was one of genuine shock and horror. If his sword had broken in his hand at a critical moment, or his horse had failed to obey the pressure of his knees, or as he set down a cup he had drained to the dregs he realised that he had been poisoned, he could not have felt more sharply the sense of having been betrayed. He'd just looked at her, asking himself what such a woman would be good for, and she had looked at him and given the answer. Made for delight! The very marrow of his bones moved and melted as he thought of the form that delight would take.

'Go now,' Malchus said, as though aware that his object in producing her had been achieved.

'You go, too! Get out my sight,' Gaspar said, trusting that the shortness of his breath would be attributed to wrath. The boy stood his ground.

'You see, she is beautiful; and she is ripe for marriage. She had been well reared; but now the jewels that she and my mother had on them at the time of our ruin have all been sold. I earn little. *What will her future be?*'

'That,' Gaspar said, 'is hardly my concern.' He was so angry, with himself, with the boy, with the girl, with the Vizier who must have connived, that he could hardly think of anything sufficiently spiteful to say. But he did his best. 'Lakma is safely married, now,' he said. 'Maybe in six months' time he could take her as his concubine.'

'Sooner than that I would kill her.' He gave Gaspar a steady look, and now the man could see the likeness between brother and sister; in the hair, the shape of the skull, the way they held their heads. A look of race, unmistakable in man or beast.

'Have I your leave to go?' Malchus asked.

'Just a minute. You . . . you work as a smith, don't you? What about *your* future? Have you ever considered joining the army?'

He had reorganised the remnant of the Jexalian army, taken away most of its privileges and trappings and officered it with his own young men who were waiting their time to be admitted into the ranks of the Five Hundred. It was now fairly efficient and growing more so every day; and he was always careful to have some part of it well to the fore when he entertained travellers or emissaries from other places. Let nobody go away with false ideas; he had taken Jexal because he was the leader of the finest fighting force in the world, and because Jexal had been ready for the taking. Nobody was going to take it from him.

'It is my intention to become a soldier as soon as I am old enough. Sons of your men are admitted when they are fourteen; the rule is that a Jexalian born must be sixteen.'

'And how old are you?'

'Fifteen.'

'Well,' Gaspar said, with sudden geniality, 'we'll make an exception in your case. I'll give the word and if you present yourself tomorrow you will be accepted. Soldiers earn more than smiths–so you'll be able to look after your sister.'

Why had he added that?

'I am indeed most grateful,' the boy said, without looking grateful at all; and Gaspar knew that nothing he did, nothing would inspire true gratitude in this cub; if he fetched out the crown and set it on his head, and bowed his own head and kissed his hand, he'd take it as no more than his just due. Such a boy could be dangerous; he must be watched!

'We don't play at soldiers, now,' he said. 'You must work hard. I shall keep my eye on you. You may go.'

'I thank you. I shall work hard,' the boy said. He turned and walked away, unhurriedly and with a lithe grace. Somewhere in the corridor he called, 'Ilya, where are you?' and it struck Gaspar that the words were an echo of words spoken only four years ago, but in fact unimaginably far away, the words of two children, silk-clad and carefree, playing in the long corridor of the Palace that was their home. Getting fanciful, he told himself scornfully.

It was a relief at the end of the day to sit down to supper with Benjamin, the old Jew who bought and sold carpets.

In the old days, if the Vizier was to be believed, supper in the Palace had occupied the whole evening and lasted far into the night. It had been a social occasion, a nightly feast, with many guests and three or four times as much food cooked as could possibly be eaten. Gaspar and his Five Hundred had come straight from a life where they thought themselves lucky if in the morning they could place slices of tough raw meat under their saddles and at the day's end remove it, flattened and softened in fibre, and find fuel enough to char it black on the outside. Often enough they had eaten it raw, tasting of leather and horses' sweat. Bread had been a luxury, so had any vegetable or fruit.

From such a life they had plunged, in a single day, to life in this city, which straddling the trade routes from East to West, offered every delicacy known to man. A wide belt about the city itself was devoted to market gardens, to farms where pigs grew fat and calves were bred to be eaten young. There were imports, too; fruits from plants too delicate to flourish even in this sheltered valley, and fish, not the well-nigh indestructible salted and smoked fish which was a rare luxury in the desert, but fresh fish, reared in great pools on the fish farms, and other fish, cunningly preserved in oil and spices, brought from far places. There was even one delicacy, fish eggs in oil, sealed into jars, that came, by painful stages, from some unknown place in the north.

For a time they had all eaten gluttonously: and if they had simply been sacking the city and intending to move on, gluttony would have been in order, even a duty, since a man should build up reserves when he could, against the hungry days, as a camel did, or a fat-tailed sheep. But they were not passing through; they were here to establish themselves, and very soon Gaspar, in whom the desert-bred respect for food was lively, had issued orders. Nowadays, even in the Palace, one main dish was served, fish or flesh or fowl, with all the bread, cheese or fruit that a man needed to attain the full-fed feeling. The horde of master cooks in the kitchens, mourning the waste of their acquired skills in rearing airy towers of spun sugar, the moulding of marzipan into flowers and animals, the making of small many-coloured cakes that melted on the tongue, had been set to useful tasks, often menial. And in the Great Hall where parasitic officials had feasted Gaspar sat down to eat with those of the Five Hundred who had no homes of their own, or preferred the company of their fellows, and any chance-comer upon whose right to be there Gaspar and the Vizier were agreed.

There had been a time when visitors showed obvious signs of nervousness. Jexal had been taken by barbarians and in many people's minds barbarianism and cannibalism and reasonless killing were closely associated. But gradually the word had spread, the new régime was different, definitely uncouth, but it was disciplined; and Gaspar was not a bad fellow; difficult to talk to, being ignorant of Greek which Alexander's short-lived Empire had made almost a universal language.

On this evening, because, despite his embargo on the many public holidays, people were still celebrating, in a muted way, the Festival of the Horse, none of the Five Hundred was present and Gaspar and his guest sat down alone; not in the Balcony Room which would ordinarily have been Gaspar's choice were the company to number less than ten, but in a small room, on the ground floor, handy for the kitchens. The Balcony Room, his chosen refuge in this place, had been spoiled for him by the morning's experience.

The old Jew, who had washed his hands and his feet in an ante-room, gave his ritual greeting, 'Peace be on this house.'

'Peace be upon you and yours,' Gaspar responded. It was curious, he thought, how, from the very first, he had felt an affinity with this old man who came from the West, who was a trader. It had been partly explained when, during their first meeting, the old man had said that his people had once, long ago, been a desert people; and they had taken a city called Jericho in very much the same way as Gaspar had taken Jexal. Another partial explanation lay in the fact that Benjamin reminded Gaspar of his grandfather, though there was no physical resemblance between that fierce old warrior, lean and leathery, all scarred from his many battles, and the plump, peaceable Jew. Yet there was a likeness; perhaps it lay in the fact that both men gave the impression that they had lived long, seen many things and been little impressed. And there was the similarity of greeting and leave-taking. True, Benjamin said, 'Peace be upon this house,' and Gaspar's grandfather said 'upon this tent', never having seen a house; but the intent was the same. And the ritual reply was identical.

'And now,' Gaspar said when the mutton and rice had been served. 'What is the news in the world?'

Benjamin had learned, on his previous visit, how limited Gaspar's knowledge was. Tell him now, for instance, about the increasing size and importance of the port of Caesarea–a thing of great importance to one who regularly shipped cargoes of carpets and rugs to Rome and a dozen other places, and what would it mean to Gaspar who had never seen the sea or a ship? He considered and discarded several things and then said:

'The news that most closely concerns me is a plague that has broken out amongst the slaves in Tyre. They are the ones who fish out the murex, from which the purple dye is made; and they have died more quickly than they can be replaced. So for a year or two there will be a great shortage of the true purple colour.'

'Our carpets then, already dyed, should increase in value,' Gaspar said, and was instantly ashamed. City talk. Tradesmen's talk!

'That is so,' the Jew agreed placidly, 'and today, in my buying, I took that into account. I paid more for any carpet with purple in it; and I warned your people of the shortage.'

Gaspar narrowed his eyes. 'Now why should you do that? They couldn't know. They'd have sold at the old price.'

'God would know,' the old man said, simply. 'And the man who profits by another's ignorance can not lie down at peace with his God.'

Possibly in its far distant and now-no-more-than-legendary homeland Gaspar's peoples had had gods, religious beliefs and ceremonies, but if so they had been left there, with everything else that could not be carried on horseback or travel on its own legs. All that remained to them as drought after drought had forced them to move farther and farther to the south-west, was a primitive kind of sun worship, strictly practical in its purposes. It was convenient to have some form of ritual to mark a permanent marriage from a passing association; it was convenient to know that when a man said, 'I swear by the sun . . .' what he said thereafter was likely to be the truth. There was no mysticism about it; nobody imagined that the sun had any interest in him or demanded anything from him. They kept one festival, on the day when the sun stood highest in the sky and meat was plentiful, since that was the time when young bull calves and rams were ready to be eaten, must indeed be weeded out to prevent over-grazing. Gaspar was about as far from understanding what Benjamin meant when he said 'God' as any man could be. He remembered that on his former visit, telling stirring tales about famous men of his race, the old Jew had several times mentioned God and some completely unbelievable things that he was supposed to have done.

They talked of other things and then Benjamin, looking grave and leaning a little forward, asked:

'Are Pella's activities known to you, or am I the first to bring the news?'

'Pella,' Gaspar repeated, knitting his brows. 'Who is he?'

'From what I hear, he claims to be a son of the old King of Jexal. There was a son, I remember, who got on very badly with his father and went to live in Armenia. That would be almost twelve years ago now. I have no liking for carrying bad news, but I thought a word of warning wouldn't come amiss.'

'A son of the King lives here, in Jexal. He was in this place this morning. He's no threat to me, so why should I be warned against one in Armenia?'

'Ah, but he is no longer there, or so they say. He is in Rome, trying to interest Caesar Augustus in his cause.'

'His cause?'

'His claim to the throne, *here*.'

Gaspar knew Caesar Augustus by name; he ruled in some place half a world away, separated from Jexal by deserts, by mountains and seas and dozens of other kingdoms; and he had won his right to rule by his sword, just as Gaspar had won his. So much he knew from talking to travellers, and that was the sum of his knowledge. He was not perturbed, but he was puzzled.

'What does it matter to the King of Rome who rules in Jexal?'

'Nothing. But that is the way the Romans work. They seize upon someone else's quarrel and march in to restore order, as they call it. They did it in my country. Order they restored, but not the ruling house. They set up a puppet king, Herod of Idumea, who is not even a Jew. Worse, he is not even a good man.'

'And you really think it likely that they would come *here*?'

'Who am I to say? Their decisions are unpredictable, their methods are not. They reach out and establish themselves and then they build a road to link the new possession with the old. And this I have noticed; Augustus sees himself as a second and greater Alexander; Alexander moved to the East; it seems to me not unlikely that Augustus should turn his eyes this way.'

Gaspar made a grunting sound. 'This needs thinking about.'

'It does. In your place I should think of it often and heavily,' the old Jew said, gravely; he liked this strange young man, this barbarian with whom from the first he had felt at ease. The next remark must be worded carefully, he thought. 'In Roman eyes Pella's claim is legitimate enough to justify action on their part–if they wish to take action. Of course, there is another possibility. . . .'

'And that is?'

'Something else I have seen done. An emissary may come to you, secretly, and suggest that you pay tribute; a ten per cent levy on all the goods that pass your custom houses. Then, if you agree to pay, you are Rome's friend, and Pella will one day be fished out of the Tiber. Body of a man unknown.'

'And we,' Gaspar exploded, 'who fight hand to hand and would never betray those who had eaten our salt, are called barbarians!'

'My people,' Benjamin said, 'were once equally scrupulous. There was a woman called Jael who killed, with her own hands, the leader of an invading force. It was a laudable action, but she is not reckoned amongst our noble women; it is held against her that she had first fed him.'

'In many ways your people and mine sound somewhat akin,' Gaspar said. 'Tell me, how do your people accept the rule of Rome?'

Like all really pious Jews Benjamin tended to overlook the vast numbers of his countrymen who had settled down under Roman rule and concentrated rather upon the few who were rebellious, the guerillas in the hills who still actively carried on the war, the civilians who thought up cunning ways to avoid taxes. Unwittingly he painted for Gaspar an entirely false picture, leaving him with the impression that Rome's hold on Palestine was infirm and feeble compared with his hold upon Jexal. By the end of the evening the conscientious old Jew realised this and tried to give his host some idea of the strength and magnitude of Rome, but it was like warning a child who had never seen water except in a jar or a goatskin against the danger of drowning. Gaspar simply did not understand. And somehow Benjamin let slip the fact that in Jerusalem six hundred legionaries were stationed. Gaspar said:

'There are Five Hundred of us. The Jexalians had an army of seven thousand.' And it was all very well to say that Rome was different. How different? And why? This man was a simple soldier from the desert, with no more imagination than the table on which he leaned his elbow, no more comprehension of politics than he had of mathematics–and five hundred seemed to be the limit of his reckoning.

The time for parting came. Benjamin said, 'I thank you for your hospitality. Peace be on this house.'

Gaspar said, 'Go in safety, and return soon. In my tent you are always welcome.'

He realised that his tongue had slipped and smiled, waving his hand. 'My tent!' he said.

Soon after he went to his bed and slept and dreamed that a thing, brute-face and very hairy, but recognisable to him in some mysterious fashion as Pella, was about to rape the girl called Ilya and that he was going to her aid, with his knife in his hand, but someone from behind hit him, a sharp chopping blow on the wrist and his knife had fallen to the floor and the noise of its falling had wakened him, short of breath and sweating at every pore.

After that she had haunted his dreams. Most often she was in some distressful situation from which, always impotently, he tried to save her; sometimes the situation was reversed; at such times most commonly he was dying of thirst and she, ploughing her way through the sand, was bringing him water. She'd stumble and spill it, or she'd reach him and the cup, the jar, the gourd she carried would be empty, or full of something undrinkable, horse's urine, mud, chaff, a crumpled silk scarf which he desperately pulled out, yards and yards and yards of it.

He never mentioned his dreams to anyone–to whom could he mention them? Outwardly life went on. He issued an order that he had been meditating for a long time. All the beggars in the city were to be rounded up, confined in one place and given one good meal a day. He'd hated the sight of them himself and he had seen them through the eyes of visitors, a blot, a scar.

The Vizier said, 'But if it is known that we *feed* beggars they will flock in, from Babylon, from Samarkand.'

'Not on *my* terms,' Gaspar said, 'when I say beggars I mean those incapable of making a living; the blind, crippled and witless. Any able-bodied fellow who wishes to eat the bread of idleness can be *made* blind, crippled or witless.'

So beggars had ceased to infest the streets and there were less than twenty in the asylum he had provided.

He had issued another order, too. Anybody coming into Jexal from the West was to be brought to the Palace and interrogated. He always asked about the Romans, and so far he had learned nothing more than Benjamin had told him; Pella's name had never been mentioned.

To the Vizier Gasper had mentioned Pella, introducing the subject by demanding why he had never been informed of the man's existence.

'Because, to us, he is no longer alive. Ten, twelve years ago, he took his portion and went away, for ever. Not only is his name never to be mentioned; in the book of records it was blotted out; it is as though he had never been born.'

'Why?'

'He was . . .' the Vizier hesitated, choosing his words carefully. 'I will not say a bad *man*, but a bad Jexalian, and a bad son and a bad prince. Always he was in opposition to his father and his family, so much so that if his father said, "It is a fine day", he would say, "Not so!" He gathered about him a few of the same mind, young men who could not agree with their elders. Then there came the time when it is necessary that he should marry and beget an heir. Since he was so high,' the Vizier measured the height from the floor, 'he has been promised as husband to a princess whose people have been our friends always. Peace and much trade had resulted from that promise. But will he marry her? No, he will not. He has fallen in love,' the Vizier's voice was edged with scorn, 'with a woman in the market, a woman who sold doves for the temples; she was a widow. On his knees his father beseeches him, saying marry the one you are promised to and beget a son, that is all I ask; the market woman can be your concubine. But that does not suit Prince Pella. . . .' The Vizier's face turned pale and sweat shone on his brow. 'If my old master could hear me, he would have my head for that! No, that does not suit him. It is his wish, his intent, to bring the market widow, the dove-seller, into the Palace and make her Queen, crowned with his mother's crown. The result of this you can imagine. Every well-born lady in Jexal insulted; the King whose daughter has been passed over, ready to make war; the market people insufferable from pride. Not to be contemplated. So he is given his portion, he announces publicly that he is no longer prince, or heir, or any connection with the ruling house and he goes. To Armenia, it is said.'

Gaspar listened to this sorry little story with a sneaking feeling of admiration for Pella, a man of some spirit, he thought, not a Jexalian at all.

'Suppose,' he said, 'just *suppose*, that he came back, with an army behind him, to claim what he claimed to be his right.'

'He renounced all rights. Between the dove-seller and Jexal he chose once and forever.'

'So you said. But if it came to choosing between him and me; what then?'

'You,' the Vizier said, 'valued Jexal enough to fight for it; he flung it away like a worn out shoe. Also, there is this to be said . . . You said I was always to speak the truth to you, and the truth now I dare to speak. We are subject to you and to your Five Hundred, but with you we feel safe. When the battle was over it was over, some lost their positions, some their mansions, but our lives are safe. With Pella nobody would be safe. He gave up Jexal once for a market woman; he would give it again to the foreign army that re-established him. He was a man of no judgement. May I ask . . . is it likely that we must make this choice? Has he, in the face of all that he vowed, some plan to return?'

'Not that I know of. I was talking idly. And still talking idly, I ask this. If Pella should ever come, the boy Malchus, the girl Ilya, where would they stand?'

'Against him, whatever that involved,' the Vizier said promptly. 'He and his mother and the two princes who were killed did everything in their power to make life miserable for the young wife and her children. Malchus, I assure you, has no ambitions; except to be a soldier. With three elder brothers he never expected to inherit the crown and now that you have allowed him to be a soldier he is content–and your devoted subject.'

That Gaspar doubted, but he let it pass, hoping that the Vizier would now speak Ilya's name, since he couldn't without betraying his interest, speak it again himself.

'For the girl I am sad,' the Vizier said, 'as I am sad for any girl for whom no husband can be found. My old master so doted upon her, his only girl child, that no offer made for her pleased him. This one was too old, this too young, this had bad teeth and the other was of known bad temper. Thirteen years old and not promised, when he died; for a Princess, and so pretty, a thing unknown. And now too late. Unless–and this I do also dare to say because you said that from me you would take nothing but the truth–if you would marry her. What a wonderful thing that would be, and how pleasing to all the people.'

'When I marry,' Gaspar said, 'it will be to please myself, not the people.'

'But naturally,' the Vizier said.

Time passed; no emissary came from Rome offering a ruinous friendship; there was no news of Pella. The year passed its peak and began to decline; travellers from the West grew fewer; soon would come the season when snow would lie on the mountains. Gaspar busied himself with his army and his defences, never naming Rome as the enemy even in his mind, but being ready because, as he had reason to know, all men are enemies to those who possess something covetable.

Then, on a crisp bright morning, the Customs Officer in the post on the north-easterly road out of Jexal reported the arrival there of an old man, almost half dead from hunger, riding a lame camel: his name, he said, was Melchior and he came from far away, from a place called Pyangyong. He seemed to be a scholar, he had spoken in two or three strange tongues before trying the one which, with difficulty, the Customs Officer had understood.

'And which tongue was that?' Gaspar asked the Vizier who had brought this report to him.

'Something between the market speech which I use to you and the speech of the Five Hundred which you use to me.'

Coming from that direction the old man could have no news of Rome or of Pella; he was not, like Benjamin the Jew, a rich and valued customer; there was no real reason why Gaspar should receive him. But lately he had welcomed any diversion which would prevent him, in the evening hours, from brooding upon his own foolishness with regard to a pale, frail girl with great dark eyes.

So he said, 'Kinship of tongue should indicate kinship of blood. Ask this Melchior to eat supper with me.'

'If the report is to be believed,' the Vizier said, 'he and his camel may be dead by supper time.'

'Where are they now?'

'A swift runner brought the message and I came straight to deliver it. They may by this time have reached the bridge.'

'Order a meal; bring the old man to me, and look after the camel.'

Had the King of Jexal given such an order in the old days it would have been relayed and subdivided and its execution delayed; but things were different now and in a short time Melchior and Gaspar made their fateful meeting. Gaspar, well used to assessing a man's physical state, saw at a glance that the old man was in the last stages of exhaustion, and near starvation point as well. But he was courteous. He put his left hand in his right sleeve, his right in his left, and bowed so that for a second his queer round hat looked like a shield. Then he raised his wasted face to Gaspar and said:

'It is charitable of you to invite me to eat with you; but you are only prolonging a useless life.'

The words, spoken in a weak voice, and, to Gaspar's ear, strangely accented, were only just recognisable. Their meaning seemed obscure.

'Sit down,' he said. 'Food is ready.'

A servant brought in a dish, hastily prepared and the old man eyed it so avidly that Gaspar said:

'Take a mouthful or two of wine first, to make way. Then eat slowly. With fasting the belly shrinks.'

'You have known hunger?'

'Many a time.'

The wine ran down hearteningly and presently Melchior began to pick at the food.

'You have travelled far,' Gaspar said. 'Where is Pyangyong?'

'To the East. By the shore of the Yellow Sea.'

Gaspar had never heard of the Yellow Sea but he was skilled now in concealing ignorance, so he nodded and asked:

'And where are you going?'

'That I cannot tell you, because I am uncertain myself. This may sound strange to you, but it is fact. In Samarkand I consulted a map, said to be new and accurate, and I think I was bound for Jerusalem or some place a little to the south of it. Not that it matters. I know now that I shall never get there. I have failed.'

'In what way?'

Along the road, making an ineffectual attempt to bargain, or–since his money gave out–to beg, Melchior had tried to explain something of his errand and its urgency; he had always been laughed at. So now he was cautious.

'I had a message to deliver,' he said. 'A message of the utmost importance, something that only I knew about. I realise now that I am an impractical man. . . .' He brooded for a moment, ignoring his food, then said in a more vigorous voice, 'On the other hand, had I foreseen the difficulties and the expense or realised how money becomes of less and less value as one moves westwards, there was nothing I could have done. I sold all I had. My own wants are meagre, but to keep a camel in condition is very expensive. And the ferries . . .'

He looked at Gaspar with his old unworldly-wise eyes and said with a thin smile that looked as though it hurt:

'Have you ever been obliged to pay for a passage, with a camel, across a wide river, by ferry?'

'No.'

'You have then been spared the worst evidences of human rapacity. I have made five such crossings and they have ruined me. It is not, one admits, easy work, and there are certain risks, especially with a camel aboard; but I can see no excuse for saying that the ferry fee is so much and then stopping in mid-stream and demanding as much again. Or, as once happened, allowing me to land on the farther bank and then pushing away, threatening to carry my camel back to the other side unless I paid more. I hesitate to say that such practices are unknown in my own country, I have led a retired life. And it is possible, of course, that strangers are exploited everywhere. Oh, not here,' he added hastily, 'here I have been most kindly received, and I am grateful indeed. And I ask you to forgive, if you can, my showing a miserable face at your hospitable table. The thought of my failure distresses me.'

'I am interested,' Gaspar said, 'in your having a message to deliver to some unknown destination. How can that be?'

'Ah yes. I am an astronomer. I read the stars in their courses; and I read this message plain and clear. It is just possible that others have read it and are now on their way, I can only hope that that is so. But I was better equipped, I think, than most of my kind, so it seemed to me essential that I should take action. Perhaps you are one of those to whom astronomy is foolishness. In that case I will not bother you with details.'

'In the desert,' Gaspar said, and he felt a pang of the old homesick feeling, 'the stars are a reliable guide. That is all I know of them.'

'In the desert, as on the sea, for navigational purposes, certainly, they have their uses. And the star I follow has never failed me. But the stars have other purposes. There are combinations, movements . . . things which, if you will excuse me, can only be properly discussed by those who understand. What I *cannot* understand,' some petulance crept into his voice, 'is my position. To this study I gave my life and a considerable fortune and I read the message. But it looks as though it would have been better had I spent my time studying what it costs to feed a camel or to charter a ferry boat, and why it is that in one place a coin will buy a whole sheep and in the next, only a few miles away, a mere bowl of weak mutton broth. It is ignorance of such things that has defeated me, *not* lack of will or weariness, frustrating as the latter can be at times.' He gave a great sigh.

'You said that your destination might be Jerusalem,' Gaspar said. He recognised it as the home of Benjamin the Jew; the place which the Romans had taken as he had taken Jexal, but the Jews had not settled down tamely as the Jexalians had done; they were, by all account, still rebellious, and he thought of them as a potential weak spot in the defences of a potential enemy.

'Do you know it?'

'Only by word of mouth.'

'Who rules there?'

'A King named Herod; but I understand that he is a hollow man. A tool of the Emperor of Rome.'

'Emperor,' Melchior repeated thoughtfully. 'It is possible, then, that my errand concerned him and his family. Does he live in Jerusalem?'

'He does not. He lives in Rome, and from what I hear he is a rogue.'

'Indeed?' Melchior sighed again. 'Oh well, no matter. Whoever was concerned, in whatever place, will have no warning from me. I have done what I could, I have spent all I had, I have begged, I have starved, all to no avail.' But even as he said it the small quantity of wine he had drunk, the food he had eaten had revived him and he was willing to snatch at the faintest hope. He looked at Gaspar with a calculating eye, and then took note of his surroundings hitherto ignored.

'You are a man of wealth and power; if you could bring yourself to believe in the importance of my errand and help me on . . . The child's family would surely repay you, since part of my errand is to warn them against his death by treachery before he is weaned. If I could be there in time, I would tell them to whom they owed the child's life and I would ask them to reward you—' He broke off, deterred by the inscrutability of the hard young face of the man with whom he was pleading. 'I am unaccustomed to begging,' he said with great dignity, 'and, believe me, for myself I would never do it. But for the sake of a child with such a destiny, and in such danger, I humble myself and ask you, sir, to lend me a camel and enough money to take me to Jerusalem!'

That word again!

'Eat, while I think,' Gaspar said and leaned his chin on his hand.

His thinking was simple and direct; he had little imagination and was incapable of visualising anything not related in some way to his own experiences. When he thought of the Roman army, said to be a great one, he saw, in his mind's eye the old Jexalian army, a great mass of strutting men with plumes and banners and silver trumpets, and remembered how easily it had gone down before the charge of his Five Hundred. And when he thought of the guerillas in the hills of Judea of whom old Benjamin had spoken, he saw them as men like those of his own Five Hundred in the days before the great battle, skulking, watchful, hard men awaiting the chance to strike.

One of the first rules of fighting that he had ever learned was that one should attack before one could be attacked, and that the battle should take place in the enemy's terrain, so that his tents, his flocks, his womenfolk and children suffered. Another thing he knew was that of all weapons surprise is the most deadly.

He sat there and remembered how, in the months before he swooped down, he had come, on this pretence or that, into Jexal, mingling with its people, marking the strengths and the weaknesses. What he had done once he could do again: and what better disguise could he adopt than that of travelling companion to this star-bemused old man?

And deep under all these thoughts, so deep that he need not trouble to face it, was another–that by absenting himself, by moving about and making plans, he would escape from the spell which the girl Ilya had cast upon him.

Finally he lifted his chin from his hand and said:

'I am minded to come with you.'

'You do not trust me?' Melchior asked haughtily.

'What? With one camel and twenty gold pieces in a bag? Do you think that of me . . .?' He had been about to tell Melchior who he was and what he owned. 'No,' he said, 'I have a fancy to see this city of Jerusalem. And I think that you would travel faster and more safely in the company of a practical man like me.'

'That is indisputable,' Melchior admitted. Hope was now lively in him; the food and the wine had had their full restorative effect, his plea for aid had not been rejected; he was himself again. 'When can you be ready to go?'

'Tomorrow morning,' Gaspar said, thinking of what he must first do. Melchior shook his head.

'Oh no! Haste is of the utmost importance. I have lost time already, with Senya so lame.'

'This,' Gaspar said, 'is a thing I do not understand. You say that according to the stars this child has a destiny, and yet according to the same stars, he may die before he is weaned. One or the other may be true, but not both.'

'Ah, that is what is so difficult to explain to one like you. The stars indicate: they do not rule. They say what may happen, not what will. There are indications, and counter-indications, always, and in this case both are very clear. It is–how shall I put it simply? A woman goes to market and buys a length of woollen cloth. Let that cloth represent what the stars *indicate*. Now of that cloth the woman may make a gown for herself, breeches for her husband, a blanket for the bed. She cannot, of woollen cloth, make a silk robe or a muslin veil, but within limits the choice is hers, and her choice can represent the counter-indications. Have I made that plain?'

'As plain as it ever will be, to me,' Gaspar said, giving up. 'So, haste is of importance; but we shall make good speed. We shall travel on swift . . .' He had almost said 'horses', but hastily substituted 'camels, *riding* camels'. It would never do to ride one of his horses, if he wished to pass unnoticed; everyone who ever came to Jexal noticed and commented upon the beauty, the strength, the spirit and docility of the horses. His tribe had brought with them from their remote Mongolian homeland all the rules governing the treatment of horses, and had preserved them strictly. It was an offence to strike one except on the rump and then only with a rod as thick as a woman's smallest finger. And if water were scarce and of horse or man only one could drink, the horse drank, which was sense, since the horse could carry the man; and a man could suck a pebble and reflect that privation toughened him.

It was an irony, Gaspar reflected, that because his horses were so good he must ride a camel.

'Even so,' Melchior said doggedly, 'I should prefer to move on today. I am already late.' If they were to travel together, on camels, and with money provided by this man it was important that from the first he should understand the urgency of the errand. It was not a question of whose will should be paramount–or at least that was not how it appeared to Melchior's dedicated mind; but it was *his* errand, *his* responsibility, therefore *his* must be the authority. He was grateful, in a fashion, but gratitude was irrelevant.

'Give me an hour,' Gaspar said. 'Lie down,' he pointed to one of the couches, hardly ever used nowadays. 'Rest yourself while you may. I will go about my preparations.'

He went out and sent for Kalim, Lakma and a third man, Temur, his three most trusted comrades. He told them that there was something to the West that he wanted to look into, that he was leaving in an hour and could not foretell the time of his return. He left Jexal to them, he said, and would not insult them by giving orders; they knew the rules as well as he did; trivial matters they three could deal with; things of importance must be discussed by the Five Hundred in solemn session, each man speaking in turn.

Their absolute trust in him was evidenced by the lack of protest, of questions. He had always led them successfully and this proposed absence fell neatly into pattern with his behaviour in the past. To the West they knew lay many petty kingdoms, similar to that of Jexal: another raid in the Spring, perhaps; or maybe at last he had taken note of their many hints, and was going to look for a wife.

'Go in peace and come back with joy,' they said.

When he came back he would find everything as he had left it; they were his brothers, bound to him by that which the boy Malchus had, in his flowery, Jexalian way put into words, 'the loyalty of the heart.'

When all was ready, the camels already kneeling in the courtyard, Gaspar went to rouse Melchior; he did it by taking the old man by the shoulder and was almost shocked to feel the bones so prominent under the faded blue robe, and the bones themselves so frail and light. Melchior, accustomed to sleeping lightly and brokenly, was awake at once, on his feet and ready to go.

'There is one thing,' Gaspar said. 'Of Kings and courts I am ignorant, but I think that if we visit this Herod he might expect gifts. What shall I bring?'

'My gift I carry in my head,' Melchior said. 'And I also am ignorant of Kings. But all men like gold.'

Gaspar had a pouchful of it, but that he might need for the journey. However, he knew the very thing–the crown that had rolled from the dead head of the old King; the crown which, before they understood his mind, some of his followers had wished to see on Gaspar's head. 'It would impress people,' they had said, and he had retorted that he could impress people in his own hat, or know why not.

'Wait here. Eat again,' he said, remembering the bones; and he strode along to the bedchamber where, unwillingly, he had slept to defy the rumour that he was afraid. The King of Jexal had died there, by his own hand–which showed, Gaspar had always thought, what manner of man he was. Seeing the battle go against him he had run to his room and stabbed himself, and the crown had fallen from his head and rolled into a corner. It and all the other pretty, womanish things he had worn, rings and necklets, armlets, jewelled pins, had been put into a chest into which Gaspar now thrust a hasty hand and brought out a crown. It consisted of three golden circlets, the largest just the size of a man's skull, the others smaller, linked by curved struts; circlets and struts were set with jewels, rubies, sapphires, emeralds. The triple crown of Jexal. A pretty thing, but no wear for a man. Now the other . . . Gaspar wasted a moment looking at the Queen's crown, a filigree coronet, all set with pearls, was the right wear for a woman; at least for some women; it was difficult to imagine it upon the head of any woman he had ever seen in the market. It was difficult, in fact, to imagine it upon any but one woman! Upon that thought he let the lid of the chest fall with a crash. The triple crown he slipped into a soft leather bag and tightened the thong. He was ready.

It was, by this time, not much more than an hour before sunset, and as they rode towards the western gate, called the Water Gate, Gaspar looked towards the mountains, measuring what remained of daylight, and because he had as yet no experience of Melchior's method of travelling, thought that really they might as well have waited until morning. But he did not resent the early start, for already he felt an uprush of relief at leaving the Palace and the city, and all that they meant, behind him.

The wide street that led towards the Water Gate was not a busy thoroughfare at this season and the people who were in it were all women, walking purposefully. Gaspar scowled at them; he knew where they were going–to the temple which stood just within the city wall. In Jexal there were nine temples, dedicated to various gods and goddesses, and Gaspar regarded them all with distrust and suspicion; but he had never issued an order that they should be closed. What he had done was to inculcate and foster the idea that no man worth the name would go running, trying, to placate an irate, or cajole a friendly, god, and his policy had worked so well that nowadays only women and a few old men frequented the temples. This had made priesthood an unremunerative occupation, not attractive to recruits. The time would come, Gaspar told himself, when this superstitious thing, conducive to fear and the shuffling off of responsibility, would die out of its own accord. Already in Jexal it was fashionable to swear by the sun, and to be married by the mingling of blood.

He was thinking this, not without complacency, when he recognised, in one of the women, the girl Ilya. Her walk was unmistakable. He intended to ride past without turning his head and he almost managed it, but in the last second the temptation to look, to see whether she was as lovely as his memory of her, was too much. So he turned and once again they looked into one another's eyes.

She made a little sound of astonishment, recognising him in his stiff felt hat, leather jerkin and baggy trousers, the horseman, mounted on a camel; then she began to move more swiftly, almost running beside him, and lifting her face. She said the word he had forbidden:

'Lord,' she said, 'Lord!'

And because he wished to conceal from Melchior, who up to this moment had regarded him, he was sure, simply as a wealthy and charitable man, his real identity, he checked his camel's pace; and because being obliged to do so angered him he said gruffly, 'What do you want with me?'

'To thank you,' she said. 'To thank you from my heart for what you have done for Malchus. He is so happy now.'

She spoke the true Jexalian tongue, removed from his own by the softening, refining influence of a thousand years; Malchus, who had worked with common men in the smithy, had seemed to lisp, and there were times when Gaspar was obliged to ask the Vizier to repeat himself; upon Gaspar's ear what she said fell with all the appeal of a woman speaking with a lilt, an intonation, just understandable and no more.

'I am glad to hear it,' he said. 'Happy soldiers are good soldiers, as a rule.' Then he added the little extra, 'Temur speaks well of him.'

Something flashed in her eyes. It said–if he read it rightly and he thought that he did–Because I thanked you for breaking a rule on my brother's behalf, don't imagine that I value Temur's good word!

Then she said, 'You go a journey?' and she looked at the camel, comparing it, he knew, with the horse he ordinarily rode.

'I go a journey,' he said.

'Then take this,' she said, 'to preserve your most precious health in evil-smelling places.' She reached up and thrust into his hand a little package, wrapped in linen. 'Ishtar will not grudge it,' she said. She stood back and raised her hand, in perfect imitation of a member of the Five Hundred taking leave.

'Go in peace and return in joy,' she said.

He was having his first experience with camels; they were more gregarious, less near-to-human, than horses. the one he rode and the one Melchior rode had always been a pair, measuring their paces. His, held back, fretted and fidgeted, and Melchior's ridden forward, was fretting and fidgeting too. In one wild moment of confusion, the package in his hand, the camel restive, the mockery of her leave-taking and his need to take one last look at her, all mingling, he could do no more than call back the traditional, tribal response to the leave-taking:

'Stay in peace; I shall return.'

Then his camel, straining forward, drew level with Melchior's, straining backward, and the two fell into even pace. And as they did so he realised the nature of Ilya's gift. The scent assaulted him, the dominating scent of what he called the city stink. It was frankincense. In a curious way it represented all the alien way of life, the ritual, the king reverence, the god worship, the decadence of the city he had made his own and yet distrusted. And having it thrust into his hand by that woman, of all women, roused such a violent distaste in him that for a moment, wishing to throw it from him, he was unable to do so; he was paralysed by disgust.

'The brazen slut!' he said to Melchior as the two camels, order restored, moved forward happily. 'Accosting me with her stinking rubbish!'

Melchior sniffed. 'Rubbish? It smells like frankincense; believe me, in many places it is worth more than its weight in gold. This King–did you say his name was Herod?–would find that an acceptable gift, I think.'

'You give it to him, then,' Gaspar said; and to his relief found himself able to move, to hand the package over. 'But so long as you carry it, try not to ride between me and the wind. I hate the stuff.'

'On which side of you I ride,' Melchior said mildly, 'is of no matter to me. So long as we move forward. Perhaps I should have told you. I am old, I need little sleep. I travel by night. Then, when the camel must rest, I take my reckonings by the star and mark my charts. You are young; you may find my way somewhat tiring.'

Never, since he was ten years old and about to be taken, as a great favour, on his first desert raid in the company of men, had anyone spoken in that mildly admonitory, challenging voice to Gaspar. And then the voice had been his grandfather's, the voice of a man tried and proven, tough as leather, tempered as steel. To hear the echo now, from this old man, so frail, so just-brought-back-from-death-by-starvation, so sharply snatched back from despair, wiped out Gaspar's mind every thought, every emotion except that of the primitive feeling of competition. Rome, Herod, Jexal, Ilya were all forgotten as he said:

'Ride ahead, my friend. And when you are tired, let me know.'

PART FIVE

EDESSA

400 miles

Upstairs, in a cool airy room overlooking the terrace, the Lady had settled down to gambling, and downstairs her slaves were hoping, even praying that her luck might be good. Her temper, at all times disagreeable, became savage under provocation, and nothing provoked her more than to lose at games–unless it was the failure of a tenant to pay his rent.

Balthazar stood a little apart from the rest with his arms folded so that the stiffened fingers of his right hand were held between his other arm and his body in a cradling, cosseting gesture. He was a scribe, an accountant, and his right hand was most precious; its gradual, increasing disablement gave him great anxiety.

He was not praying for the simple reason that he did not know to whom, or to what to pray any more. Years back, in Tyre, he tried all the gods, and one after another they had failed him. He watched, with gloomy detachment as one slave killed a dove and offered it to Aphrodite and another took four bleached bones from a bag and arranged them in a pattern and made a ritual gabble. Poor things! Upstairs the dice would fall as they would, indifferent to anything that was done down here; and if they fell unfavourably for the Lady, tomorrow everyone would suffer, more or less. He would suffer more than anyone except the Lady's body slaves, for he must every day, sometimes many times a day, go and stand in the dread presence. He cradled his right hand and a little more closely, remembering what she had done to it on one occasion, and might very well do again.

A great wave of hopelessness washed over him. Lately he had been prone to moods of miserable despair. Being a thoughtful man he attributed this, in part, to his age; he was forty years old and the last of youth's hopefulness had drained away; he was no longer capable of feeling that around the next corner something better might be in store. I have, he admitted to himself, been disappointed too often.

The first of his disappointments had happened when he was twelve, a happy though sometimes hungry boy living in some nameless part of Africa, so far inland that on maps he had studied later it was just blank space. It was near a great river, not the Nile, and his tribe had its home where the river spread out over the flat land, making innumerable wide muddy shallows where the crocodiles had lurked, one eye watchful above the water's surface, ready to snatch at women who came to fill their gourds, and at men who came to fish.

The tribe had a god, the Great Crocodile, N'Zana. They believed that the ordinary crocodiles were his minions and that if they did certain things and observed certain rites N'Zana would favour them and keep them safe from his servants. Once a year, at a time calculated by the old wise men of the tribe, three girls, virgins, without any physical blemish, were chosen and taken to a special hut where, no matter how low the food supply might be, they were fed and kept idle in semi-darkness, so that at another date they might be brought out, sleek and fat; then they were oiled and garlanded with flowers, and to the beating of drums and the yelling of their fellow tribesmen, they were cast into the river and immediately torn to pieces.

Once a favourite sister of the boy who now bore the name of Balthazar had been one of the chosen virgins and he had not accepted it in at all the right spirit. His father had rebuked him, telling him that it was an honour to give a virgin to N'Zana, but he could not resign himself. All through the fattening season he moped and pined and when the day of sacrifice came he had hidden himself away and wept. Not long after, a woman going to the river for water had been snatched and drawn under and devoured and the boy, fearful of his father's wrath, but curious and rebellious, had asked how could this be. The price of protection had been paid and where was the protection?

'You are my son,' his father said; 'but you do not always obey me. That crocodile was a disobedient son of N'Zana. He will be punished.'

The forty-year-old Balthazar could tell himself that had he had any sense he would have learned his lesson then and there and spared himself much disillusionment. But at the time he had accepted it, and when, being twelve, he had been most painfully initiated into manhood, he had received his pierced crocodile tooth–the badge of a full man in his tribe–with pride, and had worn for some months; until the slavers came, in fact.

The slavers came in the night, and N'Zana made no move to save or protect the tribe who once a year had given him their choicest virgins, and at all times the choicest joint of any beast they killed, the tribe whose chief on ceremonial occasions had worn the symbolic crocodile skull. N'Zana, said to be many times larger than the largest crocodile ever seen in the river, and to have four times as many teeth, had not come up from his hidden place and lashed about with his great tail, or snapped with his great teeth. He had done nothing. So the huts were all burned, the very young and the very old were left to starve to death with no one to care for them; the others were marched off, their necks thrust into forked sticks.

They had marched for many days, a long chain of misery; some had died. Those who lived were taken to the banks of another great river, the one which Balthazar now knew as the Nile; and there they were packed into ships, as closely as fresh-taken fish were packed into baskets, and taken to a place called Egypt where everything was strange and terrifying and the houses were as many as, and as tall as, forest trees.

There someone had rubbed powdered chalk upon his feet and he had stood on a block and several men had fingered his arms and legs, forced his mouth open and studied his teeth. Later that day, with other boys of about his own age, he had been taken into one of the tall houses and suffered something worse even than the initiation rites. The pain had been terrible and very hard to bear, with none of the hope, the pride, which had enabled him to bear the elders' slashing and slitting; that had been destined to make him a man; this was destined to make him something less than a man. All that the initiation rites had conferred this more agonising process took away.

When he recovered–which every boy so operated upon did not do–he was tested as a singer. One of the results of the operation was to preserve whatever voice a boy possessed, and a slave who could sing and play some instrument was of enhanced value. Balthazar proved to have no ear, nor any potential skill as a potter or a painter which, after singing, were regarded as the employments most suitable for the truly black, woolly haired slaves brought from far inland.

'You have no skills,' the owner of the slave-school told him, not angrily, but as a plain statement of fact. 'I see nothing for you but to be a guard and escort for women.'

By this time Balthazar had acquired a smattering of several languages and had talked to many people and learned a good deal; he knew that the life of a harem attendant was not an enviable one. It was tantamount to being a human watchdog, and who cares for a watchdog? Women, he had been told, were profoundly cunning and deceitful, and when a deception was discovered, who was beaten? The watchdog who had failed to be watchful enough. Also women quarrelled amongst themselves, and who must step between them lest they come to blows and damage one another's looks? Again the watchdog. Women, again, seemed, from the tales he had heard, to bear a curious, deep-rooted enmity against his kind. Some of the tales he had heard were quite horrifying; and although amongst his tribe he had been regarded as a courageous boy, courage seemed to have left him with his manhood. He was very sensitive now, both to pain and to mockery.

All the things he had heard were not horrible, however; there were many tales about slaves who had been clever, risen to positions of trust, managed to save money somehow and had purchased their freedom, or so endeared themselves to their owners that they had been set free. There was one whole layer of society which consisted of freed men. Some of these even owned slaves themselves. It was, however, generally agreed that once the harem curtains had closed upon a half-man, he would stay there, like the other inmates, for life.

So, timid as he had become, Balthazar thought he must risk making one suggestion. Bowing his head, he said:

'Master, I am worthless. But I think I could learn the abacus.'

The slave-trainer looked at him with astonishment. The arts of reckoning and of penmanship were regarded as too intellectual for slaves from far inland who could sing, make pleasing patterns with colours, mould pottery, mime amusingly and play the clown–all physical things, extensions or refinements of what came naturally to them, of what they would have been doing if left in freedom in their own homeland. The use of the mind was a different thing altogether; some people doubted whether they even had minds. Dubiously the old slave-trainer cast an experienced eye over the boy; a good lively eye, he reflected, and a promising forehead.

'We can but try,' he said. 'Fetch an abacus.'

Eighteen months later he was able to put upon the market a property practically unique; a young, neutered slave who could read and write and reckon accurately; who was docile and teachable and reliable; and black, with the black's well-known powers of endurance and ability to eat almost anything. Most slaves who could read and write were Greeks or Semites or half-breeds who resented their condition and were shifty or sickly; often they were men who had fallen into slavery on account of debt and tended to be followed about by hungry families, which made them attempt to be dishonest.

To the Greek merchant from Tyre, in Alexandria on business, and astonished by the price asked for Balthazar, the trainer said:

'Within three months you will think it too little.'

And within three months the Greek was almost of that opinion; for in addition to all his other qualities the boy proved to be completely honest. The Greek, himself a profoundly dishonest man, subjected Balthazar to the most subtle and cunning temptations his wily mind could devise and Balthazar never cheated him of a penny. And when a trader–bribed by the Greek to do so–offered him a bribe, Balthazar refused it, with the extraordinary excuse that there was no column for such things in his accounts book.

At the end of a year–it took so long to convince the merchant completely–he was able to say to his wife:

'Now, when I go on business there is no need for you to go downstairs and dull your pretty eyes checking the accounts. Balthazar is quite honest, or he has such a mania for accuracy that it amounts to the same thing.'

In his work Balthazar was happy; but within himself he was always aware of a yawning emptiness. The sense of loss which he had felt after his mutilation had increased rather than diminished through the years. His sleep was haunted by dreams, pleasant in themselves but dreadful to recall when he woke because he would dream that he was a whole man again, back in his home by the great river, hunting and fishing with the men by day, and at night snug and happy in his hut with a woman who was always–this was the shocking part–the sister whom N'Zana had taken.

He was now enlightened enough to see the Great God of the Crocodiles for what he was, something that men in their fear of the ordinary crocodiles, and their impotence, had invented for their own comfort. He had lost his faith in N'Zana at the same time that he had lost his freedom, but deep inside himself he had a hankering for the comfort which only faith in something outside himself could supply. As he grew older and his need for an emotional outlet grew, he began to think about other gods, the gods worshipped by all these clever busy people who had no fear of crocodiles.

In Tyre there was no lack of them; the flourishing polyglot port had much to offer to anyone seeking a god or a goddess. There was the Phoenician Baal in his many forms; Baal Tamar of the Palm Trees, Baal Perazim of the Wells, even Baal Zebub, Lord of the Flies. His groves were everywhere. For the convenience of visiting Egyptians there were temples to Isis and Osiris; for Greeks temples dedicated to Zeus, Aphrodite, Artemis and a dozen more; the Romans had reared temples to Jupiter and Venus; the Babylonian goddess Ishtar had her sacred place, and so had the god recently brought from Persia, Mithras.

They all had one thing in common with one another, and with N'Zana, Balthazar discovered; they all liked presents; and presents he was prepared to give and able to give. On certain days of the year it was customary for masters to give trivial sums of money to their slaves; females spent these sums on finery for themselves and whole men spent them on finery for their women. Then, occasionally, after some particularly profitable transaction, the Greek would toss a coin or two to Balthazar; open-handed merchants would do the same. And he earned money too, by writing letters or making a reckoning for some unlearned fellow. Many slaves, commanding such resources would have bought delicacies to eat, but Balthazar, often hungry in childhood, was quite content with the food in the Greek's kitchen, simple, monotonous, but sufficient. Nor had he any need to spend his little income on clothes, the Greek took pride in his slaves' appearance, and Balthazar, in the counting house, in the public eye, was better clad than most. And women, those ever avid, never satisfied creatures who made such demands upon a man's pocket, meant nothing to him.

So, bearing gifts, he made a slow round of the groves and temples and underground shrines; looking at first for a place to rest his heart; for something to fill the great emptiness caused by the loss of freedom, of manhood and belief in N'Zana. It was much to ask, and he never found it. After his twenty-fifth year he asked something else, something simpler, of the gods. In his twenty-fifth year his right hand had begun to trouble him.

Laying down his pen one afternoon, he had stretched his fingers as usual, and they had resisted the stretching movement and remained cramped, as though still clutching the pen he had laid aside. It had been a long day and he had written small, paper being expensive and the cramp did not cause him much concern. In an hour it was gone and his fingers were as flexible as ever. But day by day the condition grew worse until there came a time when he went to bed with his fingers still bent about an invisible pen. In the morning, for a long time, his hand was better; and then one morning he woke to find his fingers still contracted, and in the centre of his palm a curious bony bump. After that, offering his flowers, his doves, his expensive spices, he had asked of the gods not a resting place for his heart but a cure for his fingers, and the answer to the one request matched exactly the answer to the other. Nothing.

He could still write, which was something to be thankful for–but thankful to whom? His fingers were cramped into a writing attitude and clenched about a pen could still do their work. But they were growing worse, and abandoning the gods, once and for all, he took other measures. He gave his money to a man who took his afflicted hand and thrust it into a pan of almost boiling hot mud; to a woman who filled his palm with oil and gently rubbed and pressed and prodded until the oil had been absorbed; to a man who had attempted to press the fingers and the bony protuberance of the palm, flat between two boards, excruciatingly painful and quite ineffective.

He had tried to learn to write with his left hand, practising surreptitiously; and his left hand could write, but in a fashion quite unsuitable to the narrow columns of an account book. It wrote a large, sprawling hand, square and ugly, and no amount of determination, no amount of practice, could make it write otherwise. And looking ahead into the future Balthazar saw himself like a chariot horse, injured at the Races and sold, doomed to drag out a limping, ill-fed life, dragging a heavy cart until it died. He was a writing slave, and of what use was a writing slave with a crippled hand?

He was in this particularly vulnerable state when one of the house slaves died, died mounting the stairs to the living quarters and dropping, as he fell, a tray laden with porcelain dishes from Cathay in the far East, which the Greek in one of his travels and transactions had managed to acquire. Over the dead man nobody had mourned, but the Greek's wife's lamentations over the broken dishes had been loud and long.

The slave bought to replace the dead man was a Jew, named Eliezer, and he was, by his own account, a slave by choice. His aged father had fallen deeply into debt. 'He was seventy, I was his youngest son. Unknown to me he had sold all that we had, and borrowed money from a Samaritan who demanded heavy interest. He was about to be shamed and disgraced. The Samaritan agreed to take me, and to cancel the debt. So I am a slave. But my father's debt was paid and I have obeyed the law–Thou shalt honour thy father and thy mother. I was misled. By our law no slave can be held for more than seven years. Whatever his value, in the seventh year he must be set free. But other people have other laws and I have now been in bondage for twice seven years and my father, if he is still alive, is doubtless in debt again, being a fool in business. Still, I did what I could.'

Balthazar was much impressed to learn that a man could voluntarily sell himself into slavery, that hated state, and even more impressed by Eliezer's indomitable cheerfulness which was not the cheerfulness of the light-headed and thoughtless kind which seemed to be the only kind available to slaves, and which Balthazar himself had never attained. This cheerfulness, he discovered gradually, was based upon hope and faith, both rooted in a religion, which as it was revealed, bit by bit, was astonishingly different from any of those he had sampled. Eliezer's god was a spirit who had on earth no physical representation at all and who demanded not the occasional present or the bowing down in this place or that, but control of a man's whole life, from the moment he waked in the morning until he fell asleep at night. 'It is the Law,' was Eliezer's explanation of everything, down to his refusal to eat certain kinds of meat and his frenzied attempts to do as much of the seventh day's work on the sixth as was possible. The reward for keeping this law might come in this life. 'Jehovah never deserts a just man,' Eliezer said, and it was plain to Balthazar that Eliezer still, after fourteen years of slavery, was hopeful for liberating action from his god; but this life was not all, a just man could count upon life after death when he would be gathered to his fathers and enjoy everlasting felicity.

It took some time for Balthazar to learn all this, since his work lay in the counting house and on the docks, and Eliezer's kept him to the domestic side of the house, but whenever they could they drifted together and the talk took a religious turn. One evening Balthazar stretched out his right hand which he usually concealed as much as possible and laid it on Eliezer's knee as they squatted together in the dusty courtyard.

'Look,' he said.

'A handicap to anyone,' Eliezer said gravely, having looked. 'And doubly so in a scribe.'

'If it were yours and you prayed for a cure, would *your* God answer you?'

Eliezer hesitated and then said:

'No. In the old days there were prophets who could work wonders; Elijah restored a dead child to life; Moses made a dry path through the sea. But there have been no prophets for the last five hundred years. Besides,' he hesitated again, 'if Jehovah answered that kind of prayer nobody would ever be sick or blind or crippled . . . or a slave.'

'Have you ever prayed outright for your freedom?'

'As I would ask for a melon from a stall? No. I have asked my God not to forget His servant in his bondage and exile. And that prayer He has answered.'

'How do you know?'

'In my heart,' Eliezer said simply. 'In his heart a man knows whether he is forgotten by God or not.'

'How?'

'He becomes melancholy. Perhaps I can best explain to you by way of a story. . . .' He told Balthazar the story that all Jewish children knew, the story of their first King, Saul, who was forgotten by God and went melancholy-mad. And then by contrast he told another story, that of Job. He ended with a quotation, 'Though He slay me, yet will I trust in Him.'

Balthazar dimly realised that though this god of the Jews offered no remedy for the contracting fingers, he might offer some remedy for the apprehension with which he himself regarded the future, and also, almost equally important, something to fill the emptiness within him. When Eliezer said, 'In my heart', Balthazar had understood, because his need was the need of all men, all the temple-frequenters, the sacrifice-offerers, the need to feel that somebody, somewhere saw you as an individual and *cared*.

After that talk he became assiduous in his questions. Did Jehovah have a temple?

Yes, indeed, Eliezer said; it was in Jerusalem, the most beautiful and holy building in the world. It was the ambition of every pious Jew to visit it, at the Feast of the Passover, at least once in his life. Eliezer told Balthazar in great detail about the building of the Temple–which he had never seen; its destruction by Nebuchadnezzar, its rebuilding by the liberated Jews, under Ezra, by people who worked with a trowel or a shovel in one hand and a sword, a club or a dagger in the other–that made a stirring tale; and finally its enlargement and beautification by Herod.

'And here, in Tyre?' Balthazar asked. 'Your god has no temple here?'

Eliezer suddenly looked uncomfortable.

'One God, one Temple,' he said. 'In other places we have a meeting house, a synagogue, where the Law is read and expounded and the songs of praise chanted.'

'There is one in Tyre?'

'There is one in any place where any number of Jews are gathered together.'

'And you go to it?'

'When I can–which is not very often. A house slave has little leisure,' Eliezer said. 'Listen!' He jumped up with what Balthazar could only puzzledly regard as relief at the sound of the bell which summoned him.

There was then a time when Balthazar, hot foot after this, the last of his gods, found Eliezer very odd and evasive, which was strange, because to say the least a scribe-accountant by even talking to a mere house slave, honoured him. But the day came when Balthazar could say to Eliezer:

'I am interested in all that you tell me of your god. When next you go to your synagogue, tell me. I will ask leave to go with you.'

Eliezer's face took on the peculiar colour which all pale-faced men showed under any strain.

'That is not possible,' he said, avoiding Balthazar's eye.

'Because I was not born a Jew?'

He could see Eliezer wavering between tact and honesty. Honesty won and Eliezer said:

'It is not that. It would be better if you asked no more and accepted my answer–it is not possible.'

'Because I am black?' He'd never been particularly conscious of his colour; it was true that most of his kind were slaves but that was because of their misfortune, not because of their colour, and there were plenty of men, quite as black as he was, who came to Tyre to visit or to trade and were regarded as the full equal of anybody except a born Roman citizen.

'No,' Eliezer said; and he lifted his eyes and looked Balthazar straight in the face. 'It is written, it is the Law as given by God to Moses.* No man, maimed as you are, can enter the congregation.'

The forked yoke of the slave trader had fallen upon his neck, the gelder's knife had agonised him; but neither had hurt him as these words did. This was the final blow, because he had been all ready to give his heart, his whole being to this god of Eliezer's, who was a spirit and who answered prayers by gifts to the spirit and not to the body. He had been ready to say, with Eliezer, 'Though He slay me, yet will I trust in Him', and 'Yea, though I walk through the valley of the shadow of death, I will fear no evil'. That was how he had always wanted to feel, how he was prepared to feel. And now . . .

'Your god is a very unjust god, Eliezer. And inconsistent, too. If, as you claim, he is a spirit, concerned with men's hearts and minds, that is a senseless rule. This thing,' he said, in an angry voice that was in sharp contrast to his ordinary mild utterance, 'was done *to* me without my wish or consent. No reasonable man would hold that against me, far less a god who, as you claim, sees and understands all.'

'I am sorry,' Eliezer said, 'but I cannot help it. It is the Law.'

After that Balthazar had finished with gods.

About a year later the Greek came home from the docks where he had been supervising the unloading of one of his ships, on a hot day, and complained, in the counting house, of a headache and feeling of stiffness in the neck. His wife had sent for a physician who prescribed some remedies and rest in a darkened room. But next day he was worse, with high fever and pains in all his limbs.

Downstairs in the slave quarters somebody said:

'Cleo, bring your ball and look into it and tell us, will he live or die?'

Cleo was a young Nubian girl, recently brought into the household; she was a skilled hairdresser and spent most of her time in the bedchamber of the Greek's wife. She owned a ball, about the size of an egg, but rounded, of black obsidian, and she claimed that by looking into it she could see events that were yet to happen.

Balthazar, from the first, had regarded her as a fraud, and her fortune-telling as a means of gaining attention. But twice–this was undeniable–she had been right; once when one of the master's ships was overdue she had cradled the ball in her hands and looked into it and said, 'It is wrecked. It has gone down in the sea.' And once she had foretold the sex of an unborn child. Everyone else was much impressed but Balthazar considered these prognostications to be lucky guesses.

On this evening she brought her black globe, warmed it between the palms of her hands, stared fixedly at it and at last announced in a flat, dull voice:

'He will die.'

There was a general groan, for the Greek merchant was, as masters went, lenient and conscientious.

* Deuteronomy, Chapter 23, verse 1.

'All men die,' Balthazar said, a little sharply, the verdict being unwelcome to him, too.

'He will die on the second day,' the young Nubian insisted. Then she pushed the globe into Balthazar's hand and said, 'See for yourself.'

He stared and was overcome by amazement; there, pictured in the polished black surface, was the bedchamber of the Greek, his dead body on the bed and the embalmers busy with it.

After a long silence, during which he stared and stared, Balthazar protested:

'Yes. I see him dead. But there is nothing to show whether he will die on the day after tomorrow or in twenty years hence.'

'Look closer. How many white rings enclose the picture?'

'Two,' he said in exactly the voice he would have used if asked a question in the counting house.

'So!' the girl said. 'He will die on the second day.'

As she spoke the picture faded from the globe, and standing there with it, blank, in his left hand, Balthazar realised that he had just experienced something new and strange; he had seen something that had not yet happened as though it were already past. The obsidian was cold and heavy in his hand; he gave a little shudder.

'Put it away,' he said.

Two days later the Greek died and the house was filled with the mourning wails of the slaves, to which were added, for a short time, those of the widow. But she recovered rapidly and began in a level-headed way, to turn all the assets she had inherited into cash so that she could return, wealthy and independent, to her native Corinth. She had always, she said, felt an exile in Tyre.

The slaves began to plague Cleo to look into the ball again and see, if she could, what would happen to them who were to be marketed in just the same way as the ships, the storehouses and the pack animals. Several times she made unsuccessful attempts; 'I see nothing.' But one evening, having warmed the ball carefully, she looked into it, gave a moaning cry and fell senseless. The ball rolled from her limp hand and somebody picked it up and gave it to Balthazar.

'You saw our master dead. See what is in store for us.'

'It is better not to know,' he said, remembering how Cleo had cried out. But they insisted and he was curious, in a way, himself. So, almost flinchingly, he looked, and he saw himself, rather finely dressed, riding a camel in company with two other men who wore peculiar hats; one round, the crown running steeply into the brim, very much, in shape, like the roofs of the huts of his own tribe, the other a kind of cap with a white crown and a black brim. On his own head he wore a turban, made from a silk scarf, and his robe was richly red.

'You see something,' the slaves cried. Tell us what you see.'

'A happy future for all,' he said, wondering about the meaning of what he had seen concerning himself. They crowded round, demanding details, individual forecasts. In his hand the ball had gone blank again and cold and heavy.

'I had no time to see small things,' he said, handing the thing to one of the women who stood by Cleo. 'I can only tell you that you were all happy.'

But Cleo hanged herself from a beam some time during the night and what became of the black ball nobody ever knew.

The widow retained Balthazar to the very last; there was a great deal of reckoning to be done; he knew about the business, and her husband had considered him to be honest. Several times in the ensuing months he was able to save her from those who would have taken advantage of her sex and her ignorance. Every time this happened and every time he made a shrewd or useful suggestion, she said, 'You shall be rewarded,' and he would think about the money piling up, how enormously rich she was, and dream that in the end she would write him his paper of manumission and set him free. In the globe he had worn the clothes, ridden the camel, of a prosperous freedman and he knew that could he once attain his freedom he could become prosperous. He could set up as an accountant and scribe, and charge for his services. Perhaps the two men with whom, in the vision, he had been riding, were clients of his, merchants from far away, glad to make use of his knowledge of languages and of currencies.

All this pleasant speculation ceased when the widow, wearing the aspect of one who has performed a good action at some cost to herself, told him that she had sold him to a Roman.

'I could have obtained a better price for you,' she said, in warm, complacent tones, 'but I bore in mind how well you have served me lately, and the state of your hand. With your new master you will not be required to write so much, or so small. Theodor Metellus is growing old and losing his sight. You will have an easy life with him, just reading to him and writing a few letters. I hope you are pleased,' she added, changing her tone as she saw the sagging disappointment in his face.

He was bitterly disappointed, and also dismayed. The Romans, as slave-masters, had an unsavoury reputation. Hardly two generations had passed since the Roman world had been rocked by a great uprising of slaves, led by Spartacus. It had been put down with the utmost severity, but it had not been forgotten; Romans still regarded their slaves as potentially dangerous and behaved to them accordingly.

Contributing to his dismay was the knowledge that he had been sold cheaply because, in slave-market parlance, he was 'unsound'. And, as with pack animals, the way in which a slave was treated was in direct relationship with value. There was also the question of Latin; his, picked up by use in the streets and the counting house, was not of the kind that a Roman gentleman would require or expect.

He wondered once more, as he had wondered many times before, what Cleo had seen in the obsidian to make death preferable. And how reliable was information from such a dubious source? The black ball, like the gods, like the widow, had let him down.

There was nothing to be done, however, and on the appointed day he took his little bundle of possessions and moved across the city to the residential suburbs where fine villas stood, remote from the noise and bustle of the quays and the business quarters. It was with a certain amount of relief that he noticed that the slave who admitted him looked well fed, well clad and cheerful.

Metellus was a lawyer who had enjoyed a considerable reputation, both as a scholar and an orator; he was old now, and on account of his eyesight, virtually retired, though still active in a consultant capacity. His great dread was that he should become dependent upon his slave secretary–he had seen that happen with other ageing men–and for a long time he resisted Balthazar's well-meant attempts to make himself indispensable. 'I am still capable of doing that,' he would say; or 'Don't take too much upon yourself, Balthazar.' And long after he had ceased to see at all he would reach out blindly for a paper and say, 'Let me look.' In the end, however, he succumbed to his new slave's genuine ability, desire to please and gentle manner. As much friendship as could exist between master and slave existed between them; Balthazar was made free of Metellus's considerable library and they spent hours together in talk.

Metellus was a Stoic, and without in any way aiming to convert Balthazar–for how can a man be persuaded into an intellectual state–he introduced him to that stark, impersonal creed, the reverence of natural principles, the respect for reason, the uncomplaining acceptance of one's fate. They talked of Zeno, of Cleanthes and Chrysippus and of Posidonius whom Metellus tended to decry as being 'too mystical'. It was a far cry indeed from the doves of Venus, the groves of Baal, but after all, Balthazar would reflect, they had failed him. Stoicism could not do that. It had one fault, however; it underestimated the importance of a man's emotional life; it was a creed, Balthazar realised, for whole men, for aristocrats, for men whose emotional needs had been satisfied elsewhere. Nevertheless, adherence to it gave a man dignity; see how uncomplainingly Metellus accepted his blindness! In such company Balthazar found it easier to disregard his contracting hand. Also, the widow, greedy, false and selfish as she had been, had also been right in one thing. With less writing to cram into constricted spaces his hand suffered less from cramp.

This leisurely, comfortable, peaceful life lasted for five years; towards the end of that time Metellus had become entirely dependent upon Balthazar whom he called 'my amanuensis'. Fewer visitors came to the secluded house; every year there were new young lawyers appointed, men to whom Metellus was merely a name, a man whose books could be consulted in any library.

One young man, however, was a regular caller. He was a lawyer named Marcus, born of a Roman father and a Syrian mother. Partly because of his mixed blood–for though in a multi-racial Empire racial equality was paid some lip service, truly Roman Romans regarded themselves as superior to all others–and partly because he had indulged in practices not considered strictly ethical in legal circles, he enjoyed small esteem amongst his fellows and it pleased him to be received in the house of a man, who, though old and blind, was of unblemished reputation.

He was fond of saying, 'I must ask Metellus' opinion on that.'

Then his hearer would say, 'Metellus? Is he still alive?'

And Marcus would say, 'Very much so; I dined with him yesterday.'

To Balthazar Marcus always behaved with arrogance. 'I have something to ask you, but that can wait until we are alone,' he said more than once.

Most often Metellus would say, 'If you ask me something and I need to refer to a book, Balthazar can find it quickly.' Or, 'You can speak freely before my amanuensis, I like to have him near in case I need something.'

Balthazar regarded the young lawyer with a dislike somewhat out of place in a true Stoic and occasionally showed it, murmuring a correction of a date or a name, sometimes even going so far as to say, when asked to fetch a book,

'There is no need, sir. I have that passage by heart.'

Metellus would smile and say, 'You see, Marcus; he is my eyes and my memory, and, I suspect, a better lawyer than either of us.'

But the evening came when, on Marcus' arrival, Metellus himself sent Balthazar out of the room on a reasonable excuse; and as soon as he had gone, he said:

'I want you to do something for me. Write that man a paper of manumission and I can sign it now. Then you can hold it until I die.'

'I trust, sir, that that day will be far distant,' Marcus said politely, and truly, since his friendship with Metellus lent him status.

'I think not,' Metellus said calmly. 'I am older now that most men live to be; and I have had warnings.' A Stoic did not waste time describing symptoms, except to a doctor from whom he hoped for relief; nor did he invite sympathy. 'You know what to write,' he said; then, as he felt for the edge of the paper, fumbled it into position and signed it, he added. 'I am reasonably sure that if Balthazar knew of this it would not affect his behaviour one iota except to make him grateful and more doggedly devoted. And that would irk me. So you keep it and regard it as part of my will. The contents of a will should never be divulged.'

'I will hold it safe, and trust that it may prove an ineffective instrument, sir.'

'And what may that mean?'

'Only that you may outlive him.'

'Then you wish me ill. To replace him I should need a nurse and a scribe, and still be at a loss for a companion.'

A bare three months later Metellus died, in his sleep. The young man, Marcus, remembered his mother's sister, a woman of great wealth who lived in Edessa and from whom he had expectations. She was always in trouble with her stewards; free men, freedmen, slaves, she'd tried all and never been satisfied. So he destroyed the paper of manumission, and at the sale of Metellus' effects bought Balthazar very cheaply, having ostentatiously drawn attention to his afflicted hand. Then he personally conducted Balthazar to Edessa so that his aunt might thank him, face to face, for his thoughtfulness and consideration.

Knowing nothing of how nearly he had missed being set free, Balthazar could hardly be said to be disappointed. Now and again he thought that if Metellus had not died so suddenly, had he had time to realise that he might die, things might have been different. On the other hand his Stoic creed might very well have influenced him to think that Balthazar was a slave as naturally as he himself was blind; unpleasant states both, and to be borne without complaint.

He was glad to learn that although Marcus had bought him, he was not taking him into his service. Stoutly he braced himself to learn new ways, to fit into a new household, to be obliged, probably, to learn another dialect, to please, if possible, his new mistress. He was thirty-four now, the extreme adaptability, the resilience of youth had gone.

Within a week he realised that he had fallen into the clutches of a woman not entirely sane. The Lady, as everyone called her, had been so corrupted by great wealth and almost absolute power that she did not know her own mind from one hour to another and her rages were frightful to see. In a rage she had no respect for anything, not even for herself. Balthazar had seen her, in a stamping temper, pull out her own hair and throw it away from her as though it were obscene. And Marcus must have been disappointed by the reception of his present.

'I don't like eunuchs!' the Lady had said. 'They're always eating.' She rapped out, in gross terms, the reason for their thinking food so important. Then she said:

'What's wrong with his hand? What use to me is a steward who can't write?'

In happier circumstances Balthazar would have gloated over Marcus' discomfiture, and tasted to the full the irony of hearing Marcus, who had always seemed to despise him, lauding his abilities and virtues.

'I'll believe all that when I have reason to,' the Lady said. And to Balthazar, 'Straighten your fingers, man!'

'Madam, it is impossible. They have grown this way. For many years now.'

'Let me look,' she said, less sharply; almost kindly; and innocently he had extended his hand.

She took it in hers which were satin soft, plump, decorated with many rings, pretty, feminine, harmless-looking hands, but they were strong as steel as, with a quick movement, she clutched his wrist in one hand and with the other attempted to bend back the crooked fingers. It hurt much more than the pressure between the two boards, for then the contracture had not been so complete. Balthazar's black face turned grey, sweat sprang out on his forehead, he was obliged to lock his teeth to prevent the escape of a cry of agony. Worst of all, as she flung him back his hand, was the sight of her face with its look of pleasure, of satisfaction. A person who enjoys the pain of others, he thought, with a feeling of complete despair; and I belong to her!

To Marcus, immune from physical ill-treatment, she said:

'And why should you bring me a black? You know how I loathe them. They stink!'

'This one is clean,' Marcus said placatingly. He might have been speaking of a pet dog, house-trained.

Balthazar realised that never until now had he plumbed the depths of humiliation which being a slave involved. How fortunate he had been hitherto. First the old slave-trainer in Alexandria, anxious only to produce the most marketable product; then the Greek, busy with his money-making and valuing anything which contributed to it; then the Roman, reasonable and just, and in the end dependent. He had been a slave for a long time, but this was his first taste of slavery.

Now, at the end of six miserable years, he stood apart while his fellow slaves called on their gods, and worked their magic, and upstairs the Lady shook the dice-box. And he was empty, of hope, of vigour, of everything except what he knew now to be a nebulous dream. Suddenly he could not bear any longer the company of his fellow slaves, so he went to the open door and sidled out into the courtyard.

This was a very different place from the dusty, dung-scented yard of the Greek's house in Tyre. Every corner of the Lady's house was swept and scrubbed, polished, fussed-over. This courtyard was enclosed on three sides by the walls, with their arched openings, of the house itself; the fourth was the terrace with its marble balustrade, upon which, at intervals, were set marble vases filled with flowers. Immediately below the terrace the land fell away, first to the Lady's pleasure ground, and then, lower, the vegetable garden and below that again, the orchard. Still farther down the slope were the towers and the roofs of the city. On suitable days, midway between the winter's chill and the summer's heat, people would sit on this terrace with the Lady and congratulate her upon her view and she always accepted the compliments as though she had made the slight slope with her own hands.

Tonight, in the darkening, slightly purplish twilight, the rail, the struts, the vases at the terrace's edge looked black against the sky. From overhead came the sharp rattle of the shaken dice-box and the shrill voices of excited women. Balthazar moved to the edge of the terrace and stood there thinking of tomorrow, and of all the tomorrows that would follow after. To a certain extent, during the last six years, he and the Lady had come to terms, terms of her choosing. He was of value to her, he knew, and to a certain extent she trusted him; in the service of any sane woman his position would have been assured and he would have been immune from ill-usage; but in this woman there was something dark and dreadful, unreasonable and perverse; the thing which had once, when he had done her a service that nobody without a knowledge of accountancy and law could have done, had made her, thanking him, suddenly take off her shoe and hit him in the face with it, and split his lip and make the blood run.

He stood on the dark terrace, thinking his dark thoughts and, without realising it, staring at one of the black curving urns, freshly planted that day with sweet-scented flowers.

And there he was, dressed as before, with those two men, instantly recognisable; and this time they were riding into the gateway of what could only be a great city; he could see the high walls to the left and right, made of enormous blocks of stone and within the walls tall towers and the upper stories of buildings that must be either temples or palaces. The gateway and as much of the street as he could see was as crowded as the busiest parts of Tyre.

He stared and stared in amazement–not that he should be seeing a vision, for while it was happening it seemed to be real, the only thing happening in the world–but that the men with him should have been so instantly recognisable, their faces as familiar as though he had known them always. The old man, very thin, with high cheek-bones and mild, study-wrinkled eyes, the young man with a face like a hawk's: queer company for one another, and queer company for him.

From the upper room came the sound of a slight crash, followed by a cry. Balthazar gave a little start and instantly the picture was gone; there was the black, smooth-sided urn, no different from its fellows.

He at least had something to think about during the next day, when the Lady who had lost heavily, was so intent on making everyone wretched that her ill-will extended even to peasant farmers she had never seen, men who wrested a meagre living from an outlying estate of hers, two days' journey away to the East. They were all, she shouted at Balthazar, to pay increased rents, either in cash or kind, and he could tell them so when he went, at the end of the next week, to do the rent-collecting. It was not a prospect that he relished. They lived such miserable lives already, that sometimes when he left them he would compare their lot with his; a slave was reasonably certain of his next meal, at least; then, as he walked and the distance between him and the Lady decreased, his pity for them would change into envy.

Her losses on that evening had convinced the Lady that she was on the verge of penury; everybody's ration was reduced, and when Balthazar asked could he have a new pair of shoes before he set out on his long walk to the estate she said, 'No. Wear what you have,' and hit him on the head with a heavy silver comfit box which happened to be handy. 'And don't pretend that hurt,' she said as a slow trickle of blood ran out of his hair down his forehead. 'A skull of wood, and woollier than a sheep!'

That evening he went, as he had gone every evening since that of the disastrous gambling party, and stared fixedly at the urn in which he had seen the picture. He knew that by doing so he was merely inviting yet one more disappointment, but he felt drawn to the place, to the urn. He remembered Cleo and how she had often said, 'It has nothing to tell me.' What governed such things? he wondered. Were those two men–and himself–there, in the urn and he unable to see them? Had he merely imagined the experience which had now visited him three times? Or was it, each time, a dream? In which case, over the death of his master, he and Cleo had dreamed the same dream almost simultaneously.

While he was thinking in this way, something moved in the dark depths of the urn. It was a star, much larger, much brighter than any of those that scattered the heavens and it moved, perceptibly, down, down until it was very low; then it seemed to swell and splinter into something that he could never describe, a great burst of glory and beauty and wonder, very real and yet unreal, as though colour had sound, and sound had taste and taste had shape. An entirely new world, he thought, obliged to close his eyes against the dazzle of the revelation.

When, timid and dizzy, he opened his eyes again the urn was as it had been at other times, and loneliness weighed on him like a sickness. To whom could he say, I saw a star burst and the world was made new, with no more slavery, men of all colours made equal, the rich giving their goods to feed the poor? And if there had been one to whom he could say it, how feeble and ineffective the words would have been, how incomplete the other's understanding. And how, even to himself, could he explain that this vision was inextricably connected with the two men in peculiar hats. But it was. . . . And he must, somehow, find those two men.

He went to his bed and lay and gave serious thought to a subject he had not really considered since he was a boy in the old slave-trainer's establishment in Alexandria–how to run away and not be caught. In a civilisation based upon slavery this was an extremely difficult thing to do, and doubly difficult if you happened to be black. And the punishments devised for runaway slaves were deliberately designed to deter all but those already made crazy by ill-treatment. In addition to being black he was a eunuch–and no free man, save an ecstasy-drunk priest of Baal who had mutilated himself, was that.

Still he thought, sturdily, even a black man, even a eunuch, might have bought himself free, or been manumitted.

Now, he thought, pursuing that thought, if my master the Greek, or my master Metellus, or my mistress the Lady, had manumitted me, I should carry a paper, signed or sealed.

The Lady had never troubled to learn how to write her name, but she had a seal, a great square topaz set in silver, which, when she pressed it into the hot wax which Balthazar had prepared, left in the wax a sheep's head in the centre and in each corner the initials of her personal and family names. (Her father's wealth had been made from sheep; once there had been a great sickness and thousands of sheep had died; his had stayed healthy and he had been able to sell a ewe in lamb for the price usually charged for a tiger, an elephant or a fully trained performing bear.)

She never, even in a temper, let the seal out of her keeping, and demented as many of her actions were Balthazar knew that there was no hope of presenting her with a forged manumission paper, amongst several others and getting her to seal it. Where anything concerned with business or money was concerned she was very shrewd. But he had, in his possession, many of the little clay tokens which it was his duty to give to tenants in exchange for their money, their corn, their jars of oil, or wine which constituted their rent. Every quarter, as he went round he issued new clay tablets, a different colour for each new quarter, and collected the old ones. It was just possible that he could smear the face of one of these stamped tokens with oil and press it against some fresh-dribbled wax. He would then have a replica of the Lady's seal. . . .

Next day he wrote himself a document of manumission, phrased, although he did not know it, almost in the very words which Marcus, that clever lawyer, at Metellus' bidding, had used. Then he forged the seal. Transferred from topaz to clay and from clay to wax and then to wax again it lacked the sharp, immediate impact of the original; but looking at it critically he thought it would fool most people.

There were other cunning little moves to make. In the ordinary way he spent two days on his journey, two days rent-collecting, two days on his way home. But this time, before he left, with the forged document tucked into his breast, he said:

'My Lady; the increase in rents that you have ordered will bother these people and may cause some delay. The usual rent they have, hidden in the wall or under the floor, if it is in cash; put aside in barn or storehouse, if in kind. Faced with the increase most of the tenants will be obliged to run to the money-lender, or fill other sacks and jars. I say this because this may take me more than six days.'

She said, 'Did I not make myself clear? I want this increase; I *need* it. And you are to stay there until the last penny, the last grain of corn, the last drop of oil or wine, has been yielded up.'

'That might mean, my Lady, that I should be absent for two weeks.'

'What of it?' she said. 'Do you think that I shall pine for the sight of your ugly face? I know what you are thinking of. In this house you eat full and sleep soft. For two weeks you'll miss your comforts. Three even, if some of them have to sell their children to meet my demands.'

Yes, it might even be three weeks before she missed him and said, 'Where is Balthazar?' And, after that, at least two days' grace, waiting, wondering, expectant. And then the hue and cry; runaway, a neutered slave, black, the fingers of his right hand bent, aged forty, hair turning grey, when last seen wearing . . .

He knew it all, he thought as he passed from the Lady's presence for what he hoped with all his heart would be the last time. Once she knew, and the news was out, everybody would be on the alert, avid for the reward.

But he had at least two, at best three, weeks; he had, if challenged, his forged document; and he had on the one hand his hope, on the other his despair. If he failed, if his dream like everything else in his life simply led to disappointment and he was brought back, he would take his fifty lashes and his branding, and he would die. . . .

On the night before he left he gave sensible consideration as to the best direction to choose. The really practical thing, he knew, was to go to the estate at Babila, spend a day collecting the rents that were immediately available and then disappear from there; he would thus acquire money for his journey, he could buy the camel and the clothes which, in his vision, had seemed to be his. But this procedure was distasteful to him, not only because he had never stolen a penny in his life, but because it seemed wrong to start out in pursuit of something unspeakably wonderful by committing a theft. Also–and it was amazing how even a slave could find reasons for not doing what he didn't want to do–to act in this way would be to act exactly as the Lady, when he failed to turn up, would guess that he had acted. She would send first to Babila, two days' journey to the east; by moving westwards at once he would add four days to the time he had in hand. So he would go west; taking with him the few coins he was allowed to purchase food. Apart from that he had nothing, for in Edessa–or at least in the Lady's household, the charitable custom of making small money presents to slaves on certain days was not honoured; nor had she allowed him to write a letter or make a reckoning for anyone other than herself. He had attempted it in his early days in Edessa, where there were plenty of ignorant persons willing to pay for such a service. The Lady had said, simply and spitefully, 'If you can't find enough work to keep you busy on my business, just tell me, and I will help you.' He had known what that meant!

So, meanly clad, his shoes already broken, and with just money enough to purchase one evening meal, he set out, very early in the morning, and turned west as soon as he reached the city's boundary. Then, for two days, he dared not use the highway for fear of being seen by someone who knew the Lady and might recognise him and report. Walking across country in this way was a slow process, for he was traversing a belt of highly cultivated land upon which Edessa depended for its market produce and the plots were divided by walls of stone loosely piled upon one another, by fences, by irrigation ditches. Also there were no shops where food could be purchased. On the first day, except for the 'dawn-bit' which he had eaten before setting out, he ate nothing at all; on the second, seeing a woman outside a lonely little house, milking a tethered goat, he had approached her and asked could she sell him something to eat. She rose to her feet, looked at him, with fear and then, searchingly, all around; looking for his accomplices.

'I am alone,' he told her. 'And I am not a beggar; I can pay.'

Her expression did not change, but she nodded, and taking up the bowl of milk, went into the house, walking in the stiff-legged way of one who wishes to hurry but deliberately refrains from doing so. He heard the bolt on the inside of the door jolt into place.

He stood there, feeling disheartened; without eating he could not travel; and he realised again that a slave's life, though full of humiliation and, in the power of anyone like the Lady, pain, was a sheltered one; he had been used to eating regularly. Even in Edessa, when the Lady was angry or needlessly economical and the quality and quantity of the food had been reduced, there had always been something, served up at regular times.

Resolutely he cast his mind back to the days of his youth, particularly to the brief period between his initiation and his capture when he had been allowed to go with the men on their hunting expeditions. They never went out until the food supply of the village was almost exhausted, and what little there was left in store stayed there for the support of the women and children. In the morning they would say, 'Tonight we eat full.' But often enough there were days when they had no success and lay down with empty bellies. They'd thought nothing of it; nor had he, then. The forty-year-old Balthazar thought–I am not the man my father was. Then he thought–Naturally not; I am not a man at all. And he wondered whether the Lady had been right when she said that eunuchs thought of nothing but eating.

Next day, still moving west and travelling across country he was fortunate and fell in with a woman more brave, or more charitable, than the first. She sold him some wheat porridge, cold and set almost as firm as bread, two small onions and a cup of goats' milk. He carried the onions with him, and ate them just before he lay down under a wall and went to sleep.

On the third day, after a long laborious climb up a ridge or rising ground, planted on its lower slope with olive trees, above that bare and rocky and very damaging to his poor shoes, he found himself looking down upon a road, carrying considerable traffic and running–he took his bearing by the sun–slightly south-west–north-east. He scrambled down the ridge and joined the traffic that was going, so far as he could judge, away from the direction of Edessa. There were trains of pack ponies and donkeys, trotting along in a haze of dust; camels swayed under their loads. There were mounted men and ladies being carried in litters, and so many people on foot that Balthazar felt himself to be reasonably inconspicuous.

Hunger bothered him again and presently he had proved that he had no skill as a beggar; nothing came his way that day, and the situation was made worse by the fact that all along the road people were eating, and there were places where food could be bought. Bread freshly baked in a village shop smelt delicious and brought the water into his mouth; so did the sight of a pedlar resting against his pack and eating the leg of a chicken.

Towards evening he came to an inn. Poor travellers who were prudent and determined to get good places for themselves on the covered platform that ran around the yard, and good places for their beasts in the enclosure; were already settled and eating the food they had brought with them; from the doors and windows in the inn itself came the odours of the meal being cooked for wealthier people who could afford to eat indoors, in comfort. Balthazar paused. There must be a great deal of work to be done in an inn at such a moment; animals to be fed and watered, dung to be swept up, dishes and pots to be washed. He turned in and at the door asked, most meekly, whether there was anything he could do in return for a meal.

'I don't encourage beggars,' the innkeeper said. 'Puts people off if they think they're going to be accosted and bothered.'

'I wouldn't accost or bother anyone. I'd just do anything you gave me to do, whatever it was, in return for something to eat.'

To that the innkeeper did not even bother to reply; he pursed his lips and whistled, and from somewhere a dog appeared, and without a bark or a snarl or any evidence of hostility, sank his teeth into Balthazar's wrist, and held him.

'That'll do,' the innkeeper said; the dog loosed its hold and backed away.

'Now you be off,' the innkeeper said, 'unless you want another dose.'

Outside the place he was obliged to stop and tear a piece from his tunic to make a bandage for his wrist which was bleeding profusely. It dawned upon him–and this hurt more than the dog-bite, or the blisters, just beginning to break on his feet, or the hunger-gnaw in his belly–that he had come out on a ridiculous errand, hunting for two men he did not know, who might even now be travelling in exactly the opposite direction. Even at this low moment he did not doubt their existence; they were as real to him as the surly innkeeper, but he was beginning to fear that he might die of hunger, and never find them.

Miserably he wandered on, and in a short time heard, from the side of the road where there was a clump of myrtle trees, the sound of several men's voices, laughing and cursing; the scent of charred flesh reached him. He ventured cautiously around the trees and saw that he had stumbled upon a group of soldiers, Roman soldiers, who had bought, or commandeered, a sucking pig, and made a fire and were now endeavouring, clumsily, to cook it by using their swords as toasting forks. Even as he watched, it slipped and fell into the fire which spat and sizzled.

'Jupiter give you a pig for a first-born,' one of the soldiers said. 'We want it for eating, not for a burnt-offering.' He reached out and, taking the pig by its hindleg, retrieved it.

Balthazar moved forward, a shadow emerging from the shadows and said in the faultless Latin he had learned from Metellus:

'I could cook it, if you would permit me.'

At least they were not frightened and did not turn upon him eyes of fear or any of the emotions that fear engendered.

'See,' one of them said, 'didn't I tell you that this was enchanted country. We need a cook, and one walks in.'

'In disguise!' another said. 'As unlike a cook as any I ever saw–and I've seen a few. Can you cook, fellow?'

Balthazar had never cooked anything in his life, but he had seen cooking done.

'I can cook the pig,' he said.

'Then cook it,' said the man who held it by the leg, 'and shout when it is ready for eating.' He gave the greasy, half-charred little body to Balthazar and turned away. The others turned away too, towards a dim lantern that stood on the ground. They were Romans, the dominant race, and to them it did not seem strange that out of the dusk service should come and offer itself. One of them, just beginning to throw the dice, was annoyed when Balthazar came behind him and asked could he borrow his knife. No slave of the Lady's was allowed to carry a knife or anything capable in the most far-fetched circumstances of being used as a weapon of offence or defence.

Handed the knife, Balthazar cut two forked branches and planted them firmly in the ground, one at each side of the fire. Then he cut a long, stout stick and forced it through the body of the sucking pig; the protruding ends he lodged in the forks of the branches and the pig hung there, near enough the heat to cook, far enough from it not to char. He sat down by it, now and then replenishing the fire, now and then giving the long stick a turn so that another portion of the pig was brought in contact with the heat. A mouth-watering smell overpowered the scent of charring and spread about the little camp. One of the men turned and called:

'How long will it be?'

'Not long now, sir,' Balthazar called back. He thought how tender the white flesh would be, the crackling how crisp, the fat how sweet, and was obliged to wipe his mouth on his sleeve.

For the first time in many years he remembered Eliezer, who would have starved before he would eat pig-meat, or hare, or venison. At the time he had respected Eliezer's respect for his Law and admired him for it; now it seemed ridiculous. Though no more ridiculous, he thought, than casting yourself into a hostile world on account of a dream, a waking dream. Then, because every man must attempt to justify his own form of madness, he thought that after all his action might not have been so ridiculous, even if he never found the men he was looking for. If he could keep alive and stayed on this road while the Lady hunted for him around Babila, he might come to a city large enough to hide in and set himself up as a street-corner scribe. In that there'd be none of the wonder and glory he'd come out to find but one thing he'd dreamed would have come true. No more slavery. He'd thought that that had applied to the whole world, but maybe he had been mistaken; maybe it applied only to him.

Presently he tested the meat with the knife; the point ran in easily, even in the thickest part of the leg. He threw earth on the fire to deaden the heat and then carefully lifted the forked sticks and planted them again a little way away.

'The meat is ready for eating, sirs,' he said, and walked a little distance away.

'I want my knife,' said the soldier who had lent it.

Balthazar, apologising, brought it back; by this time the others had fallen upon the meat as though they were starving, and Balthazar licked his lips.

'You hungry too?' asked the knife-lender in an off-hand, but good-humoured way. 'Move over, Varro. There you are.' He turned back to Balthazar and offered him a chunk of meat from the point of the knife. Nothing had ever tasted so good.

He slept that night under the myrtle trees, and was awakened by the clatter the soldiers made as they moved off. He ran to the place where the pig had been hacked to pieces and breakfasted on the scraps of meat which still adhered to the scattered bones. The meal and a night's rest had restored his spirits and his hope of meeting the two men was lively again. He resumed his walk, studying carefully anyone who rode a camel.

On that day he made less progress for the blisters on his feet had begun to fester. By midday the dog-bite on his wrist was troubling him, too; when he let his arm hang it throbbed like the worst kind of toothache. But he refused to be discouraged by his sores, or by his marked ill-luck in begging. He was now on one of the great highways of the world and anyone who lived beside it and had a charitable heart could have stood and given away all that he possessed in forty-eight hours; and those who carried their food with them were concerned lest their supplies should not last to the end of their journey. In three days after leaving the soldiers, he ate twice, once on a half-rotten apple which a fruit-seller threw out because it might contaminate the sound ones, once on a piece of barley bread given to him by an old woman who was eating as she trudged along with a bundle of laundry on her head.

He arrived at the caravanserai at the crossroads in the dead hour of the afternoon on the seventh day. It was an imposing place, occupying the whole corner between two of the four roads that met. Just inside the yard which gave upon the wide open space where animals were stabled was a stone drinking trough, and a little girl, with one shoulder higher than the other and, he presently saw, one leg shorter than the other, was emptying a wooden bucket of water into it.

He said, 'May I drink?' Finding anything to drink had also been something of a problem on the highway; people were actually *selling* water!

'It's for beasts, really,' the girl said. 'I'm just going to draw another bucketful. I'll bring you a cup, if you like.'

'This will do,' Balthazar said, cupping his hands and drinking eagerly. She limped away. He splashed the lovely, the beautiful, the free, cleansing water over his face and head. He ripped off his makeshift bandage and plunged his wrist, with its aching, festering wound, deep down into the trough. He was about to kick off his shoes, climb to the edge of the trough and ease the sores on his feet in the same way, when the girl came limping back. His thirst slaked, he looked at her more closely; she wasn't dressed like a slave.

'Are you,' he asked, 'the daughter of the house?'

Her thin little fingers touched first the folds of her dress, worn and dirty, but in its day a dress of quality, and then the silver ornaments in her ears.

'These are for show,' she said. 'I am a slave.'

'Oh,' he said; and he was a little disappointed. She was kind, she'd offered to fetch him a cup, and a child learned its attitude from its parents, he had hoped that the father might be kindly too, and let him do a job and give him a meal.

'Could I speak to your master?'

'Not now. Not for an hour. He is asleep; or in bed with *her*.'

'I wanted to ask is there any job I could do to earn myself a meal.'

'A lot of people ask that. He always says "No"–except to fortune-tellers. After they've eaten, most people like to have their fortunes told. If you can tell them,' she looked at him dubiously, 'you would be welcome; but not otherwise.'

'I'm so hungry,' Balthazar said, 'that to get a meal I'd become a fortune-teller.'

'I can give you something to eat. Every day we cook more than enough.' She spoke eagerly. 'Wait there,' she said and pointed to a nook made by the house wall not running quite in line with the lower wall that enclosed the place where travellers' beasts were herded. 'That,' she said, 'is a good place. I go there when I cry.'

He went and sat down, eased off his shoes, unwound the dripping wet bandage and looked at his wound. It was worse; that dog must have had poison in his teeth! His whole wrist was puffy and hot and from the two punctured holes yellow pus was oozing, giving off an offensive smell.

The girl, and although she limped, she moved quickly, came and presented him with a wooden platter, heaped, piled with what was plainly the remainder of several main dishes.

'It doesn't look very appetising, but it is all good,' she assured him. 'I've lived on it for three years.'

'It looks good to me,' Balthazar said, digging his fingers into the rice, the bits of gooseflesh and mutton, the leaves of artichokes, the cabbage. Looking at the girl he judged her to be about thirteen, so she had been here, living on left-overs for three years, she must have fallen into slavery at an earlier age than he had . . . or perhaps she had been born one. . . .

'Three years,' he said, 'you have lived here for three years?'

'Three, thirty, three hundred. I lose count of time. She'–she raised her eyes to the blank, recently whitewashed wall that jutted out above this secluded little corner–'she marks every hour and one new wrinkle under her eye rocks the house. I,' she said, tapping her flat little chest, 'am a slave, but sometimes I think less a slave than my master. She is very pretty and has a heart of stone.'

'Is it because of her that you come here to cry?'

'Sometimes. Sometimes it is for my family in Antioch. Sometimes,' she looked away from him, 'it is because of the things I have to do. I have to . . . sleep with men,' she said.

Balthazar, chewing on a gristly bit of mutton, looked at her and wondered what sort of man it could be who would wish to go to bed with her, so immature, so crooked? She sensed, and indirectly answered his question.

'In the dark,' she said, 'when they are eager and inflamed by *his* promises, they use me. Afterwards they are . . . ashamed, and angry with themselves, and with me. Afterwards, when a pretty girl would get smiles and presents, I get curses, and blows. You see,' she said, simply, '*she* won't have a pretty girl in the house. She uses her bed as a stick to hold over my master; it would never do for him to have another bed to go to.' She looked at him, saw comprehension and sympathy in his eyes, and went on: 'She wouldn't have another woman of any kind in the house except that she, the wife of an innkeeper, the daughter of a pig-butcher, thinks herself a lady and must be attended in her bedchamber. And it is impossible,' she said, 'quite impossible, for anyone to work as I do, in the yard and the kitchen, and still have hands smooth enough to handle hair as it should be handled.'

Something in the way in which she had said 'pig-butcher' prodded Balthazar's memory.

'You are a Jew?' he asked.

'Yes. My father is a shoemaker in Antioch; three years ago he fell ill; more than three years ago, I have been here for three years. Jews are well liked if they are thriving; when they fail to thrive they have no friends except other Jews, as poor as themselves. He owed money, not much, but some, for leather, for thread and wax, also rent for the house, and those to whom he owed came in a body and said he must sell something and pay his debt. He offered to sell his tools but they were worth little. My brother was four years old, my sister still at the breast. If my father had sold himself they would starve. So, weeping, and in great sorrow, he sold me.' She raised her chin a little. 'Sometimes a pedlar, a friend of my father, passes this way and we send messages. Always my father says that he is saving to buy me free, to be patient and keep the Law and work well and freedom will come; always I send back a message to say that I am happy and have a good master and mistress. I think sometimes that this is contrary to the Law, "Thou shalt not bear false witness", but it harms no one and comforts my father and my mother.'

'And observes the Law about honouring them.'

'You know about that,' she said eagerly. 'You know, when you came to drink at the trough, something in my mind said, this is not a beggar, this is a prophet! And it is strange that I should think that, since you are not a Jew. But you know our Law.'

Balthazar nodded. 'A little.' He racked his memory for some words, used by Eliezer, and applicable to this child's case. He found it. 'Sorrow may endure for the night, but joy cometh in the morning!'

'Oh,' she said, her ugly little face transfigured, 'you do know! That is a saying from—' She broke off as a loud, ringing female voice called, 'Susannah!'

'I must go. I've wasted time . . .' she said, and limped hastily away.

Balthazar stayed where he was in the sheltered angle between the walls, the hidden place where Susannah came to cry. The meal he had just eaten weighed upon him with a comforting, enervating weight. His wrist, freed of the rough, bloodstained bandage and recently cooled in the trough, hurt less than it had done. He dozed. The somnolent, dead afternoon hour ended with an inrush of travellers, anxious not to be on the road after dark, anxious to secure room for themselves under the tiled awning which sheltered the platform that ran about the enclosure for animals, or, if they were rich a private sleeping chamber and a place at the table where the meal was served for such as could afford it. Balthazar roused himself, not without self-reproach. Indirectly he had justified the Lady's jokes about eunuchs; out in search of the indescribable, the wonder for which there were no words, he was still a slave to his need to eat and sleep.

He rose and stretched himself and took a step or two out of the secluded corner into the main entry of the yard. He was thirsty again and intended to take another drink from the trough.

He never took that drink, for as he emerged from behind the corner of the house, two men, on camels, sagging, exhausted camels quite unlike those he had seen in his vision, rode into the yard. And their faces, their hats, everything about them, except that they, like the camels, looked utterly exhausted, was exactly as he had seen them in his waking dream. Even the hats, about which there could be no mistake.

He ran forward with all the joy, the incredible excitement of one who finds a dream translated into fact.

'You are those I have been seeking!' he cried, in his weightless tenor voice. 'You follow the star. I beg you, take me with you!'

They looked at him with blank, uncomprehending faces. And of all the bad moments in his life that was quite the worst.

PART SIX

NAMELESS VILLAGE

300 miles

Melchior and Gaspar had not been travelling a week before the younger man had learned one very useful lesson–toughness had little to do with appearance. The old man, so frail and thin, was never the one to suggest that they had travelled far enough for one day, and to Gaspar, not yet accustomed to the motion of his camel, the days, extending far into the night, seemed very long. In the end he was compelled to protest, not on his own account–that he would have been ashamed to do–but on account of the camels.

'By the sun,' he said, 'no wonder you lamed your other camel! These will drop dead under us if you go on this way.'

It chanced that he first said this in a desolate place; had it been in a town or a village, Melchior would probably have answered that they could buy fresh camels; but even he could see that *here* should the camels fail, there would be nothing for it but to go ahead on foot. So he said:

'You were right when you said that I needed a practical man as a companion. I never thought of the camels!'

'But you must yourself be tired,' Gaspar said.

'My bones are tired,' Melchior said; 'but they have been tired for so long that I no longer notice them.'

And when they halted, wherever that might be, by the roadside, to eat food that they carried, or in the crowded caravanserais, the day was still not ended for Melchior; he must take out a chart and make his complicated reckonings, the results of which were never to his liking. 'We must move faster,' was always his verdict. The need for haste obsessed him, and soon another problem arose. 'Night by night,' he said, 'I grow more doubtful about our destination; it lies south of Jerusalem. Of that I am almost sure.'

Gaspar, who had come out with the intention of seeing Jerusalem, and Herod too, if that could be managed, always tried to console him.

'You told me, on the first day we met that this child was to be born of a royal house; and Herod is King of Jerusalem. It may be that he has a Palace for Winter and a Palace for Summer, or one in the city and one in some quiet place, suitable for a breeding woman.' The Kings of Jexal had owned a Summer Palace, on high ground above the river, and Gaspar spoke with some assurance. 'We must make first for Jerusalem, and there ask.'

When he said this for about the twentieth time Melchior, who had never denied that this might be the most sensible thing to do, suddenly said:

'And in what tongue?'

The matter of language was becoming a problem in itself. As they moved westwards the dozens of dialects and mutations of the tongue which was common to them and which had been carried by the successive waves of emigrants from their original homeland, had become less and less of service to them, and Melchior had been obliged to fall back upon his book-learned Greek, a language he had never heard used and every word of which he must pronounce in all possible ways before he made himself understood. So long as they were moving, all unknowingly, along the road which Alexander and his men had twice travelled, where wounded men, exhausted men and various camp-followers had stayed and rested, Melchior had managed, not without difficulty to make himself intelligible enough to buy what was needed, to ask a few questions and obtain answers. As they moved south-westwards they had found that nobody at all understood any variation of their common tongue, and fewer and fewer people could understand Melchior's version of Greek. When Melchior asked, with a slight bitterness, 'And in what tongue?' they had been moving, for several days, through a region where educated people spoke Latin and the common people some form of Aramaic–as varied and as seemingly universal as their own tongue was in the areas reached by successive impacts of the great Mongolian invasions.

Gaspar answered the question in his usual blunt way:

'That,' he said, 'I must leave to you, Melchior. You are the scholar. I am merely the provider.' And that, Melchior realised, was not said as a reproach, it was, like most of Gaspar's statements, plain fact. Food, for man and beast, accommodation, tolls at bridges and ferries, everything had been paid for from Gaspar's pouch. And the man himself was a good fellow-traveller; tireless, uncomplaining. And considerate. Many times he had insisted that in a caravanserai Melchior should occupy a private room. Private rooms were few and costly. Ordinary travellers slept on a kind of platform, sheltered by an awning which ran around the open space where animals jostled and brayed and scratched and moaned. Gaspar always, when they slept in a caravanserai, chose to sleep there, not in a private room. 'I like to sleep in the open; but for you I will buy a room,' he would say. 'You have your work to do, and coming back would disturb us all; also, since you sleep so little, you must sleep soundly, undisturbed by a child crying or an ass braying.' In many ways Gaspar behaved to Melchior like a son–the son he had never had. They depended upon one another, and it worried Melchior a little that though Gaspar's contribution to their journey, the gold he carried, was acceptable everywhere, his contribution, his book-learned Greek, was becoming less and less of value. Also it was evident to him that Gaspar's goal was Jerusalem.

There was something else, also, that troubled Melchior. Gaspar's curiosity and interest in people that he himself would have passed without a second glance. 'Are they soldiers? Roman soldiers?' Gaspar had asked once, with some excitement. 'Ask. Find out.' And he had checked his camel, and Melchior's had immediately slowed down too. The men had been Roman soldiers–and Melchior admitted that it was clever of Gaspar to have guessed so shrewdly; but what of it? What did Roman soldiers matter? You could waste time, most valuable time, on things like that. And some of the soldiers, not understanding what Melchior said, made gestures that even he understood, rude. . . . On the whole the standard of manners and of hospitality declined as they moved westwards, and, unless they were being grossly cheated, prices were still rising steeply. Melchior had realised before reaching Jexal that he had no skill as a bargainer; Gaspar had never bargained in his life and was, in addition, unused to handling money, and seemed not to notice prices at all.

The strain, the haste and fatigue, differences in character and in objective, even the sense of being so independent upon one another, would have resulted in bickering had Melchior not been so naturally courteous and Gaspar the heir of a long tradition of respect towards elders: but on the day when their path converged towards that of Balthazar they had almost quarrelled.

Gaspar, who had always believed that he could out-ride and out-fast any of the Five Hundred, which meant any man alive, was galled to find that this old man, skeleton thin, was not only prepared to stay on the jolting camel for at least an hour after he himself was reeling with fatigue, but that he was also more indifferent towards food. On the morning of that day, having slept in the open, they had eaten the last scrap of food that they carried, Melchior insisting that Gaspar should take the larger share; 'You are young,' he said, 'and accustomed to feeling well.' But he had waited, with obvious impatience as Gaspar gulped down the stale bread, the bit of stinking cheese. His overnight calculations had been very unsatisfactory. 'We shall be late,' he said, with dismal certainty. 'This child will be born, at latest, four days after the winter solstice, and after that there are a few days' grace. Then, if I am not there, all my efforts will be wasted. We must press on today.'

They had pressed on and just as the sun was setting had reached a point where the road sloped steeply down towards a huddle of roofs that indicated a sizeable town. Gaspar pointed to it and said:

'We stay there for the night.'

'Oh no. We shall be there before it is full dark. We must travel until moonset, at least.'

'Our food is exhausted, our water-bags are empty, our camels are spent. To go farther would be folly. Tonight we seek an inn and have a meal of cooked meat. We buy stores for tomorrow. The camels restore their strength. Tomorrow we shall travel faster.'

'I have no time to waste upon meat or stores or camels,' Melchior said stubbornly. 'I told you from the first that my errand was urgent. Nothing else matters. I must press on.'

'Then you go alone,' Gaspar said, and as soon as he had said it, realised his folly. It was now a long time since anything he said had been understood by any save Melchior; difficult as it was to find in these parts people who comprehended the old man's other language, such people were to be found, and they constituted the sole hope of making contact. Melchior, equally dismayed, remembered that Gaspar had the money in his pouch.

He said, 'This country is more thickly inhabited; if we ride on until moonset we shall reach another town.'

'That I wouldn't count on. Unless you show some sense, Melchior, you will arrive at the place after this,' he jerked his head towards the little town, 'in worse case than you arrived at Jexal.'

'There was nothing wrong with me when I arrived there,' Melchior said petulantly. 'My camel was lame, that was all.'

'You have a short memory! You were so nearly starving that I was obliged to warn you to eat little and slowly.'

'Very well, I was starving and I am prepared to starve again. A man with his mind set can endure a little starvation and take no harm!'

That was the kind of thing which Gaspar was accustomed to saying, not to hearing said, and it irked him.

'Camels can't live on their thoughts,' he said. 'Go ahead, if you wish to be stubborn, and see how far you get!'

Melchior thought that over. Something of the despair he had felt as he limped into Jexal returned and made itself felt again. From that despair Gaspar had saved him.

'You have been very good, very generous,' he admitted. 'You are hungry and you are weary, and part of my mind tells me that you are sensible. Particularly as regarding the camel. It occurs to me that Senya may have gone lame because of an empty belly. An empty belly shows no symptoms, gains no sympathy; lameness does both. If we halt here . . .' the first houses of the town were now alongside, 'will you agree to start out *very* early in the morning?'

'Very early,' Gaspar said.

So, when they reached the inn, they had turned into the yard, and had been immediately accosted by a beggar of exactly the kind that Gaspar most deplored, the kind he had banished from the streets of Jexal.

Ignoring him, he nudged his camel forward, Melchior, more courteous, even to a dirty stinking beggar, said in his rusty Greek, 'I am sorry, I have nothing.' And to that Balthazar replied in the Greek of the counting house at Tyre.

'I ask nothing, except that you should take me with you as you follow the star.'

'Star! Did you say star? What do you know of the star?'

He gave his camel the signal to kneel and dismounted with stiff haste. He was ready to think that this was a fellow-astronomer from some far, far place, who having done work similar to his own had reached the same conclusion, and the thought set his heart pounding from excitement.

Two lengths ahead, farther into the yard, Gaspar's camel in some extraordinary way had sensed that its companion had knelt and been dismounted, and since what was right for one was right for both it knelt without waiting for the signal. The innkeeper, watching from his doorway, saw two men, not impressively clad, and a third whose appearance was a disgrace, and two wilting camels, obviously in the last state of exhaustion; so before Balthazar could answer Melchior the man rushed out, crying in Aramaic:

'Not there! You block the entrance!'

Neither Melchior nor Gaspar understood a word he said, but they realised that they were being shouted at; Melchior turned upon the man a look of dignified inquiry, Gaspar one of a ferocious hauteur. The combination silenced him.

Balthazar said to Melchior:

'He says we block the entrance to the yard.'

'Only for a moment,' Melchior said. 'Would you tell him that we wish these beasts taken to the enclosure, watered and fed, as much as they can eat? For ourselves a supper, with meat, and a room inside the house.'

While Balthazar was obligingly translating these orders Melchior watched him, taking more carefully into account his poor condition: he'd share his supper with him, he thought, though it was unlikely that he would be welcome inside the house, either by the innkeeper or by Gaspar, with his so-sensitive nose. But all that could wait. They must first discuss the star.

His first reaction to Balthazar's blurted tale was one of deep disappointment.

'Ah,' he said, 'a clairvoyant! Not that I decry clairvoyance, but unlike astronomy it is an inexact science, if indeed it can be called a science at all. Still you are here, and you recognised us; and you are the only person I have met in many months who seemed to have an awareness of this star at all.' He pondered the significance of this.

'You will take me with you? I beg of you. I will serve you, wait upon you, be your slave,' Balthazar said, willingly putting his head back into the yoke from which he had so recently freed it.

Melchior thought of Gaspar and his money pouch; he looked back to the time when he had been rich and independent, and to the time when he had been poor but independent, and he gave a sigh that came from his heart.

'That is not easy. And it is not for me to say. I have nothing of my own. All I ever had was spent in the pursuit of knowledge. To accompany us you would need a camel, a good camel. . . . But wait here. I will speak to my companion.'

He went into the house where in a public room Gaspar and a few other travellers who could afford the luxury were consuming the mutton and the onions and small crusty loaves of fresh-baked bread. He intended, as he took his place, to appeal to Gaspar in much the same way as he had done in the Palace at Jexal, but looking sideways at the hard young face, he had a better idea.

'There is a man who could be of inestimable use to us,' he remarked in an almost off-hand way.

'That black beggar!'

'He is not a beggar by trade. He is a man of education. He speaks the tongue that has served me fairly well, so far, but has become less and less useful lately; and he also speaks the language of the country. It has worried me, to think that we might reach our destination and not be able to make ourselves understood.'

'That is a thing to consider,' Gaspar admitted. It was not a situation which his own mind would ever have presented to him, but now that it was put to him by someone else he was able to visualise it quite clearly. 'Are you suggesting that we take him with us?'

'It would be a convenient arrangement.'

'But he stinks! Washed and re-clad he might be tolerable. And he would need a camel.'

'He would need a camel,' Melchior agreed, picking at his food and looking at Gaspar from the corner of his eye.

'Could he fit himself to travel with us, *very* early in the morning?'

Remembering the almost wild urgency in Balthazar's voice and eyes, Melchior said with assurance:

'Oh yes; he would be ready.'

'Then he'll need some money,' Gaspar said, feeling for his pouch. How many? Unconcerned as he had seemed about the cost of things he had realised that his money had lost value as he moved westwards. But even here, surely, ten would be enough. He passed the coins, unostentatiously, into Melchior's hand. 'And tell him, from me, to do something about that running sore on his arm,' he said.

Melchior took the money with a feeling of relief and of triumph, and of gratitude.

'I hope,' he said, 'that you will have reason to regard this as money well spent.' He picked up his plate and went back to the yard where Balthazar waited, patiently, sitting against a wall.

'It is arranged,' Melchior said. 'You are to come with us, if you can obtain a camel, and fresh clothes and be ready to set out before sunrise. Also you must wash and find some remedy for the sores on your arm and your feet. Here is money.'

He held it out and Balthazar's eyes bulged. He'd seen such coins–but only on three widely separated occasions–in the counting house. The most valuable coin in the world, not only because it was so heavy, of such pure gold, but because of its beauty. It was greatly in demand, not as currency, but as a decoration. Men who could afford it hung their women with gold coins both as a means of advertising their wealth and as a form of investment; and a rose jekkal was of all coins the rarest and most sought after. Any woman lucky enough to own one wore it in the very centre of her forehead, exposing the side which showed the full-blown rose which gave the coin half its name.

'Ten! I don't need ten,' Balthazar said when he had caught his breath again. 'Two will buy all I need and leave a great deal over.'

'It must be a *good* camel,' Melchior reminded him. 'We must travel fast. And in this country everything is very expensive. When last we filled our camels' food-bags the man who supplied us took one of these.'

'Then he was a thief and you were cheated. Grossly cheated. There, also, I can be of service to you. I am an accountant, of great experience. I recognise even a rose jekkal, and know its worth.'

'Take two then,' Melchior said. 'And look, I have brought you some food.' He held out his hardly touched supper.

'That was a kindly thought; but thank you, I have eaten. Not long ago. And even had I not, I could not waste time on food just now. I have a lot to do.'

'You,' Melchior said, 'are a man after my own heart.'

'And you are one of those of whom I dreamed. I knew that once I could find you, all would be well.'

Melchior carried his plate back into the house. The fat had congealed as the food cooled and it was no longer the appetising dish that it had been; he ate it without noticing, absent-mindedly and in haste. He still had his charts to consult, his reckonings to do.

'You still here?' asked the innkeeper who had been called out of the house to settle a dispute between the two men who each claimed that the other's donkey had eaten his donkey's food. 'I don't like beggars hanging about my yard. But you did a good service, speaking for those strangers, so take this. And be off.' He pushed a penny towards Balthazar who pushed it away and said:

'I wish to buy a camel, a *good* camel. Perhaps you can tell me where to go.'

Innkeepers always knew what was for sale and where; they advised travellers, and if a sale resulted they were given their percentage.

'I myself have a camel to sell. A prime camel, young and swift. A merchant came here and fell sick; we nursed him tenderly, my wife and I, but he died.' Balthazar gave a little inward shudder at the thought of what that tender nursing had been. 'He owed us a great deal,' the innkeeper went on, 'and we shall never be fully paid. There is the camel and some clothes of the kind that there is no demand for in this place!'

'Show me the camel, and also the clothes.'

'Show me your money.'

Balthazar held out the two rose jekkals, gleaming against his pinkish palm.

Two of them, the innkeeper thought: one for his pretty wife to flaunt, one to sell!

'Come with me,' he said.

Balthazar knew, even before he saw it, that the camel would be a good one; and he knew with absolute certainty that among the dead man's clothes would be a dark red robe, and a headscarf of the same colour, striped with blue and woven with a silver thread. And they were there, together with everything else, down to the very shoes which he had seen himself wearing in his dream. Exultant, bemused, one half of him gloated and rejoiced, the other half, the accountant half, stayed unmoved and bargained shrewdly. The innkeeper craved the two rose jekkals and they were too high a price to pay for an untried camel, however good-looking, and a dead man's clothes. A full bath of hot water must be included.

'Oh yes, yes,' the innkeeper said, 'the maid shall prepare it.'

'Also,' Balthazar said, 'I need ointment for my blisters and the place where the dog bit me on the arm.'

'We have, in this town, a woman most skilled in the making of ointments and potions. She keeps her own bees, and grows the pink Cistus that yield myrrh,' the innkeeper said, thinking of his percentage. 'She lives a little way along this street, in a house with a broken fence. It is late,' he said, 'and when you are bathed and reclothed it will be later still. But if you tell her that I sent you she will open her door.'

'Very good,' Balthazar said, spreading his open palm to which the two rose jekkals were now stuck. 'The camel, these clothes, enough change to buy the ointment. *And*,' he added in a fierce tone, alien to his own, 'the freedom of the little lame girl.'

'But consider,' the innkeeper protested. 'Even for two rose jekkals that is much to ask. Also the crooked one does not belong to me. She is my wife's slave.'

'Then you must ask your wife; does she wish for two rose jekkals to hang on her forehead or not.'

For the first, for the only time in his life, Balthazar felt omnipotent; on this side the fulfilment of his dream, on this the possession of two rose jekkals. . . . And yet, thinking of the little lame girl, he was sad. Tomorrow the pretty, hard-hearted wife of the innkeeper would buy just such another and treat her just as badly. And then he remembered what he had seen when the star splintered and revealed the new world that was about to come. Save the little girl now, he thought, because it was obvious that unless something was done she would not live to see that new world; the next poor creature to fall into the hands of the innkeeper's wife might be stronger, more resistant. We must play for time, Balthazar thought. He said:

'Well?' in the stern tone he had cultivated for use with the Lady's tenants.

The girl is clumsy and is always crying, the innkeeper reflected, and Ophelia does nothing but grumble about her. The next one may not be so very unattractive and maybe when Ophelia is angry with me, and bars me from her bed, I could . . .

'It is a bargain,' he said, and stretched out his hand, itching for the touch of the two rose jekkals.

'You must write the girl her paper of manumission,' Balthazar said.

'But there is the difficulty. I shall need the services of a scribe. I myself cannot write.'

'I can,' Balthazar said. 'You, I presume, can make your mark.'

'I make a good mark; it is recognised and given credit as far away as Antioch,' the innkeeper said, with some pride.

'That is well. Now, we will have the camel tethered alongside those of the lords with whom I leave in the morning; my bath will be prepared, and these clothes brought to its side. When I am reclad I will write the paper and you shall make your mark thereon.'

'It shall be done. You wish to take the girl with you?' The innkeeper was prepared to believe almost anything by this time; for to a man who had seen two, *two* rose jekkals in the palm of a filthy, sore-ridden beggar, nothing, but nothing, could come as a surprise.

'No. Once free, she will make her own way to where she wants to go,' Balthazar said. 'Now, what about my bath?'

When he was dressed he wished that he had a silver mirror, as large as the one on the Lady's dressing-table, in which to behold himself, but there was none; however the way in which the woman herbalist received him assured him that he looked respectable and well-to-do. He smiled a little sardonically as he reflected that had he arrived at her door little more than an hour ago, begging a crust, she would have bolted it against him in terror.

She made ointments of all kinds she said; he asked for the best, and she said the best ointment deserved the best jar. She had a number of little pots on a shelf, most of them made of the coarsest, thickest clay, one or two of fine, almost translucent alabaster. As she turned to take one of these down he stopped her indicating the ordinary jars.

'What a pity,' the old woman said, fretfully. 'The clay pots break easily; these,' she laid her gnarled finger almost caressingly upon an alabaster one, 'last forever, for all they look so fragile.'

'But once my sores are healed and the ointment used I shall have no use for so small a pot.'

'This is my best ointment–smell for yourself; full of myrrh, my own. A smear tonight and another in the morning and you'll never know you had a sore. And it keeps, in fact it improves with keeping. Are you sure you won't change your mind?'

'I am sure.'

She was grieved, and spooned the ointment into the little clay pot almost reluctantly.

He went back to the inn and anointed the broken blisters on his heels and the inflamed bite on his arm and then wrote out a paper of manumission worded exactly like his own. The innkeeper made his mark gladly; his Ophelia was delighted at the prospect of wearing a rose jekkal in the middle of her forehead and had said that for such a coin she would give six slaves, had she six to give. He was anxious to get to bed with her while she was in such a good mood.

'There you are. Now you are free, child,' Balthazar said. 'You can go and find your family in Antioch. Never lose this; never part with it. It is your freedom.'

'Even if it meant nothing,' the little girl said, clutching it to her flat chest,

'I would keep it to remember you by. It smells of you.'

He had written it after using the ointment, without washing his hands.

In the morning another and less favourable comment was made upon the ointment odour.

'Yesterday,' Gaspar said, 'he stank of dirt and rotting flesh; today he stinks like a harlot.' As he said that he became aware that for several days he had not been conscious of the scent of the frankincense which Melchior carried at the bottom of his camel-fodder bag. When he had caught occasional whiffs of the fragrance he had blamed them for the way in which his mind reverted to Ilya. Yet now, with the scent forgotten, he still thought of her. This realisation made him annoyed, so he regarded Balthazar with disfavour.

'Come along, come along,' he said irritably. 'I thought we were in a hurry!'

'It was you,' Melchior reminded him mildly, 'who warned me against pushing a camel too hard early in the day.'

Yet although he regarded Balthazar as his protégé, to be protected from criticism and in an oblique way spoken up for, he watched the black man's fumbling mounting and inept management of the camel with some dismay. With money, with language, he would be a valuable companion; but if he slowed down progress he must be jettisoned at once. Nothing, nothing in the world, must be allowed to delay them now.

Balthazar was aware that he was on approbation. Melchior, so considerate overnight, seemed different this morning, preoccupied and remote; in Gaspar he sensed a latent hostility–perhaps he felt that his money had been wasted upon fine clothing. If he could have spoken to Gaspar direct he would have explained that the clothes were not new, that he had driven the shrewdest possible bargain. But he did not dare disturb Melchior's thoughtful intensity by asking him to translate; and he could see that he must give all his mind to the problem of managing this animal–he had never ridden a camel before. He must also, for as long as they were together, endeavour to be of service, to make himself indispensable.

Gaspar wished that he were on horseback. A good horse could out-run a man's thoughts. On the other hand, any man worthy of the name should be able to govern his thoughts and prevent them from dwelling on the charms of a pale, frail, entirely unsuitable girl.

'Ask him,' he said, jerking his head towards Balthazar, 'whether he knows anything about the Romans.'

'Yes, indeed,' Balthazar said, when this question had been translated. 'For many years I lived in the household of a Roman lawyer–as an accountant. I speak Latin. My Latin is very good; superior to my Greek or my Aramaic.'

Melchior gave this information to Gaspar, hoping that it would cheer him. He attributed the younger man's mood to his having been compelled to rise so early. He was a rich young man, and rich young men were not accustomed to rising at dawn. He told Gaspar what Balthazar had said, and added:

'Is it not fortunate that we should fall in with one who knows so much about the people in whom you are so interested?'

Thinking of Ilya again, Gaspar said, shortly, 'Very fortunate.'

PART SEVEN

NAZARETH

90 miles

The announcement about the new taxes came as a shock to everybody. It was made in typical, sly, Roman fashion. Probably notices were put up in public places, probably the tax-farmers, already informed, had begun to spread the news; but in Nazareth, and hundreds of other small country places, it was left to the local Rabbi to make sure that everyone understood.

Harvest was over, the heat of the summer was past when Hilliel the baker, wearing his prayer shawl, stood up to break the news. The Torah had been taken out, read and solemnly replaced; the whole congregation had joined in the last chanted praise and people were preparing to disperse when Hilliel, at the raised reading desk spoke, not in his formal, synagogue voice, but as though making a remark across his bakehouse floor.

'I have been asked,' he said, 'to tell you something. It is not a thing I wish to speak of in this dedicated place, so would you, please, go out and wait under the sycamore tree. It is,' he added, 'something of importance. Please wait.'

In the synagogue women and men sat separately; at the doorway Joseph, joining Mary, slipped his hand under her elbow and said:

'Would you rather go home? Your father or your mother can tell us whatever it is this evening.'

Anne came every evening, whether or not she had seen Mary during the day. She had been delighted, transported to learn that her daughter was to have a baby. 'So soon!' she had said to Joachim. 'To tell you the truth I always thought Joseph was just a mite *old*! But no youngster could have done better.' Then, immediately she had fallen into the ambivalent state of mind of women in her position; there was nothing to having a baby, nothing at all, no need to fuss. If you were sick, you were sick and you ran off to be sick in some private place; and if your back ached, it ached and you bore it without complaint. Bearing children was what women were put into the world for, a pregnant woman was a fulfilled woman and she should be joyful. But, there was another, a darker side to this whole business. There were women–Anne could have named three or four–who had been careless, who had pushed or pulled or heaved things and lost the baby in a welter of blood and pain; and there were women who had craved things out of season and either not mentioned their craving or been denied what they craved, and their babies had been born too early, too late, ailing, deformed, even blind. 'If you hanker for anything,' Anne had said, on the first day when she knew that with any luck she was to become a grandmother, 'you just tell *me*.

Joseph is a good man, but no man can understand these things. Tell me, and I'll sell a calf–after all I rear them, all by hand; and I'll send to Sepphoris for whatever it is, *whatever* it is.' With her managing nature she had been slightly disappointed that Mary had never expressed any desire for something which, unobtainable in a village like Nazareth, would be for sale in a great new city like Sepphoris, only a good hour's walk away, and the most completely Romanised city in Galilee. On the other hand, she had been pleased, and proud that her daughter wasn't being fanciful and whimsical. Pleased and proud. Puzzled too, by Mary's disinclination to discuss her condition or the actual date when it might be expected to end.

'But you must *know*,' Anne had insisted, and she had gone in great detail into the intricacies of that calendar which, never written, never acknowledged, yet governed women's lives. So many days and a doubt, so many more days and a certainty, so many more and a delivery. Every woman, however simple, could do that reckoning.

Mary had never contributed anything to Anne's reckonings, she had never contradicted and Anne had thought–How fortunate that she will have me, and not be dependent upon the midwife! And every evening, every single evening, she had walked down the village street, always with some excuse, in order to make sure that Mary–we mustn't fuss or treat this as anything but an ordinary happening, part of ordinary life–was well, needed nothing and was taking care of herself.

She had joined them now and was subjecting her daughter to keen but tactful scrutiny, speaking as she did so about the latest-acquired of her many remarkable bargains, a length of the very finest linen, straight from the loom and only needing to be bleached before being fit for a baby's use. 'You'll be surprised when you see it,' she said, 'it's not the kind of stuff you see every day; it's more like silk. Fit for a prince!'

What was wrong with that? she wondered, seeing what she called 'that funny look' on Mary's face. In the next second she had explained it to herself; Mary was frightened that the implied assumption of the child's sex might be unlucky. 'Or a princess, come to that,' she added.

At that moment Hilliel, divested of his prayer shawl, emerged from the synagogue and moved towards the little mound out of which the sycamore tree grew. Joseph, in a lower voice repeated his question and Mary said:

'No, let us wait. It won't be long.'

Hilliel cleared his throat and said:

'I've been asked to tell you, first that we're all to be taxed anew.' There was an outbreak of groaning and Hilliel, when it had died down a little said, 'Yes, it is unlikely that there'll be reductions–I've never known them go down. The second thing is this–there's to be a new register, and to help with its making every man is to go back and register at the place where he was born.'

This was greeted by a brief astonished silence broken by one voice saying in dismay, 'But I was born in Beersheba!'

Mary and Joseph looked at one another and each saw that the other's face had whitened. They'd never spoken about the matter–though they had both heard the prophecies read and quoted often enough to know that Bethlehem, David's city, was the destined place for the birth of the Messiah. The truth was that almost immediately after Mary's return from her visit to Elisabeth, they had ceased to talk about the baby in any but the most ordinary human terms. This reticence had not come about by arrangement, or by the imposition of the will of one upon the other; it had simply happened: as though the truth would have been too much to live with day after day and they must take refuge in the pretence that everything was ordinary and normal.

The people were now battering Hilliel with questions.

'When is this register to be made?'

'By the last day of the month they call December. For us mid Tebeth.'

Satisfaction stirred in Anne's heart. As well as she had been able to reckon–with so little help from Mary–that would mean that Joseph, who would have to walk from Nazareth to Bethlehem and back again, might be away at the time of the birth. Men were nothing but a nuisance at such times, so she'd be glad to have him out of the way; and his absence would give her perfect excuse for having Mary home; with a little persuasion she would stay there until her purification rite. It couldn't have been better arranged.

The crowd did not share this feeling.

'What's the idea behind all this?' a man asked.

'I know no more than you. But I can guess. I think the Romans are using the tax as a cover for a census taking.'

'By *our* Law forbidden. On them the guilt! But that could have been done without uprooting so many.'

'It's a scheme to ruin us all,' said the disgruntled man from Beersheba who had just counted how long he would be away from his smithy.

'It can hardly be that,' Hilliel said. 'Ruined people can't pay their taxes. It may have something to do with our names. I believe the Romans find them difficult. Maybe they thought that if all the David-son-of-Davids were together on a given day it would ease matters. But I don't know. All that I was asked to tell you I have told you.'

He stepped down.

Anne, losing no time, said, 'Mary, don't give a thought to being alone. You must come and stay at home, with me, until it's all over.'

Mary said, 'Thank you. It was kind of you to think of that so quickly; but I shall go with Joseph.'

Surprise and the deepest possible consternation held Anne silent for some seconds; then she said, in a voice that made the dispersing congregation halt and turn and stare:

'Go with . . . Are you out of your mind? Ninety miles, on foot. In your last month! Child, it's impossible. Never, in all my days, have I heard such a witless notion. Mid-winter, too!'

Even as she spoke she realised that she was making no impression. To a woman of her competent, managing nature, not to be able to manage this–after her own marriage and child-bearing, the most important event in a woman's life–seemed unbearably frustrating. The hurried, ill-attended wedding had been bad enough, but at least that had been a challenge, and to arrange things in a short time as well as most women could have done in a long one had given her a secret satisfaction. This was quite different. The possibility that her grandchild should be delivered and swaddled by other hands than hers made her feel positively ill. Angry, more vehement sentences began to form in her mind, but a glance at Mary's face informed her that railing would do no good. So she tried cajolery.

'You didn't mean that. You spoke without thinking. Suppose, just suppose that your time should come when you were far away from me.

What would you do? How would you manage? You hadn't thought of that, had you? You come back home, my dear; back to your own room, so snug and cosy, and let me look after you.' Then, without allowing Mary time to speak, she added a cunning touch. 'If for no other reason, you must think of Joseph. He could be there and back in the time it would take you to get to Bethlehem. You wouldn't want to waste his time, would you now?'

Mary knew her mother. When chiding, and coaxing and craftiness failed, she could always fall back upon that reliable weapon, a fit of weeping. It would be horrible to see Anne crying because of her. Had they been wrong not to take her into their confidence? She said gently:

'Mother, I have thought of all these things, and I still want to go with Joseph.'

This would happen! Anne thought furiously. So good the girl had been all through the early, the usually most trying days, never a complaint, never a whim: and then, this! The most ridiculous, the most senseless, the most dangerous fancy surely that any woman in that state had ever entertained.

Well, there was nothing for it. Humiliating as it was, she must appeal to her son-in-law.

She looked at him sternly, daring him to go against her, and said in a deceptively reasonable way:

'This isn't for us to decide, Mary. Let's hear what Joseph has to say.'

He'd annoyed her about the hurrying forward of the wedding day, and without knowing it she was jealous of him because he was now closer to Mary and more in control of her than she herself was, but she had faith in his good sense. He'd heard everything that she had said to her daughter, standing by, saying nothing and looking a bit sheepish; he *must*, not being a fool, give the answer she wanted. But he did not; he said:

'I'd like Mary to come with me.'

'You great goat!' Anne said. 'Can't you see what a risk you'd be taking? I thought you, at least, would show some sense. Can you give me one reason, one sound *good* reason for dragging a woman, in her last month, all that way, far from her home and her kindred?'

'She wants to come, isn't that reason enough?' he said mildly. 'I shall be there, I shall take care of her. And if the child *should* be born in Bethlehem that wouldn't be so much amiss. I was born there, and my father before me.'

'Spoken like a prince!' Anne exclaimed, losing her temper completely. 'The ancestral roof! And you told me yourself you had no kin there or anywhere else. Very well, have it your own way; and blame yourself if this baby is born in a ditch. All that walking!'

'Mary will have no need to walk,' Joseph said. 'I intend to buy her a donkey.'

'You do that,' Anne said, furiously, 'then she'll have a pair!'

She turned away abruptly, knowing that she was about to cry, and even now not wishing to upset Mary. Her way led up the street, theirs led down and when they had walked for a minute Joseph said:

'In her place I should feel just the same.'

'So should I. Poor Mother! Just for a moment I wondered, should we have told her? Ought we to tell her now?'

'She has no discretion. The kindest of hearts, the best of good sense, that I grant. But if she disbelieved she would shout her derision, and if she believed she would whisper to this one, or that. It is better that she should think you wilful and me stupid.'

For a long time, almost ever since her return from her visit to Elisabeth, they had kept up a curious pretence that everything was ordinary. It had been their defence against a truth too strange to take its place in everyday life, a light too bright to be looked at without blinking. Hilliel's announcement this morning had brought them face to face with the truth again.

Mary said, 'It is all coming true, is it not? Word for word. All the Jews in Galilee and Judah wondering why that order should be given, and only we know the answer. I have so often wondered lately how I could mention Bethlehem to you. And I need not have worried.'

'I had thought of it,' Joseph admitted. 'The truth is, and it shames me to say it, I *forget*. Not wholly, but as one half forgets a dream. Day after day, my work; I come home and there you are, with my supper ready; sleep and then work again. Sometimes I wake in the night and the full realisation smites me, I wonder, I look ahead and I sweat. Then in the morning, off to work, everything so down to earth; and the truth, God forgive me, seems like something I dreamed.'

She attempted to put into words the result of hours of thought.

'Don't you think perhaps, that that is how God wanted it to be? We're the human part; the ordinariness is our contribution; all we have to contribute, really. I fix my mind on that, Joseph. He's to be born an ordinary human child, and how could that be if all the time his parents were walking about thinking that their child was the Son of God?'

'Sooner or later, though, that thought must be faced.'

'I know. But it's like Bethlehem; there were we wondering how to mention it even, and it's all arranged for us. God will look after that part of it.' She took his hand. 'Oh, Joseph, while we can, let us cling to the ordinary. There's so much to come that won't be. . . .'

So much, she thought. All those *dreadful* prophecies about being wounded, bruised and then slaughtered. One said, 'He is brought as a lamb to the slaughter.' Surely, never before, in the whole history of mankind, had any woman conceived and carried a child whose fate she knew from the first. She'd known, of course, all along, but in the early days, especially after her visit to Elisabeth, she had been filled with ecstasy and mysticism. But day by day, as the child grew and weighed heavier, became more and more part of her, her sorrow for him, her protective feeling, grew. He would be great and glorious, he would be the Son of God; but human, too, vulnerable to pain, and she, his human mother, must grieve and suffer, for him.

But these were thoughts she could share with no one. Alone in the kitchen of the little house, laying out the Sabbath food, cooked on the previous day, she did pause for a moment, gripped her hands together and said, 'God, I must leave it to You. All I ask is strength to bear what comes.' Then, carrying the dish she went in to Joseph and said, gaily:

'Mother was annoyed, wasn't she? Calling you a donkey! If she only knew, to my mind that was a compliment.'

Smoothly, beautifully, she had made everything sound safe and ordinary again.

Chapter Two

Despite all the mutterings and the prognostications of ruin, the carrying out of the latest order from Rome caused less upheaval than had been anticipated. The order was regarded as harsh and tyrannical and, as always under any kind of threat, the Jews united. Farmers who, because they were born in or near Nazareth, need make no journey, or only a short one, undertook to keep things going on the farms of those who must face longer journeys. An old smith who lived in comfort with his well-married daughter in Sepphoris walked all the way from that city to tell the man who must go to Beersheba that he would take charge of his forge while he was away; he made no favour of it, it would be as good as a holiday, he said, to get his hands on tools again.

Joseph was less fortunate in finding a substitute and was faced with the closing of his carpenter's shop when he heard through Hilliel, who had heard from the Rabbi at Japha, half an hour's walk away to the south, that a carpenter named Aaron there would be willing to undertake any urgent job, if Joseph would leave a chalked notice on his door directing any possible customers to *his* shop.

In later days, amongst his many other worries, Joseph sometimes wondered about Aaron and how long he had done two men's work before wiping that notice off the door at Nazareth. But when he came back there were the chalked words, renewed again and again, and one of his first visitors was Aaron, carrying in his hand a small bag of money and in his head an exact amount of every piece of work he had done on Joseph's behalf.

Only men, the taxpayers, the putative recruits should there ever be a general call up, were compelled to register, but Mary was far from being the only woman to accompany her man; there were women who disliked the idea of being left alone, women whose men did not wish them to be alone, and a multitude of women to whom the prospect of a family reunion was irresistible. Relatives unseen for years could be visited, children shown off, marriages arranged. The women, less politically minded and in many cases less informed about the Law, would, with the slightest encouragement, have made the whole thing into an outing–or in the case of those who remained in their own homes, an opportunity to show hospitality. The men took a more dour view, looking upon the new taxation with dread and upon the census with distrust.

In Joseph's household the preparations were complicated by two incidental things. The first was Anne's inability to accept the idea that Mary's child might be born far away, under some other woman's eye. She wept, she cajoled, she threatened to accompany them, and then withdrew the threat when she realised that two of her own brothers must return to Nazareth for the census and would have to be looked after.

'Muddling about and walking just at that time,' she said, weeping again, 'the baby'll most likely be born by the roadside.'

'That won't happen,' Joseph said firmly. 'We intend to start early. And she won't be walking, she'll be riding.'

'And being jolted, which is just as bad!'

Mention of the riding reminded Joseph of the other complication. Over the matter of the donkey he had yielded to Mary and in his heart felt that in doing so he had made a mistake. There was a donkey, very old, more than a little lame, that belonged to a man named Micah who had a little brick-kiln, and on this sorry animal Mary had set her heart.

'But it's lame,' Joseph said.

'It wouldn't be if it had some rest. If we could buy it now and feed it up a little . . .'

Joseph's mind underwent the by-now-familiar dichotomy; this woman, my wife; this woman, chosen of God to be the mother of His Son.

'If only I could afford it,' he said, 'you should have a white pony with red harness.'

'I'd much rather have Micah's donkey, who is already my friend. I give him crusts and cabbage leaves, and though he is so roughly treated, he's very gentle. Please, if you really think I need a donkey, let it be that one.'

Joseph had given in hastily because he was afraid that she was about to cry–and in all the time he had known her he had never once known her to use tears as a weapon as so many women did. Actually she had been on the brink of tears, thinking of the hopelessness of it all. Micah would buy another donkey, younger, stronger, which soon, from ill-usage, would be as lame and dejected looking as this one. You couldn't save them all.

And then, for the first time, her mind touched upon the other side of those direful prophecies. *He* can, she thought. He will be God, all-powerful, and at the same time He'll be human. He'll know about pain and being hurt, about bruises and stripes. And when all the prophecies have been fulfilled and He emerges in glory, He'll do something for humble, helpless things. If necessary, she thought. I shall ask Him: I shall say–Please do this for me, your mother. . . .

It didn't do to pursue such thoughts, they made her feel frightened and dizzy.

'I shall take some tools,' Joseph was saying. 'You never know. Most people have a job for a carpenter and never get around to sending for him. I could shore up a beam or respoke a wheel in return for a night's lodging, maybe.' For with them, as with hundreds of other Jews, ready money was short. In the country a good deal of trade was still being done by a system of barter and many families had difficulty in gathering enough coined money to meet the demands of the tax-gatherers.

As well as the tools they would carry food of the kind that would not spoil by keeping. The task of providing this was taken out of Mary's hands by Anne who in the last few days before the departure never visited without bringing some offering. A smoked mutton ham, a great jar of pickled eggs, a cheese the size of a mill-stone; dried figs, raisins and dates, a string of salted fish; a huge honey-cake. . . .

'At least you shan't starve, you wilful girl!' she said, beginning to cry again. Then mopping her eyes with the edge of her veil she said, 'And what, pray tell me, is this that I hear about that ass of Micah's? Is it true? On that very first day Joseph said you should have a donkey to ride. Does he call that bit of carrion a donkey?'

'I chose it,' Mary said. 'And it is now not a bit lame; there's gloss on its coat too. It will get me to Bethlehem.'

'I no longer understand you,' Anne said. 'I reared you well and you were always meek and amenable. Now you are very headstrong. Rushing off to Bethlehem, without the slightest need. At such a moment, too! And on a broken-down donkey. . . .' She began to cry again.

This was all such a far cry from annunciation on the hill-top, from the moment of ecstasy in Elisabeth's garden, that one human mind could hardly be expected to contain, to deal with it all. Should I, Mary wondered, have taken my mother into full confidence from the first? But I knew then that she would think I was mad, and if I told her now she would think the same. This predicament and the discomfort it causes me is part of the price I must pay.

She said, 'I want to see Bethlehem because it was Joseph's birthplace and a place of importance in our history. You yourself told me that first children are often as much as two weeks late. The donkey is sound now. Can you not take comfort in the thought that I may go, and be back?'

'It is possible, I suppose. But I wanted you to be with me, in your own room, being looked after.'

'Then my uncles, Dan and Asher, would have had to look for lodging elsewhere. Are you sure . . .' Anne, the provider, could surely be diverted by any question concerning food, 'that in giving us so much to take with us, you have not depleted your stores?'

'I never–as you know,' Anne said, instantly diverted, 'take one mutton leg from the chimney without putting another one in. And the same with the cheese, before the ripe one is eaten another is ready. For the lesser things I still have time in plenty. They haven't so far to come.'

'Still, they'll be hungry and happy to taste your cooking again,' Mary said swiftly, for at the word 'far' Anne's eyes had filled anew. But her distress did not prevent her from being practical.

'You *may* be right about getting back to have the baby here; but don't, for pity's sake, forget to take the baby's things. And don't be brave. Oh, I know I've brought you up not to make a fuss of an ache or a pain, but there are times when a woman can be *too* brave. At the first sign of a pain, make for a respectable house with a decent woman in it. I shall hope and pray that you're not taken on the road, but if you are . . .' She fumbled in her dress and pulled out a little bag. 'Twenty sestertii,' she said, producing her horde with justifiable pride. 'Enough to pay for your lodging and the services of a good midwife.'

Overcome, Mary said, 'You are the best mother in the world!' and as though the praise had in some manner restored her to herself, Anne said, almost in her old sharp way:

'I only hope that your child will never bring you as much grief as you have me, just lately.'

They set out at first light on the appointed morning. Mary rode on the donkey which also carried two bags, one of food–the jar of eggs had been left in the house, one of clothing, everything the baby would need and one change of linen for each of them. Joseph shouldered his bag of tools. To him Micah's old donkey resembled a careful housewife's bowl, once broken and mended with strips of linen soaked in flour-and-water paste. It might look all right, but the flaws were there, and under stress it was likely to collapse.

It worried him, and he worried that he should be worried. It showed such a lamentable lack of faith. There was no *need* for anxiety, he told himself, again and again. It has been foretold that the Messiah should be born in Bethlehem, and there he would be born, even if the old donkey fell dead.

When he thought such a thought he would enjoy a feeling of relief, but the carefree moments never lasted. God will provide, he'd think, and I do believe that; but *through* me. I'm responsible; I was chosen. After all, he'd think, every pious Jew believes that Jehovah sent the ravens to feed Elijah, and could do the same any day, yet we work for our daily bread. And I believe that Jehovah will bring us to Bethlehem, but I must act and think as an ordinary, prudent man in my circumstances would do. And then, there he'd be, worrying away again.

After a while, when the donkey flagged, Joseph added the bag of food and then the bag of clothing to his own load; and that moment, which might have been one of recrimination, was sweetened by a laughing reference to Anne's sharp remark about Mary's two donkeys. Then on a long, uphill stretch Mary said she would walk for a bit and when Joseph protested she said, 'Walking is good for women in my state. Remember that one of my grandmothers was a desert woman, and when the desert people are on the move between two wells they dare not stop and risk disaster to all because a woman is about to have a baby. She walks to the last moment, bears her child, swaddles it and walks on.'

'And sometimes dies,' Joseph said sombrely.

That was another thing that worried him. The sacred writings told of an immaculate conception, a virgin birth, but they said no word about what happened to the mother. There were times, horrible almost unbearable times, when he felt that death in childbed must be the logical end. Was it possible to visualise a woman, the ostensible wife of a carpenter, going about her household tasks, with complete right to call herself the Mother of God? It wasn't possible, and the only alternative was death; and whenever Joseph thought of that he plunged deep into the pit of premature bereavement. He loved her now, with a love that was completely different from the love he had felt for the pretty young girl who had caught his eye, and most surprisingly consented to marry him. These celibate months had taught him something that very few men ever guessed, or imagined, however dimly. He loved Mary as a person, not as a woman, as a companion, not as a bedfellow. And he had come to understand, grudging his own understanding, why she had been chosen; beautiful, kind, gentle, intelligent, witty at times, knowing when to speak and when to remain silent . . .

Mary said, 'I am not going to die, Joseph; on that score put your mind at rest. This will be an ordinary human baby and God will know that he needs a mother to suckle him and rear him. I shan't die until I see him come into his kingdom. I shall be an old woman, with grey hair and nobbly knuckles, and very probably a sharp tongue, like my mother's.'

But she thought–A man of sorrows and acquainted with grief, and she knew, with deadly certainty, that she would witness the death of this child who now, vibrant with new life, kicked her in the ribs. He would be human, and as a human he would die; but he would also be the Son of God, and as such immortal. Difficult to understand, impossible to communicate, but in her heart she knew.

So they moved southwards. Every morning the old donkey set out bravely, the finished product of at least four thousand years of conditioning, from the free wild ass, stamping his hill beat, through captivity, gelding, near-starvation, into this tempered slave, this triumph of survival. But each day, when he began to sag and limp, and with any ordinary owner would have been given fresh impetus from pain, whip or stick or goad, Mary alighted. And each day she walked more heavily. Presently Joseph began to fret about the weather.

There were always a few weeks when, even as far south as Jerusalem, the rain-laden winds were chilly; about once in every three years the rain would turn to snow; even more rarely there would be frost. Such times were known as bad winters and helped to date things: before, or just after, or during the last bad winter, people would say, recalling some event. Joseph hoped and prayed that this was not to be one of those bad winters; but the signs indicated that it might be. The wind veered and came screaming down from the north, filling the sky with leaden, swollen-looking clouds. Then, in the evening, after they had found a place to sleep–and for all his anxiety he always insisted upon stopping early–he'd go out to attend to the donkey, or simply to sniff the wind; and the sky, so lowering all day, would be swept clear of clouds and the stars would shine with a frosty sparkle. There was one, particularly large and bright, which seemed to look down and say 'Frost tomorrow!' Frost or snow, and what would happen to the old donkey, already making such heavy going that occasionally Joseph lost patience with it?

'When he worked for Micah he carried heavier loads,' he'd say. Or, 'He takes advantage of you; he knows he has only to sigh and you'll get down and walk.'

It worried him greatly when people passed them in the road; and it seemed that everybody passed them, even people on foot. Mary walked slowly and heavily now and easily grew short of breath.

'If all these people are bound for Bethlehem, the place will be crammed,' he said.

Mary always replied, 'Don't worry, Joseph; there'll be a place for us.'

She said that on the last morning, just as Joseph, shouldering his bag, took the donkey's head-rope and said:

'Come on you! We're having no nonsense today!'

And at that moment he felt, on his cheek, the first, soft, almost caressing, deadly ominous touch of a snowflake.

PART EIGHT

ON THE ROAD TO JERUSALEM FROM JERICHO

11 miles

After Balthazar had joined them, Melchior and Gaspar travelled more comfortably and cheaply. He did all their shopping, took on the menial jobs of camel-tending, fire-making and cooking when they camped in the open, negotiated all the arrangements if they slept at inns. He could also have made the journey much more interesting and instructive, had Melchior not been so impatient. Gaspar was eager to exploit his ability to ask questions and explain things, but Melchior often acted as a buffer, saying, 'We have no time now. That can wait.'

The company of a third person brought the inevitable discord. Two men, however, different in character, can, unless they are unreasonable, come to terms between themselves; with two there can be no taking of sides, and in an argument it is one voice against one voice. With three it is different.

Usually, as they pressed onward, Balthazar, in any argument, tended to side with Melchior who had befriended him, who followed the star, who was a man of education, the man to whom he could speak directly, the man who, except when preoccupied or bothered about time, was friendly. But when, as they came nearer to Jerusalem their arguments were no longer concerned with such trivial things as to when to stop and where to spend the night, but devolved upon their point of destination, then Balthazar found himself siding with Gaspar.

'I know now,' Melchior said, coming back from a session with his chart and his tools, 'that Jerusalem cannot be the place. It is too far north. If we come to a road which branches off we should do well to take it. This road is crowded and leads to the city. We have no reason to enter the city at all.'

There followed one of their awkward, three-cornered arguments.

Balthazar could recall, with complete clarity, the maps that had hung upon the walls of the counting house in Tyre. On them all the caravan routes were marked, and every city with which the Greek did business was ringed in red.

'There is no large city directly south of Jerusalem,' he said with what, for him, was assurance. 'South of Jerusalem there are a few villages, sheep country, then desert and nothing else until you come to Egypt. In my dream, or my vision–call it what you will–I saw the three of us, riding into the gateway of a city, a walled city with many towers. There is no such place south of Jerusalem.'

'I'm inclined to discount what you saw,' Melchior said, politely, but firmly, 'as I told you, clairvoyance is an inexact science. The star has guided me, unfailingly, for thousands of miles. Am I now to disregard it because of something you saw in a dream or a trance? With no moment to waste, mark you.'

'What is it now?' Gaspar asked, sensing contention. Melchior informed him, briefly. And with almost equal brevity Gaspar said:

'I wish to see Herod, and Jerusalem. I do not like huckster's talk, but it is a fact that you have come so far at my expense.'

'That I do not deny,' Melchior said sourly, 'but it is of no importance.' He looked at his two companions and thought how dangerously easy it would be to hate them both, the young man with his money and his passion to see things and ask questions; the black man with his chatter about visions; both of them prepared to waste time, that most precious commodity of all, by going to Jerusalem, the one to satisfy idle curiosity, the other to fulfil his dream. Yet they were both indispensable.

Balthazar looked at his two companions and thought how easy it would be to dislike them both: the young man so arrogant because of his money, the old man so stubborn about his errand. He thought of his vision, the risks he had taken–would either of them have risked such a flogging as he would endure if recaptured? Yet, in their separate ways, they scorned, or were oblivious to, the thing which had made him risk his life.

Gaspar looked at his two companions and thought how pleasant it would be to hate them; the old man, so physically inexhaustible, with all his gabble about stars and his innate arrogance; the black man, so emasculate and servile. Yet there they were, his left hand and his right. Without them he could not ask for so little as a cup of water.

'What you saw,' Melchior said to Balthazar, 'could have been the gateway to a Palace. Perhaps with your real eyes you have never seen one. I have seen many, with great gateways and towers and turrets, easily to be mistaken for cities. . . .'

'With my real eyes I have seen palaces. In Egypt, in Tyre . . . places that you perhaps have never heard of. Believe me, I know a palace from a city as you know a radish from a melon. And I saw us, dressed just as we are and riding the camels we ride, passing into the gates of a city. I know,' Balthazar said, with the humility that has power because, being so low it cannot be struck down, 'that you ridicule my vision. But I beg you, ask yourself; but for that vision, which brought me to you, where now would you be?'

'Lost and penniless, in a strange land,' Melchior said with equal humility. 'That I admit, and so, when he understands, will he. But I still say that Jerusalem is not my goal and I am positive that to go into Jerusalem will not only be a wicked waste of time, but, because of the waste, dangerous to the child.'

'Now I beg you to consider,' Balthazar said, 'you look at the stars and see a child, connected with a star. I–dreaming, or tranced, what you will, see a star and the gateway of a great city. In ordinary terms, which of us, I ask you, carries most weight? He'–he nodded towards Gaspar–'has seen nothing, but he has paid and paid and paid. And he wishes, you tell me, to see Jerusalem. Could we not oblige him?'

'It is the waste of time,' Melchior said. 'That is all I deplore. You have been useful, he has been useful. I would gladly oblige you both. If you asked my right hand I would lay it on the block, willingly. But for nine months now I have followed this star and it does not, I swear, lead to Jerusalem. And time matters.'

'What are you gabbling about?' Gaspar asked in the voice that often called the Five Hundred to attention. Melchior told him, shortly, honestly. And that gave Balthazar time to think up a really clinching argument.

'Suppose,' he said to Melchior, 'you had not decided to halt at that inn where you found me. There was the twilight hour left; you could have ridden on, and five miles along the road found a better inn. Then you would have missed me and by now every one of his rose jekkals would have been spent, people cheating you as they did. Is it not possible that, leaving the intervention of gods and goddesses aside, there is *something* that governs our lives? Your stars, my dreams, his . . . what has he, poor man, except his money? A wish to see Jerusalem. To see Jerusalem he has travelled far and hard. May it not be that his will as much significance as your star and my dream? May it not be that we are to go to Jerusalem because something awaits us there?'

'I do not understand such talk,' Melchior said coldly. He added, with reproach. 'I thought you were a sensible man.'

As he read it, the place for which he was bound was only a short distance from Jerusalem; he could travel so far without the help of Gaspar's money; what he feared was that he would reach his destination and find that nobody understood his message. Very soon Balthazar might be of the utmost importance, and he set himself to argue, to cajole, anything to win Balthazar round to his way of thinking. But in his humble, unaggressive way the black man was adamant. The fact that he had found these companions, was riding a camel, wearing the very clothes of his vision, fortified his stubbornness.

'I shall know the gateway when we reach it,' he said. 'And we must ride in.'

Then, soon, there was another trouble; the roads became crowded, not with the ordinary traffic, designed for speed, but by slow-moving groups of people on foot, mainly men, but enough women and children to be noticeable. A few rode inferior donkeys, here and there there was a cart with slow-turning, creaking wheels; everywhere, there were bundles. To Melchior they were merely a nuisance, but to Gaspar, who was interested in everything and only too willing to halt and order Balthazar to ask questions, they were a prod to curiosity.

'One would think,' he said, 'that they were fleeing from the sack of a city, but that they go in both directions. Ask him to ask who they are and where they are going.'

The first question Balthazar could answer immediately.

'They are all Jews,' he said and hoped that Gaspar would be content with that, and not insist that he stop and ask questions and thus provoke Melchior even more. But Gaspar insisted; so Balthazar gathered as much information as he could in the shortest possible time, and reported.

'They are going back to their places of birth in order to be taxed.'

'By whose order?'

'By the order of the Emperor, Caesar Augustus.'

Gaspar looked at the throng, moving this way and that, and gave his verdict.

'Then he is a fool as well as a rogue. What a way to organise taxation! In Jexal, when I . . .' He paused, on the brink of betraying himself. 'When I lived there the whole tax system was reorganised from top to bottom.

People were ordered to stay in their homes and the officials went round. It was quiet and orderly. And all over in a day.' He looked more closely at the people, finding, on the whole, little likeness to the one Jew he knew.

'A miserable-looking lot,' he commented. Melchior passed this remark on to Balthazar–as he passed, almost without thinking, these days, any remark made by either man.

Balthazar said, 'I think they are unhappy. Not only about the new taxing. They believe that they are being counted and that is displeasing to their God. I was once well acquainted with a Jew who told me many interesting things. One of their own kings numbered them, long ago and their God was angry and killed many people–to put the numbers wrong again!' He allowed his voice to be tinged by ridicule, remembering the time when he had been anxious to give himself to Eliezer's God and been rejected with contempt.

'If they really believed that, or in their God,' Gaspar said, thinking of the old carpet merchant's honesty over the purple dye, 'they would rebel.'

'Rome is mighty,' Balthazar said, 'Also the Jews have no leader.' A long-buried loyalty to Eliezer, and the memory of the stories with which that fellow-slave had entertained him, made him say, 'When they had leaders they fought well and won many battles.'

Melchior, remembering that fantastic horoscope that he had worked out at the top of his tower in a long ago Spring, said:

'The child who is about to be born might lead them. If only we arrive in time. Which we may not if you insist upon wasting time in Jerusalem!'

The three-cornered argument then began again and went on until, just north of Jericho, something happened to give Gaspar a temporary ascendancy.

Lately they had abandoned any attempt to sleep in caravanserais; they were too crowded and uncomfortable. This was well-watered country and it was easy enough to let the camels drink their fill at some public watering place, and Balthazar could shop, well and shrewdly, for what food they needed; he could also cook. Sometimes the nights were chilly but an unspoken competition in hardiness prevented any one of the three from complaining of that.

On this evening, when Gaspar pointed out as he so often did, that the camels were exhausted, and the truth of that was apparent even to Melchior, they were on a narrow road which wound in and out and up and down in bare, hilly country. The road, for once, was clear–which made Melchior all the more annoyed by the necessity to halt at all; none of the three was informed enough to know that this stretch of road was notorious and that nobody in his right senses would be anywhere on or near it after sunset. Looking for a place to camp they came upon a break in the rocks which for a long time had enclosed the road like a wall and Balthazar, the one who felt the cold most, and also regarded himself as being responsible for most of their practical arrangements, pointed out that if they pulled off the road here, they would be sheltered by the rocks on either side; that he could hear the noise of one of those curious little waterfalls which in this country appeared from nowhere and disappeared again; that this would, indeed, be an ideal place in which to spend the night. Melchior, raising his eyes to the heights on either side the little opening, agreed that it would be a good place; on either side the rocks rose sheer, unclimbable, but straight ahead was a steep incline, covered with scree up which he could make his way and so gain a clear view of the sky. Gaspar, though accustomed to flat, open spaces, relished the loneliness of the place, and looking at the hard, inhospitable terrain, felt respect for the men whom Benjamin had mentioned to him: the nameless men, the night-walkers, the rebels who had taken to the hills.

Earlier in the day Balthazar had bought some goat meat and he was soon busy, making a fire and rigging up his makeshift spit. He now carried the two forked sticks and the cross-piece with him, having learned that there were places where one could not count on finding even a bush. He was glad that the duty of provisioning the party had fallen to him, for Melchior and Gaspar, though willing enough to eat when food was handy, never gave it much thought beforehand. It seemed, at times, as though they were trying to outdo one another in their indifference to it. Balthazar, for the most of his life, had been accustomed to regular meal-times; even when the Lady's temper had resulted in a reduction of slaves' rations, there had always been something to eat when meal-times came round. And he had enough to contend with in the mere riding; he never complained, was never the one to suggest a halt, he had no intention of being a drag on his company; but the stiffness in his fingers had often, by the end of the day, communicated itself to every bone in his body and sometimes when he alighted from his camel the whole earth would swing and sway and reel around him.

He made the fire, lighting it with a little bundle of sticks which he prudently carried, and then in the fading light began to hunt about for something to keep it going. Evidently, at some season of the year, even these barren rocks bore some short-lived vegetation; all withered and scorched and dead now, but with roots, waiting the winter rains and the soft warmth of a brief spring. He grubbed out an armful of them and carefully replenished the fire. Soon the savoury, peculiarly pungent scent of roast goat meat filled the narrow place. The camels grunted and groaned as they slept. Gaspar indulged in one of the short naps which Balthazar envied; he could sleep for a few minutes at any time, in any place and wake instantly, with all his wits about him. Melchior unrolled a chart and holding it close to the fire–so close that once the sizzling meat spat fat into his eye–studied it, gloomily.

They ate, pulling the meat apart with their fingers and passing from hand to hand the goatskin of cheap wine mixed with water which Balthazar had provided, each one careful to wipe his mouth on his sleeve before drinking, and the mouth of the container afterwards. They were half-way through their meal when Gaspar lifted his head, listened, seemed to sniff the air like a dog.

'We are not alone,' he said to Melchior, and getting to his feet, put his hand to his knife which he carried thrust into the belt of his baggy trousers, under his leather jacket. 'See,' he said, and pointed towards the slope of scree up which, as soon as he had eaten, Melchior proposed to scramble. Neither Melchior nor Balthazar had heard anything, and looking into the darkness outside the fire's range, they saw nothing for a minute; then they did, and it was a frightening sight. Three men, all looking larger than normal, clad in tatters that fluttered as they moved, all carrying clubs, all with wild, desperate faces.

'Robbers,' Balthazar said in a breathy whisper, recognising the breed. His legs had turned numb, his stomach quaked; one blow from a club like that and you'd be dead, or hopelessly disabled.

Melchior, alarmed, but still thinking clearly, said:

'The camels. They must not take the camels. Gaspar, give them everything we have. The camels they must not take.' Lose the camels now and all would be wasted.

To Gaspar these were the men he wanted to see, members perhaps of that nameless, un-numbered army of rebels who might one day be his allies.

'Do not be frightened,' he said. 'I am here. Melchior, tell him to speak civilly. Tell him to ask them what they want.'

The men were now within hand's reach and arrogance hung about them, palpable, unmistakable. One old, frail man, a soft, flabby merchant, obviously rich and as obviously terrified, and one, younger and capable of giving trouble but prepared, from his attitude, to be placating. A hired guard, perhaps, with no intention of risking a cracked head to protect the interests of those who had hired him.

Balthazar asked the question and one of them replied:

'To begin with, a share of your meal.'

'They wish to eat with us,' Balthazar told Melchior, and Melchior said to Gaspar:

'Let them take the food, the gold, everything; but *not* the camels.'

In the desert the rules of hospitality were strict; it came easily to Gaspar to say:

'Tell him to ask them to sit down and eat.' But it was plain that these men did not know the rules. They were already helping themselves. Most unmannerly!

'I have many questions to ask them,' Gaspar told Melchior. 'Tell him to ask them where they come from, how many they are, how they feel about Herod and about the Emperor of Rome.' Never yet in all this journey had Gaspar so much regretted his inability to speak strange tongues.

But with these men even Balthazar's skill was unavailing. They understood his quavering questions, that was plain by the way they laughed and nudged one another and laughed again.

They gave no proper answers. One said:

'We have no names; we are not numbered. We know nothing of Herod, or the Emperor of Rome.'

Wary and dangerous as wolves, they squatted by the fire and ate all that was left of the goat meat and the bread which Balthazar had bought from a village bakery at midday, and they made short work of the wine.

One of them said, 'Tell the young one to sit down and take his hand off his knife handle.'

Already terrified, Balthazar felt considerable dismay in being ordered to give Gaspar such a curt command. The young man with his haughty looks and his money was still, to the slave, a figure of awe. He said to Melchior:

'The one with the most hair wishes that Gaspar should sit down and remove his hand from his knife.'

Melchior passed on the words and Gaspar sat down in an attitude that any of his own would have known to be potentially dangerous. He sat with his legs crossed and the outer edges of his feet resting on the ground. It looked relaxed enough, but the slightest pressure against the sides of his soles would bring him upright. His arms were crossed too, but in such a fashion that in a blink of an eye his hand would be back on his knife.

Such precautions were second nature to him; he felt no fear; only a burning interest in the men who looked so hardy, who gave such cautious answers; and a maddening frustration because he could only communicate with them through Melchior *and* Balthazar. How could he be certain that the questions were rightly put and the answers rightly returned? He tried again.

'Ask them their names,' he said.

The answer came back from the same man who had spoken before.

'We have no names.' All three laughed.

They were remarkably uncouth, Gaspar reflected; a good deal of discipline would be needed to turn them into anything like a useful fighting force. But they looked hard and tough, quite unlike the harassed, tame Jews who were hurrying about in obedience to Caesar's command. Something could be made of them, if it came to the pinch.

'Ask them if they follow a leader.'

'We have no leader,' the answer came back.

The wine, though watered, was still potent–Balthazar was a careful shopper; and in the hills wine was a rarity. The three men grew hilarious, laughing at nothing. One of them reached out and snatched off Melchior's hat, set it on his own shaggy head, and exercising some peculiar gift of mimicry, composed his body and features into a caricature of the old man.

Melchior, unaffected by the mockery, said to Balthazar:

'Tell him he can have my robe as well. Anything but the camels.'

And why, Balthazar asked himself, as he translated this statement, should they spare the camels? It was plain to him that these were robbers, bandits, who would take everything. They would certainly take the camels, drive them away over the hills and sell them somewhere, cheaply.

But the laughter, the mocking of Melchior's dignity, affected Gaspar; leaning forward a little from the hips he said to the shaggy-haired man:

'Stop that; and give back the hat.'

The shaggy-haired one, without understanding the words, sensed the protest, and replied, mocking Gaspar:

'Yack-yack-yack! Yack-yack-yack!' And they all rocked with laughter.

'We'll have all your hats! And everything else you have!'

Balthazar said to Melchior, 'These are robbers; they will strip us of everything.'

Melchior said to Gaspar, 'They are bandits. They will take all.'

'They will take nothing! Wait. Leave this to me.'

It had dawned upon him, with the snatching of Melchior's hat, that these were not the dignified, dedicated men-of-the-hills of whom old Benjamin had spoken with such respect, and whom he had come so far to see.

And there were three of them, men in their prime, armed, against him alone. At a moment like this he couldn't count upon the frail old scholar, or the easily terrified black fellow. And what could one knife do against three clubs? Strategy was called for.

Suddenly he swayed back, laughing, laughing; his teeth bared in a grin as wolfish as any of theirs.

'Laugh,' he said to Melchior. 'Tell him to laugh. Laugh, I said, this is important!'

Melchior, wildly distressed at the prospect of losing the camels, managed only a death's-head grimace; Balthazar, trained in obedience, creased his face into a smile that was in ill-accord with the terror in his eyes where too much white was showing.

'Now tell him,' said Gaspar, pretending to hold his sides with amusement, 'that when I move my hat he is to offer his turban to the one nearest him; but to loosen it first. Say this as though you were joking with him!'

Smiling pallidly Melchior passed on this order.

Still laughing loudly, Gaspar took off his hat, held it a second in his hand and looked at Balthazar, who immediately removed and loosened his beautiful turban. Gaspar clapped his hat on to the head of one of the men, pushing it down, still acting as though it were a joke. Balthazar put his turban upon the head of the third and a fold fell. . . .

They were still laughing, the two temporarily blinded when Gaspar got to his feet, drew his knife across the throat of the one who wore Melchior's hat, and in less than a breath's space dispatched, in similar fashion, the other two. It was done so quickly, so surely, with such deadly savagery, that neither Melchior nor Balthazar could believe that it was done. One second the throats were emitting laughter and the next gushing fountains of blood.

Gaspar wiped his knife on the rags of the last man he had killed and straightened up, his face impassive.

Melchior, that civilised man, felt a single queasy heave of the stomach, but it died away under the thought–The camels are safe. He said:

'By my father's grave, you are quick.'

'In my country,' Gaspar said, 'a man is either quick or dead.'

Balthazar, who had seen blood spilt before, was far more affected; he hadn't the strength just then to stand up, so he shuffled backwards a little on his haunches and, turning out of the firelight, threw up his supper.

Then something extraordinary happened. From the top of the rocky wall to the left of the enclosed space in which, by the fire, three men in grotesque attitudes lay dead, and one live man calmly sheathed his knife, and one thought of his errand, and one vomited, something came hurtling down, stumbled as it fell, recovered itself and made for Gaspar.

It was a boy, quite a small one, no more than six or seven years old, but in such a blind, murderous rage that he was momentarily as dangerous as a tiger. Had he worn shoes the kicks he aimed at Gaspar's shins would have done real damage, the will to damage was there, but he was barefoot. And his teeth, directed at Gaspar's throat, were defeated by the collar of the leather jacket. He had launched himself, made the assault in silence, but under the double frustration he began to scream. Gaspar took him by the nape of the neck and held him at arm's length, as though he were a puppy. The boy's legs and arms thrashed about and he went on screaming. Gaspar dispassionately cuffed him about the head until suddenly he hung, limp and quiet.

'One of their cubs,' he said, dropping the boy to the ground, and looking about. 'There may be others.'

But all was quiet.

'We must go,' Melchior said, standing up on legs that were not quite steady. 'This is a dangerous place.'

Balthazar wiped his mouth and his sweat-drenched face and turned back into the firelight, carefully avoiding looking at the dead men.

The boy, who had stood, dazed and dizzied where Gaspar had dropped him, moved and went to the side of the shaggy-haired man who had taken Melchior's hat. He said:

'You killed my father. I wish I could kill you.'

Balthazar, falling into place again, said to Melchior:

'That man was the boy's father.'

'The boy's father,' Melchior said to Gaspar.

'A spirited boy,' Gaspar said; but Melchior disregarded the remark. They must get away from here.

'You killed him,' the boy said again. 'He was only seeking food.' He began to cry. 'He was bringing me my supper. Look!'

He fumbled in the dead man's rags; and Balthazar, the only one who understood what the boy said, forced himself to watch, and it was true. Under cover of the ravenous eating, the greedy drinking, the horse-play, the man had remembered the child and secreted a good hunk of goat meat and some bread.

'He had saved some for the boy,' Balthazar said. This remark Melchior considered not worth passing on.

'Come,' he said, 'let us go.'

But Gaspar and Balthazar seemed to be fascinated by the boy. He held the food in his hand and he looked at it with a tragic expression, tears streaking his dirty face; but he was hungry, plainly very hungry, for though he wept with his eyes, his mouth began to drool like a dog's. Then, suddenly he ceased to cry, his mouth folded in on itself, and he flung the meat and the bread straight at Gaspar's face. Gaspar, with one of his swift movements, ducked and the two missiles went over his head.

It was sad; so much Melchior admitted, in his mind. But the men were robbers and might have taken the camels and rendered his whole errand abortive. The boy had made his gesture; and probably, as soon as they had gone, would hunt for the food, find it and eat it.

He said again, 'Come. Let us go.'

But Gaspar said, 'I like this boy. Ask Balthazar what other food we have.'

Impatiently, Melchior asked, and Balthazar said that all the meat was now eaten; they still had bread and some cheese.

'Give him some.' Gaspar said. And while Balthazar opened the food-bag, he retrieved their headgear; Melchior's first; the old man took it and with an impatient gesture, slapped it on his head; then his own, unsullied; the extreme end of Balthazar's turban, hanging down over the robber's face, was damp and dark with blood. Gaspar, with a delicacy of feeling that nobody would have given him credit for, took out his knife, cut off the soiled portion, threw it on the fire, and tucked the raw edge back. Balthazar, returning with the food, accepted the turban with fastidious suspicion, but it looked all right. . . .

The boy took the proffered food with a look in which sullenness and something else warred for mastery.

'Ask him to ask the boy's name.'

'Such a waste of time!' Melchior said. 'What does his name matter?' But he passed on the question and Balthazar asked it, gently.

The boy said, 'I am the son of my father. My name is Barabbas.'

Melchior, moving towards the camels, tossed this piece of worthless information, as he had tossed many similar pieces, to Gaspar.

'Tell him I wish I had such a son and that I am sorry his father is dead. But it was necessary.' As he spoke Gaspar fumbled in his pouch and brought out a rose jekkal. The boy took it and said something. Balthazar spoke, Melchior spoke.

'He says his father is dead but he is alive and he will be avenged.'

They mounted their camels and turned them, and as the weary, unwilling animals moved, grunting and protesting, down the defile towards the road, the boy pelted them. Two crusty loaves, a piece of cheese, a rose jekkal and then lumps of rock, thrown with unerring aim, and with all the impetus of impotent fury, hit the camels' hindquarters, so that their pace, for a few moments, satisfied even the impatient Melchior, who had just realised that with all this fuss he had failed to take his nightly reckoning.

Next day, thinking over the incident calmly, he realised that but for Gaspar they would have lost their camels; and that even Gaspar's speedy trickery could not have succeeded without Balthazar's gift of tongues. So his opposition to their desire to enter Jerusalem was rather less obdurate than it might have been. He gave in, grudgingly and petulantly. 'One hour, then. That is all I can spare. And that is an hour wasted,' he said.

And then, of course, when they reached the great city, with the massed towers, the many roofs showing above the walls of hewn stone, and thousands of people going this way and that, halting progress in the most infuriating way, Balthazar must choose to be difficult. He said, 'This is not the one, I'm sorry,' at gateway after gateway. Gaspar, all agog, was quite willing to ride all round the city, but Melchior, though the day was very cold, felt hot sweat prick out all over him, even to his eyelids as they wasted time and wasted time.

Then, as they came towards the Gate of the Fountain, Balthazar said in a tranced, ecstatic voice, 'This is it! This is the gate through which I saw us riding.' He halted his camel and would have sat there, staring, had not Melchior said peevishly:

'Let us ride in then, and get it over with.'

Gaspar had been assessing the city with a soldier's eye. It was a strong, fortressed city which, properly provisioned and held by resolute men, would withstand a prolonged siege. Not, compared with Jexal, a beautiful city, but certainly strong.

To him, Melchior said in the same peevish way:

'*I* have not come so far to sight-see! There will be time to stare later.'

So they rode into Jerusalem; and even Melchior was slightly pacified to find that Balthazar had chosen the gate that was nearest to the Palace of Herod.

PART NINE

TYRE

200 miles

Ephorus, Greek by birth, and once a sailor had been stranded in Bethlehem for eleven years, and knew that he would die there: yet there never was a morning when, blinking his gritty eyes, licking his dry swollen lips with a dry swollen tongue and throwing back the shutter, he didn't think–What a place! How did I land here? Why do I stay? The answers to both questions would pour into his momentarily sober mind, smooth as oil, and he'd take a cup, draw some wine, add a few drops of water and drink. The first drink of the day. Then he felt better, able for about an hour to make himself useful about the place. An old sailor–he called himself that, though in years he was far from old–was handy, could turn his hand to almost anything; one hour of his time, every morning, every morning for eleven years had made a great difference in the appearance of this place which, though the smaller of the two inns in Bethlehem, was much the more attractive because of the way in which he had made and mended, plastered, painted and applied his natural Greek talent and his experience to decorating.

But an hour in the morning was as much as he could bear. Then, back to the wine, this time without water; wine, more wine, and soon the real Ephorus was drowned again. Dead for one more deadly day. Sometimes, sheltering behind his own recognisable shape, but never one with it, he was a merry man, ready to quarrel and, if necessary, fight; sometimes he was a sullen man, brooding in silence. None of these men was Ephorus. Ephorus woke, took a drink and worked for an hour because after all he owed Eunice something; and then he took himself off. And what the merry, the aggressive, the sullen men did or said concerned him very little.

Once, only once, had he struggled up out of his drunkard's happy anonymity and tried to talk sense and truth to a fellow being; and that was when a neighbour, a man named Josodad, suffered a bereavement and began to come to the inn in search of comfort. He'd heard himself–to his amazement–speaking in metaphors, like a poet. He'd told Josodad that there was no comfort lying in the bottom of a wine-cup; and that a loss might make you a cripple but drunkenness made you a social leper. It seemed to have worked, Josodad ceased to frequent the inn; and now, after years, still looked as wretched as ever.

There'd been a little trouble with Eunice over Josodad; they hadn't so many customers that one needed to be driven away, she said. She also said, 'I heard you. Talking about that whore! After all this time! After all I've done for you!'

He said, 'I was only warning Josodad not to try to drown his sorrow or he'd end as I have.'

Eunice gave one of her short, rather cruel snorts of amusement, and said: 'He'd be lucky! What's wrong with where you ended, you silly drunken clown? What's wrong with this bed, eh?'

He could have told her–everything! It was a trap, a cage, a baited hook: it was the battlefield upon which he was always defeated; it was the sandbank upon which his barque lay stranded. But Eunice was not to blame for that–or at least only in a small degree–so he'd gone stumbling to the bed. At that time he'd still been able to give Eunice what she wanted, and the carping quarrelsome day often ended in reconciliation. Later on things had grown worse.

On this morning, in the middle of his eleventh winter in Bethlehem, he rose, thick-headed and tremulous, opened the shutter a crack and looked out. The sky was greyish purple and hung just above the roof-tops. Snow, he thought, unless the spiteful, bone-chilling wind succeeded in driving it over. He shivered, and thought, What a barbarous country! How did I land here? Why do I stay? He looked back over his past, boyhood and youth, before he came to Bethlehem, and saw it all in sunshine, with the exception of one spell in the middle of a voyage. Byblos, Tyre and Sidon, Delos, Crete and Rhodes, Alexandria, Carthage, Marsala, dozens and dozens of places, and always in the sun.

He was born in Byblos, born an orphan, one might say. Somebody must have fed and protected him during infancy, but he had no memory of whoever it was; he had come to self-recognition, awareness of his own identity, and to the beginning of his memory, in a hovel, with a lot of other boys, all older than he. The owner of the hovel was an old crone, and when there was anything to cook, she cooked it. It was not a home; his home always seemed to be the quayside. Somebody must have taught him a few professional begging phrases and as a small boy he had haunted the places where sailors, just back from voyages, were paid off. They were always generous. Possibly their seeming wealth and their good-nature had inspired in him the desire to go to sea as soon as he was old enough. Possibly his unknown father had been a sailor. Anyway, to be one himself was his earliest, his lasting ambition. There'd been an interval when he was rather too big to beg; and during that time he'd run with the other boys, stealing if a chance offered, doing odd jobs and errands. The old woman ran things in a simple way; if you went home once with no loot and no coin she'd grumble and give you a bit of whatever there was to eat, but if you were unlucky on the second day then you were unlucky indeed, you got nothing. It was a hard, haphazard life, but he'd known no other, so he never felt sorry for himself. And somehow, he grew up to be big and strong and remarkably good-looking. Whoever his parents had been it seemed that they had both been Greek, of pure blood; there was nothing of the mongrel blur and conflict about his features or his colouring.

When he was twelve he went to sea for the first time in a very menial capacity, a fetch-and-carry boy, even his name lost. 'You' they called him. Do this, you! Look sharp, you! You, get out of the way! His upbringing had sharpened his wits, and while he fetched and carried, and looked sharp and got out of people's way, he'd learned a lot. At fifteen he was a sailor. And he, too, was always open-handed with small coins for small beggars.

At twenty he was working on a ship which plied regularly between Byblos and Alexandria. From Byblos they carried the Eastern goods that had already travelled for months on the overland caravan routes; spices from the far islands, silk from China, from India jewels and a very fine, almost transparent material which women liked for veils and head-dresses. To all these was added a certain amount of the precious Tyrian purple dye. Out from Alexandria they carried papyrus. Byblos and the papyrus trade were so firmly linked that the town had given its name to the books made of the papyrus; Byblos softened down to bible, meaning a book. Also from Egypt the ship brought objects made of glass, and from one of his voyages Ephorus had brought Dorcas a string of glass beads which had cost far more than he could afford, but were beautiful, curiously mottled, pink, purple and rose-coloured. A wonderful present, but of course, unworthy of her.

Unworthy . . . that was the key word; it ran like a song theme with many minor variations, through all his dealings with her. Women like Dorcas weren't caught young and trained and schooled for the delectation of common sailors. They were the *hetaira*, designed for the delight of men's minds as well as their bodies; they could all converse with wit and intelligence; some could sing, some could dance or play musical instruments. They did not ply for hire, like the common prostitutes who flaunted themselves on the quayside and in the streets; they were not compelled to consort with any chance comer like the girls in ordinary brothels. Money was involved, of course, the *hetaira* were a luxury, but the business side was very discreetly handled; and because the girls were allowed freedom of choice, and were all so beautiful, elegant and clever, an association with one of them was a thing to boast about.

Ephorus knew nothing of this when one evening he saw an open door and heard music, and saw men coming and going, and followed a group of men in. Once inside he knew that he was, as he termed it, off-course; his pay was heavy in his pocket and he'd braced himself defiantly, thinking–My money is as good as the next man's. In the paved and pillared atrium, prettily arranged with urns of flowers and singing birds in cages, he'd braved some curious, some hard, some almost amused glances, and then all at once he'd found himself in such company, enjoying such happiness, as he had never dreamed existed. He had never talked to anyone, leave alone any woman, as he could talk to Dorcas.

She had never set foot on a ship, yet she seemed to be conversant with nautical terms, with sea routes. She had never been to Tyre or Carthage or Alexandria, yet she knew as much about them and a dozen other places as he who had visited them all. He was astonished and enchanted and at the same time humbled. She was so lovely, so clever, that she seemed to him almost like a goddess, and at first the idea of using her as he had used other women here and there was inconceivable. Later his astonishment and enchantment grew at finding her just like other women, but infinitely more skilled.

She said, 'What are you doing in a place like this?'

'You mean that this is no place for a common sailor?'

She laughed. 'Don't be so touchy. That isn't what I meant at all. I meant that you are so young and so handsome. Why should you pay for what any girl would gladly give?'

He said, 'After tonight there will never be another girl for me.'

'I should have added a flattering tongue when I listed your attractions,' she said.

After that his sea-going life, hitherto his whole life, his chosen life, his achieved ambition, meant nothing but enforced absence from what he loved. The voyages were vast desolate stretches between brief joys. He fretted incessantly. To whom was she talking, now? To whom, at this moment, was she opening Paradise? It was terrible to have set the private mark of one's heart upon a public thing. But he had done so, and there was no help for it.

There came a time when he could bear it no longer; he asked her to marry him.

He was not surprised that she should look amazed: he was amazed at his own audacity.

'Don't laugh at me,' he begged her. 'That I couldn't bear. I've nothing to offer you except my love. I know. But don't laugh.'

'Why should I laugh? Ephorus, how old are you?'

'I'm not certain. If the old woman reckoned rightly, and she's all I have to go by, I'm about twenty-one.'

Dorcas said, 'I'm thirty. Eight years from now you will be in your prime and I shall be an ageing woman, with no beauty left.'

He had never thought of her as being of any age and by this time he was not particularly conscious of her looks. There was the beautiful façade, but that was largely artificial; hair elaborately curled, white skin that the sun never touched, eyes made to look large and languorous. The real Dorcas, the woman he loved, lived inside this pretty shell and was a different person altogether. He often caught glimpses of her behind all the decoration. He tried to put this into words and failed.

He said, 'If you went bald, or were pitted by pox, you'd look the same to me. I love you.'

She didn't say what he yearned to hear–that she loved him, though he had sensed the possibility that she did, otherwise he would never have dared to mention marriage.

She said, 'I think you are a poet, Ephorus. And that means you could be dangerous to yourself. You make statements like this inside your head, and they sound well. But you mustn't believe them.'

'But it is true. Let me prove it.'

'By losing my hair and getting pox-pitted? Dear Ephorus, what a thing to ask.'

'I'm asking you to marry me.'

She moved, restively. 'Nobody marries women like me. Well, now and then perhaps; some old man, already provided with heirs. You see, we are barren. The precautions we take, the draughts we drink if they fail, offend the gods of fertility and we become barren.'

'I don't want children,' he said with great vehemence. 'I want you.'

'But, my dear, you can't afford me. I am a plaything, a toy. I can neither cook nor sew. I have never in my life been in a market. Until I have it on a plate before me I can't tell a melon from a cucumber or beef from mutton. I sleep till midday. Just imagine what a wife I should make.'

She spoke with sincerity, honestly hoping to dissuade him. In her life he struck almost as strange a note as she had struck in his, and for the first time in many years she was unsure of herself. He was young and handsome, his devotion was very touching; it would, she knew, be all too easy to love him; but what then? Poverty, ugly in itself with an infinite capacity for making everything it touched ugly too. Could love compensate? Would it last?

Could a woman of thirty, reared and trained as specially as a chariot horse, make the necessary adjustments? She didn't know; she wished he had not disturbed the nice balance of their relationships by his simple forthright question.

Ephorus said, narrowing his eyes, 'Suppose, just *suppose*, that I made some money. Not a lot, but enough. Enough to hire a little white house, and to buy you a slave who could tell melon from cucumber. What then?'

Why must he mention a little *white* house? A lifetime ago, when she was young, thirteen, fourteen, rebellious against her lot, a little white house had been visible from the window of the room that had been allotted to her. It was gone now, torn down to make room for a great tenement building; but she remembered it. A small white house, a woman, several children, a man who came home every night. The woman was always busy, cooking, washing, wiping a child's nose, picking up one that had fallen, occasionally dealing out smacks all round; but the girl Dorcas, busy then with mastering the Latin tongue and the playing of the lute and how to look, how to speak, how to arrange her hands and feet, had watched, often with envy, the simple domestic life in the little white house.

A lifetime ago.

Now she said, 'Ephorus I do not know. I was taught early to avoid four things: obesity, pregnancy, boredom and sentiment. It may be that on the last I have failed my teacher. I do feel for you what no woman of my kind should feel for any man. But I am afraid. It could so easily be as it was when Psyche lit her lamp. For us the lamp would be the light of common day; in that light what should we see? I should see a young man and count my years and be sad. You would see an ageing sloven and feel defrauded. Leave it as it is, for a time at least. Visit me when you can. And look about for a girl of your own age and kind. Teach her, if you wish, something of what I have taught you, so that kneading her dough and chopping her onions she will think of the night's joy and feel her bones melt. That way you will have a faithful wife and may remember me with gratitude. Better still, forget me altogether.'

Ephorus said, 'That is nonsense, and you must know it. I could *never* forget you. I told you, on that first night, that there would never be another girl for me. And it is true. You know how sailors are welcomed, set upon, wherever they go. I swear that for me they might be apes or goats or stone statues for all I care.'

And that was how she had been trained to look at men. Not as people. Her indifference had been cultivated, but she understood exactly what Ephorus meant. Out of a world populated by shadows, one person emerged, whole, real, as real and as dear as oneself. So easy to give in, to let oneself be carried away, to say yes, and yes, and yes, to pledge oneself with a kiss and begin to make plans. But there was this eight years gap which poverty would only emphasise. Oh dear, she thought, I was taught so much, but never how to deal with such a situation.

'I know,' he said, 'how to make some money. Real money.'

'You're not to do anything dangerous, or illegal. Please, Ephorus, I have to live with myself, and if I thought that because of *me* you had run into trouble, I should never sleep easily again.'

He said, 'It isn't dangerous . . .' and whether that were truth or a lie he couldn't tell; the whole thing was so shrouded in mystery and in silence that nobody knew. 'And it isn't illegal. It is the one way in which a sailor can make money.'

And although he had, from the first, appreciated her sharp intelligence and wealth of information, he was startled, somewhat displeased, when she said:

'The tin trade! Ephorus, no! That is suicidal. Do you want to saddle me with the responsibility for your death?'

He asked, truculently, 'What do you know about it?'

'More than you do, I'll warrant. Do you realise, Ephorus, that on a tin-trading ship you have not only the elements, the wind and the waves, lightning and thunder against you, but your own ship's master? The secret is so valuable, so precious, that men swear to keep it, even if it costs them their lives.'

'How do you know so much about it?'

'Never mind that. I know. I could, but I won't, give you the name of a shipmaster who, finding that he was followed by a spy ship, marking his course, deliberately ran his ship aground. Half his crew died, drowned; he and those who remained with him walked for a month through Iberia and many more died of starvation and exhaustion. He survived–and he was rewarded; a ship had been lost and many men had died; but the secret had been kept and that was all that mattered. I *know*,' she said, reaching out and taking his hand and beginning to weave her smooth white fingers with his, 'that set in the scales against possible profit a man's life weighs lightly anywhere, but in the tin trade it does not weigh at all. The tin ships are in the charge of men who set no value on themselves, much less on their crew.'

He thought that she exaggerated. In his time he had known several reckless men, but they were, really, men who trusted their luck and were inwardly sure that the risks they seemed to take were not risks at all. A deliberately self-destructive man he had never yet encountered; frankly he doubted whether such a one existed. Men owned ships for profit, and other men sailed them for pay. True, the whole of the tin trade was a mystery, but he could not believe that any ship's master would sacrifice his life to preserve his secret.

However, Dorcas appeared to believe it and to lift the look of trouble from her face he said:

'Why are we talking about the tin ships? That may be one way to make money, but I know another, and much safer, way.'

'What is it?'

'That is a secret, too.' And though she teased him and tried to trick him into telling her he remained obdurate. Had he been quick-witted enough to invent a believable story–believable to a woman of her intelligence–he would have told it; so he teased her back, saying that she knew too much already and that no woman could keep a secret. Then he came back to his original question; if he were lucky and returned with enough money to hire a house and buy a slave, would she marry him?

She looked at him, her eyes very clear between their artificial darkened lashes, their artificially lustrous lids.

'You are absurd,' she said, 'And very young, and very sweet.'

'Good enough to wait for?'

'Oh, I shall be here,' she said. 'I shall be here when you return, and we'll talk of it then. How long will this mysterious, profitable voyage take?'

'It could be a year,' he said, knowing nothing about it but feeling that in the circumstances it was better to guess at too long a time, rather than too short a one.

'A year. To me that will seem a short time. Did you know that, Ephorus? As one gathers years, each one seems shorter than the last.' She put her hands on either side of his head, digging the tips of her fingers into the crisp close curls. 'Swear to me,' she said, 'that you are not embarking upon any dangerous or difficult enterprise.'

'I swear that. It's a simple easy way of making money which would cease to be profitable if more people knew about it. And you will wait for me?'

'If, during this voyage which will last a year, you promise to think over what I have said. And promise to consider yourself free; not bound in any way to a woman who would make a bad, barren wife.'

He said, 'You are the one woman in the world for me. As for children; you can buy them, you know, in any market, choosing the sex, the size and shape, the age, even the disposition that you prefer. In Delos I saw children with labels about their necks; one label read "This boy bites if provoked". He fetched a good price.'

'Oh, why must we bother about the future?' she asked. 'To go, to stay, to wait upon the morrow, which the gods hold in their careless hands. This is now, and you are here and I am here. Let us make the most of the moment that is ours.'

So they made love again, in the small, pretty, scented room. And then he had gone straight out and sold himself into the tin trade.

The place that one sailed for was called the unknown destination; the world's end; the hidden place. And before he was accepted he had to subject himself to a strict inquisition, ominous in its implications and very enlightening. When he emerged from it he knew why the shipmaster whom Dorcas had mentioned had wrecked his ship rather than allow himself to be spied upon and followed–his family was his hostage. The tin-traders had a monopoly and they guarded it unscrupulously; no man ever took ship on this enterprise without knowing that not only his life was at stake, but the life of someone beloved.

In the office where Ephorus offered himself, the man asked why he wished to make this venture; and he gave an honest answer; he wished to make money, so that he could marry. Marry whom? He gave her name, just as every other man who sailed for the unknown destination, had given the name of someone who mattered to him.

'Come back tomorrow,' the man in the office had said; and when, on the next day Ephorus presented himself, he knew that there had been a check, to make sure that Dorcas existed and was there, in Byblos, easily available, to be tortured, killed, if he should fail in any way, or should utter an indiscreet word. Tin was the most important commodity, scarcer than gold, and the few Phoenicians who held the trade in their hands knew the value of the secret.

The man in the office was quite blunt, as he could afford to be.

'A complaint,' he said, 'or a misplaced question, a comment, a hint, an unconsidered word, and . . .' He made the gesture of a man slashing a knife across a throat.

Ephorus thought–With other men, no doubt he makes different gestures; Dorcas is particularly vulnerable in this respect. Any man with a knife could enter that house. . . .

He said, 'I understand; no complaints, I promise; no questions, no loose talk.'

'Very well. You are hired. Take this.' He handed Ephorus a small clay tablet, with, inset on its upper side, a tiny thread of tin, not much thicker than a hair and in length the eighth of a man's thumb, 'to Appolodorus, on the *Dido*.'

When he handed the clay tablet to Appolodorus that stout cheerful man had said, 'Oh. One in two hundred! Well, boy, if we're lucky you won't be able to buy up Byblos when we get back, but you should have what it would take you ten years to earn in any other trade.'

And that was exactly what the dockside whisper had said–one voyage on a tin ship paid as well as ten in any other kind. Ephorus, settling down amongst his fellows, all for some reason desperate and committed men, thought of the little houses, the busy slave, and Dorcas, enshrined.

He had known, for this was common talk in all the ports, that voyages made to the secret place were not very pleasant. Ships that went in search of tin faced unimaginable dangers, places where the sea was a sheet of flame and sails scorched; places where two-headed monsters rose from the sea and crunched a ship in their jaws; places where there were women with snakes for hair, and kisses that were irresistible and fatal.

He'd heard all the stories; discounting some and believing others, he had been prepared to risk all for Dorcas' sake. When he had been aboard *Dido* for a short time he began to suspect that old seamen were paid to sit about in taverns and tell such discouraging tales. *Dido* sailed due west, holding roughly to a course that he knew; but she did not go south to Carthage, or north to Marsala. Soon they were in waters farther west than any he had known, but the sea was not on fire and there were no snake-haired women. Finally they came to a place of which Ephorus had heard but which he had never seen, the Pillars of Hercules as it was called, where the known sea ended in a narrow passage between high escarpments, Calpe and Abyla. This was, to sailors, the end of the world. But not to Appolodorus. He pressed on, through the straits and into the sea beyond, which was ordinary sea, though rougher than any Ephorus had yet sailed. And–this was what Ephorus, years later in Bethlehem, remembered–there was no sun. They moved now between a grey sea and a grey sky, a curious twilit world. Soon they took a northerly course and then, turning East, headed for the land which lay, tiger-coloured, on their starboard side, but they did not make port. They anchored and a swarm of little boats came out from the tawny land, boats manned by men with Phoenician faces, clothes and tongues. This, then, Ephorus said to himself, is the unknown destination, the source of tin. But he was wrong. What the swarming boats carried were fresh supplies of perishable foodstuffs, meat, vegetables, fruit and cheese. With stores replenished, they headed out into such a sea as Ephorus had never imagined, a sea which–by a fine irony–took away the appetite of even the most hardened. The grey sea reared and tumbled, and every wave bore a crest of white foam which often blew free and with the wind behind it stung faces and hands. *Dido* plunged and rolled and every man in her, even Appolodorus, was grimly sick; the wind flung foam, and rain, and worse than rain, small pieces of ice at the sick, dizzy, reeling men who manned the tortured ship. But she survived, and so did they, and presently the seas smoothed out, the wind eased, the belly muscles ceased their spasmodic contractions, and Appolodorus, his face coloured as no human face should be, green around the mouth and purple around the eyes, said, 'We've made the Bay. And that is what we're paid for.'

There was still no sun; a faint golden glimmer around mid-day sometimes, a pink glow at dawn or sunset, but on the whole a grey, cool, sad light divided from dark. Spirits were low. Even the inevitable quarrels seemed muted and half-hearted. Ephorus was the only member of the crew making the voyage for the first time, and experienced men said that often it was worse than this; sometimes the grey sky sank until it joined the sea and progress was halted and men walked about through a clammy cloud.

At last they sighted land; it rose from the sea, a blur of solid grey in the greyness, and then slowly it revealed itself in colour and shape, a red and rocky coast, with waves beating high and hard at the foot of the cliffs and creaming over the small rocks with which the sea was sown. There seemed to be no harbour, no houses, no people. The jagged, rose-coloured coast, and as they came nearer, inland a wonderful green became visible. Ephorus had never seen a green so vivid, nor quite such an inhospitable shore.

Appolodorus nosed the ship nearer, the man with the plumbline calling soundings every few minutes; then, just short of the outmost fringe of rocks they anchored and a man ran to the ship's bows and blew a horn. Blast after blast sounded through the sunless air, apparently into empty silence.

And then, suddenly it seemed, the narrow fringes of the shore at the places where the sea had beaten the red cliffs back, there were men, running, running into the water and dragging with them dark, circular objects which floated upon the sea, and into which, once they were afloat the men jumped, took up paddles and came, with what seemed incredible speed, towards *Dido*. Ephorus stared with interest at these boats, if boats they could be called. What brave crazy people these must be, he thought, to venture out, in such a sea in what were no more than round baskets, fashioned from boughs over which hides had been stretched. These men were not Phoenicians, as the men from the tawny-coloured land had been; they were a different breed altogether, with round dark heads and very light skins, so light that the blood showed, red in their faces.

Appolodorus opened the chest which had laid, locked, in *Dido*'s hold. There were knives and arrow heads, some lengths of brightly coloured cotton cloth, copper bracelets and anklets, some articles of pottery of the coarsest, cheapest kind, boxes of dried figs and dates and raisins; a sack of almonds. There were only three things of any real value; one was a lump of amber on a silver chain, one a silver brooch set with a piece of turquoise, and one a highly polished silver mirror such as rich men used for shaving and rich women used for self-admiration.

The natives, very quietly and shyly, loaded *Dido* with lumps of tin, some freshly mined and shining, some grown over with moss, as green as the inland meadows, some white with encrusted sea-salt. A year's hoard at least.

It took some time since the flimsy round boats could carry only small amounts.

Appolodorus said, 'This could be done in half the time if everybody dealt with them as honestly as I do. There was a time when the women used to come out too, then some wretched fellow grabbed a few, thinking they'd fetch a good price at Delos–they're very pretty. So now, when they hear the horn, they hide their women, and only men come out. And grabbing them, everybody knows, is sheer waste of time. They can't live in captivity.'

There was no attempt at communication. When the last lump of tin was delivered a man who seemed to be the leader of the group–he wore a wolf skin around his middle and his chest, upper arms and legs were stained with a blue dye, simply spread his hands to signify that that was the end. Appolodorus with a similar gesture indicated the chest and man after man took the object nearest to hand without any discrimination.

'They share it out, later, amongst themselves,' Appolodorus explained.

Carrying their payment–pitiable in comparison with the worth of what they had delivered, the men paddled back to shore; but Appolodorus did not immediately give any order. He waited; and soon the little round boats were heading out again. This time they brought fresh meat and fish, baskets of berries, some horns hollowed out to make drinking cups, ornaments of bleached bone, curiously carved. These were presented with eloquent gestures of the hands, and with the first smiles Ephorus had seen on the pink and white faces.

'They always do that,' the man standing nearest to Ephorus explained. 'They're very generous, gentlemen, in a savage sort of way. It's a pity they're doomed.'

'Are they?'

'It's my guess that in twenty years or less this'll be Roman territory.'

'Then what about the tin trade?'

The man shrugged. 'All organised and taxed! But by that time I shall be done with it. I had six daughters,' he explained. 'I've dowered four and married them. This trip should take care of the other two. . . .'

Heavily laden, *Dido* headed south. In the Bay the weather was rather worse and she was no longer buoyant; everyone in her was–which would have seemed impossible–more nauseated than before. Then she slipped between the Pillars of Hercules, this time so close to Abyla that one could see the apes bounding about on its rocky face, and then they were back in the known world, making for Byblos.

There was a waiting time–to the impatient Ephorus a long, interminable time–while the tin was assessed; then, according to his term of contract, every man was paid off.

Walking so fast that he was almost running, Ephorus began to make his way along one of the narrow alleys that led from the quay, one of his childhood's haunts. And there he was accosted not by a painted harlot or a mendicant child, but by a young man, wearing the toga of Roman citizenship, neatly groomed, well shaven, but apparently exuberantly drunk. He said, barring Ephorus' way:

'Welcome home, sailor. I'll warrant you have a thirst. Come and take a cup of wine with me.'

'I've no time,' Ephorus said brusquely. 'Let me pass.'

The young man reeled against the filthy wall and hiccupped. Then he turned about and was walking as near alongside as the narrowness of the alley permitted.

'You think I'm drunk, don't you?'

'What is that to me?'

'You're right. I am. So would you be. I've just come into a legacy. All made out of sailors' sweat, so I thought I'd spend a little on sailors.'

'Find one who isn't in a hurry. I am.'

'Wife waiting? Ha ha! You been long away?'

'Six months,' Ephorus said, untruthfully.

'Tell me; did you ever see a mermaid?'

'No.'

'They say there's a rock off Sicily, where they sit and comb their hair. You ever been to Sicily?'

'In my time.'

'Not this time? What a pity! I dote upon sailors' tales. Come and drink wine with me and tell me a tale.'

'I told you,' Ephorus said impatiently. 'I have no time; I have no desire to drink and no tale to tell.'

'Uncivil,' the young man said in a maudlin, reproachful voice.

They had reached the point where the narrow alley opened into a wide busy street, and stumbling as he turned, the seeming drunkard began to retrace his steps. Within three paces Ephorus heard the change in the rhythm of the walk, and glancing back saw the man making for the quay with a purposeful and completely sober stride.

It might have been a serious attempt to get him drunk and make him wag an incautious tongue; it might have been a deliberate trap, laid by the ship-owner. Dismissing it thus, he hurried on.

It was still early in the day. The house was shuttered and dark, and very quiet. A slave was apathetically swabbing the floor of the atrium and hardly bothered to look up as he entered. He said:

'Rouse Dorcas. Tell her Ephorus is here.'

Now that the moment had come his heart beat with such excitement and exultation that it shook him to his finger-tips. All through his absence–ten months and eighteen days–he had exercised a Spartan self-control, knowing that it was useless to tantalise himself with dreams and hopes and plans. He'd gone from this place with the object of making money, knowing that he might perish in the attempt.

He was back; in a few minutes Dorcas would come; he would show her his money; assure her of his ability to provide.

He stood waiting; staring around the place which he had never before visited in daylight hours. For all its grandeur it had the sleasy, somewhat furtive look of a place devoted to the pleasures of the night. She would be glad to be out of it.

The slave came back, gave him what he called a silly look–but she had, by nature, a silly expression–and resumed the floor-washing. Then, through the arch came, not Dorcas, but another girl named Lydia, known to him by sight and by name but hardly recognisable. She had just been roused from sleep and her unpainted face looked almost phosphorescent in the gloom. But she was a professional; she made an effort, said, 'Welcome back, Ephorus,' and laid her henna-tipped fingers on his arm.

'Where's Dorcas?' he asked. The dry-leaf rustling whisper was not his own voice.

'She's gone.'

'Gone,' he repeated stupidly. 'Gone where?'

'I don't know.'

'Then fetch somebody who does.'

'Oh, if she'd told anybody, she'd have told me,' Lydia said. 'But she wouldn't tell me. So nobody knows.'

'When did she go?'

'A little more than three months ago. I miss her very much.'

'*You* miss her!' he said brutally. 'I came back to marry her!'

'Oh. Then that is why she left you a message.'

Stupid bitch, he thought. Of course Dorcas would have left a message for him; and anybody with any sense would have said so, at first.

'What was it?'

She closed her heavy eyes and said, like a child dutifully repeating a well-conned lesson:

'She said–If Ephorus comes, tell him I wish him well and not to be unhappy because he will live to thank me. That is what she said.' She opened her eyes and blinked.

'And that is all? Think. Try to remember. Nothing else?'

'Nothing else. Ephorus, you are distressed. Let me get you a drink.'

'Who'd she go with?'

'Oh, a man.' The way she said that indicated what a stupid question it was.

'What man? What was his name?'

'How should I know? He wasn't my customer. He wasn't a regular. He came–twice I think. The second time he gave her a bracelet. She said, 'Look what my fat friend gave me.' He was fat. Then she told me she was going to live with him. But she didn't say where, and she gave me the message for you. Oh, and she's gone to a palace.'

'How do you know that?'

'When she packed. She was in a strange mood, not like herself at all, half laughing, half crying. She took things out of her chest and said, "Is this fit to wear for a palace? No!" and then she'd fling them on the floor. She took hardly anything.'

'And you haven't any idea where the palace is? Lydia, even if she vowed you to secrecy, tell me. I must know.'

'She didn't tell me anything. It was all very sudden; and I had my own customers. She just told me she was going and gave me the message for you. What she said about the clothes told me that she'd gone to a palace. And that, Ephorus, truly is all I know. Except that it is a *red* palace.'

'Red? Who told you that?'

'She did. At least, I guessed. You see, she had a red dress; new; she'd only worn it once. She threw it on the floor with the rest. She said she wouldn't take it, there was enough of that colour where she was going; even the stones there were red. . . .'

She was more widely awake now, recovered from her abrupt wakening.

She said, 'If you really thought of marrying her, I'm sorry, Ephorus. And I think you need a cup of wine. Come with me. She's gone, but we're still here.'

Business as usual!

Repulsed, with no word spoken, simply reading the look on his face, she hunched a shoulder and said, not without malice:

'The way she went was understandable. She's gone with a rich man, to live in a palace; she wouldn't want anybody who knew her here to go seeking her out. Would she?'

Something must have happened inside his head. He had no memory of taking leave of Lydia or of leaving the house. But here he was, in a tavern, and pretty drunk too. Folding his arms on the table, putting his head down on them and crying. Everything wrapped in a red mist.

And there was the tavern-keeper saying in a quiet, tactful way, 'Go elsewhere to weep, please. It is such a bad advertisement.'

The man was fat. Noting this, through the red mist, Ephorus said:

'I hate fat fellows. A fat fellow robbed me. A fat fellow in a red palace. She said a year would go swiftly, but when I was sick in my belly it seemed a long time. And how many *red* palaces are there in the world? Because I shall find her if it takes the rest of my life.'

The tavern-keeper, experienced and reasonably honest, helped him to his feet. 'You go home and sleep it off. And look out for that money.'

'I shall,' Ephorus assured him. 'I spewed it up, every coin, out of my guts.'

And so began the timeless time when he was never sober from the moment he woke until he fell into sodden sleep again. But in every day there was a time when, sober enough to be coherent, drunk enough to be confidential, he'd ask anyone who gave him a moment's attention if they'd ever heard of a red palace. And the day came when a man said:

'That'd be Petra, surely. Red as a rose, they say it is. Red as a rose.'

'They say? Who say so? Have you ever seen anybody who's been there?'

'Yes, I have,' the man said a little truculently. 'A man I do business with. If you want to know, it's the capital of Nabatea, a very busy place, with caravan routes to Gaza and Boara and Damascus. And it's all cut out of red rock: houses, palaces and temples. Quite a sight to see. But it's a long way away.'

Ephorus asked a few questions about direction and received unsatisfactory and conflicting answers which worried him little. It was only a question of navigation, he told himself; he had a Greek tongue in his head, and on none of his voyages–except to the tin island–had he found a place where he couldn't make himself understood. Money didn't bother him either; he still had some; less than he should have had, for he had been drunk in dubious company more than once; if the money gave out before he reached Petra he would have to earn some, or beg or steal.

What exactly he intended to do when he reached the distant city, found a red palace and Dorcas in it, he didn't know. Shock and steady drinking had rendered him incapable of making any coherent plans. He felt under a compulsion to see Dorcas again, to reproach her to her face; he wished to do some real damage to the fat man who had, he felt, robbed him. Meanwhile he walked.

He was still drinking; his hearty appetite had vanished, and at the end of the day's march he was often too tired to eat. So he drank and slept, woke in the morning with a queasy stomach and walked on. The weather was hot, and this was the first time he had experienced the inland heat. At midday or about then he'd buy bread or fruit, find a shady place, eat and rest a little, then on again. He was aware, in a dull kind of way, that his hitherto superb health had deserted him; there were times when he turned dizzy, times when he shook as though he had palsy, times when he lost his sight for a few minutes.

He had such a spell one afternoon, just after he had resumed walking; and the next thing he knew, he was lying on a bed and being tended by Eunice. She told him–oh, how often–how a decent honest man with two camels had deposited him at her inn, senseless and naked but for a breech clout. 'Nobody but me would have taken you in,' Eunice said. Over and over again.

Somebody must have robbed him, even of his shoes. And probably hit him over the head, too, for he was now disabled in a fashion which did, he knew, result from some head injuries. His left arm and leg were almost powerless, seemed to weigh heavily and were afflicted, every now and again, with a maddening tingling.

Eunice couldn't have been kinder. She was Greek, which made a bond; she was eight or nine years older than he, and not uncomely in her way. She was so sympathetic that she invited confidences, and to her he told what, drunk or sober, he had never told in full to anyone–the story of his love and his betrayal.

She said, 'You're young. You'll get over it. Your mind will mend with your body.'

His mind, if not mending, was clearing, because for the first time since his talk with Lydia he was sober; and he could see the sense of Eunice's argument when she said:

'Maybe it's a good thing you never got to Petra. What could you have done there? If the man's rich, he's powerful. You couldn't have hurt him, and he could have hurt you. Got you locked up for being a nuisance if nothing else. As for her, she made her choice, didn't she? She'd laugh to think of you trudging all those miles just to have a look at her. That's all you'd have had, you know. Just a look.'

The room where he lay, with its thick mud roof, its thick, sun-defying walls, its vine-shrouded windows, was as cool as Eunice's reasoning.

'You just lie and get better,' she said. 'I'll look after you.'

Getting better took a long time, and when he could stand, and had learned to walk again, the left leg still dragged and the left hand was not to be wholly trusted. He was in no shape to continue his journey and no longer felt the urge to do so. Nor could he ply his old trade again. What should he do?

He talked this over with Eunice, and she had the answer. For her it couldn't have worked out better; she had always helped her father with the inn, and he had died only a short time before the good-hearted man had brought Ephorus to her door. She'd been waiting for a purchaser for the place, since innkeeping wasn't a job for a woman alone. Why shouldn't Ephorus stay and help her?

She did not, at that point, make any mention of what she had done for him or imply that he'd owed her anything. Ephorus, however, realised that he was in her debt and felt that now he was almost able-bodied he should stay and help her for a bit.

Eunice wove her net cunningly; she made him very comfortable, and Ephorus, who had never known a home, was susceptible to domestic order and ease. She coddled him and flattered him, listened, seemingly entranced, to his tales of his sea-faring days, forbade him to over-exert himself; it was his presence about the place that mattered, she said.

He drifted on; and when by little signs and hints she indicated that her objective was to get him into her bed, he drifted there, too. Grateful, not unflattered. She was surprisingly good in bed. He never asked, never even wondered, where she had learned such tricks. What he did tell himself was that in the ultimate act one woman in bed was very much like another. And out of it there was nothing, not a turn of the head, not a tone of the voice, to rouse an unwelcome memory or a hurtful comparison. When Eunice revealed her next objective, marriage, he drifted will-lessly into that, too.

There was no visible reason why they should not have become just another married couple, moderately happy, more than moderately comfortable; but almost immediately after the marriage their relationship deteriorated. Neither he nor she changed overnight, yet the changes came. Some obscure dissatisfaction in her turned her sour, she became a nagging scold; he sought refuge in the wine-jar and in dreams, which even as he entered them he knew would come to nothing, of making his escape. For several years there was the bond of bed, but that failed at last. Under her nagging his indifference changed to active dislike, and that made him impotent; and that gave her something else to taunt him with.

The inn prospered, however. Eunice was a good manager, and Ephorus, though he worked slowly and only a little each day, had improved its appearance. It was known as a respectable place, and Vatinius, the centurion in charge of the small barracks not far away, always recommended it to the newly arrived legionaries, at the same time tactfully avoiding it himself since men off duty are off duty and do not care to be overlooked.

It stood at the end of the street, set back in what, before Ephorus' time, had been a yard, dusty, unshaded, uncared for. He'd planted trees around it, made stands for lanterns, set benches and tables under the trees. He'd sawn old casks in half, painted them green, and in Spring and Summer kept them filled with flowers.

Behind this pleasant courtyard stood the house; one big public room, the kitchen, and opening off the kitchen two small rooms, one where the two female slaves slept, one where Eunice and Ephorus fought their more private battles and Eunice, when she was not otherwise busy, made and mended clothes. Above there were five rooms, one the connubial chamber, the others for letting to travellers who could afford to pay for privacy.

At the back of the house, accessible from a side entry was a yard with a large water-trough in the centre of it. On two sides the yard was enclosed by a low platform, roofed over, and it was on this platform that most travellers slept. The third side was open to the orchard and garden; the fourth was occupied by a stable in which, in winter, the house cow and the ass, which was used for serious marketing, and for carrying firewood, lived. In summer they were turned into the orchard, often enough with a calf, a young pig, or a sheep, which Eunice, careful housekeeper that she was, was fattening up. The inn animals were never allowed to mingle with those of the travellers; transient animals had all kinds of diseases, from footrot to the itch; and many of them were so perpetually hungry, so accustomed to shouldering others aside in order to eat themselves, that any well-behaved animal in the enclosure would have starved. Eunice had explained that to the ignorant Ephorus years ago when he had suggested that their animals should share the yard and that the stable should be floored, opened on the side facing the yard and made into extra sleeping space. That was in the days when she still explained things; now she would merely have shouted and called him ignorant; but he'd stopped making suggestions long ago.

The snow, which he had sensed when he opened the shutters held off until almost sunset. By that time the animal enclosure and the platforms were almost full and Eunice was in a raging temper–and in her element. People who, had the weather been clement, would have hoarded their pennies and slept at small cost under the awning, came and asked for room in the house. Poorer people who, had the weather been clement, would have slept in the open, came and asked for room under the awning; the good manager, the bully who shared Eunice's hide, had enjoyed themselves hugely, Ephorus thought to himself. She had anticipated this invasion at about this time; she had heard about the new tax rule some time before, and talking about it had betrayed her latent scorn and contempt of the people amongst whom she had spent her whole life. 'They'll obey,' she said, 'like sheep. Such a silly order, given to *our* people, would have led to rebellion.' She had laid in stores; enough to feed an army. She could feed all comers, and their beasts. But space she couldn't make, though she did her best. She went to the edge of the platforms and cried, 'Move along there! Move along, I said. You there, move along. You're taking up room for three. It's a bad night, shelter must be found. Take that child in your lap. Make room.'

She was having a wonderful time; she came back into the house, the snowflakes melting on her still-dark hair, and went into the room where supper was being served.

'Eat up! Others are waiting. I have many more to feed. Eat up, please.'

With swift competence, aided by the panting slaves, she served supper three times over, and then set about converting the big room into an extra sleeping space.

During all this haste and confusion and noise Ephorus stayed, as was his habit, inactive and apart. It was a curious thing, but never, even at her busiest, did Eunice make any demands upon him for help. She'd say, 'Oh, get out of my way,' in an irritable tone if she happened to pass within a yard of him, but she did not suggest that he should carry a dish, full or empty, or go out into the yard and by shouting, pack one extra body on to the platform, or crowd one extra donkey into the enclosure. Her attitude towards his drinking was similarly negative; she would remark, nastily, that he was drunk again, would say that he had better lie down before he fell, but she never made any attempt to persuade him not to drink, seemed to ignore the frequency of his visits to the small, half-subterranean store where the wine was kept. A shrewd, impartial observer might have deduced that as he was, idle, drunken, will-less, she wanted him to be.

Tonight he had no place to sit; the house was crammed; his bed and Eunice's and those of the two slaves would presently be spread in the kitchen. In every other place people, weary from travel, or, wishing to make sure of their sleeping space, were lying down. Because of the weather it was impossible to have any shutters but two on the leeward side of the house open, and very soon the air was foetid, the stink of human bodies mingling with that of food. He must have air, he thought. He stepped over and around the recumbent forms on the floor of the public room and went to the wine store and poured himself not a cup but a jug of wine, and carrying it in his hand went to the door. He'd had some intention of sitting on the bench under the trees for a few minutes; but the wind was too bitter and snow was still falling; so he stood in the shelter of the doorway, braced against the jamb, staring into the night and lifting the jug to his lips every now and again.

There were lanterns on the two posts which he had set up at each side of the entry, and another hanging from a hook over the door. Each had a faint golden halo of light in which the slow, spiralling flakes were visible. Like life, he reflected, his thoughts as idle and aimless as the snow; out of the dark, a brief space in the light, and into the dark again. No permanence, and no point.

From the kitchen, where one of the shutters was open, he could hear

Eunice's voice, railing away. He could catch no words, but he knew her tirades so well that he could have repeated them perfectly. She was an ill-done-by woman who worked her fingers to the bone and had no consideration from anybody, nor a word of thanks. Customers were demanding and greedy and prepared to be dishonest if given half a chance; the slaves were idle and clumsy. Why she should be expected to work herself to death, she really didn't know and she swore that tomorrow she'd sit down, fold her hands in her lap and see what happened then.

She was capable of expressing these few simple statements in such a variety of ways that she could grumble on for an hour.

He could hear, too, the clatter of dishes and bowls being washed and stacked; once something fell with a thud and that sound was immediately followed by that of a good smart slap.

He shivered, huddling in the doorway and lifted the jug. He'd wait a little longer; then he could go in and help arrange the beds, and Eunice, exhausted, would fall asleep. That would be another day done.

Then, on the edge of the forecourt, the darkness between the two lanterns took on solidity, and shape, and movement. Silhouetted against the grey and the shift of the snow-filled air the figures showed up black, surprisingly clear. A man and a woman, their heads bowed against the blizzard, and a donkey, limping so badly that only the man pulling at its head-rope kept it in motion at all. The woman had her hand on its flank, whether to support herself, or to help its sagging progress it was impossible to say.

They stopped. The donkey dropped his head and looked as though it would never move again. The woman walked to the end of the bench and sat down as though she, too, had expended her last bit of strength. The man came towards the door, walking with a step that told of weariness and haste.

He was quite near the door when he realised that Ephorus was standing in its shelter.

He asked, in a deep, pleasant voice, 'This is the inn?'

'It is. But you're too late. Not an inch left.'

It occurred to him that he had never seen a more worried-looking man; no ship's master, in the most hazardous situation, had ever looked more anxious, more eaten up by fearful concern.

'Oh, please,' the man said. 'Just room for one. For my wife. That's all I ask. I know we're late; the donkey went lame. But you could find room just for one surely.'

'We're full,' Ephorus said. 'Packed like fish in a barrel.'

He saw the expression of sheer despair wrench the man's face and in a laconic, wine-muffled way he was sorry for him; but he thought–We all have our troubles. Still, he roused himself enough to say:

'There's another inn on the other side of the town.'

'I tried there. We came in that way. They were full. They suggested a private dwelling. I've tried dozens. All full. My wife . . .' He looked at the woman on the bench, and back, pleadingly, at Ephorus. 'She can't go farther. She *must* have a bed. I can pay. I'll pay anything.' He was prepared, tomorrow, to go and sell himself into slavery; anything so that Mary should have shelter and a bed tonight.

His insistence exasperated Ephorus.

He said, 'Well, I'm sorry; but I tell you, we're full. No room for a dwarf. We've been turning people away.'

The man said, 'Oh God! God!' It sounded as though he were praying;

and Ephorus thought sardonically that he was wasting his breath; it'd puzzle even the Jews' God, that powerful Jehovah, to find a spare bed in Bethlehem at this time of night, on such a night. With that thought he turned himself and took the handle of the door in his free hand, which was his infirm, left hand, so he fumbled and was about to shift the jug and lift the handle with his good hand, when the woman stood up and came forward.

She said, 'Joseph' and the man turned and said in a defeated voice: 'There's no room here, either.'

She said, 'Don't fret. I'm rested now. We'll find a place. . . .'

And by that time she was within the radius of light cast by the lantern over the doorway; and Ephorus' heart, quiescent for so long, gave a great jump, and seemed to stop. He had to put out his right hand and catch at the door-jamb to save himself from falling, and the wine-jug, entrusted to his untrustworthy left hand, did fall, and broke.

The face inside the blue hood was so like that of Dorcas–not the Dorcas he had known, but a younger Dorcas, untouched, unsullied, the girl whose existence he had always sensed, under the paint and the fine clothes.

It seemed a long time before he could find breath to speak. Then he said: 'Wait here. I'll see what I can do.'

In the kitchen the dish-washing was finished; the slave girls were laying out the makeshift beds; Eunice, having talked herself to a standstill, was rubbing her mixture of honey and rose-water into her hands. She looked hot and flushed and formidable.

He said: 'Eunice. There's a woman wanting a bed. Do you mind if she has my place?' Before she could protest he added cajolingly, 'That way you'd be all females together. Better so.'

'And where,' Eunice asked, 'do you propose to sleep?'

He had not given that a thought, but he scrambled about in his mind and found an answer.

'In the stable,' he said. 'Her husband's with her. We'll sleep in the stable.'

'Alongside the donkey!' Eunice's voice took on its sharpest cutting edge. 'Very right and proper. You and a fellow with a wife, hunting a bed at this time of night. You and him and the donkey–and the donkey with more sense than either of you. Well, if you don't mind, why should I? They'll pay. But I want to take a look at her first.'

They went to the door. The man and the woman stood under its shelter, the donkey had hobbled forward and joined them.

'The best we can manage . . .' Eunice began, and then she rounded upon Ephorus. 'You great fool! I knew you were a fool, but I didn't know you were blind! It isn't a bed she needs, it's a place to give birth in. And you'd have landed me with her, in my kitchen! You daft drunken sot!' She drew in her breath with the peculiar hissing sound that punctuated her worst tirades. 'We have no room here. No room at all!'

Ephorus began to shake. Amongst all the other thoughts that battered him at that moment, a horrible memory came. Once, at Byblos, there'd been a beggar woman, one of those who came, purely to beg, when a ship was about to sail. Women who met an incoming ship were all intent to sell themselves; those who begged from an outgoing ship were old, with no shadow of attractiveness left; they simply hoped that men with a few remaining coins, men who had just left wives, sweethearts, mothers behind, would be generous. This particular woman, holding out her hand with an imploring, ingratiating smile, had suddenly taken on an agonised expression, bent over, groaning, and dropped to the gutter. Most of the other women had drawn aside, but two old hags had gone to her aid, and there in the gutter she had given birth. Ephorus, fifteen years old and safely aboard his ship, had watched it all; and it was that experience as much as anything else that had made him glad when Dorcas had said that she was unlikely to bear a child. If Eunice, on the other hand, had ever fallen pregnant he would have been pleased. But how a man could knowingly doom a woman he loved to such agony he could never understand.

And now, here was this woman, with the face of young Dorcas, about to face that ordeal, with no roof, no shelter.

He said, 'There is room. There is the stable.'

'Shut your mouth!' Eunice said. 'Once get her on our premises and who can say where it'll end? Childbirth fever. Milk fever. She might lie in our straw for weeks. I ask you, would any decent woman be in such a pass? Let her bear her child in the ditch, where, like as not, it was begotten.'

He said, 'You shut *your* mouth! I've done with you. D'you hear me? Done!' He lifted his hand, which shook like a leaf, and unhooked the lantern from over the door.

'Allow me,' he said, 'to conduct you to the stable. It is at least sheltered and warm.'

'And it's mine!' Eunice shouted. 'So is that lantern and I absolutely forbid—'

He said, 'Eunice, I never yet have struck you; but another word and I will hit you, hard!'

Both he and Eunice were completely bi-lingual, switching effortlessly, sometimes even in mid-sentence, from Greek to Aramaic, from Aramaic to Greek. Ephorus, assuring Joseph that there was no room, had used Aramaic; Eunice had spoken the same language when she said, 'The best we can manage . . .' But the altercation between them had been in Greek. Joseph, the much-travelled man, had followed it, and in his heart been deeply affronted; but the innkeeper had mentioned a stable, and even the shelter of a stable would be welcome now. So he had held his tongue, tried to control his face and been thankful that nothing this horrible woman was saying meant anything to Mary.

Eunice, quelled by the threat, opened the door and went in, banging it behind her; and the three of them, with the donkey, were left in the wind and the snow.

'If you will come this way,' Ephorus said, and, holding the lantern in his quaking hand, led the way to the side entry and the stable door. It was a low building, but deep and wide, with a manger along one side. To the left of the doorway were some neatly ranged tools, to the right a great heap of straw. A cow and a donkey stood by the manger, and their bodies had heated the place so that, coming in from the night, it felt warm. It smelt sweet too, of straw and the breath of the non-carnivorous animals.

'It isn't much,' Ephorus said, 'but it is the best I can do. It's quiet,' he said, consoling himself, 'and you'll have it to yourselves.'

The woman turned to him with a smile, which, because it reminded him of Dorcas, he tried to analyse. If you said it was sweet, he thought to himself, you'd wrong it, because sweet sounds insipid; yet there was a sweetness about it, and a radiance which lit up her pale tired face.

'We're extremely fortunate,' she said. 'And you are very kind.'

'I meant it all to be so different,' the man said. 'I aimed to get here yesterday, or the day before. But we're thankful to be under cover.'

Ephorus' desire to serve outran his caution.

'I'll bring you a blanket,' he said. 'And what about supper?'

She said, 'Thank you. We have some food left.'

'Cold food,' he said. 'You need more than that on such a night. I'll be back. . . .' He looked round for a hook on which to hang the lantern, and hurried away, his lame leg dragging a little less than usual.

When he had gone, Mary said, 'I knew that somehow a place would be found for us.'

'But what a place!' He looked around him with distaste. 'Suppose your time should come, here on a bed of straw.'

She said, 'It must be the right place, the place God chose. The pains began hours ago, and they're getting harder now. He'll be born by midnight.'

Something seemed to burst in his brain. 'You didn't tell me!' he said, almost angrily. 'You walked and walked. And all on account of that damned donkey! I didn't want to buy it in the first place. It's ruined all my plans. What baby was ever born in a stable . . . leave alone such a baby as this. . . .' And his thoughts ran about; in a crowded inn there must be some kindly, experienced woman who could help; and how curious it was that they'd been without any shelter until he'd said, 'Oh God, God!' Then the innkeeper had relented and he'd thought that God had them in His keeping, after all. But the end was a bed of straw, in a stable. Mystery added itself to mystery, enough to make a plain, ordinary man run mad.

'It is the right place,' Mary said confidently. 'For me, for *him*. Look at that!'

Their old donkey had limped in behind them and made for the manger, snuffing eagerly. It had made for the manger and Eunice's well-fed animal had edged away, making room for the newcomer at that portion of the manger that contained food.

'He's prepared to share,' she said. 'And the man is kind. Where better could a child be born?'

She'd tell him, she thought, when he was grown and Lord of the world, just how he had been born, and ask him to look out for humble people and animals.

In the kitchen the two slaves were abed and asleep. Eunice was abed, but not asleep. When Ephorus entered and went towards the great black pot which held the remains of the mutton stew she reared up and said:

'Oh, so you've done with me, but you come crawling back for your supper!'

He heard only the chiding, not the relief in her voice. He said, 'I don't want your supper! It's for her . . . for them. They're customers, aren't they, like all the rest? They're entitled to supper. They'll pay, don't you fret about that.'

Ordinarily he defeated her by his apathetic silence, the best buffer a man could rear between him and a nagging woman. Now he was answering back. Happily she threw herself into what promised to be their first real quarrel in years.

'That's right,' she said. 'That's just like you. Stand like a stuffed man when I'm serving proper people, then hop about like a flea to serve a couple of feckless no-goods that turn up late and happen to take your fancy.

Threatening to hit me, too; after all I've done for you. And that's about all you're good for, biting the hand that's fed you all these years.'

He moved the black pot on to what remained of the fire, took two bowls and two spoons.

He said, 'You can stow that talk, Eunice. I've had about enough of it. You've fed me and housed me, but you did it because you wanted to. Don't deceive yourself about that. Out there, just now, you said things no man could bear. *Your* lantern, *your* stable. Try that in a court of law and you'll soon learn whose this place is, down to the last spoon! But I want none of it. It's all yours. . . . I give it to you, with a glad heart and you can enjoy it, all by yourself, tomorrow. But tonight I'm dishing out *my* mutton stew and I'll also have *my* blanket.'

Astonishingly, she was silenced. In silence she watched him dish the stew into the bowls, cover them with a cloth and set them on a serving tray. In silence she allowed him to take the blanket, fold it over his arm and go out. When he had gone she turned on her pillow and cried into it. She cried and cried, weeping for the man whom she had seen in that stripped, unconscious body, the man who had eluded her, never coming to life, however coaxed or provoked, until now, when after eleven years of skirmishing he was about to elude her for ever.

She was still crying, and her candle was still burning, when Ephorus came hurrying back. His face was bleached and distraught. He spoke her name, 'Eunice,' in a way he had never said it before. Ha! she thought, he's had time to think things over, and has come back to apologise. She steeled herself. Never let him think that he had got the better of her!

'What is it?' she asked coldly.

'I want you to do something for me.'

As she had guessed; he wanted to be forgiven and taken back, fed, sheltered, kept in idleness. This was what she wanted too, for him, but it would never do to relent too quickly.

'Things'll have to be very different around here,' she said.

'Oh, they will be,' he promised hastily. 'I'll do anything you want me to, Eunice. I'll work, I'll stay off the wine. I'll do everything I can to repay you, if you'll do this one thing for me. . . .'

She was tired, she had been upset, she had been crying, and her ordinarily sharp wits weren't at their best. She could only think of times in their earlier life when quarrels had been mended in bed. Tonight, for the first time in several years, they'd had an open quarrel, and he had been angered; he was now seeking what had formerly served as a remedy. A deep satisfaction moved within her; she had won after all! She had known from the first that their unions had meant more to her than to him, that she, in a fashion, had always been the supplicant, he the obliger. And when the bed bond had been broken under her nagging and his apathy, she had been, very decidedly, the loser.

Even his threat to strike her, earlier in the evening, helped now towards her self-deception; so did his behaviour over the stew and the blanket. That was real man's behaviour. So was this.

She cast one look at the slaves; they were sleeping soddenly, worn out by all they had done that day. Her sense of propriety was satisfied, and desire, the more powerful because so long unappeased, began to move in her. She gave in. She smiled and lifted the blanket.

'Come, then,' she said, invitingly.

He recoiled as though she had spat in his face.

'Not that,' he said, 'I want you to *do* something for me. A favour. I know it's a lot to ask. The woman out there–you were right; she is having a baby; it's started. And, Eunice, she's so young; it's her first. She'll need a woman's help. . . .'

It was her turn to recoil.

'I never had a child,' she said in a small, bitter voice.

'But you'd know what to do.'

Her eyelids were swollen, still damp from her tears, but between them her eyes were stony.

'I know nothing about it,' she said.

'I'd tell you what to do,' he pleaded. 'I'd help you. And the man carries carpenter's tools, so he's a handy man, too. We'd help.'

'If you're both so clever, do it yourselves. Why bother me?'

'A woman should be there; for decency's sake.' While he pleaded he reckoned the alternative; there was a woman, in the crowd on the sleeping place beside the yard; a woman with a child. But to rouse her he'd have to wake a score of people; and he had no idea what kind of woman she was. Then there were the slaves, young, silly, heavy-handed. Eunice, with all her faults, was sensible and competent; he thought of how well she had tended him when he was helpless.

'Eunice, *please*! If you'll just do this one thing for me, I'll . . . I'll love you for ever. I know you've had a bad bargain in me, but I'll be different I swear. I'll *love* you, Eunice.'

Her whole life had been spent in trading one thing for another; you handed over so much money and bought so much wine, so much food and fodder, then you parcelled them out into smaller portions to be exchanged for smaller coins. Only once had she given something for nothing, and that was when she nursed Ephorus–and she'd received exactly nothing in return. Upon that thought, her sound good sense halted; had hadn't cared for the stranger for nothing; ill as he was, starved as he seemed and poor, she'd seen possibilities in his youth and good looks; so that had been a bargain, too. All the same, she had dreamed of something that wouldn't be mere payment, of something that would have been an offering, a flower laid in the lap. It had never come.

Now here he was, promising what she had dreamed of, not as a gift, another bargain. But as things were, and at her age, a sensible woman must compound for the best she could get. She pushed the blanket aside and heaved her weary body to its feet. As she reached for her outer clothing Ephorus gave a great sigh of relief.

'I've heard plenty of talk,' Eunice said. 'There's nothing much to birthing a baby, really.'

'And you're so clever,' he said. 'There's nothing you couldn't do, if you tried.'

She gave him a sidelong, sardonic look, intended to let him know that she wasn't taken in by his flattery; and she was startled by the expression on his face. Never, not even in the early days, when he had most reason to be grateful to her, had he looked so grateful, so admiring, so almost . . . almost adoring.

'It's cold out,' he said. 'You'll want this.' He turned and unhooked her cloak from the door and held it open for her. As he folded it around her, his hands lingered for a second, touching her; a middle-aged body, a trifle too solid, but a good comfortable armful of woman still.

She bustled into the stable, with all her vigour and energy suddenly replenished.

'Well,' she said, briskly, but not unkindly, 'this is a fine to-do. But don't fret. We'll manage. I don't want you, or you,' she said to Joseph and Ephorus. 'Go in the kitchen, make up the fire and heat some water. I'll call when I need it. Better warm some wine, too.'

In a momentary respite Mary unclenched her teeth and said:

'You are kind. God must have sent you.'

Eunice, the Greek, thought–What a typically Jewish thing to say! She felt like retorting that Ephorus had sent her. But if faith in her God was a help to the girl, let it go; she was going to need all the help she could get.

'I don't think this will be a long job,' she said. 'And if you want to yell, yell. There's nobody to hear except me.'

PART TEN

A FIELD

2 miles

This would be his fifth winter of tending another man's sheep–and to that he was not resigned, and never would be. This would be the fifth winter since his bereavement–and to that he was not resigned, and never would be.

People, meaning well, had said, 'You have other children; another son.' But a heart once given is given and cannot be retracted and bestowed elsewhere. People, meaning well, had said, 'Time is a great healer.' So it might be, for small wounds; but had time, he asked himself, ever enabled a man to grow a new limb to replace one sawn off? People had also said, 'It was a hero's death.' And the reply to that, in the depths of his heart, was always, 'It was the wasted death of a fool.'

The would-be consolatory remarks had ceased within a year. It seemed to him sometimes that he was the only person who remembered at all; and he thought that even he might have remembered less, had he taken on a job where he had to be busy and bustling. A shepherd, even a good one, giving his flock every care, could think with a part of his mind, and on the journeys from pasture to pasture, and between watering holes, he must dawdle along with little to do but think.

On the other hand, what could he have done? Nobody could learn a trade overnight; to set up in business one needed money. He was forty-three when ruin came upon him, a big, slow-moving, seemingly slow-thinking man, marked by weather and a scar or two–not everybody's idea of an employee. Except as a shepherd. Sheep he knew about. He had lived with them and for them since he was seven years old. Also, he had wanted to stay in the district where Martha, his wife, had family and friends. Being a shepherd's wife could be a lonely business.

He had not been forced to the humiliation of actually asking for a job. He had sold his flock–a magnificent one–to a man named Ezra, and as soon as the transaction was made, Ezra asked:

'And you, Josodad, what will you do now?'

'I must get to Jerusalem, and move heaven and earth to save the boy. Beyond that I can't think.'

Ezra had been the first, or almost the first, to remind him that he still had a family.

Josodad said heavily, 'I know.' He was fond of them all, two little girls and a boy of two, but he had never felt and could never feel for them the wholehearted love that he felt for Nathan, his first-born, who had for a long time been his only child, who had toiled beside, watched with him, through at least twelve lambing seasons, who was at once like him, often so much like him as to seem his other self, and yet endearingly unlike, being merry, and musical, and gregarious. The girls and the little boy were his children. Nathan was his son.

'They must eat,' Ezra reminded him.

'I shall leave their mother enough for their needs,' Josodad said, and was turning away. Ezra understood that at the moment the man should think only of his errand–in Ezra's opinion about as hopeless a one as any man ever set out upon; but he was thinking of himself, too, and what a pity it would be if, when Josodad was trudging, defeated, home, somebody else should step in and offer him a job.

'If you want a job with sheep I can offer you one. Be glad to.'

'But I can't say when I shall be back.'

'I can wait,' Ezra said, with apparent generosity, knowing that the waiting time would not be long. 'So long as I have your word.'

'You have it,' Josodad said.

He came back, in just about the time that Ezra had reckoned, with his empty purse, and his empty heart, a lie in his mouth for the boy's mother–that was how he thought of her, the boy's mother–and a memory like a white-hot iron in the brain. And without wasting an hour he had gone to work tending Ezra's sheep.

He knew, almost at once, that he had been forced into the wrong job. For twelve years he and Nathan had worked together, so everything was a reminder. And there was so much time. . . . In the morning you looked the flock over. One not getting to its feet? One coughing? One walking on three legs? Any sign of fly-blows? Should there be anything wrong, you dealt with it, glad of the break in the routine. Then there was the nice judgement of pasture, of water supply, and, in winter, where the wind lay. But there were great tracts of time when there was nothing to do but wait and watch, listen to the monotonous bleating, and think, and remember. . . .

He was working with other men now, he who had worked only with his own father, by himself, and with Nathan. He worked with two young men, Arad and Ibri, hirelings, as he himself was now a hireling, but of a different kind; men who had never been anything else. For a week or so they had borne his gloom and his silences. They were local men and they all knew his story and what had happened to Nathan. Everyone in and around Bethlehem knew. Nathan had been crucified. Josodad had come home and given Martha his carefully prepared lie, 'It was all over in an hour.' It had lasted for sixty and all that time Josodad had stood by the foot of the rough-hewn cross and prayed a single prayer, 'God, of thy mercy, let him die!' and even as he prayed, had had flitting memories of the things he had done to make this boy strong, solid of bone and muscle. More than once, when Nathan's plate was empty and clean he had said, 'Have this; I've made my growth.' And more than once in summer he'd said, 'Go and swim. I can manage.' In winter he'd been careful to see that Nathan's fingers were not frost-bitten, as his own had been. And the end of all his care, his occasional self-denials, had been a strong body, dying slowly and inevitably.

Arad and Ibri had tolerated him for a time; then they had decided that he was surly and unsociable. And that mattered little to them, they were company for one another. Then he made himself unpopular with them.

In any flock, however tended, there were losses, but to Josodad, the former owner of the flock, the attitude of his fellow-hirelings was shocking.

A lamb was lost, and Arad said, 'The kites'll find it,' and settled down to trim his nails with his knife.

'That is a sure thing,' Ibri said, and settled down to play with his five stones. Five stones, polished from much handling, which he held in his palm, and then threw upwards, and tried to catch all five on the back of the hand which he had turned palm downward; never yet had he caught all five, but four, on the few occasions when he caught them, made him jubilant; three was fairly good, two disappointing, and one a mere inducement to try again.

On that occasion Josodad had gone to hunt for the lost lamb and found it straddled over a rock which it had failed to jump. It was exhausted and he had lifted it, set it across his shoulders and carried it back to the flock.

Then there'd been the time when three ewes, old enough to have known better, had gorged themselves on a patch of vetchling and blown up, huge, helpless, lying on their sides and gasping with glazing eyes.

Arad had regarded them dispassionately. 'All old; they'll be tough eating.'

'You'd let them die?'

'They always do,' Ibri said.

'Not in *my* flock,' Josodad said, with a vicious snap in his voice. He drew his knife and went to the nearest ewe, set his left hand like a fork over her neck and with his right made the small incision in the blown-up belly. The gas had rushed out with an audible hiss; the ewe struggled and Josodad helped her to her feet before turning swiftly to operate upon the other two.

Ibri said, 'I never saw that done before.'

But a few seconds later Arad said, 'Did you hear that? *My flock*, he said. He looks on these as though they were his.'

'You'd think,' Ibri said, catching Arad's mood, 'that he was *married* to them!' And in that remark lay the germ of a joke.

'The Old Tup,' they called him, behind his back, but, as such things do, the nickname reached Josodad's ears, and hurt and was resented.

But for a long time, surly, resentful, scornful of their attitude as he was, he tried to be tolerant; but the time must come, and it came, when he was bound to think–They are rubbish; they work for pay and whether they earn it or not is a matter of indifference to them. My boy, a shepherd boy, is dead. They flourish, and hundreds like them. Maybe this is a world where only rogues flourish.

There were other petty annoyances, too. Ezra, once he had him safely hired, seemed to enjoy putting him in his place, in opposing him, senselessly, in small things which merely said, *my* flock. Lambs that he, with his knowledgeable eye, had marked as good breeders were sent off to market or to slaughter, others, of less potential value, retained. And there was a constant running warfare about the amount of pitch needed to treat fly-blows.

'You must be heavy-handed with the stuff,' Ezra said. 'A quarter of the amount served in the old days.'

'Because half the blows were left untreated,' Josodad snarled.

The little he had of home life was no happier. Martha had vented her grief over Nathan noisily, for a day or two, maybe three; then, exactly as she would have drawn together the edges of a torn place in a garment, she had set to work to mend her life. Nathan was gone. Martha, named for her, and

Mary, and young Lazarus remained. The girls were the cleanest, the most tidily dressed, the most well-brushed of all the girls in the village and the boy was being spoiled rotten, in Josodad's opinion. 'You are fortunate; you still have a brother,' Martha had said to the girls once, in his hearing, 'you must cherish him.' Josodad had recognised it as a back-handed slap at him, the father who had failed to take comfort in his second son. He had tried; he had waited, trying not to make comparisons. But the boy was seven now, afraid of the dark, afraid of a thunderstorm, afraid of his father, a timid shrinking creature, liking to sit in his mother's lap, to play girlish games with his sisters. When Nathan was that age, Josodad had fashioned a miniature shepherd's crook for him who was stamping with impatience, and then watched, how proudly and happily nobody would ever know, how the boy had mastered the use of it.

These thoughts, and the memories of Nathan's final hours, occupied his mind during the long days, the even longer nights. He would wake, abruptly as though disturbed by something, lift his head and listen, as he was paid to do. Arad and Ibri, Arad or Ibri according to rota, similarly paid, slept on; and Josodad would stand up, survey the sleeping flock, dark humped shadows and know that all was well and that whatever had roused him came from within his mind. Then he would know that the torture hour was about to begin, and he would do his best to fend it off. In winter he would mend the fire, but winters were short. He would walk, with a shepherd's slow, noiseless steps, around the sleeping flock; he would wet his finger on his tongue and hold it up to find which way the wind was blowing. He'd look at the sky and forecast the next day's weather. And all the time he knew that he was doing these things in a completely futile effort to avert the evil hour when in the hollow, the sharp-thinking night he must face his memories, and his God.

He'd been a happy, a most fortunate and blessed man until the season of the Passover when Nathan was seventeen. It had been arranged, far ahead, that Nathan should then go to celebrate the Feast in Jerusalem. He was to travel with others of his age, and older people who had either never been before, not being able to afford it, or a few who were going for the second or third time. Josodad had been once, and so had Martha; they had remembered it and spoken of it often. Then she, busy with house and children, and he, busy with the sheep, had kept the Passover at home. Nathan had been very much excited by the project.

Non-Jews, of whom there were a few in the neighbourhood–the inn-keeper was a Greek, the blacksmith a Roman veteran who had learned his trade in the army–had the wrong idea about the Feast of the Passover; because it was solemn they thought it dull and dreary, and thought the word 'Feast' mis-applied. But it was a feast, even for those who stayed at home, and for those who went to Jerusalem it was an expedition, a sightseeing visit, a holiday and often a family reunion as well.

That year Josodad had enjoyed the Feast a little less than usual. Martha had put all the traditional things on the table, the unleavened bread, the mutton, the eggs, lettuces and radish, and the sweet dish made of raisins and nuts and spices; all the traditional things had been said; but Josodad's mind, instead of being fixed on the Escape from Egypt which the Feast celebrated, had been all the time marking the vacant place and wondering how Nathan was faring, whether he had fallen in with congenial company, whether he were being robbed or cheated by the rascals who haunted the outer precincts of the Temple, fattening on inexperienced pilgrims.

Nathan had come home changed in some subtle way. He was still merry and lively, but with thoughtful spells. He seemed older, which was right, he was growing up; and perhaps, the father thought, the Temple had impressed him. His mother had produced the obvious feminine reason for the change; somewhere a girl had taken his eye; and she hoped that it would be a daughter of one of the family's friends or distant relatives to whom he had been charged to give messages, should he see them.

This explanation Josodad could not accept. Nathan would have told him. He was not the kind of boy to cast his eye on an unacceptable girl, and he knew that all he had to do was to mention his preference to his father who would at once begin to make inquiries and approaches. Then they would build an extra room on to the house, prepare for and celebrate the marriage, and as a gift Nathan would receive part of the flock. Josodad had already selected the breeding animals whose progeny in a few years' time would form the nucleus of a new flock. That was how it had been in his family for generations, ever since the return of the Jews from the Babylonian captivity; Josodad hoped that so it would always be. He was a Jew of the old-fashioned orthodox kind.

But although their relationship was as sound and easy as it had always been, there was no mention of any girl. What there was a good deal of talk about was a young man named Dan whom Nathan had met in Jerusalem and who had proved to be almost a neighbour, coming from Tekoa, a village within an easy walk away. Dan played the pipe, too; he made songs; he was altogether congenial. His father was a shoemaker and he himself had learned that trade.

All through that summer Nathan, whenever he had any spare time, set off for Tekoa to visit Dan.

Martha said, 'You must invite him back.'

Nathan said, 'I will,' but never did so until she began to nag.

'Why must you always go to him? Isn't your company worth a walk?' 'Are you ashamed of your home?' 'Do I not cook as well as *his* mother?'

Thus pressed, Nathan had issued the invitation, and Josodad and Martha, without knowing exactly what they had expected, were disappointed in Nathan's new friend. A hulking, awkward, dumb young man who seemed at first painfully shy, and then suddenly, over supper, came to life when he began to talk of the iniquity of the Roman occupation and the even greater iniquity of the Jews' apathy. Once his silence was broken, words poured out of him; he spoke bitterly about the Hippodrome that Herod had built in Jerusalem, and of the Jews who attended it. 'In ten years' time,' he said, 'you won't be able to tell a Jew from a Roman or a Greek.'

Nathan, looking very uncomfortable, listened, and when Dan, from lack of breath, not invective, paused for a second, said:

'Don't talk politics over supper, Dan. It spoils the taste of the food.'

Then, for some reason, Dan had looked contemptuously at Josodad and given a little grunt and relapsed into silence.

Next day, out with the sheep, Josodad said, 'Your friend, Dan, is a Zealot.'

'He is that way inclined. I think he'd be in the hills by now, but his father's sight is failing and he has several sisters. So he's needed at home.'

'Then I hope he doesn't say in the open what he said last night in our house. Such talk is dangerous.'

'Maybe. But everything he said was true. And such things should be said.'

'That I doubt,' Josodad said, mildly. 'I've never known talk like that do anything except stir up trouble.'

'What would be your remedy, then, for our present situation?'

'Patience; faith in God; and the strength to survive, holding to the Law and keeping our blood pure.'

'You think that is enough?'

'It has served, in similar situations in the past. We were slaves in Egypt, but we came out as a people; we were captives in Babylon, but we came out as a people. Now we have the Roman heel on our necks, but we shall emerge, as a people.'

'How long is it since you were in Jerusalem, Father?'

'Eighteen years.'

'Then forgive me if I say that you can have no notion of the changes that have taken place. Life here goes on the same, so you think it is the same everywhere. Do you know what Dan calls people like you, Father? Happy-do-nothings.'

'But what is there to do–except what I have just said? Wait. In His own good time the Lord will deliver us.'

'With what? That is what Dan asks. Who could free a whole nation of happy-do-nothings, and worse?'

All around them the sheep were quietly grazing and Josodad jerked his crook towards them.

'My boy, if God so willed he could turn that flock, in a blink of an eye, into an army, ready and girded.'

With some awe, but also with some curiosity and a slight disdain in his voice, Nathan said, 'You really believe that, don't you?'

'If I didn't I should not have said it.'

'No. You are a man of integrity,' the boy said. 'And you are happy in your faith.' It was as though, suddenly, their ages had been reversed. This thought stung Josodad and he summoned all the parental authority which in families like his seldom had to be called upon because it was so implicitly acknowledged.

'Look here,' he said, 'I don't want that boy to go putting crazy notions into your head. Talk of resistance and of guerillas is all very fine, but what do they *do* except make things worse for ordinary people? So, they kill one Roman, or they steal three horses. The Romans can spare what they lose, but in the subsequent inquiries in all the nearby villages we lose what we can ill spare. The lesson taught at Sepphoris wasn't wasted on sensible people, and, on a smaller scale, every bit of revolt is similarly punished. If I thought that you,' he said, very confident of his power over this beloved boy, 'went to Dan's house to listen to such inflammatory nonsense as he talked last night, I should forbid you to go.'

'Often enough,' Nathan said, 'we hardly talk at all. We make songs and sing them. He has many friends. And he plays the harp. It's easier for us to go to him, carrying our pipes.'

Hundreds of times later Josodad was to reproach himself for being over-confident, too easily satisfied, blind. It hurt him sometimes, even now, to remember that in her unwitting, female, jealous way, Martha had been nearer the truth than he had. The little group of musicians had achieved a certain local fame and been asked to make music for a wedding in Zilgah.

'Oh,' Martha had said sharply, 'he can carry his harp so far!'

'There is a harp in the house of the bride's father,' Nathan said.

On that occasion he had been absent for two days and a night–and why not? He was young, and when he worked he worked; he was entitled to his recreations.

For two years it had gone on, had become part of life; a wedding, a Barmitzvah, a circumcision feast, all in need of music.

Looking back, in the light of hindsight, that most vivid and dreadful illumination of all, Josodad could see that often around the times of Nathan's absences, there had been incidents. But what was there about them to make connection with a boy who was always home exactly when he had said he would be, who never had a mark on him, who never showed any sign of excitement, or of interest in the incident; and who could always supply, in the detail so dear to women, exactly what had been worn and eaten at the wedding or whatever it was which he had witnessed?

In the end what had happened was plainly the result of a thought-out plan, a carefully laid trap.

Rachel's sepulchre lay to the north-west of Bethlehem. It was regarded by pious Jews not exactly as a holy place, there was only one holy place and that was in the heart of the Temple, but as a place of reverence, a landmark in their history. There the patriarch Jacob's favourite wife had died in giving birth to Benjamin, his favourite son, and he had buried her and reared a pillar over her grave as a memorial.

A small contingent of Roman soldiers, out on patrol from the subsidiary barracks just outside Bethlehem, had chosen to camp by Rachel's tomb–there was water and firewood handy. They had leaned their standard against the weather-worn pillar and two of them had succumbed to that perpetual disease of soldiers–the necessity to leave their mark, to carve their meaningless names. The Rabbi of the nearest village, accompanied by three elders, had gone out and asked civilly that the standard should be shifted and that the pillar should not be further defaced. Some of the men had not understood a word, but one had, and he had said, 'Old men, go shave yourselves!'

How had the ill word spread? Tekoa was even farther from the sepulchre than Bethlehem was; who carried the news? On what swift and fatal feet it had travelled, how instant and unthinking had been the response.

Nathan, Dan and a third boy had taken axes and hacked the standard to pieces. The Romans had pounced; two had been killed and one injured. The boys, outnumbered four to one, had been hauled off.

For Josodad the time immediately after had been a blur of misery, self-reproach and conflicting advice. Had he been able to feel surprise he would have been surprised to find how many people in the immediate vicinity had known what was going on under the pretence of music-making, and believed that he did, also. To the remarks of such people, knowledgeable after the event, he paid no heed at all; but he did listen to the wildly varying bits of advice.

There were those who said, 'Do nothing. To take any action now will be to inculpate yourself.' Those he ignored.

There were those who said, 'The Romans are great on law; even boys like this will be properly tried. Go to Jerusalem at once and hire a good lawyer, one who will plead that the boys were taking a short cut home and that the Romans, alarmed, attacked them first.'

'Does such a lawyer exist?'

Dozens, they told him, men who would stand up and plead any cause, with eloquence and passion, for a price.

There were others who said that in such a crisis the only possible hope lay in the High Priest. He was very powerful; even the Romans, even Herod the King, never wittingly went against him. And the only way to his ear was through a venal priest named Ephraim.

There were those who said, 'Keep religion out of it. Once mention religion and you're done. Hire a lawyer who will plead that Nathan is younger than Dan, completely subservient to him and simply did what he was told.'

In any other circumstances Josodad would have questioned the ethics of such pleading. But he knew that he would sacrifice a dozen Dans to save Nathan. A dozen? A hundred. A thousand.

Plainly the one thing that all the advice had in common was the need for money; money to buy, money to bribe. So he'd gone to Ezra and sold all that he had to sell, his flock.

Often now, in the slow-dragging nights, he could see that in love, in panic, he had rushed into folly. On the day after Dan's first visit he had to Nathan decried desperate action and praised patience and trust in God. But when the moment came when he must choose between the two, he'd gone into action that was just as futile, as anything those boys had ever done. And so he had injured his cause with God.

He had offered bribes, thereby breaking the law against not causing another man to stumble. They'd stumbled very eagerly, taken his money, promised impossible things. He'd lied too, borne false witness, sworn that Nathan was a near simpleton, completely under Dan's thumb.

It was unavailing. Afterwards, when he came to his senses, he realised that men who had taken his money and given him promises and hope had known how it would end. Had Nathan not been concerned he would have known himself. The boys were guilty, the Romans could have killed them, there by Rachel's sepulchre, and committed no outrage; the meticulous mockery of a trial, with its inevitable end, was designed as a warning. Nothing was left but to go to the Wailing Wall and ask one favour of God–that the boy should die quickly. And even that had been denied.

These had been his memories for almost five years as he walked about by day, or woke, with that abrupt jolt, in the night.

What followed the memories, grew out of them and seemed inseparable from them, and were even more torturing, were the doubts which the whole business had bred. He'd always been a devout Jew, with the religion of his fathers woven, firmly he would have said, into the fabric of his life. But he'd prayed that agonised prayer for one last small mercy for his son, and the prayer had not been answered. Had God no mercy? Was there no God? And if no God, then no life hereafter; which meant that Nathan was not gathered to his fathers, safe in Abraham's bosom, but a dead thing, rotting in the ground. To think thus meant despair.

Night by night he fought that thought. He would remember that psalm of David's known as the Shepherd's Psalm. . . . There was a passage in it that ran, 'Lo, though I walk through the valley of the shadow of death, I will fear no evil.' That seemed to imply that death was only a phase. Then not far away was a place called Endor, where in the distant past a witch had summoned up Samuel's spirit and Saul, who had known Samuel well, had recognised him. If that wasn't proof of a life hereafter, what was?

Hopes and questions and speculations span round and round in his mind until finally he reached the most dreadful thought of all. That over the years the poems and the stories and the whole business of belief had been invented by men, bereaved as he had been bereaved, who could find no comfort on earth.

In the quiet dark the stars so far away, so uncaring, the night wind blowing, it was dangerously easy to harbour such a thought: to see men as sheep, of no real importance, born only to die.

Sometimes from exhaustion, he would reach this point and sleep again; sometimes the torture lasted until the stars faded and the darkness paled and the dawn lay rosy in the sky. And never once, no matter what dark paths he had trodden through the night–and might tread again, two or three times during the day, had he ever failed to make the good Jew's first prayer of the morning–'Blessed art thou, O Lord our God, King of the Universe who hast sanctified us by thy commandments.'

In part this was habit, but it was a great deal else beside. Truth for one thing; by the commandments of God the Jews observed them were sanctified. Nathan's friend might say that Jews were being corrupted and absorbed and that might be true of a few, in cities; but the great majority of them resisted the temptation to run after strange gods, attended the simple, clean service in the synagogues, believed that God was a spirit, kept the Law and were the Chosen people. Josodad, even in his despair, had no wish to cut himself off from them. There was a certain amount of caution, too, in his attitude; no man could fully understand God's ways, and despite everything–and by that he meant his doubts, his unanswered prayers–it was possible, more than possible that Nathan was with his fathers, and there, when he himself died, Josodad hoped to join him. So all day and every day, he still lived exactly in accordance with the Law, just in case his thinking had gone a little awry through grief.

So, day followed day, and now it was winter again, his fifth of tending Ezra's sheep and the flocks were in their winter quarters, near enough to Bethlehem so that should snow fall and cover the ground for any length of time, they could be fed from Ezra's well-stocked barns. Josodad did not appreciate, as Arad and Ibri did, this proximity to the little town; it meant that he could make frequent visits to his home. The boys–as he called Arad and Ibri in his mind–were rigorous about claiming their free hours, and if he abjured his, always thought he was doing so from the intention of presently cheating them; and everyone knew where the flock lay, so if he didn't go home there would be talk.

So on this particular day, very cold he noticed as he climbed down from the sheltered place where the sheep were, he had gone home. And he had had a very miserable visit.

He blamed himself. Something like hostility had long existed between his wife and himself. She had, very sensibly, mended her life and unconsciously blamed him for not mending his, and read into his not-mending a criticism of her for having made almost a perfect job of hers. She was wrong there, he was glad to see her happy; but he could never bring himself to say so. The children, awed perhaps by his face which grief and the constant thinking had scored deeply, or perhaps warned by their mother, were always too well behaved in his presence. He was the stranger; the father who came and went; came–they must sense it–without joy, and left without regret. And for him the small, comfortable house was haunted by Nathan's invisible presence. On the door-jamb were the marks which Josodad had scored with his knife, measuring Nathan's height from time to time. He had said, 'Yes, you shall sit up with me through a lambing, when you are so high!' And he'd marked the height, against which the boy would measure himself, standing on his toes, stretching his neck. And hanging on a hook in the wall there had always been, until this day, Nathan's pipe. There were other reminders too; but this cold day, entering by the door he had looked at the notches and then towards the pipe. He always did, he always would. But on this day the hook was empty.

He greeted his wife, and his elder daughter, named for her mother, who were in the room; the girl her mother's very image, even to the way she stirred a savoury-smelling pot on the hearth. Then he said, 'Where's Nathan's pipe?'

His wife said, 'Oh, the pipe, Lazarus has it. Mary went along with him to Ebenezer; he is going to teach him to play.'

'*Teach* him!' Josodad said. 'Nathan taught himself to play. What is more he made that pipe himself. If Lazarus wanted a pipe he should have made his own!' And then, all at once, knowing that nothing but disharmony could result, but feeling something beyond his power to control, a mental scab which itched, and must be scratched, he said, 'And Mary must go along, to guard a boy of seven. Two hundred yards along a village street. What did he think would get him? Wolves?'

The elder Martha said to the younger, 'Go and see if the little brown hen has laid yet. She's our only hope today. If she hasn't and is on her nest, stand by her.'

'You must watch this pot, then,' the young Martha said, 'its bottom is wearing thin and unless you stir the beans stick.'

'That's my good sensible girl,' Martha said; and she took the long spoon her daughter had been using, but did not employ it. Instead she pulled the pot to the side of the hearth and squared herself, facing Josodad. She said:

'You are my husband; but I have had enough of this!'

'Enough of what?'

'Many things,' she said. 'The constant criticism of Lazarus for one. So, he is seven years old, and at that age, we all know, Nathan was a shepherd with short legs and a short crook and he wasn't afraid of anything. I know, I'm tired of hearing it said, by word or by look. Oh, you may think I cannot read your looks, but I can. And every time I think–One family could not expect to breed two such wonders. One we had, and we lost him–through his own folly. Now we have one ordinary little boy who happens to be timid. Remember, to get to Ebenezer's he must pass the inn, and that Ephorus is always drunk. Nathan thought him funny, but Lazarus is scared of him; and I for one see nothing wrong with that. Nor with his taking the pipe. Nathan made it; but since there it is, made already, why should Lazarus risk cutting his fingers making another? Tell me that!'

And then, before Josodad could frame an answer, if there was one, she ran on:

'There's another thing, too. And that is why I sent Martha out of the room. . . .' The mention of the good sensible girl reminded her of her duty to the cooking and she turned, gave the savoury mess a perfunctory stir, and went on, her words hitting Josodad like little hailstones.

'You may not have noticed,' she said, 'but the girls are growing up. Martha is fifteen, and if she isn't betrothed soon she never will be; Mary is almost fourteen. Have you ever asked yourself what will become of them? In the old days men came to the house, asking your advice, wishing to buy your sheep; anyone with a flock which he wished to improve might very well have taken one of your daughters and a few choice sheep as dowry. But it is very different now. . . .'

He said harshly, 'I know that!' He'd realised on his return from Jerusalem that it had been a mistake to sell the whole of his flock outright; he should have sold them and then raised money on the rear, bear, shear and share basis by which he would have been able to claim one lamb out of two, and half the price of the fleeces; but he'd thought of nothing except laying hands on the money and getting away to Jerusalem as quickly as possible. And this woman, fluffing herself out like a hen defending chicks from a hawk, was right to reproach him. He had sacrificed three to one. And uselessly.

'So,' Martha's voice was relentless, 'you know. That at least is something. What I am asking is, what do you propose to do about it?'

'What can I do? You know my wage. You know what it costs to live.'

'Who better? So there will be the girls without dowry and they'll die unwed; Martha, my true daughter, who would make an excellent wife, and Mary, less good in the house, but sweet and gentle. And then,' she said, her voice sharpening, 'you blame me for treating Lazarus as I do!'

There must be some connection–Martha, even in anger, did not talk incoherently–but he could not see it, and was obliged to say:

'What do you mean by that?'

'That I want him to stay alive; to recognise danger, and be careful.' Then she added, '*You* reared Nathan!'

In the three final words he recognised a twenty-year-old jealousy. Justified, in a way; from the time that he could toddle the boy had always wanted to be with his father, had been as Martha said, 'a shepherd with short legs'. And that would have mattered less if another child had been born, or on the way. There was a gap until young Martha was born.

Alongside the jealousy there was blame. *He* had reared Nathan to be hardy, to minimise risks . . . and so indirectly he was responsible for what had happened. A dreadful accusation, and one he could not accept, but the idea added one more twist to his misery.

Young Martha returned, cradling an egg in her hand. He viewed her from the aspect to which her mother had drawn attention. It was true; somewhere, imperceptibly, she had passed the borderline between childhood and womanhood; and what was going to happen to her?

'Good,' his wife said, seeing the egg. 'Put on the pan and begin to cook it when your brother comes in.'

'Is the boy sick?' Josodad asked, knowing that the question was a return to a sore subject, and yet unable to hold it back.

His daughter answered, saying gravely, 'He isn't sick, but he would be if he ate that,' she indicated the bubbling pot. 'I think the grease upsets him.' She took the long spoon and stirred. 'He has a delicate stomach,' she said.

Then Lazarus and Mary came in and Josodad eyed them as though he were seeing them for the first time. Mary, only a year and a few months younger than Martha, was still a child, thin and angular with beautiful, dreamy, almost sleepy eyes. The boy was tall for his seven years, taller than Nathan had been at that age, but fragile-looking; and, at the moment, wearing a sulky look.

Josodad roused himself and made an effort.

'Well,' he said, 'and how did the lesson go? Can you play the pipe, Lazarus?'

'No. Ebenezer was horrid to me. He said I had no ear.'

Why that report should please him Josodad could not have said, but it did; and the fact that it did proved that there was something very wrong with him.

'I tried,' Mary said. 'When Lazarus had done,' she glanced at her mother as she made this explanation. 'And *I* have an ear. Ebenezer said so. And he said it was a pity because pipe-playing is not for girls.'

'I should think not!' her mother said.

Martha boiled the egg, cracked it and put it into a small bowl and set it before her brother. Her mother began, rather slowly, Josodad thought, to dish the savoury mess of mutton, onions and beans into the plates. Then, with a plate in her left hand and the spoon in the other, she turned her head, looking at the door and listening; it was all right, her expression said; and in a few seconds in walked her brother Lazarus, the one for whom the second boy had been named. He was a big, handsome, jovial man who up to four years ago had made a humble but adequate living as a weaver. Then his wife, a childless woman, had died and soon after he had married a widow who owned a prosperous vineyard. Upon her he had begotten a child, but she was too old for successful breeding; she and the child had died, less than a year ago. Since then he had eaten, several times a week, at his sister's house, and once he had said to Josodad that he now knew that it was God's will that he should be childless. 'So I look on these as my own,' he had said, indicating his nephew and his nieces. Josodad had known a moment's envy for the cheerful man who could suffer two bereavements in a short time–three if you counted the still-born boy–and find comfort where it was to be found. Lazarus, like his sister, was sensible; they mended up the hole in their lives and didn't go about with great, raw-edged wounds in their hearts.

For the first time Josodad noted, but without the least feeling of envy, the difference in the quality of the welcome extended to the uncle and that which he, the father, had evoked. His own presence cast a gloom, with Lazarus the sun entered and they all basked in its radiance.

The boy recounted, for his uncle's benefit, his unsuccessful attempt at pipe-playing and Ebenezer's verdict; and Lazarus said:

'No ear? That can't be right. You have two; I can see them. One, two!' he said, pulling each ear in turn, and the boy's sulky expression lifted and he laughed.

Then Mary made her report, and Lazarus said, 'Well, there I agree with the old man. You know why? To play the pipe properly you have to screw up your lips and in time that'd spoil the shape of your pretty mouth.'

To the younger Martha he said, 'Something tells me that you had a hand in this delightful dinner, my dear.'

Josodad's wife said, 'She did; she was almost entirely responsible. How did you know?'

'By the seasoning,' he said. 'It is exactly how you used to cook, Martha, when you could think of the taste and not how long the salt and herbs must last.'

He pleased them, effortlessly. Josodad, eating his own tasteless portion–all food tasted the same to him these days–felt like a stranger in his own house. And the worst of it was that he didn't mind at all. They were happy. They gave the impression of being a happy, united family with the uncle as its centre. And that, even if he had resented it, was so natural that resentment would have been absurd and unworthy. Of course children clung to those who amused and approved of them and made simple little jokes. And of course a woman like Martha, who had mended her own life, felt more at home with her brother, who had mended his, than with a man whose grief was unassuageable.

It occurred to him suddenly, just as the elder Lazarus said:

'It will snow before sunset; of that I am sure,' and he himself had said:

'Then I must be getting back,' and sensed that his going would be a relief, I might as well be dead!

He regarded that thought for a minute and then revised it–They'd all be better off, if I were dead.

Lazarus, a good brother, as well as a pious Jew, would do his duty, take his sister and the children into his house, exert himself to find husbands for the girls, leave his vineyard to the boy. And when sometime Uncle Lazarus said–as he surely would, being a man of sense–That is a ruinous way to bring a boy up! the mother would take heed. She couldn't turn on her brother with the unanswerable words–*You* reared Nathan!

He left them. Uncle Lazarus was in no hurry to get back; there was nothing he could do about the snow if it fell, except be thankful that it had come instead of frost. His winters now were easy and leisurely and he was prepared to spend the rest of the day in the cosy house where young Martha had mended the fire and they were all about to roast apples. There was nothing wrong with the leave-taking, he was their father and the children were reared to be mannerly; Martha asked when he would next be home and he told her truly that he did not know; much depended upon the weather. Lazarus said the snow was certain but he hoped that for Josodad's sake it would be a light fall.

Then he was out in the cold air, alone; but no more alone than when he sat amongst his family.

His house stood a little apart from the village and he had to descend a slight slope, cross the end of the street and then mount again to where the flock lay in a sheltered valley between two hills. The last of the houses in the street was the smaller of the two inns in the town, the one kept by Ephorus the Greek, if the word 'keep' could be used in connection with Ephorus who, as Martha had said, was usually drunk. It was curious, and ironic, but it was true that the idle, drunken sot of an innkeeper, Greek by birth, was the only person who had ever come near seeing the depths of Josodad's desolation. He had also, by a timely word, prevented Josodad from becoming a sot, too. For there had been a time, during the first autumn after Nathan's death, when Josodad, having tried every mental form of self-consolation, faith in God, prayer, joy in his living children, and dismally failed to find what he sought, had experimented with drunkenness and found that to lie down with one's head spinning, one's stomach slightly sickened, did at least mean that one slept. Then, when one waked, grief, denied its nightly outlet, clamped down more fiercely, and a feeling of guilt because one had slept and forgotten, mingled with the sorrow; and the only remedy was more wine.

But one evening, Ephorus, quite drunk himself, had said, 'Don't do it, Josodad. Comfort is not to be found at the bottom of a wine cup. I know. I sought it there myself.' And Josodad, so lately a flock-master, and still a respected member of his own community, had been shocked back to sobriety by the thought that a drunken, Greek innkeeper should feel compelled to speak to him like that. That had been his first reaction. Then Ephorus said, 'We all have our losses you know, and they cripple us. But a cripple would be a fool to invite leprosy as well. I know,' he said, 'I did it. Grief made a cripple of me and then I made myself a leper–I'm speaking metaphorically, of course, and I'm a fool to do it. You Jews don't understand metaphors.'

'We call them parables,' Josodad said, thinking of the prophet Nathan . . . Nathan . . . Nathan . . . who had rebuked King David for taking Uriah's wife by telling him a parable of the man with one ewe lamb.

'Use you own word,' Ephorus said, concentrating so fiercely that he was almost cross-eyed. 'And don't go saying I'm a leper. I'm not a leper; nor a cripple as anybody about here understands the words. I'm just trying to tell you, because I feel for you, Josodad, I feel for you. I had a loss and it crippled me, I lost Dorcas and then I took to wine-bibbing and so I'm a leper, socially. Don't you travel the same road. I'm just warning you . . . warning you.' He'd tossed off another cup of wine and relapsed into his usual silence. And Josodad had left his cup as it was, and had not, as he had intended, asked to have his flask filled to buffer him against his night thoughts.

He'd never been inside the inn since, but he'd always remembered Ephorus with a kind of affection; the one man in Bethlehem who understood what a loss was, an amputation that could cripple a man.

On this evening, so busy with his own gloomy thoughts, he noticed, with a distant, impersonal satisfaction on Ephorus's behalf, that the inn was very busy. Bethlehem-born men coming back in accordance with the new order, to put their names on the tax register. He'd registered that morning, before going home.

Name? Josodad, son of Nathan.

Occupation? Hired shepherd.

Place of residence? Bethlehem.

Age? Forty-eight.

As the questions were rapped out, the answers given, he'd thought, Nathan should have been here beside me, and the answer to the second question should in both our cases have been, 'Flock-master'.

Thinking about the tax register had been some slight relief and carried him on, in the teeth of the biting wind, to the top of the hill from which point he could look down upon the sheep, just visible in the gathering dusk. They were huddled together and he thought–They know. Lazarus was right; it will snow before dark. And almost instantly a few flakes, slowly, indecisively, seeming sometimes even to ascend, filled the air.

He thought–I chose the spot well. If I'd listened to Arad or Ibri we should now be lying nearer the town, with nothing between us and the snow-bearing wind. Not that I was thinking of snow, only of the wind; sheep don't like the wind from the north.

Arad and Ibri had collected plenty of fuel and made a good fire. They were playing with Ibri's stones, the light danced on their moving hands, and on their laughing faces. He could hear the laughter and the loud talk as he approached; but when he joined them they fell silent and took on glum expressions, as though his presence were a rebuke to their merriment. He thought–Here too I cast a shadow. He tried to think of something to say and could only think of a question, 'Is all well?' And that, he knew, would strike a wrong note, as though he thought that in his absence things were bound to go wrong. Yet he could have asked Nathan that question as unthinkingly as he breathed. So he thought again, and produced a remark about the weather.

'It looks as though we're in for a nasty night.'

Ibri–recently married–said, 'All nights apart from Ruth are nasty for me.' Then he said, 'Your turn, Arad,' and the game went on, but in a muted way.

A kind of contrition made itself felt in Josodad; he thought–I have resented them because they are live while Nathan is dead. And he remembered the perverse pleasure he had felt over Lazarus' failure to manage the pipe. He thought of wounds: some healed, leaving no mark, or only a dry, healthy scar, some went festering on and on until they had poisoned the whole body. That was what grief had done to his mind, to his very nature, poisoned the whole. He was now fit company for nobody, not even himself.

He opened the bag of food which the two Marthas had packed for him, small loaves of sweet crusty bread, some fresh cheese, some of the salted, smoked mutton which the Jews prepared in the same way as unbelievers treated pig-meat. And as he opened the bag he saw that the food was exactly the same as that which Nathan had carried with him on the fateful journey during which he had fallen in with Dan. So although he had intended to offer the food in a pleasant, conciliatory manner, his voice, when he said, 'Help yourselves,' came out harsh, off-handedly as though he were offering food to animals.

Arad said, 'But if we eat this, what'll you do tomorrow? And the day after?' He was reminding Josodad that he and Ibri both had their home visits to make, and he must be on duty.

'There's more than I shall need, even if you eat your fill.' And he thought–Never to be obliged to eat again, mumbling the tasteless stuff! Never to think again; or to remember . . .

He knew then what he meant to do. The thought–I might as well be dead–had fallen, like a seed, into fertile soil. The first sign that it had rooted had been the next thought–They'd be better off if I were dead; and now, springing to full life the growth had revealed its nature, a determination to be dead. To end it. To have done with everything.

There was plenty of time; he must wait until Arad and Ibri were asleep. He felt restless and would have liked to say–I'll just walk round; but if he did that they would misinterpret his motive, think that he suspected some neglect on their part. So he sat down, within the fire's radiance, but a little apart, and watched the snowflakes spin down.

It would be, as Lazarus had wished that it should be, a light fall. Already in the west the low clouds were breaking up.

He sat wrapped in his thick cloak and thought of what he intended to do; he thought of it from every aspect. Family first. He was sure that they would be better off. His brother-in-law was a good man, and his business brought him many contacts. The girls would be seen, admired, spoken for; the boy would take kindly to his uncle's business, there being nothing in a vineyard to frighten him, as a ram had once frightened him when Josodad had tried to introduce him to the flock. Martha would be happy.

He then thought about God, who, though He had failed him, could not be ignored without condemning Nathan to oblivion. (And the strange thing here was that though for himself he desired nothing more than complete oblivion–Let Josodad be blotted out as though he had never been–he couldn't accept oblivion for Nathan, that merry laughing boy.) There was nothing in the commandments against killing yourself. He ran them through in his mind, and there was nothing. He then called to mind such of the stories of the past as he had heard and could remember. After his defeat on the Mount of Gilboa Saul had fallen upon his sword. But Saul had been mad, deserted by God. Then there was the story of Elijah the prophet and how he had gone into the wilderness and sat down under a juniper tree and prayed, 'Now, O Lord, take away my life.' His life had not been taken, because he still had work to do; but the prayer had been suicidal, and he had never been rebuked for that. And there was an account of somebody–the name escaped him–turning his face to the wall and willing himself to die.

He considered it all quite calmly, and reached the conclusion that if Nathan were now in the safe-keeping of God, his own self-destruction would be no barrier against their reunion.

And what was the alternative? Years and years more of this life, days during which he would steadily alienate himself from his fellows, nights when he would doubt his God.

But he would, he thought, give God one last chance! And then, for all his doubts, his orthodoxy rose in protest. A blasphemous thought. He'd ask God one last favour.

So he made his last evening prayer, 'Blessed art thou, O Lord our God, King of the Universe, who at thy word bringest on the evening twilight . . .' and then he added his special request: that he might die as he slept.

It was usual for shepherds to draw lots for the order in which they should watch; but he and Arad and Ibri had long ago abandoned that custom. If he slept at all it was always in the first watch, then he'd wake with that jolt and spend most of, if not all, the rest of the night awake. His two companions, after a very short time, had turned this to their advantage. No need, they said, for two people to stay awake. So one of them, or both of them officially, stayed awake and watched while he slept the brief sleep of exhaustion and then he watched for the rest of the night. Most often, when he woke, they were both asleep. In winter there was danger from wolves that would sneak down from the hills, and always there was danger from sheep-stealers, and these were not all men-of-the-hills, hungry and stealing for food. There were professionals, very skilled and soft-footed, who could snatch a sheep from the edge of a flock–the more easily if it were a large flock, like this, smother its head in a cloth and bear it off and sell it to a butcher.

There was no outcry, no trail of blood. In the morning there was a sheep missing, and somewhere, far away, an unidentifiable carcase on a hook.

Tonight, however, there was little danger from thieves. Men who lived by sheep-stealing were, fundamentally, men who liked ease and comfort without working to earn either; the cold and the snow would deter them. A visitation from wolves was unlikely, too, with the flock lying so near to

Bethlehem, it would take a prolonged spell of bad weather to make them desperate enough to venture so near a town. As for the men-of-the-hills, their raids had in the past two years been so infrequent that it seemed to Josodad as though the resistance movement, which had cost Nathan his life, was dying down. So the flock was safe, and it wouldn't matter if he died in his sleep and Ibri and Arad slept on, as was their habit.

As he thought these things he was aware of the absurdity. At this crisis of his life, what did the flock matter? If the flock were stolen or ravaged, he'd be out of reach of any blame or chiding. Still, even now, he reckoned the risk to the flock carefully, because at heart he was still the good owner shepherd, not a hireling, like Ibri or Arad. And when, dead to this world, he woke in the next–if there was another, and faced the judgement of God, he hoped that it would be taken into reckoning that though as a man, as father and husband, he was a failure, as a shepherd he had been reliable.

So he looked over the flock before he lay down. All was well. The fire was bright, and beside it the two men were still engrossed in their game.

He couldn't in the traditional manner, turn his face to the wall, but he turned it towards the rock, under whose overhanging edge they had made their little camping place. And as he lay down he thought with a profound feeling of relief that now he had done with it all, done with the grief and the toil, the searing doubts, the consequent self-recrimination. As he composed himself for sleep, faith came flooding back; he had prayed and he believed that this prayer would be answered. So he began to sink down into darkness and softness and not-knowing as gently as he had done in the happy days. His last thought was that he had not approached sleep by such a pleasant path since he had shared night watch with Nathan. . . .

Shortly before midnight he woke, with the old familiar jolt. Something wrong? He raised his head and listened and, as usual, knew that with the flock all was well, with him all was wrong. The feeling of loss and disaster fell upon him again. Not dead. Alive and wide awake, back with his misery.

He stood up and looked around him. The snow had ceased; the sky had cleared and overhead the stars were brilliant. Arad and Ibri were sound asleep beside the fire which had died down to a pinkish glow under a shroud of ash. The sheep were sleeping too, lying close like the boulders in a dry riverbed. It was all as usual. He thought–God has failed me again; and this time felt no self reproach. It was simple truth. God had failed him all along. He'd kept the Law, done his duty, paid his dues, made his prayers, and never, until tonight, asked a favour for himself. On Nathan's behalf he had prayed for an acquittal, then for swift death; both denied.

He thought, in plain peasant fashion, that if you knocked on the door of a human friend, once and again and again, and had no answer, you'd conclude that he was not there, or that he was, for some reason, no longer your friend. Did not the same apply to God?

The wind blew coldly and he stood there between the great empty space of earth and the great empty space of heaven, between a vast flock of senseless sheep and a vast flock of unheeding stars and knew the ultimate loneliness. He faced–for the first time without recoil or protest–the fact that Nathan had gone for ever, the strong merry, bright-eyed boy who had made music and cracked jokes and loved his food was now just a dead thing, rotting; what he had been had vanished into darkness.

And I will follow, Josodad thought. I will make an end. He knew just how to do it. His knife was sharp; one firm slash across his left wrist would suffice.

Even now, in this moment of no faith, of dead belief, his mind reverted, from habit, to the Law by which he had lived all his life. Thou shalt not kill. That was plain enough and any believer in the Law would understand that suicide as well as murder was forbidden. Yet it was never held against Saul that he had thrown himself on his sword after his defeat at Gilboa. His suicide, indeed, had inspired one of the most beautiful of David's songs. But Saul had long before lost touch with God. Like me, Josodad thought. He drew his knife and saw the starlight sparkle on the clean bright blade.

Then he paused. He had lost touch with God, but not with man, and not with sheep. Arad and Ibri didn't like him, he knew that; to his face they were sullen and suspicious, behind his back they laughed at him and called him Old Tup; but it would spoil their breakfast if they woke and found him here by the dead fire, lying in his blood. And the sheep would be upset, too. All animals were sensitive to blood; carnivores liked, were excited by the smell of it; sheep, oxen, horses abhorred it. So he must go away to do what he had to do.

He began to scramble, making as little noise as possible over the sheltering rocks. At the top he walked a hundred paces and then looked around for some hidden niche in the broken ground where he could lie. The boys would wake in the morning and look over the flock in their casual fashion, have their breakfast, remark upon his absence, and wait. Eventually one of them would report to Ezra and a search would be organised. Maybe by that time the kites would have picked his bones clean. His death would cause nobody any bother, or any grief.

Up here the stars seemed even brighter and there was one, very large, very golden, hanging low in the sky, a star which he had never noticed before in his sleepless nights. Once he had thought of the stars, as of the sun and the moon, that they were all part of the miracle of creation, the result of God's order, Let there be light! But tonight the courts of heaven were untenanted, and the throne was empty.

Searching for what was to be his last bed he turned his eyes from the sky to the ground and was startled to see his own shadow very black and sharply defined, stretching ahead of him. No amount of starlight could cast such a shadow. He turned and saw that behind him the sky was luminous, filled with light that was not of the moon or the stars, light without origin or focus, visibly brightening. It was, he thought, as though the sky were opening.

A fearful terror came upon him, terror so complete that he could not move, or breathe, or even tremble though the marrow of his bones vibrated. The light grew dazzling, and shifted, and took shape. Then suddenly, brighter than the light, more beautiful than anything ever seen or imagined, there was the angel, leaning down along the shafts of radiance and speaking with a golden voice.

The angel said, 'Fear not; for behold I bring you tidings of great joy, which shall be to all people. For unto you is born this day in the city of David, a Saviour which is Christ the Lord. And this shall be a sign unto you; ye shall find the babe, wrapped in swaddling clothes, lying in a manger.'

The Saviour. The Messiah. Something in Josodad's mind shouldered fear aside. He said in a loud, almost angry voice, 'Didn't I tell him so?

Didn't I say that in His own time, in His own way, God would deliver His people. He had only to wait. The waste of it!'

He had felt that his misery was absolute, that nothing could add to it. But he had been wrong. There was this extra bitterness to come. 'Too late,' he said. 'This is too late for Nathan who is dead, and too late for me, who have denied my God.'

Then he saw that the angel was not alone. Around him there was a multitude, a great host, all with bright, beautiful faces. But of the host Josodad had eyes only for one familiar, beloved face; and in the chorus of voices singing, 'Glory to God in the highest, and on earth peace, goodwill toward men', he heard only the voice of his own son.

They vanished and he was alone in the starlight. He stood there knowing that Nathan was not a dead thing in the ground, but alive, recognisable and happy, part of some inconceivable glory. He was filled with joy, and mingling with the joy was remorse because he had allowed grief to sour him, to estrange him from his family, from his fellow men, from life itself. All those years wasted in grief and bitterness, with Nathan, young and beautiful, safe in the hands of God all the time. He said aloud, 'O God, maker of the Universe, forgive me. How could I know?' The answer came from his own mind: no man could *know*, but a man should have faith.

He began to shake then, realising how nearly he had escaped final calamity. Moving like a palsied man he hurried, not caring how much noise he made, over the rocks and down into the sheltered place. Arad slept the sleep of the carefree single man, but Ibri was awake, blinking and bemused.

'I saw a great light,' he said. 'I heard voices.' He spoke as though the light and the voices had been things he had dreamed.

Josodad said, 'Come, let us go to Bethlehem.'

PART ELEVEN

JERUSALEM

8 miles

Except on state occasions, when he must appear as a king, it pleased Herod to wear the simple toga that was the mark of the Roman citizen. This he was entitled to do, for the first Caesar, Julius himself, had conferred full citizenship, with all its privileges, upon his father, Antipater, forty years earlier.

On this day, however, he wore his kingly, almost Oriental robes, with jewelled clasps and a jewelled belt, a coronet of emeralds on his head, where the hair was still plentiful and crisp, the black only just frosted with white at the temples; on his wrists he wore bands of gold, set with other emeralds and rubies and sapphires, and his fingers were stiff with rings.

He was about to go out and show himself to his people, so that those who loved him and those who hated him might see for themselves what rumour was worth. His friends had been grieving, his enemies rejoicing, over the state of his health; and both had had good cause. He had been gravely ill: but he had made a most painful journey by litter, across the Jordan, to a place called Calirrhoe, and there he had taken medicinal baths and drunk immense quantities of revolting, bitter-tasting water, and been not only restored to health, but rejuvenated. The pain that had gnawed, a wolf in his belly, had gone; his ravenous appetite was now normal, and his complexion, lately the colour of beeswax, had regained its smooth, faintly tanned Idumean hue.

He had come back, jubilant, just in time for the Feast of Saturnalia, and inside his palace he had celebrated, merrily: but he was far too cautious, far too wary of the High Priest and his following, and of the orthodox Jews, to make any public appearance during the Festival. So on this day he intended to ride out.

The gentleman-attendant, whose duty it was, held open his cloak, purple velvet, lined with fur and embroidered with gold thread. Parosh was a Jew, of the Hellenised kind whom Herod found tolerable, so to him he could say, 'Solomon in full glory could not have been better clad!' and be sure of provoking a smile.

'I am ready, now,' Herod said, shrugging his shoulders into the cloak. 'And if Archelaus keeps me waiting, I shall disinherit him.'

The threat to disinherit was one of his slightly sour, self-mocking jokes; he never for a moment deceived himself about the extent of his power. He was King of Judea because his father had been a friend of the Romans and because his own personality and abilities had recommended him to Mark

Antony and Octavius while they were still friends and shared the government of Rome. He had remained King of Judea because he had been wily, and because even when Antony and Octavius had fallen out, and Antony was dead and Octavius supreme, the latter had had the good sense to see that there was nothing to gain and much to lose by deposing a man who was managing well, who had put down civil war in Judea with a heavy hand, who was a good friend of Rome, whose half-Jewish blood made him acceptable to at least part of the nation he ruled. But when he died, even though he made a will and showed clearly which of his sons should succeed him, there was no certainty that Archelaus or any of his other sons would be chosen by Octavius–now Caesar Augustus, to occupy the throne.

Of his five remaining sons–Archelaus, the youngest, was his favourite; most like him in appearance, and though, only sixteen years of age, most compatible in mind. Unless something very regrettable happened, Herod intended to use all his influence, even his posthumous influence, on behalf of this boy; and with that in mind often appeared with him in public, frequently sent him on visits to Rome, and while he was in Jerusalem never failed to bring him to the notice of any visiting Roman.

Archelaus was punctual and Herod, looking him over, was satisfied by his appearance; he was dressed as befitted a prince, but not in such a way as to offer any competition to his father. Herod, who had on at least three occasions placed policy before paternal feelings and murdered his sons as though they were enemies, was fond enough, at this moment, to say:

'No cloak? They tell me the wind is very cold.'

The escort waited; six members of the palace guard, a body of men whom Herod had organised very much upon the lines of the Emperor's Praetorian Guard in Rome; imitation, so long as it was not tainted by competitiveness, was a useful means of flattery. It often seemed to Herod that many men of intelligence failed to succeed because they lacked knowledge of human nature. In one of the long, rambling complaints which the priests were always sending by delegation to Rome, one charge was that Herod copied the Emperor; and Augustus had given the reply that any sensible person could have expected. 'Whom better could he copy?' Augustus had asked.

Herod had felt well when he wakened, well as he was robed; now with a horse between his knees again, he felt even better. Before his visit to Calirrhoe he had been able only to ride in a litter, and even that was painful. Now he rode a superb horse, one of Arab breed, brought up from his native Idumea.

They rode through a wide courtyard where the grass was always green, even in the height of summer, because it was intersected at regular intervals by small irrigation streams. There were many fountains, too, bronze or marble figures of boys and girls, holding bowls of torches out of which the water spouted, horses and deer and strange mythical beasts with water pouring from their mouths. Such things were detestable to the pious Jews who took the first commandment literally. But there was no need for any Jew to enter this way; there were other entrances, some containing nothing likely to offend. In this as in other things Herod had been willing to compromise between what he wished and what was acceptable. About the water supply, so essential in a civilised city, compromise had been impossible, one could not build an aqueduct secretly, nor cheaply, and there had been a short, sharp rebellion when it was discovered that some of the Temple funds had been appropriated for the aqueduct. But to balance that,

Herod could point to the immense amount of work he had done to embellish the Temple itself. It was now finer than the one that Solomon had reared, which had been destroyed by the Babylonians. At the return from exile, the Jews under Ezra had rebuilt it, but small and plain. Herod had greatly enlarged and beautified it.

Behind him, as he rode out this morning, was the Palace, upon which he had lavished money and planning genius, and across the huddled roofs of the city, as he gazed ahead, he could see the Temple.

He said, 'I intend to do something generous and spectacular to show my gratitude to Calirrhoe. The waters there are as good as any in the Empire, but the buildings are nothing, and the place is amateurly run. I think I shall build a great new bath with a musician's gallery and a library and rooms for massage and amusement. To make the place popular would be an investment. As the roads improve more people will travel. That fellow Quintilius who dined with us the other evening, was on his way there.'

The old man talked as though he had years of life ahead of him, Archelaus thought; and really since his return from the baths, he looked as though he had.

Aloud he said, 'Now what did you make of *him*, sir?'

Herod thought–I could tell you exactly. He's an independent observer, in other words a spy. Augustus had heard of my illness and was beginning to plan ahead. Reports from officials are always biased. . . . But it was unwise to be too open, either of mouth or heart, even to your favourite; so he answered by asking:

'I don't know. What did *you*?'

'It struck me that either his gout was very mild, or he has found some very powerful opiate. He ate and drank everything that was put before him.'

'That was very observant of you.'

'Also,' Archelaus said, 'his appetite for information was as insatiable as his greed. He seldom asked a direct question, though. I noticed that. He had a way of bringing the conversation round, so that the way was open for you to *tell* him things.'

'Did you tell him anything? I saw you in conversation for a considerable time.'

'I told him nothing–at least nothing he wanted to know. He told how badly he and his brothers agreed when they were young; and the way was wide open for me to tell him how Antipas and Antipater and I hate the sight of one another. But I did not do so. In fact, I think, sir, that I left him with the impression that I was somewhat slow in the uptake.'

'Never fear that! It's the slow-witted ones who gulp down the bait, my boy.'

From under their hooded lids his bright eyes looked at Archelaus with something like approval. The boy had his wits about him. From Herod's point of view there was only one thing wrong with him–apart, of course, from what was wrong with every human being, untrustworthiness–he was the son of the wrong mother! Whenever he approved of Archelaus he was bound to reflect that if he could breed such a boy upon an ordinary woman, how exceptional his sons by Mariamne would have been. They, however, Alexander and Aristobulus, had allowed their untrustworthiness to become blatant, and he had been obliged to have them murdered.

This, however, was no moment to think of Mariamne or her sons. He gave his attention to his capital.

Most of the streets they rode along were narrow and steep, presenting, under the heavy grey of the sky, a dull, ancient, rather grim appearance. The people, huddled against the cold, looked dull too. In many places the sullenness of the sky was reflected in the faces turned towards the clattering little cavalcade. To many Jews Herod was a semi-barbarian, a usurper, a man who endeavoured both openly and secretly to bring them, their city, their way of life, into line with the pagan ways that masqueraded under the term 'civilisation'.

'I often think,' Herod remarked as they passed a group of men who stared, silent and hostile, 'that of all rulers, he who governs a theocracy has the most thankless task. People are so busy praising God for his mercies–mainly invisible–that they can't be ordinarily grateful for tangible advantages.'

Archelaus privately decided that when he was King–as he fully intended to be, by craft and corruption if qualification was not enough–he would do something about these surly, stubborn people. If they wouldn't smile and cheer from loyalty and gratitude, they should do it from fear. He looked at his father and thought, with some bewilderment, that you couldn't honestly say that he was a soft man; he'd killed hundreds and would not hesitate to kill again; but he was oddly careless about the attitude of the ordinary man towards him.

Once, on a similar ride, a man, safely anonymous in a crowd, had flung a taunt; 'Son of Esau!' he had shouted, referring to Herod's ancestry. Herod had turned in his saddle and laughed and shouted back, 'Thank you!'

Archelaus, younger then, had said, 'But sir, that was an insult.'

'From a Jew, a compliment,' Herod said. 'If you must go picking over your pedigree like a race-horse, who wouldn't rather be a descendant of Esau, the first-born, the good hunter, than that lying, cheating, mother's darling who spawned this lot?'

Archelaus remembered that incident, and thought–Well, that's one way of looking at it; that's one way of governing, so completely to despise those you rule that whether they cheer or not doesn't matter: all the same, when I ride these streets as King, people will cheer or I shall know why!

In places they were cheered. Anywhere where there was building going on. Even a Jewish builder knew the value of full employment and over the rebuilding of the Temple alone, ten thousand workmen had been employed steadily for six years. There were loud acclamations, too, from people about the theatre, the amphitheatre and the Hippodrome where the workers were mainly Greeks or half-breeds of one kind or another, with some Jews who were prepared to accept civilising influences in the proper spirit. In places where the reception was warm and friendly Archelaus responded with a guarded enthusiasm. To be popular for yourself alone, and to endeavour to foster popularity was not a safe thing, if you were Herod's son. Antipater, at the moment, enjoyed great popularity, simply because he and his father were always quarrelling. They would have a row in the Palace overnight, and somehow the word would spread and be all over the city by morning and on Antipater's next appearance he would have a tumultuous greeting. But that kind of thing merely worsened the situation between father and son, and Archelaus was clever enough to realise it. He was risking nothing; after all, Herod was seventy, and the Romans had enough respect for his judgement, and enough awareness of all he had done to keep this province of the Empire peaceful and prosperous, to take some note of any wish he expressed on his deathbed. Archelaus intended to wait.

When, with the wind growing colder and the grey sky darkening towards twilight, they passed the Royal Portico of the Temple, on their way back to the Palace, Herod said:

'I have the High Priest and five other Sanhedrin members dining with me this evening. It's amusing to think that they have probably spent most of the day composing a complaint to send to Rome because I allowed Saturnalia to be celebrated. Unless Octavius lost his sense of humour when he became Augustus, he must often have a good laugh over these deputations.'

'They show such poor judgement,' agreed Archelaus who had once been in Rome when such a deputation arrived. 'One deputation, I remember, complained, hardly pausing for breath between, that three men had been unjustly tried and sentenced to death and that you wore the toga. Augustus did smile–he seldom laughs outright–and he said, "Which of these is a serious crime? One I commit regularly myself!"'

'They have too much money; too much money by far,' Herod said darkly. 'Jews scattered all over the face of the earth, prosperous some of them, many poor, but all sending back money, sending back money, for the Temple funds. But when the harvest failed–oh, long before you were born–and pestilence broke out; did the damned priests lift a finger or give a sesterci to help the people? Did they even remit their tithes? They did not. I remitted my tax, my income, for a whole year. I also sold treasures from my Palace that I have never been able to replace. My best gold candlesticks ended up in Pontus, I believe; and there was a table of lapsis lazuli. . . . I bought corn from Egypt, they'd had a good harvest, and I gave it away, free. And what thanks did I get? I was trying, they said, to pauperise upright Jewish citizens by imitating the dole-giving in Rome. They said that with their mouths full of my bread. Ingrates!'

There again, Archelaus thought, the contradictory streak; if when he ruled a year of famine came, he wouldn't sell a candle to help, leave alone a candlestick!

'Well,' Herod said, 'that's over. They know I'm alive and well, and early next week I can go to Caesarea.'

That was a new town, his own creation, a beautiful place. It was cosmopolitan too, and the heavy leaden hand of the Jewish faith lay there so lightly as hardly to be felt at all. There he would not be expected to dine with six priests and spend the evening in solemn conversation.

Archelaus said, 'May I come with you?' eagerly.

'It's about time you went to Rome again,' Herod said. 'You can do a double errand there. You can give Caesar a first-hand account of my health. I think you'll know what to say about *that*! And you can find out his favourite sculptor and his favourite pose and order a statue, twice life-size, to go in the atrium of the new baths at Calirrhoe. I owe my throne to the Emperor and my life to Calirrhoe, and that would be a suitable way of combining my expressions of gratitude. You can let that information fall in a casual way. Even flattery profits by a touch of subtlety; always remember that, my boy.'

'I know exactly what you mean,' Archelaus said, thinking–That's clever!

'I believe you do; otherwise I should not be sending you. You can come to Caesarea and take ship from there. Now I will go and don my detested toga, so that the High Priest's disapproval lends *some* flavour to this dismal meal.'

It would be, as always on these occasions, as nearly meagre as could be served at a King's table. The Jews had all these ridiculous rules about what could and what could not be eaten or drunk; let them abide by them. The meal this evening would be just that served in any well-to-do Jewish family's household; mutton and beans, onions and horse-radish. And the wine would be a cheap local product, from grapes grown on Jewish soil, gathered by Jewish hands, the wine of *Kiddush*. Herod himself much preferred Falernian.

There would be one bright spot in the evening, too; sooner or later the priests were bound to mention the new taxes and the census; and there Herod would be on very sound ground. He could say, 'Caesar gave that order; I had nothing to do with it. You should have sent a deputation to Rome if you had any valid objection.'

There was another comforting thought. On the last occasion when he entertained the Sanhedrin members, he'd been in the throes of his illness; ravenously hungry; the miserable meal had done nothing to appease the wolves gnawing in his belly and he had hardly been able to wait until the priests left and he could order another, better meal, knowing all the time that it would merely feed the wolves and strengthen them for tomorrow's assault. Tonight he would be able to eat normally.

He was hardly inside the Palace when one of the stewards came bustling up to say that three travellers had arrived and humbly craved audience. They were insistent and were waiting.

'From Rome?' Herod asked, instantly alert.

'No, my lord, from the East. Only one of them speaks a recognisable tongue.'

The East? Parthia?

'Who sent them? What credentials do they carry?'

'None, my lord.'

'You are sure of that?'

'Dumah questioned them and is certain they have no mission–except their own, which is a wish to see you, my lord.'

'Then why should they imagine that I should receive them? If I opened my door to every chance traveller I might as well be on show in the menagerie! Send them away.'

'My lord, Dumah did gather that a prince is concerned.'

Herod made a sound of exasperation. Antipater again. Women? Debts?

'Is one of these a merchant?'

'So Dumah thought. A black man; better dressed than the others, and the spokesman.'

Herod could guess what had happened. In one of their recent quarrels he had absolutely forbidden Antipater to obtain credit in any city under his jurisdiction; he had a generous, a wildly generous allowance, and he must keep within it. But Antipater had simply taken advantage of the words 'within my jurisdiction' and had gone to the free cities of the Decapolis and there run up debts. Now a black-faced fellow, probably a freedman– and they were the sharpest traders in the world–had come, with two witnesses, to ask payment. And his daring to come showed how highly those citizens of the independent Greek cities valued themselves. Insolent upstarts! He was on the verge of saying that the men should be hustled off, roughly; then he remembered that the Decapolis was under Roman protection. The next thing he knew *they'd* be sending a deputation to Augustus complaining that

Herod had no control over his own son.

He said, 'Tell the Treasurer to deal with it, whatever it is,' and strode angrily along to his own apartments where the attendants waited to disrobe and dress him again. But his anger with Antipater had opened the old wound in his heart: his true sons, his real heirs, had been Mariamne's sons, and they were dead. So was she. And the fact that he had been responsible for their deaths, planned and ordered the executions, did nothing to lessen his grief. A man with a rotting limb might be driven to cutting it off with his own knife, that he performed the operation himself would not lessen the pain, nor the loss.

Brusquely he waved aside those waiting to serve him and went to the high, bronze decorated door that separated his rooms from those of Mariamne.

Her sleeping chamber, a large room with a silver and ivory bed on a dais, was warmed by braziers that gave off sweet scent as well as warmth, and the air was also full of the scent of roses. A slave had already lighted many candles, at the sight of Herod he scuttled away. The light shone on the flowers and on the dressing table with its silver mirror, its flasks and pots of rose-crystal, jade and alabaster; it was just as she had left it. Easy enough to delude oneself that this room's occupant, a fastidious woman, superlatively served, had just been robed, had painted her face and dressed her hair and gone out of the room for a moment and would, in a moment, be back.

His attitude towards his murdered wife was the most evident sign of that contradictory streak in Herod which those close to him had noted. He had loved her, distrusted her deeply, and had her killed. Immediately after he had given orders that her rooms were to be kept exactly as she had left them, that she was always to be spoken of as though she were alive. He had never cancelled the order for the daily delivery of roses; during rose-less seasons in Jerusalem they were brought from far places, cut in bud, wrapped in damp cotton fibre, transported by the swiftest means, and arranged. On any occasion when, alive, she would have shared a meal with him, her place was set; he visited her apartments once every day as a matter of routine, and frequently at other times when he was worried, puzzled, exultant, or sorry for himself. Often he spoke her name, a thing to which his courtiers and staff were accustomed but disconcerting to strangers.

There were some who worked in the Palace who were not so sure that the whole thing was a mere foible. When Herod called 'Mariamne' there was no answer but an echo; her wraith was never seen, but occasionally someone walking a hall or a corridor where there were no roses would become aware of the sweet scent which had been her favourite. Once a slave, dusting the table where Mariamne had been used to sit, beautifying beauty, had dropped and broke a glass phial and then reeled back, her hand to her face, screaming. Later she had a bruise to show to corroborate her story that she had been slapped. Nightwatchmen, too, told uneasy stories of the behaviour of the hounds which made their rounds with them. Over the years the Palace had become a place where few men willingly walked alone after sunset.

Herod was as jealous of these hints that other people as well as himself were aware of her as he had been jealous of anyone who approached her when she was alive. He, the sceptic, the murderer, the extremely rational man, liked to believe, did believe, that somewhere she lived on, entirely his at last, understanding why he had done what he did, and full of sweet forgiveness and deeply concerned with his well-being. This imaginary Mariamne bore little resemblance to the haughty, intractable Asmodean princess whom he had married from expediency and who with a glance or the movement of a hand could convey her scorn of him, a half-breed upstart and usurper. In her lifetime she had never forgiven a misplaced word, much less a wrong, and when he had killed her brother, who was High Priest at the time, she had immediately turned to plotting, with her mother, the old Queen Alexandra, and then with Cleopatra of Egypt, another deadly enemy of his. Yet their life together had not been without its good moments; there had been times when his passion had seemed to evoke an answering passion in her; and it was around these rare and lovely times that he had built his fantasy, softening and changing the character of his love into what he would have wished her to be.

He invariably came to this room and laid his problems before her; he sat on one particular couch, emptied his mind, called on her name and waited.

He did so now. 'Mariamne!' he called; then he told her that he was angry with Antipater, stared at the nearest bowl of roses and waited.

To his attendants the waiting time seemed long; to Melchior, his nerves shredding with impatience, it seemed interminable. But finally Herod emerged, moving briskly, a slight, puzzled frown on his forehead.

'I've no time,' he said to the man who moved forward to begin the disrobing. 'Three strangers asked to see me. Run, tell Dumah I will receive them; in the small Silver Room. If they've gone, they're to be followed and brought back. Run!'

To a second attendant he said, 'Find Prince Archelaus and ask him to receive and entertain the High Priest and his staff until I can join them. I won't keep them long.'

To yet a third he said, 'I want no attendants at this interview.'

That was unusual; when Herod received visitors he liked to do so in pomp, surrounded by his lords.

'With guards at the door, my lord?'

After a second's thought, Herod nodded. The room was called small because it was so compared with other audience chambers, but it was sixty feet long, and whatever these strangers had to tell him could not be overheard by the guards in the doorway.

And what, he wondered, as he strode, rustling, towards the Silver Room, could three strangers, without credentials, one a merchant, have to tell him of such importance and urgency that Mariamne had seemed to persuade him to change his mind and receive them? That it was urgent and important he was sure. Only once had he acted against the inspiration which seemed to flow into him as he sat in that quiet, flower-filled room, and then the result had been regrettable.

As he crossed the shining tessellated floor upon which were portrayed the seasons of the year, and took his seat in the great silver chair under a purple canopy, his mind reverted to Parthia where there were scores of petty kingdoms, loosely knit, some of them chafing under the Parthian yoke. It could be that these men 'from the East' were emissaries of so secret a kind that they carried no credentials. He was known to be Caesar's friend and an intriguer with skill and experience; somebody might have had the idea of making an approach to Rome through him. If so it was fortunate that Archelaus was about to go there and could be entrusted with a verbal message. And then, thinking of Archelaus, he was reminded of a tale the boy had brought back from his last visit. From somewhere farther away, eastward even of Parthia, some fellow, Pella, Pelli, Pello, no matter, had appealed to Augustus for help in regaining a throne he had some kind of claim to. Archelaus had recounted how Caesar had called for maps and studied them and then said, 'The place is not even marked. . . .'

The three men were brought to the door and there left to make their own way towards him.

Certainly two of them came from some very distant place; their clothes were most outlandish.

There was an old man, frail and brittle as an autumn leaf wearing a curious black hat, like a pent roof, and a stained coat of quilted cotton cloth, with wide sleeves. He looked neither to right nor left as he entered and he was the first man, in Herod's experience, to enter this room with the beaten silver panels on the walls, and the beautiful floor, and not to show either admiration, envy, disapproval or awe. He walked straight forward, moving swiftly, his eyes fixed upon Herod's face. A king paying a visit to a king was the thought that flashed through Herod's mind before he turned his attention upon the second man. He was younger, a man in his prime, just as freakishly clad, but with an air of arrogance. He showed more awareness of his surroundings; as he walked his glance took in the room and its furnishings, and Herod under the canopy, as though he were summing them all up. And then, into his eyes, very blue and bright, there came an expression which suddenly and sharply reminded Herod of Mariamne at her most scornful. This man walked with the gait of a man who spent more time in the saddle than on foot. The third Herod summed up and dismissed; black, emasculated, well-to-do, typical freedman.

Melchior halted when he was within about six paces of the chair; the others took their places, one on each side. Melchior put his right hand into his left sleeve, his left in his right and made a slight, formal bow. Gaspar, stiffly upright, raised his right hand in the desert horseman's salute which Herod, the Idumean, recognised. The open palm, turned to face the one greeted, said, 'See, I come in peace, unarmed'. Balthazar, very conscious that he was in a palace, in the presence of a king, and that he must do the talking, bowed his head and bent his knees as he was accustomed to do when entering the Lady's room.

Herod, with the cordiality which endeared him to people who were not on personal or political grounds prejudiced against him, said:

'You wished to see me? What is your errand?'

Melchior put his hand on Balthazar's sleeve. 'Briefly now. Just ask where the child is and the quickest way to get there.'

Herod leaned his hands on the elaborately wrought arms of the silver chair and said:

'Ask me yourself! Your Greek is like mine or near enough, learned from a book and not much used. Where do you come from?'

'Pyangyong; but that does not matter. Where is the child?'

'What child?'

'The child whose horoscope I read, nine months and more ago. I am an astronomer. He is of ancient lineage, royal, and will be born, if he is not, as I fear, already born, no more than ten or twelve miles from where I stand. I assure you that it is of the utmost importance that I should have speech with his parents.'

Herod rapidly reviewed his family, his household. Two sons named

Philip, Antipater, Antipas, Archelaus . . . secret liaisons? Ancient lineage? Had he overlooked some Asmodean princeling who had gone into hiding and spawned?

He said, 'There is no child here.'

'What did I tell you?' Melchior, said, speaking to Balthazar but sharing his look of malice between him and Gaspar.

To Herod he said, forcing himself to courtesy:

'We are sorry to have troubled you. It was a mistake. My friend here was under the delusion that the child would be born King of the Jews.'

'Nobody can be born to that title. I hold it by favour of Caesar Augustus, who will choose my successor.' And even as he said the words something clicked into place at the back of his mind. Ancient, royal line, King of the Jews. . . .

His attachment to the Jewish faith was purely formal and expedient; in public he kept the law, in public he observed the rites. Of Jewish history he was ignorant, and of Jewish literature. His mother had been a Jewess, but he'd spent no time with her; his father, a brilliant soldier and a shrewd politician, had been his hero, and from the moment that he was safe on a horse he had been his father's companion. Mariamne, however, was as learned as any scribe, and she had often entertained him with stories; it was she who had told him about Esau and Jacob, about Solomon whose glory had stunned the Queen of Sheba, about Samson slaying a lion barehanded, and Baalam's ass which had spoken with a human tongue. He had always welcomed such stories because Mariamne had related them in moments of friendliness.

What he remembered now was not a story and it had not been told in a friendly mood; it had been flung at him, in the middle of one of their quarrels, like a stone. Something about a Messiah, of the house of David, who would deliver the Jews from their enemies, 'of whom you are first and foremost!' Mariamne had said.

Melchior said, 'If you will excuse us. Time is of importance, and we still have some distance to travel.'

'Wait,' Herod said. 'It is possible that I may be able to help you.'

Experts are handy. By this time the High Priest and his companions would have arrived, been received by Archelaus, and be waiting for their dinner. They would know all about the legend, the prophecy, as Mariamne had called it.

He was about to clap his hands and call and attract the attention of the guards when caution intervened. Mariamne again?

The priests were all sensible, hard-headed fellows, as professionally priests as he was professionally King; but you never knew; there might be one amongst them who was susceptible to Jewish myths, who might go out and talk, who might even see some way of turning this information to his own advantage. It would be far better to keep this trio and the priests apart.

There was another thing to consider, too; the High Priest's dignity, the respect that he considered due to his office. He might very well already be offended at being received by Archelaus, instead of Herod himself; he would almost certainly be incensed to be sent for. Hating the High Priest, and all his works and ways, liking to annoy him as far as it was safe, Herod was never blind to the fact that the man had power. Everywhere that the Romans went they liked to use the existing mechanics of government and they had recognised that to a very religious nation like the Jews the priesthood was a source of authority. Twice during his early reign Herod had asserted himself against a High Priest, and though he had survived, he had learned to be careful. Cold, formal, just-sufficient civility cost nothing.

'I shall not delay you long,' he said to Melchior, and rose to his feet and rustled away, his wily mind already busy with the question of how to extract information without giving any.

'Perhaps we have not, after all, wasted time,' Balthazar said. He spoke timidly, still feeling guilty about his obstinacy over the gateway, and also deeply disappointed because nothing had happened. He had recognised the gateway as surely as he had recognised Melchior and Gaspar, and the robe and the turban and the sandals. And he had seen the star, with which Melchior's errand was involved. All the ingredients were now assembled and yet nothing had happened. And–with shame he admitted this–he was terribly hungry again.

'We shall see,' Melchior said non-committally.

Gaspar said, 'I shall give this man no gifts; he is already decked like a kept woman, and he smells like one. Also he is ignorant. Water was not offered us. Nor food!'

All the time that the incomprehensible talk had been going on he had been watching Herod, and like many other men, far more sophisticated and experienced, had been deceived. Another dressed-up jewel-hung figure-head, with soft hands and nails trimmed like a woman's, he had thought, no ally for a man like me. His thoughts had reverted to the wild men of the hills, of whom he had so far seen no sign at all.

'To wash, to eat, would have wasted more time,' Melchior said.

'Not if food and water had been offered, as they should have been, when we arrived. Of all that talk, I understood one word. Caesar Augustus, he said. What did he say of him?'

Melchior dredged up the remark, unimportant and therefore already half forgotten.

'Oh, he said that he held his throne by favour and that the one who follows him will be chosen, not born to rule. Which confirms what I said; this is not the place and we should not have come here. How long is he intending to keep us waiting?'

Gaspar began to prowl about the room, noting the great urns of jaspar, the braziers exuding scent as well as heat, the marble troughs, the hanging baskets, filled with flowers, the silken draperies, the soft–he prodded them with a stiff finger–cushions in the silver chair. All familiar, all contemptible. Jexal all over again. The city rot, the city stink! He swung on his heel and turned to Melchior.

'Ask him one thing for *me*. How many rebels are there in the hills.'

'Three less than there were,' Melchior said with his thin smile. He really must remember not to allow his exasperation with Gaspar to show; but for him the camels would have been lost. Balthazar had his uses too; but Melchior wished once more that it had been possible for him to make the journey alone. . . .

He began to twist his hands together, pulling at his fingers so that the joints gave off little brittle snapping sounds.

'They were not the true men,' Gaspar said. 'They were robbers, and witless ones at that.' His lips moved in a smile as he remembered the speed and efficiency with which he had done the killing.

'I shall now count up to a hundred,' said Melchior who had spent his youth in an ordinary house and the rest of his life in a room twelve feet square and had no notion of the distances in palaces, 'and then I shall leave. No information he can give is worth this delay. The star is my guide.' He began to count and had reached twenty when Herod came back.

Neither Melchior nor Balthazar noted any change in his appearance, but Gaspar knew the symptoms of fear as well as any man alive. He saw that just at the base of Herod's strong, arched nostrils there were tiny white patches as though fingers had pressed there and been withdrawn. He thought–Something has frightened him, and he is a man who might be dangerous when frightened. He changed his stance.

Herod had wasted no time. He had taken a short cut to the opposite side of the Palace, the side entered from a court in which there was nothing likely to offend the most fanatical Jew. The room in which he always entertained members of the Sanhedrin was likewise void of anything offensive. The tiles on the floor were plain, the walls lined with cedarwood and undercoated, the candlesticks of solid, unchased silver. There were three low tables of green marble, arranged to make three sides of a square, and on the outer side of the tables were divans covered in green velvet. Herod had learned in Rome that the ideal number for an intimate dinner was nine; tonight there were six priests, himself and two government officials, both Jews and both from priestly families.

In Roman fashion, too, this dinner was beginning with wine and a selection of small delicacies at which early guests could nibble while awaiting later arrivals, but the wine was sweeter than any Roman of taste would have drunk before a meal, and the variety of titbits was limited because of the dietary rules.

The greetings on Herod's side were a shade more cordial than usual because he had kept them waiting, and must keep them waiting again. Time mattered, but he must not appear hurried. So he sat down in the place which Archelaus had vacated and accepted the cup of wine which the boy, forestalling anyone else, poured, asking as he presented it, 'May I go now? I have an engagement of my own.'

'Yes, go. I'm sorry you have been delayed. I apologise to you all for this delay. Three men arrived, unexpectedly. They are on their way to the Essenes at Quram.' That was a cunning touch. Mention the Essenes to an orthodox priest and he flinched as though touched by a red-hot iron. The Essenes lived apart, were celibate, owned nothing, everything being the property of the community; in many ways their beliefs and their ritual did not conform to the Law by which ordinary Jews lived; they claimed to be at once better informed and more holy than secular priests. Herod disliked them every bit as much as the High Priest did, but he had hit on the use of their name both as cover for his question and as a means of quelling before it arose any interest the priests might feel in his visitors.

'These three,' he said, having watched the effect of the word, 'are argumentative amongst themselves; only one speaks Greek; they have no Latin, no Aramaic. So far as I can make out they are arguing about the Messiah and his prophesied birthplace.'

As he had aged the High Priest's face had dropped into jowls below his jaw, small, well-filled pouches which at the word 'Messiah' seemed to fall lower and go limp. Other faces altered in other ways. They were all Jews, all, in theory at least, believers in the prophets and their prophecies, but the word inspired no welcome. Consternation rather. They were professional priests, very comfortably situated, enjoying less authority than they considered to be their due, but protected, respected, provided for, easily performing their set duties, happily collecting their set dues. The actual arrival, on earth, of the promised Messiah, the Son of God, could only disrupt their lives.

The High Priest recovered himself quickly. The mention of the Messiah, made by, of all people, Herod, had disconcerted him for a moment, but it was, he reflected, just the kind of thing which curious strangers, bound on a visit to an Essene community would wish to discuss. He said:

'The place, by tradition, is Bethlehem.' His voice took on the note of one who quotes, knowledgeably. 'And thou Bethlehem, in the land of Juda, art not the least among the princes of Juda; for out of thee shall come a governor that shall rule my people Israel. That is the prophecy; does it settle the argument?'

Herod remembered the certainty with which the old man in the curious hat had said, 'No more than ten or twelve miles from where I stand.' Now the High Priest had said the place was Bethlehem, the city of David. It was at this moment that the white patches made their appearance beside his nostrils and they were not, as Gaspar was presently to suppose, the brand of fear, they were signs of a deadly determination.

He said lightly, 'Armed with that information from the highest authority, they can go and argue with the Essenes.' He took a sip from his cup and set it down. 'I shall be with you before the first dish is served.' He rose and rustled away.

The priests began to talk amongst themselves, about the Essenes, and then, free of Archelaus' presence, about Herod. Only one of them took no part in the conversation, but sat brooding.

He was a friend of Zacharias, had actually been on duty with him in the Temple when the older man had stiffened and stared and seemed to go into a cataleptic trance from which he had emerged completely dumb. Some time after that Zacharias' wife, a woman far past child-bearing age, had become obviously pregnant, and in the previous midsummer, she had borne a son. On the eighth day after the birth the child had been circumcised and named, and Elkanah had been invited to be present at the joyful ceremony. And a very curious thing had happened. Everybody had taken it for granted that the boy should be named after his father, but when the moment came, Elisabeth, a very quiet and retiring woman, had suddenly raised her voice and said: 'Not so; he shall be called John.'

The fact that at her age she had borne a child at all had attracted attention and there had been many neighbours present and practically every relative on both sides of the family except Mary, a cousin married to a carpenter in Nazareth, who was pregnant herself, and when Elisabeth said 'John,' all the families had burst into protest. In neither family had there ever been a man of that name. Boys were always named for their fathers or some respected elderly relative or friend. Why John? everybody asked. But Elisabeth was adamant, the child must be named with the name which she had chosen. It seemed arbitrary and someone had suggested that Zacharias should be asked. They had made signs at him, assuming, as everybody always did, that a dumb man must necessarily be deaf as well. Zacharias had written upon one of the prepared tablets which since his affliction he had always carried, and he had held it out to be read by the nearest literate person, who happened to be Elkanah; and what Elkanah had read out was, 'His name is John.' Not should be, or will be, or even must be, just, 'His name is John,' as though in another place the child had already been named.

So the alien-sounding name had been given, and that was no sooner done than Zacharias recovered his power of speech and burst into a chanting song, declaring that this child should go before the face of the Lord to prepare his ways. That was six months ago. Now there were men asking where the Messiah should be born. Elkanah had a great deal to think about. . . .

To the three waiting men Herod said:

'I have wise men in my household. I have consulted them and there is a general agreement that a child of some importance may be born in Bethlehem.'

'South of here,' Melchior said, not asking a question, stating a fact. 'Thank you, we know now what road to ask for in leaving the city. That will help.'

His hands moved towards his sleeves, he was about to take hasty leave when Herod said, 'Wait,' and at the same time Gaspar said:

'Ask him *my* question!'

'This one,' Melchior said, past all patience, 'would be a good companion were he dumb. Now before we can leave he must ask, how many unruly men live in the hills?'

Momentarily diverted by this inconsequent question, Herod said:

'Six hundred; debtors hiding from their creditors, men hiding from their wives.'

'Six hundred,' Melchior said to Gaspar in the tongue they shared. And again he made the preliminary gesture of polite leave-taking.

'I wanted to ask you a favour,' Herod said. 'If this child is as important as you say . . .'

'Nothing that I could say would tell you how important,' Melchior said. 'And for that reason I must go.'

'Go,' Herod said, 'go swiftly; search diligently; but when you have found him, come back and tell me where and in what condition you found him. Of such importance and born in my realm, it would be only right that I should make some sign of recognition. You will, in any case, be returning this way.'

Something in his speech struck Melchior as being very odd. If the man had his own soothsayers, Chaldeans or whatever they were, who could pin-point the very place of birth for the child, why should he make that request? It didn't make sense; and all his life Melchior had dealt with things which, properly regarded, did make sense. This man, he thought, consulted nobody; he looked at a map, came back and gave me a name within the right distance, and is now relying upon me to return and tell him where the star led me. . . . And the baby is not of his lineage, or he would not need to be told. Such a pity, the old man thought, looking at Herod with his study-dimmed eyes; I have never yet deceived anyone, even myself, but this man could be dangerous, and to him I must lie.

He did it as evasively as he could. He said:

'That is indeed little to ask in return for the help you have given us.' The sad truth was that once you came down from your tower you had to deal with people, and in their own currency. He had made what sounded like a promise, while privately determining that neither he nor either of the others would come back this way.

Then Herod, all unwittingly, confirmed Melchior's worst suspicions. Anxious to ingratiate himself, he belatedly offered refreshements.

'Thank you, no!' Melchior said. 'We must be on our way.'

Time was now more pressing than ever. If Herod had looked at a map, pinned one leg of the compass on Jerusalem and set the other leg at ten or twelve miles, he would already know roughly where that baby was. And Kings had enormous resources, men on horseback, men on foot. . . . Then why ask us to return? Oh, I see, because I know; I might be dangerous too. . . .

'We thank you,' he said, making his bow. 'Come, we must go.'

Outside the brisk cold wind had cleared the clouds and their star shone, with a myriad others, lighting the night.

Melchior said, 'We must ride now as we have never ridden before.'

Balthazar, very humbly, said, 'The visit was not all wasted time. We know the place now.'

'We know what place he named,' Melchior snapped. 'I place no faith in that man. I shall go where the star leads; and by the shortest road.' He slapped his camel with a hand that trembled a little more than it had done.

Herod sat for a little time in the great silver chair in the room where never before had he been alone. He said, softly:

'Mariamne. Mariamne.' And when he felt, in that inexplicable way, that contact had been established, he said, 'I thank you!' The danger had been so narrowly avoided. If he had sent that old man, with all his dangerous knowledge, away, to go blabbing about royal lineage and great destiny . . . If he hadn't remembered, as willingly or unwillingly he remembered every word that Mariamne had ever said to him . . . what might have happened was horrible to contemplate. If that story had once reached, in however garbled a fashion, the ears of the religious patriots amongst the Jews almost anything could have been expected. More than once during his reign Herod had seen what religious frenzy could do to a crowd. Unarmed, they had lain down in the streets and allowed themselves to be trampled to death in the attempt to hold up the progress of something obnoxious to their faith. Give them a fulfilled prophecy, a glimmer of hope in Jehovah's direct intervention, and they would rise in full-scale revolt; and that would mean military action on the part of Rome, a proconsul established in Jerusalem, the end of Herod.

However, thanks to Mariamne that had been avoided. The child would be identified and, as soon as identified, slain. The three men would return, and once they had entered the Palace they would never leave it again. Herod, who had never shrunk from killing even his nearest and dearest when policy dictated such action, would think nothing of adding four more murders to his score. Killing was effective. Once, long ago, when he had seen Mark Antony falling under Cleopatra's spell, he had advised him, 'Kill her!' If that advice had been taken, how differently things would have turned out.

He realised that he must not sit here, thanking Mariamne and inviting her approval of the way in which he had handled things; it would be injudicious to keep the priests waiting any longer.

So, ruthless and determined, Herod went in to his dinner. Melchior, Gaspar and Balthazar, pressing their camels hard, rode through the starry night, the old man turning every now and again to make certain that they were not being followed. In and around Bethlehem little children slept in their beds, or in their mothers' arms.

PART TWELVE

A ROMAN BARRACKS

Half-mile

By Balthazar's reckonings–he had inquired in the city which gate of exit and which road to take, and how far to Bethlehem–they had done three-quarters of the last lap of their journey when Melchior, who had been constantly urging his camel, halted it and made a moaning noise, like an animal in distress.

'Are you ill?' Balthazar asked. It seemed likely to him that the old man's frail body, so ill-fed and subject to such strain, might at last have given way.

'This is the wrong road,' Melchior said. 'Look!'

The star was now low in the sky, and did appear to be to the left of them, while the road ran straight ahead.

'But there is only the one road. I inquired most carefully. I asked in the city which gate, and at the gate I asked again. This is the road to Bethlehem and all we can do is to follow it and then turn left to seek the place indicated.'

'I can go across country,' Melchior said and began to edge his camel towards the bank which divided the tilled land from the road.

'That is cultivated land.'

'Nothing grows in mid-winter.'

'I was thinking of fences and irrigation ditches, and hard going over the ploughland.'

'And I am thinking how little time is left.' He struck his camel, which baulked at being asked to mount such an obstacle, but, guided inexorably, gave in and scrambled awkwardly up the bank, balanced at the top of it for a precarious second and then plunged down. The others followed.

Gaspar had understood no word of the talk, but its tone had been argumentative and he guessed that his companions were once again wrangling over direction. He was indifferent. He'd come out to see what was to be seen and though his observations had been impeded by Melchior's impatience, and by the need to have every question, every answer twice translated, he had learned a lot. He would have been willing to have turned back towards Jexal upon leaving Jerusalem; but two things held him fast to Melchior. One was that without him he would have been as helpless as a stray dog; in this country he could not ask for a bite of bread or a cup of water, he the leader of the Five Hundred, the ruler of Jexal. His second reason for sticking to Melchior was that he had been impressed by the old man's powers of navigating; far away in Jexal he had spoken of Jerusalem as a possible destination, and with a few tools and his charts, he had found

Jerusalem, grumbling all the time that the city was not in truth, his destination, and in that he seemed to have been right. In Jexal he had said that he was seeking a child, and if–as Gaspar was now inclined to believe–there was a child at the end of the journey, he would know that Melchior had the ability to use the stars in two ways. Such a man could be vastly useful to a ruler. Melchior was penniless, and far from home; it was reasonable to suppose that he would welcome an offer of honourable employment. Nonetheless the proposition would have to be put tactfully; the old man had a tough character. Gaspar remembered how, when the robbers came, he had shown no fear for himself; he hadn't cried 'Save me' he had said 'Save the camels.' The members of the Five Hundred wouldn't laugh and jeer at him, as they did at the scholars and so-called wise men of Jexal.

The black fellow could be useful too. Amongst other things that this trip had taught Gaspar was the disadvantage of knowing only one language in a multi-lingual world. Suppose the worst came to the worst, and Rome by supporting Pella, provoked him to strike first, if he could, and he came this way again, with his Five Hundred, strings of spare horses and an abundance of arms and tried to make contact with the men-in-the-hills. (He still had faith in them; and if Herod, the fop, admitted to the existence of six hundred you could safely double the number.) What use would it be if nobody could speak to them? He wanted Balthazar to go back to Jexal with him too, and give lessons. The lessons should be compulsory for the young; older men could please themselves, but he himself would set an example by trying to learn, and he knew that every man of the Five Hundred who valued his good opinion–which meant five hundred–would follow.

Balthazar was keeping close to Melchior because it never occurred to him to do otherwise. Events in Jerusalem had disappointed him, and he was conscious of a great gulf between what the star meant to him and what it meant to Melchior; what connection could there be between a flashing vision of a whole new world and a child, however famous that child might live to be? Yet behind all the confusion something glimmered. His insistence upon entering Jerusalem had proved useful; muddled as things seemed some pattern might yet emerge. And even without this hope he could not have left the pair who without him couldn't have managed; Melchior often spoke sharply to him, Gaspar, he knew, despised him, but a lifetime's slavery had inured him to sharp speaking and dis-esteem.

So they rode close; and presently as Balthazar had foreseen they came to a thickset thorn fence, a living wall, as high as a man. As far as they could see in the bright starlight it stretched across their path. Melchior said, 'To the right,' and they skirted the fence which presently, at a corner, ended. From somewhere within the closed space a dog barked, geese cackled and a man's voice shouted.

They rode on, and there was a drystone wall, built of stones picked from the fields it divided. In many places it was bound and reinforced by leafless brambles.

'Right again!' Melchior cried, and they followed the wall until presently they reached an opening, closed by a stout hurdle held in place by ropes tied to the thickly thorned bramble stems.

Without hesitation Balthazar made his camel kneel, and while the other two were struggling to keep their animals on their feet, he untied the rope, scratching his hands, opened the makeshift gate, held it while Melchior and

Gaspar rode through, led his own camel through, and tied the hurdle in place again.

After that they came, in quick succession, to two irrigation ditches, one narrow enough to be crossed by a camel's stride, the other wide. But the camels were unaccustomed to water except as something to drink. At the first ditch they drank, against Melchior's wishes, but Gaspar said, 'Be reasonable; a drink will keep them going.' At the second ditch the camels sidled and danced grotesquely and had to be cajoled and forced into crossing.

But after that it was remarkably easy going, a flat, hard, uninterrupted space at the far edge of which there were lights.

'There, you see. We have saved time. There is the star and there are the lights of Bethlehem!'

But Balthazar had his doubts. The lights were indisputable but he had never yet seen a village where every lighted window was exactly in line with its neighbour and exactly the same shape and size. Village lights were haphazard; poor men had low houses, rich men higher ones; on the ground floor women cooked supper at about this time, on upper floor ladies dressed their hair.

He said, tentatively, 'This might not be a village. Only Romans build so straight. And it's all one building, I think. It could be a barracks. We should do well to avoid it.'

'Look how low the star is now. We have no time to make a detour. Even if it is a barracks we can ride past it.'

'Not if we are on their ground,' Balthazar said, arguing as he had argued about fences and irrigation ditches, from his greater knowledge of the country. 'I think we are already trespassing. This flat ground is where they march and exercise. We had better turn back to the ditch and seek another path.

'I am not going back,' Melchior said stubbornly. 'I have come from Pyangyong to deliver a message and I have hardly any time in which to do it.'

'What is it now?' Gaspar asked.

'He thinks it is a barracks, a place for soldiers. Romans.'

'Oh,' Gaspar said, his interest quickening, 'that I should like to see.'

'By the grave of my fathers,' Melchior said, forgetting absolutely that Gaspar had paid for his journey from Jexal and dealt with the robbers, and that Balthazar's insistence upon entering Jerusalem had enabled him to pinpoint the source of the threatened treachery, 'I am tired of you both! I care nothing for his caution, or for your wish to see things. I go where the star leads and you can please yourselves whether you come with me or not. . . .'

He slapped the camel and rode headlong into a sentry who cried, 'Ho. Who goes there?'

It was Latin, it meant nothing; no more to Melchior than the voice of the man shouting above the noise of the dog's barking and the geese cackling inside the thorn fence. With one hand he guided his camel to avoid the man who shouted, with his other he slapped it, to hasten its pace. But the sentry had resources that the old man hadn't dreamed of. He let out another, louder, roaring shout and suddenly the night was full of men, of bobbing lights, noise.

After that it was all confusion. Balthazar was prudent enough to make his camel kneel immediately, so he escaped rough handling; but his heart sank. Romans had a passion for law and order; they'd ask who you were and where you came from, they'd inspect your papers, if you had any.

Gaspar thought–They're alert, which is as it should be; and we have done nothing wrong; this will enable me to see them at really close quarters.

Melchior said, 'Take me to your chief. Your khan. Your head man,' and realised with a lurch of the heart that nobody understood him. Once again dependent upon Balthazar whose advice he had disregarded, once again wasting time. He looked at the star, moving, moving. . . . In a thin voice he said, 'Balthazar, speak to them. Ask for the head man.'

Balthazar said, 'We ask to have speech with your officer.'

'You shall have it,' one of the soldiers said. 'Here he is, now.'

Caepio, who, with his century, had come to do a two months' tour in Bethlehem and had arrived a few days before, came out, treading heavily.

He was in a cheerless mood, missing his drinking companions, the lively girls he knew, the opportunities for amusement that Jerusalem offered. Here there was nothing except duty, boredom and Vatinius, the permanent centurion-in-charge who acted as though he owned the place. Caepio knew all the gossip about this man; he had a blunt tongue and an inflexible nature, and so, though an experienced and reliable soldier, had missed the aim of all centurions–to be *primus pilus*, and had instead been promoted downstairs and put in charge of this dismal backwater. Caepio had expected to find an embittered, disappointed man, and since he himself was a man with a grievance, he had expected that they would have a good deal in common. But he found a contented man, apparently unaware of how he'd been pushed into a backwater, apparently pleased with himself and his job, holding himself a little aloof, and on good terms with several Jews. There'd been, so far, none of the long, grumbling sessions which Caepio had anticipated; nor had there been the one thing that compensated for the dullness of the place, leisure. Vatinius went about finding jobs to keep everyone busy, and if he couldn't find one, he'd invent one, like a captious housewife.

That was bad enough; but this evening Caepio felt that he had been insulted. A visitor had arrived, not a Jew, a Roman, with a train of slaves, including a skilled cook, and Vatinius had not invited Caepio to join them at dinner.

So the centurion was in no mood to be sympathetic to three men who had come, after dark, and from the rear, on to barracks property. Balthazar did his best, explaining how they came to be trespassing, assuring Caepio of their harmlessness, begging to be allowed to proceed. He was lavish with the word 'sir' and when that did no good, substituted 'lord'. All to no avail. Had they been three stray sheep Caepio would have impounded them, if only for the pleasure of proving to Vatinius that while he was feasting–the gentleman's dinner had smelt delicious–*his* sentries had been alert, *he* had been available and prompt to act. He could see himself, in the morning, saying, 'Oh, by the way . . .' and relating what had happened. Vatinius would be almost certain to ask, 'Why didn't you inform me?' and the answer to that was civil and correct, yet conveying a slight rebuke, 'I thought you would not wish to be disturbed, *sir*.'

He issued his order.

'Search them.'

Melchior, who had nothing to hide, only understood the order when he saw a soldier advance upon Balthazar; then he cried:

'This is intolerable! Even the cow-worshippers and the mare-milk drinkers never treated me thus.'

Gaspar did not understand the order either, but the action spoke for itself. His knife! He carried it, in its sheath, stuck into the waistband of his baggy trousers, inside the belt. He drew in his stomach muscles sharply and under pretence of a willing raising of his hands, knocked his wrist against his leather jacket and the knife fell into the pouch where his trousers overhung his boots. He had been standing watching the soldiers with an unwilling admiration; they seemed well disciplined, they looked hard and tough and clean. But when the soldier slapped his hands under his arm, around the waist and at the knees and said, 'Nothing, sir' he thought–These people can be fooled, too! And he felt happier.

'What about the camels?'

'Fodder-bags, sir. And . . . these.'

'Balthazar,' Melchior said, 'tell them not to touch my possessions. Is there no law in this country?'

Balthazar said, 'Lord, they are the humble tools of his trade. Without them he is ruined.'

'You'll all be ruined in the morning,' Caepio said. 'All right; take them away. Lock them up, separately.'

Melchior cast a despairing look at the star and began to protest, angrily, in his own tongue. Gaspar said:

'There are too many of them,' and he was speaking to Melchior and himself. He had quickly calculated their chances of escape by violence and seen that there was no hope even had his knife been ready in his hand. A good soldier must take chances of course, but part of being a good soldier was knowing when you were hopelessly outnumbered. And to give no sign of dismay; so he stalked, a little more arrogantly than usual, as he was led away. Melchior went on protesting until he realised that by doing so he was inviting rough handling; then he subsided, knowing that a wise man bows to the inevitable once he knows that it *is* inevitable. And this, he had, in a way, brought on himself; he had insisted, against advice, in riding across country. He called to Balthazar:

'You were right, I was wrong. I am sorry.'

Balthazar let himself be led away like a sheep.

Even the indignity of being searched had not prepared Gaspar for the sheer horror of what happened to him next. They pushed him into a tiny space, nothing more than a hole in the wall; six feet wide, less than six feet long. It was built of brick and whitewashed, and along its length there was a ledge, also of brick, upon which a man might lie or sit. Nothing else at all. When the door was closed he was walled in, and once he realised it he began to go mad. His own simple language had no word for the peculiar thing he suffered from, the mental quirk which made him feel uneasy when he rode into Jexal and even more uneasy when he entered the Palace, that made him prefer the Balcony Room to any other apartment, made him sleep–once he brought himself to sleep there–with the door and window of the bed-chamber wide open. There was no torture that the Romans could have thought of that would have hurt, hurt, hurt so much as being shut in, in this tiny airless space.

For a time he went frantic, behaving much as a newly captured wild bird thrust into a small cage will behave. He tried to break out, throwing himself against the walls, against the door, against the built-in bench. He emitted loud hoarse cries. He beat his hands bloody, he bruised his shoulders, his elbows, his thighs. Then, spent, suffocating, about to die, he thought of his knife; better to slit your throat and die quickly than to suffer this torment and be stifled. One small remaining grain of sanity told him that this was a desperate remedy, was there no compromise? High up in the door was a grating, could he jump and set his fingers in it and push his nose close, breathe, control his panic, and live? Could he?

The grating was set at a level from which anyone in the passage, which was higher than the cell, could look in upon the prisoner. Gaspar jumped and jumped, several times missing his hold; but at last he managed the jump-and-clutch that was necessary and had his fingers through the grating and hung for a moment against the door, like a carcase suspended from one limb. Then he tautened his bruised muscles and had just succeeded in bringing his face level with the grating when the guard, attracted by the noise, noticed the protruding, clutching fingers and dealt them a paralysing blow with the flat of his sword. The fingers loosed their hold and inside the cell Gaspar fell like a sack, striking his head on the floor.

And he was back in Jexal, easy in the saddle, riding in with Kalim and Lakma and several others, on a sunny morning along the wide street, dappled with shade from the trees, all in flower. Their water bags were empty and he was thirsty, looking forward to a long cool drink. They came to the Fountain of the Maidens, and there Ilya was waiting, with a great, two-handled silver cup in her pale hands. As he came level with her she offered him the cup, and this time there was no accident; he took the cup in his hands and drank and drank and drank. . . .

Outside, the guard thought–That was the noisy one, and I've quietened him.

Balthazar, pushed into an identical cell, went and sat on the built-in bed, and thought–This is the end!

The soldier who had searched him had either missed, or not been interested in the manumission paper which he carried inside his robe. But tomorrow it would be taken out and studied and its falsity would be detected. Tonight's search had been perfunctory–they had missed Gaspar's knife. Balthazar knew, from his experience in Metellus' household, how meticulous the Romans were about property and ownership; if they had the slightest suspicion about his forged paper they would get in touch with the Lady and she would claim him, and punish him so severely that he would die.

He looked back, calmly over the event that had brought him to this situation, and finally he thought–I deluded myself. Once and once only did I truly see the future, and that was in Cleo's black ball, after she had conjured up the vision. She was a real seer, what she saw was the truth; she saw the Greek dying, and I, for a moment, shared her vision. What I saw afterwards was what I wished to see; a waking dream, of no more substance than the dreams of sleep. I wished myself free, finely clad, in the company of free men. So I saw what I wished, and it meant nothing. . . .

Wait a bit, he said to himself; and he remembered that Metellus had always said that every bit of evidence must be weighed. And against this theory of self-delusion, he must, in fairness, set the fact that he had found Melchior and Gaspar, he had found the very clothes in which he had seen himself; in Jerusalem he had recognised the gateway. . . .

But all to what end? The star had been the link between him and Melchior, and now, outside in the night it was dying, while in one little brick cell Melchior fretted over his wasted errand, and in another Balthazar saw his vision as nonsense and faced the possibility of death. And he thought, it might be that it was death that I came out to seek. I thought it was the death of the world, but it might be only my own. I thought I saw an end to slavery, and death would end my bondage. When I die, under the lash, a whole world will die with me; my world; my youth; my mutilation, my ability as an accountant, my gift of tongues, everything that made me *me*, and not the other fellow, all my thoughts, my hopes and disappointments. The death of a man is the death of a world. And in death my dream will be fulfilled, for death does put a slave on the level with a soldier, making all men equal, death does stop the mouth of hunger, and puts an end to heartbreak and homesickness.

Thinking these and a multitude of other tumbling thoughts Balthazar was quiet and gave no trouble.

With Melchior it was otherwise. He sat down thankfully, and he was glad to find himself alone in a quiet place, conducive to thought. He cast back, in his mind, to the moment when, at the top of his tower, he had seen this journey as something that must be undertaken, and for the life of him he could not see that he had at any point made a miscalculation of such immensity that it resulted in his being incarcerated here while the star moved on, came to its appointed end and the whole thing was made nonsense. In very circumstance he had been sensible, reasonable, and meticulous. In turning off the road perhaps a little impatient, but surely impatience then had been justified.

He sat very still, but his heart beat so fast and so hard that he could only breathe in little shallow gasps and his whole body quivered. There must be some way out. There always had been, hitherto. He thought of how he had arrived in Jexal, penniless on a spent camel–and there had been Gaspar. Then, when he arrived in a country where nobody understood him and Gaspar's money was dwindling at an alarming rate, there'd been Balthazar. True, outside the walls of Jerusalem he'd wished he'd never seen either of them, but even that waste of time had been justified. Now this!

Inside his distressed old body the trained, obedient mind worked on. He thought of his own attempted protests in the faces of the grinning soldiers, the hard-eyed officer; of Balthazar's pleading voice and subservient manner. Something had been missing, one decisive, propulsive word. A catalyst. There must be one. There must be something–and it must be a word, since there was nothing to be done. A word known to him, and recognisable to these barbarian men.

Of course; he had it. Herod!

He took off his shoe, stood up and went to the door and rapped smartly on it, just below the grating so that the sound would carry. He had a little trouble with his breathing, but he mastered it, drawing a deep breath, counting while he held it, ten the first time, then twenty. And when he felt sure of producing a firm clear sound he said:

'Herod.'

Then he rapped again, breathed, repeated the word. The name sounded and died along the whitewashed passage much as the name of Mariamne sounded and died through the halls and corridors of Herod's palace. Even in this extremity Melchior realised the absurdity of calling the name as though he expected Herod himself to answer; so he began to make sentences.

'Herod will be very angry,' he said in his abominable Greek. 'I was with Herod this afternoon. Herod is expecting a report from me. I am on an errand from Herod. Herod is waiting for me. Herod, the king in Jerusalem. I was in Jerusalem with Herod this afternoon.'

He rapped with his shoe, waited, repeated his simple uninformative sentences, resolutely keeping his voice steady; it would never do to sound hysterical.

'Herod will be angry. I was with Herod this afternoon. . . .'

The soldier on duty at the end of the passage said to another, 'The old one is carrying on now. Listen! All gibberish, but it sounds to me as though every now and then he says "Herod". What do you think?'

'I am on an errand for Herod. Herod is waiting my report. . . .' Melchior chanted.

'Right enough. It's Herod he's talking about.'

'I reckoned they looked a funny lot the minute I clapped eyes on them,' the one on guard said. 'And Herod's pretty touchy. Think *he* ought to be told?' He nodded his head in the direction of the place where Caepio might be expected to be at this hour.

'If I was you, I would.'

Caepio came out and listened, and for a moment there was no sound, Melchior was drawing breath. Then he rapped and resumed his chant. Caepio recognised the one important word and it occurred to him that if the King of Judea was in any way, however remotely, concerned with these mysterious men the responsibility for retaining them had better be shuffled, as soon as possible, on to Vatinius. So he turned, and went quickly, though still heavy-footed, towards the little room which Vatinius regarded as his own, his home.

PART THIRTEEN

A ROMAN BARRACKS

Half-mile

Earlier that day, just as the daylight was fading, a very elegant litter, borne between two mules, had come to a standstill before the small barracks from which Eunice and Ephorus drew so much of their custom. The litter's occupant was obviously a well-to-do man who travelled in style; there were three pack mules and four slaves in his train. The mules were all plump and sleek-coated, the slaves, young, plump and well dressed; and when from inside the litter a hand moved and pushed back the bronze-coloured velvet curtains, it was seen to be a plump hand with a large ruby ring upon the forefinger.

'Ask,' said a voice, well used to issuing orders, 'for the centurion, Vatinius; and say that Quintilius is here.'

Vatinius was inspecting stores. The last day of December had seen a fresh century of soldiers come marching down from Jerusalem to occupy the barracks for two months, and the stores had, as usual at the change-over, been delivered. As usual they had been stored, all in confusion, and Vatinius had waited, tactfully, until Caepio, the centurion who had come with his men, had had time to settle in and get things into order. Like many before him, he had done nothing, so then Vatinius had said, 'This is a filthy mess and muddle; you can't tell wine from vinegar, honey from oil. Set a couple of men to put it straight.' Caepio had heard something of Vatinius' fussy ways–and his other peculiarities–before he came to Bethlehem; he had given the order, muttering to himself that he was a soldier, not a housewife. Now Vatinius was viewing, with only mild approval, the job the two men had made of the store-room. The point was, he said to himself, that in an orderly store-room a depredation was so much more quickly detected.

When the message reached him, he exclaimed, 'Quintilius, *here*?' and not waiting even to snatch his cloak, had gone out and stood by the litter. The curtains parted more widely and in the failing light the two men, once comrades-in-arms, closest of friends, had looked one another in the face for the first time in sixteen years.

Quintilius said, in an easy, jocular way:

'You seem dumb-struck, Vatinius. I assure you, I am no apparition. I am bound for the baths at Calirrhoe–for my gout. Being in the neighbourhood and hearing that you were here, I proposed to spend an evening with you, and cadge a night's lodging.'

'A barracks is not a hostelry,' Vatinius said; 'but there is one, a good one, kept by a Greek, only a short distance along the road. I'll send a man to guide you.'

'But this, I understand, is your *home*. I have come to visit you in your home. Is this a way to receive an old friend?'

'I told you, long ago in Areta that if you did . . . what you did . . . you were no friend of mine.'

Lowering his voice a little, Quintilius said:

'I am now Caesar's friend. I *think*, that if I need to, I could commandeer this barracks. But I would prefer to be invited.'

After a perceptible pause Vatinius said, 'You are invited.'

'Good!' Quintilius said and snapped his fingers. Two slaves ran forward, and with tender care, unlashed the litter, lowered it to the ground, then lifted it–the other two slaves having led the mules out of the way–and staggering a little under the weight, carried it to the entry and there set it down, and assisted their master to alight.

Quintilius stood up cautiously, his left foot, swollen and bandaged inside the soft velvet shoe, barely touching the ground.

'That will do,' he said. 'Hand me my stick. Now, Vatinius, if you will lend me your arm, I shall manage very well.'

With obvious reluctance Vatinius bent his weathered, heavily muscled arm, and held it stiffly, keeping as much distance as possible between him and the weight, the warmth, the scent of this man, beside whom he had once marched and drilled, sweated and laughed and slept, and swum in the waters of a faraway river called the Rhône.

'Gout,' Quintilius said, 'is not a contagious disease.'

Damn you, Vatinius thought, you miss nothing; you never did.

They made slow progress along a straight, lime-washed passage towards the rear of the building where Vatinius had his quarters.

Quintilius said, 'I am well provided; if my fellow can have the use of a hearth he will prepare a meal which I hope will please you–unless you have fallen victim to this Oriental nonsense about only breaking bread with your friends. Not that I have ever entertained any but friendly feelings towards you, Vatinius. Every word you said was fully justified; I knew that at the time. . . .'

'If you don't mind, I'd prefer not to hark back,' Vatinius said. He made the opening of a door an excuse for releasing his arm. 'These are my quarters,' he said.

It was a fair-sized room, with walls of whitewashed brick. There was a heavy wooden table, a chair, and against the wall a wide bench with curved ends, upon which from time to time, a soldier lay to submit himself to such rough surgery as an experienced centurion could perform. There was a set of shelves upon which maps and rolled records were ranged with precision, and there was a row of hooks which held weapons and equipment. An oil lamp, just lighted and emitting a faint, disagreeable odour, stood on a wall bracket, and a candle burned in an iron stick on the table. An uncurtained alcove in one side wall was furnished with a hard-looking bed and an iron tripod holding a basin and ewer. In the outer wall a shutter rattled in the wind. The general effect was neat, soldierly and cheerless.

'How familiar it smells,' Quintilius said. 'So this is your home.'

It had been his home for a little more than three years, and Vatinius had never before entered it without a small secret feeling of satisfaction. His ultimate goal, to become *primus pilus*, he had never achieved, but out of the shifting, homeless thing that was army life, he had made his little niche for himself, and for three years he had enjoyed more independence, more privacy and more authority than most of his kind could hope for.

Tonight, however, viewing the only home he had through Quintilius' eyes, he saw it as stark, devoid of comfort, and impermanent. It was not his own; it was government property and his tenuous hold upon it could be ended tomorrow by a word spoken by a man he had never seen, and to whom he, Vatinius, was not even a name.

He said, 'You'll need a cushion, even on the chair.'

'I shall need three,' Quintilius amended, glancing at the bench where Vatinius had pulled aching teeth and set broken bones. Two of the big cushions from his litter along its length and one between its head and the wall and it would be converted into a couch of moderate comfort.

'I'll have them fetched,' Vatinius said. As he went into the passage to shout the order, he thought–He's had a long experience in making himself comfortable. Unwillingly he remembered various occasions in the past when Quintilius' genius for finding the easiest way, the best place, the little bit extra, had contributed to his own well-being.

Propped on his stick, leaning his hip against the table as he waited for the cushions to be brought, Quintilius said, when Vatinius re-entered:

'So you are in charge here? Permanently?'

'You should know that in the army nothing is permanent. I've been here rather more than three years. The place is occupied by one century, for two months, turn and turn about, and there was always trouble about the state it was left in, or a discrepancy in the stores. So the tribune decided that it would be best if one man was made wholly responsible, and stayed here. I was chosen.'

Quintilius remembered the gossip in the Antonia in Jerusalem; blunt tongued, inflexible by nature, and thirty-five years old, *and* without a single black mark on his charge sheet, Vatinius had been steered into this backwater by very willing hands; and here would stay, if authority had its way, until he reached retirement age, or became infirm.

'If the appointment pleases you, my congratulations,' he said. 'And I think it does please you. You have the look of a contented man.'

Vatinius realised, with a slight shock, that up to the moment of Quintilius' arrival he had been contented. Too easily contented?

The entry of an orderly bearing the three cushions, gave him an excuse for making no reply. The cushions were placed and Quintilius arranged himself. Then one of the slaves came in, soft-footed, to say that the meal would be ready in an hour; another brought in a tall flagon, made of glass, in a filigree net of silver and two wine-cups, silver, decorated with a pattern of vine-leaves, the tendrils making the handles. A third brought a flat silver dish containing salted prawns, sardines and anchovies, olives and almonds, delicacies calculated to provoke appetite without allaying it, and to keep thirst lively.

'I have brought you a really prime Falernian,' Quintilius said to Vatinius. To the slaves he said, 'Bring the table nearer to me, then you can go and I will pour. Now Vatinius, turn the chair about and make yourself comfortable.'

He reached out his plump, beringed hand; and Vatinius saw the lean, brown calloused hand of his young fellow legionary. The mental vision shifted and expanded, and he saw two young men, walking back from the

Games in the arena at Areta; heard himself say, 'Then you choose between him and me. Nobody's boy-wife is going to be a friend of mine. If you take up with that turd, Marius, I shall never speak to you again!'

All long ago and far away. And it was crazy to think that now, by eating and drinking and talking with him, one was condoning. It was crazier still to feel that in some subtle way the food and the wine were contaminated. He'd eaten, in his time, what was practically carrion, drunk out of filthy ditches.

There was also–and this he must face, rationally–the practical considerations. Quintilius had said something about falling victim to Oriental nonsense; and Vatinius knew what was said of him in Jerusalem–'as near Jew as a non-Jew can be'. It needed only one malicious remark, which Quintilius was capable of making, and somebody was going to say, 'It's high time Vatinius was shifted.' On at least two occasions, when soldiers had come into conflict with the natives, he had tried to be impartial; that would not have escaped the sharp eye of authority, or done him any good. Better be careful. He took up his cup and deliberately chose one of the salted prawns.

Quintilius, before drinking, tilted his cup a little and spilled a few drops, a libation to the gods.

'Good fortune, Vatinius! Now, let me look at you. You have worn very well. Very well. I swear that had I met you in Sabatra, I should have recognised you. You could hardly say, I fear, the same of me.'

'I might have blinked twice. But I should have known you. Inside every fat, middle-aged man, if you look close enough, you can see the young man he once was.'

'You never learned, did you? That blunt tongue of yours! Fat, middle-aged. True, most regrettably true; but such things should not have been *said*. You should have remarked that my hair has not receded, and my teeth are sound.'

The words, though a rebuke, were spoken with such charm, such good nature, that something in Vatinius wished to respond and say that indeed the hair, the teeth were as beautiful as they ever had been; but he stiffened himself and said:

'I'm too old to learn such civilities now.'

'You were always,' Quintilius said, 'the most honest man I ever met. I fear you always will be.' His bright glance cast about the bare rooms and made a silent comment–This is where an honest man lands!

'Yes,' Vatinius said, 'you are right. Not about the honesty; if I'm honest it's no more to my credit than the length of my foot. I have, all along, tripped over my tongue.'

'Not for lack of warning.'

That was dangerously close to harking back; so Vatinius said, again gruffly and bluntly:

'What exactly are you doing here? You spoke of Caesar's friendship–but even that would not empower you to commandeer barracks, unless you had some special errand.'

'How very indiscreet of me to have said that! The sight of you, after all these years, and wearing such an unwelcoming look, must have disarmed me. Still, between old friends . . . Or is *that* harking back? . . . here and there along my route I have paid more attention to Caesar's business than to my own. Gout, oddly enough, is a most useful travelling companion; it comes and goes. There are days when even the jolting of my litter would be intolerable. So I can always halt when I'm interested and move on when I'm bored.'

Vatinius was on the point of asking what there was of interest in a subsidiary barracks just outside Bethlehem, but that might be twisted by Quintilius into sounding self-important. He'd find out in another way, if he could, if there was anything to find out. Quintilius as he remembered him had a better appetite than head for wine; and he had already emptied his cup and refilled it.

'Let me not be egotistic,' Quintilius said. 'Tell me something about yourself. You were at Colenus, were you not?'

Nobody ever spoke of that engagement as a battle; rightly so; it had been a bloody massacre of trained Roman soldiers by ill-armed barbarian Germans.

'I was there. Of our maniple fourteen survived, all wounded. And of that fourteen I am the only one still serving.'

'I heard of it, and wondered about you. It was quite a time before I learned that you had been fortunate and that I had wasted my grief.'

Vatinius remembered the nightfall on that green meadow, where the grass had slowly shed its round flowers of blood; and how, as they counted their dead and did what they could for the wounded, he had wished Quintilius among the dead, a friend who could be rightly mourned and remembered with respect. A curious thing to remember now, with the man, so sleek and prosperous, here in his room. He made no comment upon Quintilius' mention of having grieved for him, though he believed it. He sat looking at the grain in the scrubbed table top. The silence grew.

'I went to Alexandria, and to Corinth, to Rhodes, Crete and Cyprus. Marius died there, poor man, at Paphos. Apart from a tactful, token legacy to Caesar, he left me all he had; he was richer than anyone guessed. But, as I explained to you at the time, mere money was never my objective.'

That was true, Quintilius had said at the time–I'm not doing it for money; I'm doing it to escape, to have some pleasure and comfort and status. What have we to hope for if we aren't killed? To reach centurion's rank, and be honourably retired and granted a few acres of land to grub a living out of, like a peasant. Straighten out your ideas, Vatinius, and as soon as I am established I'll find you a rich gentleman friend in Marius' circle, who'll do as much for you. And to that Vatinius had replied–I can tell you where *you'll* end, with a painted face, soliciting outside the baths!

He now said, 'Did you break your journey here for the purpose of showing me how well things had gone with you?'

Quintilius said pleasantly, 'Well, I thought that if the years had brought you tolerance you might like to know that your *direst* predictions had not been fulfilled. And if they haven't you might be interested to hear that I have rehabilitated myself. The means was to hand. A widow, very well connected. Her husband–as I have reason to know–was impotent; can you imagine a woman married for twelve years and still a virgin? There's not the slightest doubt in my mind that, tiring of her state, she poisoned him. She was not young, and she died in childbed. No condolences are necessary, she was not of an amiable nature. The boy is all I could wish, almost thirteen years old. Handsome and intelligent. And though his father was merely rich, his mother was a Flavian, so he'll never have the troubles *we* did.'

'Upon *him*,' Vatinius said, 'I congratulate you.'

He was not–or at least not consciously–envious of this success story; but as Quintilius told it he seemed to realise something that had hitherto escaped him. The job in which he had been so happy and satisfied was virtually a sinecure; he was nothing but a figurehead. Each century that marched down the road brought its own centurion with it; every duty was known and assigned; he was treated with respect, he was in charge but he was nothing but a caretaker, a stock-keeper. There wasn't, for example, a single thing which he could at this moment claim called for his attention so that he could get away from this man, out of this room. If fire broke out, or a wall fell down, or twenty men fell sick at the same moment Caepio would deal with the crisis and report it in the morning. By this time everybody in the place would know that he had a guest: they'd say–A Roman, *for a change*! and respect his privacy all the more for that.

So here he was, stuck with Quintilius, and the endless evening stretched ahead.

'I had a very interesting stay in Jerusalem,' Quintilius said, moving to another subject with the skill of a socially expert man. 'Herod has made vast improvements. The Hippodrome is one of the best I have seen. Well patronised, too. A surprising number of Jews seem to have come round to the idea. Of course, at the gateways an even greater number were expressing disapproval, groaning and making peculiar hissing noises. Strange people, don't you think? Or are you, like most Romans, oblivious to them so long as they behave?'

'I know several Jews. The ones in this district are simple people, inclined to credit me with powers I don't possess, so they come with complaints and pleas. If I can deal with the matter I do so, if not I explain, or advise, and I must say I've always found them very reasonable and responsive.'

'You have friends amongst them?'

'So that's it!' Vatinius set down his cup with a jolt which slopped the wine. 'That's why you came. To spy on me. By the blood of the bull, who'd have dreamed that I warranted so much attention? Very well then! Ebenezer's cabbage field *was* ruined and I said so in my report; and that lout Crassus *did* attempt to rape Caleb's daughter, and I punished him to the utmost, not for the attempt, which could never be proved, but for being late back, for being improperly clad, for dumb insolence and everything else I could find against him. *I* know what stories get back to Jerusalem, but I don't care. We're supposed to be an occupying army, not an invading rabble.'

'You sound very heated,' Quintilius said. He leaned over and filled Vatinius' cup. 'As for spying upon you, my dear man you must know there is no need. A hundred men and a centurion go back to Jerusalem six times a year. Clever as I am, could I learn in an evening what they had failed to see in two months?'

'Yes; that was absurd. The thing is that over the cabbage field and the girl what I did was extremely unpopular. I have made friends here. Ask yourself what my life would be, if I hadn't. A hundred men come, after two months they go. I can't consort with the men and every single centurion who has ever come here has resented me, openly or covertly. So they go away and call me a Jew-lover.'

'I sympathise with you,' Quintilius said, and he sounded sincere. 'It's strange, isn't it, how unpopularity centres around nationality; in Jerusalem they still call Herod "*that Idumean*". He's a character, if you like. I dined with him one evening. He complained bitterly of the Jews' ingratitude towards him; he knows he is unpopular, yet he never does anything to endear himself to his people.'

'What could he do? A murderer many times over.' Vatinius remembered the light way in which Quintilius had accused his late wife of murder, and felt bound to explain. 'Jews–the pious sort–have respect for human life; that is why they don't like the Games or the chariot races.'

'At least Antipater is popular.'

'Is he? Is he? I should say that most people cheer him as a means of knocking Herod on the nose. And it's dangerous for him. My friends never expect to see him on the throne.'

'Indeed; why not?'

'To be popular isn't healthy, if you're Herod's son.'

'About that, I must tell you a joke.' Quintilius poured wine. 'Caesar made a pun, in Greek–Better Herod's pig than his son, meaning that Herod would kill his son, but being half-Jew, wouldn't touch a pig. The point is that when Herod has no Jew at his table, he eats just as you and I would. And what do you think his *favourite* food is? This is true, he told me himself. That hard, pork-and-garlic, Danubian sausage that you and I used to carry to supplement our rations.'

Sliding back, Vatinius thought, back to the pleasant, rambling talks that we used to have, the kind of talk I've never had with anyone else. He was always so interested in everything. And it was his mind I loved, not his body, splendid as it was. Yet when he sold his body–for that is what it amounts to, and he sold it twice, to Marius for money, to the widow for position–I cut him off, disregarding his mind.

'If your friends don't expect to be ruled by Antipater, what do they look for?'

'How should I know?' Vatinius asked, with a return to his old gruffness. 'The Jews I know are not politicians; they're poor simple men whose main concern is to make a living. And if they had political opinions they would conceal them from me, out of courtesy. I can tell you this. It'll interest you. Their main hope centres around a bit of folklore. They believe that their subjection is the result of their god's displeasure and that in his own good time he will deliver them by sending them what they call a Messiah. But neither Caesar nor Herod need tremble, because this Messiah is to be born of a virgin. So by my reckoning they have a long time to wait.'

'Oh well, how was Minerva born? Or Mithras? He was born of a rock we are told. As a putative parent, rock or virgin, I'd wager on the latter, wouldn't you? Remember how we toyed with Mithraism? In those days I thought that the rock birth was symbolic. One says, sound as, solid as, immovable as a rock. Qualities that make Mithras superbly suitable to be a soldier's god. I understand that more and more go over to him every day. Now a god born of a virgin sounds unlikely to be a deliverer of a subject people, don't you think? Very innocent, pretty, pure and sentimental. I've noticed that at the Games the Vestal Virgins–though their virginity is largely a matter of nomenclature–are always the first to turn *up* their thumbs and lead the crowd to spare the defeated. If symbolism counts this Messiah would be a curious kind of god.'

'Ah,' said Vatinius, throwing himself into the argument, 'according to my friends, he'd also be the son of Jehovah; and about him there is nothing pretty or sentimental. He's a god of battles, and he laid down a code of behaviour, stricter than any . . . I ever heard of.' He had paused and added the last four words in a trailing voice, for he had remembered what one of his Jewish friends had said about Jehovah and men like Marius and Quintilius. 'They shall surely be put to death.' And when Caleb had told him that, Vatinius had thought–Well, that would be a way of putting a stop to it, this thing, which like a disease was spreading rampantly, was no longer disapproved of, was used as a ladder by ambitious young men.

And here he was, with the man to whom he had sworn never again to speak, succumbing to the old charm. He folded his hands into fists and pushed the knuckles together, wishing with all his heart that something, anything, might happen that Caepio couldn't deal with and that he might be called away.

Relief was at hand. The slaves came in and began to reset the table. Quintilius reached for his stick and stood up.

'The bog,' Vatinius said, 'is next on the right.' Without thinking he had used the old army word. 'And if you want to wash . . .' He indicated the tripod in the alcove. 'I'll get a clean towel.'

He made no attempt to help Quintilius along the short length of passage to the latrine; he laid the clean towel on the edge of the bowl and then made a rapid survey of his small domain, still hoping against hope that there might be something that would give him an excuse for not sitting down to eat with his self-providing, self-invited guest. Too many memories were involved; all the meals he had eaten with Quintilius; hasty meals on the march, dull regulation meals in barracks, and those happy times, when, their free times coinciding, they could take a loaf, some cheese or meat, a little fruit and if Quintilius had succeeded in one of his little schemes, some wine, and walk away and find a place, sheltered in winter, shaded in summer, and throw themselves down and eat and drink and talk, and be not soldiers, rigid and purposeful, but two young men, interested in everything and involved in nothing.

But in the whole of the little barracks there was not one thing which justified a moment's absence. He went back to his room, and saw Quintilius drop the used towel on the floor and begin to hobble back to his couch, and then the slaves, with nice timing, brought in the first dish.

'These mullet,' Quintilius said, 'were alive this morning in a pool not far from the Antonia. And if Plautus, my flat-foot, has smothered their delicate flavour with a sauce too highly spiced, he'll smart for it.'

Fresh fish, as opposed to the salted and smoked kind upon which inland places were bound to depend, offered Vatinius an impersonal subject for talk. He had theories about diet. He said that he was certain that the irritable skin lesions, the softening of the gums which so often afflicted soldiers–and it was said, all sailors–was caused by too much eating of preserved, easily portable food. It could be cured, he said, and he had proved it time and again by the eating of fresh meat, fruit, vegetables. Especially cabbage.

'To my mind the least pleasant vegetable; but as a medicine, maybe acceptable,' Quintilius said. 'Tell me, are you much bothered by guerillas?'

'Very little. There have been incidents. Fewer of late.'

And he thought–Curse you for bringing that subject up, ruining what little appetite I had. He saw that in becoming the friend, the near-intimate of a few Jews, he had put himself in a well-nigh untenable position. Ebenezer and Caleb and Reuben were tactful in the extreme, but there had been mention of a man called Josodad whose son Nathan, a wild young man, had with other wild young men, been convicted and executed for the killing of a Roman soldier. It was impossible for Vatinius, a soldier and a Roman, not to feel that the sentence had been just and right; it was equally impossible for anyone who was a friend of the Jews not to see the whole thing as a tragedy. There was no doubt about it, life was easier if you ran on the orthodox lines; you could then say, I am a Roman and whatever the Romans do is right. Vatinius had once held that view; but a ruined cabbage field, a nearly raped girl, had opened his eyes. He'd come to know the people of the countryside, and sometimes he had asked himself–What are we doing here? In Gaul, and by the banks of the Rhine, by the banks of the Danube you could at least give yourself the answer that you were a civilising agent; but here, no. The Jews were civilised.

Caleb had once said to Vatinius, 'My friend, Jerusalem and Jericho were orderly cities when Rome was a haunt for wolves.'

Vatinius had refuted that with a sturdy answer. 'Age has nothing to do with it. Babylon was an orderly city when your people lived in tents.'

Then Caleb had retorted, 'In the tents the Law was kept.'

'How many are there?' Quintilius asked.

'Nameless ones? The official reckoning is, I believe, six hundred; but you could treble that and still be short of the mark.'

'How would you, or your friends, give their numbers?'

With a brusque return to caution, Vatinius said:

'How should I know? I'm acquainted with four or five Jews, all respectable, settled men. None of them is a guerilla, or related to one, or likely to become one, so far as I can judge. They're just ordinary fellows who do what they're told–and pay their taxes.'

'And await a miracle, eh?'

'Not entirely without reason. They have, more than once, been saved by what they call miracles and you and I would term lucky accidents. Once they were besieged by the Assyrians, and plague broke out in the camp. They were slaves in Egypt, and in Babylon, and both times, for some reason, set free and sent home. But you see, the orthodox Jew, from the moment he fastens his shoes to the time when he takes them off again, in everything he does, down to killing a chicken, is in the hand of his god; to him there are no lucky accidents. All is Jehovah's will.'

'As Herod said, fanatics. So according to you, the worst thing he, or Caesar, has to fear is some simple Jewish girl who had, shall we say, an *unlucky* accident and couldn't or wouldn't name her seducer and claimed that her conception was Jehovah's will.'

'I don't think that could happen. For one thing the genealogy of the mother is known, and girls who are eligible belong to good families, and are not only well guarded, but extremely prudish. That I know for a fact. I was four years in Jerusalem, and I've been here three, and in all that time I've hardly seen a *loose* Jewish woman, who wasn't left without a single male relative. Take my friend Caleb; he's a shoe-maker, he earns pitiably little, but as well as his own family he supports his own mother, his wife's mother and his widowed sister, and thinks nothing of it. It is the Law.' Vatinius thought, too, of Ebenezer, with his two poor fields; when he grew corn every ear counted, yet he always left some to be gleaned by those who had no field at all; that was the Law.

'Very admirable. I think you do admire them.'

'For those I know I have profound respect,' Vatinius said. He could not tell Quintilius, he could not tell anyone, that when his time for retirement came, he hoped to settle in this country, have a small white house, an orchard and a vegetable plot. A typical old soldier's dream, except that most men dreamed of returning to their homeland, not of staying in the place of exile.

The slaves came in with the next dish; breasts of pheasant cooked in wine. When the door was open Vatinius lifted his head and listened, his trained ear seeming to catch the sound of some faint commotion somewhere. Then he heard what was certainly Caepio's tread. Better not to interfere. Caepio had resented the store-room incident and would need tactful handling for a few days. So he sat still and Quintilius chatted on, saying how highly Herod had spoken of the waters of Calirrhoe, and what a beautiful city Caesarea was. Seemingly aimless talk which yet persisted in returning to the Jews. Once Quintilius, who seemed to have wasted no time in Jerusalem, mentioned the Sanhedrin. 'They struck me as being mercenaries,' he said of its members, using the word as only an ex-legionary would do. And Vatinius thought–How odd, that is exactly how Ebenezer and the others regard them.

Then Quintilius said, as a more than usually vicious gust rattled the shutters:

'Travelling South I did not expect such barbarous weather,' and gave a little shiver.

'I am at fault,' Vatinius said, 'I should have ordered a brazier.' He rose to go and shout in the passage; but before he called he listened. The place was not silent; there was the noise, so familiar as to be unnoticeable, of a hundred men busy with their evening routine or relaxation; there were voices, talking and singing, the twang of a stringed instrument, laughter, the rattle of dice, footsteps. All just as usual, and yet . . . Then he knew that it was not his ear that sensed something out of the ordinary, it was his nose. Mingled with the odour of leather, men's sweat, lamp oil and whitewash and cooking there was something else. My scented visitor, Vatinius thought, simply by walking in he tainted the air.

He said, 'Bring a brazier,' to the man who came running in answer to his call, and unwillingly went back to his room.

When the brazier had been brought and they were alone again, Quintilius said:

'I hope Calirrhoe will do as much for me as it has for Herod; but after all he is seventy or thereabouts; and he is only human. Of his sons which would your ordinary Jew choose to take his place?'

'The younger Philip,' Vatinius said, after some thought. 'He's reported to have frugal tastes and is what the Jews call a just man. But the truth is, the Jews don't take very kindly to kings at all. From what I hear, when they had their own, there was always a prophet busy keeping them in order.'

'Soothsayers?'

'Not exactly, they use the word differently. Certainly they foretold events, but that was a sideline. Holy men is the nearest word.'

He thought how eagerly, in the old days, he would have told Quintilius some of the fascinating stories which in Jewish households were spoken of as sober fact. Elijah, regarding as a miracle, a feast, a few scraps of carrion dropped from the beaks of glutted ravens, for example. It was too late, now; such talk could only be shared with friends.

The dishes were changed again; the slaves brought in small cutlets on a mound of rice, perfectly cooked, each grain separate and fluffy.

Indicating that he had already eaten his fill, Vatinius said, not entirely without malice:

'Small wonder, that you have gout, if you eat like this every day.'

'This!' The surprise in Quintilius' voice was genuine. 'Why, this is only a makeshift meal, easily carried, quickly cooked. At home eight or nine courses is the rule. After all, Vatinius, eating is one of the *certain* pleasures, and should be made the most of while it is available. Barring the dubious blessing of early death we're all going to end without teeth, or appetite, mumbling slops. A fearsome thought. Do you ever feel time seeping away, like water from a leaky goatskin?'

Vatinius remembered that even as a young man Quintilius had been unusually aware of passing time; the awareness had contributed to his decision. He'd said–I'm twenty and what have I ever had? Half my life or almost, sped, with hard work, hard food, hard beds and hard words. . . .

'I've thought of it; I shouldn't think there's a man who hasn't, at some time or another.'

'The thought *haunts* me,' Quintilius said; he spoke almost peevishly, and something of his worldliness seemed to drop away. 'I look at my boy and see him bald, with a paunch. I take a bath, am well-scraped, freshly clothed, but I *feel* the skeleton there under the flesh and the silk. But I try not to brood. Out of the dark we came, and into the dark we go and all we can do about it, all anyone can do, is make the best of the little time we have.' He took up his cup and drank deeply.

'There,' Vatinius said, 'the Jews have the advantage of us. They hold that this life is no more than so much,' he measured a tiny space between finger and thumb, 'in a life as vast as the sea.'

'Have you ever contemplated turning Jew?'

'Jews are born. I suppose one could adopt their beliefs; but my credulity has limits.'

'Mithras promises immortality, too. All these Eastern faiths are much the same.'

'I might have taken to Mithras when I was young, but for one thing . . .'

'I remember. Your mother!'

With all that he had seen and been and done and heard, he had remembered, across the years, those conversations on the banks of the Rhône. There was something so disarming, so almost touching, about this that Vatinius felt embarrassed. His voice was gruff again as he said, repeating what Quintilius remembered:

'I couldn't have truck with a faith that excluded my mother who was worth any ten men. Let's talk about something cheerful. Your son; nearly thirteen you say. What is his name?'

'His name?' For a second Quintilius looked down at his food, then he lifted his eyes and looked straight at Vatinius.

'Oh, I called him Vatinius, after a friend I once had, in Gaul.'

To his complete chagrin Vatinius felt a pulse leap in his throat, and the red blood pour up under his weather-beaten skin. He said in a half-choked voice:

'There was no need for that!'

'No need at all,' Quintilius agreed, deliberately misunderstanding, 'but boys must have names. And I . . . well, write me down as a sentimental fellow.'

No sound he had ever heard had been so welcome to Vatinius as the sound of the door opening behind him. He turned in his chair and said, 'Oh, Caepio! Enter. What is it?'

Caepio reported, in clipped formal phrases, the arrival of the three trespassers. 'There seemed no need to disturb you, sir. I locked them up and intended to report it in the morning. Now one of them is causing a disturbance. He mentioned Herod. I thought you should be informed, sir.'

'I'll come at once.' Deliverance. Just when the situation had become unbearable. Another minute, and they'd have been weeping on one another's shoulders!

'Wait,' Quintilius said, quietly, but with authority. 'This could be of interest to me. Have them brought here.'

Vatinius hesitated. A curious coincidence that in this unvisited place, in one evening, there should arrive Quintilius on some mysterious errand from Caesar, and now three men on Herod's business. It was an axiom that spies were always spied upon.

'What sort of fellow is this? Likely to be violent?'

'Oh no. Very old. Very frail.'

'A Jew?' Quintilius asked.

Caepio acknowledged the source of the question by giving Quintilius a glance, but he punctiliously addressed Vatinius as he answered.

'None of them is a Jew, sir.'

'Bring him in,' Vatinius said.

Melchior, having attained his aim by being noisy, was quiet again. He put his hands in his sleeves and bowed and said in a voice in which politeness, impatience and petulance mingled:

'Please, who is chief here? I asked, when we were arrested, to be brought to someone in authority.'

Vatinius stared, uncomprehending. Quintilius, stirring a little on his cushions, said:

'It is a form of Greek. He asks who is chief here.'

I wonder myself, Vatinius thought, angry at having been baulked in his attempt to escape.

'Tell him I am. Caepio, would you fetch Atticus; he's a Greek.'

'We came,' Melchior said, 'to the back of the house, like thieves. I am to blame for that. We are not thieves, we are harmless men on a very important errand, and we are already late. I beg you, let me and the black man proceed. Hold the other as hostage if you must. It is of the utmost importance that I should reach Bethlehem without delay.'

'He says,' Quintilius said, 'that he has an urgent errand in Bethlehem.'

'Ask him why he mentioned Herod.'

'Simply as a means of gaining attention. I meant nothing. I shouted the most important name I knew.'

Melchior was now in quandary such as he had never imagined. His suspicions of Herod had so worked upon his mind that he felt it would not be safe to divulge his real errand; and yet these men must be persuaded to let him and Balthazar go. And how could that be done?

'What is your errand?' Quintilius asked.

'Harmless. Of no importance to anyone but me. I have to ask for the release of the black man because he speaks for me.'

Caepio returned, bringing Atticus.

Glad to exclude Quintilius, Vatinius said, 'Now Atticus; ask this old man where he is going, and why, and why he mentioned the name of Herod the King.'

Atticus spoke; Melchior answered. Atticus said:

'I'm sorry, sir. I don't understand a word he says.'

'I'm not surprised,' Quintilius said, 'pure Greek is worse than useless. An ear accustomed to attuning itself and a mind capable of making leaps are of more service. Shall I try again?'

'Do,' Vatinius said, grudgingly. 'Ask him how he has made his needs known, speaking a tongue that only you seem able to understand.'

'He says,' Quintilius said, 'that the black man speaks for him.'

'All right,' said Vatinius. 'Atticus, go back to your dice. Caepio, fetch the others. We may as well see them all.' He looked at the old man, saw that he was deeply distressed, tremulous and confused, and that part of him which had sympathised with Caleb and Ebenezer, and at second-hand with Josodad, came uppermost.

'Tell him not to worry. Tell him to take the chair and calm himself. Tell him he's in no danger and that I've sent for the friend who speaks for him.'

Translated, these sentences drove Melchior to the very verge of panic. Balthazar knew that his errand was with the child. He'd blurt it all out, in this place where Herod's name meant so much. It seemed to be a place for soldiers and it was on the very verge of Bethlehem. Oh, what had he done, acting always–except that he had implied to Herod that he would return while determining not to–in a straightforward, honest way? A simpleton, that is what I have proved myself to be, he thought, and I thought I was the wisest man in Korea.

Caepio, thinking–He treats me like an errand boy, but I'll show him that I am at least an efficient errand boy, released the obviously harmless fellow first. To Balthazar, roused from sleep and still dazed, he said, 'Walk straight ahead, turn right and wait by the first door.' Then he released Gaspar who only two minutes before had regained consciousness, groped for his knife and was on the point of going crazy again. When the door opened he had been thinking that death by his own hand, by his own knife, would be better than enduring the torture that being shut in this dreadful little cell inflicted upon him. Then the door opened and he thrust the knife, with one of his rapid movements, into the front of his jacket; and his heart rejoiced because, if he were to be locked in again, and thus forced to kill himself, he would kill one or two of his captors first.

Caepio opened the door, and having recognised Gaspar as the dangerous one of the three, would have taken him by the arm; but Gaspar said, 'Don't lay your hand on *me*!' with such vehemence that though the words were without meaning, the tone and the look that accompanied them was perfectly clear.

So, let Vatinius, the storekeeper, the fussy housekeeper, the Jew-lover, deal with him, Caepio thought, and he beckoned and pointed, and finally ushered both Balthazar and Gaspar into the room where Vatinius awaited them.

As soon as Melchior saw Balthazar, he said, in a low, sibilant whisper, 'No mention of the child. Say anything, but not the truth.'

And he was fortunate, for Caepio was, in the same moment, saying:

'I think, sir, that this one has a knife.'

'You think! Weren't they searched?'

'Yes. This one, I think, concealed his weapon.'

Vatinius looked at Gaspar and saw him for what he was, and knew that had he been called, when he *should* have been called, he would have had such an obviously dangerous man stripped to the buff. Caepio, like every other centurion who had ever come here with his century, had made some fumbling, futile attempt to undermine *his* authority. Well, he must learn.

He said, almost casually:

'If you think he has a knife, take it from him.'

Testing me, Caepio thought; but alongside that thought ran another. Men returning from their two months' boring sojourn, all agreed that Vatinius was fussy, strict, a Jew-lover; but they'd add that he never asked anybody to do what he wasn't willing to do himself, that he was brave, a good soldier.

So, with complete confidence that should aid be needed, Vatinius was there to supply it, Caepio went to take away Gaspar's knife–if he had one, if that sudden furtive movement as the door opened had meant what Caepio was almost certain that it did.

But he had reckoned without any knowledge of Gaspar, in whose country one was either quick or dead. There was a brief scuffle; then the centurion, solid and heavy as oak, went reeling back against the wall, pain painting a white band about his mouth and in his mind the certainty that his back was broken. So swift and cunning a throw had never been seen in any arena. Gaspar had not even drawn his knife; but, having thrown Caepio, he leaped upon the table, and stood there, knife in his hand, his teeth bared in a wolfish grin, his eyes like a cornered rat's.

Before anyone else could speak or move, Melchior turned, and with a movement swifter even than Gaspar's brought the edge of his thin old hand down on the desert man's wrist with a gesture of a woman chopping meat for a stew. At the same time he screeched some kind of rebuke or instruction. The knife fell to the floor and Balthazar retrieved it and laid it before Vatinius.

'Get down from there,' Melchior said to Gaspar in the tongue that only they shared. 'Things are bad enough!' To Quintilius he said, 'I beg you, pardon this barbarian; he suffers from claustrophobia, he cannot bear to be shut in. But he is a good man and intends no harm.'

'He means no harm,' Quintilius translated, sardonically.

'No harm,' Caepio said, still leaning against the wall, 'he's well-nigh broken my back.'

Vatinius thought–If you'd made a thorough search in the first place . . . But his voice was kind and concerned when he spoke, reaching for a flask which stood, with others, on the shelf under the maps, 'This is good strong liniment. Get somebody to rub you, *hard*, as he would a horse. And tomorrow rest. I will undertake your duties.'

Moving like a cripple Caepio departed.

Balthazar had had time to think, to muster his forces, and when Vatinius said to him:

'You speak for this old man, I understand. Tell me, as briefly as possible, where you are bound and on what errand,' he said, smoothly, meekly.

'Sir, my master is an astrologer; he casts horoscopes and he has been asked to go to Bethlehem to predict a favourable day for a wedding.'

Melchior, anxious and trembling, had no idea of what story Balthazar was telling, but he saw with great relief that it was received with some amusement.

Astrology had enjoyed a brief and lucrative hey-day in Rome, but charlatans had exploited it and gradually it had fallen into disrepute;

nowadays only slaves and the most ignorant, credulous people gave it any heed.

'An astrologer?' Vatinius said, looking at the old man. And suddenly he knew that whatever the man claimed to be he *was*, integrity was written all over him, just as servility was written over Balthazar.

'And who's this hothead?' he nodded towards Gaspar.

'Oh, he rides with us, sir, for protection against robbers.'

All three fitted the characters assigned. But Vatinius was nothing if not careful.

'Your master spoke of Herod the King. Why?'

'Because the King received us this afternoon and wishes my master to call upon him as he goes back through Jerusalem.' Sheer inspiration visited Balthazar; he knew that he was in a tricky position. Melchior wouldn't be understanding any of this; if the one who could communicate with him asked a question and received an answer that didn't match . . . 'It is in order to get back to Jerusalem, to the King, that my master is in such haste.'

That sounded reasonable, too. But in Vatinius' mind something jarred a little. Jews, so far as he knew, did not dabble in anything that savoured of necromancy or magic or fortune-telling.

'The family that plans the wedding,' he said, 'of what nationality are they?'

'Greek, sir,' said Balthazar without hesitation. It was a safe thing to say; there were Greeks everywhere. 'I speak Greek, too; that is why he needs me.'

'And why did you arrive at the rear of this barracks?'

'We were taking a short cut, having been delayed in Jerusalem.'

To Vatinius it all sounded satisfactory enough; the old man was what one would imagine a professional astrologer looked like; the black man was somewhat finely clad for a servant, but many people took pride in their servants' appearance, and a servant who spoke Greek and Latin was a valuable one; the third man looked like a guard–and a good one. He was about to say that it was all right, they could go, when Quintilius said softly:

'Very plausible. A little too plausible, don't you think?'

'In what way? What do you suspect?'

'Everything and everybody, except you, Vatinius. May I take a hand here? You,' he addressed Melchior, 'take your companions and go and stand by the door. Close to the wall.'

Balthazar, understanding, moved without prompting; Melchior spoke to Gaspar who had been standing with his arms folded, hearing the talk as senseless gabble, but ready, at the first sign of danger, to take action. Here, he thought, as he moved without taking his eyes from the two men behind the table, it was exactly as it had been in Jexal, while he watched and waited. It was always the ones clad in silk, the ones with the soft hands, who gave the orders. And that was not as it should be; that was bad.

Quintilius swung his feet to the floor and patted the place where they had been.

'Sit down; and listen to me.' He lowered his voice so that Vatinius had to bring his head very close in order to hear. 'It could be a trick. Herod is very wily. Practically every day deputations go to Rome complaining about him, and he may be planning a counter-attack. I suppose it never struck you that your nice little sinecure here is a frontier post. What lies between here and Egypt? You take my point? Three men, apparently harmless, come to the rear of a barracks, at night; they tell a garbled tale. If you wave them away by the front door, how does that look? How will it sound? Herod might very well complain that security measures were very slack; and that is something Caesar would take note of.'

'How does it sound if I hold them? They say they were with Herod earlier today.'

'I've no doubt they were. Cooking up his fairy-tale. Truly, Vatinius, the one sensible thing to do, the thing that would vindicate you however it was looked at, would be to send a fast rider to Herod, saying that three mystery men have arrived here and you are holding them until you have word from him as to the validity of their errand.'

Vatinius backed away, looking at his one-time friend in horror.

'You want to ruin me? I, a Roman, a soldier, take orders from Herod? Are you in this damned plot, too? The planted, independent, civilian witness?'

'Oh, don't be silly,' Quintilius said, a little wearily. 'I'm advising you. Send two men if you wish, one of the tribune.'

All at once Vatinius felt dizzy. What had seemed to be solid earth under his feet, the daily round of an obscure man in an obscure place, was so swamped with suspicion, trickery, uncertainty that it had turned into a quaking quagmire. It was quite possible, *now*, to imagine Quintilius reporting somewhere to somebody–I arrived, I was received without question, we drank together, and when a decision was called for he obeyed me like an ox. He is not fit to be in charge of a strategic post.

And to be honest, he had never until now, regarded his post as being of importance, except as all places where soldiers were stationed were important; places to be manned, kept in a sanitary condition, always alert. Only a very short time ago he had, in a moment of depression, thought that he was nothing but a caretaker; but when Quintilius had asked–What lies between here and Egypt? he had realised that he held and had held, unknowingly for three years, one point of a great empire's frontier. Not that there was anything to fear from Egypt, that was part of the Empire; but to the South East there was the whole of Arabia. Well might somebody in authority think it worth while to test his alertness, his integrity.

He looked at Melchior and Melchior looked back at him with the urgent, dumb appeal of an animal, endeavouring to convey something, wordlessly. Whom can I trust? Vatinius asked himself; the old man with his look of integrity and other-worldliness; the black man with his facile tongue; my one-time friend?

Well, he thought, if I go down, I go down, making my own decisions; if I'm to be ruined I'll do it myself, by my own calculated error.

He said to Balthazar:

'If your master is an astrologer he should carry the tools of his trade. Where are they?'

'On his camel, sir, if they have not been removed.'

'Go and fetch them. The man on duty at the door will show you the way. Bring them here, and be quick.'

Balthazar scuttled as all his life he had scuttled in obedience to orders.

Quintilius said in a detached way, 'They'll be in perfect order. Herod is no fool.'

That thought had not occurred to Vatinius, and hearing it expressed undermined his self-confidence still further, made him feel that he was a simple-minded fool, ill-equipped to deal with a world in which nobody could be trusted.

But he was equipped to maintain an unruffled demeanour in awkward situations, to remaining calm, seemingly confident, however he might feel. He said:

'I am in charge here, Quintilius. I'm ready to take responsibility for what I do.'

Balthazar, breathless and sweating, for all the night air was so cold, came hurrying back and laid on the table with the uncleared dishes and Gaspar's knife, the cane chart case, the compasses, the piece of lodestone, the tube with its end of glass, even the bit of sharpened chalk.

Melchior gave a sharp cry, as though someone had stabbed him. He came forward to the table and spread his thin shaking hands over his treasures; they fluttered like distressed parent birds over a threatened nest.

'No! No!' he cried in his native tongue. 'They are all I have. All that are left to me. To you they would be useless.'

He looked at them, the pitiable remnants of that great fortune, which would have kept any ordinary man in comfort and happiness all his life.

The slow, difficult tears of an old, usually well-controlled man, rose to his eyes and stood there, unspilled, between the scanty lashes.

Nobody, not the best, the most celebrated actor in Rome, however schooled, however bribed, could have put on such an act, Vatinius thought.

He said shortly, 'You may go!'

'We may go,' Balthazar said to Melchior: Melchior said to Balthazar, 'We go.' Then he looked from his possessions to Vatinius, and Vatinius answered with a nod. In furious haste Melchior gathered his things, stuffing them into the front of his robe, holding the cane case in his hand, as though it were a wand of office.

For a second the knife lay there. A beautiful knife with a keen, bright blade and a handle of gold shaped to the hand, and with, between blade and hilt, a hand shield, curiously worked. Nobody saw it as a symbol, the knife between the barbarian and the towering might of Rome.

Then Gaspar, thinking that if Melchior could take his gear, he could claim what was his, snatched it up, asking no one's permission.

Balthazar was the only one to take civil leave. Bowing his head, bending his knees, he said in his beautiful Latin:

'Sirs, we thank you.'

He was grateful to them because they had been instrumental in restoring some trace of his self-esteem; he couldn't read the stars, he couldn't kill robbers; his dreams seemed to come to nothing; but apparently he could tell, on the spur of the moment, and with no help from anyone, an acceptable tale.

'Come along, come along,' Melchior said, now in a frenzy of impatience. 'We haven't a moment to lose.'

PART FOURTEEN

JOURNEY'S END

'This,' Melchior said, 'is the place.' Exhaustion, varied emotions, and that desperate need for haste made his voice shake a little, but he spoke with complete confidence.

The dying star, hanging like a luminous apricot, was now so low that it was possible to pick out from the uneven huddle of roofs, exactly the one which he had crossed a continent to find. The whole inn yard was awash in mellow light; and looking round he was inclined to hope that, despite all his fears, he might still be in time–but only just.

The end of the long journey appeared to be a shed or stable; very low, built of clods and roofed with mud and boughs. That a journey planned at the top of a stone and glass tower which had cost a fortune should have ended in this humble place neither surprised nor troubled him. His business was with the child and its parents; the surroundings were quite irrelevant.

He tapped his camel's neck and it knelt willingly. He alighted briskly, defying his weariness; one more effort, the greatest and the last, then he could lie down and sleep; he felt as though he could sleep for ever.

Gaspar and Balthazar also alighted, less briskly; they also were pent.

'Now,' Melchior said, addressing Gaspar first. 'I want no interruptions from you. You will not understand anything that is said, so stand quietly and do not bother us with any foolish questions.'

Gaspar grunted. The place where he had hit his head when he fell was beginning to ache and throb, but he ignored the pain, as he had been bred to do and fixed his mind once again on the extremely satisfactory way in which he had thrown that great hulking Roman. He also thought about his plans for the future and began to wonder how best to place his proposals before Melchior and Balthazar, and how long, if they bought fresh camels, it would take them to ride back to Jexal.

Balthazar was now dazed by hunger and fatigue and the speed at which so much had happened, and all so inexplicable; but when Melchior, moving towards the low doorway, said, 'Balthazar' his lifetime of slavery, of pushing himself and his thoughts into the background and of concentrating on other people's business, enabled him to say, brightly and attentively, 'Yes?'

'Now this is most important. It is unlikely that anyone here will understand me, so you must speak and you must say *exactly* what I say. You must repeat it word for word, and watch their faces. If they look confused, or ask a question, or make a protest, stop me at once. Do you understand? I rely upon you absolutely.'

'I will do my best,' Balthazar said. Melchior opened the door which moved silently because Joseph had re-hung it and oiled its hinges.

It was, as the old man had thought, a stable. A lantern hung on the wall, but compared with the light of the star outside the illumination it gave was poor and dim, and he was obliged to close his eyes for a second or two, screwing them up, to accustom them. Then he looked around and all the vital organs in his body seemed to fall away, leaving him hollow. The disappointment was not to be borne; he would die here of sheer misery, of the knowledge that he had been completely fooled.

For there was no child.

There was a heap of straw and on it two people lay asleep. One was a girl, very young with what even Melchior's old eye recognised as a virginal look. The other was a man, much older. Father? Brother? He was wrapped in a brown cloak, and he was not sleeping peacefully; he tossed and muttered. There was a long manger, occupied at its farther end by a cow and two donkeys.

No child!

'But this is impossible,' Melchior said aloud, in a voice shrill with incredulity.

Then the man awoke and with a movement as swift as any even Gaspar had ever seen, was on his feet, between them and the woman, alert, defensive; he had a chisel in his hand.

Balthazar said hastily, 'We come in peace.'

The woman woke then, raised herself and looked anxiously towards the unoccupied end of the manger; Melchior's gaze, following hers, found what it sought; there, wrapped like a cocoon, lay a baby, fast asleep.

'Then you are welcome,' Joseph said; but he still looked wary.

Melchior acknowledged this with his most formal bow; and Gaspar gave his salute, because he respected a man who could be asleep, awake, armed and ready all in the same breath space. He approved of the brown, sinewy hand. This was a man more like those legendary men-of-the-hills than any he had yet seen: and he must be some sort of outlaw, if this was the best place he could find for his woman to give birth in.

Balthazar bent his head and flexed his knees.

The girl on the straw acknowledged each salutation with a smile and a curiously dignified movement of her head. She looked very pale and very frail, and Melchior regretted that the message he carried would compel her into instant action. Still, it must be done; and there was no time to lose.

'Who are you, and what do you want?' Joseph asked.

'Balthazar, say this. I have come to congratulate you upon the birth of a wonderful child. A child of great destiny. And I have come to warn you.' He spoke slowly, and paused to give Balthazar time to put the sentences into Aramaic; but there was no need. As soon as he had begun to speak the man had poised his head as though listening to some distant, just recognisable sound; he frowned in concentration, and at the word 'warn' shot Melchior a glance which, though startled, was not surprised. It was almost as though the word confirmed something that he had suspected. And before Balthazar could begin to speak he asked quietly, in bad Greek:

'What is the warning?'

'I can speak to you direct? Good. That will save time. I have come to tell you that this is a very special child.'

Joseph said cautiously, 'To their parents all children are special.' He had just wakened from a terrifying dream; and though these men said they came in peace, and looked harmless–at least two of them looked harmless, he felt it best to be careful.

'But this is different,' Melchior said. 'I am an astronomer and I read his destiny in the stars, nine months and some days ago, at the time of his conception. I was astounded. You can have no idea of the importance of this child. *If he lives*, he will govern all the world we know, and places as yet unmarked on any map.'

He was amazed because the man's face betrayed no astonishment. Surely this was–to put it mildly–an unusual destiny that he was foretelling. Perhaps after all the man did not fully understand.

'Do you understand what I am saying?' he asked.

Joseph nodded. 'I travelled a bit when I was younger, and Greek worked anywhere. I know what you're saying.'

I will astound you yet! Melchior thought. It was essential to make the man understand the importance of the child before issuing the warning. So he tried again:

'Kings,' he said, 'will bow down before him. Great armies will march behind his banners–occasionally defeated, but in the end triumphant. He will rule an Empire compared with which that of Alexander was nothing, for his will reach to north and south, to east and west.' All innocently, anxious only to inspire belief in a future which present circumstances made almost unbelievable, he moved his thin hand as he named the compass points.

Mary, watching and listening, understanding nothing of what was said, had thought that with his grave dignity, his outlandish garb, his glittering eyes and impressive way of talking, the old man was very much as she had always pictured the prophets to be. When he made his gesture she knew that he was making a prophecy; and he had drawn on the air the sign of the cross. Despite all her faith, all her acceptance, in her heart she cried, Oh no! No! Not that lovely little body, flesh of my flesh, nursed at my breast. But begotten of God, she reminded herself; with every day of his life planned and foreseen, a man of sorrows, and acquainted with grief. . . .

She thought again that no other woman had ever been called upon to bear what she must bear. She looked back upon that moment amongst the flowers, when Elisabeth had hailed her as blessed among women, and she had answered that her soul magnified the Lord. A moment of ecstasy, and such came all too rarely. However, God had chosen her, and would give her strength to face what must be faced; but even that thought could not prevent her being sorrowful.

Even the mention of Alexander had not, Melchior observed, moved this father to giving any sign of excitement or surprise. Such words, spoken of a royal baby, lying in a golden cradle in a palace of marble, would have aroused some wonder, surely.

'People who know nothing of him but his name,' he said, 'will hold it in awe. And his Empire will not split up at his death; if anything his death will *consolidate* it. He will die young–I regret to be obliged to tell you that–thirty-two or three years will be his life-span. *If he survives now*. And here I come to my warning. There were very strong counter indications, with influences of the utmost malignancy. Unless precautions are taken he will die by treachery before he is weaned.'

Maybe the man's face changed a little then, the anxiety becoming more marked; but still no surprise.

'Until this afternoon,' Melchior went on, 'I did not, of course, know from what direction danger threatened. Now I am suspicious of a man called Herod, a King in Jerusalem. Most misguidedly I mentioned something of my errand to him, and he knows my destination.'

Now he had made an impression. The man's face was that of a man who knows that his worst fears are confirmed; it lost colour and every line in it stood out darkly as though drawn by one of Melchior's sharp chalk sticks.

Melchior said quickly, 'But we have a full day. I was not followed, or forestalled, and I think he is depending upon me to go back and tell him where the child is. Tomorrow, when he realises that I have tricked him, he will act, and swiftly. By that time you should be as far away as possible.'

There, he had now said it all. His mind presented him with the kind of picture–the whole lifetime in a flash which drowning men were said to see. (But who could *know* that he had asked himself when first he heard that theory, since no drowned man had ever been able to relate his final experience?) He saw himself, as a young man, knowing that astronomy was the only thing he cared about, he saw the long years devoted to the study, the fortune spent upon it, the decision taken on a cold spring night at the top of the tower, and then the journey, probably the longest journey any man had ever yet made. Now it was done; and he was an old, incredibly tired man; and he knew that unless he sat down quickly his legs would give way under him and he would fall.

He looked about and saw the stool.

It was the one which Eunice had allowed Ephorus to borrow from the house in order that Mary might sit on it and the more easily nurse her child. Once long ago, it had been a fine piece of furniture, with a cover of crimson silk and legs inlaid with mother-of-pearl. Now the cover was shredding and many pieces of the inlay were missing, but Eunice treasured it, and had said, 'Even to please you, Ephorus, I wouldn't lend my stool to just anyone. But I know courage when I see it, and that slip of a girl is brave. I could see she was in for a hard time and I told her to yell if she wanted to, there would be nobody to hear her but me. Yet when the time came, and she had good cause for yelling, she remembered that this was an inn and it was night, with people asleep all around. So she stuffed her sleeve into her mouth and bit on it hard. She can have my stool.'

So there it was, and Melchior sat on it.

Joseph stood for a moment, thinking about his dream. In it the same angel had come to him again, bringing not comfort this time, but a warning. He was to take the young child and his mother and flee into Egypt because Herod was planning murder. The dream had been so real that Joseph had thought how small his resources were. Fleeing he would not dare to stop, look for work and earn money. He had been on the very point of asking the angel's advice, asking how this was to be done, when these men had arrived and he had wakened.

Now here was this old man, first confirming all the prophecies about the child being the Messiah, and then issuing exactly the same warning as the angel had done; naming the same enemy; setting safety's limit.

Mary, seeing the trouble on his face, said, 'What is it Joseph? What did he tell you?'

He crouched down in the straw beside her and told her, softening everything, trying not to alarm her, yet unable to conceal his mounting anxiety.

Then the three men watching saw her put out her hand and lay it on Joseph's shoulder in what was recognisably a comforting and sustaining gesture.

It reminded Melchior, oddly enough, of old Senya. Not that she had ever touched him; but she had a way of knowing when something in his work, all a mystery to her, had gone wrong; at such times she would put his food bowl before him in a special way, a way that said–Don't worry; you'll manage. This woman's hand on the man's shoulder said just that.

Gaspar noticed the gesture and he stared at the girl who made it with fierce attention. Her hand was small, finely boned, though the skin of the fingers showed that it was the hand of a working woman. The wrist was delicate. So was the girl's neck. She was a pale, frail creature, with great shadowy eyes, in no one way measuring up to his ideal of womanhood. Yet the movement of her hand had not signified weakness or dependence; on the contrary it was strong and heartening, conveying exactly the reassurance which even the most self-sufficient man felt the need of at times. And she had borne a wonderful, strong-looking, beautiful baby, in circumstances as comfortless as any desert woman ever knew.

He thought of Ilya, but in a different fashion from the way in which, at the back of his mind, he had thought of her since the moment when, in the Balcony room, their eyes had met; not with yearning lust, strictly governed, not with defensive scorn, but with love. The last rational barrier between him and what he wanted went down. Melchior had weakened it, by proving that when necessary a frail body could be indomitable; this girl, with a movement of her hand had demolished it altogether. It had been his last defence, the thought that a delicate creature must needs be a bad breeder and a clog on a man. It wasn't true; and he knew, with a great uprush of joy that he would go back to Jexal and stand up in the sun's eye and mingle his blood with that which in his bigoted folly he had called dregs. And what, he thought, would Lakma say to that? He knew that *he* would say–You great fool, I wanted her for myself, all along. Probably they'd fight again, and Lakma would break another finger for him, and he'd give Lakma another crack over the skull. And it wasn't by any means all sentimental nonsense either; there'd been some truth in what the boy, Malchus, had said; this marriage would unite the old and the new, so that if trouble came Jexal would stand undivided. He could hardly wait for the moment when they would head back for home.

He said to Melchior:

'Have you said all that you came to say?'

'I have said it. And now we must be practical.'

Balthazar had also noticed the gesture, but it was rather as though he had seen it through a sheet of glass. Once, long long ago, he had loved his sister; and they'd taken her, kept her in a dark hut, fattened her up and then with flowers and the beating of drums, thrown her into the great river, a living sacrifice to N'Zana. Wasted. And for many years, to him there had been little difference between men and women, and the hand of the woman on the shoulder of the man had stirred nothing even remotely sexual. He had listened to what Melchior had said– the first time that he had heard the whole story–and seemed to have nothing to do with what he had come out to seek, about that he was more confused than ever. In a vague way he felt sorry for this couple, who must now leave this poor shelter and go into the night, into the world that was so hostile to humble people. Also it couldn't be a very pleasant thing to be told, when your child was only a few days old, that he would live so short a time, whatever glory he might achieve in a few years. Considering their plight he studied the animals and hoped that they owned them, though a cow would slow down their flight and the nearest donkey was extremely old, more likely to be a liability than an asset. Balthazar had a shrewd eye for a donkey; the Greek trader had owned many and had been quick to discard a faulty animal.

Melchior addressed Joseph.

'You have told her? She understands? She is fit to travel?'

'She is willing,' Joseph said, and the change of word spoke volumes.

'I can see that you are poor. I am poor myself, but I am trying to find a way to help you.' He turned to Gaspar and spoke his name. Gaspar came out of his dream and said:

'Yes?'

'If this child is to be saved, he must be removed. They are poor and travel is costly.'

'Travel is costly,' Gaspar agreed; and he thought–I hope you will remember that, and how much I have spent on you, when I lay my request before you.

'The gold you carry,' Melchior said, 'which you did not give to Herod–very rightly. Will you give it to these people?'

Just that, the simple request, no reasoning, no pleading; the old man spoke as casually and with as much certainty of getting what he asked for as though, at table, he had suggested that somebody should pass him the salt. A really remarkable old man, old and poor and star crazed, but with the manners of a king.

He said, 'Herod didn't get my gift because I could see that he was useless to me. You, on the other hand, could be very useful. I will give what I carry to these people if you, in return, will do something for me.'

And as soon as the words were out he thought–Spoken like a true huckster! Unless I soon get back to my own place and my own people, I shall be thoroughly corrupt.

'And what in the world could *I* do for *you*?' Melchior asked, looking at the man who had financed him, and saved him from the robbers.

'You could come back to Jexal with me and use your skill on *my* behalf. A man who can read the stars as you can is not met with every day.'

Nor every century, nor every millennium, Melchior thought with the supreme satisfaction of a man who has proved himself right. But there was no time for self-congratulation, nor for argument, or even for consideration. These humble custodians of the future Lord of the Earth were like conies, their only safety lay in flight, and the sooner they started the better. When, at the top of his tower, he had visualised himself giving that warning, Melchior had seen armies alerted, guards set and fortresses manned; now he saw a worried man bundling his wife and the precious baby on to a donkey and making off through the night. Not that it mattered. If the threatened danger could be averted the destiny was quite sure.

'Very well,' he said, after what had seemed only a second's thought, 'I will do that. But I must ask you to remember that I am no hired Chaldean. I cannot promise to tell you only acceptable things.'

'Am I the man to ask that? That is settled then. But there is another thing

I must ask you to do for me. I want him, too.' He jerked his thumb at Balthazar. 'I want him to come and teach tongues to my young men.'

'That can wait, surely.'

'I want it done now. This is as important to me as your business is to you.'

A really remarkable young man, Melchior reflected; ignorant, in many ways uncouth, but issuing orders like a king.

With his own innate courtliness he looked towards the man and the girl and said:

'Excuse us, please. It is your business that we discuss,' Then he passed on Gaspar's request, as hastily as was compatible with clarity, to Balthazar, who faced with this in addition to all that had happened and had not happened, seemed to suffer a lapse from sanity.

'It is not possible,' he said. 'I have been thinking; I have been wrong. I came out to witness some great thing, and to do that I committed a crime; so I have seen nothing. I am a slave, the property of a Lady living in Edessa. Money was paid for me, so by running away I robbed her. I must go back and make full restitution . . . and take my punishment.'

He could hardly believe that he was saying these things, but he was, and in a far more firm and positive voice than he had ever used towards his fellow travellers. Even when he had urged the necessity of entering Jerusalem, the slave wheedle had tainted his voice; now he spoke like a free man.

Irritably now, because of the delay, Melchior translated. And, Gaspar turned and looked, for the first time with any real respect at Balthazar, and gave him a cheerful man-to-man blow upon the shoulder, a gesture he reserved for the chosen few of the Five Hundred.

He spoke and Melchior spoke.

'He says you are to reckon your worth, double it, and this woman in Edessa shall have it, in rose jekkals. Also he says that from this moment you are free, because a teacher must have status and authority.'

How Balthazar took this astounding piece of news he did not stop to see, for he turned straight back to Gaspar and said:

'Now please, the gold.'

'And what,' Gaspar said, 'about the stinking stuff you carry? You said it had value, equal with gold. Couldn't they have that, and sell it?'

'Oh dear,' Melchior said, pushing himself to his feet, angry at the oversight. 'Of course, of course.' He had tried so hard to be practical. He said to Mary and Joseph:

'We have thought of a way to assist you.' But they had asked for nothing; they were decent poor people and had their feelings and their pride; so he added, 'They are birth gifts for the baby, and you will honour us by accepting them.'

In Balthazar's stunned mind only the word *gifts* made any impact. Of course, to a new baby one brought gifts, and Melchior and Gaspar had come prepared. He had nothing. The child's father, understanding Greek, would know that he was a slave–*had* been a slave, who did not even own himself; but the sweet-faced woman wouldn't know. Judging by his clothes she would think him well-to-do, and mean.

Why he should mind what she thought was as mysterious as the impulse which had prompted his confession; and he had no way of knowing that he was the first of many millions who would wish to please her and shrink from her disapproval. He knew only that he had no gift, and shooting her a humble, apologetic smile, he followed the others into the yard, meaning to stay there and hide his shame, while trying to work out why his venture had been on the one hand so rewarding, making him a free man and a teacher, and on the other, so disappointing.

Neither Melchior nor Gaspar glanced at the star as they used its last light to fumble for what lay hidden at the bottom of their bags of camel fodder. For Melchior its work was done; for Gaspar it had never mattered much; it was not his star.

But Balthazar stared at it, and it was he who saw its end. Just as in his vision, it gathered itself into a great burst of glory, and was gone.

Now the only light in the inn yard was cold and came from a distance, from the ordinary stars and a young, thin crescent moon.

And then, to Balthazar, understanding came in a flash. Melchior's errand and his merged and made sense. It was in the reign of this child, and under his influence, that the old world would end and a new one be born, and the bad things, like slavery, be done away with.

He wished with all his heart that he had a gift to offer this wonderful child; and even as he wished it, he knew that he had. A small gift but useful. He had the pot of myrrh ointment, stuff of such potency that only two dressings of it had healed his festering sores and the wound the dog had made. And every child had rashes and scratches, fell when it took its first steps and bruised its face, grazed its knees. The old woman had said that the ointment improved with keeping. Remembering her he wished that he had bought an alabaster pot.

So the gifts lay in Mary's lap; the jewelled gold crown that had rolled from the head of a dead king; the frankincense that had been intended for the altar of an unknown god; the pot of myrrh that had eased a slave's sores. She read their meaning plainly: gold for kingship, frankincense for priesthood; and myrrh for the anointing of a dead body. Just as it was written. But of what she knew she gave no sign; she thanked each man as he made his gift and smiled with a smile intended for him alone.

'And now,' Melchior said to Joseph, 'you will leave at once.'

'At once. Nothing that I can say can express the thanks I feel. You came from God!'

Gratitude and another un-nameable emotion choked him. In the last few days he had lost faith, regained it, lost it again.

Mary had always held that the baby would be born just an ordinary human baby, but privately, in his heart he had hoped for some sign, something out of the ordinary and reassuring, even if it came secretly, to them alone. The birth had been like all others, a painful, bloody business, and Eunice had treated him as the women in charge always treated the man regarded as responsible for such an unpleasant procedure; coming to tell him the news she had said, 'You have a fine son; better than you deserve, keeping her on her feet till the last minute, you thoughtless, feckless fool!' And Ephorus had said, 'We must drink to the boy.' What could have been more ordinary? It had been impossible to shake off the sense of something lacking. Then, when Mary was sleeping, three shepherds had arrived; one of them had seen angels, and heard heavenly voices; one had seen and heard something, the third knew nothing.

But Joseph had taken their coming as a sign, and so had Mary, until Eunice, bringing a bowl of gruel and seeing the shepherds depart, taking with them Joseph's cautious warning not to say anything about this to any but faithful, trustworthy Jews, had said, 'Was that Josodad, the shepherd?' Joseph said that he did not know the names of any of them.

'I recognised him,' she said. 'Poor man, he is demented; he lost his favourite son and has never been the same since. And he drinks. Not here, Ephorus discouraged him; but he drinks.'

And the shepherd had talked about seeing his son, dead these five years. So what did one make of that? Drunken men did see strange things; Joseph knew a fellow carpenter who had seen snakes, bright blue ones, in his bed. A man crazed with grief and full of wine, might have had an hallucination and communicated his hysteria to his companions, seen a light, felt the urge to communicate, and then, being a Jew, knowing the prophecies, seeing a new born child, said all that the shepherd had said.

After that there had been the ordinary days; until tonight when he had had his dream, been about to ask how the journey could be managed and then these men had arrived, bringing the answer. And the old man had spoken with the true prophetic voice.

It seemed to Joseph that he was always falling out of the hand of God, falling, falling, only to be caught again in the hand of God. So, standing there, he uttered a brief prayer, extempore–Lord God of my fathers, I do believe; help me when next I doubt.

But even as he did that he was thinking about Micah's old donkey. Standing idle and well-fed, it had again taken on that deceptive appearance of roadworthiness, and Mary, he knew, would insist upon taking it. And he thought about Anne's jibe that Mary owned two donkeys; it was justified. His faith, like the donkey's gait, flagged, was restored, and then failed again.

Another thought assailed him, had it not been for the broken-down donkey they would not have landed in this place, with the innkeeper so attentive, his wife so competent and both so kind. Nor would they have been here tonight, to be found by this old man who confirmed all the prophecies and who had brought the answer to the question he had been about to ask in his dream–How is this to be managed? It was all–he thought–far beyond the understanding of a plain simple fellow like himself, and the most he could do was to blunder along, doing his best from day to day.

'We will go at once,' he assured Melchior and looked at Mary, who, as though she understood, rose up, straight and strong.

'There is no reason,' she said, 'to rouse the house at this hour. I'll fold the blanket and leave it on the stool, with the coin that Elisabeth and Zacharias gave us. Eunice and Ephorus will understand. But first, I think our friends should see him. I must wake him anyway.'

She went to the place where the child lay, lifted him and turned, holding the baby towards them, as though offering them a reward for their journey, for their gifts.

And suddenly they were all smiling. Joseph with his faith restored, Melchior with his errand done, Balthazar who had seen this wonderful thing and Gaspar who had found his heart. Even Mary, burdened with the weight of knowledge, knowing the end at the beginning, troubled by so much that must be kept locked in her heart, smiled, as any woman does, feeling the weight and warmth of her child, smelling the sweet, clean, milky scent.

So she held him towards them, and the beam from the lantern was caught in the soft fuzz of baby hair; so that to those who watched it seemed for a moment that he wore a halo of light.

TITLES IN THIS SERIES:

GEORGES SIMENON
10 Maigret Stories

MARY STEWART
The Crystal Cave The Hollow Hills Wildfire at Midnight Airs Above the Ground

RUDYARD KIPLING
The Just So Stories Stalky and Co. Puck of Pook's Hill The Jungle Book The Second Jungle Book

ERIC AMBLER
The Mask of Dimitrios Passage of Arms The Schirmer Inheritance Journey into Fear The Light of Day

E. M. FORSTER
Where Angels Fear to Tread The Longest Journey A Room with a View Howards End A Passage to India

MONICA DICKENS
One Pair of Hands The Happy Prisoner Mariana Kate and Emma One Pair of Feet

CATHERINE COOKSON
The Round Tower The Fifteen Streets Feathers in the Fire A Grand Man The Blind Miller

IAN FLEMING
Dr. No Thunderball Goldfinger On Her Majesty's Secret Service Moonraker From Russia With Love

ERNEST HEMINGWAY*
For Whom the Bell Tolls Fiesta The Snows of Kilimanjaro The Short Happy Life of Francis Macomber Across the River and into the Trees The Old Man and the Sea

H. G. WELLS
The Time Machine The Island of Dr. Moreau The Invisible Man The First Men in the Moon The Food of the Gods In The Days of the Comet The War of the Worlds

GRAHAM GREENE
The Heart of the Matter Stamboul Train A Burnt-Out Case The Third Man Loser Takes All The Quiet American The Power and the Glory

GEORGETTE HEYER
These Old Shades Sprig Muslin Sylvester The Corinthian The Convenient Marriage

EVELYN WAUGH
Decline and Fall Black Mischief A Handful of Dust Scoop Put Out More Flags Brideshead Revisited

C. S. FORESTER
The Ship Mr. Midshipman Hornblower The Captain from Connecticut The General The Earthly Paradise The African Queen

DENNIS WHEATLEY
The Devil Rides Out The Haunting of Toby Jugg Gateway to Hell To the Devil—A Daughter

14 GREAT PLAYS*

MORRIS WEST
The Shoes of the Fisherman The Second Victory Daughter of Silence The Salamander The Devil's Advocate

AH LOFTS NORAH LOFTS NORAH LOFTS NORAH L
ORAH LOFTS NORAH LOFTS NORAH LOFTS NORA
AH LOFTS NORAH LOFTS NORAH LOFTS NORAH L
ORAH LOFTS NORAH LOFTS NORAH LOFTS NORA
AH LOFTS NORAH LOFTS NORAH LOFTS NORAH L
ORAH LOFTS NORAH LOFTS NORAH LOFTS NORA
AH LOFTS NORAH LOFTS NORAH LOFTS NORAH L
ORAH LOFTS NORAH LOFTS NORAH LOFTS NORA
AH LOFTS NORAH LOFTS NORAH LOFTS NORAH L
ORAH LOFTS NORAH LOFTS NORAH LOFTS NORA
AH LOFTS NORAH LOFTS NORAH LOFTS NORAH L
ORAH LOFTS NORAH LOFTS NORAH LOFTS NORA
AH LOFTS NORAH LOFTS NORAH LOFTS NORAH L
ORAH LOFTS NORAH LOFTS NORAH LOFTS NORA
AH LOFTS NORAH LOFTS NORAH LOFTS NORAH L
ORAH LOFTS NORAH LOFTS NORAH LOFTS NORA
AH LOFTS NORAH LOFTS NORAH LOFTS NORAH L
ORAH LOFTS NORAH LOFTS NORAH LOFTS NORA
AH LOFTS NORAH LOFTS NORAH LOFTS NORAH L
ORAH LOFTS NORAH LOFTS NORAH LOFTS NORA
AH LOFTS NORAH LOFTS NORAH LOFTS NORAH L
ORAH LOFTS NORAH LOFTS NORAH LOFTS NORA
AH LOFTS NORAH LOFTS NORAH LOFTS NORAH L
ORAH LOFTS NORAH LOFTS NORAH LOFTS NORA
AH LOFTS NORAH LOFTS NORAH LOFTS NORAH L
ORAH LOFTS NORAH LOFTS NORAH LOFTS NORA
AH LOFTS NORAH LOFTS NORAH LOFTS NORAH L
ORAH LOFTS NORAH LOFTS NORAH LOFTS NORA
AH LOFTS NORAH LOFTS NORAH LOFTS NORAH L
ORAH LOFTS NORAH LOFTS NORAH LOFTS NORA
AH LOFTS NORAH LOFTS NORAH LOFTS NORAH L
ORAH LOFTS NORAH LOFTS NORAH LOFTS NORA
AH LOFTS NORAH LOFTS NORAH LOFTS NORAH L
ORAH LOFTS NORAH LOFTS NORAH LOFTS NORA
AH LOFTS NORAH LOFTS NORAH LOFTS NORAH L
ORAH LOFTS NORAH LOFTS NORAH LOFTS NORA
AH LOFTS NORAH LOFTS NORAH LOFTS NORAH L
ORAH LOFTS NORAH LOFTS NORAH LOFTS NORA
AH LOFTS NORAH LOFTS NORAH LOFTS NORAH L
ORAH LOFTS NORAH LOFTS NORAH LOFTS NORA